SPECTRUM
COMPENDIUM
archival documentation of the post-industrial underground

Spectrum Magazine Archive 1998–2002

by Richard Stevenson

A Headpress Book

CONTENTS

Acknowledgements by Richard Stevenson

4 FOREWORD
Eye and Ear by Justin Mitchell
Editor and Critic by Klaus Hilger
First-hand information by Mikko Aspa

6 REFLECTIONS OF A BYGONE ERA
A Pillar In Time by Rene Lehmann
Age Of Dissent by Jason Mantis
The Past Is Alive by Henrik Nordvargr Björkk
The Times Without Pitchfork: Trend-Free Underground Journalism by Stephen Petrus
Tyranny Of Distance by David Tonkin

10 INTRODUCTION
Influence & Inspiration: The Spectrum Magazine Story by Richard Stevenson

14 SPECTRUM MAGAZINE ARCHIVE ISSUES No. 1–5
Spectrum Magazine — Historic Chronology
Issue no.1: Hazard, Malignant Records, Megaptera, MZ.412, The Protagonist, Sanctum
Issue no.2: Endvra, Iron Halo Device, Raison D'etre, Shinjuku Thief, Stone Glass Steel, Stratvm Terror
Issue no.3: Caul, C17H19No3, Deutsch Nepal, I-Burn, Imminent Starvation, Kerovnian, Tertium Non Data, Ordo Equilibrio, Slaughter Productions, Schloss Tegal
Issue no.4: Bad Sector, Black Lung, Cold Spring, Der Blutharsch, Desiderii Marginis, Dream into Dust, Gruntsplatter, Ildfrost, Inade, Law, StateArt, Warren Mead, Yen Pox
Issue no.5: Brighter Death Now, Crowd Control Activities, Death in June, Folkstorm, House of Low Culture, IRM, Middle Pillar, Nový Svět, Tribe of Circle, Skincage, Spectre, Vox Barbara

311 SPECTRUM MAGAZINE ISSUE No.6
Overview and cancellation statement
Interviews: Genocide Organ (profile), Isomer, Militia, John Murphy (Knifeladder/Shining Vril), Navicon Torture Technologies, Terra Sancta, Toroidh
Reviews: 2001-2002

368 ARCHIVAL MATERIAL
Richard Stevenson Interview: October 2001
Spectrum Magazine Promotional Flyers
Live Performance Photo Archive
Personal Correspondence Archives

A note on the archive section: The original print files for most back issues have been lost, and so this section is comprised of page-scans for the most part. Also note that some of the contact information in these pages may no longer be in service.

ACKNOWLEDGEMENTS

This book is dedicated to my wife Melenie Stevenson for support and encouragement.

Thanks and respect to the artists/projects/labels featured in *Spectrum* over the years, and, for their reflections on *Spectrum* and the era in which it was created: Klaus Hilger, Mikko Aspa, Jason Mantis, Henrik Nordvargr Björkk, Justin Mitchell, Stephen Petrus, David Tonkin and René Lehmann.

Thank you to Jennifer Wallis for her initial encouragement in pitching this book to Headpress, as well as invaluable input with proofreading and editing suggestions. And to David Kerekes/Headpress for his support and enthusiasm in making this book a reality.

Thank you to Gaya Donadio for providing Hinoeuma the Malediction show flyers from her archives, and to Marco Deplano for confirming details of select performances.

Gratitude to Scott Van Dort for his part in generating the initial creative spark that spawned *Spectrum*, and for the ceaselessly entertaining music-related conversations over the past twenty or more years — long may they continue!

Thanks to those who provided assistance during *Spectrum*'s activity, including: James Leslie (for the use of his PC on issues 1, 2 and 3); Michael Stevenson (building the PC that helped to create issues 4 and 5, and ongoing computer support); Joseph Aquino (proofreading issues 4 and 5 and running the mail order between 2001–2002 when I was overseas); Chris Forth (proofreading issues 4 and 5); JC Smith (contributing reviews, plus the Inade profile in issue 4).

Thanks to the labels and distributors for their support in getting *Spectrum* out to a global audience: Jason Mantis/Malignant Records, Klaus Hilger/Tesco Organisation, Justin Mitchell/Cold Spring Records, Knut Enderlein and René Lehmann/Loki Foundation, Mikko Aspa/Freak Animal, Stefan Knappe/Drone Records. Not forgetting smaller labels and distros who stocked copies!

A final thanks to all contributing artists, as well as those who supported *Spectrum*, purchasing copies and providing words of support and encouragement. Greetings also to those I have met along the way (online or in person). By naming none, no one is forgotten.

Richard Stevenson portrait by Melenie Stevenson. At Ron Mueck's 'MASS' sculpture (2017), National Galley of Victoria, Melbourne, Australia.

 A HEADPRESS BOOK
First published by Headpress in 2019
headoffice@headpress.com

SPECTRUM COMPENDIUM
Archival documentation of the post-industrial underground Spectrum Magazine Archive 1998–2002

Text © RICHARD STEVENSON & respective contributors
This volume © HEADPRESS 2019
Cover image : Warren Mead : design : Mark Critchell
Layout & design : Ganymede Foley & Richard Stevenson

10 9 8 7 6 5 4 3 2 1

The moral rights of the author have been asserted. The views expressed in this publication do not necessarily reflect the views of the Publisher.

All Rights Reserved. No part of this book may be reproduced, stored in a retrieval system, or transmitted, by any means, electronic, mechanical, photocopying, recording or otherwise, without prior permission in writing from the publisher.

A CIP catalogue record for this book is available from the British Library

ISBN   978-1-909394-62-9 (paperback)
ISBN   978-1-909394-63-6 (ebook)
NO-ISBN   (hardback)

HEADPRESS. POP AND UNPOP CULTURE.
Other items of interest are available at HEADPRESS.COM

FOREWORD

Eye and Ear
Justin Mitchell (Cold Spring Records)

Spectrum was a rarity, even in 1998, ten years after the start of Cold Spring, it was invaluable. Through the established underground networks, it brought information of releases to a public eye that, to my mind, only the genius of Donna Klemm's (RIP) *ARTWARE* catalogues ever did. A feast of treats for ear and eye, a little 'where do I start?' for the neophyte and a gap-filler tome for the established. It was heavy and it was expensive to fly in bulk halfway around the world, but we did it anyway. So thorough, there was stuff in there I hadn`t heard of (I now get forty demos a week — I got four last Xmas day alone!). Before the internet it was genuinely word of mouth, mail-art, and postcards, but *Spectrum* bridged that gap, if you were IN it, you were seen — that made the difference between selling just fifty tapes or 1,000 CDs or vinyl. The 'industrial' world, for labels at least, is tenuous at best — a sliver of the marketplace, hanging by the hopeful consideration that someone, someplace, buys that record and secures your future. *Spectrum* did that, so this book is more than justified.

Editor and Critic
Klaus Hilger (Tesco Organisation Germany)

Spectrum was one of the publications that completely fulfilled the demand for a magazine in its time. Richard Stevenson was an editor and critic in one person, but was well disposed towards the subject of his work. This makes him very close to the ideal critic, someone who manages to assess and describe facts, based on generally accepted standards. At the same time, he has created a tool that counteracts the zeitgeist, that being fast-paced internet journalism. The effect and the information content of *Spectrum* in its diversity is still present today, and these carefully prepared publications are still worth reading. With *Noise Receptor,* however, a worthy successor was also created.

First-hand Information
Mikko Aspa (Freak Animal Records)

It is clear that many people have abandoned the idea of fanzines. Why bother spending months on writing something, if it will be seen by mere hundreds of people, when in another context you can casually reach thousands of them online! Nevertheless, in the last decade, not only have we seen a new wave of magazine culture in various fields and topics, but also the rising popularity of printed industrial and noise fanzines. Despite the abundance of possibilities to post content online, it simply doesn't fulfil the craving for getting something *completed*. Something that is not just one fragment in a stream of endless information which never ends. Nothing is ever completed. Eventually your daily information feed is filled with more possibilities than hundreds of people could fully digest.

Fanzines return to the idea of slow digested reading. Longer features. Something to return to. Making an impact that results in perhaps a lasting landmark and even a reference point in the history of the genre. Allowing artists or editors to speak. To introduce ideas behind their work. Not merely firing another promotional campaign towards jaded consumers. So what if thousands of people flipped through a recent social media one-liner and audio link? How many of them remember it tomorrow? And how could they re-visit the long-gone content? In recent times it has become a more frequently asked question: What is the point of popularity if it happens at the expense of substance?

This is the question more people should ask themselves. What if one forgets the plain number values and focuses on experience, its quality and meaning? The conclusion we may form, is that despite the fact that magazines or books are seemingly a medium of the past, and their validity may have been tested, but it not only survived, it triumphed. While industrial music seems to have an intrinsic connection to technology and multimedia, these are most of all a means to an end. However, the things that may result are at risk of being trapped in the same potential shallowness and meaninglessness of technology, material that artists may have originally opposed.

To refer to the years 1998-2001, when *Spectrum Magazine* existed, it was a time when the internet also existed, but didn't yet dominate everything completely. At the time a magazine was not the product of nostalgia, therefore my assumption is, the editor did not need to consider options at length, as a printed magazine at the time was a very natural format. The choice of *Spectrum*'s core coverage was the flourishing post-industrial movement that was at the time conquering vast numbers of new listeners. It was also a time that was not only a peak within the genre itself, but it was a moment of new things happening. Also a time that witnessed material being pushed further toward crowds in metal, gothic and other subcultures. While there may not be an abundance of magazines focusing on this particular field, at the time it felt very much expected that there be a magazine that covers it. Now looking back to this era, if longing for the first-hand documents, what can we find? It is not much!

We have books and widely circulated articles covering many of the biggest names of original industrial music. We have detailed memoirs of some of the early days of industrial culture. Academic experimental music may be the matter of studies and documentation. But what happened to various email groups, discussion forums and websites dealing with the post-industrial underground? Decades-worth of information has disappeared into the void of cyberspace. Some interviews and reviews scattered in the pages of fanzines that focus on other styles of music. Only a very few genre fanzines that are remembered by the fanatics.

At the time one could not predict the future importance of a magazine like *Spectrum* fifteen years later. Efforts of what may have been merely an attempt to introduce interesting artists and recent noteworthy releases, have contextually now mutated into rare pieces of preserved history of an entire genre and era. Thanks to the work of a relatively young Richard Stevenson, almost two decades later we have a rare opportunity to read first-hand information about many dark ambient, death industrial and related projects — without the clouding perspective of nostalgia. We find interviews with artists that have disappeared or become something else. Artists who were in the shadow of bigger names, but nevertheless created noteworthy albums. Artists who were taking their first steps and later became household names in the worldwide post-industrial genre. A rare opportunity to be able to either return to or discover late-nineties albums and read what the artists said about their work back then.

A handful of established names barely create a whole genre of music, and with the handful who may have reached to the pages of the bigger press, that is only the tip of the iceberg. Besides a handful of individual creators, the overall atmosphere of musical style, as well as infrastructure of the entire genre, demands more. Individual bands or artists barely make the same impact as phenomena. Many times, the underground flourishes in its collective spirit, where personalities can flourish when the atmosphere enables it. Some may remember the headliner of a festival, but the fact remains that there could not be a festival without a greater number of bands. Some can name noteworthy record labels, not based on a couple of great artists they had released but their ability to create a phenomenal roster. Some can even remember distributors who didn't merely sell the safe top ten, but were able to cover unheard artists and those bubbling just under the surface. Most people may simply come to easy conclusions, that these were artists that stood out as most crucial in certain eras. It is more difficult to fully analyse to what extent it was purely their own achievement instead of the zeitgeist of the time!

While focusing on already established classics has its positive sides, so has the rejection of popular opinions of what artists are noteworthy. To throw oneself into the actual experience. Look at the unknown and for the unheard. Connect, commit, listen, read and observe. And perhaps, like Richard Stevenson, find a way to passionately introduce discoveries to other people who could potentially be interested.

REFLECTIONS OF A BYGONE ERA

A Pillar in Time
Rene Lehmann (Loki Foundation)

■ If one has to write about something that is already twenty years old, then it can be determined that a lot has changed. This however does not inevitably mean the changes went from good (back then) to bad (the present), but the larger point is we are now one generation further on. During the end of the nineties labels like Cold Meat Industry, Tesco Organisation or Staalplaat functioned as the consistent 'alpha' labels, while many other smaller labels started to release CDs or vinyl more regularly. With our own label Loki Foundation we were on the threshold of becoming much more recognised, while we played many concerts with Inade during this time as well. From these activities a large network was built up for our projects and the label. Many listeners of our music became friends and long-standing companions, yet equally some of our friends (in both labels and music projects) were lost over the years and did not return to the same path. Some of the minor details may now be fading in our memory, but the reality of the bigger picture is consistently with us. We travelled through England, France, Belgium and Russia and played our first North American tour in 1999. These were personal milestones for us, and the scene we were operating within was already well covered by *Spectrum*.

In reflecting on the whole scene of yesteryear, it some ways it was like today, where lots of projects came and many of them disappeared with time. But the functional operation of the underground then was totally different to today, where it was much more difficult to obtain information for new releases. Thus a new printed catalogue in the mailbox caused much more excitement and interest than a Facebook post that promises the next 'genre-defining album' can today — when the same sort of statement is made again the next week. Likewise before online web-stores you had to call in mail orders by phone to be among the lucky ones to obtain an in-demand release. Now the number of 'likes' for a release post on Facebook can be disproportionate to the number of actual orders made. Yet around the millennium the ability to release a CD or vinyl was much less of a financial risk, where this made it easier for labels to support and release new and unknown artists, while the 'half-life' of outstanding releases was much longer than it is today.

At the time the activity of various key labels was flanked by a vital concert culture which includes the now legendary festivals in Lille, Erlangen or Rostock (MS Stubnitz) — just to name a few. Who of us still remembers when Roland Freisler of Genocide Organ ran through the audience with a burning hand; or Bad Sector setting up his impressive gear on a large stage and playing his *Ampos* album for the first time with full force to our ears; or Anenzephalia and Con-Dom/The Grey Wolves setting new standards in noise-electronics at Deadly Actions Festival in Lille (which was held in a dark brick walled and oppressively claustrophobic old stable building). We also drove 300 miles to see Whitehouse (again), playing in a small fucked-up venue, but with a good PA where Peter Sotos sprayed beer over just twenty people. This was absolutely worth all the effort to witness.

To then ask, has there been much pathos during noise concerts? The answer is there most certainly there was, but its rougher and unpolished effect also did not seem too pretentious at the time. This may then be a quite subjective point of view, but everything acted exactly at a point where it caused positive and influential friction within the post-industrial underground. It is amazing how many remarkable things have come from the post-industrial movement of those years. A lot has changed and the influence of noise and ambient music reached into the mainstream as well. The aesthetics of sound has changed massively, and what could be found in the last hidden corners of underground music, has partially made it into chart productions as well as film scores.

Spectrum's vital role was in its ability to distill and process much of this activity in its coverage, while being presented with outstanding design for its time. It was much less a fanzine based on standard or repeated questions; Richard went much deeper and related information and background on project's activities that could not be read elsewhere. In the years following *Spectrum*'s demise, nearly no publications have followed in those established footsteps, and it is difficult to find something similar now. Today *Spectrum* seems to be like the content of a time capsule, reminding us that many releases of this time were personally as impressive as the original classics from the first industrial era. Yet in today's context just a few releases with the same background could generate similar effect. But you cannot turn back time and, in reflecting on the past today, it is perhaps a bit like having seen the other side of the moon. The time span covered by

Spectrum was maybe the most important for us as artists and as a label. We set many important contacts, found our footing and conquered the world with a kind of trial and error tactic and in the process helped shape a subculture that no longer exists in the way it once did. But there is no reason to mourn, the world turns on again and *Spectrum* stands as a pillar of its time. Chapeau and Salut!

Age of Dissent
Jason Mantis (Malignant Records)

Faced with the task of contributing to a foreword drove me to dredge up not only past issues of *Spectrum*, but also issues of the magazine I published from 1992–1996, *Audio Drudge*. *Spectrum* came about a few years after *Audio Drudge* ceased publication, and Richard has stated that that was an early template and inspiration. As much as I'm honoured by that, there was always a small part of me that was resentful, just because he did it so much better than I ever did, from the layout, to the writing, to the coverage and printing. That high quality certainly continues to this day with his work via *Noise Receptor Journal*, but that's the present. *Spectrum* is the time capsule.

In the age of the cynical, jaded, and easily distracted listener, it's perhaps easy to forget the fervent enthusiasm and appetite that existed for underground electronic music in the late-nineties, and even harder to remember a time when everything seemed so fresh and utterly compelling, unfettered by trends and a sound re-treaded. Devoid of social media and with primitive websites to work with (if you were lucky, and if they loaded within twenty minutes), information wasn't always easy to come by, and magazines like *Spectrum* were paramount for discovering new releases, new acts, or just news in general. Richard deftly managed to capture the spirit of the time and it's reflected in the pages of *Spectrum*. It's fascinating to leaf through them now and reflect on a scene that had reached or was just reaching its pinnacle. I was active in the early- to mid-eighties tape trading metal scene, and as that dwindled and I moved on to what I then perceived as more fertile and untilled ground, the industrial scene was able to capture some of that dark magic and allure. It became imperative that every release on Cold Meat Industry, Loki Foundation, Praxis Dr Bearmann, Tesco Organisation, or Slaughter Productions, HAD to be in the collection, and once it was, it was devoured with clawing fingers, my mind desperate for scraps of information about a swathe of artists that remained cloaked in mystique and mystery. For shit's sake, how else can anyone ever explain the hype and popularity of Mortiis? But, those grey hued photos in the Cold Meat Industry catalogue caught your attention, and helped build something that in hindsight, perhaps never really should have existed. A symbol of the time, though. Conversely, much of it DID justify the hype, and releases like IRM's *Red Album*, Brighter Death Now's *May All Be Dead*, Con-Dom's *Colour of A Man's Skin*, the *War Against Society* 3LP (among many others) are now tried and true classics, and symbolize an underground movement that comes around once in a decade.

Count me among the jaded and cynical now, my ears hardened and calloused over the years, and while not entirely immune to enthusiasm, now distracted by life's mundane rituals and shiny things that catch my attention on the internet. Let's face it, I'm getting fucking old and it gets harder to impress me every year, but what remains, and what will always remain, is a gratitude for living through several musical movements that will never exist again, but live on through audio relics and in the case of *Spectrum*, print. Never forget.

The Past is Alive
Henrik Nordvargr Björkk (Mz.412/Folkstorm)

Having been involved in the 'industrial' scene since the eighties, experiencing the migration from printed zines to today's digital counterparts has been a depressing experience. Nothing can quite match the feel of the printed medium, and if there is one specific zine that stood out for me it was *Spectrum Magazine*. I can't remember how I initially got in touch with Richard, but I would think that he asked me for an interview and that way got my attention. I do remember the first time the zine was sent to me as it stood out from many other zines of that time, at least to me. I will go deeper into this topic, but let me give you a little flashback to the late-nineties first.

The years that this particular zine was active were personally maybe the slowest and most boring period of my musical career. We had been recording a lot with Mz.412 up until 1997 or so, but after that things slowed down and I found myself restless, full of ideas, but not having any proper outlet for it all. This eventually ended up with me starting Folkstorm, which to this day is still going strong. At about the same time I also lost interest in the scene in general as not much was happening that inspired me; the reason for this could have been personal issues or that there just was a little gap in general creativity, I don't know, but there were not many things that piqued my interest. I could also go on and tell you all about the whole mythical Swedish industrial scene that more or less was all linked to Cold Meat Industry in some way, but I will leave that to my memoirs (or possibly my grave as all things do not need to be known).

Spectrum Magazine was at this time one of the few really good zines out there, and the main reason for this was the choice of bands that were featured in combination with the vast review sections. The latter was very helpful to me as a source of finding new music to check out. At that point in time there was not a lot of info online to be found, so this was extremely helpful in hunting down new music. Another thing that stood out was the fact that this was produced on the other side of the planet, far away from the 'real action'; not that this scene ever was very lively, but still. Flipping through the oldest issues is also quite fun as they are clearly done by someone who really is committed to the scene and this style of music, the enthusiasm is extremely evident.

So in conclusion I am very happy to have been a part of this zine, as I was interviewed three times including as Mz.412 for issue 1; as Folkstorm for issue 5; and as Toroidh for the unreleased issue 6. I am also very happy that this archival release is being completed so we can preserve a part of musical history that is still alive, albeit mutated and evolved, for a new audience.

The Times Without *Pitchfork*: Trend-Free Underground Journalism

Stephen Petrus (Murderous Vision/Live Bait Recording Foundation)

When Richard first asked me to chime in with my impressions of the dark industrial movement that inspired his essential fanzine, Spectrum, I was, by proxy, actually invited to explore a very fond time of my life again. Ah, an old man's classic nostalgia! As I combed through my personal archive of items I've collected, and quite literally protected with my own life, I started to really feel the weight of what occurred between the years of 1998 and 2001.

Underground music was at the very cusp of a huge change on many levels: changes in how people interacted and exchanged their art, changes in how releases were distributed, and brought to the audience of one's intent, not to mention changes in how the art form was covered in relation to the upcoming decline of print media covering the industrial underground. When Spectrum and all the other essential zines of the period closed up shop, it seemed to create a massive shift in how coverage of the industrial genre was conveyed. As I scrolled through the back issues of Spectrum as well as mail order catalogues by Cold Meat Industry, and even my own label Live Bait Recording Foundation, as well as various correspondence and pieces of ephemera and classic handbills, I was reminded of how it was the best of times for any underground musical movement. The introduction of the internet was still new. It was still only a supplement to an already thriving, and real world based network of individuals who enthusiastically exchanged releases, zines and mail order catalogues. The internet made it easier to connect to one another as, only a few short years before, communication was executed exclusively through letter writing. Being able to seal a trade deal with a label on the other side of the planet in a few hours, instead of waiting a couple of months for a snail mail letter to arrive was a fantastic development. It was also a time where it cost about one US dollar to mail a CD internationally, and three US dollars to mail an LP. It was a perfect climate combination for an underground movement to thrive.

Death industrial was no exception. It was such a vigorous time, as far as the volume of quality physical medium that was being exchanged throughout the world. It was also still very much expected that a physical medium for coverage of industrial music existed, just as a physical copy of the music was pretty much still the only option at the time. As luck would have it, fanatics had zines such as *Worm Gear*, *Degenerate*, *Judas Kiss* and of course, *Spectrum*.

Richard was always trusted to deliver the goods. Receiving your copy in the mail was like pulling an art book from your mailbox, as opposed to the usual flimsy, photocopied zine. It was always a welcome treat to leaf through the pages of Spectrum and read interviews of many friends and colleagues. Almost like catching up over a few beers. Not to mention seeing the ads for labels and bands whose albums you were dying to get your hands on. The advertisements could be almost as exciting as the words printed within. Reading the qualified reviews, that either helped you decide what was next to hunt down, or confirm or antagonize an already formed opinion on a current release, was always a pleasure. There was a perfect hybrid of print and digital media in those days, in that musicians and fans could further pick up the conversation online in places like the Malignant Records Tumorlist, or the Cold Meat Industry Yahoo! Group. All the charms of physical media, backed with the instant interactions with both the subjects and the authors of the coverage, was a real bonus.

As postage rates steadily went through the roof, costs became incredibly unmanageable for most labels, zines and any other purveyors of high quality physical items. I assume as much for *Spectrum* too. Honestly, I have to lay more blame on postal rates than I do on the easier and immediate distribution tactics and dissemination of materials digitally that occurs with the internet for the decline of physical medium. Now, the audience that enjoys music that I suppose is pretty similar to what *Spectrum* covered is quite a bit larger, the amount of people who would still purchase a high quality physical item I guess is nearly the same, despite the larger numbers who prefer digital content, both in terms of music releases and written word.

The deal killer is the postal rates. Since inflation, many people who did the amazing genre classic releases featured within have disappeared. Certainly all are not due to this reason, but I think the impact is enormous. Through it all, plenty of classic acts like Deutsch Nepal, Genocide Organ and Brighter Death Now refuse to give up and are still active and waving the flag, stronger than ever before. Of course, there are bands developed after 2001 who certainly embrace the foundations as well, not exclusively, but definitely most notably due to Malignant, Cold Spring and Tesco Org keeping the flame alight.

I am absolutely delighted that this era, which has meant so much in my personal life, and so many others, is being historically preserved in this edition. So many albums featured throughout this volume, in reviews or even advertisements, are now pillars of the genre. For lovers and historians of the darkest electronic music on the planet in the 1990s, these issues best documented the death industrial underground.

The Tyranny of Distance
David Tonkin (Isomer)

Flicking through my copies of *Spectrum,* I'm reminded how closely my formative interest in industrial music seems to have aligned with Richard's. Twenty-five-odd years ago, I suspect I discovered the same artists and labels he appears to have, despite our interests converging from different starting points. Living in different cities, we rarely see each other in person, but when we do it's like catching up with a family member with shared past experiences.

I think I stumbled across *Spectrum* Issue no.1 either at Peril Underground or Heartland Records, both Melbourne goth/industrial/experimental record store mainstays of the early 2000s. Polyester Books' small CD and zine sections were also a goldmine for weird and inappropriate material (much more so than sister shop Polyester Records down the road), along with Missing Link and Au Go Go Records. A couple of times a year I'd make my pilgrimage to these stores during family visits from Adelaide and stock up on releases from many of the projects that feature heavily in the first few issues of *Spectrum*: Brighter Death Now, Deutsch Nepal, Gruntsplatter, Der Blutharsch, Yen Pox, Schloss Tegal and their ilk. Issue nos 3 and 4 in particular are like a mirror held to my mid-twenties. Around the time that *Spectrum* published a lengthy interview with Death In June, I discovered Douglas P. lived in my hometown, throwing me further down the rabbit hole.

It was during these years I started self-releasing my own Isomer material on tape, and struck up trades and correspondence with various Australian artists and labels: Magnetic Storm/Unstable Apes Records (Matt Niedra), Near Earth Objects (Alan Lee), Smell the Stench (Leigh Julian), Shame File Records (Clinton Green) and Screwtape/The Taped Crusaders (Andrew McIntosh). Soon after, Melbourne-based Dorobo Records (Darrin Verhagen) — Shinjuku Thief and Alan Lamb's wire music in particular — obsessed me for some time.

The nascent Australian scene had already come and gone, many years prior. Ulex Xane's personal reflections in Jennifer Wallis's publication *Fight Your Own War* capture that zeitgeist particularly well, and are a recommended read. That's all outside the scope of my own reflections here, but I've wondered about Richard's contribution to Australian industrial culture, or otherwise. Location doesn't automatically influence output, whether you are an artist, label or zinester, but environment and context surely does. This is particularly so if you take into account the background hum of live activity, and the tyranny of distance means most gigs here are local.

Thankfully, 'Strayan' output has grown apace since the years of *Spectrum*, and the country has a long history of producing an inordinate number of projects and labels more popular overseas than at home. Richard supported many Australian artists in his *Spectrum* reviews, and continues to do so in *Noise Receptor*. And yet — much like local label stalwarts Cipher Productions, Fall of Nature and Trapdoor Tapes — his focus has always been staunchly international. I imagine there's a common thread in any country with decent-sized industrial communities: once you cast the net wider than small city-based scenes, national definitions are largely meaningless and you may as well catch it all.

And Richard does that well. I'm especially impressed with his willingness to make lengthy and costly trips overseas to attend live events, and his concert write-ups are always worthwhile. Personally, I've always found his interviews to be the most rewarding reads: they are informed, well researched and pry out some interesting responses. He rarely asks the hoary old chestnuts seen countless times elsewhere, and interviewees at times sound surprised they've opened up as much as they have.

I've also admired Richard's commitment to the format. While he maintains an online presence for *Noise Receptor* — saving his premium content for print — *Spectrum* brought a professional approach to zines, and he's never apologised for that. *Spectrum* never aimed for the intoxicating DIY cut and paste aesthetic, but rather, the zine displayed a decidedly austere and minimal design approach. Richard has refined this approach over his years of activity, to the point where, in presentation at least, *Spectrum* and *Noise Receptor* probably hold more in common with zines like *Audio Drudge* and *Descent*, active just a few years prior.

Of course, in underground music all physical formats and releases should be celebrated, and *Spectrum* is a bright light in that lineage. They demand effort and investment, both from the creator and the believer. But if you're reading this you already knew that. We should be thankful folk like Richard Stevenson carry that torch. Here's to many more years to come.

INTRODUCTION

Influence and Inspiration: The *Spectrum Magazine* Story

Richard Stevenson

■ Well, here we are, twenty years on since the release of the first issue of my self-produced and self-published magazine in 1998. As much as it is a cliché to say it, it does not seem like two decades have slipped by — but the years have disappeared all the same. However given that the process of self-reflection and 'nostalgia' appears to run in broad cycles of a couple of decades it is, then, an opportune time to re-visit the late 1990s and early 2000s post-industrial underground through the prism of *Spectrum*'s pages.

With five issues produced between 1998 and 2001, the magazine was a relatively short lived affair in the overall scheme of the history and development of industrial and post-industrial music, but still made an impact during its limited timespan. At the time I was quite surprised that *Spectrum* was extremely well received within the international underground scene, with particularly positive attention coming from mainland and northern Europe, the UK, Ireland and North America. This was all the more unexpected since *Spectrum* was produced in isolation and distributed from a relatively far flung corner of the globe: namely Melbourne, Australia. Prior to starting *Spectrum* I had no direct (or indirect for that matter) connections with any of the groups being covered (be they local or international), meaning all contacts were effectively established at the time and as required through postal and later email channels. With the various contacts made through *Spectrum*, over the years I have been lucky to meet quite a few people in person at various shows and festivals; equally there are many others who I have never met or had a verbal conversation with, but still feel a personal connection to through our shared interests. This is clearly a positive and pivotal trait of the network of artists, labels and fans which make up the post-industrial underground.

As to the reason for this book, given that all back issues of *Spectrum* have long been sold out, this led to the idea to have all back issues republished as a 'compendium' in order to give *Spectrum* a new lease of life, with the back issues documented in book form as an archive of the period. To highlight the thematic coverage and focus of *Spectrum*, each issue was furnished with a tagline of 'ambient/industrial/experimental music culture magazine' which was intended to give an immediate idea of genre coverage. But with expanding personal musical interests over time, perhaps this tagline should have evolved to include heavy electronics/power electronics, neo-classical/martial industrial and neo-folk as well, given there was a greater focus on these genres in later issues.

In terms of its original intent, *Spectrum* was clearly a product of an underground fanzine ethos, driven by a personal obsession with the music of the broad post-industrial scene and a desire to document this often maligned but also more broadly ignored genre of music. So on the one hand *Spectrum* functioned to document my own rising interest in this sort of music, while with the benefit of hindsight it is clear that it was also a case of *Spectrum* 'being in the right place at the right time'. I was therefore able to assist in documenting what was an extremely active period in underground post-industrial music including the rise of some very influential music labels (but more on that later).

In order to properly tell the back story of *Spectrum*, it is perhaps important to outline how I personally became acquainted with this sort of music, particularly as there are multiple ways and divergent music scenes by which people tend to find themselves listening to the sounds covered in the pages of *Spectrum*. Some of the most obvious pathways are those via goth-related music, or the electronic/experimental spheres, or EBM club-related music, or the commercial end of 'industrial' rock, and perhaps the less obvious route being via extreme metal (which was in fact my own experience).

Back in the early 1990s and still in my mid-teens, it was through heavy metal that I discovered grind-core and death metal, which were both soon to be eclipsed by the now notorious second wave of black metal which made a huge impact on underground metal at the time, and for me spurred on my obsession with the black metal scene playing out in Norway and northern Europe. That second wave of black metal happened just prior to the internet being what it is today, so the main way to obtain music and information about the bands was through the global underground of tape trading, and the demo and fanzine networks that were the lynch-pins of the underground network before the internet took over this role. For those who did not grow up in this era, I can imagine that it is quite difficult to fathom today, given there was a degree of dedication required to be involved, which included obtaining foreign currencies, posting it to far flung corners of the globe, and then waiting literally weeks or months for demo tapes and zines to be sent back in reply.

Yet as brightly as the initial flame of the second wave of black metal burned, by the time 1997 rolled around this had diminished somewhat due to the sheer volume of carbon copy projects and the rise of keyboard-heavy 'symphonic' and 'experimental' black metal bands which only served to dilute much of the initial raw and individualistic spirit. But as I was still on a personal search for darker and more intense forms of expression, I had become aware of dark ambient and death industrial music. From my first introductions, dark ambient and death industrial seemed to embody a far greater seriousness in attitude and approach, which was also not obsessed with the whole charade of who was 'true' that plagued most discussions about black metal. My declining interest in black metal was further spurred on by a certain 'cheese' factor that had crept in to all of the 'eviler than thou' posturing (which some might argue was there in black metal from the very start); at least within post-industrial circles there appears to be a greater sense of self awareness, and on occasion a strong streak of pitch-black gallows humour at play, which I found refreshing and far less po-faced than black metal tended to be.

My awareness of these other forms of darker-veined music came about via black metal, where Mortiis (the former bassist of Emperor) had created a project under his own name playing self-described 'dark dungeon' synth-based music, and had duly released his debut album on Malicious Records in 1994. Around the same time, through the black metal tape trading scene, I had been made aware of Lustmord, Shinjuku Thief, Archon Satani, In Slaughter Natives and Raison D'être, with the latter two particularly stimulating my early interest in the legendary (but sadly now defunct) Cold Meat Industry label from Sweden (Mortiis had also found a home there). So by the time 1995 was over and we were moving into 1996 my interest in dark ambient and industrial music was in full flight, with underground magazines such as *Audio Drudge* (written by Jason Mantis of Malignant Records) and *Descent Magazine* (written by Stephen O'Malley of Sunn O))) and Tyler Davis of The Ajna Offensive) being particularly useful in schooling me in this new obsession. The *RE/Search Industrial Culture Handbook* also provided a greater depth of understanding of the history, context and development of industrial music from its earliest phases in the late 1970s.

Another key creative influence was in the years between around 1995 to 1997, when I assisted a close friend, Scott Van Dort, with artwork and reviews for the third issue of his underground metal *Blood Inscriptions* zine. It was this involvement that was pivotal in sparking my interest in creating my own magazine, but the flame was ultimately lit in early 1998 when I heard that *Audio Drudge* had ceased and would no longer continue after seven issues (Jason advised he had decided to quit the magazine to focus more on his growing Malignant Records label). Given that I was heavily obsessed with *Audio Drudge* at the time, upon hearing the news of its demise it generated a sort of personal sense of needing to fill the void left behind, by creating a magazine focusing exclusively on the music I wanted to read about. With this point of inspiration, from there it was just a matter of sourcing the means to create the magazine, which was realised through borrowing a housemate's computer and learning to use a desktop publishing programme. Less than six months later the first issue was released. Given that its small print run of 150 copies was distributed globally and sold out rapidly, it functioned to immediately spur me on to

INTRODUCTION

producing the next issue and the ones that followed. With the first issue being released in late 1998 and the fifth issue in the early months of 2001, it meant I had written, published and distributed five issues in a two and a half year period. Looking back on it now it was a rather huge undertaking, given pretty much all aspects of the writing, production and distribution of the magazine was handled by myself (I was also working a full time job and still managing to have a social life).

Following the release of issue 5 I was able to make good on my plans to head over to the UK and Europe to work and travel, when in mid-2001 I finally headed over to the London. With the initial plan being to be away working and travelling for a year, plans changed as they have a habit of doing: my time in the UK ended up extending through to the start of 2006. Being based in London for the majority of that period gave me the opportunity to see some amazing industrial shows in London (many at the monthly Hinoeuma the Malediction events at the now demolished Red Rose Club, Finsbury Park, organised by Gaya Donadio), as well as numerous other shows in mainland and northern Europe (see the Live Performance Photo Archive within this book). Although when first moving to London in 2001 there were plans to continue with *Spectrum* and release the sixth issue in late 2002, residing in a city like London meant that life and the enjoyment of living simply got in the way, and due to lack of both spare time and funds resulted in me deciding to formally quit *Spectrum* in mid-2002. Although admittedly I was sad to end *Spectrum*, it felt like the right decision as I didn't have the drive and dedication to keep it going at the time, which is perhaps a tell-tale sign that I was suffering from a degree of creative burnout. Although a large amount of preparatory work had commenced for the sixth issue during 2001 and 2002 (which included the completion of a series of interviews and reviews), these did not go to waste and were mostly published through *Degenerate* magazine from Finland and via the UK-based *Compulsion* online magazine in 2003. For the sake of completion and posterity, all of the completed interviews and reviews intended for issue 6 have been reproduced herein.

In reflecting today on the five issues of *Spectrum*, I can see they are statements which reflect my youthful passion and enthusiasm, and for the most part I feel they have stood up well to the test of time — despite the fact I lacked any sort of technical skill or training in graphic design at the time they were produced. Although I have always had an interest in art and design, this is not something I have studied beyond high school, so with *Spectrum* it was really a case of teaching myself computer-based design. I will admit that some of the layouts are a bit clumsy or over-complicated, and clearly not what I would produce today, but then again they are a product of their time and my evolving design skills. Likewise, upon reflection there are clear instances of the overzealous use of text over background images, which at times give rise to contrast and readability issues. This was particularly pronounced within the review section of issue 5, where, due to small text size over a background image, the text was virtually unreadable. In this instance I made the decision to 'rebuild' those pages from issue 5 for this volume, so as to make the text clearer and more readable. I had also hoped to be able to republish all back issues from the original PDF print files; however, due to lax file archiving and degraded hard drives, in the end I could only locate the original digital PDF print file for issue 4, which has necessitated all other issues being reprinted from scans of the magazine. Perhaps another irksome aspect for me is the sporadic poor spelling and grammar throughout (most pronounced in the review sections). Although not really an excuse, this was merely a by-product of producing the magazine myself, and for the most part I had to do everything on limited timelines, where spelling and grammatical errors simply slipped through as a consequence. I have made no attempt to rectify these errors, as the intent has been to republish the magazines 'as is', as a product of their time and in the spirit in which they were created and published.

But beyond these technical aspects, on reflection I do feel that for the years *Spectrum* was active it was perfectly positioned to cover an extremely active period in post-industrial circles, including the rising global prominence of key labels such as Cold Meat Industry, Malignant Records, Tesco Organisation, Cold Spring, Loki Foundation etc. *Spectrum* was also there for the initial explosion of the neo-classical/martial industrial scene, as well as the renewed activity in neo-folk circles, with interviews being conducted with key artists at the time. To mention one interview in particular, I was extremely proud to feature Death In June with the longest interview ever featured in the pages of *Spectrum*, where I was simply stunned by how seriously Douglas P took the interview (especially considering that *Spectrum* was a much smaller magazine than he might normally deal with). It remains one of the best interviews to re-visit from the *Spectrum* era.

Perhaps of further contextual relevance, the later issues were produced during a time that the Malignant Records 'Tumorlist' and Cold Meat Industry Yahoo! Group email networks were fully active. These functioned as critical information portals and provided a global focus and hub for post-industrial music, and would no doubt have greatly assisted in spreading awareness of *Spectrum* well beyond the usual mail order catalogues and lists. Looking back at the coverage today, inevitably there are various projects and labels which have ceased operations (and in some instances mysteriously disappeared, as was the case with LSD Organisation). But of those which are gone, equally there are numerous projects, artists and labels which are still active and have gone from strength to strength. To my mind it only serves to highlight the serious artistic nature of the music that Spectrum covered and how, for the most part, it has managed to maintain interest and an audience over the years (even if some artists and/or albums may not have stood the test of time all that well).

Although in the years following the demise of Spectrum I have continued to write about and promote post-industrial music as a guest writer via various publications (most recently since 2012 via my current publication Noise Receptor Journal, a print magazine and blog), I still look back on Spectrum and the era in which I created it with a particular fondness, and I am proud that it has proved to have longevity beyond being simply a long forgotten fanzine.

Whether you choose to approach this book with nostalgia, or as an archival document, or perhaps even as a form of education of what was happening with post-industrial music in the late 1990s and early 2000s, I hope you find something of interest and that it highlights the types of music covered as both having strong artistic intent and being something more than mere entertainment.

www.spectrummagarchive.wordpress.com
www.noisereceptor.wordpress.com

SPECTRUM MAGAZINE : HISTORIC CHRONOLOGY

SPECTRUM MAGAZINE no.1
Released September 1998. A4 magazine size, professionally printed in greyscale and forty pages in length. 150 copies published. Featuring interviews with: Hazard, Malignant Records, Megaptera, Mz.412, The Protagonist and Sanctum. Plus: review section (50 releases reviewed).

SPECTRUM MAGAZINE no.2
Released March 1999. A4 magazine size, professionally printed in greyscale and fifty-six pages in length. 250 copies published. Featuring interviews with: Endvra, Iron Halo Device, Raison D'être, Shinjuku Thief, Stone Glass Steel, Stratvm Terror. Plus: review section (45 releases reviewed).

SPECTRUM MAGAZINE no.3
Released January 2000. A4 magazine size, professionally printed in greyscale and sixty pages in length. 330 copies published. Featuring interviews with: Caul, C17H19No3, Deutsch Nepal, I-Burn, Imminent Starvation, Kerovnian, Tertium Non Data, Ordo Equilibrio, Slaughter Productions, Schloss Tegal. Plus: Death In June/Der Blutharsch show report and extensive review section (90 releases reviewed).

SPECTRUM MAGAZINE no.4
Released October 2000. A4 magazine size, professionally printed in greyscale and seventy-two pages in length. 500 copies published. Featuring interviews with: Bad Sector, Black Lung, Cold Spring, Der Blutharsch, Desiderii Marginis, Dream into Dust, Gruntsplatter, Ildfrost, Law, StateArt, Warren Mead and Yen Pox. Plus: Death In June show report, Inade profile, and extensive review section (150 releases reviewed).

SPECTRUM MAGAZINE no.5
Released May 2001. A4 magazine size, professionally printed in greyscale and sixty-eight pages in length. 500 copies published. Featuring interviews with: Brighter Death Now, Crowd Control Activities, Death In June, Folkstorm, House of Low Culture, IRM, Middle Pillar, Nový Svět, Tribe of Circle, Skincage, Spectre and Vox Barbara. Plus: extensive review section (130 releases reviewed).

SPECTRUM MAGAZINE no.6
Cancelled before publication. See details on page 313.

INTRODUCTION

SPECTRUM
ARCHIVE ISSUES 1-5

SPECTRUM
AMBIENT/INDUSTRIAL/EXPERIMENTAL MUSIC CULTURE MAGAZINE

ISSUE 1

MALIGNANT RECORDS

MEGAPTERA

THE PROTAGONIST

SANCTUM

HAZARD

MZ 412

Malignant Records & "DJ" Stone Glass Steel Present:

IRON HALO DEVICE
The Collapsing Void

IHD The Collapsing Void
DEBUT FULL-LENGTH CD

"a dark cinematic mesh of epic percussion & samples... revolutionizing the Industrial DJ"

GRINDING — SURGING — SWIRLING — ABRASIVE ELECTRONICA

North American Distribution: Projekt (1-800-CD-LASER), Metropolis Records, others.
European Distribution: Tesco (Germany), Cold Meat Industry (Sweden), Cold Spring (UK).

www.concentric.net/~saul/mlgnantweb/

MALIGNANT RECORDS
P.O. BOX 5666
BALTIMORE, MD
21210 • USA

PLEASE WRITE FOR A FREE CATALOG OF THE BEST IN DARK AMBIENT, DEATH INDUSTRIAL, & POWER ELECTRONICS

INADE — The Flood of the White Light 10" — 3 Tracks (over 24 minutes total) of sweeping electronic doom from this intense German outfit. Immense factory drones and dominating repetitive rhythms that wield unspeakable power. Limited 500 copies

FORTHCOMING:
STRATVM TERROR - Pain Implantation CD (side project of Raison D'Etre)
STONE GLASS STEEL - Dismembering Artists CD (rare unreleased first album)
YEN POX - New Dark Age CD

FROM MALIGNANT:

ORPHX - Fragmentation CD — Over the top tribal rhythms, bludgeoning percussion, intense screams, swirls of heavy electronics and dark atmospheres. Ferocious and unbridled aggression. "5/5" - Alternative Press. "Fragmentation is a well constructed sculpture of sound that will pummel you, and leave you wanting more" -Outburn 3

HAZARD - Lech CD — 11 tracks of disorienting dark ambience from Benny Nilsen (formerly of Morthound). Some tracks drift along in a liquidous dream state, others are more structured and feature loops and slight rhythms interacting with various electronic treatments. See review in current issue of Outburn!

ALSO AVAILABLE

MAIL ORDER
CD
$13.00 ppd (N. America)
$16.00 ppd (Overseas)

10" Vinyl
$10.00 ppd (N. America)
$13.00 ppd (Overseas)

SPECTRUM

AMBIENT/INDUSTRIAL/EXPERIMENTAL MUSIC CULTURE MAGAZINE

ISSUE 1

EDITORIAL

WELCOME TO THE FIRST INSTALLMENT OF SPECTRUM. IN YOUR HANDS YOU HOLD MY DEBUT EFFORT AT A PUBLICATION SO I HOPE YOU FIND IT WORTHWHILE. AFTER BEING INVOLVED PREVIOUSLY WITH A FRIEND'S FAN-ZINE (IN ANOTHER MUSIC GENRE) I FINALLY GOT INSPIRED TO CREATE A DOCUMENT OF THE MUSIC AND ARTISTS THAT I HAVE IMMENSELY ENJOYED OVER A PERIOD OF TIME. AS YOU WILL SEE THERE IS A SPECIFIC FOCUS ON THE STYLES OF MUSIC CONTAINED WITHIN (AND IT IS INTENDED TO KEEP TRAVELLING IN THIS DIRECTION) HOWEVER QUALITY OF MUSIC/SOUNDS WILL ALWAYS BE THE PRECURSOR FOR INCLUSION. WHILE THE BASIS OF THE MAGAZINE IS ESSENTIALLY A 'FAN-ZINE' I HAVE ATTEMPTED TO BLUR THE LINE BETWEEN THE CUT AND PASTE PHOTOCOPY JOBS AND FINANCED COMMERCIAL MAGAZINES. ALTHOUGH I AM EXTREMELY PLEASED WITH THE RESULTS HEREIN (BOTH TEXT & IMAGE WISE) THERE IS ALWAYS ROOM FOR SELF CRITICISM AND IMPROVEMENT. AS COMPUTER PACKAGES PROGRESS ALONG WITH MY DIGITAL SKILLS (BY NO MEANS AM I A COMPUTER GENIUS) SO WILL THE LAYOUT AND PRESENTATION. I ANTICIPATED THIS ISSUE TO BE OUT WITHIN A MONTH OF ITS MENTAL CONCEIVEMENT, HOWEVER THAT BLEW OUT TO A LITTLE OVER FIVE....JUST GOES TO SHOW AMBITION AND FINAL RESULTS SO OFTEN DIFFER. GIVEN THIS, THERE WILL BE NOT SPECIFIC TIMEFRAME FOR THE RELEASE OF SUBSEQUENT ISSUES - ONLY WHEN THE RIGHT ARTISTS ARE CONTACTED AND I AM SATISFIED WITH THE RESULTS. GIVEN TIME CONSTRAINTS (CAUSED BY FULL TIME PROFESSIONAL EMPLOYMENT) IT IS OFTEN DIFFICULT TO FIND SPARE TIME TO WORK TO ON A PUBLICATION LIKE THIS, SO IF ANY OF YOU READERS ARE INTERESTED IN CONTRIBUTING CONTENT GET IN CONTACT AND PUT FORTH YOUR IDEAS. (PLEASE REMEMBER THAT I WILL ALWAYS HOLD THE OVERALL DIRECTION OF THE MAGAZINE SO ANY PROSPECTIVE CONTRIBUTORS WILL HAVE TO ADEQUATELY FIT INTO MY VISION). ANY RELEASES FROM LABELS AND ARTISTS WILL BE GRACIOUSLY ACCEPTED AND WILL MORE THAN LIKELY RECEIVE A REVIEW (BE IT GOOD OR BAD) IN SUBSEQUENT ISSUES. IF YOUR WONDERING, THE ENCLOSED ADVERTISEMENTS WERE PROVIDED FREE OF CHARGE FOR THE LABELS AS A MEANS FOR ME TO NETWORK THIS THING TO GET IT OFF THE GROUND. THIS MAY CHANGE IN FUTURE ISSUES, BUT BY IMPLEMENTING A CHARGE IT WILL HELP OFFSET THE COST OF PRINTING WHICH AGAIN WOULD RESULT IN MORE COPIES BEING PRODUCED AND BEING MORE WIDELY AVAILABLE...A FAVOURABLE SITUATION FOR ALL. IF YOU HAVE ANYTHING INTERESTING TO SAY (ESPECIALLY WORDS OF PRAISE!) OR IF YOU WANT TO OBTAIN WHOLESALE COPIES FOR YOUR SHOP/MAIL-ORDER PLEASE DON'T HESITATE TO GET IN CONTACT. BEFORE I FORGET THERE IS THE OBVIOUS DISCLAIMER - "ALL OPINIONS EXPRESSED ARE NOT NECESSARILY THE SAME VIEWS HELD BY THE EDITOR". IF YOU HAVE A PROBLEM WITH ANY OF IT DON'T COME BOTHERING ME WITH YOUR COMPLAINTS. ENOUGH OF MY RAMBLING, JUST SIT BACK AND ENJOY THE READ. RICHARD STEVENSON — SEPTEMBER 1998

EDITOR/INTERVIEWER/
REVIEWER/LAYOUT DESIGNER/
COVER IMAGE ETC.

RICHARD STEVENSON

SPECIAL THANKS:

JAMES LESLIE (FOR TECHNICAL SUPPORT & ASSISTANCE - OF WITHOUT THIS ISSUE WOULD NOT HAVE EVENTUATED), SCOTT VAN DORT (FOR THE INSPIRATION TO GET THIS MAGAZINE OFF THE GROUND), JASON MANTIS (FOR THE FREE ITEMS AND QUALITY RECCOMENDATIONS), MAGNUS SUNDSTROM (FOR SUPLY OF SELECTED IMAGES), THE ARTISTS/INDIVIDUALS WHO CONTRIBUTED INTERVIEWS AND FOR THE LABELS WHICH HAVE SHOWN INTEREST IN THIS MAGAZINE THUS FAR (MALIGNANT RECORDS, CROWD CONTROL ACTIVITES, RED STREAM, COLD SPRING, SELF ABUSE RECORDS). ALL THOSE FORGOTTEN - OUT OF SIGHT OUT OF MIND......

TEXT, LAYOUT & COVER IMAGE © SPECTRUM/STEVENSON
ALL OTHER IMAGES © THE RELEVANT ARTISTS

SPECTRUM MAGAZINE C/- RICHARD STEVENSON
346 CHESTERVILLE ROAD, EAST BENTLEIGH
VICTORIA, AUSTRALIA 3165
STEVRICK@HOTMAIL.COM

CONTENTS

MALIGNANT RECORDS

MEGAPTERA

THE PROTAGONIST

SANCTUM

HAZARD

MZ 412

SOUND REVIEWS

END.......

MALIGNANT RECORDS

Within the underground music scene there are always individuals who believe enough in the music they enjoy to put their money where their mouth is (..so to speak), and run an active campaign of promotion through record labels & 'zines (hey that would also include me....!). Here is an interview presented with one Jason Mantis of Malignant Records (also formally of Audio Drudge magazine). Malignamt Records is a label that has quickly gained recognition for releasing the music of respected artists within the general feilds of ambience & industiral.

Jason I would like to welcome you to the first issue of Spectrum. Please introduce yourself, your music label and the intentions for its general activities.
Jason Mantis, 29, sole head honcho at Malignant Records in Baltimore Maryland, since 1995. Intentions...I guess world domination is too lofty of a goal, so I'll guess I'll go with to release evocative, dark, sometimes agitating music that's original and worthy of more than 5 spins on the record or CD player!
Apart from the running of your music label you previously produced an ambient/industrial magazine namely Audio Drudge (now defunct) which saw the release of seven issues. One of the great features of the magazine was that each issue included a tape with tracks from the groups interviewed. Was the release of the magazine with the tapes the precursor to the birth of Malignant Records?
Yes, very much so. The original intention was in fact to release a sort of best of' Audio Drudge on CD as culled from the cassettes, but I was worried about it lacking the flow I look for in a compilation, thus the idea for Invisible Domains was born. You'll notice that a lot of the bands that appeared on Invisible were the same that appeared in issues of AD though (Contrastate, Illusion of Safety, Stone Glass Steel, Voice of Eye, Vromb, Maeror Tri, Lull), so in that sense it really was an extension of the magazine. As far as being a precursor to the label...a resounding yes...I don't think I'd have gotten anwyhere without the contacts and distribution already in place thanks to the zine! It really was just a natural progression.
Why did you choose to discontinue the magazine? (I will say that it was most defenitly a gem of magazine and was almost solely responsible for enlightening me with a more extensive knowledge of the general ambient/ industrial scene). Do any of your future plans include the production of another magazine in some form or another?
Not to discourage you from producing what will surely be a fine piece of journalism, but magazines pure and simple are a pain in the ass. An exausting process in which all time loses meaning and the brain turns to jelly just trying to think up new and imaginative things to say about releases. Believe it or not, by the seventh issue I actually started to plagiarize from my first two issues (based on the premise that I didn't think anyone actually still owned the things!), that's how fried I was getting. So, it really was just a matter of getting burnt out on the whole process and severly lacking the time to devote to another issue (what with the label kicking into full gear, getting married etc etc). Usually, 6 months after an issue came out I found myself itching to do another one, but the last time the inspiration just never came, and I took that as a sign that it was time to pack it in. So, to answer your question, it's very doubtful that there will ever be another issue. Sorry!
As I am aware many of the above mentioned tapes included exclusive tracks from the groups as part their interview contributions. Is there any plan to revisit these tapes for a potential compilation release as a historical document of Audio Drudges activities?

No, simply because a lot of the submissions I received were on regular chrome cassettes, so the quality would be pretty shoddy. Plus, again, the lack of focus would really drag it down I think...not what I want in a compilation CD.

At what point did you become first become interested in the ambient/ industrial/ experimental field of music and how were you originally introduced to it?

I got into probably around 1988 or so (10 years now ...a rather scary thought) from the friend of a girlfriend at the time. He turned me onto some Test Department, SPK, and probably the most influential song of all time for me, Hamburger Lady by Throbbing Gristle. From there I started exploring and discovered things like Jeff Greinke's 'Cities in Fog' LP (now reissued by Projekt!), some early Illusion of Safety cassettes, Sleep Chamber etc and I was hooked. I still cherish the 'More Violence and Geography' LP from IOS that I got on a trip to Boston and hold it in high esteem as one of the greatest industrial LPs of the '80s and '90s. Anyhow, back in the mid '80s I was still really into death metal, but was growing increasingly bored with the lack of originality and posturing in the scene and was looking for something darker more cerebral, and 'industrial' (or whatever you want to call it) really filled the void.

I believe that Malignant Records had its first release back in 1995 and has since produced a handful of quality CD's and a vinyl EP. I would imagine that you have now gained a respectable reputation within the scene, but how difficult did you find it at the beginning to start a record label and negotiate deals & distribution contracts with established groups/ labels?

Believe it or not, I think I actually had an easier time finding good distribution when I started than I do now...maybe I've become complacent, maybe I've weeded out a lot of the people that didn't pay (which I guess doesn't really constitute good distribution, but it does constitute distribution!), I don't know, but that's just the feeling I get. Sometimes it feels like I'm still trying to establish myself in the grand scheme of things. Part of this may be due to the current, shit-poor state of distribution in the United States, which has really slipped in the last couple of years since I started Malignant. Soleilmoon pays very little attention to stuff outside their own label, Anomalous has phased out nearly all darker death industrial stuff, and that leaves me with few choices outside of Projekt and Metropolis. Both are decent, but I can't help feeling I'm missing out on a big chunk of my potential audience. Case in point; just a few days ago someone posted a note on one of the internet usegroups asking if Malignant was still around and stated that they hadn't seen anything since Invisible Domains. So really, I thought that said a lot, since Invisible was probably the most widely distributed of all my releases, and yet it was my first release! Unless you get into a huge outfit like Dutch East or Cargo you're stuff really has little chance of making it into stores and out to a broader audience. Sad but true. But you know, I look at a label like CMI or Ant-Zen, that are now up to 70 releases or so and really just starting to gain *full* recognition...so with Malignant only having 9 releases out I guess I really should be happy with the position I'm in.

How good is the distribution of your products? I noticed that from your web page a number of items are out of print. How many copies of each product do you produce and are they specifically limited?

Yes, both Invisible and Yen Pox are now out of print with the Inade 10" going very very close. Distribution in Europe is strong as Malignant seems most widely appreciated there... the US again lags far behind, much to my frustration. So really, what I've tried to do is just build up the mail order business where I can skip the middle man all together. Slowly but surely it's starting to come to fruition. Most CDs are limited to 1000 copies, and vinyl to 500...though there are exceptions. The Hazard was 1200, the Blood Box CD just 500, and the Stratvm Terror and next Yen Pox will probably be 1500-2000. All depends on the release really.

In relation to CMI, Roger Karmanik plays a pivital role in the aesthetics and production of the artwork for his releases. What is your involvement in the production and co-ordination of the products that you issue?

My design sense and skills are fairly sub par so I'm not in the position that Karmanik is, in that I'm able to do all this stuff myself. Thus, I'm at the will of people gracious enough to help me out...usually Phil Easter of Iron Halo Device/Stone Glass Steel and Brett Smith of Caul. That's not to say I don't oversee, critique and approve everything that's created....just the opposite. Nothing goes out without mine and the bands stamp of approval. I guess I'm lucky to have people working for me that are understanding and committed to doing what I feel is an outstanding job....which makes it that much easier. Outside of the artwork and layout, everything else pretty much rests on my shoulders in terms of distribution and promotion etc etc. **Upcoming released include a disc from Stratvm Terror (of which I highly anticipate) and there is also word of second discs on Malignant from Hazard and Caul. What other products do you have planned for imminent or potential release?** Right...well, next up is the Stratvm Terror, which I'm finishing up right now for a likely June release. It looks really incredible and sounds just as good...can't wait for it to be unleashed. Following soon after that is a CD from Italy's Cazzo Dio, which will be released on the side label Black Plague, run by my friend Butch Clough and distributed by Malignant. After the Stratvm there's the release of a rare and previously unreleased recording from Stone Glass Steel called 'Dismembering Artists' (nice pounding rhythms and a dirgey web of recontextualized samples), then follow up CDs from Hazard and Yen Pox. Caul is definitely in the mix sometime in '98 as are releases from Law, C17H19N03, a SALT 10" (look out!), and a Swiss band called Skalpell. Should be a busy and fruitful year! **What does a group or formation have to possess to gain your interest? Is there any specific quality which must be present for someone to be signed to your label?** Um, I've been asked this before and sort of stumbled through the answer...it's mostly a matter of knowing when I hear it, rather than some concrete trait. I guess I look for a fair degree of professionalism first and foremost....something that doesn't sound like it was created by a bunch of teenagers making a bunch of fucking noise (and believe me, I get tapes of the stuff every week). Secondarily, a high amount of texture and mood...something that's evocative and creative. I like to think that there's a definitive Malignant sound being nurtured, even while the releases may be varied. You'll see this become more evident with some of the upcoming releases this year, I hope at least?! **If you had the opportunity to have released any bands within the genre what releases would you have wanted to put you label name on? (I always find this one of the interesting questions!).** I'm going to narrow this down and not do it so much by certain bands, but particular releases by particular bands...which is basically the same as listing some of my favorite releases: Illusion of Safety - Historical (brilliant music with the packaging to boot), anything and everything from Genocide Organ, Mental Destruction's Straw CD, Deutsch Nepal's 'Deflagration of Hell', and a few others that don't spring to mind immediately. **To date what would you class as your favorite release on your label and who / what group would you ultimately like to release in the future?** You know, a few years ago when I interviewed Karmanik for an issue of Audio Drudge I asked him the same question and his response was 'whatever I'm currently working on is my favorite release'. At the time I didn't quite grasp that concept...but, as I've released more stuff I've found that really to be true, if only because I've got to get myself pumped up to promote the thing, and listening to it alot and 'convincing' yourself how good it is will help in the process. But, to give you a more concrete answer I think I've got say to say that my favorite release to date is the Iron Halo Device, followed by the Orphx. As far as future releases...well, I like to think it's a band that's yet to be discovered, as that's really the premise Malignant was founded on. With the exception of Stratvm Terror and Hazard I really try and go outside of the current scene and find a band no ones ever heard of and help build them into a recognizable name. I could easily have gone the path of least resistance and done some big names from the get go, but that never appealed to me as I wanted to build a solidified roster of bands that people relate to and immediately think of as a Malignant artist (unlike somebody like Aube or Merzbow, that will spread their legs to any label willing to stick their dick in between!). It's also precisely why Orphx will never have a release on Malignant again). That to me is how you build up a name for true name for yourself and gain a true following...people may not have heard of the the band, but they see that it's on Malignant and have faith in knowing it's probably something they'll enjoy and have a general idea of what to expect. So anyway, there's really no band I could think of I'd like to worth with that I haven't already signed...with the possible exception of doing something like a Genocide Organ 10" maybe?!

In addition to the label you also run a distribution company that sells a wide range of items from a variety of well known and obscure labels. It would appear to me that only the items you really appreciate personally are stocked for sale. Is there any major reason behind this if my assumption is correct?
That's a fair assumption yes...though less so than in the past, since I've tried to build up the number of things I carry. But, I'm still fairly selective and really just try and bring in things that I really enjoy and know other people will enjoy as well. Being able to track down some of the more obscure European releases and offer them to a wider audience is one of the greatest joys and challenges of doing mail order. I've built my reputation on getting those limited edition items and it's what keeps a lot of people coming back in a lot of cases. In one sense, it's all rather selfish because these are items that I want to get my hands on for my personal collection as well, so ordering them wholesale saves me quite a bit of cash in the long run.

What types of people tend to be your biggest customers and are they isolated to certain countries?
The normal assortment of freaks, psychos, degenerates, mass murderers, florists, and hairdressers. No really, most of the people that order big are just kind enthusiasts living normal lives with a penchant for the darker, more extreme side of life. The majority of people ordering can be found within the confines of the U.S., and while I've never really done a demographic study, most of the business comes from California, New York, Washington State, Pennsylvania and believe it or not North and South Carolina (not much else to do down there I guess). A nice amount of people from the desolation of midwest America too, where I guess there's not much to do outside of staring at rows of corn and listening to The Grey Wolves (sort of a scary thought actually).

I gather that the label stands as a monument to your interest within the given scene, however are you able to make any sort of a living from the label? Is the label a full time job or do you have other full time commitments?
Nah, I don't really have any interest in doing this as my full time job...I have a pretty comfortable standard of living thanks my full time job in the wine business (believe it or not) and doing Malignant full time just wouldn't allow me to up keep that. Not that I'm raking in the dough by any means, but it's nice to have a stable income. I never take any money from Malignant...it all goes right back into the label. The more I make the more I release is the formula I stick to, which allows it to remain tax free and actually means I get some money back come tax time...a beautiful thing really, but I don't know how much longer I'll be able to keep that status!

What does a standard contract involve with the groups you sign? Do they get some royalty or payment or is itt simply the pleasure for them to release their music?
Well, I'm not all that comfortable divulging what artists are paid, but they do receive royalty payments, yes. How much depends on the artists demands. Would be nice if it were simply for the pleasure of making music (still looking for that band!), but alas, it wouldn't really be right.

Have all elements of the operations of Malignant been as you planned thus far? Are there any points you would like to change looking back on the labels short history? How do you envisage the label evolving and growing in the future?
I don't think I'd change too much and I guess the only thing that's never gone as planned has been release dates that I set ...I can look back at some of the early catalogs (a year and half to two years ago) and see myself hyping things that still haven't come out! Pretty sick...but, defi-

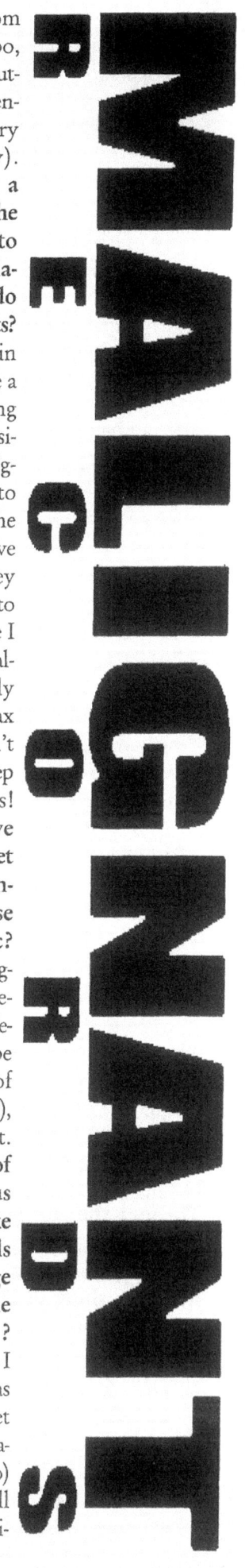

nitely getting better. I don't want to be like CMI or Staalplaat and have three things come out within a weeks time and flood the market because I think that takes away from a release, but once a month or once every two months would be nice. I'd say that I'm pretty much on schedule now (with some glitches)though and hope to continue that. Some things I would have changed would be to have perhaps done some special packaging...not stuck with just the jewel box format, which has me bored to tears at the moment. Also, doing a few more vinyl releases would have been nice. Musically, I wouldn't really change anything, except to maybe have done some more power electronic releases...not so much dark ambient stuff, which is what most people associate the label with. But, all that will change over the next year or so I hope.. though I'll definitely keep the dark ambient purists happy with releases from Yen Pox and Caul, and to some degree C17H19N03. Where do I see the label going? You know, I've never really thought about it as I'm too caught up with the present to think about the future....I guess I can just hope for better distribution and a wider appreciation of my releases. I always want Malignant to stay firmly entrenched in the underground, but that doesn't mean I don't think there's plenty of room for growth.

Through the interviews I have read in issues 6 & 7 of Audio Drudge it would appear that you embrace and/ or tolerate a wide variety of beliefs however show disdain for politically extreme views. Are you one to be interested in philosophical, political and religious views and if so are there specific traits of though you subscribe too?
Um, tough question for me to answer.....as it stands at the present time, I actually think I'm very open to extreme political views but pay very little attention to any of it outside of the musical spectrum. It doesn't mean I condone it or embrace it by any means, but having been through a very angry and hate driven period in my life I think I can relate better than most. But, I went through a more liberal time in my life too, which I think you'll see in something like issue 6 of Audio Drudge, where I was less forgiving and less open to oppposing views. But the pendulum swung back again and now it rests somewhere in the middle, which is a nice safe place to be. For now, I prefer to remain rather complacent in my views on politics and philosophy and rather than stand in the way of someone elses political views, I prefer to just let them speak their mind freely and not stick my nose in places it doesn't belong. What I absolutely detest is a strong ideology not backed up by strong music...and I speak specifically of bands like Puissance, Blood Axis, and that sort. For Christs sake, if you're going to have a right wing agenda, then make some music with some fucking balls to stand up to it, not that bull shit light weight neo-classical drab. As for religion... bah, if that's your gig, more power to you, just don't shove it my way.

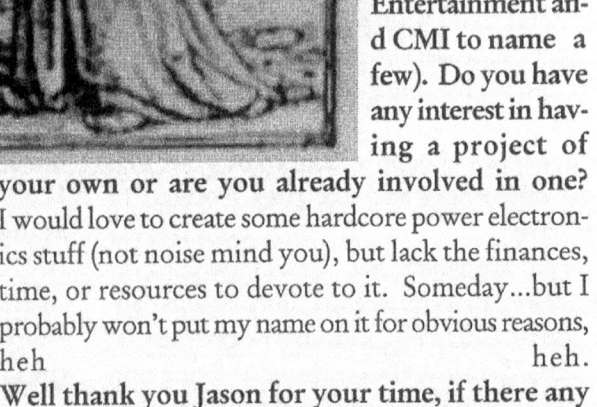

Often the individuals behind labels have their own musical projects (Slaughter Productions, Release Entertainment and CMI to name a few). Do you have any interest in having a project of your own or are you already involved in one?
I would love to create some hardcore power electronics stuff (not noise mind you), but lack the finances, time, or resources to devote to it. Someday...but I probably won't put my name on it for obvious reasons, heh heh.

Well thank you Jason for your time, if there any thing that I may have missed speak now or forever (or 'till you die!) hold your piece!?
Nope, thanks for the interview and keep spreading the disease!

- J a s o n   M a n t i s

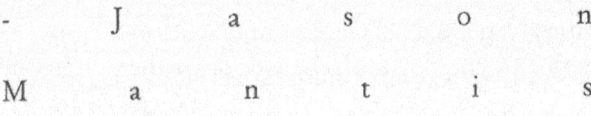

[megaptera]

For me Megaptera was one of those groups that I knew the name but had never got around to buying one of their CD's. A number of years ago I tried to order the 'Disease' CD but gave up as a number of distributor's I order music from were out of stock. Since that time I have now become formally aquainted with the all encompassing industrial darkness of this obscure group. I finally managed to obtain a copy of the 'Disease' CD through the sole member of this group Peter Nystrom which also led to this interview. Here we go ....

Being one of the longer standing groups from the early CMI/Sound Source days you still remain one of the more obscure and unknown groups. Can you please give us a history of your involvement in ambient styled music?
I have been making industrial music since 1991, but I don't do it for the fame. Since I started taking music seriously, I also got a big interest in collecting records. My biggest dream in the late 80's was to make a record of my own. That dream now has come true.
How did you first become introduced to the music of the ambient/ industrial scene as opposed to becoming an active member of it?
Around 89/90 one of my friends played some new music to me. It was BDN and Controlled Bleeding, I think. I really liked the music, so I joined my friends Mikael Svensson and Magnus Pettersson, who already started Megaptera.
When Megaptera formed in 1991 you were not actually a member but joined at a later date. How was it that you became a member of the group?
Before that, I was in a band with Magnus Sundstrom called First Aid, but we decided to quit. I liked the music Mikael and Magnus were doing, but I was bet-

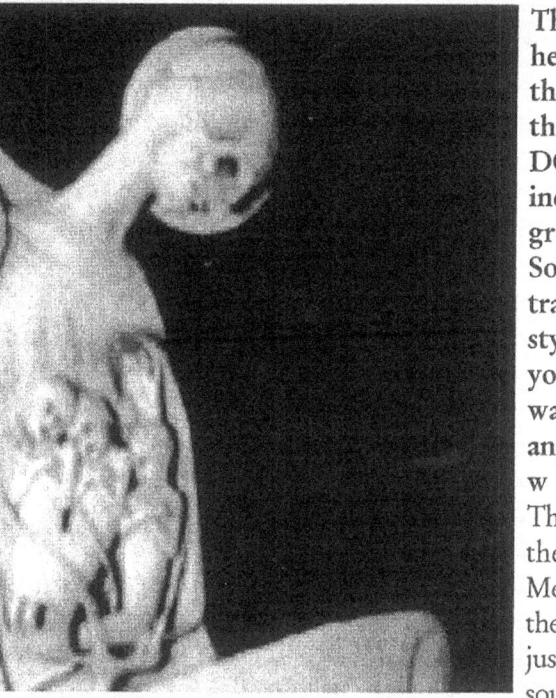

ter with some of the equipment they were using, so I started to experiment together with them. After a while, I was a full time member.
The current status of Megaptera sees you being the sole remaining member. How did this situation arise and is this the most productive way for you to work?
Mikael and Magnus just lost their interest in making music. I had really got the taste for it, so I decided to continue alone. Sometimes it's boring to be all alone, but it's positive too, because I decide everything on my own.
The earliest music I have heard from Megaptera are the tracks included on "in the Butchers Backyard" DCD (a compilation which included material from the groups on the Sound Source label). As these tracks (of an ambient EMB style) are a far cry from your current works I wanted to ask if you had any contribution to these works?
The tracks you mention were the first ones of the new Megaptera sound. They were the first tracks where we used just a sampler. No analogue sounds are used. During that same period, we also made "Shadowland" and "Sodom" on Death Odors. At that time, Magnus Pettersson had quit the band.
As many of the early Sound Source tapes have been re-released on CD are planned to be re-released, do you see any chance of this including the Megaptera tape 'Near Death'? Are you satisfied with the results looking back on it now?
"Near Death" will be re-released as a double CD together with "Songs from the Massive Darkness" some time this year on Cat's Heaven. I still like our old productions. We had a lot of fun recording them.
Thus far your releases have tended to be limited to the more obscure/ underground labels of the genre. How did you first gain contact with the

labels who have released your music?
After releasing "Songs from the Massive Darkness" in 1992, we got a letter from Marco Corbelli of Slaughtr Productions. He was very thrilled about this release, and he asked if we wanted to participate to on of his compilation tapes. This together with the first contact with Roger Karmanik is the most important in the history of Megaptera.

Your upcoming CD "Curse of the Scarecrow" is to be released soon on Release Entertainment, however at one point this was to be released through CMI. What exactly is the history behind the interest in the CD vs the label who finally obtained the rights?
I didn't get any response from Relapse for a while, so I thought they weren't interested. I asked CMI instead and Roger was positive but he wanted to check with Relapse one more time. Then they were interested. I'm signed to Cat's Heaven, so they also are involved in this release.

Is it true that the "Curse..." is actually an album recorded back in 1994 when other members of Megaptera were still present? If this is so what led to the lengthy delay and how does this material compare to current works and previous releases?
It was written in 1995 as a follow-up to "Beyond the Shadow". It was supposed to be released by Anomalous Records, but too much trouble got me looking for another label. The track "Don't Desecrate the Dead" on The Absolute Supper is from this album and I think it's one of my best tracks ever. I don't think you can hear if it's new or old material.

The track which was solely responsible for evoking my interest in Megaptera was the apocalyptic death industrial track "Final Day" (included on sampler tape of upcoming releases on the Fever Pitch label - the track was to be included on the 'Beautiful Chaos' 10" EP). This 10" EP was meant to be out in 1997 but yet to be released and current word has it will now be a mini CD. Furthermore an excerpt of the track "Final Day" was included on the Death Odours II compilation. What exactly is the storey behind this release and the tracks to be included on it?
It was my idea to release it as a 10", but as time went on, Fever Pitch asked me if it was ok to release it as a cd-ep instead. It was fine with me. I had made two tracks for this release, "Final Day" and "Sleep". I also made the shorter version exclusively for "Death Odors II". Two more tracks are included on the cd-ep, "Massmurder Part II" that carries the old sound, and "The Passage" a shorter and remixed version from "Disease". It has finally been released.

When referring to the current Megaptera Magnus Sundstrom's (The Protagonist) name has appeared on more than the odd occasion. What exactly is his relationship to your workings as Megaptera?
He helps me with computer programming as I am very bad with that kind of equipment. As he is my best friend, and we share the interest in experimental music, it's only natural that he gives a helping hand.

With a number of current releases appearing over the last few years and the quality of works becoming more intense and dark Megaptera finally appears that they will break through and gain a much wider following that they deserve. What outputs can we expect from Megaptera in the near future?
At this moment, I just want to release the delayed stuff. I have no plans for a new fullength album. Meanwhile I work a little with Obscene Noise Korporation, a noisier side project.

Although you have stated that there is no political or religious motives being your music your works still remain intensely dark and foreboding. Where exactly do you draw your inspiration and what do see that your music represents?
I am inspired by TV, films, newspapers, reality. I try to mix those things with dark atmospheres and heavy machine rhythms. A reflection of our time.

Much of the vocals included in your music are in fact sampled from various known and obscure movies? Are there any plans to incorporate real vocals to your music and have you struck any copyright problems with the extensive use of dialogue?
There will never be vocals in Megaptera, there for I have all these diaolgues. They create the atmosphere even better than real vocals. I haven't had any problems yet with copyrights.

What music are you personally listen as opposed to what may have given you inspiration for the works you create?
I listen to all kinds of industrial/noise music, old EBM as Front 242, Skinny Puppy, Front Line Assembly etc. I also like soft music like Enya and In The Nursery. All the music gives me inspiration to form my own style. There is a piece of every style in my music.

I do know that you were a member of the group "Each Dawn I Die" which released a fantastic CD some time ago. As it looks set that the groups will release a second CD, are you still

an active member of the group? Magnus Sundstrom has taken my place for the second CD. Each Dawn I Die is a project focused around Marten Kellerman. The tracks on "Notes from a Holy War" we did together in 1993. A couple of years ago Magnus and Marten started to collaborate. I don't have a clue when the new CD will be out.
Apart from Megaptera you also have a number of side projects (Negru Voda, Instant Cold Commando, Obscene Noise Terror). What is the reasoning behind have so many projects running concurrently? Can you please describe each project, what it represents and how you see that they differs from eachother? What releases by these projects should we be aware of?
Megaptera is the main project. Instant Cold Commando was my first sideproject, which released a tape on Slaughter Productions. It sounds like the first Megaptera tracks. Negru Voda is my machine rhythm project. A new CD is coming out on Old Europa Café, and a re-release of a split tape with third EYE. Obcene Noise Korporation is my latest project. It's pure noise experiments. An LP is released on Slaughter Productions. The reason for running all these projects is that I don't want to mix different styles under the Megaptera name.
Do you have any other projects in the pipeline than the above mentioned ones?
No new projects are planned.
When working on previous project collaborations how difficult is it to achieve productive results? Is this part of the reason for your numerous solo side projects?
No it's not difficult. As I said, the reason is that I don't want mix styles.
How do you go about producing your dark ambience/ death industrial of Megaptera and what types of equipment do you utilise? Are your works improvised or does extensive preparation and planning go into the production of the tracks?
I improvise a lot, but often I have sounds that I want to sample ready. The equipment I use include sampler, analogue synths, drum machine and background tapes.
As you are an individual that takes to the stage where possible, what is the attractionbehind this? What encompasses a Megaptera performance and are the tracks improvised or live versions of recorded ones? Do you use video visuals or other props and what reactions from the audience do you receive?
I have only performed live twice, and I don't like it much. My music is difficult to play live. We used video backdrop, all music is on DAT but I try to add lots of improvised noise and sounds. I haven't received any special reactions.
A new Megaptera track is included on the CMI compilation "The Absolute Supper". Although you have never released anything on this label (except for a tape on the side tape label 'Sound Source") is it likely that we will see a full length on this label?
I don't know if I will release anything on CMI. Nothing is planned.
Well Peter, thanks very much for your interest and input into this magazine. Anything else to say to before we conclude?
Thanks and no..........

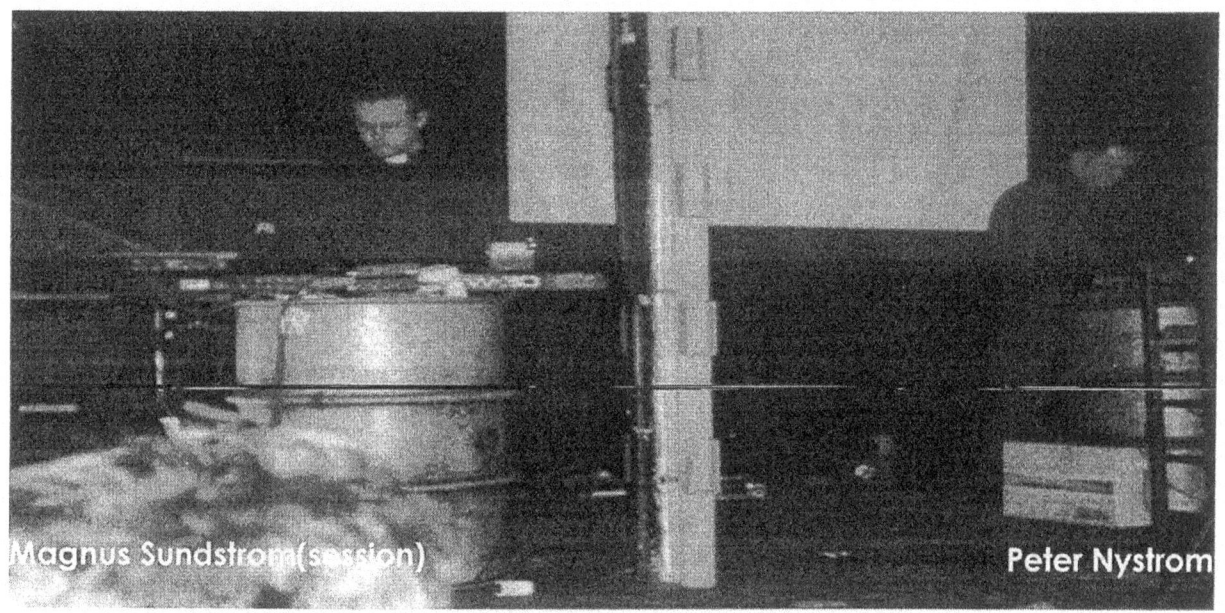

Magnus Sundstrom(session)　　　　　Peter Nystrom

The Protagonist

Magnus Sundstrom is one of those artists that have been lurking in the wings of the ambient/ industrial scene for quite awhile, but whose recognition up until now has been limited. Since the formation of his new project "The Protagonist", Magnus has gained a noted reponse over a short period of time. This will surly explode into full blown respect once his debut CD is released this year on CMI (it should be out by the time this goes to print). Now onward with the interview...!

Your history with the ambient/industrial scene harks back to when groups such as Megaptera & Morthound were just beginning however it is only in the last year or so you have become a major contender? Can you please detail your history with music which led to your current solo formation?
1987 I started Fiskebatarna with Peter Nystrom of Megaptera. We wrote silly synth-pop songs with even sillier lyrics in Swedish. After a while our music making became more serious, we changed name to First Aid (and later on Commorium) and the music became darker. Around 1990 we got bored and Peter joined up with Megaptera. I didn't write any music until two years later when I started the band TWAT. What first sounded like something by early Laibach, ended up as a one time performance in the vein of Ministry and Revolting Cocks. Two years later I began making music again, now under the name third EYE. Mainly influenced by Klinik, SPK, Skinny Puppy and Test Dept. I made a few songs that appeared on a split tape with Peter's side project Negru Voda.
Although I am aware that your chosen pseudonym has only been changed recently, for me I find it holds quite an atmosphere. What was the reason behind choosing this name?
Some compilation appearances later I found out that there was a German band called third EYE, so when I was supposed to participate to the "Palace of Worms" CD I decided to change name. The reason for choosing The Protagonist is that it's a rather neutral name not typical for the genre, it's more suitable for my music's new direction, and it's a homage to one of my favorite bands, Dead Can Dance. Unfortunately, there is a Norwegian synthpop-band called Protagonist, but since we don't have the same audience, I don't care.
As you are now signed to Cold Meat Industry it appears that it has been a long time coming from your original contact with Roger Karmanik. Can you please detail this history with the label that led to you current signing?
Roger Karmanik contacted me after listening to the split tape. He thought that my music was fantastic and wanted to hear more. I told him that my music had turned more orchestral and I sent him a tape with three tracks, "Imitation", "Zoroaster" and one more. After a while he told me that he wanted "Imitation" on his next compilation (...and Even Wolves Hid Their Teeth). After that nothing happened, and I didn't want to bother him, so I released the song on the compilation "Palace of Worms" instead. We lost contact, but when it was time to release "The Absolute Supper" he contacted me again.
CMI will have the honor of releasing your debut CD however are you signed for more releases than this?
No, I am not signed for further releases, but Roger / CMI has told me that I am "sentenced to eternal suffering" on CMI, or as long as I please.
How appropriate do you see CMI for the music you create? If you could be signed to any label which label do you feel would be most suitable for you?
I think that CMI probably are the most suitable label for me right now, and it's good to know that someone believe in my music. However, I want the music to sound as good as possible, and in my case I would need to involve people from a classical orchestra. This is rather expensive and the money CMI gave me only cover the studio costs. A dream is that someone would give me the money I need to realize the orchestral project, but until then I just try to make the music sound as good as possible with the available equipment.
Thus far the only material of yours that I have heard is your contribution to the "Ahisma" compilation and your two tracks included on the CMI "The Absolute Supper" compilation. For me the sound/ structure of the compositions greatly improved between the "Ahisma" track and the CMI

compilation tracks. If you agree with this statement what in do you see as the reasons behind this?
All three tracks were written in 1994, but they have been recorded at different occasions. "Spirits of the Dead" on "Ahimsâ" was the first to be recorded, and at that time my equipment wasn't as good as it is now. I also think that my composition skills have improved during the years. So yes, I agree. I still like "Spirits of the Dead" though, so it's not impossible that some day I will record a new version.
You have also been included on a number of compilations prior to the above mentioned. How many and which compilations have you been included on?
Well, as The Protagonist I have been included on the following compilations: "Palace of Worms" CD [Palace of Worms Records, Italy] 1996. "Riefenstahl" 2CD [VAWS, Germany] 1996. "In De Ban Van Tiwar" MC [GEENS, Belgium] 1996. I have also done two remixes: Statemachine "Happy Endings" CDM [October P., Sweden] 1996 and Les Jumeaux "Cobalt" CD [ITN Corporation, England] 1997.
Are the above mentioned tracks (and/ or other compilation contributions) to be included on your upcoming CD? Are these to be considered representative of what to expect of you full length debut?
The track on "Palace of Worms" is an early version of "Imitation", which will appear in its final version on the album, with spoken word by Marten Kellerman of Statemachine / Each Dawn I Die. "Riefenstahl" contains my song "The Puritan" which also will be found on the album in a new and improved version. The Belgian tape includes a Skinny Puppy cover which will not be used again. I think that my contributions to "The Absolute Supper" are the most representative tracks regarding the forthcoming album, but the sound will be much more authentic.
The release date for your debut was scheduled for early this year however this has obviously been delayed. What are the reasons for the delays & do you think that Roger Karmanik is committed to releasing your CD quickly when complete? (I ask this as there has been some extreme delays with some CMI items being recorded to being released).
The recordings should have been finished before the end of 1997, but the collaboration with Mark Ellis of Elijah's Mantle was delayed, so it was a good idea to take a break and repair some studio equipment. Unfortunately, the maintenance has also been delayed, but the equipment just got back. This means that everything will be recorded within two or three weeks. There are two songs left, which include Mark Ellis on spoken word, a new acquaintance called Psychonaut on cello and hopefully Peter Pettersson of Arcana on vocals. The CD will probably also contain an exclusive remix of "Zoroaster" by In The Nursery! Roger has told me that the album will be released as soon as possible, and I think that means August or September. We'll just have to wait and see.
Do you have any ideas or concepts on how you want your music presented? Do you have any aspirations to play a role in the production of the art for the visual presentation?
I try to let the music speak for itself, but a CD need a cover. I don't have any particular concept, but I think that Roger and I will come up with something suitable.
As your music is quite militaristic in style/ struc-

ture this could lead to certain assumptions & interpretations on potential philosophies/ideals behind the music. **What do you see as what your music represents and is there any specific intrinsic meaning?**
I assume that you refer to right wing philosophies, but I don't see the connection that so many other people do. I make bombastic / militaristic music because I like it to be dramathurgical and not because of my beliefs. I guess that all my impressions are reflected in the music in one way or another, however, there are no deeper meaning behind them other than the fact that I want to create both dark and beautiful music at the same time. In the future I would like to write music for film, so I guess you could say that my music is the soundtrack to my inner self.
Your music being classiclly structured and executed would lead me to believe that you have had formalized music training. Is this the case?
I studied classical music theory one year. That has helped me a bit, but most of the songs on the forthcoming album were written before that. I think you could tell which songs are the more recent ones, because they seem to have become more melodic.
What styles of music do you personally listen to and who are some of you favorite artists?
I can't say that I listen to any specific styles, but some of my favorite artists right now are: Dead Can Dance, In The Nursery, Shinuku Thief, Soma, Contrastate, Test Dept., Current 93 and Death In June. I also listen to a lot of film music, by composers as Wojciech Kilar, Elliot Goldenthal and Christopher Young.
CMI plays host to many groups crossing a wide spectrum of religious and political beliefs. I do know that you show distaste for some of the groups who have a pseudo evil attitudes. Is this dislike of image/ attitude someway related to that you may not be taken seriously as a musical artist if you are affiliated with the said groups?
The only thing I have in common with most of the bands on CMI is that we are on the same label. Personally I like the wide spectrum of artists, but the label has become something more that just a label. People seem to expect certain things from the artists; that they are extreme in one way or another. I'm not saying that I'm more serious than any other band on the label, but I focus on the music and nothing else.
From my knowledge of the CMI roster it would appear that most groups have at least a knowledge of each other to a certain level. Which groups are you in regular contact with and do you know the members of the groups that you dislike their image/ attitudes?
The people I talk to once in a while are Benny / Hazard, Tomas & Chelsea / Ordo Equilibrio, Mikael / Inanna, Magnus / ConSono, Hakan / Sanctum and Lina/ Deutsch Nepal. I have talked to most of the others, including the bands that I find less interesting, but they are all very nice people. The different beliefs and opinions don't affect our relationship.
Your personal involvement within the general Swedish Ambient / Industrial scene goes beyond your musical endeavors as you maintain a number of web pages for some other no table groups. Exactly whose web pages do you maintain and what is the ethos behind doing this?
I maintain websites for my self, Hazard, Megaptera and the American label Crowd Control Activities. I do it because they are my friends and I think they deserve more attention. I guess you can see that no money is involved, because they are very simple.
An upcoming label Crowd Control Activities is to re-release a spilt tape of "third EYE" (pre Protagonist material) and "Negro Vodu" (a Megaptera side project) on CD. Will this include additional unreleased tracks from each group? Looking back on this material now are you satisfied with the results?
That tape actually was my first appearance in the industrial scene. I can't say that I'm satisfied with the result, but I think that the music definitely deserves a CD release. The re-release will contain two bonus tracks from each band, Peter's are both unreleased, but one of my tracks is from a compilation called "Life After Fallout / Ödland", released by Blaster Records. The other one is written especially for this CD. It will probably be out in August.
One of your friends projects Megaptera is now

essentially a solo outfit however you have been recruited as a contributing member for live performances. I have also noted that you name popped up on the Megaptera -Deep Inside 12" EP. What is your actual contributions to the group and are you in fact a member (de facto or otherwise)?
I started helping Megaptera when Mikale still was in the band, but after the recording of the soon to be released CD "The Curse of the Scarecrow", he decided to quit. My involvement came naturally, since Peter and I knew that we work quite well together. I'm not considered a real member, I just help Peter with sampling and programming of the computer.

As you have graced the stage before, have you performed under your current moniker? If not are you planning to take to the stage in the near future? How difficult would it be to transform your music to the stage?
I have not performed as The Protagonist, but once as third EYE and twice as part of Megaptera. Actually, two performances are planned for this summer, June 21st in Stockholm, Sweden and July 24th in Waregem, Belgium. I find it impossible to appear alone, therefor I will be assisted by one person on percussion and one on cello. I think there will be no problem to transform the music to the stage, but I can assure you that it will be even more powerful than on CD.

Currently you are working on the second CD of Each Dawn I Die however you did not contribute to the first CD? How did you become involved in the groups and are there any of the original members left?
The people responsible for the first album was Marten / Statemachine and Peter / Megaptera. Marten and I both live in Stockholm but Peter doesn't, so when he said that he wouldn't be able to participate, Marten asked me instead.

What are your plans for the music for the second Each Dawn I Die CD and when can interested persons expect it to be released and on what label?
The album is entitled "Frozen Smiles on Faces Forgotten" and will be more orchestral than its predecessor, and much better produced. However, both Marten and I have lots of other things to do, so we don't know when we can finish it. The label will as far as I know be Dark Vinyl.

Are there any other side projects we should be made aware of?
After my debut album with The Protagonist, I will start working on a side project in the vein of third EYE; more noise, less music and more improvisation. The project is untitled at the moment.

I gather that you would not be able to undertake music as a full time endeavour. Would this be your ultimate plan or would you prefer to make it simply an interest/ hobby? What occupation do you have to support your musical interests?
Right now I am studying economics. When I'm finished I will try to begin making music full time. I want to compose for TV, film, theatre, art exhibitions and also remix other artists. I hope this will work out, because music is what I have to do. Hopefully my forthcoming debut album will help me find customers.

Once again I would like to thank you for completing this interview. Is there anything you would like to bring up before the interview concludes.
No, sorry...

What can one say about Sanctum? They are surely one of the most innovative bands within any genre of music at this point time as they cover so many styles and themes within their music. For me, I do believe that there is a certain commercial potential for this group with their perfect mix of theatric music combined with enough industrial sensibilities and a heavy does of moving melodies. (yes, if your wondering I used the above blurb in the Sactum review also - pretty slack hey...! - ed). To say I was pleased when I snared this interview in an understatement, so sit back and enjoy this indepth and informative interview as much as I did writing & recieving it..

Hello Jan Careklev and welcome to the pages of Spectrum. Sanctum to me are one of the more elusive acts that are signed to CMI, so could you begin with introducing the groups members and what their role is complete within the group.

Well you have Marika on cello, and Benny on drums, he is the one who joined Sanctum last, he studies music in Linkoping. Lena sings and writes lyrics and she just moved to Stockholm to join a theatregroup. Then you have Hakan he stands for the main graphics of the sanctum, he is also writing some lyrics. Hakan also works with graphic design. Now it is my turn, I have written all the music so far and I'm also doing most of the programming. I have quit my studies at Uppsala University to be able to focus on the music. At this moment I have four projects going on besides Sanctum. Hakan and I work together in a dancegroup caled Agnes. We have made a few performances together so far and are at this very moment working on a performance that will take place in Stockholm in May and Jonkoping in June.

I'm also working on a composition that was originally created for an exhibition with a Photographer. It will be a 45 min soundscape that maybe can be explained as slowindustrail-neoclassic-ambient-music. And then you have a project where I work with Hakan and our live sound engineer, it can bee described something like this. Exprimental-harsh-doomindustrial, We experiment much with the way of creating sounds and always seek new ways of bringing the sound that we want. I am also is working together with a former member of my sleeping band Nov Com, Andreas Matsson called Chromedragon.

I first became aware of Sanctum through a live gig review from 1995 (that was on the original version of the Cold Meat Industry Web page), but did not manage to hear any of your music until your debut CD "Lupus in Fabula" was released in 1996. There was an original version of the track "Dragonfly" on the US version of "& even wolves hid their teeth" sampler CD (which I am still yet to hear) but what, if any releases did you have before this?

Lupus in Fabula is Sanctums first release and the music on L.I.F was created over quite a long period. I have made music for some theatre projects that I rewrote for Sanctum when the idea to start the group arose. The main reason to start up Sanctum was that Hakan and I wanted to create music without limitations. We had a group before called Nov Com (the november commandment) but we felt that we had to many limits in that band and that we had done all of what we could (I think I have lost the line:-) So certainly, L.I.F is our first release.

You mentioned a previous band Nov Com that you and Hakan were involved in. What style of music did this group incompass and did you have any releases under this moniker?

It was some kind of EBM, I don't like that label but I aspome that is what people would have called it. We worked much to create a rockfeeling. It was in that group that Hakan and I started to work together in late 80's. There was two other members in Nov com, Andreas Matsson that I have already mention concerning my band Chromedragon and Pär Gustafsson. He is now studding at the same university as Sanctum. We released some recordings back in 92 (a complete showtape) and a single (Exile station) in 93. I can also tell you that Nov Com will release the complete works on Flaming Fish this summer.

How did you manage to come in contact with Roger Karmanik and were you previously aware of CMI when Sanctum formed? How closely are you involved with the Swedish industrial scene as a whole?

Samuel Durling that is one of the members in Mental Destruction (a band on CMI) is an old friend of ours He thought that I should start a group with the kind of music that I have done for theatre and other audio-visual projects. And like I said before Hakan and I wanted to broaden our minds and not have any limits in our creation of music. Hakan and I felt that Lena (a friend of Hakan) should fit into our concept so we asked her and she was really exited of the idea thus Sanctum was formed. Our first gig was together with Roger Karmanik's "Brighter Death Now" and we had have some contact with him before. After he had heard us he was willing to have Sanctum on his label. Concerning how we are involved in the industrial scene here in Sweden, I think that all the good industrial music lies on CMI, like Raison D'etre, In Slaughter Natives and Mental

Destruction. Sanctum has been touring with some of them and I think the atmosphere is quite good among the bands. Of course there is a lot of different thoughts and beliefs but as long you have respect for one other and can see the reason for each persons ways, when we are together it is no problem.

I will comment that overall there are "CMI" elements within your music, but at the same time I feel that it has the potential to be well received by a larger audience than simply individuals from the industrial/ ambient scene. What are your thoughts on this and was it by any means a deliberate attempt to produce such a diverse release?

Yes I think you are right that we are a little bit more "easy listening" then the other bands on CMI, and I think that we could have a different audience if we had the opportunity to let them know about us but it is hard to reach them. But I must say that I'm very satisfied with the fact that we have reached that many people with our first album. The reason for the diverse release that is "Lupus In Fabula" is like I said before that we will do music we find interesting and hopefully people haven't heard before. And another reason is that the material on L.I.F was produced over a long period. I think that the next album is going to be more of a unit.

After hearing your contribution to "the absolute supper" compilation (with the track also being included on your recently released 10" picture disc) to me it sounds even more commercially oriented with its straight forward structure and short length. Was this a consious effort on you behalf and is this a preview of the future direction of Sanctum? Furthermore is there any cryptic meaning behind the song having a title on the compilation but only being referred to a symbol on the 10" EP?

No we have no intention to do more commercial music, and the tune on "Absolute Supper" can not bee taken as a preview of future Sanctum. It is a tune that we like and we have played it for quite awhile We actually recorded the music just after the release of LIF for our European tour 96. It was the opening act and we got so great response on it but we felt that it would not fit in our next album (maybe we will make a rearaged version on the album). The idea to have it on the Absolute Supper comp.arose so we included it as we are very satisfied with the tune. Concerning the title, something went wrong in the communication between CMI and us. The title on the comp. was our working-title however they also spelled it wrong, so on the second edition it is nameless. The tune is nameless because the lyrics tell about a man that seeks for something that he doesn't know what it is. I'm sorry but it was not anything cryptic, maybe I should not tell you the reason and pretend it was ;-) To go back to our music, I talked to a guy a couple of days ago and he also told me that the tunes on the 10" was more commercial. We discussed it because I don't agree and we come to the conclusion that it is commercial compared to the other bands on CMI. We have the intention to work with the lyrics as much as possible and that is something that I think separates us from other CMI-bands and that could be experienced as commercial. I don't know. Our new tunes is longer and more harsh but with the orchestral delicateness still there, it is maybe more of it compared to LIF but the samples is also more harsh to make the contrast bigger.

Which scenes or countries have shown the greatest interest in Sanctum and how may units of your debut have you manged to sell?

We have had quite good response from many different kinds of people and of couse the industrial scene is the one we see the most response from because of magazine with reviews and articles and for the reason that we are into that. It is also due to the fact that our label is CMI that brings us into the industrial scene. If we had another label behind us with a broader audience I think we could have reached more people. For example we recently played as an opening act for a celloist that had a string and brass section backing him up. I can tell you that the audience was quite varied, we had very good response from all different kinds of people from the age of 15 to the age of 60. I have noticed this phenomena several times when we have played live. I think we have sold around four thousand copies of L.I.F until now.

The artwork of the CD is quite fantastic with the group being credited for its production. As the Karmanik family plays a vital role in the artwork of CMI groups did they have any participation in the production of your sleeve? Furthermore have any of the members had formalised artistic tuition?

The sleeve was completed fully on our own responsibel, with no interpretation from CMI. Hakan with his job works with these kind of things and has done some other sleeves for groups. I'm very interested in the visuals and try to get

some time to paint and do some "computer art" so it felt natural for us to do our sleeve by ourselves.
Are you also responsible for the stunning images on the 10" picture disc? Is there any actual meaning behind these pictures other than being aesthetically pleasing?
We have made the artwork on the 10" as we try to bring something with our music (and the same goes with the artwork). But I can't say it has an actual meaning, it is just like our music. It is up to the listener/viewer to put a meaning to it.
As the 10" has just been released how do you feel about its presentation and the music contained within? Are you big fans of vinyl releases and was this a specific request to CMI from the group?
I'm very satisfied with the 10" both the visuals and the music. The strongest tune on the 10" is called 'Madelene'. If you listen to the lyrics and try to transform it together with the music into a unit it is quite scary. It is so great when the lyrics fit in the music totally. I created the music like a year ago or so and Hakan wrote the lyrics after I was finished with the music. At first I didn't feel that strong about the tune but it has grown to be something special for me. I hope that the listeners to the 10" will feel something like I do because it really deserves that. I don't want to be pompous ore something but if I had not liked what I'm doing I had not going on doing it. Concerning the vinyl-thing, we felt that we wanted to release something to our listeners, after all it is two years since LIF came out. We wanted to do something more than just a cd-ep so we brought the idea up with CMI and as you know they are into odd releases so they liked the idea. But we have no special love for vinyl it just seemed to fit in our concept of what we wanted to bring. I'm glad that it has sold so good as there are just a few copies left. When we got the vinyl in our hand I was afraid that it would be difficult to sell, but it didn't. So after all I'm very satisfied and hope the work with the next album will go the same way.
Quite a number of industrial groups take a satanic approach to both concept and music while Sanctum seem to (from my interpretation of the lyrics) bypass the 'evil' trappings and focus more on the duality of the human mind/ human nature. Is this a correct assumption/ interpretation on my behalf?
We are interested in existential issues. That's why the lyrics have a spiritual touches and deal with contrasts like light and darkness, good and evil for example. We can't stand for the satanic or other extreme thoughts that sometimes appear in this scene. I don't agree for any reason in these kind of beliefs or thoughts but as I said before that's not a problem for us as we respect the other bands on CMI if they can respect us. The bands want to do something and they are doing it just like us.
What are your personal views on traditional organised religion and do you subscribe to any specific ideas of individuals or trains of thought?
I can't agree to the organised way of practising the Christian belief but I have a belief in God, good and evil. I think that it is important to care for one other and make the life as good as possible.
The above question and answer has led to the gossip and rumors that Sanctum is a Christian band. Do you want to confirm or refute this claim?
We all have different thoughts and beliefs concerning this. As said before I have a belief in God and so does Hakan but we also have questioning in our life. I can't say that Sanctum is a Christian band if you mean that we have a mission for God with the band. We try to bring feelings and experiences from life, put a light on the human kind (that sounded pompous). We just create music that we can express ourselves in, in one way ore another. I don't think it has any importans what label you put on a band the main thing is what the listener gets out of the music and the lyrics. The listeners must be alert and active when they listen to music and put their own experience into it and transform it to something that is unique for him. When you just put a label on the band as Christian and then it is all right to listen to it is so wrong. I have noticed that people do so, I have had the question many times, and I've got e-mails from people that wonder if we are Christian. Is that important, don't they have their own will to analyse the lyrics and music and like I said before, make it to something that they can stand for? The important thing is the way we practise life that we try to do our best in our own oppinion.
Sanctum have managed to grace the stage on quite a number of occasions and from reports received you

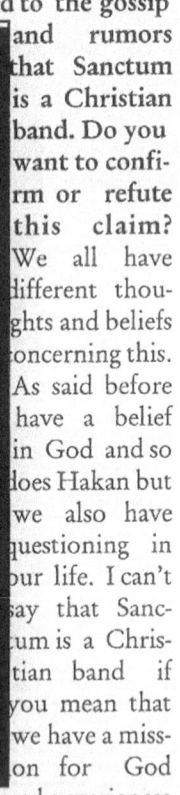

are an act which has to be seen live. How important do you see playing live is to the group and do you use samplers or programmers when playing live?
I think it is very important to play live because it is a chance to meet people that like our music and helps to bring our music further with visual elements that we try to use as much as possible. It is hard to bring that feeling on a small CD disc. Live we work with video projections and sometimes we have dancers on stage and we try finding new ways to bring the visual experience closer to the music. We play live as much as possible. I play some hand drums and odd instruments that I have collected from different sides of the world and some of them have we made by ourselves. I also play on samplers. Hakan plays some keyboards and sings, Lena sings and Marika plays the cello and sing some background. In a way I don't like to play live because I can never reach the feeling that I can get in our studio when I create the music. That is quite frustrating for me as I've got a picture of how the music should and when you hear the live sound you often gets disappointed. But I can't deny that the feeling when you get good response from the audience is wonderful, that make my worries worth it. And the fact that the other members just love to perform live also makes me going on.  
How do you present yourself in the live arena and do you employ any visual/ video imagery to enhance the symbolism of the performance?
In our video projections we reflect our music and we want it to bring the experience further in a way that we can't do with only the music as medium.
In future do you see yourselves having the opportunity and/ or aspirations to produce a video clip? If so what would you see as a potential song to use and how would you present/ represent it?
We have had the thought for awhile but we have not had any particular tune in mind. As you had noticed we are very much into the visuals and try to make the visuals united with our music, so making a video is something we really should enjoy doing. We have plans to work together with a woman; her name is Ulrika Carlson. She is studying to become, what do you call it...? a photographer for movies. She has really good ideas and we have worked together with her before when she took care of the lights on our live performances. If I should pick a tune now to make a video of I thing I should take 'Madelene' that I mention about before, or another tune that will appear on the new album. After all you always feel most for the tunes that has been made recently. How I would represent it is hard to tell, I have many ideas but as for everything else concerning our music we had tried to mirror our music as good as possible and tried to bring our expression further with the elements the video gives.

As your music ranges from sweet/ sorrowful orchestral ambience to harsh industrial I gather the musical field you would draw inspiration from would be quite extensive. What styles of music do you listen to and which bands/ groups have gained your attention recently?
Yes, we have a very broad music field within the group. I listen to a great variety of music and I thing that is important to be open-minded, one reason is that if you don't, you miss so much great music and I think when you create something artistic it is good to be open-minded. So as said before I listen to many different styles. I have grown up in a home where classic music had a central place and I have been listening to classic music since then. I listen to everything from hard heavy metal to ambient dance. If I should mention some of the music I listening to now, you have Hans Eklund a modern classic composer, Neurosis, Neubauten, Radiohead, Portishead, Blackhouse, and a band called Delta Files that I had the opportunity to see on a festival in France where I joined Mental Destruction. I must say that I been listening very much to Mental Destruction's last CD "Straw" lately. For me it is very important that the band have a very good hand with the sounds they create and that the rhythm is intelligent and Mental Destruction sure has that element.
With such diversity, maturity and complexity displayed on your releases I gather that the members would have been involved in other projects in the past. How did you first become involved with industrial/ ambient music and how did you progress to your current workings within Sanctum? Furthermore, do any of the members of Sanctum have formal musical or compositional training?
Yes everyone in the band has had one or more projects going on. But I don't know how I became involved in the industrial scene. I/we have no intention to be an industrial band, you can say that we became one when we agreed working with CMI. It was at this time I got involved in the industrial scene. I got in contact with the ambient scene earlier and have been a "musician" (am I a musician!? ;-)) for almost 12 years now. I have always been atracted to the elements that is contained within the ambient music. When I started it was not called ambient, I think. The reason way Sanctum has become reality is because of the above mentined band nov com It was in that band Hakan and I started to work together. But we started to feel that it was to many limits in that band, and we had already started to work on a project called "Pale Session" where we used music and visuals. Pale session had a performance caled "Totale age" that you can say is the mother of Sanctum. At this time I also worked together with some theatres, doing music and soundscapes for plays. I brought some of my work from

these plays into Sanctum. Concerning our musical or compositional training, Lena has taken some vocal courses and Marika is studying music now (espessialy the cello). Hakan has no training behind him. "Unfotunately" I don't have any training in composition either, besides that I have done this for a couple of years now. I feel at this point that t could be of use, but I also think that you should have a solid ground to stand on. To know what you want atchive with your music, without that musical training could bee a trap. I often see musical trained people waist there creativety because they are limited within their training. Like I mentioned before Hakan and I had a group together with two other guys and we have also done some other more project based happenings. I have, like I said before done some music for theatre and I have played drums in a couple of bands. Hakan play keyboard in a hardcore band called Counterblast. Lena has never been into this kind of music at all, but has sung in some "cover bands" I don't know what you call them, but it is a band that plays tunes of other artists. Marika has played guitar in a band in the goth scene and drums in a Latin-American band. Hakan and I have this project together with our live-soundengeneer caled "The year of the Parrot". I'm working on my own in a 45 min composition at this very moment. And then I have Cromedragon together with Andreas Matsson.

I hear that you are currently involved in the production of a sound score for an exhibition. Can you elaborate on the actual music and the nature of the contribution to the exhibition? Further, will this be made available to those who what to experience it who are not able to attend the original instalation?
The tune or the soundscape was created for and photoexhibition, it was the artist Mattias Wreland that had taken the pictures and they were taken in a factory where the exhibition took place. This was back in 93 I think. This factory was shut down and a cultureproject was started in some parts of it and the exhibition was a way to mirror a past time in the factorys history. It was great to work on mirroring this pictures with sounds, I really admire his work. The idea to do something with the soundscape arose about a year ago, Sam (Mental Destruction) and I discussed the exhibition and the works I had done for it. Sam thought that I should do something with it. When I listened to it (which I had not done for a while) I thought that I had to rearange it a bit and the rearangements have grown to something completely new. There is not much left of the original sound. I'm confused if this is bad or good, I really enjoy to work on the tune and I think it can turn into something great. From the beginning I had the intention to include so-me of the artwork on a possible cd-cover but now I don't know the music differs so much compared to the original. The music can maybe be described li- ke this, slow-harsh-neoclassic- industrial mu- sic. I really hope that I together with Ma- ttias can work out some kind of

collaboration to join the music and the visual, the time will tell.
A new project of yours has also surfaced under the know how "TYOTP" work when they create their music you get a hint on the meaning behind it, I think hmm.... I don't know. It is hard for me to explain the music of TYOTP if I make it easy for me I would say Strange-industrial. I really hope that it will be avalible for those who are interested in a near future.
Are any of Sanctum's members able to involve themselves in music as a full time occupation or do you have the standard type jobs/ careers so as to support your musical endeavours?
No unfortunately not, we all work or are studying
What are Sanctum's current plans for the future and are any new releases currently in works? Will you remain signed to CMI or have any other labels shown intrest?
We work hard on the new full-length album. I hope CMI is still interested.
Do you see your future music further exploring the sounds and themes on your debut or will you branch out and explore other musical ideas which were not previously touched upon?
I hope that we can bring our sound further and also explore some new grounds, now we have found a sound that we like but we still have the intention to do just what we like to do so it is hard to say where we are going to land.
As I have been made aware that the new CD has been delayed due to the members being located in different places for study purposes when can the finished product of your second full length be expected?
I really don't know, but I hope in a near future.
I will now finish this interview here but is there anything you would like to be said before we conclude?
I hope that the one who read this will listen to Lupus In Fabula and maybe they can join us in our journey. And I will thank you and your mag for showing interest in Sanctum.

Envy
Sed Diabolus in invidia sua Istud arrisit
Una nullum opus Dei Intactum dimisit.

Only the Devil laughed honour to scorn
In his envy he left no work of God untouched.

Benny Neilson, (better known at this point in time for his previous works as Mortho(u)nd who released three CD's on CMI) has returned with his new musical formation otherwise known as "Hazard". With one CD 'Lech' already under his belt (out on Malignant Records), Benny is pushing the definitions of minimalistic ambience into more 'active' realms than his current contemporaries. With 'Lech' having received praise in it's respective genre the upcoming Hazard CD's will surely give Benny the same acclaim as what Morthound received.

To begin this interview I guess I will have to ask some inevitable historical questions relating your previous musical project Mortho(u)nd. How did you first become involved in music and the industrial / ambient style?

I have always been messing around with sounds since I was little brat! I remember hearing a Klaus Schutze live concert on the radio. I guess that was my first introduction into ambient type of music. Later on me and some friends discovered bands like Neubauten, DAF, Cabaret Voltaire, NON, Laibach, Zoviet France, Nurse with wound, SPK, Big Black, Sonic Youth... Ordered records from Staalplaat and Cold Meat. The compilations QED and A Bead from an small mouth was the two most important records for inspiration.

Why did you choose to end Mortho(u)nd? Even on the Karmanik Collection CD (before the release of your 2nd & 3rd CD's) the bio tended to hint that you where going to end the project (quote: "I present to you the last feature made by Morthond"). Was this in fact the intention or was it related to the changing of spelling of Morthond to Morthound?

I was tired of the project and wanted to start up a new one.

Exactly what does the name Morthond/Morthound mean and what was the reason for the change in spelling?

To separate the first things from the later ones.

After the release of the 3rd & last Morthound disc there was a slight break before you resurfaced under the Hazard moniker. After the conclusion of your first major music project did you always intend to continue with making music?

Yes, I'm completely devoted to this. During the break I did some other things, like wasting my time in a couple of bands. Gained some hearing loss.....

Can you describe the intents and purposes behind Hazard and how do you see it differing from Morthound?

It's more abstract and intense, hypnotic, feverish, almost close to explode or..... implode. Try to stretch time and space, the usually stuff!

Your debut Hazard CD was released by the upcoming label Malignant Records. As your previous works were released predominantly on CMI did you specifically choose to find a new label for you new project? Was CMI at all interested in releasing the debut Hazard disc?

Yes and no. It happened that way, I guess it's the way it worked out. I even continued doing some thinking while recording. Some of the tracks were meant be as Morthound but since CMI didn't like the stuff, I was fed up and decided to leave the label. Then I sent some stuff around and also to Malignant/Jason who was very positive about it.

The CMI compilation "The Absolute Supper" featured a new Hazard track (titled: Who blew out the northern lights?). Was this included as a tribute to the label and your past works on it? Are there any plans in future to return to the label?

I didn't know that I was to be included on that CD, I sent some stuff that's all. I don't make plans for which label I gonna do recordings for. Anyway, I think that I'm to surreal and minimalistic for CMI.

What is the meaning behind the above mentioned song title and it at all related to some sort of northern European "pride"?

No, there is no special European pride. We are as much assholes as anyone! Such things just makes me wanna throw up. The Northern lights are beautiful to watch at though.

The track titles on the debut Hazard CD "Lech" do not seem to follow a specific concept. Do the titles represent what each track is about?

Only in my head, I would prefer to not use them but at the same time I think that it can add some extra sense to it.

Most of the time you choose to remain anonymous leaving your music at the forefront. Why do you choose to do this and do you portray any actual meanings, concepts or ideas with your music?

I got some concept ideas for a couple of records, Like more field recordings and such stuff. I'm a big fan of old elevators and fan-systems and generators at the moment.
Track four on the CD "Wrapped in Plastic" features a voice stating words that via some technique gradually morph into another word. How did you achieve this unusual effect?
I changes the start point of the loop sample gradually, by moving the modulation wheel slowly forward.

experimentation?
Yes..
Latest news would have it that you have been commissioned to produce soundtrack material for an Australian film maker. Who exactly is the film producer and what types of films will you be working on? Did this interest in your music evolve from that individual hearing your compositions? Will you have free rein over the music you produce or there guidelines you must work within to create

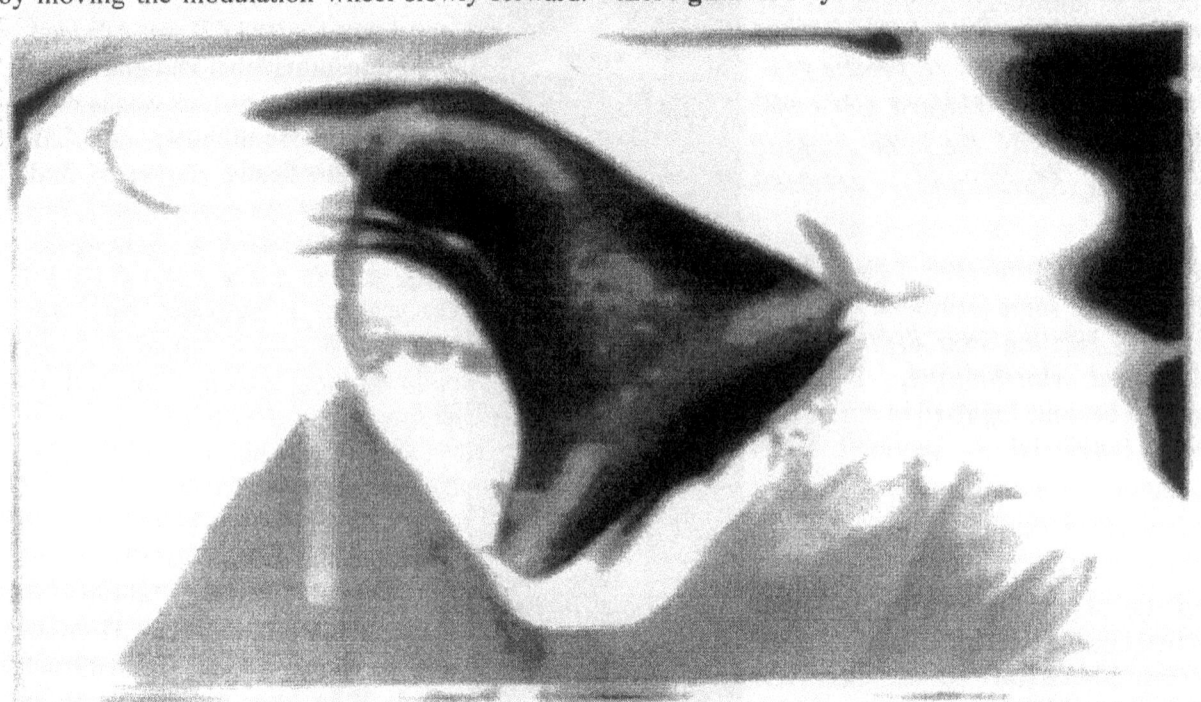

How has the reaction been to your new incarnation, is it predominantly the same audience as before. How many units have you managed to sell of the "Lech" CD?
Around a thousand copies. I don't know if I have reached a new audience or not.
Could you say that there is there a typical type of "fan" of you music?
No, Please let me know!
As your "music" would not consider traditional in the true definition of the word how do you go about producing it and what types of equipment do you use?
I use anything that can produce or reproduce sound: Analogue synths, Samplers, Bass guitars, Guitars, Pedal boxes, Wood, Water, Generators, Metal, Elevators, Radios, Paper, Glass, My own voice, Other peoples voices...and so on. I start with an idea, then collect the specific sounds I think will fit in. Records it onto an Sampler, Macintosh and/or the A-DAT. Mess around with it for a while until the sounds have found their place in the mix, then mix and record it. A very old school way of working.
Do the tracks evolve out of specific ideas/ compositions or do they evolve from improvisation and

music for a certain scene/ passage? Will the music be recorded under one of you group names or will you choose just to use you real name?
They had heard the Karmanik collection CD and liked the Morthond track so much that they wanted to use it in their movie called "Bloodrush" I don't know any more about it because they seems not to be able to manage to send me any copy of it. Tricky people. I don't wanna lose energy for nothing. So if anyone has got a copy of it please send it to me.
Would this be your ultimate goal to pursue music on a full time level?
It would be ok to work on it full time for awhile. I'm working now on some music with M Stavöstrand from Inanna/ Archon Satani on some TV-scores. Which is fun because we can do what we want (Almost).
You are currently collaborating with Lina of Deutch Nepal on a side project. What is this project and what style/ form will it encompass?
It's Psycho Kraut amongst other things..
Can we expect any sort of release from this collaboration?
We have recorded a few hours of material that is going to be a couple of records. The first is an old collaboration between Morthound/ Deutsch Nepal. It´s

about a Boy called Richie Beacon who kills his parents and then fly out of the window. Out soon on Lina's own label: Entartete Musikk. About the second one I don't know. It has got some Nico covers on it and some really nice atmospheres. A release year or label is not decided yet.

There was rumor that a new Morthound CD has been recorded. Is there any truth to this and if so do you have any plans to have your two projects running side by side? I started on it but got bored. However I have started some other projects / collaborations. One with Rich and Christie from Orphx. We did some recording when the played in Stockholm. It turned out really good I think. Then there's some other unfinished stuff, I record alot of other groups in the studio where I live & "work".
Hazard has performed live on a number of occasions. What is involved in playing live? Do you play recorded tracks or new improvisations? Do you utilize any sort of stage prop installation as part of the performance?
Mainly new improvisations even though I have certain passages I have to get through. No installations so far but as everything else I'm working on it. It's always tricky to do something interesting live with this sort of thing. The gear is Guitar, Microphones, Metal, Loops and loads of effects. It tends to be very droney.
It would appear that 1998 will be quite a prolific year for you as there are three CD's planned to be released under the Hazard moniker. Are these albums yet recorded and who will have the privilege of releasing them?
First one on Malignant " Battery Slave"-Louder than the rest, Collection of live sessions from the past few years. Second one: "The law of a world without a future" on Cold Spring Records. It's more subdrone and ambient(That word again) Third one: "North in various capacities" on Sentrax Corporation, It is the best so far I think: Static, Hypnotic and...
As each Morthound album differed extensively while retaining certain styles/themes will this be the same case for Hazard? How do see the upcoming albums differing from the Lech CD and how will Hazard evolve and change in the future? Hazard can evolve in whatever direction seems interesting, We'll see.
What are your views on the current ambient/ industrial scene & the growing interest in it from other sub-cultures of music? How do you see it evolving and expanding in the future & how far can experimental scene go? The only way to survive is to mix genres and be open for new things or at least be aware of them. I do listen to a lot of music but seldom do I get surprised (until this year) when I got introduced in the Mego scene which I really really like. For the first time in years I've got that feeling of not knowing exactly what it is that you hear. It is a beautiful feeling.
What are your personal tastes in music? Fennez, Bowery Electric, Neu, Faust, Ashratemple, Sonic Youth, MX 80 Sound, Main, Tomas Köner, Project Dark, Jim O'Rourke, Nurse with Wound / Stereolab , : Zoviet*France:
Well thank you Benny for being a part of Spectrum's first installment. I will now pass the floor over to you to conclude the interview. Thank you and good luck with the mag. Cheers, Benny.

MZ. 412

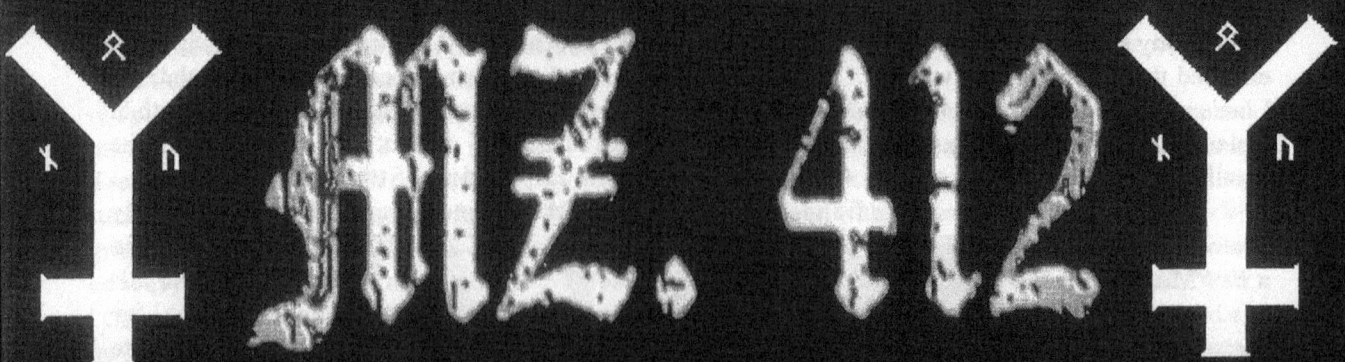

Mz.412 are one of those projects that have been medling in a few styles/ sub cultures of music for a number of releases, with quite interesting results. Below is the interview with Kremator the main vocalist for the group that was first conducted late in '97 and further updated in May 1998.

Mz.412 have been in existence for nearly 10 years but it has only been over the past 4 to 5 years you have again emerged as a major force In the industrial scene. What was the reasons for the groups dormant phase during the early 90's?
We had some difficulties with the line-up, and we lacked interest. people left the band for other projects and everything was difficult to maintain, so Maschinenzimmer 412 was not functional for almost 5 years...

Satanic symbolism plays quite a role in the bands imagery along with some norse elements. How compatible are these two concepts of heathenism and satanism? (as essentially one is an honor based life code while the other focuses on the destruction of all life/ mankind).
Our beliefs are in the development of mankind as a natural beast. We are basically just animals... And only the strong survive, survival of the fittest! We do not prefer the destruction of all life, just the unworthy, weak and dirty lowlifes. Satanism is more symbolic, representing the strong individual.

So it would be correct to assume that you are not childish enough to believe that there is in fact a real conscious entity named Lucifer? If this assumption is correct why not reject the term "Satan" (which is inexplicably linked to the bible and the Christian ethos) and simply focus on the extension of mankind through an individual belief code?
Well, I agree with you... but the term "Satan" is more a symbol of individuality than an entity with a pitchfork.

With your use the term "Satanism" and your somewhat extreme image, is it not that you are simply adhering to what others think a "Satanist" should be? Wouldn't it be more extreme in itself to portray "normal" everyday look/ image which would makepeople more susceptible to listening and understanding your viewpoints?
We don't look that normal/everyday anyway... and to be frank with you, I don't care that much what people think.

What is your opinion of groups such as "Ordo Equilibrio" that are clearly "anti Christian" however promote themes of love & peace to your close brethren?
To begin with i can tell you that i am a very dear friend of Ordo E. and we get along fine... they might even join us in the studio when we record the final pieces of the new album. "love peace and understanding" is great as long as you share it with your own kind.

Corpse paint also plays a heavy role in your imagery but as many black metal bands are currently choosing to drop its use, will mz.412 follow suit? Furthermore how important is the black metal image for the group?(considering that many other industrial artists choose to remain anonymous).
The image is not the most important, the music will always be the thing that counts. We will not drop the war paint as we prefer to be anonymous.

The latest offering ('burning the temple of god') delves into some traditional elements of black metal fused with harsh industrial noise. I also have been led to believe that the upcoming release will feature a heavier focus on the black metal elements. What was the initial reason for choosing to embark on this style?
Basically because we do the music we like... The new album, Nordik Battle Signs, will have some BM elements, but I don't think its going to be the main focus. We are a hybrid band, playing the best of both worlds............

I have noted there has been certain backlash against black metal in the past year or so. Do you think this may reflect badly on mz.412 being taken seriously in the long term as an in-

dustrial project, since you have taken aboard some black metal elements?
No, I think we will do fine whatever the "public-BM-opinion" is, we're still basically an "industrial" band (whatever that means).
It has been stated that a human bone drum was used during the recordings of "burning the temple of god". As it is not easily definable on which tracks this was used, was its use more related to the ritual aspect of the music's creation than the actual sounds it created? The bones used are from New Guinea and are made from the big hip bones (I think). Shaman Behemoth bought them on a vacation trip several years ago. They are used on "submit and obey" in the ritual we performed during the recording of this track. **The ritual aspect of your formation has cropped up a number of times when referring to the production of your music. What types of rituals do you form and have you had extensive experience with magic?** We do not like to discuss this subject as it is no ones business except our own. **Further to the above question, it is noted that when spelling words that you constantly replace the letter "c" with "k"? Is there any major significance in this and is it in any way related to Aleister Crowley's spelling of the word "magic" with a "k"?**
No, its just a nordik tradition. **With the vinyl version of "burning..." (due to length constraints) the track "vampiir of the north" was omitted. As this was one of the track that displayed black metal elements, why was this track dropped instead of one of the more traditional industrial compositions?**
That was Cold Meat´s choice, not ours... I would have preferred a double 12" gatefold vinyl release instead.
As you are the pioneers of a new genre/hybrid style of music do you believe other groups will follow the lead you have shown and if so what is you opinion of this?
There are already bands copying our style... As long as they do it good and not just are cheap assholes with nothing new or original to offer, its ok by us. Just remember who started it......
There has been mention of a collaboration between puissance and mz.412 to create a 20 minute track(from what i can imagine the results would be truly apocalyptic!). Is this still to take place and do the two groups have set ideas on what they want the track to sound like or will it be improvised in the studio?
Unfortunately we never recorded something together, but we are "partners-in-apocalypse" and I think that a future collaboration is not impossible. **Although in the cover of "burning..." It states that your role in mz.412 is vocals, are you limited only to this input? Also does any one single member have a pivotal role to play in the music's production?**
Basically we all do the music/rituals, but our main tasks in thegroup are the one printed on the album. **Further to the above question I believe that you obviously have a good understanding on how to create dark industrial music as you have your own side project/collaboration called "Kremator Nordvargr / Hirdman Drakh ".How will this project differ from the music of mz.412 and when is a release expected?**
The first "Nordvargr/Drakh" (northern dark supremacy) release will be released in the end of 1998, hopefully on some strange new CMI sublabel. It will be a limited vinyl only release. The music is more industrial/ambient than mz.412. I also have my very own projekt "volkssturm", which is more harsh noise Sado industrial. (if someone is interested in releasing it, please contact me! Serious (labels, please)).
As the collaboration is with the entity called 'Hirdman Drakh', who exactly is this individual and does he play a role in any other musical project that the underground would be aware of?
He is drakhon of mz.412....
I believe that the last time mz.412 undertook a live performance was in 1990. As it has been mentioned that ritual improvisations plays a part in your music's production, did this live performances reproduce recorded tracks or consist of new improvised compositions? Did you use any stage props or video footage/visual material and what

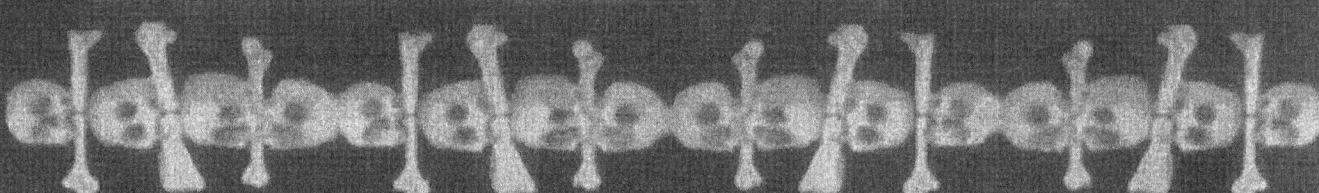

was the reaction of the crowd when you performed?
That live performance sucked.... There was no "special effects" or props involved at all. The music was partially improvised & partly on DAT.
Was this the live performance that was released as the first half of the "Macht Durch Stimme" CD by Dark Vinyl? Looking back at that live material are you still pleased with the results?
Yes it was. No, I don't like that recording.
Seeing that you have played live before do you have future aspirations to take to the stage again. If so, what type of a performance do you have planned?
We have no plans for live gigs, so we haven't thought much about it... but I guess it would be a bloody performance.
Previously it has been mentioned that the "Malfeitor" album from 1989 will be re-released. Is this still to occur and will it be re-worked for it's new pressing? Does any of the material on the "Macht Durch Stimme" CD contain any of the tracks from the "Malfeitor" LP?
Roger Karmanik told me last week that he is planning to re-release Malfeitor spring 1998... It will contain the original album + some old Unreleased tracks + maybe some unreleased new songs, time will tell. Yes, some of the live tracks on Macht... originates from Malfeitor, but the live versions differ from the LP..
The latest track you have released is the "n.b.s. act 1-begravning" track contributed to the CMI compilation "the Absolute Supper". This track appears to hark back more to the more slower & harsher industrial sounds of the "in nomine..." CD from 1995. Is this track represetative of the material you are preparing for your new release?
Yes and no, some of the new songs are slow, some are very noisy and some are very militant(!). In the above mentioned track a repeated vocal/voice sample is used. For those of us who do not speak Swedish (I gather that is what language it is) can you translate what it is saying?
Actually its in German. No, I will not translate it... I will not spoil the fun!!!
I believe that the upcoming mz .412 recording "Nordic Battle Signs" is currently in production. What can listeners expect from this new release in comparison to previous offerings? Also as it appears that the release will be a double CD (now for the all important question!), Will it be pressed onto vinyl?
Nordik Battle Signs will be more majestic and harsh than "burning...". Also, as menioned above it will be more militant. I hope their will be a vinyl release also, I just love vinyl.
This is one question I just had to ask!! On your web page there is picture of the mz.412 logo/symbol tattooed on your calf. Now that a new version of your symbol has recently been released what will you do with your tattoo?
There is no new symbol for mz.412, only for the album, so there is no problem with that. (besides, I wouldn't mind an other tattoo...)
Ok Kremator, than you very much for completing the interview, is there anything that you would like to say to finish up?
Thanks for your support, keep the faith in darkness and you shall never Fail!
Hail victory!

REVIEWS

Well, here we are at the obligatory review section where I get to air my personal tastes and general grievances in music for all to read and assess! Well apart from that, I hope that you will be able to read about a release that you might otherwise have never been aware of and be able to find something in it similar to what I have (I guess that is the ultimate aim of a review). Please note that no numbered/ star rating systems have been used. Each album can exist independently of another and not need to be converting to a common scale for comparison purposes...only the words and descriptions are of i m p o r t a n c e .

Also, for whatever reason if you do not agree with what I have written please do not write and complain...it is only an opinion expressed, as is yours. Some releases may seem a little old for a 1998 review, however that all depends on when they were written (originally intended for publication elsewhere), when I obtained it (my list of releases I want always out weighs my budget) and that I thought it warranted a review anyway (no better excuse with a debut issue). I have attempted to give all reviews adequate length as short reviews can never do an album justice, be it good or bad. You may also note that most reviews are positive, however there is specific reason for this. As I know what sounds I like, more often then not when I order something I already know what to expect, or at a minimum have been given a good recommendation. Here's hoping that record labels will come to the party to help diversify the contents of the review section for subsequent issues (and that others may want to also contribute reviews). For now read on and enjoy.

Allegory Chapel Ltd. (USA) "When Angels Fall" 1995 Charnel Music

Not being a huge fan of the overall noise scene I found this CD quite refreshing in its stylistic approach. While less intense and harsh than the previous cassette 'Demimonde Voices' this still owes a lot to its noise roots. On the opening track waves of mid range white noise swirls and evolves while composed keys are interjected giving a solemn feel. Track two "Trajectory Calculations' steps up a notch in harshness however retaining the swirling noise structure which is then continued into the next track (after a brief interlude provided by a short spoken intro). A highly processed voice makes an appearance through the waves and layers of sound with a young girl screaming "please let me out" which is quite unnerving in its pitch and intensity. Deeper noise elements in mid to low range embody track five "Escalate the Violence!" that is incessant in its more straight forward noise attack. The final track "Requiem for Thee Possessed" takes a more death industrial guise in it's low rumbling vibe and sampled female vocals. It then converts back to low harsh noise late in the piece, only for haunting female vocals to sweep the CD into a numbing c o n c l u s i o n . The width of sound has been well presented and the pieces of the total structure omitted from opposing speakers has been extremely well produced for an all encompassing effect. The contrasts present (via the use of both noise structure and composition) gives this a unique feel that works surprisingly well. Even without the more composed moments this release tends to hold more of a more listenable middle line that avoids the 'head fuck' scenario generally associated with noise.

Arcana (Swe) "Cantar De Procella" CD 1997 Cold Meat Industry

What can one say about Arcana that hasn't already been said?... like Dead Can Dance circa "In the Realm of a Dying Sun"....most anticipated debut album ever on CMI etc, etc.... Besides all this, everyone within this scene should know of or at the very least heard of Arcana's epic and sorrowful gothic classical music. Here we have the second CD from the duo and while it is a progression in overall sound from the debut it is again somewhat of a let down as was the case with the first album. I don't know if it is just me, but I have held this group in such high regard since their first few compilation tracks that I think I have come to just expect too much. Anyone thinking I am speaking poorly of this is clearly getting the wrong idea as this is truly a superb release. The dynamics of the songs gradually build as does the intensity of the male and female choral vocals which rise to soaring heights. Some tracks are based on the sounds and motion of the voice alone while others use the full epic structure of an orchestra especially focussing on the brass, wind and string sections. Two tracks here were also featured on the preceding 3 track MCD, but I guess that was always intended to be a taster for this full length (too bad I got stung the price of a full length for a 3 track single CD.....). All of the 12 tracks presented tend to focus on the one theme and expand on it slightly over an average track length of 5 to 6 minutes. Maybe this is where the problem lies in that the tracks do not evolve and change enough to take the listener on the epic medieval journey that they so often promise, but somehow fail to fully deliver. I'm sure if the musical ideas and themes were merged over fewer songs Arcana would deliver an absolute masterpiece. Stand out tracks include the title track, the medieval folk tinged "the Chant of Awakening", "The Dreams Made of Sand" All that is left to be said, is that one must wonder why the more talented an artist is, the more critical the fans are.......... As the reader you know the answer to if this should be included in your collection.

Archon Satani (Swe) "The righteous way to completion" CD 1997 Cold Spring

Archon Satani (Swe) "The final way to completion" 10" Pic disc 1997 Cold Spring

I have chosen to review these two releases in one, given that the tracks were recorded at the same time. These works essential form the final ever recordings from this notorious group (although older works are scheduled to be re-released in the future). Since the early compositions of Archon Satani as a duo, through to the split and solo continuation of the project, it has become more minimalist oriented. (note: Tomas Peterson left to later form Ordo Equilibrio and Mikael Stavostrand formed Inanna and also continued with Archon Satani). Treated waves of flowing sound rise and fall in a subtle rhythmic style (ala Thomas Koner) however these releases see the introduction of repetitive looping beats (not dance beats of course) at various points in the tracks. These tend to break up the monotony, as there is not a hell of a lot happening over the combined 70 odd minutes of music. The passages where the beats are not utilized is somewhat like being trapped in a deep subterranean location where the only audible sound is the bedrock of the earth slowly being warped and cracked by tectonic forces. Overall I tend to prefer the earlier works of Archon Satani as a duo which where more varied and had a much more engulfing dark atmosphere. This point is further substantiated by the quality of the Archon Satani track featured on the new CMI compilation 'the Absolute Supper'. This track saw the reformation of Archon Satani as a due to record one final (and great!) song as a tribute to the ultimate completion of the group. The members will now lay the Archon Satani legend to rest and to continue with their respective projects. Although I would not consider these to be the releases to be introduced to Archon Satani by, they would be a worthy addition to a music collection for anyone who has prior knowledge of the groups music. (note: the 10" is almost in certainty sold out by now as it was limited to 500 copies).

Archon Satani (Swe) "Memento Mori" CD & limited picture LP (399 copies) 1997 Memento Mori
Well, here we have a historic release from when Archon Satani were still a duo with the music being taken from a live performance on the 25th of May 1991. The music itself differs to the groups other studio outputs as the recording in essence is quite harsh. When I first obtained this on LP I figured some of the rawness of the sound was due to the vinyl format, however when I also picked this up on CD the harsh rawness was still present.
Mid range harsh frequencies hum along with cavernous factory sounds, rhythms and noises reverberating underneath. Distorted vocals sporadically make appearances while each tracks flows forth merging into the next composition. Tracks "Insane with fear", "Ritual Murder" & "Hymn of Despair" make up the first three tracks which are all worthy live performances of material from the Virgin Birth (Born Again) CD. To my knowledge the remaining three track have not been included on other albums (however I could be proven wrong!).
Track four "Pater Miles" (when it gets going) has a bludgeoningly heavy rhythms with vocals and sounds buried underneath. "Lost Souls of Eden" (track 5) gradually builds with the echoed drum sound, vocals and vocal samples to a passage with sampled choirs to then fall back to the repetitive drum loop and sampled classical radio tune and mid range frequencies. The final tracks begins with a sparse sound that again build to a harsh rhythms/ tune with what appears like radio static introduced into the mix. At 35 minutes this a reasonable short, disc however it remains as a document to the early death industrial scene giving those of us who will never get to experience such groups live a chance to at least hear what it would be like.

Blood Box (USA) "A World of Hurt" CD 1998 Malignant Records/ Katyn Records
If the name of this group sounds slightly familiar it may be that you are thinking of 'Yen Pox', and not without good reason. Jason Hensley the name behind this project is actually half of the ambient/ drone group 'Yen Pox'. Whist being on a solo mission Jason treads on familiar ground covered by 'Yen Pox' but also tries to ensure that 'Blood Box' has its own character and quality.

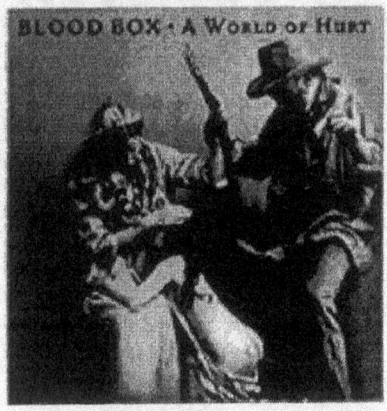

The opening track 'Paradise' is stylistically 'Yen Pox' all the way, except for its focus on slightly more electronic/ keyboard feel. Track 2 gets even more electronic with its make up of sampled and treated sounds meandering and evolving over a 10 minute span. 'Mother of Dust' includes a sampled spoken passage, whilst track 5 'Dawn of the Hunter' sees a composed keyboard passage and sampled acoustic guitar used to good effect which then employs a minimalist neo-classical passage to round out the song. Both themes of electronic and organic styled dark ambience are further explored over the remainder of the album. The final track 'inhale' is a short and strange piece of distorted factory noise/sound which actually sounds more akin to the latest Vond CD.
As has been said previously this CD is less organic and more electronic than 'Yen Pox' having an overall more disturbing undercurrent that can aptly be aquatinted with the release. Highly recommended dark ambient passages with other influences thrown in for good measure. The only other thing I can say about this CD is regarding the strange image that was chosen for the cover.... make up your own mind.

Brighter Death Now (Swe) "Innerwar" LP 1996 Cold Meat Industry (CD on Release)
Mr R. Karmanik the brain behind CMI returns with his project to torture us with themes of moral decay and decadence. On this album we find Roger in a very angry and aggressive mood. For those who are unaware of the music of BDN it is generally termed 'death industrial' using horrific low ambient noise and percussion periodically being punctured by unworldly voices and chants. "Innerwar" is quite a departure from previous recordings, much more into the realms of noise music and power electronics but still retaining a structured industrial edge through repetition and looping drones. In this respect I feel it is one of his strongest releases to date. Overloaded looping drones grind on incessantly some at a high pitched velocity others at lower levels but no means less powerful. Sampled voices make periodic appearances throughout the record, some audible others indistinguishable. The track entitled "Sex or Violence?" in brief seems to sum up the themes behind BDN quite well. Further more side two opens with the track "little baby" which includes a sickening intro of a teenage girl recounted sexual abuse as a young child. This track obviously is in reference to the picture on the back sleeve which has a young girl reclining in a somewhat sexual pose (For those who prefer gore images the CD version is definitely for you, having select napalm and autopsy slab photos). The finally of the album comes with a track entitled "WAR" with an extreme and distorted voice chanting the word over and over accompanied by the trademark overloading looping noise.
As I have the LP version I have been told that it does not pick up much of the high end noise present on the original recording. If this is true all I can say for anyone who chooses gets the CD version prepare for your ears to bleed!

Brighter Death Now (Swe) "Pain in Progress" CD 1998 Cold Meat Industry
The master of death industrial returns with a re-release of his first tape (CMI 03) ten years on as a tribute to the legacy of BDN, and what a release it is! Seven of the fourteen tracks made up the original "Pain in Progress" tape while the remaining seven are included for our pleasure/ torture taken from various compilation contributions from the late 80's to early 90's. Although being a decade old the tracks here still sounds fresh and undated and at its time "Pain in Progress" would have been milestone release. Although the current workings of BDN are moving towards power electronics/ industrial, the sound of this disc encompasses a more slow death ambient/ industrial style. Much here is in common with an earlier tape/ CD release entitled "The Slaughterhouse" with slow distorted noise rumbling along with the trademark sparse sound and grinding metallic rhythm. Some distorted and ghastly vocals are interjected through a number of tracks as though announcing some unspeakable horror while other dialogue samples outline some of BDN's themes. The only complaint I have is regarding a track entitled 'meat processing' which has a heavy yet tinny mid paced percussive rhythm that is too up front and runs in contrast with the overall BDN sounds and themes. This track is repeated at the end of the disc with a slightly heavier mix but my main point of complaint remains.
The minimal black packaging is stylish and simplistic as an obvious homage to the original artwork which compliments the obscure nature of the project.
Now all there is to do for the BDN completeists is to look forward to the final completion with the release of "Greatest Death" CD. (This is essentially a compilation of tracks from the "Great Death" trilogy of which those owning all three parts were able to vote for their favorite tracks).

Caul (USA) "Crucible" CD 1996 Malignant Records
Well "Malignant Records" have done it again proving that there is much more to the ambient scene than what CMI has to offer by releasing the debut CD of the dark ambient artist Caul.

The works of Caul delve into minimalistic ambience as well as more structured compositions. The 70+ minute CD is quite filmic in nature and could almost be described as background music to the haunting elements of motion pictures. Subtle melodies, low droning percussion and haunting chants flow effortlessly throughout the length of the disc. The opening track 'Aurora' is a short dark ambient piece which flows into the next track which has slow rumbling percussion with floating noises and vocals siting in the mid range. 'Behold' contains again sparse noises but this time with violins holding the feel and flow of the track. This concept of using strings is used in the following track 'Reduviid' and other subsequent tracks. The heavier mid paced percussion of 'Cluster' breaks the predominant feel of the proceeding tracks while the music stays stylistically the same. Comparisons can be made to the more minimalistic works of Raison D'être while the dark ambient elements lean towards Lustmord. Once again another great album to create dark atmospheres for those appropriate times.

Caul (USA) "The Sound of Faith" CD 1996 Katyn Records
Hot on the heals of 'Crucible', Brett Smith is back with his second CD release under the 'Caul' moniker. Opening with a very 'Lustmord'ish brooding passage, the CD crawls out of the depths of the void with desolate organic sounds and processed synth atmospheres over a seven + minute span. Track two launches into a short composed piece with plucked strings, chimes and marching rhythm. Track three 'Nature and Grace' takes the same string sounds to continue the themes of semi-composed and minimalist compositions over the CD's length. An overall religious type aura surrounds the music with space and distance being a common aesthetic between the dark ambient tracks and more composed ones. The tunes where present in certain passages remain sparse in delivery, conveying a somewhat dreamlike state. For want of a better comparison (or due to shear laziness) Lustmord's name invariably comes up with the 'deeper' elements of the disc. (To be fair this release does have a character of it's own, I just guess that minimalistic and dark ambient music always tends to have that common thread normally associated with the long time standing works of Lustmord/ Brian Williams). For me this disc slips up and lets me down with track eleven "Ankou" which is a full on "new age" style piece complete with sampled doves in the background. Apart from this "The Sound of Faith" is a strong body of work but has a little way to go before I would class this classic.

Caul (USA) "Reliquary" CD 1997 Eibon Records
Continuing the trilogy of reviews this is Caul's third CD, and I must say it has finally reached the level that this project has hinted on over the first two CD's. Overall the vision here is more focussed which has resulted in a more composed body of work. This is not to say that the dark minimalistic passages have been totally forsaken of course. Textured and layered synth passages act as the undercurrent while slow melodies are accentuated by piano keys and other sampled string and wind instruments. All in all this has a less "new age" feel than the last disc overall being darker and bleaker. Some of the passages here are quite reminiscent of some of Graeme Revell's Hollywood soundtrack offerings, with the works from the movie "the Craft" partially coming to mind. Track four 'A sigh is the sword of an Angel' focuses on a deep percussive rhythm with a haunting oboe tune and waves of atmosphere rising in the background. Track five 'the soul rising out of the vanity of time' is more in the dark ambient vein but also quite a bit more active that the standard type track in the genre. The pinnacle of the album is reached in track seven 'lights in the firmament of heaven' where the slow plucked tune bursts into crescendos of soaring angelic voices. The themes of dark ambience and minimalistic classical music are explored throughout the remainder of the disc with even some slight middle eastern influences fused into a few of the melodies. The packaging in itself is quite different with a get black slipcase that folds out into a fiery picture of cloud landscape. Caul are one group to keep an eye on as the prolific individual behind this project already has another couple of discs in the pipeline for upcoming release. I look forward to them.

Cernunnos Woods (USA) "Awakened: the Empire of Dark Wood" 1998 Cruel Moon International
This disc was meant to have seen the light of day all of 2 to 3 years ago but has only surfaced at the beginning of 1998 for unknown reasons (This was meant to be first off the mark for Cruel Moon International but ended up being their third product). This CD takes guise under the form of medieval/ folk styled ambience that seems to be forever increasing in popularity since the rise of the Mortiis empire (and I mean both concept & business!). Although this lacks extensively in the realms of full compositions and well executed instrumentation (incidentally this is all produced on the keyboard) it most certainly makes up for these areas in atmosphere. Horns, flutes and drums trudge forward with Bard Algol narrating stories through a number of tracks. For an American the spoken vocals come off especially well with flair and without a hint of a cheesy accent. Some tracks (ie: track four) don't work well at all as playing seems out of time and all over the place, however other hit the mark perfectly with mildly stirring and majestic pieces. I must also fully complement the digi-packaging that suits the music perfectly in its portal of a medieval atmosphere via photos and drawings. As I hear the entity behind Cernunnos Woods is now unhappy with this release in light of when it was recorded and in reference to current compositions. If this is the case all I can say is I look forward to future recordings.

Coma Virus (Usa) "Hidden" CD 1996 Side Effects
What can one say when it comes to the dark ambient genre? At the moment there are some truly great artists working in this field as is shown by some of the other reviews in these pages, with Coma Virus being no exception. As Lustmord is primarily Brian William's brainchild, he however does gain input from other people - one being Paul Haslinger. On the same note Coma Virus is primarily Paul Haslinger who also gains input from Brian (not to mention both Coma Virus and Lustmord are signed to the same label). Confused yet? Well for another interesting fact Mr Haslinger was a once a member of Tangerine Dream, so it certainly shows he has been in the ambient game for some time now. Coma Virus sits in the same realms as Lustmord frequents but does have a charm of it's own.

Self Abuse Records

Dealers in Extreme, Abstract, and Unusual Sounds Worldwide.

Write for our free Catalog, or check us out on the web at
http://www.mv.com/ipusers/selfabuse

Self Abuse Records
26 S. Main # 277
Concord, NH
03301, USA

When I first heard this I actually thought it was a Lustmord release using a different name. But with close concentration on the music, it tends to be more rhythmic and composed. The standard dark ambient elements are included, being sparse spacious sound, deep evolving rumbling noise and subtle melodies. Amongst the rumbling ambience keyboards have been mixed in (disguised very well) akin to a half remembered tune being played in the dark recesses of the mind. Dynamics are also important with the levels rising and falling in volume throughout the metamorphosis of the disc. Only four tracks are present but with a play time of fifty minutes the tracks range in length from seven to fifteen minutes which directly points to the slow evolving style that it encompasses. Vocals make an appearance on a few occasions but are used in a low chanting manor or have been electronically distorted so no actual words can be deciphered. Concept wise the release uses the theme that any creation of the mind can be considered a virus as it can only exist solely within the host. The theme is elaborated on in the cover with a very thought provoking passage. While other dark ambient artists use ideas of 'deep space' Coma Virus uses the ideas of the inner spaces of the mind and when viewed from this perspective while listening, it is truly fascinating. As always I am truly in awe of how this dark ambience is created as it is so far removed from other forms of 'music'. Both Coma Virus and the label Side Effects will be of great interest for any fans of this genre.

C17H19NO3 (USA) "Terra Damnata" CD 1996 Fifth Colvmn Records
For anyone who is fanatical about In Slaughter Natives yet is frustrated by the slow progress of J. Havukainen in recording I.S.N CD's, I urge you to get a copy of this. What we have here is foreboding compositions that span electronic and orchestral realms which have mutated into a supreme blend of apocalyptic industrial. The themes and sounds presented on this release are quite foreign to what is normally associated with it's country of origin, being much more akin to a European release. Sampled voices and processed vocals interjected throughout, outline the concepts of the merging of man and machine, via a macabre evolution of the human species. Gothically influenced the orchestral compositions and atmospheres are presented in an eerie and at times a quite romantic guise. Owing a great deal to the paths previously forged by I.S.N, all comparisons are easily forgiven when apocalyptic industrial is done this well. Watch out for the upcoming CD scheduled for a late '98 release on Malignant Records.

Darrin Verhagen (Aus) "Soft Ash – Seven treatments of lethal atmospheric inversions (with a drifting narrative sense)" CD 1997 Dorobo
Now the title of this CD says it all…only to an extent. Darrin Verhagen, better known for his works as Shinjuku Thief has produced this concept CD under a solo guise. The actual concept of the disc is the common thread here, as the music contained over 48minutes/ 7 tracks has more the feel of a compilation. Darrin has taken inspiration from six historical points in time where humans have suffered death from airborne pollutants – from the killer fogs of 19th Century London through to Chernobyl. Further each track has been composed in a specific style, from isolationist, electro-acoustic, organic to romantic. Each track also has a recommendation for a listening volume depending on which style it was produced in. The opening track stylistically comes across like Tomas Korner while tracks two and three resemble more radio static in low frequency tones. Track four (composed under 'romantic') comes across somewhat like Shinjuku Thief's "The Scribbler" CD with a poetic spoken interlude included. 'Chernobyl' (track five) is highly active with it techno/ tribal beats, while things calm down on the final two tracks. Track six is a low fi atmospheric piece that has utilized a basis of field recordings of thunder. The final track is filed under 'organic' with an anti-structure of simple and repetitive tapping sounds that are gradually overlayed to create a more complex beat pattern. This CD commands close concentration from the listener and does not work particularly well as background music, given its changes in direction from track to track. It is good to note the growing interest in experimental forms of music as two of the tracks were actually commissioned by the Australian Broadcasting Corporation (Government based TV/ Radio) for a program called "The Listening Room". A highly interesting concept CD with the cover living up to the look and presentation of the label.

Decree (USA) "Wake of Devastation" CD 1997 Decibel/ Off Beat
This is another gem of a release that I probably would have never been made aware of if it wasn't for the strength of recommendation that came from Malignant Records. This CD walks a fine line between harsh noise, death industrial, dirty techno and industrial (in the industrial 'band' type definition). Spanning 45 minutes over 10 tracks & consisting of both live and studio recordings, this is an immensely strong release that is varied yet relentless in it's approach and delivery. Starting with a track "Delusion" this is quite apt in misrepresenting what the CD is like in it's entirety. A strong mid paced dirgy techno beat surges onward with sampled noise flowing throughout the mix. Track two continues in much the same vein however the mix begins to get slightly harsher with the integration of aggressive processed vocals. The noise element becomes much more evident in track three "Who Dares?" in the form of a live instrumental recording where the noise flows in a mid ranged region with a reasonable depth of sound. The cavernous sounds of the beginning of "Madness Unveiled" gradually increase in intensity (that when played at high volume) surely threatens to destroy the undeserving sound system which the CD is being playing on. The driving machinelike rhythms, processed into a barrage of sound (while being kept coherent by the undercurrent of bludgeoning beats) draws certain comparisons to the likes of Stratvm Terror & Mental Destruction yet not being derivative of any group in particular. Ultimately heavy in all aspects of the delivery (related to the genre's covered), this comes as highly recommended release.

Desiderii Marginis (Swe) "Songs over Ruins" CD 1997 Cold Meat Industry
Sometimes I really don't understand the rational behind the release schedules of CMI. I had been waiting for this since 1995 when first hearing the track of "…and even wolves" CMI compilation CD, however this disc did not see it's release until mid to late 1997. Even CMI made a statement to the effect that "it had taken them ages to release this and that it should have been out much earlier considering the great response it got". I can only hope that the wait for the second disc is not as long! Of the music herein, much harks back to the CMI sounds of the early 90's, which in itself is quite refreshing. Of anyone familiar with the CMI sound will recognize the trademark Swedish industrial/ ambient sounds. When I first heard this I knew next to nothing of the individual behind this project and still know relatively little (not that this should affect the music of course!). To put it simply this CD reminds me of a mix of raison d'être's early CD's mixed with the darker sounds of Archon Satani's 'Virgin Birth' CD. All of the necessary elements are present, dark flowing rhythms, choirs, bells and undercurrents of minimal orchestral compositions. Apart from the obvious influences this is a very strong disc with multitudes of its own character. This would have to rate as one of my favorite ambient/industrial disc's of '97 and originally I even felt that it was bounds ahead of the new raison d'être CD (I now consider both albums to be on the same pedestal). All I can say is that I am getting a little sick of CMI doing it once again!

Drape Excrement (?) "Born Dead" LP 1995 Art Konkret
Taking a leaf out of the Brighter Death Now camp this is 'death industrial' at its darkest presented here. Deathly heavy and dense noise drones slowly on with tortured and distorted vocals buried under many layers of sonic sludge. Some tracks utilize sampled voices (which don't really make reference to anything in particular), while each track tends to sustain a certain style over their short lengths. Again the comparisons to Brighter Death Now are to be made with this sounding somewhat similar to the "Great Death" sound (however I might ass that at times this makes B.D.N sound sonically 'clean'). 'The Lost Age' being the first track on side two is quite impressive with its overall depth of sound being more akin to the Lustmord style of ambience. The simple styled black and white LP cover compliments the obscure music with scattered images of religious decadence and decay. I will say that this is not overly a highly original release due to the obvious sources of inspiration but in this circumstance I won't hold this against the project when it is done this good.

Each Dawn I Die (Swe) "Notes From A Holy War" CD 1997 Dark Vinyl Records
Have you ever brought a CD simply on the strength of the members works in other groups? Well this was the case with this CD. The two members making up this project had previous workings in or are currently part of Megaptera, and with a title such as this one I thought I could not go wrong. All I can say is that this disc is so far from what I expected! The closest description I can come up with would be 'weird Euro-

pean electro/ ambient music' if that is anything to go by! At first I really disliked this, as it was not what I had expected but as I accepted it for what is was its true potential was realised. The concept of the album is based around the Spanish inquisitions and the witch trials of the 14th Century with the original inspiration being taken from the book "The Talisman of Death". The first track begins with a 'dub' style tune but a heavy bass kick keeps the beat dark and heavy. The vocal are done in a surreal talking manor describing a fantasy type world while the electo rhythms/ sounds float forward at a mid pace. Track two starts with an ominous and bombastic orchestration which could be compared to In Slaughter Natives however about 3 minutes into the song the music changes direction to a mid paced keyboard acoustic tune with deep/ clean male vocals. After another few minutes the track changes direction again where the music stops for two & a half minutes of text sampled from directly movies detailing the above themes. The tune floats in again for a short time only to return to the sampled spoken pieces. Once the music returns again a dark and brooding orchestral piece finishes off the track. Electro beats and rhythms return for track three to the point of if the music was slightly sped up it would constitute quite a dark dance track!. Sampled text/vocals and again the electro beats make up the lengthy 10 minute track four where the music fades in an out through stages of text and music. The finally of the album is embodied in the 22 minute track 'Trader of Life" where the overall feel is more ambient although background looping and beats give it a 'driving' feel as it gets into a 10 minute groove. Low fi ambience filters in for the middle section before the electro elements return to complete the disc. This release is definitely not for everyone and no doubt by reading this review you will have a good idea of if you would like this sort of thing. Although 'Notes from a Holy War' is not half as dark as I expected and does contain many non standard ambient elements, for me it is one obscure release I am glad I found.

Endvra (Eng) "Great God Pan" CD 1997 Elfenbut
As you would realize by now by reading my reviews, for me the aesthetics of a release are just as important as the strength of the music (there is nothing worse than a great release with cheesy packaging). Well this CD packaging is no exception. Encased in a black gold embossed cardboard box, the jewel case CD comes with 11 tarot cards whose graphics are truly dark to behold. And after all of this the music also measures up - what more could you ask for!? Endvra have certainly been busy over the last few years but the funny thing is 'Great God Pan' was their first CD to be recorded but was released as their fifth CD in 1997, some four years late. The infamous individual behind Candlelight Records delayed the CD by two years before Endvra severed all ties to find a more suitable label. Misanthropy Records came to the party but due to the rearranging of that label and the setting up of the side label 'Elfenblut' the disc was further delayed. As the CD represented the groups first major effort I initially was expecting a release which would show a group in their formative stages of composition arrangement but after hearing it, I feel that this is their strongest release yet. Some remixing and reworking did occur but ultimately the songs have remained the same. By far it is there most orchestrated release with dark totalitarian compositions mixed with dark brooding ambient moments. There is a definite archaic, mysterious element to Endva's sound which could be put down to the groups interest and involvement in magick. This element is emphasized with the track 'Hymn to Pan' being adapted from a Aleister Crowley poem. The disc open with a dark orchestral marching type track with a large emphasis on the heavy beat. Track two slows down slightly but continues in essentially the same feel. Track three 'Dark Face of Eve' has angelic soaring female vocals together with low male vocals and a dark undercurrent flowing through the song. Continuing on minimalist ambience with vocal chanting constitute track four 'the sickening skies' The spoken piece which constitutes the vocals for 'The truth is a sharp knife' are made even more convincing as the liner notes states that they were recorded on Holy ground - within Durham Cathedral. An almost 'baroque' feel is embodied 'Saturn's Tree' with the light overture and deep string sections. The finally of the fifty five minute disc comes with bombastic 'The Battle Song or Endvra' with a deep type vocal chanting words in the background. This release has certainly found the middle ground for the mixing of orchestrated industrial and minimalistic ambience. Endvra are definitely one group that all CMI fanatics should be taking notice of.

Hagalaz' Runedance (Nor) "When the trees were silenced" 7"ep 1997 Elfenblut
Here we have an essentially a solo project of Andea Myer Haugen aka Nebelhexe of the now defunct Aghast. Anyone expecting a rehash of the ghostly atmospheres of Aghast will be rather taken aback by this 7". Taking on Viking folk aspect two slow marching type tracks are presented. The title track has tribal type drums with female vocals and a choir in the background with a light acoustic tunes added for atmosphere. Side two basically again consists of Andrea speaking/ singing while the drums and choirs drone in the background with the tune also being carried with a folk violin. All in all not at an amazing release but worth a listen if the ambient/ folk thing is for you.

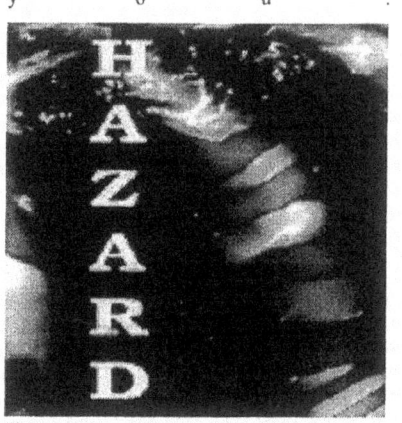

Hazard (Swe) "Lech" CD 1997 Malignant Records
For those of you unaware this is the new project of Benny Neilson, infamous from theMorthound project of a few years back. Since dissolving his last project Benny has since resurfaced with a new project and new vision of where he wants to take his music. When first hearing this, it would be advisable not to be expecting a reincarnated Morthound. However if one had to compare this, it is more along the lines of the highly minimalistic work of 'This Crying Age' and the more low droning tracks off 'The Goddess how could make the ugly world beautiful'. Low washes of sound are complemented by slow evolving percussion, while light textures of melodies are interwoven into the sound scapes effortlessly. Liquidous motion and hazy electronic treatments exemplify Benny's overall vision of a surreal dreamscape. Certain parts threaten to evolve into more harsh sound scapes however this never actually eventuates. Light dreamy dub like rhythms emerge sporadically but tend to only meander in the foreground in an effort not to be totally dominant. Dualities in sound are forever present with soothing and relaxing sounds being juxtaposed next to claustrophobic and suffocating atmospheres. Overall this is dreamy and surreal which makes it particularly hard to review track by track as it works best as a complete body of work. Hazard also promises to be quite prolific with a number of new releases scheduled for this year and if his track contribution on the CMI 50# compilation is anything to go by Hazard should expect to go far.

Ildfrost (Nor) "Natanael" CD 1997 Cold Meat Industry
Well Ildfrost return with their second CD although admittedly I did not get to hear their debut effort. However I did hear one of their tracks of "...& even wolves hid there teeth" CMI sampler CD (which was quite good I might add). I do know that originally Ildfrost consisted of two member, one male, one female. On this disc it appears that the female member has left the fold, leaving the male counterpart to keep the Ildfrost flame alive. Now what about the music I hear you ask. Well all in all the music held within in not overly dark but more akin to orchestrated sorrowful/ dreamy music. The primary instrument is the keyboard but it is used in such a fashion that a rich sound is attained, being almost real (well as close as you can get in my book). The fourteen tracks flow forwards at a slow pace over fifty seven minutes, but periodically burst into moments of symphonic crescendos. The instruments include the full wind and string section of an orchestra, bells, timpani's, marching drums etc giving the release a very "classical" type feel. Vocals are included in most tracks where the delivery is presented in monotone style, with the male voice talking in a European accent. The vocals are quite low in the mix and have a slight echo effect on them so following what is being said becomes quite difficult. In this respect the vocal tend to just blend into the background of the music as it flows along. The start of track three sees the Norwegian Black Metal influence infiltrating the music with some horrific high pitched shrieks. All in all I think the use of these vocals somehow undermines the validity of the release and in my opinion it would have been better to leave this out altogether. As the group does not have any real distinctive ties with the Black Metal scene, those outside of it would not understand such vocals thus the screams are likely to work against the release more than in its favor. Not to say that Ildfrost is music only, the packaging is also quite brilliant. It is presented in card gatefold sleeve (like a mini LP cover), but there is also a written booklet inside the gatefold. Now it is this booklet that is the interesting part. Not

only does it have the lyrics it also has a written conversation between two individual discussing the ideas and philosophies behind the work of Natanael. This approach I found refreshing as it is not simply someone preaching their ideas. Furthermore it also gives the opportunity for arguments and questions to be raised within the conversation. This is as much the same way that Friedrich Nietzche present his philosophies in "Thus Spoke Zarathustra" by means of storytelling and the trials/ situations that Zarathustra faced.
Again another fine release from the Cold Meat deli!

Iron Halo Device (USA) "The Collapsing Void" CD 1998 Malignant Records
The names associated with this Iron Halo Device CD (namely Stone Glass Steel & Phil Easter) have been familiar to me for awhile however I had not heard any output from the said project/ artist. After hearing this CD I most certainly will be searching out some of the related releases! If it wasn't for the opening announcement that the disc forms a live performance (and the first one for that matter) I would have never picked it This has to be one of the most well conceived and executed live performances for this genre that I have had the fortune of hearing. Opening with quick paced rhythmic percussion and doomy layers of background rumblings and textures, these gradually take over as more and more layers of suffocating swirling sounds are introduced over a 12 minute length. From a audile sense you have to take this a full piece of work as there are no breaks between sections other than the segmented pieces denoted by digital track insertion points. The merging of sampled sections of music, beats, instruments and vocals are juxtaposed perfectly with the artists own contributions to piece together a flawlessly flowing piece of live art. Static yet flowing deconstructionalist ambience, doomy bass riddled industrial and composed rhythmic electronics are just a few of the descriptions that come to mind, but by no means does this come close to doing this justice. There is just so much going here that my mind is spinning! Harsh yet beautiful, extreme yet calm, subtle yet energetic - the music has so many facets to it. The live portion of the disc fades out after nearly 50 minutes leaving me feeling numb and detached wondering what the section of the CD will present? Taken from home recorded demo's from 1995(I would hardly class this material as 'demo') the second part is also broken up into four 'tracks' Not as openly energetic, the tracks take a more straight forward doomy, ambient industrial route whist travelling at a slower to mid pace. At one point I do believe I picked a noise sample has been taken from Lustmord's "Heresy"? I might be wrong on this but it sounds awfully close to the unearthly wails on the said record. Some truly heavy sections of slow orchestral keyboards help to elevate the foreboding atmosphere of "The Expanding Void" whist a textured and electronically treated vocal sample cuts in and out of the mix during the beginning passage of "Red Memory". Leading the disc into its conclusion is the electronically treated ethic/ middle eastern inspired sounds of "A Passion Vessel". The packaging is top notch (also coming from the genius behind this) and has a particularly interesting excerpt from a court case where it appears that Phil was subjected to a court trial for alleged breach of copyright regulation(related to the sampling and deconstruction aesthetic technique of his music production). For an artist who deserves much wider recognition than he actually has you wonder why a corporation would bother? I gather that both the artist and label would have risked further legal persecution with the issuing of this release, therefore I commend both for being brave enough to bring this to the masses(albeit however selected those masses actually are!). I am truly glad I have experienced the sheer energy and power of Iron Halo Device.

Lustmord (Eng) " Strange Attractor/ Black Star" 12" 1996 Plug Research
When I ordered this I was only really buying it for its collectors value not for the music. That being said, the reason I did not expect much was that I assumed that the sparse dark ambience that Brian Williams presents would be lost amongst the static of an LP. Boy was I wrong! This has to be the most powerful LPs I own (and the artwork suits the release perfectly). The two track present are extended remixes of some of the material from "Where the Black Stars Hang" CD however some source material from an earlier release "Heresy" has been mixed in. For those unfamiliar with Lustmord, he does not create music as such, but dynamic flowing and evolving darkness. Track 2 (black star) totally blew me away first listen and is undoubtedly one of the most apocalyptic pieces that Lustmord has produced thus far.
Words can not even come close to describing the all consuming darkness of this release thus it is best to leave this review short and obscure like the mastermind behind Lustmord.

Macronympha (USA) "Intensive Care" CD 1998 Self Abuse Records
Now before I begin with the review I will make it known that I am not a huge connoisseur of the noise genre so any points made here are purely from my stance on this style. This disc is one of the first perks that I have gained since starting this magazine, with this promo CD coming my way after doing the rounds looking for advertisers. To start with I can say that this lives up to what I have come to expect from noise music, both from a sound and visual perspective. The full colour 10 page booklet has various morgue and hospital patient pictures intermixed with extreme pornographic imagery. Obviously these have been used to present the 'music' for their shock value (they certainly hit the mark there). And what of the sounds? Well the 72 minute disc is broken up into 4 'tracks', but you are hard pressed to pick the change from one to the next. This is to say two things - one that they generally sound the same and two – that each track is all over the place in terms of focus and direction. The basis of the noise is extreme in its delivery with full on obliterated frequencies and electronic squeals in a mid to high pitched sound range. The attack is incessant and brutal with little let up, apart from a few lulls to give the listener a short lived reprise before it hurtles headlong back into 'headfuck' territory.
As was said before I feel that this lacks focus as it sounds as someone is flipping through channels of static frequencies on a radio. Some parts hint at becoming structured with looping noise only to change just as quickly, moving off on another tangent.
I may have not fully got the point with this style but I guess if simply extremities is the basic concept behind this, structure and direction become incidental. One thing I do find interesting about this music is just how do these artists go about creating the noise in such an angry guise? For anyone more versed in noise than I, would probably get a real kick out of this.

Megaptera (Swe) "Deep Inside" MLP 1997 Slaughter Productions
Here is a limited mini LP from Megaptera that features one unreleased track and two tracks that were previously featured on two Slaughter Productions Compilations.
Track 1 "Brian Ghost" (being the unreleased one) is heavily rhythmic with a variety of treated sounds and almost upbeat percussive sounds. This track is quite a lot more straightforward in style than the haunting atmospheres I have generally associated with Megaptera. Track 2 "Lurking Fear" does not disappoint with its more classic type Megaptera sound and structure. Washes of sounds rise and fall gradually building giving off the exact impression of the tracks title. Midway through the sounds become more structured as the track consolidates itself into a slow coherent atmosphere.
The last track (being also the title track) begins with a more 'wet' floating type structure which is more sporadic in its delivery. A sampled piano tune makes a brief appearance before the track again lurches back to the sparse void of ambience. Towards the end of the track some angelic chorale vocals and injected into the mix along with some rantings of a religious nut. The packaging of this goes to show that now all 'dark' type music needs to be encased in black. The white foldout sleeve is complimented with a simple grey boarder and the obligatory pictures of mummified bodies.
This is one of just a few current Megaptera releases that will surely propel them to the front the dark/ death ambient genre – a position which has wrongly eluded them thus far. A worthy addition to any record collection.

Megaptera (Swe) "Curse of the Scarecrow" CD 1998 Release Entertainment
The CD first conceived and recorded back in 1995 has finally seen its proper release and not a moment too soon (don't the cliches make you sick!). Opening with a highly atmospheric yet extremely bass heavy track called 'Disturbance', this adequately sets the tone for the 50 minute CD. Claustrophobic swirls of sound merge and evolve while ultra slow pounding beats reverberate underneath. Track two is slightly more focused with a slow machine like drone gradually making way for more clattering sampled sounds and slow beats that aptly reflects the track's title (Cog-Wheel Machinery). 'Don't Desecrate the Dead' (track three) ups the stakes yet again forging headlong into some the most foreboding death industrial that has ever been produced. Taking a middle line with sustained tones and a repetitive beat/ sound the track is broken up with sampled voices taken from one movie or another. Sampled choral voices also make an appearance giving the perception of being part of the proceedings of a macabre church gathering. Things are toned down on the title track and, being more minimal death industrial with obscure vocal samples included and partially buried in the mix. During the track 'More Disturbance' in amongst the swirling atmosphere and voice samples a repetitive middle eastern type tune plays out its part as the track gradually builds in intensity. The remainder of the album does not disappoint keeping the flair to the well worn death industrial structure, using intense atmosphere and repetitive clattering noises and beats. The cover art suits the CD perfectly being presented in black and silver featuring various images of skull/ bone collections. The most unusual thing about the photos is that they appear to have been taken inside a church with the bones and skulls being the major focal point of the interior design. Strange indeed! All in all a great CD that should get Megaptera the recognition that they duly deserve.

Necrophorus (Swe) "Yoga" 10" Pic. Disc 1997 Yantra Atmospheres
The always productive Peter Anderson (of better known Raison D'etre/ Stratvm Terror fame) has returned for his second release (after a debut CD) under the Necrophorus moniker. As much as I liked the debut CD I found it patchy in places and some of the vocal treatments got slightly on my nerves. Nevertheless the sounds presented on this vinyl are much more to my liking. For a bit of background, this item is actually released on Peter own label, with this being his first product. Drawing away from predicable inspiration Peter has dedicated this 10" it to his dog with some of the source/ sound material actually having been taken from his pet! Further tribute is shown to "Ronja" by being featured on both sides of the picture vinyl!! As for the music this generally fit in the slow minimalistic school, with washes of sounds and strange noises flowing and evolving. Track one begins with manipulated sounds with a minimalistic rhythm structure which flows forth for about five minutes. A this point a rising/ falling 'spacey' type sound sample is introduced which extend to the completion of the track. Track two is basically an extension of track one in style & sound except it has slightly more going on with the movement of the atmosphere. Towards the middle to end of the song a light middle eastern composition is overlaid to good effect. Generally both tracks follow a similar construction (titles Yoga 1 & Yoga 2) and could potentially make up the one composition if included on a different format. In reference to the source material some of the strange noises that I could detect in the background included his dog breathing, eating & pushing a food bowl around on the floor! As much as this sounds like it wouldn't work it gels surprisingly well. (I guess no one may have picked these sounds if Peter hadn't announced this was dedicated to his pet). Anyway, anyone interested in getting this better move quickly if they want to obtain this as it is limited to only 315 copies!!

Ordo Equilibrio (Swe) "I4I" 7" Pic. Disc 1997 Cold Meat Industry
Once again CMI never cease to amaze with the artistic production of their products. This picture 7"EP is impressive enough with its runes, roses and symbols, but you are also treated to a full colour sleeve. Both tracks included on this are exclusive to this release and showcase two sides to the 'Ordo' sound. Track one ("In the grassy fields where the world goes to sleep. We kissed this world Goodbye") features the always impressive basis and inclusion of a repetitive acoustic guitar to build the backbone of the sound. Keys, noises & sampled sounds complement the acoustics and monotone male/ female vocals. Track 2 ("War for the Principle of Balance. Nature seeking Equilibrium") is more sparse and focuses on a more post-industrial approach which comes across as quite moving and anthemic. Beginning the track are bell chimes, slow snare beats and commanding spoken vocals which then breaks into a militaristic semi-composed neo-classical tune only to fall back to the beginning structure. This format of the song is repeated throughout it's five odd minute length. My main love in Ordo Equilibrio has always been the use of acoustics to build atmosphere and this release further cements their brilliance in this style. And finally the title represents "eye for eye" and not 'one hundred & forty one' as some have coined it!! Oh, and limited to 1313 copies of course.

Ordo Equilibrio (Swe) "Conquest, Love & Self Perseverance" CD 1998 Cold Meat Industry
Well here we have it, the long awaited third sermon from the male/ female duo Ordo Equilibrio. And where have they chosen to take the listener with this release? Their disdain for the Christian faith has not been dulled however they have further expanded on their interest in S& M via their lyrics. Thirteen tracks are showcased here over a 50 minute span however this time all of the tracks feature lyrics and vocals. This is as opposed to the previous two CD's that had ambient/ industrial passages intermixed with more composed tracks. Opening with a foreboding horn section and looped laughter a marching snare drones on whilst the spoken monotone vocals of both Chelsea and Tomas present the lyrics in a cold and unfeeling manor. The acoustic side of Ordo is presented on track two with the looping acoustic riff and light keys filling out the sound. Track three expands on some of the ideas explored on the first album, with the cracking of a whip utilized to form part of the sample rhythm used. The acoustic track found on the previous 7" is featured here, being a good inclusion due to its sheer quality and atmosphere. The track from the CMI 50 compilation is also included, however has undergone a slight remix with an echo effect on the vocals being the most obvious part. In my opinion this is the epitome of Ordo's sound and will remain one of my favorite tracks that they have produced thus far. Track 8 ('The blind are leading the blind are leading the blind are leading the blind') is quite up tempo with its looping industrial beat and repetitive vocal lines and tune. In amongst the honing of their sounds some more folk elements have made an appearance in the form of folk marching drums and the use of a mouth harp on one track.

With the cover artwork we are treated to a somewhat humorous 'band' photo. The picture shows a naked female on all fours with a skull and red candle balanced on her back whilst Chelsea (holding an teddy bear) and Thomas (holding a whip) are kneeling behind her. The front cover shows a picture of Chelsea dressed a school girl posing with dagger and lollipop (with a black background, red roses and the Ordo logo filling out the visual). Although the CD is not as progressive as I may have initially hoped this is a solid CD that remains focused throughout its entirety without loosing its direction. Another essential items for your CD collection.

Proiekt Hat (Swe) "Lebensunwertes Leben" LP 1998 Cold Meat Industry
Here we go with a review of quite an obscure release from the Cold Meat camp. Admittedly I know next to nothing about this project however when it was billed as 'old school Swedish industrial' I could not resist. Overall in structure this is very minimalist 'factory' styled industrial. The record starts with a mid paced semi distorted machine rhythm that flows forward but does not really get anywhere over the distance covered. Track 2 'Dislocator of the Souls is probably my favorite track as it is a bit more structured in the B.D.N style and sound. The next track is more cavernous than its predecessors that rounds out the first side with a short and slow piece of ambient industrial. The second side starts with a lo-fi distant rumble

with more mid range sound rising and falling in the mix over a lengthy track. The final track of the LP remains slow moving but has a more electronic feel with some laid back soothing yet harsh type noise(if this was sped up and more forceful it could possibly pass for power electronics). The tracks that make up this release are taken from various recording between 1992-97 but if these tracks have ever appeared elsewhere is anyone guess as there is little to no information included on the sleeve. Glancing over the artwork it is easy to see why it is limited to 500 hand numbered LP's. It would be guaranteed that any politically correct individual would most certainly take offence to the anti-Semitic cartoon & symbol, photos of abused children and a person of the 46+2 variety. Overall this LP is good however I find it slightly unusual for CMI given their current directions of releases.

Orphx (Can) "Fragmentation" CD 1996 Malignant Records
Orphx taking on a tribal power electronic/ death industrial guise this remains one of the interesting CD's that I own. Sounding like a small piece of many groups it is blended together suitably to be able to retain its own character. A very "B.D.N" styled track opens this with the low rising factory industrial vibes and processed vocals. "Layers of Dura" has static harsh and heavy beats that are produced to the point where the whole mix threatens to collapse under the heavy distortion. Text and spoken word passages float somewhere in the middle of the mix being indecipherable amongst the infernal clatter. Early mz412 comes to mind more than once especially during the heavy tribal beats of "Ekstasis", complete with its screamed and distorted vocals. Hard listening is abound during the start of "Sepsis" with its highly disorientating use of the balance dial whilst when it calms down to the percussion brings to mind the repetitive nature of some of Deutch Nepal's noisier efforts.

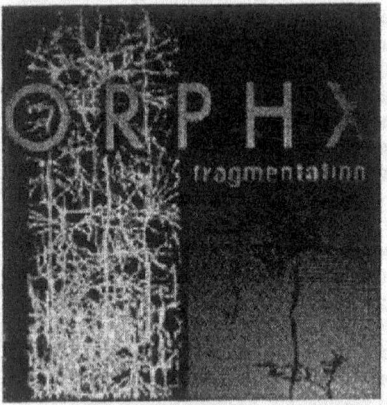

The screeching vocals of Christina and Richard are used in number of tracks to add an unnerving effect. While not being so up front & in your face they are mixed into the background of the aggressive tribal percussion and distorted electronic attack. There is some let up during lengthy 9 minute "Words Once Spoken" track where it takes a slightly nosier take on the Yen Pox styled drone ambience only to evolve into a full holocaust of fried frequencies. The final track hints again at the use of the drone ambient genre, which in itself is a relief after the ear damaged sustained from the preceding tracks. Throwing in other names such as Mental Destruction and Memorandum for further comparison this should be leading you in the right direction of what to expect. Being aggressive, punishing and repetitive, the music manages to retain its full focus of force over the 70+ minute length. This is music to be played loud for full harrowing effect.

Puissance (Swe) "Back In Control" CD 1998 Cold Meat Industry
Well, as the title suggests Puissance are back with their second full length offering and are supposedly "back in control". First off I will question to if the wait for this disc was worth it and sadly I must admit the answer is no. However this is not to say this is at all a bad disc. My major complaint is of the eight tracks only three are new. Two tracks were originally featured on their limited 7"EP "Totalitarian Hearts", along with their contribution from the CMI Anniversary compilation. Further, as the disc is only 40 minutes in length it seems a little short for the time frame between discs. Well anyway on with a review of the music. I will admit that there has been a definite progression since the debut effort with the duo delving further into a mix of militaristic

---

RED STREAM MAILORDER
DISTRIBUTORS OF AMBIENT, NOISE, DEATH INDUSTRIAL, EXPERIMENTAL SOUNDS AND OTHER GENRES OF EXTREMITIES.

SELECTED TITLES:
- **Blunt Force Trauma**-"Bled Out" CD (Malsonus) $14.
- **Coma Virus**-"Hidden Soul" CD (Side Effects) $14.
- **Deca**-"Phantom" CD (Old Europa) $15.
- **Endura**{UK}-"Black Eden" CD (Red Stream) $13.
- **Megaptera**{Swe}-"Curse of the Scarecrow" CD (Relapse) $14.
- **Nightmare Lodge**{Ita}-"The Enemy Within" CD (Minus Habens) $15.
- **Nightmare Lodge**{Ita}-"Negative Planet" CD (Minus Habens) $15.
- **No Festival of Light** {Swe}-"Enter the Realms of Satan" CD (R Eskimo) $15.
- **Of Unknown Origin**{US}-"Seven Ovens of the Soul" CD (World Serpant)$16.
- **Ordo Equilibrio**{Swe}-"Conquest, Love & Self Perseverance" CD (Cold Meat)$16.
- **Ruhr Hunter/Gruntsplatter**-split CD $14.
- **Wejdas**-"Wejdas" CD (Red Stream) $12.

AUSTRALIA: ADD $9 FOR 1-10 CDs. USA: POST PAID.

CREDIT CARDS ACCEPTED. WRITE OR E-MAIL FOR FURTHER INFORMATION ON ORDERING AND HOW TO OBTAIN A FULL CATALOGUE OF ITEMS.

RED STREAM
PO BOX 342
CAMP HILL PA 17001-0342
USA
FX: 717 774 3747
EMAIL: MAIL@RSTREAM.COM

AD DESIGNED BY SPECTRUM INC.

neoclassical orchestral music and dark industrial styles. The first track is a low-key industrial piece with some composition included in the background. The disc takes a leap forward with track two into a more composed orchestral track with heavy slow marching drumming and a slow moving yet stirring melody. As track three arrives I will crown it as being the best track of the disc (which was the same song from the CMI 50# comp). This song is a full classical piece that begins with a sad & somber tone but then periodically breaks into apocalyptic crescendos over its 5 minute length. Spoken word vocals are included in both tracks 2 & 3 which gives the listener some interesting insight into the philosophy of the group. Track 4 falls back in a dark minimalist industrial vein with vocal samples of a controversial nature being intertwined (i.e.: detailing subjects of recreational murder, torture, bondage, a police interview with the British serial killer who buried victims under the floorboards in his kitchen etc). As the samples are kept low in the mix and have a slight effect on them, half the fun is trying to make out exactly what is being said! Track 5 (also featured on the 7") is a great listen with is full distorted production, fast and heavy marching drumming and the ranting vocals. Much of the charm of this song lies in the sustained notes and sounds in the background with the heavy rhythm drumming moving it forward at a fast pace. Tracks 6 & 7 yet again play around with the juxtaposition of orchestral and industrial styles further cementing their own style and sound. The final track "Totalitarian Hearts" (which takes its name from the title of the previous 7" EP) will be very controversial due to the lyrics and I can say without a doubt they will definitely be misinterpreted. Again this song is an orchestral marching type song but has a more folkish element due to the accompanying flute tune. The vocals in this song are less commanding, possibly being even a little condescending in style and tone. In regards to the last line of the lyrics of this song, from my knowledge of Puissance's stance it appears to be at odds with other lyrics and ideas contained on the album. (As I don't want to fall into the trap of misinterpretation, give the lyrics in the booklet a read and see if you can determine exactly what I am getting at). As can be seen the album is basically split between industrial type tracks and neoclassical orchestral tracks. As much as this sounds like a contradiction in sound the two styles work suprisingly well. Although far from being a classic release it is yet again a solid offering from the Cold Meat camp.

Raison D'être (Swe) "Reflections from a Time of Opening MCMXCI" CD 1997 Bloodless Creations
I imagine that the upcoming Australian label of 'Bloodless Creations' would have scored quite a coup with the release of this disc. As the label is relatively unknown in the ambient field it would be an understatement to say that many other ambient labels would kill to have opportunity to release an artist of Raison D'etre's caliber. Somber sounds and dark atmospheres are what Raison D'etre does best by utilizing a deep spiritual undercurrent and dark twist on the catholic religious type sounds. Slow rhythms and beats are complimented by lush compositions that don't rise to spiraling heights but choose to keep a minimalist evolving tone. Predominantly this disc is a collection of Peter Anderson's early works when Raison D'etre first surfaced early in the 1990's. The majority of tracks were originally released by 'Old Europa Café' on an MC from a few years back entitled 'Conspectus', however the 8 tracks from this are mixed up with a 5 previously unreleased tracks. All tracks have been reordered and remixed to complete quite an impressive document of how Peter has evolved with his compositions & is a strong representation of both past works and future directions. A disc for fans of Raison D'etre and the Cold Meat Industry sounds alike.

Raison D'etre (Swe) "In sadness, silence and solitude" CD 1997 Cold Meat Industry
With little fanfare surrounding the release of this disc I was quite surprised when the promo disc arrived in the post. Before this time there was absolutely no rumors or mention of when to expect a new CD, but here it was! Peter has managed to be quite diverse with his releases while still encompassing the trademark sounds, with this disc being no exception (this is his 4th – not including the 'Reflections... CD). To say the music enclosed on the album is sparse is an understatement. Peter has definitely mastered the art of subtly knowing that what is left out is often more important than what is left in. Stylistically Raison D'etre has previously been reasonable composed, however this release sees a departure more towards the realms of dark isolationist ambience. I was very disheartened when first experiencing this to the point of writing it off but it wasn't until after five or so listens that I really began to appreciate it's sparsity. The backbone of this album is a flowing current of evolving sound (akin to Lustmord) that works on a multitude of levels. The sounds evolve and metamorphosise over the length of the disc with some more composed moments of keys, bells, rhythms and catholic type chanting sporadically placed throughout. It would also appear that some of the darker, harsher sounds have been influenced by another of Peter's side projects namely Stratvm Terror. Of the six lengthy tracks, track two is the most composed with it's mid paced rhythm flowing forward with lush keys and vocal chants. This feel is also again reproduced towards the completion of the album. This album is dark yet ultimately beautiful to the point of being indescribable, which one must hear to fully comprehend. Undoubtedly Peter Anderson's best work as Raison D'etre yet. (note: I only recently discovered that this disc is compromised of both live recordings and studio works – unbelievable!).

Sanctum (Swe) "The answer to his riddle" 10" pic. Disc 1998 Cold Meat Industry
What can one say about Sanctum? They are surely one of the most innovative bands within any genre of music at this point time as they cover so many styles and themes within their music. For me I do believe that there is a certain commercial potential for this group with their perfect mix of theatric music combined with enough industrial sensibilities and a heavy does of moving melodies. After such a stunning debut album as 'Lupus in Fabula' this 10" is a bridging release to their upcoming album. The title track here has also recently been featured on the CMI "Absolute Supper" compilation, which is easily their most commercially viable song to date. Beginning with a classical type vibe, when the track hits its industrial phase the powerful female vocals soar over the driving and distorted samples. Heaven forbid if I was to refer to this as 'pop' music buts that's exactly what it is in its own quirky way. 'Madelene' is the next track to follow that is more laid back and theatrical in presentation with strings and wind instruments making up the majority of the structure. A dark twist is taken in the song when earth shatteringly heavy beats enter and eventually take over the mix along with harsh aggressive spoken vocals and more sweet female vocals. Side two begins with a stunning remix of 'in two minds' (a track from the debut) to which I am still unsure to which version I like better as both are stunningly great. This is emotional industrial band music at its best. The final track 'euphoria' is almost a throw away piece as it is very short with a repetitive sample and vocal overlay. Not really worth a mention in comparison with what else is on offer here. Apart from the stunning visual presentation of the picture disc EP the cover is more artistically personal than CMI's normal output with its transparent 'tracing paper' over wrap. Might I add this is limited to 1000 so I suggest you act fast.

Shinjuku Filth (Aus) "Raised by Wolves" MCD 1997 Iridium
The nastier, dirtier and more technology & techno orientated alter ego of Shinjuku Thief returns with this second offering of a mini CD. The music contained within actually made up 35 minutes of the musical backdrop of the Handspan Theatre Company's show (also entitled 'Raised by Wolves') which was performed in Melbourne, Australia in October 1997. A harsh rhythm/techno type structure makes up the predominant sound however none of this is remotely commercially orientated. A certain 'junk' type style is evident with vocal snippets, sounds and samples entered randomly into the mix giving it quite an unstructured cut and paste sound at times. Heavy rhythmic techno drumming moves many of tracks along at a blistering pace with some distorted guitar saxophone and keys added in certain sections. Other tracks slow things down slightly with heavily manipulated distortion rounding off the chaotic mix of beats & sounds. Track six has a slight departure in sound more akin to the classical type sounds of Shinjuku Thief's 'The Scribbler' which morphs into a techno dub song towards the end. Taken out of the context of the stage show this release sometimes appears to be patchy and disjointed without the complimentary visuals, however there is still merit to be found within the music. Although mostly very removed from the sounds of Darrin's other works, this is nonetheless an interesting release and worth a listen if you are a little open minded to more varied sounds of a techo mix with a dark undercurrent.

The 3rd & The Mortal (Nor) "In This Room" CD 1997 Music for Nations
(This review may not be typical of the rest of the albums presented here but I still think it is worthy of a listen for those how listen to a wide variety of styles of music). Well, well. Since the departure of Kari Ruslatten after the bands debut CD this band have really changed direction and not for the worse I might add. Gone are the folk influence replaced by prog rock, blues and jazz influences. This is the bands third full length and the second with their new female vocalist Ann-Mari Edvadsen. (not including the MCD "nightswan") As fantastic a vocalist Kari was I feel Ann-Mari's style of singing better suits the type of music the band are currently writing.

Many of the songs have a floating, emotional feel to them and just meld one into the other like travelling in a dream. The track "So pure" sees the band in a full jazz mood with Ann-Mari experimenting with the vocals rather than just having the passive sweet female voice. This experimentation is taken further in the tracks "sophisticated vampires (to the point of being disharmonic) and "did you" which has her screaming in an aggressive voice asking "did you kill me, did you bury me?". On some tracks no vocals are present, with them simply acting as a musical bridge to float you to the next piece on offer. This makes the CD progress really well as a single piece of music rather than just a collection of tracks. Distorted & acoustic guitars, grand piano, keyboards, tapes, and samples (& drums of course) have been the main ingredients of choice but as the band have six members all active in the song writing process one can be assured they are not one dimensional. The music has a top notch production and the studio has been used extensively to produce a rich an diverse album that is not just a taped live representation of the band. I will admit this band will have lost many along the way from the more extreme scenes but they certainly won't shake me that easily. It is the bands willingness to experiment with influences and styles which helps them remain fresh and undated to my ears.

....the Soil Bleeds Black (USA)"The Kingdom & its Fey" DLP 1997 Cruel Moon International
Firstly to anyone thinking of buying this, act quickly and get the double LP version as it has 10 bonus minutes of music not on the CD, not to mention it being limited and the layout being heaps better. I'm sure not that many people are aware of this strangely titled group but anyone who knows a thing or too about the record label CMI will have at least heard the name. Most of the music on this release is not actually new to me as I was lucky enough to snare a copy of their two earlier tape releases (limited to 100 each) which comprised most of the tracks herein. The first time I heard this I was a little taken aback by the upbeat folky elements as I was expected mostly dark music akin to what Mortiis is doing. Over a number of listens the actual ingenuity is revealed. It is heavily based on synthesized percussion and melody but used in manor to express folkish beats, cymbals, horns, flutes, trumpets etc. All of the tracks are fairly short (there are 30 tracks on the DLP) but this means an ample amount of variety. Many different themes are explored through slower tracks but also many uptempo sections can be found. Male vocal in a talking/chanting style enter on a few occasions but there are also female vocals interwoven more periodically. The use of background sound effects and vocal samples add to the atmosphere and help carry the feel of a concept and story being played out. Admittedly this folk inspired medieval style of music will not be for everyone but if this review sparks your interest, do make an effort to seek out this unique formation.

...the Soil Bleeds Black (USA) "March of the Infidels" CD 1998 Draenor Productions
Back with their second full length CD (I hear that there has also already been another tape album and third CD, with the fourth and fifth in production) the highly productive ...the Soil Bleeds Black continue where the last CD left off. There has been minimal if any change in style, sound and production from the last album, thus the above review is still typically applicable. Background dialogue and sound samples used to illustrate battles and other themes have been sampled from Braveheart and other movies I can't pick. Bard Algol of Cernunnos Woods also pops up on one of the tracks with his distinctive vocalizations. Now for a couple of gripes. My main concern with this project is the lack of progression and sound between albums. If it is simply a matter of churning out tracks with little thought to constantly progressing, they risk loosing the interest they have generated thus far. Furthermore I wonder in it's current guise how far this style can be taken. Spanning 16 tracks over 37 minutes this is significantly shorter than the first album which questions if the amount of proposed albums could be shortened by consolidating material. These are just a few minimal concerns so if previous material caught your attention this won't disappoint. As with the last album the cover art is distictive and impressive strait from the hand of one of the members.

Trial of the Bow (Aus) "Rite Of Passage" CD 1997 Release Entertainment
After the exceptional "Ornamentation" MCD from 1995 Trial of the Bow return with their debut full length. In the few years between the two recordings it appears that the duo's stylistic approach to their song writing has altered slightly. While the MCD flowed together as a piece of ethereal/ tribal ambience the new CD seems to consist more individual tracks. Ten tracks are on offer all being of a different nature and theme while still using the common threads of middle eastern sound and structure. Trial of the Bow have managed to use the middle Eastern sounds to create dark brooding and emotional music without giving the feel of being in a Budist temple. A definite highpoint for the group is that no keyboards or electronic instruments are used. What is heard are the all real thing which gives a natural and authentic flavor that is so often lost with synthesized sounds.
The CD opens with the track "Father of the Flower" and is a mid paced tune with tabla drums, acoustic guitar, eastern and western string instruments and soaring background chanting vocals. "Ubar" is the next song which is slightly more up tempo with the basic structure being of percussion and wind instruments with the accompany again of an acoustic guitar. Track three "the promise" resembles the floating feel of the MCD in it's slow moving pace which has a cello brooding under the strong percussion. This theme flows into the next track "Serpent" this time with a sorrowful flute tune carrying the tune.
Track five is a departure from the other songs as for me is one of the highlights although it has the least happening. Being extremely hypnotic the songs floats along by the sounds of bowed instruments without using an actual tune. Notes/sounds flow into one another and evolve over the length of the 6 minute track.
Track 8 uses a recorded to my ears which sounds more of a Baroque style while the percussion remains firmly rooted in the middle eastern style. The finally of the album comes by the name of "Alizee" with it's deep reverberating bowed double bass rumbles while male vocals chant a haunting tune.
In comparison to the MCD many more themes have been explored with this release, but at the same time it seems the flow of the album has been sacrificed for the stature of the individual tracks. One theme will be experimented with but before you can get fully engrossed within it moves on the next track where another theme will be explored. In this respect repetition is avoided. This is a minor complaint on my part and by no means reflects on the quality of this release. Obvious comparisons can to made to elements of Dead Can Dance but Trial of the Bow have definitely managed to carve themselves a niche within the world music realms. It will be the darker elements of this group that will attract interest from the dark ambient and metal scenes but still an open mind is a definite prerequisite for this album. Great interest has been shown in this group in the international sphere but sadly they still remain relatively unknown within their home county. A definite shame if they do not gain the expose in Australia that they so deserve.

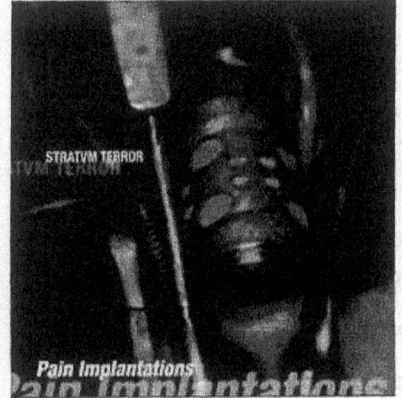

Stratvm Terror (Swe) "Pain Implantation" CD 1998 Malignant Records
Fresh off the press this is the brand spanking new CD on Malignant Records further solidifying the high standard of releases that has preceded it (Cheers Jason for provided me with a promo copy!). For those unaware this is the second CD from Statvm Terror, after the 1995 "Pariah Demise" CD and two previous tape releases preceding that. This project is a side project of Peter Anderson (better known for outputs as raison d'être) who works with another individual by the name of Tobias Larsson to bring forth the sounds of decadence presented here. Whilst Peter's out-

put in other projects has been sorrowful and beautiful this steers well clear of that territory driving headlong into inspiration derived from aggression and pain. The aptly titled CD "Pain Implantation" is probably a good description of the music, given the focus of the approach. Sparse and suffocating atmospheres float forth while distorted noise samples are injected, taking not so much a noise angle but a more sicken tone in their frequencies. This is an intensely harsh listen - but I do mean this in a good manor. While the previous recordings took a bit more structured pummeling rhythmic focus this has veered off into harsh electronic/ ambient territory. Selected tracks included sections of distorted industrial beats but this focus remains somewhat subdued. People familiar with Statvm's sound will find the distinctive tones are still present it is just the style has been slightly altered. The distorted vocals and voice samples of previous efforts are also absent, but in no way does this detract from the overall effect. The opener "Nerve Short Circuit" lulls the listener into a false sense of relaxation before the distorted frequencies leap out to reek havoc on the listeners cerebral area. The ambient noise of "Intravenous Pain Injection" whist could not be described as true noise, the ever incessant mid to high pitched static certainly reflect the track's title. Some parallels in the overall background structure can be made with the latest raison d'être CD, which gives rise to the question - which project is inspiring the other? There are no real standout tracks as all are of a high quality and they work well as a complete body of sound over a 70 minute length. This is pinnacle of technological decadence put to sound, being an impressive addition to the catalogue of the productive Peter Anderson & Co.

Various Artists (Wld) "Death Odors II" CD 1997 Slaughter Productions
Compilation CD's are always an unusual thing. On one hand they can showcase a wide variety of artists but can lack focus and direction. On the other hand the can work extremely well as a complete body of work, without appearing to have the contribution of many individuals. In the case of this release it falls somewhere in between. Common threads of sound and structure are evident but it also works well to showcase both known and unknown groups. Opening with a track "The Final Day": from 'Megaptera', I find it annoying that it is only an except as I have had the pleasure of hearing the complete track on a 'Fever Pitch' sampler cassette. Low droning base rumbles while minimalist monk type samples are interjected occasionally. This except version concludes just prior to the track exploding into rhythmic death industrial, so if you want to hear the track in its entirerty you will have to also purchase the "Beautiful Chaos" MCD! Up next is well know and respected 'raison d'être'. Using the 'less is more' concept Peter continues the themes touched upon on his latest CD. The track is quite minimal in structure with muti-layered slabs of organic sound and treated keyboards. The result is no less than what we have come to expect from this artist – a track which hauntingly dark yet extremely beautiful. The 'Deutch Nepal' track opens with a quirky keyboard melody with the input/ collaboration from 'No Festival of Light' being quite evident when a bass heavy looping sample comes clattering into the mix. This continues throughout the remaining 10 minutes while keyboards and the trademark distorted vocals of Lina pop in for a visit. All in all not a bad track but tends not to hold my interest for it whole length, given its repetitive nature. 'Archon Satani' don't do anything other than what has been showcased on his latest and final releases with a track of the trademark low-fi 'void' type ambience. Although quite standard still worthy of a mention. The next track "dark territory" being my first encounter with 'Negru Voda' (a Megaptera side project) I am highly impressed. What we have here is noisy and harsh death industrial at its best! Agonizing high pitch squeals introduce this before a factory noise 'beat' surges into the mix and are gradually overlaid to meld into pummeling finally 'Statvm Terror' (another raison d'etre side project) are included with an unusually titled track called 'Another Thong'. The project being more industrial and technology oriented, the track has quite a lot going on. With the basic structure of layered sound a variety of looping samples and mid paced beats blend in and out of the song's makeup. Heading into the second half of the disc the names of the groups become less familiar and I can't say I have heard any of their collective outputs before. For a quick rundown 'Soldnergeist' feature a pretty standard looping death industrial track with repeated vocal samples to boot. 'Discipline' take a more neo classical approach and although not a bad track, they have a fair way to go before this would stand up next to 'In Slaughter Natives' of 'The Protagonist'. 'No Festival of Light' have their own track included here and while their sound is fairly unique within the ambient definition (somewhat like early 'Archon Satani' but less orgainic and more beat/ keyboard oriented) it is not more than slightly above average. 'Memoria's' track seems to lack focus over the first half with sporadic factory industrial sounds, which is held together better when a 'raison d'être' type keyboard passage is used. From the second half of this track this might be a group to keep an eye on. 'Crepuscule' who hail from America sound distinctively European with comparisons to be made to early MZ 412, with a track of rumbling bass and tortured samples and vocals. Rounding out the CD is 'Keimverbreitung' from Italy with a cavernous ambient sound not unlike 'Tombstone' (also from Italy). Light tunes from a piano and wood wind instrument float in the background of the mix avoiding being the focal point. In conclusion this is a good CD which features well known and well worn artists amongst upcoming talent. With deluxe packaging this comes with a good recommendation.

Various Artists (Wld) "The Absolute Supper" DCD 1997 Cold Meat Industry
The reasoning behind this deluxe double gatefold digi pack release is the celebration of CMI's 10th anniversary/ 50th release. With 20 groups spanning two discs, 22 tracks and 2 hours & 14 minutes this could turn into a marathon review. This is exactly why I will try to keep this short and sweet! The whole range of CMI's "sound" can be found here from the lo-fi floating ambience to structured neo classical industrial through to harsh grating death industrial. The well know groups, In Slaughter Natives, Ordo Equilibrio, Sanctum, Puissance, Arcana, Mortiis, Raison D'etre, Brighter Death Now and Archon Satani all put in solid and impressive efforts. Newcomers to the label being The Protagonist, Sephiroth, Hazard, Megaptera, Frozen Faces and Nacht all have really impressive tracks. *(By newcomers I mean that they are new to having music released on CMI with their current projects- this also excludes the involvement in previous projects). The remaining groups Desiderii Marginis, Frozen Faces, MZ412, Deutch Nepal, Ildfrost and Cintecele Diavolvi are also worthy of a mention. All I can say is that anyone with no interest in the ambient/ industrial scene would still find something to like here. Priced as a single CD and with detailed information of the history of the label and groups included, you can't go wrong. Do not hesitate to purchase this extremely well presented and well realized release.

Vond (Swe) "The Dark River" CD 1996 Shivadarshana
Mortiis has definitely lost the plot. With all the hype that has surrounded him over the past few years it appears he has lost any inkling of self criticism. Here he is back with his second full length by the side project Vond. While normally

I have enjoyed Mortiis's previous works under whatever name, I can no longer say this is the case. He seems to be churning out whatever he records without giving it much thought to if it is of quality or not. This Vond CD has average songs (of the ones that sound decent sound more like Fata Morgana than Vond), shit vocals on two tracks and blatant mistakes in track 4 (take a listen, you can hardly miss it). The title track is an attempt at a dark ambient piece (ie no keyboards, just low rumblings, vocals and predictably the sound of running water). This comes off really weak and I find myself jumping for the skip button.

For a bit of advice Mortiis needs to simply practice his compositions a bit more before recording so he can get all of the keys played in time, not a milli second off (as is the case here), which has resulted in an amateurish sound. Hence again the comments on self criticism. Musically he can write good songs but stylistically and technically his playing of the keyboard leaves a bit to be desired.

Furthermore Mortiis obviously has not studied economic rationalism as he would realise that the consolidation of his projects would result in a stronger unit that is more varied and diverse. Granted not everything he writes would fit the music under the Mortiis banner, but having four side projects is testing the fans loyalty a bit much. Some will say this is great simply because it is from the hand of Mortiis (probably why Shivadarshana licensed it) but I am going to be more skeptical of his outputs from now on. I just fully hope that this disease is limited only to this second Vond CD and that Mortiis will prove me wrong with future releases, but at this point I am just fining it hard to swallow this piece of dross.

Vond (Swe) "Green Eyed Demon" 1997 Extreme Subterranea
After reading the above review of Vond's previous disc I gather you are wondering why I would even bother with this. When this first came out I had absolutely no wish to purchase this however when Jason at Malignant Records gave this a good recommendation I could not resist. (note: Jason has always had a general distaste for all of Mortiis's outputs, so when he said this was good I was willing to take this on face value). If anyone gave this to me to try and guess who it was, Mortiis would have been the last person I would have picked. Gone is the heavy keyboard basis replaced with a 'death ambient/ industrial' sound. The album is broken up into seven tracks with five being structured pieces with the final two being short vocal samples. The disc begins with a low frequency track that rumbles along with some sort of vocals buried underneath the various layers of distortion. The track also includes dialogue detailing the process

involved the electric chair execution of a condemned individual. This track is generally limited to a dark repetitive hum while although track two begins much the same ends up more varied due to the layered structure. Again a story/ dialogue samples of a necrophile/ cannibal/ serial killer is included which I believe was taken from an old movie entitled "Deranged". Track three ups the disc another notch with a cavernous sound complemented with a slow rhythmic foundation. Various vocals are again included to encompass a good effect. Track four "to the dreamer dead & the dreamer dying" is the closest this disc gets to previous outputs of Vond however the new styled dark ambient backbone is retained with light keyboards included as a backdrop. Further a 'Raison D'etre' like chant/ choir has been sampled. When this track picks up it mildy soars with its orchestral composition (which still has the slight Mortiis like sound).

It has been quite a while since music has really unnerved me however the final 'musical track' on this disc "(beyond hope): Hell starts Now" really hit a nerve on the first few listens. With its extreme blugoning layered vocals & sound it actually coming off somewhat like "Brighter Death Now's" new musical approach. This release (along with the new & improved sound and structure that Mortiis portrays on his track on the "The Absolute Supper" compilation) I can finally say that we will yet see some true quality from the Mortiis camp.

Wejdas (Lit) "Wejdas" CD 1998 Red Stream
Containing only three tracks over 47 minutes we are subjected to lengthy passages of unusual pagan/medieval/ folk styled 'new ageish' music. Starting off with a promising keyboard passage the scene is set whilst low chanting vocals rise in the background. After about 4 minutes this fades out to be replaced by various field recordings of "nature" sounds intermixed with light beats, sections of keys and slow drumming, treated vocals and other sounds, all generally kept to the background. They way this is presented gives the listener the feel they are listening to a movie without being able to see the images. The direction of the sounds tends to be quite sporadic and unfocused which doesn't help it to retain full interest. Heading to the 30 minute mark of the opener the original keyboard passage is reintroduced to take the track to it's conclusion. The shorter 10 minute track two has an unusual electronically treated rhythm that is not unlike some of the left of centre quirky tracks Deutch Nepal has produced. Remaining structured and repetitive the track cyclically moves through its sounds that sees a flute run included towards the end for good measure. The final track is very dreamy and new age styled complete with a sorrowful wind instrument passage. One gripe that I have is that I find the use of electronically created sounds tends to detract from the overall aesthetic of which is trying to be created. By trying to project a sound of the past the electronic sounds tend to be too sterile. Possibly if the keyboard instruments were made to sound more authentic this would not be as much of a problem As interesting CD nonetheless that certainly showcases creative ideas.

Yen Pox (USA) "Blood Music" CD 1996 Malignant Records
After a tape release and 7" I believe that this is the groups first offering on CD. Yen Pox create what is coined as 'dark ambience' which is an

over simplistic yet relevant term. I don't think what is on this disc could be called music as such but should rather be referred to as atmospheres. Predominantly minimalistic in style, noises and sounds flow and evolve over the length of the six track, 70 minute disc. This is similar in what is on offer from another dark ambient project 'Lustmord' but the sounds present here have a more 'wet' underwater element. No keyboards are used, rather source material recording are processed by electronic means to create the ambience on offer. Besides this point of being created from an electronic medium the atmospheres sound very natural, evoking arcane visions and primal fears of something utterly dark, yet hidden & incomprehensible.

For anyone not skilled in listening to this form of ambience will ultimately call this release boring due to it's minimalistic nature, but it is not something that you listen directly to. Put this CD on in the background or while you go to sleep and let it grow and evolve around you to gain the full effect.

Yen Pox with "Blood Music" definitely prove they are a force to be reckoned with in the dark ambient realm, as is the up and coming label "Malignant Records" who have released this gem.

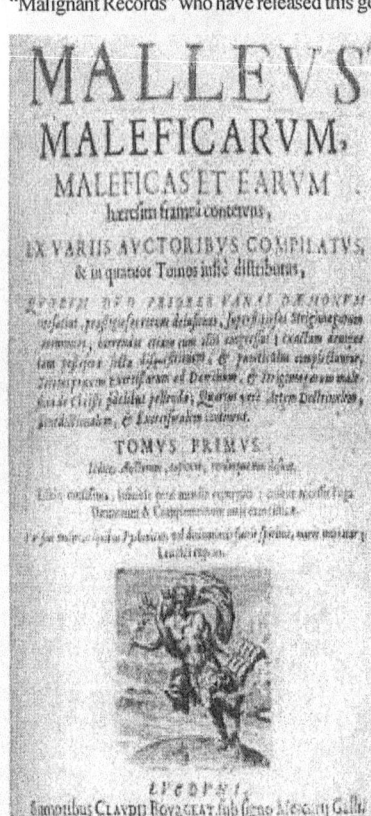

ADDRESS LIST

ART KONKRET:
C/- Markus Kropfreiter, Linkenheimer Weg 5, D-76646, Bruchsal, Germany
E-mail: Art.Konkret@t-online.de
WWW: http://home.t-online.de/home/Art.Konkret/

CAT'S HEAVEN RECORDS:
P.O. Box 170 116, 47181 Duisburg, Germany
E-mail: vuz&vuz.du.gtn.com.
WWW: http://www.badlands.de/vuz

CAUL:
Brett Smith (No postal address)
E-mail: caul@concetric.net
WWW: http//www.concentric.net/~Caul/enter.html

COLD MEAT INDUSTRY:
PO Box 1881, S-581 17 Linköping, Sweden
E-mail: Order@coldmeat.se
WWW: http://www.coldmeat.se

COLD SPRING,
87, Gloucester Avenue, Delapre, Northampton, NN4 9PT. England, UK.
E-mail: coldspring@thenet.co.uk
WWW: http://www.thenet.co.uk/~coldspring/

CROWD CONTROL ACTIVITIES:
821 White Elm Dr. Loveland, CO 80538 USA
E-mail: crowded@ezlink.com
WWW: http://www.ezlink.com/~crowded/controlcenter.html

DARK VINYL
P.O. Box 1221, 90539 Eckental, West Germany
E-mail: Darkvinyl@T-onlime.de

DOROBO
Darrin Verhagen P.O. box 22 Glen Waverly, Victoria, Australia 3150
E-mail: dorobo@werple.net.au
WWW: http://werple.net.au/~dorobo/dorobo.html

DRAENOR PRODUCTIONS:
C/- Max Vordernberger, Str.20., A-8790, Eisenerz, Austria
E-mail: Napalm@computerhaus.at

WWW: http://www.geocities.com/Vienna/Strasse/4765/

EIBON RECORDS:
Via Folli 5, 20134 Milano, Italy
E-mail; rberchi@galactica.it
WWW: http://www.this.it/eibon/

FEVER PITCH MUSIC:
1108, E.Capitol Drive, Appleton, WI 54911, USA

HAZARD:
Benny Nilsen, Villavägen 37, 610 50 Jönåker, Sweden
E-mail: hazard @hotmail.co
WWW: http://home3swipnet.se/~w-30139/hazard/home.htm

MALIGNANT RECORDS:
Jason Mantis. PO Box 5666, Baltimore MD 21210, USA
E-mail: mlgnant@earthlink.net
WWW: http://www.concentric.net/~Caul/mlgnantweb/

MANIFOLD RECORDS:
PO BOX 12266, Memphis TN. 38182, USA
E-mail: manifold@manifoldrecords.com
WWW: http://www.manifoldrecords.com/

MEGAPTERA:
Peter Nyström, Runebergsgatan 38, 611 37 Nyköping, Sweden
E-mail: salome@hem2.passagen.se
WWW: http: //hem2.passagen.se/salome/home.htm

MEMENTO MORI:
C/- Dark Vinyl, P.O. Box 1221, 90539 Eckental, West Germany
E-mail: Darkvinyl@T-onlime.de

MZ 412
(no postal address)
E-mail: nordvargr@swipnet.se
WWW: http://members.tripod.com/~vampiir/index.html

OLD EUROPA CAFE
C/- Rodolfo Protti Viale Marconi 38, 33170 Prodenone, Italy
E-mail: oec@iol.it
WWW: http://www.stack.nl/~bobw/music/OEC/

THE PROTAGONIST:
Magnus Sundström, Nybohovsbacken 43:232, 117 64 Stockholm, Sweden
E-mail: protagonist@swipnet.se
WWW: http:/home3swipnet.se/~w-30139/home.htm

RED STREAM:
P.O. Box 342 Camp Hill Pa 17001-0342 USA
E-mail: mail@rstream.com
WWW: http:/www.rstream.com

RELEASE RECORDS:
C/-Relapse Records, P.O. Box 251, Millersville, PA 17551, USA
E-mail: relapse@relapse.com
WWW: http://www.relapse.com

SANCTUM:
Jan Carleklev Norra Bogesundsgatan 3A, 554 73 Jönköping, Sweden
E-mail: sanctum@coldmeat.se
WWW: http://sanctum.coldmeat.se/

SELF ABUSE RECORDS:
26 S.Main Street #277, Concord, NH 03301, USA
WWW: http://www.mv.com/ipusers/selfabuse

SLAUGHTER PRODUCTIONS:
c/o Marco Corbelli, via Tartini 8, 410 49 Sassuolo (MO) Italy

SOLEILMOON RECORDINGS:
PO Boc 83296, Portland OR 97283 USA
E-mail: mailorder@soleilmoon.com
WWW: http://www.soleilmoon.com

END......

A NEW MALIGNANCY

THESE AND OTHER RELEASES NOW AVAILABLE FROM MALIGNANT RECORDS

$16 u.s. / postage pd / Overseas
$13 u.s. / postage pd / North America

EUROPEAN DISTRIBUTION:
Tesco, Dark Vinyl (GERMANY), Cold Spring (UK),
Cold Meat Industry (SWEDEN)
and others

NORTH AMERICAN DISTRIBUTION:
Metropolis, Relapse, Soleimoon,
and others

ALSO PROVIDING MAIL ORDER FOR:
AntZen, Tesco, Hands, Cold Spring, CMI, Slaughter,
and others

FORTHCOMING RELEASES:
Stone Glass Steel: "Dismembering Artists"
Hazard: "Battery Slave"
Yen Pox: TBA CD

PLEASE WRITE FOR A FREE CATALOG
www.concentric.net/~caul/malignantweb

MALIGNANT RECORDS
P.O. BOX 5666
BALTIMORE, MD
21210 • USA

FIRE + FLESH

DJ Stone Glass "Steal" Presents:
IRON HALO DEVICE
The Collapsing Void

"a slithery and all-encompassing sonic octopus
of diverse samples manipulated into cohesive,
illusive, mind-altering songs" - OUTBURN

From the mind behind Raison D'Etre:
STRATVM TERROR
Pain Implantations

...a horrific excursion into
the darkest depths of human depravity.
Volatile • Hypnotic • Brutal • Corrosive • Industrial

SPECTRUM ISSUE 2

AMBIENT/INDUSTRIAL/EXPERIMENTAL MUSIC CULTURE MAGAZINE

RAISON D'ETRE - STRATVM TERROR - STONE GLASS STEEL

IRON HALO DEVICE - ENDVRA - SHINJUKU THIEF

MIDDLE PILLAR
MUSICAL ESOTERICA

DARKAMBIENT • EXPERIMENTAL • INDUSTRIAL
ELECTRONIC • NEO-FOLK • ETHEREAL • RITUALISTIC

2500 titles available, including:

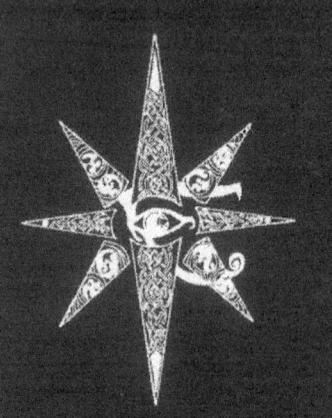

COIL
ARCANA
ENDVRA
CURRENT 93
BLOOD AXIS
SOL INVICTUS
GOLDEN DAWN
RAISON D'TERE
DEATH IN JUNE
STRATVM TERROR
LEGENDARY PINK DOTS
MOON LAY HIDDEN BENEATH A CLOUD

Specializing in World Serpent and Cold Meat Industry
Please send $2.00 or Four IRC's for full catalog.

MIDDLE PILLAR PRESENTS
"WHAT IS ETERNAL"
limited digipack CD out now featuring exclusive cuts from:

THE MACHINE IN THE GARDEN, 4TH SIGN OF THE APOCALYPSE, UNTO ASHES,
MORS SYPHILITICA, QUARTET NOIR, LORETTA'S DOLL, DREAM INTO DUST,
THE CHANGELINGS, THE MIRROR REVEALS, BACKWORLD,
TOR LUNDVALL & TONY WAKEFORD, JARBOE, ATHANOR, ZOAR

THE MACHINE IN THE GARDEN : NEW ALBUM DUE MAY 1999
Haunted female vocals and woeful ambience
mixing neo-classical elements and ethereal electronics.

MIDDLE PILLAR, DEPT S.   PO BOX 555, NY, NY 10009
FAX LINE: 212-378-2924   TOLL-FREE ORDER LINE : 1-888-763-2323
complete catalog online at: www.middlepillar.com
email: info@middlepillar.com

SPECTRUM
AMBIENT/ INDUSTRIAL/ EXPERIMENTAL MUSIC CULTURE MAGAZINE

EDITORIAL: MARCH 1999

Well here I am, back with the second installment of this magazine and what an issue it has turned out to be! The interviews are all longform, informative and extreemly interesting, there is a more extensive review section and the design layout/ visuals have gone well beyound my initial expectations (I even surprised myself with some of the layouts I came up with). I will say that this issue eventuated much sooner than I anticipated, given that issue 1# was only released in September, 1998. The response I recieved to the first issue was flattering to say the least, which I guess stirred me on to get another issue out. As a general rule, there won't be a set date for upcoming issues, but I do hope to continue with this, to make it an essential source of information, as support and promotion for this genre of music is something sorely lacking. As a final note, given that everything in here is done by myself, extensive proof reading is something I don't have the time nor inclination for. If there are gramatical errors, I sure you can read between the lines and work out what I was meaning to say..........read on and enjoy. Richard Stevenson - March 1999

EDITOR/ INTERVIEWER/ REVIEWER/ LAYOUT DESIGNER ETC...

RICHARD STEVENSON

SPECIAL THANKS:

James Leslie & Mick Stevenson for technical support & assistance, Jason Mantis for constant support and promotion, the artists for their dedication to providing lengthy & quality interviews, Stephen Pennick & Phil Easter for supply of images, Stephen Pennick (again) for allowing me to use the cover image, all the labels who have spent their dollars advertising in this issue, groups and labels who have sent promotional items (sorry if not everything was reviewed), The chester street boys (Shane, Damian & James) for antagonistic criticism of this music, and finally to family & friends for interest and support. all those forgotten - out of sight, out of mind......

SPECTRUM MAGAZINE C/- RICHARD STEVENSON
346 CHESTERVILLE ROAD, EAST BENTLEIGH
VICTORIA, AUSTRALIA 3165
STEVRICK@HOTMAIL.COM

Spectrum Magazine is distributed by: Malignant Records, Cold Spring, Middle Pillar, Arcane Recordings, Slaughter Productions, Maintenance & others.....

Cover image by Stephen Pennick - "Collage 04" (from the Death & Resurrection Collection 1999)

CONTENTS

RAISON' DETRE

STRATVM TERROR

STONE GLASS STEEL

IRON HALO DEVICE

ENDVRA

SHINJUKU THIEF

SOUND REVIEWS

TEXT & DESIGN LAYOUT Ó SPECTRUM/ STEVENSON
ALL IMAGES Ó THE RELEVANT ARTISTS

Raison D'être are almost beyond words...... (anyone who has heard this project's albums will know what I mean). Encompassing a pure meditative aura via music & sound of shifting beauty and sorrow, this is the type of music that in the right setting and mood can take the listener on an journey to the core of the inner psyche. The sole member, Peter Andersson was obliging enough to grant me this interview, conducted via e-mail in January 1999.

Welcome Peter Andersson to the second instalment of Spectrum Magazine. As Raison D'être have been creating music since the early 90's, can you please give us a history of the project and how you came to be involved in the style of music you produce?
Ok, I started raison d'être in early 1991 as a tool for expression and introspection. I have been doing music on my own since 1988 but it wasn't until 1991 I began composing music seriously and with my new thoughts about music and mind. I think that my music is an expression of my inner self, a reflection of my mind. When listening to the composition I can, through introspection and meditation try to understand myself. Raison d'être (and my other projects) is part of my self-realisation, and the maturation of my psyche.
So, through my music I try to understand myself in order to reach my goal, which is to feel entirety, harmony within myself and in the world. This process is designated the striving to individuation and is part of the psychoanalyst Carl Gustav Jung's theories of our psyche.

I think I was born into this type of music I'm making. I began listening on music (bought my own records) when I was very young. The first group I really enjoyed was Kraftwerk, and then I listened to Tangerine Dream, J-M Jarre and Klaus Schülze. I enjoyed their meditative and electronic sound and I often painted the imaginary landscape my mind that this music generated. After that I discovered most of these well known industrial bands, sure they were really amazing bands, but something essential was lacking: the special meditative state music could generate. But when SPK released "Zamia Lehmanni" I found that this type of music was perfect for me and led the way to other similar groups. I guess all these groups influenced me when I started raison d'être. I think I have to thank my oldest brother for much of this because he led me into this type of music in the first place.

Your first album 'Prospectus I' was a reasonably composed body of work while over the subsequent albums the overall structure has become more minimal, seeming to be subscribing to the 'less is more' theory. Has this been a conscious effort whilst planning for your recordings?
I usually don't plan what to do before I do anything, at least not musically, as I think it can block my creativity. The latest years I have been more interested in the structures of the sounds, instead of pure melodies. If you take a piano and hit a key one time you'll hear a note, but did it express any feelings. No, not much. But if you play a melody on the piano it will express a feeling. I try to create such sounds with structures that express feelings without playing melodies. It's difficult, but more powerful than melodies as no one can imitate theses sounds. A melody can be imitated quiet easy. I still use melodies and I will continue with that because melodies can express things that sounds can't do, and they complement each other. After all melodies are easier to remember than structures of the sounds, if they want to hum on some raison d'être melodies. I think I have been quiet minimal

all the time, but yes I have indeed become more minimal, because the use of less melodies. Also I don't use more sounds then I need. A sound must have a reason to be in the composition. I just can't have plenty of sounds, they would destroy the overall atmosphere and the meditative ability. There is a possibility that my minimalism is a reflection of my bad thoughts towards the mass consumption society we are living in.

With all of your works there is a definite spiritual aspect to its aura and sound. This leads to the question of are you religious individual or have any specific beliefs on such matters?
I am not religious, but I have a personal belief and I believe in my self.

While Caul recent CD ('Reliquary' on Eibon Records) seems to be heading in the direction of the 'light' (with his religious styled compositional works), with Raison D'être your compositions remain firmly entrenched in the shadows. Can a parallel with your music be drawn to mans need to seek out spirituality but not necessarily in the traditional Christian sense?
Sure, I seek. Not any religion, but my self. I digging deeper and deeper into my inner universe and as most of this place is unknown for me it must be a dark place. Perhaps that is the reason why my music is in the shadows. Darkness is a much more interesting thing than light. Darkness leaves much more for imagination and excitement etc.... than light does.

Why have you chosen to base your focus on the production of non-collective listening music?
I think that is because I'm a quiet introvert person, so this non-collectiveness only reflects my nature. I haven't chosen this, it's just the way it is. Music has a better ability to stimulate the mind when it is listened in a private and silent place, during relaxation and meditation etc....

Personally I find your music to work best when I am almost in meditative dreamlike state. Given that your music is intrinsic to your inner being/self, thus being very personal what do you expect from your listeners?
I make music because I need to. It helps me to mature as an individual and to understand my self. I don't expect anything from my listeners. I am only happy if they enjoy my music, and it seems they do. I have received letters from people who can't think about a life without raison d'être. At the same time it's pretty scary, what happens if I retire?

Given that Raison D'être translates to "justification/ reason for being/ existence" how did you first come to choose this project name? Has its personal meaning grown in significance over time or has it remained the same from the outset?
I took the name from a sentence I read in a book by C G Jung. It says "Entirety is the goal for the Self (the core of our psyche). This particular and lifelong process is designated the striving for individuation, and individuation is the raison d'être of the Self; its intrinsic aim is to attain the highest level of

self-realisation as ever possible in the psyche and in the world." Many of my personal philosophies is based on Jung's ideas so it's an appropriate name I think. For me it means the meaning of life(except for breeding), which, for me, is to reach a state of entirety (harmony within my self). I believe the meaning of raison d'être is growing in significance all the time, as it is always in progress.

How do you approach recording an album or track? Do you taken vocal samples and composed sections first and then flesh out the sound or do you start the approach from manipulation of noise/ sounds to create the background?
I have no rules what I do, but mostly (the latest years) I sample a bunch of sounds and processing them. Then I pick one or two processed sounds, which I use as background. Then I start with some short of melody or drone sequence. Sample some more sounds, adding some layers and so on. Every sound in my music is carefully selected. I think every sound must have a "soul" and they must have reason to join the composition. The "soul" of the sound I pick must be close to my nature.

Where do you record your music and due you employ the use of a traditional studio? Also what types of equipment, samplers, computers etc. do you use?
I have my own recording studio in my apartment. "Prospectus I" and "Enthralled by the wind of Lonelines" were recorded in other studios. I have changed equipment a few times, but right now I have a fully digital studio including a PC with hard disc recording and CD burner, a digital mixer, a Dat recorder, a few samples, some synthesisers and effect processors. To be more specific I have in my studio a PC PII 233 Mhz CPU, E-MU APS Soundcard, Cubase VST Audio, Wavelab, Yamaha Promix 01 digital mixer, E-MU ESI-32 sampler, Korg Wavestation A/D synthesiser, Roland JX-8P synthesiser, Yamaha SY 22 synthesiser, Yamaha TX16W sampler, Yamaha EMP 100 effect unit, Alesis Quadraverb effect unit, Sony DTC-690 DAT recorder, Onkyo A8200 amplifier Mission 760i monitors and Denon AH-D350 headphones. I also have a few metal plates, bells and some home made equipment/instruments.

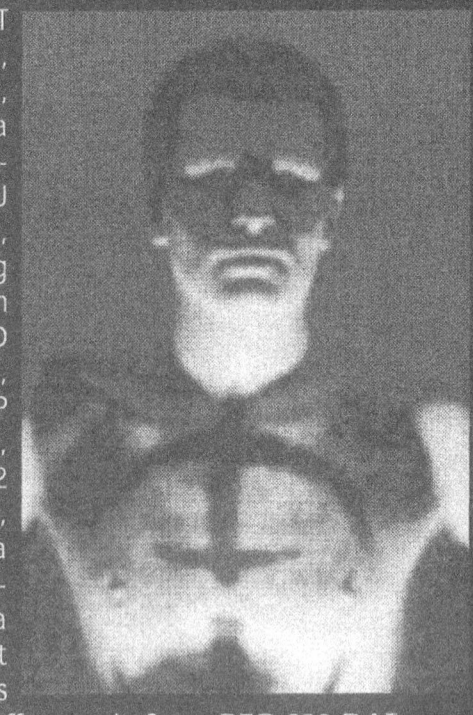

Each of your albums have had their own distinct style and sound and approached the composed sections slightly differently. Have any of your Raison D'être CD's been concept albums or worked with a specific idea/theme?
"Prospectus I" was built around a concept of the past. I was trying to evoke some collective archetypical memories of the past. On the other albums I didn't work after a specific concept, at least not that sort of concept. Musically every album is a new concept, because I use different methods which are almost identical to all tracks on the album. For example on " In Sadness, Silence and Solitude" I uses a sheet of metal which is included in almost every composition. The whole album derives from that piece of metal. It gave me inspiration, and I succeeded to bring very different and many sounds from it. For the next Necrophorus CD I will use ice instead.

As you are able to juxtapose elements of beautiful sorrowful moments with ghastly

outbursts, how do you see this as a contraction in focus?

I believe these contradictive elements make my music very exciting, but I don't see them has contradictions, more like a complement to each other. The world is built up of this black and white, positive and negative elements, just according to Yin-Yang, so I don't feel this strange at all. When my music contains these juxtaposed elements its like a war going on between Heaven and Hell. Perhaps raison d'être could be a soundtrack for Armageddon, the only thing you have to is to imagine the visuals.

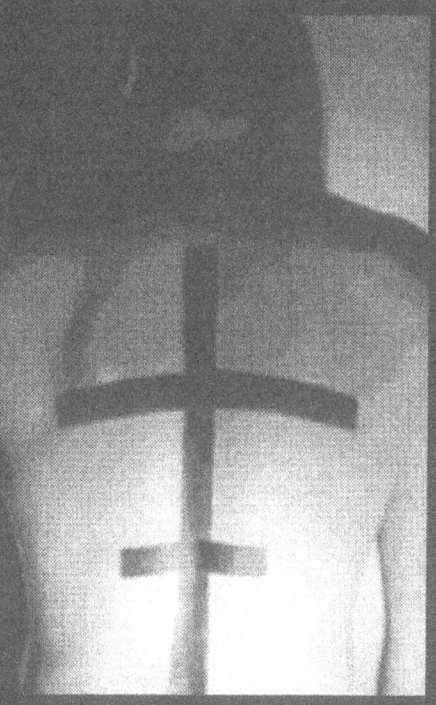

All of your works have featured both male and female coral vocals which is undoubtedly where the catholic religious type comparisons originate. Where have these vocals been sampled from and have you created any of these samples with your own voice or have you employed the services of vocalists to get the desired results?

Most of the them has been sampled from a number of CD's, then they have been manipulated a bit. On "In Sadness, Silence and Solitude" I did the mourning vocals on "Falling Twilight". If I could sing I would probably record my own voice. I have been thinking of employing a choir but it's a too big step right now. Also on the Necrophorus CD I did some choirs.

Raison D'etre have undertaken a number of live performances, where also parts of your latest CD "In silence, sadness & solitude" were recorded in a live setting. Can you detail some information on how you approach a live show and what it involves? Are stage props/ video footage utilised? How many times/ and where have you performed? Are the results what you desired and are you pleased with the results?

I have not worked on a special live show. Personally I think it's quiet boring to see raison d'être live. I think the music is more important, but of course a good live show expands and excite the whole performance. Mostly I use some video sequences projected in the background, very dark blue or red colours. I stand somewhere playing and making some sounds and drinking alcoholic liquids every once in a while. Most of the music is on a background tape, so I concentrate myself on my stage made drinks. "In silence, sadness & solitude" were not recorded live, it's a pure studio recording. But I did create the music for the live shows in 1996.

In amongst working as a musician you also have recently started a record label "Yantra Atmospheres". Thus far you have released only you own music in the form of a Necrophorus 10" EP, Raison D'être rarity CD (limited to 100) and the upcoming second CD of Atomine Elektrine. What are your plans & goals of this label? Will you branch out into releasing music of projects other than your own?

The nearest future I will only release my own stuff, but later, within 2 years or something, I hope I will be able to put out some other peoples music. I have no plans to be a big label, I just want to release a few records every year. For 1999, there is first the second CD of Atomine Elektrine, which should have been out 2 years ago. After that I will release a limited edition CD of early (from 1992-1994) unreleased songs of Atomine Elektrine. I will probably do the same with

Necrophorus and an early project I had in 1992 named Cataclyst. So there will be 3 limited edition CD's this year with unreleased material. I will also work more on the sleeve design of these limited edition CD's than on the raison d'être CD that looked quiet cheap.

Given that you are signed to CMI there has been certain interest in your music from black metal fans due to the 'cross-over' factor. However, given that you have recorded a number of intro/ outro tracks for an Australian black metal band Abyssic Hate what is you actual involvement with this sub culture genre?
I'm not involved in the black metal scene at all, I do not listen to it and I'm not interested in it. Quiet funny because I have just accepted to do a re-mix of a song by a Norwegian death metal group. I have free hands to do whatever I want to do with the song, so I will probably destroy it as much as possible. Anyway, I accepted because I wanted the experience.

Incidentally you also released a CD of a collection of older Raison D'etre tracks on the Australian label Bloodless Creations (run by the individual behind Abyssic Hate). How did this CD release eventuate?
Bloodless wrote to me that he like raison d'être very much and was surprised that the "Conspectus" tape wasn't released on CD. He thought that the music was deserved to be released on CD so he offered to release it on his own label. I didn't have the idea to release it on CD at all, but after I while I agreed with some minor adjustments. I wanted to release the first side of "Conspectus" plus some more songs from 1991. He agreed and released it.

It would appear that most musicians tend not to listen to music in the genre's of music that they create. Would this be the same in your case? What music/ styles do you typically listen to and does any of the music you hear inspire you compositional works?
I almost only listen to industrial and ambient music and their varieties. I prefer listen to Alio Die, Robert Rich, Lustmord, Nocturnal Emissions, Zoviet France, Rapoon, Voice of Eye, Jeff Greinke, Vidna Obmana, Coil, SPK, Dead Can Dance, Lycia, Download, Future Sound Of London, Tangerine Dream, Klaus Schülze, Brian Eno, Cranes and Daniel Menche only to name a few.

A statement has been made that you have not composed any new material for Raison D'etre since August, 1997. Are you currently working on new material at the moment? Do you have any pre-conceived ideas on what direction you plan to head in? Do you have any firm ideas of when a new release can be expected?
First I will finish the next Necrophorus CD, before I will do any raison d'être, perhaps I will do some Stratvm Terror in between. I have some ideas of how it will turn out, but we'll see. I will not tell you anything, more than I want it to be released the 1st of January the year 2000. I will work on the album the whole summer and autumn and I think I want to add a few new elements in the music. Actually I have already some plans for the CD next after that, but that's a big secret too.

(continues with the Stratvm Terror interview...)

Stratvm Terror

Not being content with one project, Peter "raison d'être" Andersson has a number of side projects to express a variety of moods. My discussions continue with Peter about Stratvm Terror - the uglier and noisier musical alter ego, which exclusively takes inspiration from themes of aggression and pain. Read on to receive your pain implantation.....

Peter Andersson, hello again! Given that you have quite a number of side projects I thought I would focus some questions on Stratvm Terror which has received quite a bit of interest of late. Stratvm Terror is essentially quite different to the output of your other projects due to the fact that it is a lot more harsh and it involves the collaboration of another individual. Can you detail the necessary historic details and some information on your co-collaborator Tobias Larrsen?
In fact, Stratvm Terror derives from another band named "Swelling Itching Brain" I had together with Tobias and one more member. We did split up after a short time and Tobias and I started Stratvm Terror in 1993. We have released two tapes and two CD's at this moment. Tobias Larsson uses to sing and play the drums in few rock bands or whatever it is. We have known each other since 1991 from school. He is more into the rock scene, the closest industrial he comes is Skinny Puppy and Klinik, but he likes to make noises just like me.

Early tape releases and the debut CD of Stratvm Terror, whilst still very harsh had a heavy focus on pummelling beats and percussive elements. The latest CD 'Pain Inplantations' has moved away from the beat oriented/ composed elements to a harshness and noise manipulation. Why the move away from more composed elements to harsher territory? Will this continue with future releases?
Well, we have already composed about 30 minutes of new material and this new material is like "Pain Implantations" but feels harder and containing some harsh beats. We have moved more to harshness and noise manipulation because we want to make noises and the name Stratvm Terror deserves more harshness and noise we think.

Stratvm Terror has performed live, with these performances having been recorded to be part of current and future releases (including the live track on the recent 'the Book ov Shadows' compilation LP). Is playing live essential for the concept of Stratvm Terror or is it a simple release of anger in a live setting? When you play live is the music live interpretations of studio tracks or new improvised pieces?
To perform with Stratvm Terror feels much better than with raison d'être. I think that Stratvm Terror music is more suited for live situations than raison d'être which I feel is more suited for strange installations. Both projects are suited for CD of course. It feels like we release a lot of anger on stage, at least Tobias. His instruments are always broken after a performance (he plays too hard). We play some improvised pieces but the mainly we making some sound layers, improvised or not, upon a background tape. In the meantime we get drunk and have fun.

Early this year you will be travelling to the USA for a small 'Malignant Records' tour featuring Raison D'etre/Stratvm Terror, Hazard & Deutch Nepal. Do you have preconceived ideas on how the tour will turn out and how your music will be received?
US is a bit different than Europe. There is another culture, totally mixed every culture in the world it seems. I guess they like to dance on the beach more than going on an industrial show. Anyway a lot of people have shown tremendous interest in this. Not so much of the Swedish industrial bands have played over there. We will do the tour in June and the performances will be in Washington/Baltimore, Philadelphia, New York City, Boston and Albany etc.... It's big places

so I hope the people will show up. Some clubs seems to be a little bit afraid of arranging an event like this because they don't know how many people will come. But we are trying to marketing us as much as possible, and I think Malignant does a great job over there.

There would appear to be a number of Stratvm Terror releases on they way including re-releases, live material and studio recordings? When can these be expected and on what labels?
First, there will be a CD release of the tape "The Only True Septic Whore" plus a few tracks from "Germinal Chamber" and one unreleased. This will be released in spring by Slaughter Productions. Then we have some new material, both studio and live recordings, which will be released by Old Europa Café. Title and release date is unknown.

Your debut CD 'Pariah Demise' was released in a limited run of 1000 on Old Europa Café. Personally this fantastic CD seemed to go by relatively unnoticed apart from 'those in the know'. It now seems that the interest in your past releases is gaining momentum given your current 'Pain Implantations' release on Malignant Records(I have recently seen the Pariah Demise CD fetching upwards of $25 US on a few mail-order catalogues). Do you think that 'Pariah Demise' may not have gained a wider recognition at the time of release given it's limited numbers?
Old Europa Café has talked about a second edition of "Pariah Demise". This release was, at least in 1996-97, the best selling CD of OEC releases. Personally I prefer unlimited editions, as more people would be able to get it, and without paying an enormous sum of money. I believe that "Pariah Demise", if it was unlimited, would have sold 500-1000 copies more. But then there is also a matter of marketing and distribution, I don't know how good distribution OEC have.

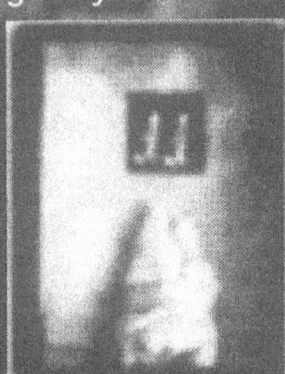

The cover image of "The Only True Septic Whore" MC features a picture of a hammer and a head shot of a political leader (I believe). I was interested in finding out the meaning behind both the picture and the title of the tape?
The pictures are unknown for me. Slaughter prd put something together, which I didn't have anything to do with, or had a chance to see before it was released. The title shows the danger to fuck whores, you never know what diseases they have. But one whore must be the most dangerous, and that's her we thinking at in the title. (I have no personal experience of fucking whores.)

When referencing music you have put your name associated with, there is quite a roster of releases under various monikers. What is the reasoning behind so many projects? (at

last count it included: raison d'etre, Stratvm Terror, Necrophorus, Atomine Elektrine, S v a s t i - A y a n a m) . There are different sides of my personality which I feel I must express, that's the reason for why I have so many side-projects. I simply can't do different kinds of music with the same project.

What upcoming releases do you have planned for these projects and are any of them defunct at this point in time? For raison d'être there is a double CD "Collective Archives" containing compilation tracks, "Aprés nous le déluge", re-mixes of a few tracks from "Prospectus I" and some more. I've already mentioned Stratvm Terror. Necrophorus will have a CD out on Crowd Control Activities late this year and titled "Tundra Stillness". With Atomine Elekrine is nothing new planned yet, first I'm waiting for "Archmetrical Universe" to be released. After that CMI has talked about a second edition of the first CD "Elemental Severance", but I don't know if it will happen. Svasti-ayanam was only a temporary project, and there is nothing planned at all with that project.

At what point do you feel that you will stop creating music or possibly scaling down your operations to a few select projects? I'm not sure. I haven't felt that yet but I think I will always have a number of projects, but perhaps not as many as today.

Speaking of new projects it appears that another collaboration project is about to surface with Lina of Deutch Nepal. What is the name of the project, what style does it encompass and are any releases planned at this stage? We call this project "Bocksholm" which is the old spelling of the town we both had our childhood. The reason for this project is the many and strange things Lina and I have in common. We are both from the same town (Boxholm), we release records on Cold Meat, and we have identical names. His real name is also Peter Andersson. That's quiet confusing and many seems to think that we are the same person. Staalplaat thought that raison d'être was a side project of Deutch Nepal. We have finished our recordings, almost every sound is sampled in Boxholm, we will only add some voices for some recordings. So far there is both a CD and 12" LP release planned, on what label we don't know yet. CMI, Old Europa Cafe or we might release it by ourselves. Musically I think it sounds strange, it's a mix of all our projects, but it doesn't sound like any of them.

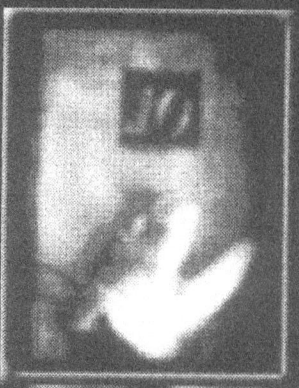

Well, I must thank you for taking time out to complete such a marathon double interview. Is there anything else you would like to ad? Thanks. It's my pleasure.

AVA/ES1 RECORDS

label, distributor, online zine

RELEASES:

Conception-the dark evolution of electronics Vol.1 CD (compilation featuring: Contagious Orgasm, Stratvm Terror, Aube, Merzbow, Deutsch Nepal, Atrax Morgue, Sshe Retina Stimulants, Taint, TAC, Frozen Faces, and Seelenlarm)

Cellar + - CD (psychedelic techno; triptechnoise with beats, melodies, and samples in die cut package)

Atrax Morgue-Woundfucker CD (the 1994 tracks remastered with new material; swirling synth-noise, white feedback, and disturbing vocals; themes of rape, murder, necrophilia, and bloodletting...as extreme as it gets)

The Decay of Cities 3cs Boxset (Dead Body Love; Deison, BaaL: 3 cassettes packaged in a hardshell vinyl case with inserts etc... each band offering 23 minutes of harsh structures & 23 minutes of ambient soundscapes for the downfall of a society and the chaos that follows; 3rd Edition Print)

Lunar Blood Rituals-the dark evolution of electronics Vol.2 CD (compilation featuring: Inade, Chod, Zwickau, Melek-tha, Tombstone, BaaL, Idpa, In Death's Throes, The Epiphany, Arkanyus)

UPCOMING RELEASES:

Aube-Comet 2CD (March/April)

Contagious Orgasm-Seven Sounds Unseen CD (June)

Two Minds of Murder-the dark evolution of electronics Vol.3 CD (August) (Contagious, Schloss Tegal, Slogun, Morder Machine, Bloodyminded, Pain Nail, Deison, Grunthuster, Boss Monster)

BaaL-The Innocent Corrupted:Self Destroyed CD (October)

Also Available (lavishly packaged 2cs collector's Deiscqs 11PD=50):
Azoikum/BaaL-In Memory of James Maybrick
BaaL/Francois Douris-Electroimpulse Therapy
Boss Monster/Deison-Hospitalised

INDUSTRIAL TECHNOLOGIES

AVA/ES1 Records
P.O.Box 605488
Cleveland OH 44105
USA
Email: BaaL7Ava@aol.com

website: http://www.angelfire.com/ny/scriptureszine/avaes1.html

Ad assisted by Spectrum Inc.

stone glass steel

Stone Glass Steel is a musical gem that has been dormant over the past few years, except for a few select compilation appearances. Even with the musical ravages of time both full length CD's of this project remain just as powerful and evocative now, as when they were released. Given the future of this project looks considerably more active, I undertook this extensive chat with Phil Easter about all things of Stone, Glass & Steel.

Welcome Phil Easter, please introduce yourself and your musical project Stone Glass Steel. Greetings. Thanks for having me. The Spectrum H.Q. is actually larger than I expected. I like what you've done to the place. Very comfortable furniture. Anyway, I'm the guy behind Stone Glass Steel, one of the original "Ambient Industrial" pioneers of the early 90's. I guess I've probably grown a bit obscure these days, but perhaps a few of your readers remember my records.

For someone who had your last two CD's released back in 1992 & 1993 respectively, you have still managed to retain quite a high profile through a number of compilation appearances. Which compilations have you appeared on over the years? My first notable compilation was for Audio Drudge, the zine Jason Mantis ran before founding Malignant Records. I did a couple tracks for the cassette that was packaged with Issue #5. Seems like Lull was on that tape as well. The next compilation of note was Ant-Zen's "Xerosma." That was really a wonderful record to be part of. Excellent packaging as Ant-Zen has always been know for, blue and silver metallic printing on the sleeve and insert and a clear blue vinyl LP. Still proud to have tracks on that one. When Ant-Zen put together their anniversary release "Ant-hology" last year, Salt was kind enough to include "Circle Of Sound" of my Stone Glass Steel tracks from Xerosma. I suppose it serves as a bit of documentary track, since it features a sample of Joachim Kohl of Tesco Organization calling my answering machine and leaving an order for a box of Stone Glass Steel CDs. After that, I did tracks for the two Beautiful Records compilations. A track called "Beneath the Skin" appeared on Theme Beauty and "Pain Hope & Pining: The Drowning of Swans" was for Theme Desire. I always enjoy the process of creating music to fit a theme. It makes a compilation seem less random. It creates some vague sense of collaboration with the other artists. I'm not really sure what has happened with Beautiful Records. Things seem to have gone dormant. I'm not sure if they still exist. Which would be a shame, since the label's founder is one of the nicest people I've worked with. At least, I think a few copies of Theme Desire are still available, so your readers might want to track them down. It's a project worth supporting. The other significant compilation I contributed to was "Invisible Domains," the debut release from Malignant Records. This was a theme-oriented compilation about viruses. Every artist on the compilation chose to compose tracks about biological viruses. I, on the other hand, created a track about computer viruses. When Invisible Domains finally came out and I saw that I was the only one who went the technological route, I felt a bit silly. It looked like I had missed a meeting or something. Actually, my track "Violent Grace: Parts 1-3" is really more about a metaphysical infection, but that message is less overt than the technological theme. There were a few other comps and projects that never quite came together. I ran into some legal problems that effectively tied up my ability to release any material under the Stone Glass Steel name for a few years. Everything I started during that time period pretty much died on the vine. The one project I still regret having never finished was a split Stone Glass Steel / Deutsch Nepal release. The plan was for each artist to record tracks, and then do re-mixes on each other's work. Lina sent me his material, and I was never able to follow through on the project. It was a big disappointment for me.

With the music you create what proportion is composed by yourself compared to utilising sampled sections of other artists music?
That can be a loaded question. I think determining the answer depends on your aesthetic standing on sampling as an art form. I'm stridently pro-sampling, so I have a very biased view. With Stone Glass Steel, I take credit for the entire composition, even though nearly all of the sound you hear has it's origin in samples of commercial recordings. I treat these source recordings as sound generators. With Stone Glass Steel, the art form is not the initial sample, but the manipulation and shaping of this sounds into something completely new. It's all about deconstruction and recontextualization. It's about messing with the fundamental building blocks. Sampling is just a starting point.

Things are different with my side project Iron Halo Device. IHD was designed to blur the line between the sampling artist and DJ. The samples are far more recognisable and yet the artwork is more conceptual. It's about juxtaposition and contrasts. It's the way a DJ thinks, the combinations and selections he makes, that makes the performance worthwhile. It's about being a filter, or a navigator, the way only a DJ can be. With IHD I don't take credit for the sources, though I think the overall product is obviously of my design. Ironically, IHD is less sampled than Stone Glass Steel. Most of the background textures and noise are being performed in more conventional ways.

Given the nature of you musical works using samples of others music do you consider yourself an artist or a DJ?
A bit of both, depending on the project. As Stone Glass Steel I function as an artist, albeit a sampling artist. When I record as IHD I serve more as a DJ a filter for other music. Of course, in a few years all DJ's will be using samplers, so then it will be even harder to answer your question.

How do go about picking the various samples and do you have any process to 'personalise' them?
I'm a huge music fan. I collect all sorts of CDs. I try to stay current on all the experimental artists, but I also collect lots of indie-pop records. With Stone Glass Steel, I often just pick samples based on the music I like and am listening to at the time. In a way that makes my Stone Glass Steel recordings very personal snapshots of my life at that particular time. I think it lends an extra level of meaning to the work. On the other hand, my IHD project is more targeted and deliberate as far as the actual sample. Those IHD samples are collected to make a point. If anything, that point is the reflection of me, more so than the specific sound. As far as personalising the samples. I use a variety of techniques to manipulate and destroy the source material. Mostly delays, distortions, effects, and real-time filters. Also I believe the combination and layering of samples is a big part of the personalisation process. Why one person chooses to layer one sound with another is unique to the artist.

Is there any specific concept inherent in how you operate with the production and manipulation of sound?
Well, philosophically I am a recontextualist first and a deconstructionist second. I suppose that

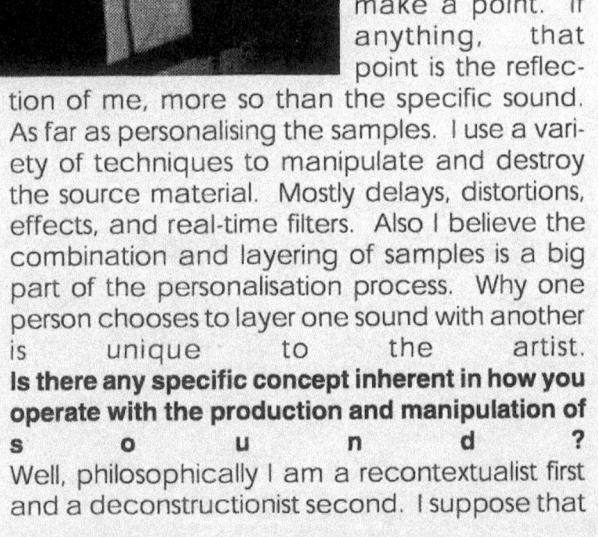

makes me a post-modernist with neoist leanings... er something. I guess in real terms, I believe that art and music should reflect the times we are living in, because obviously, it's all that any of us will ever have. It's fine to preserve and study the creative works of past generations or ages, but never at the expense of the creative expression being made today. I don't care if it's a classic symphony, 60's rock, late 80's goth, or early 90's industrial-dance. You should not substitute it for what is going on today. The core of all creativity is experimentation, so once you figure something out, it's time to move on. Musically speaking, I used to label my music as ambient-industrial, but somewhere over the years it turned into something I've been calling "cinematic isolationism." It's evocative and ambient, but also dark, bleak, and introspective. As the times change, I'm sure the music and label will change again.

All of the your song titles and some vocal samples tend to point towards various ideas, concepts and thoughts (including your well used sample/ quote "take it apart, put it together again, mold it like putty"). Is this case or are the titles simply there to 'name' each track?
Yeah, there's definitely a philosophical and conceptual base to everything I am doing. The "take it apart, put it back together again" quote is part of my so-called Recontextualist Manifesto. The fundamental concept behind being a sampling artist, but also a reflection of being a cultural deconstructionist as well. All of my titles have very intentional meaning, both as individual track names, and as a group within the context of an entire album. When I am working I give each composition a working title. But those are almost always replaced with a more meaningful names once the recording is finalised. Usually there are several levels of meaning, literal, philosophical, impressionistic, personal, etc. I like to leave it a bit vague to let the listener find his own connection and meaning. If you are a nuts and bolts type of listener you will read one meaning, but if you are more impressionistic you will find another. Both are correct. An example would be "The Drowning of Swans" on the Theme Desire compilation. On one hand, the title is a reference to the samples I used from Soundtracks For The Blind, the Swan's final studio album. But the title is also impressionistic, and captures a sense of mourning and implied violence that fits the overall feel of the music.

Your next release is a release of a rare 'unreleased' first album. Why was this recording never officially release and what is the history surrounding it?
The first full length Stone Glass Steel recording, "Dismembering Artists" was completed in 1991. In the last stages of making this rather harsh and aggressive record, I become more interested in dark ambient soundtrack music. Rather than stopping to putting out Dismembering Artists, I continued recording new material and wound up with what became the first release, Industrial Meditation. My initial plan was to put out a double CD, the first disc being the harsher more aggressive Dismembering Artists and the second disc being a more soothing moody counterpart, Industrial Meditation. The reality was that I couldn't afford to release both, so I went with the newer stronger material and shelved Dismembering Artists for a later day. That day never came, until now, nearly ten years later.

What can be expected from this release in terms of sound and in comparison to your other works?
The material on Dismembering is considerably more structured and noisy compared to my later material. About 80% of the sound is sampled, while the more musical parts are actually performed. There's also quite a bit of guitar-type noise which I stopped using after this record, There are a few odd influences sprinkled in here and there. The original master for Dismembering Artists was incredibly lo-fi and bathed in bad effects like reverb and flanges. I had no idea what I was doing when I made it. So when Malignant asked to release the work, I dug out the original mixes and remastered the tracks. It's still low-fi compared to today's music, because I was using a cheap 1 MB sampler, but the new master is remarkably louder and cleaner. The listener will at least hear what it sounded like while I was recording. Also, this release will feature the original working titles for the tracks. Far more cryptic than impressionistic.

Given that it seems you have not recorded a new full length Stone Glass Steel release since 1993, are there any new albums in the pipeline? Do you have any ideas or concepts of sound that will lead your future direction?
There were at least three full-length Stone Glass Steel records that never made it to completion, 1994's "Dissecting Laura," 1995's "Consumer Grade," and 1996's "Garden of Wires," All of those recordings were thwarted by the legal problems I mentioned earlier. I started tracks, got frustrated and shelved the projects. I'm sure I really frustrated the labels who were interested in those projects, like Tesco and Ant-Zen. Only the people around me at the time were able to hear that material. Nothing exists of it today except disk after disk of samples. Currently I have a few new Stone Glass Steel projects in the works. The more immediate is tentatively entitled "warez" and will be released on Malignant. This recording is just the next natural chapter in Stone Glass Steel, bearing in mind that several in between chapters have been lost. It will be louder, cleaner, more complex noise. I also have a couple of tangents I'd like to work through, one is a elaborate remix project for Malignant, and the other is something I've been calling "Music For 2 Rooms." Everything is still in progress so there are no set release dates.

There is quite an interesting story involving a Hollywood music business type who had plans to start a mainstream label specifically for ambient/ industrial music. As you were one of the prospective artists this individual was interested in, would you be able to elaborate on this?
That business type would be the animator Gabor Csupo of Klasky Csupo fame (creator of The Simpsons, Rugrats, etc). A very wealthy and bereft human being. He was a fan of my first two Stone Glass Steel records. He contacted me in early 1994 and asked me to help him with a record label he was planning. The idea was to run a experimental indie label with a mainstream Hollywood budget. I was running my own indie at the time, TypeToken Records, and I guess I seemed like a suitable candidate. The company was legitimate and they willing to pay top dollar. So, I signed up and moved out to Hollywood to work on the project I also enlisted every artist I knew at the time. Jason Mantis, then still running Audio Drudge, helped me design and put together a themed compilation project for the new label that included a stellar list of artists including Shinjuku Thief, Deutsch

Nepal, Alio Die, Lustmord, Paul Schutze, Caul, C17H19NO3, Fibre, Waste Matrix, Hungry Ghost, Alien Farm, etc. It was an auspicious and lucrative start for us all. All of this wonderful underground music was going to be brought forward for the world to hear. But it all came crashing down before anything was ever released.

I believe that the above scenario then led to a legal battle and court case released to the unauthorised sampling of other artists works? Could you also expand of these circumstances?
Everything you've ever heard about big business and experimental art not mixing, is completely true, and you can multiply that by a thousand in this case. I was young and naive and blinded by the money. What started out as a wonderful idea quickly disintegrated into dirty politics, agents, lawyers, and heavy handed contracts. I had to work with clueless men in suits who wanted me to explain how a project like Caul was going to compete for market share with their other major label clients. It was absurd. I woke up one morning and realised that I was being expected to screw all the artists and colleagues I'd made while slaving to start my own label. I got up, drove to work, and quit. Over the next few weeks, most all of the artists I'd brought on board followed me out the door. The label fell apart.
The owner, Gabor Csupo was caught off guard by my sudden departure. His dream label was wrecked. He was embarrassed, angry, and looked like a fool. He vowed revenge on all of us that left, especially me. The result was a 3.5 million dollar, 13 count lawsuit filed in federal court. It was a serious attack designed to drain, if not destroy all parties involved, just by our attempting to mount a defence. It was a six figure nightmare just to defend myself at the federal level. Every charge you could think of was thrown at me, breach of contract, sampling copyright violations, even RICO charges for international wire and mail fraud. It was crazy stuff. Luckily I found a powerful team of lawyers who were willing to file a counter suit and fight the charges on contingency. Even so, it was an ugly and expensive two year battle. I was damaged in every way possible. All of my existing projects and creative outlets were put on hold. I was quite paranoid and at times feared for my life. As one of attorney put it, "it would be cheaper if he just had you killed." It was a very black time. But finally in 1997 a federal judge threw out the most damaging charges. The lawsuit was effectively disarmed and my attorneys settled the remaining case out of court. I had won the war, but it was a worthless period in my life.

While Sweden and the associated CMI artists seem to have a thriving scene, is there any such scene within the States where you live?
I think most big cities in the US have small pockets of artists doing what I do. It's not quite what you could call a scene. These groups tend to be very insular and frustrated. I'm not sure if this is because they feel oppressed in their environments, or if experimental artist just tend to be bitter hermit-like people. Probably a bit of both.
I currently live in Minneapolis, which is more receptive for this style of music than most places. There are several ambient improv projects here, though only a couple have made waves outside of the city. These artists are more into live improv performances, than recording. There are shows literally every week at tiny clubs and cafes. One project called Ousia has shown up on a few international playlists. I've also seen some vinyl by a local DJ / noise artist called Lost In Translation. At least a few are making records and getting out there. But as far as the U.S. as a whole, I have no idea if there is a centralised spot that you could legitimately call a scene. It's a very dissipated market. Sometimes it seems like we only band together on the internet.

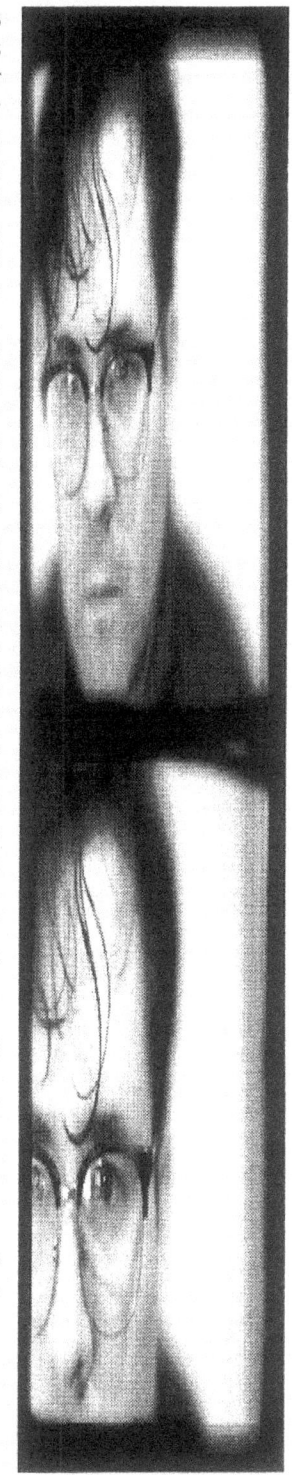

(this lengthy chat with Phil continues over the page with another of his projects, namely- "Iron Halo Device").

"DJ" Stone Glass Steel Presents:

IHD

iron halo device: the collapsing void

Iron Halo Device is another brilliant musical face of Phil Easter aka "Stone Glass Steel", whose live CD of last year received an extensive amount of praise and acclaim. With the CD shaping up to be a genre defining pinnacle of the late 90's ambient/industrial scene, here I continue the conversation with Phil regarding this excellent collaborative project.

One of your more recent releases is the Iron Halo Device CD. Given this was yourself in collaboration with other artists, how many people where involved in the performance? As it seems that the other collaborators did not put their names to the CD for fear of legal ramifications, would you be willing to name the said individuals?
Iron Halo Device was originally formed during my time in Los Angeles. It started as a collaboration with Robert Salchak & Nels Brown of Waste Matrix. Until I saw Waste Matrix, I had always been content to be a studio musician. Then I saw them create amazingly complex layers of electronics and noise, all live and all improvised, with no help from sequencers or tape. Iron Halo Device pretty much started as a way for me to study and learn their performance secrets and techniques. When all of my legal troubles started, I had to cut things off and leave Los Angeles. I relocated to Kansas City where Brett Smith of Caul and John Bergin of C17H19NO3 were living and working. I was still in the frame of mind to do Iron Halo Device, so I enlisted Smith and Bergin to join the project. At the end of 1995 I did a number of demo sessions with both of them sitting in, though independent of each other. In 1996 I did a string of live shows with Brett Smith providing Caul-type back up textures, and then in 1997 John Bergin joined in and we performed as a three piece. Both Brett Smith's Caul and John Bergin's C17 were involved in that Hollywood lawsuit. Even though I had my attorneys protect them, Smith and Bergin viewed me as a bit of a legal lightening rod. I guess they blamed me for their involvement. While they both seemed content to participate when Iron Halo Device was just demos and live shows, they were unwilling to risk being part of an official commercial release. They were convinced I would bring another lawsuit down on them. I guess everyone was a bit paranoid during that period. When I finalised a deal with Malignant to release the first record, both Smith and Bergin bailed in a very ungraceful manor. It was bad timing and I was pissed, as evidenced by my under-the-tray message. It was their loss.

Given that you have personally received all the praise from the disc would it be correct to assume that you are the main driving force of the group? If this assumption is correct what role did you play in the live setting, as opposed to the others input?
Yes, I guess I qualify as the driving force behind Iron Halo Device. I created the underlying concept and provided the framework within which the improvisation and composition occurred. I drove the theme and tone of the compositions. I also mixed and mastered the recordings. Most importantly, I was also the only one willing to put my name on it. In the first set of live shows, Brett Smith provided background noise and undertones to my sampled loops, and drones. On The Collapsing Void performance you can easily hear the Caul influence on the in-between bit and pieces. By the time we Bergin joined started performing live with us, it was slowly becoming more of a collaborative effort, almost a "band." Sadly, non of those shows were ever recorded.

Did any of your live collaborators also partake in

the second studio half of disc? If not, why the need for a new project name if it was only yourself? Also what do you see as the main differences between Stone Glass Steel and Iron Halo Device?
Yes, Bergin makes his only appearance on the record in the Abduction of Winter. His drudgey pulsing rhythm opens the track. That part is very similar to a piece from one of his early C17 pieces. Smith helps out on the other three demo tracks. His contribution is similar to that of the live show. Background textures, Caul-like fills, that sort of thing. Also, I purposefully chose to work under the Iron Halo Device name during this period, instead of Stone Glass Steel, because of the lawsuit. It was a project name that the lawyers didn't know about, so it was safe to use.

I also noted that on "The Collapsing Void" CD you did not formally associate your real name with the music instead opting for 'DJ Stone Glass Steal'. Was this taking advantage of a legal loophole by using an alias, therefore not specifically formalising your involvement?
It's a complex matter. The IHD recording pushes the boundaries of copyright infringement and I didn't want to take any unnecessary risks. As you will notice, there is no copyright being claimed for the music. I really do view it as a DJ performance. I'm just spinning samples you might say.

As details of your previous legal proceedings where included in the Iron Halo Device cover, did you encounter any legal turmoil over "The Collapsing Void" release?
Nothing yet. Nor do I expect there to be. In legal terms it's a small release. No one is making any money worth counting. I'm not claiming a copyright. There's really no foundation for anyone to get upset. The release is about art not commerce.

Was Iron Halo Device a once off live collaboration, or will the future see more releases? Are these likely to be in live or studio form?
The foundation of IHD is based in improvisation and evolution. The project is designed to weather the changes. So, it will continue. I've already been approached by a couple of potential new members, but I'm not quite ready to do another run just yet. Most likely, the next IHD release will be a studio work. But the big change may be with the project name. It will always be IHD, but the actual words may change. That was always part of the original idea. Something similar to what SPK did.

Given that the Iron Halo Device CD is reaching cult status, what was involved in the actual live performance? Was there a large audience in attendance and how was received?
Cult status? Really? That's rather flattering. The show was at a rock club in Kansas City. Iron Hàlo Device was brought in to play after the headliner of an "industrial showcase" cancelled out. It was not an ideal setup. My original concept for IHD was to play low key performances in galleries or art spaces. It was a bit unnerving to launch the project by headlining in front of an audience that had come to see Nine Inch Nails style rock bands.

It was a hot and sticky July night and the club was packed with a industrial/goth type crowd. The stage was in an enclosed outdoor courtyard. It was threatening rain, lots of deep rumbles from the sky. I adjusted the set list to include lots of industrial type samples in an attempt to both pander and mock the audience. Brett Smith provided back up. Neither Smith nor I had rehearsed the material outside of the Collapsing Void track, which we had done as a demo the previous year. So, the sounds we made were completely new to us. The stage setup was rather simple. Just two samplers, lots of fog, deep red and blue lights, and disturbing abstract video images being projected across the back of the stage. We went on stage around 11pm and played for about 45 minutes. I was working in a recording studio at that time, so I invited one of the engineers to run sound and tape the show to DAT. This was a lucky break for two reasons, first we had an extremely loud mix, and second it created a tape that was good enough to release. The crowd was response was really quite strong. I don't think they had any idea what they were seeing, but they enjoyed it. Even a few people starting dancing, which was rather peculiar to see. Other people just stood there looking quite disturbed, which was more expected. The sound pressure was really rather intense. You would need to turn up the volume on the CD all the way to even get a hint at how loud this show was. We even had the police taking decibel readings out in the parking lot at one point. At the very end of the show we actually blew up the monitor amp. You can hear it pop lightly on the CD and then all the sound cuts out. That track wasn't supposed to end quite as quickly as it did. But that's all part of improv. Happy accidents.

Did any manipulation or production occur afterwards to prepare it for official CD release?
Actually, you hear the complete show, just as it unfolded. The only post production tweaking was in mastering. I applied some gentle compression and EQ. Just the normal stuff you do before pressing a CD. Keep in mind, the source recording was a two-track DAT, so there wasn't any way to adjust the mix or something like that. I thought it was important to keep the performance intact. It's intended to be a document of a real event.

Your Stone Glass Steel CD's 'Industrial Meditation' & 'Industrial Icon' were released on your own label Type Token Records. Is this label still in existence and what releases have you had thus far?
TypeToken is the umbrella name under which I work. It started out as a record label in 1990 when I released my first cassette release under the name Black Beach Moonrise. The tape was called Chapter 24: Night Shades. It consisted of a black plastic box that held the tape and a series of postcards that featured B&W photographs illustrating each track on the cassette. After that I released a CD under the name Death In Arcadia, which was a more beat-oriented project with lots of cut and paste voice samples. Death In Arcadia actually got a fair amount of attention and airplay. Most Americans hated it but the Russians loved it. In fact, a TV station in Moscow actually used one of the tracks as a theme song for a music video show. Weird, but flattering. After that I focused on the Stone Glass Steel recordings. They did far better commercially than I had expected and dramatically eclipsed the other two projects. That success helped me develop a very large mailorder audience and very solid distribution network in North America, Europe, and Asia. It even got to the point where I was running regular ads in large US magazines like SPIN. It was this success and impact that got me noticed by that fateful Hollywood company. Just before I moved out to Los Angeles, TypeToken was branching out into distribution, just a handful of small hand picked releases by artists I admired. That all was placed on hold

after I moved. **You are also obviously well versed in other digital mediums as you have created the layout and artworks for a number of Malignant Records CD's and you have also mastered the Stratvm Terror-Pain Implantations CD and the debut CazzoDio CD under the name of Type Token Special Projects. Have you had formalised training in any of these digital mediums?**
I studied aesthetics in college. So pretty much everything else is self taught. I think that's the norm for most of us really. Formal training tends to muck up creativity and exploration. For the last three years or so I have been making a living working for recording studios and doing freelance graphic design. So, while I may not have formal training, I've learned on the job and become a paid professional. It's an odd mix of things, but the computer is the centralised tool for both.
I think you can see evidence of my on-the-job training when you look at my Malignant album covers. The difference between the early covers like the Orphx CD and the newer artwork, like Stratvm Terror is obvious. I've also greatly enjoyed the post production audio work I've done for Malignant and Black Plagve. Besides the Stratvm Terror and CazzoDio discs, I also mastered the Blood Box "World Of Hurt" recording.
It still amazes me what a little mastering can do for a release.
Right now I'm in the process of setting up a home studio in which I can edit, master, and burn red book CD masters. The going rate for renting a mastering suit in a recording studio is around $1000 a day. That's an impossible expense for a tiny label or artist who can barely budget that amount for manufacturing their CD. But if they leave mastering up to the manufacturing plant, which a lot of labels do, you are guaranteed to have a quiet flat sounding disc. Once my studio setup is complete, I will be able to provide hi-end mastering services to other like minded artists and labels. I really think there is a need out there for that.
Is Type Token Special Projects an extension of the record label or is it a metamorphasized version of it? (if the label is now defunct).
The suffix attached to TypeToken, like "records" or "special projects," is pretty much interchangeable depending on what type of work I'm doing. The "special projects" name is usually reserved for projects that are directly related to the type of music and work I personally support. More generic projects I do for local recording studios get labelled with TypeToken Media or In House Design (I H D).
Outside of your involvement with music and Malignant Records, what are you interests and what are your career movements even if it is not associated with the music?
Career wise I just would like to keep doing what I have been doing, but perhaps make a little better living at it than I do now. If anything, I would like to steer more towards editing and mastering music. That's my realistic short term view. In an ideal world, I'd love to devote myself full time to making records and producing/re-mixing other people's music. But that's a rare situation to be in. As far as outside interests go, I spend a great deal of time messing with Macintosh computers, warez, and the internet. I'm not sure I qualify as a hacker, but I probably come close. Close enough to get into trouble anyway. I also watch lots of bad TV, play video games, and travel when I can. Someday I'd like to move back to Los Angeles so I'm closer to an actual music scene and the ocean.
Speaking of Malignant Records, even though Jason Mantis is the founder of the label, your name had been associated with your CD's as well as for creating artwork, mastering releases, working on the Web Page and helping set up an information e-mail chat service. Given this level of involvement what is your actual role with Malignant Records? Are you an official employee or is your input for the love of the music?
I'm horning in on his biz, I think is what you call it! No seriously, I've known Jason since the early days of Audio Drudge. When I went out to Hollywood I tried to hire him on as my employee, but he was smart and stayed in Baltimore. We've always been working on ways to collaborate and support each others interests. This past year Jason visited me in Minneapolis and I was

inspired to take things up a notch or two. After his visit I came to him with the idea for an expanded webpage and creating an online community around the style of music we all support. Jason was very supportive and gave me his blessing to work on it. Our goal with the website is to make Malignant the portal for this style of music. Not the only place you go, but the first place you check. All the artists and labels in the scene should benefit once we get to that stage. It's not about competition, but about pulling the scene together so that we might take it to the next level. Of course we also hope to do quite a bit of online record sales so that we can increase the number of records Malignant releases. To get back to your question, I'm working with Malignant for the love of the music, but more and more, I am becoming an employee. I suppose by default I am serving as the labels creative director or some such a thing. **On a totally different note, given that everything about your music and images makes reference to computers and technology, what are your views and thoughts on the risks that the Y2K 'Millennium Bug' poses for the operation of modern society?** On January 1st, 2000 the lights will go out, chaos with abound, and men with guns will rule the day. Well, maybe not. But it makes a good point. Probably the fear of what might happen is the biggest threat facing us. Just suppose the Y2K bug does actually knock out the power in some areas even for just an hour or two. The obvious risk is that these gun toting survivalist types may see it as something much bigger and go haywire. Word to the wise, steer clear of grocery stores and banks. But by and large, I think we humans are a clever lot. We created and spread the bug and we can probably find a way to contain it. I'm not making any special plans for the turn of the century. I'm certainly not stockpiling food or learning to make clothes out of rabbit fur. But I probably will stay home with the doors locked, or if I'm lucky, vacation somewhere warm. That's not to say that we won't see some disruption somewhere on the planet. It will probably be some Asian or Eastern European country that didn't have the resources to test all the embedded chips in some ageing part of their electrical infrastructure. It's completely possible that the grid may go down in some country. At least for awhile. It will certainly be a hugely hyped news story. Lots of worry and panic. We could easily start the new millennium deeply soul searching our reliance on technology. I expect most of us that live in larger cities around the world will only see a few minor annoyances. Maybe a few taxi cab meters will malfunction here, and an ATM will lock up there. At worst, a couple places might have blackouts when older power substations work out their kinks. Poor under-populated rural areas might have a lot more problems, but maybe not. **That about wraps up all I have to ask. Is there anything you would like to ad?** Just that Spectrum has had a very auspicious start and I hope that you manage to stay at it and grow this zine into a recognised source of information. The day is coming for our musical genre. Without resources like Spectrum, it could be an opportunity missed.

Thanks again for checking up on me and my work.

C h e e r s .

< take it apart. put it together again. mold it like putty >

endura

The forever prolific Endvra with thier constantly evolving sounds have caught the attention of many dark ambient fans since their emergence in the early 90's. And rightly so, given their music ranges from brooding ambient ritualistic passages to neo-classical compositions & everything in-between. Having just released their excellent 6th full length album, as well as a limited 10" EP, I decided to contact this extremely interesting group for a bit of a discussion....

Endvra being a musical duo featuring two individuals, (Stephen Pennick and Christopher Walton) how did you two first come in contact & were there initial difficulties in working collaboratively? Was there a specific style and concept inherent from the outset?
CHRIS:-The band that is now called ENDURA began when I, Chris Walton, met Stephen Pennick in January 1993. We were put in touch by a mutual friend from London, Hassni Malik of the Work In Progress label, who had known Stephen for a number of years through tape trading and through recording, and I had recently been in contact with him through a fanzine I had published, "Wisconsin Death Trip". We never really agreed to "form a band", we just began messing about on Stephen's equipment and from there we recorded the first demo tape, "Hexe", which was self released in the Summer of 1993. At that time we were called AbRAXAS, we soon dropped that name in favor of ENDURA, for the simple reason that there are too many other bands, organizations and groups also using the name of Abraxas - most of, which were either musically inept or politically abhorrent. I think changing our name to ENDURA was one of the best moves we ever made. That was in the autumn of 1993, from there we have kept moving, making new contacts, recording material for lots of different labels, just continually striving for bigger and better things.

STEPHEN:-There have never been any difficulties working together. Although our starting blocks are far apart we usually find a mid-point on which we both agree. This is the whole concept of the collaboration. We are each strong personalities and we each pulling in our own directions. We knew we wanted to keep the music dark. All the material leaned in that direction anyway simply because whenever we come together, the clouds blacken and it starts to rain!!

I believe that the meaning of the word 'Endura' relates to a form of religious self-sacrifice by starving oneself to death. Could you shed some further light on the meaning behind the name, and how you feel it fits into the concept of the group - religious or otherwise? Also what is the reasoning/ meaning behind it's spelling with a 'V' instead of a 'U'?
STEPHEN:- People who believe in a flat earth, despite tremendous evidence to the contrary, are mo-

rons. People who deny the holocaust ever occurred, despite incontrovertible evidence to the contrary, are morons. People who disagree about the relative moral implications of one sick, tortured individual doing painful things to another individual are people who just don't agree. And people who need to believe in a higher being to justify their existence, in my mind, are just weak. Everyone has different opinions about faith and religion. My faith is that of complete disbelief. As for the use of the "V" instead of the "U", it is purely for aesthetics.

The two members of Endvra appear to be equally opposed in inspiration and interests. Whilst you seem to be more interested in music for music's sake, Christopher appears to be more involved in the formulation of the concepts and ideals of Endvra. How does the partnership work in terms of musical ideas/focus, compositional production & direction and inclusion of lyrics/ concepts?
STEPHEN:- Whilst on the surface, it may appear that we are opposed in inspiration and interests, I don't think we are too different. Chris and I agree on many things. He may call it "occult" I call it "life experience". I have an image of occult meaning secret enlightenment, which has been passed down through the ages in an elitist movement. A hierarchy of individuals thriving on the knowledge that they are worthy of the few. Instead of using pre-digested ideas, which may have been tainted through translations, I prefer to create my own. It may mean that I am ignorant of other information, but that only streamlines my focus. Knowledge is like baggage. Too much only serves to slow you down. I need only enough to get me to my destination, upon where I will change it, like a suit of clothes.

New 10" EP of yours features a track "Vestigial Horn", where a 1 minute 49 second excerpt of it is featured on the new Misanthropy compilation "Presumed Guilty". Why was such a short length excerpt of this track included on the compilation rather than longer one(or not at all for that matter)?
STEPHEN:- I think that question would be better answered by Misanthropy Records. We sent the complete track down with the understanding that it was going to be included in it's entirety then we get word back that they didn't like the whole track and were going to cut it to ribbons. What can you do? Our child was being manhandled by the kiddie-porn king. I think we made up for it in the long run though. Misanthropy had wanted a specially recorded track – we gave them one. They ripped the soul out of it without our consent so we released it again in a far superior form. Life goes on and on and on and on.

Your latest CD 'the Watcher' sees a total reversion in style from your last disc "Great God Pan". The new CD is very ambient and minimalist whilst the last CD release was quite composed. Admittedly G.G.P was originally recorded back in 1993 (but only released in 1997 with the 'first' four CD's recorded after but actually released before G.G.P), however since it seems to be your best distributed and most widely known release to date, do you think this will cause confusion with fans/ potential fans?
STEPHEN:- Those who know us will understand that we don't record music for our "fans", we record purely for ourselves. Although acceptance is always a nice feeling we don't yearn it. The minimalist stage is something, which we have to go through. It is something which Chris and I both wanted to explore and the album which Old Europa would also appreciate. I recently heard back from a guy on an Internet newsgroup. He had asked the question about another Endura album and someone had come back with "What – another one, those Endura guys are certainly prolific". We are. We are because we usually like what we do. We please ourselves.

Further to the above all of your CD's are slightly if not vastly different from each other. What are the main reasons you see behind this?
STEPHEN:- We just need to keep ourselves interested. Usually, as you have already pointed out, our albums differ in theme as well as content. In both aspects, we explore all avenues. To keep repeating those themes soon grows old so we use one release as the springboard for the next. "What did we do on the last album?, right, I'm sick of that already, let's do something different".

Could you give a brief rundown of the styles and inspiration encompassed on each of you releases and what are your personal thoughts regarding each one?
STEPHEN:- "Dreams of Dark Waters". This was our first real attempt at recording together. The first 20 minutes still impress me. That is usually the case with any new band. The early recordings reflect an enthusiasm and a mass of ideas. Not that nowadays we are short of any but those early recordings were the start down a new road, musically and mentally.
"Liber Leviathan". I'm not sure what order our CD's were recorded/released in. After a while, one recording session merges with the next. LL was a continuation in the use of 'space' within the recordings. The concept that the gaps in between the tones are just as, if not more so, important than the tones themselves. This is one of the things I like about the first 20 minutes of "Dreams ..."
"The Dark is Light Enough". This is a bit of a hitty missy album in my book. We tried to be all things to all people and maybe spread ourselves a little thin. Looking back, I wish we had done it all in one style instead of switching between three or four. The material on there is excellent, but it doesn't seem to follow any thread. Ah well, we live and learn.
"Black Eden". In my book, probably our most accomplished release to date. This is where it all started to come together for us, the mix was right and the timing was perfect. The artwork was a bit lacking but added a little mystery to the release by not giving away anything. People would listen to the music instead of reading the liner notes. "Great God Pan". Musically, this release was a pain in the arse for me. All the spontaneity and life was sequenced out of it. Too much time was spent dotting the "I's" and crossing the "T's" and as a starting point for our music I wouldn't suggest this album. Recording and mastering of this one certainly took it's toll on me and I don't think I've listened to the bastard thing since we sent the DAT down to Misanthropy.
"The Watcher". I think this album is great and I'm not just saying that because it is our most recent. Gone are all the over sequenced percussion and stabs. We stripped everything down to it's absolute minimum. We had talked about doing a true ambient album for a couple of years but the timing wasn't right for us. The CD for Old Europa Café was the perfect opportunity. They had access to the audience, which could appreciate what were wanted to do, so we went ahead and did it.

The 49 minute 'the Watcher' release is said to have been recorded in real time. How much compositional planning/ work was undertaken prior to entering the studio? Was any overdubbing or 'filling out' of the sound undertaken after the initial recording?
STEPHEN:- I think that the Watcher album works because it was recorded practically in real time. To create an album like that, with multiple layered tracks, drop-ins, overdubs etc. just wouldn't seem right. Music doesn't need to be that complicated. We were trying to create something, which would work on a primary level. Anyone can go into the studio and, providing they have enough time and money, make something sound halfway decent. We wanted to prove to ourselves that we could do it without all the sleepless nights, laboring over the mixing console. Although the CD is 49 mins long, we recorded the left and right tracks separately

and the stereo image was only created during mastering. The intent was to create an album, which could be used by the listener in mono mode, and he/she could mix the left and right tracks to create their own sound.

The concepts behind 'the Watcher' being related to states of dream & sleep paralysis merge very well with the musical content. Can you please elaborate on the concepts explored on the album?
STEPHEN:- The human mind has almost unlimited powers of creativity; both a great painting and a great thought begin as a concept seen as a whole in 'the mind's eye' – To become conscious of this process of creative visualisation is the first step towards harnessing its extraordinary power, whose secrets have been jealously guarded by magical adepts through the centuries. Mental creations can, depending upon the single-mindedness with which they are called into being, impinge on the reality of others. The adept conjures up thought forms or tulpas that achieve a degree of ideoplastic solidity and are, it is claimed, perceived as real by others. Werewolves, vampires and other legendary monsters may be deliberate magical creations. Encounters with fairies, demons, angels, and the Virgin Mary and ufonauts may be part of a similar process, whereby a culturally determined belief is externalised as a vision. Ordinary people can learn to utilise the extraordinary creative powers of the mind through the modern therapeutic technique known as, 'creative visualisation', which refers to the viewing of internal pictures in the mind. It is a simple, sensitive and effective way of communicating with the unconscious. These pictures occur naturally in dreams, daydreams and fantasies and have a wide application in psychotherapy. It has been suggested that there is a continuous internal picture-show projected beyond conscious awareness. One can enter this 'movie house of the mind' and utilise these films in many positive ways. Imagining a successful outcome to some situation seeing a future picture of the desired outcome may well influence activities in a positive way to secure this result. One form that these pictures may take is an inner journey into the unknown. The visualiser is led through a variety of encounters with frightening challenges. Often he comes face to face with monsters, dragons, waterfalls, tunnels and caves - just as classical heroes traveled the world overcoming powerful enemies. In therapy the visualiser confronts such challenges, and in the process automatically overcomes problems, on the 'surface' in his real world. There is no need for translation or interpretation of the visions, as they are already metaphorically linked with reality. The theory involved with this form of creative visualisation suggests parallel worlds in the mind - By confronting the fears in the fantasy world the adjoining worlds of the personality gain in strength. To achieve benefits from creative visualisation one initially needs the non-interfering support of a therapist or friend who guides from the outside, using , clean language' -words that will not imply or suggest any imagery. The visualiser sits quietly and comfortably, with eyes closed, allowing himself to drift into a day-dream trance state by focusing on any internal pictures that may occur. The direction of the journey may be determined by 'going into' a feeling and imagining what it looks like from the inside. The monsters, dragons and devils commonly encountered on such journeys are initially terrifying, but almost inevitably change into sensitive and powerful allies if the visualiser approaches them as a friend. These internal pictures are spontaneous, not directed by the conscious mind, and apparently random; yet they are as real to the viewer as the waking state.

Thus far over 6 full length CD's and a vinyl EP you have not had two releases on the same label. Why have you chosen to work with such a variety of labels and do you think it poses any problems for fans to track down your releases? Would you ever consider every exclusively working with a single label?

STEPHEN:- And so it shall remain until we land upon a label who can guarantee to do what we want. In the past we haven't wanted to be bound by contracts. Album, tour, promotion, sell your soul, make money for the man. No thanks. Most of the labels we have worked with in the past have been quite small and haven't minded our butterfly-like approach to the music world. And if people can't find our material then they are not looking hard enough. It's readily available on mail order list all over the place. Hell, they are even selling Black Eden in Peru!! The obvious thing to do, if anyone is having difficulties is to write to the label of the release which they presently possess. All the labels we have worked with have a mail order list of some description, most of our releases are on them.

Where do you plan to take Endvra's sound with upcoming releases? As you have been quite a prolific and productive group in past years, will this trend continue towards the end of the millennium? What releases do you have planned at this point and if none have you formulated ideas/ concepts?

STEPHEN We generally only plan loosely, six months in advance. We have a couple of compilations in the pipeline and the foundations are in place for the next album "CONTRA MVNDVM". It will include lyrics and texts by UK serial killer Dennis Nilsen. I have been writing to him in prison and ran past him the idea of appearing on our next album. He's actually a very eloquent individual who is able to translate his thoughts to paper through clever poetic style. So far he's sent over a number of poems which will certainly be on the next album. I am probably more excited about this release than I have been about anything we've done before. We are also talking to Red Stream Records - the label that released our Black Eden album, to work on a double CD This will be a re-release of the material from "Dreams of Dark Waters", "Dark is Light Enough" + all our compilations track to date. This will be packaged with a 12 page booklet and a full colour poster. We are looking at ways and means of including a CRr track on there as well, but we will have to see how much it will all cost. As you can appreciate, this will certainly be a release to look out for.

I am also working on my next Ontario Blue album "Waiting For Rain". Displeased Records (Holland) will release it, around the latter half of 1 9 9 9

As has been stated that each album has it's own distinctive style and sound (but still retaining the trademark Endvra aura) was this dictated by how you approached the studio and recording process.

and what types of equipment and sound sources do you typically utilise?
STEPHEN:- I think the 'sound' is always going to be there. Certain studios add their own distinctive flavour to a sound simply by the equipment used and how it is used. Abbey Road – London is said to have it's own sound and people are willing to pay highly to get it. Certain artists work on their own sound for ages and once they have it, work trying to get rid of it. Over the last few years, the sound may have changed a little because most of the equipment has been upgraded to digital. In my constant quest for the pure signal, I've dumped the old tape system and started hard disk recording.

I believe that Endvra played live in 1995, (with only Christopher in attendance) where the performance and complimenting video visuals caused quite a stir. Can you detail a bit of information about this performance and to what extent was it a 'live' show? Have you performed since this time and if not are there any plans as such?
STEPHEN:- Live. Why does everyone want us to play live? Frankly I can't see the fascination with it. Neither of us is really into the concept of entertaining people so if we did play live we'd probably do something really torturous. From a production point of view, playing live is a pain in the arse. I am a control freak, I have to have everything under control. To introduce the element of chaos into the equation just seems to spoil everything. I prefer to think of our releases in the same terms as a painter would his canvases. To tour the galleries of the country and reproduce versions of the same painting for a different audience seems a bit old.

CHRIS:-I was totally surprised by the reaction the ENDURA performance received, I was shocked by the way the audience was shocked. The ENDURA performance in Lille was a last minute thing, we had been approached by Nuit Et Brouillard but had declined their offer to play, unfortunately the communiqué never reached Lille and they were still under the impression that ENDURA could play. I decided to go ahead with the performance in Stephen's absence, this meant that the original performance had to be re-thought. As I was travelling to France on my own I could no longer carry all the equipment I needed for a full live show, instead we prepared a DAT and a video, and luckily I was helped with some live sounds from Marcus Schwill, without whom I would have been in deep trouble. The piece I performed was called "The Infernal Current", an evocation of the darker, sinister forces that exist, the video reflected this. The Belgian magazine TDR called the performance "disastrous", while I will be the first to admit that the circumstances, both with ENDURA and with the festival, were not the best and the performance was not all it could have been, I think the word "disastrous" misses the point. "The Infernal Current" was a ritualised performance, a magickal rite, and as any act of magick should produce a "change" in the status quo I think "The Infernal Current" was successful. A change certainly occurred, both in the way I viewed the world after the event and in the way certain members of the audience behaved.
Did the ENDURA performance traumatise people? I certainly hope so as I have no concern what so ever for the sensibilities and the fragile egos of people more used to the play-act pose of pseudo-ritual "homage" rather than the nitty gritty of practical magick. Shocking as some people may have found the video I think the reaction was caused by the totality of the event, the fear that arose when people realised they were the unwitting participants in an act they may not have chose to be a part of, and fear is often to be found hiding behind the skirts of anger and indignation. Speaking of those who hide behind the skirts of others, we got a vigorous critique from a certain vulgar little Belgian, indeed he was so incensed by ENDURA he skulked in the shadows and threw things, sent his girlfriend in to do his dirty work and even grabbed Marcus Schwill to scream in his face that ENDURA was nothing but a cheap copy of his band. It is telling that he never made any of these points to me, perhaps he was too traumatised? I have no regrets about the Deadly Actions festival at Lille, I thoroughly enjoyed myself, met some very nice people and enjoyed some excellent music. Nuit et Brouillard made me very welcome and I enjoyed a civilised weekend in the charming city of Lille. I think it would be wrong to assume Stephen was resting in Crete. Drinking so much alcohol in such

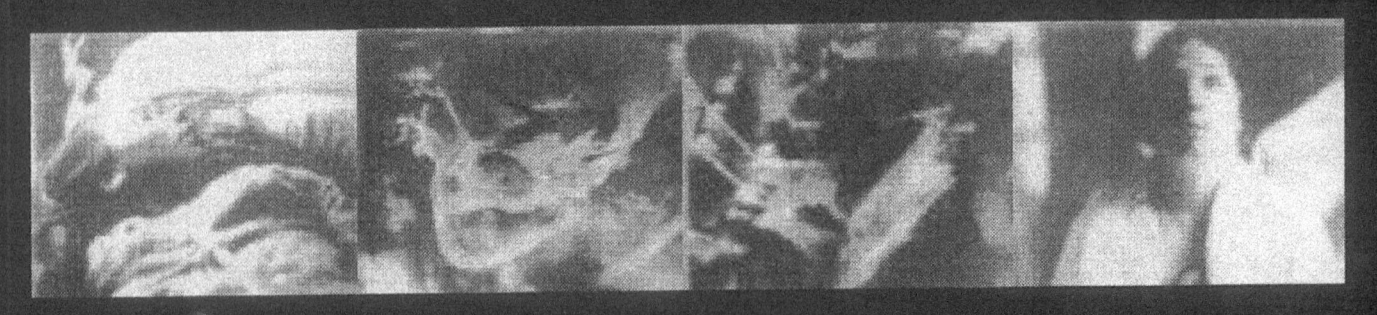

a short space of time in such a hot country was very tiring, he needed another holiday when he came back. Actually he was doing some research, when we have made our fortune through ENDURA we plan to retire to some sunny Mediterranean resort and open a strip-club.

Whilst on the topic of video footage you have produced a video for "He Knows the Gate" taken from the "The Dark is Light Enough" CD. I take it this would not be widely available nor even have had a mainstream screening. How was it produced, what types of visuals were filmed and are you satisfied with the results?
CHRIS:- The video was shot for the "Macrocephalous Compost III" compilation released by Old Europe cafe a few years ago. Before you get too excited let me tell you that it was shot for £50 one cold afternoon and is not the sort of thing any TV station would be happy to show. It was fun to do but video is still outside the reach of bands like us, to make a professional video, even for a small band is expensive and unlike the audio medium, video looks tacky if it is not done with a nice budget. Saying that though I think we made the most of our limited resources but don't expect to see something from Hollywood.

The Internet in recent years has played a reasonably vital role in the spreading of interest and knowledge in this style of music (given this magazine wouldn't exist without the contacts and the availability of relevant images/ information). How do you see its role now and in the future?
STEPHEN: I see the Internet or some technological offshoot as the future of communication. As something of a gadget collector, the Internet never fails to amaze me. It has so many uses. At the moment it is a bit restricted by bandwidth capacity, but as compression rates increase, it will not be too long before the average user is able to use their home computer as their only link with the outside world. I am hooked on computers. They do exactly what you tell them without question. A perfect digital instruction, clinical and precise carried out without loss. The master and his slave.

Peter Lechaise has been involved in the art and art direction of 'the Watcher', 'Great God Pan' & 'Black Eden' CD's and has been referred to as the third member of Endvra. Who is this individual and is the third member reference meant purely in an artistic sense?
STEPHEN:- Peter contacted us years ago, after he had heard our Hexe cassette. He comes over to the UK every couple of months to visit his daughter and we usually use the meeting as an excuse to go down the pub and get drunk. We discuss the various projects we have been working on, books we have read and talk of how things are going in Paris. Chris & I have been over there a couple of times but prefer to venture outside the city and into the old countryside. I don't know about you, but I absolutely hate cities. All those damned people rushing around, in your face like swarms of bloody insects. The dirty air, the media driven masses, the noise, aaghh just thinking about it makes me want to have a shower. Anyway, where was I? Oh yes, Mr Lechaise. He's pretty much like an old headmaster type and owns an old bookshop on the banks of the Seine. He can get hold of any book you can think of, as well as a keen eye for design, he also has a penchant for absynthe.

You yourself are personally involved in art, both traditional painting & computer generated. Do you ever plan to take over the whole design element of your releases? As you have stated you don't perceive yourself to be a 'musician' as such, on the same token do you consider yourself an artist?
STEPHEN:- I agree, I don't recognise the distinction of musician. I am an artist, and as such I don't want to be categorised or pigeonholed. I drift into different mediums as often as the weather changes and have already assumed the graphic designer role in the band. I think the artwork of a release is just as important as the recording on the disk.

As you have also recently released you debut CD of your side project Ontario Blue, could you tell us a little about this more personal project?
STEPHEN:- I have always enjoyed creating music, even from the age of about 15; I would mess around with two tape decks and some old microphones. I found it fascinating how the stereo image could be manipulated to such a great extent

to gain all kinds of textures, even if in the early days, my equipment was quite crude, I managed to get some interesting results, recording makeshift "demos" (more like catalogues of ideas). After 8 years plodding along, amassing ideas which I never really saw through to completion, I met up with Chris in 1993 and we decided, almost by accident, to record some stuff together, firstly as AbRAXAS then as ENDURA. By then, I had built a small studio and was craving new inspiration. Chris proved to be an abundant supply of fresh ideas. He's an avid reader and introduced me to the world of Lovecraft and Crowley; a mystical world, which seemed to be crying out for musical exploitation. This was the backdrop for ENDURA and everything seemed to fall into place. Our work as ENDURA has become quite successful but over time I feel we have been exhausting the same themes, the music has become secondary to the 'occult' image and I have been returning to my own experimentation for inspiration. I suppose, this came to a head in 1996, while we were still recording "Great God Pan". I was getting really pissed off with the album and wanted it over with as soon as possible. The recording sessions were like "pulling teeth" and seemed to last forever. Chris will agree with me on that score. It seemed like we were no longer recording for ourselves; somewhere along the line, we had ceased being individuals and became a "band" tied to deadlines and giving people what they wanted. Whenever we received interviews, they were from stupid "metal long hairs" more interested in the 'occult' and how to 'suck the Devils cock' than what we were supposed to be about - recording music. I would try my hardest to piss them off - and still do. During that period, I took some previous ideas, which were not realised in ENDURA and used them as the basis for my own material, after all, if they don't go into ENDURA, there's nothing to prevent me using them elsewhere. I already had a load of material, which was shelved and was encouraged by others to circulate it to see if there was any interest. There was, and ONTARIO BLUE was resurrected. I suppose, In some ways I've managed to retain a kind of child-like enthusiasm for things. If I like something, I rave about it and it totally consumes me, however, my imagination needs to be constantly fed to maintain my enthusiasm.

From listening to the Ontario Blue, it holds a few parallels to Endvra and for me tended to indicate that you would therefore be the main musical composer in Endvra. Am I correct or is this a huge blunder of an assumption?
STEPHEN:- Well, the studio and all the equipment in it is over at my house, so I just have more time to commit to the actual recordings. I might tinker around with the material in Chris's absence and on his return he'll say if he approves or not. If he does, the changes stay, if not, I think "what the fuck have I been wasting my time for, I may as well have been working on my own stuff instead".

Also a few years back you had a small label that you and Christopher ran entitled "Enlightenment Communications". Is this still in existence and if so are there and solid plans for its marketing and growth?
STEPHEN:- Personally, I would like to see Enlightenment Communications grow into a multi-media communications network, releasing material by other bands. I would also like it to include publishing so we could print books and magazines. At the moment it is all on hold because we don't have the time to do the things we want. Maybe in the future, when we are not too busy recording our own stuff, we'll make this pipe dream a reality.

Handing the final question over to you, anything you would like to add?
STEPHEN: -Thanks for spreading the word. You can view our website for updates or write to us for insertion to our mailing list.

SHINJUKU THIEF
the witch hunter

Shinjuku Thief being the premier Australian ambient/industrial group I could not pass up the opportunity to feature them, in these pages. Originally meant to be featured in Issue 1, at the time the sole member Darrin Verhagen was inundated with work on various other musical projects, thus the inclusion of the interview was put back to issue 2. When the time arrived for Darrin to complete the interview for this issue, it went precariously close to succumbing too the same fate however was managed to be submitted just days before the d e a d l i n e . Having heard some of the new Shinjuku Thief tracks at one of Darrin's DJ sets I can assure you that no fan will be disappointed by the wait for the third instalment of the Witch Trilogy when it finally released. In the meantime this interview will have to suffice.........

Shinjuku Thief are quite well known as a musical formation however its member and origins remain quite obscure. Can you please detail the members, history and other relevant information about the group?
The group began once I returned from Indonesia with an armful of DAT recordings in 1991. At that stage Franc Tetaz (percussion), Charles Tetaz (toys, guitar & Mexican flute) and I were interested in composing a Fourth World style album, that avoided the precious white-boy gloss of other fusion type projects. "Bloody Tourist" was the end result. Franc and I worked on the arrangements for "The Scribbler" together, thereafter, I've been flying Shinjuku solo.

Further the name Shinjuku Thief is quite unusual. Can you please explain it's meaning and why it was chosen? Do you think it adequately represents what you portray in a musical sense?
The title was taken from an Oshima film from the '60's. "Diary of a Shinjuku Thief" was part of an experimental wave of cinema from Japan, and (apart from other things) concentrated on challenging the audiences expectations as to the genre and techniques employed. Those jump cut approaches seemed appropriate to what we were attempting in those early sessions (mixing up tribal ambience with noise, jazz, funk, rock and the like). Given the high rate of sampling involved, and the much of the source material which I had collected, the use of the word "thief" was a reference to that whole school of 'cultural appropriation' argument which the west often shuffles its feet about. Whilst, ultimately, the background behind a name slips away as the title becomes established, I guess

you could make the link between the cinematic approach which unites all the Shinjuku albums and the filmic origins of the band name. Thereafter, the other shifts (filth vs thief etc) simply exist as signifiers to ward of stylistic shifts, with 'meanings' almost becoming academic.

I am yet to hear your first offering "Bloody Tourist" however I do believe it is at great odds with what you ended up producing on 'The Scribbler' and the first two parts of the 'Witch' trilogy. What is you opinion of your debut disc today in light of the other Shinjuku Thief works?
I heard "Bloody Tourist" for the first time in ages a few months ago, and really enjoyed it. I think that the humour and energy which went into the recording sessions right through to the production stage with Paul Schutze has helped to keep the work quite 'fresh' sounding. And whilst stylistically it inhabits quite a different realm from the albums which were to follow, many of the techniques characteristic of the Shinjuku sound (right angle shifts, sound design, dynamic range, sound bites etc) are certainly grounded in this release.

The music on 'The Scribbler' CD was originally included on a different tape version titled "Darrin Verhagen: The Trial/ a musical reinvention".(The music on the CD is the same as on the tape yet has been rerecorded in a more professionally sounding form). Which format was included as part of the stage installation & can you also detail the history related to the music on the 'The Scribbler' CD?
"The Scribbler" was originally written as a musical reinvention of Kafka's novel. The structure was taken from the locations of the various scenes throughout the narrative, with vocal extracts taken from all but the central character. The version on the original tape plus some additional interludes formed the soundtrack. Given the stripped back approach to the concept - essentially reducing a great literary work to a checklist of scenery - I chose the orchestral minimalist style of artists such as Philip Glass, Michael Nyman and Wim Mertens. On the CD, this 'flat' musical approach was augmented by a more sinister use of industrial elements in the sound design (referencing Kafka's day job as an industrial accident claim's assessor) but the approach was fundamentally the same.

For me 'The Scribbler' was the album that began to hint on what was to come with the 'Witch' series. How important was this release in leading you to the themes included on subsequent albums?
I guess, if one is to view "The Scribbler" as a stepping stone from our debut to the Witches, the main shift comes in the use of traditional orchestral instrumentation. In "The Scribbler" this was piano, organ, oboe and small string ensemble. Obviously once we hit the supernatural belt of the Witch trilogy, the orchestra is blown out into a much fuller set - large string sections, brass, percussion, with solos (where necessary) carried by violins and cellos rather than woodwind. "The Scribbler" was completed before I had a sampler, hence the approach was more straight and musical. With my sampling option on the K2000 came the ability to extend the sound palette into both more lush, as well as more experimental realms. Exploring this use of samples, lead almost inevitably to the "Witch Hammer".

As an overall observation your music has great depth, being multi-layered using both sampled sounds and real instruments. This would lead me to believe that extensive planning would go in the writing and production of your music. How do you approach the composition process and what is involved from moving from the 'idea' stage to the final recorded product?
The main ingredient in moving from the idea stage to the finished product is just time. The final in the trilogy, for example, has been on the drawing board for about 5 years, half finished for almost 3. It's simply the time demands of losing money (Dorobo) and making money (commissions) which keep seeing it getting pushed aside. Once a piece is begun, the majority of the time spent on its completion is generally in the detailing. Usually, I take two to three times as long on sculpting the final work to a level where I'm happy than in constructing the initial skeleton.

As much of the orchestral sounds you produce have an "authentic" feel I would like to ask exactly how much of the music utilises real instruments vs synthetic sounds? What types of equipment do you use to gain your depth of sound?
One of my great aversions is to overly synthetic sounds being passed off as 'realistic' representations of acoustic instruments. In some cases, such as with string ensembles, one can make allowances - but if you're talking about something like a violin solo, a synth patch, or note by note keyboard sample stinks for miles. To that end, if I want a melody to convey some impact or emotion, I'll often attempt to get it

played by a real instrument. And with just that one element of authenticity, it then becomes easier to get away with all the electronic approximations which support it.
The equipment I'm currently using includes and Kurtzweil K2000, an Ensoniq ASR10 sampler, with, more recently, additional tracks of audio on Logic sequencing software.

What is that you want to portray with your music to the listener and exactly what do you see Shinjuku Thief representing? Also what inspirers you to create your 'audile' paintings?
Ultimately what the listener brings to/or takes away from my music is up to them. Generally, my pieces will be a personal exploration of a particular genre, mood or timbre, often (in the case of Shinjuku) grounded by a concept I find interesting. I think, when writing your own music, second guessing what the audience wants or will find interesting, is a very quick road to insincerity and second rate material. In that regard, I've been fortunate, as even the commissions I've worked on - where consideration for an audience is more important - (eg. Starship Troopers computer game, strange dance company productions and experimental theatre) have all been projects which have interested me, and which have fallen into my musical interests of the time.

Can you please also detail any of the tuition you may have had in general field of music technique, composition & production?
My background was in piano, clarinet, and harmony and counterpoint theory in High School. At university I studied Indonesian, African and Indian music, and started playing shakuhachi (Japanese flute). Musical technique, composition and production though has all been learnt incidentally through a combination of listening and writing.

Ever since I originally viewed the Dorobo Video compilation (I+T=R) I was always intrigued by the choice of songs taken from 'The Witch Hammer' CD. The two chosen tracks "warm as the blood beneath the clods" & "in the path of walpurga's ashes" (which are complemented with video footage) are two of the most minimalistic tracks on the given album. The video footage basically consists of a slow panning shot of what appears to be an old European town in a modern setting. For me the footage seems at odds with the concepts & themes behind the album. Why did you choose these particular tracks (as opposed to more composed ones) and how do you feel the footage is representative of the chosen works?
Those pieces and that footage was chosen by Richard Grant (Mr I+T=R). The images were actually film of a graveyard with landmarks from the city of Prague in the background. Given the sense of depth and reflection the in the last two Hammer tracks, I actually enjoyed the rather surreal use of the graveyard shots (and thought the link back to "The Scribbler" through the geography was also nice). I think, had Richard chosen any of the more bombastic pieces it would have been difficult to have constructed clips which would do justice to the existing concepts already developed in the audience's imagination (short of burning through a cast of thousands, buckets of make-up and massive silicone graphics FX budget).

The last track on the video 'the year of silence' is another Shinjuku Thief track which I do not believe is included on any of your albums. This track sees the slight evolution of your sound with the incorporation of a more middle eastern/ ethnic basis. Where does this track originate from and can it be considered representative of the angle that may be taken on the next Shinjuku Thief CD?
Not really - it actually appeared on our debut, "Bloody Tourist", hence the indigenous influence.

Late in 1997 one of you side projects "Shinjuku Filth" collaborated with "Handspan" theatre company to produce backing/ theme music for a stage performance. Although I did not get to see the final product much of the advertising kept mentioning "Shinjuku Thief". Was there any reason behind this or was this simply a marketing blunder?
Essentially, the distinction between the two Shinjuku's is there for the initiated. It's certainly "Filthy" music, but we felt that most people, if they'd heard of either, would have heard of Thief. Hence Shinjuku Thief in the advertising, but Shinjuku Filth stipulated on the soundtrack.

Did you perform the music for the production live or was it simply used as a recorded backdrop? How happy are you with the results of you contribution and could you describe for us the overall theatre production from your perspective?
The music I wrote was as pre-recorded backdrop.

One of the tradeoffs with material as densely written as Shinjuku, is that it's never practical to perform live. Whilst I enjoy the version on CD, it was rush-released to coincide with the production, hence lacks some of the additional detail to be found in the performance mix. The production itself was an attempt at fusing my music, live input and collaboration from Regurgitator, with Handspan's massive theatrical staging (8 foot cockroaches, cherry pickers weaving throughout the audience, pyrotechnics etc etc). The space itself (Shed 14 down at the docks) was about 200 x 50 metres, and whilst the size and its use allowed them to play with the audience's expectations and sense of space, it did diminish some of the impact of aspects of the work. The only other unfortunate component was Regurgitator's "take the money and run" attitude, which was disappointing given that the original intention was to feature the band in a more integrated and collaborative manner. (Rock'n'Roll)

The music mentioned above has been released as a limited mini CD as "Shinjuku Filth: Raised by Wolves" on Iridium (Dorobo's side label). How has the response been to this disc and is there any truth in the rumour that it will be re-released as a full length CD once additional music is composed and recorded?
Response to "Raised by Wolves" has been most enthusiastic from folks who are into experimental industrial dance. It was interesting given that it ended up being released at the same time as "Soft Ash" (the markets for each album being virtually mutually exclusive). Not surprisingly, the full assault tactics of "Raised by Wolves" have proved more popular than the delicate nuances of "Soft Ash". The full length version of the stage score was to be completed in time for the Adelaide Festival production of the work, which never eventuated. At this stage there are no plans to reissue the CD with more tracks.

Whilst on the topic of playing live, have Shinjuku Thief ever taken to the stage? Are there any plans in future to undertake live performances?
Thus far, although Shinjuku Thief has been used in theatre and dance, we've never attempted the full live thing. As I mentioned earlier, attempting to recreate the complexities of the albums would be next to impossible on a shoestring budget. And playing lead lines over a DAT backup wouldn't impress anyone. Eventually I'd like to work towards something live with a string ensemble, but it's still early days for that. In the mean time, I've been doing some DJ work (including premiering the forthcoming "Witch Haven"), and David Thrussell (Snog, Soma, Black Lung) and I have some plans to collaborate on some material which will end up on stage - but I suspect that will be in a more poppy electronic direction than the dark side of Shinjuku Thief/Filth.

Currently two of the "Witch" trilogy CD's have been released, however the third instalment has taken on almost mythical proportions, given the years that have transpired since the second was released. Is there any specific reason for such a lengthy delay and when (if ever!) can fans expect this disc to be completed and released? Furthermore how will it differ from the music on the first two parts?
Well, I'll avoid boxing myself into a corner, because I've been saying "it'll be finished within the next couple of months" for the last 2 years. Let's just say "by the end of '99". (Fingers crossed) Preparing for these DJ sets has seen me work on mixes of a number of tracks, so things seem to be progressing nicely. The delay simply comes down to juggling too many things. Initially it was just attempting to keep on top of Dorobo. Then, as it became clear that the label was unsustainable as any sort of an income stream, it came down to finding music work which I could survive on (commissioned works for radio, theatre, dance etc) Given that most of these commissions were for projects I really enjoyed - not to mention the fact that they also got me back in the studio, my own personal projects just started taking more of a back seat. Musically, thus far, "The Witch Haven" follows the path suggested by the development from the first to the second - but with much of the sound design yet to be completed (and some fairly radical plans in the back of my mind in that department) not to mention the bombastic "Starship Troopers" music I've been working on, it's difficult to say where the whole thing will end up.

Once the final part of the trilogy is released do you have any preconceived ideas on what directions do you plan to push Shinjuku Thief in? Will you remain in the 'gothic industrial' type vein?(which appears to have been your most popular direction to date).
At this stage, I have to say that I have no specific plans for Shinjuku Thief after the completion of the trilogy. Work for theatre has recently involved Russian Circus Music (Handspan), delicate glitch fused with degenerated blues - grounded in bees ("Stung" for DW98), Japanese percussive fusion (closing Melbourne Festival ceremony '98) "Soft Ash" style electroacoustic radio works ("Here's to the death of one over 'f'", ABC Classic FM), the delicate electroacoustic shakuhachi suite for "New Music Australia" ("p3") , and most currently, nasty techno/glitch/drum&bass/electrothrash ("Bodyparts" for Chunky Move '99). Current projects include feral and suburban soundscapes (Playbox's "A Few Roos" and "The Dog's Play"), Japanese ambience with traditional drumming ("Miss Tanaka", Handspan), bombastic orchestral/military ("Starship Troopers" CD ROM) and more experimental dance pieces for a variety of choreographers.

Dorobo Records (being your label) was originally

conceived for a one off pressing of the Shinjuku Thief CD "The Scribbler'. Since that time it has blossomed into a quality and respected label. Why did you choose to continue with releasing music after the first disc pressing?
I was mad.

What are your personal goals for the label and what visions do you see for its continued future?
Well, the last year has seen my attempts to find a solution to my current label vs studio dilemma. (Which saw 3 albums released manufactured by Projekt USA, and Matt Thomas' "_remodulations" handled by Staalplaat, Netherlands. Stylistically, the trend suggested by releases from Lamb's "Primal Image (Dorobo 008) onwards - general more subtle, less theatrical works - will, I think, continue. Our most recent releases have been dark and delicate experimental excursions - Philip Samartzis' "Residue" (Dorobo Limited Editions 1), Darrin Verhagen's "p3³" (DLE2), Matthew Thomas' "p3³" (DLE3) and Philip Samartzis's "Windmills Bordered by Nothingness" (DLE4). The next Iridium release will probably be the soundtrack to Chunky Move's "Bodyparts", with the next Dorobo release being Shinjuku Thief's "Witch Haven".

Dorobo has released a variety of styles of music which are not typically related. What overall style do you see that your label represents and what attributed does an act have to hold to be signed to Dorobo roster?
I think a certain dark undercurrent and an obvious love of sound unites most of the releases on the label. Personally, I don't find that there's much of a leap of faith from a Shinjuku orchestral CD, to an Alan Lamb noise exploration of wire music, or even the Japanese soundscape dub of "Document 02: sine". My exposure to and love of a wide variety of music has certainly shaped my tastes, but I've tried to keep some degree of musical continuity across the label (hence the establishment of the two sub labels - Iridium for industrial dance/ experimental techno, and Dorobo Limited Editions for more delicate electroacoustic material.

As Shinjuku Thief has shown a flair for presenting a wide variety of styles from release to release does this pose problems for Dorobo from a promotional & marketing perspective?
I have to admit the stylistic freedom I enjoy pursuing artistically can become a source of frustration from a marketing point of view. But ultimately, I'd rather adopt that particular balance than the other way around (where the music becomes a cynical arm of the marketing operation). To that end, I've presented cues - whether they be in the Thief/Filth/Verhagen distinctions, or in examples such as the "Witch" trilogy (where expectations can be reasonably fulfilled from one album to the next).

Even if the music on Dorobo is quite diverse the label has definitely its personal 'look' with the presentation (with this also including the video compilation). Who is responsible for the overall production and realisation of the art and what role do you and the relevant groups play in the final visual product?
Our designer is Richard Grant (I+T=R). And it is his talent which has provided a solid label identity. Generally, the groups and I will have a general idea as to the type of look we want, or at least the sorts of elements we'd like involved. Beyond that, Richard is given a large amount of freedom. He'll often generate a selection of starting options, which we'll then pick and choose from - but generally, he can be credited with all the sexy design/layout. (As a result of his Dorobo profile, he was recently employed by Cold Meat for the Protagonist CD.)

Are the releases on Dorobo typically limited and which particular products have been licensed overseas/ & by who?
That usually depends on the financial viability of repressings – with the dual components of the label's liquidity and the artists ongoing saleability determining the outcome. Recently, we've explored the notion of collectors editions in the Dorobo Limited Editions sub label – which has its own delicate acousmatic focus - and those 4 CD's are definitely limited to runs of 500. We'll probably not repress most of the Dorobo backcatalog from here on in. The only title which is reaching dangerously low levels however is Ikeda/Koner/ Lustmord/Gunter - "Night Passage: demixed" (with only 20 copies left). As regards licensed works, here's a run down -
Dorobo 001 v/a - Document 01: trance/tribal (Fifth Colvmn, USA)
Dorobo 003 Shinjuku Thief - Witch Hammer (Projekt, USA)
Dorobo 005 Black Lung - Silent Weapons (Machinery, Germany)
Dorobo 012 D.Verhagen - Soft Ash (Projekt, USA)
Dorobo 014 F.Tetaz - Motionless World (Projekt, USA)
Dorobo 015 Matt Thomas - _remodulation (Staalplaat, Netherlands)
Iridium 193.2 Black Lung - Depopulation Bomb (KK, Belgium)
Iridium 193.5 TCH - Sinflower (Projekt, USA)
P305 Shinjuku Filth - Junk (Fifth Colvmn, USA)

Apart from the label you have a well established and extensive mail order catalogue. Are you able to make money from the mail order component or is it simply there to finance the operations of the label?
(Verhagen clutches chest, wheezing with laughter.) Sadly neither alternative record manufacture or alternative music distribution actually make money. The distribution arm is primarily there for our own protection. After being done over a few times by overseas distributors, we now favour trade over cash

payments (owing to the latter being difficult, if not impossible to secure). As a result, we then need to find an outlet for the traded material, hence offer it into the modest Australian market. Both the label and the distribution are now financed by my music commissions.

Are you able to make any sort of reasonable profit from the operations of Dorobo & is it a full time operation? If not, what occupies your life outside of music & the label?
Well, the balance certainly now seems to be improving - with music writing now taking up most of my time. Dorobo has the nature of expanding to fill up any time I allow it - but from a hard nosed business point of view, the time spent can never be justified by the returns it generates. That's not to say I begrudge the label - there are certainly fun aspects to releasing material - but I have needed to keep things in perspective, as a fun hobby won't put food on the table.

The 'Soft Ash' side project released under your own name, again showcases your skills to produce music in a number of given styles and fields. Rather than this disc coming off as a complete work it has more the sound and feel of a 'various artists' compilation. Can you detail for the readers the themes behind the concept of the album and some notation of the styles within?
The album was based on the concept of lethal atmospheric inversions (essentially when one atmospheric system caps another, trapping the pollutants below). The most exotic ones, which first piqued my curiosity, concerned killer fogs in Belgium and London - where the population's response to the cold and poor visibility, was to burn more oil/coal, further increasing the particulate matter in the atmosphere, and so the deaths. That starting point was then combined with a gentle swipe at the academic approaches of some of the contemporary composers - with each scenario from history assigned its own interpretative genre, polluting documentation, and listening level. The styles covered electroacoustic, industrial ambient, dark orchestral, with the tags becoming more surreal as the album unfolded - through to "rhythmic minimalism (with sporadic ambient techno / glitch residuals and an unnecessary flair for hyperbole)" - an obvious pisstake on the love of categorisation which can accompany writings about music.

Two of the tracks included on the above album were actually commissioned by the Australian Broadcasting Corporation. What exactly were these tracks produced for and how did you come to be in contact with them?
I approached "The Listening Room"(on ABC classic FM) shortly after leaving full time retail employment. I presented them with a proposal outlining my ideas for a "Soft Ash" suite and played them the first track I had already composed for the Japanese compilation "Statics". Whilst my style was different from the sorts of works they usually commissioned, the concept I think stood me in good favour, as they had already planned to schedule a fog work by Gregory Whitehead.

There has also recently been a new solo release of yours under the working title P3 (a three inch mini CD). This displays a technological cut up collage type of ambient aesthetic. Exactly what principles of music experimentation/ presentation were utilised? Also as the 20+ minute release appeared to have its debut on an Australian radio station can you elaborate how it eventuated and if it was a live or prerecorded performance?

p3 was a suite of studio pieces I composed for "New Music Australia" (ABC Classic FM) utilising shakuhachi as a source instrument. The end result places the raw footage alongside artifacts of contemporary recording (digital and analog clicks, pops, and hiss) in a delicate electroacoustic study of texture. The end result fuses a musique concrete approach with a glitch aesthetic, on occasion presented over a post-industrial ambient bed. I then gave the soundfiles I had constructed to Matthew Thomas, and his "p3" companion CD has also just been released on Dorobo limited editions.

I believe that you also have plans for further solo releases under your own name. What can we expect from these and will their contents be dictated by the whims of your interests at the given time of writing and release?
I can only hope. The last thing I'd want is my output to be dictated by the whims of someone else's interests! At this stage, I'm not too sure what will be released next. Apart from the immediate focus of the third in the witch trilogy, the only other work I'm keen to get out is the recent soundtrack to Chunky Move's "Bodyparts". Whilst I'm on that bill under my own name, I suspect the nasty techno/drum'n'bass component of that work will warrant a "Filth" for marketing purposes. Ideally, I'd like to keep my own name for the more 'personal' projects. Given that I'm pretty much booked up for the next year however, I'm not too sure what sort of personal material I'll have time to work on....

I would have to say that you clearly have the conceptual ideas and talents to work in a professional field of sound design and production. As other artists such as Graham Revell & Brian Williams have been able to make inroads into Hollywood soundtrack territory does any of your goals see you seeking a career in the fields music production & design?
No plans to jump ship yet. Thus far I've been really fortunate in the sorts of scores I've been asked to write. All have been for interesting projects which have allowed me a fair degree of latitude to explore my own ideas. Moving towards the homogenised world of Hollywood would be fairly artistically dispiriting (despite the obvious pecuniary rewards). That said, should any interesting film work present itself (locally or from o/s) I'd certainly keep an open mind.

I also hear that awhile ago you (and other noted experimental artists) were targeted by a certain Hollywood music business individual, to be part of a new mainstream ambient/ experimental music label. Would you care to shed a bit of light on this situation?
I'm afraid I'm not up with all the juicy details on that score. I'd imagine Jason Mantis may have more goss there.

Well thank you Darren for being part of the magazine. As the interview draws to a close do you have any final comments?
Sorry for taking so long to finish this!

Should anyone want a free mail order catalog (Cold Meat, Malignant, Manifold, GROSS, Dark Vinyl, Staalplaat etc) feel free to drop us a line -

Dorobo
P.O.Box 22
Glen Waverley
Victoria 3150
Australia
dorobo@werple.net.au

Thanks again.
C h e e r s .

SOUND REVIEWS

Alan Lamb (Aus) "Original Masters – Night Passage" CD 1998 Dorobo
After having the 're-mix' CD 'Night Passages' released a few years prior to the original work, this had a lot to live up to given the sheer quality of the interpretations/ re-workings done by Lustmord and Thomas Konor (among others) on the former CD.
On the first two tracks (of three) Alan Lamb has done little other than collating and compiling the sound sections into coherent pieces, letting his 'wind organ' do the rest. And what is a 'wind organ' I hear you ask? Well in this case, during the mid 70's Alan stumbled across a stand of old disused telegraph wire poles in the outback of Western Australia. Discovering that the wires would 'sing' with the movement of the wind he proceeded to tap into the old wires with contact microphones and record their sound at various points from 1976 through to 1984. All sounds created and recorded on this release are a direct 'cause and effect' of nature upon the wires. From temperature fluctuations, wind & rain through to birds and insects coming into contact with the wire, have all shaped and created these evocative pieces. The depth and breadth of sound is astounding, coming across as powerfully as any manipulated and composed dark ambient release. From low flowing sections rising to clattering levels, the ambience of the wires takes on life of their own. The third track on the CD is taken from a recording of purpose built 'wind organ' in Kobe, Japan, as part of a festival held in October 1987. Alan played a slightly more proactive role here where a vertical nylon wire was attached to the horizontal wires and then played with a bow, much like a giant instrument. Although on a different 'wind organ' the result has much the same sound and effect, although more subdued and crystalline with less sporadic moments.
The sheer dynamics and intensity of this form or experimental wire music is testimony to the archaic forces of nature managing to manipulate and affect mans technological advances. This original 'wind organ' has long since collapsed but this final release remains as a legacy to the original instrument. I sincerely hope that Alan Lamb will continue to explore the dynamics of wire music through purpose built facilities. Get this!

Ataraxia (Ita) "Historiae" CD 1998 Cruel Moon International
Although I have been aware of this group for a number of years, this is the first time that I have had the opportunity to appreciate their music. On the surface of both music & imagery this is similar to Arcana in its use of layered male/ female vocals, but overall it is less orchestral and more folk oriented in composition. For those who have a background in doom metal music may be interested to know that the female vocalist of this group appeared on the Monumentum CD a few years back.
The opening track uses the said layered vocals with guitars, harps, marching drums and various medieval styled instruments which results in a mildly rousing piece. Track two is much more operatic in the presentation of the female vocals complimented by lute guitar, light percussion and flute all floating along with the vocals. "Filava Melis" (third track) reminds me very much of the approach used by a band called Summoning (Black Metal) who produces epic Tolkein inspired hymns. The lack of electric guitars and with the addition of female vocals sets this apart with epic horn sections and more folkish interludes.

Another classical guitar and operatic (female) ballad is found in track 4 which runs the following composition which is a very traditional sounding celebration dance song.
"Antinea" begins with overlaid male/ female chant styled vocals used in a foreboding manor. Later a slow marching beat is introduced with a classical guitar following the vocal lines. Before the track reverts back to the opening vocal chants late in the piece a mid paced section is used.
The remainder of the tracks use the same sound aesthetic approach of the preceding compositions but are taken from a live recording (in a medieval court) during the Spring Equinox(whereas the studio tracks were recorded in the Autumn Equinox) As all songs are of high quality is hard to pick the difference from the former studio songs to the later live ones.
Overall the music is showcased with a full and rich sound production, that is very authentic in the medieval age that it was inspired by. Not really a disc for dark ambient fanatics but for those inspired by traditional European folk sounds.

Blood Axis (USA) "BLOT: Sacrifice in Sweden" CD 1998 Cold Meat Industry
One of the more controversial modern electronic/ industrial acts of our time present a live CD recorded at the CMI 10 year anniversary party held late in 1997. Led by Michael Moynhan, many accusations have been leveled at the ideology behind the music, however I will leave this up to the individual to sift through the imagery and lyrical hints to work it out for themselves. On a personal note, having read a non-fiction study of the Black Metal movement written by Mr Moynhan it is easier to dissect certain viewpoints from analyzing the editorial perspective.
Well enough ideology and politics- what of the music? Beginning at a funeral march pace, a slow organ hymn is presented with a spoken word overtone. The organ continues into track two "Herjafather", but now includes low vocal chants and a slow backing beats.
Via the introduction of howling wolves an emotive and folk like guitar and violin are presented on the third track "Seeker" along with a half sung, half spoken vocal line. The dynamics are again increased on "Electricity" with sampled operatic vocals and orchestral violins. The vocals are presented in a totally spoken manor but always forceful and sometimes distorted. The foreboding drum beat increase along with the anger of the vocal chanting "Heil Victory (x3).....Electricity".
"Lord of Ages" again uses spoken vocals, violin and slow drums but midway explodes into a fist raising marching tune. The well known "The March of Brian Boru" (played on the violin with traditional Irish drum percussion) is utilized well as a bridge to the more bombastic and forceful half of the live set.
Continuing, the original version of "The Gospel of Inhumanity" is further filled out with the use of the violin, which is a good contest to the electronically produced samples and keyboards. The electric guitars, keys and vocals are forceful and focused on "Eternal Soul" which are juxtaposed against the more sorrowful and poetic track "Between Birds of Prey".
"Reign I Forever" can not help but be a classic track, sampling the main musical theme from a Prokofiev piece, being also complimented by sermonistic lyrics focussing on nordic mythology. A newer track "The Hangman & the Papist" is highly anthemic with a more traditional guitar based structure, still retaining the marching folk feel.
Rounding out the 60+ minute set is the bombastic "Storms of Steel" which again verges on topping the original version.

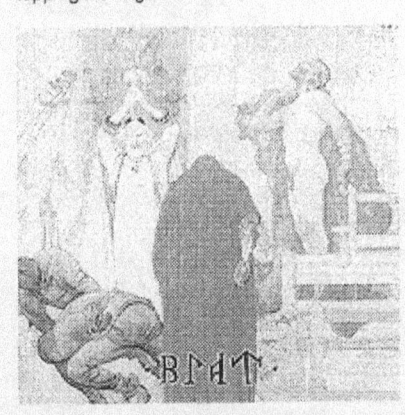

From listening to this, there is something definitely at work below the surface of the music, something which you can't put your finger on immediately. The most obvious is the focus to the strength of the European Archetype – or more subtly a spiritual summoning if you will. Again I will leave this to the individual to interpret as they see fit.

For a live performance (and one of Blood Axis's first major shows) this is a highly focused and skilled presentation of the past, present and future directions of the group.

I'm not sure if any major re-mixing and or overdubbing was undertaken after the performance, but for a group to be able to eclipse a studio version of a song in a live setting is no easy task(which is achieved here on a number of the tracks).

This is an album containing modern electronic elements and traditional orchestral structure, melded perfectly via a live medium, creating a stunning musical release.

Brighter Death Now (Swe) "No Salvation/ No Tomorrow" 10"ep 1998 Anarchy & Violence

Released on a new, yet very obscure side label of CMI comes a two track vinyl EP. As you would expect the cover is a simple black sleeve with a black and white corpse picture, however the gimmick is that the cardboard sleeve has been intentionally scratched and damaged by Roger/BDN/Karmanik. Talk about personalizing your work!

Up first is a new track "No Salvation" which was reportedly recorded during 1996 (no liner notes exist on the cover). This has quite a psychotic edge with it's ranting vocal sermon (treated and processed to become indistinguishable). The rolling marching beat has also undergone a extensive distortion treatment with other stabs of noise included. Quite repetitive in structure it is still enjoyable over its 7-10 minute (approx.) length.

Track two "No Tomorrow" was originally featured on the "Innerwar" release but has gone through a slight remix here, being a repetitive slow paced beat driven dirge with over the top processed vocal and piercing screeches – just the way I like it.

Limited to 500 copies you can't half tell that I am a bit of a BDN complete-ist!

Brighter Death Now (Swe) "Greatest Death" CD 1998 Cold Meat Industries

Containing no new music what so ever, Roger Karmanik continues on with his re-releases of BDN material for those of us unfortunate enough not to have obtained a copy of the real thing (don't think for a minute that that includes me!). For those who don't know the story The Great Death Trilogy began when 'Great Death I' was re-released along with new recording of 'Great Death II' in 1995(delux cardboard box packaging with embossed tin logo & limited to 1500). Those who obtained the box set, were then invited to order the exclusive third part of the trilogy. Those then owning all three parts were further invited to vote for their favorite 5 tracks for inclusion on a best of compilation(& also purchase another exclusive 7" picture vinyl). So, basically what this release ends up being is a 'best of' the complete works spanning the trilogy (let it be known that all five tracks that I voted for are included here).

As I already own all of the music included on this disc I really own obtained it to further complete the set. However I must say I was surprised how well it worked as a compete body of work for an album as well as a great representation of the three CD's. Being compiled in the order that the tracks were voted for, it appears that the ultra heavy noisy death industrial was what which struck a chord with most voters. Despite this tracks such as the cavernous industrial piece 'Laudate Dominum I' have found there way to the forth most popular in the play order. With the music being recorded over a period of the first half of this decade it still remains timeless in it's own haunting and deadly way. For the new listener this release will only serve as a contemptuous twist of the rusty blade that they did not manage to obtain the complete work that this derived from.

After a few years of silence on new full length BDN releases it finally looks as though that Karmanik is soon to be ready to unleash a brand new double CD entitled "May all be Dead". May it be worth the wait!

Brighter Death Now (Swe) "May all be Dead" DLP 1998 Cold Meat Industry

Mr Karmanink must be commended for this release. Limited to only 1000 copies, this heavy weight double vinyl set has been kept to the price of a single LP. Having been waiting for a new full length BDN release for over two years, this is nothing but astounding with its giant fold out LP cover.

The sounds of this DLP are not really like any particular album that proceeds it but more of a mixture of elements. Taking the repetitive droney elements of 'the Great Death' era and mixing it up with the harsher elements of 'Innerwar' you might get some idea. Given that the DLP contains only 6 listed tracks, the cuts are mostly very lengthy and somewhat repetitive – not to say this is a bad element at all.

With a brief electronic clatter the chugging/ surging tape loop of 'I Hate You' kicks in with considerable force containing also tape processed vocals and sporadic stabs of sound. Repetition is in order and by the track hitting it's plateau early, it is content with it's position. "I wish I was a little girl" (formerly of the CMI 50# comp.) is included here and is a personal fav tracks of BDN, with it's feverous vocals, incessant loops and pure aggression of the noise tones. Side B of LP 1 brings the track 'Behind Curtains' which is atmospheric in tone with high end wavering sound and a mid ranged distorted rolling beat. Spoken vocals are again included but have a more psychotic edge which becomes more noticeably aggressive as more layers of noise is introduced. It would appear that there is a bonus track on this side of the vinyl with an unnamed/ unlisted track. I'm yet to confirm if this is on all copies, but it is a good track that yet again manages to contain a different sound without forsaking the traditional BDN elements. Here, there are no tape looped beats, just sustained noise tones & indecipherable vocal samples. An interesting guitar solo also finds it's way into the track.

Side A of LP 2 is introduced with yet another vocal snipit before the apocalyptic waltz loop and industrial clatter of 'Pay Day' enters. 'Oh What a Night' has a slower dronier edge but does contain some more ear piercing elements, again using simple dynamics of increasing vocal and music intensity as it progresses. The final side of the 2LP set comes with a very lengthy track 'fourteen'. A slow pounding beat compliments the more subdued electronics going on in the background. The vocal and samples are distorted in such a manor that they simply become another layer of electronics within the whole track dynamic.

For those unlucky enough to miss out on the bonus clear 7" EP (only in a limited number of the 1000 DLP sets) the tracks are two short pieces that only sweetens the whole feeling of this release. One track is purely a high pitched squeal with only a distorted vocal ranting, while the other side has another mid to high pitched tone with an electronic stabbing beat. All in all, the bonus 7" is quite distinct in sound to the 2 main LP's.

For the most part putting words to BDN's sound is an arduous task. Karmanik having been at

LUCIFER RISING   cd

athanor's new anthems dedicated to the "free spirits"

featuring: endura, chod, blood axis, der blutharsch, dawn dusk entwined, allerseelen, ernte, bobby beausoleil, changes, waldteufel and ain soph

[120 ff ppd]

athanor

B.p. 294
86007 poitiers cedex, france
ursprache@wanadoo.fr

ad assisted by Spectrum Inc

CazzoDio (Ita) "il tempo della locusta" CD 1998 Black Plagve
Here we have the first release on the mutation of Malignant Records, with the rise of the new side label Black Plagve (which promises to be as inventive and original as Malignant has proven to be).
Opening with screeching samples and a rhythmic, metallic percussive affair, the tone of the album is laid down early. Whilst some power electronic opt for a bass driven sludgy production, this is at the total opposite of the scale, being load and crystalline (the emphasis on load!). The overpowered frequencies are pushed to the optimum fiery temperature where only the searing heat of sound can be felt by the listener. The majority of vocal samples have been overloaded and processed beyond any reasonable recognition and is much the same when vocals are presented (on two tracks), in the form of a ranting lunatic warning of the coming plague.
On the title track swarms of locusts have been sampled (or replicated immaculately!) over the factory rhythm clatter, giving a modern equivalent of a prediction of a pestilence to befall man. Amongst the metallic power electronic focus, this does not at any stage venture into the piecing noise territories of it's counterparts. The noise frequencies (although harsh & high pitched), are kept bearable in tone having been produced to their sonic capacity (with thanks to the production skills of Phil Easter aka Stone Glass Steel).
One of the favorite tracks for myself comes late in the album with "among the corpses of the servants of drabness" which employs a darker bassier edge but still retaining the rhythmic metallic percussion.
In parts this can draw comparisons to the harshest moments of Decree and also to the non melodic/ percussive focus that Mental Destruction have perfected. If grating, driving, surging power electronics is your weakness, bow to the new sonic master.

ConSono (Swe) "iGNOTO dEO" CD 1998 Crowd Control Activites
One of the very early CMI acts has finally returned with a new release and also signed to a new label. Where they were previously a dark ambient styled group incorporating a few more composed elements (& vocals), this time around all songs are fully composed, complimented with gothic styled vocals. I guess that since their first disc was a collection of early recordings and compilation appearances they did not really get to showcase their total musical vision, thus why the two discs seem quite apart in structure.

The vocals being sung/ spoken in a low gothic fashion draw some comparison to Controlled Bleeding and/ or In Blind Embrace and the like. Unusual percussive sequences often form the background structure with pianos, keys, bells, chimes and other sampled sounds etc all used sporadically to certain effect. Other real instruments such as guitar, bass and sitar are also utilized on a number of songs.
None of the tracks really enter up-tempo territory preferring to stay sparse and minimally composed. One of the standout tracks is "Winter Tale" with the haunting background tune before another unusual percussion sequence is introduced. There is certainly an unusual aura and feel surround the songs and production which is both archaic and mysterious; akin to tapping into forgotten times and cultures.
As this does not fit entirely into the dark ambient mold nor the pure gothic style, I gather there would be quite a overlap in the fans of this CD. I suggest you get this if you enjoyed the first or if you are not afraid of vocals incorporated within darkly melodic tunes. As the label who released this is slowly gaining momentum they are surely to go far if they keep up such quality.

Crepescule (USA) "Music for Decay:Part 1 metamorphais of life" CD 1998 Tegal Records
When I ordered this, (given the name of the project and the title of the CD) I was expected some death ambient or death industrial stuff, but I was quite wrong with this assumption. It does have some of these said elements but overall it is much more subdued, intrinsic and mournful than I anticipated. Track 1 ('Created') has a variety of static oriented frequencies with radio and keyboard modulations cutting in and out. 'Mother' again takes a similar approach to the first but is a little more minimal in its longer flowing format. Track 3 ('love') is a nice classical oriented passage that is melancholic in a way to twinge a element of unsubstantiated sorrow. The sound here has attempted to be full and rich but either due to specific purpose or the limitation of the mastering the sound tends to distort. 'Childhood theif' is quite weird as it has the repetitive 'phaser' effect that tends to drown out the quite nice ambient manipulations floating underneath. Track 5 although starts off quite subdued, with the inclusion of some light keyboards, it has some quite dark undercurrents of sludgy buried sound that gradually builds in intensity – somewhat akin to Vond's last industrialized CD.
The start of 'Father' is nothing less than a surreal listening experience with what seem to be farmyard samples of all things?! As the track is quite long it meanders off into other territory soon enough, but the damn phaser effect makes another appearance. Luckily is disappears again from whence it came being replaced with some more just plain weird, noises, vocal samples and the like.
The partial classical approach is again taken up in (tack 7) mixed in with more vocal samples and even a distorted guitar piece that is manipulated well enough to fit the concept sound. One of the better tracks on the CD is 'matricide fantasy' (track 8) with ominous sounds, engulfing wave like effects and the angry ranting of a woman.
For the final track ('matricide reality') it is 9 seconds of silence which must have some relevance to the 9 tracks on the CD-but who knows??
Throughout the CD there is quite a heavy use of vocal snippets and samples, which help to flesh out the concepts of the release, but sometimes I find these misplaced and overloaded and taking way from the musical backdrop. Also some of the musical ideas are there but do not come to full fruition or suffer from some of the scattered sounds techniques utilized.
The cover includes a written passage from the individual behind this (incidentally a mortician) and is a nice piece of short literature looking at the ideals of childhood, love, innocence and human nature. Given the 'deathly' nature of the title, it's meaning is actually reflected in the written piece, in by death is described as a gradual process and not just a moment in time. In fact the CD runs as if a narrative to the cycle of life from the womb to the grave, illustrated by the many vocal samples. The packaging is only a card sleeve but is presentable enough not to be a detraction.

C17H19NO3 (USA) "1692/2092" CD 1998 Malignant Records
The eagerly anticipated new C17 CD has finally been unleashed after some talk of it originally to have been released on the Side Effects label. Considering the great debut 'Terra Damnata' CD I was really looking forward to some powerful and bombastic neo-classical works, however this CD is much more subdued than I anticipated. This being the first obvious change I also think due to the very full commercially oriented soundtrack styled sound, along with the inclusion of vocals on a number of tracks, many traditional dark ambient fans will take some adjusting in getting used to this. As this CD is the soundscore for a non-existent motion picture, the music follows this format very closely and is quite convincing in portraying an actual movie to support it.
The opener 'the room of ice' is a slow brooding piano piece that sees the low key vocals of Jarboe slip in well alongside the plucked strings and violins, as if being a storyteller setting the initial scene. There is some hint of some more forceful work on track 2, however it is mildly let down with the sound that is a little too synthetic in places. The clanging bells and horn sections give rise to visions of a chase scene with all the dynamics associated with such

musical passages. Some more dark ambient sections are employed at the start of 'harvest of souls' before consolidating into a mild cello, tympani and vocal choirs orchestral epic. The final minutes uses a very nice and darkly dreamy classical guitar solo to send it into the next track – the lengthy romantic and bombastic sounding 'metatron'. This track melds together very well an undercurrent of a classical composition with an electronic focus on the beats drumming and sound effects. As the electronic sounds fade into the distance, the classical components remain, before the electronics mount a second wave of attack in the latter half of the track. A lowly dark ambient passage is the fair for 'the burning of the black waters' which is both atmospheric and evocative which has some very nice cavernous effects.

'A spell for breaking an opening into the sky' is another track that contains vocals, but here Bukeka uses her voice in a much more up front style which I personally feels detracts from some of the nice brooding musical backdrop. There are other vocals in the form of background chanting and spoken passages which work fine, it is just the 'stage show' presentation of the main vocal that does not do it for me. 'Excision' is very low in tonal sound that floats and meanders through caves and chasms on its slow sinister journey. 'Deep Flesh' has a nice spooky echo beat effect over some more dark ambience, that soon explodes into quite a distorted industrial song with little hint of classical sounds. As this track has more of a 'song' structure the vocals work really well, rather than sounding above and/or removed from the sound.

'I cover the waterfront' has a spoken (rhyming) poetry piece included at the start (which I am not too partial too), prior to a sorrowful orchestra rising forth over a slow heartbeat. The vocals (when used again) are sung in a low fashion and work quite well until the more sung/spoken style is utalised over what would have been a great dark ambient passage to finish the track(if the vocals in this part were dropped). The brooding and pounding of 'my bones rise above' set visions of a suspenseful scene while there is a more structured slow factory industrial sound to 'breathe'. 'Electric Air' holds a sound very familiar to the debut CD however in the guise of this CD the sound is much more fully produced and professional sounding. 'Broken Soul' again uses the acoustic guitar to great effect with a backing of wind instruments and a rolling marching drum that uses sorrowful dynamics that gradually fade out into the abyss of ambience.

As with most soundscores these days that include a dance remix (as opposed to those soundtrack CD's which are nothing more than compilation CD's), a remix track can also be found here. This is the final unlisted track which is a remix of 'a spell....' and I must say if vocals are to be used it is here in this format they work much better. I'm sure this will have many fans jumping for the stop or skip button, however I do enjoy the contrast in the two versions of the song.

Overall I think that the sung vocals on the CD have been somewhat overstated as they are only contained on 6 of the 13 tracks, with the remainder being instrumental (or with low key spoken male voices). The select vocals that I initially had concerns with(not all of them), do present themselves better with subsequent listens, however I am still of the opinion that some passages would have been improved if the vocals had been dropped or reduced in the mix. Other than that, while this may seem to be a challenging listen to some fans of this genre, I feel both the concept and fully produced professional sound make this a CD very worthy of you attention.

Daniel Menche (UK) "Vent" CD 1998 Hold
The first thing I will have to comment on about this CD is the packaging. While a friend commented "that would have been cheap to produce" I found it more aesthetically interesting. The case is the standard jewelcase with clear inlay, with a one sided circle (the same size as a CD) placed in the CD tray. There is little if no graphics and minimal info provided (no titles or listings for the 7 tracks), however I find this as a simple yet ingenious take on CD presentation.

Anyway, enough of my graphic design ramblings and onto the music. Well Mr Menche has been at his organic noise releases for quite some time now, so if you have heard his stuff you should know what to expect. I admittedly steered clear of his releases for far too long due to the 'noise' tag, but his works are much more sound technique/ manipulation oriented than the standards generally associated with noise. Don't be a fool like me and be swayed by such a description.

The short 2 minute opener is quite obvious as a raw contact mic recording of a heartbeat and is a subtle introduction to the album. Track 2 scared the sonic shit out of me on first listen with short but intense blast of static to introduce the track. From there, the scratching/scrapping sound taken on a boiling writhing form and layers of tones are effortlessly guided through various levels of sonic depth and intensity.

Track three is less active in sound source, being content with slowing rising tones giving off the felling of the temperature rising from comfortable warmth to searing burning pain.

An 'itching/ picking' organic sound opens track four that fades away into pure silence before a cavernous sounds rise from the depths. The subtle dynamic are very impressive gradually building a sense of growing dread and the waves of sound rise and fall, forever increasing

SPECTRE RECORDS

Out now:
Asche / Templegarden's 10"
"Cenobites In The Ballroom"
"Hidden Places"

90 copies in carton cover w/ diamond saw blade
10 copies in metal package and large diamond saw blade

Also available: "The Book ov Shadowz" compilation LP

dixit MALIGNANT catalog:
"A wet dream of a compilation for death industrial enthusiasts featuring all new material from MEGAPTERA, STRATVM TERROR, DAGDA MOR, INADE, PREDOMINANCE, TORTURA, SOLDNERGEIST and AH CAMA-SOTZ. Each bands contribution represents some of the strongest material any of them has ever recorded and released. Compiled as they are here makes THE BOOK OV SHADOWZ one of the most definitive death industrial compilation to be released, ever, period. A must! Luxuriously packaged with postcards and two mini posters."

vinyl fetish
10 x 100 - 10-inch series
10 different releases each on 100 copies - 90 copies in special cover and 10 copies in luxurious package

Spectre Records
P.O. Box 88
2020 Antwerpen 2
Belgium

spectre@skynet.be
http://users.skynet.be/spectre

in strength as the seconds pass.
The 20 second track 5 is a short prelude to track 6 which although uses the same composition esthetic still manages to come up with tones and sounds distinctive from the preceding tracks. Here the sounds are not broad and deep, but more intense (yet somehow subdued) in a mid ranged sound frequency, akin to a fiery furnace.
The final track is the first time I have heard the artist use a musical sample included (only at the intro). The overall sound could be oriented to distant howling storm winds with some foreground heatbeats and wood knockings and other subtle scrapings and sounds. Towards the 4 minute halfway point the sounds is relatively clean with an almost sustained 'keyboard' like drone which sees both the track and the CD out.
Even though Mr Menche is not really heading into uncharted waters, but staying in the harbour of his previous releases (still in the more subtle experimental vein), this is still a really good CD. As there is little info on the sound sources utilized I'm not sure if this is still a purely somatically inspired release or that new sources have discovered, but either way this is still up to the same high standards.

Darrin Verhagen (Aus) "P3" 3"miniCD 1998 Dorobo limited edition

Coming from the mind behind Shinjuku Thief this is an intriguingly obscure release. Looking more like a computer disc in its size and packaging we are treated to some of Darrin's 'cut up' experimental collage ambient works. The majority of this 21 minute work is highly minimal with a few sporadic nosier moments. Glitches, crackles and bleeps are all included through/ and create part of the mix, giving the feeling of changing levels of electronic static with some more constant floating notes. Parallels in the sound and structure can be made to another of Darrin's solo works namely the 'soft ash' CD. This is not something that works at all as background music but requires attention and focus whilst listening. The liner notes are included as part of the blurred cover art, but what I can make out is that this appears to have been originally broadcast on Australian radio on 11 August, 1998 and has been reissued in a limited quantity of 500. Surely not everyone's taste due to it's highly experimental edge but still very enjoyable in the field of artistic experimentation.

Dissecting Table(Jap) "Life" CD 1998 Release Records

This is the first time I have heard Dissecting Table, but if the reviews I've read are anything to go by it seems that Ichiro Isuji's compositions have become more over the top with each release. Listening to this CD I could assume he has done it again with this new recording.
Opening "the needs of the body" with an upbeat industrialized bass riff and drums a looping squeal soon kicks in to then be disbanded just a quickly into an erratic noise composition (with a sampled bleating of a sheep??!!). Just over three minutes in, the noise is cut back to a low tone and mild dub rhythm before a way out psychedelic
beat and noise collage takes over. There also seems to be an obsession with natural tones are sampled frogs and crickets make their way into the mix. The opening passage is again reintroduced for another quick run before the tracks runs off on yet another tangent. Industrialized apocalyptic machine like noise gets a look in as well which nearly rounds out track 1, prior to one final foray into a low-fi rhythm and beat.
"I would like to be…" starts on a low frequency tone with a slow pounding drum beat Demonic howls which almost sear the speakers are introduced before a machine gun like drum and noise attack ambushes the listener. The structure of the song reverts back to the low tone and slow beat before the noise attach (now in a different guise) reappears. Things are slowed down yet again into a manipulated beat and tone to finish the track.
The beginning of track three "past" reminds me of some of the nosier, live decomposition tracks on 'Decree's' "Wake of Devastation" CD, that later takes in the blast beats, noise distortion and growling vocals. With this track I found it is strange that two totally different/ unrelated music styles could end up at pretty much the same result. Here we have extreme noise music with hyper beats and screamed vocals which is not too far removed from the structure and sound of grindcore music. (Furthermore the main label behind Release (Relapse Records) were quite big on releasing Grindcore in the early '90's. Quite weird to think about actually!) The more structured dark rhythms & beats also get their fare share on this track and is where I feel that 'Dissecting Table' works best. The final track "no future" low end bass rumblings and erratic noise distortion that gains its structure when the beat and rhythm kicks in. The most forceful and extreme vocals of the CD are on here almost reaching self combustion temperature. Again comparison's between Decree are applicable but this is even more extreeme than the former act.
At least this CD stands as testimony that not all noise music from Japan is Mezbow derivative noise. As a final note, let it be said that between all the dark rhythms, noise and beats, this is very over the top in its quirky, original and strange way.

Dissecting Table (Jap) "Why" 7"ep 1998 Suggestion Records

Having heard this earlier 7" after the newer CD (reviewed above) I can say that Ichiro Tsuji has surely been a pioneer in his crazy over the top industrialized percussive affairs.
Track one 'Why' starts with a grinding bass tone then blasts into hyper beats, fast paced mid ranged rhythms with the almost death metal styled vocals. This track is forceful and focused and works really well an actual song.
Track 'Camouflage' is more mid passed with the heavy drum machine beats, but the whole noise, rhythm, bass & guitar esthetic is retained. With a few time changes and sound manipulations this comes across more as a band song than a music/ noise project, that is admittedly very enjoyable.
Although it seems that Ichiro has gone more along the paths of erratic compositions with current releases, this 7" shows him in a very structured form with short focussed tracks, which I find much more to my liking. With a glossy gatefold cover this is worth your effort in tracking down.

Endvra (Eng) "the Watcher" CD 1998 Old Europa Cafe

Endvra not being one to ever back themselves into a musical corner, have still admittedly managed to come up with a very unexpected release. Now, they have had a habit of changing styles, sounds and focuses between releases but this is goes beyond all expectation. Presenting only a single track with a play time of 49 minutes this is a journey that requires the right state of mind and a dose of undivided attention. The actual music is slow evolving dark ambient pulses and drones, that in a few places flirts (ever so slightly) with some minimally composed elements. Shifting tones and frequencies morph and evolve in a hypnosis enduing style. Floating subtly on cloud like waves of sound, there is both light tones and more deep bass orientated tones, giving a cavernous and bottomless effect to the ambience. As the various passages and sections effortlessly flow and evolve, the listener is left stranded wondering how they got to the particular musical point and where it is all heading from there on. For a single track pushing 50 minutes it is as though time itself has been altered as the time passes in a blink on an eye. Or maybe it is the music's ability to draw the listener in and disorienting their perception of time via its engulfing hypnotic form.
Concluding the minimal review (for a minimal release), let it be said that I think that Endvra have managed to create their strongest piece of work to date, despite being totally different to the styles they have become known for. Recommended for any dark ambient/ drone fan, but beware to the reader expecting anything like what was presented on the last CD Great God Pan.

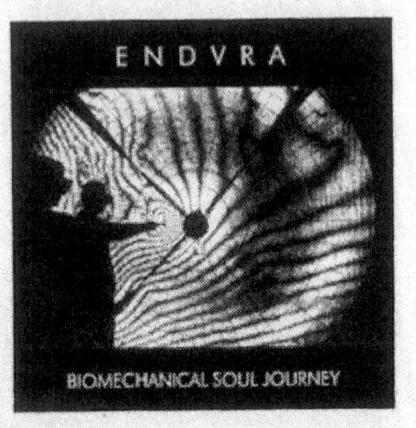

Endvra(Eng) "Biomechanical Soul Journey" 10"ep Power and Steel 1998

Endvra are back again with yet another release! A limited edition of 400 this 10"ep features two lengthy tracks from this group. While one track is relatively new the other is an older track taken from a various artists cassette released in 1994. Given that many would have missed the compilation track ('Biomechanical Soul Journey') it is good that it can be obtained on a more official and exclusive format. The second newer track ('Vestigial Horn') was originally meant to be included in it's entirety on the latest Misanthropy Records Compilation CD, however as the label did not like the full version (what!!!!) a measly 1 minute and 49 section excerpt was included. Endvra not being one to allow one of their songs to be bastardized, the full version in all its glory is included here.

Starting with the title track this is a nice piece of ominous and unnerving ambience with encompasses shifting clanging sounds and other sustained notes and tones. One of the main features is a vocal/ text sample as if someone is recounting an alien abduction. The introducing elements fade out after 5 minutes or so and when the vocals make a second appearance, a slow bass strobe, with shifting background sounds complete the track.

'Vestigial Horn' starts with a stirring piano tune and slow rousing horn section, however these composed elements are soon engulfed in the rising storm of flowing ambience. The sounds are generally mid range and very cavernous, emphasizing the depth and breadth of sound. Tortured vocal wails rise and fall periodically as if channeling spirits trapped within the walls of time. This track treads a middle line somewhere between the sounds of 'Black Eden' and 'Great God Pan' which is to say it is nothing less then great.

The gold and black packaging is quite impressive being simplistic and visually pleasing. Another essential item for your collection.

Final (UK) "Urge/ Fail" 7"EP 1998 Fever Pitch Music

Although this was originally released in 1995 a second pressing of 400 has bee made so there still should be a few copies floating around (I got mine in September, 1998).

Well, Final work with manipulated guitar distortion to create the ambient/ noise music on offer. Quite similar to the improvised guitar compositions of KK Null, this however takes a slightly more subdued approach not reaching the intensity of noise of the above mentioned. Track 1 'Urge' has a moving deep space void ambience low in the mix, juxtaposed with overlaid disharmonic noise movements. Although quite short (due to the format) I imagine this would work extremely well over a longer drawn out space of time.

Track 2 'Fail' does not disguise the guitar distortion as well the first, with it being quite easy to visualize the artist recording the track(not such a good thing in ambient music). Despite this it's dredging & heavy bass guitar distortion is complimented with piercing frequencies swooping in on the listener. Again it quite short at around 5 minutes.

If this is of interest it would be worth the search.

Gruntsplatter/ Slowvent (USA) "Gruntsplatter/ Slowvent Split Release" CD 1998 Crionic Mind

It appears that the US is finally getting its act together in terms producing some good death industrial projects.

On this split CD Gruntsplatter is up first, opening with some damn heavy bass rumblings manipulations and slow keyboard tones, before exploring some noisier, semi-structured textures on the following track 'Ascending Marrow'. 'Bloodsoil' is slightly more atmospheric, holding a somewhat random sound held together again by the use of a slow keyboard passage, reminding me slightly of Vond's 'Green Eyed Demon' CD. 'Gravemound' has a more ominous sound that is gradually raised on a base of sound akin to a distant tornado. Some deep factory sounds and manipulated electronics help to fully flesh out the track, however I feel the track is a little muddied overall because of the amount of sound sources used. Despite this small criticism this is one of the best tracks Gruntsplatter have on offer. The final track for Gruntsplatter is 'the Prophetic Maw' which again uses a basis of multi layered muddied sound that has comparison to the German project Drape Excrement.

The second half of the 60 minute disc is by Slowvent and from the self titled explosive volcanic opener, it shows a great mixture of death industrial and more noise ambience. Here the track is looped and repetitive over it's 6 minutes. 'Spectral Violence' has a random experimental noise edge, not unlike what Atrax Morgue is producing with his Morder Machine side project. 'The Cold Slugs' uses a subdued repetitive death industrial basis while random factory clangs and rumbles appear sporadically. Gradually the looped structure subsides leaving the sporadic tones, as another loop gradually rises up. 'Rust Resurrection' is short and simple again using a straightforward repetitive guise. The final track for both Slowvent and the CD is 'Impaired Descent' which chops and changes from noisy Attrax Morgue styled electronics to more death industrial moments.

For a debut CD for this label the packaging is well presented and laid out, using the obligatory black and grey tones. Given the promise that these two projects show, I will be interested to see what both of these projects come up with in future releases.

Hollow Earth (USA) "dog days of the holocaust' CD 1998 Crowd Control Activities/ Malsonus

This project is a collaboration between Michael J.V Hensley & Jonathan Canady of the groups Yen Pox and Deathpile respectively. I do believe that this was meant to have been released a number of years ago on Malsonus but for whatever reason it has been delayed until now, where the musical collaboration has been released as a label collaboration! As I have not had a chance to hear any of Deathpile's music I can't formulate any opinion on potential comparison's in sound, however I am able to do this in terms of Yen Pox.

The opener 'floor of hell' has a manipulated vocal section before it kicks into some extremely dense and heavy death/dark ambience. Within a couple of minutes there are definite comparisons to be made with Yen Pox (or Michael's other project 'Blood Box' for that matter), however while Yen Pox have an atmospheric take on drone ambience, here the sound and tone seem all the more dense, heavy and overtly sinister. There is also quite a bit more movement in the sound exploring more territory than the drawn out elements of Yen Pox. 'Scrawled in Blood' stands out somewhat, as it opens with a multi layered accelerating tones that gradually level out but still containing quite a bit of force and movement.

Of the 5 tracks totaling 63 minutes, this has resulted in all compositions being lengthy, spanning times of between 10 to 15 minutes. The manipulated tones of this are not cavernous, as much as they are suffocating, being condensed to an extreme level within a mine shaft barely wide enough to give the listener unrestricted passage. Given that there are many groups that have tried their hand dark ambience (as some with not more than average results) it is always instantly obvious when someone has come up with a good take on this style. It is hard to become sick of this form of ambience when there are CD's such as this being produced.

As the title, text and selected pictures of the cover don't leave much to the imagination, it will undoubtedly cause a stir with someone, who will make a judgement on the content without actually finding out what the members purpose is for using such themes. I guess the antagonism of the politically correct mob is half the fun. If I had got this CD prior to making my 1998 release picks, this would have definitely been one of them. Lets call this a late inclusion.

Inade (Ger) "the Axxiam Plains" 7"EP 1998 Drone Records

Going for the simplistic packaging we are greeted with a plain white cover with reverse print writing within a large black rectangle. The inner slip is much the same however features a picture of a solemn looking figure, which I assume may have some political significance. The notes on the inner slip might have shed some light on this assumption, but alas as my German skills are not up to scratch I'm unable to formulate a clear idea. And speaking of clear this edition is pressed on pristine clear vinyl, with three tracks being featured. Opening with 'Breaking the Walls' (incidentally which is a collaboration with Dagda Mor) a guttural vocal sample pitch shifted beyond recognition leads the way into some spare tones and metallic clangs and sporadic factory noises. Up next is 'Above The Plains' which is a more hypnotic ambient affair with floating tones and manipulated sounds that does not really have a starting point or clear direction, simply holding the same feel from the outset. Side two only has a single track ('Movement and Construction') which is more noisy than the first side. An electronic looped sample holds the forefront while the ambient backbone and waves of sampled static fill out the soundscape. Given that this music was recorded back in 1994 and originally released in 1995 this 300 copy repress is a good document of the evolution and changing focus of Inade's sound.

Kirchenkamph (USA) "Nebula/ Parasite" 7"EP 1997 Fever Pitch Music

Here is another older Fever Pitch 7" which is still kicking around if you are interested. Track 1 'Nebula' is a spacey type new age-ish piece (in a 2001 a Space Odyssey kind of way) which I find to be a bit of a strange listen. Not quite keyboard inspired 70's space music and not quite minimal enough to pass as ambience. The keyboard predominantly high in the mix and sounds both improvised and composed, which also throws the focus off a little. Track 2 'Parasite' reflects its title in the slowly rising and evolving affair. The washes of semi composed keyboards are still evident, however remain more subdued giving the track an overall darker aurora and is much more to my liking. Comes packaged in a simple yet visually pleasing blue and silver card sleeve.

Manipura (Nor) "vessels for the infinite" 7" 1998 Spreading across my hemisphere

This is project of I have not heard of before, but who seem to subscribe to the space ambience esthetic. The 7" contains 2 tracks being part 1 and part 2 of the title track, however as the 7" is not labeled it is anyone's guess to which side is which....but no matter.

Track 1 (the one I put on first anyway!) contains some light spacey keyboard tones at the high sound range while the lower sound range is taken up half organic/ half mechanised factory rhythmic drone.

Track 2 starts with a mid paced drone while a semi composed keyboard tune does it's bit. This track is a bit more subdued overall and holds much more of a atmospheric floating ambient edge. In the final seconds of this track there is a quick succession of bleeps as if to represent a satellite's signals forging their way through the expanses of deep space. I don't think I would call this music typically dark, however it does have a nice atmospheric aura as if the listener is floating the vast empty void of the universe.

The packaging complements the aural images given, with a fold out picture of the horsehead nebula and the outer images taking on a psychedelic edge with the manipulated colors. All in all quite a nice product.

Megaptera (Swe) "Beautiful Chaos" MCD 1998 Fever Pitch Music

The long awaited Megaptera MCD finally sees its official release. Originally meant to be a 10" vinyl EP, many delays were evident with it was finally being released in digipack CD format. As I mentioned last issue this MCD features the track which was solely responsible for turning my interest to Megaptera via the apocalyptic death industrial track "Final Day" (which is the opener of the 4 tracker). Low droning base incessantly rumbles, while minimalist monk type samples are interjected occasionally. At about 2 minutes in, without so much as a hint, the track explodes into harsh yet rhythmic death industrial. Factory sounds and beats pulsate with the heightened keyboard/ vocal sample rising and falling periodically over the structure and layout of the composition.

The second track "Sleep" works with washes of keyboard drones and swirling wind type noise prior to veering off on another tangent with the trademark Magaptera industrial death rhythm vibes and keyboard frequencies. Not so "terror inducing" than some of Peter's other compositions this is quite a relaxing track with a sinister edge.

Track three (Mass Murder Part II) holds the very early sound and style of Megaptera without the focus on subtleties of frequencies. Much less composed and more industrial factory sound oriented, indecipherable vocal samples are used along with a drawn out four note melody. The final track "The Passage" is a shorter remix of various sections taken from the "Disease" CD, and no matter how many times I hear the opening vocal sample it still has the same creepy effect(I think it is taken from The Exorcist III). As I have said before this should be just one of a few recent releases of Megaptera that will see them prosper with the recognition they deserve. With top notch packaging this is worth tracking down for any current or prospective Mepaptera fan.

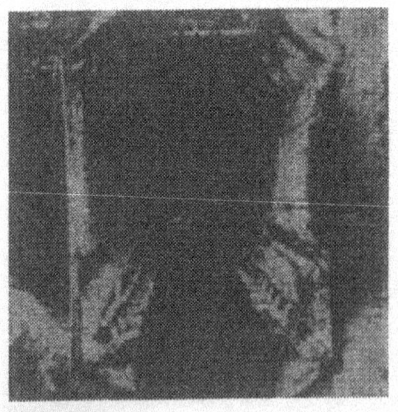

Megaptera (Swe) "Live in Rostock" CD 1998 Bastet Recordings

As the title suggests this a live recording of one of the few live performances that Megaptera have undertaken. This one dates back to late in 1996 from a show in Germany I believe. With what would appear to be the use of background tapes and samplers, various improvised metallic clangs and tortured screaming vocals are included on the opener (obviously relate to the tracks title "Intro: the Squire goes insane part 1-warmer"). From what I can see the majority of the tracks are live interpretations of existing tracks (ie: track 1, 'Deep Inside' & 'The Passage'). Despite this, there are no real standout tracks as they all tend to blend one into the next over the 40 recording.

The crew involved in the live performance is of course Peter Nystrom as well as the session input of Magnus Sundstrom (The Protagonist). As Peter stated in his interview in Issue 1# (still plugging it!) his live performances are manly based on pre-recorded tapes with various other elements and sounds integrated during the show. The overall sound is pretty raw and has that improvised element and sound throughout. The final mix isn't as bass heavy and load as what I have come to expect from Megaptera, however this may relate to the recording quality and not the actual live mix. With special cover packaging and limited to 200 hand numbered copies this is likely to become a well sought after collectors item for fans.

Merzbow/Genesis P-Orridge (Jap/Eng) "a perfect pain" CD 1998 Cold Spring

Well, I'm note quite sure of the background and input into this disc, but on face value this is obviously a collaboration release between the above two artists. The cover tends to allude to the point that Genesis P-Orridge have provided the text and spoken vocal passages, whilst Mezbow has simply done his thing over the top. I could be totally wrong but this how it appears from my viewpoint.

Of the five tracks, they range in length from a little over 3 minutes to up to 25 minutes totaling a full length of around 56 minutes. All of these tracks feature spoken text and come across very much as a theatre or a spoken word performance. There is also some light distortion placed over them giving their presentation a slight surrealistic edge. The complimentary noise backing is overall more subdued than the searing electronics noise normally aquatinted with Masami aka Merzbow, but this is not to say that his compositions are not noise music. The starting track 'a perfect restraint' is the shortest track at slightly over 3 minutes, containing mid pitched squeals and a looping noise manipulation. Track two's musical backing is quite low in the mix with the vocals forceful and up front. Some scattered electronic beats and noise make up most of the experimental backing, leaving the spoken vocals to do their thing, but once the vocals are out of the way the noise manipulations gradually rise in intensity for the final 4 minutes.

The 24 minute track 'Source are Rare' the pulsing noise is much higher in the mix adding an edge of intensity to the spoken vocals. In some parts the vocals taking on searing tone becoming indistinguishable through the distortion. Again once the vocal passage is complete the noise experimentation becomes more freeform and in part includes some structured backing beats. Given that this track is so long, Masami manages to push the noise to all it's searing glory, just to show us he has not lost any intensity. The track entitled 'Kreeme Horne' is almost industrialised with the beats and drones, but balances on the knife blade between composition and unstructured noise. 'All beauty is our enemy' is a great cacophony of high and low pitched noise manipulations to finish off the album and what is left of my inner ears.

I can say that I have never been a Merzbow fanatic however increasingly I have been warming to his sounds. This disc goes a long way to solidifying me as a fully fledged fan, and with the collaborative vocals of this CD adds a further dimension to Masami's sound. The packaging and imagery is nothing short of brilliant, however in my opinion does not typically match the noise music of this CD.

Morder Machine{feat: Atrax Morgue} (Ita) "Death Show" CD 1998 Slaughter Productions

Coming from the mind behind Atrax Morgue and Slaughter Productions this is Marco's foray in the territory of death industrial. A slow rumbling beat opens the CD with cavernous background ambience with distorted, processed & treated vocals. With the aura surrounding this track you could not ask for a stronger opening to the CD. Track 2 keeps the vibe of the slow death industrial pounding, but has a more high pitched looping screech to compliment it. Some points of the release tend to point towards Marco's nosier efforts featured in Atrax Morgue, yet they do not become too prevalent. The vocals when present, are always pushed well over the top for that extreme effect whilst some elements are more akin oppressive electronics than straight death industrial.

The opening track "I'm So" gets a reworking in the middle of the album but apart from the vocals the remix is really a separate entity. Track six with its lack of vocals and low vibe comes across very much like Brighter Death Now's opening track to Great Death I.

The final track "Music for Dead Brains" is a low fi trip down repetitive lane that is although interesting for the first few minutes, drags by the finishing 12 minute mark.

The packaging of the CD comes with an A5 fold out card sleeve, which is simplistic but has a well designed layout.

Given that this release was partly programmed & partly improvised (whilst Atrax Morgue has always been totally improvised) this manages to come of as more focused and sophisticated than Marco's other project. Common comparisons to Brighter Death Now are inevitable given the chosen style and production, yet this is a quality release and not some pale comparison. Recommended.

Mortar(Ita) "Emperor's Return" CD 1998 Fuoco

Strange, Strange stuff this is indeed. Demented, creepy and surreal are a few descriptions which first come to mind. The sound is kept purposely lo-fi, flawed with static and under produced which all adds to its surreal charm. And I quote from the sleeve "For best results, play load on the worst audio equipment you can find". Certainly a different perspective in music and it's presentation/ intended listening quality.

The starter to the CD has an oddly disjointed looped piano and keyboard run and is the most 'composed'(if you want to call it that) track on the CD. 'Dead fanfare' uses a looped timpani beat with sustained horns notes and sounds that rise and fall out of the mix periodically giving off a slight militarist air. As with a lot of the dark ambient stuff I have heard from Italy this has quite a cavernous sound that is common with quite a few groups from that country. The comparison to this generalization is found in the depth of sound present within the track entitled "Crypts", while the sounds on "Scream of undead" are more ritualistic with unearthly moans, bells and minimal percussion(with a wavelike layer of sound taking up the high end of the mix). Track 5 "Labirinth" features what I think is a noise sample taken from MZ412, however slightly manipulated (or maybe the two groups used the same sound source). The remainder of the sound is more wide in breath than depth which somehow has a lo fi orchestral sound to it. 'Lunar influence' is a very creepy sounding dark ambient track extending over a 10 minute span that could have a possible comparison to "Amon" (also from Italy).

The title track is a more lively dark ambient piece with gradually building sustained keyboard tones with the following song 'Decadence' using a sorrowful looped violin passage to good effect. 'The fall of the gods' is a great mix of dark ambient and mild death industrial that works perfectly while the following track reminds me quite a bit of "Caul" flowing moments. The finishing track is a mere 1 minute 32 seconds long back creates a decent slow keyboard aura within that time.

Similar with the other Fuoco CD I have seen, the back panel is used for the main cover image, with the actual sleeve being plain white on the outer panels and info and images taking up the inner panels.

As was mentioned earlier this has a very surreal and creepy charm to it that is hard to describe with words as it covers quite a bit of ground in its 71 minute length. Nonetheless a very interesting and enjoyable release.

Mo*te (Jap) "Stash" CD 1998 Solipsism

Another 100 pressing limited CD (actually a burned recordable CD) released on the Self Abuse side label. The packaging of the CD is not up to a professional standard, but it would seem that the spirit of this label has more to do with the tape label philosophy than relating to commercial success. I imagine that tape labels will gradually disappear over the next few years to be replaced with labels and releases such as this one.

This CD is by an unknown (to me anyway) Japanese Noise Artist and is everything that you have come to expect from the connoisseurs of that scene. Extreme in its attack and delivery with little let up or breathing space provided, only the most hardy of noise addicts will venture into the realms of this CD. The slabs of distortion are kept middle to high range but without entering piercing territory. Walls of screaming and wailing vocals are present but almost become fully obliterated with the remainder of distorted and swirling tones. Five minutes into track one ("borrowed bone") the middle tone are removed to make way for a bass oriented cascading sound before....(you guessed it).....back to the noise attack. Track 2 "Equipment" works more with modulated harsh mid ranged tone with the same intensity as the preceding track. Some sort of TV music/ voices are forced through the waves of noise. "Bad Habit" has an annoying frequency as it's intro while an scattered noise effect rises in the background up until the 5 minute mark where the harsh noise returns yet again. However this time it is more intense, focussed and angry in its delivery. Much of the same is explored over the remaining two tracks (5 tracks over 60 minutes). By no means will this change your opinion of Japanese noise if you didn't like it before, but will surely get those going who are fanatics of the scene.

Murder Corporation (Ita) "Death Files" CD 1998 Fuoco

Featuring 10 nameless 'files', we find ourselves in the executive suite of the corporate headquarters, trapped with the crazed chief executive, who is ready to inflict his will on the unsuspecting victims (namely us). If you hadn't gathered the intent of this release, it should be obvious by now that this is harsh murderous noise.......... but done with focus and flair! Although heavily harsh and abrasive I found the opening track is still bearable at high volumes as it avoids the high pitched tones rather opting for the 'weight' of sound(however later tracks do go for the ear piercing charm). Much of the background and underneath sounds of each track appear to be specifically programmed with the more sporadic and scattered harsh and high pitched tones laid over the top.

From a production perspective, the sound is sterile and clinically clean which only adds to the overall intensity. The tracks span a length of between 3 to 10 minutes and move around within certain confines set down for each track(back to the point about the underlying programmed elements).

File 4 has a very quiet start of a programmed sounds but there is always a low rumbling in the background akin to the sound of distant thunder alerting the individual of the chaos of the storm to come. While the storm never actually blows our way, the faith in the power of the storm of noise is reinstated on the next file. A low bass sound pulses while scattered and searing high pitched notes a introduced one by one until they merge into one huge noise feast. The remainder of the album does not stray from the noise pastures but all files are all distinct enough in sound to not merge into one unidentifiable mass of deceased humanity.

Packaging wise the main focus for the 'cover' is directed to what is actually the back.....quite different from a design perspective. And if the music's intent was not easily understood before the sleeve pictures make sure nothing is left to doubt with assorted black & white morgue, skeletal and suicidal shots complimented with plain grey backgrounds.

For the majority of the time when listening to this, it sounds as though the culprit planned each step, just as if was a calculated murder and not simply a bloodied frenzy. When noise is produced this well I can't but help appreciate is audile velocity. Who knows, maybe I will become a fully fledged noise connoisseur after all?

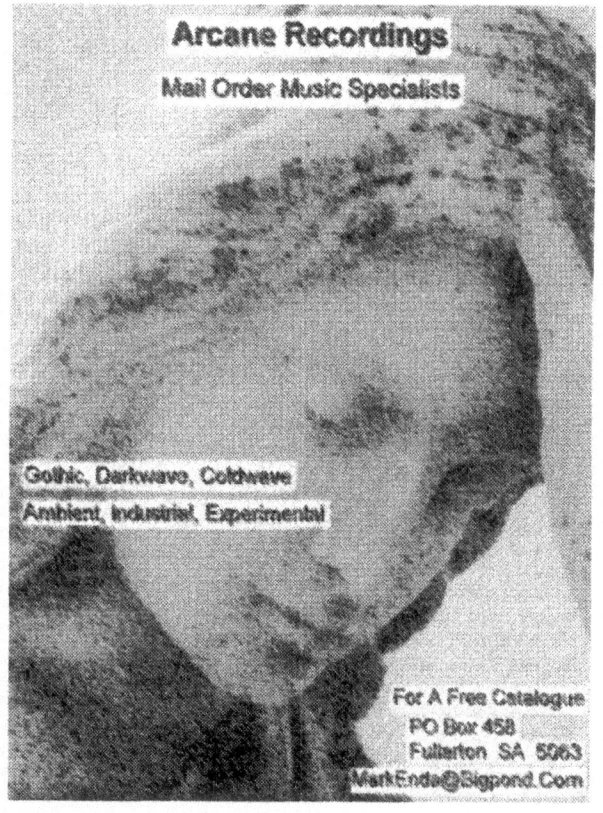

Arcane Recordings

Mail Order Music Specialists

Gothic, Darkwave, Coldwave
Ambient, Industrial, Experimental

For A Free Catalogue
PO Box 458
Fullerton SA 5063
MarkEnde@Bigpond.Com

MZ412 (Swe) "Nordik Battle Signs" LP 1998 Cold Meat Industry

When MZ412 were interviewed in issue 1 of this mag, they indicated that the next album was to be more of a crossover of black metal and industrial that had been explored on the 'Burning the temple of God' CD. As I really thought the Black Metal elements they utalised on the last album were more of a low than high point, I was hesitant to what this album may have been. Thankfully this is not the case at all as there are not traditional drum and guitar parts associated with the said scene. It is even to the point that the LP has no band photo's so I don't even know if they still embrace the war paint concept(the answer to that may come when the CD version of this is released early this year). Also it would appear that one of the members has left the group leaving this album credited to a three piece.

The intro to the album ('MZ412/Introducktion') is a very quick piece of load and dirgy rumbling static with a buried vocal sample. This track cuts out as quickly as it began moving into track two 'Algiz-Konvergence of Life and death' that has an unusual choice of intro vocal sample before the dirgy electronics cut in again. This track is credited to a collaboration between MZ and Ordo Equilibrio however from listening to this it would be fair to assume that MZ412 provided the musical backdrop whilst Thomas Petterson provides a poetic spoken vocal passage.

When Thomas's vocals commence, there sound changes to a cavernous echoey tone with a tribal drum cacophony. In-between these spoken moments the trademark harsh and grinding electronics and screamed vocals of MZ412 act as a bridge to the more subdued elements. Toward the end of this track Tomas's vocals join the extremes sounds with his vocals being manipulated and overlapped over themselves. 'Satan Jugend' is a good track but it is the vocal sample that repetitively praises you know who, that for me detracts from an otherwise good track. The rumbling industrial storm gradually increased in intensity and dynamics before abruptly cutting out. 'Der Kamph geht weiter' sound quite militant with a very nice looped and distorted drum roll as vocal snipits and wavering tones rise in and out of the composition. Some traditional excellent 'factory' sounding industrial sections are also used within this track before becoming much more focused and composed when all the elements come together with a slow marching styled beat. Later some sampled chants are used as the musical backdrop gets much more atmospheric and ritualized with floating tones and somewhat sporadic beats. This track merges well some of the best sounds to be found on the 'In nomine....' & 'Burning...' CD's.

'Tyranor' being the first track on side two is sonically clear and load with it's electronic jugular attack that harks back to the deathy heavy sound on the 'In nomine....'CD. A nice high pitch droning tone is used over the top that delineates the sound from the early comparison and as great as this track is, it is just too damn short! 'NBS act 1: Begravning' which was originally featured on the CMI 50# comp is a much stronger track here in its full form, alongside the other intended compositions. Atmospherics', factory clatter, deathly drones and repetitive German vocals make this a very sinister track indeed. MZ412 have a knack of tracking seeming unrelated elements, used all together is a mass of sound and then in a blink of an eye miraculously merging them into rhythmic passage – as is the case in the above track. The extended ending (not featured on the CMI comp version) when I first heard it, had me thinking the LP was scratched as it sound as if the needle is jumping within a groove. The final track 'NBS act II:14W' begins as another nicely sinister atmospheric track again using all the trademark sound and a manipulated vocal passage talking about the beauty in death.

This album is far above what I expected due to the lack of any Black Metal elements and will surely go down well with any established MZ412 fan. Having not timed the length of this release I tend to have the feeling that it is too short, but I guess that is more of a compliment, than being criticised for an album that drags due to it's excessive length.

This LP is pressed on white vinyl (is that a bad joke on the 'black industrial' tag?) and limited to 412 copies. The CD version is scheduled to be released early this year and is to included a bonus track that it to be recorded from source material sent to the group by fans. Not a bad concept at all.

Negru Voda (Swe) "an impulse of fear"/ third EYE (Swe) "raudive experiments" split CD 1998 Crowd Control Activities

A good introduction to this CD would be a bit of background info. This was a split tape released a number of years back on Slaughter Productions and features works by Peter Nystrom/ Negru Voda (better known for Megaptera) and Magnus Sundstrom/ third EYE (now known as the Protagonist). The tracks which make up the two spilt halves are also complimented by two bonus tracks from each artist.

Negru Voda is up first with distorted poundings, clangs and factory loops (complimented by a mild tune) to be found on "Death in Your Eyes". The beat and drum poundings are a bit more forceful on "Hide your Face" while "Metal Feedback" starts with a quiet vocal sample only to explode into a fully clattering metallic composition. The low beat vibe of "Tribes of Cannibals" is quite foreboding with more movie text sample being interwoven underneath. The unnerving edge of the track is further exacerbated with the half audible background violins and horns. "Incinerate" ups the sound level from more bass oriented tones to sustained low to mid range sounds. About three minutes in the bassier keyboard tones return giving off a low claustrophobic vibe sounding quite a bit like Peter's other work as Megaptera. "Impulse of Fear" has a huge death industrial sound to begin with, evolving it's sound into tribal beat oriented death industrial.

The 'Vodka Remix' of "Psycho Voodoo Killer' (one of the bonus tracks) is a little more harsh in sound and tone but retains a similar structure, while the final Negru Voda track "the Forth Coffin" is more crystalline and less sludgy in sound the preceding tracks.

As an overview when listening to Negru Voda, on more than one occasion the tribal rhythms of the defunct Memorandum come to mind with the heavily doom laden beats and factory clatter, along with some tones and sounds baring similarities to Megaptera (I guess that is inevitable being the sole member in each project and utilizing the same equipment).

Having not heard Magnus's work other than as 'the Protagonist' I was not quite sure what to expect from his works under the 'third EYE' moniker. This is quite different even to my initial assumptions and the closest descriptions I could think of was imagining the structure of 'In Slaughter Natives's' "Sacrosanct Bleed" CD without the bombastic neoclassical edge. On the first third EYE track 'Black Friday' Structured beats and sounds are interwoven with scattered sounds, musical snippets, movie dialogues and buried vocals. The somewhat ad hoc unstructured clatter of various sounds, samples and noises of "The Enigma of Death" gradually pulls itself together into another heavy rhythmic beat affair with the unstructured edge being audible underneath. "Lucid Dreams" has a much darker focus on the undercurrent tone with tortured mid paced poundings of the drum machine. Inaudible male and female vocals add to the hypnotic effect along with the wavering keyboard tune. "Precognition" follows a similar darker path and even hints at what Magnus would go on to produce as 'the Protagonist' with the somewhat classical undercurrent (with the industrial sounds and beats overlaid).

"Hypnago State" is a huge departure in style and sound of the former tracks partly due to it being one of the bonus tracks recorded 2 years after the original tracks. This has a very similar aura to raison d'être's works which isn't helped by the sampled manipulated tones, keyboard sounds and monk chanting vocals on the 7 minute 41 second track. Despite the comparison this is very dark, being one of my favorite tracks on the CD.

The final track for the album and Third EYE is 'Insomnia' and is a new track recorded during 1998 which is a low key death industrial droning sound which actually reminds me of Megaptera of all groups!(Magnus is an occasional session member of Megaptera).

To finish up what has turned into a very long review I will say that overall this is a really good CD and is definitely worthy of your attention.

Negru Voda (Swe) "Dark Territory" CD 1998 Old Europa Café

Coming from reviewing Negru Voda's earlier work above (from 1994), I'm now jumping forward to Peter's newer works from 1998, being his first full length CD. It seems that the focus of overall structure and sound has changing in the spanning years with this bearing little resemblance to the earlier works.

A much more harsher and aggressive focus has been taken forsaking much of the rhythmic death industrial sound. Simple put if I was to hear some of these tracks without knowing the artists I would have had a tough time identifying the culprit.

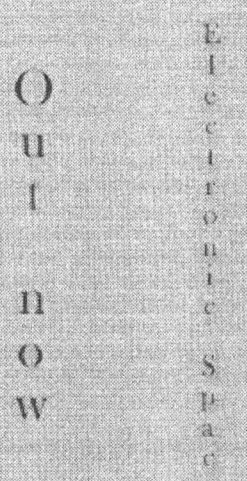

From the outset the new abrasive tone is evident, owing more to power electronics or structured noise. The mid range 'whitish' frequency of 'radio tronic' is modulated into various levels of intensity over approximately 5 minutes. 'Silent Force Entry' utilizes movie dialogue and subscribes to the same technique used on the first track but in a slightly less noisy guise. The title track (also featured on the Death Odors II compilation) probably best mixes the old sound with the new with the high pitched frequency squeals and guttural bass poundings. Gradually different clangs and beats are added into the rhythmic death industrial chaos.

"Suction" is a very forcefully looped 'factory machine' track albeit very short at just over 2 minutes with the following track being a little under three minutes with a more experimental and improvised sound with its modulated noise.

'The Institute' brings to mind being in a cavernous insane asylum where electro shock therapy is administered to all unwilling patients via the high pitched noise frequencies, while "Please, don't steal my head!" sounds like Stratvm Terror if they employed a very dirty sound production. The final track (mono/ stereo) is much quieter than the rest of the disc being a straight forward tone modulation and manipulation to see the disc to its conclusion. Overall the music is quite straight forward retaining a reasonably simple structure or focus on each track which even gives rise to a partially improvised sound (maybe akin to some of Atrax Morgue's work). This is not to say that improvised sound is a letdown as here it done extremely well from a seasoned professional. Although this is a very good CD for it's style and focus, on a personal note I still think I prefer the earlier incantation of this group. Packaging wise this is in an A5 cardboard slip cover with simple layout and graphics, hand numbered in a limited edition of 500.

Noxious Emotions (USA) "Symbols" CD 1998 ADSR Musicwerks

Here is a release from both a label and band I have not come across before (who incidentally got in contact with me). This CD, encompassing a style I do not normally listen to nor buy, I still found this somewhat enjoyable.

The bio coins this as "Elektro-Body-Music and Dance Industrial" but I still find that this does not give a whole and clear perception of what this is about. The music contains vocals in a semi aggressive spoken distorted guise while a background of electro sounds and beats make up the medium paced compositions. While certainly this is much more commercially oriented than most industrial groups, there is a dark enough current flowing through for me to find value within. The vocals and electronics bring to mind the standards set by NIN while there is some comparison to Rammstein's sound - just without the guitars. Other moments (although limited) of the disc lean more towards experimental industrial when the beats are not included and the random sounds are left to do their thing. One of my flat mates stated that this sounded like "Lithuanian Step Aerobics Music" whilst singing "step one, two, your going to die", however I only include this comment for it's joke value and not as a detraction from the actual music. In most part the vocals work well within the whole sound, however in some points, especially in track three when the dual, back and forth yelled chorus really lets the song down. As the songs contain a traditional straight forward composition structure, with the use of a drum machine the sound comes across as very clinical and robotic. At some points (such as in the track 'Mass") a terrible 'hokey' styled keyboard runs ruins the song and ultimately loosing some of it's industrial credibility, but luckily these are fewer than more. The cover with it's use of contrasting colours (incidentally which reminds me of the cover of Sanctums debut CD) and traditional art is well presented. Given that this is the fifth release of this group and the last CD is reputed to have sold over 5000 copies I'm sure both existing fans and other industrial goth types would really get into this.

Ontario Blue (Eng) "Shine" CD 1998 Fluttering Dragon

Having been quite a fan of Endvra for a number of years I was quite interested to hear the solo offerings of one of the members - namely Stephen Pennick. Whilst some of the trademark sounds and vocals of Endvra are here, the overall tracks are less dark & foreboding being more composed in both a tribal and romantic manor, depending on what track is on rotation.

I was in total awe once the opening track "New Beginnings" burst into full flight with sorrowful yet uplifting piano melody with background synthesized string and wind orchestra. "Chant of the Forgiven" uses the layered droney half sung vocals of Endvra with tribal middle eastern ethnic hand percussion.

A quick dreamy keyboard interlude in the way of "Mara's Daughter" floats forward before the track "Lost City" makes it foreboding entrance. Here we have a merging of tribal percussion with a more classical keyboard melody and gothically chanted vocals which works to great effect.

Introspective elements can be found on the track "Change" where the monotone vocal lines make statements such as "I often wonder how it would be, to change the word to my dreams" and "I often wonder if I am mad and those around me are in my head" this being complemented by a slow violin tune, slow beat and layers of light sound.

Some of the chosen keyboard sounds and treatments at the beginning of "Shadows" are not totally to my liking, but this is a minor gripe as these sounds are soon eclipsed by the drum beat, piano melody and vocals once the track gets going.

A painfully depressing acoustic guitar with sadly chanted and sung vocals commence "Don't Weep for Me" to further build to a number of small crescendos with the synthesized backing orchestra.

Other highlights include the slightly baroque influenced composition "This Mortal Coil" which at first holds quite a similarity to the compositions on the Endvra "Great God Pan" album, however this track ends up even more up tempo and composed than any track of the former musical project. The vocal lines stating "Living is easy, dying is hard....I want to live" comes across as a personal catharsis without a hint of cynicism.

This CD being the forth release on a label I have never heard of before (Fluttering Dragon) has not stopped the packing being top notch with full coloured 8 page booklet and inlay tray image. A number of the enclosed paintings/images are also credited to Stephen meaning he is talented in more areas than simply music. It would appear that the next Ontario Blue CD will be released on Displeased Records so while waiting for the next release make sure you track down this gem.

The Protagonist (Swe) "A Rebours" CD 1998 Cold Meat Industry

The long awaited and highly anticipated debut CD of Magnus Sundstrom aka the Protagonist was finally released in the dying months of 1998. And what is the foundation of this release? Through the merging at art and literature set to a classical backdrop and having derived inspiration derived from Joseph Thorak, Percy Bysshe Shelly, Leni Riefenstahl & Edgar Allan Poe, this release could be seen as a modern interpretation of classical art, music and literature.

"The Eternal Abjectness of Life" opens the album with an ominous string section, soon fading out to a vocal passage recital, only to be introduced again with more forceful orchestration and tympani drumming at the conclusion of the spoken section. Overall this track is somewhat subdued, but the true intentions of the album are better exposed on the second track "Kamphfene Pferde". With its more majestic and mildly bombastic composition the music could be said to convey an aura surrounding the progress in preparation for battle with it's militaristic air of pounding drums and stirring horn sections. Mark St.John Ellis (of Elijah's Mantle) provides the spoken word guest appearance on "Mutability" where dynamics are used to their utmost. Towards the middle of the track where the intensity is built via an angelic choir & plucked string section interlude, that blast back into the full flight of the orchestra. "Zoroaster" originally featured on CMI's the Absolute Supper, has undergone some minor changes, but still showcases the underlying militaristic and bombastic nature of the compositions. "Song of Innocence" is a somber affair with consisting of only slow voilin, cello and horns, accompanied by the sorrowful vocals of Peter Pettersson (of Arcana).

The highlight for myself is encased in the track "The Puritan" purely on the sheer intensity of dynamics encased within. Foreboding and ominous in its string opening gradually the whole orchestra is introduced, always retaining underlying feel that at any moment the could explode into war mongering anthem. While this does not fully eventuate the rolling marching drums of the track preclude the inevitable battle that is presented on "Imitation" in its full bombastic glory. The shrill violins, forceful trumpets and horns, incessant cello and pounding percussion increase in their intensity as the track surges forward. Juxtaposed against the previous track the album has its fitting conclusion with a track entitled "The End". Featuring an acoustic guitar with the orchestral accompaniment, the tune picks up the listener sweeping the individual away from the battle field to a fitting resting place of serene calm and contemplation.

The sound quality and production can not be faulted and had been layered and produced in way that it is not blatantly obvious that a keyboard is the main sound source. Furthermore the sound has been enhanced with the use of real cello, acoustic guitar and vocals on a number of the tracks.

On a different angle, when I first viewed the packaging I was surprised how much it resembled Dorobo's releases. Upon closer inspection the answer was revealed as it was in fact the design firm I+T=R that designed this along with many of the Dorobo titles. Normally this would not even matter, but as Karmanik has always played a pivotal role in all his released it was interesting to see him handing over the mantle to another designer (on Magnus's request). This CD made my top 10 releases for 1998 and is surely destined to become a classic both within CMI's roster of releases and the scene in general.

Raison D'etre (Swe) "Lost Fragments" CD 1998 Yantra Atmospheres

Now this is a gem that I'm damn glad I got my hand on. Limited to a mere 100 and only available directly from Peter 'raison d'être' Anderson, it is assured that only the most astute of raison d'être fans will track this down. The premise for the limited nature of this CD is that it contains both rare and unreleased recordings that Peter deemed unsuitable for regular release(as he was unable to rework or remix the tracks, ultimately being unsatisfied with the sound quality). The strange thing was how moved I was by these tracks of supposed "unsatisfying sound quality". Given I have the ear of a fan and not of the artist I am not being as critical, however to me the sound is well balanced and not patchy or substandard at all. To be honest if I had a label of my own I would be honored to officially release this.

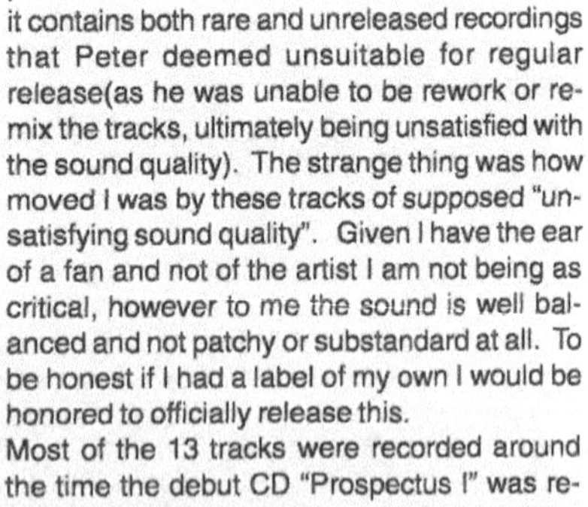

Most of the 13 tracks were recorded around the time the debut CD "Prospectus I" was recorded in 1992, with the general song structures being testimony to this. Where as Peter's compositions have become more and more minimal over time the basis here is generally beats, slow drum loops, disjointed factory noises, voices/ dialogue with overlaid keys and samples. Given this is a compilation of tracks, the flow of the CD is slightly disjointed rather than having a specific flow or direction, but this is really a minor point and only points to the grandeur found on 'true' albums. A couple of tracks here were originally featured on a rare "raison d'etre/Svasti-ayanam" split tape entitled "The ring of Isvarah", released on Slaughter Productions from a few years back. While the focus on industrialized catholic sounds have been Peter's forte, it is unusual to hear on one track "Carnificina" the use of a more eastern oriental feel with the tune and sampled gong.

In various sections there is also some early experimentation with the inclusion of chorale vocals which would become a main feature of later works.

The artwork is nothing to get exited about, being printed out on a home computer and having the bare essentials of musical/ recording detail, however is stylish in its simplistic way. Again this is not the point, as just having this collection of rarities is reward enough. Get this if you can!

Sian (Jap) "Still/ Act" 7" EP 1998 Fever Pitch Music

Fever Pitch of late have been quite big on the repressing of older 7" releases, with this receiving a second print run of 200 hand numbered copies on white vinyl. Not being totally familiar with all aspects of the Japanese noise movement I do know that this release is a collaboration between the well known artist Aube and the lesser known Monde Bruits.

Rather than going for the standard Japanese noise assault this is more akin to experimental ambience focussing on the ebb and flow of treated sound in a transcendual manor. The two tracks follow a very similar feel and theme and the label description of trance/ ambience is right on the mark.

With track 1 sounds gradually build with quite a hollow void feel akin to what Yen Pox is creating (this was before I realized I was playing it on 33 rpm and not 45rpm as required!). Well anyway the track is a little more alive and forceful on the correct speed with not so much of a hollow sound (yet still very like Yen Pox), but as both speeds sound good you take your pick! Track two experiments slightly more with the composition of treated sounds and tones with less focus on the ambient flow. Again a slightly more composed Yen Pox comes to mind.

The cover consists of a well designed gloss over wrap sleeve with obscure yet interesting images in tones of black, grey and silver.

Skin Crime (USA) "Live" CD 1998 Solipsism

Skin Crime is the project of Patrick Oneil, the individual behind Self Abuse Records (and the smaller side label Solipsism). This CD features three lengthy live tracks from Patrick in collaboration with other individuals on each live track that were recorded between June 1997 to November, 1998 (the Nov, 98 tracks is a live studio take).

The first track starts of quite subdued in a electronic ambient way that gradually increases in intensity as the layers of distortion gradually loop into the mix. At a sudden point mid to high range squeals and static jump into the mix and the intensity is all go from this point on. A destroyingly load bass rumble later kicks in with oscillating frequencies scattered over the top. Various fazes of the music both static and load and more soft and subdued are followed through the improvised technique. However it does seem that the collaborators have a good knowledge of what they are doing and have the ability to push the distortion to certain effect and direction. Overall track one is tolerable in reference to the piercing sound elements meaning that one can sit and enjoy this at both load and soft volumes.

Track two starts off more intensely with mid ranged factory frequencies and higher pitch distortion. There are some vocals or voice samples included but are barely at an audible range being buried in the mass or swirling factory static. The basis of the track is quite repetitive with a pulsing undertone, where as the actual noise changes and alterations get lost in the mix. The pulse of the track gradually evolves into a wavering tone and sets the composition off down a side alley (but not too far from the main road). Later in the piece the mid range frequencies are fade out leaving the high and low end squeals and rumbles, only for the mid range sound to build again. Heading towards the 18 minute mark things are qui down substantially with some sort of classical sample being fed into the light swirling noise loop over the next 6 minutes or so. After some further general experimentation the track abruptly finished just shy of 30 minutes.

Track three (the live studio track) has quite unusual opening with what sounds like a metal ball being rolled around in a ceramic bowl (continued at intervals through the track). The tone set after the introduction is more akin to organic/ technological ambience of Alan Lamb or Daniel Menche. Heavy metal clangs and scrapes with bass rumbles are the tone with not so mush as hint of harsh/ high toned frequencies. A mid paces machine pulse enters the mix while some other more organic water sound and scratching noises are used. I could even use the comparison of a less dark more free form of Brighter Death Now(in his early days). Some oscillating tones make an appearance later down the track but remain somewhat subdued until they evolve into a full fledged noise frequency. The intensity gradually builds in both layers and experimentation to conclude the track around the 23 minute mark. By far this is my favorite composition on the CD which overall is quite an intense listen.

While this CD is essentially live noise music and does have an improvised sound quality (to an extent), it still manages to hold direction and focus. Ordinarily lack of focus is a common complaint of mine regarding noise music, however I was able to appreciate the direction of these tracks. This could be put down to the collaborators having a good knowledge of what they are doing and have the ability to push the distortion to certain effect and direction. Furthermore the premise of the works seems to be more focusing on tones, sounds and frequencies then going for pure aggression and harshness.

The cover art is a collage of the live equipment utilized which appears to be a total maze of wires, feedback units and distortion pedals to create the cacophony of sound found on the CD. Given that Solipsism was set up to release limited quantity items I believe that this is had a pressing of 100.

Slogun (USA) "The Pleasure of Death" CD 1998 Death Factory

As it now seems CMI's side label is latching onto the current trend in power electronics/ noise we have a re-release of an older tape of Slogun from 1997. This CD is billed as "True Crime Electronics" which is not a bad description I guess. The packaging is white with black writing including various mug shots of criminals, overall looking somewhat like a scrap book.

Despite being static oriented in mid to high frequencies it manages to retained an overall droning, highly intense edge that gives some focus and direction. The vocal that are included on all tracks are not totally buried in the mix but are treated and distorted to a point where they are quite hard to follow. Other snippets of news reports and the like are used further detailing various crimes and re-enforcing the CD's themes. The total of 8 tracks are generally around 7 minutes in length (total 58 minutes) and set a certain tone within a short time frame. From there the tracks surge forward in a repetitive searing and noisy style where vocals, static and noise fade in and out sporadically.

Given that this does have some direction I find it enjoyable in short sections however at extreme volume and over extended periods this is surly to incinerate more than your eardrums. With no letup whatsoever for the total length, the defiant and monotonous white noise is incessant in its unbridled rage. Definitely not a CD for the meek.

Sutcliffe Jugend (Eng) "When pornography is no longer enough" CD 1998 Death Factory

Now, before I have some noise fanatic coming after me for what I about to write I will let it be known again the noise music is not really my forte.

Given that the members of this groups are almost cult figures because of their past recordings and involvement with other foundering groups of this genre, I was expecting something really extreme. This is not to say that this is not extreme (as in places it is brutally shocking) but in other parts I found it hard to take seriously.

Opening with a dirgy death industrial vibe an overloaded vocal piece rises in anger and screeching intensity over its two minute length (detailing the theme from the CD's title).

For me it was track two where this release fell down. The modulating harsh frequencies are mid ranged to high pitched with a highly audible vocal which is presented as if taped during a murder taking place. As intense as it is, it is a little too over the top and I can't help but imagine Vivian from "the Young Ones" presenting the vocals. During the first rotation of track two I was actually laughing which I guess was not the desired result, however as the disc moves on in a similar fashion the smile was quickly wiped from my face. By the conclusion of the disc (including the last track with its supposed calm finish which explodes into harsh noise for the final minute), I was feeling utterly empty and browbeaten.

Not much new ground is covered here over the 34 minute length, but when it comes from one of the scenes founders what else do you expect. Basically it is the standard extremely overloaded noise music/ power electronic with multi-layered stabbing static.

Aesthetically there are no shocking images to go with the 'music', but simply presented in a well laid out white digi-pack. Even without my above review, if you are into this style you already know if you want it.

Svasti-ayanam (Swe) "sanklesa" CD 1998 Crowd Control Activities

As an artist such as Peter Anderson has too much creative vision to house under a single musical project, he has spawned offshoot projects from the main tree commonly referred to as 'raison d'être'. At last count Peter currently has six active musical projects! Well for this release Peter has taken a spiritual journey (be that in body or just in spirit) to the regions of the Himalayan Alps to present us with composed tribal styled Tibetan Monk hymns.

Opening with low male vocal chanting the track evolves into a mid paced tribal drum affair that is repetitive and looping in structure. Much of the sound of the slow 'Varna-Sankara' (track 2) is based around gongs, bells, synthesized chants and sampled and 'found' background sounds to fill out the picture.

Track three 'Ugra-Karma' is a meditative affair with a more industrial approach with the manipulation of a collage of sound, however this is used with a warm sound production tone to portray a spiritual state of mind over its 9 minute length.

'Zar' (track 4) sees a return to the repetitive ethnic styled drumming with sustained notes and samples filling out the structure. The remainder of the tracks follow under similar descriptions of the above not straying too far the visions laid down early in the album.

From an analytical breakdown of the album, the basis of music's structure (as with most of Peter's projects) is a backbone of industrialized sampled sounds. What sets the sound of the projects apart is how the sounds are manipulated and overlaid with more composed elements – the case here being ethnic tribal drums/ beats, gongs, bells and sampled & synthesized chants. The sound production never reaches cold or harsh territory giving a warm and meditative feels throughout.

Of the 11 tracks presented I have been familiar with 6 of them for a number of years as they were included on Slaughter Productions split tape (also with 'raison d'être') entitled 'The Ring of Isvarah'. All tracks included have specially re-mixed for this release along with simple yet well designed jewel-case packaging.

The relatively new label 'Crowd Control Activities' will no doubt be one to look out for in future if their products continue along with the same quality of releases such as this.

Turbund Sturmwerk (Ger) "Turbund Stermwerk" 1998 Cold Spring

Here is another group that I am not even going to begin to try and dissect the political content and inspiration. Furthermore as my German skills are below par (OK non existent) it would only serve to further complicate the task.

Anyway, this CD is a re-release of this groups debut LP that appeared on the L.O.K.I Foundation in 1995, however the opening track 'Sic Transit' is a newer track from 1997. The music found on this release is in the industrialized neo-classical vein and ranges from passages of brilliance to moments of mediocrity.

'Sic Transit – salvation through blood' contains a slow beat with stabs and swirls of electric sound being overlaid with a low spoken German voice over the repetitive 7 minute length.

'Cupio Dissolvi -staying alive was your fault- now remain' is longer at 17 minutes and interestingly uses the loading of cartridges and cocking of guns for the basis of it's opening beat. The atmosphere here is more rousing with slow clanging bells, ominous horn sections and buried vocals, however as the track goes through a number of stages and passages, it has the feel of a number of tracks than a single one. It is when a more scattered high speed electronic beat keyboard run is introduced that this track looses me, but thankfully this section does not last too long and the horn and industrial passages return to my applause. The closing minutes are quite impressive with a more slow anthemic keyboard passage and distorted vocals.

'Hagakure-what time will not heal-iron will' is very impressive, beginning with a slow marching hymn with flute, rolling drums and chanted vocals, but when things hype up in a more electronic fashion including supremely sung/ distorted vocals this track can do no wrong. Soon after the tracks reverts back to its starting intentions containing parts of both the first and second movements resulting in a solid third segment.

'Styrmsal – what iron will not heal-fire will' is by far the most bombastic and forceful track containing a looped marching snare roll, guttural brass horns, electronic keyboard passages and rising string sections, whilst scattered sounds and vocals writhe underneath. At about the halfway mark of the 12 minute track it is stripped back to a totally new slow keyboard passage with sampled choir vocals. In the final minutes all composed elements are removed leaving only the scattered sounds that have been lurking in the background for much of the track.

The mid paced industrial rhythm of 'Lichtschlag!-through fire into the light' is contrasted against another passage of a sampled choir over a repetitive five minutes. The final ploding keyboard track 'Gloria Mundi' would be alright if it was not for the awfully sung/ spoken vocal which are nothing but purely annoying.

The packaging is encompassed in black, white and red containing runes, symbols war imagery & written text that gives some insight into the group but raises more questions than it answers. Apart from a few select points of the album that I quite dislike, this is overall a very good release. Certainly for those who have appreciated the certain sounds of Blood Axis and Puissance.

Valefor (USA) "Invokation of Forneus" CD 1998 Momento Mori

Being the second CD from this American duo it seems this time around they are aiming for a bit more credibility. The corpse paint has been dropped and pseudonym names of Barron Drakkheim Abaddon & Drakat St LeJeune have been changed back to their real names of Michael Ford and Shanna LeJeune.

As for the music while last time it was basically death ambient drones (pretty impressive at that) here they have invested in and heavily utilized a drum machine/ sampler.

Introducing the album is a mildly distorted track "Fenrir" (with a comparative B.D.N beat) which quickly hypes up into an a pretty harsh drum oriented affair including vocal snippets, looping frequencies and almost black metal styled harsh vocals. This track alone set apart quite heavily the atmospheres presented on the first CD.

"Progression of Aiwass" has a low deathly chant and 'wet' sounding ambient backing before a treated mid paced beat and female chanting makes their appearance. A few sections are worked through were the beats temporarily fade to the back with new configurations and vocals to be introduced.

The title track is more towards the former low key droning sound but still has more of a focus to the bass heavy pounding beats and the use of almost cheesy demonic voices.

"Undead" quickly reverts to the repetitive ritual/ tribalized drumming at the forefront, again with the scattered background noise and deadpan vocal chanting. Strangely this track is dedicated the English group Bauhaus.

My favorite track on this collection is "Caverns of the Mind" and as the title suggests it is a droning death ambient hymn with no added percussive elements. Over the remainder of the final two tracks much of the same sound (as described earlier) are explored.

I'm still not entirely sure about Valefor's new found direction and I think that their debut is more my preference given its heavy atmospheric, yet regressive low key tone. Throughout this CD the occultic/ ritualistic edge is evident in sound and structure and the imagery and text further reinforces this. Overall I guess some common comparisons could be made to a noisier mix of both Archon Satani & No Festival of Light. As for the label, this is another addition to growing roster of Dark Vinyl's "black ambient" side label.

Various Artists (Wld) "the Book ov Shadows" LP 1998 Spectre Records

Certainly the thrill of limited vinyl was not forsaken on this release and featuring the best of the globes 'death industrialists' this promised to be an instant classic.

The first chapter is presented by Dagda Mor with 'the Voice of War' being a strong and surging sermon which includes a rumbling distorted bass sample and overlaid rising/ falls noise tone. Vocals make an appearance but are rendered indecipherable due to the production treatment. Stratvm Terror is featured next with 'Worms' which is quite a short track but is the nosiest and schizophrenic track produced from this group to date. Abrasive, harsh and pulsating, this is certainly flesh sheering stuff. The velocity of this track is partly explained but it being taken from a live performance from June 1998 and damn it, I wish I could have been there to witness this ear punishing performance! Pure power noise electronics at their best.

Soldnergeist continue proceedings with 'Hidden Powers of Nature'. A variety of spoken samples are included over the monotone bass pulses and tones. The basis of the track is set down early with the monotonous approach being the pick of the day. Slight dynamics are utilized with layered sounds but true progression is kept minimal. The track hits its peak late in the piece where a half remember tune rises into the mix and takes it to completion.

Ah Cama-Sotz round out side A with a fantastic atmospheric yet extremely dirgey piece on 'Till Death Do Us Part'. The breadth of sound is truly amazing with bass tones so load they threaten to jump the needle out of the groove. Wind and wave like swirls take up the high sound range with a radio static voice ranting on about someone being executed. The sustained keyboard notes don't go as far as providing a tune, but do assist lightening the crushingly heavy slab of sound.

Side B sees Megaptera going for a regressive sound on 'Frozen Corpse' which is reminiscent of the death industrial 'factory' sounds which were prevalent in the early '90's. Shattered tones, clangs, rumbles and stabs of sound are the order of the day, served up cold and bloody just the way we like it!

Predominance certainly amaze with their track 'Cathedral of Light, which is incidentally the most composed on the album. Anthemic and militant the slow pace of the beat and rousing keyboard sections give an air of pride and strength. The vocals are a wonder within themselves being presented in a commanding and monotone guise which are only enhanced with the pitch shifting effect (to slow the vocals down). Themes of sprit, strength and pride are all touched upon and while not being blatantly obvious on stance, it will certainly have detractors scratching their heads trying to decipher what the music is actually advocating.

Inade open with an ominous tone of unearthly vocal wails akin to the brilliant atmospheric work on the Alderbaran CD of 1997, however things take a change of direction when a Aztec tribalised drum beat is introduced into the sound collage. This track ('Tat Twam Asi Pt II') is as strong as any of Inade's past works and only goes to show that many styles and sounds can be explored without forsaking original intents.

The finale of the LP is from Tortura with 'Resistance is Futile'. The sound quality is quite crisp which emphasizes the forceful intent of the track. The style is quite reminiscent of the sounds that MZ412 have been producing on the last few releases. A vocal sample is included and repeated throughout stating "this evil man came to our community and took all away from her" along with other ranting distorted vocals hidden in the static.

After the sheer quality of the music, the packaging is also superb with a full colour slip sleeve, two mini posters and various postcards, all containing stunning visuals..... supreme! A classic release limited to only 500 copies which I'm certain would have lost some of its aura if it was pressed on normal CD format. Congratulations to Spectre Records for keeping the vinyl spirit alive. Oh did I mention that this is limited to 500!?

Various Artists (Wld) "Machines in the Garden:(part 1 of the Cataclysm Singles)" CD 1998 Blacklight Records

This CD was sent to me from a label I had not previously come across, with the disc itself featuring only one project that I am familiar with (the opening track presented by Caul).

Now the compilation itself is quite diverse covering many styles from industrial, ambient and experimental sounds to more e.b.m, darkwave styles.

One thing I can say is that the majority of sounds presented here are to my liking, even if I wouldn't go out of my way to search out all or many of the projects other releases.

A total of 16 tracks is included by 16 different acts (all appearing to be residents of the U. S of A). Proceedings are keep formal and to the point with the tracks ranging in length from under three minutes to no longer than six. This ensures that more tracks are featured and the tracks that a listener is not that interested in passes quickly. Given there is too much music to individually review I will focus more on the tracks which caught my attention.

As stated Caul opens the disc with 'Metempsychosis' being a good manipulated electro-acoustic slab of dark ambience. Signalbleed sound if they have taped a static inducing, malfunctioning machine hence the tracks title 'Broken Transmitter'. Red Rum Trance start with an ad hock composition('out of the ashes') that gradually reduces to a slow plucked guitar tune. Torn Skin are of the industrial band variety (ala NIN) and do not cover any ground that hasn't already been heavily trampled. A semi static manipulation by Autovoice evolves into more death industrial territory with a mildly pounding beat and some semi buried music and vocal snipits. Thymikon's track 'Steel' impressed me as it sounds as though a finished composed track was taken and forced through an effects unit creating a totally new version(whether this was actually the case is incidental when the ma-

---

Self Abuse Records

Dealers in Extreme, Abstract, and Unusual Sounds Worldwide.

Write for our free Catalog, or check us out on the web at
http://www.mv.com/ipusers/selfabuse

Self Abuse Records
26 S. Main # 277
Concord, NH
03301, USA

COLD SPRING WINTER / SPRING 1999

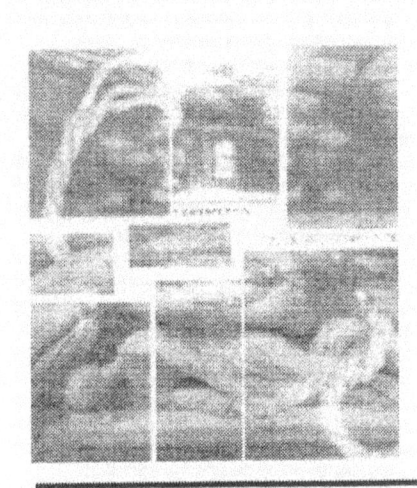

MERZBOW / GENESIS P-ORRIDGE - `A Perfect Pain` CD (CSR23CD)

The two grand masters of industrial sound together for the first time - exclusively for COLD SPRING! 5 brand new tracks - one hour of extreme sonics, devastating rhythms and dark voices. First pressing sold from COLD SPRING in the first week - second pressing available now!

MELEK-THA - `De Magia Naturali Daemoniaca` CD (CSR22CD)

One of the most brutal, beautiful and dark albums we've ever heard! Massive orchestral power meets screams from Hell - an enormous soundtrack of killing - warring armies, clashing of swords, explosions and death! This unique CD of hate music is available now!

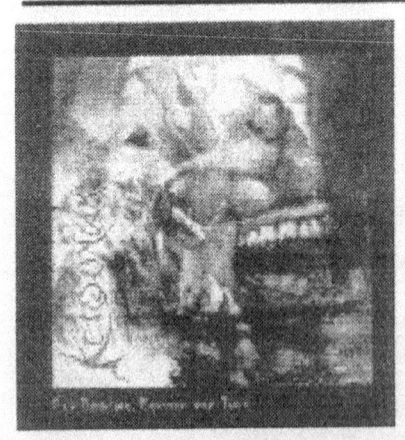

KEROVNIAN - `Far Beyond, Before The Time` CD (CSR24CD)

The debut album from the master of ultra black ambient industrial - and signed to COLD SPRING for a five album deal! Hailing from Croatia - KEROVNIAN is smothering black sonics, with very low vocals, speaking in the KEROVNIAN tongue, a mixture of 1000 year old Greek and Persian - a language of dark angels.

PRICE OF EACH CD INCLUDING 1st CLASS / AIRMAIL POSTAGE:
UK £12.00 - EUROPE £13.00 - REST OF WORLD - £14.00

COLD SPRING, 8, Wellspring, Blisworth, Northants. NN7 3EH, England, UK. Tel/Fax: + (0) 1604 859142 - Email:coldspring@thenet.co.uk / www.thenet.co.uk/~coldspring
Write for our free 40 page quarterly newsletter and catalogue, containing hundreds of titles (including some rare or out of print) from the many labels we distribute.

FORTHCOMING:

SCHLOSS TEGAL - "Black Static Transmission" CD

PSYCHIC TV - "Were You Ever Bullied At School - Do You Want Revenge?" CD

NOVATRON - "New Rising Sun" CD

MARK SNOW - "Death...Be Not Proud" CD

ENDVRA - "Contra Mvndvm" CD

nipulation sound this good). Twitch are heavily into the distorted bass rumbling experimental ambience. Cradle->Grave present a middle eastern twinged piece that gradually builds in sorrowful intensity via the introduction of compositional elements of percussion, keys and vocals.

The darkwave'ish track 'the Elven Moon' by Evonica sounds similar to Anatome Elektrine with sampled choir vocals and real vocals. Comparisons could also be made to those tunes featured in 80's horror/ drama movies (this is used in a complimentary not derogatory sense). Blackhouse are content with providing erratic experimental sound and vocal sample manipulation. Bringing the CD to it's conclusion is Dopple Hode that is a dark keyboard piece that has dub oriented undertones that make their intentions known towards the close of the track. As an overview this CD is basically the first in a trilogy of compilation CD's that are to form an independent international boxset of sub cultural styles of music. The artwork is top notch and recognition to the label is deserved for putting together a compilation which will surely increase the knowledge and interest in non-main stream forms of music. (Note: I did receive the other two parts of the series, however they arrived too late to receive a full review within this issue. From the brief listens I managed to have, they encompass a similar focus to the above CD however probably tend to have more a focus on the darkwave and traditional industrial bands than experimental sounds. Still worthwhile none the less).

Various Artists (Wld) "Middle Pillar Presents - What is Eternal" CD 1998 Middle Pillar

Well, after having a well renowned mail order business for quite a number of years, Middle Pillar have branched out into starting their own label, with this being the first release off the ranks. This is a stellar collection of neo-gothic, ethereal, classical, ambient type tracks from a variety of quite well known (and not so known) artists working within these fields.
Proceedings start with The Machine in the Garden (not to be confused with the V/A album of a similar name reviewed above) with a Dead Can Dance type track entitled 'falling softly'. A gothicially oriented piano tune is solemnly played with a angelic and operatic female vocal accompaniment. Cello, violin and background percussion are utilized making this song a great introduction to the CD. 4th Sign of the Apocalypse have quite a ominous start (on 'lady doe') with a dark brooding violin and vocal (female) piece however things fall down when the male vocals are introduced late in the track(Try to imagine a gothic singer trying to yodel and you might be half there). Unto Ashes have a very romantic baroque sounding song with spoken male/female vocals a bit like Ordo Equilibrio which later break into mild singing. A similar feel is exuded from the following track by Mors Syphilitica however the female vocals are sweeter and more operatic. A nice classical guitar tune is the basis for Quartet Noir's song 'petals from a rose' which obtains quite a folky feel with the use of flute, harp and female vocals (with this group incidentally featuring Tony Wakeford).

Loretta Doll start off very much like the vocal songs of Arcana before a movie dialogue is introduced along with a mild guitar tune that gets more technology oriented in sound as it progresses with processed percussion and sounds. The Arcana like vocal melody is reduced a final time to see the track out.
Dream into Dust have a more dark ambient feel with the 'noises from the cellar' background that fleshes out the picture with a classical piano/ guitar tune and orchestral violins. This is a very good track being somewhat reminiscent of Caul's works.
The Changlings manage to capture a very eerie classical feel with a dub oriented ethnic mix with Portisehead like vocal accompaniment. The sweetly sorrowful tune/ female vocals of The Mirror Reveals song 'let all the poets sing' is very radio friendly in sound, while still being a good song.
A mild comparison could be made again to Ordo Equilbrio with the repetitive acoustic guitar of Backworld's 'leaving the isles of the blest (remix)' however the male vocals are vastly different being both spoken and sung in a more lively manor (almost akin to David Bowie).
Tony Wakeford appears again on a track with Tor Lundvall (who is better known for his macabre art) who have their track starting out with a pretty poor 'chop sticks' piano tune. The track does add a bit more background instrumentation however the two finger piano playing still gets on my nerves. Jarboe have a pretty average gothic type song which has a reasonable 'witchy' atmosphere due to the vocals. Athanor on their track 'for whom the bell tolls' (….and no it is not a Metallica cover) start out with a dark ambient styling (including a repeated radio voice), that becomes more neo-classical in sound with the introduction of violins and piano and spoken lyrics.
A great finisher to the CD is the track from Zoar that is if the backing was taped within a mad scientists abode with the musical component being dark guitar electronica with an almost In Slaughter Natives edge at times.
In conclusion the packaging is also top notch with a three fold digi-pack with stunning complimentary visuals. After the decent quality of this debut release I'm interested to see what this label will come up with in future.

Yen Pox (USA) "Deliver/Remove" 7"EP 1998 Drone Records

Now given I missed the first limited pressing of 250 (released in 1995) I have the ability of hindsight to make comparisons with their debut CD released also in 1995. The demand for this was such that Drone Records were warranted in repressing a second edition of 300 copies (which I'm sure will sell as fast as the first). I believe that the packaging is much the same as the original with a simple yet effective image gracing the cover and giving some hint to what musical slab is held within the wax. Stylistically anyone familiar with Yen Pox's sound will pick this sound straight away, however given the shorter format they are presented on has resulted in the tracks being more dense and dynamic.

On Side A 'Deliver' grasps the listener by the throat and slowly drags you into the dense engulfing void as the waves of droning layered sound build in intensity. A few more dynamic mid range sound elements are utilized, giving rise to visions of unearthly orchestra in the throes of warming up for a final performance. It is literally as if the air in the room has become stale further emphasizing the suffocating intensity.

Side B delivers the track 'Remove' while although not an densely heavy, the atmospheres are however swirlingly dynamic with the tonal qualities being in the mid to high range.
Gradually forcing upwards in twisting spiral the track levels out to again starts on its downward decent into the chasm and to its conclusion. As much as I appreciate this release, it has done nothing but to leave me salivating for the new upcoming album scheduled for a 1999 release on Malignant!

THE END....

ADDRESS LIST

ADSR MUSICWERKS
1106 E Republican, Seattle WA 98012 USA
e-mail: adsr@adsr.org
WWW: http://www.adsr.org

ARCANE RECORDS
C/- Mark Endacott, P.O. Box 458, Fullarton, South Australia 5063
Phone/ Fax: 08 8357 5008
e-mail: markenda@bigpond.com

ART KONKRET
C/- Markus Kropfreiter, Linkenheimer Weg 5, D-76646, Bruchsal, Germany
e-mail: Art.Konkret@t-online.de
WWW: http://home.t-online.de/home/Art.Konkret/

ATHANOR
C/- Stéphane, BP294, 86007 POITIERS, Cedex, France
e-mail: Ursprache@wanadoo.fr

AVA/ES1 RECORDS
P.O.Box 605488, Cleveland OH 44105, USA
e-mail: BaaL7Ava@aol.com
website:http://www.angelfire.com/ny/scriptureszine/avaes1.html

BLACKLIGHT RECORDS
P.O. Box 6552, Kokomo, IN 46904, USA
e-mail: label@blacklight.com
WWW: http://www.blacklight.com/releases.htm

CAT'S HEAVEN RECORDS
P.O. Box 170 116, 47181 Duisburg, Germany
e-mail: vuz&vuz.du.gtn.com.
WWW: http://www.badlands.de/vuz

COLD MEAT INDUSTRY
PO Box 1881, S-581 17 Linköping, Sweden
e-mail: Order@coldmeat.se
WWW: http://www.coldmeat.se

COLD SPRING
87, Gloucester Avenue, Delapre, Northampton, NN4 9PT. England, UK.
e-mail: coldspring@thenet.co.uk
WWW: http://www.thenet.co.uk/~coldspring/

CRIONIC MIND
4644 Geary Boulevard #105, San Francisco, CA 94118 USA
e-mail: crionic@pacbell.net
WWW: http://crionicmind.org

CROWD CONTROL ACTIVITIES
821 White Elm Dr. Loveland, CO 80538 USA
e-mail: crowded@ezlink.com
WWW: http://www.ezlink.com/~crowded/controlcenter.html

DARK VINYL
P.O. Box 1221, 90539 Eckental, West Germany
e-mail: Darkvinyl@T-onlime.de

DOROBO/ SHINJUKU THIEF
Darrin Verhagen P.O. box 22 Glen Waverly, Victoria, Australia 3150
e-mail: dorobo@werple.net.au
WWW: http://werple.net.au/~dorobo/dorobo.html

EIBON RECORDS
Via Folli 5, 20134 Milano, Italy
e-mail; rberchi@galactica.it
WWW: http://www.this.it/eibon/

ENDVRA/ ENLIGHTEMENT COMMUNICATIONS/ ONTARIO BLUE
C/- Stephen Pennick, 4 Verdun Terrace,West Cornforth County, Durham, Dl17 9ln, England
Fax: +44 01740 654356
e-mail: Stephen@encomm.freeserve.co.uk
WWW: http://www.encomm.freeserve.co.uk

FEVER PITCH MUSIC
1108, E.Capitol Drive, Appleton, WI 54911, USA

MANTEINANCE / I- BURN
Gabriele Santamaria, via Gen. Pergolesi 21, 60125 Ancona - Italy
+39-0712811423
e-mail: mantein@tin.it
WWW: http://space.tin.it/musica/gasantam/index.html

MALIGNANT RECORDS
Jason Mantis. PO Box 5666, Baltimore MD 21210, USA
e-mail: info@malignantrecords.com
WWW: http://www.malignantrecords.com

MALSONUS RECORDS
C/- Jonathan Canady, P.O. Box 18193, Denver, CO 80218, USA
e-mail: malsonus@milehigh.net

MANIFOLD RECORDS
PO BOX 12266, Memphis TN. 38182, USA
e-mail: manifold@manifoldrecords.com
WWW: http://www.manifoldrecords.com/

MEGAPTERA
Peter Nyström, Runebergsgatan 38, 611 37 Nyköping, Sweden
e-mail: salome@hem2.passagen.se
WWW: http: //hem2.passagen.se/salome/home.htm

MEMENTO MORI
C/- Dark Vinyl, P.O. Box 1221, 90539 Eckental, West Germany
e-mail: Darkvinyl@T-onlime.de

MIDDLE PILLAR
PO Box 555, NY, NY 10009, USA
e-mail: info@middlepillar.com
WWW: http://middlepillar.com/mainmenu.html

OLD EUROPA CAFE
C/- Rodolfo Protti Viale Marconi 38, 33170 Prodenone, Italy
e-mail: oec@iol.it
WWW: http://www.stack.nl/~bobw/music/OEC/

THE PROTAGONIST
Magnus Sundström, Nybohovsbacken 43:232, 117 64 Stockholm, Sweden
e-mail: protagonist@swipnet.se
WWW: http://protagonist.coldmeat.se

RAISON D'ETRE/ STRATVM TERROR/ YANTRA ATMOSHERES
Peter Andersson, Bondegatan 20 c, nb S-595 52 Mjolby, Sweden
Fax: Int. code + 46-142-17886
e-mail: raison.detre@swipnet.se
WWW: http://home9.swipnet.se/~w-90779/index.htm

RED STREAM
P.O. Box 342 Camp Hill Pa 17001-0342 USA
e-mail: mail@rstream.com
WWW: http://www.rstream.com

RELEASE RECORDS
C/-Relapse Records, P.O. Box 251, Millersville, PA 17551, USA
e-mail: relapse@relapse.com
WWW: http://www.relapse.com

SELF ABUSE RECORDS
26 S.Main Street #277, Concord, NH 03301, USA
e-mail: Selfabuse@selfabuse.mv.com
WWW: http://www.mv.com/ipusers/selfabuse

SLAUGHTER PRODUCTIONS
c/o Marco Corbelli, via Tartini 8, 410 49 Sassuolo (MO) Italy
e-mail: slaughter@mail.dex-net.com

SOLEILMOON RECORDINGS
PO Boc 83296, Portland OR 97283 USA
e-mail: mailorder@soleilmoon.com
WWW: http://www.soleilmoon.com

SPECTRE RECORDS
P.O.Box 88, 2020 Antwerpen 2, Belgium
fax : ++32.3.238.38.46
e-mail : spectre@skynet.be
web : http://users.skynet.be/spectre

STONE GLASS STEEL/ IRON HALO DEVICE
Phil Easter, 2311 West 50th Street, Apt. #2, Minneapolis, MN 55410, USA
e-mail: eyespark@bitstream.net

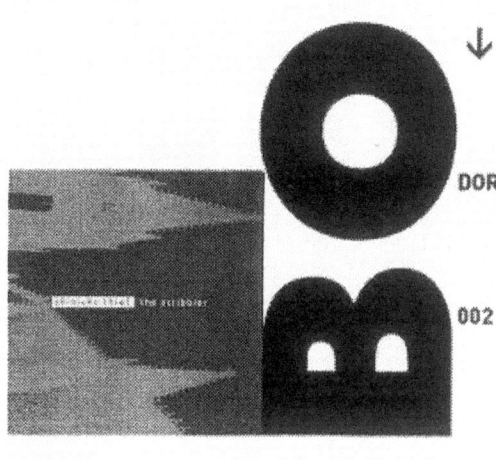

DOROBO 'records'
P.O.Box 22, Glen Waverley, Victoria 3150 AUSTRALIA Fax: 61-(0)3-9756-0341
email: dorobo@werple.net.au   http://werple.net.au/~dorobo/dorobo.html

002   Shinjuku Thief - The Scribbler AUD$25
Originally composed for an oblique stage reworking of Kafka's "The Trial", this album features a series of orchestral minimalist pieces (a la Nyman, or Glass) set into filmic soundscapes (including portions of Kafka's original German text, and occasional backdrops of industrial noise)

003   Shinjuku Thief - The Witch Hammer AUD$25
An impressionistic rendering of possession, exorcisms, ergot poisoning, witchtrials, pagan ritual and pacts with a fyfe player. A homage both to expressionist films of the 1920s and the supernatural horror from the turn of the 19th century. The end result is a classic Gothic Industrial album - dark orchestral timbres, rich soundscapes interspersed with outbursts of violence and power. Intense reverberations of sound, veiled walls of deceit, thundering crashes of vigor and trickling brooks all permeate throughout this symphonic, ominous Neoclassical work.

009   Shinjuku Thief - The Witch Hunter AUD$25
The thematic sequel to "Hammer". East European violin, reflective passages of brooding ambience and occasional moments of hope are undercut by sheer orchestral violence and a chillingly bleak filmic soundscape.

lr193.6 Shinjuku Filth - Raised by Wolves EP AUD$20
"Verhagen's new soundtrack throws caution to the wind and rips out the pancreas with a grapefruit knife. Massive industrial dance grooves underpin vicious soundscape cut-ups scanning from Italian short wave transmissions through Australian police CB confusion. Power mix of industrial, rock distortions, passages of disturbed strings and the Shinjuku Filth approach to sonic slash and flame make this soundtrack just as comforting as the theatrical production." - David Hodgson, PBE/USA

Professor Richmann - Succulent Blue Sway AUD$25
Shinjuku Filth - Junk AUD$25
Darrin Verhagen - Soft Ash AUD$25
Darrin Verhagen - p3 AUD$15

Shinjuku Filth - Bodyparts

MALIGNANT RECORDS

C17H19NO3: 1692/2092 - Malevolent neo-classical orchestral arrangements brimming with sorrow and epic majesty. A soundtrack for the dark ages of the past and future. 'The Room of Ice' & 'Electric Air' featuring Jarboe (Swans). **TUMOR.09** NEW

STONE GLASS STEEL: DISMEMBERING ARTISTS
The long awaited release of a lost gem. A raw, highly complex assemblage of recontextualized samples, climactic atmospheres, and shimmering passages of dark grinding noise. **TUMOR.10** NEW

music for dissipated cultures

STRATVM TERROR: PAIN IMPLANTATIONS - From the mind behind Raison D'Etre. A horrific excursion into the darkest depths of human depravity. An unrelenting attack of corrosive, violently explosive electronics. Hypnotic, & Brutal. **TUMOR.08**

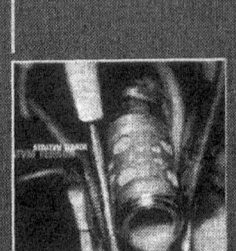

CAZZODIO: IL TEMPO DELLA LOCUSTA - A thick entanglement of metallic percussion, white noise, voice samples, and overdriven, saturated power electronics. Debut release from new Malignant side label **BLACK PLAGVE**

IRON HALO DEVICE: THE COLLAPSING VOID
"A slithery and all encompassing sonic octopus of diverse samples manipulated into cohesive, illusive, mind altering songs"
TUMOR.07

a record label
mailorder distributor
& online record store

introducing:
www.malignantrecords.com

INCUBATE YOUR OWN PERSONAL MALIGNANCY Join the Malignant Tumorlist
- EMAIL < infect@malignantrecords.com > **(automated subscriptions only)**
- PLACE IN MESSAGE BODY: SUBSCRIBE tumorlist your_name

SEND NON-LIST EMAIL TO: < malignant@malignantrecords.com >

FREE PRINTED CATALOG - SEND ADDRESS TO: _____
P.O. BOX 5666 • BALTIMORE, MARYLAND 21210 • USA

SPECTRUM ISSUE 3
AMBIENT/INDUSTRIAL/EXPERIMENTAL MUSIC CULTURE MAGAZINE

ORDO EQUILIBRIO/ SLAUGHTER PRODUCTIONS/ CAUL
DEUTSCH NEPAL/ TERTIUM NON DATA/ C17H19NO3/ I-BURN
KEROVNIAN/ IMMINENT STARVATION/ SCHLOSS TEGAL

CROWD CONTROL

TERTIUM NON DATA: "THE THIRD IS NOT GIVEN" CD
Notably diverse and tense, cinematic pieces blending seamlessly with haunting soundscapes. A cold, black atmosphere with an elegant and commanding pervasiveness. From John Bergin and Brett Smith (C17H19No3, Caul, Trust Obey).

DISSECTING TABLE: "KAIBOUDAI" 3CD SET
The most complete look into the apocalyptic psyche of Ichiro Tsuji; contains the long-lost first LP and 7", as well as essential compilation tracks. Highlighted by Ichiro's most recent works, "Kaiboudai" culminates with 45 minutes of contemptful industrial noise. Limited to 500 numbered copies.

INANNA: "SIGNAL/OR/MINIMAL" CD
The final album from Mikael Stavöstrand (Archon Satani, Entarte) as Inanna. The dark ambient master intermingles subtle, spectral lows with complex, imaginative highs to create an album that is surely the pinnacle of his compelling artistry. "signal/or/minimal" will infiltrate your senses and subdue your conscious mind.

VARIOUS ARTISTS: "THE SOUND OF SADISM" CD
Prepare yourself for the beast that means to destroy your pathetic taste in noise-pop and oriental dime a dozen static nonsense! The most violent, hateful, and perverse 70 minutes you have ever heard. A lesson in aural blood and moral violation. Exclusive tracks by: Deathpile, Con-Dom, Slogun, Discordance, Taint, Iugula Thor, Gruntsplatter, Hydra, Sshe Retina Stimulants, Skin Crime, Stahlnetz, Atrax Morgue, Bloodyminded, and Black Leather Jesus.

5000 SPIRITS: "MESMERIC REVELATION" CD
Stefano Musso (Alio Die) teams up with Raffaele Serra for the second album from 5000 Spirits. Undertake an arcane journey that travels through different psycho-acoustic environments and atmospheres. Truly a subtle, melodic study of mesmeric proportions.

ALIO DIE / ANTONIO TESTA: "HEALING HERB'S SPIRIT" CD
Antonio Testa adds a tribal, shamanic approach to Alio Die's intimate and droning revelations. While mixing sonic disturbances with a multitude of hand-made instruments, "Healing Herb's Spirit" captures the soul as the mind wanders endlessly in an abyss of ambient consciousness.

COMING IN JANUARY:
NECROPHORUS: "TUNDRA STILLNESS" CD
GRUNTSPLATTER: "THE DEATH FIRES" CD

All CD's $12 ppd except Dissecting Table "Kaiboudai" which is $20 ppd
please send cash or money order payble to James Grell

CROWD CONTROL ACTIVITIES
821 White Elm Drive • Loveland, Colorado 80538 USA
Fax 970.472.1167 • crowded@ezlink.com • http://www.ezlink.com/~crowded

ALSO DISTRIBUTED BY: ARCANE RECORDINGS, MALIGNANT RECORDS, DARK VINYL RECORDS, METROPOLIS RECORDS, AND SOLEILMOON RECORDINGS

MIDDLE PILLAR

DISTRIBUTION
MUSICAL ESOTERICA

ethereal
electronic
darkambient
experimental
industrial
neo-folk

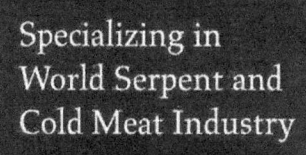

Specializing in
World Serpent and
Cold Meat Industry

brand new catalog of over 2500 titles
available sept. 99 send $2 to:
MIDDLE PILLAR, DEPT M.
PO BOX 555, NY, NY 10009
FAX LINE: 212-378-2924
TOLL-FREE ORDER LINE
1-888-763-2323

complete catalog online at:
http://www.middlepillar.com
email: info@middlepillar.com

MIDDLE PILLAR PRESENTS

A MURDER OF ANGELS
While You Sleep

A drowsy yet unsettling blend of dark neoclassical and eerie electronic ambience that defines the style of Damnbient.

THE MACHINE IN THE GARDEN
One Winter's Night

Haunting vocal melodies, dark electronics, acoustic soundscapes, shadows and dreams. An ethereal masterpiece.

Coming Soon:
ethereal musings from THE MIRROR REVEALS,
and the TREE OF LIFE compilation.

Middle Pillar Presents
Dept M, P.O. Box 555, NY, NY 10009
1-888-763-2323, Fax: 212-378-2924
http://www.middlepillar.com
info@middlepillar.com

Spectre — PoBox 88 — 2020 Antwerpen 2 — Belgium
spectre@skynet.be — http://users.skynet.be/spectre

KRAKEN
"Aquanaut"
LP
transparent blue
heavy wheight
500 copies
NA01

The debut release of CMI-list member Ricardo Gomez and Joris Vermost. This new belgian musical duo creates on this album a perfect blend of lucid ambient tunes with manipulated samples. The result is a strange abyssal journey through the realm of neptunal underworlds.

TORTURA
"Mental Agony - Victimm"
7-inch
heavy weight
399 copies
Noc3

Known from their blistering contribution to "The Book ov Shadowz", Tortura now invades with powerfull interpretations of control and domination. Two tracks two faces. One rhythmic electronic side suited for darkened dancefloors and another side designed for nightly graveyard sessions.

PAL - AH CAMA-SOTZ
"Audiowall - Guilty"
7-inch
heavy weight
399 copies
remix collaboration
Noc2

Ah Cama-Sotz and Pal were invited by Spectre to organise this collaboration. Each artist made a basic track which was re-mixed, re-edited and re-shaped by the other artist. This resulted in two very different songs, the one being very rhythmic and dynamic - almost technoid - the other being a true wall of sound designed to penetrate the brain.

Vinyl Fetish

SPECTRUM MAGAZINE ISSUE 3

ORDO EQUILIBRIO / SLAUGHTER PRODUCTIONS / CAUL / DEUTSCH NEPAL / TERTIUM NON DATA
C17H19NO3 / I-BURN / KEROVNIAN / DEATH IN JUNE-DER BLUTHARSCH SHOW REPORT
IMMINENT STARVATION / SCHLOSS TEGAL / SOUND REVIEWS / CONTACT LIST

EDITORIAL: DUSK 1999/ DAWN 2000

What to say? Well, finally a new issue is released, albeit a bit later than I anticipated but still within a reasonable time frame from the last issue. The visual side of things has again been taken up a notch from the first two issues, whereby I hope there will be a constant improvement in this department for each new issue. When I originally started, I figured I might do one or two issues and just see where it took me. I will say that given the responses I have been receiving on my efforts so far, it makes all the time and effort spent on this thing worthwhile. The point I have currently reached tends to brighten the horizon (or be it illuminate the cavern) for an extended future of this publication. Who knows, with the way things are progressing maybe one of these days I will actually buy a computer of my own and stop hassling my flat mate for use of his! This time around the net has been cast just that little bit further in terms of who is featured and the content of the review section, which only indicates broader and evolving musical interests. Speaking of the review section it is getting to a point where it is almost spiraling out of control....not that I am complaining of course, rather that it is a bit daunting that there were nearly 100 items to review, that were received over a time frame of approximately 8 months (the time elapsed from the last issue). This is exactly the reason why I have enlisted the writing talents of JC Smith as a contributing reviewer. There is a marked difference in style between our writing, but this should only add to the diversity of opinions expressed. Given that this is predominantly a one man show I have made my best endeavors to ensure it is free of mistakes, but given I know exactly what I am wanting to say, upon proof reading sometimes stupid grammatical errors slip though. If any are enclosed herein I'm sure it is reasonably clear of what I was getting at, and not that I am a complete ignoramus. In conclusion I have already got my eye on a number of artists I want to feature in Issue 4# but they will remain a secret until further confirmation can be obtained. For the moment enjoy issue 3# and expect a new issue in around mid to late 2000.

O'vr'n'out.....Richard Stevenson

EDITOR / INTERVIEWER / REVIWER / LAYOUT DESIGNER ETC: RICHARD STEVENSON
CONTRIBUTORS: JC SMITH - REVIEWS / MIKE RIDDICK - COVER IMAGE

SPECIAL THANKS

As always James Leslie for providing the means, Mick Stevenson for technical support, Jason Mantis & Phil Easter @ Malignant Records for ceaseless support and promotion, Mike Riddick for the fantastic cover image contribution, JC Smith for the enlightening words of review, friends and family for bemused (& occasionally feigned) interest, Scott Van Dort for the forever entertaining 'metal' conversations, all contributing labels for their promotional products and advertising support, to the artists for their contributing efforts, to the individuals/ artists that I'm in regular contact with (for general inspiration) and all others I have somehow forgotten.

SPECTRUM MAGAZINE C/- RICHARD STEVENSON, 346 CHESTERVILLE ROAD, EAST BENTLEIGH 3165, VICTORIA, AUSTRALIA
SPECTRUMMAGAZINE@HOTMAIL.COM

TEXT & DESIGN LAYOUT COPYRIGHT SPECTRUM MAGAZINE
ALL IMAGES COPYRIGHT THE RESPECTIVE ARTISTS

Cover image by Mike Riddick - "untitled" 1999
Contact: yamatu@erols.com, http://www.coldburialsystem.com/riddick

Ordo Equilibrio

The male/female duo Ordo Equilibro has reached a well respected level with the CMI (and affiliated) scene by the utilisation of folk oriented acoustic guitars, orchestral & industrial sentiments and apocalyptic/poetic lyrics with evolution and maturation having occurred over the span of three albums. At the time of writing, news has come to hand that discontentment in the Ordo Equilbrio camp has resulted the female half of the group (Chelsea) removing her presence. While this is disappointing news of the project and even prior to this announcement, consequence. Following some light past achieve- it does not appear that this is the end though this interview was conducted certain parts allude to the later below Tomas Pettersson sheds ments and future activities.

Ordo Equilibrio have been an entity that has produced three albums thus far, but rather than me making an assessment of your success, I think I would rather hear of how you view Ordo Equilibrio in the context of sound, concept and relevance to the current scene.
The sound of OE is the audible unveiling of my individual disposition and personal preferences; nothing more nothing less - a genuine & conceivably distinct hybrid of purportedly customary/traditional dark ambient & neo folk industrials.
The conjectural concept/abstraction of OE that is unveiled throughout the tangible as well as metaphysical essence of Ordo Equilibrio is coequally akin to the disposition of the music itself; merely being an aesthetic reflection of my personal preferences and individual nature. But much rather than me trying to ascertain the hypothetical importance & relevance of OE as part of the contemporary industrial/neo folk scene, I would much rather enjoy the possibility of hearing your assessment of my alleged success; particularly as this is something I am yet relatively unfamiliar with.
Through the being and operations of OE I do not deliberately seek either praise or acknowledgment for any of the appointed subjects; but if people find a premeditated and conceivably more profound signification of my intent in that which I spawn, I can merely relish in gratification.

Ordo Equilibrio = Order and Equilibrium. Please elaborate as you see fit.
Order & Equilibrium or optionally The Order of Equilibrium depending on which interpretation you wish to assign Ordo Equilibrio, serves as an operative and illustrious signification by which to portray and dispute any variety of becoming and contrary perspectives related to Balance & Order; War/Peace, Life/Death, Love/Hate, Male/Female, Light/Dark, Good/Evil, Left/Right etc.etc., religiously and sociologically & socio-politically fabricated terms & valuations that most people apparently take for granted.

There has been a clear establishment of style and sound across your three CD's with the third arriving in a format of having an apocalyptic folk sound with generally being more 'song' structured with a reduced reliance on ambient passages. Has these been a clear vision from the start on what realms of sound you wanted to explore and directions to head in?
At the time of founding Ordo Equilibrio I had the inconclusive apprehension of what instrumental setting I desired to utilise, but the appointed evolution into a designated disposition of Apocalyptic Neo Folk Industrials was never something I consciously endeavoured or believe that I have suffered.
Each individual working that I spawn; separately and collectively as part of OE, is an invariable and aesthetically veritable evidence of my psychical, spiritual and emotional person/condition over a particular duration of time – the time betwixt its origin and completion. So alongside the invariable variations of all conceivable conditions akin to the setting of my individual persona, each aesthetic evidence of Ordo Equilibrio is e n g e n d e r e d .

I believe that you are currently working on your forth album. What can be expected from this album and is there a tentative release schedule? Likewise what poetic accomplishments will we find manifested in the album and song titles?

At this time there is a forth and a fifth working scheduled for late autumn/winter 1999, optionally early spring 2000; but the factual instant of their respective releases are yet dependent on the contemporary unfolding of aspirations and individual premises. Naturally, and judging from a personal perspective, the contemporary and yet unreleased material is my most competent achievement thus far – melodically, lyrically and technically. And granted that you appreciate any of my foregoing workings, I believe each of the anticipated accomplishments will prove equally satisfying.

It seems pointless at present time to announce either of the appointed workings designated titles, but some song titles are nevertheless – 'Harvesting the Crop; The chaste Verdict of Negligence', 'Passing eyes' in Mimer's Well' & 'Hunting for the Black September'.

One element that has been used in establishing a more folk oriented sound has been the use of repetitive acoustic guitar throughout selected tracks, with this tending to draw a comparison to the long standing works of Death In June. Would you site this pioneering outfit as a direct influence? Also by virtue of the repetition of the acoustic riffs, I wanted to ask whether these parts were sampled or played by yourself?

Naturally I can not disavow the importance of Death in June and Douglas's indirect influence on my musical preferences, and therewith my ensuing musical spawnings as the foremost pioneer of the designated scene. But rather than supposedly apprehending a sound which is apparently belonging to DIJ, Current 93 and Sol Invictus, and subsequently stagnating in a pre-contrived aesthetic pattern established by others, I seek to utilise and explicate these unintentional influences into something which I ultimately believe will be conceived and recognised as Ordo Equilibrio.

While anyone within the scene should be well aware of you past workings in the group 'Archon Satani' I do not feel it necessary to delve into the past, however I do have a question in relation to a particular liner note statement on the 'Conquest, Love & Self Perseverance' CD. While it is clear from your statement on the liner notes of 'Reaping the fallen... the first harvest' that the split of Mikael and yourself was less than amicable, the liner notes on 'Conquest, Love & Self Perseverance' indicate that friendship has now been restored (referring to the statement "Mikael Stavostrand for continuing friendship and erecting the tombstone"). Is the later part of this statement in relation to Mikael ceasing any further works as Archon Satani?

To bury the past and ensue with the present towards the future, it can be stated that I was quite disappointed with Mikael's seemingly rabid claims and behaviour back in 93, and which consequently ensued with my departure from AS. Disappointment & hostility as a consequence of consequences withstood for some time following my departure, but passed as we finally decided to confront each other and ultimately resolve the erstwhile situation. Consequently explaining each of the above mentioned liner notes.

We have since discussed the possibility of releasing one final and conclusive AS working featuring all previously unreleased material conceived prior to my departure; conceivably in association with one first and final AS performance, and thence put the entity of Archon Satani to rest once and for all. But when and whether either of the appointed aspirations will ever be realised yet remains to be resolved, as Mikael currently seems apparently inclined to put his erstwhile activities behind him. And consequently the liner note on 'Conquest, Love & Self Perseverance' was not relative to Mikael's cessation of releasing records as Archon Satani.

I will comment that I found the inside cover art of 'the triumph of light...' CD to be quite profound in the ability to conveyer your stance against Christianity. My interpretation of the images would be twofold, in that on one hand it is representative of taking away the ability of Christianity to communicate its message and on the other hand showing it to be an empty vessel in terms of the value of its teachings. Do you agree with this assessment and was the original idea one of yours or the result of Roger Karmanik's handy design work?

One intention of the allegedly 'sacrilegious' aesthetics of 'The Triumph of Light' was trying to establish Christianity's deficiency of verbal capability and significance, alongside the establishment of Christianity's veritable self as that of herd indifferent to whom is its shepherd. And consequently your assessment of whether or not the appointed interpretations are manifested throughout the artwork of 'The Triumph of Light.... and Thy Thirteen Shadows of Love' is correct, but there is likewise the assessment of my sincere conviction that Jesus certainly could use some head.

Throughout certain lyrics and particularly on more recent photo shoots, there is a strong sense of irony, playfulness and dry humor. How important are these elements to the group and is it yet another means of getting the point of your ideology across without appearing to be the constant misanthropist?
Notable parts of the industrial scene, with the exception of a few bands and individuals, are to all appearances extensively deficient of distance, irony and perspective. And applying irony as an application by which to divert unnecessary attention, and perchance impose contemplation, is an underestimated exercise.

Constant themes of the celebration of both sexuality and the female persona are present in Ordo Equilibrio's lyrics, and likewise I view both the male/female elements as equal in the overall musical presentation. However it seems that you have taken the role of spokes person for the group with myself being unaware of Chelsea having ever conducted an interview. Is this something, which a conscious decision was made on?
Without attempting to reduce or trivialise Chelsea's participation under any circumstances, the situation is such that Ordo Equilibrio is my entity. It emerged as a consequence of my aesthetic yearnings, and consequently it was neither a conscious decision, nor any question that I was to respond on behalf of OE; but more accurately something that resolved naturally.

Likewise to the above question, is there a main composer in the group and what are the individual roles of Chelsea and yourself in the creative process?
Once again, and without attempting to reduce or trivialise Chelsea's participation in OE in any way, the situation is such that I am the spiritual and aesthetic catalyst/instrument/essence of Ordo Equilibrio. I write all lyrics, I compose all music - without me there is no Ordo Equilibrio - past, present & future.
Chelsea's participation has indeed been rewarding in the significance of correlating and complementing my aesthetic inclinations; but as far as the essence of Ordo Equilibrio is concerned, OE is affiliated to me. I suppose the concerned acknowledgments sound cruel and unrelenting, but conclusively they are solely veritably honest.

Having a very poetic style of lyric writing, it adds a certain dimension of ambiguity when you write about topics of nature and the demise of society and modern man. Do you profess to have some sort of solution to the current predicament that the human race as a species is facing, or do you view yourself an artist/individual who is content with being the narrator of this downward spiral into oblivion?
What I narrate through OE is merely an individual observation of the contemporary terrestrial predicament; a condition that I personally do not relish, but neither a condition I wish to see resolved through the settlement of complete terrestrial ruin. And consequently I feel hesitant to behold myself as a minstrel of terrestrial miscarriage towards ruin and oblivion, as this is not the resolution I desire. But do I however profess some sort of solution to this contemporary predicament?
Not unless something seemingly dramatic occurs and changes the entire condition of this world. Intellectual awakening perhaps. Initiated through the reawakening of reasoning, as within its reapplication resides the resolution to considerable human & terrestrial anguish. Thereafter we need to evaluate the contemporary status of this world, revise the moral principles that permeate our surroundings, and consequently retrieve the essential rectitude and understanding of ancestral and preceding generations. All life can not be spared at what seems to be any cost; especially as every being does not intrinsically; solely by virtue of being alive, comprise the same equitable aptitude and unconditional right to subsist. All human beings throughout this planet comprise an individually distinctive aptitude; and every human being does not intrinsically by virtue of its mere being, comprise the imperative aptitude to become an astronaut solely because they retain the aspiration. People are intellectually, physically, genetically & competently distinct; any other conviction is intellectually deceiving oneself.
The strong and ingenious have to be permitted to prevail in favour of the weak and frail. This condition is not an option or a matter of either elitism or humanitarianism, it is an imperative requirement for the world to persist and

flourish.
Incompatible and short-termed monetary motives may not be recognised as the dictating incentive of the terrestrial procession and its outcome; there are far greater and more important issues besides negligent and improvident financial gain. Nature and the environmental settings throughout the world in which we subsist, need to be nourished and protected from senseless defilement. Nature will affirmatively persist without mankind, but mankind will not endure without nature; but which sadly seems to be a comprehension that transcends the understanding of numerous people throughout this day and age. Infraction requires equitable punishment; punishment befitting the severity of the infliction. Justice is not necessarily or exclusively served by the ruling of an eye for an eye, but there should nevertheless be conspicuous infliction for conspicuous acts of needless transgression; acts of serial and multiple rape should equal death without exception; and so forth.
Mankind should thus be conscious and responsible for its individual actions, and/or consequently liable to suffer the consequences of its conducts. Man should experience and realise him/herself; as within the comprehension of our very being rests the answer to the riddle of our very existence and individual salvation.
Love conquers all.
We should love ourselves truly, literally, passionately and extensively; as are we indeed capable of loving someone else, unless we are intrinsically capable of loving ourselves? Sex necessitates recognition and utilisation as an unconditionally imparting exercise; unreservedly linked with process of life, creation and procreation; farther akin to an infinite magnitude of physical and psychical gratification. And so forth....
These are briefly some elementary thoughts on how I believe the contemporary predicament could be improved.

Ordo Equilibrio are a group that does take to the stage on select occasions and it would seem that you put on a 'show' as much as simply performing your music. What entails a typical Ordo Equilibrio performance and what instrumentation is used?
Performing live I try to present an act that is aesthetically affiliated to the philosophical, spiritual & aesthetic aspirations of Ordo Equilibrio; whether it is akin to contemplated irony, militia or fetishism; further accompanied by drums, banners and flaming fires. But as I am still investigating the possibilities and disadvantages with regard to performing live, and still am learning about the necessary constituents to appropriately succeed according to my aspirations - the performance will most certainly evolve as I proceed. And in conclusion I can merely say - Do not expect anything, and you won't be disappointed.

There has been talk of an Ordo Equilibrio video as far back as when your debut CD was released and more recently in the pages of the September, 1998 CMI newsletter. Can you provide some detail on this item?
An official OE video release is likely to be available in the winter of 1999 or in the spring/summer of 2000. It is currently being accomplished in association with video artist Mikael Prey a.k.a. Fetish 23, and will likely feature an assortment of distinctive video clips akin to the aesthetic, sexual, spiritual & symbolical preferences of me & OE. But as it is currently being developed it seems pointless to estimate the date of its release.

Your use of symbolism is another reaccusing theme, with the main one being in the form of your logo and to a lesser degree through the representation of the rose and use of runes. Can you elaborate on the reasoning behind using each of the above elements?
The seal utilised throughout the aesthetic revelation of Ordo Equilibrio is initially from Aliester Crowley's deck of tarot - the '4 of Wands'. The seal serves as an ideal representation of Ordo Equilibrio and my philosophical, ideological and spiritual conceptions and inclinations; converging and signifying both Balance and Completion along with the force of Will - the inner circle of eight flames - four doubled - signifying the flames of energy in play; asserting balance and uniting Completion and Limitation through the seeds of disorder.
The symbolic affiliation of the rose is figuratively complex, incarnating a diversity of symbolism relative to its color, status, application in context, number of petals etc., etc., and its application in OE is equivalent; significant of beauty, desolation, life, death, prosperity, perfection, creation, blood, sensual pleasure, mortality, completion, etc., etc. The rose is the flower of gods, and understanding its signification in affiliation to OE, is realising its application in complete context.
Implying the application of runes tends to indicate a recurrent utilisation throughout a variety of workings, but which I believe is an evidently deceptive assertion.
Runes have merely been applied once, and at which instant solely one particular rune was utilised - Algiz. This particular rune was however deliberately conscript and applied as to symbolise the convergence & divergence of paths, life & death, victory, protection alongside war & peace. All of which are signified through Algiz in one way or another.

Well, Tomas here is the obligatory thanks and conclusion. What words of wisdom shall we part on?
Realise yourself.

CHTHONIC STREAMS

ON THE BRINK OF INFINITY

TONY WAKEFORD & MATT HOWDEN, 4TH SIGN OF THE APOCALYPSE, EMPYRIUM, DREAM INTO DUST, BACKWORLD, ARCANE ART, KEROVNIAN, and others reflect on death and rebirth, endings and beginnings, destruction and creation. a journey through neoclassical, industrial, experimental, & neofolk in twelve exclusive tracks.
$12 US / $14 WORLD

THE WORLD WE HAVE LOST

first full-length CD released on ELFENBLUT/MISANTHROPY records. waves of dark orchestral strings, pounding rhythms, dissonant acoustic guitars, and chunks of distorted noise are the apocalyptic backdrop for lyrics of sadness and decay. experimental sounds flow into songs as part of a larger whole. $17 US / $19 WORLD

T-SHIRT

white printing on heavy black 100% cotton. available in large or extra-large. a requirement for your wardrobe to show your allegiance. $13 US / $15 WORLD

A PRISON FOR ONESELF

7" and cassette with numbered i.d. card (out of 500) and insert. inspired by tv series THE PRISONER.

"...strange loops, unconventional percussion and a classical overtone... strikes a strong film score vibe of suspense, atmosphere, obscurity and terror."
CURSE OF THE CHAINS
$6 US / $8 WORLD

NO MAN'S LAND

"gothic / industrial / doom best describes this little piece of depression...a bleak and sorrowful landscape with beautiful yet at the same time horror-filled keyboard and vocal movements..."
NJ NOISE SCENE
$8 US / $10 WORLD

ALL PRICES INCLUDE POSTAGE. CHECK OR M.O. IN US$ ONLY TO DEREK RUSH.
several other other itmems also available.
write for free catalogue of dark obscure music or visit

www.chthonicstreams.com

CHTHONIC STREAMS P.O. BOX 7003, NEW YORK, NY 10116-7003 USA

SLAUGHTER PRODUCTIONS

Slaughter Productions are certainly worthy of the title of a cult label given their commitment to releasing music from known artists and truly underground projects over the past 7 years. Although the release schedule side of things has slowed down somewhat due to the tape releases being faded out, the quality has remained extremely high with the CD and vinyl titles, which includes the well respected compilation CD's Death Odours I & II. Read on with what founder Marco Corbelli had to say about his label & musical activities...

When did the label begin & how did you become involved in this style of music which led to the foundation of the label?
I create the label in 1993; I was always interested in experimental/industrial music since 1989/90, I listened to early Current 93, coil, Ptv, Zoskia, Whitehouse, NWW and more like the first productions of Cold Meat Industry that really hit me. Originally, the label's birth begin with the release of the first cassette of my personal project Atrax Morgue "In Search of Death". The first release on CD was the compilation DEATH ODORS featuring some Swedish bands like Megaptera, Archon Satani, raison d'etre...

Is there any specific direction or label philosophy that you adhere to?
I just try to release the stuff that I like and consider particularly interesting; I don't release any stuff just for a commercial profit, this is sometimes a risk, but I like risk, I think every artist must be risk.

In the early days how hard was it to establish contacts within the global scene?
It was a bit hard, but if you have energy and you want to let your label and your products known by people, nothing is i m p o s s i b l e . . .

Are your items widely distributed on a global scale? Which countries have shown the greatest interest in your products?
In the last time, I really do very few promotion to my products; it seem that my label has been something as a phantasm label, and this is related to my self-destructive character and to my constant state of depression and hate for working.... but please you all know that my label is still alive and every contact is well accepted.

It seem that you are re-releasing a number of early tape releases on CD format. Is this due to you perceiving that the said tapes did not gain the full recognition they deserved due to the format?
Yes, I have stopped definitely the tape production. I will release some of the more interesting tapes in my catalogue in CD or CDR; this is a more selective and tasteful way to continue the production.

What cd and vinyl releases do you planned for 1999?
I will release soon a series of limited CDR with new projects that I consider really interesting: TODAY....I'm DEAD - Anatomy of Melancholy will be the first to be released, its death-industrial obscure harsh-electronic project really powerful....the others will be: SUBKLINIK - Cremator CDR, STRATVM TERROR-The only True Septic Whore CD (re-issue of the tape with re-worked and re-mixed + extra tracks) ATRAX MORGUE - Overcome LP.

Who do you feel are the most promising artists are of your current roster?
I'm very satisfied with the work of TODAY...I'M DEAD and SUBKLINIK and I really like to produce project like them. I also like very much CREPUSCULE, a very particular experimental project, maybe I will release a cd by this one in future....

What does a group/project have to possess for you to be interested in releasing their music?
O r i g i n a l i t y .

How do you go about approaching an artist to commission a release? Do the artists receive any money from releases, be it for CD's/vinyl or tape?
Depending, in some cases I give money and in some cases I give royalty copies of the release.

As Slaughter Productions is a perfect example of an "Underground" record label do you plan to stay underground of aspire to become more "commercial" label? (meant in the sense of making the label/ mailorder a large profitable b u s i n e s s) .
I don't know. Depending also by how goes my life....I

have a style of life really deranged and unforeseeable, I don't have plans for the future and this is also reflecting about the label activity....But for the moment i prefer to remain an Underground Cult label, and possibly i will stop with distribution mailorder.

As the Internet is playing a vital role in the networking, distribution and sales of sub-cultural music do you have plans to harness the Internet to expand Slaughter Productions?
Yes, I have a site now on the Internet, so people can take a look to my catalogue and news in a very easy way.

With over 100 tape releases under your belt and the majority of the packaging being hand made and overseen by yourself, do you find it difficult to come up with new ideas and inspiration?
Yes, sometimes it's difficult to create a new original design for a cover, but i have a lot of fantasy and this is not a real problem for me.

So far your cd releases have been in limited quantities, also features deluxe fold out cardboard sleeves. Are there any plans to utilise the standard jewel case cd format and move away from limiting the quantities?
The new releases will have a standard jewel box package, this because i noticed that more people don't like the fold out cardboard sleeve for a cd; and to be honest, the jewel case is really more handy.

Can any money be made out of the running and operation of such label in its current scale?
Yes, obviously.

What are your favourite releases in tape, CD and vinyl formats thus far?
tapes: Die Sonne Satan - Fact-totum, Crepuscule - Closing Wounds, Taint- Justmeat, Atrax Morgue- Homicidal . Vinyl: Megaptera-Deep Inside mlp, Obscene Noise Korp - Primitive Terror Action. CDS: Atrax Morgue- Cut My throat, Morder Machine - Death Show , Atom Infant Incubator - Quantum Leaps lost soundtrack.

Given your beginning as a tape label, do you see tape labels currently being as valid before?
At the time, I don't see exist more tape label in the network, maybe just fews and I'm not particularly interested in them.... I don't deny my past as a tape label, but the past is the past and don't exist any more....there must be always an evolution.

I have also noted that have been a few labels set up that use the "tape label" philosophy but now use new technology to burn their own limited quantities of CDs. Will this be an option that you would consider for Slaughter Productions?
I don't know, i think it depending also by money....I'll try to release only material super-selected and supervised, and I'll try to release only few limited editions CDs and CDR.

Do you intend to continue with tape releases or redirect your efforts into vinyl and cd releases?
As I said before I stopped with tape release. I'll release only vinyls and CDs.

Aside from being the sole individual behind Slaughter Productions you also have a number of personal musical endeavours. The most well known will be the power-electronics/noise terrorists "Atrax Morgue". When did you start with this project, what is it's aims and how many releases have you had?
My project ATRAX MORGUE started in 1993 with the beginning of the label; it is always a solo project because it is a reflection of myself, my obsessions, my desires, and my sickness.... Since my beginning the sounds has changed, has become more minimal and structured it has reached a sort of perfect imperfection.... With Atrax Morgue I simply made an exorcism of my inner self, when I'm recording I feel incredibly energies, and I feel to put out the obscure side of myself, my demon, what I never known about myself. Since 1993 I've released tons of tape and seven compact discs from different labels.

You also have another project under the name of Morder Machine which incidentally features Atrax Morgue. What are the differences/similarities you see with the two projects? why was its necessary to associate Atrax Morgue with Morder Machine, rather than keeping the two totally separate?
Well, MORDER MACHINE and ATRAX MORGUE is always played by me. ATRAX MORGUE is more improvised and less structured, instead MORDER MACHINE's sound is more obscure, structured and not completely improvised; in more tracks there is a distorted drum machine rhythms....this project is more influenced by one of my favourite industrial band: BDN. I don't want to keep the two projects totally separated cause in some cases one is the reflection of the other one and vice versa. There are similitude's in these two projects, like the vocals, the obsessively, and the subjects. What changes is the structure.

What future releases can we expect from these two projects and which labels will be releasing them?
I am working on the new ATRAX MORGUE cd; "Paranoia" it will be released on the Italian label Old Europa Cafè later this year....What I can say about this is that I think it will be the best work I ever made.... it's completely deranged and it's deal with change sex disorders and other psycho sexual thrills... I will also release some new MORDER MACHINE stuff and a re-issue remixed version of the first MM tape maybe on my own label.

---

contact:

Slaughter Productions

via Tartini,8 41049 Sassuolo (MO) Italy
tel fax 0039 (0) 536 872999

e mail: slaughter@mail.dex.net.com

website: welcome.to/slaughter

Caul

Caul have become a well respected name in the ambient scene over the past five years, having released four CD's thus far that explore spiritually tinged dark ambient passages. Given that the new & most accomplished Caul CD to date 'Light from Many Lamps' (and incidentally the most composed) has recently been released on Malignant Records (mid '99), I contacted sole member Brett Smith for a bit of a chat.

To start with what originally led you in the direction of starting up the musical project 'Caul' and when was it officially established?
Well, I've making my own music since I was in high school and I had been working at various styles for some time. While most of it didn't sound like anyone else and I was happy with some of it, I hadn't stumbled upon something that really came together. Around 1993, I started making music as CAUL. It was something that began as a communication with God (though at the time I didn't realise that this was the case) and I was suprised by the situation because I felt (and still do) that I wasn't the one who was making this music. It think it was established right from the start, I knew this was something completely different than what I had been doing before.

There has been a clear direction in the focus of your music taking on more an more composed elements with each new CD, however similar groups such as raison d'etre have in fact gone in the opposite direction becoming more minimal over time. Was this direction into more full compositions clearly intended or just a by product of your creative process?
I think it's just a natural direction to want to try new things- as your abilities expand you try to express things in more various ways. I started out minimalistic, so it's probably natural I moved towards a more elaborate style. The music has always led the way, however- I made some conscious decisions towards a particular style and I've had plenty of ideas of what I would like to do but the final direction is pretty much out of my hands.

Much speculation has been made between your personal musical journey and your discovery of religion, when juxtaposed against the evolving dark sounds of early tape releases, through to each subsequent CD having a more religious slant in terms of composition and track titles. Can you detail your thoughts on this?
The music I make as CAUL is a direct expression of the relationship I have with God, that's the main reason for the evolving sound. "Crucible," is a document of the birth of the situation, "The Sound of Faith," a document of my growing realization of the aspects of that relationship. "Reliquary," is a document of my discovery of the more mystical aspects of that relationship and "Light From Many Lamps," is more of an expression of my emotions towards certain personal events.

I have read in an interview that you consider yourself a spiritual person but not necessarily a religious one. What are your thoughts on how these two elements are separate yet ultimately intertwined?
When I think of someone being "religious," I tend to think of someone more concerned with the "rules," not the "spirit," which is what I tend to more concerned with. I think that's the problem with many religious movements or groups, they tend to get caught up what they think the rules are and then they try to force them upon others instead of trying to impart the spirit of their religion to others.

In relation to your reference to God in the above answer, in an old interview with

Douglas P of Death in June (Dark Angel Magazine Issue 20#) he referred to his meeting with God in London, 1988, but then rephrased the term 'God' to 'Life Force' deeming it a more appropriate description. Would this be similar to your point of reference?
Not as I understand his view of spirituality. I've read other interviews with him and I can say that our viewpoints differ greatly. Basically, I'm a Christian and he's not- I can't remember what he's into (Astaru?) and I know he's been open about his hatred of Christianity, so I can't see us having similar points of reference.

Given that you make a personal distinction between being spiritual or religious in comparison to the often dogmatic teaching of organised religion, does your belief system exclude you from listening to certain groups within the ambient/ industrial felid when related to the group's beliefs or the inspiration encompassed within the music?
No, not really- I listen to music I find interesting or moving, regardless of where it comes from. There's a great deal of supposed Christian music I find offensive. It's so poorly done and they just try to sound like any other top 40 bands. There's plenty of other music I've found offensive for various reasons, racist agendas, etc. I just don't listen to it if I don't want to but I give things a chance first.

Recently I have read an article on the philosophy of 'Second Religiosity' which in essence is taking the recognisable and identifiable figures of a religion (Christianity for example) yet subscribing a whole new thought and value system to them. Are you aware of this concept and do you think it has any relevance to the ideas and philosophies behind Caul?
I don't really know about this, actually, so I can't answer your question. It sounds interesting, though.

Those who have read Spectrum 2# (and particularly the Phil Easter interview) will be aware of a court trial which somewhat revolved around a now lost, original version of Caul's 'Crucible' CD. Do you want to provide some background information on this, your level of involvement and your overall thoughts on the situation which transpired? How much did the original recording of the 'Crucible' differ to the version later released on Malignant Records as your debut CD?
Well, basically Phil got screwed by the label, it was an unfortunate mess. The charges brought against him were so ludicrous, it was mind boggling. I had turned in a version of "Crucible" that was close to being finished, there was still some work that had to be done on it. I don't think of it as being a "lost" version, however, as it wasn't quite finished to begin with. I do have some tapes with that material on it and it differs in ways from the final release. It's more minimal I think. It's also more muddy, the fidelity isn't near as good. It sounds more directionless as well. In the end, it has some good and bad aspects to it.

It would also seem that you were involved in the live recording of Iron Halo Device (released on CD by Malignant Records in 1998) yet you chose not to credit your name on the liner notes. Do you regret this decision given the critical acclaim in has received in the underground scene? How long was your involvement with Iron Halo Device project?
I'm sorry, but this is a situation I don't feel that it would be right for me to comment on.

Thus far you have worked with Malignant Records, Katyn Records and Eibon Records for your releases and additionally with Harmonie for an upcoming re-release of early demo material. Will you continue to label hop in future and do you think that you are too much of a prolific artist to be affiliated with a single label?
Probably the reason I haven't stuck with one label is that it hasn't worked out that way for one reason or another. The situation, however, is a good one. I've gotten to work with a variety of great people which wouldn't have happened otherwise or if I would have had my own label.

Regarding the upcoming CD re-release of earlier material, will this be put through extensive re-working/ re-mixing or kept true to the original

sound? I also believe that the CD is to be limited to 200 copies? Why is this? (as surely there will be many disappointed fans who will miss out given the limited number). When is a release date expected?
It'll be remixed/reworked. It's not going to have everything on it, there'll be nothing from "Whole" on it at all. It will mostly be tracks from "The Golden Section" and then the balance of tracks from "Epiphany/Fortunate." It'll be recognisable, though, I'm not going to rework it that much, I just want it to sound better.   As far as the 200 copies goes, that's a label decision. It probably has to do with the way it's being done, I believe they're actually being run off one at a time. It should be out by this winter, probably December.

What are you currently working on musically and not specifically limited to Caul?
At this point, I'm currently working on a collaboration between John Bergin, Jarboe and myself. It's called Black Mouth and will be released by Crowd Control. Also, a collaboration between John Bergin, Chris Snipes and myself. We don't have a name for that yet, we recorded about 45 minutes of live material a few months ago which turned out well. It's more electronic than the stuff I do and was a lot of fun. We had someone playing didgeridoo along with us, as well.   Aside from that, I have more personal interests I'm pursuing.

You come across are seeming to be a very self critical artist and in relation to another of your projects 'Tertium Non Data' you made a statement to the effect that while people had given quite positive comments on that work, you however seemed to only see the holes in the musical tapestry. How do you view Caul CD's now with the benefit of hindsight and what changes would you make if any?
I tend to be pretty self critical, I think most people are when they are dealing with something that's important to them. I would either change many things or nothing at all, I'm not really sure. If I had the chance, I would probably try to improve the sound quality, above anything else. Maybe add and extra sound or two, maybe some extra instrumentation. It would be fun to mix them down again and send that to a high quality mastering facility and have someone who really knows what they're doing work them over.

Much (if not all) of the artwork on your CD covers is of your own hand, as well as having done other design work for select CD's on Cold Spring, Crowd Control Activities and Malignant Records. Do you have any formal qualifications in art, and generally what are your preferred mediums to work with?
I don't really have any formal qualifications. I've don't artwork of somekind all my life and I took most of the art classes offered at my high school, though I didn't excel in them at all. I like working on the computer, though it has an incredible amount of limitations as a tool for art. I like building things- the picture on the front of "Light From Many Lamps" is part of a piece I made, as well as the face in the "Crucible" CD booklet.

Is there an underlying philosophy to your artwork other then the obvious aesthetics of the images needing to suit a certain release? Is art something you are heavily involved in independent of your musical projects?
As far as a philosophy behind the images I make for others, no. I just try to do something that fits and that satisfies who it's for. Art is something that is a large part of my life. I was a cook for ten years, which a form of art (though most might not think it so). Now I work in the art department of company that does commercial artwork and printing. It's more of an "industrial arts" atmosphere- we don't come up with the designs for clients, we just replicate them on various products. I write from time to time as well.

Although it seems that the American audience for music such as yours is sparsely located, has playing live with Caul been something that you would like to explore? Would this even be an option given your multi-layered compositions?
At some point, I would like to do some live shows. I think there's some people here in town that I could do it with and could pull it off. I wouldn't really try to play stuff off of the CD as much as come up with material that I was comfortable playing live.

Well, thank you Brett for your time and input. Last words?
You're welcome and thank you! No parting words I can think of, however...

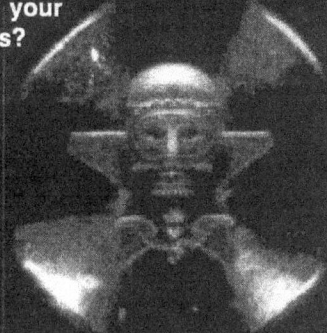

Deutsch Nepal

Deutsch Nepal?.....eccentric solo project of Lina Der Baby Doll Genera AKA Peter Andersson.....forefather and favourite son of the current Swedish ambient/ industrial scene.....creator of dark eclectic soundscapes.....collaborator with artists such as Hazard, Raison D'etre, Der Blutharsch.....founder of the up & coming label Entartete Musikk.....no further introductions necessary & on with the interview.....

Welcome Peter. Firstly to avoid confusion I will state for those who don't know that there are two Peter Andersson's: one of raison d'etre and the other being yourself of Deutsch Nepal. While over time you have been better known as Lina Der Baby Doll General (or variations of that), was the use of this alter ego a direct response to the potential confusion that could be caused by members of two groups associated with the same label, having the same name?
No it had no connection to Peter of Raison d´être....Lina is an old nickname.. thinking of it my sister called me Lena as I was a Baby at that time she used me as her Doll.... and she got really mad if anyone called me Peter...but it have no connection to this either... I prefer LINA as there are so many male Peter around and I hardly respond to it any longer...

I would have to remark that you have the distinction of being one of the fore-fathers of the current post industrial movement. How do you view this distinction – with cynicism? Would you like to give any historic document into your introduction to the style that you now create music within and then leading onwards to your current position?
hard question!! It started with that one of my friends recorded some songs on cassette for me with TG...a group I heard on radio some month earlier.. and if I remember correctly it was Discipline... there was a connection to them through The Leathernun that was kind of punk cult in Sweden at that time sometime round 1983... later I started to record stuff myself and also I had like small tape labels ....the first one was Slave State...in this way I got in contact with a lot of strange people Roger Karmanik was one of them....he was already by that time extremely cult in Sweden and lived his anonymous life as Döds Roger (Death Roger)... at a party we talked about starting a real label for Swedish Industrial Music because there was nothing around anymore as the Konduktör Rekords had fallen asleep... I proposed the name Cold Meat Industry and he liked it.... I disappeared into outer space while Roger worked on hard and I only did small printing works for him as I worked in a printing house...and later on I moved to Göteborg during this years I played with a group called Njurmännen that I later left because the musical direction of it didn't suite me....When this happened I had already had released some albums with Deutsch Nepal.....hmmmmm I don't know if this answer your question.......

I have always viewed Deutsch Nepal as a predominantly CMI artist that happens to release discs on Staalsplaat. I believe that you have recently signed a 5 CD with Staalsplaat with 'Erosion' being the first of these How did this deal come about and does the deal preclude you from working with other labels in the interim? Do you have any 'elitism' regarding labels you would prefer to work with?
No, I just release where I want to but I must say I prefer Cold Meat Industry and Staalplaat. Also there was kind of contract with Staalplaat for 3 CD;s .....I don't know why they're so keen with contracts as there already is a deal by mind that I release one on CMI and then one on Staalplaat continuously ....

Prior to this deal you have released CD's, tapes and vinyl's on various labels such as CMI, Staalsplaat, Old Europa Cafe and Ant-Zen among others. Was there any context to your decision on which label was able to release what material?
Behind these labels there are people I like.. and if anyone like to release something ..and have the time to wait, normally I send them some material as they ask..... but as I don't record that much any longer, it might take years.

I will comment that a staple diet of most ambient/ industrial groups is a heavy dose of 'darkness'. Deutsch Nepal have at times used dark themes and ideas, but also mixed with many weird and quirky elements, including highly obscure vocal samples. Where

does an idea for a track generally begin and what evokes you into choosing a vocal sample?
The darkness within has its own sound...it's more a question of finding it in the chaos around ....outside yourself. It also have its own language ....and you could hear it every time you put on the TV-set ...just make a pick....but do it right. I mean who cares about screaming women any longer.?

How about shattering some of the mystique and revealing the source of some of these vocal sample? (especially "gouge free market").
I could hardly remember have to put on the CD......hmmm sounds like an English movie... have hundreds of KZ:s with samples and ...it's impossible..... anyway the first famous vocal sample of Deutsch Nepal being released on the first cassette was as follows "..you shall hear nothing, you shall see nothing, you shall think nothing, you shall be nothing..." was a Peter O'Tole-sample from a movie called "Svengali"...an awful American movie....but the voice was good!

Taking the sampling element to the extreme there is one track on the new CD called 'you're just a toy' which is just confusing in what it represents and to why it was included. Do you care to shed any light on this?
The song is a homage to myself...I think there are just a little bit too few of them around...

Do the track and CD titles have a clear connection with the tracks they relate to, or are they simply there for naming purposes?
Sometimes one could think so .....but thinking in this way...the music is an archaic imprint of me in the environment ,meaning I thought it should sound like this...without any reason I could explain also thought that this title suite for this track....just another imprint.. but sure there are connections...inside....

As opposed to using vocal samples, your own vocals have been creeping >into the composition structure. Is this to be a future direction for Deutsch Nepal with more utilisation of your voice?
Yes I start to like my voice and I suppose there will be more of it.....thinking of the previous questions maybe it will be easier for people to understand the idea of Deutsch Nepal..

The track "gouge free market" off the 'Comprendido!...Time Stop!...World Ending' album has the distinction of being one of my all time favourite Deutsch Nepal tracks. Have you even considered pursuing a full album in this style?
I have to put on the CD again...you see I never listen to my own music.....hmmm I'm not sure, as it is now it feels like it going in another direction but I haven't started to think about next album yet.....

The was quite a gap between the release of the above mentioned CD and your newly released 'Erosion' CD. Is this likely to also occur with upcoming releases? Are there and firm details you can give at this stage?
It use to take about 2 years between the albums but also I have released some other things in between like Kz:s and Vinyl's...but honestly I'm a very lacy person.....I'm more into drugs these days and it far more interesting than recording music..it seems....hmmm I'll try to get an album out next year maybe....if I live that long.

Referring to the preoccupation of many groups on presentation and image, photos of yourself seem to indicate somewhat of (if a can paraphrase a quote from 'the Absolute Supper' booklet) an 'alcoholic playboy' rather than a morbid individual. What is your opinion of other groups who reply heavily on their presentation and image and how would you categorise yourself within the scene? (if in fact there is even a scene – apart from the assumption that is invariably made by myself living on the other side of the planet).
Most groups do present themselves like something they want to be or want their audience to believe them to be....I don't know if it's the audience or the groups that are stupid......I like to present me as I am......I'm a person demanding respect and giving respect to others I am not a teenager playing around for some years before getting married starting a new life on my parents request trying to forget these "things" you did in "the life before". I want to give

people something to believe in even though they might not like it....I'm not a part of a cheap trend or fashion I wont change the image of me because the wind turn the other way... I will be like this forever...because this is the only way I can be.... Anyway the quote 'alcoholic playboy' is a nice thing that Roger put there to fresh up my representation a bit.... I wish I should stop with that..... alcohol is not that enticing any longer...there's better stuff around...hehehehe

What do you personally find inspiring and not being typically limited to music?
Drugs, Zarah Leander.......

On prior occasions you have made statements to the effect that there is no meaning or hidden message behind the works of Deutsch Nepal – essentially that it is 'music for music's sake'. Do you still stand behind this statement?
I don't remember...I think there is no message that you could put a finger on.... also... I'm a good liar..hahaha one could think I'm almost human.....HAHAHA......no, no, seriously one of the basic ideas behind industrial music is to rule people....and Deutsch Nepal is an industrial act sooooo.........what I meant was that I didn't need to put some piercing in my balls and scream about Adolph Hitler and pretend to be religious to manifest the music of Deutsch Nepal....or to sell some hundreds extra of my albums...though I know it work in that way.....

Further to the above your have an association with Albin Julius of Der Blutharsch and have recorded music with this project. Regardless of whether or not Albin intends to have an agenda with Der Blutharsch, there are certain implications with his style and presentation that will 'brand' him with an agenda amongst certain factions. Do you see a difference between the stance of your project having 'no stance' as opposed to working with Der Blutharsch?
I never thought of it in that way....I just do things together with Albin as i like him a lot and he's a good friend of mine... and it´s just music we make so .....I don't know anything about Der Blutharsch ..I mean about his ideas or Albin's political intentions as we meat we more like walking around in Wienna or the Swedish woods hunting and smoking cigars from Checkia drinking wormwood spiritus or whiskey.....recording some music..fighting with taxichauffeurs......drinking beer with Jurgen and Ulla...having a coffee with Elisabeth.......messing with my brothers children.....crashing with Rogers car.

Can you detail some information of the releases of Der Blutharsch that you have been involved in? Will this be an ongoing collaboration?
We did some things together and then there are some things I don't really have control over but officially I've done "The Night in Fear" together with Elisabeth and Albin..I was on some other releases also speaking Old Swedish then there is the 10" "Apocalyptic Climax" and the Video with "Sad Songs Singers" and the 7"-Box with Der Blutharsch....singing something "beautiful".... We'll see what the future have in it's hand....at this moment Albin is travelling allot ....round the world and I'm lost inside.

You also have many other projects including: 'Frozen Faces' (solo), 'Janitor' with Beni of Hazard and 'Boxholm' with Peter Andersson of raison d'etre. Can you please detail some information on these groups, including (upcoming) releases? Do you have any additional projects not listed above?
Frozen Faces have just released a 7" on my label Entartete Musikk and before that a LP and a Kz.... Janitor just released a documentation of our work since 1996 titled "richie"....it's like something between Deutsch Nepal and Hazard still different.....and maybe more variated Bocksholm is an project where me and Peter only uses sound from Bocksholm - our hometown were we both grew up..we finished an album some month ago and I just should make an artwork so that we could release it on vinyl.....for the hate we feel for this awful place...

'Entartete Musikk' is your own label which has had 4 releases thus far (with 3 in the past 8-10 months). What is the overall concept and future plans with the label?
It's just something I do for fun...and it's mainly only releases including some influence of me....but that will change as i found some projects that might be interesting to release....It have been a much bigger interest than I ever could believe there should be..so there is plans to release..... Frozen Faces -CD, Bockxholm -LP, Njurmännen-7" "Von Däniken", Thurnemans-7" "Wilhelm", Psykadelische Jugend -7" "Lacerate your mothers Neighbour",, Janitor-CD, Cyclotimia....something....but only plans so to say......

The obligatory 'thanks' questions is upon us. Anything else to add?
..........I could be your Neighbour......so be really careful......the way you close your door...........

TERTIUM NON DATA

Tertium Non Data might be a new name in terms of CD releases but are in fact a project which has been in existence for a number of years now. being a collaboration between the members of none other than Caul and c17h19no3. This fact sould give some idea of the territory the music inhabits &needless to say they come up with some amazing results. John Bergin steps forward to answer a few questions...

First up for those not in the know, Tertium Non Data is a collaboration project of both yourself (John Bergin) and Brett Smith, who would probably be better known for your solo outputs as C17H19NO3 and Caul respectively. Has recognition via the other projects assisted in gaining interest in Tertium Non Data or is it like building a new name/ fan base all over again?
Recognition of our other projects has made getting attention for TND easier. However, a few recent reviews I've seen were from writers who were not aware of our other work. Hearing the thoughts of people who are completely new to TND was a nice change of pace. I like seeing people come to the music with no expectations or preconceived notions derived from our history.

Tertium Non Data translates to "the third is not given" which is also the title of the debut CD. What is the meaning behind the name/ saying?
"Tertium Non Data" translated from Latin means: "the third is not given." it is a term from Alchemy which refers to the process of combining two disparate elements to create a new, third element. The process of transformation is a mystery - an unknown. The title refers to the collaborative process between Brett and myself. We combine our different musical talents and...something happens. We can't explain what.

The debut Tertium Non Data CD has been released on Crowd Control Activities however the tracks span being created from 1995 through 1999. It would seem that some of the tracks were included on releases under the titles 'the vacant chair' & 'lust'. Were these early demo releases and what other information can you convey about these release?
They were cassette-only releases that were sold exclusively via mail order. There were three. They are not available any more, but most of this older material will appear on forthcoming TND albums.

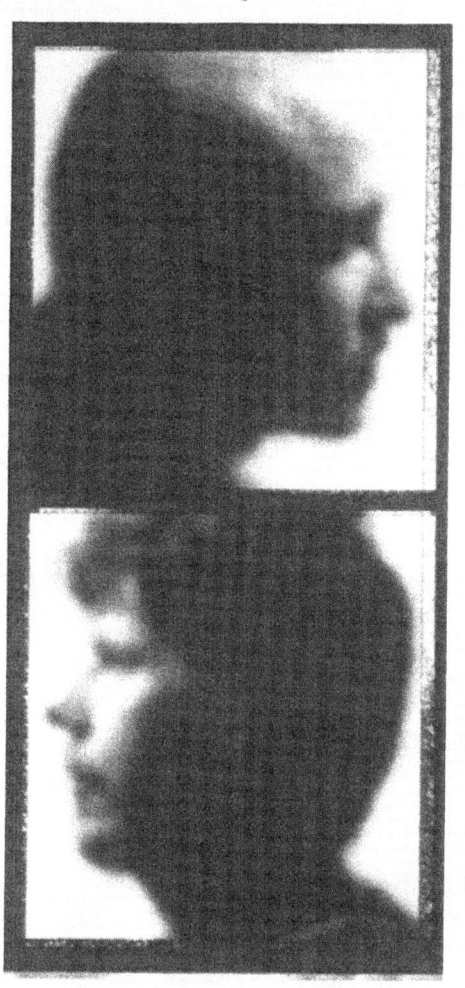

A statement is made on the CD cover that the music derived from improvised live recordings. Is this meant in the sense of 'live' jamming in the studio or actually playing live?
Both. Everything is improvised in one take - either in a studio setting or live on a stage. Most of the work is in a studio setting. We occasionally play live in front of an audience. A few months ago we did a show at the Kansas City Art Institute. Some of that material will be on our next album. Christus from Iguns Fatuus participated. Brett and I have also started swapping digital files - improvising a "live" performance without being in the same place at the same time.

As the Tertium Non Data stands as a monument to quite an eclectic collection of ambient/ ethnic and dark industrial sounds and compositions, I wanted to ask you about the recording process. At the point of preparing to record was there any clear discussion on what was attempting to being achieved, or was the way gradually felt out as the compositions evolved?
No, there is no agenda or plan. Brett and I have worked together for many years. When we perform together, we always try to make room for each other. The music is always left to go in whatever direction it takes. We never know what it will sound like. We are often surprised. I suppose you could say this is our agenda: a willingness to let mystery happen... a desire to hear that which is "not given." I think that is why the album is so eclectic.

Further to the above, there are distinctive sound frameworks that can be pinpointed to both yours and Brett's solo works. Do you personally view Tertium Non Data as a full musical entity in its own right (without wanting to complicate intents with comparisons with your other

projects), or was it more "lets mix our solo sounds together see what we come up with"?
We view TND as a singular endeavour. An understanding or awareness of our solo projects is not necessary to enjoy or understand TND. TND obviously falls within many of the same categories as our other work. That's unavoidable. We are who we are. I suppose it might be very interesting for people who _are_ aware of our separate projects to hear a collaborative improvisation. That sort of project usually doesn't work very well, but I'm very pleased with the results here.

As essentially Tertium Non Data is one project among a myriad of others you have (including two others also with Brett), where does Tertium Non Data fit in the hierarchy of importance?
All of our projects are equally important to us. There is not a hierarchy of importance, rather a hierarchy of 'time'. We both have only so much time to devote to certain projects... and that changes every month depending on what's scheduled. Right now Trust Obey and Paved in Skin are taking most of my time. Brett is very busy with his next Caul album. In a few months I will be immersed in Black Mouth... Everything we do is important to us.

More than being simply being a one off collaborative project, at this stage there are plans to release another two Tertium Non Data CD's. Are these to be again released on Crowd Control Activities and what is the anticipated schedule?
Yes, we plan to release more work with Crowd Control. The next TND is about 80% complete. Release date is not scheduled at this time - probably early next year...

Given that the first CD was recorded and compiled over 4 years, which inadvertently resulted in a wide array of sounds, what directions will Tertium Non Data head in and will the music remain as eclectic mix or focus more on certain ideas and concepts?
There will be more early works included on the upcoming albums. Excerpts from the live performance I mentioned earlier will also be included. The remainder of the album will be comprised of new material. The early tracks sound a lot like the material on our current release. The live songs are a lot more percussive and beat-orientated. We used a lot of sampled beats and harsh, gritty, lo-fi sounds. We also had a friend performing digideroo. Christus added some amazing choir and string samples. So, yes, it will be eclectic again. I think the wide variety of sounds isn't necessarily caused by the time span between each song, but rather it is due to our willingness to let the music go wherever it will. Like I said, we never know what to expect.

As stated earlier Tertium Non Data is one of three projects that you collaborate with Brett Smith on. Can you give a brief run down of these, their movements, intentions, future plans and how you see that they differ with your other projects?
Trust Obey: I just finished assembling the remix/re-release of Fear and Bullets, our Crow comic book soundtrack. It will be released by Invisible/Deezal Records October 28. This re-release is a remixed + re-recorded version of our 1994 album, Fear and Bullets. About a year ago we completely reworked the album. Black Mouth Collaboration between Brett, myself, and Jarboe. Everything has been recorded - I'll be mixing the album soon. This one is a little different for all of us... which was the intention - to stretch things a little.. Jarboe did some amazing work... as usual. A lot of beats, heavy bass, sparse... Should be out by the end of the year on Crowd Control.

(NOTE: interview with John Bergin continues on with c17h19no3).

c17h19no3

Continuing on from the Tertium Non Data interview I decided to subject John Bergin to a bit of an interrogation about his apocalyptic orchestral/ industrial solo project C17H19NO3. He was more than happy to oblige....

John, continuing on with the interview, I would like to take the focus off Tertium Non Data and ask you a few questions about your solo project C17H19NO3. Your solo workings under this name could be broadly categorised as neo classical/ ambient compositions with an ever so slight electro influence. Two CD releases have come out under this name (the debut on Fifth Colvmn called 'Terra Damnata' in 1995 and the second '1692/2092' in 1998 on Malignant Records), however how long has the project been active?
Since 1992. Before the Fifth Colvmn album I self-released 8 or 9 cassettes.

Initial comparisons with C17H19NO3 (and especially on the first CD) could be made with the apocalyptic and bombastic neo-classical compositions of In Slaughter Natives. Were you directly influenced by this group, and if this was not the case who did you consider were influential on your musical style of composing at the time?
I first heard ISN when I was about halfway through composing Terra Damnata. Enter Now The World was the perfect validation for what I was doing at the time. I have enjoyed all ISN albums and don't mind the comparison at all. I listen to so much music, so many different kinds of music, that I couldn't even begin to unravel my inspirations...

Your second CD '1692/2092' CD took a turn in style and sound into slightly more subdued, brooding and ambient territory (although the not all bombastic moments were forsaken), while the sound production quality was greatly improved in cinematic terms. Was the modification of style a conscious effort on your part or something that simply evolved that way?
Both. It's been about three years since Terra Damnata was released [and the material on that CD was already a year or so old]. My work has changed, evolved... I'd like to think it's matured and improved. It would have been easy to release an album that was similar to Terra Damnata. Instead, I made a conscious effort to update C17H19NO3's sound to the point where I felt it best represented where I am right now. I could have made a smoother transition from Terra Damnata to the second CD... but, I found it to be much more rewarding [from a composer's point of view] to challenge the familiar... to ask listeners who are familiar with C17H19NO3 to keep up with me.

The '1692/2092' CD was originally scheduled to be released on Brian 'Lustmord' William's Side Effects label, however this obviously fell through. It also seems that the track listing for the Side Effects release did not end up exactly the same as featured on the actual Malignant Records release. Can you please shed some light on this situation surrounding the CD?
My album was the last scheduled for Side Effects, a little sooner and I would have made it under the wire before Brian shut down operations. Brian and I are good friends. no animosity in the situation at all - it was completely out of _both_ of our hands. Sales were just so incredibly bad for all of Side Effects releases going through Soleilmooon, that Brian just saw no reason to continue with his label. My album wasn't the only one left hanging - there were some great releases scheduled (I did all the artwork and design for Side Effects, so I was up-to-date with everything Brian had planned). It was just an unfortunate situation, that's all. Brian was moving his label in a new direction. It was getting very interesting... check out "Lustmord VS MetalBeast", Lagowski's "Ashita"... Brian was moving the label into more of a beat-orientated direction. Still dark and ambient... but with a new, deep-beat sound.

The final track listing for Malignant's release of 1692/2092 is different from what I had originally planned for the album when it was with Side Effects. Like I said, Lustmord was moving his label in a new direction and 1692/2092 reflected that. Originally, there were a few more songs in the vein of track 14: "A Spell For Breaking An Opening Into The Sky." That is to say: the usual C17H19NO3 sound: evil ambience, pounding rhythms, dark visions... but with a lot of breakbeats and hip-hop sounds introduced into the mix. Brian called it "evil-hop" and "doom and bass." Which is an apt description.

When Jason Mantis (from Malignant) sent demo mixes of 1692/2092 to some of his European distributors they found the "doom and bass" a little too challenging... too much of a departure from the first C17H19NO3 album. So I removed or remixed some of those songs. At first I was a little disappointed... I didn't want to rework the album... but really, all that matters to me is having an opportunity to make

in my eyes - fire   in my hands - a knife   in my heart - a snake   in my mouth - a spe music. So this was a nice challenge for me... to see if I could steer the album in a new direction, but keep the original intent intact. I succeeded. In the end, I'm glad I had a chance to re-work the album. I like the new, ambient remixes a lot. Much more lush and subtle than the original breakbeat versions.... I think the album is much stronger. The Europeans were right.

The most recent release '1692/2092' the cover has the information original motion picture soundtrack music composed and produced by C17H19NO3. I initially got duped into thinking that there was an actual movie with somewhat embarrassing results at the hand of Phil 'eyespark' Easter on Malignant Records chat groups 'the TUMORlist'. While Phil gave quite an eloquent run down of the story of the alleged movie, I do think this was more at the hand of his creative wit. I wanted to ask, if there was a clear concept of story that you were narrating via music, or was this more of a marketing gimmick/ t o o l ?
I didn't have a very concise story concept when I was working on the score... I had a few vague notions, scenes, and moods in mind. I didn't develop a story because I want listener's to fill in the blanks. The sound, the song titles, the artwork... the entire project is designed to give the impression of a story, but not the actual story. The details are up to you. The film I had in mind would be something like The Crucible, but with a science fiction edge. A story where events which take place during the Salem witch trials cause a disaster in the future. I enjoy stories where seemingly minor events echo through time and impact the future in ways that could never have been imagined at the time when the events occurred... A person suspected of being a witch is hung in 1692, causing the universe to implode in the year 2092. Broken Soul was written to score the final scene... which takes place in 1692... in a forest, during a slow rain storm. A man hangs from a gallows pole (you can hear the rope creaking as he gently swings back and forth). Camera pulls in to a close-up of his hands. You can see his dead hand clutching an odd piece of machinery. Something completely anachronistic for the year 1692. Is this man from the future? A light is blinking on the device... It falls from his hand... and is buried in the mud. The end. This is not a happy ending. This quiet scene holds incredible power... the lost device spells doom for the future... I don't know why, the details are up to you. Again, I enjoy stories where quiet scenes like this hold the power of a full-blown over the top special effects sequence...because the audience knows what is coming by making the connection between a small, quiet event and complete and total destruction. Watch the film Threads... watch the whole thing (as dated and clunky as it is). Watch it all the way to the end. The last few seconds of this film are exactly what I am talking about. 1692/2092 isn't a film... yet, but acclaimed sci-fi author A. A. Attanasio is currently working on a proposal for a novel loosely based on my s o u n d t r a c k . Scoring a film also gives musicians a chance to use a variety of styles...which was another reason for calling this album a soundtrack. I was able to go from ambient to hip-hop and the album held together.

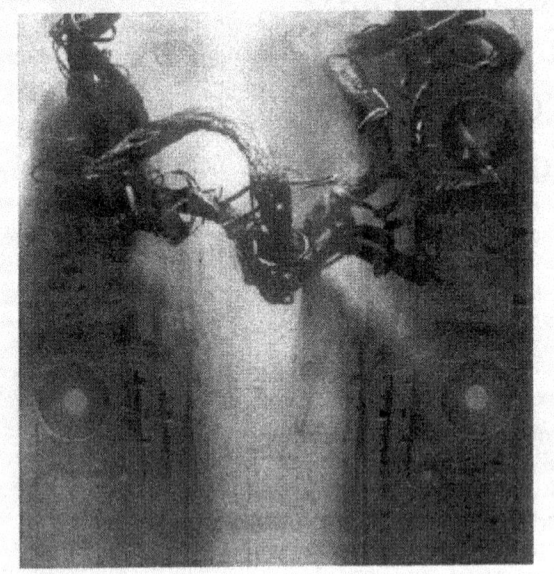

Further to the above, the '1692/2092' CD plays out very much in the same way as selected soundtrack works of Graeme Revell. Do you have current aspirations to work with movie sound scores, as I am lead to believe that there may have been some attempts to secure the rights to produce the musical score to 'the Crow'? Can you elaborate on this?
Thanks for the compliment. Graeme and Lustmord have done some great soundtracks. Yes, of course, I do have aspirations to do an _actual_ film soundtrack. I've had a few opportunities come my way - independent films. Nothing solid yet. The Crow soundtrack? Are you referring to "Trust Obey : Fear And Bullets?"

With the seemingly extreme amount of musical projects you are involved, I would imagine that you are somewhat of a 'full time musician'. As one of my constant intrigues is seeing what people into ambient/ industrial do in their lives apart from music, are you involved in some sort of standard 'day job' which finances your greater i n t e r e s t s ?
Financing greater interests... I don't know where to begin. I'm involved with so many different things. I had a pretty good career drawing comic books until the

comic book market collapsed a few years ago. I do a lot of graphic design and illustration; I've had a dozen or so graphic novels published... tons of CD covers, book covers... I also do a lot of multi-media work. CD rom design, digital video, computer animation... right now I'm working on a huge project for Hallmark Cards (if you can believe that). I'm doing a lot children's music, animation, and videography for a non-profit division of Hallmark called Kaleidoscope... So, yes, I do have a day job which supports everything; freelance artist. Most of the jobs I get are pretty cool. No corporate brochures.

What are the future plans with C17H19No3, what new directions do you plans to take the project in and are there any releases imminent?
The next release will be on Invisible Records/Deezal. A double CD. One disk will compile older, previously released and self-released songs from 92-present. The other CD will be new material (including the songs which were cut from the original 1692/2092). The new material sounds like what I mentioned earlier. >evil ambience, pounding rhythms, dark visions... but with a lot of breakbeats and hip-hop sounds introduced into the mix.

Well, thank you very much John for completing this dual interview, anything that you might want to add?
web site: www.grinder.com. The site includes a gallery... News about upcoming releases... A catalogue. etc etc....watch for new projects:
*Black Mouth: a collaboration between me, Brett Smith, and Jarboe. Brett and doing all music, Jarboe vocals and lyrics. Out on Crowd Control before the end of the year.
*trust Obey : Fear and Bullets
*new TND... also on Crowd Control sometime next year.
*check out Invisible Records' Ministry Tribute "Wish You Were Queer." Includes a Paved In Skin track. I did the album artwork as well.... New Paved In Skin is still available. "Box" A 2 CD boxed set. We also have a live Internet radio broadcast coming up in a few weeks courtesy of 3WK.

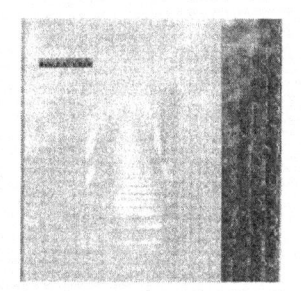

REMANENCE - `Apparitions`
CD (CSR26CD)

Beautiful, dark neo-classical and melancholic ambient.

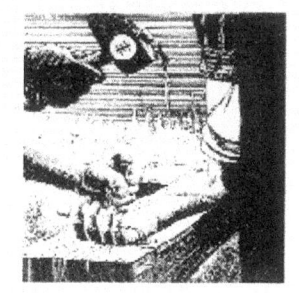

PSYCHIC TV - `Were You Ever Bullied At School - Do You Want Revenge?` 2 x CD (CSR27CD)

Double CD set of never before heard live shows. Unique and powerful!

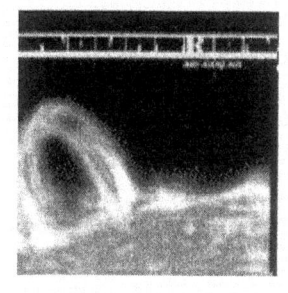

NOVATRON - `New Rising Sun` CD (CSR28CD)

Black Sun cult music - sub-bass sonics and solar winds.

COLD SPRING
AUTUMN WINTER
1999 / 2000

PRICES: SINGLE CD - UK - £12, EUROPE - £13, REST OF WORLD - £14. DOUBLE CD SET: UK - £15, EUROPE - £16, REST OF WORLD - £17. ALL PRICE INCLUDE FIRST CLASS/AIRMAIL POSTAGE.

BE PREPARED FOR THE NEXT SEASON:
FOLKSTORM - `Victory Or Death` CD (CSR31CD)
HAZARD - `The Law Of A World Without A Future` CD (CSR29)
VON THRONSTAHL - `Imperium Internum` CD (CSR32CD)

COLD SPRING, 8, WELLSPRING, BLISWORTH, NORTHANTS, NN7 3EH, ENGLAND, UK.
FAX: + 1604 859142 - Email: coldspring@thenet.co.uk - www.thenet.co.uk/~coldspring
WRITE FOR OUR 60+ PAGE NEWSLETTER AND MAIL ORDER CATALOGUE.

I-BURN

Although relative newcomers to the scene, I-Burn have managed to make quite an impact with only 1 CD and a vinyl EP of dark disorienting noise/ industrial experimentations. The 10" vinyl release of this year (reviewed elsewhere in these pages) ensured that featuring this group in Issue 3# was a definite necessity.

Hello Gabrielle, to start with can you please introduce the project I-Burn, the members behind the moniker and the basic philosophy of which it entails?
Hello to you, Richard, and thanx for having this interview with me/IB. I BURN is an Italian project to be filed in an hypothetical postindustrial/ambient global directory, me and a guy called Maurizio Landini are part of the project. Basic philosophy? Being a musical project, nothing less & nothing more than an attempt to portray via audio-metaphors the way our minds relate to the "everything" outside + to exorcise our obsessions/ fetishisms.

I have been led to believe that the project I-Burn came about unintentionally via collaborative studio experimentations, which has since become a fully fledged project. Can you detail how I-Burn came into being, and how do you view its importance today, or is it still viewed as a side project to your other activities?
I BURN began "accidentally", or I'd rather say luckily by chance: me and Maurizio, after having had years of musical experiences in more "band/guitar oriented" projects (in a way or another, we both tried to infect our previous "bands" with germs of industrial music, however, and anyone willing to disclose the secret - willing to investigate who these projects were - can easily understand), on early 98 by chance we've been suddenly lucky enough to have access to good digital sound editing softwares + good samplers - this situation led to the situation of being addicted to a monitor for a long long time and being completely addicted to several unconscious late night PC sessions where almost unintentionally (since at that stage it was just a "learning process" thing, learning how to use and abuse HD recordings and digital stuff, after years of analogic life!) we where laying the foundations for a 100% satisfying/involving musical project. After about a month of hard work we finally realized that more or less an entire IB CD was created, and it was good enough to be released semi-officially: so, we released the first I BURN record as 100 copies limited CDR with our own label, and then everything started - Eibon/Amplexus reissued the CDR in a more complete way, and so on... IB has become since then our MAIN project, and all the other musical project we still are involved in have been faded into background, mainly because the music we have the chance to develop with I BURN is the real thing for us, the real thing we like to play and the real thing we direct our attention to, listening-wise.

Comparisons with your first cd were made to Brighter Death Now, but with I-Burn being on a more lo-fi and simplistic tangent. Was your intension from the start to emulate a certain 'style' (ie: death industrial) with adherence to associated sound production and concepts?
Well, without doubt Brighter Death Now and a good part of the early swedish death industrial (Archon Satani, NFOL, Negru Voda above all) have strongly contributed to our "musical moulding" - but on the other hand I have to say that during the first CD's compositive phase no kind of sound has been predominant to another, inspiration-wise: all the songs have been written in a "random" way, that's to say, we built all definitive songs starting from shapeless masses of sounds/samples - and all the work has been done in a quite "unconscious" way, or better, the initial part of the creation has been absolutely unconscious and randomized, while the final assembly phases (when all the definitive sounds have been glued together in actual songs) were 100% logic in terms of rejects or selections. It would have been really hard trying to start from an already shaped kind of sound and from there beginning an attempt to recreate the same thing with instruments we were handling for the first time ever - so, if ever there's been a BDN influence, it's been a totally unconscious influence.

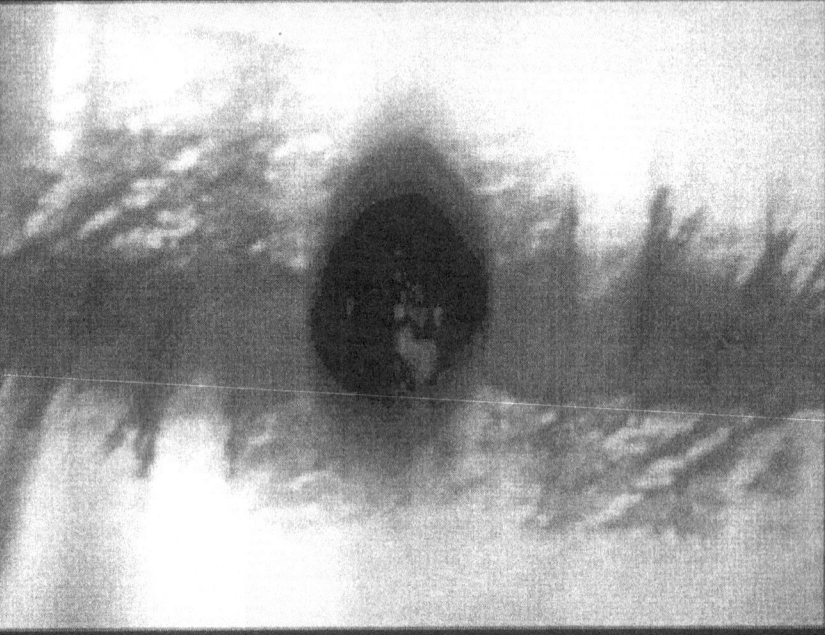

What sounds (if any) have influence you in the creation of your brand of industrial ambience, and alternatively what types of music inspires you but not necessarily in creating your own music?
We listen to such a wide variety of bands/musical styles that it would be hard to make a complete list of what kind of sounds influence us (even non-directly)...I'm a very very dogged listener of early 80's hardcore punk music (bands such as Black Flag, Minor Threat, SSD..) but would you even dare thinking of it only

judging by the music I make?? However, we swim into an ultrawide range of listenings: my personal faves/tastes ranges from Caul, Thomas Koner, Coil, Francisco Lopez, Meira Asher, Pan Sonic, Surge, Cazzodio, Craig Armstrong, Hazard, Final, SPK, Genocide Organ, Morthound, to bands as Pixies (probably one of my 5 favourite bands ever!), Celtic Frost, Don Caballero, Flying Saucer Attack, Sonic Youth, June of 44, Husker Du, and lots more... While Maurizio is absolutely more martial, under this point of view, and he's an addicted to the Ant Zen & Hymen rythmical/distorted stuff, and I must say some of his influences coming from these fields have showed up in at least one track of our 10", the rythmical remix of "Prophesyng Non Motion" (off the first CD) is definitely and declaredly in the vein of this very kind of sound!

The first CD showed I-Burn dealing with reasonably minimalist noise and drone manipulations while your second release (the Ipertmia 10") took these experiments into more solid moving territories, with a slightly harsher edge. Is this showing a clear progression in the project's sound, or are the types of tracks you produce likely to alter drastically from release to release?
It is progression, definitely. As you can listen in the 10", the harsher edges of our sounds have become even more harsh, while the "minimal" elements of the sound shall become more "shining", thick-sounding and clean - we're trying to leave the more "droning-for-the-sake-of-being-droning" initial approach on the back and try to build a kind of ambient sound seen from more angles - something less constantly droning and more varied. The material of the new forthcoming CD on OEC are definitely a step further in our musical achievement, due a finally reached awareness and confidence with the machines - just a couple of tracks will still remain on the path of the older material while the 80% of the new tracks will display a marked renewed approach and, why not?, quality.

I do believe that you through your music you attempt to convey certain ideas, in particular related to illustrating searing temperatures via sound. While many tracks give off the feeling of gradually boiling and vapourers temperatures, others (to my ear anyway) encompass a more cold, glacial feel. What is the basic premise for sound presentation and what are you attempting trying to illustrate to the listener's ear?
Yes, more or less the background of all the records is based on the combustion, the fire, the high temperatures...Well, it all started from me turning my attention to some books focused on fortean phenomena as self-combustion and at the same time reading articles regarding the application of infraharmonies as weapons in books as "The Amok Journal", that lead us to the idea of trying to conceive a sort of laboratory simulation of an hypothetical series of field recordings captured during a body's process of (self)combustion, so we tried to create a fake combustion-field recordings work, simulating the process of amplifying the sounds flowing from the body while burned...all started there. From there we developed the concept and focused on several kind of phenomena related to fire - the track "HCE" off the "Ipertermia" 10" is a sort of sonic description of the Cerebral Hyper Electrosis phenomena, more or less a brain-focused self combustion that makes your head explodes if your head and brain are too electrically active! However, I think that the main purpose of the music we play is of having no-purpose and let anyone take out of it whatever he feels to, and the fact that you see a glacial side of I Burn its 100% legitimate, obviously the way the way you experience the sound is extremely variable and depending from your own mental wavelengths and your own ways of approaching it - there's no sharp point of separation between the several kinds, even opposite kinds, of sound reception - as for I Burn, I think the point of separation is only clearly established by the visual and "lyrical" elements we surround the records with (colors used, song titles) - the new CD will be visually focused on ultra-cold colours (unlike the old records based only on the yellow and red colors) such as the blue or the azure, so it will be quite interesting to see how a record actually focused on fire-related arguments could be seen (and listened) under a totally different point of view only because it's wrapped on a visual interference.

It would seem that much of I-Burn's material is derived for PC manipulated and synth treated guitars. While there is a tonal quality that can be associated with a guitar the actual sounds are far removed form the original source. How do you go about the process of formulating the basis and basic structure for a track and is it likely that you will widen the 'palette' of sound with other instrumentation manipulation?
All the I Burn's music is entirely assembled using PCs and sound editing softwares, we just plug samplers and guitars in the audio card and record all kinds of stuff and sound source, my guitar, any kind of environmental sound that could result interesting, other CDs, and any kind of thing – and we start working on the single sound with effects, if the sound is good enough to be left as it is we just clean it up a little bit, apply reverbs and nothing more, while with other samples we start processing the sounds for hours or days 'til we reach a good point where the sound is completely transformed in something else (and consequently from there we actually begin to put together several samples in a logical consequence until we finally have built something with the shape of a song), or until we reach the point where the sound is literally destroyed and we cannot use it anymore, so we throw it away. The guitar recording process is more or less the same, but at the end it always leads to more "harmonic" song structures, because of the instrument, of course. At the end, everything (and I mean EVERYTHING - we have an archive of tons of samples and unfinished songs, from excellent to absolutely cheesy stuff, that probably won't ever be used anywhere!) is burned into CDRs. As you can see, nothing too alchemic!
Widen the palette of sound? Yes, of course, any kind of sound source will be reviewed, but if you mean, widen the palette of sound in a more traditional way, with a keyboard or something more "classy"...no, definitely. I think the prerogative of using only PCs give us a certain kind of sound that we probably could not have whenever decide to use a normal keyboard or synth.

It would seem that you have come to your current musical direction via a path from the early 90's death metal scene. While I don't what to taint the opinion of those readers who have yet to hear your music into some sort of view that I-Burn is simply a metal crossover project(and not that I would want to insinuate that either), however do you see your musical past as a positive or negative experience in view of your current workings?

Well, even if, at this stage, I have almost no connections at all with that kind of musical scene (if not the still intact love and admiration for some metal bands), I just look back at it and see a necessary step for me to slowly understand and gradually approach a musical conception 100% open to any kind of extremism, and probably if now I can have shivers while listening to a power electronics band is because I've once had no fear in listening Carcass in the early 90s...do you know what I mean?? The death metal was a lap, not the point of arrive...maybe a "childish" lap, however, necessary to understand better what does (and what doesn't) the definition "musical extremism" mean

What is on the current horizons for I-Burn at the moment with upcoming releases and do you anticipate trudging a path out of the studio and onto the stage for some live interoperations of your material
We have our 2nd full length CD out now, "3rd Degree Burns Ambience", out for Old Europa Cafè in a limited edition of 470 copies; 2 CD compilations with I Burn (as well as other related side-projects) tracks + a full 12" are planned to be out within the end of the millennium for Oktagon Records, and our collaborative I BURN VS SSHE RETINA STIMULANTS CD is planned to be released in January 2000 by State Art...phew! We still haven't ever performed live but it seems that June 2000 could be the time for a big style debut, no anticipations for now..

The first I-Burn CD was originally released in a limited run of 100 on your own D.I.Y label 'Mainteinance'. This label accommodated only CDR releases with special hand made packaging, but has since been made defunct with your new label 'Pre-Feed' taking its place, which will move into the realms of manufactured CD's. While maintenance was operating you were very adamant about its focus, direction and underlying concept and philosophy. Can you detail a bit about its history and what factors contributed to its demise?
Well, the Manteinance history is quite linear - in February '98 we finished the I BURN debut CD (at that time it wasn't supposed to be a CD, it was created as a something to be sent out as professional demo, or something like that) and we decided to do an "experiment" releasing the CD by ourselves in two consecutive editions of 50 copies each (with different packages) - with the original intention keeping the thing strictly on a DIY basis but as more "professional" as possible; the I Burn CDR's have been appreciated and requested by several other labels, and we've been able to establish contacts with a lot of other people, and seeing how positively the situation was developing we decided to attempt in releasing other artists/bands in the same sonic field, all of them keeping the same politics based on limited quantities and handmade packages
In about a year of existence, Manteinance have released: M001 I BURN "s/t" CDR 1998, M002 NO FESTIVAL OF LIGHT "Virtue O' Selfishness" 1998, M003 MSBR "The Final Harsh Work #4" CDR 1998, M004 HPP "hpp" tape/CDR 1998, M005 PARAPHILIA WORSH[WH]IP compilation CDR 1999, M006 SSHE RETINA STIMULANTS "Monitors" CDR 1999.
Concept and philosophy...there were no actual concepts behind Manteinance, if not the way of conceiving a "label" without any kind of business attitude - it's been our total "do it yourself" 5 minutes utopia! The demise has been as natural as its birth - at a certain point I've decided that I was bored with homemade CDRs, bored of releasing them and bored to take care of all the technical problems such format involved, so, it was the time to start something new and leave the Manteinance experience on the back (as well as hoping that this demise will not contribute to the birth to the undredth collector's mania!!). Simple as that.

Now that 'Pre-Feed' has been established, how does its philosophy differ that that behind 'Mainteinance'? What are the overall aspirations for this label and what releases do you have planned?
PRE-FEED is a more "square" label but with no major differences from Manteinance...the only different aspects are that the Pre-Feed edition will be larger, 500 or 1000 copies, or more, who knows, the cover packagings will not be anymore artistic and "un-regular" as the Manteinance packages were, and the main difference is that with Pre-Feed I have no CDR releases planned...That's all. A sort of more professional and less DIY version of Manteinance
>I've released on September 99 a new FRANCISCO LOPEZ CD, "Untitled #90", which is gone sold out a couple days after it's been published; I'm currently discussing with a few artists for a 2nd release to publish in December, while I have a 3rd release already planned for February 2000, SIGILLUM S "Happening whenever" new CD

Well, that about concludes my questions relating to the world of I-Burn and Pre-Feed. Is there anything you would like to add in conclusion? Thanx for the interview and for the effort you put into Spectrum

PRE_FEED / I Burn
Gabriele Santamaria
via Gen. Pergolesi 21
60125 Ancona ITALY
mantein@tin.it
http://move.to/Pre_Feed

new/forthcoming
I B U R N
"3rd Degree Burns Ambience" CD
- out in late September on OLD EUROPA CAFE
- first pressing limited to 350 numbered copies

KEROVNIAN

FEW GROUPS HAVE MANAGED TO CAUSE SUCH A STIR WITH A DEBUT ALBUM, YET KEROVNIAN HAVE SEEMINGLY COME FROM NOWHERE TO HAVING RECEIVED SUBSTANTIAL CRITICAL ACCLAIM FOR THE DARK AND OBSCURE ATMOSPHERES EVOKED ON "FAR BEYOND, BEFORE THE TIME". GIVEN THEY HAVE SIGNED AN EXCLUSIVE 5 ALBUM DEAL WITH THE COLD SPRING RECORDS, KEROVNIAN ARE SURELY DESTINED TO BECOME AN EVEN MORE WIDELY KNOWN NAME. FOLLOWING BELOW IS AN INTERVIEW WITH ONE OF THE ENTITIES BEHIND THIS MYSTERIOUS ULTRA BLACK AMBIENT GROUP....

Welcome Vlad K. Please introduce your project Kerovnian and the individuals it contains. In addition what meaning is held within the groups title?
Well, it has always been hard to "introduce" the project, hard to describe what it actually is or what it represents... as it came from Chaos, it changes its shape constantly, but always remaining the Portal to the Uncreation residing, as it says, far beyond, before the time...in other words, Alall Natrah Utwas Bethud...

As has been indicated above, Kerovnian accommodates a number of members, however your debut CD was recorded by yourself only. What was the reason for recruiting new members and how will it alter the overall vision and sound of the group?
The debut CD was recorded by myself alone, yes, but not made by myself. The beings that you mention came LATER to the manifestation of Kerovnian. The Far Beyond... was made by an unspeakable being from beyond the Chaos...Obliveon is his name...I simply assembled all He gave me, with a touch of my own. The new members are actually consultants on the project concepts. M. Empress Sigyn is contributing with some music also, but it is again all done by Obliveon and me. The reason I introduced them under the name of Kerovnian is that we are forming the Triangle of Chaos, a chaotical magickal ring of some sort; the triple manifestation of the omnimorphed Chaos...Regardless to this, Kerovnian remains the same Kerovnian as it was during Far Beyond was being recorded.

How did you come to be in contact with Cold Spring which led to your 5 CD deal? Is this something at all that you expected when you started creating music for Kerovnian?
I've sent them a demo tape, asked them to listen to it, and they found it very interesting. They offered me a 5 CD deal. It is something that I never expected, but I was glad to see that Chaos and Obliveon will manifest afterall!

The artwork of your "Far Beyond, Before the Time" CD uses many nightmarish images by the medieval artist Hieronymus Bosch. Personally I feel these images suit the atmosphere presented by the music exceptionally. Were these painting that you specifically requested to be used in the presentation of your debut CD? If so, does your interest in Hieronymus Bosch run deeper than simply the artwork he produced?
The images of Hieronymus Bosch are of the closest resemblance to the pictures I had in my head while recording the album. I always have a vision that Obliveon gives me, and then comes the music...The pictures themselves were hard to paint, and designer's idea, which I accepted, was to put Bosch's images. The painted artwork means alot to me in presentation of the album, it is like a second dimension to the whole concept. This is one of the additional reasons I asked M. Empress Sigyn to join me, since she is an artist, and we shall together assembly all the future releases.

Your music contains vocals (but are heavily treated and low in the mix) which are reported to be a language of your own creation. Can you provide some details on this?
The vocals are mostly dry (without effects except reverb), which we consider as additional instrument. There are also parts which are actually vocals heavily treated, which give some sort of background to melodic passages, for example the whole "Before Obliveon" song is concepted with two channels, the heavy vocals as background, and melodic passage atop. The search for the "dark side" of the sounds is one of Kerovnian's spiritus movens. Those vocal parts that are understood as vocals are in Kerovnian

language, a sort of mixture of ancient Greek and Persian. It is their morphology that builds Kerovnian language, but the words themselves are invented or "channeled".

As your country of origin is Croatia I wanted to know how (or if at all) the Balkans conflict has affected you personally and has this potential altered the outlook you illustrate through your music?
The war has nothing to do with Kerovnian. We are not bothered by the Earthly problems. The inner psychical inertia has alot to do with the completion of our sound. More like the dark side of human's dark side....the "un" to negation. The reflection between two mirrors, the shadow of the shadows...The un-undead is not dead, but something else...what? The un-un do not annihilate each other, but transmute into something unspeakable by the sane ones. The same formula is applied to the sounds. The un-unsound.

As Croatia is not all well known in terms of having a thriving music scene, your project comes across as being somewhat exotic and mysterious. Do you think that being a Croatian project helps or hampers the project? What is the scene (if any) like over in Croatia?
I don't know. I never thought about it. The scene in Croatia does not exist. It is mostly pop-rock (a copy of a copy of a copy of each other), the underground exists, but it is then rave, techno, and allot of rock, punk and metal bands.

The ambiental dark atmospheres that you create, for me transcends any childish representation of the concept of 'evil', rather that it is if you are musically illustrating other dimensions of sorts. What if any concepts are inherent in Kerovnian's music?
Well, what I said before would be the perfect answer: The searching for the dark sides of sounds....the unnegation of sounds. Beside vocal and melodic parts, other sounds are sampled from our common day-to-day activities....those common, mostly unnoticed sounds have a great dark side....probably because they are so neglected, and mostly unnoticed...well treated, and they become demonic manifestations of abyssal pits and hellish landscapes....what, hell is uncomparable to the Chaos waiting to be conjured. Treated like this, the sounds reveal the basic integration and their "roots" as it was before the beginning of Time....

How did you become interested in dark/ black ambient music and what other artists would site inspiration and/ or respect to?
I recorded a couple of songs that simply emerged from my soul, and later I found out they belong to the black ambient scene. But I must admit I am heavily influenced by J.M. Jarre, by his first albums, regarding to melodic parts. The rest is merely the inspiration I get from behind the Chaos.

Can you provide any details on how you approach the recording and composition process?
Well, it is hard to describe. I simply record what comes to me....

Do you have any other musical projects, regardless of if they are in another style of music?
No. I used to play in a black metal band, previous to releasing the Far Beyond....

Cold Spring's release schedule indicates an upcoming 10" EP and another CD? What information can you give regarding these? Have they already been recorded and how will they differ from you debut CD and do these recordings feature the new members?
Yes, there should be a 7" single coming up next, probably by the end of this year (99), and another CD, the sequel to Far Beyond..., by the end of next year. Sound? Well, I can say we introduced more death industrial elements, but the Kerovnian atmosphere is still the writhing same!

On a parting note is there anything you would like to additionally add?
What remains when you turn off the light?

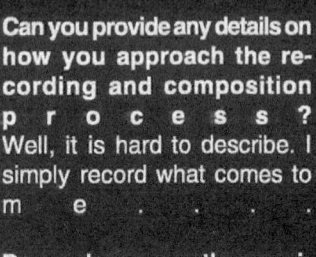

DEATH IN JUNE/Der Blutharsch
show report, 9 july 1999, melbourne, australia

When I first got word of this gig there were certain rumours flying around that it was also going to feature a performance with Der Blutharsch (which obviously then promised to be a great gig). However, even on the evening of the show I was still not certain to if Der Blutharsch were playing as it was stated in an interview with Douglas P (conducted that week) "I co-wrote the album with World Serpent labelmate Albin Julius of Der Blutharsch who recently supported me with Boyd on my European tour of this year". Regardless of the final outcome of if Der Blutharsch would play or not, I was still going to attend to see Death in June, as we all know their live performances are far an few between!

As for the gig was held at Chasers Nightclub (Chapel Street, Melbourne, Australia), which is more known as a danceclub venue than an association with industrial music, and while the venue might not be the best setting for such a performance I was not exactly about to boycott the event. While the nightclub had a very 'clinical' feel with its strobes and lazer lights, quite a bit of effort had gone into the setup of the stage and surrounds. The stage was presented with a large backdrop banner (the DIJ 'death' skull logo) a large gong to the back right hand side and a standing drumkit in front, a sampler/ synthesiser to the back left hand side, a central microphone flanked by floor toms and a row of chines below the mic. All the instruments were further adorned with a number of banners and the whole setting complimented by red drapes radiating out from the stage to the upper level of the venue.

It was a bit hard to tell when the Der Blutharsch gig actually started given that there were DJ's mixing it up (including David Thrussell of Black Lung/ Song), however the mood with the background music became very low key and 'folky' for around 10 minutes, prior to the lights being dimmed and a smoke machine being utilised to great effect. On the shrill cry of a wailing air raid siren Der Blutharsch finally took to the stage a bit after 11.30 pm. While the session drummer (John Murphy) took his position, Albin slowly walked to the stage with a flaming torch held high and took stand at the centrally positioned microphone, being clothed in black army gear. The actual performance of Der Blutharsch consisted of constant marching drumming from the session drummer and Albin providing live vocals over a backdrop of pre-recorded DAT music. Despite the lack of actual playing of the music Albin kept a militant stage presence that was still captivating, presenting a commanding aura of pride and strength. Albin at certain points provided some additional floor tom drumming or recited text from an archaic scroll, which both added to the overall effect.

The performance itself was relatively short covering only 35-40 minutes, however it was certainly worthy for the quality and present. I was only able to recognise a couple of tracks off the "Der Seig...." CD being of the up beat highly rousing percussive marching songs (in the neo- classical vein), with the remainder of the set consisting of similarly bombastic tracks. I also managed pick some reworked tracks of the group 'the moon lay hidden beneath a cloud' (which was Albin's previous project) within the set list.

When it was time for DIJ to commence their performance, again the smoke machine was working overtime. Firstly Albin and the session drummer (again John Murphy) entered the stage in swirling smoke holding flagged banners high and dressed again in army blacks with a gas mask and leather mask respectively. When Douglas arrived on stage thrashing his flag around violently he was wearing his trademark mask and hooded jacket and barely visible through the cloud of smoke. The whole entrance and setting was far beyond simply viewing just another band....this was a real performance.

Many tracks of the new album were given a live rendition and more often than not coming off even more powerful than the studio version, especially when all three members partook in providing pounding anthemic drumming. The theatrics were again heightened on "Dispair" with Douglas striding around the stage arms held high shaking a ritual percussive instrument. The first half of the set consisted of Douglas presenting vocals and general percussion where the second half Douglas was unmasked and utalised the acoustic guitar for the remainder of the set. As I am not fully versed in all of DIJ's back catalogue, I did note that they did pull out tracks off such albums as "Rose Clouds of Holocaust" (including the title track) and other tracks such as "Giddy Giddy Carousel". The first half of the set came across as much more powerful that the later acoustic but all in all it was a good representation of the DIJ sound. The show ended quite abruptly (after being on stage a little over an hour) with the infamous noise sample that got quite a run through on the new album....as quickly as it had began it was all over.

Although as previously stated the venue had a very 'clinical' in feel (as it is normally a techno/ dance nightclub), the professional stage props and performance were good enough to evoke a very suitable atmosphere.... that atmosphere being resoundingly militant. The sound and production for Der Blutharsch was both clear and load with no elements being subject of complaint, however DIJ simply overpowered them with a much more full and bombastic performance.

Throughout the night it was also quite amusing to see some normal nightclub people turning up expecting the standard danceclub and wondering what pro-European/ eurocentric celebration they had walked into. The attendance was a bit disappointing (not more than 100 I would think) and there appeared to be more people watching Der Blutharsch than DIJ, which I found odd considering it was only billed as a DIJ show.

To conclude, I'm glad I finally had an opportunity to witness a gig of such high calibre groups (of which rarely tour these shores) and although I was I would have liked to have stayed around to meet Douglas and Co. after they packed up, given the late hour and my work commitments the following day I had to call it a night (Nonetheless I managed to get a copy of the new DIJ CD signed by both Douglas and Albin). Overall the gig was well beyond expectation and I hope to have the opportunity to do it all again sometime soon.

imminent starvation

Imminent Starvation being a total powerhouse of corrosive, overdriven technoid beats and rhythms (intermixed with cold oppressive soundscapes) has quickly flung them to the forefront of the Ant-Zen power/ noise movement. After hearing their more than impressive Nord CD from 1998 I contacted solo member Olivier Moreau for an interview (however actually retrieving it turned out to be quite a task given his many other studio & live commitments at the time!).

Hello Olivier and welcome to Spectrum Magazine. Imminent Starvation has thus far released two CD's (both on the Ant-Zen label), and while this project is essentially a solo formation, I don't believe that it is your first involvement in the current technoid/ power noise movement. Can you please detail some historic documentation of your involvement in the scene leading to the formation of Imminent Starvation?
Well, I formed Imminent Starvation 8 or 9 years ago and it was my first solo project, so everything started with it. But it's true I let Imminent Starvation on the side for a few years. At that time I was more busy with all the techno stuff (94/96) and it's only later that I came back to the roots of Imminent Starvation to develop it to what it is now.

Your debut CD was a mixture of both low key ambient moments and the more hyper techno/ beat oriented power tracks, however your latest CD has totally avoided any ambient type passages opting for a much more melodic (yet harsh) beat driven affair (or industrial strength techno as Ant-Zen like to call it). Particularly this new focused direction lends itself to the much more harder edged DJ set, but I wanted to ask whether this was the intention to market yourself more towards a club arena?
When I made the second CD there was absolutely no direct intention to be more DJ friendly. The fact that there is less ambient piece is due that Nord is in the first place a collection of tracks I made for my concert and so which are more beat oriented as I avoid ambient tracks during my concert. Unfortunately the audience has no or very low interest in ambient concert, they want beat to dance, so I give them what they want. Nord is a witness of that situation and a victim of the tyranny of the beat. But this is not a problem for me as if I want to make something more ambient I will make it under a different name, I keep imminent Starvation for the more heavy stuff.

As your music has a harsh yet ambient undercurrent as well as structured industrial techno edge, there is a certain crossover appeal between music scenes. From which scene have you had the greatest response and which scene do you feel most affiliated with?
The greatest response at the moment come from the industrial scene, but this is very easy to understand. I am on an industrial label, so my audience is industrial. If I was on a techno label (like before with re-load) it should be techno. It's a pity but the frontier between the scenes stay strong and it is very difficult to cross them.

Within Swedish dark ambient scene there is a certain sense of community which revolves around the Cold Meat Industry label, likewise it would also seem that there is a similar one surrounding the German label Ant-Zen and associated groups. Is this the fact case?
In a way yes. Salt has very good contact with all bands and he tried to avoid jealousy between them. He put the same energy and enthusiasm with everyone so that nobody complains. We have no rivalry at ant-zen, all bands are equal and together we are stronger. You don't have that feelings with all labels, too often they ripped you off and you are angry against them which lead to a bad atmosphere. The keywords with ant-zen are trust and respect.

How did you come to be in contact with Ant-Zen and are you permanently signed to this label with Imminent Starvation?
A few years back, Salt (label manager of ant-zen) contacted me for a track on a compilation (C-lektor), and later he asked me for a full length CD. What I accepted. Since as I am quite happy with his work and as it's a very nice and honest guy, I stayed there releasing almost all my stuff on his various labels. But no I am not permanently signed to him, I am free to go where I want. For example there are 2 albums going out at the moment which are not on ant-zen. The Urawa on Foton and the Ambre/Mark Spybey on Hushush.

Along with the standard release of your new CD there was a limited edition boxset, which contained actual pieces of your mixing board (along with a T-shirt, pin, 7"ep etc). Why dismantle and give away an integral piece of Imminent Starvation's equipment? As a result will your sound change with new equipment? Also what recordings was this mixing board used on?
The mixing board was used on all my solo releases and on some parts of

Urawa, Torsion and Axiome. I dismantled it because it really start to malfunction a little too much. I was using the malfunctions a lot but with the time these became too strong (funny when you have to wait 6 or 7 hours before the mixing desk is warm enough to work correctly, or when you have to open it and solder some cables just before a concert). It had a unique sound I never find back on any mixing desk. By breaking it, I wanted to mark the end of a period, a way to say I have done this in the past, now I want to make something different. And to get away from the influence of my equipment I simply destroyed it so that there is no way back. I put it in the box because I think it's nice for the people when listening to the records they can feel a part of the machine which produce it. It makes the record more personal and less anonymous than a vulgar piece of plastic which has no soul. For sure my new equipment will change my sounds, this was my main objective when I decide it, not repeating myself and making something new.

I have heard the new album had some chart success on the independent charts in Germany. Can you provide some details on this?
I heard the same rumors as you but as I am located in Belgium (where nobody cares about Imminent Starvation) I don't really know what's happening in the charts of my German neighbors. So I don't have any details and it seems quite surrealistic to me that my records enter the charts. In fact I don't really care about it, I just find it funny, nothing more.

Playing live seems to be another essential part of the Imminent Starvation experience. Do you normally play music festival shows or more club DJ type sets? If you play both, do the reactions different between the two (i.e. people standing and watching at music festivals as opposed to dancing at the club sets?).
In the past, when I was quite busy with Delta Files and Torsion (which were released on a techno label), we used to play the most in club with DJ. But since I am on Ant-Zen the situation has change and I play more now in industrial festival. The audience is very different between the 2 scene and depending the kind of music you play you can get better reaction in one or another. But in general I have to say that I prefer playing at a festival than at a party. Just because the audience most of the time come to see you and so know what to expect from you. Which is not always the case if you play at a party where there are always people who don't care about who's playing.

What consists of an Imminent Starvation performance, and in essence how 'live' are the shows? (i.e.: are DAT recordings heavily utilized?).
I use no DAT, minidisc or CD for my live performance. Everything is played live by a sequencer and I am making as much live as electronic music allowed me to do it. I would never dare making such a live act with a tape in the background and just adding a few sounds, I would feel ashamed because this is a real betrayal for the audience, it's considering them as idiot. But I have to say that as electronic musician I feel me very limited during my gig, when I see a jazz musician improvising for example I feel very humble and jealous. I really miss that freedom of improvisation when I am in front of my machines.

Are there any concepts/ themes surrounding Imminent Starvation, as the slogan on the 'nord' CD cover 'please contact us we are your friends!' (and also featured on the last track) would tend to indicate this?
No there is no particular message behind my music. I am not very interested in telling the people what they have to do, in music the only element which is important is the music itself. All political messages or concept only disturb you from the essence of the music itself. I hate to dislike music just because I don't agree with the idea behind it. The contrary is also true, I will not like a music just because I do agree with the idea. Having a concept is nice if it works, but I am tired of all the bands having a concept just because it is cool to have one. The please contact us sentence is more of a joke because I used that sampling during my concert and I thought it was a funny idea to finish the CD, as I am not completely a psycho as some people would think when hearing my music.

Personally, how far do you think the power noise style can be taken without becoming derivative or generic?
It is already derivative. Unfortunately there is really few people who wants to make the things move and go deeper into it. Most have find a formula which works and they keep themselves to it. I hate that attitude, you have always to prove yourself and the other than you can do better or different than what you made before. On an artistic level, the repetition kills the creativity. It's why I destroyed my previous equipment, I was used to it, and it had become a routine to make a track. I wanted to stop that and go further by looking into the future and not into the past.

What other projects and/ or collaborations do you have besides Imminent Starvation? How do these projects differ in sound style and concept?
Well I have many. With John N. Sellekaers of Xingu Hill I make Torsion, Urawa and Ambre, all very active at the moment as all get fresh releases. Torsion was in fact the follower of Urawa, a few years back we had some legal problems with KK records which own the Urawa name, so we had to find a new name and it was Torsion. So this is basically the same project as the original Urawa. I say original Urawa as we now have back the rights for Urawa, so we did bring it to a new live but in a completely different

approach. Urawa is now our open project where everything can happened and with which we invited guest to work with us. For Ambre c-drik join us, and we just finished an album with Mark Spybey (of zoviet france, download, etc) which is part of trilogy called Threesome. The next part of the trilogy will be early next year an album with Mick Harris (of Scorn) (more information on www.hushush.com). Still with C-drik there is Axiome which was my first musical project.

How prolific are you as an artist when in comes to composing tracks and when can a future release be expected? Do you have any initial ideas of how your new recordings will sound?
There will be no new Imminent Starvation before the end of 2000. Not because I am not prolific enough but in the next 6 months I have no time for working on that stuff. I have a few new collaboration which should be finished before I start working on my own new material. I don't know how it will sounds. At the moment I just finished my new live act but I don't think I will put it on my next CD. It's nice stuff for live but not for my next album, maybe for a maxi. So I am still unsure about the future sound of Imminent Starvation.

Well, thank you Olivier for giving some insight into Imminent Starvation and also being a part of Spectrum 3#. Is there anything you would like to add to finish?
Take care of penguins.

SLAUGHTER PRODUCTIONS
sounds from the dark side of human sickness

[SPT114] 15 DELIGHTS OF DIONYSUS "The Lament of Virtue"
46 mins A5 sleeve [USA], L.12000

*dark and meditative deep sounds
contemplations of religious animosity
and self annihilation*

Prices do not include postage.

Payments only through:
. International Money Order payable to Marco Corbelli (to avoid problems with the local post office, please do not mention the Slaughter Productions name).
. Cash in a registered letter at your own risk! Currencies accepted:
Italian Lire / German DM / US Dollars.
Do not send money in advance. Contact us listing the items you are interested and wait for your invoice.

All items listed in the invoice will be shipped immediately after receiving your payment.

Overseas: please, specify which method (Surface, Air) you would like to receive the stuff to get the exact rate.
Many items listed in the distribution page are limited in the stock.
Please, always ask for alternative titles.

All cassettes are real-time copies in good quality tapes.

Slaughter Productions • Via Tartini 8 • 41049 • Sassuolo (MO) • ITALY
Fax: + 39 0536 872999 • Email: slaughter@mail.dex-net.com

① ⑤ delights of dionysus

The Lament of Virtue

schloss tegal

Schloss Tegal are a group that for some unknown reason alluded my attention for far too long. All I can say is that after finally tracking down one of their releases I became an almost instant fanatic for their highly unique soundscapes. Read on to see what duo Richard Schneider (RS) & Marc Burch (MB) had to say about the dark & bleak anti-world realms of Schloss Tegal where occult, science and extraterrestrial sounds converge...

Schloss Tegal is a dark ambient group that has been in existence for quite some years, with your fifth full length CD Black Static Transmissions having recently been released on Cold Spring Records. First things first, could you give some basis background information on the formation of the group?
MB: Richard and I met at KJHK, the student operated fm radio station, of the University of Kansas in 1982. I was the host of a Sunday night special program called, The Debraining Machine, which featured music and interviews with groups and individuals involved in the initial wave of what has become known as "industrial music". Richard had a shift, which followed this program. His program was called, The Death Disco and featured a variety of industrial music. We became good friends with similar interests in music and art and after sometime decided to create our own music. Our first attempt at this was called Louis Lingg. It was a name taken from a poem by Aleister Crowley. Louis Lingg was made up of John Gleason, a good friend and fellow KJHK DJ, on Fender bass which he ran through a Roland guitar synthesizer, Richard Schneider on Arp Odyssey synthesizer and Marc Burch on tapes and noise generator. Louis Lingg played two shows. The first performance was opening for the German group MDK and the second performance was with Hunting Lodge, William Burroughs and Whitehouse. After these shows and some deliberations between the 3 of us, i.e. John moved to Kansas City to pursue a career and then Louis Lingg became Schloss Tegal and went from 3 to 2 members. Bass and percussion were done away with and a more intrinsic approach to creating music became the aim of Schloss Tegal. With the discovery of Casio samplers (SK-8) in the Wal-Mart toy section during the summer of 84, this ambition became actualized, with digital loops replacing the many tape loops, which we once used. On Sept.24, 1984, Schloss Tegal played their first show, "Escaping Lobo Tech", at the University of Kansas's Helen Spencer Museum. From there they have gone on to create a substantial body of work and have earned themselves some notoriety /recognition as masters of dark ambient soundscapes.

As I do not own your full discography could you give a rundown of details of each CD and the concepts on each?
Discography of Schloss Tegal: Procession of the Dead/Dreamtime EP Tegal Records 1989, Musick from Madness Cassette State of Flux 1991, The Soul Extinguished LP Tegal Records 1991, The Grand Guignol CD Artware 1993, The Garbage Sandwich Cassette Compilation"The Beast" 1993, Oranur III "The Third Report" CD Artware 1994, Treat the Gods As If They Exist CD compilation Auf Abwegen 1996, Human Resource Exploitation CD Noise Museum 1997, Mind of A Missile CD Compilation Heel Stone 1997, Kontrast 5x7"EP vinyl boxset Duebel Advanced Sonic processing 1997, Black Static Transmission CD Cold Spring 1999.
MB: Procession of the Dead, The Soul Extinguished, Musick from Madness and The Grand Guignol were investigations and attempts at understanding the nature of good and evil. Why people do the things they do? What is the catalyst that decides a person's course of action? This was our scary Evil Tegal phase, as we investigated both the occult sciences and sanctioned religious activities.
RS: That is why we used actual serial killer themes for The Grand Guignol. We wanted to capture the serial killer in his mental state glory. The Soul Extinguished even goes into aspects of poltergeist phenomenon, religious flagellation and Abductions. So there are a lot of things going on if you can pick them out.
MB: Oranur III was an investigation inspired by the studies of Wilhelm Reich as well as our own interests in the Universe. This was when Richard and I really started getting into digital recording and began exploring through sound some of our favorite interests UFOs, aliens and the "things" that are out there.
RS: It also expressed the persecution that Dr Reich received by the hands of the Food and Drug administration for his orgone theories. I think Oranur III tests your belief in under standing what is real and what is a hoax especially with the new Internet explosion hoaxes and getting people to believe things will be easy. The cover of Oranur III is of two hoaxed UFO photos.
MB: Human Resource Exploitation is a study in global mind control and manipulation by governments and corporations upon the consumer. It is a reaction against the homogenization of the world. Humanity must remove its blinders so we aren't sheep to be culled.
RS: It goes even deeper into the conspiracy of HAARP and mind control via electronics and futuristic extrapolations into what our planet would be like when the rich elite leave our depleted planet and control us from outer space to be mere protoplasm for their gain hidden from our consciousness.
MB: Mind of a Missile is Schloss Tegal taking the listener on a flight of destruction. Digital destruction experienced via digital audio. Put on your headphones and cruise to target zero.
MB: HRE and MoaM represent our investigating control mechanisms in their various forms be it subliminal imbeds in commercials to the HAARP project and various audio signals broadcast by black ops networks throughout the world, with the intent of manipulating or controlling people.
MB: Black Static Transmission is a journey to the anti-world. The realm of the dead the flip side of what we call life is the subject of this latest CD. Inspired by the research of Konstantin Raudive and our own personal experiences with death. This is a study not only of death but also of cataclysm. This is a message from the universe itself. We cannot avoid the inevitable end of things. It's a natural occurrence and we shouldn't be afraid. Death is not the end.
RS: Yes, the realm between oscillations seen only if we possess the appropriate mirror, may we view this antiword or otherworld. It challenges our pheble primitive human perception mechanisms.

Schloss Tegal appear to consist of two individuals on your past two releases, but has this been the case from the beginning?
RS: Schloss Tegal has always been two but we have been working with other artists such as En Lewellyn who brought us the scientific more literal side of EVP, and plan to work with others in the future. We have also begun releasing other artists on our label, which was primarily for ST works only. We plan to work with other artists in the future.

It also seems that you had assistance from En Llyellyn of Crepescule on your new CD? How did you come to be in contact with him and what was his involvement with the release?
RS: I'm not really sure? I think it was by email. He sent some cassettes and his music was striking, wonderfully eerie and mysterious. We had talked about releasing a 10 inch record of a piece he sent us but decided to do the "Music for Decay" CD instead because this was a project he had been working on for quite some time and needed to be released to the public. We were just interested in what each other were doing. Since he is an EVP researcher I asked if he would contribute some tracks for a collaboration with us. The result was part one of BST.

With such an unusual name I wanted to know its meaning and significance to the concept of the group?
RS: The name Schloss Tegal comes from one of the first mental patient hospitals out side of Berlin. The name Black Static Transmission represents the

antiworld a world existing between oscillations and neutral black static and transmissions from other dimensions. Its a way to witness something we thought could never be, like transmissions from the dead, strange happenings and miracles.
MB: We became aware of Schloss Tegal while employed for a publisher of scientific journals. It was mentioned in an article in the Menninger Bulletin about the history of mental clinics. Schloss Tegal was one of the first clinics, which utilized art and music therapy and actually made attempts at treating patients rather than just locking them away. Schloss Tegal was founded by Ernst Simmel and was located outside of Berlin. Most of this activity took place throughout the time frame of WWI and dealt with the treatment of shellshock victims. We thought it was a great name and idea for a band. We saw the planet as an asylum and we were the therapists. We were leading the way to escape the lobotomy system that comprises the day to day routine. It was no longer time to clock in. It wasn't until we went to Germany to perform that we discovered the darkside of the psychiatric clinic known as Schloss Tegal. Klaus and Jochim of Tesco and Genocide Organ told us that during WWII that Schloss Tegal became the antithesis of a hospital and "treated" enemies of the Nazi regime until it's destruction at the end of the war. Naturally, we were concerned about this but we kept the name for it's original intentions and in no way are we interested in politics or ideology that advocates hatred. Schloss Tegal is a vehicle for creative freedom and attempts to create or arrive at new ideas or concepts regarding sound stimuli hence the term neoteric. Utilizing technology we attempt to redefine what music can be much like the Dadaists and Italian futurists of the early 20th century. As we prepare to enter a new century Schloss Tegal along with others is ushering in new potentials and directions in the realm of creating music, not just as a form of entertainment but as a means of communication.
RS: We even found out later that the Menninger Psychiatric Clinic in Kansas was modeled after the Schloss Tegal in Germany. We went there and searched through thier medical library. That is where we learned about Ernst Simmel.

You personally describe your music as "tachyons and psyonics". What does this descriptive terminology mean?
RS: These are terms for sounds that are actualized from power electronic intrinsic sound sources on a specific subconscious level and specific purpose bombarding the senses for a mind response.

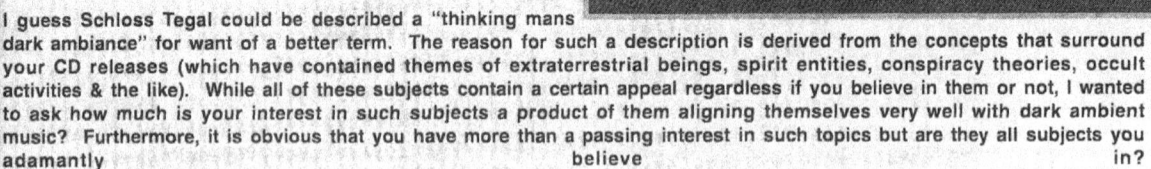

I guess Schloss Tegal could be described a "thinking mans dark ambiance" for want of a better term. The reason for such a description is derived from the concepts that surround your CD releases (which have contained themes of extraterrestrial beings, spirit entities, conspiracy theories, occult activities & the like). While all of these subjects contain a certain appeal regardless if you believe in them or not, I wanted to ask how much is your interest in such subjects a product of them aligning themselves very well with dark ambient music? Furthermore, it is obvious that you have more than a passing interest in such topics but are they all subjects you adamantly believe in?
RS: We have always been attracted to the unexplainable. It really isn't our intention to have concept CDs. Its just that we have some many subjects that are inter linked that our records seem to be about a single concept when there are many themes and concepts that can be interpreted from our records. It keeps it intriguing for us to hear new concepts arise even we didn't perceive them the first time.

Further to the above, it is stated that your new CD contains EVP recordings (Electronic Voice Phenomena) which is essentially is voices recorded on radio frequencies who claim to be spirits who used to inhabit the earth but now reside in another dimension. Can you please give a detailed summary of this subject and how you became involved with its research?
RS: We have always been interested in EVP transmissions but never really had any experience with it until I received recordings from En Lewellyn. There are many EVP researchers Constantine Raudive and another Swedish scientist were the first noted to explore trying to record spirit voices from another dimension on magnetic tape. En's recordings were very intriguing, whispers of voices and poltergeist clangings. It reinforced our interest in other dimensions beyond life and death. There are many sites on the Internet dedicated to EVP research to visit and listen to sounds and voices if you search them out.

The actual dark ambient you create has a cavernous and somewhat improvised feel to it, which totally avoids any tones that could be associated with a synthesizer. Likewise the overall compositions tends to lean towards sounding like you are conducting a scientific "sound" experiment than specifically trying to compose dark ambient music. How much truth is in this assessment and what types of equipment and processes do you use during composition?
RS: We mainly go by instinct and then work from there. There are always some idea or basis in the beginning but it evolves as it advances through the creative process. The sound processes we record are much like an laboratory situation at first. I've never really liked the term experimental music because the term means that it is still in the process of experimentation. We consider our music finished experiments and results. I don't even consider our music to be ambient either. I think its in your face more than ambient which is something in the background.
MB: I utilize a Roland S-10 sampler, a Boss SP-202, an Akai S20 and a Roland DEP-5 as his primary pieces of equipment. Richard uses a Roland W-30 workstation and Macintosh G3 Computer. Of course the fun part is collecting the various field recordings and sound sources and then taking them into the studio for further processing.
RS: A lot of our field recordings are very important when selecting what to use it must have some intrinsic nature to the psyche which makes the sample important rather than just sound. Like a filmmaker who shoots a scene in the actual location to capture the essence of the environment and location we try to do the same thing with audio. I have been working with visuals to place on our web site as soon as they are finished and audio.

Your CD covers generally have written passages which detail the themes contained on the release. Are these written by yourself or derived from other sources?
RS: Most are written by us some are obtained from other important sources and then written by us. The text plays an important role in giving the listener something to read about the ideas while the music is playing and gives them a reference point to understanding where we are coming from.

One of the passages in the cover of Oranur III "The Third Report" is clearly referencing the writings and Cthulhu mythos of H.P Lovecraft. Where do you stand in opinion to if H.P Lovecraft's writings were merely science fiction or if he had discovered some deeper spiritual knowledge?
MB: We have always liked his work. His depiction's of cosmic evil and his entire pantheon of entities are just brimming with possibilities. Is it fiction or some primal religion that has long been buried in the furthermost recesses of our minds and somehow HPL was able to recall these primordial beings and thus write about it? Throughout the BST sessions, "In strange eons even death may die," was a constant thought or mantra for the project. In Oranur III, we mention Yuggoth and the Outer Beings and in BST, R'lyeh rises in a great geophysical sound piece. We acknowledge the vast unknown that we exist in or perhaps it allows us to exist.

The image print on the Oranur III "The Third Report" CD details an image of the Virgin Marry, baby Jesus and an angel. As this seems at odds with the themes on the CD (extraterrestrial phenomena & Wilhelm Reich). I wanted to ask of this images relevance to the overall concept of the CD?

RS: This photo is a mural painting from the 15th Century that has images that depict a UFO in the background. Was Jesus Christ an extraterrestrial? Many early paintings depict images of alien origin. Is religion of alien origin? It added a lot of mystery to the artwork.

The new CD Black Static Transmissions has 7 tracks listed but only two digital tracks. While the first digital track is the title track, the remaining 6 tracks play together in one mass of sound. In this second digital track, deciphering where one track finishes is almost impossible, as there is a hell of a lot going on throughout the 41 minutes. Does this indicate that in your view the actual tracks and titles are irrelevant in the greater context of how the listener perceives the sounds?

RS: Yes that is right. It seemed hard to decipher all of the track with this work which is why it is in two tracks and it forces the listener to list to both tracks as complete works. The first track is the title piece and the second track takes you into heaven and hell and the dark oblivion

MB: Black Static Transmission: This is our best project to date. Not just because of the quality of the recording but also because of the support we received from Cold Spring. BST took quite awhile to compile the sounds and then put everything together into a cohesive package. Justin was very patient and let us take our time and this allowed us to really get into this project when it came to the final mixdown. I think that Black Static Transmission is probably our best CD in terms of studio usage and it really possesses a power that effects the listener. Justin also introduced us to Vlad of Kerovnian, who put together the artwork we sent him and made our job of composing the musick that much easier. We are very grateful to them. The actual title track for BST is imbedded throughout track #2 in the form of the soviet woodpecker signal and a certain pulsar's radio signature. As to the various track titles that comprise track 2, we felt that these compositions really didn't need to be designated a specific numerical code. The compositions would simply flow in one continuous stream of digital signal and the listener would be able to distinguish the subtle changes leading into each piece.

Is the music of Schloss Tegal improvised during a performance or is it some kind of audio experiment that is being conducted upon the listening audience?

MB: During a Schloss Tegal performance there are parameters that we try to follow, but we often try to push the levels if we can on the sound system so the audience can get the full effect.

RS: We like to try to achieve this for ourselves as well so we can actually experience the power of the sounds we generate in a live situation. It's not about trying to replicate exactly what is on our CDs. We want to go further with our compositions when we perform them live. We are attempting to alter perceptions and sensations through the manipulation of sound.

You have recently come back from a European tour in support of you new CD. What were your overall impressions of how the tour went, and what was the attendance and crowd reaction measure up to your expectations?

RS: The Black Static Transmission tour was the best thanks to good organization by Ars Morta Universum. All of the venues we unique to say the least. Especially the MS Stubnitz Club a ship docked in Rostock Germany that looked like something from the movie "Beyond Thunderdome". We played in the bottom hull of the ship converted into a stage with an incredible sound and video system and The Spider Club was an underground bunker/bomb shelter used during WWII in Kladno, Czech Republic. The highlight was the Arsenal festival in Poland with many supportive Schloss Tegal fans. Another European tour is planned for June 2000.

Also I believe that there may be a live CD from recording taping during the tour. When is this likely to eventuate?

RS: I am currently in the process of compiling all of the live shows and putting it together sometime in the near future with Ars Morta Universum. Also a lot of video footage was shot on the tour. Hopefully we can put together a live video also.

What plans are currently on the cards for Schloss Tegal and likewise with your record label Tegal Records and your music store Interzone Music?

RS: Our record store has been doing well, now open for 6 years. Most of our releases in the future may only be available directly through our web site and a few small distributors. We are planning to release Kid 606 "Merzboy" in early 2000 who is a hardcore gabber artist who performed at Interzone. A lot of it will be live material some recorded here at interzone and some studio material with cover songs of Whitehouse and Throbbing Gristle. This CD will be on fire. We also plan to release the live CD of the tour with VOID and Skrol in conjunction with Ars Morta Universum and hopefully a video of the tour highlights. Also a new Schloss Tegal CD is in the works now for 2000 also. Keep an eye on the web site for release dates.

In regard to Tegal Records, what exactly is the depicted in the label's logo?

RS: The logo is a photo of a lingum (religious crystal egg that glows with divine light) taken from religious leader Sai Baba's stomach. He would do magic or religious miracles to amaze the audience. He would cough up one of these lingums in front of the crowd. It was kind of a hoax to make people believe he would hold it up and it would glow with divine light. That is what the Tegal Records logo is, the egg shaped lingum in his hand. It is a symbol of challenged belief systems.

It seems that Interzone Music stocks quite a range of musical styles. Is this dictated by you own taste in music and what are the main styles you personally listen to?

RS: We are primarily and electronic music store with lots of vinyl and dance music for Djs and clubs. The selection is very diverse with a lot of dark ambient industrial and power electronics along side of electronic experimental and dance music. We are building a shopping cart for the web site that should be available before 2000 and real audio will be available soon for each of the catalogues and Tegal Records sections.

With Interzone Music you recently held instore shows with the Swedish industrial/ ambient group/ Sanctum. How did these shows come about and were you involved in the planning and preparation of the tour? Overall how did the shows go?

RS: We have had some great performances here in the store/performance space this year. Sanctum was a very successful show and had a good turnout. The shows come about by various direct contacts in the underground network by email and Internet. I wasn't involved at all in the planning of the Sanctum tour. I'm not sure exactly who was. Its comes about mostly through correspondence. We also had Inade and Ex Order from Germany it was set up by Malignant Records. It's really nice to introduce this kind of music here in the states. It was like being in Europe again.

Well, that just about concludes my exploration into the 'anti-world' dimension of Schloss Tegal. Anything to add in conclusion? What is next for Schloss Tegal?

MB: We are planning more releases for the next century and are looking forward to more live performances. We would also like to do some possible collaboration with other artists. Schloss Tegal will continue the process it has embarked upon...the healing of the mental state via tachyon bombardment and psionic therapy.

RS: This will be your next ...Humans.

SOUND REVIEWS

ALL REVIEWS BY RICHARD STEVENSON UNLESS INDICATED OTHERWISE

AH CAMA SOTZ (BEL)/ PAL (GER) "GUILTY/AUDIOWALL" 7" EP 1999 NOCTURNUS/ SPECTRE
A nice concept on this collaboration 7" where both artists recorded a separate track each then swapped to rework and remix them as they saw fit, finally coming up with two very different but rewarding tracks. The Ah Cama Sotz track is up first being wildly atmospheric and stylistically harsh with an overdriven tribal beat that is almost techno in final production. Harsh swirls of noise add to an almost non structured backing as the beat kicks in an out of a few minor segments. PAL on the other hand steer clear of any beat territory going for a much harsher sound manipulations. Landing somewhere in between power electronics and death industrial, the mid paced noise pulse throbs incessantly as layers of looped static, noise and treatments are multiplied into the mix. Without either going for a densely heavy sound nor high end squeal that track retains a positive flair throughout, heating up for a nice and noisy finally. Heavy weight vinyl and quality slip sleeve packaging (+insert) round out a very nice item.

ALLERSEELEN(AUT)/ BLOOD AXIS(USA) "KAFERLIED/ BRIAN BORU" SPLIT 7" EP 1998 STATEART
As this item was released to commemorate the groups European tour, it was interesting to read that the label who released this item was subjected to some incidents of violence/ aggression. As it turned out, a certain 'P.C' faction had made assumptions on the ideology behind the label and groups and decided to partake in some rock hurling. With all of this being an attempt to halt the live gigs, the police stepped in on the side of the bands to ensure the gigs went ahead, so certainly the actions of the instigators did not achieve their aims. Now where was I?....ah yes the music.....the Allerseelen track hurtles straight into a repetitive bass loop that is almost funky, however the background synth tune keep the mood down to a reflective sombre feel. Spoken vocals are included but are low in the mix with a mild echo effect. Although I am not all that familiar with Allerseelen's output, I can say that this is one of the best tracks I have heard from Kadom's project.
Blood Axis have taken the traditional Irish song 'the march of Brian Boru' (as featured on the live release 'Blot: Sacrifice in Sweden') and given it a going over with a bit of distortion. The track still features percussion from a Bodhran and the standard violin part, but the backing is a distorted electric bass and some general feedback. This may not the best song Blood Axis have ever covered, but it still fits well into the groups evolving neo-folk sound.

ANTONIO TESTA/ ALIO DIE "HEALING HERB'S SPIRIT" CD 1999 CROWD CONTROL ACTIVITIES
Earthy and shamanic (organic), rich textures slither, coil around the ears (embrace), leading the listener into all the remote pockets of unexplored terrain, a full-bodied excursion, and yet the sound is not cluttered or overwhelming. Quite the contrary, the fascinating collage of instruments (including Woodblock rototom, bone flute, rainstick, Tibetan bowls, water pumpkin, bamboo... stones, shells and leaves...electronics, samples, etc.) helps to create a diverse canopy under which the mind fills with images of forests (trees sighing...), wind and sky, of the residual ambience of eons long dead but still infused with vitality. The result is an expanding array of sounds enmeshed in the fabric of ritual, of sonically soothing spiritual diversions that lead to transcendence, peaceful and yet invigorating. Ah, but within this framework, the heart of the disc grows quite dark, leery, more mysterious...it is a prismatic travelogue incorporating many sonic colors or lacks thereof (reds, yellows, grays...blacks...) in a haunting and sporadically time-resistant cocoon...time standing still...losing meaning. A nice transition that keeps the listener always attentive. Calm, though quite invigorating...—JC Smith (Reprinted by permission from Sideline Magazine: www.sideline.com)

ASMOROD (FRA) "DERELICT" CD 1999 TESCO ORGANISATION
Asmorod create dark sonic scapes with a power electronics radiance, a scintillating balance of ancient, cathedral ambience (quite cavernous) and tension-laced noise. "Suspended Motion" opens with looped female vocals of a foreign (to me, at least) disposition. The darkness resonates, low hum shadows, pierced by a light that slashes, the wound secreting radiation. The exquisite sonic clarity (I'm thinking Stratvm Terror—Pain Implantations, though the impact is of a more restrained, insidious design) heightens a plethora of sonic possibilities: dense, moody clouds that shroud one in futility; the fluttering wings of unknown beasts; skittish, elastic tones that split the sonic belly, the dull throb of blood and viscera spilling forth...The track is held together via the despairing, underlying synths; synths that carry immense, mood-altering weight-a cocoon of melancholy. "Vaporscreen" follows, another foreboding synth backdrop unveiled, this time augmented with a sound akin to the slo-mo smack of wood to the back of the head and mysterious, layered samples that lead into torturous desperation samples—something hideous is about to transpire...An ambience of unease is achieved, tension again (so much tension), taut and stretched to the tearing point, static voices threaded underneath, threatening to snap...The sound of a thunderclap as heard from some buried vantage point opens ""Glass No Kamen II: Vitreous Structures," before sonar blips introduce one of the most hunkered down in the heart of darkness synth lines imaginable—this one is so despondent I can feel the itch of the razor against my wrist. Brittle bones are then crunched underfoot as the listener is led through moist terrain, the moisture seeping through my speakers, reeking of blood, urine and tears, so many tears. The scope of hopelessness conveyed by these sounds is beyond comprehension...and then, distorted vocals into distortion loops and more samples...This is such finely honed music, every iota helping to weave tale of impending doom and imminent defeat. Finally, the track ceases amidst static, the sonar blips gone spastic, screams of feedback, strange, haunted voices...Brilliant, worth the price of admission, go out and buy this disc NOW! "Anaesthetic Season" is a change of pace, a less tense endeavor (a downshifting of aural gears), afloat on a rickety boat, courting a watery (back to the womb), somber ambience that eventually grows a bit worrisome-hesitant, uncertain-toward the end, no comfort found in the gentle tide as enigmatic synths and a disturbing, repeated sample ("scandal, murder, insanity, suicide") address the listener with tones of unease...The bonus track, "Glass No Kamen I: Collapse," re-establishes the Asmorod mandate of overwhelming tension, no respite for the curious, amidst whining feedback, brooding synths, static and distorted noise that sounds like laughter...An astonishing release-what more can I say?! —JC Smith

ATARTAXIA (ITA) "LOST ATLANTIS" CD 1999 CRUEL MOON INT'L
On Atartaxia's follow up CD to the last Cruel Moon offering, much the same musical territory is covered here, hence depending on you thoughts on the former album (and most probably the albums preceding that released on different labels) I imagine that you would come to the same conclusion here. Exploring all aspects of ethereal medieval styled folk song writing (or pagan opera as the band describe it), on this album the group delves into the mythos and mystery that surrounds the legend of the sunken city...Atlantis. All in all 11 tracks are featured ranging in length from as short as 40 seconds up to 11 minutes, giving the CD an overall length of just over 50 minutes. Stand out tracks include the sorrowful acoustic tune and operatic soaring vocals of 'Aperlae' and again the acoustic guitar is used on 'Agharti' but now having a more classical/ folk approach and more richly scored background. 'Oduarpu' has the sound of a doom metal type song minus the vocals & heavy guitars, yet arriving at a similar depressing emotion.
On minor complaint is in relation to the occasional use of programmed drums and overly synthetic keyboards. Given that the majority of the music is sung or played on real instruments it gives the overall pieces a rich organic flavour which is slightly diminished via the use of synthetic sounding programming. This case is illustrated where the title track has the opportunity to be a powerfully sounding marching

folk tune, however the programming simply lets it down with a weak drum sound. I personally am not going to say that I am totally enthralled with this group (or this style for that matter), but this is more to do with my slant on what music I myself appreciate. In their favour the group is genuine and sincere in all aspects of their art being accomplished in writing, playing & singing departments. Certainly seek this out if the above description is at all enticing.

ATOMINE ELEKTRINE (SWE) "ARCHIMETRICAL UNIVERSE" CD 1999 YANTRA ATMOSPHERES
Keeping up with all of Peter "raison d'etre" Andersson's outputs with all of his projects is almost becoming a bit of a challenge within itself, but that is not to say the results are not rewarding! This is the second CD by this project but sadly I missed out on the first CD released on CMI which has now been long deleted (I can only hope for Mr Karmanik or someone else to furnish it with a repressing). This disc being released on Peter's own label could be broadly defined as space trance, electronic ambience, but can be further categorised into two types of tracks ie: those with simply a space ambient trance focus, or the others with electro/ techno beat styled focus. While there are melodies tinged with elements of sorrow, mostly speaking the music is hypnotic and soothing lulling the listener in the womb of the vast cold void of space. Track one sets the scene of the space trance focus gradually leading into "Sagitarius Cloud" which has second above mentioned characteristic of the album. Although it may appear that the two described styles would be diametrically opposed, they do fashion themselves very well together to created a highly positive result. Of the tracks with the more techno beat elements are not really fast enough to be categorised for dance floor use, however would be more suited to a 'chill out room' type setting. Not much more to say, but if you know any of Peter Andersson's work you will be well aware that whatever he touched musically, does indeed turn to gold. Definitely one of the modern day alchemists...

ATOMINE ELEKTRINE (SWE) "ATOM EXTENSION" CDR 1999 YANTRA ATMOSPHERES
Given that the title of this is "Atom Extension" this review is going to be essentially an extension of the review above. Not being an official 3rd CD, this is a limited release (100 CDR copies) of a collection of tracks broadly composed under the Atomine Elektrine moniker. As the cover specifies it is split into two section: the first being recording around the time of the first Atomine Elektrine CD and with the second half stated as not being specifically Atomine Elektrine compositions (rather that they are mostly suited to this project more than any other of Peter's projects). Further to the above review I have also since managed to track down a copy of the debut Atomine Elektrine CD, which obviously assists in providing a review from a more knowledgable perspective.
The first section entitles "The Elementary Section" certainly has the overall aura of the debut CD with more groove trance and ambient beat driven moments than the more space ambient electronica of the second CD. Mostly the programmed beats and rhythms take to the forefront with the layers of synth treatments filling out the underlying elements of the compositions. The flow of the CD is also more based on the moment and mood of each track rather than a clear connection between one piece to the next, with this opposing to the "Archimetrical Universe" CD which is almost the opposite on all of the above accounts. One unusual element (or for Peter's works anyway) in one of the tracks ('Shining') is a distorted guitar riff, but is mixed very low in the mix along with plenty of keyboard, thus and does not become an obvious elements, whilst a vocal sample from the plays over throughout (where else but from the move 'the Shining'). 'Hyperion End Theme' takes a slightly different angle with a looped Gregorian speech and vocals, with the backing being almost neo-classical in style. "Earthly Delights in Eden of Rusty Shells" has plenty of subdued groove but composition wise it has a certain medieval, tribal, folk feel which again differs greatly from the more tech ambient feel of the following track 'Hypotension'. And it is the brief description of the above three tracks which characterised the quite eclectic nature of these recordings and the mildly changing style between compositions on the first half.
"The Extended Section" as an overview tends to be more ambient dub with a trance strain, but tracks such as "Electrokinetic" go all out (or a least more up beat than any of the other tracks) with synth generated strings and a mid paced beat and rhythm. 'Core Meltdown' works with heavy distortion to generate static driven beats and a phased out and manipulated backing which takes its time to meander through its allotted time – which in itself would be characteristic of the later half of the disc. The tracks are generally longer and more drawn out in introducing each element, whilst the earlier compositions usually get straight into it and obviously concludes more quickly. With a total paly time of around 73 minutes there is quite a bit to explore but mostly this will be one for the Peter Anderson completist fan who is willing to take the time to track a copy down.

ATOM INFANT INCUBATOR (ITA) "QUANTUM LEAPS LOST SOUNDTRACKS" CD 1999 SLAUGHTER PRODUCTIONS
First off, this disc has nothing to do with actually being lost soundtracks for any television show or movie or what-have-you; according to Marco (head of Slaughter Productions), it was just a title they (the band) decided on. Weird? Yes, it is. But the music does carry a distinctive soundtrack quality that I would like to hear more in movies; it also incorporates the pristine production and overwhelming sense of peripheral shadows subtly moving about that some of Nightmare Lodge's work embodies. "Escape" rides wood pounding against steel barrel echoed percussion and ominous synths before it all disintegrates, stumbling into a fit of cluttered ricochet percussion. The dense, fallen angel synths of "To Burn Away" lead us into a world that is beautiful and mysterious; the nervous slingshot cadences are most alluring. "Spacewalker" orbits the earth, skittering beats tethered to a satellite, the tether eventually snapping, the skittish beats subsiding as the spacewalker drifts helplessly off into the cold void of the universe. The crisp, delicate piano line of "Timeless Sonata" opens a doorway to an exotic locale cloaked in mystery, but the cloak is open for one's observation, the sounds drawing one in...Stark, anxious synths decorated with fluttering sounds grow dense in the brief, compelling landscape of "Incedere Maestoso." "The Jewel Case" contains dripping icicle synths, freeing frozen insects in the process, upon which lovely, brooding synths are layered. The whole CD is not so much dark as mysterious, a collection of compact soundtracks that trigger the brain, allowing the grey matter celluloid to unravel, images embracing emotions on the bone white cranial screen within us all. —JC Smith

AUBE (JAP) "108" CD 1998 OLD EUROPA CAFÉ
Of the Japanese noise/ experimental movement it is good to see not all groups are obsessed with S&M fetish subjects. With Aube their concept is quite simple – use a different sound source material on every release. While other Aube releases have used somatic sounds, lava lamps, steel wire etc, this release uses only sounds generated from bells. Figuring from the sound source you could wrongly assume a fairly organic sound palette, however given the electro acoustic treatments the sounds are more clinical in execution. 'Gen-Shiki' opens the CD using a resonating bleep like sound as the sound rises and falls rather than being specifically flowing. Minimal and repetitive in approach the aesthetic of adding and subtracting sound elements it the main technique utilised. Apart from the low throbbing texture 'Ni-Shou' has a spacious glacial air prior to elements of a looped reverberating gong leaping in and out of the mix. The overall sound production has avoided being load and attacking to the ear (as Japanese noise is most notorious for) and while some tones verge on being ear piercing, have been reduced in capacity to better suit the more subtle background sound textures. 'Zetsu-Mi' contains quite a warm textural flowing piece of ambience that ever so slightly gains moment over its 9 minute length, with the following track 'Shin-Soku' being similar yet containing less warmth and more looped (subdued) structures. An eastern spiritual edge is alluded to via the cover with Japanese letters and an pair of hands in prayer with the music certainly suiting (in most part) a meditative state.

BEEFCAKE (GER) "POLYCONTRALE CONTRA PUNKTE" 1998 HYMEN
With only my recent discovery of Ant-Zen and sub labels (probably discovery is the wrong word– more that I decided to start obtaining some of their items) this is one brilliant gem that I have had an extremely hard time prying out the CD player.
Also for a note, forget the name and don't let it turn you off, as I'm sure this group chose it for reasons other than related to a certain

cartoon, as any images conjured up from the name are probably far removed from cinematic break beat and cut up techno tunes on offer. Much of the music works on dual levels with a relaxing drone and flow with sometimes moody beats but more often in the cut up, sporadic, scatter gun approach. Scathing noise also make sporadic appearance but are always well placed and by no means overused. Angelic vocal flow through the backing of 'enjoy the silence' over the base of static beats, with the track 'beefcake' taking things up a notch in energetic stakes with the hyped beats accentuated by the light keyboard plucks underneath. 'In uns-hope' uses a well placed female vocal sample and brooding keyboard tune, over what is probably the most standard and retro beat on the disc, but the fazer and echo make it far from cliche. On one track (phenylethylamin) mixes superbly a classical violin passage (which I know but can't quite pick), along with a no frills lounge beat. A total orchestral sample is used for the opener of 'sein' complete with a classical piano solo with not a hint of a beat in sight throughout the whole track – a cinematic piece at its best (although I get the feeling it might have been totally sampled). Break beats are again on the menu in the next track being morphed through a variety of treatments and the flow string orchestra plays out a suspenseful piece with German radio voices entering the mix at radon. 'Wake up and believe' is a calling to all who have not been awakened to the brilliance of this DJ duo, containing a schizoid & rabid beat again over low keyboard washes, with the remaining tracks of the CD playing out in various combinations of the above described elements. While the beats contained within the music do give it a techno edge they are by no means constant repetitive base kicks of the derivative kind, and in fact in most cases don't have enough flowing passages that would make this close to danceable. These compositions are much more suited to lounging around where they can hype the mood from an otherwise stagnant morbid trance and likewise clearly demonstrates that techno can be done brilliantly without having any association with the rave type culture. There is one last thing to say about Beefcake and that is that they keep a constant focus on how they produce the compositions but the wide array of samples, sound sources and beats utilised, means each track as a very distinct sound with a crystal clear studio production. Although a release from last year this has quickly become a stable favourite of this one.

BEYOND DAWN (NOR) "IN REVERIE" CD 1999 EIBON RECORDS
The third release by Norway's Beyond Dawn (though recorded in 1996, so it actually qualifies as their second endeavor) is a refreshingly somber affair, the music stripped down to an acoustic foundation upon which the (now familiar) trombone as well as violin and other assorted sonic accoutrements decorate. Add to that the restrained, gothic-tinged vocals and the groundwork is laid. Opening with 'Need', the feel is somehow reminiscent of early 70's Bowie, not the glam eccentricities, but the acoustic dalliances, the clear, weary vocals nudged by the insistent trombone drone and sporadic guitar. The piano of the resigned "Rendezvous" paces the slow strummed guitar, a melancholic violin that feigns joy, crying over the trombone. Squiggly electronics nervously tickle the despondent guitar of "Prey." The cold, droning atmospherics of Joy Division's "Atmosphere" are heightened by the processional call of the trombone (I tell you, it's a strange, unfamiliar addition-the ubiquitous trombone-but it works, somehow, within the realm of what Beyond Dawn creates), a doubling or more of the vocals adding to the cold...atmosphere. The off-kilter "Chameleon" contains processed vocals that mingle with the somber jangly guitars, building dramatically, the more regular vocals moaning in response, injured, uncertain (and maybe a little Michael Gira inspired). Forget genre, here is a band that is, quite simply, trying to construct songs in an original manner, no matter what it takes. I can't tell you where they are going, I can only venture that whatever creative path they take, the results should be most interesting. —JC Smith (Reprinted by permission from Sideline Magazine: www.sideline.com)

BLACK LUNG (AUS)/ XINGU HILL (GER) "THE ANDRONECHRON INCIDENT" 10" EP 1999 ANT-ZEN
Stated to contain selected tracks from an upcoming movie, I'm not sure of the exact details of this flick, but essentially the release contains two long tracks, one for each side of the vinyl. Having not heard any of the outputs of Xingu Hill before I'm not sure how relevant this release is to his normal sound, but the dark atmospheres of Black Lung are still evident, albeit with a bit more of a focus on the beats & groove. Starting with some gliched noise the first track ('crimson skies and vapour trails') soon finds its elements in the mid paced dub/ techno/ beat and the groove laden backing. Easily accessible the polished sheen of the beats works on one level, while there remains an extensive underlying layers of sounds & noise to be explored on subsequent listens. The beat remains the constant in the lengthy & flowing track, with the various layers added and subtracted, gradually morphing & evolving the overall atmosphere. The glitched opening element makes another (late) appearance before the dark grooving beats and atmospheres kick in for one last round. Side two contains 'spiders web end theme' that starts with a clawing and droning sequence before the uptempo bass heavy techo kicks in. About 3-4 layers of bass lines, breakbeats and the like are used to make a complex structure, again utalising layers of background textures. Later in the track the dark cavernous background atmospheres rise to the foreground (as the beats are gradually removed), leading the track into its ultimate conclusion. Dark, trancelike beats and grooves and uptempo techno break beats ensure a great listen complimented by obscure cover art that suits the music very well. Recommended.

BLACK LUNG (AUS) "THE WONDERFUL AND FRIGHTENING WORLD OF BLACK LUNG" DCD 1999 ROLLERCOASTER RECORDINGS
New recordings from this aussie project spanning 120 minutes of music over 2 discs, and with the conspiracy theories still being part of the sleeve text they provide interesting reading whilst listening to the music. As for the music Black Lung have always been somewhat of a chameleon changing from low key ambient moments to other beat driven techno sections, covering allot of ground in between. More soundtrack oriented overall, standard formats of song structure are less evident with the music looping in and out of segments, exploring every alley and highway it sees fit to traffic along the way. Hard edged distortion & purposeful glitches play a part in characterising the music, with beats presented as being clinical, robotic & emotionless as the bleeps, blips & looped samples round out the schizophrenic

---

CRIONIC MIND
Bludgeoning Bipeds Everywhere With The Extremes of Sound

GRUNTSPLATTER/SLOWVENT
"Split" $11(us) $13(wld)

GRUNTSPLATTER provide 30 minutes of grim Noise Ambient and darkened isolationist textures. Rich with subtlety and introspective horror. SLOWVENT make their debut appearance with 30 minutes of viscous Death Industrial. With thick, low end electronics, sluggish rhythmic distortions and subterranean atmospheres. Limited to 500 copies.

COMING JANUARY 2000

LEFTHANDEDDECISION - "Instinct and Emotion"

For a listing of our full distribution catalog of Experimental, Dark Ambient, Metal and beyond visit our website or write the address below

All orders in U.S. Funds only, well concealed cash or M.O. payable to Scott Candey

CRIONIC MIND
PMB 105 | 4644 Geary Boulevard
San Francisco, California 94118 USA
crionic@pacbell.net | www.crionicmind.org

sound structure in its entirety there are less ambient sections (or at least lurking low in the mix), with the majority of pieces giving birth to twisted & deformed noise/ beat mutation. Harshness has also seems like a well loved savoury snack of David Thrussel of late as a few tracks veer into blistering pure white noise stabs, that assault the listener at various times without warning. Although I personally would have liked more chilled out & bleak, ambient segments I guess there is not much to complain about when David is behind the mixing desk as the results are destined to be more than worthwhile.

BRUME (FEAT: VRISCHIKA) (ITA) "S/T" CD 1998 OLD EUROPA CAFÉ
Admittedly I don't know anything at all about this group, other than I am slightly familiar with the name 'Brume' (but not likewise with 'Vrischika'). From first listens, the overall impression appears to be a CD within the ethnic/ esoteric realms that Old Europa Cafe have had a penchant for in recent times. Mystical elements of low distant chants, hazy background textures, traditional tribal type flute passages and chimes make up some of the many elements of these experimental and somewhat improvised sound collages. Radio cut up voices are also spliced into the textural weave along with bangs and clatters of struck and manipulated (sporadic) percussion. The first track is a 19 minute meandering sprawl through the netherworld of sound that becomes more forced in certain passages which reveal scattered guitar plucks and wails (which to my ear jolts me out of a dream/ meditative state up until this section – not the best of things in my opinion). The general mild guitar sound, noise, and random percussion clatter continues well into the midst of it before returned to more ambiental pastures, where the guitar is still quite audible but retains more of a flow into the last gasping minutes. The second offering takes an approach of a more traditional tribal percussive backing, intermixed with again radio voices, a much more floating backing of washes of Indian type guitars giving off an aura of a peaceful drug soaked haze. Heavy ethno rhythm influences are abound in 'Huescha' containing various tape loops and found sounds with the following track taking a similar yet stripped back stance, containing a more menacing undercurrent. 'Lost in Molecular Electronic' might indicate a sound palette quite removed from the other tracks, and rightly so being solely based on charged static loops and manipulations. This more electronic type sound is continued into 'Fanehuset' while 'An Introduction to Stability' gets an almost cut up techno feel (without the 'doof' beats) much like some the backing noise sections of Beefcake's music. The final track chooses to take a more introspective feel with the haunting tune and folding and overlapping backing, ending what is a diverse and varied journey in music exploration and experimentalism. Black A5 card sleeve and limited to 500 means your will have to search via the normal suspects for this one.

CANAAN (ITA) "WALK INTO MY OPEN WOMB" DCD 1998 EIBON RECORDS
The second release by Italy's Canaan expands on the style (darkened, pristine doom) and format of their exquisite first release, Blue Fire, an expansion presented on two discs: The Apathy Manifesto Chapter 1: Slavery, and Chapter 2: Deception. The finger-picked, crystals on black ice guitar-lines may be the distinguishing element here, but it's the instrumentals (almost every other song on each disc) that raise Canaan above the abyss of which most doomsayers reside, and I don't mean just some little filler link between songs: these are fully sculpted excursions down different dark sonicscape paths that pack depth, power and mood-altering despair—they are of a quality most creators of black ambience would envy. Slavery is highlighted by the cavern scoured eeriness of "The Glass Shield" and the restrained power and majesty of the title track, a power accentuated by vocalist Mauro's (he's also the head of Eibon Records) varied, assertive yet somber approach. Deception opens with Mauro in melancholic disillusionment while tombstone caressing waves of thick guitars fill the "Codex Void"; further in, "The Rite Of Humiliation" features the bloodless timbres of shadows sliced by glass.
Throughout, the clarity and focus—be it sung or sonically whispered—are most alluring to the connoisseur of richly conceived doom and darkness; an essential release for anyone truly willing to taste the night's foreboding, sonic elixir. —JC Smith

CATACLYST (SWE) "MONUMENTS OF A RUBICUND AGE" CD 1999 YANTRA ATMOSPHERES
Another collectable CDR from Yantra Atmospheres limited to a mere 100 copies (mine is number 2 don't you know!) and yet another side project to rasion d'etre, although this does not really count as it is a defunct collaboration project from a few years back (the other member being Johanna Rosenqvist who is now part of the power electronics project Institute).
Almost tribal EBM the first track contains manipulated female vocals keyboard washes over a slow beat pulse, drawing a fleeting comparison to certain tracks of Atomine Elektrine's first CD. The tribal beat focus continues with 'The Verge of Mortal Ground' now being is the main focus with only looped sound & vocals as the backing. 'Elwes in Sheeting Wind' slightly resemble early raison d'etre works with layers of looped factory noise, synth generated vocals and minimally sorrowful atmospheric keyboards. More dark and depressing keyboards are used on 'Rubicund Age' but are complimented by slightly forceful tribal percussive beats. 'Rubicund Cloister' is quite busy piece with many looped layered elements, including looped vocal snippets, choirs, beats and drones, being totally repetitious (not a bad thing though). Predominantly noisier textures and beats are utilised on 'The Serpent's Fang' almost stepping into noise territory, but held in check with some sporadic keyboard drones. The opening tracks makes a second appearance with a slight remix (in the beat and backing texture departments), yet it manages to remain faithful to the first version. The final track of the CD is the lengthy, 19 minutes, 'Dwarves in Hidden Realm', which is a little disappointing given a shoddy and very repetitive beat. Things barely pick up in the backing department with barely audible keyboards and a treated and looped vocal snippet (not in English). This as the ending track is a shame given the nice atmospheres evoked on the preceding tracks. This CD is not really a place to start with being introduced to Peter Andersson's music, rather for the completist fanatic. Obtain a copy if you can......

CATHARSIS (FRA)/ DRAPE EXCREMENT (GER) "HOMO HOMINI LUPUS" CD 1999 BLACK PLAGVE
I've always been a little sceptical of split releases, but possibly this is due to the affiliation that these have had within the metal scene(by where two shitty demos would be slotted on the CD format for the label to make a few bucks). Luckily this is not the case here as both sections of music were specifically recorded for this release and compliment each other pretty well. To start with a general overview, the sounds comprise of monstrous death industrial vibes tinged with elements of mild power electronics. Many tracks form both groups brought to mind the works of Megaptera and now seeing that that project is defunct these two are left to duke it out for the title.
Catharsis take to the stage first with the track 'Holywar', consisting of low machine drones prior to a slow crushing beat sequence and other manipulated noise textures. Far off in the background some tortured wails and synth tones are evident as the composition is gradually thickened with various layers of sound. Non distinguishable vocals are also presented in a wailing voice akin to BDN as the monotonous textures take the track across a 7 minute span. "...and silent sins" gives some respite with a more prominent synth passage and a swirling rhythmic backing prior to heading back into the factory driven, machine like pulse of "XI-nihil". Catharsis put the title track to sound, and while begins very distant and minimal, this is short lived as a mid ranged sustained squeal and pounding beats enter the mix and become incessantly angrier as the track unfolds. The final track for Catharsis ('fire wind') is a mid ranged swirling factory drone, again using the overlaid/ overlapped layers in the make up of the composition – no melodic moments to be found here and probably the most simplistic track on offer from the project.
Drape Excrement (who are reported to be a Soldnergeist live collaborator) take up the second half of the disc, with a rather mixed take on the death industrial vibe. Mind you they have come along way since the muddied death industrial tunes of the 'Born Dead' LP. Here the sound have a much better clarity adding to the atmospheric of the production. 'Dark Skies' has wealth of depth and breadth to the sound as it slowly rises and falls in circular drones gradually bringing new elements into the mix. A heavily treated (slowed & echoed) vocal sample remind me slightly of Inade, and with the musical backing seems indicative of some of the awesome sounds coming from the German scene at the moment. 'birds, only birds?' is more straightforward containing mildy forceful drones and a typically repeated 'true crime' type narrative snippet (which is nicely placed at various levels & points within the sound collage). Underneath the cavernous

textures of '_____ society' the track becomes somewhat orchestral with a half-played tune, symbolising the fate of the damned that it is dedicated to. Both elements of the mix become more urgent toward the finally, where chimes and church bells solidify the prophecy of the musics termination. 'Sudden Death' is a atmospheric calamity, composed by a multitude of layers of writheing sonic waves while 'Engram' has chosen to plunder a monastery, taking hostage a lone vocalist, as the serene moment of his singing is gradually it crushed under an increasing factory drone. The power electronics element is at the fore on 'anger, remember to my words' where a scathing processed voice spews forth a sermon of hatred as the static looping vibe acts as amplifying sound board – but as quickly as it starts it is over, being just over a minute in length. The final two tracks that Drape Excrement have on offer mix it up with medium dosed tones, half rhythmic beats and a distant underbelly of synth and noise treatments (being much the same as Catharsis's last track) where the tracks are all but stripped back to basics for the final moments.

To conclude grab this disc in the commemoration of the passing of Megaptera and bask in the darkness of the groups that are destined to rise to fulfil the legacy left behind.

CAUL (USA) "LIGHT FROM MANY LAMPS" CD 1999 MALIGNANT RECORDS

Arriving at the forth CD from Caul, the music finds itself in its most complete and composed form. The emphasis on dark layers has been somewhat minimised whereby they have been pushed to the background, letting the minimal and slow evolving sorrowful keyboard melodies take charge. String and wind sections replicated on a keyboard are mainly used as the basis for the compositional structure, (but are not derivative or in any way cheap sounding) along with piano and percussive elements. Distant chimes and howling winds usher in the first track as void like drones & angelic wails engulf the background (and eventually the fore) with the pinnacle reached with a single thunderous rumbling mass of sound dragging all down with it as it fades away. 'The Blood Within the Veil' takes a simplistic yet effective piano tune intermixed with a solo violin and oboe creating a suitable atmosphere. 'Thine Is The Day, Thine is the Night' uses deep percussive structure with angelic vocals, completed with distant and minimal strings which becomes more tribal in beat someway in. The following track has a more sinister tone and can be attributed to the darker drone elements allowed to make up the majority of the structure. Bleak vocal textures and noises add to the rising tension. 'By the Breath of God, All the Stars' is a mildly rousing slow classical piece based on deep horns and shrill string melody. 'Midnight's Tongue' features from memory the first spoken vocals of Brett Smith within a Caul composition. The music contains minimal backing with mainly acoustic guitar and keys, however in terms of the vocals I don't feel that they sit all that well in the mix and would have been better left out. The cavernous darkly glistening tones reappear on 'A Tapestry of Bone' prior to an extremely bleak organ hymn taking over, further continuing into 'The Twelfth Golden Swan' that is introduced and completed with shrill, unnerving tones. Just as the CD is introduced with distant howling winds, thus they returns to conclude the disc and bring the work full circle. Overall this is certainly the class of CD Caul has been threatening to make given the rate of progression between previous releases, but although I still guess some fans will be disappointed in the move away from the darker droning elements. Nonetheless a fantastic body of work and in common with past Caul CD's it is quite lengthy at over 70 minutes.

CHIRON (AUS) "EVE" CD 1999 ENERGEIA

To write a band off on one sweeping comparison is not fare to any group and lazy on a reviewer's part, but yet I am compelled to do it regardless and particularly for good reason. The comparison to be made with the music presented would be to 'the Cure' especially around the 'Disintegration' period (however I don't use this is a negative comparison I use it as a benchmark of quality musicianship). Delving more into the sound, this is high class gothic rock with enough pop sentiments to be highly accessible coming across as fresh and catchy, being far removed from the standard goth groups wallowing in there self imposed misery and depression....all for the sake of image. Also not being overly versed in this genre this has caught and held my attention over numerous listens which is very complimentary in itself and making another distinction the vocals are none similar to Robert Smith, rather that they range from commanding low, half sung sections to higher melodic parts. The second track on the disc "Ascent" accentuates the catchy motion of the song writing in the elements of drums, guitar and bass while the keys meander through the background. "Point of no return" has an almost middle eastern edge to the guitar tune giving an exotic sound which also seems to be a trademark of the guitarist as it exemplifies quite a large portion of his style. "Screaming" is slower and more of a progressive rock guise which an experimental tinge while "Night in Cairo" has a catchy bass riff as the main basis with layers of clean guitar floating lightly above and a flowing up tempo beat.   The title track "Eve" contains a nice dark atmospheric guitar, bass and keyboard layered track flowing into "Burn" that has a subdued swinging dub beat and melody and swirling guitar and keyboard treatments. A late track in the album "Into Sin" uses a heavy focus on both a quick programmed beat and keyboard, with guitars playing a minimal role rather being used to flesh out the sound scape. All in all there are 12 tracks over a play time of just over 50 minutes, which only falters slightly on a couple of tracks were a mild case of gothic pretentiousness gets the better of them. As a last note I believe that members of this group used to be part of another band by the name of Ikon, which should give some of you a bit better idea of the genre this inhabits. Even is this is not a style you would normally listen to check this out anyway as you might be surprised.

CHOD (FRA) "ISHTAR AUX ENFERS" 7" 1999 ATHANOR

Chod is a fairly new project of which I was first made aware on the exceptional 'Lucifer Rising' compilation CD. While simplistically you could call Chod a death ambient group, that would not do them justice as they hold quite a complex sound. Probably 'archaic ambient' would be a much better term by the atmospheres they present as there is nothing 'modern' sounding in any of their works. Track 1 (title track) starts with a sampled female choral vocal and throbbing undertone, prior to chime percussion and roaring, fiery tones being presented in a very primal/ ritualistic guise. Track 2 ('le deluge Babylonien') uses slow and heavy tribal drums, braying of wolves and a flute tune over what sounds like a field recording backdrop (which certainly adds to the breadth and scope of the soundscape). Towards the conclusion of the piece some more rhythmic hand percussion is used along with a looped foreign vocal sample. Pressed on clear brown vinyl and with a nicely designed card cover these two tracks are exclusive to this 7", with a debut full length CD on Athanor planned for imminent release.   Seemingly coming from nowhere, I'm sure Chod will become a well known name soon enough.

COMPULSION MAGAZINE ISSUE 3# (ENG) 1998

Another fine publication which has no linkage to the standard 'fan-zine', other than in concept & philosophy. Having the appearance of a handbook rather than magazine it is a professionally printed with gloss cover and glued/ bound spine. The visuals, layout and presentation are simplistic yet effective with the main brilliance of this coming in the form of the interviews, articles and reviews. With a sub-title of "surveying the Heretical" it gives an idea of the slant, maintaining a non-censored forum for the expression of ideals and concepts. I found the interviews to be particularly well informed and the answers to often be very thought provoking especially the one with R.N Taylor (of the band Changes). The review section is jam packed and gives a snapshot of what has being going on over the past few years (with older reviews mixed with newer ones). While there is allot of music & subjects covered that I am well informed on, it also covers a wide array of topics which I am not so versed with, adding to the reading experience. To give an idea of content it features: Blood Axis, Somewhere in Europe, James Manson's Universal Order, Jim Rose Circus Sideshow and many others. All in all a great read that will keep you engrossed for many hours on end.

CONVERTER (USA) "SHOCK FRONT" CD 1999 ANT-ZEN

Converter is the noisy, rhythmically annihilating half-brother to the doused in darkness industrial disarray of Pain Station, both fathered by Scott Sturgis. Opening with the seething rumble and squeal of angry machines, "Conqueror" is then stomped under the heavy percussive stomping of giants; once the percussion kicks in, an exercise in slingshot rhythm dynamics overlaid with a coat of fuzzy distortion. The relentless assault is on and there is no mercy to be had. "Cannibals" devours the speakers via a rabid steel-brush scouring of an unknown machine upon which raw metallic rhythms continue to chomp and grind, chewing, digesting and excreting in cannibalistic glee. "Sacrifice" gnaws in a subtly abrasive mode, rhythms multiplying as the track progresses, joined by hacking static and an exhalation loop, as if the machines are alive-so much of this incorporates the machines as a sentient entity, as if they really are alive! (And then there is the humming beehive towards the end of the track, an image of bees the size of dogs, adorned in metallic armor, fervently buzzing, attack impending...) "Memory Trace" resides in a vacant alley, the ambience of acid rain corroding iron fire escapes and steel garbage dumpsters. "Deadman (Perdition)" scalds the senses with catastrophic eruptions of noise lubricated with machine oil and sweat, fuel-injected adrenaline and blood pulsing through the metal pipe tunnels of the post-apocalyptic wasteland. The percussive typhoon presented here fits perfectly into the harsh Ant-Zen sonic mindset, seeping into power electronics, but with purpose and a rhythmic foundation. Comes in a metal 'booklet' (two slabs o' metal, my friends) encased in a standard jewel-case, most appealing; the weight feels good in my hands, and perfectly compliments the enclosed music. —JC Smith

CRADLE-GRAVE (AUS) "SAPER VEDERE" CD 1999 HEARTLAND RECORDS
With too few Australian releases reviewed in these pages I am glad to say this is an item that I have been highly impressed with and incidentally does come from these fine shores. Cradle-Grave being a group that I had not previously been aware of play an evocative form of industrial/ electronica which swiftly grasped my attention on initial listens. Generally dark and brooding there is a lot of interplay between synth generated lines and drum sequenced sections, alongside more traditional sounds of piano, violins chimes, bells and the like (albeit still synth generated). Loosing the sequenced drums (not that you would really want to) would give rise to pure dark ambient works that could draw a distant comparison to Desiderii Marginis or other similar groups. Some of the moods evokes also tend to be slightly gothically tinged without any hint of pretentiousness. Vocals are kept sparse in the mix (only on 4 tracks) where the vocalist whispers or half sings a few selected lines & passages in the background. One track ('you are of the broadest skys') becomes more tribal/ classical in approach being akin to the recent Sephiroth CD with this lineage to CMI is also evident with the cover art, being quite similar in aura to that certain look – dark images, dark blue/grey tones, foreign text etc. The album containing 10 tracks, two bonus remixes of two of these are included at the end which are obviously slightly more beat oriented. Given I got this right on deadline I thought a short review was better than none at all. I recommend this CD highly.

DAGDA MOR (GER) "AGENT PROVOCATEUR" LP 1999 TESCO ORGANISATION
Having not heard any of Dagda Mor's earlier material (other than a compilation track) I must say that they have come up with a very good blend of death industrial and power electronics which is definitively German is sound. "You will not ridicule, you will not argue with me, you will not be friendly, you will be aloof...watch me suspiciously" is the repeated vocal sample of 'Kollaboroator' with low throbbing textures that introduces the first side of the heavy weight vinyl. Next up 'Filled with Hatred' takes a power electronics aesthetic with agitated processed vocals and mid ranged yet slightly subdued sound attack. Scaping narcissistic sounds and drones encompass a total aura of disdain on 'G.M.R', again utalising processed vocals and sample drowning in the sound mix. Incessant pounding beats and gradually tweaked noise/ drone layers & echoed/ processed vocals illustrate the themes of 'we observe and we kill' however this is purely from a sound perspective as there is little if no opportunity to follow the lyrics given their presentation. 'E-D-O-M' is both cavernous and atmospheric with most tones being presented in the 'distance' of the mix. Cascading waves and warped sounds fill out the breadth of sound yet never becoming to overpowering, making it a classy slab of pure death industrial. The title track and opener to side two is nothing short of brilliant being a very militant sounding industrial anthem due to the percussive/ marching basis, as slabs of sound are thrown in for good measure, all whilst a lone voice informs us "you have 15 seconds to comply". Static overlapped and overdriven noise makes up much of the sound of 'Night', with much the same being found on 'Mind Scan' except for a bit more of a storming/ whip lashing structure and distorted vocal snippets. 'Sturmruf' takes yet another sound approach using a slow repetitive neo-classical type key tune, low spoken German vocals, scattered crowd cheering, vocal samples and underlying deep atmospheric tones (mind you it is a very good track if I didn't already mention it). The final offering on the wax ('The Coming Race') is an attacking noise loop & processed vocals which brings the sound of the LP full circle, showing a great mix of the earlier mentioned power and death elements. Another solid quality release in all aspects from the hands of the Tesco Organisation.

DECA (ITA) "PHANTOM" CD 1998 OLD EUROPA CAFÉ
This is another Italian project I know little of apart from the name and I am at odds to how to describe this music. The opener is literally all over the place being entities "Extraterrestrial" and split into for parts. Synth generated low key noise gradually breaks into flight with a space inspired keyboard run and programmed up beat drums which seems to remind me of a Mortiis side project Fata Morgana (I'm not sure yet if this is a good or bad thing). Part two reveals more textural sound manipulation prior to another composed keyboard tune/ drum sequence which is not really dark in terms of ambient styled music as it is almost like listening to only the keyboard & drum machine section of a goth metal band. The distant and discordant piano tune of part 3 work better to my ear as does the keyboard drones of part 4. 'Vision of Faith' has drawn out sinister edge but the obvious snyth generated noise textures and again the programmed beats, this time with vocals tends to give visions of a guy in a studio rather then painting a picture for the mind. While the title 'Vision of Flesh' of one of the tracks conjures up some dark imagery, this composition is far from dark, being unfortunately quite cheesy in the style of a keyboard goth band. The final two tracks do a little better with some dark sound manipulations and an understated keyboard tune. Neither fantastic nor downright awful, this CD falls somewhere in between.

DESCENT MAGAZINE VOLUME 5 THE DEATH ISSUE (USA) 1999
Just flicking through the pages of this mag has me wondering what exactly I am doing with this thing! Descent 5# has a pristine and immaculate layout with stunning images and background textures, the majority in dark shades of grey and hearty serving of black. The size has slightly altered from previous efforts in more of a square than rectangular size, with the cover presented in shades of blue and silver print and the whole lot printed on quality heavy weight paper (and card for the cover). In terms of content I have watched this magazine over the past few issues shift focus from death and black metal to more a eurocentric slant by including ambient, industrial, neo classical/ apocalyptic folk sounds coming from those territories. While there still a handful of metal bands featured the main interest for people into Spectrum would be the featured artists such as: Blood Axis, Coil, Der Blutharsch, Dream into Dust, Ernte, Genocide Organ, Turbund Stermwerk, Valefor, Boyd Rice among others. This is filled to capacity with information and reviews, to the point where it only gives rise on one criticism...and that is in relation to that the majority of the text has been reduced to such an extent it sometimes becomes difficult to read, especially when overlaid over changing background textures. However given the magazine is still 64 pages in length I gather the text reduction would have been a necessity to retain all interviews and keep printing costs in check (regardless, really a minor point in the grand scale of things). Both angles of music and philosophy are contained in the line of questioning and come across as extremely well informed and thought out. The abundance of contributors likewise assists in providing different styles of focus between interviews and reviews. This is a supreme issue beyond any comparison to fanzines and likewise to a swag of other 'professional' magazines out there.

DER BLUTHARSCH (AUT) "DER SIEG DES LICHTES IST DES LEBENS HEIL" CD 1998 WKN /WORLD SERPENT
After gaining quite a bit of notoriety in his last (now defunct) duo project "..the moon lay hidden beneath a cloud", Albin Julius has gained

quite a bit of respect with his new solo formation 'Der Blutharsch'. For those unfamiliar, Der Blutharsch are essentially one of the main rising acts in the neo-classical/ apocalyptic folk movement, which has been gaining rising recognition of late. This CD is not Der Blutharsch's first release as there has been a 10" ep, 7" ep and 5x7" box set, however as these items were ridiculously limited (between 2-300 copies each) this will be most easily obtainable item for a new listener. I believe that this CD contains most of the tracks off the 5 x 7"ep box set with reworked version and other songs not featured on that set. The music itself is very varied in tone and composition ranging from rousing marching hymns juxtaposed against more brooding classical/ folk moments, even to the point that the CD opens with an original recording of a traditional German folk type song. On a whole, the compositions consist of a varied mix of synthesised sounds, sampled & looped classical pieces, pounding marching drumming, Germanic voice samples and monotone spoken vocals. Overall I don't think the music could be described as anything other than 'historic' in feel, with the sound and aura being highly convincing in production particularly heightened with the use of era recordings. Almost no information is provided about the disc whatsoever, with no title details, track listings, or recording information being printed (other than a label address). All I can really tell you (other than not much!) is that the disc contains 16 tracks over a 66 minute length. The artwork of the cover is printed in silver on high quality stark black card, detailing a historic battle illustration. Over this image the Der Blutharsch logo is cleverly printed in clear gloss and can only be viewed from certain lighting angles. Although the CD is varied in sound and theme, it is brought together in such a way that it has an impeccable flow, engulfing the listener in a celebration of elements of past European history. For those who already know the music of Albin's previous project, this will not disappoint, and for the rest this is a great place to start with his current musical direction.

DER BLUTHARSCH (AUT) "GOLD GAB IAC FUR EISEN" VIDEO/MCD 1999 WKN/ WORLD SERPENT
Seems as though the neo-classical/ neo-folk movement is constantly trying to outdo itself with packaging and presentation (with the fan ultimately paying for these indulgences). This little number is housed in a military green leather replica, silver and black embossed box, containing green slip cases for both the video and CD, and additionally with a booklet of live images. All items are immaculate in presentation and featuring such images as spear endowed warriors, sigal runes and an iron cross. Opening the CD is a shrill whistle and someone announcing "Actung...Der Blutharsch" in a commanding yell (which is credited to being Boyd Rice). The first actual track is the era recording track (which also opened the "Der Seig...." CD), then it is onto the real live section which consists of a DAT background recording of samples, keys and vocal snippets, overlayed with live militant drumming and live deadpan spoken vocals. Most of these tracks I seem to remember from when I saw Der Blutharsch live (see the gig review elsewhere) but obviously not all of them as this live recording only spans 26 minutes. The CD does include two tracks of 'Der Sieg...' CD and the anthemic reworkings of a couple of 'TMLHBAC' tracks (but now with more vocals than the original), however I am not sure if the other tracks are renditions of new or older compositions. In terms of sound production, while the following in not really a major complaint, there does seems to be separation in the sound with the live drumming and vocals tending to stay load and high in the mix while the DAT recordings get somewhat buried. The set list on the video features the same tracks as the CD but being complimented with footage shot throughout the Der Blutharsch 1998 European tour. The visuals for the opening track (the era recording) take on somewhat of a 'holiday shoot' with various shots of Der Blutharsch and Co. (which includes Douglas P, Boyd Rice and others) in various cities and locations. With the actual live stuff it is filmed from many angles and heavily bathed in dark glowing lights to add to the atmosphere. Post production has then spliced and overlaid the footage, finally finishing it with a grainy presentation. For the live shows it features John Murphy on percussion and both Albin Julius and Klaus on vocals and again with Albin contributing some additional percussion (This slightly differs to when I saw them live as only Albin was present out front with vocals). Again the separate gig review elsewhere will give a good idea of the groups stage presence and presentation. Overall this is quite a pricey item but I'm glad all the same that I purchased a copy.

DEUTSCH NEPAL (SWE) "EROSION" CD 1999 STAALSPLAAT
After signing something like a 4 or 5 CD deal with Staalsplaat, Lina Baby Doll has finally got the first of these CD 's off the ranks after quite a lengthy break from his last release on CMI. This does vary quite a bit from the established Deutch Nepal sound however still holds a distinctive style inherent in Lina's work. While I would dearly like Lina to pursue a style like the sounds on an earlier track entitled "Gouge Free Market" it would appear that he is both developing as an artist an is willing to explore a lot more territory with his works. The opener (and incidentally the title track) uses a creepy distorted horn and keyboard sound with low deathly wailing type vocals which are very much like what Roger K has used in BDN works. Never failing with providing totally weird and indescribable vocal snippet samples, "Surgery II" features one such vocal snippet over a background of a slow heartbeat pounding and scattered hypnotic sounds. "Collapsing Surface" spans over 13 minutes and on face value is straightforward and repetitive, but on closer audile scrutiny it shows the lightly composed clanging sounds are gradually overlayed and shifted to create a myriad of shifting rhythms as elements are gradually introduced and subtracted. We are treated to some croonings by Lina himself on "How Low..." and while not a true singer by any means it does result in a nice atmosphere with the undertow of keyboard treatments and vocal chants. "Your Just a Toy" is nothing but a totally off the wall sample of a 1930's-40's musical complete with a dreamy orchestra and male/ female duet. With absolutely no treatments or alterations this just has me scratching my head in disbelief at the reasoning behind it inclusion, but I guess that is Lina for you?! "Static" is featured as a highly repetitive yet rousing rhythmic track, which is much more akin to Deutch Nepal's earlier works than the remainder of this album. The conclusional track "Faint Retard" somehow manages to portray its title very, very well, with a dark yet slightly off centre composition of sounds, pounding beats and quirky rhythm. The packaging is definitely homage to Lina's statements that there is not content in the music other than artistic merit, as the CD photos do not point to any established look or themes prevalent in so much of post industrial/ ambient culture. No doubt with future releases Lina will again take us on an weird journey into his avantgarde world of music.

DEATH IN JUNE (ENG) "TAKE CARE AND CONTROL" CD 1998 NER OZ
Well, DIJ have certainly taken off on quite a different and interesting tangent with their latest release. On this album Douglas P has enlisting the services of Albin Julius from Der Blutharsch, with this certainly shows in the direction change. While much of the trademark DIJ sound has been brought about via acoustic guitars and understated half sung vocals, this is much more in the neo-classical/ apocalyptic folk guise. The vocals however are still present in most of the tracks and as always poetic and insightful.
"Smashed to Bits (in the Peace of the Night)" opens with a searing noise loop before distant horns usher in an orchestral string section, setting the classical tone of much of the album. "Little Blue Butterfly" is still very DIJ in flow with a chorus/ verse/ chorus of morose vocals, but instead of a main acoustic guitar it is substituted with pound of a tympani heartbeat, folk percussion and synth generated tune. A heavy basis on the lower ranged stringed instruments of the orchestra, only lightly filled out with samples, vocals and piano repetition "the Bunker" is quite a slow track, more ambient than aggressive and incidentally is featured twice on the album, one with and one without vocals. "Kameradschaft" simply by virtue of a full and rich production has taken the traditional DIJ acoustic guitar based track to new heights, overlayed with various layers of vocals, bells, chimes and keyboard generated instruments, being both tragic and sinister in subtle anger. Both romantic and militant in morose celebration, "Frost Flowers" has both a low industrial vibe and classical flow and kettle drums and floor toms pound away somewhere in the distant background alongside samples and choir like vocals. The militant sentiments of the proceeding track are fully realised on "A Slaughter of Roses" with the heavy martial percussive basis, provocative samples, scattered industrial noises and poetic vocal sermon. "The November Men" is a surreal ambient and somewhat experimental passage with both vocals and backing being purposefully subdued. Other gems that contain the classical/ apocalyptic sounds are to be found on tracks "Power has a Fragrance", The Odin Hour" and "Despair" with the later being a supreme orchestral number with soaring female vocals with the forever present martial percussion. Classic DIJ, complimented with a new direction......

DREAM INTO DUST (USA) "THE WORLD WE HAVE LOST" CD 1999 ELFENBLUT
This CD is quite hard to put into words.....the sound seems to be constantly changing & evolving, yet at the same time has the perception of being a photo that has frozen a moment in time forever (as if to represent a forlorn image of the past). Probably much of this perception comes from both the mix of style contained in the music and the images of the cover which are although early wartime shots, don't seem to be celebrating or condemning the concept of war, rather illustrating its pure reality. (Or alternatively maybe they are a symbolic representation of the philosophy behind the CD's title?).
On with the music..."Maelstrom" (the opener) is a swirl of plucked & bowed violins, menacing horns and a creepy undercurrent of industrial chaos, prior to flowing into the cleanly strummed guitar, cold half sung vocals of "Cross the Abyss" which then gradually morphs into an industrialised gothic/ doom type song (but which is not derivative of either of the said scenes). And there you have it within the first two tracks.....it is this said intermixing of styles (be those from ambient, industrial, slight goth and doom tinges to subdued neo-classical/ apocalyptic folk) makes for almost new genre in which I can't really compare this to much at all. It is as if you took away half of any of the compositions makeup it would could potentially be placed into any of the above categories, yet when overlaid together makes appropriate descriptive terminally quite elusive. Poetic vocals are included in many of the compositions, but never being overstated, rather acting as a minimalist narrator with the words being spoken or at other times half sung. Such an example is "Mercury Falling" with a marching drone sequence, drudging bass that seeps into the plucked & strummed acoustics and myriad of overlapping sound textures of "Nothing but Blood". Crescendo type moments are attained on "Farewell to Eden" which has a heightening effect to the more sombre mood of the other compositions and particularly in this instance sounding off against the factory industrialised sinister tones of the preceding track "Enemy at the Gates". Overall I would characterise the mood of this CD to be bleak and introspective yet it still remaining a challenging and always an interesting listen that is definitely worthy of your time.

ENDURA (ENG) "ELDER SIGNS" DCD 1999 RED STREAM
Stephen Pennick and Christopher Walton are the sonic alchemists behind the paradoxical ruminations of Endura, transforming rich, illusory tones of an ancient, eclectic design into insidious, deceptive tapestries of malignant, Lovecraftian eeriness...and vice versa. Their treks into the unlit caverns of the unconsciousness inspire wonder as well as dread (another Lovecraft reference, from The Call Of Cthulhu: "The most merciful thing in the world, I think, is the inability of the human mind to correlate all its contents"-this seems to be a starting point for Endura...). Elder Signs is a masterful 2CD set collecting the first two releases (Dreams Of Dark Waters and The Light Is Dark Enough) along with compilation materiel derived from the same period; there is also, as far as I can tell, one track ("Stay Not The Tides") exclusive to this release.
The title track from Dreams Of Dark Waters opens disc I, moist and dripping with ritualistic atmosphere, vocals summoning dark specters of the mind via unknown languages, storms brewing discontent on the bleak horizon; tormented, guttural mewling from the throat of one who has seen too much, one in touch with the animal within (primal codes...deciphered) follow...According to the press release, the first 30 minutes of Dreams Of Dark Waters is the first 30 minutes of music Endura ever recorded; there is a rawness, an uninhibited nature to the random progression of the disc: there are no barriers, only vast mindscapes and a willingness to peer into the shadows, seeking secret knowledge and a grim understanding of the black mysteries of our world, and of one's self. The disc flows like a dream, loosely threading together the illogical wanderings from within the corridors of the mind: bombastic music augmented with crying babies, sacrificial gifts to the memory (or hopeful resurrection) of Cthulhu, in "Intra-Uterine Sabbat"; peering into the prismatic, hallucinatory, sample-laden haze of "Colours"; stern synths dancing with moaning apparitions during the restrained percussion of "Stelluris"; the tattered, cloaked in incense percussion and haunted vocal accompaniment mocked by the slithery, cobra charmed synths of "Dance Of Qulielfi"; the nails in the shaven scalp wail and cluttered ambience groan of "The Frozen Moon"; the cascading shadow synths and hollow whispers of the ghostly "Twilyte Language"; the rabid legions of demons and dead souls in a cannibalistic frenzy at the foot of whatever is "Nailed To The Cross Of Pluto." As a first release, Dreams Of Dark Waters is nothing less than a phenomenal introduction to the idiosyncratic nuances inherent in Endura, laying out a blueprint that has been expanded and refined on future releases. Disc I is fleshed out (and then skinned alive...) with a few compilation tracks, including the cataclysmic mind eruption/disruption interrogation (torture) of the horrific "Biomechanical Soul Journey," as well as the ancient folk musings overtaken by brooding synth swells that promise to raise unknown monstrosities intent on devouring the musicians whole during "The Last Pylon."
Disc II commences with desolate wind chimes (which are threaded throughout) before taut, dramatic synths and marching percussion lead us confidently through the shadowy terrain of "The Stars Are Right." The Dark Is Light Enough is a more gothic tinged (not in the traditional sense, more in the ambience that prevails throughout) and direct exploration, still rich with the ebony textures initiated on the first release, but the refinement, as well as a stretching of the wings of gargoyles perched on the rim of Endura's abyss-like imagination (vast, bottomless...impenetrably dark), has begun. "Nevers Gift" contains somber, down-trodden vocals reciting solemn, mysterious lyrics ("Show me everything and nothing/open doorways within my mind/beyond the long forgotten thoughts/are the answers to mankind"), and layers of midnight synths, some doused in rays of beauty, some in the questioning reason of Trepidation' s furrowed brow; the tribal insistence of "Listen To Wolves" is driven by the deranged ramblings of priests of the netherworld (Stephen and Christopher, of course-conduits of treacherous incantations, or some such diabolical purpose); a suffocating, ominous synth hangs heavy on the shoulders of "He Knows The Gate"; scattered, mysterious tones reverberate amidst the declaration that "What has drowned will rise/what has risen will rule" during "In The Sea My Lord Lieth," a call to Leviathan; the title track anxiously ambles before stern synths punch through, strong vocals proclaiming "The child will endure/the dark will endure," an impression of evil heritage growing more prominent as the track climaxes. The compilation tracks on disc II begin with the distraught flute/synth and dour vocal harmonies of "The Fall Of Amor," and include (amongst others) the

---

WE DEFINITELY THINK THAT AMONG THE FORMS OF EXPRESSION THERE IS A PLACE FOR CLANDESTINE DIRECT ACTION

EXPECT NOTHING, PREPARE FOR THE POSSIBLE!
stateart@t-online.de
http://home.t-online.de/home/stateart

seething orchestral stomp augmented with a voice intoning (in dread realization) "She's a venomous child" during "Child Of Fire" and the desolate, cinematic denouement of "Stay Not The Tides," stark and so alone. Thirty exemplary tracks in all, beautiful booklet to match, a most astonishing presentation, by a most astonishing band, the enigmatic Endura. -JC Smith

EX. ORDER (GER) "THE INFERNAL AGE" CD 1999 POWER AND STEEL
"Don't speak. Don't move. I kill you." The Infernal Age is a collection of subtly sinister sonicscapes that unfold like an interrogation. The first track, "Force 77," opens with swirling, fluttering electronics upon which the sample in quotations above is barked; other samples are interlaced, all amidst an ambience that takes us into the callused heart of war, below the shrapnel sprays and reek of blood, and into the heart of cruelty, of pure evil. "Under Command" follows, radio static vocals, a plodding, dirge-like beat, and electronics spiraling into the brain like a corkscrew-a slow digging descent into complete disarray. (I can feel the wire digging into my wrists, I can feel the rusted nail tearing at my scrotum as I squirm-there is no escape.) "Logic Bomb" devours logic, a looped wall of crackling distortion over which bombs are dropped, repetitious by design, a Chinese water torture put to sound. The whole CD courts this venomous strategy, unrelenting and mind-numbing. The pure mental corruption of "Kemper Ballad" signals that all hope is nullified: a menacing low hum is augmented with samples of one who speaks of the power and confusion and perverse enlightenment of premeditated murder; the story unravels, cold and dead (think Illusion Of Safety, circa Historical), the sounds growing more prominent as the track progresses, yet never reaching critical mass.
Unnerving and brilliant, a masterpiece of psychological depravity, an audiocumentary of lucid insanity. "Test Area L.A." is constructed around surging waves of simmering, hostile ambience, just on the brink of power electronics; the ending speaks of God and violence and the melding of both. "Pain Amplifier" pulses with neuro-inflammatory insistence, the controlled, calculated design forged by the samples and sounds, rendering the listener hostage. Eight tracks of psychologically incendiary ministrations cluttered with devious samples. (Of course, as this is a side-project from Rene and Knut of Inade, one would expect nothing less than the absolutely mesmerising presentation here.) —JC Smith (Reprinted by permission from Sideline Magazine: www.sideline.com)

EXOTOENDO (FRA) "ENDORCISM PROCESS" CD 1998 OLD EUROPA CAFE
Seems as though France is stating to generate a few class acts for this scene with the above being one such group. Containing both a mystical and esoteric edge this is sinister dark ambience done with original flair. Roaring out of the abyss, the CD envelopes the room in bleak sound textures having a depth of sound seemingly stretching from the infinite point of origin to the earthly realms of listener's ear. In amongst the subdued chaos and catacomb depths, a lone male vocalist chants for redemption being gradually blanketed by waves of sound. Pan pipes and wood flutes seem to make up the start of track two underscored with a light tribalised beat and distant vocalisations as the thunderous layers pound their way into consciousness. Version 3 of 'inner picture' uses chimes and layers of vocal chants and voices being both serene and sinister, somewhere between salvation and damnation. Maybe a comparison to a less bleak early Achon Satani would be fitting for this composition. 'Between' marks the mid point of the CD being (you guessed it) in between the two parts of the disc, the earlier three versions of 'inner picture' and the later three versions of 'outer picture'. Playing out like a suspenseful tolling chime, it gives the perception of something being evoked and the inevitable change to follow. Version 1 of 'outer picture' is less dark than proceeding tracks being more tribalised with vocals hand percussive beats, chimes rattles and wind pipes. This is probably the most evident change between sections, in that the former tracks contain more dark elements while the later more tribal, however it is good to see on the last track it takes a 14 minute spiralling journey back into the silent depths. Parallels could be drawn to the likes of the spiritual minimalist ambience of raison d'etre's last CD and to other pioneers such as Lustmord, however this is yet another interpretation that intermixes various sounds to good and original effect.

FIVE THOUSAND SPIRITS (ITA) "MESMERIC REVELATION" CD 1999 CROWD CONTROL ACTIVITIES
Five untitled tracks, no guidelines for perception (no tracks entitled, say, "Into The Mystical Valley Of Petrified Dreams," or some such concoction, which could possibly influence one's perception of the sounds incorporated therein, as opposed to the bungee drop approach of untitled tracks) except in the ears of the individual listener. Raffaele Serra and Stefano Musso (Alio Die) specialize in rich, full-bodied sonicscapes that swirl and surround, tethered to crevices in the void, whether via chips of plastic crumbling off of the drone-chiseled facing of a radiant sonic plateau (track three), or sailing on obsidian waters, the horns of night extinguished by wooden mallet on steel thunder strikes (track five), or simply capturing within the layered synth net, the cadences of resolute, comforting solitude (track four). A subtly powerful journey into synth augmented silence made palpable that opens one's ears to the vast unexplored landscape within the mind...—JC Smith (Reprinted by permission from Outburn Magazine: www.outburn.com)

FROZEN FACES (SWE) "RELIGION OF HATE" 7" EP 1999 ENTARTETE MUSIKK
The first LP from the project came about by Lina of Deutsch Nepal creating a number of compositions that were too noisy for his main project, thus this side project was born. While the tracks on "Broken Sounds for a Dying Culture" were reasonable noisy industrial type tracks, the title track of this 7" is pure unadulterated power electronics. High end modulated static and drudging clatter ring out with proceeded and looped vocals sitting mid region, spewing forth words of hateful condemnation, being more threatening in intent than hell bent of delivering an all out assault. The second track on offer on the wax is a track that I guess only Lina could get away with, and it is an understatement to say that the track is far removed from the power electronics moment found on side A. Highly experimental looped rhymic beat clatter this is far more playful than it is dark with Lina's processed voice (being barely audible) ordering us to go "over the barricades" (hence the tracks title). Comes with a simple slip case, adorned with images of bullet and blade weapons just to be nice and ambiguous. Worth it for the title track alone.

GENITOR LVMINIS (SWE) DEAM ADESSA 10" EP 1999 STATEART
This new group which I know next to nothing of has been billed as an extension to the groups like Der Blutharsch. While I agree with this to an extent (and mainly due to the homage paid to a neo-classical style) the two groups are quite removed with this not being in the slightest a cheap copy of the former mentioned group. The packing of this is very nice, housed in a olive military green slip sleeve and nicely sized booklet inset, which is only really provided for aesthetic value than to give information about the recording. That aside the music itself is mournful and sinister classical compositions, using the obligatory marching snare, deep horns, stringed sections and occasional distant choirs. The compositions choose to mostly stay low key and understated rather than revealing an all out bombastic marching attack (although one track does choose this strategy). Of the four tracks presented (no titles provided) repetition is the main basis laying down the theme and gradually building on it over somewhat lengthy passages, becoming gradually more stated in overall atmosphere. It seems from the short passage provided on the insert that this release has drawn inspiration from studies in the field of esoteric European history, coming up with a nice musical result in the process.

GRUNTSPLATTER (USA) "PEST MAIDEN" 7" EP 1999 TRONIKS
Well well, Gruntsplatter on this new release have reached the level of which was hinted at on previous recordings, now being a fully fledged contender to the heavy weights of the death industrial genre. The first thing which is evident is in regards to the clarity of the recording which has more breadth and atmosphere, steering clear of being partially muddied and one dimensional. Fiery storming atmospherics make up the first track "All Fall Down" intermixed with singular sustained notes, distant tortured voices and some hefty non-descript bass rumblings. Quite ominous overall, mainly due to the track having a very solid width and decent depth to the sound

spectrum. Side B ('the watchman, the visited & the under-sexton') has an even greater level of atmospherics, interspersed with factory type death industrial with more dark droning elements. Sweeping through various phases the sound textures rise and fall in a subdued yet heavily threatening manor, being akin to listening to a hurricane muffled by bunker walls. Housed in a cover with bleak imagery & text makes this a very nice taster to the full length debut CD to be released on Crowd Control Activities early next year. Check it out…

HAZARD (SWE) "NORTH" CD 1999 ASH
With this CD I just happened across it in a store (that incidentally I rarely visit) a week after its release. To say that finding it was a surprise is an understatement, as I had not even caught wind of its imminent release. Benny had this CD scheduled as his fourth Hazard CD after two upcoming releases on both Malignant Records and Cold Spring, but it seemed these other two were pushed back in favour of getting this CD out first. For those not up to speed with this project it is the new musical face of Benny Neilson of Morthound fame (who has released one CD under the Hazard moniker on Malignant Records). Again Benny has shown with all of his musical projects he is willing to change focus and direction as he sees fit. From the outset of viewing the bleak grey packaging with writing almost indistinguishable through colour and font size, it gives an indication of the cold and bleak atmospheres held within. It is if Benny has trapped the temperature of the Antarctic within the sounds presented. Gone is the emphasis on liquidous flow of sound rather replaced by slowly creeping and unnerving tones intermixed with random low level noises and mild clatter giving off an overall atmosphere of if you were listening an impending snow storm far off in the distance or visualising a baron lake freeze with the onset of winter. Seven lengthy tracks are presented and on initial listens appears to cover a lot less ground than the debut Hazard disc, but on repeated rotations this is where the ingenuity lies giving off a hypnotic trance like effect. Between the backbone tones, subtle noise & clatter some tracks use more composed slowly repeating bass rhythms such as on "Tangled mass" while the track "The vibrating room" uses both a low vocal sample (not in English) and a 'dubbish' type beat towards its conclusion. The other two upcoming Hazard CD's are meant to again vary quite differently from this CD with one including mostly live material. I for one will be interested in whatever Hazard comes up with given the quality of the first two releases thus far.

HOLOCAUST THEORY (USA) "INCEPTION OF ERADICATION" CD 1998 POSSESSIVE BLINDFOLD RECORDINGS
A powerful release from America's premier purveyors of doom industrial cum apocalyptic fury cum pummelling ferocity, Holocaust Theory. The veil has been removed: the soul-wrenching darkness of their first release, Proclaimed Visions, has been modified, mutated, and grown quite aggressive on their sophomore release, Inception Of Eradication. A more noisy ambience is present, infiltrating everything from the prevalent, looped, militaristic machinery percussion; to the blood-soaked synths; to the distinctly distorted, uniquely enunciated (though sparse) vocals. "Rain Phase 5 (The Six Stages Of Holocaust)" sets the stage, a turbulent downpour of torrential electronics, both beautiful and fierce. "As Death Approaches" comes in the standard, ominous stomp and clattering electronics version, and the shattered glass sheen of the completely manipulated into indistinguishability "vacuum mix" by Gridlock. The "Man Vs. Machine" trilogy ("1A," "2A," and "3A") portends an epic, futuristic playground/battleground in which man and machine duel for supremacy; the caustic electronics and shellshock percussion of this masterpiece renders the listener weary from the audacious onslaught. That's only a sampling of the 13 tracks to be perused on this outstanding disc, easily one of the finest examples of American industrial with European flair (specifically, the aggro-noise found on Ant-Zen—in fact, there is a great, spitting bullets remix of "Cig" by one of A-Z's favorite noisemeisters, Noisex's Raoul Roucka); most American bands do not have the testicles to chew up this much shrapnel splattered noise, spit it out and chew it up again. Holocaust Theory bare their canines and demand more…—JC Smith (Reprinted by permission from Outburn Magazine: www.outburn.com)

I-BURN (ITA) "IPERTERMIA" 10" EP 1999 STATEART
This is the second release of this very promising project from Italy, after the release of their debut CD (which was incidentally in two different versions on two different labels). The material presented here are tracks of nicely dark and foreboding layers of death industrial/ manipulated noise (derived from guitars, samples and PC's) that gradually rises to elements of overloaded intensity. While this does get quite noisy in parts I would not say that it gets forceful enough to be passed off as power electronics. The first side of the 10" (which contains the title track) commences with building pulsating and throbbing tones complimented with mild static frequencies. A guttural pounding beat towards the middle of the track takes to the fore before the second wave of more forceful static noise kicks in to lead the tracks to its conclusion. Side B opts for three shorter tracks and the first track 'HCE' has more of a cold glacial sound that is not a static driven as the opener. 'Corticate' being a little over three minutes consists of a number of simplistic noise loops (overlapped at various points) and again static interludes. The last track to be featured ('Re-Prophesyng Non-Motion') takes a slightly different take on I-Burn's sound via the inclusion of a mid paced pounding rhythmic beat over the gradually boiling background tones. This release is quite a bit louder than the debut CD and gone are any initial comparisons initially made between I-Burn and Brighter Death Now. With a number of CD's and collaborations in the pipeline I look forward to future output with baited breath.

IMMINENT STARVATION (GER) "NORD" CD 1999 ANT-ZEN
There was a hell of lot of hype that surrounded the metapophysis of Imminent Starvation's sound from their debut CD to this, the second release, and while I have not yet heard the debut CD 'Human Dislocation' I have nothing but praise for this disc. Starting with the packaging it suits the music perfectly, presented in tones of silver and blue, and might I add that only S.Alt has the ability to use pictures of river reeds and to fit them perfectly into the overall look of a CD such as this. For those unaware of the music Imminent Starvation produce corrosive, over driven, energetically structured, industrial strength technoise (hey did I just invent a word?!). The albums opener 'Nor' starts as more of an alarm bleep than an actual track, but more than anything this track is representative of why Imminent Starvation works so well. Using one noise sample on it own may be nothing of consequence but aligning it into a gradually building, overall rhythmic beat driven soundscape makes it part of the exceptional whole. Also on face value it is the overdriven rhythmic beats that grab you at first, but more so it the underlying cold oppressive soundscapes that gradually weave their way into your subconscious after repeated listens. Furthermore it is the length and repetition of the track that achieves an almost trancelike, cinematic feel even with the harshest of beats and loops. While all tracks are of a extremely high calibre, standouts even above these would have to be 'tentack one', 'lost highway (exit)', 'vni', 'arles', 'ire' & 'parle' (hey, wait a minute I just picked over half the album as highlights…sheeez…..the more I think about this the better a release I realise it is!).
While there is no doubt that this will have a crossover appeal to dance floor types who are into harder, heavier edged techno, this also contains core elements of dark industrial music to appeal to a wide spectrum to those both in the scene and those not affiliated with it. Without a doubt one of the highlights of 1999! (note: since reviewing this I tracked down the debut CD and while in itself is a great release it is only a taster of what excellence that is found on this album).

INADE (GER) V.I.T.R.I.O.L 7" EP 1999 LOKI FOUNDATION
Inade do it yet again, managing to attain some of the darkest atmospheres through the use of a huge variety of sounds and styles from release to release. Having used a more death industrial and dark ambient focus on past compositions, the two tracks presented here delve much more into ethnic and occult sounds. Track 1 opens with a Tibetan monk chant and an underlying metallic clatter that has the ability to creep up on the unaware listener by the dynamics being kept simple with the sounds and tones gradually looped and overlapped to create the echoed and rising feel. Track 2 is again foreign to any sounds I have heard from Inade before, being very occult influenced

that would not be out of place on a soundtrack to a susspence/ horror movie (and by that I don't mean cheesy b-grade stuff). Discordiant shrill strings set the unnerving tone as the background gradually metamorphosis's to the fore of weighty throbbing and drone percussion. Despite the eventual focus on the percussion the orchestral string feel is not lost, rather that it tends to lurk in the background as the other elements take over. Although a short track it is probably the most intense tracks Inade have created thus far. This is one release you should not miss….

INANNA (SWE) "SIGNAL/OR/MINIMAL" CD 1999 CROWD CONTROL ACTIVITIES
Similar to Benny Nilsen becoming more of a serious sound artist on his latest CD, this is how I would view Mikael Stravostrand's move with his latest Inanna release. Glitchy, sporadic elements of the sound would tend at first tend to indicate the compositions as being total improvised, however regardless of this being the case it is easy to tell that a genuine artist is behind the mixing desk. As much as I loved Mikael's past works as Archon Satani I must confess that I did not expect much from this CD, especially after Inanna's mediocre 'Not.thing' CD from 1994. All I can say that this release has totally taken me by surprise! A certain parrel could be drawn between Alan Lamb's 'wire compositions' in which Alan placed contact mics on a series of telegraph wires and collated the results into full sound works. On this CD the tracks seem to have a life of their own running off on various tangents with it giving off much the same feel as Alan's works yet in a more clinical than organic guise. In this it is meant that Mikael appears to be not much more than a collator of various living sound textures ranging from clinical, to subconsciously intrusive, to barrenly cold, to somewhat alien. Mostly consisting of high end textures & (flawed) static they never reach a point of being ear piercing or annoying, rather retaining an electronic feel throughout subdued drones and muti-layered elements. No track listing was provided, however it does not really matter as the 60+ minute disc flows forward at a minimalist pace morphing and evolving through various segments as if one total sound piece. Quite minimal yet highly detailed in texture has resulted in a very worthwhile listen.

JAALPORTIT (FIN) "KAUAN KOSKEMATON" MC 1999 NOITAVASARA DISTRO
Probably a project know only by a few at this point but this is likely to change with the quality of this debut tape release (however in which musical scene it becomes popular remains to be seen). I tend to get the feeling that this project has strong links to the black metal scene given a number of factors. Firstly the cover and logo look very black metal in style and concept (including a silhouetted corpse painted face), secondly the music is very much like those intros or keyboard segments black metal bands compose (even to the point it is written like symphonic black metal without the guitars) and thirdly it is very much in the league of other crossover groups such as Mortiis, Penitent & Cernunnos Woods. In terms of these comparisons it is not intended to give a bad impression of the tape, but rather give a perspective of what to expect. Back to the comment in the opening sentence, surely most black metal fans would find little of complaint as this contains all the necessary dark medieval sound structure, however how much the ambient/ industrial scene embraces this is the real question (given an evident dislike for such projects as Mortiis). The overall music is flowing, well structured classical/ medieval music composed solely on a keyboard. While it does result in a synthetic sound, the production is decent giving a rich, multi layered sound. Usually a central theme is picked and built upon with representations of the various elements of an orchestra, all slighter differing in approach giving a good breath of sound. Compositions are kept at a mid to slow pace with each track meandering through various passages but ultimately arriving back at the main structure. The composer does have a good grasp of the instruments (or be it keyboard) being above one finger playing. The overall feel is majestic yet mournful rather than being overly bombastic.
All in all the tracks presented are of a high quality calibre running for a total length of around 30 minutes, complimented with a pro-printed cover. The overall result is a more than commendable effort for a debut cassette. It is a bit of a shame that the CD format could not have been used (or even CDR) as quite a few people these days can no longer be bothered with tapes.

JANITOR (SWE) "RITCHIE" LP 1999 ENTARTETE MUSIKK
Janitor is the collaboration of two of Sweden's premier dark sound manipulators, being Lina of Deutch Nepal and Benny of Hazard. The four tracks which make up this LP (or more of a MLP with its overall length) take a pretty straight path, then for me only to realise that the path is running through collective weirdness created by this collaboration. "Skinned Knees" takes a middle line between the two projects intermixing somewhat recognisable soundsources from each – being the more low key dark ambient elements. In this I would attribute the minimal quirky looped beat to Deutsch Nepal and the creeping atmospheres to Hazard. With the elements of the dark throbbing beat and serpentine undercurrent it makes for a strong opening cut. In part, interview vocal samples are included seeming to refer to the title of the LP. Rather then being content in producing many tracks of this ilk, the next track is a cover of a Nico song "all that is my own". Having not heard any of this groups works it is a bit hard for me to comment on the effectiveness of this rendition, however the beginning section had me quite fooled. A number of mild sonic layers are built up having me think that Nico might have also been ambient music but that incorrect assumption was soon to be shattered when the more programmed song structure made its entrance. Chimes, beats and percussive sounds are produced into a darkened mix with dual vocals of Benny/ Lina being a deadpan singing style really throwing this track out there in the quirky stakes. While neither of the artists are fantastic vocalists they make a commendable effort which suits the overall weird atmosphere the track manages to create. Side B offers up a slightly driven dark ambient piece on "Like an Angel" which is much nosier than the proceeding ones as it contains a overtone of power electronics via a hefty slab of looped and manipulated static. Vocals attempt to rise out of the swirling molten mass but are quickly drowned and rendered indecipherable through the noise element – all the while the pulse beat gradually become angrier to match the writhing loops. The final track "Traktor" takes more interview/ movie samples to illustrate the title theme and inspiration with the music back to a focus on dark ambient/ industrial driven manipulations of the more factory/ cavernous kind – with there being no real need to point out that it is done extremely well.
The tracks on this are indicated that they have been record over a period of three years from 1996-1999 making quite a bit of sense when related to the shifting style and sound of the tracks. The record itself is pressed in black vinyl housed in a grey/ white slip sleeve complimented by a nice cover image.

JILAT (ENG) "JILAT9902" CD 1999 JILAT
"A long drone-like piece of music made with synthesisers, samplers and digital delays which attempts in its minimalism to be a thing in itself without external reference, having an analogue in certain states of consciousness where being in experienced also as a thing in itself and not a contingent on meaning or purpose". There you have it, the statement printed both on the promo document and the back of the CD slip sleeve describes the release in a nutshell. Sounds interesting? It did to me it did when the CD arrived unexpectedly in the mail one day. As I placed the disc into the player it revealed itself to be one single track with a playtime of 70 minutes ….thus far staying true to the intentions of the above statement. Atmospheric, synthetic yet somehow containing an organic edge, the sound make up sits in the mid to high range, with a flowing, mildly droning, yet slightly wavering edge to the notes explored. As much as it enthralled me on initial listens, I soon found my mind wandering away from the music rather than into it…which is not really a positive. Giving this some thought I found the answer was simply due to the shear repetition and non movement of the overall sound work. Part of the problem is that piece is not minimal enough to get away with being so repetitious. The recording level and sound tone tends to give the hint that at any moment it will soar off into the horizon, but as this never eventuates it dashes the obvious expectation, causing subsequent disappointment, soon followed by boredom. A shame really as if this was say a 10-15 minute piece it would certainly be a pearl. With move movement and sound exploration I'm sure this group could come up with something quite interesting (as I have not heard earlier CD's I can't compare) but unfortunately this disc falls a little flat.

KEROVNIAN (LIT) "FAR BEYOND, BEFORE THE TIME" CD 1999 COLD SPRING
The nature of weird (occult-laden, Lovecraftian...) darkness is explored on the first release by Croatia's Kerovnian. The sound here is vast, a shroud stretched taut along the heavy wings of eternity; and eerie, never comforting, always uncommon, often monstrous, suggesting demonic conspiracies and appalling resolutions. The vocals are uncanny, sometimes highly processed, bellowing from the heart of the abyss, a marriage of the monstrous and the human, invoking the dead language of Kerovnian, a combination of Persian and Greek ("a language of dark angels"). "Those Beneath The Howling Castle" resonates with the aforementioned eeriness, sounds rising from a place of immense, fathomless loneliness—the soul stripped of everything but dour, torturous existence. The next track reaches even deeper into the black pool, delicate, distraught, trepidatious timbres corrupted by disturbing, highly processed vocals and a discomfiting, overdriven drone. Every track requires dissection as unknown organs are plundered within the process, the anatomy of darkness couched in the body of each song, new sounds for the dark age: cold, lifeless, unearthly....Utilizing desolation as salvation, the music leads one down a rarely trodden path littered with the remains of those who have succeeded in cavorting with the arcane messengers of darkness, finally ending up in a place Kerovnian call home. The barren scope of "Before The Oblivion" is (so very) devoid of life, and yet something gurgles underneath, teasing forth from the shallow end of the black pool; toward the song's end, more strange vocalizations and hurried exhalations, all fading into...oblivion. The closest comparisons would be Inade (for the unique take on the manipulation of shadows) and Endvra (the eclectic, occult-tinged elements), but to be quite honest, Kerovnian veer far from any other black sonicscape creators to a place that is solely their own; a place of hollow hope, ebony horizons and the undetermined sonic territories of dread. —JC Smith (Reprinted by permission from Outburn Magazine: www.outburn.com)

KRAKEN (BEL) "AQUANAUT" LP 1999 SPECTRE
Opening the packaging containing this release I was first taken aback by the stunning dark turquoise imagery of the cover, with the record being pressed in transparent blue vinyl. Given these elements and the title, they should be somewhat of a hint of what this encompasses...(and for those not willing to take a guess), that would be a liquidous dark ambient state. Seething drawn out tones introduce the LP as slow looped (and sparsely placed) rhythmic textures add to the hazy mood, as repeated female vocals reference the tracks title: 'liquid enchantress/ lured underneath'. Still minimal but more forceful than the first, the second track 'demagogic journey' it slightly more claustrophobic with singular tonal drones and treated bells & textures. Other less dense swirls lighten the outlook (but only just) passing through minimal then more noisy phases. The singular drones continue through 'point of submersion/ maelstrom' yet in slightly higher tone, as much heavier guttural textures sit underneath, (partially audible) in the murky darkness. Side 2 begins as less drone oriented, rather opting for shifting, minimalist, glacial sound with other drawn out textures scattered throughout, resulting in quite a suffocating aura. Seeping in late in the piece darker droning elements push the piece toward 'descending into the abyss'. This track is much nosier than those preceding it yet still quite minimalist overall. Looping whirlpools of sound radiate against the sides of the underwater cavern, amassing the sound inward rather than outwardly, enhancing the addition of electronic noise textures. The final piece 'cerebral core of the Octopus/ Hynotic preassure' is reasonably short (in comparison to the other drawn out flowing tracks) and is on a different tangent given it has a recognisable looped keyboard/ piano run and freezing background drones...essentially being a fitting ending to what is a great release. For reference a passing comparison to Hazard should give you an idea of the quality, meaning that on what is only a debut release, Kraken have hit the mark spot on in terms of creating original, darkly submerged atmospheres. (I might also add that the recipes for two seafood dishes printed on the postcard inserts are an novel idea!).

LAW (USA) "WADING KNEE DEEP IN YOUR BLOOD" LP 1999 OLD EUROPA CAFE
What more can I say other than then this release is truly superb! Having heard of the name Law, and for some reason having the perception of the group being in the leagues of power electronic such as Con-Dom or the Grey Wolves, I was totally flawed by the music bled into the groves of the red vinyl.
Corrosive atmospheres, controlled noise elements, unbridled anger smouldering just below the surface (of the calmer moments)..... this release has it all in terms of diversity, dynamics and sound make up. The overall sound owes somewhat to the European tradition of power electronics and in part may sound something like Stratvm Terror if they went for a more power electronics tone than an industrial edge. Certainly being much more subdued than a typical power electronics release, this is exactly the reason why it has caught and held my undivided attention. Overall it comes across as being intelligent, always containing purpose, focus and direction. Tracks gradually morph and flow into one another with the dynamics blending between controlled hateful anger and quieter misanthropic disdain. The use of vocals whilst minimal at best, when used on 'Sacrificial Key' are such, that while not in the distorted/ yelling guise of most power electronics, the static/ echoed whisper boosted to the forefront of the sound production gives a very flesh crawling effect. They certainly scared the crap out of me the first time they burst out of the speakers to address my unsuspecting ears! The music although released in 1999 is credited to having been recorded in 1997. There have been other releases recorded since and now are awaiting imminent release (one on Malignant if I am not mistaken). Given this is limited to 350 copies I would suggest you act quickly as you will certainly be disappointed that you didn't, at the instant you hear the corrosive power on one of Law's future (& less limited) offerings.

LES JOYAUX DE LA PRINCESSE (FRA) "PARIS 1937 EXPOSITION INTERNATIONALE" 7" EP 1999 LGDLP
There is art within music and then there are groups such as this who take even that notion to the next level. The time and effort that has gone in the concept and packaging is almost justified with the hefty price tag this item was fetching upon first sale (around $20 US when factoring in postage and surely destined to rise dramatically given this is limited to only 370 and is from a group that fetches exorbitant prices for all his releases thus far). The packaging is a full colour oversized fold out booklet with a very art deco styling of the illustrated images of Paris. Upon opening the booklet is has a clear circular cut out in the left hand panel which holds the 7", surrounded by written text. The right hand panel shows a photo of a grandiose example of classic architecture, void of any human presence. The whole packaging is completed with a tracing paper insert separating the two panels and a piece of gold twine tied along the spine edge. Side A ('Arts & Techniques') is split into two sections, being introduced with a sampled French voice before sweeping into a subdued section of a neoclassical composition of horns, strings and controlled percussion. The sampled voice enters again to mark the change, with the music being much more distant and forlorn in both sound and production, again being classically driven which unfortunately fades out all too quickly. Side B ('Dans La Vie Moderne') begins with an unusual yet very short, somewhat musical section before the shrill strings, horns and pounding timpani rise to the fore now very much more forceful and militant than side A. Underneath this is what starts as a slow hiss but gradually rises into the mix (being or a very much a searing power electronics tone) sweeping the track into oblivion of static. Despite what described to be conflicting musical elements it is indeed a great track but again simply too short. The overall concept of the release is somewhat lost on me given that I can't read the text, but it still leaves a lasting impression on me nonetheless. The only real complaint I have here is the shortness of the release, but the packaging does counteract this. Expect to pay a high price if you mange to track one of these down.

THE MACHINE IN THE GARDEN (USA) "ONE WINTER'S NIGHT..." CD 1999 MIDDLE PILLAR
Being the second CD off the ranks for Middle Pillar this offering falls into the gothic/ ethereal type vein with 'one winter's night' encompassing a sorrowful journey through electro generated atmospheres complimented by soaring female vocals and occasional brooding male ones. In terms of overall structure the tracks are presented in a song format guise, including composed tunes, lyrics and sung vocals that explore various moods and sounds. Given the territory covered the CD crosses and entwines many musical styles such as electonica, moody industrial, gothic, composed ambient and darkwave.

Light keyboard runs (& sounds), grand piano, programmed beats and multi layered female vocals introduce proceedings on 'Falling, Too', setting the scene for the album. The industrial guitar drive of 'Control' quite simply rocks, being held somewhat in check by the female counterpart while 'Miserere Mei' sits as slow industrial beat oriented track, however feeling slightly off centre due to the classical/ baroque style of the female singing. Being always a fan of a good piano dirge 'Fear no More' comes up with the goods sounding akin to Dead Can Dance or Arcana. Tribal percussive elements of 'Ex Oblivione' again alter the perceived style, whilst still retaining a groove oriented industrial beat and atmosphere. The playful gothic elements of 'The Sleep of Angels' sees lightly strummed (clean) guitars, programmed (rock) drumming, keyboards and both male/ female vocals coming up with a great track and yet again redefining the sound of the CD. The doomy bass and sitar like guitars of 'Everything Alone' along with the ever present (female) vocals results in nicely depressing tone that hypes up slightly with the introduction of some echoed marching snares. 'Lullaby' is just that being another piano/ vocal combo, flowing into the gothic/ darkwave fields of 'Midnight' with a strong basis on programmed beats and distorted/ clean guitars. Given that this is the groups third release (or so I am led to believe) they have come up with the goods that is likely to appeal to fans from a number of genres.

Arcane Recordings
Mail Order Music Specialists

Gothic, Darkwave, Coldwave
Ambient, Industrial, Experimental

For A Free Catalogue
PO Box 458
Fullarton SA 5063
MarkEnde@Bigpond.Com

MELEK-THA (FRA) "DE MAGIA NATURALI DAEMONIACA" CD 1999 COLD SPRING
Pandemonium's infernal orchestra is unleashed on the second release by Melek-Tha, De Magia Naturali Daemonica. Spilling forth like intestines from a sword slashed belly, "Diabolical Diatribes (Hell On Earth Prelude)" opens the gates to an orgy of nefarious samples that copulate and breed demonic ministrations; chaos personified, the hordes of darkness, of evil, adorned in the skins of the sacrificed and dancing to a black celebration. Everything that follows, including the buried under ashes' synthesizers, is drenched in sanguine hues, blood everywhere, necessary elixir for the black mass ambience that infuses all of the music here. There is an air of madness, a tenacious scratching at the inside of one's cranium, as Satan's cloven hooves gallop mirthfully ahead of an onslaught of sonic battles and scorched sanity, of the joy of anarchy as priest's burn and tongues twist to and fro (and frontwards, backwards...back down [no backing down here!] the swollen gullet of excess overload, constant regurgitation of sonic clutter and confusion). There's even a looped Godzilla roar throughout the background of the title track, confirmation that, despite the overriding aura of evil, a mischievous heart beats merrily along. Devious....—JC Smith (Reprinted by permission from Outburn Magazine: www.outburn.com)

DANIEL MENCHE (USA) "RUSTY GHOSTS" 2 X 7"EP 1999 DUEBEL
Prior to the music getting a look in I feel I need to comment on the packaging. Encased in a textured grey/ blue print sleeve the 2 x 7"s are further wrapped and folded in dark blue tissue type paper, which gives a very nice personalised feel to the whole release. It seems that Mr Menche has moved away from his angrier, more noisy releases and is occupying a niche in explore the subtleties of sound manipulation. Overall organic in feel, the four tracks play out in a definitive sound that is associated with this artist, but I'm not sure what types of sound sources have been used given there is no details provided on the cover. Also as the four sides of the EP's are not marked, reference to the sound of each track is destined to be difficult. Not to matter as the collective sounds presented (retaining the always organic textures) gives rise to mentally illustrating the following descriptions via the medium of sound.... (and those descriptions are?). This is the amplified sound of: the Ebola virus at gradual dissolves its victim from the inside out; the leach engorging itself on its host, the swarming of an insect plague; the carcass being consumed by maggots; the starving rats in the walls gnawing at the wires and cables, the soul being swept into oblivion (leaving behind the quickly cooling & fragile mass of flesh behind)....whatever mental images perceived this is classic Menche, always evocative & never boring or derivative.

MORGENSTERN (GER) "ZYKLEN" CD 1999 ANT-ZEN
In regard to the cover I must say that S alt never fails to impress with his flair and eye for design, gaining darkly appropriate imagery out the most unlikely subject matter. In terms of sound, scrapping, throbbing, droning aurally piercing textures are used in a way which mixes both death industrial, dark ambient and subdued power electronic elements. For a ball park comparison the most obvious would be Stratvm Terror and selected more low key elements of Brighter Death Now (but having a cleaner sound production than the latter). 'Anfang/ende' encompasses sinister electronic noise manipulations running between low drone and mid ranges probing sounds being both confronting and relaxing. 'Hymn' is much more of a death industrial vibe that retains a distant pounding sound structure and haunting cavernous elements that includes a sweeping treated like choir vocals. Noise looped elements open 'soar' and distant (engulfed) human screaming give off a suitable apocalyptic vision of peeking into the fiery abyss of hell. After about the 3 minute mark the track morphs into a looped tribal/ industrial pound fest that is swept in and out of many cryptic regions until the conclusion after the 10 minute mark. Restless distorted beats and undercurrents are the flavour of 'ravished' containing what seem to be vocals but are so beyond distorted they simply add to the clatter (which incidentally reminds me of mental destruction) with the following 'Not am sein' is heavily looped with subdued and relaxed distant factory clatter containing a hypnotic surrealistic edge. Dreamy drones and atmospheres solidify early in 'stormy battle ode' but from the title it is clear that this will soon be allot noisier. Slipping into the background the dreamy elements sit below a gradually building structure of more corrosive drones, tortured vocal wails and mid paced industrial clatter (only to periodically float up to the surface). 'Flake' is a ceremony of distant rhythmic beats and intermixed vocal snippets that rise into a total distorted noise/ power electronics cacophony and would seem to suit the title of the preceding track. Haunting and sweeping textures, choir vocals, bass riddled cavernous drones ensure that 'rodion's dead souls' is the darkest track on offer coming across as a highly cinematic piece of dark ambience/ & death industrial. 'Welt' offers up a less dark but just as sorrowfully haunting cinematic piece interspread with distant chants and ritualistic beats. Not that all of the darker elements are contained at the start of the album the corrosive textures and demonic vocals of the final track (ende/ anfang) give rise to the vision of passage out of hell being rendered unpassable as

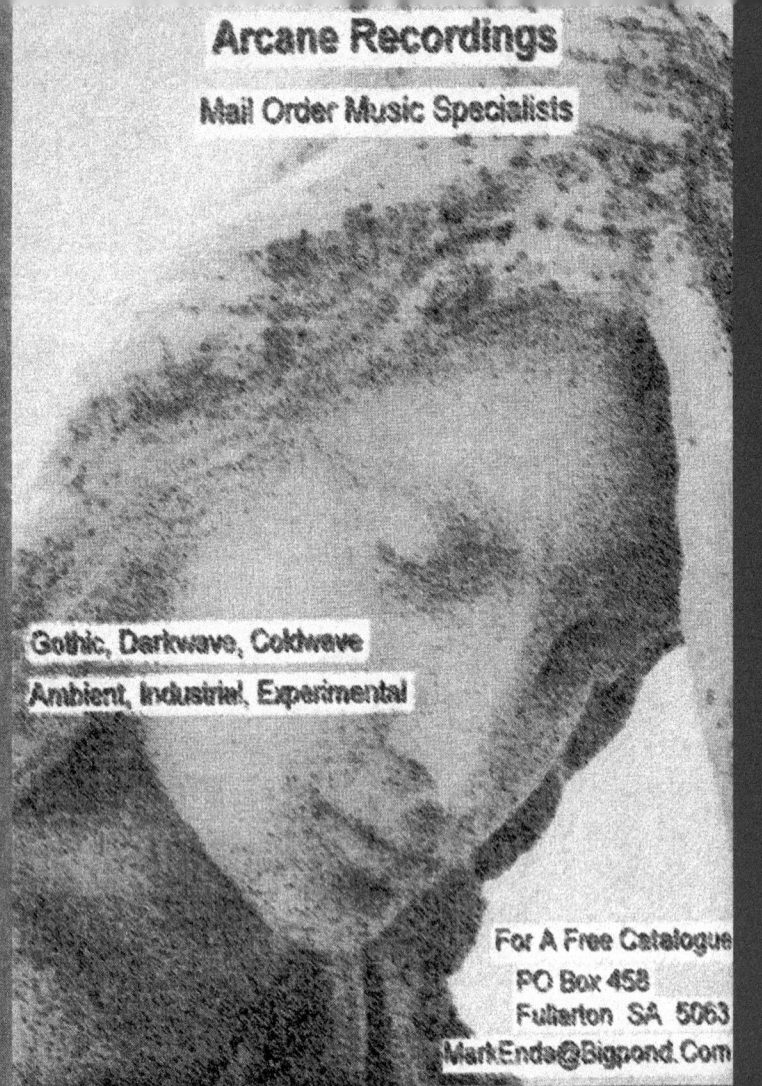

the angels above lament the soul's damnation. Very dark indeed....
Morgenstern is credited to feature one Andrea Border who is also part of templegardens and a previous member of ars moriendi (assistance is also provided from members of synapscape and asche) ultimately coming up with a solid and stunning offering. As a final note it great to see a female that can mix it with the best when it come to dark corrosive atmospheres.

A MURDER OF ANGELS (USA) "WHILE YOU SLEEP" CD 1999 MIDDLE PILLAR

From the collective talents behind Dream into Dust & 4th Sign of the Apocalypse this almost guarantees a superb piece of work, with the CD definitely delivering on this promise. Dark ambient and neo classical styling have been intermixed into a category coined 'damnbient' by the group & while I find this to sound a little cheesy it represents only a minuscule hurdle to overcome given the quality of the music. Mystical and ritualistic elements inter-spread with classical and cinematic overtones give a surreal yet nightmarish aura which has more than suited if not totally enhanced the background atmosphere of my recent HP Lovecraft readings. Distant wails and drones are scored with violin passages (and later with ritual beats) on the opening offering 'Necrosis Reversal', ultimately succumbing to oblivion only to be resurrected again in 'Manuscript' which spans full and rich orchestrations (although distant) and more sinister, otherworldly atmospheres in the foreground. 'Wandering Soul' has elements similar to Caul's compositions where layers of sounds/ textures build the basis, complimented by subdued classical tones and a lightly played piano (4-5 notes played sparsely throughout). The sound of 'Lurking Gentleman' although starting quite relaxed becomes more urgent mid way in yet returning again to calmer waters for the conclusion. 'Melting Across the Night' while might not have the same weight of say Mepaptera it does contains a death ambient vibe in the pounding undertone, later altering to a highly cinematic orchestral section which is comparable to possibly Shinjuku Thief's gothic tinged releases (however differing with the inclusion of a spoken section/ story). Subdued urgency is perceived on 'Tribunal' with male/ female coral elements rising over a surging horn section and sweeping sound textures. Again a passing comparison to Caul could be made on 'Suspended in Frozen Misery' continuing into 'Opaque Atmosphere' which is much more of a straight dark ambient droning/ ritual piece. Not to go quietly the disc exists on a high (and louder) note, where 'the Ninth Circle' is repeated cinematic orchestration with nosier high end tones bordering on white noise. Within only three releases Middle Pillar have cemented themselves a quality label in terms of both music and packaging. On this CD (as with the others) it is housed in an immaculately presented digi-pack, with bleak images in tones of black and red. Overall given that the tracks are between 6-8 minutes in length the CD (63 minutes in all) is in no sort of hurry, rather being content with gradually hypnotising the listener into its nightmarish, cinematic void.

MZ412 (SWE) "NORDIK BATTLE SIGNS" CD 1999 COLD MEAT INDUSTRY

As the LP version of this was released in late 1998 and reviewed in last issue I have reworked that original review for this issue. While the LP contained no Black Metal elements as alluded to during an earlier interview (and previously featured on 'Burning the Temple of God'), there were no band photo's to indicate which way the image had gone. This time around one of the CD covers inside panels confirms that the black metal makeup has not been fully forsaken, featuring a close up of lone corpse painted member (Kremator) overlaid against a black and white scene of fallen warriors (The remaining panel images are much the same taking on themes of death and blasphemy).
In terms of the digital CD format it has only heightened the searing and flesh tearing sonic warfare being declared on the listener's psyche, threatening to destroy both soundsystem and mind alike, but giving some respite by further expanding the depth of cavernous echo of quieter moments. The intro to the album ('MZ412/Introducktion') is a very quick piece of load and dirgy rumbling static with a buried vocal sample. This track cuts out as quickly as it began moving into track two 'Algiz-Konvergence of Life and Death' that has an unusual choice of intro vocal sample (Charles Manson) before the dirgy electronics cut in again. This track is credited to a collaboration between MZ and Ordo Equilibrio however from listening to this it would be fair to assume that MZ412 provided the musical backdrop whilst Thomas Petterson provides a poetic spoken story like vocal passage. When Thomas's vocals commence, there sound changes to a cavernous echoey tone with a tribal drum cacophony. In-between these spoken moments the trademark harsh and grinding electronics and screamed vocals of MZ412 act as a bridge to the more subdued elements. Toward the end of this track Tomas's vocals join the extreme sounds with his vocals being manipulated and overlapped over themselves. 'Satan Jugend' is a good track but it is the vocal sample that repetitively praises you know who, that for me detracts from an otherwise good track. The rumbling industrial storm gradually increases in intensity and dynamics before abruptly cutting out. 'Der Kamph geht weiter' sound quite militant with a very nice looped and distorted drum roll as vocal snipits and wavering tones rise in and out of the composition. Some traditional excellent 'factory' sounding industrial sections are also used within this track before becoming much more focused and composed when all the elements come together with a slow marching styled beat. Later some sampled chants are used as the musical backdrop gets much more atmospheric and ritualized with floating tones and somewhat sporadic beats. This track merges well some of the best sounds to be found on the 'In nomine....' & 'Burning....' CD's. Not featured on the original LP release is a new track entitled "Satan Jugend II: Global konquering" which was record using source material sent in by individuals specifically for this purpose (after a request was put out by the group). Layering of many droney bass soaked textures are intermixed with static loops and outburts and a lone individual tries to scream his way out of the sonic chaos. This is a bit more noiser (did I say MORE nosier?!) and straight forward than what I normally associate with MZ, but I guess it as how they would sound giving their hand to trying power electronics (but still retaining some distinguishable elements). 'Tyranor' is sonically clear and load with it's electronic jugular attack that harks back to the deathy heavy sound on the 'In nomine....'CD. A nice high pitch droning is used over the top that delineates the sound from the early comparison and as great as this track is, it is just too damn short! 'NBS act II: Begravning' which was originally featured on the GMI 50# comp is a much stronger track here in its full form, alongside the other intended compositions. Atmospherics', factory clatter, deathly drones and repetitive German vocals make this a very sinister track indeed. MZ412 have a knack of tracking seeming unrelated elements, used all together is a mass of sound and then in a blink of an eye miraculously merging them into rhythmic passage – as is the case in the above track. The final track 'NBS act II:14W' begins as another nicely sinister atmospheric track again using all the trademark sound and a manipulated vocal passage talking about the beauty in death.
The overall play time of the CD is longer than the LP at around 45 minutes but I am still tend to have the feeling that it is too short (but I guess that is more of a compliment, than being criticised for an album that drags due to it's excessive length). This album is far above what I expected due to the lack of any Black Metal elements and will surely go down well with any established MZ412 fan.

N (ITA) "AUTOFAGIA" 4 X MC 1999 SLAUGHTER PRODUCTIONS

Although Slaughter Productions stated they were no longer doing tape releases this obscure item landed in my letterbox. Housed in a black video box, with photo attached to the cover, little if no information is provided on the group or the recording, nor containing a track listing or titles. 4 tapes with a combined length of around 180 minutes this is a hell of a lot of material to take in and condense down into a review. Landing in the general arena of 'power electronics' mostly analogue manipulated sounds are presented in a guise of menacingly cold nihilism. Generally more subdued than forceful, some compositions are such that broad comparisons could be made to death industrial, just minus the thick & sludgy production. Looking at a comparison between being partly composed and totally improvised, I tend to get the feeling most works are in fact improvised given the spatter schizophrenic changes in the noise layers. While sometimes this works really well in other parts it sounds as just that ie: someone in a studio playing around with feedback & distortion equipment. Given the amount of material there is not enough variety to keep constant interest compounded by the fact that some pieces don't seem to have progressed past rudimentary experimentations. I'm sure if the material over the four tapes was culled down to a single CD it would be overall more powerful and focused.

NO FESTIVAL OF LIGHT (SWE) "OFFICINA GENTIUM VAGINA NATIONUM" CD 1999 FUNCTIONAL ORGANISATION

NFOL having been around for quite some years yet seem to be a under recognised element in the Swedish death ambient/ industrial scene(with even myself having only picked up the last two releases of this group in the past few months). Certainly the gradually improving infamy of this groups will not be stifled with this recording. This CD is the follow on the 'Enter to the Realm of Satan' CD, and from initial appearances the artworks and presentation has greatly improved (although this is on a different label to the former CD). The first deviation from the previous CD would be in relation to the minimalist element of the recordings and the distinct lack of martial percussion present on a number of the tracks on the 'Enter…' CD. Very quiet and low cold droning elements build the (slightly electronic) ambiental textures over extended time frames of each of the 6 compositions. Bleak and sinister tones are the prevalent staple in each of the tracks in which Fredrick Bergstrom is heavily involved in the exploration of many aspects of his ideals & philosophy via a sound medium. Comparatively speaking Archon Satani come to mind when the mysterious far off factory sounds puncture the soundscapes along with (minimal) orchestrally elements. (As Archon Satani is only now a fond memory, NFOL are doing a more than comendable job of plugging the massive void left behind). One track tends to differ in that it makes use of a glitched electronic/ experimental framework which is more artistic then specifically dark. Dynamics play a positive role in that (given the minimalist structural elements) when things do occur they tend to much loader and up front adding to the overall breadth of sound. The only real complaint that I have is that I would have preferred more percussive elements to break up the bleak soundscapes and given that they were a particularly positive element of the preceding disc (they are found on the opening track here). No matter as this is still an enjoyable release that will hopefully help furnish this project with a bit more respect (& notoriety) that is definitely due.

PARCA PACE (SWE) "PARCA PACE" CD 1999 FLAMING FISH MUSIC/ STRUCTURE

Here we have a single 50 minute flowing, morphing and evolving piece of industrial ambience (with selected classical touches) from Jan Carleklev, better known at this point for his work in the group Sanctum. Factory noise, scattered beats and guttural almost tribal rhythms are used in various sections, with faint classical strings injected at appropriate moments. Gruff, distorted vocals are used at one point, when the beats and noise are particularly load which then leads off into the first full blown classical section (which is comparable to some of the sections of Sanctum's debut CD) including shrill strings, choir like vocals and the undercurrent of noise beats. The CD has the feel of rotating in a circular flow moving through segments of noise, rhythms and classical compositions, not necessarily repeating itself, rather following along a set out framework. This is particularly evident with four main sections utilising classical sentiments, with the other noise and rhythmic elements acting as a bridge to the more composed elements. In regard to the packaging I was a little disappointed given it is not much more than a cardboard slip sleeve with two inserts and a sticker on the cover. Nice imagery but a little expensive given the price being charged. (On the other hand the quality of the music is more than enough to make up for this complaint). This is quite a stunning release but that should be no surprise considered when considering whose creative element this has come from.

PENITENT (NOR) "ROSES BY CHAOS SPAWNED" CD 1999 MEMENTO MORI

For me Penitent have been a bit of a hit and miss affair. Not really being too taken in my the debut CD I was surprised how impressed I was with the superb, free form grand piano tunes on the second CD "the beauty of pain". Following that, I never got around to getting the third CD "as life fades away", picking up the trail again with this, the forth CD. Straight out I can say that this CD is a great disappointment….gone are the longer form tracks, being striped back to the style and flow of the debut CD. While is seems that Penitent on previous albums have had different members, (apart from the constant of Karsten Harme) this may be part of the reason for the changing stances between albums (on this release Penitent are credited as being a solo group with Mr Harme writing all music and lyrics). Mostly consisting of medieval piano/ organ dirges (keyboard generated with others various background 'classical' synth lines) slow and repetitive percussion (drum machine) crawl along with the mildy rousing yet repetitive tunes. Vocals also present a problem for me here being sometimes sung, sometimes half spoken or whispered. This is mainly due to Karsten pushing his vocals down a couple of notches past its normal register, resulting in a forced, half cheesy commanding tone. Redemption is somewhat gained in selected moments where the music attains a feeling and atmosphere that I could get swept way with, but again the vocals just tend to get in the way (as is the case on "A Bleeding Heart of Desire" which also makes use of female vocals). I am probably being more harsh than deserved, and others will probably heavily disagree with me, but I still can't help but feel that Penitent can come up with a much stronger album than this. On a final note I have always wondered how the hell bullet belts have ever fitted into medieval concept of many metal bands, with the cover of this CD paying homage to this baffling question by providing an image of a sword ringed by bullets. Please explain…

PLAN 10 (AUS) PROJEKT 1 CD 1999 PLAN 10 CONCEPTS

This CD while of Australian origin is credited to having been co-written with Noh-Ji-Satsu (Japanese noise artist perhaps?). Low noise, static and droning keys kick things off and continues in a similar fashion over the first three short tracks, however the third becomes quite noisy with technological driven swirls of pitch shifting feedback which tend to be more confronting than melding into the background ambience. Checking the track counter it becomes evident that that tracks have skipped forward at a rather quick pace, with the sounds giving no indication of where one track starts or finishes. (I guess in practice they really only serve as insertion points into the mix rather than indicating actual tracks). Some dark and quite deep, subterranean droning atmospheres are found on tracks 7 through 10 which are not too dissimilar to that of what Hollow Earth have produced…in other words quite classy. About 4-5 minutes into track 10 (which has a total play time of over 60 minutes) silence is used for a good 50 minutes before the scrapping dark atmospheres return now with demonically processed vocals. Some bleeps, modem sounds and tech type overdriven noise is fed into the gradually rising madness which continues into the end of the track. No-Ji-Satsu's imput seems to be limited to the final track which is almost a full death industrial track with its guttural pounding, scaping textures, scattered machine gun fire and slow pitch shipped vocal wails. In terms of the cover imagery is not at all dark, rather looking like the product of a bad acid trip (in my opinion not at all suiting the music). The CD does have quite a bit of merit but I still have mixed feeling on it overall. Analysing this further I think this is specifically due to the technological sounding elements which just don't seem to fit in with darker background textures and drones. Although the disc has a play time of over 70 minutes there is under 20 minutes of music on offer, but after hearing this I am interested in seeing what future works will offer.

PREDOMINANCE (GER) "HINDENBURG" MLP 1998 LOKI FOUNDATION

Opening with a sample from Led Zeppelin (a nod also given with the cover artwork), Predominance proceed to erase any connections with the music that follows, a six track collection of brooding sonicscapes, quite dark, dramatic, and of a doom-laden nature: sinuous, hushed shadows utilized in the creation—via music and samples—of an aura of bleak mystery, of dreadful circumstances and foreboding consequences. "In Through The Eyes Of Heaven" seems to breathe and almost laugh amidst an imperceptible synth shroud. "Under The Blackened Sun" consists of machines in battle, the spit and fire of warfare coursing through its sonic veins. "Encoded Pages" is constructed from sound/noise hieroglyphics, the cadences of other lands mingling with the subtlety uneasy scrapings of steel on static. "Lakehurst—A Tragic Moment Frozen In Time" wields a catastrophic ambience, destruction and chaos aside a somber synth line—heightened by the samples of an anguished reporter at the sight of the Hindenburg tragedy. A truly powerful presentation, and reason enough to seek out other Predominance and Wolverine (their former namesake) releases. Essential! —JC Smith (Reprinted by permission from Sideline Magazine www.sideline.com)

PROPERGOL (FRA) "CLEANSHAVEN" CDR HERMETIQUE

I can just see the members poring over the mixing desk on the final mastering "you call that load?? No it needs to be loader..boost it as

Alchemie
...the Soil Bleeds Black

MEDIEVAL COURT MUSIK

Inspired by the themes and sounds of authentic medieval music, The Soil Bleeds Black return with a fourth full length offering of middle age art and custom.

"Alchemie" is a musical and lyrical tract for the sacred spiritual gold of the intellectual. Acoustic bows, wooden flutes, mouth harps, dulcimer, penny whistles, and percussives bring to life hymns of olde atmosphere.

Featuring a special guest appearance by Cold Meat Industry artists, ARCANA.

THE SOIL BLEEDS BLACK • 3308 Stone Heather Ct. • Herndon, VA 20171 • USA
Email: yamatu@erols.com • Web: http://www.coldburialsystem.com/TSBB

WORLD SERPENT DISTRIBUTION • Unit 7-I-7 Seager Buildings • Brookmill Road, London • SE84HL • ENGLAND
Phone: 0181.694.2000 • Fax: 0191.694.2677 • mailorder@worldserpent.demon.co.uk

high as you can!". Looking at the graphic equalisers on my stereo it is rare that all the bars are maxed out simultaneously without causing a total wall of distorted chaos (...wait a minute this is a total wall of distorted chaos & excellent at that). I guess the point being made is this is damn LOAD!

Track one is quickly written off as a movie sample quote with the real action commencing on track two. After a flurry of low volume static vocal sample, the tracks hits full force as a pulsating, throbbing mass of bass industrialised tones and high end vocal static. Bordering somewhere between power electronics and some damn heavy death industrial bringing to mind some of the most anger filled moments of Brighter Death Now. Masses of what appear to be movie dialogue samples are interspersed throughout, being feed through the corrosive sound mass which barely puncture the surface only adding to the distorted squealing frenzy. The track continues in its all out assault in a variety of looped formats for its extended 17 minute length. 'Dans les veines...' uses a more chaotic sound makeup that sits in the swirling (yet mildly ear assaulting) atmospheric range giving off a broad comparison to Stratvm Terror. The tones gradually become more threatening moving away from atmospherics to a fiery mass, of creeping bass and higher end corrosive scrapping textures again ended in an all out aural reaming. The juxtaposed elements of power electronic and death industrial are used to great effect on the title track with screeching acidic static and echoed/ distorted vocal anguish taking out the high end, with the lower sound regions taken up by a slow monotone bone crushing (programmed) beat. Things do quieten down on 'Hotel Earle "a day or a lifetime" taking a more sinister death ambient vibe. Basically taking a whole scene/ dialogue excerpt out of a movie, it includes some orchestral textures which I'm not sure if they originated from the movie or the project itself. Not that it matters as either way it greatly adds to the atmosphere, with the echoed and left/ right balancing of background noises (ie: doors slamming) gives a very disorienting feel. The buzz saw noise and demolishing weight of 'wood trash' is a storming electrified mass, running the fine line between structure and chaos... composed yet improvised. Power drill bursts and storming/ droning industrial undercurrent of 'signal h', comes across as quite sparse despite being a full composition of dark sonic textures.....I guess this only points the absolutely overloaded sound quality of the majority of the other tracks! 'Joshua's day' includes a dark jazz/ dub groove of all things (which works extremely well I might add!) intermixed with controlled minimal industrial sounds and again a full movie dialogue excerpt.

Of the 9 tracks (over a 72 minutes) span the compositions takes on predominant characteristics of being sometimes subdued, more often chaotic, yet always fiery and angry, with the disc solidifying as an excellently weighty soundscape. Given that this is a CDR all I can say is that I am more than impressed. Packaging is DIY (yet commendable), but as for the music I would surprised if this group is not signed for a major deal rather quickly. Track one of the 200 copies down if you can and add it to the list of quality releases from the expanding French scene.

PUISSANCE (SWE) "MOTHER OF DISEASE" CD 1999 FLUTTERING DRAGON

I guess you could say that this is the direction that Puissance has been heading in over the past few releases...much more neo-classical and bombastic in structure with less elements on nosier industrial interludes. The opener "Light of A Dead Sun" sets the tone early with soaring synth generated choir and orchestra complimented by a pounding snare & tympani undercurrent. Straight away a parallel comparison is drawn to the stand out track of the last album "Love Incinerate" with many of the tracks taking on this quality. A more brooding moment is found on "Reign of Dying Angels" where while there is still rolling drums, the wind section and soothing piano set a serene yet menacing tone. The title track plays out again very much in the style of "Love Incinerate" with the bridging passages intermixed with bombastic outbursts. Over the music a montane 'radio' like voice reads yet another page from the book of Puissance philosophy and while crude in description I guess illustrates how they could potentially achieve their aim. For the first time within Puissance's music, real singing vocals are employed on "In Shining Armour", with a mixture of militant male vocals and more coral female vocals. The only track which really represents past compositions of dense industrial sound is "Post Ruin Symphony", however is hardly that, unless it is the orchestra playing a morbid tune from under the rumble of a ruined city. Hands down I would state "Core of Revelation" to be the highlight on the CD with the massive pounding beats and orchestral symphony, which barely lets up throughout its length. "Human Error" bypasses the industrial sounds of past CD and takes it even further back to the production of the second demo, where this track is much more based on beat rhythms and an ever so light undercurrent of synth atmosphere, piano and a vocal sample. As the CD chooses to commence with a roaring neo-classical tune, much is the same with the conclusional passage "The Voice of Chaos", utalising all the trademark sounds for such a track.

I will say that I imagine that Puissance are attempting to get a sound similar to groups as Der Blutharsch, LJDLP or to an extent Blood Axis however there is a marked difference in the former to later groups. I don't know if it is the synthetic edge prevalent in Puissance's music as opposed the sampling and looping of the comparative groups, but as much as I like this it just doesn't hit me on the 'other level' as the other groups do. As you will note, this is released on a non CMI label so I don't know where that leaves them in terms of the previous label affiliation, however Fluttering Dragon have done quite a nice job with the layout and presentation – gold packaging mixed violent renaissance art.   I will say it again, this is a CD I do enjoy and is the best Puissance have produced to date, but it just does not bridge the gap to the next level. Wait and see what the future brings for them (apart from the obvious oblivion).

RAISON D'ETRE (SWE) "COLLECTIVE ARCHIVES" DCD 1999 COLD MEAT INDUSTRY

Where do you start with a review of a double dose of raison d'etre? As I don't have a real answer to that, the packaging seems to be as good a place as any. Immaculate as always (thanks to Roger K), the cover is simple in its layout, letting the complimentary desolate and archaic artwork of Alexander Nemkovsky take effect (who is reported to be a huge fan of this project).

Disc 1 of the set takes us through a collection of many of the compilation tracks (and selected cuts off limited tape releases) produced from 1991 through 1996. The trade mark sound elements illustrating emotional desolation are evident throughout all tracks, yet are marked in sound via the evident evolving compositional abilities of Peter over time. Stages of his working sound are played out from the early sounds of tribal and rhythmic based compositions, to later tracks that are less based on rhythms, consisting of minimal compositions filled out with waves of treated ambient tones. And as always religiously inspired choirs and chants have been sampled and injected (in fleeting doses) to great effect. By the time the later tracks such as "Saifeiod" (from 1995) commence, the spiralling heights which this project has risen to can truly be appreciated. It seems that the less the music is based on actual tunes the more tragic, desolate and all encompassing the pieces become – true works of sound art.

Moving on to the second disc, this consists of the infamous MC "Apres nous le Deluge" (released on the pre CMI sound source tape label), two demo tracks from the 'demo' version of that tape, 5 remixed tracks off the debut CD "Prospectus I", with all of that being all kicked off with a short live composition from 1997. The live composition still retains a desolate tone, yet is mildly menacing which is a mood I would not oft associate with raison d'etre, however as it is only a minute and half long it is unknown to how the whole live set would have sounded. The remixed tracks off the "Prospectus I" CD at first do not appear at all different from the originals, yet I assume Peter would have planned it that way. The subtle differences I detected is in the actually flow of the songs, which overall seems just that much more smooth in orchestral undercurrent and more accentuated in the sparse snare drums, bells and vocals. Although I would not hail the "Apres nous le Deluge" tracks as brilliant, it does show an artist in his formative stages of fleshing out concepts and ideas, whilst mastering the tools in his trade – essentially a master craftsman in his apprenticeship days. It is actually quite interesting to fathom the leap which occurred from some of these early tracks, to only a year later when the debut CD was released. Here many of the tracks do have fleeting moments of the overall religious aura to come later, but are more stepped in the European industrial traditions of the use of programmed beats and sounds – good? - yes but slightly derivative. In passing, this is a superb documentation of the journey of an artist through his continued emotional catharsis, evoked through the elements of composition and sound.

REGARD EXTREME (FRA) "VAGUE A L'AME" CD 1998 WORLD SERPENT
Referencing the project's title, it is a name which would have more of a connotation to the power electronics movement to that actual style it represents. Having become aware of this project from a collaboration with LJDLP I figured that this might be down the neo-classical ally with my assumption being pretty much spot on. Stylistically it is easy to see where half of the sound of the LJDLP collaboration CD "Die Weike Rose" came from. Contained here are mostly richly scored synthetic orchestral movements occasionally underpinned with ominous tympani percussive sections. In reference to one element, this CD differs from the collaboration CD whereby the actual flow of the compositions tend to be somewhat understated and subdued, opting for a mournful romanticised sound than being powerful and bombastic. Opening with a semi powerful track and opting for a slower second, the third track "Apres L'eternite" reminds me of, and is stylistically like the calibre of the slower tracks of Arcana's debut CD, minus the vocal elements. "Songe D'une Nuit" begins as a beautiful grand piano piece that later expands into a variety of other instrumental interludes including droning cellos, shrill string sections and other traditional classical elements. "Grain De Sable" eluded me for quite some time in what it actually reminded me of, but finally it struck me as I reviewing it: the dark orchestral compositional style of Shinjuku Thief's 'the scribbler' CD.
In itself an overall comparison to that said CD along with some elements of Arcana and LJDLP would give you enough clues to what this music is about. Much of the tone of the CD is well established early on without any real great surprises to be found other than a consistent CD in both writing and production. I do remember having read a pretty poor CD of this groups debut solo CD (and having not heard it cannot specifically compare), but from the words written it would seem this would be an almost different project this time around.

PHILLIP SAMARTZIS (AUS) "WINDMILLS BORDERED BY NOTHINGNESS" CD 1999 DOROBO LIMITED EDITIONS
Being very much on the theory and academic end of experimental electronic work Phillip Samartzis has produced a CD containing a single track at just under 40 minutes in length. Opening with a 'wet' sounding clatter the sound quickly sinks back into very minimalist depths to almost the point where the volume has to be extremely increased to pick up what is going on. If one ignores playing around with the volume the insectile scrambling textures slowly rise to an audible level before being axed in favour of a lone bell toll and a gently multiplying warm drone. Later in the piece things become more sporadic and scattered jumping between high pitched tones and rampant clatter and what sound to be uncut field recordings. Overall not really a CD you can loose yourself in due to the sporadic nature but interesting nonetheless. The cover probably says more in a glance than this review can.....basically detailing a splash of distant colour and texture in an otherwise background of bleak nothingness (stark white).

SCHLOSS TEGAL (USA) "BLACK STATIC TRANSMISSION" CD 1999 COLD SPRING
Arriving at their 5th full length the well renowned Schloss Tegal take us into their dark and bleak realms where occult, science and extraterrestrial sounds converge. Schloss Tegal I find to be one of the most unnerving groups to listen to and likewise one of the hardest to describe. While many groups specifically compose dark ambient music, whenever I listen to Schloss Tegal the actual music does not really seem to be the main focus. Am I making sense?...probably not. What I am trying to get at is while the CD is very much a dark ambient CD it does not sound as being a product of a composition process, rather that the artists are conducting a variety of sound and scientific experiments that ultimately on completion resembles dark ambience. This recording is reported to contain EVP recordings which adds to the experimental guise of the recording (more on this topic in contained in the interview elsewhere) and while heavily overloaded with these and other samples they do not get in the way of the overall soundscapes (although others have given complaint on this element).
Seven tracks are listed on the CD with only two digital tracks programmed in the disc, ensuring that the listener must take the full journey into the anti-world of Schloss Tegal and not just skim the surface by playing individual tracks. Delving further, 'Anti-world' sounding ambience is probably a very good description for the music, as comparisons 'deep space' or 'void' ambience does not really give the full feeling of the claustrophobic & sinisterly surreal, all encompassing sound of this release. Shifting sounds move from one moment to the next throughout a multi-layered tangled web of textures, clatter, drones and vocal snippets. The first digital track appears to be the title track (running for a little under 22 minutes) being quite sporadic and chaotic in its ambience and layers vocalisations yet always retaining bridging and connecting undercurrents. The second track would then obviously be an amalgam of the remaining six tracks in a 40 minute slab of soundscapes. Less chaotic and more subdued, the bass loaded textural rumblings forge forward slowly before sweeping off into more middle range atmospheric noise territories, complimented by a lone voice describing the 'eye' located at the centre of the universe. Given this track works as a complete piece picking where one 'track' starts of finishes is next to impossible. Again with the use of bridging elements the composition forefront uses an almost cut up style with the addition and subtraction of various sound and vocal layers. In the midst of the piece a single satellite like 'blip' chirps incessantly, indicating some sort of attempt at communication.....with what exactly?, I think I'd rather not know. Very late in the piece a looped female chant rise from the abyss giving a serene moment from the preceding (subdued) madness and chaos. Given the amount of textures and sounds covered, trying to describe all elements is both useless and futile. The only way to really experience this CD is to completely surrender to a total sensory overload and enjoy being engulfed in the hypnotic and unnerving journey. I hear that the majority of this pressing from Cold Spring is already sold out, thus some searching will be required to track this down from another distributor who might have copies left. Just think of the search as the first part of the journey......

SEPHIROTH (SWE) "CATHEDRON" CD 1999 COLD MEAT INDUSTRY
Sephiroth is a new signing to the CMI roster and is the solo incantation of the artist Ulf Soderburg who has also released two CD's under his own name (one of these CD's is also reviewed in these pages). While the music between his solo

PRE-FEED records

out:
FRANCISCO LOPEZ "Untitled #90" CD
PFCD001
(ultra highpitched field recordings made only using the natural sounds of insects and forests - in the vein of the highly acclaimed "La Selva" CD) Limited to 500.

coming:
PFCD002 - MOLJEBKA PVLSE - debut CD after the appearance on the "Esthetiks Of Cruelty" CMI compilation!
PFCD003 - SIGILLUM S "Happening whenever" new CD

PFCD001 is available in the US via:
MALIGNANT
ANOMALOUS
SOLEILMOON
+ others
Available in Europe via:
DEMOS (Ita)
TESCO (Ger)
STAALPLAAT (Hol)
+ others

get in touch for infos:
PRE_FEED c/o Gabriele Santamaria
via Gen. Pergolesi 21 60125 Ancona - ITALY
mantein@tin.it
http://move.to/Pre_Feed

offerings and this namesake is highly comparable, there is one clear difference that Sephiroth has opted for having a more brooding dark edge with less intertwining of many composed elements. With his solo efforts I immediately sat up and took notice of the highly composed tribal/ ritual percussive tracks, however it was the lack of this factor that initially caused me to be slightly disappointed with this CD. Nonetheless this just meant that there were more subtle tones & textures to be discovered and explored over numerous rotations. Evident on the first track is the trademark ominous dark ritual tones, that gradually rise up from the depths to explode into the tribalised percussion that Ulf has such a penchant for (and might I add does a splendid job of evoking the aura of its title "wolftribes"). Toward the end of this track it sinks back into the depths to flow forward into the slowly brooding title track, which is broken up into four segments which explores elements of ethnic ambience, customised ritualistic percussion and 'Lustmordian' like tones. Haunting nightscapes of forgotten times are summoned in the imagination throughout much of this CD, tempered with scattered moments power and exhilaration and mixed with subtle, unnerving terror. It been indicated that field recordings from such exotic places as Cairo, Iceland and Nordic forests are included within the soundscapes which only adds to the depth and visual presentation of the sound production. Vocals in the guise of low ritual/ choral chanting are also sporadically intermixed, being just enough to hint vivid mental pictures of mourning worshipers gathered amongst scattered ruins.

A minor complaint of this CD would be that I would have liked to have seen a longer overall play time (not nearly long enough for me at 45 minutes when the music is this good) and possibly the inclusion of the track off the Absolute Supper (which would have nestled quite nicely here with the other tracks). In conclusion this has been claimed by some to be the most professional recording that CMI have released thus far, and if it is compared to some of the big budget soundtrack stuff coming from the hands of the likes of Graeme Revell you would not be far wrong.

SHINJUKU FILTH (AUS)/ DARRIN VERHAGEN (AUS) "ZERO/ STUNG" CD 1999 IRIDIUM

Combining two separate pieces of music specifically composed for stage/ dance productions, this comes across a surprisingly coherent and complete body of work. In terms of previous works of Darrin, (be it under the Shinjuku Filth or solo guise) he delved heavily into various forms of ambient/ industrial/ experimental styled pieces, that while on their own were great tracks, tended not to lend themselves fitting together like a complete and flowing album. This is where this CD transcends the previous soundworks. The technological bent on ambient/ beat driven tracks is particularly emphasized by the predominant sound glitches, crackles and cut up noise that is used in such a way that becomes as much a part of the composition sound makeup as the other elements. Given that these tracks were used as part of contemporary dance performances, it might give the impression that the tracks are highly composed and up beat which is not in fact the case at all. I was actually surprised how minimalist and dark the majority of tracks were, but given that one of the performance groups (Chunky Moves) explores modern dance via jagged movement, the experimental minimal aspect of the music plays off the experimental nature of the dance company.

The lengthy opening track with is quite minimal with a scattered plodding bass and cut up sound palette lulls the listening into a hypnotic state prior to the heavily beat and glitch driven section kicking in. This juxtaposition encompasses much of the interplay of the album, jumping from load to soft textures, essentially exploring the atmosphere of sounds and beats in between these parameters. Track two with its heavy driving industrial guitar would almost fit on Stone Glass Steel's 'Dismembering Artists' CD, while a glitched jazz/ dub type track is toyed with on track three, where a single sampled female voice repeats the title of the first segment of the CD. A nice hip hop/ breakbeat is utalised on 'Trismus' where a background vocal scream becomes gradually more rabid throughout as the beats increase in intensity. Dark hip hop/ dub beats are forged on the next track 'E.B', complete with a looped gunshot of all things!

In terms of the second half of the CD (entitled 'Stung' and credited to a solo work) the main difference is in the more minimal, less beat oriented style. Again having a heavy basis in the glitched cut up sound and production technique the first track of this segment (track 9 of the disc) has a middle eastern flair in tone and slightly classical backing, almost coming off as an outtake of a Shinjuku Thief piece. Again referencing juxtaposed elements, the machine like pulses and static frequencies play off against the distant and minimal orchestrations and piano floating in the background, while the last two tracks of the CD jump back into dub/ beat territory to complete the cycle of the album. In total the CD runs for around 50 minutes and is housed in a cover faithful to distinctive characteristics of Dorobo/ Iridum releases. Yet again another very worthy item to explore from Mr Verhagen.

SKROL (CZE) " MARTYRIA" 10" EP 1998 POWER AND STEEL

Having heard some good things about this groups neo-classical/ apocalyptic works I must say I was a little disappointed when I finally obtained this. Not that the music is all that bad it is just that I feel that I expected more. Side A contains a pounding apocalyptic anthem but feels a bit too rigid and programmed which results in loosing the aura it was attempting to achieve. Interesting in itself is to hear a female out the front presenting the anger filled spoken vocals, they are a bit more venomous than the female vocals of TMLHBAC, (although do break into some commanding type singing). By the end of it all the shrill strings deep horns, crashing symbols and pounding marching drums do evoke a militant atmosphere, but I just know that this could have been all the more powerful. Side B is a little more sparse and subdued with distant factory type echos and slow kettle drums (credited with a title of 'Insomnia') which later encompasses minimalist orchestrations and half operatic female vocals. The final track 'Dei Irae' is a darkly atmospheric piece of slow drones and sparse factory noise injected with programmed orchestral elements, being quite reminiscent of ISN's 'Sacrosanct Bleed' CD. A pretty good track but a sound that has already been done better elsewhere. Being part of the Power & Steel 10" series= gold slip sleeve+information insert.

SNOG (AUS) "THIRD MALL FROM THE SUN" CD 1999 ROLLERCOASTER RECORDS

Clever, ingenious, humorous, insidious, thought provoking, insightful,......are just some of the words flying around in my head when listening to this. David Thrussel as Snog (AKA: Black Lung & Soma) has come up with a massive album which I would be astounded if it did not receive some sort of wider recognition than purely in underground circles and "those in the know". Most people probably have at least an idea if what musical genre Snog inhabit – being industrial/ techno hybrid of sorts. Decidedly more polished and commercial sounding than the plethora of other releases here within, this may not appeal to all, but the philosophy behind it has parallels with much of the anti-establishment sentiments in the wider experimental music scene. Glitched techno, snippet voices, driving samples, spaghetti western sentiments, big beat electonica, dark undertones, grating guitars, classical orchestrations etc make up the many diverse sounds which still retain a level of flow and coherence. The utterance of the trademark husky/croaking vocals are included in most tracks acting as a focal point for the dissemination of ideals against modern corporate society (& those who are a slave to it) and the constant struggle against these elements by the non conformist/ individual. Other sampled vocal segments further enhance what is being said throughout the lyrics and shine light on what people should be commonly aware of – but choose to be blissfully oblivious. The artwork is ironic in one sense yet quite dark and disturbing on a totally different level. It even seemed that the Australian licensed version nearly did not get released due to the potential legal implications related to the cover art. There is no point in highlighting the best tracks given the amount of fantastic moments throughout the 16 track 75 minute journey. To finish up, I will simply say that this album has been on high rotation in the dying weeks before this issue finally went to print.

ULF SODERBERG (SWE) "TIDVATTEN" CD 1998 NIGHTLAND RECORDINGS

Ulf Soderberg is the mastermind behind this solo project and also the group Sephiroth who has an upcoming CD on CMI (at the time of this review being written anyway). This CD is nothing short of brilliant and only has me salivating for the soon to be released Sephiroth CD. Both rousing and sorrowful cinematic soundscapes are presented here with such conviction and feeling, that it hard not to get drawn into the whole atmosphere of the time that the CD is depicting. Taking on a ehtho-ambient concept this is done on such a grand scale

I wonder of this is the type of atmospheres that someone like Mortiis is aspiring too? Not to taint this review with a comparison to Mortiis, this music is far less folk oriented and much more in an ethnic European tribalised fashion, in a much more professional guise. A heavy emphasis to put on sections of complex hand/ percussion rhythms, intermixed with an undercurrent of dark classical keyboard tones, far off voices, chanted vocals, bells & sounds (appearing to be field recording which gives off a very authentic feel). Further comparisons could be made to selected works of Dead Can Dance but this still retains a darker edge, with the whole CD flowing effortlessly and giving a prevailing aura of a ritualised twilight setting. Even though this disc has 10 tracks I see no point in a segmented review as this works as total body of music, where justice to it would not be done if it was presented or listened too on the basis of selected tracks. This item may be hard to track down but it is ultimately worth the price and time that you will invest (Might I add that Ulf's first solo CD from 1997 would also be a worthy investment). As the Sephiroth CD should already be out by the time of printing check out the review in these pages to see if it lived up to the expectations furnished by this CD.

SOLDERGEIST(GER)/DRAPE EXCREMENT(GER) "HUNTING FRENCH TOURISTS/ VILLAGE ON FIRE" SPLIT 7" EP 1998 STATEART
Not a bad split 7" from two of Germany's premier death industrial/ powers electronics groups. No complaints to be had with the music, however I was a little disappointed with the cover. Image wise it is fine, but I feel more could have been done with the font styles, layout and colours.....nonetheless on to the tracks. Soldergeist open with a variety of buried and semi-buried vocal samples as the pulsing loops gradually builds its intrinsic velocity. Threatening to explode into overdrive a slow pulse like beat kicks in as the sound become more powerful with not necessarily more movement. The tracks charm is held within its overall threatening tone that chooses not to fully deliver. Immediately on Drape Excrement's first track, its more forceful nature is evident. Throbbing pulses of overdriven tones take the middle to high end noise spectrum with distorted and echoed vocals and scattered noise stabs filling out the remainder of sound. 'Keine Reue', the second of D.E's tracks is a little more straight up with a central 'roaring' noise tone with flecks of alternating sound evident around the edges. It will be interesting to see what this group comes up with on the on the upcoming Catharsis split CD on Black Plague.

SPATIUM SAEVUS SONITUS (GRE) "THE RITUAL OF THE BLACK SUN" CD 1998 CREEPY AWESOME PREDACIOUS PRELACY
Not knowing much about this project I did note that they were included on the roster of the recent CMI festival held in Greece (October, 1999). The opening track (being the title track) is a lengthy 20 minute track with heavy ritualistic overtones. Deep reverberating drums, bells, percussion, sporadic agonised vocals set the scene and move forward at a snails pace with various alternating background sounds and elements. At about the five minute mark things turn off on another tangent becoming more spacious and droning complimented sustained keyboard notes, retaining the ritual overtones. At around the 10 minutes mark the deep percussive elements, bells and vocals return and seemly at the next 5 minute mark thing again alter heading into cavernous & echoed territory which then continues through a minor few transitions into the tracks conclusion. Coming off a 20 minute track the next one ("To the Unknown God') is a tenth of the length, sounding not unlike the deep sound structures and synthetic strings of a number of Caul's compositions. Tortured vocal wails mark the beginning of track three, with the music having the similar characteristics of the preceding track yet with added elements of sporadic organ dirges and experimental noise sound structures added at random giving off again an improvised, ritualistic feel. Another dark keyboard hymn/ drone formulates part 2 of 'To the Unknown God' being a very slowly forming tune. Part 3 is a little more lively organ tune which promises a bit but never really gets going and much is the same with parts 4 & 5 (although part 5 decided to go for some 'spacey' keyboard tones). Overall given what appears to be improvised parts intermixed with pre-planned or pre recorded sections results in a sporadic finished product....sometimes it works really well but in other parts falls a little flat. A bit of a hit and miss affair I'm afraid. Packaging D.I.Y looking (but pro –printed) fold out card sleeve...imagery and text being nothing spectacular. 'Tis strange that I would probably would gain a better overall impression of the music if the packaging was more professional in text presentation and image choice. Probably a pointless complaint but I guess I have been a bit spoilt when it comes to immaculacy dark artwork, all thanks to a few key labels.

STONE GLASS STEEL (USA) "DISMEMBERING ARTISTS" CD 1999 MALIGNANT RECORDS
Somewhat of a pioneering artist in the field of recontextulised ambient industrial, with the release of this CD Phil Easter shows us just how advanced and ahead of his time he was. While the packaging may state 1999 the recording itself dates back nearly a decade to 1991 consisting of the first (yet never released until now) Stone Glass Steel CD. For myself already being familiar with, (and a big fan of) SGS's first two officially released CD's, this really acts as a percussor to the listening experience to be found on the 'later' albums. All trademark productions trickeries of Mr 'eyespark' Easter are to be found: the seething and boiling sonic magma, the sweeping textural waves, the digital throbbing, the cinematic overtones, it is just that all of these elements are intermixed with more up front sampled elements of industrialised guitar loops and percussion. In terms of this focus I believe the context of when this was recorded is also quite important given that Industrial music (in the sense of the American definition) was just starting to make both inroads and impacts on the mainstream music market. I assume that this factor in the rise in commercial acceptance of industrial guitar bands would have played somewhat of a role in shaping the sampling palette of SGS at the time. All of this talk about historic elements may lead you to believe that this would sound somewhat dated, but this is far from the case. Throw this in the hand of any industrial fan and defy them to pick when this was actually recorded. The production values, the sound makeup and the sonic layers are as current as any album recorded by an artist armed with today's digital equipment (if not in fact exceeding the quality of current contemporaries). In passing it is almost scary to fathom what exotic sonic delicacies will be served up by Stone Glass Steel with new compositions, given the break even from his other more recent CD's (all the way back to 92 & 93 would you believe!). Whist we eagerly await any new offerings, feast on this historic morsel as a taster.

TERTIUM NON DATA (USA) "THE THIRD IS NOT GIVEN" CD 1999 CROWD CONTROL ACTIVITIES
Tertium Non Data is a collaboration between John Bergin of C17H19N03 and Brett Smith of Caul; both have worked together before in the bleached, guitar weary Godflesh terrain of Trust Obey. TND seems a perfect melding of disparate sonic visions (Bergin conjures rich cinematic, almost pristine, soundtrack influenced music, while Smith relies on a more internal sonar, sonically eviscerating the soul via spiritual explorations), though I would say the all around feel directly relates to the latest C17 disc on Malignant, 1692/2092 (the imaginary soundtrack disc; there's even a remix of one of the vocal tracks from that disc here, the vocals seeming to placate instead of intrude as they did on the original). Brooding, apocalyptic, immensely vast in scope and dense with imagery filled sounds that take one on a journey to places of the mind and spirit that provoke mystery, melancholia and magic, the music on The Third Is Not Given translates to wonderfully desolate (Brett Smith's music seems bred in the empty hearth of desolation…), cinematic industrial sonicscapes brandishing serrated, metallic edges. CCA will also be releasing a CD later this year by Black Mouth, which combines the duo here with Jarboe (of Swans [R.I.P.]…as if I needed to remind you of that), a tangled web completion to the disjointed trilogy, as Jarboe sang on two of the best tracks from the aforementioned C17 CD… —JC Smith (Reprinted by permission from Outburn Magazine: www.outburn.com)

TEMPLEGARDEN (GER) "CULTURE VS. NATURE" CD 1998 ANT-ZEN
Opening the card like packaging (complete with wax seal) the esoteric element of the disc is felt even prior to the index finger hitting the start button. Reading some of the titles such as 'trance', 'transition' & 'tranmission' further establishes this aura. Given that the CD runs over 70 minutes with only 6 tracks the equation equals long drawn out tracks. Rather than dissect each individually I think that one overall description will suffice and still do this justice. Being at the mercy of the sound textures, murky drones rise to the surface of the underground lake only to find echoing darkness radiating to the edges of the vast cavern. Occasionally more earthly elements of distant vocals, gongs, flute and natural sounds are heard but still seem all to foreign within the compositions. Shimmering electronic drones and

slightly urgent electronic loops become more spacious heading into less claustrophobic territories, where some of the drones take on an almost angelic choir like spiritual quality (however you can alway be assured of a more sinister texture lurking behind to be revealed soon enough). Textured minimal rhythms (more than specifically beats) round out segments in a semi tribalised guise, whilst others have drones which paint mental pictures of the exotic far-east. The music is credited to having been recorded over a 4 year period from 1993-97 and having input from no less than 6 individuals – some being notables of other Ant-Zen acts. Part ambient, part tribal and part spiritual equals another worthy release.

T.G.V.T (GER) "PARALYSIS" 10" EP 1998 POWER AND STEEL
Dark, minimal, ritual ambience is what we have here and while this group has been around for some years they have not been the most productive of projects (given that the last release was back in the early 90's). A low bass driven pulse makes the predominate backing for side A ('Archaic Mementos Parts 1 & 2') with underneath sweeping tones, minimal clatter and distant treated vocals. The pulse dropping out mid way in, is replaced with ethnic styled atmospheres with a mildly noisy edge. Things become even more ethnic in sound with ritual percussive hand drumming, chimes and sustained tones (derived from wooden flute) that all build to a climactic moment and subsequent conclusion. The tracks on side A are credited to being remixes of early works from 1994, while side B offers up a more recent composition to give a hint of where the group are heading. The track 'Meditation' on Side B still holds an ethnic/ ritual feel but is more sparse & focussed that totally eclipses the earlier tracks. Heavy claustrophobic ritual drumming gives a stated atmosphere with fleeting tones and distant dark drones taking up the background. Mid way the drumming and background in stripped back to only atmospheric sweeping tones and treated female vocal snippets, while choir like vocals rises and falls high in the mix. Dynamics being again on the move bring to the fore nosier mid ranged 'storming' elements that sweeps the piece to its end. Simply a stunning multi-layered, dynamic piece of music. Given the sheer quality of this track, let's hope the project will have a new full length offering out before to long. In regard to packaging is the similar to others in the series being housed in the gold slip sleeve with information insert. Definitely worthwhile.

THIS MORN' OMINA (BEL) "NEZERU ENTI SEBAUEM NETER XERTET" CD 1998 OLD EUROPA CAFE
A common thread through quite a few of OEC's CD releases has been the mystical/ spiritual edged groups, with This Morn' Omina being another such project. Overall you could probably coin this esoteric atmospheric & experimental ambience however the twist comes when the rituallistic beats are used in more of an industrial programmed sense. This gives a duality to the sound intermixing the modern and the primitive or the archaic atmospheres blended with technological driven sounds. For reference purposes this could be comparable to a less aggressive Memorandum as well as not being as dark and the aforementioned group. Another group that a parrallel could be drawn would be Svasti-Ayanam (a raison d'etre side project). 'K'hai' works particularly well with dark noise and subdued rhythms and ritualistic beats. The ethnic flavour on 'the fifth incarnation of vishnu' is very strong, including the main elements of ritual programmed beats as well as whispered/ spoken vocals. Given that the programmed production is less evident on 'the stars are like dust' enables the dark flowing background to evoke a suitably dark, middle eastern tinged atmosphere. Again with the beats not being over-produced or synthetic sounding the uptempo ritual elements of 'Dragon – flies/ samarrkand' the group really hit their element. The final track is a 25 minute sprawling effort that is dark ambient in intent, inter-spread with the beat ritual elements (which pervades the majority of the album) as well as some cinematic classically oriented keyboards. I find this overall to be an interesting CD in the ideas utalised and sounds explored, however the overall finished product has not held my attention that has encouraged multiple listens.

MATTHEW THOMAS (AUS) "P3" 1999 DOROBO
This mini CD is basically an extension the Darrin Verhagan release in the same format and title (reviewed last issue). Here Mr Tomas has taken the source material from Mr Verhagan's works and given them his personal treatment and manipulation. This angle of being an extension of the original is emphasised as the starting track is digitally noted as being 'track 6', with there actually being only 4 tracks (and a play time of a little over 20 minutes). The atmospheres are highly experimental utilising digital glitches, cut ups and intentional flaws as much as deep bass tones and glacial sonic waves. Built on a minimalist basis, it is music that you hear as much as you feel, with the bass tone attaining those window rumbling frequencies even at low volumes. Sonic textures throb crackle & moan, with a comparison being something like listening to a scratched and jumping Korner CD. Sonic textures, ambient as much as they are dark, provide a nice little collectors disc from a rising Australian experimental artist.

TORTURA (BEL) "MENTAL AGONY / VICTIMM" 7" EP 1999 NOCTURNUS/ SPECTRE
Previously having only heard one death industrial track from this reasonably new project (the track off 'the book of shadows' compilation) I was looking forward to some new output from this group to see what else they could serve up. 'Mental Agony' is beyond anything that I would have expected, given that is has a high energy looped noise beat creating some very interesting rhythmic dark electronics. As the repetitive beat elements forges forward some 'true crime' type voice snippets are injected into the convulsing patient in a failed attempt at sedation. 'Victtimm' being the second side of the vinyl is far removed from the first side being a densely heavy dark ambient piece. Lacking the more guttural and harsh tones normally associated with death industrial the low repetitive drones and loops evoke a similar feel. The heavily manipulated voice samples are included throughout which add to the dark calamity, as the backing tones gradually muster up further strength. Although the results are quite different than what I expected this 7" shows Tortura is a master of many dark sounds.

UNCONDITIONAL LOATHING (USA) "S/T" CD 1999 PRODUCT WHORE RECORDINGS
Noise with a sense of humor, and yet also with the testicles to taunt and seethe with relentless abandon. This self-titled release contains 22 terse, contaminated injections of overloaded sonic fury that actually display a keen sense of variance, of dynamics that, despite their caustic, speaker flooding approach, kept this listener's ears pasted to the side of my head throughout its duration. Highlights? Well, there's the aggressive, steel wool scraping of mental debris from the inside of my skull during "An After Death Mint"; the corrosive, raging storm in the sonic vomitarium of "Battered Persistance"; the looped airplane landing and lifting off, punctured valve ejaculation of unknown squirming, squiggly, semen-like monstrosities, all under a brooding veil…and then, a more stealthy stream is pumped out, all during "3"; "Strobelight Sodomy" which rhythmically assails the sonic anus, a pummel of an excrement coated design, all with a bit of variety to keep the victim amused; the indistinguishable samples ably assisted by church organ and choir, upon which abrasive noise (a baptism in unholy water?) is indelicately poured over the top during "God's Retirement Party (4:54 a.m.)"; the diarrhetic onslaught of noise, like drowning in a storm of watery excrement, of "Shinimasho Pt. 2"; and so much more. If one likes one's noise in bite size pieces, Unconditional Loathing definitely deliver a rabid, foaming mouthful. Fun stuff! —JC Smith

VOX BARBARA (USA) "THE FIVE SENSES" CD 1999 LITTLE MAN RECORDS
The Five Senses takes organic sounds (household objects, human voice) post-manipulated debris (handmade paper/steel sculpture) and manipulates them into wonderfully lucid sonicscapes that are further manipulated via the mixing process and an ear for constructing mesmerizing, hypnotic rhythms. "Spirit Musk" is full of clattering, clanking, distinct noises, driven by a muddled (but not muddy in tone), looped percussion that would be right at home on a Deutsch Nepal release. Sounds shamble about like rats in the walls, pipes being struck, stinging slashes of indecipherable noises lashing like leather on flesh, low scraping cadences like rubber being scratched by sharp nails…and more. The way the music evolves, I am in awe of the textures as each claims its space, then slinks back to a hiding place within the contours of sound. Each of the five tracks follows this pattern, but it is a pattern that travels down unexpected sonic avenues. The fluid

sheen of "Liquidity" escorts the listener to a realm of thick, overwhelming pensiveness, and then through a space of repetitious, disjointed and yet perfectly sequenced percussion. "Resonance" starts noisy (but with clarity), looped, squiggly sounds vying for attention, a whole jumble of nervous tones rising to stake a claim to their individual space within the song, the resonance of weird elements sprinkled masterfully throughout-excellent. Machinery breathing opens "The Stickiness Of Colors," followed by a boiling liquid that sounds like rubber, or at least rubbery (?!), as slabs of indecipherable sounds grow heavy...there's even a sound that is vaguely vocal (maybe; yes; no...hmmmmm); this leads into the crunch, rip and tear of "Membraneous Absorption," polished to a sandpaper rubbed sheen...and more, so much more. The whole project is inspired by Anaitre Tellsos' novel, Ravings Of A Madman. I don't care where Frank Smith's (the man behind Vox Barbara) inspiration comes from (well, actually, I do find fascination in what inspires the creative process, I'm just making a point-read on), just as long as he keeps creating wonderful, full-bodied, sonically explorative CDs like The Five Senses. (Point made.) Again, excellent! —JC Smith

VARIOUS ARTISTS (SWE) "ESTHETICKS OF CRUELTY" DCD 1999 COLD MEAT INDUSTRY
Cold Meat Industry has gathered, under the corrosive noise umbrella (yeah, that's the one with the serrated edges and nuclear glow), a plethora of little or unknown bands from their homeland, Sweden, for this percolating collection of tympanic membrane destroying music. This massive 2CD set, twenty-nine tracks in all, showcases an abundance of methods in which one can sonically ream the labyrinth-like cavities and canals of the ear, of which any one of the following will suffice: the caustic, incendiary, war-laden Iron Justice; the squeal and excrement loop of Dodsdomd; the crumbling, speaker disemboweling onslaught of Irgun Z'wai Leumi; the mind-shifting clutter that punctures the deep oscillations of Bad Kharma; the little girl samples sucked into the white noise tornado of Blod; the punishing hammer drive, volatile vocals and swirling, sandpaper in a blender massage of IRM (LP on CMI out soon); the wrapped in plastic, convulsive decay of Apostasia; the ear to the ground secretions from the inside of the skull of Persona...okay, I'll stop (I think you get the point). There's even worthy appearances from some of the CMI roster's alumni, though they wear masks here (and I've probably missed some...Richard? Ed: yep..the ones missed also include: Peter from Magaptera on Obscene Noise Korporation & allegedly Lina of Deutsch Nepal on Thurnemans,); Benny from Morthond/Morthound/Hazard appears as the static reverb radiance dissolving into pools of putrefying flesh of Tape Decay and, along with Lina from Deutsch Nepal, as the fluttering, spastic, urine-rusty needle in the eye Janitor; and the sinister, low key seduction/interrogation of Bodies Drowned Natural (BDN), obviously sprung from the decadent mindscape of Roger Karmanik, the man behind Brighter Death Now as well as Cold Meat Industry's esteemed curator. Cataclysmic noise from the label that specialises in variations thereof. Mandatory!—JC Smith (Reprinted by permission from Outburn Magazine: www.outburn.com)

VARIOUS ARTISTS (WLD) "THE FLATLINE COMPILATION" DCD 1999 FLATLINE
I believe that this was put out by/ and or in collaboration with An-Zen and while the Teknoir DCD (reviewed also this issue) featured the harder edged industrial/ noise oriented club music being produced, this is focused more on the melody based EBM industrial/ electronica out there. There is some crosser into the nosier areas here with groups such as, 'imminent starvation', 'synapscape' etc, but overall the beats tend to be more dance friendly with many layers of dark but hyped keyboard lines, such as done by 'the galan pixs' who open the CD set. 'Snog' produced a dark slab of programmed electronica complete with trademark vocals and cynical lyrics. 'Biopsy' create some great lounge breakbeats but unfortunately head into over-programmed beat/ guitar/ yell territory.
In terms of a short overview: 'netz' - breakbeat sentiments mixed EBM elements, 'If project' – hardcore industrial electronica, 'it' — schizoid beats and keyboards, 'mother destruction' – dark ambience mixed with dark electonica, 'beefcake' – awesome drum & bass breaks and cinematic soundscapes, 'generation x-ed' – big beat industrial attack, 'hanzel & gretyl' - ramstein styled guitars mixed with electronica elements, 'torsion' - ambient passages & industrial beats juxtaposed against harsh guitars, 'Pail' - noisy & abrasive break beats with melodious keys, 'equinox' – dark soundscapes and partially buried beats, 'vnv nation' – dark classically inspired electro EBM. Other groups featured but not mentioned include: 'spahn ranch', 'ichor', 'the agression', 'rx', 'dive', 'haujobb', 'pain konsept', 'tower II', 'skorbut' & 'das ich'. Personally I would go for the Teknoir DCD compilation first, but from the list of names associated with this comp you should have a reasonable idea of if this release is for you.

VARIOUS ARTISTS (WLD) "LUCIFER RISING" CD 1999 ATHANOR
Certainly a top notch release both musically and visually in the esoteric realms. The CD is furnished in it's own full colour slip case, complimented by an oversized A5 full colour 16 page booklet with fantastic imagery (cover by Franz Von Stuck). While a variety of sounds are covered by the groups on the disc, the common thread is the compilation's theme of focusing on the Luciferian mythos.
Proceeding are commenced with Endvra who produce a rousing yet sinister track "Parzifal" which would not have been out of place on the 'Great God Pan' CD. A newish group Chod are featured next with a very nice dark ambient track, including wind, fire & choir samples alongside a pounding timpani drum, background atmosphere and distorted vocals late in the track. Everything I have come to appreciate about Blood Axis is reinforced with their reworking of one of their early tracks "Electricity". Both sampled classical sections and composed neo-classical elements are mixed with commanding vocals and a variety of interludes, making this one the CD's highlights. Der Blutharsch's track begins in a low key industrial guise but later becomes more militant with a repeated German vocal sample. Dawn & Dusk Entwinded have a reasonably well composed neo-classical track and while is not at all a bad song it just tends to be overshadowed by some of the other groups. While admittedly the Allerseelen track is the first I have heard from the group it is pretty much what I expected with it's bass driven avangarde industrial focus, however I do not feel that the female vocals sit very well overall with the song. Ernte have a unusual track with sporadic beats and horns overlaid with European vocal, thus some of the intent of the track would be lost on an English speaker like me. Bobby BeauSoleil features an except from his soundscore to the move "Lucifer Rising" (incidentally where the title of the release was taken from) with the track being a nice reflective piece of classically inspired music. The 12 string acoustic guitar and mild vocals of the apocalyptic folk group Changes builds a retrospective feel that proves that not everyone in the late 60's early 70's was into the prevading themes of peace and love. Waldteufel feature a whistling tune with sung/ spoken vocal which unfortunately are far too upfront in the mix. The whistling suffers from poor execution and the backbone of the tune is barely audible over the high mix of vocals, both being factors that have impeded on what otherwise may have been a good track. The long standing group Ain Soph finish off proceedings with a lengthy and very dark death ambient type track which although is very different to the rest of the compilation is still a great ending to it. Overall this is a high quality release for the eye, ear and spirit....

VARIOUS ARTISTS (WLD) "ON THE BRINK OF INFINITY" CD 1999 CHTHONIC STREAMS
This is simply a beautifully conceived and packaged item in all aspects. Firstly the 'recycled' card packaging suits the stunning archaic imagery, with the chosen artists presenting a fantastic collection of track. This is especially to the point where there are no stand out tracks as all are of a similar calibre. Also the actual flow of the album need a mention as the tracks have been compiled in such a way the CD has an impeccable flow...starting from a folk perspective, gradually heading into darker noisier territory with the middle tracks and finishing tracks being more neo-classical.
Howen/ Wakeford open the disc with a track somewhere between an actual song and piece of ambience, given that it contains spoken vocals and plucked bass, with the remainder of the backing being quite free flowing. Empyrium have a beautiful piece featuring classical/ folk acoustics, piano and vocals ranging from a whisper. to growls to commanding tenor like chants. Given that Arcane Art is a Penitent side project, I can't see any huge difference between the two other than this track of medieval classical sentiments is a little more up tempo than the average Penitent. It might also be worthy to add that this Arcane Art track manages to eclipse the quality of the tracks on the latest Penitent disc. Anima in Flamme are grounded very much in medieval classical vein using only violin and piano, and

with the recording making use of the real instruments rather than a synthetic reproduction gives the track a very authentic aura. Funerary Call makes the change in direction into darker realms with a death ambient type piece that could be somewhat like a mix between Megaptera and early raison d'etre. Nothus Filus Mortis use a heavy dose of vocal snippets, dark drones, cavernous percussion and keyboard textures to good (obscure) effect. Following on Kerovnian just keep getting better with their ultra black ambient works, and with the quality of this track, the forthcoming second album will certainly be a highly anticipated one. Like Kerovnian, Gruntsplatter keep upping their level creating a multi layer and extremely dark ambient piece that ever so slightly touches on noisier more grating sound textures. 15 Delights of Dionysius (being ...the soil bleeds black side project) create a stunning tribally tinged dark ambient slab of sound. Atmospheric keyboard treatments and sound waves swirl overhead whilst deathly slow tribal percussion helps ground the composition. 4th Sign of the Apocalypse heralds the move toward more neo-classical sound works, which includes a partly sorrowful, partly romantic violin passage along with a sporadic undercurrent of sound and vocal snippets prior to cutting back to a clean guitar line and lone voice talking of resurrection and religion. Dream into Dust create an impressive stated atmosphere on their track with a militant pounding introduction, proceeding into a slow dark orchestral passage that gradually builds in stature and anger. This passage is then suddenly all together removed as it proceeds to move into quite minimalist territory akin to hearing horn players from afar across the battle field. Last up is Backworld giving a feeling of completion with an almost celebratory acoustic guitar, piano/ keyboard & vocal track. Nothing more to say than this is beyond recommended.

VARIOUS (WLD) "THE SOUNDS OF SADISM" CD 1999 CROWD CONTROL ACTIVITIES
Aural extremity and depravity is what is show cased on this little number, being far from friendly listening for the whole family, rather detailing some of the nastier elements of power electronics. Deathpile start things off presenting a track (holding the title of this CD), consisting of a scattered low and high end backing which is surprisingly subdued given the high flanged vocal treatment going on. Improvised, high end, wall of sound and semi-buried vocals are the go for Iugula Thor, while more mid ranged factory type rumblings & buried vocals are the trademarks for the Taint track. Skin Crime in all their massively overloaded 'wall'o'noise' intensity, ironically become almost ambient if only not for the treated vocals pushing things way over the top. Atrax Morgue have the absolutely insane ranting of Marco making the majority of the track with the backing being little more than a mid ranged hum. Not being familiar with Hydra has a quite horrific real scenario type passage over multiplying static frequencies which leads into yet another class Gruntsplatter effort. The track tends to be quite heavier than the majority of the others, opting for a low grating edge rather than a straight high pitched attack. It is still quite a bit more rabid and noiser than what I am used to from Gruntsplatter, with this potentially related to the concept of the compilation. Bloodyminded don't really do that much for me, with this being particularly related to the vocals which lack any sort of treatment (other than straight yelling and growling). The backing also seems to be alittle simplistic, consisting of a couple of repetitive elements and sporadic squeals. Con-Dom have an eloquently titled track ('gagged by my own genitals') which is a classy piece of multi layered mid range liquidous loops, inter-spread with flesh burning, searing white noise and vocal snippits. Just when you think the track is going to pass without the trademark static driven vocals they arrive in the mix, taking the track to an even higher intensity level. Correct me if I'm wrong but do Con-Dom get more venomers and angry with each new piece? Last I heard Black Leather Jesus was a defunct project, but with a track here maybe they have again resurfaced? Being the first output I've heard, this is a chainsaw grating slab of noise that tends to have a looped sound to all the chaos. Sshe Retina Stimulants attempt at cleaning the listener with a sermon of white, high end noise, that has the sonic sharpness equivalent of a scalpel. Very nasty indeed.
The 'true crime electronics' artist Slogun have a powerfully modulated, mid toned storming track. The inception of the heavily treated vocals ensures the noise attack soars off on the high end tangent as another layer of sound, rather then being specifically decipherable. Discordance have a heavily scattered piece of sporadic high end static intermixed with low pulse elements and searing vocals. Quite a good track if it were not for the lone high pitched squeal present throughout the whole piece. The final attack comes from Stahlnetz which serves up quite a speaker punishment with the crystalline blistering static. Having a certain improvised edge the electronic tone scatter off on various tangents and at some point disappearing altogether revealing buried vocals. Overall maybe too many of the tracks head into 'noise for noise sake' territory for my own personal tastes, this is still extremely well presented overall in both packaging and group/ track selection.

VARIOUS ARTISTS (WLD) "TEKNOIR" DCD 1999 HYMEN
Anyone familiar with the more techo/ industrial side of Ant-Zen (namely the Hymen label) should have a good idea of what is encompassed on this double CD set. Housed in a slimline double CD case the sleeve is impressively simple with textured/ stamped grey card. A good majority of the tracks contain techno/ glitch/ beat/ noise sounds ranging from straight forward non commercial industrial dance to other tracks inter spread with darker undercurrents. On the first disc great tracks are provided from the likes of: orphx (dark & driving yet somewhat subdued beats), imminent starvation (all out noise/ rhythmic pummellings), synapscape (fantastic beat/ noise/ groove combo), p.a.l (glitched beat/ noise), lustmord vs. metal beast (beat/ groove oriented cavernous dark ambience) & seekness (noise/ beat atmospheres). The other artists featured on disc one include the likes of: black lung, monolith, icon zero & vromb (among others). In terms of disc two much the same territory is covered with worthwhile tracks from: architect (hypnotic & cinematic breakbeats), beefcake (soaring cinematic glitched dark techno), somatic responses (industrial strength factory noise & beats), it (harsh groove beats), snog (techno/ guitar warfare) & hypnoskull (power/ speed hyper techno). Other groups on disc two include (selected): oil 10, bochumwelt, esplendor geometrico, winterkalte & silk saw. A release which is a good representation of the sound and direction of this Ant-Zen side label and likewise a great introduction tool if you are not familiar with many of the above mentioned groups.

VARIOUS ARTISTS (WLD) "WE'RE ON THE PLANET: COMMEMORATION OF THE DEAD" CD 1998 CREEPY AWESOME PREDACIOUS PRELACY
Every so often a CD lands in my letterbox from groups/ labels that I have not previously heard. This is the case with this CD and apart

Self Abuse Records

Dealers in Extreme, Abstract, and Unusual Sounds Worldwide.

Write for out free Catalog, or check us out on the web at:

www://www.mv.com/ipusers/selabuse

Self Abuse Records
26 S. Main #277
Concord, NH
03301, USA

from not knowing the label I have not heard anything at all of the 11 projects featured. The cover itself gives little to no information on the featured groups but as the label is based in Greece I am assuming most groups are from this region (but I could also be quite wrong!). A reasonably bland spacey/ new age type keyboard piece starts proceedings, being credited to an unusually titled project 'The Narrator Mr Cricket'. 'Decadence' showcase a DIJ inspired acoustic song, including gothic tinged female vocals, backing piano & classical acoustic guitar solo. Overall maybe not unlike Ulver's second acoustic folk CD? 'Into the Abyss' are acoustic guitar based group with clean male vocals and some backing synths) being more folky darkwave than ambient, but managing to come up with a refreshing sound (here I might mention I have always been a sucker for dark acoustic guitar work). 'Glaufx Garland' mess around with some dark drones and experimental textures, however some badly placed cheesy discordant keyboards ruin any atmosphere gained. 'Snowskyn' produce some nice classically tinged apocalyptic dark industrial that hypes up with a snare breakbeat mid flow whilst retaining the dark undercurrent. As for some of the remaining groups: 'Ding An Sich' – dark keyboard tune with Nick Cave like vocalist, 'Density of State' - dark programmed industrial in the vein of NIN, 'Viridian' – tribal industrial ala This Morn' Omina, 'Alpha-Omega' – cheesy gothic EBM, 'Slow Motion' – medieval classical comparable to Ataraxia, 'Cpinalonga' – spacious & lengthy dark ambient experimentations, Overall quite a nice surprise of a disc in terms of projects featured…. pity the packing does nothing to spark interest if you were to spot this on the racks.

CONTACT LIST

ANT-ZEN: C/-S.Alt. Lessingstr. 7a, 93049 Regensburg, Germany, salt@ant-zen.com, www.ant-zen.com
ARCANE RECORDINGS: C/- Mark Endacott, P.O. Box 458, Fullarton, South Australia 5063, markenda@bigpond.com
ASH: 13 Oswald Road, London SW17 7SS, England, ashnp@touch.demon.co.uk, www.touch.demon.co.uk/ash.htm
ATHANOR: C/- Stephane, BP294, 89007 POITIERS, Cedex, France, ursprache@wanadoo.fr, www.multimania.com/wiligui/athanor/accueil.htm
AVA/ES1 RECORDS: P.O. Box 605488, Cleveland OH 44105, USA, baal7ava@aol.com, www.angelfire.com/ny/scriptureszine/avaes1.html
BLACK PLAGVE: C/- Malignant Records, tortured@magnus1.com, www.malignantrecords.com/blackplague.html
CAUL: C/- Brett Smith, caul@concetric.net, www.concentric.net/~Caul/enter.html
CHTHONIC STREAMS: P.O. Box 7003, New York NY 10116-7003 USA, chthonic@chthonicstreams.com, www.chthonicstreams.com
COLD MEAT INDUSTRY: PO Box 1881, S-58117 Linköping, Sweden, order@coldmeat.se, www.coldmeat.se
COLD SPRING: 8 Wellspring, Blisworth, Northants, NN7 3EH, England, UK, coldspring@thenet.co.uk, www.thenet.co.uk/~coldspring/
COMPULSION MAGAZINE: P.O. Box 36 Enfield, En3 4ZX UK, tonycompulsion@hotmail.com, www.callnetuk.com/home/compulsion
CREEPY AWESOME PREDACIOUS PRELACY: Lisiou 8 GR – 11146, Athems, Greece
CRIONIC MIND: PMB 105, 4644 Geary Boulevard, San Francisco, California 94118, crionic@pacbell.net, www.crionicmind.org
CROWD CONTROL ACTIVITIES: 821 White Elm Dr. Loveland, CO 80538 USA, crowded@ezlink.com/~crowded/controlcenter.html
C17H19No3: C/- John Bergin, grinder@unicom.net, www.emerald.net/grinder
DARK VINYL: P.O. Box 1221, 90539 Eckental, West Germany, Darkvinyl@T-online.de
DESCENT MAGAZINE: P.O. Box 2339, Stuyvesant Station, NYC, NY 10009 USA, s@khanate.org
DEUTSCH NEPAL: C/- Peter Andersson, bsb015v@trinet.se, http://user.tninet.se/~bsb015v/
DOROBO: C/- Dorobo, P.O. box 22 Glen Waverley, Victoria, Australia 3150, dorobo@werple.net.au, http://werple.net.au/~dorobo/dorobo.html
DRONE RECORDS: Baraka (H) S. Knappe, Gneisenaustrasse 56, 28201 Bremen, Germany, dronetroum@aol.com, http://members.xoom.com/dronerecords,
EIBON RECORDS: Via Folli 5, 20134 Milano, Italy, rberchi@galactica.it, www.this.it/eibon/
ENTARTETE MUSIKK: C/- Peter Andersson, bsb015v@tninet.se, http://user.tninet.se/~bsb015v/
FEVER PITCH MUSIC: 1108. E.Capitol Drive, Appleton, Wi 54911, USA
FUNCTIONAL ORGANISATION: C/- Hilger, Gralssstr 8, 68199 Mannheim, Germany, tesco-org-ma@t-online.de
HEARTLAND RECORDS: P.O. Box 126, Baladclava, Victoria 3183, Australia
HERMETIQUE: C/- Jerome Nougaillon, 48 Rue Leonard Danel, 59000 Lille, France, hermetique@nordnet.fr
HYMEN: hymen@gmx.net, www.klangstabil.com/hymen
I-BURN: C/- Pre-Feed, Gabriele Santamaria, via Gen. Pergolesi 21, 60125 Ancona – Italy, mantein@tin.it, http://go.to/I-Burn
IMMINENT STARVATION: C/- Olivier Moreau, Kolenmarkt 97 / 1d, 1000 Brussels, Belgium, om@ant-zen.com, www.ant-zen.com/imminent
IRIDIUM: C/-Dorobo, P.O. box 22 Glen Waverley, Victoria, Australia 3150, dorobo@werple.net.au, http://werple.net.au/~dorobo/dorobo.html
JILAT: 13 Wells Road, Walsingham, Norfolk, NR22, 6DL UK, www.jilat.demon.co.uk
KEROVNIAN: kerovnian@hotmail.com, www.geocities.com/Area51/Portal/2579/
LITTLE MAN RECORDS: P.O. Box 45636, Seattle, Washington 98145-0636, USA, vox@speakeasy.org, www.speakeasy.org/~vox/noise/barb.html
LIVE BAIT RECORDING FOUNDATION, 423 Seventh Street, #3, Fairport Harbor, Ohio 44077 USA, livebaitrecording@hotmail.com, http://crionicmind.org/livebait
LOKI FOUNDATION PSF 241321 04333 Leipzig, Germany, loki-found@t-online.de
MALIGNANT RECORDS: PO Box 5666, Baltimore MD 21210, USA, malignant@malignantrecords.com, www.malignantrecords.com
MALSONUS RECORDS, C/- Jonathan Canady, P.O. Box 18193, Denver, CO 80218 USA, malsonus@milehigh.net
MEMENTO MORI: C/- Dark Vinyl, P.O. Box 1221, 90539 Eckental West Germany, Darkvinyl@T-online.de
MIDDLE PILLAR: PO Box 555, NY, NY 10009 USA, info@middlepilar.com, www.middlepilar.com
NOITAVASARA DISTRIBUTION: Väinämöisentie 35, 96300 ROVANIEMI, FINLAND, noitav@hotmail.com, http://hp.ic.ru/achtung/ordo/
OLD EUROPA CAFE: C/- Rodolfo Protti Viale Marconi 38, 33170 Prodenone, Italy, oec@iol.it, www.stack.nl/~bobw/music/OEC/
ORDO EQILIBRIO: C/- Tomas Pettersson Box 497, 114 79 Stockholm Sweden, hybris@flashback.net, http://hp.ic.ru/achtung/ordo/
PERIL UNDERGROUND: Basement, 17-19 Elizabeth Street, Melbourne 3000, Victoria, Australia, phone (03) 96142040, fax (03) 9614 2050
PLAN 10 CONCEPTS: P.O. Box 4179, Footscray West 3012, Victoria Australia, dogface@lnug.com.au
POWER AND STEEL: C/- Loki Foundation PSF 241321 04333 Leipzig, Germany, loki-found@t-online.de
PRE-FEED: C/- Gabriele Santamaria, via Gen. Pergolesi 21, 60125 Ancona – Italy, mantein@tin.it, http://move.to/Pre_Feed
PRODUCT WHORE RECORDINGS: 3010 Hennepin Ave, S-PMB #555, Minneapolis, MN 55408-2614 USA, pda101@hotmail.com
RED STREAM: P.O. Box 342 Camp Hill Pa 17001-0342 USA, mail@rstream.com, www.rstream.com
RELEASE RECORDS: C/- Relapse Records, P.O. Box 251, Millersville, PA 17551, USA, relapse@relapse.com, www.relapse.com
SCHLOSS TEGAL/ TEGAL RECORDS: Interzone 215 N.Market Street Fredrick Maryland 217001 USA, orgone23@interzonemusic.com, www.interzonemusic.com
SELF ABUSE RECORDS: 26 S.Main Street #277, Concord, NH 03301, USA, www.mv.com/ipusers/selfabuse
SLAUGHTER PRODUCTIONS:C/- Marco Corbelli, via Tartini 8, 410 49 Sassuolo (MO) Italy, slaughter@mail.dex.net.com, www.welcome.to/slaughter
SPECTRE RECORDS, P.O.Box 88, 2020 Antwerpen 2, Belgium, spectre@skynet.be, http://users.skynet.be/spectre
STATEART: C/- Koch, Roseggerstr, 2, 30173, Hannover, Germany, stateart@t-online.de, http://home.t-online.de/home/stateart
SYNAESTHESIA: P.O. BOX 7252 Melbourne, Victoria 3004, Australia, atomic@vicnet.net.au, www.vicnet.net.au/~atomic/
TERTIUM NON DATA: C/- John Bergin, grinder@unicom.net, www.emerald.net/grinder
TESCO ORGANISATION: C/- Hilger, Gralsster, 8-68199 Mannheim, Germany, tesco-org-ma@t-online.de
TRONIKS: P.O. Box 4055, Berkeley, CA 94704-0055 USA, tenebrae@jps.net, www.troniks.com
WORLD SERPENT: Unit 7 i-7 Seager Buildings, Brookmill Road, London SE8 4HL, England, mailorder@worldserpent.demon.co.uk, www.worldserpent.demon.co.uk
YANTRA ATMOSPHERES: Bobdegatan 20C, nb s-595 52 Mjolby, Sweden, raison.detre@swipnet.se, home9.swipnet.se/~w-90779/index.htm

MALIGNANT RECORDS
MUSIC FOR DISSIPATED CULTURES

YEN POX
NEW DARK AGE

as if the sun was suddenly eclipsed by a looming, blood red orb and the world was cast under a liquidous murky glow

Suffocating and expansive drones spiraling into the blackened void...

YEN POX: NEW DARK AGE

$13 ppd
TUMOR 12 - CAT# MLG1-0202-2

also available:
CAUL LIGHT FROM MANY LAMPS
$13 ppd
TUMOR 11 - CAT# MLG-0301-2

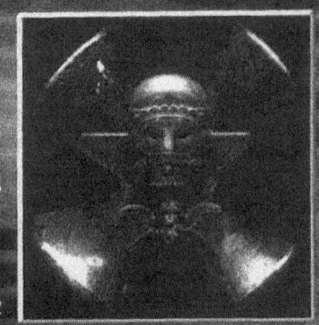

new from our sister label...
black plague

Catharsis / Drape Excrement
Homo Homini Lupus
(split CD) Infest 002 / $13 ppd
CAT# BLK1-0201-2

www.malignantrecords.com
DOWNLOAD OUR ORDER FORM - http://www.malignantrecords.com/services/orderblank.pdf

INCUBATE YOUR PERSONAL MALIGNANCY >> Join the Malignant Tumorlist
a) **EMAIL** >> infect@malignantrecords.com >> (automated subscriptions only)
b) **PLACE IN MESSAGE BODY** >> subscribe tumorlist your_name
SEND NON-LIST EMAIL TO >> malignant@malignantrecords.com

COMING SOON:
LAW . HEID . IRON HALO DEVICE
NAVICON TORTURE TECHNOLOGIES
STONE GLASS STEEL

FREE PRINTED CATALOG - SEND ADDRESS TO: P.O. BOX 5666 • BALTIMORE, MARYLAND 21210 • USA

ISSUE 4 SPECTRUM
AMBIENT/INDUSTRIAL/EXPERIMENTAL MUSIC CULTURE MAGAZINE

LAW
YEN POX
ILDFROST
STATEART
BAD SECTOR
BLACK LUNG
COLD SPRING
WARREN MEAD
INADE PROFILE
GRUNTSPLATTER
DER BLUTHARSCH
DREAM INTO DUST
DEATH IN JUNE LIVE
DESIDERII MARGINIS

VEINKE: COLLECTION III • *THE BLACK SUMMER*
DISSECTING TABLE: *POWER OUT OF CONTROL*
LAW: *VINDICATION AND CONTEMPT*
LAW: *OUR LIFE THROUGH YOUR DEATH*

COMPACT DISCS: $13.00 ppd. EACH.
Money order, credit card, cash.

• TRIUMVIRATE •
triumvirate@datacruz.com
P.O. BOX 6254 | SOUTH BEND, IN | 46660 USA
ph: (219)254-0180 | fax: (219)254-0901

MIDDLE PILLAR PRESENTS

BUTOH
Various Artists

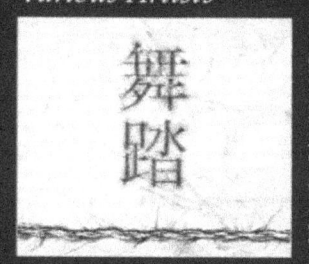

Celebrating the Japanese dance of darkness with new music by the Machine In The Garden, A Murder of Angels, The Mirror Reveals, The Unquiet Void, Mors Syphilitica, Sumerland, Thread, Wench & Zoar.

THE UNQUIET VOID
Between The Twilights

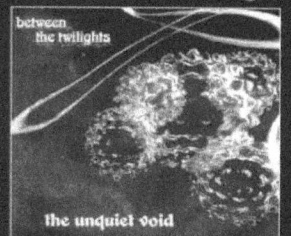

Instrumental waves of synthesized unconscious energy, visions that surface before the waking hours, building from ambience to grand sweeping arcs.

THE MIRROR REVEALS
Frames of Teknicolor

Lush and evocative female vocals dreamily weave poetic tales through torch-songs entwined with shimmering guitar melodies and ambient atmospherics.

A MURDER OF ANGELS
While You Sleep

An unsettling blend of dark ambient, neoclassical, and eerie electronics that defines the style of "Damnbient." A languorous soundtrack for your nightmares.

THE MACHINE IN THE GARDEN
One Winter's Night

Haunting vocal melodies, dark electronics, acoustic soundscapes, shadows and dreams. Siren vocals glide over technological enchantments. A 13-song ethereal masterpiece, now re-pressed.

WHAT IS ETERNAL
Various Artists

Limited Jewel Case re-pressing. Featuring The Mirror Reveals, Tony Wakeford & Tor Lundvall, Jarboe, the Machine in the Garden, Loretta's Doll, The Changelings, Mors Syphilitica, and more.

COMING FALL 2000
THE MACHINE IN THE GARDEN *Out of the Mists*

Multimedia CD-Rom includes full length album with twelve new dark and ethereal songs, plus the video for "The Unaware".

Middle Pillar, PO Box 555, NY, NY 10009 Fax: 212-378-2924
American Distribution via Middle Pillar Distribution
http://www.middlepillar.com/mpp/
email: info@middlepillar.com
212-378-2922
European Distribution via World Serpent Distribution
www.worldserpent.com

COLD SPRING
Release Schedule Summer 2000

PSYCHIC TV — Were You Ever Bullied At School...... Do You Want Revenge?
Limited double CD set of two fantastic live shows from 1984, both diverse in style, showing the range and ability of this incredible group.

Esoteric ritual music.

NOVATRON — New Rising Sun
Focussing on the concept of the Black Sun Cultus - a simmering mix of dark noise, pounding percussion, and subsonic bass rumbles. Links with RAMLEH and SKULLFLOWER, this stands head and shoulders above their contemporaries.

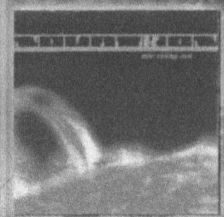

Packed in beautiful foldout booklet, with full colour art and metallic silver texts.

REMANENCE — Apparitions
Debut of this beautiful neo-classical act. Stunning classical arrangements and dark winds create a journey of melancholic, poignant emotions, and dark intentions.

Packed in a stunning eight page textured book with opaline outer.

FOLKSTORM — Victory or Death
Harsh noise, slamming rythms and heavy, gritty vocals makes for an uneasy listening experience that will blow you away!

The first side project from the cult band, MZ412.

VON THRONSTAHL — Imperium Internum
The long awaited debut from this incredible band is now here! Massive orchestras and military marches, anthems for an old land - this is one of the most powerful recordings COLD SPRING has ever released.

Fans of TURBUND STURMWERK, BLOOD AXIS, LAIBACH, etc should take special note! Out now!

BAND OF PAIN — Sacred Flesh
Incredible original soundtrack from the movie `SACRED FLESH`, which is released by SALVATION FILMS May 2000. The mastery of the dark ambient genre is brought to the fore by BAND OF PAIN, as each of the smothering, claustrophobic pieces bring alive the cinematic images of Nigel Wingroves film.

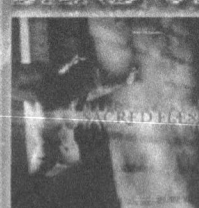

Packed in a stunning full colour 16 page book featuring stills from the movie. Out now!

All CDs listed are £12 - UK, £13 - EUROPE, and £14 - REST OF WORLD (except Psychic TV : £15 - UK, £16 - EUROPE and £17 - REST OF THE WORLD) inclusive of first class Airmail / postage and packaging

WRITE WITH 52p A5 SAE FOR OUR 80 PAGE CATALOGUE (FREE WITH ANY ORDER) OR VISIT

http://www.coldspring.co.uk

TO VIEW OUR COMPLETE ONLINE CATALOGUE AND PURCHASE THROUGH OUR NEW ONLINE STORE.

We Take Credit Cards (Visa, Delta, Master Card and Switch), Cheques, Money Orders and Carefully Concealed Cash (sent at mailers risk)

Distribution Allies:
- **GERMANY**: Tesco / Dark Vinyl / Triton / Artware / Vaws
- **ITALY**: Demos / USA Dutch East / Malignant / Manifold / Soleilmoon
- **HOLLAND**: Staalplaat / Sonic Rendezvous
- **UK**: Shellshock
- **SCANDINAVIA**: House Of Kicks
- **FRANCE**: Athanor / Nuit & Bouillard
- **ROMANIA**: Totalitarian Archangels Foundation

COLD SPRING, 8, Wellspring, Blisworth, Northants, NN7 3EH, England, UK.
Tel/Fax: 01604 859142   Email: info@coldspring.co.uk   VAT: GB 623 38 6726.

SPECTRUM MAGAZINE ISSUE 4: EDITORIAL SEPTEMBER 2000

Well, first off I would like to extend my greetings and likewise gratitude to you for picking up a copy of this, the forth instalment of Spectrum Magazine which has been released with 9 (or so) months elapsing since the last issue. As always general improvements have been made and additionally you might note that there have been some minor changes to font size and layout. Obviously I hope there alterations have been for the better, but basically the reduced font size was a prerequisite to keeping the publication's overall length in check.

In regards to the review section I took up the offer of one Chris Forth to undertake proof reading of the review section, to ultimately combat the nagging spelling and grammatical errors that slipped through in previous issues. I will say this assistance has been invaluable and I extend my gratitude for his input and suggestions. Also as with last issue, JC Smith has again enlisted his services in the review department. I do grudgingly admit that he often puts my 'literary' efforts to shame, BUT, where JC may focus on a providing a few select high quality contributions, I took to the quite mammoth task of tackling the remaining 140 or so reviews!. While on the topic of reviews, if you contact any labels pursuant to their herein enclosed advertisements or otherwise seek out any releases after reading a written review, it would be greatly appreciated if you could mention this publication to the label/ artist/ mailorder that you obtain it through (thanks in advance for your assistance on this!).

As for the interview side of things there are a swag of great artists and labels featured in this issue, and just so you are aware all response transcripts were typed and submitted by the relevant individuals. Thus, in the interest of retaining the original flavor of each contribution I have generally not undertaken any corrections to grammar or style (unless requested otherwise). Additionally, while I never envisage to implement any sort of censorship regime with the content of this publication, if anyone feels like taking issue with any statements herein, do keep in mind that by publishing words and exploring ideas (or even displaying images) does not automatically equate to belief in, or endorsement of such matters. This publication will not accept responsibility for any offense caused, as essentially how could I personally (or anyone else for that matter) ever legislate to accommodate every individuals' own filters and perceptions that may subsequently taint their ultimate reactions? So if you aware that you are at all prone to being offended, why not trying keeping your legs straight to avoid those embarrassing knee jerk reactions!! (hmmm....could that in any way be also read as a metaphor?).

At this point in time I don't know exactly when Issue 5# may eventuate as this really depends on my current (albeit vague) plans of doing a bit of extended traveling through Europe sometime in 2001. Personally with my limited spare time, this publication may seem to some to be a sporadic endeavor, however thus far I have managed to have an issue released every 6-9 months. But then again only time will tell if the next issue will arrive before the commencement of my global trek or has to wait until my return. All I can add on this front is that patience is a virtue….

Also making reference to promotional items, I ask that if you are planning on sending material for review please consider what you send in relation to its relevance to the general content of this publication. For example, I have never been (nor never will be) a metal magazine, but from time to time such items still turn up in my mailbox. As much as I have got better things to do then to be constantly sending back unsolicited material (so I therefore don't..), I'm likewise sure these labels/ artists don't have money to burn by sending out promotional items that simply to not serve their intended purpose (…and just so it is said, this policy is not limited to metal only). If you do want to send something along, but are at all unsure, your best bet would be to get in contact via e-mail first. Likewise with the amount of music I now obtain between issues (either purchased or gained promotionally) I can now no longer guarantee review space for every item, HOWEVER the more recent the release, (and more importantly if sparks my positive interest), it puts the said item in a much better position for me being motivated to write something about it!

To flag any potential inquiries, all back issues are sold out directly from me, although some of my distributors may still have some copies. Also at this point there is no plans on furnishing them with a repress, as basically I would prefer to put time, effort and money into new editions.

Lastly as I can't really think of much else to ad (other than unnecessary mindless ramble, or statements of "I hope you enjoy the issue"), so I will taper…off….. about……… here………………

O'vr'n'out…….end transmission…… - Richard Stevenson

EDITOR - INTERVIEWER - REVIEWER - LAYOUT DESIGNER & GENERAL WORKAHOLIC ETC: RICHARD STEVENSON
CONTRIBUTORS: JC SMITH - REVIEWS AND INADE PROFILE/ CHRIS FORTH - REVIEW SECTION PROOF READER/ WARREN MERD - COVER IMAGE.

Greetings and thanks:
To all artists/ labels/ distributors & shops who have supported this publication via providing interviews, promotional items, advertisements and (heaven forbid!) stocking copies! Your collective input and support in invaluable and particular gratitude is extended to all @ Malignant Records. JC Smith and Chris Forth for their input & assistance. Mick Stevenson for general tech assistance and likewise for building the PC that birthed this 4th issue. James Leslie for allowing me the use of his PC that solidified the 'Spectrum' vision via Issues 1# thru 3#. Joseph Aquino for the P. Kerr quote. Lastly all other family members and friends for interest and support (even if you don't always 'get' the musical path on which I travel).

This issue is dedicated to the loving memory of Betty McClure. (29 October, 1919 – 18 March, 2000).

TEXT & DESIGN LAYOUT: COPYRIGHT SPECTRUM MAGAZINE
ALL IMAGES COPYRIGHT THE RESPECTIVE ARTISTS

(no section of this publication may be reprinted without prior permission - all rights reserved)

SPECTRUM MAGAZINE: P.O. BOX 86, ELSTERNWICK 3185, VICTORIA, AUSTRALIA
SPECTRUMMAGAZINE@HOTMAIL.COM

The cover image is a cropped version of the photographic artwork entitled 'Soldiers' – captured by Warren Mead and featured (un-cropped) in the 'Dark Poland' exhibition of June, 2000.

CONTENTS:
- WARREN MERD
- DER BLUTHARSCH
- DREAM INTO DUST
- DEATH IN JUNE LIVE
- LAW
- STATEART
- DESIDERII MARGINIS
- BLACK LUNG
- INADE PROFILE
- ILDFROST
- BAD SECTOR
- COLD SPRING
- GRUNTSPLATTER
- YEN POX
- SOUND REVIEWS
- CONTACT LIST

"The greatest irony is that man passed his day of judgement completely unawares. The nuclear bomb that exploded in 1945, and for everything that happened since has just been fallout. For most people this is old news, and no one is bothered very much. How can you be bothered by something that has already happened, that still exists beyond your control, that defines you? The future - any future, even one of the kind once described in science fiction - no longer exists. There is the status quo and not much else. All of which perhaps explains why there is no imperative - social or scientific - to do anything about changing things. Armageddon, Apocalypse, End Time, Holocaust - call it what you will, it's been and gone and nobody really cares" - **Phillip Kerr** (excerpt taken from and deliberately quoted out of context of its source 'The Second Angel' 1998).

WARREN MEAD

Rather than provide some long winded introduction, the images created by photographic artist Warren Mead say immensely more than could ever be expressed by words (and personally speaking I was so taken by his 'Dark Poland' exhibition I am now the proud owner of the original piece "ócjów" shown adjacent). Anyway, peruse the accompanying pictures to see exactly what I mean and read on to gain some insight into their creator…

Starting with the rudimentary, can you please introduce yourself and provide some details on what studies have you undertaken in your pursuit of artistic photography? I am a creator of images that to some are deeply disturbing and to others, are perceived as being mystical and profoundly beautiful. My work is in no way the prodigy of formal study. My style and technique as a photographer has been developed by acknowledging a vision and chasing a particular look through experimentation which I feel I have now mastered.

Given that your recent exhibition 'Dark Poland' centres around a series taken during your 2 years of travel through the country, I wanted to ask what initially drew you to Poland as a place? Did you expect to discover you had such a profound interest in the country when you first chose to travel there? I was initially drawn to Poland after discovering the Polish artist Beksinski. Beksinski's work is extremely haunting and had a depth to it that I could not comprehend mainly because I had never seen anything painted with such concise vision and dedication to genre before. I explored Polish art further and discovered a wide array of artists who were painting dark imagery and decided that it would surely be an interesting country to visit if not just for the art. I guess I was expecting to find an artistic depth in Poland that I couldn't find in Australia and on this level I was far from disappointed.

It now seems that you have such a deep connection with the country that you hope to half your time living between Australia and Poland. Is being a photographer (freelance or artistic) a viable pursuit for you if splitting your times between these countries? Living in Poland opens up the German as well as the Scandinavian markets for me and offers an abundance of opportunities in both fine art and commercial photography. As an artist, it is essential for me to institute and maintain radical contrast in my life and living between 2 countries as diverse as Poland is to Australia offers this. Whether or not this is a viable pursuit depends purely on my determination to make it so and sustain it as a lifestyle. I have a base in Krakow and in Melbourne and as long as I'm not away from either country for too long I can easily slip into the groove and get on with it.

As your 'Dark Poland' collection in your exhibition has specific parallels with the imagery underground gothic and dark ambient scenes, alternatively I wanted to ask the response has been from the more 'high brow' artistic community? Indeed. I wasn't sure what the response was going to be to "Dark Poland" and I have to tell you that I did not specifically aim it at any particular market. I received a lot of media coverage prior to the exhibition and the opening night proved to be a real eye opener for me. The gallery was packed with up to 300 people from such a broad cross section of the community. I noticed that a huge contingency of very rich looking, well dressed people were in attendance and it was there and then that I knew I'd appealed to a much wider audience than I had expected. The cheapest piece in "Dark Poland" was $500 and a lot of the exhibition sold to very wealthy people.

With your exhibition encompassing 20 finished pieces of a variety of imagery, yet broadly categorized under the 'Dark Poland' theme, how many images did you have to sift through to compile it down into the finished collection? "Dark Poland" was shot on only 7 rolls of film. I am not an artist who fires away with the shutter and then wades through thousands of images to pick out the gems. I know I've got a winner as soon as I shoot it. I am extremely selective about what I photograph and can usually pull 3 to 4 exhibition quality shots from each roll. I will go to any length required to get the shot I'm after and if for some reason I fail due to whatever reason, I suffer incredibly from it and spend at least four days murderously brooding. The fact that it took 2 years to compile the images for "Dark Poland" was largely due to the weather conditions. I wanted a still, Winter look with snow and ice and this is not always available during the Polish Winter.

The titles of your works seem to reference a simple description of the pieces (ie: 'Krakow', 'Teutonic Ruins', 'Soldiers' etc) rather then attempting to imbed some deeper meaning with a poetically phrased name. What is your view on the images you create from the point of assigning them with titles? There was a time when I did attempt to imbed a deeper meaning in my images with titles such as "Dawn of the Iconoclast" which was a popular poster that I produced a few years ago. I scrutinised the finished pieces for "Dark Poland" with the idea of also embellishing each one with a poetically phrased title but reached the conclusion that the majority of these images projected an ambiguous quality and to thrust them into a definitive direction would have possibly taken away from this.

Without simply placing the finished pieces in sterile metal frames, your choice of framing with deeply textured wood added an archaic/ organic resonance to the pictures themselves. I believe there is even a story behind the choice and discovery of this framing material? When I take on a project of this scale I have the whole concept from start to finish swimming around in my head. "Dark Poland" looks at a time in history when building materials were very heavy duty such as stone and massive timbers. I wanted the frames to have this medieval resonance to them and held the project off until the appropriate timber turned up. I happened

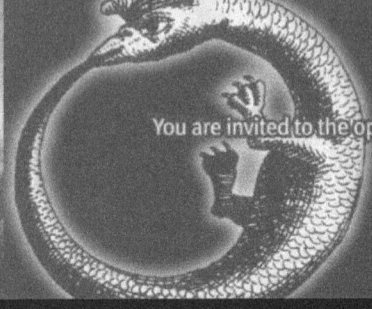

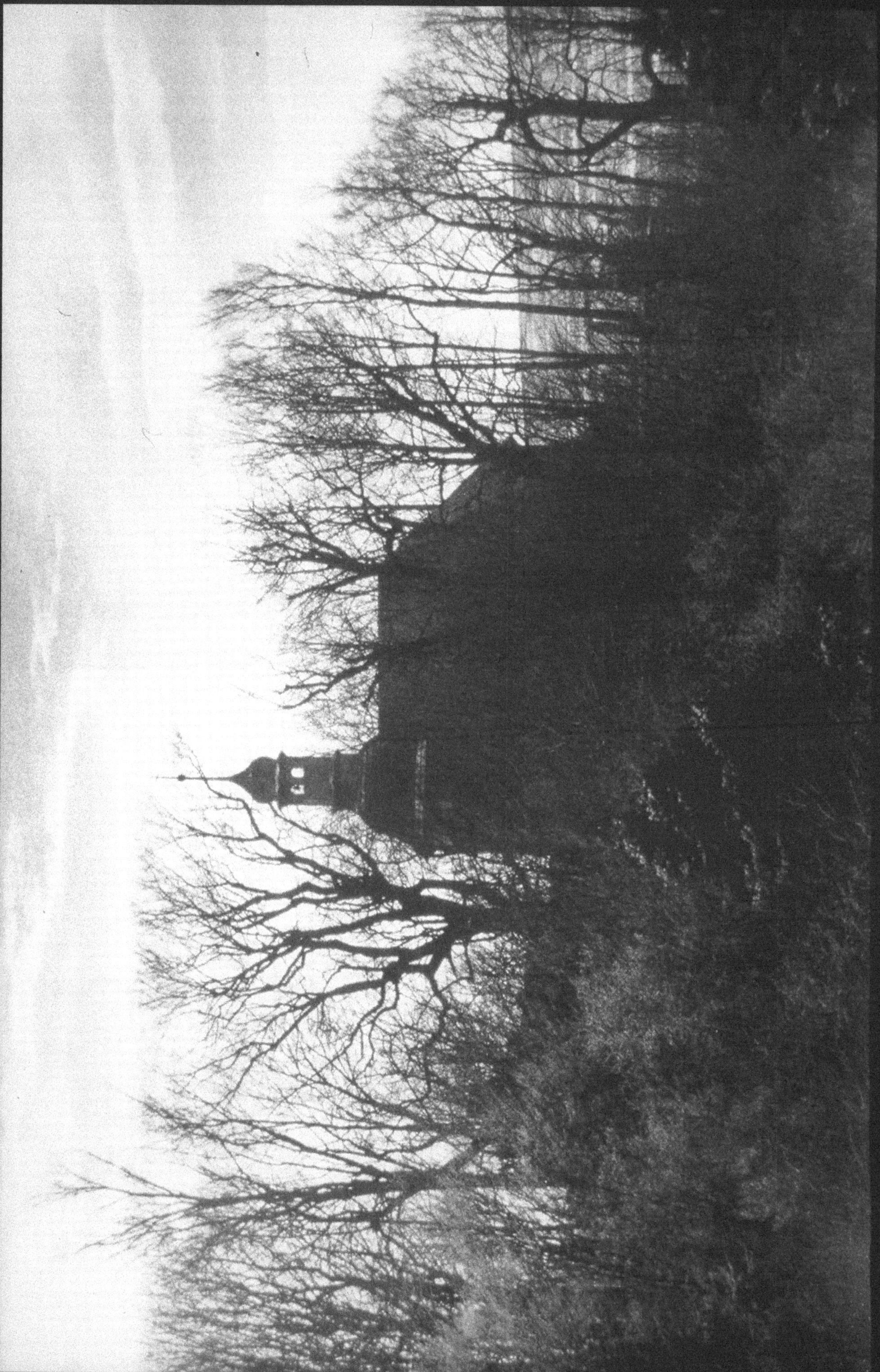

upon an old demolished building one day in Melbourne and discovered to my delight a plethora of beautiful old hardwood that I had identified as being Messmate and aged at around 80 years. The construction of the frames from this timber required the Supreme Effort and nearly killed me. By the time the frames were finished with glass and everything else, they weighed as much as 16kg each.

Initially I became aware of your exhibition as the imagery had specific parallels with dark ambient music and then was then quite surprised to find you were a fan of the said scene. How did you come to be aware of dark ambient styles of music and is this a scene you still follow? I became interested in dark ambient music after reading several years ago of research that had been done by the US Military into psycho-acoustic weaponry based on the theory that sound frequencies, particularly subs, could alter moods and even kill. This reading led me to "Lustmord" who was doing things with military tone generators and after working my way through "Heresy" and "Monstrous Soul" I began to discover that what I really enjoyed listening to was pure subs and this led me to Thomas Koner whose album "Permafrost" is to me a masterpiece and a great source of inspiration. I can't listen to dark ambient that is structured any more. I'm purely into works that are devoted to ominous sub frequencies and I have some really serious speakers with extended sub frequency range that could easily smash windows if I let loose on them. I have discovered a greater appreciation for the natural sounds around me from exploring dark ambient music and tuning my hearing to low frequencies that most people would probably filter out. Living in Poland isolated me somewhat from the dark ambient scene.

In another general conversation you stated that the aura of Poland as a place negated the need to listen to dark ambience. Can you describe this further and likewise some of your general experiences taken from and places visited during your travels? I live in Krakow which is an intact medieval city. There is a suburb of Krakow called Kaziemierz. Kaziemierz was once a bustling centre for Krakow's Jewish population but today stands as a desolate memory to the thousands of people who were murdered there by the SS during WW2. Auschwitz is only 65km from Krakow and was the site of mass murder and misery for nearly 5 years. It is not a well known fact that 5 million Polish civilians were also murdered along with the Jews. There is reference to WW2 everywhere in Poland and each point of reference is an insight into the horror that went on there. Dark ambient music for me is a method of inducing a certain mind set that effectively triggers introspection. Due to Poland's tragic past, an omniescent, sombre aura hangs in the air like a morbid fog and I found the presence of this awesome and also inspiring and no dark ambient music that I had with me could come even close to producing the depths of introspection that I experienced in that country.

The subject matter of 'Dark Poland' centres around focusing on the past architecture and likewise the spirit of the country, ultimately shrouding everything in a regressive historical light (created via your photographic techniques). Given this assessment, what historical epochs interest you, if not inspire the images you create? I am deeply interested in medieval Europe. A desperate amount of fear is apparent in the architecture and not only fear of physical invaders. The fear of spiritual attack is apparent through the addition of gargoyles and other entities on the roof tops and the crucifix is everywhere. I find this era extremely evocative and loaded with mythic resonance.

A dark religious aura is evident in your works, rather that it is unavoidable given the subject matter, however what role does religion, (organized or otherwise) or even personally spirituality play in your life? Ostensibly I am an atheist. I do identify with a higher entity but I do not support any doctrine or definition of just what that might be. My interest in the symbolism of the Catholic Church is purely derived from my perception of it as being a source of fear and foreboding for those who would dare to stray. I feel disturbed and restless in churches and have never experienced a religious calling of any kind. I am attracted to the crucifix there is no doubt about it. I think it is a beautifully powerful symbol but its call is purely aesthetical.

Looking at a technical aspect of your image creation, how much are they a product of meticulously laboured dark room techniques once the actual framing and capturing of the shot has been completed? My work is predominately shot on black & white film and the high-contrast look that I capture is a product of many different combinations. I always shoot on TMax 3200 which is an extremely high speed film and which produces a grainy high contrast look. I usually underexpose the negatives to increase the contrast and print the images on cold tone paper to increase the starkness. I really apply my stamp by bleaching the prints in a solution of potassium ferrycyanide and potassium bromide and then if necessary, air brushing particular areas to either highlight clouds or to add subtle colour. The result is often something bordering on a painting.

There appears to be very few photographic artists (or other artists for that matter) which focus on dark gothic type imagery that are respected as 'serious artists' other then being perceived to be derived from certain subcultures of music. Do you agree with the assessment and how would it apply if at all to you? In Australia this is certainly the case. Australia is all fluff and colour which is a reflection on how easy life is here. I believe however that there is a strong market for the type of imagery that you describe and I have just proven it. My experiences and adventures in life have led me to a deeper understanding of humanity and this was made evident by the success in "Dark Poland's ability to attract a very conservative and wealthy audience. I believe my work has now matured to the point whereby what I'm really trying to say is being felt by those who see it and this must be the path to being accepted as a credible artist.

You made mention to me that your commercial success as a photographer has been slightly marred by the infiltration of your dark, gothic styled influences. Is your direction and vision of aesthetics so imbedded in your subconscious that you find it happening as a natural instinct? Absolutely. I am for some reason driven to take the kinds of images that I do. My fine art photographic style is way too strong for commercial agencies and the slightest sniff of it coming into my commercial work definitely goes against me but I find it hard to turn off what it is that enables me to take photographs and this is sometimes a dilemma.

What are your future plans and aspirations for future series and exhibitions and do you hope to explore different topical matter? I'm having an exhibition in Krakow in October of much lighter material. It's all futuristic, impressionist type imagery that I am presently photographing here in Australia. What I really need at the moment is a holiday. I'll be back in Krakow until June next year and plan to have an exhibition in Melbourne or Sydney at least once a year. In regard to exploring different topical matter, I will journey to wherever my vision takes me.

Thanks you extremely much for your participation. Is there anything you would like to ad in conclusion? I believe all points have been covered.

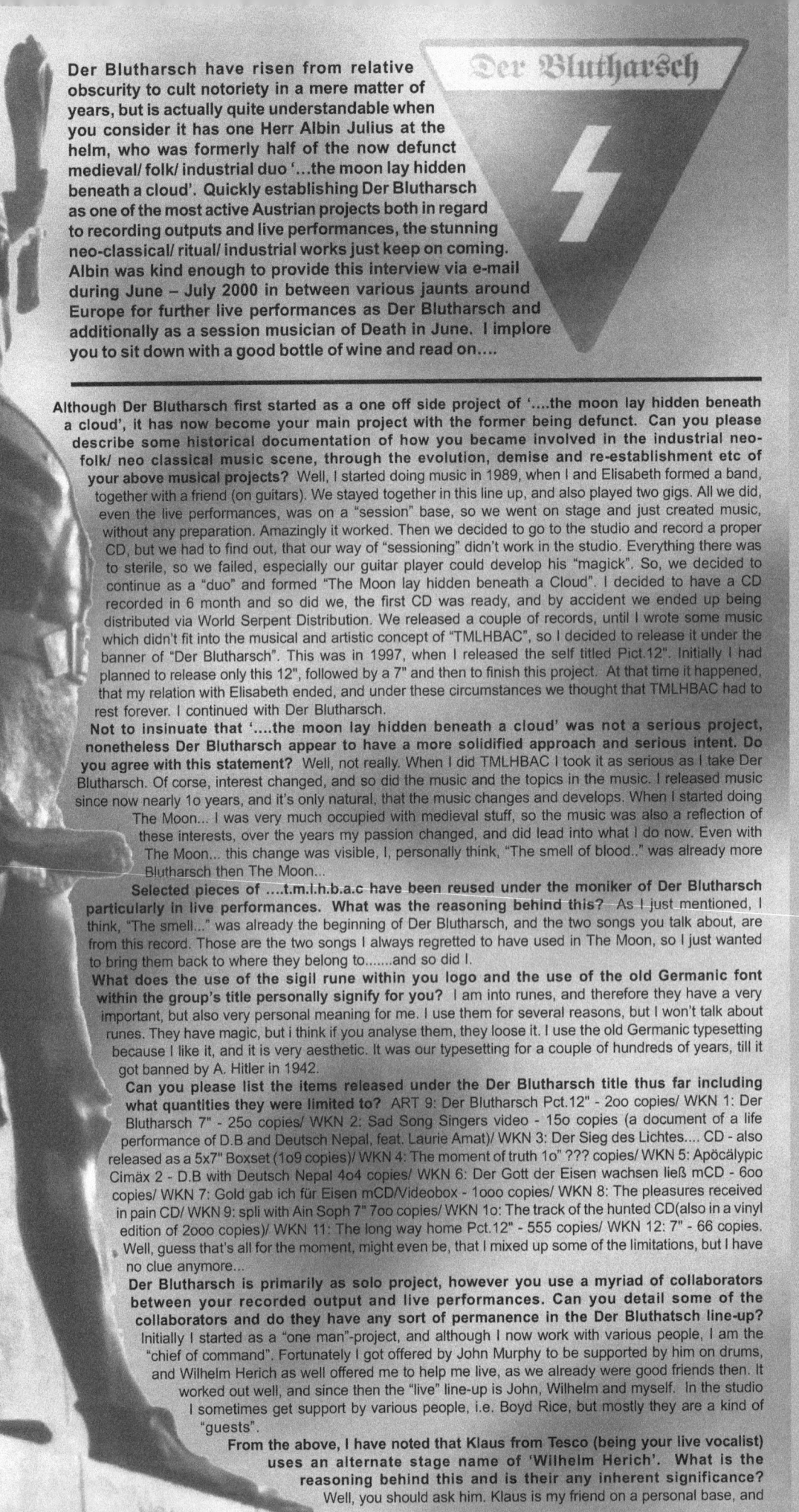

Der Blutharsch have risen from relative obscurity to cult notoriety in a mere matter of years, but is actually quite understandable when you consider it has one Herr Albin Julius at the helm, who was formerly half of the now defunct medieval/ folk/ industrial duo '...the moon lay hidden beneath a cloud'. Quickly establishing Der Blutharsch as one of the most active Austrian projects both in regard to recording outputs and live performances, the stunning neo-classical/ ritual/ industrial works just keep on coming. Albin was kind enough to provide this interview via e-mail during June – July 2000 in between various jaunts around Europe for further live performances as Der Blutharsch and additionally as a session musician of Death in June. I implore you to sit down with a good bottle of wine and read on….

Although Der Blutharsch first started as a one off side project of '….the moon lay hidden beneath a cloud', it has now become your main project with the former being defunct. Can you please describe some historical documentation of how you became involved in the industrial neo-folk/ neo classical music scene, through the evolution, demise and re-establishment etc of your above musical projects? Well, I started doing music in 1989, when I and Elisabeth formed a band, together with a friend (on guitars). We stayed together in this line up, and also played two gigs. All we did, even the live performances, was on a "session" base, so we went on stage and just created music, without any preparation. Amazingly it worked. Then we decided to go to the studio and record a proper CD, but we had to find out, that our way of "sessioning" didn't work in the studio. Everything there was to sterile, so we failed, especially our guitar player could develop his "magick". So, we decided to continue as a "duo" and formed "The Moon lay hidden beneath a Cloud". I decided to have a CD recorded in 6 month and so did we, the first CD was ready, and by accident we ended up being distributed via World Serpent Distribution. We released a couple of records, until I wrote some music which didn't fit into the musical and artistic concept of "TMLHBAC", so I decided to release it under the banner of "Der Blutharsch". This was in 1997, when I released the self titled Pict.12". Initially I had planned to release only this 12", followed by a 7" and then to finish this project. At that time it happened, that my relation with Elisabeth ended, and under these circumstances we thought that TMLHBAC had to rest forever. I continued with Der Blutharsch.

Not to insinuate that '….the moon lay hidden beneath a cloud' was not a serious project, nonetheless Der Blutharsch appear to have a more solidified approach and serious intent. Do you agree with this statement? Well, not really. When I did TMLHBAC I took it as serious as I take Der Blutharsch. Of corse, interest changed, and so did the music and the topics in the music. I released music since now nearly 1o years, and it's only natural, that the music changes and develops. When I started doing The Moon… I was very much occupied with medieval stuff, so the music was also a reflection of these interests, over the years my passion changed, and did lead into what I do now. Even with The Moon… this change was visible, I, personally think, "The smell of blood.." was already more Blutharsch then The Moon…

Selected pieces of ….t.m.l.h.b.a.c have been reused under the moniker of Der Blutharsch particularly in live performances. What was the reasoning behind this? As I just mentioned, I think, "The smell…" was already the beginning of Der Blutharsch, and the two songs you talk about, are from this record. Those are the two songs I always regretted to have used in The Moon, so I just wanted to bring them back to where they belong to…….and so did I.

What does the use of the sigil rune within you logo and the use of the old Germanic font within the group's title personally signify for you? I am into runes, and therefore they have a very important, but also very personal meaning for me. I use them for several reasons, but I won't talk about runes. They have magic, but i think if you analyse them, they loose it. I use the old Germanic typesetting because I like it, and it is very aesthetic. It was our typesetting for a couple of hundreds of years, till it got banned by A. Hitler in 1942.

Can you please list the items released under the Der Blutharsch title thus far including what quantities they were limited to? ART 9: Der Blutharsch Pct.12" - 2oo copies/ WKN 1: Der Blutharsch 7" - 25o copies/ WKN 2: Sad Song Singers video - 15o copies (a document of a life performance of D.B and Deutsch Nepal, feat. Laurie Amat)/ WKN 3: Der Sieg des Lichtes…. CD - also released as a 5x7" Boxset (1o9 copies)/ WKN 4: The moment of truth 1o" ??? copies/ WKN 5: Apöcälypic Cimäx 2 - D.B with Deutsch Nepal 4o4 copies/ WKN 6: Der Gott der Eisen wachsen ließ mCD - 6oo copies/ WKN 7: Gold gab ich für Eisen mCD/Videobox - 1ooo copies/ WKN 8: The pleasures received in pain CD/ WKN 9: spli with Ain Soph 7" 7oo copies/ WKN 1o: The track of the hunted CD(also in a vinyl edition of 2ooo copies)/ WKN 11: The long way home Pct.12" - 555 copies/ WKN 12: 7" - 66 copies. Well, guess that's all for the moment, might even be, that I mixed up some of the limitations, but I have no clue anymore…

Der Blutharsch is primarily as solo project, however you use a myriad of collaborators between your recorded output and live performances. Can you detail some of the collaborators and do they have any sort of permanence in the Der Bluthatsch line-up? Initially I started as a "one man"-project, and although I now work with various people, I am the "chief of command". Fortunately I got offered by John Murphy to be supported by him on drums, and Wilhelm Herich as well offered me to help me live, as we already were good friends then. It worked out well, and since then the "live" line-up is John, Wilhelm and myself. In the studio I sometimes get support by various people, i.e. Boyd Rice, but mostly they are a kind of "guests".

From the above, I have noted that Klaus from Tesco (being your live vocalist) uses an alternate stage name of 'Wilhelm Herich'. What is the reasoning behind this and is their any inherent significance? Well, you should ask him. Klaus is my friend on a personal base, and

Wilhelm Herich (from Genocide Organ) is a supporter on stage. nevertheless I love both of them.

You yourself have now become the main collaborator with Douglas P in Death in June on the past two albums. How did this come about, will this continue and are you satisfied with the results to date? Well, I met Douglas a couple of years ago, after a concert of D.i.J. We stayed in touch, he visited me a couple of times in Wien, and we became friends. He liked what I did with The Moon lay hidden... and when I went to Australia for holiday he invited me to visit him and stay at his house. He liked what I did with The Moon lay hidden... and when I went to Australia for holiday Australian summer, and just see what happens. We didn't kill each other, but ended up with "Take Care And Control" after 1o days. We toured twice together, and when we played Australia, we had 6 days in between Sydney and Melbourne, so we just went back to this nice little studio in the Adelaide hills, and, well, ended up with "Operation Hummingbird". I would have to lie, if I would say that I am not satisfies by the result. It was a pleasure and big fun to record the records, and I still like to listen to them sometimes, although I can't hear the songs at the moment anymore, after 35 times of playing the songs live. Nevertheless, I never felt as part of D.i.J. and I never will. D.i.J. is Doug's baby, I have my own. It always was just working/creating with a friend. I know that we will work together in the future, but I don't think (and I don't want to...) on a permanent base.

Between your collaborations with Death in June, and the new distribution deal for both groups with Tesco Organisation (and also considering that Klaus one of the individuals behind Tesco is a live and studio vocalist for Der Blutharsch) it would seem that this is more than mealy music networking, rather the formation of a close knit brotherhood. Please comment as you see fit. Yes. That's how it is. Klaus got to know Doug via me, being on tour together, and they as well became friends. So, one day, in Italy, Douglas mentioned that he would like to do something on TESCO, which finally did lead into his, and our (Ian Read as well) distribution deal. Klaus and I were friends, and sooner or later this had to lead into this relation as well. Yes, it is a really good situation. It's easy and a pleasure to work with them, they know exactly what to do, from packaging to other things. If I have an idea, they know how to realise it, etc..# But also it's fun to be with them, to go on holiday or just to do crazy things. Being with them is being with "kamerads", yes, it is kind of a brotherhood. "They are ours!".

The close knit circle alluded to in the above question has further relevance as it has been mentioned that you recently assisting Genocide Organ (fronted by Klaus) in their live performances in England. Was this a one off occurrence or are you now part of this cult act? No, this was just a one off. They played London and Leeds, and I joined them, initially because we afterwards went for holiday together in Scotland. So, they asked me, if I would like to join them on stage, and I wanted. Anyway, it ended up in a disaster. The sound on stage was so bad, that I couldn't hear any of the sounds, and I initially was meant to do percussion and rhythms, but in finally it ended just in "big noiz's".

One element of Der Blutharsch is the live performance side of things with a number of small tours having been undertaken over the past two years. Where have these travels taken you and what has the response been like? (controversial or otherwise). It did lead me/us through whole Europe. We played nearly every European country and Australia. I am talking about more than 40 gigs in 1 1/2 years! The reactions were always phantastic, only Athens audience was a bit cool, very goth and I think they were not amused by the two Germanic guys shouting at them :-). But everywhere else the audience was absolutely enthusiastic.

Where will your current and upcoming tours take you and which other groups will you be touring with? For summer there is only one concert with D.j.J. scheduled. I have a lot of offers for Der Blutharsch, but don't want to play Europe that soon again. We are talking about an Australian tour followed by a tour through the USA, but this are only plans at the moment. If, it would be the "rat-pack", aka: D.i.J/Non/Der Blutharsch. I would like to tour Europe again next year (this year I have enough other plans) and then with D.i.J. again. Touring with Doug and Boyd is more than touring, it's big fun, and always the funniest and strangest things happened to us. Boyd wrote a really good tour diary in an US-mag called "Panick". If you can find it somewhere, get it!!!

Last issue when I interviewed Deustich Nepal I questioned Lina about his collaborations with you. The point I was quizzing was that considering his project has no meaning behind it (his description), did he see any anomalies with working with Der Blutharsch (given that certain implications with your style and presentation would 'brand' you with an agenda amongst certain factions). As I can now ask you directly with no need for assumption, what agenda if any is inherent in your music and inspiration? Well, I accord to Lina Baby Doll: Alcohol, Sex and a little bit of Fun.... :-)

The neo-classical compositions of Der Blutharsch certainly contain little if any modern elements, therefore what historical time periods interest you? Likewise what philosophies and ideologies are reflected in Der Blutharsch's works? There are no specific ideologies or political views reflected in my work. I am interested in various things, but Der Blutharsch is not a vehicle for dogmas or whatever. If there are several specific topics to be seen in my work, they are simply a reflection of my interests and my occupation with several things. I am interested in all time periods, sometimes more in recent times, but as well in the very past.....

To what extent does paganism, heathenism, Christian mysticism (grail myth, knight templars etc) interest you? I was very much occupied by these a couple of years ago, but meanwhile I went forwards in history.

An image associated with your interview in Runen Magazine Issue 1# depicts the burning an American flag. Did you supply this image for use with the interview, and if so I wanted to ask to if this a statement against the country itself or more of a symbolic gesture against the capitalist western ideal that the us embodies? This picture was enclosed by the editor, and was not provided by me. It has nothing to do with the interview or my person. Nevertheless I dislike the politics of the USA as a "world-police", and personally think they should "Fuck off" Europe. But, as I said, that's my personal opinion.

The use of samples of Charles Manson speaking about topics of strength, honour and pride have cropped up more than once within Der Blutharsch's musical framework (and likewise have also been utilised by affiliated artists such as Blood Axis and Turbund Sturmwerk). What attracts you to the ideas being put forward by this media demonised individual? He's evil, the personalised devil...

:). It's a phenomenon of so called civilized culture - the rebirth of the eternal victim.

Do you subscribe to/ follow the ideas and philosophies of Charles Manson's organization A.T.W.A (Air Trees Water Animals)? No.

With your music containing a blend of real and synthetic instrumentation, I wanted to ask exactly what types of equipment you employ and how you approach the construction of a track? Do you write material prior to recording sessions or are the tracks entirely constructed in the studio? I use everything sounds and noises can be produced with. Sampling machines, effect machines, tape-loops. I record loads of sounds with Dat-machines outside, but I as well use authentic instruments, such as "dulcimer", "hurdy gurdy", flutes, pipes, drums and so on.....To record a track I simply just start, I take a noise or sound or even just a rhythm and then start constructing around, add some things, take some others away, and if I am happy, i get a result I like.

Some people have criticized Der Blutharsch's sound as being below par, however I get the feeling that the production is intentionally flawed to give a timeless feel to the compositions. Opinions? Also why do you avoid using track titles let alone providing any information on recordings? Is this again to enhance a timeless aesthetic? Well, I have no idea. There is no special reason behind this. I mean, I do not do it for a certain purpose, it's just the kind of sound I prefer. I don't use any track titles, as I don't see a CD simply as a collection of songs. For me the CD is one piece of music, and the CD title reflects the main atmosphere I see in it. I mean, does a movie title each scene???

All of you releases have been produced on your own label WKN and often ridiculously limited in quantity, which now fetch insane prices on internet auction sites. If there is an obvious demand why are many of your releases still limited in quantity? When I started with Der Blutharsch, I never expected the phantastic response. I released the Pct. 12" in an edition of 2oo, and I sold 15 to a local record store. After half a year they still had 2 copies left, which I (fortunately, heheheh...) bought back then. I never expected that people pay such ridiculous prices for my releases. I heard, that the WKN 1 7" sold for $ 8oo.- on eBay. Some people seem not to have to care about money, for this I could have nice holiday. Meanwhile I increased the quantities, but everything I release already sold out even before I have it from the pressing factory. I released the new CD also as an edition of 2ooo copies in Vinyl, and they already nearly sold out, so what shall I do??? On the other hand, I like to release vinyls, they are something special for me. CD's are for the masses, vinyl for special people, and the smaller the edition, the more I love it myself. My fav baby is the WKN 12". One day I will release a 7" in an edition of 16 copies, and I will love it.....

Cost also seems to bear little consideration in packaging and presentation of releases, particularly with reference to the deluxe "Gold gab ich fur Eisen" video/ MCD box set. Why do you choose to go to such lengths and are you even able to break even with costs when releasing such items? Yes, at least I get the money back. The mentioned boxset is another story, as it was totally overpriced by WSD, but unfortunately I had no influence in their price politics. In the shops it ended for DM 1oo.., which is ridiculously high. The 5x7" box I did was sold to people for less then $ 18.- incl. P+P. For this I just got back the costs and made a little bit of money to buy a couple of bottles of wine. But, I don't care. I made enough money on the CD. WKN 12 for example was never sold, I made it and gave it away for free. Sometimes it's nice to do these things. I will also do such things in the future.

How satisfied are you with the finished presentation of the video/ MCD packaging and additionally the actual live video footage? As both the live set on the video and MCD were 26 minutes each (& encompassing the same tracks) was this the full set list of the majority of you tour shows? Are you absolutely sure??!! Caught!! But, please don't tell Roger. His Royalty requests will be immense. I never could afford that much beer we would like to get...;):) I am nearly 100% satisfied with the result, except some small things. For example, the green colour is not exactly the same for the video/booklet and CD wallet, but that's due to different cardboard. Besides that, I like it, although I think it was overprized by WSD. The video/mCd features the whole set we played on this tour. As me and Fire+Ice were the support for D.I.J. I thought it would be a good idea not to play more than 3o minutes. For support this is fair enough. Although I never would play too long, as we never did with TMLHBAC (the longest gig we played was 38 minutes), I prefer it short but brutal. Attack!!!!!!

Listening to you second full length CD "the pleasures received in pain" I could not help but get the feeling that you had sampled Brighter Death Now for part of the background noise. Is this at all correct? Well, not from my knowledge.

Well more specifically I am referring to the last track on the album and giving it further listens I am almost positive that there are pitch shifted loops taken from B.D.N's 'Innerwar' album. I have even gone as far as quizzing others on this with them holding the same opinion. Are you absolutely sure??!! Caught! But, please don't tell Roger. His Royalty requests will be immense. I never could afford that much beer we would like to get....;):)

Other samples contained within you music include (euro centric) era recordings, speeches, choir vocals and classical loops. What is the general process in firstly locating these sample and secondly determining their suitability for use within Der Blutharsch? I don't analyse. I just construct. Normally I start with a loop, a sound or a rhythm. Then I start building up things around. Mostly it happens by instinkt. Very seldomly I hear a sound/cut-up and safe it for later use. I don't store sounds.

What releases are you currently working on between new Der Blutharsch material, your other collaborative projects, new items for issue on you other label Hau Ruck etc? I recently released WKN 1o, "The track of the hunted". There are no other plans for D.B releases for this year. In autumn I hope to start recording new material, also I have an offer to write the music for an American theatre-play. We'll see what happens. On Hau RucK there are several releases planned, first a mCD (HR! 7) of "La Maison Modeme", a piece of pure dance music, followed by a 7" (Tribe of Circle) and a 1o" of an Austro-Australian project named Novo Homo. They all will be out before summer. In autumn I will have two Cd's be released on Hau RucK, the second CD of Novy Svet, followed by the debut-CD of a French band called "derniere volonte". Also I received material which shall lead into 3 new 7" for winter.

With this theatre play you mention above, can you expand on this a little? Are you at all aware how they came across your music? (considering you are an artist working within a relatively obscure underground scene). To cut a long story short, I met the director somewhere in the hills outside Vienna, and all ended up in a big party. We noticed that we had a lot of things in common and good times. As well as she liked my music, as she is preparing a play of Shakespeare, well, I think D.B. would fit. As well, meanwhile I wrote a song for a Spanish Fetish designer m(F) which will be used on his next catwalk at the "Torture Garden". So, as you might see, I am very much interested to work also outside the so called "scene". It's always a new experience.

In passing anything else you would like to add? No.

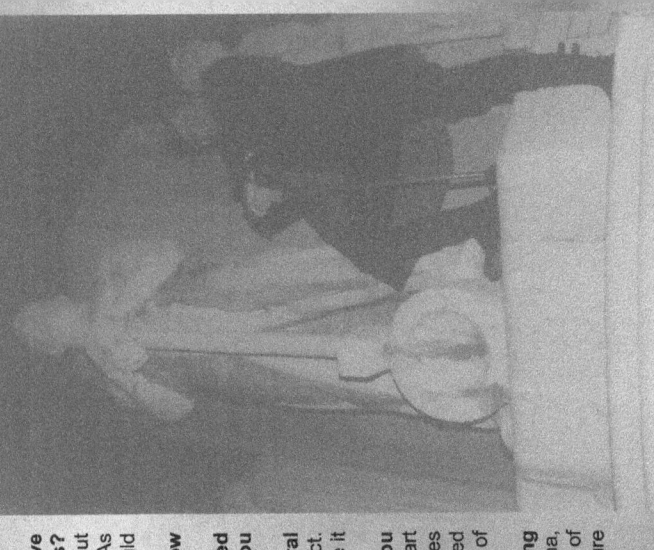

If it isn't Suffering, it isn't Art!

SONGS OF INNOCENCE AND OF EXPERIENCE
Musical interpretations of the classic books by William Blake.
Double CD in Limited Edition full-color Book.
All exclusive tracks by 30 artists, including:

AMBER ASYLUM	ORDO EQUITUM SOLIS
ATTRITION	ORDO (ROSARIUS) EQUILIBRIO
BACKWORLD	PENITENT
COIL	THE PROTAGONIST
DREAM INTO DUST	PSYCHONAUT
4TH SIGN OF THE APOCALYPSE	ROSE MCDOWALL
GENESIS P-ORRIDGE & BUNNY BLANCA	SOL INVICTUS
ILDFROST	THAT SUMMER
LORETTA'S DOLL	THE SWORD VOLCANO COMPLEX
TOR LUNDVALL	THE UNQUIET VOID

4TH SIGN OF THE APOCALYPSE
Frolic of the Demons

A journey begins penetrating emotions best expressed by the id while travelling through shattered kaleidoscopic memories of love, betrayal, and chaos. Also available in the limited edition box set *Box Full of Demons*, with exclusive CD *Left Over Demons*.

THE SWORD VOLCANO COMPLEX

A world of lush strings, experimental soundscapes, spoken word passages, and electronic dance pieces that reveal the innermost torment of a man's soul.

THEE MAJESTY
Time's Up

Spoken word by Genesis P-Orridge (THROBBING GRISTLE, PSYCHIC TV) framed by Bryin Dall's avant-garde guitar. Designed to open your mind to the beauty of words and sounds. Limited edition of 1000, in foil-stamped cover.

OF UNKNOWN ORIGIN
Seven Ovens of the Soul

Alchemy and chaos influences combine to create dark soundscapes ranging from tribal-industrial to deepest ambient and beyond. a collaboration between members of DREAM INTO DUST and 4TH SIGN OF THE APOCALYPSE.

4TH SIGN OF THE APOCALYPSE
Lost Hour World

Dark and humorous sentiments share equal time in eclectic visions coupled with unconventional electronics. Travelling through the subconscious via illbient loops, bizarre soundbites and an experimental tapestry of sound.

GOLDEN DAWN
L.V.X.

The actual rituals of the magickal order set to a modern musickal score. Includes 20-page instructional booklet and a song about the history of the order.

The Order of the Suffering Clown
PO Box 2124, New York, NY 10009 USA • sufclown@aol.com

Manufactured and Distributed by World Serpent Distribution. Available in America through Middle Pillar Distribution.

www.worldserpent.com • www.sufferingclown.com • www.middlepillar.com

APOPTOSE
NORDLAND
TESCO 041

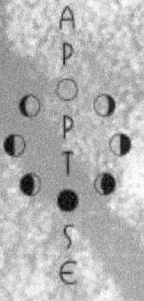

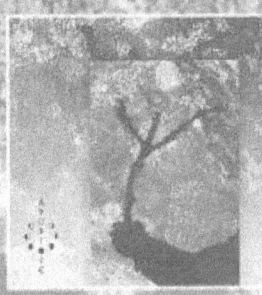

Comes in special digi-pak, German project working in the field of ancient myths. Subliminal drones and beautiful soundscapes remembers us to long forgotten rituals.

**DER BLUTHARSCH –
TRACK OF THE HUNTED, CD/LP**

3rd and probably the best album by this Austrian band.
The colored vinyl edition comes with poster.
WKN 10 now only distributed via Tesco.

**FIRE+ICE –
BIRDKING, CD**

New release by Ian Read, featuring J. Budenholzer, M. Cashmore, M. Fallson, A. Karlsdottir, A. Lee, M. Moynihan and Ostara. A journey with echoes of the ancient northlands and the journey into the yet-to-be.

**FIRE+ICE/DEATH IN JUNE –
WE SAID DESTROY, 7"**

Ltd. 2000, the first 1000 are in coloured vinyl. Presents two previously unreleased tracks. F+I plays a beautiful folk ode and DIJ surprises with a track which will find lovers in the industrial field as well.

**LADY MORPHIA –
RECITALS TO RENEWAL, CD**

A wide range of percussive instrumentation lends a martial feel to some pieces. The sound always remains exceptionally evocative and darkly compelling. The lyrics are very much influenced by the writings of E. Jünger.

**MATT HOWDEN –
INTIMATE & OBSTINATE, CD**

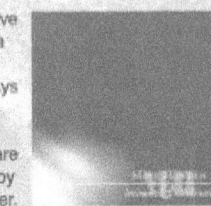

He has produced and worked with Sol Invictus on "In a garden green", "The blade", "In Europa". The result is a Sol Invictus like ambience, a light Coil, Stratosphere or Namlock electronica and a Graeme Revell like soundtrack!

**STURMOVIK –
FELDWEIHE, LP TESCO 042**

L.ed.500, dark arrangements of broding noises and slow evolving rhythms reflects the atmosphere of a submarine ready to attack. With samples and noise loops of classical instrumentations, it sounds like a soundtrack to WWII.

**DEATH IN JUNE –
OPERATION HUMMINGBIRD, CD**

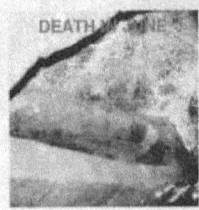

The new studioalbum brings seven new songs in cooperation with "Der Blutharsch", held as a mini-album as intention to follow the "Take Care And Control" release.

**DEATH IN JUNE –
WALL OF SACRIFICE, PIC-LP**

This ltd. 2000 picture-disc is the third in the series all designed by Enrico Chiarparin.

This hard sought after record brings back one of the best DIJ albums ever.

**TEHOM –
THERIOMORPHIC SPIRITS, CD**

Douglas P. presents the 2nd TEHOM release. Siniša Očurščak the man behind TEHOM died shortly after completing this work.
These recordings are outstanding in the fields of mystic ritual music.

Available again: Brighter Death Now - The Slaughterhouse, Con-Dom - All In Good Faith, Dagda Mor - The Border Of The Light

TESCO DISTRIBUTION · P.O.BOX 410118 · D-68275 MANNHEIM · GERMANY
FAX: +49(0)6 21/8 28 07 42   E-MAIL: TESCO-ORG.-MA@t-online.de

DREAM INTO DUST

For a short introduction, DREAM INTO DUST are one of the best American exponents of dark evocative music. Spanning genres of industrial, neo-classical & neo-folk (to name but a few), DREAM INTO DUST are none of these individually yet taking parts of each to create a highly original and distinctive sonic tapestry. Derek Rush the creator and driving force behind the group (not withstanding collaborative input by close friends) answered some of my queries via e-mail in the middle of 2000....

What was your musical journey that lead to your interest in and ultimate recording within an underground culture of obscure music? if you want to start at the very root of things, there was an old upright piano in my parents' house which i abused horribly as a child. i would bang on it, hold the sustain pedal down with books, and open up the front to play the strings with kitchen utensils. i composed and later recorded short pieces in near-total naiveté, since the only music which was played in the house was classical on a tinny-sounding radio or ancient record player. then there was "music class" in school, which made no sense to me. to me, written music has always been about as inspiring and understandable as calculus. this drove me away from music for years and i pursued visual arts. i slowly got back into music_ once the visual side became restrictive in itself. by the time i went to art school i was constantly taking my breaks in the piano rooms. i re-taught myself music from a standpoint of different types of chords, and timbres of sound, as opposd to scales and keys. i learned a few rules and broke them immediately if i thought they were stupid, and let the final judgement be whether or not it sounds good. by this time i'd been exposed to both mainstream and underground music. i thought there was just music that was easy to find and other music that was more obscure, but for me the difference became clear when trying to send demos to labels and managers. i realised how differently these people approached music, and how much they would influence and warp it to suit the needs of the current marketplace, and that they were unable to understand certain things about the artists and the audience. it made more sense to follow the underground culture i was exposed to in books like 'cassette mythos' and RE/SEARCH's 'industrial handbook'. not only was working in this way more feasible but more attractive to me as an artist. i'm not against commercial success but it should happen on the artist's own terms.

For a brief history DECEMBER was your first project (of subdued industrial gothic tinged songs) that was then laid to rest in favor of DREAM INTO DUST. In particular DREAM INTO DUST has progressively become more instrumental and neo-classical with each release. Has this been a conscious effort or an inevitable progression? not conscious at all. given the classical music in my background i'd say it's inevitable, even atavistic. i still can't get into most classical music because it doesn't sustain a mood or key long enough, or i dislike certain conductors or playing styles. but there are segments of it that are just amazing. those are the moments i try to capture and extend for a piece, or work into another context. i wouldn't describe what you said as a progression, at least not the final progression. i wouldn't be surprised if some elements from the older material began creeping back in. i'm reluctant to classify it as "gothic" since that brings to mind a certain bass guitar-driven sound that we only briefly touched on with the "river of blood"/ "venus in chains" single. i like to think it was a unique take on that, and had other elements which point the way to other things. there's constant growth and change depending on what's necessary. there's a lot of variety if you're open to the numerous subgenres of dark music, but our work all stays within a framework that defines the sound.

Do you personally consider DECEMBER to be the starting point for DREAM INTO DUST, or did the name change mark a total shift in attitude that ultimately required a new beginning? it's pretty much the same attitude and feelings in that they come from me, but my life was different then. when things changed, the stylistic shift was enough that the name change was appropriate. besides the fact that several other bands were using an exact or similar name. i think DREAM INTO DUST is more unique and personal, and not provoke as narrow or prejudiced a reaction. i probably should have picked it in the first place.

Having already indicated that you are increasingly working within the neo-classical genre, DREAM INTO DUST still have the ability to transcend mere categorizations of a particular style, drawing from numerous sources (folk, doom, gothic, industrial to name a few). Has this ever created compositional difficulties for you in which direction you pursued? (consciously or otherwise). i try to balance between letting the song go where it wants and trying to make sure it stays true to the sound i want to portray. a perfect example is "farwell to eden". it's almost entirely classical in arrangement, and the voice is very melodic. i really didn't want to go that far in that direction, since there was a possibility that track would be played separately and misrepresent us as a purely neoclassical band. but that's how it turned out. in the end i have to trust my feelings about it.

Although your music has a very European flavor, you actually live in New York (and what I'm sure is a very urbanised construct) I wouldn't think this would be an inspiring setting for the music you compose. Do you find your surroundings a hindrance to your creativity? new york would be wonderful if not for all the people. i try to exist at hours to come in contact with as few people as possible. that's not always an option. i'm not in an especially "urbanised" area, although it is getting worse all the time. i would say the negative aspects of the environment are inspiring in a sense. if i felt there were more interesting things to do, great people to go out and meet, i'd be out spending my time on that sort of thing. instead, there are more yuppies, corporations, and tourists than ever blundering around town, strip-mining each community and turning everything into a bastardized disneyland. so mostly i try to stay in the studio and work. there are other advantages though, so we'll stick it out here as long as we can.

Many people spout on how they would ultimately love to go live away from the majority of human contact etc, however what is your opinion on this? i think i forsee that in the future for myself. however you have to be careful not to become so cut off you aren't aware of what's going on, or you become unable to function around people because they're so alien to you. ingesting a little of this poisonous society at a time helps keep you immune to it.

What musical groups/ scenes, writers, philosophers have played a role in the shaping of DREAM INTO DUST as we see/ hear it today? there's always influences coming in from everywhere, but i do my best to weed out those not relevant to the band, and distill those that are. industrial, classical, dark metal, experimental, neo-folk are all represented in what we do. if something seems like it's leaning a bit too much towards a certain style i try to throw a spanner in the works that no one else would. that might sound like a hodgepodge, but it does seem to coagulate into something other than the sum of the parts. as for writers and philosophers, nietzsche, sartre, kundera, and perdurabo has all had influence as well as mirroring concepts i already had. everything is filtered through my perception though, the band is not following any doctrine, unless it is that of the individual.

Given the images you have used on your releases have a historic euro centric focus, what aspects of European history interest you the most? i wouldn't say history of any sort interests me per se. to me it's all just ideas, concepts, alternate ways of thinking and living than the bland and obvious path that's set in front of us from birth. i'm drawn to european culture as an aspiration to something higher than the crass generic american lifestyle. others would also say it's because some of my background is european - more atavism i suppose! perhaps a bit of both reasons. it's a part of me that i've been separated from and thus am attracted to as a result.

"Not above but apart" is a song title off your 'the world we have lost CD. Can you detail how this if at all pertains to the overall philosophy of either yourself or the concept behind DREAM INTO DUST? i think the title is self-explanatory. i almost didn't feel the need to write any more words than that. it's a fitting end for the CD. given all the negative lyrics and the album title, one might think the finale would be blowing everything up, or claiming to be superior. instead you get, "not above but apart."

Likewise when exactly was our world lost? Is this a metaphor for loss of a certain mindset or referencing specific historic events? that depends on how you define the term "world". it could be the planet earth, a particular way of life, a "scene", a circle of friends, a certain time frame...the possibilities go on. like the name DREAM INTO DUST itself, it's loaded with multiple connotations for people to consider. i want people to think as well as listen to the music. even if they only get something years later - in fact when that happens to me, it makes me appreciate the piece more.

A sense of timeless nostalgia and sorrow permeates much of the atmosphere of the lyrics and music, but the photographic representation of your releases represents an era of past history (approximately the 1930-40's). Do the photos you have used reflect a deeper meaning other than for their aesthetic appearance? i became interested in war photography several years ago. the fact is, there was more film shot in WWII than any conflict ever before or since. so a lot of images are going to come from that. however the photos we've used have come from various wars since the late 1800's. it's not meant as an historical reference, or in support of any country or political party. it's to show the horror it can bring, and unfortunately, the sick and strange beauty the destruction can provide the photographers with. it's a reminder of how close we all are to that state, how fragile humans and our creations are. it's also a metaphor for the battles all of us fight every day with ourselves and the outside world, and the feeling of desolation we can have after fighting for so long. however, after the 'no man's land' and 'the world we have lost' we're moving on to other types of images. the music and lyrics are about more than just those things.

You seem to be involved in a scene of ethereal/ folk noir groups centered in New York and increasingly solidifying around the MIDDLE PILLAR label. Is this a correct assessment or totally off the mark? it is somewhat correct in that we all know each other or are aware of each other. several people have switched bands over the past few years, or work with each other from time to time. at one time or another various bands have worked with MIDDLE PILLAR, either contributing to compilations, making distribution deals, or signing recording contracts. they're doing a great thing, but for the most part, the bands exist independently of each other and the label. MPP simply recognizes talent and know what to do with it – kudos to them for doing so. it should be mentioned that before MPP, there was an event called "a night of misanthropy" which bryin dall used to present, which did a lot towards helping a live dark music scene coalesce here in the 1990's.

Can you provide some detail into your involvement in your various side projects? (of which there are many!). well, speaking of bryin. he's the one i work with most of the time on other projects. although he contributes to DREAM INTO DUST as well sometimes. i first helped him on a country song a few years ago, which led to a remix of a track by his band LORETTA'S DOLL. since then i actually joined them, playing bass and other noises and mixing half the new album. meanwhile, he and i did an even noisier experimental/industrial project called OF UNKNOWN ORIGIN. i sometimes do mixes for his main project 4TH SIGN OF THE APOCALYPSE as well as the powerelectronics outfit URSUS NOIR. i helped on two tracks for THEE MAJESTY which he does with genesis p-orridge, as well as one track for THE SWORD VOLCANO COMPLEX album. recently we collaborated on a dark ambient project A MURDER OF ANGELS, and then applied some of the same techniques in postproduction to the first album by THE MIRROR REVEALS. we've started work on a full album of dark country songs. i still plan to do other things and work with more people. but bryin and i work well together and he's lives nearby! as enjoyable as those projects are, i'd like to slow things down in those areas for awhile and concentrate on DREAM INTO

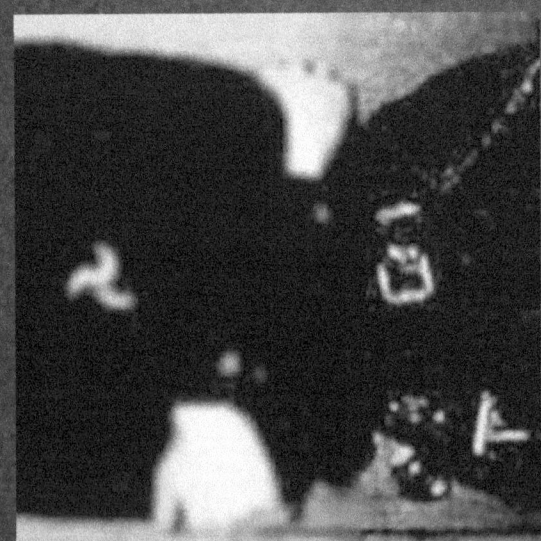

DUST more.

ELFENBLUT were responsible to introducing DECEMBER to the masses and later bringing forth the debut DREAM INTO DUST CD. How did you get in contact with the label and are you satisfied with the results? as i mentioned before, my previous dealings with labels were frustrating at best, and i had given up on such a route and released the 'hope for nothing' cassette myself. it attracted some attention in the underground dark music press, and i was trading it with other artists' tape releases. one of these was ENDURA, who dubbed a copy for a friend at MISANTHROPY RECORDS, who liked it and wrote about working with us. they then started ELFENBLUT as a non-metal counterpart label to ENDURA. AIN SOPH, ENDURA, BLOOD AXIS, HAGALAZ RUNEDANCE, DREAM INTO DUST, and others. they didn't actually release the debut 'no man's land' MCD which came out first due to a scheduling conflict at the time. they did come through with the release of 'the world we have lost' though. it came out exactly as i'd envisioned it. i'm satisfied with their efforts, however unfortunately they decided to fold because of the tedious side of the record business. even though their releases were very much respected and selling quite well. we were one of the last three releases and i believe we suffered a bit timing-wise because of that. no fault on their end, but there was a slight perception and profile problem because the label's closing was known, as well as some distribution problems, especially in germany.

Your other releases being in the form of a 7" and MCD were produced on your own label CHTHONIC STREAMS and I believe was originally started to release the 'No Mans Land' CD. What is the future plan for this label and how does DREAM INTO DUST fit into its continued vision? Do you prefer others to release your music or yourself apart from the obvious cost factor? in some ways i'd prefer to have others release DREAM INTO DUST, since i concentrate on so much of it. it takes the pressure off and gets some perspective to have someone else handle a few details. of course doing it all yourself means more control, so it's a tradeoff. the cost factor is a slight deterrent to releasing everything on CHTHONIC STREAMS. however, i'm very serious about releasing good music, so if i didn't believe in something i wouldn't put money into it. besides the MCD and "a prison for oneself" 7", you mentioned, there has also been the compilation on the brink of infinity', which came out at the end of 1999 and featured 12 artists' reflections on endings/beginnings/death/rebirth/cycles. i've already been speaking to a few other artists about releasing their material on CS. it's just a question of time and money.

What future items are currently in the workings, be those for DREAM INTO DUST or other projects and which labels are they destined to be released on? there will be another MURDER OF ANGELS album sometime in 2001. there's a great 4TH SIGN OF THE APOCALYPSE 2CD box set coming that i have some interesting mixes and a lot of artwork on. and by the end of 2000 COLD SPRING should be releasing the URSUS NOIR album, which i mixed over half of. LORETTA'S DOLL has completed the sixth album 'creeping sideways', which will hopefully be out on WORLD SERPENT by the time this is printed. there's a lot of compilations that DREAM INTO DUST has done tracks for. By now the following should have been released: WIDERSTAND (STATE-ART), interpretations of the title's meaning; TEN YEARS OF MADNESS (ACHTUNG BABY!), about socio-political changes through dark post industrial expression; SOL MAGAZINE #3, by tony wakeford. coming soon should be SONGS OF INNOCENCE AND EXPERIENCE (SUFFERING CLOWN), musical recordings of the william blake books. we're winding down on these projects and preparing for the next DREAM INTO DUST release. it will be a 7" picture disc dealing with the holiday season, religion, and related issues. that will be out in december 2000.

As you prepare design artwork for your own label/ releases and for other labels such as MIDDLE PILLAR, is this something you have trained in and is this your career as such that allows you to finance your other endeavours? that's the way it is at the moment. the covers and ads are only part of it. i do a lot of freelance design and layout which helps fund the creation of music and the inherent expenses of that. the mailorder and label sales help a bit as well, but none of it is making me rich.

Last comments? thank you for the interview, richard. keep up the great work on SPECTRUM. DREAM INTO DUST MP3s can be heard at http://www.mp3.com/dreamintodust CHTHONIC STREAMS website: http://www.chthonicstreams.com mailing address: PO BOX 7003, NEW YORK, NY 10116-7003 USA

(NOTE: photos of derek rush by dawn of the dead. all other images by derek rush)

DEATH IN JUNE

Show Report: 24th May, 2000 Melbourne/ AUSTRALIA

Although Ikon were the headlining act with Death in June as the special guest, admittedly I was really there to see the later rather than the former. However, mentioning the headline act first off, while Ikon are not of a genre I normally frequent, I can appreciate that they are solid performers at what they do. Basically they play (heavy) uptempo gothic rock - instumentation ranging from electric to acoustic guitars, bass & drum rhythm section and the occasional keyboard/ programmed backing track. Ikon playing for around an hour, the set included mostly originals, but the audience was treated to their stunning uptempo version of Death in June's 'Fall Apart' for this special occasion. Further reviewing the night in rewind, the gig was held at the Esplanade Hotel (affectionately referred to as the Espy) being an icon (not Ikon...?!) of the Melbourne pub/ band circuit. Having the Death in June gig billed as "unplugged" I assumed this would mean the attendance of Douglas P and John Murphy only, as it was likely that Albin Julius still over in Austria. In short this assumption turned out to be correct. While the stage setup of this show was less visually impressive than the one the previous year at Chasers Nightclub in Melbourne, I guess this time there was less equipment required, complicated with more stage area to deal with. Nonetheless it contained the obligatory DI6 symbol banners strategically draped to the front and rear of the stage, also covering the standing floor form off to the side (also flanked by chimes, snare and symbol).
On the call of the shrill squeals of pigs and braying donkeys (intro to 'Ku Ku'), Douglas and John entered the stage at approximately 9:50 pm. Both were clad in full camouflage army garb, with John wearing a full leather fetish mask and Douglas shunning the trademark clay face mask, opting for an army helmet with rope camouflage attached to the front. This ensured both individuals' faces were fully obscured, resulting in a faceless performance and reflected the ethos of Douglas not being interested in any form of rock star status. This entry and subsequent rendition of 'Ku Ku Ku' saw a number of camera wielding people rush the front stage to immortalise the moment (me being one of them)– with the camera flashes being somewhat symbolic of night time warfare explosions.
Straight away it was evident that the sound was much more powerful than I anticipated, and that even when armed only with an acoustic guitar, mournful vocals and a minimalist standing percussion setup, the overall power and subdued martial sentiments were not forsaken, particularly enhanced via expertly executed pounded rhythms.
Due to the acoustic format unfortunately we would not be treated to any live renditions of the more industrial/ neo classical sounds on the last two albums, thus the set list revolved mostly around the mid eira of Death in June particularly the apocalyptic acoustic folk sound. The overall atmosphere of tragedy and despair that permeates Death in June's live offerings was certainly felt through lyrics such as 'to love is to loose and to loose is to die" off 'Fall Apart' and "Europa has burned and will burn again" off 'Giddy Giddy Carousel'. For myself one of the highlights was the inclusion of 'Kameradshaft' which lost nothing in the delivery, despite lacking the programmed backing. The set list likewise included live versions of 'Of Runes and Men', 'But What ends when the Symbols Shatter?', 'Leper Lord' and others which escape me at the moment (much akin to the quickly escaping aura of DI6 at the conclusion of a performance). Being on stage for only a brief time, the 30-40 minutes passed all but too quickly - but I guess a glimpse is better than no vision at all...
Talking with John Murphy after the show it seems that later in the year after overseas shows are dispensed with, Death in June may be back in full entourage with Albin for further shows. I certainly hope this occurs as I really would like to see how the new tracks off 'Operation Hummingbird' translate to the live medium.
(Words, live photographs & background image by: Richartd Stevenson).

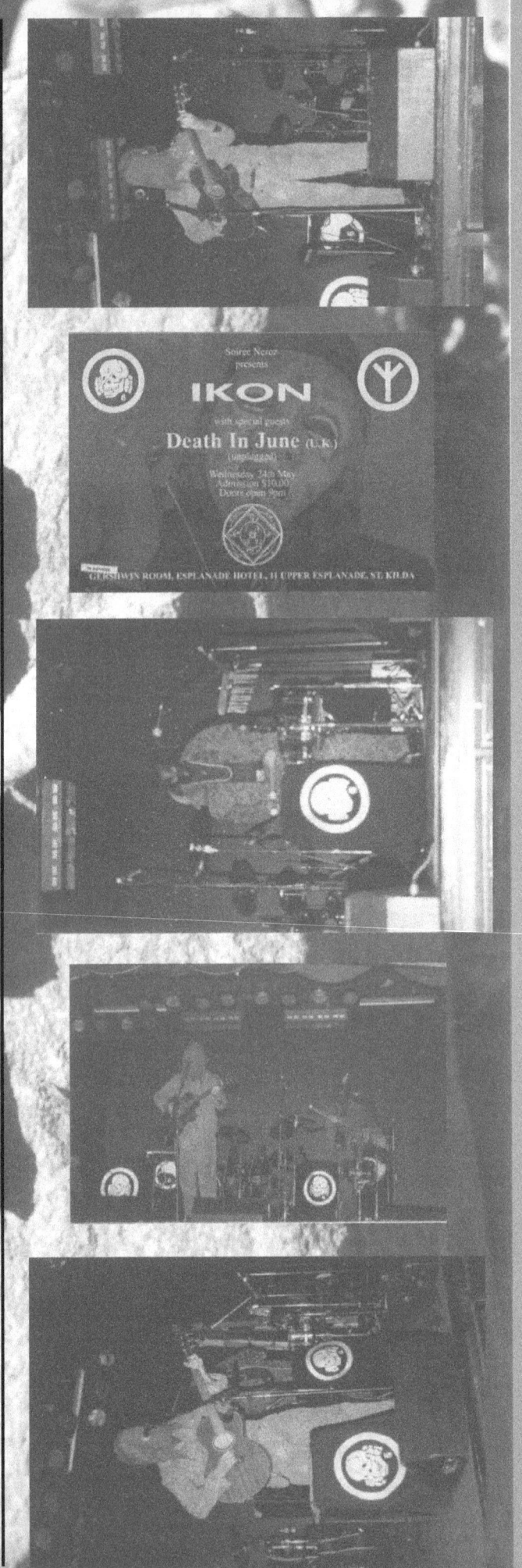

LAW

Having only been introduced to the power of LAW in mid 1999, I must say I quickly became a devote to the abrasive yet intelligent sound/ noise-scapes. The corrosive anger & smouldering contempt of sole member Mitchell Altum has now manifested itself in his response to my interrogation undertaken during mid 2000.

Can you give a summation of the history of LAW and the recorded output thus far? I decided to attempt creating my own audio at the beginning of 1993, and within a few months my partner of the time and I had a very basic studio set-up. Within one year Law's first release was completed. Here is a brief LAW discography: + MALEDICTION - Self-released in 1994, this was the first sonic declaration of Law. + OKTAGON - Law had three new pieces on this double-LP compilation put out in 1995 by Germany's ANT-ZEN. Oktagon was specially packaged, and pressed on red vinyl. + NUCLEAR ASSAULT - Released in early '96 by Art Konkret in Germany, this specially packaged (housed in a sealed metal canister) tape comp. featured one new Law track. + PARIAHS AMONG OUTCASTS - From 1996, this full length album was released by ANT-ZEN, and held within a special 12"x12" booklet made up of intense artwork, photos and text. + WAR AGAINST SOCIETY - An ambitious three LP compilation put out in 1997 by Germany's Praxis Dr. Bearmann, and containing an album's side worth of new work from Law. + WADING KNEE-DEEP IN YOUR BLOOD - Full length album from 1999 on Italy's Old Europa Cafe. Pressed on red vinyl and packaged in an elaborate four panel folder. + VINDICATION AND CONTEMPT - Released in January of 2000 via Triumvirate, this material marked the first appearance of Law on compact disc. + OUR LIFE THROUGH YOUR DEATH - This long-delayed title (completed in 1996) will finally be detonated in autumn 2000 by Triumvirate. A CD of diverse audio tactics and blast patterns. + THE BLACK LODGE - The final material to be released under the banner of "LAW", this CD will be housed in an elaborate folding package and released at the very end of 2000 by France's Nuit et Brouillard.

In the past year or so LAW have really made quite an impact with the LP on OEC and your CD debut incidentally on your own label, but when the recordings are scrutinised they both date back to 1997. What if any current recordings have or are you working on and likewise what was the reason for the delays of all said items? The recording of "The Black Lodge" was finished in autumn 1998. I'm currently collecting and programming the vast array of samples and sounds needed to construct the next full length block of material, which should be ready in the first part of 2001. To fully program, compose, record and mix a new Law work can take from 12 to 18 months. After my work is completed, in the past I had to begin the process of finding and securing a label to produce and distribute the material. Once a release agreement could be made, there was the wait as the label had the title manufactured, then fit it into their release schedule. In some instances, release dates had to be repeatedly pushed back by the labels for their own reasons — which I'm often not aware of until after the fact. "Vindication and Contempt" was finalized at the end of '97, but it wasn't until fall 1999 (after declining a few release offers for the work from various labels) that my partners and I decided to make it the debut Triumvirate CD. I programmed the packaging artwork, had the audio mastered, and secured a production facility all within the next few months. The disc was unveiled January 2000. I've come to the conclusion that all future audio works will be released either through Triumvirate, or solely by myself, without being within the structure of a "label".

How has your involvement in the underground scene eventuated and at what point did you think you had something to offer in the way of a power electronics project? Actually — not to be picky or oversensitive about genre labels, because it doesn't concern me that much — I don't think LAW has much of *anything* to offer the power electronics field. I personally don't consider my sonic output to be in that realm, and I'm sure most fans of power electronics wouldn't either. That said, I wouldn't have originally attempted creating my own music if I hadn't felt I could do a justifiable job of it, and the initial, strongly favourable reception from many quarters of the "Malediction" cassette helped affirm my convictions.

Working within the broad confines of abrasive noise there always contains a level of focused direction. What musical compositional background do you have? No formal or classical training. However, I began actively listening to music and seeking out unconventional styles and artists in the late 70s, and always tried to recognize what sound techniques worked to create a certain mood or effect. Almost as importantly, I came to realize what methods were overused clichés and cheap tricks. When I decided to create my own music I tried incorporating some of the techniques I understood into Law, and made every effort to avoid the mistakes of groups or artists in my general field.

What is the basic concept of constructing/ composing LAW tracks and how has your equipment altered over time? I often let the raw, unstructured sounds and samples partially dictate the form and composition of an individual piece. I have eight digital tracks at my disposal, plus numerous "virtual" ones via the sampler and midi techniques, so when it's appropriate to the song I often try filling all available parts of the sonic spectrum to give the audio a dense, heavily layered impact. I usually sketch out a kind of "schematic" for the structure of the track, plotting start and end points, duration, levels, etc., for each separate element, all in an effort to build the piece into a purposeful sonic journey, rather than a random collection of sounds or drifting haze of meandering improvisation. When LAW started back in 1993 the core equipment was an 80s-era sampler, a basic drum machine, a multi-effects processor, a compact mixer, a four-track analog cassette recorder, and a DAT recorder. Whenever finances have permitted over the years I've upgraded each piece of gear, and added a small number of new ones. Right now I have a rudimentary, yet fully functioning digital "studio". I still haven't made the shift into computer based synthesis and recording, and don't think I will anytime soon.

What music encompasses your listening time and to what you may find inspirational for LAW. Likewise what sources of literature and motion pictures have you found merit in if not taken inspiration from? I listen to a broad range of musical styles, and the dark ambient/hard electronics genres make up only a portion of my interests. Music that is unique, powerful, and evocative is what inspires me to try to bring the same qualities to my own work. Part of my motivation for being involved in Triumvirate lies in the fact that music at it's best has a power beyond just notes and melodies to inspire and energize, or to act as a catharsis and refuge. Triumvirate can act as a conduit for bringing a small fraction more of such music to a larger audience. I look for similar characteristics in films and literature — works that are thought provoking, effective, that temporarily draw you into their reality and force you to consider what you would do if faced with their scenarios.

The liner note of "Vindication and Contempt" contains a scathing reference to "two-bit hobbyists and delusional tinkerers". Is this aimed at anyone in particular or a general statement to the experimental scene? No, it's not an indictment of any one artist or even the larger scene, but instead a reference to and dismissal of a general category of losers attempting to live out some sorry fantasy that they have anything meaningful to contribute to the world of music. Let me preface any further comments by saying that I DO NOT claim to be making the best dark electronic music in the field — I'm rarely entirely satisfied with Law, and there is an endless road of improvement to travel down. However, with high power sound equipment, recording gear, and CD-R burners affordable to virtually all above the lowest economic classes, in recent years there has been a sickening, sludge-like flood of utterly worthless, unoriginal, talent less "releases" sloshing over the landscape. This goes across nearly every genre, but is especially prevalent in the electronically dominated styles, particularly where one or two people can do everything from calling up factory pre-programmed drum loop #B17 on the affordable keyboard, to slapping the crappy label fresh out of their inkjet printer onto the face of a 75¢ CD-R. It takes more than an obligatory website or a flaccid performance at a local teen dance club to be a legitimate audio label or group/performer. Many people who think they're going to make it big by mailing out a few demo CDs and getting "signed" by ***A RECORD LABEL***, or impress their obsessive record collector friends with the sleek new synthesizer plugged into the back of their Radio Shack stereo would be well served to pull two or three discs from their own collections by their favourite artists working in genres remotely similar to what they think they're going to do. If after seriously, objectively comparing the output from those established artists with their own, they can truly say that their work holds up (and most of them will *still* be kidding themselves), then there's justification to proceed.

Likewise the statement "All hail mini-van-Wal-Mart-America" is used for sarcastic effect, however does this reflect the surroundings you live in? Middle class, middle America (as with many Western countries) is populated by a soulless citizenry whose highest aspirations include finally making the last payment on their rusty, five year old mini vans, breeding miniature replicas of themselves with spouses they can barely put up with — and have long ago lost all passion for, and occupying the dead hours between the job and the television with all-consuming pilgrimages down to the local mega-warehouse discount chain store to purchase useless goods they can't really afford. The sight, sound, smell, and very IDEA of them is a perpetual mental drain and source of disgust.

With your reference to the American Middle Class above, where would you place yourself in the class scale of American Economic Society? (If America is anything like Australia, the middle class is being marginalised and being replaced by a smaller grouping of upper class and burgeoning mass of a poor underclass). I'd say my income would place me in the lower-middle class of the American economic structure. However, since to date I've done a fairly good job of avoiding the worst socio-economic traps most people fall into, my money goes farther. First and foremost, I do not have children, and will never father or raise offspring. There's no demanding wife, expecting to live an illusional life of convenience and comfort beyond our financial means. I don't have a lease on a ridiculous sport utility vehicle or high end Japanese sports car, so there are no crushing monthly car payments for me. I'd prefer a larger dwelling, but I always strive to keep the rent for my living quarters in line with what I can realistically afford. I don't fill my small domicile or drain my wallet with worthless, overpriced consumer goods.

Have you read 'the Redneck Manifesto' by Jim Goad? What are your opinions of this publication and would you display any sort of affinity to the portrayal of this class of American (particularly since Jim states he feels closest to the 'redneck' than any other societal group). Yes, I've read the book. Goad is often an entertaining author, and this work was well written and accurate for the most part. The last few chapters seem to be on the verge of filler, Goad having already made his point, and perhaps needing enough additional words to bring the book up to full length. No, I don't identify with the "redneck" class — they're ignorant, self-defeating, and intolerable for the most part. With each additional year I find myself farther removed from all the classes and subcultures around me. I didn't name the Law album "Pariahs Among Outcasts" solely because I like the way those words sound.

Certain lyrics seems to convey a level of regret and discontent. Do you have regret and not necessarily in relation to LAW? Naturally I regret actions I've taken, and things I *haven't* done in my life, but I don't try to express those thoughts in the music. At most, I might be in that general frame of mind when programming or recording a given passage or song, and some of that mood might be reflected in part of the music.

What is the law of LAW as you see it? No dogmatic or overblown laws for public consumption or adherence. Instead, "Law" refers more to my personal values, principles, guidelines and goals. I attempt to live life as a unified whole, using the same principles and judgments whenever possible in all situations. Not necessarily a world of only black and white circumstances and decisions, but rather ideally one comprised of very dark grays and very light grays, where I strive to push everything as far as possible towards one end of the spectrum or the other. The few things that fall in between make up acceptable compromises, and sometimes, for brief periods, balance is achieved.

Image hasn't seemed to be a huge factor in the representation of LAW (except for the obscured image in the War Against Society set & Wading Knee Deep..LP), but then again no image can be just as constraining? Thoughts? I don't expend all this time and energy constructing audio so I can get my face plastered in magazine articles or advertisements, or my name endlessly dropped and jabbered about among hordes of online dimwits. My personal appearance has nothing to do with the music I create, so my image has not, and never will be featured on any of my releases.

In much of what you say (or at least how your come across in e-mail) you are a forthright person who likes to "tell it like it is". Now a trait of certain genres (particularly metal) is that people will put forward an image via an interview but resemble little of what they portray in real life. What is you opinion of this and how does this relate if at all to LAW? I'm not a talent less, insecure cunt who starves herself for two weeks just to squeeze into a leather jumpsuit for the big photo shoot, or a pudgy, middle-aged computer nerd trying to convince listeners I'm as "dark" and "dangerous" as the image of the music I'm slapping together, so I don't need to construct some stage persona or artificial mystique. I live my life, pursue my interests and goals, and create the type of music that appeals to me. Whether observers find my tastes and activities "controversial" and "extreme", or boring and just disagreeable is irrelevant to me. Long ago I realized it's far easier and satisfying to simply speak the blunt truth whenever possible, regardless of possible hurt feelings or perceived unfriendliness. Over the years a number of people have told me that the way I speak, act, write and dress, both privately and publicly, all seem to mesh together naturally, with no pretension or artifice on my part.

In one interview of yours I read, you stated you planned to drop the moniker 'Law' after the release of an upcoming album 'The Black Lodge'. Exactly why would you choose to do this and would the name change likely see a change in musical direction? I've been working as "Law" for seven years, and while the inspirations and references that lead me to chose that title are still important to me, the word itself as a creative shell has become less important. I've even considered just using "Mitchell Altum" as the identifier for the music, but I guess I still fall prey somewhat to the aesthetic appeal of one ambiguous word to act as a creative edifice. That, and using something other than my own name also reinforces my belief that the music is more important than my personality. The name change will not have any direct effect on the nature of the audio.

What to make of the distinction of living in the heart of the most decadent nation to ever exist? Would you prefer to live elsewhere if given the opportunity? I've never lived in another country, so I don't have any direct comparisons to make. I'd certainly be interested in traveling through many other nations and geographic regions, but even as bad as much of American culture and society is, it's still far better than much of the rest of the world. Let's pause for a moment while non-American readers swear and clench the sides of the magazine with indignation... I'd say that virtually ANY part of the world would be more liveable if it were massively depopulated. As much as I dislike the cold, from time to time I've thought it might be interesting to live for a short while in Antarctica.

Given that America does not have a mandatory voting system such as the one in place here in Australia do you choose to vote in your 'democratic' election process? For the past few years, only when there has been a worthwhile Libertarian candidate on the ballot. Mandatory voting — there's real liberty and "democracy" in action for you. Just as blatant censorship and confiscation of private property represent modern democracy in Germany, and the decimation of "civil liberties" in the name of the "War on Drugs" and "safety of the children" qualify as democracy in the United States.

Triumvirate is your own label and obviously contains the input of two other individuals. Who is the triad forming the label and how are responsibilities for production allocated? Likewise how far do you plan to take the label and what are the planned outputs? Eric D. and Erica Hoffman are my two partners in this endeavour. I handle most of the technical audio and visual details involved in constructing a release. I brought my base of contacts and first hand experience acquired during working in this field for seven years to the label, and do a great deal of the networking for promotion and distribution involved. Eric & Erica bring their business acumen and experience to the effort, having run their own small, successful business in the past. Eric tends to be more adept at friendly social interaction than I am, so he often handles most of the direct or phone contact needed with potential artists and distributors. He also supplies most of the ammunition and mind enhancing chemicals. Erica is skilled at running the numbers and keeping the books, so she usually tends to keep the records and bills straight. She's also in charge of constructing the Triumvirate website. We all review audio submissions, and there's some amount of overlapping of duties in general. As long as there's enough interest and support generated by the listeners of unorthodox, obscure music to keep us from sinking into bankruptcy, we'll continue. This issue of "Spectrum" is slated for publication just as Law's "Our Life Through Your Death" CD will be hitting the market. We have four other releases in varying degrees of readiness scheduled from autumn 2000 through early 2001, but since I'm writing this in summer of '00, I prefer not to go into detail since those items are not yet cast in stone. Fact and action over hype and empty promises...

Lastly for those who have not heard any of your output why should someone listen to LAW? Someone should listen to Law if they're interested in having their expectations challenged, and are willing to actively absorb unsettling music. They should listen to Law if they're tired of aimless, thoughtless electronics. Someone should listen because I TELL THEM to listen...

LAW • TRIUMVIRATE: triumvirate@datacruz.com, P.O. Box 6254, South Bend, IN, 46660 USA

KK NULL / MOZ
"A Split Release" CD • CM007 - $11(us) $13(wld)
KK Null presents five new tracks of frenetic electronics and rhythmic experiments, ranging from cacophonous to an almost tribal atmosphere. Ever evolving within a sphere of obscure tension the details reveal themselves with a stalwart elegance. Moz delivers 6 tracks of socially introspective Death Industrial and Dark Ambient. Drifting slabs contrast sharply with vitriolic sonics to render this misshapen pillar of sobering electronics. Limited to 500 copies.

DEISON
"Dirty Blind Vortex" CD • CM006 - $11(us) $13(wld)
A fuming miasma of desiccated frequencies and oppressive atmospheres from this Italian purveyor of Death Industrial & Dark Ambient. "Dirty Blind Vortex" is a cryptic snarl of emotion and obsession, impulse and lethargy. Features contributions from Sshe Retina Stimulants, Govt. Alpha, Baal, R.H.Y. Yau, Lasse Marhaug and more. Limited to 500

LEFTHANDEDDECISION
"Instinct & Emotion" CD • CM005 - $11(us) $13(wld)
"Instinct & Emotion" is a guttural deluge of constrictive Heavy Electronics, thick, grinding sonics & acidic vocals, that maintains an underlying subtle darkness beneath it all. A monolith of contemptuous, and unforgiving Noise... Limited to 496 copies.

GRUNTSPLATTER/SLOWVENT
"Split Release" CD • CM003 - $11(us) $13(wld)
Gruntsplatter provide 30 minutes of grim Noise Ambient and darkened isolationist textures. Rich with subtlety and introspective horror. Slowvent supply 30 minutes of viscous Death Industrial. Thick, low end electronics, sluggish rhythmic distortions and subterranean atmospheres. This release is limited to 500 copies.

COMING SOON • WILT - "Wither" CD • NEVER PRESENCE FOREVER - "tba" CD

CRIONIC MIND

ORDERING INSTRUCTIONS: All prices are postage paid, payment by well concealed cash or money order made payable to SCOTT CANDEY, NOT CRIONIC MIND. All payment must be in US funds only.

PMB 105 : 4644 Geary Blvd. : San Francisco, CA 94118 : www.crionicmind.org : crionic@pacbell.net

In the relative short amount of time that STATEART has been in operation as a record label, it has gained a healthy level of notoriety & respect in amongst 'those in the know' of the general industrial underground. I am more than pleased to further assist in raising the profile of this very worthwhile label by featuring this interview with label boss Marco Koch...

Can you give some details about personal status and the path you travelled that eventuated in your involvement in subversive music cultures? By being a subversive nature myself, I've always felt a certain tendency for the "extreme". Since my early youth I received musical influences that ranged from 80's Pop, over Punk and all extremes in Metal music, until I finally found the phenomenon of Industrial music. I've definitely not taken the "classical way" to my discovery, the prime of THROBBING GRISTLE or SPK was long since gone in the early 90's and I was young, as I'm still not too old. In the meantime, my personal musical taste has evolved a lot... The extremity is not anymore of great importance to me, rather the explicit expression and transmission of ideas through music. Thus I can confess, even a good Pop record or songs from ADRIANO CELENTANO are able to ennoble my day, because they radiate a lot more honesty than most of these evil clowns...

STATEART have become quite a cult label over a short amount of time. What exactly made you decide to start a record label? Thank you for the ascertainment of STATEART being a cult label. Of course I'm satisfied with the status we reached within barely 4 years, although I wouldn't overrate the same. I decided to start a record label with my first recordings under the name IDPA and close contact to the individual behind THOROFON, who was part of the clan until the release of his "Littleton" project, as well as my general plans to become active as a label. This is, in short, my former motivation to start with STATEART.

Have your early aspirations for the label changed and thus far have you achieved what you initially aimed for? Where do you want to take the label in future projects? I consider STATEART as some kind of independent „organism" and after all I've achieved a lot more than I was able to dream four years ago. My early aspirations for the label have changed drastically. At the beginning there was only our desire to release and work with the music we liked, but the guidelines that take our struggle ahead are now far different from what we've done before. Music as bearer of ideas and alternative influences is an important key point for our present and future work. Where STATEART has just been one amongst several other Post-Industrial oriented labels worldwide, we'll now take a rather personal and different direction. Music, as bearer of ideas, is a tool that has to be formed. Industrial music, at the other hand, rather became a dogma that tells us, how the music has to be shaped to become successful within a scene, where a certain narrow-mindedness unfortunately is the daily order. Where is the revolutionary spirit of Industrial music today? There's not much more left than a subculture copy of any equal mainstream culture. And this takes us to the point of where I want to take the label in future projects... At the moment we're trying to give our "New Guidelines! A New Path! NEUE MUSIK!" profile a living form. NEUE MUSIK (New Music) doesn't mean we're striving to create something generally new and never seen before. That is almost impossible to plot out of the ground and it will lead to a blindness towards the truly important aspects within our concept! Of course we're trying to see STATEART as a family of musicians, who are sophisticated and innovative. NEUE MUSIK generally is a powerful synonym for "consequent music". I don't know where STATEART will walk in the future, if the label will some day disappear from the surface or if we grow... For now I'm trying to organize my work in a clearly arranged manner. With certainty, the only functional dictatorship STATEART won't remain a one man dictatorship any longer and I'm planning to give away competence to some of my closest friends, concerning organization, design and propagandistic work.

STATEART have released items from what could be considered the elite of industrial noise/power electronics and neo-classical artists. Did you personally know any of the groups prior to starting the label and if not, was it difficult to make the contact and convince the groups you have worked with of your serious intentions with STATEART? Yes, I've known some of the groups prior to starting the label. The scene is rather meager and to keep it functional and active, flowing contacts are a necessity! It has never been difficult to establish contacts, nor was it necessary to convince anyone to be part of the STATEART history. "Natural Order" was, in the case of talking about an "elite", a maximum of concentrated popular artists. I'm very proud with the fact that it was possible to win the trust of everyone and I hope there has never been a disappointment between the groups and STATEART. It's not anymore of importance to profile our work with "big" names. We have and always had a very close and friendly relation to all groups we've worked with so far, except for a few who represent an exception. The most interesting part of my work with STATEART has always been the support of newcomer groups with intense profile and aim.

Is provocation on the agenda for STATEART as an entity partially with the label title, advertisements you have run and the content of selected items released? As previously said, provocation is not anymore one of my principal concerns! Of course we use provocation on different aspects, especially if the concerned project demands the use of a good portion of flogging... The agenda of STATEART is to be as explicit as it gets and as effective as it gets! Radical and constructive!

I remember you telling me that you consider all advertising of STATEART to be propaganda. Can you expand on this statement? Yes indeed, you remember correctly... Advertising is propaganda! There's no difference, except the economical and political terminology. And because of the fact that STATEART is more than just a common music label, we don't want to propagandize our products, we propagandize our view! And even if we propagandize a product, it's not more than propagandizing propaganda itself... Propaganda is nothing negative, but radical! Propaganda is a monologue and only one side of the coin. To view the other side, people have to look behind the curtain. STATEART propaganda is an order to think!

What does an artist/project have to offer for you to sign them to your label and of all of the releases you have produced thus far. What has been the most successful and in comparison what has been your favourite? The most successful release, considered from the sales angle, certainly was the ALLERSEELEN/BLOOD AXIS 7". In opposite, my personal favourite so far is "Sad Finger" by COLUMN ONE, a lovely piece of music and explicit in expression. You see, the character of STATEART itself is different from what one could expect. I already said before, our work is comparable to an organism, STATEART is a continual development. Therefore our present profile is far different from what we've done in the past. I'm still very satisfied with all releases, which were satisfactory at their time. But we look ahead and not even I know which point STATEART has reached after the next four years! What an artist/project has to offer me...? First of all, a friendship! A close relationship to all who I consider being a part of the family is first priority. The artistic expression does it's own... A convincing concept and music, worth to be part of STATEART's aims and demands! In fact, it's a difficult composition of different factors.

I hear the political system in Germany allows little room for alternative political ideas and subversive subject matter. As I would class STATEART as releasing many items of 'difficult' subject matter, have you had any issues with the authorities, CD pressing plants, printing companies etc? Don't all existing political systems have this effect in one or another similar way? We haven't had any problems with authorities, pressing plants or printing companies yet... This fact could be analyzed from two different viewpoints: We're either too subtle for anyone to recognize our subversive potential, or we're simply not subversive enough to be taken serious by the authorities... Both versions have no effect on the progress of our work. STATEART has found it's true destination for the future. Where we could have been classified as merely a music label so far, STATEART does more and more become a cultural movement of explicit utterance! The family consists of people who follow a serious vision and music has always been the inner expression of mankind, even if the modern mainstream model of "music" can't be considered as that. Further on, STATEART doesn't only focus on musical basics in the future. The written word, picture and film are effective forms of expression as well! At last we leave the classification of our work being part of the addressee. He's the individual from whom we think he's able to form a clean and sophisticated perception, and he's the one who finally decides to reflect upon our work or declares to be our enemy...

I believe that there was some certain incidents involved surrounding your release of a split BLOOD AXIS 7" and their tour of your part of the globe. Can you elaborate on this? Boring old stories! Honestly I don't want to comment on this, to not show these idiots too much attention concerning their silly actions... I hope this is acceptable for you!?

STATEART has recently moved into the forum of organizing a live festival, this being the COLLAPSE Festival of 18th & 19th of August this year. Is this something you are simply assisting in or coordinating this entirety by yourself? The COLLAPSE festival was and is a collaborative work between STATEART and ARS MACABRE, a shop, mail-order service and further a label, located in Rostock (Germany). We coordinated everything together, due to our contacts and skills. The audience was a bit disappointing this year, we expected many more people to come and see this exclusive line-up. None the less, we're going to continue with our COLLAPSE festival series next year and hope this could be held at the MS Stubnitz again, an unique place for this event, and possibly in Rotterdam (Netherlands), where the ship is located and invited in occasion of the "Kulturhauptstadt Europas" (cultural capital of Europe) event during that time next year. This will of course demand a lot more stress and effort from ourselves, but we hope to reach a lot more and hopefully different people than the typical uniformed German audience.

Who is playing and do you anticipate recording any of the live performances for future release? We were trying to find an exciting as well as exclusive selection of bands: ULTRA UNITED (Switzerland), NOCTURNE (France), MZ.412 vs. FOLKSTORM (Sweden), AXON NEURON/VAGWA (Germany), EX.ORDER (Germany) and PREDOMINANCE (Germany). All bands are either close to STATEART or share a good friendship with us. A performance of HEID was also planned, to which I refer later on, that we had to replace, what finally lead to a spontaneous live collaboration between COLUMN ONE, MZ.412 and me as WHITE. The entire festival (except for EX.ORDER and PREDOMINANCE, who technically needed the TV monitors for their own films) was professionally filmed and recorded on DAT, but at the moment we don't know if a retrospective as release on video or CD is possible or necessary, since we haven't seen all filmed material yet. Of course it'd be a nice offer to everyone who haven't had the chance to attend to our first COLLAPSE. So far I've heard my personal mixers cut of the COLUMN ONE – MZ.412 – WHITE performance, which sounds really interesting and worth to be released. I'm now awaiting the reactions of COLUMN ONE and MZ.412, maybe I'm going to remix the recording together with COLUMN ONE...

As with many underground label owners they have music project to release their own sound works. I am aware you have a couple of not so known projects on the go and I also heard that you recently became a member of the newish project HEID. Can you divulge some information on your recording projects and also to you perceive problems being a member of HEID considering K. Olsson is a resident of Sweden? Well, in the past I've worked on a solid musical project called ÌDPA, from which a split 7" with THOROFON and a complete 7" called "Stream" were released via STATEART, plus one track for AVA/ES1's compilation CD "Lunar Blood Rituals" and a contribution of about 2 minutes length to MILITIA's not too old "The Black Flag Hoisted" 2CD (TACTICAL RECORDS). I'm not anymore active as ÌDPA, yet the project hasn't died – it's "on ice"... Currently I'm working under the name WHITE, which I don't consider as a solid project in the common sense. In September 1999 I absolved a live performance with exclusively recorded material at the 3rd BRAINATTACK Festival in Rostock, organized by our friend Frank of ARS MACABRE. A German 2CD compilation called "Immortal Legends" (ARBORLON MUSIC) is featuring the first ever released track of WHITE. At the moment I consider WHITE as a collaborative project, i.e. it's only appearing as such in cooperation with other artists. In this sense I performed together with COLUMN ONE and MZ.412 during our COLLAPSE festival. Future collaborations are planned, but nothing is fixed yet.

Concerning HEID... K. Olsson is one of the closest comrades to STATEART and during the time of being in contact we found many views that we share, as well as the method of working in musical and aesthetic aspects. Finally the idea of working for HEID together came up and we both were fascinated from the idea of working together on such a long distance. There are no audible results yet, except for the track "Grundgeweiht", which is featured on our COLLAPSE festival CD, for which I submitted him raw sound material. The German live performance of HEID during our festival was actually planned to be the very first real sound collaboration between K. Olsson and me for HEID, but unfortunately private reasons prevent him to play and we cancelled the show. None the less, another opportunity is planned for a show in Berlin next year, but here also nothing is fixed as well. I don't see any problems being a member of HEID, because the work in distance is leading to new and exciting, not at least to innovative aspects concerning the music of HEID. We both have the chance to record new material for our own or together, either with raw sound material from the other part, or simply with own material. Then we're presenting the result to the other part and decide then if it's good enough to be released or not. Also the possibility of doing remastered and remixed versions of the other member's material is an exciting method of working. STATEART is going to re-release the first album of HEID, which was released as a CD-R limited to 200 copies via BASTED RECORDS. We both consider this album as being released in a very unsatisfactory way, the artwork was changed to something very terrible and also the sound quality suffered due to an obvious remastering. However, the re-release (probably as LP format) will certainly contain one bonus track and maybe we're going to remix the entire sound material.

What upcoming items can we expect to surface from the STATEART in the immediate future? At the moment we work on the two next items, the first full length CD of NOCTURNE called "Kapitulation", COLUMN ONE's "World Transmission 3 & 4" 2LP set and the first CD "Ultra Audience" from ULTRA UNITED. There are further things planned, such as the long awaited 2CD compilation "Widerstand", releases by SRP, DREAM INTO DUST, GENITOR LVMINIS, SURVIVAL UNIT and more... Too many rumors and uncontrolled information in the past convinced me to be careful with information concerning the future. Details shall be unleashed in time!

Last comments? Nothing of personal concern – all is said, more can be said... Thank you, Richard, for this interview and all time good luck with your work for Spectrum, a promising magazine!

End! STATEART c/o Koch, Roseggerstrasse 2, 30173 Hannover, Germany. Phone: +49.(0)511.9886673, Phone (Mobile): +49.(0)715.9446213, Fax: +49.(0)511.9886673, URL: www.stateart.de, eMail: info@stateart.de

Discography:
SA001: idpa/Thorofon – Split 7", SA002: Profane Grace - ...In Death's Silent Embrace... 7", SA003: Ex.Order/Predominance – Split 7", SA004: A Swarm Of Locusts/No Festival Of Light – Split 7", SA005: Ìdpa – Stream 7", SA006: Thorofon – Maximum Punishment Solutions LP, SA-P1: Various Artists – Natural Order 2LP Box, SA007: Fir§t Law – Revelation 5:2 MCD, SA008: Drape Excrement/Söldnergeist – Split 7", SA009: Allerseelen/Blood Axis – Split 7", SA010: Column One – Unrealizer LP, SA011: I Burn – Ipertermia 10", SA012: Lamia Is – Flesharvest 10", SA013: Genitor Lvminis – Deam Adessa 10", SA014: Profane Grace – Ages In Dust CD-R, SA015: Thorofon – Littleton 7", SA016: Various Artists – How Terrorists Kill CD, SA017: Column One – Sad Finger 7", SA018: Cyclotimia – New Death Order MCD, SA019: PPF – Propagande Par Le Fait LP.

desiderii marginis
(close your eyes and die a little.....)

After raving about Desiderii Marginis's debut album 'songs over ruins' way back in issue 1#, out of the blue Johan Levin (the single member of the project) got in contact to see if I would mind the utilisation of the review on his web page. Not only did I not mind, I likewise jumped at the opportunity to interview his project. This could not have come at a better time considering a new album entitled 'deadbeat' had been recorded and recently submitted to Cold Meat Industry for imminent release. Certainly not being able to wait for the official release I obtained an advance copy of the album and it is an understatement that I was utterly flawed. Hopefully it will not be too far off release after this goes to print, as it is an amazing release that is even leaps ahead of the stunning debut. If this album does not place Desiderii Marginis at the top of the genre nothing will! Until the fateful day that will herald the release of 'deadbeat' continue on dear readers…

Desiderii Marginis in my opinion is an under recognised group considering the stunning debut and the even more stunning upcoming follow-up (yes I have been privy to an advance copy). How do you view your involvement in the underground ambient scene and what is the perception of the status you have within it? Frankly I'm not very involved in the scene at all and I have no idea what kind of "status" I may have. Since the first album was favourably reviewed I can't say that I feel at all under recognised though. It doesn't really matter anyway, I'm not doing this for the recognition. I'm simply exercising my freedom of expression. If I like the music myself that's enough, if someone else likes it - well that's even better. Personally I can understand if some people play a waiting game when new acts pop-up seemingly out of nowhere. I mean, it's always interesting to know where bands come from, who they are and where they started out musically.

Taking a basic definition of the conversion of the projects name (Marginis=Margin, Desiderii=Desideratum) it would roughly translate to "on the edge of something lacking but desired". How does this if at all relate to your use and interpretation of the moniker? Desiderii Marginis means "the edge of dreams". I want my music to be a little like that. In our dreams familiar elements blend with the forgotten or unconscious producing a strange experience of fear, pleasure or comfort.

There is an obvious influence in your compositions, most markedly in reference to the early 90's sounds of many CMI and affiliated artists (I would mostly point to raison d'etre, morthhound, archon satani). At what point did you get involved in the scene and from whom do you personally feel you took inspiration from when you first started composing music? I discovered Cold meat industry via Peter Andersson (Raison d´etre). He worked in CMI's store in Linköping and he brought my demos there and made Roger Karmanik listen to them. Of course I've listened a lot to the artists mentioned, especially Morthound's "This crying age" and "Spindrift", Raison's "Prospectus I" and more stuff like that. The early CMI sound reminded me a lot of what I was experimenting with at the time so it felt like coming home really. Anyway, I believe the above to be were I've found most of my influences.

What do you consider your influences were on the debut album compared to those influences you would acknowledge on your second full length? How do you feel that the two albums differ and did you approach writing them in a different way? (Particularly as there is a certain compositional ridged-ness to the tracks on your debut 'songs over ruins' to the more flowing freeform works of your upcoming second album 'deadbeat'). I think the new album represents a step forward in composing and sound quality. I've spent a lot of time trying to create more elaborate rhythmic patterns, as well as a more dynamic spectrum of sound. On "Songs over ruins" I used quite conventional percussive timbres like snare drums and timpani for example. That I have been avoiding on the new album, instead I've used more diffuse or distorted elements for drums. I didn't experiment very much with odd beats either, something I've done on "Deadbeat" to a greater extent, and with a great result I think. I also definitely believe the new material to be a whole lot darker than the old one. More despair… I wanted the new songs to be noisier, more flowing and less immediate than the first ones. That was my starting point at least. Regarding my influences I can't say they differ much from when I recorded the first album. Actually I haven't taken in very much musically at all lately. At least I can't come to think of anything or anyone in particular.

How would you respond to the comparisons you received in relation to raison d'etre. Particularly since CMI seemed to play up this angle in your bio of the Absolute Supper compilation with matters further complicated by none other than Peter Andersson of the said group assisting in the mixing of your upcoming album? I don't mind being *compared to* Raison d´être but I feel that some people tend to stress the similarities between us. I believe we do our composing in quite different ways and with different results. You could say that we both work in a common musical field - and the early CMI sound remains my creative refuge - but if one think that we're extremely alike one should listen more carefully. There's a lot of big differences between us. When Roger Karmanik wrote the bio for the Absolute supper I'd say that was about as much as knew about me at the time - that I lived (and still live) on the same street as Peter Andersson and that we're both involved in dark-ambient industrial music among others. I can't imagine that he wanted to accentuate any similarities. By the way it's a slight misunderstanding that Peter assisted in the mixing of the new album. He helped me with the mastering from DAT-tape to CD but had nothing at all to do with the sound per se. Peter is frequently asked to assist in the making of CD-masters for various CMI artists simply because he has done it many times and he's good at it. However it doesn't seem to complicate matters in those cases.

How drastically does your study for your masters degree in philosophy, history, art and literature influence Desiderii Marginis (or could it be that Desiderii Marginis sparked your interest in such study?). What do you hope to achieve or pursue (musically or otherwise) once your study is complete? Well, I find my studies enriching and inspiring in many aspects. To learn how artists have broken new ground over the years for example. It feels like I've got access to a rich source of ideas. Ideas not necessarily concerning music but ways to deal with creativity that I couldn't have come up with on my own. My aim is not to make music that is particularly clever or something like that, I want it to be atmospheric and ambient. Actually I think that some modest insight in the history of art and philosophy can help you avoid falling into the most common artistic traps. But that's just my personal opinion.

Your tracks have certain religious connotations inherent in the titles "the core of hell II" & "solemn descent" off the first album and "God's shadow on earth", "Angelus" and "souls lost" off the new

album, along with a partial religious aura to the sound. Are these utalised to simply bolster the atmospheres being created or is their some deeper personal ideal being explored? I think that exciting tensions arise in the music when you mix high and low elements, such as sacral Gregorian chants with noise and distortion, or electronically artificial sounds with sampled atmospheres from reality. Maybe the religious influences are an expression of my feeling that music (much like faith I imagine) is searching and exploring. Maybe the religious themes are simply the most convenient and obvious allusions for the kind of feelings and ambience I deal with. I'm not a religious person however. I just try to match the titles with the mood of the song, but I don't know where these allusions come from.

With the skills you possess in music written I'm sure you would have had some prior musical recording experience. Is this the case and does music composing come easily for you? I've been composing and recording music for at least ten years now. Some friends and I have built up a rather decent studio together over this period of time and hopefully acquired some sort of skill in working there. I still find it easy and inspiring to be in the studio and I can't spend enough time there really.

In terms of actual sound there is the obvious use of synths and associated programming equipment within your works, however do you infuse the use of any real instrumentation? On the new album I choose not to use any real instruments at all. Basically I wanted it to be less orchestral than it's predecessor. I have tried to minimise the use of horn sections, timpani and such - even though I still make use of strings to some extent. Of course the term "real instrumentation" can include some of the contraptions I put together to sample, but if you mean playing guitars, drums or the likes I have no such plans for Desiderii Marginis. I am currently involved in an experimental (and so far nameless) project with a guy who plays Celtic harp (among others) and we'll see what comes out of it. It sounds very interesting and quite unique I think, not neo-folk at all.

In a listener submitting to Desiderii Marginis what expectations do you have for their choice of listening environment? (The reason I ask is that your web page has the phrase "shut your eyes and die a little"). I don't care were people choose to listen to my music. I wrote that phrase because I know that some people don't actually listen, they just play the record. I want people to shut down everything else and actually listen. Hopefully the music will lead your mind astray. I want my music to trigger some kind of mental odyssey, it is not meant to be a humming background. If a musical wallpaper is what people want they might just as well open a window and listen to the birds singing or the traffic roaring.

From your web page it seems that the covers of you previous demos where quite aesthetic in presentation, thus I was wondering did you have input in the covers of the demos and your debut album/ upcoming album, or are you happy to leave this up to the skills of Kaptain Karmanik? The demo covers were made by me, since that was way before my signing to CMI. I also made the tape copies myself and sold them which might explain why they are so few and far between. The cover for "Songs over ruins" were made entirely by Roger Karmanik since I had no proper idea of how it should look. For the "Deadbeat" album I have made the cover and Roger looked at it and had his saying about some of the details. I safely rely a lot on Roger when it comes to these kind of things since he's been creating amazing artwork for so long.

In regard to these demo's, these are no longer available as stated on your web page. In hindsight are you happy with them in relation to Desiderii Marginis today and is it likely these may be re-issued (perhaps re-mastered on CD) for historical purposes? It's always with mixed emotions I look back at earlier songs. I can't say that I'm not satisfied with the music and it remains a documentation of where I stood musically at that time. On the other hand I can't help wondering how I could have done things differently to make it a little better. A lot of people have been inquiring about these demos so I feel it would be a good idea to put together some sort of retrospective album. I have actually begun re-mixing and re-mastering my first two demos 'Consecrare' and 'Via Peregrinus'. Eventually this will result in a release including about ten tracks. Plus, most likely, some entirely new track(s) as well. I try to be as true as I can to the original recording in this process, although some minor changes and some fixing-up is absolutely needed for the sound quality to become (at least) acceptable.

Are you a vinyl junkie and would you like have your releases pressed on this format? What do you consider are the advantages and disadvantages you see of vinyl both generally and in relation to your compositional works? No, I'm not a vinyl junkie even though I sometimes miss those big inviting sleeves. Vinyl records are a bitch to carry around like when you move, but so are books, and pianos... I know there are lots of people out there whose hearts bleed for the old 12" so I wouldn't mind releasing on vinyl, maybe some special edition or picture disc could be an idea. Come to think of it, it might be funny to release some early Desiderii material on vinyl, like a 2x12" or something like that... I'll most certainly talk to Roger about this!

Has Desiderii Marginis had the opportunity to perform live before and if not is this something that you would like to pursue? No Desiderii haven't done any live performances. Hopefully there will be some opportunity in the future, it depends on the circumstances. From what I've heard (and seen) being on the road with the CMI-circus can be really hazardous to your liver. But I'd gladly expose myself to that kind of unhealth!

As it seems most projects at least dabble in other music output do you have any side projects on offer or are you able to achieve your full musical vision via the one recording name? I mentioned before that I'm collaborating with a harpist right now. It remains to be seen if it's ever released at all and whether it turns out to be a reappearing project. Apart from this I play in a eight members strong medieval band where I can vent my aggressions in traditionally acoustic form playing cittern, bombarde, shawn, and bagpipe. I have no other plans or project for the moment. Maybe I'll do a 'guest appearance' for one of CMI's other acts but that is still an unwritten chapter...

Anything to add in conclusion? No that's it really.   http//home.swipnet.se/desiderii/

black lung

Like an insidious malignant cancer on the underbelly of the electronica scene, the anti-corporate/ anti-capitalist sentiments of Australian project black lung are set against a flurry of noise, samples and way out techo(ish) beats. I must also say that with a lack of Australian projects that align themselves with the content of this publication I am honoured to bring forth this feature. The following transcript details the sharp (and sometimes concise) responses of black lung's lone protagonist David Thrussell, that were submitted a mere few weeks before publication....

Firstly can you introduce the black lung phenomenon, how long you have been recording under this name, how it eventuated and you musical output thus far? ...the first black lung record was released in 1994... it was called "silent weapons for quiet wars" and was basically a collection of snog 'ambient' or atmospheric b-sides and out-takes... the 2nd black lung album "the depopulation bomb" was created as a deliberate concept album and was released in 1995 along with it's companion single "the more confusion...the more profit"...1996 saw the release "the disinformation plague"... 1997 "the psychocivilized society"... 1998 "extraordinary popular delusions" and late 1999/ early 2000 "the great architect"...

Given the Melbourne underground electronica scene has on numerous occasions been big noted by travelling artists, how do you see that black lung fits into this scene (if at all), and what is your overall opinion of the Australian and specifically the Melbourne scene? black lung is a fierce beast that lives isolated and degenerate in the distant hills!!! it has neither the time nor the temperament to deal with shabby, shallow beings... beware the intrepid traveller who seeks out contact with this slumbering beast...

Further to the above black lung is not something you seem to take out into the live medium much. Is this by choice of the lack of interest in your music from the rave and techno fraternity? actually i do quite a few black lung shows...26 in europe last year, 6 in the usa ...and a hand full in australia...last local black lung show was in perth early june 2000...next is an anti-olympics gig in sydney september 1st...mainstream rave, mainstream "alternative" and pop scenes have no interest in black lung and the feeling is mutual...

Considering that most of you musical output is feverously embraced internationally, yet barely makes a ripple in you home country, can you express some of your thoughts on the Australian industry (both labels & music store outlets), availability of venues that offer more underground musical styles and the music buying public in general? ...well, australia is a good place to live in many ways...but the music scene is not one of them...even the so called "alternative" "scene" is bizaarly conservative and bitchy...so be it...

Also you have a close association with many Ant-Zen artists and affiliates, which are obviously located overseas. How did this come about and what do you see are the advantages and disadvantages of living in Australia yet have closer ties to an overseas scene than the local one? ...met most of these artists and labels touring internationally...ant-zen are nice people delivering good music and it works fine...the majority of the australian "scene" is diabolical...so no great loss there...

Are you currently officially signed to any label in particular? (given the various labels which have had a hand in producing your releases). ....metropolis in the u.s.a, ant-zen in europe for snog and black lung, kk records and atomic reactor in europe for black lung...etc...

The title of your latest black Lung CD is 'The Great Architect' obviously refers to Charles Darwin due to the title of the first track ('darwinian mind web') and likewise I believe it is his image on the back cover, however knowing that you never like to be totally obvious could the CD's title likewise have any connotations regarding Freemasonry? ...well close, but no banana!...it's h.g wells on the back cover...i've been reading a lot of his non-fiction books in recent times..."the new world order" from 1940 is chillingly accurate in many ways..."the open conspiracy" is another interesting tome...consider this...herbert george wells wrote "the new world order" in 1940 imploring a worldwide economic confederation to eliminate corporate waste, environmental damage and uncontrolled corporate power!!...the fine details of his theory have been implemented now almost to the letter, but minus his social concerns...who re-invented his phrase and concept in the public eye?...u.s president george herbert walker bush(walker was the name of a famous u.s imperialist general at the turn of the 1800/1900's in central america)!!!!...interesting choice of names there!!!......and as you know "the great architect" is the masonic term for god...globalization is global elites playing creator...and there's more...

Regardless of the above, how do Darwin's concepts align themselves with your worldview? ...while darwin had some interesting things to say, i have a hard time believing in evolution...too many gaps...too many "if's"...most lifeforms on this planet are far too complicated and deliberate to have been purely accidental in my opinion...does that make me some kind of perverted quasi-christian?...no not really...our own capitalist society makes a mockery of "survival of the fittest"...often those with the shortest attention span and most limited world view "prosper"...

The latest CD has quite a few bouts of intentionally intense noise in amongst what is otherwise a very accessible electronica album. Is this internally used as a deterrent to those not willing to explore the more experimental facets of electronic music? ...it's not that designed...the audio signal is created through a process of improvization and late night psychosis...if nothing else it should reflect the world around us and some of the ideas that might shape it...

Although the sounds you create have a very cutting edge studio trickery sound, I hear that in actual fact you are not overly a technology buff. Can you take us through the creative process of black lung? ...some effects boxes...some samplers...some other gadgets...stuff happens...sounds and atmospheres......often start with some crazy sound or kinky beat...and have a little experiment...

Being a member of 'Musicians Against Copywriting Of Samples'('MACROS') what does this involve on your part? Likewise I would have thought that amongst your other projects this would have been the least applicable to black lung? ...i have a profound interest in sampling and appropriation culture......but it's not an academic interest...in a very down to earth sense artists have a direct moral right to recycle sound and other media that are broadcast at us, most often without our permission...if advertisers and broadcasters assume they have the right to bombard us with incredible amounts of mind-numbing crap, then we must assume we have the right to re-use it however we choose...mental self-defence, satire, profound re-contextualizations, whatever...black lung has it's fair share of sampling, but often from obscure sources and heavily treated...

Awhile back I read that you are to be presenting material at the Melbourne Underground Film Festival (orgainsed by one Richard Wolstencroft – the man responsible for the much anticipated movie 'Pearls before Swine'). What exactly does your submission cover? ...they played a couple of snog film clips...and some of our music is in the film "pearls before swine"...unfortunately i was out of the country at the time...

Referencing movies, you (as black lung) along with John Sellekaers (as Xingu Hill) have recently scored the soundtrack to an Italian science fiction movie by the name of 'The Andronechron Incident'. How did this eventuate, and what sort of brief were you given to work with? (ie: did you see footage prior to the compositional process). What other information can you divulge about this movie and is it likely to receive a wide release? ...italian sci-fi film...bit like "pi"...actually pretty good plot!...has had a wide release in italy...but not australia!... yeah, saw a rough cut when composing...

Will your full soundtrack of this motion picture be furnished with a release considering only two cuts have been released this far on a limited 10" ep? ...not completely sure, bit tied up with some other things...

Recently you the were nominated as one of 30 young, up and coming individuals (picked from a variety of creative fields) to watch out for in an article run by The Age newspaper (one of the major Melbourne daily newspapers). While this is certainly a noteworthy achievement, surely you would approach this with some cynicism? What is the story behind this feature? ...yeah, that was pretty stupid...they tried to censor my responses to their interview questions and assign me a "stylist" for the photo shoot...i refused on both counts...and gave them hell...it's just fluff to fill in the gaps between advertising...but my mum liked it!...

Having DJ'ed at the Death in June/ Der Blutarsch gig of July 1999 under the guise of a reformation of a previous club you were involved in ('Hellfire' that ran in both Melbourne and Sydney), I wanted to ask whether you had any interest in or followed the musical scenes associated with the above groups? ...i have a passing acquaintance with douglas and do enjoy some music that comes out in that area...especially boyd, "death in june", "current 93","nurse with wound", etc...

What musical genres, sounds, artists etc specifically interest you and do you hold any sort of preconceived bias that if something is popular that it couldn't possibly be good music? ...well, i'm not completely prejudiced against popular music, although one can't help being a little suspicious!!!...statistically speaking there probably hasn't been any decent pop music since 1969!!!...personally i listen to a whole slew of music, the darker, more poignant country music (johnny cash, lee hazlewood, porter wagoner),italian film musics, mid period electronic music(morton subotnick is my current fave)...i don't get exposed to much popular culture , but i did see a sickeningly fascinating video on a plane the other day...aqua's "cartoon heroes", the lyrics were "full on", a blatant insult to their audience...check them out...

Within black lung's inspiration there are prevalent themes of conspiracy theories, media manipulation and non conformity themes, often twisted with a sly sense of humor. What if anything are you attempting to achieve philosophically with black lung as in comparison to Snog which are much more blatant and upfront in the anti-capitalist sentiments? ...black lung is instrumental, so for better or worse one has to be more "subtle"!...snog is centred around traditional song structures whereas black lung is more experimental(?) and certainly more free-form and spontaneous...b.l is unsurprisingly more soundscape orientated, like a sonic map of my inner cranium...may the good lord help me!...

Of your own making is 'International Mind Control Corporation' which would seem to be another creation of your sly humor. Has there ever been serious thought in making this into a proactive information dissemination forum to educate/ inform of the topics explored through your music? (I note that your web page does this to an extent already). ...you think the i.m.c.c. is creation of my "sly humour"?...indeed, my friend, the joke is on you...

In a previous interview I have read with you ('Wounded No. 6') you listed books 'Holy Blood, Holy Grail' & 'Spear of Destiny' as sources of influence. What is exactly your interest in the Grail Myths, Christian Mysticism and the Templar Knights and do you have any held opinions on such matters? ...i've read a lot of those type of books...i like a good "real life" mystery and have deep interest in "alternate" histories, and the development of our present malaise in an historical context...actually visited rennes le chateau (the site of many "grail" mysteries) recently...most enjoyable!!!...

What movies productions and books have you experienced lately that you feel have some merit and worth? ...actually i think "hollywood" is in much better shape than top 40 pop music for example(or am i more slyly manipulated?)...chopper, arlington road, fight club, american psycho...been reading a lot of non-fiction and a lot of ray bradbury/phillip k dick etc...

In concluding what can we expect from black lung in the near future? ...crazy stunts...nude vegan tupperware parties...learn to love your real fruit festival...new 12" "sickly seratonin squeeze" in november (i think)... cheers....dt

DREAM INTO DUST

THE WORLD WE HAVE LOST

"...from ambient, industrial, slight goth and doom tinges to subdued neoclassical tracks...it is as if you took away half of any of the compositons' makeup it could potentially be placed into any of the above categories, yet when overlaid together makes appropriate description terminally elusive...always an interesting listen that is definitely worth your time." [SPECTRUM]

"...a powerful collection of apocalyptic folk-cum-neoclassical songs with a decidedly experimental edge...contemplative, observational lyrics both poignant and well-crafted ...one of 1999's finest releases!" [SIDE-LINE]

"dirge-paced percussive noise, acoustic guitar, viola, and washes of background sound make the kind of music to which the deepest of human emotions are vulnerable...beautiful and engaging from start to finish." [OUTBURN]

A PRISON FOR ONESELF

3-track 7"/cassette with numbered mirror i.d. card (out of 500) and insert, inspired by cult tv series THE PRISONER.

"...strange loops, unconventional percussion and a classical overtone...strikes a strong film score vibe of suspense, atmosphere, obscurity and terror." [CURSE OF THE CHAINS]

NO MAN'S LAND

"gothic/industrial/doom best describes this little piece of depression...a bleak and sorrowful landscape with beautiful yet at the same time horror-filled keyboard and vocal movements..." [NJ NOISE SCENE]

"...a deranged and depressive nightmare...strangely ambiguous...highly atmospheric/industrial..." [FLUX EUROPA]

ON THE BRINK OF INFINITY

DREAM INTO DUST, BACKWORLD, HOWDEN/WAKEFORD, EMPYRIUM, ARCANE ART, KEROVNIAN, 4TH SIGN OF THE APOCALYPSE, and others with 12 exclusive tracks. limited to 985 copies, nearly sold out.

T-SHIRT

white printing on heavy black 100% cotton. available in large or extra-large.

CHTHONIC STREAMS P.O. BOX 7003, NEW YORK, NY 10116-7003 USA

www.chthonicstreams.com

ALSO AVAILABLE FROM:
WORLD SERPENT DISTRIBUTION(UK), PLASTIC HEAD DISTRIBUTION(UK),
MIDDLE PILLAR DISTRIBUTION (USA), DARK VINYL(GER), PROPHECY(GER),
COLD MEAT INDUSTRY(SWE), ATHANOR(FRA), EIBON(ITA)

inade

masters of the unknown, the sonically obscure.....

When listening to Inade, one is captivated by the fact that, in the realm of all that is sonically dark and explorative, Inade go to places that even the most vivid dark sonicscape practitioners have yet to traverse. The edge of the universe is but a starting point, the perimeters of unknown dimensions, but launching pads, for the dense, ultra-panoramic creations of Inade's sonic cartographers, Rene Lehmann and Knut Enderlein. Since 1991, they have reveled in the creation of music that is limitless, bound to nothing, not even the fathomless reservoir of imagination that overflows from the minds of its creators. As explained by Rene: "The main focus is to transform ideas, concepts or legends which are congruent with our own thoughts and interests. Inade is like an echosounder into unseen/unheard plains and abstract spheres where the anonymous becomes alive. We want to place traces into inter-dimensional spheres from where the listener gets a sonic silhouette, a puzzle of innumerable pieces. The development of the music was probably half calculated and half have elements of chance played a role. During the first years we have changed our equipment quite often and mostly we worked with very limited sources. That is why the final results were more or less depending from what the sound sources gave. Later the conditions became much better and we were able to control and influence the process in the way we wanted." 2000 sees the band shifting into creative overdrive as a plethora of re-issues and new materiel peers over the horizon. "At the moment we are in the process of recording the new full length album. Although it is quite difficult to describe [one's] own recordings with words, we can say at this point that the new material becomes more intensive and physical. The Crackling Of The Anonymous will be our most complex single work, and we hope that we can finish it during the summer of 2000. We are going to release this CD on our Loki label." Also on the forefront: "The Colliding Dimensions Live LP, with material from the shows we had in the States, the UK, and recently in Prague. Other plans are to reissue the Burning Flesh MC onto a limited CD edition through Loki. That tape was released in 1993 and we are just remastering it and we will add also 30 minutes of unreleased material." How did the shows in the states go? Any highlights…or lowlights? "Before we [traveled to] the States we have been warned that the conditions to play live Overseas are pretty bad. Maybe we had luck but we cannot agree with that. The whole tour and all the shows went very well and we were absolutely satisfied with it. Jason Mantis [Malignant] and many others did great jobs to organize the events and we felt very welcome there. Beside a mono P.A. in Toronto and some tiring and long driving, there were no real lowlights during the tour." Also just out or forthcoming: the re-issue of 1996's Aldebaran CD, probably the definitive Inade experience (so far), shattering one's meager perceptions of what to expect from dark sonicscape music, a roiling confluence of space and time, dream and dimension, myth and mystery, all channeled through a textural skin of human, alien and insectile design (then again, 1999's V.I.T.R.I.O.L. 7" showed the band expanding on previous sonic notions, an awe-inspiring tour de force that is nothing less than phenomenal!); and the just released Quartered Void 7", one of the innumerable puzzle pieces, the link between Aldebaran, The Flood Of The White Light 10", and the V.I.T.R.I.O.L. 7". As they continue to meld the seemingly known (though each of our perceptions of 'the known' may differ greatly, as constructed by each of our personal psychological and sociological inhibitions) with the seemingly unknown (though each of our perceptions of 'the unknown' may be hampered by denial, by the fear of allowing 'the unknown' any substantial foothold in each of our singular realities), the work of Inade is, ultimately, designed to open doorways into the possible, in which the dark and the light, the past and the future (as well as the 'roiling confluence' of aural impressions gleaned from Aldebaran's vast sonic portfolio), embrace. Because Inade is the key. It's up to the daring listener to unlock the door. The sonic possibilities are infinite…
(Reprinted by permission from Side-Line magazine: www.side-line.com)—JC Smith

ildfrost

Ildfrost had been somewhat quiet since the release of the 'Natanael' CD back in 1997, yet have now returned with a new album and a new label. Likewise with a new sound and direction being explored, the music significantly veers away from the medieval/ neo classical sound of the first two releases towards intelligent tribal/ neo classical tinged electronica. Questions and answers were passed back and forth between myself and single member Jens Petter Nilsen during July/ August 2000, both before and after I obtained the new album 'you'll never sparkle in hell' issued on Fluttering Dragon Records.

Hello Jens and welcome to Spectrum 4#. To begin with you seem to be quite a well educated individual in both the realms of art and philosophy (evidenced through the writings/ quotes included on the 'Natanael' and 'You'll never sparkle in hell' CD covers). Are these areas you have undertaken higher study in or are simply facets of your personal interests? I have studied philosophy at the University of Oslo for a couple of years. I have no formal 'art-education' as such, but I think literature/ philosophy/ art are quite closely linked in modern philosophical though. In postmodernism, there isn't even any difference between the 3. I have a somewhat defective disposition for philosophy, meaning I don't think I have the stamina for professional philosophy, but I still have a great interest in philosophical literature. And literature. I think of myself as a bricoleur. To me, philosophy/ art/ literature is a puzzle, only one is not combining pieces; one is taking them apart.

How do you personally view Ildfrost from an artistic and likewise philosophic stance? It's changing all the time. I think of it as a playground. A forum for which I may pour my ideas and gibberish nonsense.

There is quite a lengthy written passage/ conversation styled transcript on the 'Natanael' cover, and although there is no credit I am assuming that this was penned by you. I know that you are wary of interpreting what is written and the concepts behind it, however angling a question from a different perspective, what you wanting to achieve by the passages inclusion? I wanted to approach a very difficult theme. And I did not know how. By directly addressing it, I felt trapped. By directly describing it I felt I lost the plot completely. Only as a storytelling, or a play, I was able to somewhat find a plane where I could engage in a meaningful discourse about the subject. I had to remove myself to a third person, to obtain the proper distance. Let me quote from the booklet of 'You'll never sparkle in hell': "Death defies any possible approach". So I cannot communicate my intentions, only delineating them by comparison.

Within the written passage of 'Nataenel' and the exploration and argumentation of the concept of sin, yet with the writings on the cover of 'you'll never sparkle in hell' they seem to be written from a very apathetic viewpoint and often focusing on the concept of 'nothingness'. How have your personal values altered over time resulting in the revaluation of your writing viewpoint? I don't know. There is an obvious development towards a stern cynicism, or nihilism if you like, I guess that's what you mean with 'apathetic', in my work with Ildfrost. But I am not flatly stating the meaninglessness of life as such. Autumn Departure had a certain naiveté over it, Natanael was more focused and cynical, while 'You'll never sparkle...' debates the very essence of cynicism. Cynicism is where all fancy dreams ends and melancholy starts; it's where creatively really has to start.

For me it is not clear where the title 'you'll never sparkle in hell' fits into the concepts, ideas and song titles of the album. Can you expand a little on its meaning and significance in the overall framework of the release? The title of the album is an hommage to a great musical pioneer and artist that I really respect. I had the idea of the album title a long time ago, and when the album was finished I could not decide if it was the rigth title or not. And after I had read, and re-read the text I thougth it fitted. It describes a hopelessness and a uselessness; it indicate an insignificance. So it was somehow a case of 'art-by accident'. It's a bricolage of ideas with a storyline. Whereas the music on the two first albums was somehow direct linked with the lyrics, the music of "You'll never sparkle" could be seen as a soundtrack to the concept of the album. The overall idea is expressed in the booklet by text. It occured to me in making this album, the text was written a before the music, that I should try a different route. The musical pieces are assosiations in reading the text. Filling holes, trying different paths and maybe blurring the feeling of an 'overall' concept, because 'meaninglessness' as a concept really isn't any concept. If that makes sense. I think it would have turned out rather strange if I had set out to directly compose music to this text. It would be like trying to compose a work for Becketts 'Endgame'.

Back in 1998 there was a scheduled MCD to be released on Cold Meat Industry entitled 'the neverlies'. Obviously this item has to date not eventuated, thus I wanted to ask if these recordings have anything to do with your latest CD 'you'll never sparkle in hell'? «The Neverlies» was never released. And I don't think it ever will be. It has absolutely nothing to do with «You'll never sparkle in hell». It's very old material, and quite frankly I am not sure I like it much anymore.

Also what was the circumstance surrounding your departure from Cold Meat Industry to now be signed to Fluttering Dragon? I got fed up with delays of all sorts. Everything took so much time. It was not only regarding Ildfrost, but business in general on Cold Meat. Add that to the fact that I did not actually favour the 'new' musical direction on Cold Meat. I got an offer from Fluttering Dragon Records on exactly the right time, and I was very happy to change base.

Ildfrost started as a two piece (or at least two individuals where present on the debut 'Autumn Departure' album). Given that Jane Christina Aasterud left the group prior to the 'Natanael' album, I wanted to ask what were her musical contributions to the group and did she play a part in the writing of any of the compositions? Jane was only a voice. She did not contribute with anything. I think she might have come up with some song titles on Autumn Departure, but that's about it.

It is quite obvious the actual music of Ildfrost became overall much more rich, lavish and filmic between the debut to second album. What was the difference in approach when recording each of these albums? I really don't know. On Autumn Departure I had to borrow everything. I didn't even have my own synth. I had to borrow Violins, Saxophones, Microphones, Synths and what not. The only thing I owned was an old 8-track analogue recorder with "1\4 tape. On Natanael I had got my own gearpark, and the whole album was recorded digitally in a studio in Oslo. The technical aspects aside, I obviously had very different ideas and intentions with Natanael than I had with Autumn Departure. I had a much clearer idea of what I wanted to do on Natanael, as well as I felt the lyrical backdrop had become so much more important. And the workspace was so much more relaxed.

Now with quite a large passage of time having passed between the releases of 'Autumn Departure' and 'Natanael', how do you view each piece in hindsight? I think they're both charming, and very sincere. And while they both definitely have their moments of genuine brilliance, I am not really such a huge fan of those albums today. They represent a period of my life I am over and done with.

It appears that both of the above mentioned albums were recorded in a Studio setting. What are your current surrounds in which you write and compose music and has this altered over time? It has altered immensely! Autumn Departure was recorded on borrowed equipment, in my cousins basement. Natanael was recorded in an OK studio in Oslo, with a 100% jack-off of a technician. 'You'll never sparkle in hell' was recorded in the process of setting up my new studio. Today I have a top-notch studio surrounding me in my bedroom. I have access to live recording facilities, if I should need violins, or choirs or whatever. I am very happy with my current set-up. And I have become quite a bit nerdy tech-head over the years. I even now work in Norwegians biggest music magazine as a gear tester (i.e. New samplers synths etc).

I assume that you mostly reply on synths/ keyboards/ programmers to compose your music, and considering you compose neo-classical/ neo-orchestral type music scores do you have any grand vision of having you music played by a full orchestra? Well, yes.......it would have been nice. Especially some pieces from Natanael. I have access to a full orchestra, so it's not impossible for me to do this, it's just not something I would invest that much an amount of time in doing right now. In the 2 last years I have been dabbling more and more into a technological sphere. "You'll never sparkle in hell" is hardly a neo-classical piece of work.

Talking more about the new album 'you'll never sparkle in hell', it certainly shows an even more drastic change then that from 'Autumn Departure' to 'Natanael'. While it retains an orchestral/ classical undercurrent your sound is now infused with both a tribal and electronica elements that makes for quite an eclectic & cinematic listen. How do you deem a musical piece to be suitable for Ildfrost, or is it that there are no real limits you place on what the project can be? I don't feel that there are any musical limits as such, but I have to feel that the music\song fits into a concept. For instance I am planning a completely acoustic album, a 100% electronic album and even more jazzy songs. **As long as I feel the mood of the song is right, whatever that may be, I'll go with it.**

If your own words how would you describe your current sound and direction that has been pursued on 'you'll never sparkle in hell'? Where do you think you will take Ildfrost's sound next? That's a hard one. Ildfrost probably sound like a drunk vangelis meets a harsh version of Portishead, in a Dead can Dance setting. Maybe? How the next album will sound?? Well, probably more like 'You'll never sparkle' than the two former albums. But then again, I am entertaining the idea of an 100% acoustic album as well.......we'll see.

Without including any photos of yourself on the cover of the new album, nevertheless the photos that you both supplied me and others that I have seen show yourself to be somewhat of a chameleon with your image, that obviously begs the comparison to the chameleon characteristics of your music. Thoughts? He,he......as I said, I am a bricoleur. I like playing with images, sounds, text, and ideas all over. I saw an ad for some obscure product on TV the other day, it said: "Time changes, do you?". That doesn't neccesary mean that one abandon everything one was involved in before. The most funny part is how people are hung up in appearances. Images are obviously a manipulative tool, a lot of people need to feel their buying a 'package' to fit. And when you're involved in music everone expect you to have an 'image'. I like to have several images...........I really don't have any idea of what my image is really. It's a mesh of things I guess.

I wanted to inquire what music you grew up listening to? Would you acknowledge any of this as inspiration for your own music and likewise what encompasses your listening time currently? I grew up listening to Metallica, Whitney Houston, Top of the pops shows, Venom, and a lot of Norwegian music. I don't think this music inspired me much. It was first when I got a serious interest in film that I started listening to more experimental music. I think that my early interest in horror movies have had the greatest impact, and I still loves a lot of those scores today! Today i listen to everything by Amon Tobin, some rap, Cinemathic Orchestra, Brian Eno (Old and current), Lori Anderson, DJ Food, A lot of Ninja Tune acts really, Coil , Miles Davids...a lot of old jazz stuff.....a vast mixture really.

On the 'Natanael' cover the contact address is listed as Northern Contemporary Compositions (N.C.C). Exactly what is this organization? I have nothing to say.

Is this brief response at all in relation to your current compositions no longer being very 'contemporary'? No.

With another question relating to the 'Natanael' CD, track three contains some horrific high pitched shrieks for a small segment of the vocals. This begs the question that considering you reside in Norway, was this at all a reference to the black metal explosion going on in your country at the time? Did you take much/ any interests in the extreme actions of factions of the black metal underground? (as I believe there was quite a bit of media coverage). No, the vocals was just aimed to indicate desperation. It had no referance to the BM scene in Norway. But I can understand how one would presume that! That aside, I had an involvement in the BM scene. Back in 90-92. Quite some time before the recordings of Natanael. I was actually a vocalist in a band. I had to sing that way ALL THE TIME! Can you imagine that? One get's all dizzy when singing\screaming in such a high pitch. I had not that much an interest in the actions though. It was a purly musical engagement.

Having started Ildfrost back in something like 92-93, at that stage were you aware of the underground music genre that revolves around labels such as CMI? Have you aims changed drastically from inception of the project? Yes, I was aware of the genre or scene if you like. But Ildfrost did not actually fit into that genre did it? It was something new, at least on a scandinavic scale. While that scene had the most horrible and harsh dark ambient on one side and Dead Can Dance on the other, Ildfrost was something in between. My aims have changed drastically, indeed they have. Sadly I have lost a lot of the naivety.

Is there much archival work from the time prior to the debut release that you would ever consider releasing? Yes there is. I think some of it may find its way into a release. In fact, there will be an LP version of 'You'll never sparkle in hell' which will only contain 2-3 songs from the CD. The rest of the songs are brand new. These are songs that did not quite make it to the album, but still have something on offer.

Considering that both albums are quite serious in sound and content, I was surprised to hear that the two tracks of yours included on 'the Absolute Supper' compilation were less so, actually being quite playful. Knowing that these tracks predate both albums, I wanted to ask if there was a change in intent and focus on both the type of music you were composing the ideas behind it? I have always stressed the playful nature of Ildfrost. Ildfrost is more playful today than it ever was. it just doesn't always appear that way. But I am serious too, dead serious.

Conclusional remarks? Thank you very much for this interesting interview. If people are interested in Ildfrost they should contact Fluttering Dragon records at: Fluttering Dragon Records: P O Box 182, 03-700 Warszawa 4, Poland (++48 22 813 21 92), webpage: www.serpent.com.pl e-mail: xak@serpent.com.pl and watch this space for further info: www.ildfrost.com thank you. end int.

With so many projects floating around in the underground, some artists (rightly or wrongly) simply get overlooked. For myself Bad Sector were one such group, but all that changed when I heard the 'Plasma' CD (and later the 'Dolmen Factory' & 'Polonoid' CD's). Well, all I can say is that the error of my ways was quickly noted as all releases contain expertly produced experimental sonics that bridge the gap to more structured dark ambience (incidentally of which there are few if any groups that have a similar sound). Sole sonic manipulator Massimo Magrini filled me in regarding all the important facts and concepts surrounding his project.....

Bad Sector do not seem to have the profile of other similar acts, however you are certainly deserving of wider recognition. What are your thoughts on your achievements and level of success you have gained in the 8 years recording as Bad Sector? I simply recognize that the music I make cannot have a larger audience. Nevertheless, if I could have more time to spend in promoting the project I could spread it better.

Can you list your main releases (both out and upcoming) from Bad Sector and the labels you have thus far been affiliated with? Ampos, my first CD was printed in 1995 by God Factory (at that time it was a sub-label of StaalPlaat). Even if it was recorded using very poor equipment it is still the most appreciated work. The Dolmen EP, printed on 1996 by Drone Recs, have a "cleaner" sound. It had a rather good success, too (remember we are talking about underground products), so that a second edition was made later. In 1998 Old Europa Cafe printed Plasma, a little more "experimental", with a set of interesting sources. In the same period Jesus Blood 10' was printed by Loki/Power and Steel. In the end of that year Bastet/VUZ printed Polonoid on CDr. It was a too limited edition, respect to its good quality. A very limited edition tape, with a set of tracks in the style of Dolmen was sold out in few days, so that Membrum Debile Propaganda reprinted it on CD with a very nice digipack in 1999. It had a good "success" in the middle-europe countries. The new CD will be out on AVA/ES1, an American label. It 's rather harsher and "electronic", respect to previous works. Then, before the end of the year I'll print a 7" on Pre-feed and a 3" CDr on Cohort recs. Also, the collaboration tape with Contagious Orgasm will be reprinted on CD by OEC with two new tracks, in the next weeks.

How did you come to work with these various labels and are these associations more than just related to your music output? Likewise are you satisfied with the results? There are pros and cons working with rather small underground labels. It's good that most of times you have no restriction in the sound you have to record. Cons (in some cases) are no larger distribution, not so professional graphics and packages. As far as money gained for the releases: it's another story, difficult to explain in few words. Here I just say that some labels are not so honest (or too much... "home-based").

You yourself describe your music as "structured noise, dark ambient and iterative minimal". Can you elaborate of you personal interpretation of this description? I think it's a very simple and good description of the sound you can listen to, putting a Bad Sector CD in you player. Much of the sound matter I use is very noisy and fuzzy (as my life...). But it's not a free-form noise, I usually use noisy element to build ambient-like structures. I use the term "ambient" to describe a sound which create an overall atmosphere, instead of telling a sequential story (like a song, or...a symphony). And most of time it's a dark atmosphere, I am not an optimist. To reinforce these atmospheres I usually use some very minimal and deep "melodic" patterns.

Your project manages to produce some great dark ambient atmospheres, however there always seems to be an intent involved in using interesting source material such as hospital equipment, fluorescent tubes electrical pulse etc to enhance the material. Can you describe some of these unusual sound sources used? Of these sound sources can you describe each and the inherit atmospheres each of them possess? In most part how do you go about collecting and collating such source material? Can you also describe your composition process? I tried to use additional unusual sound sources, trying to catch its character, before its sound. Normally I contact specialists in fields related to the object, for obtaining sources or their recordings. For example, on Plasma I used sounds generated by the interaction between particles coming from the space and the earth's electromagnetic field. Stephen McGreevy, an American expert in these field, gave me some of its recordings. I followed the same process for some of the other sounds. Some times I personally do the recordings by myself. For example, in the forthcoming CD I used a geiger counter and a small amount of Radium, a radioactive element. I processed the signal generated by the counter in different ways, and I used it for triggering samples and musical patterns, too. Normally I use sources that have relations with technology and science, with a "negative" feeling inside (war, sickness, death and destruction), or with a cold, non human character (e.g. sounds on Plasma). Anyway, sometimes these sounds have a very interesting sound, besides its origin, and they suggest to me the structure of the whole track. In all my works I started from an overall concept, deciding at first the main roads I have to take. However, I do not like "pure" conceptual musical: sometimes very good concepts will take to a very boring audio result. If you want to make listenable music, even if "experimental", concepts cannot have the total control of the creation process. Instead, I use a concept trying to build an atmosphere related to it. And all these "concepts" are parts of global meta-concept, which reflect my personal view of reality.

Does the composition or alternatively the sound source make up the initial framework of a new piece? How do you view/ treat you music writing process - as a partial experiment or simply songwriting? The creation process have always

BAD SECTOR

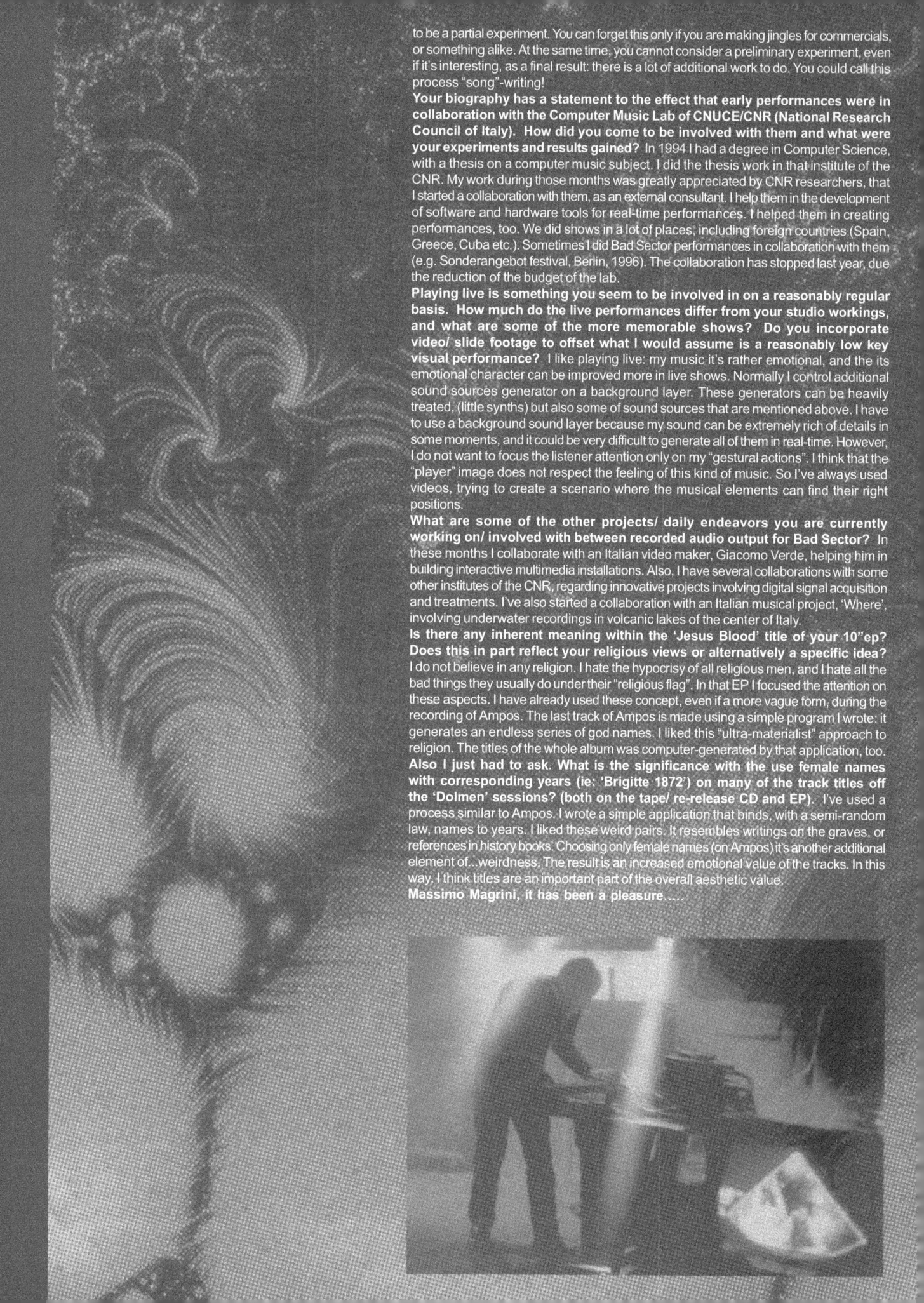

to be a partial experiment. You can forget this only if you are making jingles for commercials, or something alike. At the same time, you cannot consider a preliminary experiment, even if it's interesting, as a final result: there is a lot of additional work to do. You could call this process "song"-writing!

Your biography has a statement to the effect that early performances were in collaboration with the Computer Music Lab of CNUCE/CNR (National Research Council of Italy). How did you come to be involved with them and what were your experiments and results gained? In 1994 I had a degree in Computer Science, with a thesis on a computer music subject. I did the thesis work in that institute of the CNR. My work during those months was greatly appreciated by CNR researchers, that I started a collaboration with them, as an external consultant. I help them in the development of software and hardware tools for real-time performances. I helped them in creating performances, too. We did shows in a lot of places; including foreign countries (Spain, Greece, Cuba etc.). Sometimes I did Bad Sector performances in collaboration with them (e.g. Sonderangebot festival, Berlin, 1996). The collaboration has stopped last year, due the reduction of the budget of the lab.

Playing live is something you seem to be involved in on a reasonably regular basis. How much do the live performances differ from your studio workings, and what are some of the more memorable shows? Do you incorporate video/ slide footage to offset what I would assume is a reasonably low key visual performance? I like playing live: my music it's rather emotional, and the its emotional character can be improved more in live shows. Normally I control additional sound sources generator on a background layer. These generators can be heavily treated, (little synths) but also some of sound sources that are mentioned above. I have to use a background sound layer because my sound can be extremely rich of details in some moments, and it could be very difficult to generate all of them in real-time. However, I do not want to focus the listener attention only on my "gestural actions". I think that the "player" image does not respect the feeling of this kind of music. So I've always used videos, trying to create a scenario where the musical elements can find their right positions.

What are some of the other projects/ daily endeavors you are currently working on/ involved with between recorded audio output for Bad Sector? In these months I collaborate with an Italian video maker, Giacomo Verde, helping him in building interactive multimedia installations. Also, I have several collaborations with some other institutes of the CNR, regarding innovative projects involving digital signal acquisition and treatments. I've also started a collaboration with an Italian musical project, 'Where', involving underwater recordings in volcanic lakes of the center of Italy.

Is there any inherent meaning within the 'Jesus Blood' title of your 10"ep? Does this in part reflect your religious views or alternatively a specific idea? I do not believe in any religion. I hate the hypocrisy of all religious men, and I hate all the bad things they usually do under their "religious flag". In that EP I focused the attention on these aspects. I have already used these concept, even if a more vague form, during the recording of Ampos. The last track of Ampos is made using a simple program I wrote: it generates an endless series of god names. I liked this "ultra-materialist" approach to religion. The titles of the whole album was computer-generated by that application, too.

Also I just had to ask. What is the significance with the use female names with corresponding years (ie: 'Brigitte 1872') on many of the track titles off the 'Dolmen' sessions? (both on the tape/ re-release CD and EP). I've used a process similar to Ampos. I wrote a simple application that binds, with a semi-random law, names to years. I liked these weird pairs. It resembles writings on the graves, or references in history books. Choosing only female names (on Ampos) it's another additional element of...weirdness. The result is an increased emotional value of the tracks. In this way, I think titles are an important part of the overall aesthetic value.

Massimo Magrini, it has been a pleasure.....

コールド・スプリング
COLD SPRING

Cold Spring Records shouldn't really need any introduction considering the high caliber of releases that have emerged from the label over the past few years (thus I will keep this brief!). In amongst the general interview banter with main man Justin Mitchell, some interesting revelations surfaced regarding current opportunities that may have major implications on the future direction & growth of the label. In short the future for Cold Spring looks bright! Intrigued?....read onwards....

The items you release span items from true pioneers such as Phychic TV through to discoveries of new talent such as Kerovnian, likewise with all releases spanning a variety of genres. How do you dictate the focus and direction of the label? Is it meticulously planned or simply follows the paths of your various musical taste? A bit of both. It is planned to such an extent that anybody who buys a COLD SPRING title can be guaranteed an item of incomparable quality, and that the music does not lean too far away from dark ambient / soundtracks so people pretty much know what to expect. Most of the acts have a political or occult drive too, and to me to gives their projects more depth and a richness that is rare, especially in today's in mainstream music. I personally like all the titles released, and so often when dealing with a new act, I consider - would I buy it myself? And if not, why would anyone else want to?

Given the wide ranging releases from classic artists and new talent, I wanted to ask how long have you been involved with industrial music and how did you become introduced to it? I was aware of the symbols of THROBBING GRISTLE (though not the music) when I was about 12 in 1979, but the first venture into buying records was about 1983 when I bought PSYCHIC TVs incredible 'Dreams Less Sweet' album, as I thought Marc Almond was on it, and I was collecting SOFT CELL records back then. I'd never heard anything like it, and so that was my first introduction. It completely changed the way I understood music.

Having spoken to a number of indie label bosses, it is obvious that running a label is not all cash and praise for all the time and effort you put in (much like this damn magazine!). Exactly what made you decide to start and what currently keeps you motivated in running it? It was started in 1988. I was running one of the nine Access Points of THEE TEMPLE OV PSYCHICK YOUTH, and wanted to raise some money so we could afford to print the infrequent new letters. Genesis P-Orridge gave me two live tracks for a compilation cassette ('INRI') and a recording of a Psychick Youth Rally, 'THEE ANGELS OV LIGHT MEET THE ANGRY ORCHESTRA'. They sold out of their tiny runs, and I started with vinyl in 1990, and CDs in 1992. The pressing quantities have obviously changed from hundreds into thousands. Like anything else, some aspects of running it I don't like, but there's enough to keep me enthusiastic about it every day - and I genuinely feel we release some of the best music out there today. All the releases are snapped up eagerly by the fans of the label (with the VON THRONSTAHL - 'Imperium Internum' CD just selling out of its first pressing in 5 weeks!), and so there's a feeling of the label growing more and more. I'm about to start working more in TV and film so there's plenty of uncharted territory to explore!

How difficult was it setting up the label in its formative days as opposed to now and essentially what has changed? In the first days, it was difficult to get the message out there as there wasn't many magazines dedicated to any scene, so it was hard to get support and reviews. Also, the distribution network is a lot different. 'Industrial' music is taken seriously now by even mainstream distributors, which means that COLD SPRING titles are now available in all the main chain stores across Europe and the USA. Also, it takes a long time to get a fan base. When it started I used the TOPY mailing lists to try to attract attention. The mailing list now contains over 3000 people.

Does Cold Spring and the associated mail order business encompass what you call you full time job? Yeah, I couldn't do it at all if I had a regular day-job.

Of all of the releases you have produced thus far what has been the most successful and in comparison what has been you favorite? Hmmm....some titles have sold very, very quickly - MERZBOW / JOHN WATERMANN - 'Brisbane / Tokyo Interlace' CD (released in 1995) was limited to 1000, and that sold out in about 3 - 4 weeks. The biggest seller of the catalogue is the MERZBOW / GENESIS P-ORRIDGE - 'A Perfect Pain' CD, which has sold thousands, and is still in constant demand from the distributors. Like I said, the VON THRONSTAHL - 'Imperium Internum' is also a very fast seller. I couldn't say what my favourite is - though they occupy the same territory musically (in the eyes of the distributors, anyway), they are very different and have their own qualities. I do like VON THRONSTAHL and INADE a lot.

Like a number of other labels you seem to delegate the design work to others. How closely do you work with both the musical artists and art producers in reaching a final design solution? It's different for every release. Sometimes the band already have their ideas sorted for artwork, with others we have to employ a designer to start from scratch. Most of the time, this is Richard Cronin, who is a genius. Images are emailed between myself and the designer and the band, until they are happy, and we go to press. It's a smooth operation, and every band on COLD SPRING has been more than delighted with the outcome. It's one aspect of the label I'm particularly proud of.

One upcoming CD which has created quite a buzz for the label (mostly outside of the 'scene' I hear) has been the full length CD by Mark Snow (of X-Files soundtrack infamy). This appears to have suffered numerous delays no thanks to selected 'input' from X-Files affiliated lawyers. Where currently is this release at and what has been the background to it thus far? MARK SNOW is a really nice guy. I've spoken to him via phone many times, and he was impressed with the CDs I mailed him - he particularly liked INADE and was blown away by the MASONNA CD we did, he'd never heard anything like it. He was excited about doing a full length album, and everything was fine. Then his lawyers and management discovered what was happening and it became very difficult. Initial contracts were 12 pages long in 8 point type, with the minutest aspect of the deal detailed. Then, last summer, Warner Bros, via his management, told me to back off while they released the terribly titled `THE SNOW FILES`, a `best of` MARK SNOW which I don't believe was distributed outside of the USA. They didn't want any other MARK SNOW title out there, as they feared it would influence sales. After this, Mark began working on the X FILES again, and so the COLD SPRING album was postponed yet again. That pretty much brings us up to today, with one positive. MARK SNOW has written and submitted a track to be used on a forthcoming, as yet untitled, 4 band only, compilation which will act as a statement from COLD SPRING, and also a taster for TV and film companies. The album is finished and the tracks are fantastic. It really does show how far we have come. The line-up: MARK SNOW - `Intonation`/ ENDVRA - `Theme For An Imaginary Obsession`/ REMANENCE - `Dark Moon`/ BAND OF PAIN - `November 1970`. It should be out at the end of the year.

Another CD which caused quite a bit of interest was the now release Band of Pain soundtrack work for 'Sacred Flesh'. Can you provide some information on this motion picture and how Cold Spring became invoked to release the soundtrack? Lee from JUDAS KISS magazine had interviewed the film's director and writer, and Lee mentioned to me that the film was nearing completion and some parts of the soundtrack weren't complete. I always thought Steve from BAND OF PAIN was an excellent composer and his music would compliment a dark film wonderfully, and we spoke and he agreed to let me represent him. I approached SALVATION FILMS, and after they heard the material Steve had written, they cancelled the other music that was in place, and we got the deal on the entire soundtrack! It's a great piece of work and was a satisfying feeling sitting in a West End cinema in London 8 months later, to watch BAND OF PAIN and COLD SPRING slowly crawl up the screen. The soundtrack is out now, and we've been approached by other film and media companies, so begins the entry into the film world.

Obviously your main prerequisite for releases is to be of a high quality standard whatever the genre, however was there a conscious effort to release items such as the Band of Pain CD and Mark Snow CD to generate interest in the label from the standard scenes? Has this given the label the ability to grow to a level it might not otherwise have been able to do? Mentioning MARK SNOW certainly has opened a few doors and created interest, especially with press and distributors - like I knew it would - but its all part of the plan to bring COLD SPRING to the attention of the public, but at the same time maintain the fact the COLD SPRING delivers extreme, often disturbing, music. MARK SNOW, obviously being immediately related to the X FILES, is a perfect bridge between the grassroots 'industrial' scene and the mainstream. Also, it must be kept in mind that the bigger publicity acts sell quantities enough to keep COLD SPRING financially viable so we can still release smaller acts who contribute immensely to the industrial scene.

Your web page lists you an official citizen of Elgaland-Vargaland, with the proclamation that that the Kingdoms of Eagaland-Vargaland as a state occupies *"I: all border frontier between all countries on earth, and all areas (up to a width of 10 nautical miles) existing outside all countries territorial waters. We designate these territories our physical territory. II: Mental and perspective territories such as the Hypnagogic State (civil) and the Virual Room (digital)."* What information can you divulge about this nation state and citizenship? Is it essentially a state of mind? I became a citizen of KREV a few years ago, when they opened the London Embassy. It`s really just an art experiment - but it has some nice touches - at the embassy opening they had a video loop of the founders of KREV waving to their adoring citizens. When you joined, you receive the official passport and a CD of the national anthem (which all official citizens can re-record or remix). There's quite a membership now, including some famous names.

An elder German project Satori has in the past few years been resurrected with you taking seat as co-pilot. What is currently on the cards for this and how did you become to be a member? What recordings outputs if any have you produced prior to the involvement in this project? SATORI is an English project that started in about 1984, and released a few cassettes on the influential label, BROKEN FLAG (ran by RAMLEH). I'd been a friend of Dave of the band for years. In 1994 TESCO, the great German label, were interested in a retrospective CD, which they released titled 'INFECT'. Then SATORI were asked to play at the TESCO DISCO festival in 1995, and so I suggested to Dave that he reform the group. Dave was in a dance band at the time, and hadn't listened to industrial music for years, so I took control in creating the set and the sound that we played at the festival. That was released as part of the incredible 4 x CD set that TESCO made as a document of the festival. Since then, Dave has vanished and I've written much of a new album, with 2 labels interested in releasing it. I'll keep you posted about that one, but it's taking a lot of time to get right.

In the recent past both you and Malignant Records were scheduled to release a CD each by Hazard (both of which were recorded soon after the debut disc also released on Malignant). However I heard that Benny J Nilsen of the group requested that you both hold off on releasing these in favour of him getting a newer CD issued on his now main label 'Ash International (R.I.P)'. Now that newer recordings 'north' and 'wood-field/bridge' releases have been issued on Ash, I wanted to ask if your scheduled Hazard disc is still going ahead? If so, do you have any concern that as the early material of Hazard differs greatly from his current direction it may cause confusion with those who have only picked up on the project with the recent releases? I'm not sure what the full story is with the MALIGNANT CD, but basically, Benny asked if I wanted to release a HAZARD album and sent a DAT master with some excellent dark ambient pieces on it - in my opinion, it's some of the best material he's recorded. Then he signed to ASH for a few years, but decided he didn't want the HAZARD album coming out as a HAZARD project as he's moving away from dark soundtracks, to more experimental noise recordings, which certainly suit his new label. Hopefully it will be released at some point, the sleeve is beautiful - we're considering releasing it under the MORTHOUND name, to distinguish it from HAZARD and his new musical direction. Hopefully, it'll be resolved soon.

Speaking of new releases, what tasty items do you already have in the wings for release on Cold Spring in the next 12 months? Well, there's a couple of *big* names that are considering allowing releases via COLD SPRING, but I don't want to jinx my chances by mentioning them just yet. Things I will mention - the FOLKSTORM - 'Victory Or Death' CD is out now, with massive interest from all areas, and then we have the INADE-'Aldebaran' CD reissue, the original sold out years ago, and its still in demand. Then, we release the GENESIS P-ORRIDGE & Z'EV - 'Direction Ov Travel' CD, with new text from both of them, and never before seen photos. KEROVNIANs second album, 'From The Depths Of Haron', will emerge soon, the debut completely sold out straight away. The second album from VON THRONSTAHL. ENDVRA - 'Contra Mvndvm' is still being recorded, and I know that many people are looking forward to that, some new PSYCHIC TV albums featuring never before heard material, plus reissuing PSYCHIC TV - 'Those Who Do Not' and 'Themes Two' albums, as they're long sold out. We've just signed a fantastic new project, called SLEEP RESEARCH FACILITY on the strength of a demo. Their album is called 'NOSTROMO' and is based on the first 8 minutes of the film ALIEN, with the massive deep-space haulage vessel drifting through space. The album is divided into 5 tracks titled DECK A - E, and is absolutely immense dark soundtrack music. This will be a big one. Also, talking to Adi Newton of CLOCK DVA / THE ANTI GROUP about releasing new ANTI GROUP material. So, lots to come….

Justin, thanks for your input. Last words? Thanks for the interest, and please check out the revamped website at http://www.coldspring.co.uk - all the latest news is on their or join the discussion group at www.onelist.com/subscribe.cgi/coldspring - that's where the latest news is posted, and also rare mail order items are first offered.

MATT HOWDEN
HELLFIRES
REDROOM 002 CD
Second tour-de-force solo album from violinist Matt, a member of Sol Invictus, and The Raindogs.

LUPERCALIA
SOEHRIMNIR
WSCD 030
Lupercalia are classically trained guitarist & violinists whose debut album is inspired by mediaeval art and themes.

BACKWORLD
THE ORCHIDS
HCDEP 01
The EP you would have bought at the Wave Gotik Treffen 2000...

CHRIS CARTER
AMBIENT REMIXES 1
CTEAR 1 CD
A radical treatment of The Space Between from the multitalented Mr. Carter

NEW AT MIDPRICE
The World Serpent mid-price campaign continues with 8 classic CHRIS & COSEY/CTI releases.

HEARTBEAT
CTICD4
The instrumental crossover album, the first after the breakup of throbbing Gristle.

TRANCE
CTICD5
A groundbreaking album, sampled more than any other C&C ablum

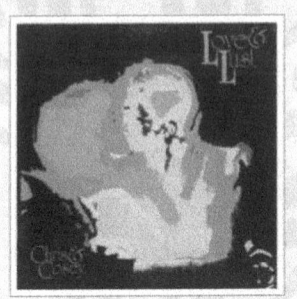

LOVE & LUST
CTICD6
The first song based C&C album

TECHNO PRIMITIV
CTICD3
One of the most accessible & commercial C&C albums

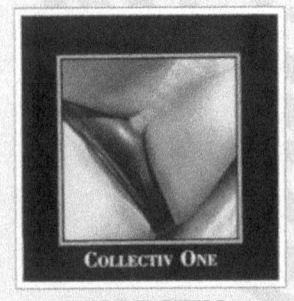

COLLECTIV 1
CDICD1
With Glen Michael Wallis & Brian Lustmord

COLLECTIV 2
The Best Of Chris And Cosey

COLLECTIV 3
Elemental 7 & European Rendezvous material on 1 CD

COLLECTIV 4
Archive recordings

Back Catalogue of all the above artists and many more, plus badges, T-shirts & merchandising, is available direct from World Serpent Mail-Order. Contact us:
Unit 7-i-7 Seager Buildings, Brookmill Road, London SE8 4HL. Tel: (44) 020 8694 2000 Fax: (44) 020 8694 2677
e-mail mailorder@worldserpent.demon.co.uk   web: www.worldserpent.com
When writing, please send an IRC.

Visit our website for fully updated listings: www.worldserpent.com
We accept: Visa; Mastercard; Maestro; Switch; Solo & JCB

WORLD SERPENT DISTRIBUTION
New Releases

DAWN & DUSK ENTWINED
FOREVER WAR
WSCD 028
The second excellent album from David Sabre; neo-classical soundscapes conjure visions of a people in decline under the relentless march of American globalisation. It is time to wake up to who we are and how we have become so.

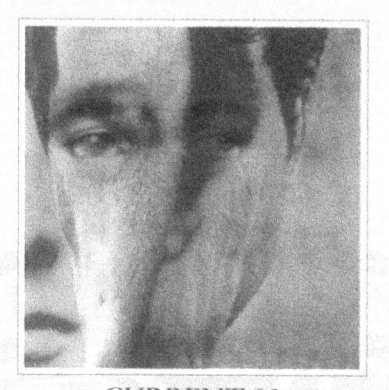

CURRENT 93
FAUST
DURTRO 060 LP/CD
Music inspired by Count Eric Stenbok's tale of Faust, which is presented here for the first time in a lavish package with artwork by Steve Stapleton. The limited LP comes on clear vinyl with the full text plus a poster in a screenprinted sleeve.

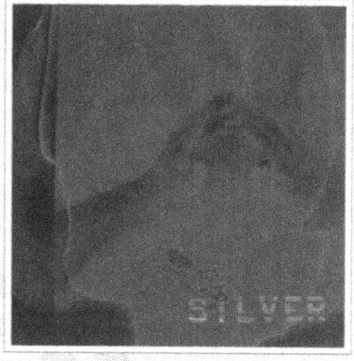

UNVEILED
SILVER
WSCD 029
The solo project of Of The Wand And The Moon's Hansen, assisted by Kim Larsen, the mainly electronic Silver contains nine ritual songs of magical darkness recorded over the long nights of the Scandinavian winters and inspired by the runes and folklore.

OZYMANDIAS
KARNAK
RAMSES 03 CD
12 hauntingly original piano compositions features on this, the third album from Switzerland's Ozymandias. Inspired by the Egyptian site of the same name, Karnak is a trip of discovery where every piece reflects a different atmosphere corresponding to one room of the temple.

ORDO EQUITUM SOLIS
A DIVINE IMAGE
SIN11 7"
OES are the latest band to contribute to the ongoing World Serpent 7" picture disc series with these exclusive two tracks. Both are new compositions; A Divine Image being from the metaphysical poetry of William Blake, while before The Morning Rose is from the *Metamorphosis* sessions.

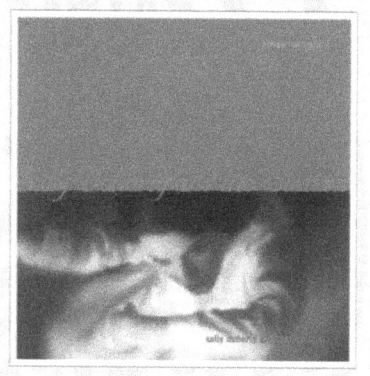

SALLY DOHERTY AND THE SUMACS
SLEEPY MEMORY
TIG 01 CD
Sol Invictus and Orchestre Noir member Sally Doherty's first solo album in now available via WSD. A dreamlike album, it features Sally's haunting vocals backed by an eclectic range of instrumentation - piano, cello, violin, double bass, flute, cornet, harp, classical guitar & tabla.

COIL
MUSIC TO PLAY IN THE DARK VOLUME 1
GRAAL 03CD
The brilliant mail order album now finally generally available!

COIL
MUSIC TO PLAY IN THE DARK VOLUME 2
GRAAL 05CD
A second issue of Coil's mail order masterpiece.

CROWD CONTROL ACTIVITIES

TERTIUM NON DATA: "THE THIRD IS NOT GIVEN" CD
Notably diverse and tense, cinematic pieces blending seamlessly with haunting soundscapes. A cold, black atmosphere with an elegant and commanding pervasiveness. From John Bergin and Brett Smith (C17H19No3, Caul, Trust Obey).

DISSECTING TABLE: "KAIBOUDAI" 3CD SET
The most complete look into the apocalyptic psyche of Ichiro Tsuji; contains the long-lost first LP and 7", as well as essential compilation tracks. Highlighted by Ichiro's most recent works, "Kaiboudai" culminates with 45 minutes of contemptful industrial noise. Limited to 500 numbered copies.

INANNA: "SIGNAL/OR/MINIMAL" CD
The final album from Mikael Stavöstrand (Archon Satani, Entarte) as Inanna. The dark ambient master intermingles subtle, spectral lows with complex, imaginative highs to create an album that is surely the pinnacle of his compelling artistry. "signal/or/minimal" will infiltrate your senses and subdue your conscious mind.

VARIOUS ARTISTS: "THE SOUND OF SADISM" CD
Prepare yourself for the beast that means to destroy your pathetic taste in noise-pop and oriental dime a dozen static nonsense! The most violent, hateful, and perverse 70 minutes you have ever heard. A lesson in aural blood and moral violation. Exclusive tracks by: Deathpile Con-Dom, Slogun, Discordance, Taint, Iugula Thor, Gruntsplatter, Hydra, Sshe Retina Stimulants, Skin Crime, Stahlnetz, Atrax Morgue, Bloodyminded, and Black Leather Jesus.

5000 SPIRITS: "MESMERIC REVELATION" CD
Stefano Musso (Alio Die) teams up with Raffaele Serra for the second album from 5000 Spirits. Undertake an arcane journey that travels through different psycho-acoustic environments and atmospheres. Truly a subtle, melodic study of mesmeric proportions.

ALIO DIE / ANTONIO TESTA: "HEALING HERB'S SPIRIT" CD
Antonio Testa adds a tribal, shamanic approach to Alio Die's intimate and droning revelations. While mixing sonic disturbances with a multitude of hand-made instruments, "Healing Herb's Spirit" captures the soul as the mind wanders endlessly in an abyss of ambient consciousness.

COMING IN JANUARY:
NECROPHORUS: "TUNDRA STILLNESS" CD
GRUNTSPLATTER: "THE DEATH FIRES" CD

All CD's $12 ppd except Dissecting Table "Kaiboudai" which is $20ppd
please send cash or money order payble to James Grell

CROWD CONTROL ACTIVITIES
821 White Elm Drive • Loveland, Colorado 80538 USA
Fax 970.472.1167 • crowded@ezlink.com • http://www.ezlink.com/~crowded

ALSO DISTRIBUTED BY: ARCANE RECORDINGS, MALIGNANT RECORDS, DARK VINYL RECORDS, METROPOLIS RECORDS, AND SOLEILMOON RECORDINGS

gruntsplatter

For those unaware Gruntsplatter are one in a growing scene of American artists exploring the sonic territories of death ambience/ death industrial, yet with the recent release of his debut CD (on Crowd Control Activities) it has solidified the project as a leading flame within the bleak darkness. Taking a slightly different angle on the genre, Gruntsplatter take quite abrasive sounds and transform them to create a deceptively ambient air (that could likewise potentially signify the birth of yet another sub gene entitled 'noise ambience'). Scott E. Candey offered up some thoughts and opinions in response to my line of questioning.....

It appears that you (not you specifically but your project) have the dubious distinction of being named in the Dodgy Group Names column of The Wire Magazine. In my mind there could be both a violent or sexual connotation to the moniker, of which neither of these seem totally relevant to the actual output of the project. What are your thoughts on the use of this name? Gruntsplatter surfacing in The Wire is certainly nothing I ever would have expected... I took the name in 1994/95 when I first started doing purely noise/experimental tracks, and back then I had next to nothing for gear, and the tracks were more violent and abrasive because of the means of recording and my general inexperience. Most of the first Gruntsplatter release, a split cassette with Torture Chamber (who eventually fractured into Deathpile) was done with a mic and couple distortion pedals and my voice. I think some of the depth that I have always tried to incorporate was there then, but the atmosphere was harsher overall. The name fit then much more so than it does now at least at first glance. After I started developing my sound more I briefly entertained the idea of changing the name, but I like the name, and the more I thought about the other connotations the name could have beyond the obvious non-descript violence I decided I needed to keep it. Recently I've had a few people tell me they always thought it was a grindcore band or a gore band or something because of the name, but whatever. I like that it's not typical of what I do, and if not being easy to figure out costs me a few listeners because it doesn't jump out at them as being dark ambient or something, I don't really care honestly.

While some might think that your track titles simply adhere to certain aspects of what is expected with death industrial type music, and while I believe that this may be the case for some titles, there are others which have a much deeper personal meaning. Can you elaborate on this and the specific titles in question? Particularly on "The Death Fires" this is true. The titles are actually more typical on the that record I think, but the whole release ended up being a vent for a couple of recent deaths in my family. For instance, "Against The Dying of The Light" aside from the obvious literary reference relates to my grandfathers last days alive. He was describes to me as angry and resentful that his time was up. Even though he was sick and weak he wanted more time to think about whatever it was he thought about and to just live, and when he realized that time wasn't coming he was upset. Conversely, "Waiting On The Body" relates to my grandmother, who survived him, but in doing so seemed to have just given up on life. She began obsessing on dying and ultimately I think willed herself to death. "When They Go" was recorded immediately after getting the call that my grandmother had died. That sunken feeling that comes with the news that someone you care about has died, even when you expect it and even when it may even be a good thing, there is that sunken, thick tongued resignation. Other tracks on the album have significance as well, but those three in particular are probably the most personal of anything I have done thus far.

Likewise what is your normal process of writing - does track title influence sound or vise versa? Sometimes one sometimes the other... I keep a list of title ideas that I think up, or see or hear in books or films or whatever, evocative phrases etc. and sometimes I'll choose one I want to try and personify. Other times, I'll write a track and have to listen to it several times before I get an impression of what the title should be. In those instances it's usually whatever visual impression I get from the music at the time. I think titles are important, despite being completely arbitrary for this style of music, it's another way to shape the presentation of the project.

The progress that you have shown between your early split CD's to the 7" and now to the debut full length CD has been quite impressive. Has this been a case of simply honing you skills or an improvement in equipment or both? I'd say both... the biggest difference between the two split CD's, with Ruhr Hunter and Slowvent respectively, is that both of those were recorded on a 4 track. And the "Pest Maiden" 7" and "The Death Fires" were recorded on hard disc so I had access to more tracks and it allowed me to do much more than I could have on the 4 track. So that more than anything is what helped me develop the sound further, I was finally able to do things that I'd wanted too do all along. Another thing, particularly on the full length was that I started playing live, and in doing that was reminded of techniques I hadn't used in a long time, going back to when I had bare bones for equipment. So that reintroduced some things that weren't on the previous split CD's and it definitely expanded the sound I think. And of course the more you do the more tricks you learn.

How did you become involved within the underground death industrial/ noise scene? The first Noise record I bought if I remember correctly was Controlled Bleeding's "Hog Floor" I'd been involved in the Metal Underground, and liked allot of the Industrial music at the time, and punk from way back so I just kept looking for new things to listen to. I had always been partial to discord whether it be raunchy Greg Ginn guitar solos in Black Flag, or VoiVod's odd riffing, to Neubauten's junk industrial majesty. Noise was just the natural evolution of all of that for me and I warmed right up to it. Already familiar with the letter writing, flyer spreading, tape trading ideals from the metal underground I took it all in stride, and started contacting people and digging for releases wherever I could find them. Eventually I started recording as Gruntsplatter when I realized I'd made more noise tracks for my guitar project than guitar tracks. And a lot of that ended up on the "Bisect" cassette with Torture Chamber. I still love Black Flag and VoiVod and Neubauten, and allot of the other stuff from before I found noise. As most people in this scene I imagine, I am just a fiend for music, and experimental music for me is the most pure, it allows for things that structure can not, that scales can not and it is visual and personal, no one walks away with the same thing from a noise track.

The abrasiveness of many of the tones of your work are uncharacteristically ambient for their tone and pitch. Was this a conscious effort on your part? Yes definitely, I for the most part, have always tried to use more grating textures in an ambient way. I think that it allows for more detail in the sound when you use harsher textures atmospherically, straight tones and synth sounds can only carry so much I think and by incorporating the more abrasive stuff you get all the sizzles and frequency manipulations and whatever else that's more common to harsher noise but I restrain them a bit and try and generate a more dark ambient sort of atmosphere. It keeps it more interesting for me to make, and ultimately it's what I personally want to hear.

Do you have a clear concept or sound in your head prior to recording or do the tracks form themselves over periods of experimentation and improvisation? Occasionally I have something more concrete in mind when I sit down to work on music, but more often than not it's just a vague idea that I want to capture and then as I start putting the rudimentary sounds together it begins to take direction. Recently I have been doing a lot of "live in the studio" stuff that is pure improv and some good things have come of it I think, so in the future I may use improv as foundation and build from there or something I don't know. Taking Gruntsplatter into the live show realm has really done a lot for my recording process, that surfaced somewhat on "The Death Fires" but I think it will become an increasing part of what I'm doing. The energy and spontaneity of being on the spot and improvising everything and still trying to capture the feel of my recorded stuff has forced me to look at the way I do things and seek new ways to go about some of it, which to some degree I had stopped doing. It also shifted my thinking back away from "electronics" to more organic types of things which has been great, I started doing things entirely organic out of necessity and as I got a little equipment I stopped using allot of that sort of thing, now I'm trying to integrate them a lot more.

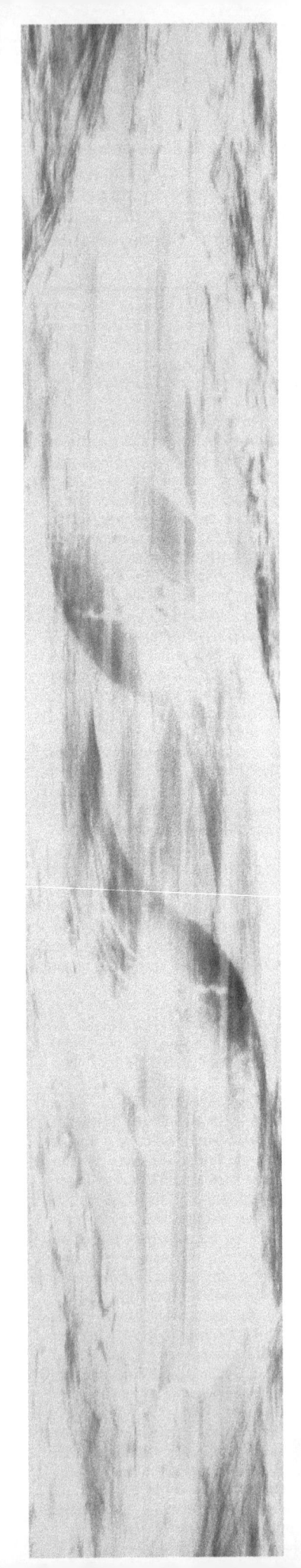

The first track off 'the death fires' saw the introduction of a subdued keyboard passage. Is this more melodic approach something you will more thoroughly explore on future works? Well, this isn't really the first time I'd done that, the split with Slowvent had a couple of pieces that had some obscured melody, and I have a couple tracks that were never released that use it as well. I'm sure I will use it more in the future, sometimes I just feel like their needs to be something like that to help shape my intent. And it ads another dimension and element of depth to the tracks I think which I'm all for. I don't see myself doing that stuff exclusively anytime soon, but it will always have it's place.

It would seem that you are officially signed with Crowd Control Activities for Gruntsplatter output. Does this preclude you working with other labels and prior to signing with CCA did you have other label interest? My arrangement with Crowd Control is that we have agreed to an unspecified quantity of multiple releases, in other words there will be more, but I don't know how many. When he asked me to sign with CCA he was looking to start building more long lasting relationships with his artists rather than just a bunch of one offs. You see it in every other style of music but this one and it is something I have always thought was a good idea. You begin to associate bands with labels and labels with bands and ultimately I think everyone benefits. The arrangement is that CCA will release all Gruntsplatter CD's until whenever one of use decides to terminate the relationship, but I am free to do any vinyl or cassettes that may come along. Prior to my agreement with Crowd Control I had a split release on Glass Throat, which is the material that got CCA interested in me. And I released the Gruntsplatter/Slowvent in-between the CD on Glass Throat and finishing anything for CCA, plus the 7" on Troniks.

As your music does not align itself with or tend to express any political views or specific agendas, but could you divulge some aspects of your worldview? My worldview... basically I guess I see things like conviction, intelligence, strength, inquisitiveness, responsibility, loyalty, honesty etc. as being valuable traits and I see much of that lacking in the world. As a general rule, I don't like people, and find them all to frequently to be a waste of energy, so I have a close group of people that I associate with and leave it at that. Speaking in a larger sense, my political views reflect, my personal views ultimately. I don't like the professional victims and whiners that are spawned by the social systems that the United States keeps in place, I don't like seeing people who do nothing and take no responsibility sitting with their hands out talking about what they are entitled to. I pay attention to current events with a fascination, particularly relating to environmental issues, unrest and creepy big government stuff. It's a bit difficult to summarize concisely I guess...

What type of recording process do you utilise and do you particularly work within the studio medium? If not do you think this would provide you with advantages you might not otherwise have? My studio is basically just a corner in my apartment. Within the last year or so I upgraded to Hard Disk recording from a 4 track, so that has helped monumentally. I began recording via my computer which allows me many more tracks to play with, and a much cleaner production. The benefits this new situation has birthed I think are obvious when you listen to the depth and sound quality of the newer stuff next to the older material. I just recently bought a new mixer for live applications, but in messing with it I definitely see it as a useful recording tool as well. I feel like I'm finally getting to a point where I can do what I've been trying to do all along. Obviously the 4 track had limitations and those limitations aren't an issue anymore and that coupled with the live stuff and reassessment of approach I mentioned earlier is keeping the recording process interesting and expansive for me right now.

When you reference playing live above, I wonder to if there is much interest let alone opportunity for such a project as yours to perform in a live medium? (given interest in death industrial music is quite sparsely spread across the globe). What entails a Gruntsplatter performance both sonically and aesthetically? I think the interest is there, at least enough so to make it worth the effort. Certainly not frequent shows like a metal band or industrial band might be able to maintain. But for occasional performances I've seen pretty good turn out for this sort of thing. At this stage I have done 2 Gruntsplatter performances, and one show under the Umbra moniker when Stephen Petrus, who I do the project with was out visiting from Ohio. The Umbra and the first Gruntsplatter show was basically me standing at a table, but the last Gruntsplatter show I was able to do some video stuff that seemed to go over really well, from the reactions I got afterwards. Ideally I'd like to always have something for people to watch like that because it makes the whole thing much more engaging and ads and entirely different atmosphere to the set. As far as music I improvise everything, I don't do album tracks or anything so each one is completely unique. I generally use an atmospheric loop for foundation and then everything else is made up on the spot. My set from Troniksfest I is going to be released in an edited form as a split LP with Control, who also played Troniksfest. I have another show August 19th with Blood Box, Nothing, Control, Sickness and Petit Mal that I'm really looking forward to. I am planning to have a couple new gadgets for that so that I can give the stuff even more depth and I'll be using video then as well.

Also what is the local 'scene' like in the area you reside and generally what type of reaction can you expect/ or have experienced from audiences? San Francisco is more supportive of experimental music than most cities I think. There are two venues here that host regular noise shows, and a couple others in the area that have them from time to time. Turnout varies, at the first Troniksfest the estimate was that over the course of the night there were about 150 people there which is damn good in my mind. Reactions have been great to the Gruntsplatter shows, there is a core group of people that seem to really try and come out and support what is going on. My first show I opened for the Industrial bands Scar Tissue and SMP, and even that crowd was pretty receptive to what I did, so I think I'm pretty fortunate to live somewhere where there are opportunities to play and an audience that will support it.

Earlier in the interview you mentioned that the first Gruntsplatter recordings consisted of contact mics, distortion pedals and your voice, yet current output is all but void of vocalisations. Were you vocals used as merely a sound source or actually conveying lyrics and ideas? Actually this isn't true, the new record has layers of vocals on many of the tracks. They are obscured considerably, but in the right listening environment they do creep out here and there. I wanted to essentially treat them like another texture, keep them very subtle, but I think "Below the Stones" has something like 7 layers of vocals that actually have lyrics, all improvised, but it's not just non-descript noises. But yes there are no obvious vocals. The old material used both abstract vocalizations and obscured lyrics. I can see myself bringing vocals more to the forefront on rare occasions in the future. But I like having them buried among the other textures because they give more depth to the pieces than if I'm just shouting over the top of it all. And by burying them I can make the tracks as personal as I want without pointing the listener in a specific direction, which is something I like. You listen to Whitehouse or something, while I love them, there is little room for interpretation. I generally try and make it so if there are vocals that are discernable it is only fragments, not something spelling out the concepts.

What are you views of utilising vocals/ speeches or even samples in Gruntsplatter's current sound and direction? On the first cassette I used a fair amount of samples, and I haven't used them at all since then. It was basically a way for me to fill holes left by my lack of equipment. I don't have anything against them, they can be used very effectively, but I think in my more recent stuff I've avoided them, and this goes back to what I was saying above, I just don't want to be too literal with what I'm doing, and samples are something concrete that anchors the sounds to an idea. Some of my other projects have included them, though not by my hand, and I think they work great in those tracks. They just don't really fit into what I want to accomplish with Gruntsplatter as it stands more recently. Vocals as I said I will continue to use in some form or another.

What is your status of your living environment and does this play an influential role in the sounds of Gruntsplatter? I don't think my living environment plays a direct role in my music, but indirectly I'm sure it does. I live in San Francisco, and there are allot of people here, there are all the problems you expect to find in a big city, and that certainly riles my contempt which eventually finds it's way into my music I think. Our environment influences us whether we expect it to or not, If I was living in the middle of no where without the constant stimulus of the city I'd imagine things would sound a bit different. I don't look to my environment for influence, but it's natural impact on my opinions and emotions is undeniable.

What drew you to seek out Thomas Dimuzio to master you debut full length? What were the impressions you got when working with him and are you satisfied with the results? I had been to a "pro-studio" to master the Gruntsplatter/Slowvent Split CD and felt like the guy just wanted to be done with it because I'm sure in his mind it wasn't "real music". So when it came time to do my full length I wanted to use someone who would give it the appropriate attention. Thomas doesn't live far from my house, and while I had never spoken with him previous to this I knew that his experience with the genre would greatly benefit the mastering process. I sat with him through the whole thing and was able to make suggestions and see that he very clearly knows what he's doing. I'd have no hesitation in going to Thomas again for my material, and have used him to master releases for Crionic Mind in the time since he did "The Death Fires". He's professional and fast and focused on what you have in mind for your music, not what he has in mind for your music.

In that most artists within the underground scene seem to work with a side-project or two, in your example they come in the form of collaborative works. Can you provide some details of these groups you are currently working with as opposed to those that may be defunct? What you are able to, or aiming to achieve via these projects that you feel cannot be covered by your outputs with Gruntsplatter? I have done 3 collaborations with releases available so far. The first was Blunt Force Trauma with Jon Canady of Deathpile. This was a Harsh Noise collab that we did back in 1997, and it's still available from various distributors. This one is definitely in hibernation, but I hesitate to say it's defunct. We haven't done anything since the "Bled Out" CD, but I'd like to see one more release from this project at some point. Triage was the next, and least from a planning stage, this is a collaboration with Chet Scott from Ruhr Hunter, the focus of this one is more analog driven, sterile cold atmospheres and pulses, and this project is alive and well. The first release "The Cessation of Spoil" has done really well, and generated a bit of label interest, so Chet is working on his portion of the follow up right now and then I get it and we'll see if those that were interested are still interested I guess. And the last one is Umbra, this is with Stephen Petrus of In Death's Throes, and its focus is on a sort of low fi dark ambient/death industrial. This one is probably most similar to what I do as Gruntsplatter, but I think it carries a completely different feel. This project is still alive as well, Stephen is working on his stuff for a follow up to "Unclean Spirit" and I'll start on mine soon. I just found out a couple days ago that some one is interested in releasing the next Umbra disc, so that will hopefully have a home when we are done with it. Currently I'm working on a project with Jason Walton of Nothing, we are still solidifying ideas, but the general direction for this one will be almost like electronic Doom Metal - with a heavy dose of experimentation. Derek Rush of Dream Into Dust and I have discussed doing something together as well, but we can't seem to work it into our schedules because he's got just as many things he's working on as I do... I have a side project called Grimes as well, that's just me, that one is more beat focused than any of the other projects. The thing I like about the side projects is the freedom to wander into things that I don't feel quite fit what I want to present as Gruntsplatter, and of course I get to work with people that I like and respect, which is always interesting.

Lastly do you want to give a bit of information on the background and future direction of your label Crionic Mind? Crionic Mind is finally getting to the point where I feel like I'm starting to do what I set out to do. This year will be the first time that I'm consistently able to put out releases, and have some things I'm really excited about doing. I released Lefthandeddecision's "Instinct & Emotion" in April and it's over 3/4 gone already, next up is Deison's "Dirty Blind Vortex" which will be going to the plant anyday now and should already be available by the time this makes the presses. Right after that will be a split CD from KK Null and Moz, which also may be out by the time this is, depending on how quickly the art comes together. Around late October I'll be releasing "Wither" from a project called Wilt, that I'm really looking forward to, and then finally around February or so I'm planning a CD from a relatively new project called Never Presence Forever. After that I don't know exactly, but I have a couple ideas taking shape. I have been doing the distribution for 5-6 years, and released a couple of cassettes, and the Gruntsplatter/Slowvent CD, but being able to maintain a steady release schedule and do releases beyond my own music was the goal from the beginning.

Scott, thanks very much for your imput...

YEN POX

When trying to think what I could write for a Yen Pox introduction, all that popped into my mind was the first review I read of their music before I actually heard their awe inspiring dark ambient sonics. Thus, rather than reinventing the wheel (void!?) why not simply quote some of those words? *".... you're transported off into a vacuumous black hole, deposited and left to swim in an endless downward spiraling void....Dense, droney and radiant with dark energy – as if the sun were suddenly eclipsed by a looming, blood red orb and the world were cast under a liquidous murky glow."* (Audio Drudge 7#). Steve Hall and Michael JV Hensley being both members of the group contributed to this quite lengthy transcript soon after the release of their second stunning CD "new dark age".

First up can you introduce yourselves and provide some brief background information regarding your who/ what/ where statuses? (just so the readers and I can better analysis and dissect you later question responses!). STEVE: Hello. I'm Steve Hall, I'm from New Paris, IN (about 2 hours out of Chicago, IL). MICHAEL: I, michaeljvhensley, live in Seattle, WA. When Steve and I began Yen Pox, I also lived in Indiana, but I had to leave, or lose my mind. I saw no reason to let distance keep Steve and I from recording together.

Why the name Yen Pox and what if anything does you music have to do with the opium trade? STEVE: It has absolutely nothing to do with the opium trade. When Mike and I were in the process of creating the first Self-titled cassette, we were reading quite a bit of William Burroughs works. I lent my copy of "Junky" to Mike, who upon reading the book, pulled the term from it. In Burroughs' book, it refers to the opium ash (which supposedly has just as much chemical potency as heroin), which is cooked and injected just as heroin would be. The words themselves had a certain ring to them and the drug reference was fitting as well. A soundtrack to the visual of someone shooting a thick black ooze into their vein. I think music itself can produce altered states of awareness, to a certain level. Put on your headphones and shut everything else out and you'll feel it.

Given that you have taken the classic Lustmord dark ambient sound and elevated it further, I wanted to ask if Lustmord was a specific influence that you would acknowledge? What other groups would you mark as inspiration for Yen Pox? STEVE: Michael first introduced me to Lustmord's material, it was "the Monstrous Soul". Great stuff, but I wouldn't really say that it was an influence. I've always had a penchant for music that has a dark, minor key sound, whether it be metal, classical, ambient, etc. Probably on of the biggest influences for me was SWANS. That's the band that really pushed me over the edge into a truly dark realm musically, particularly "Children of God" and the "Raping a Slave" e.p. Aside from that, and Mike may or may not agree, our perception of our own surroundings have a big influence......"The empty blue Indiana sky". MICHAEL: Actually, I don't think my surroundings influence my sound much these days. My surroundings when I record are just my cramped, claustrophobic apartment, which affects my work habits more than anything. With this music, I don't really feel like I am particularly influenced by much of anything, besides the voices in my head. Perhaps when I first started, I'm sure I was influenced by something, but now I just do what I do, it just comes naturally to me. I must admit that I've never completely understood the numerous Lustmord comparisons we get. I won't deny that was an early influence, inasmuch as it was among the many noise and ambient bands I was listening to before I started creating my own sound, but I don't consider this a major inspiration, just one amongst many. It would seem that the comparison is just an easy way for people to label our sound, when the reality that I see is that while we may definitely create a similar style of music to Lustmord, in the same genre, I really don't think our music sounds the same at all. Actually, the closest I think we've come to sounding like Lustmord is his collaboration with Robert Rich, "Stalker", but as that was recorded at about the same time as our "Blood Music" CD, it obviously had no influence on us. I think Robert Rich added some density and emotional depth to their collaboration, qualities I feel we have, that I have found lacking in much of Lustmord's music. Of course, I'm just guessing, as I have heard very little of Rich's music before. Other early influences for me were Coil, C.T.I., The Art Barbecue (anyone remember that album?) and a lot of compilations like the Dry Lungs series, although none of this is obvious in our sound.

I believe that you both live extreme distances from each other, but was this always the case? How did you come to meet and at what point did you decide to collaborate on a dark ambient project? STEVE: Yes, we now live about 2200 miles apart, however, there was a time when we only lived a few miles apart. We were introduced to each other by a mutual friend, Joel Bender (BELT). At the time, we were both working on other musical projects, but about 2 years later, we decided to get together one afternoon and collaborate and see what happened....that afternoon, YEN POX was born. MICHAEL: Actually, before we collaborated on Yen Pox, I have vague, smoke-obscured memories of going over to Steve's house while he and his "rock" band, Used, were practicing, taking my sampler over, and just recording improvisational, feedback, rhythm 'n noize freakouts, or sometimes I'd just throw out some vocals for the band. I can't really attest to the quality of these sessions (although I think I have a tape somewhere), it was just good clean fun. It was a natural progression from there for Steve and I to start getting together to record what would become the Yen Pox s/t cassette. This was really just "something to do", for ourselves, we didn't have a particular agenda in mind, just a way pass the empty Indiana weekends. It was this process that caused Yen Pox to come to fruition sooner than my solo material, which I spent more time "honing" and testing to see which direction I wanted to go with it. Much less thought went into Yen Pox, just get together and record. I think we were lucky with these early recordings, we really didn't know what we were doing, everything just came together perfectly, it was very natural.

Further to the above can you both please list your musical backgrounds that lead to the formation of the group? STEVE: I studied classical piano and organ for 5 years, when I was living in Oregon. Upon moving to Indiana, I quit my musical studies and attempted the formation of a couple of rock bands with high school acquaintances, which failed miserably as they usually do. After high school I moved to New Paris and was introduced to Joel Bender, who was interested in doing something serious musically. We met up one evening, Joel with his guitar and myself with my keyboard and nothing really inspiring happened. The next time we got together, I picked up a bass that Joel had at his place and that's when the inspiration started to flow. BELT was born. We did the first 7" e.p. "Exposure to Gunfire" (500 copies) which sold fairly well, mainly thanks to AJAX records distribution, and got some BBC airplay, thanks to John Peel. Prior to Joel's exodus from Indiana, I quit BELT, to continue the rock-based sound that Joel was now moving away from (eventually I did as well). It began with myself, a bass and drum machine. After a few months I met up with guitarist Traig Foltz and soon after we incorporated a live drummer named Marc Cupp. We called ourselves USED. We released an e.p. "How to Crawl", played a few shows locally and eventually played the Lab Stage at one of the Lollapalooza dates in Michigan in 1996, after which our drummer disappeared and the band fell apart, a common scenario among bands with more than 2 differing personalities fueled by excessive pot smoking and alcohol consumption, ultimately leading to a lack of focus, to which a band cannot survive without. MICHAEL: I had a couple of other friends making their own noise-ambient-electronic music, Joel Bender was one of them, and this really inspired me to buy some equipment and try it myself. Basically, I needed a hobby, some sort of creative outlet, or I was going to literally lose my mind, I had spent 3 years doing nothing but testing the limits of intoxication, and needed something else. Music was it.

Much like the slow movement and evolution of Yen Pox's soundscapes, your release schedule has been similarly at a snails pace. What is it with the compositional process that results in such large expanses of time elapsing between recordings? STEVE: Some of this has to do with the distance between us. I think if Mike and I lived closer, things might move a little faster, but this is only minimal. The main reason the process takes so long is that we become increasingly critical of our work with each new release, in an effort to exceed the level of musical content as well as the sound quality. In addition, the mixing aspect of the process has been left to Michael as he's the one who has the superior recording equipment. MICHAEL: Yeah, things would definitely be different if we still lived in the same area, we'd probably have a couple of more lps to our credit. After the "Blood Music" cd, I wanted to take some time to work on Blood Box, which I felt had been unintentionally eclipsed by Yen Pox, so I wanted to get that out there. Then I moved from Denver to Seattle, which disrupted me for a while. At this point the recording process had completely changed too, the next album would be recorded completely apart, trading tapes in the mail. This process ended up taking a year longer than we had planned to finish, then over a year after that to get released. So if both we and our label had been able to do this as planned, we would have had this cd out a couple of years ago, though it would have sounded completely different. It's also true that I've gotten really picky in the past few years, it can be a real problem for me, I spend so much time on production and recording, that it gets to the point that nothing sounds good to me anymore. Then I get burnt out and lose interest for a while, it's become a pattern with me. Also, over the past couple of years, we've both been getting new equipment, which takes time away from the recording process while we learn to use it. I foresee more regular output from Yen Pox, as well as our respective solo work from this point, we both have better tools now.

Typical of almost all underground music there is a dark quality to output, with Yen Pox certainly adhering to this principle. What are you attempting to convey with your soundscapes as both your titles 'Blood Music' and 'New Dark Age' would tend to hint at some inherent philosophy. Is this the case? MICHAEL: I don't believe in putting forth any kind of message or philosophy or dogma or belief system with the music, I really don't like that trait in bands and music. I really hate it when bands lay out some grand statement or obvious message with their music, using it as a podium to transmit their unsolicited opinions. For me, music is purely an emotional, sensory, aesthetic medium, and the titles we use are chosen more for their aesthetic value than anything, we just try to use words that sound good, look good, and represent what the music sounds like to us. I don't think it's possible to do much more when you are creating music without lyrics. This is not to say I don't think much about the titles, exactly the opposite, all too often I hear great music with bad song titles that sound like no thought was put into them at all, and it's really important to me that the song and album titles are as powerful as the music they represent. I like the music to be cinematic, tell a story, sometimes fantasy, sometimes reality, just as long as you go somewhere else for a while.

Please details what are your personal thoughts on your two full length releases thus far and what do you think are their strengths and weaknesses of each? MICHAEL: Mmm, that's a tough one. I guess I like Blood Music more, unlike the cassette, I don't think we had any filler on this one, it's more layered, and I feel, a little more emotionally intense. I like how there's always something new to discover on these, lots of subtle transitions and sounds that are not always obvious. On the other hand, some would say this music is too subtle, this music is not for the impatient or those demanding instant gratification. I remember taking some copies of Blood Music to a store here that specialized in noize and whatnot, but the guy there was unaware of our music, wanted to hear a bit before agreeing to sell it. So he threw a copy in, then starts fast forwarding to random points on the cd, listening to about 10 seconds, then skipping some more. Really frustrating, I had to tell him he wasn't going to learn anything that way, it's music that needs a focused listen to appreciate. I often wish I was able to create more instantly commanding music, something that doesn't take so much concentration to enjoy. Probably, for my tastes now, the only thing I would change on these releases, would be the production, there's a lot of room for improvement there, and we will actually be doing that sometime soon, remixing and mastering both of these, it should really revitalize these, creating very different albums while retaining the qualities and sounds that made them great in the first place. I do think we've perfected our sound on the New Dark Age cd, I'm really happy with the sound quality and mix on this release, it's heads above our previous output in terms of sound quality.

Given that the 'New Dark Age' CD was in the 'forthcoming' release pipeline for quite a length of time, have you forged ahead in compositional writing for future release? STEVE: No. There is still a collaboration between YEN POX and TROUM which will be out soon as well, however the recordings have been done for some time now and it's being mixed down now. Mike and I are both working on our solo projects now that "New Dark Age" is completed. It may be another 2-3 years before any NEW Yen Pox material is completed, however, we plan to rerelease the 1st Self-titled cassette in the very near future. MICHAEL: I definitely hope that it doesn't take that long to get our next album finished, I could be dead before then, I don't want to waste so much time on the next one. Basically, when Steve is ready, I'll start recording material. Maybe even sooner. STEVE: Sounds like we're ready.

Your song titles do reflect their atmospheric qualities, however which eventuates first - sound or words? STEVE: Most of the titles are Michael's creations, aside from the Drone 7" and maybe half of the 1st cassette. As far as the titles I have come up with, it's always the sound that comes first. From there, I can sit back and absorb the sound and see what concepts/daydreams/nightmares come to mind and cull the titles from those images. MICHAEL: Anytime I think of, or read, something that is good title material, I'll write it down, then when the music is finished, I'll look through these to find a good match. With the New Dark Age cd, the titles were sort of independent of the music, and were rearranged freely to create a literary construction that appealed to me, and more accurately matched the "story" that I felt the music projected to me, personally.

Is work on Yen Pox material an even 50/50 split? Do either of you specialize on particular facets of the writing/ recording process? STEVE: As stated earlier, the mixing process has been left to Michael in the past, however, since I've recently upgraded to a digital system, there will be more delegation of this in the future, which may or may not help speed the process a bit. Michael is the visionary when it comes to the artwork also. I've concentrated my efforts more toward the sound. MICHAEL: Yeah, I've kind of been on the tail end of the arrangement and mixing in the past, and I'm really looking forward to letting Steve take over some of that now. As with every other release, it will really change the way our next album is recorded and constructed, it will be interesting to see how this changes our sound.

How much improvisation if at all is part of Yen Pox's works? STEVE: A majority of the material I create for Yen Pox is improvised. I find that when the inspiration is there, it just flows. Maybe a second take sometimes, but usually I'll be playing around with a sound on an instrument, which then becomes a pattern, then hit record on the DAT. MICHAEL: Depends on your definition of improvisation. I continue to spend more and more time on my sounds and tracks, and a lot more preparation goes into my music, but sometimes I'll just be messing around, get a sound, turn on the multi-track and go, and not mess with things too much. Especially since I've started getting into analog synths more, and I'm not trying to create specific melodies or patterns, these lend themselves more to the "twist-some-knobs-and-see-what-happens" mindset. I'd say it's a good mix of improvising and calculated construction.

Where do you derive your source material from that forms the basis of Yen Pox material and what are some of the more unusual sound sources you have found/ used? Likewise do you use traditional equipment such as synthesizers and samplers? STEVE: Do we give away our trade secrets Mike? For "New Dark Age" I used a couple of old Ensoniq samplers and a Synth module....this release was created with more electronic equipment than in the past. For the prior releases, we used various string instruments, vocals, percussive objects along with a very limited amount of samples, mainly just looped sounds. I guess some of the more unusual sounds sources were a milk jug and the sound of traffic. Any others you can think of Mike? MICHAEL: For me, it's always been about samplers and effects, and more recently, I've been getting into synthesizers. Early on, my sampler was pretty limited, but I had a great effects processor, so we focused on using sounds, any sounds we could, to trigger the effects. Some of our sounds on there own sounded, well, not very good, but it didn't matter as long as the effects hid the sound. Now though, I'm much more focused on using a good sound and just using the effects for enhancement. Up till "New Dark Age", samples accounted for only about a quarter, at most, of our material. Mostly we would use processed bass, vocals, and like Steve said, anything we could use to make a sound. Even now, using more samples, we don't just rip things off, if we sample someone elses music or movie stuff, we'll transform it into something different. You'd never catch me sampling similar music, I prefer to sample things that have no comparison to what I do, like Journey or the Beach Boys, and force it to do things my way. **Do you currently work with a digital computer medium for your new recordings, and has this differed from early material?** STEVE: "New Dark Age" was recorded on a digital medium, not computer based though, and the sound quality far exceeds "Blood Music". Very clean. **How has changing equipment changed how you approach writing for the group? What types of equipment to you hope to utilize in future and would a formal studio setting be of any benefit?** STEVE: Changing musical equipment really doesn't change my approach to the writing process. As we have gone to using a little more electronic instruments (i.e. samplers/keyboards/sound modules), the only aspect of the process that changes is the extra time involved in programming, whereas, early on, we made sure the recording equipment was hooked up properly, checked the levels, and dove in head first. I think we could end up blowing a lot of money in a formal studio setting. It would be fun to see what could become of it. If we had a good engineer that was familiar with recording the kind of music we're making, it could turn out very well. If, in the near future, I upgrade to a computer-based recording system, I think we'll be able to do just fine on our own. Since Michael and I both have digital equipment now, I think there will be a noticeable difference in the next recordings as well. **Given the slow evolving process of your track it appears that there are melodies within however are extremely difficult to grasp in their entirety given the catatonic pace. Is this in fact the case and if so are these firstly composed at quicker pace then slowed appropriately into the finished compositions?** STEVE: Actually these melodies are performed at a catatonic pace. You have to just breath deeply, relax and let it crawl. I can't speak for Mike, but when I'm playing I allow myself to become entranced by the sound to the point that I'm able to play at such a pace and still keep the timing tight. It's almost meditative. MICHAEL: I'm glad you hear the melodies. I happen to be drawn to melodic music, and it's important to me for there to be, on some level, some of that in our music, otherwise it would just be noise. The pace is not necessarily intended, just the way it naturally occurs, it's just the way we work. **Michael, you have a solo project by the name of Blood Box which has released one CD thus far. How do you feel this differs from Yen Pox material given that it does inhabit similar territory? Also which project was operational first and was the similar in sounding names a bizarre coincidence? What can we expect from Blood Box in future?** MICHAEL: I'm glad you called this a "solo project" and not a "side project" as I often hear it referred to as. Blood Box began basically the day I got my first sampler and recorded my first music, though I didn't come up with the name at first. And it's a complete coincidence that these names rhyme, I don't remember which name came first, but I wasn't thinking of this at the time. With Blood Box I feel more freedom to experiment with different sounds, if I want to be brutal and psychotic one day, and beautiful and angelic the next, then I will, as long as I can create some natural continuum between these styles. There will probably always be some similarity between Blood Box and Yen Pox, because my primary goal with both of these projects is basically the same. If I decide to try something too far removed from this, I will present it under a different name. Right now, I am working on a couple of different Blood Box full length releases, one will be a mix of material culled from the past 5 years, and the other will be all new. I'm really excited about getting this out, I think this is some of the best stuff I've done, hopefully I will have these finished by the end of the year, then I'm going to shop around for labels. **Michael, as I believe that you have played live with Blood Box are there any plans for both of you to present Yen Pox in the live medium?** MICHAEL: At one time, I would have flatly stated "NO", but I've reconsidered that, and there may be a chance of it happening sometime, the opportunity would have to be just right. We were asked to play at this noize fest that Malignant is setting up in New York this fall, but I can't afford to go to New York right now, and it would just be very difficult to arrange. If we do a show, it would not be a chance for people to come hear our recordings played live, it would be something very different, as the semi-improvisational nature of our music would make it nearly impossible to recreate much of our work. I don't know, it could happen, we'll see. **Michael, another of your side projects was the Hollow Earth collaboration with John Canady which has released one CD thus far. Likewise is this an on going project and how did the recording/ writing process differ from your other outputs?** MICHAEL: The Hollow Earth cd was recorded in much the same fashion as the Yen Pox cassette, on the weekends, purely for enjoyment, just a way to pass the time, we didn't really expect to release anything when we started. We will probably start working on some new material soon, with the addition of Tom Garrison from up-and-coming power electronics act Control. Which is not to say that our next release will power electronics, it's far to early to know exactly what will happen, though I'm sure we will have a heavier sound this time around. **Steve, do you have any side projects in the working that you would like to mention/ promote?** STEVE: I'm currently working on a set of tracks that will ultimately be a full length V.O.S. release. There was talk of a split Bloodbox/V.O.S 7" as well! We'll see what becomes of it. **There was talk of re-releasing the debut Yen Pox tape on CD as the debut item via your own record label Circle 9. Obviously to date this has never eventuated however is there still plan to issue this? Has Circle 9 been birthed beyond the formative concept stage?** STEVE: The rerelease will be a reality, soon. MICHAEL: Circle 9 has only been birthed if you count the first Yen Pox and the first Blood Box releases, which were officially on Circle 9. Other than that, the only thing I've done is had a nice logo designed for it. We still plan on remixing and mastering the first release, as well as an extensive reworking of the the Blood Music cd (remix, remaster, "new" music, new cover), and I'm not sure if we will release these completely on our own, or as a co-release with another label, depends on the money situation, I seem to spend it all on equipment, never have any left for a label. **Do either of you follow the underground scene of which you are derived from and who would you acknowledge as being worthwhile? Likewise what other sounds, genres etc encompass your listening time?** STEVE: Lately I've been listening to MZ412's "Nordik Battle Signs", Brighter Death Now's "The Slaughterhouse", Dream into Dust's "The world we have lost" and Coil's "Music to Play in the Dark 1 and 2". Aside from these, some titles that are in frequent rotation are Soundgarden's "Badmotorfinger", Dimmu Borgir's "Spiritual Black Dimension", Alice in Chains "Jar of Flies", Skin "The World of Skin", Swans "Children of God", Sonic Youth's "EVOL", Current 93's "Thunder Perfect Mind", Nick Cave (any up to and including "Let Love In"), Death in June's "But What Ends when the Symbols Shatter", Dead Can Dance's "Within the Realm of a Dying Sun", Jerry Goldsmith's "Planet of the Apes" filmscore, and Nancy Sinatra's "How does that grab you". As far as worthwhile artists within the "scene".... Dream into Dust, Inade, IRM, LAW (Mitchell's sound has really matured with "Vindication and Contempt"), Heid,

Bloodbox, BELT (S/HE & Killing Verdict era), Maeror Tri/Troum, Voice of Eye, and Gruntsplatter are the acts who have either made a big impression in the past or recently. MICHAEL: I would probably know next-to-nothing about the "scene" if not for friends keeping me informed, I just don't buy too much of this type of music anymore. I find that I am very picky about this stuff, even when I started, one of the reasons was that I was tired of buying what I found to be crap, there was a small handful of great releases out there, and a surplus of average, uninspired and just plain bad music in this area, I decided I could do better myself, so I did. From what I hear, at least as far as dark ambient goes, we have more competition now than when we started, there are other bands doing some great stuff in this area, but I still don't feel that there's much out there worth spending my money on, at this point in my life, my attention span is too short, and I need something more from music. Which is not to say I've abandoned it completely, lately I've been listening to Brighter Death Now, Raison D'Etre, Caul, Voice of Eye, and Ordo Equilibrio, but for the most part, my tastes tend to an ever revolving and evolving diet of more "mainstream" and often conflicting styles. Lately it's been a mix of mellow trance-inducing electronic rhythms, 70's European Sleaze soundtracks, and brutal-yet-melodic teen-angst metal (and I'm really getting too old for that) and blackened metal, as well as a staple of old-school faves like Laibach, Nick Cave, Swans, Jarboe, and Foetus.

Are their any local underground/ experimental scenes to speak of in the areas you inhabit and are you at all involved in them? STEVE: Nothing much. Every blue moon a show might be organized by an enthusiastic individual trying to generate some kind of scene other than the typical lame bar band activity, and there may even be a surprising number of people in the crowd, however there's just not enough of it. I did a V.O.S. performance in the fall of last year, just over the state line in Michigan and there was a descent crowd. Maybe as time goes by things will get better, but I'm not getting my hopes up. I'm just a couple hours out of Chicago though and there are some good shows there on occasion. I was fortunate enough to have had the opportunity to see Death in June when they came to the states a couple years ago. You just have to keep your eye's and ears open and use your resources to find out what's going on. MICHAEL: Not much that I know of, but I don't really seek that out, and they don't look for me either. Most of that "scene" here is inhabited by free jazz musicians, improv noisicians and the like, which I couldn't care less about.

What is your opinion of the vinyl verses CD format? (either related to or separate from your own releases). Also does vinyl present inherent problems when say Yen Pox is working on particularly subtle segments that may be compromised with the associated hiss and static? STEVE: As far a sound quality is concerned, there's no comparison....the CD far exceeds vinyl, particularly with the type of music we create. If the vinyl quality is good, then the sound will be pretty damn clean, however, the quality of the vinyl medium as become neglected to a point, at least in the U.S. because it just doesn't sell as well as it used to. In Europe, they seem to take vinyl a bit more seriously. I've bought some really good "quality" vinyl releases recently, from European labels. I would never reject the opportunity to do a vinyl release, but if I was flipping the bill, I'd do the CD. Vinyl seems to have become more of a collectible item unfortunately.

Thanks for your participation. Have I missed any topics you would like to cover? MICHAEL: No, I was thinking of going on at length about Steve's disgusting personal habits, but instead I'll just give out our e-mail address in case anyone wishes to contact us. It is: circlenine@mac.com STEVE: Hey now!

---

vox barbara

The Five Senses

"The Five Senses takes organic sounds...post-manipulated debris...and manipulates them into wonderfully lucid sonicscapes that are further manipulated via the mixing process and an ear for constructing mesmerizing, hypnotic rhythms."
 - Spectrum #3

"The five tracks...are astonishing for their candid approach to noise...the result is distinctive and I suggest you to listen to this experimental work full of sincerity."
 - Chain DLK #7

Available for $8 (US/Canada) or $10 (world), ppd., from
Little Man Records, po Box 45636, Seattle, WA, 98145-0636, USA
vox@speakeasy.org
http://www.speakeasy.org/~vox/noise/barb.html

LIVE BAIT RECORDING FOUNDATION
BRINGING YOU THE FINEST IN DARK MUSIC SINCE 1996

423 Seventh St. #3
Fairport Harbor Ohio
44077 USA

OUT NOW

LBRF010 - In Death's Throes - Infernal Deities Transcending cd
Seventy Minutes of Sonic hell and Abrasive textures.
Black Ritual based Ambient mixed with destructive Noise Interludes.
$12.00 US
$14.00 worldwide

COMING SOON

LBRF013 The Hollowing - Sepsis CDR
Intense Rhythmic Treatments awash in White Noise Textures and Demonic Vocals.
Available soon...

LBRF015 Salvation Bloodletting Compilation CD
AMAZING COMPILATION FEATURING EXCLUSIVE TRACKS BY:
AMON, BAAL-BERITH, THE HOLLOWING,
NO FESTIVAL OF LIGHT, ORIGAMI ARKTIKA,
AZOIKUM, NOTHYS FE HYS MORTIS, DEISON, NOTHING,
SIDWYEM, GRUNTSPLATTER, IN DEATH'S THROES,
RAVENS BANE AND LEFT HANDED DECISION.

On the web -
livebaitrecording@hotmail.com
http://crionicmind.org/livebait
http://www.mp3.com/MurderousVision
http://www.mp3.com/InDeathsThroes

SOUND REVIEWS
ALL REVIEWS BY RICHARD STEVENSON UNLESS INDICATED OTHERWISE

Ah Cama-Sotz (Bel) "Poison" 10" EP 1999 Old Europa Cafe
Topics covered on this blue vinyl include the legacy of political assassinations under Stalin's rule and the poisoning experimentations undertaken by Lavrenti P. Beria (lovingly referred to as 'Stalin's butcher'), presented as versions 1 and 2 of the EP's title. Side A presents abrasive sweeping noise inter-spread with ominous treated keyboard sounds and treated/echoed radio voices, creating a juxtaposition of deep atmospheres and intense sounds. Retaining the same sound throughout, the layers of sounds and intensity of tones are explored over the lengthy piece. This track reminds me to an extent of the noisier tracks that Predominance have created (minus the vocals) on the Hindenburg 12" EP. More subdued overall, "Poison II" works on the same dual sound principle, yet has a more drawn-out drone production and fewer abrasive sound textures explored over its likewise lengthy course. Lastly, the cover is nothing really to get exited about, with reasonably plain visuals printed on blue card.

Ah Cama-Sotz (Bel) vs. Frames a Second (Bel) "Ankh-Deceptive Rate" 7" EP 2000 Nocturnus
Another release by this Spectre side label that sees the collaboration of two artists (each providing the other with source material, from which a track is then recorded). Ah Cama-Sotz is up first, with 'Ankh' being a mid-paced noise and beat fest, containing a certain groove to the static and programming. Sounds waiver in the mid to high sonic spectrum, acting as a backing to the increasingly overlapped beat and rhythm layers being created. Pulsating drum sequences and non-harsh static make what could certainly be an industrial dance floor number. Hitting its peak at the midway point, the track continues in this hyper fashion for the remainder of the 6 minute piece. Frames a Second's track ('Deceptive Rate') is instantly more harsh and grating, static noise outbursts and scattered vocals popping in and out randomly, with a faint hint of a beat sequence in the background. This beat element gradually claws its way to the fore, presenting as a mid to fast paced segment that is constantly built upon with more sound, static and voice samples. Running a ragged line between beat and noise, neither element ever gets the upper hand, both threatening a takeover at any point. Printed on heavy weight vinyl, complemented by a sepia-coloured cover and three insert cards (and limited to a mere 399 copies), this will surely sell fast.

Ah Cama-Sotz (Bel) "The House of the Lordh" LP 2000 Ant-Zen
This new LP encompasses the style in which I most appreciate Ah-Cama-Sotz - solemn death industrial sounds devoid of beat programming, etc. (this is not to say that his beat oriented tracks are at all bad, but that this is the sound that I tend to prefer). Slow and massive orchestral sentiments are quickly laid down with track 1 and, being rife with movie samples and deep catacomb atmospheres, the horrific nightmare aura is soon established. Scattered chiming bells, orchestral string layers and smatterings of vocals and noise layer embellishments, create another tense track on 'The Gathering'. Things really hit the mark on 'Crucifixion of the Flesh', a track that is quite comparable to In Slaughter Natives. Slow pounding percussion and deep horns are the main musical elements, also containing the obvious sinister industrial backing sounds. Atmospheres morph in intensity, shrill and warlike in intent...and I ask does it get better than this!?. The last track on side A ('Bleeding Crosses'), despite being a quite mid to fast paced composed keyboard number, does retain a dark stylistic approach to the tune, and sparse backing of noise elements. Side B features only two tracks, the first one 'Prophetic Vision' being an extremely lengthy piece. Dense and heavy in sound production, the dark ambience structure sees the sporadic use of percussive sounds and orchestral elements all thick and resonating with cavernous darkness. The extremely distorted and treated vocals that arrive mid-way through sound as if they are being spoken by the dark lord himself, and thus add quite a bleak touch. Towards the end of the track a programmed keyboard rhythm injects some urgency to the proceedings, leading into the finally with 'I:Believe'. There is certainly no disappointment either with a track of massive sweeping death industrial qualities. More vocal samples sit amongst scattered segments of dark orchestral melody that puncture the otherwise barren and desolate sonic landscape. With Salt always going that bit further with packaging and despite this being housed in a simple slip sleeve the presentation is impeccable as always. Limited to 500 I'm sure most have already missed this one.

Amoeba (USA) "Watchful" CD 2000 Release Entertainment
With the involvement of Robert Rich in this project (along with Rick Davis) I was expecting some excellent organic drone soundscape works, but I was off the mark altogether. This CD still has a very organic/earthen feel (and dare I say slightly 'new age' tinged), however this aura is evoked via traditional song structure, and the use of steel/acoustic guitars, percussion, vocals, synth, etc. The use of these elements on most of the tracks see the layers swirling in dreamy unison as the far off and fragile echo of the vocals resonate throughout the sphere of sound, all creating a sound production that is embracing and enveloping in its warmth. The cello accompaniment to 'Skin' works particularly well, solidifying the organic vibe of wood and bow against that of plastic and steel. The mood of 'Origami', although quite wrought with sorrow, has a certain prog-rock tone to the guitar without ever being a fast or uptempo song; rather it forms a short interlude to the more straight forward acoustics and highly atmospheric drumkit percussion of 'Footless'. This progressive rock sound surfaces again on the lengthy 'Ignoring Gravity', which relies much more on bass, guitar and light drumming (created with the use of brushes). 'Desolation' is introduced with drones akin to Robert's main works, here mixed with guitar and mournful vocals while 'Big Clouds' is devoid of any guitars, rather containing deep drones, scattered hand percussion, outbursts of sounds and treated vocals being the closest to an experimental track on display. 'Saragossa' is the most up-tempo and folk oriented piece with flutes, tribal hand percussion and that special crisp resonance that can only come from a steel guitar, all collated in the very warm, dreamy, atmospheric sound production. One comparison I could definitely make would be to the beautiful works of the group "The 3rd and Mortal", and while this lacks the soaring female vocals of said group, the aura evoked is quite similar insofar as the songs are focussed on capturing and portraying selected moods. Although this is somewhat different than I expect to see coming from the ranks of Release, given their past noise/industrial offerings, this is still a great listen.

Amon (Ita) "The Legacy" CD 1999 Eibon
Andrea Marutti's third venture as Amon (he also navigates through darkened territories as Never Known) is, unquestionably, his finest, most complete work to date. A passageway carved from humming drones opens 'Sandstones'. Brittle, clamoring machinery ambience patiently moves to the forefront, as the humming drones grow more tonally rich. The track furtively shifts from its brittle beginnings, to being almost boisterous, a leviathan of unwavering sonic audacity. There is a thickness to these tones, as layers congeal amidst a murky, all-enveloping fog. The following four tracks constitute the four chapters of The Legacy cycle, exploring different facets of the drone territories. The darkness shimmers, grows more prominent during 'The Legacy I: Enter Darkness', as low rumbles are massaged by aching winds that sink deep into the landscape of soft gray matter. Desolation of mind is featured here, midnight in the desert of decaying dreams, erosion that leads to isolation. 'The Legacy II: Machinery' really escalates the tension, as the multi-layered engines of the drone machinery grow more kinetic, tightly wound motion of a foreboding origin. The murky fog thickens to malleability, seductive in its blindfolding embrace, hinting at melodies buried way, way underneath, breathing ominously, a stentorian resonance. Pure undulating darkness, the darkness from the earth's core (or, at least, the core of the most oppressive nightmare), full-bodied, dense, and yet spacious, as sounds skitter underneath, scampering toward the furthest horizon, toward oblivion. 'The Legacy III: Domes/Colonies' is bathed in crystals whose luster is radiant, offsetting the darkness, but not the inherent solitude. It gives the solitude a chilling companion, a mocking hope awash in false light and promises unfulfilled. The crystals carve a serrated edged cavity into the drones. 'The Legacy IV: Exit Light' leads one back to the light, but this is not a comforting ascent, rather alien to be quite honest. A distinctive, piercing drone seems reminiscent of a like-minded, somber drone from The Day The Earth Stood Still, or some such science fiction movie that I cannot quite place, but it's there…I know it's there… The final track, seeking refuge beyond the Legacy quartet, 'Amunhaptra,' is not a peaceful finale. The ambience seems haunted, as jittery tones reflect off of abandoned machinery, all the while swelling and mutating, rising like defiant shadows in a warehouse graveyard (mysterious, hinting at deception and discomfort)… With The Legacy, Amon solidify their status as one of the finest purveyors of drone-infested darkness, the magnitude of which can shatter souls… An awesome display! — JC Smith

Anima Mundi (Cze) "Another World II" CD 1999 Old Europa Cafe
Fitting somewhere in the 'esoteric' sound category of Old Europa Cafe's output, this release takes that baggage and updates it with sounds of modern studio production. A treated classical sample (commanding violins) introduces the album only to slip into the mystical Middle Eastern atmospheres and sampled vocal mantras of track two. The third piece, 'Conquest of Paradise', again turns the album on its head, as groovy drum and bass beats are found intermixed with sweeping exotic sounds, backing percussion and the odd chant. 'Forgotten Soul' takes a similar path with vocal chants, sweeping strings, harp tune and groovy lounge beats creating a significant comparison to Atomine Elektrine (which is by no means a bad thing anyway!). 'Automation' strangely includes a sampled conversation taken from "2001: A Space Odyssey", referencing exchanges between the computer Hal and one of the astronaut crew (in which Hal turns against him), the conversation placed over a heavily treated sounds and hyper tribal beats. 'New Horizon' is a fantastic fusion of old world tribal beats and sound, mixed with trance inducing electronics, the following tracks 'crusade' reverting to complex fast paced hand percussion and Gregorian type chants. 'Truce' starts very traditional in sound, containing the continuance of the segment of prior vocals, and deep percussion and tense atmosphere, suddenly jumps a few thousand years ahead by bursting headlong into programmed break beats and classical inspired keyboard layers (strangely enough it works without stilting the atmosphere one iota!). Textures and sounds of Middle Eastern flair are explored throughout the remaining tracks both traditional and modernist in sound. Despite the diversity of sounds the album of 17 tracks has been produced to play out as one flowing filmic and atmospheric piece, which is very visual in sound (drug hazed images of a vibrant trading town of bustling noise located on the edge of desert oasis certainly come to mind). Nodding towards the sounds of Atomine Elektrine (more in regard to the first album) and somewhat towards Raison d'être, Anima Mundi have taken these influences on a vibrant and exotic Middle Eastern journey, ultimately infusing this with their own character and sound. Recommended.

Antony & the Johnsons (USA) "Antony and the Johnsons" CD 2000 Durtro (via World Serpent Distribution)
When I reviewed the introductory split single (with Current 93) of this group, I made mention of the melodrama contained within the vocalist's voice, which makes more sense when looking at the pale white androgynous figure of the cover (Antony himself). Being very different to any album I really own (likewise very different to what most would expect from World Serpent), this has still grasped a special place in my collection with its dark emotive cabaret-type songs. Consisting mainly of elements of vocals and piano with complementing violin, cello, flute, clarinet, saxophone, drums, bass may give you some inkling of the types of tracks that would be produced with such instrumentation. Vocals of mid to falsetto range heighten the real vehicle driving these songs and often strike a sorrowful chord. 'The Atrocities' is a number that particularly stands out with a sweeping cinematic feel of piano and violins that remains throughout despite quite heavy progressive drumming and bass sounds in the middle section. Mostly I am at a loss for descriptive words here, and as this is likely to appeal to only a select audience of this magazine, I will leave it up to the individual to determine if this is for you.

Apoptose (Ger) "Nordland" CD 2000 Tesco Organisation
With elements of dark ambience and martial neo-classical, Apoptose infuse inspiration from both into thier own sound, subsequently creating a great album in the process. To describe further, there are no tracks that could really be considered neo-classical in their own right, yet it is the use of ritual/martial percussion and solemn classical tune that give this in part a similar aura. Crowd noise, mid-paced pounding martial beats and solemn keyboard layers are found on the opener, 'Uter Bewusstsein', while the sorrowful yet rousing atmospheres of 'Abschied Von Der Sonne' are accentuated by selected outbursts of sharp drum rolls (that become more prominent mid way through to take the main focus). The sampled female choir vocals of 'Nidstang' give a broad comparison to Raison D'être (at his most composed), with the backing music containing shifting bass soaked noise and classically inspired keyboard layers. The classical type movement continues into 'Horizont' with a deep cello being the most discernable element of the melody. Mid-way in, heavy martial drumming pounds into contention creating a much more aggressive aura over the unchanging musical backing. The drawn out concluding track 'Erntewod' is content with slowly forging forward with a repeating tune and fluctuating backing consolidating the pieces focus. The only thing left to mention is the fold out digipackpack that complements the music perfectly - a great merging of visuals and sound. This release is definitely recommended.

Arcana (Swe) "Isabel" CDS 2000 Cold Meat Industry
Isabel is the barest sliver of music, three short tracks, a teaser for the latest full-length CD, "...The Last Embrace." What it is meant to do is create anticipation, as the three tracks showcase Arcana, circa 2000...which is very much like previous Arcana, but the astute listener can discern stylistic refinement. What Arcana create is beautiful, majestic music full of sweeping tonalities and rich, textural vocals. In refining their work, the sound has grown denser, more concentrated, the focus unwavering. My only criticism would be that, as with most of Arcana's music, the tracks sometimes feel incomplete, as if Arcana have honed each song down to its prime structural impetus. That said, Isabel has succeeded in its purpose, as the barest sliver of music here leaves me anxiously awaiting more. -JC Smith

Arcana (Swe) "...the Last Embrace" CD 2000 Cold Meat Industry
One of the brightest stars of the CMI roster shines even brighter on this, their third release of sweet sorrowful medieval neo-classics of the highest order. In the culmination of the themes explored on all tracks thus far, the style may not have changed drastically, but the sound now soars upwards to spiralling heights, the summit barely visible to mere mortals who remain at the mercy of these emotional hymns. The opening title track lulls the listener into thinking it is less then three minutes in length (with a deceiving 13 seconds of silence) only to burst back into contention more commanding then ever before stretching out to close to six minutes, male and female choirs complementing each other perfectly as always over a backing of rolling tympanis and orchestral sentiments. The slow brooding string sections and church bell chimes, whispered and sung vocals have never sounded better as when presented on 'Diadema', which in part nods to the track which introduced Arcana to the world - namely 'A Song of Mourning' (which caused such a stir as the opening track on the ".. and Even Wolves Hid their Teeth" compilation of 1995). 'Love Eternal' formerly from 'The Absolute Supper' DCD compilation set is even more glowing alongside its brethren, shining magnificently with Ida's solo vocals weaving their magic. 'March of Loss' starts very subdued with light notes strung together, prior to sharp rolling percussion commencing the epic passage of french horns and deeper brass instrumentation, hitting the peak with chimes and chanted male vocals. 'The Ascending of a New Dawn' sees the introduction of an acoustic guitar, ritual chimes and an absolutely massive resonating drum sound, again set against the obviously brilliant vocals. The morose piano piece 'Sono La Salva' is slightly more subdued than many of the other tracks, but no less epic in medieval classical feel. Not content to go quietly, the marching hymn of 'Lorica Vite' sees the album to its ultimate conclusion, with Ida and Peter chanting words in a vain attempt to appease the elder gods. It would appear the increased use of real instrumentation such as cello, percussion, the occasional guitar and an additional male backing vocalist has helped bolster the massive sound, yet the immaculate layering of orchestral keyboards has always ensured (and most evidently on this album) that the sound is as close to a real orchestra as you are likely to achieve via synthetic means. With 10 tracks in all, (two off the previous CD single and the track from 'The Absolute Supper' compilation), the disc is a little short at 45 minutes, but is still another amazing CD from this group.

AsiaNova (USA) "Burning the Blue Sky Black" CD 2000 Influx Communications
With no cover (well mine is a promo) and no details on the CD itself, all I can say is that this release consists of great swelling, bloated atmospheres of massive drone proportions slanted toward a tribal aura. In track 1 tribal flutes processed through reverb and delay add to the slow drone backing with a deep mid paced monotone (and monotonous) beat adds a slight urgency to an otherwise slowly-evolving piece. Elements build, direction is focussed, and the results are stunning. When concentrating quite hard on detail one may detect tones of guitar and resonance of female vocals, but these are mostly disguised within the drawn-out drone process. Vocals again used as an instrument (or drone element) usher in track 2, mixing drone, tribal and classical atmospheres superbly. With a tribal hand percussion set against a bed of dark orchestral drones, this transcends any mere drone categorisation. Over the lengthy third piece, deep fog horn drone atmospheres and disembodied voices make for a tense yet ambient listen of Lustmordian quality. Tribalised elements again add the urgency of the drone textures of track 4, firstly starting somewhere off in the distance of the listening plain, slowly accelerating to the fore of the speakers. Here the swirling non verbal vocals ensure that this piece offers an excellent mix of dark ambience and drone sentiments. Having the feel of being more composed than 'droned', the last track reveals the use of slow orchestral atmospheres, quick percussive wood textures and vocalisations that are neither sung nor drawn out - rather, they recite unintelligible sounds. When slowly introduced other orchestral atmospheres add to the knife-edge of relaxed/urgent sound. With significant additional ground covered in the remainder of the piece, sections of more subdued dark ambience appear (which is by no means a disappointment, by the way!), cavernous in its reverberating textures. There is some involvement in this from Ure Thrall (also a member of the Smooth Quality Excrement project) thus reference to the reviews of these other groups in these pages will reveal that there is a definitive high standard at work here (and likewise very worthwhile).

Baal (USA) "Selections for Biblical Studies and Multiple Orgasms" LP 1999 Troniks
With a cover image that I would more expect from the likes of Cradle of Filth, the packaging further aligns itself to the picture of fetish wear clad females on the back cover by it being encased in a black plastic sleeve. With the release being ridiculously limited to 80 copies, if you don't already have this chances are you will have difficulty tracking one down. As for the music side of things, this is a good slab of industrial noise. Abrasive mid ranged static opens proceedings ('Free Dom'), infused with what sounds like porn dialogue/scenarios (which incidentally continue throughout the album). The sound texture sets a mid-ranged grinding pace, acting as a vehicle for the sexual conversations played out, and varies only slightly in intensity before becoming maddeningly chaotic and frantic with obliterated mid to high end static. 'Pretty Pink Swastikas' has a doom-laden atmosphere of low-end industrial sound, drones and intensifying noise, again acting as a basis for the conversations. The third and last track on side A mixes the elements of noise and deep drones quite well, applying a searing edge to the monotonous wavering static at the high end, with deep ominous sounds taking up the low end. Becoming more freeform to the middle of the track, dialogue takes the main focus (referencing domination and submission) as slow synth programming gradually solidifies, along with what sounds like a looped bass tune. This section has a very nice subdued atmosphere, only rendered tense by the included voices (but all the better for it!). Side 2 offers up massive grinding noise with a mid-paced distorted beat that partly reminds me of Brighter Death Now on the "May All Be Dead" release. The incessant noise and forceful pounding beats makes the opening segment a highlight. The track soon moves off into more brooding noise territory, and maintains an ominous atmosphere over the lengthy format. The last track ('Underneath Hot Wax') starts with weirdly treated repeated vocal samples and a break beat (of all things!), with the only noise sitting within the background. This format is retained for the whole piece, making it an unusual conclusion to the album. From the initial misconceptions when I first viewed the cover, this is a surprisingly solid and impressive release. If you want this, have fun trying to obtain a copy!

Backworld (USA) "The Tide/A Vagrant Thought" 7" Pic Disc 2000 World Serpent Distribution
This is quite a beautiful looking picture disc, though I'm not sure to how many copies this is limited. A complex and emotive acoustic folk ballad is what we have with the track 'The Tide', on side A. Deep cellos reverberate against the acoustic guitar's warmth and understated male vocals. A lone violin is added sporadically to accentuate the mid-ranged classical sounds...... quite a sense of celebratory sorrow to be found here. Side B offers a darkly folk acoustic guitar and keyboard/flute piece with spoken male vocals. The sung female vocals add another level of depth to the sound over the repetitive guitar tune and meandering flute. Both are very pleasing songs that are simply too short, leaving me anxious to hear more from the group.

Backworld (USA) "The Orchids" CD EP 2000 World Serpent Distribution
A two track CD-EP is what we have here, originally meant to be only available at the Wave Gotik Treffen 2000 festival (or so the press release goes). The title track is billed as a cover of a Psychic TV number, yet as I have not heard the original I can't provide any sort of real comparison. Anyway, it is a very uplifting celebratory folk oriented track that highlights beautiful cello accompaniment with the intricate acoustic guitar work and multi-layered, clean, and softly accentuated male vocals of Joseph Bundenholzer (incidentally, the song revolves around the spiritual joys of genital piercing). The second track, 'Flowers in Flame', is a re-mix of a track off a previous album, but yet again my review suffers from lack of a comparison. Working more as a soundscape than a song, drawn-out layered female choir vocals and distant chimes shimmer in unison without gaining or losing pace over the four odd minutes. Nice psychedelic colours and patterns adorn the cover of the card slip sleeve.

Bad Sector (Ita) "Dolmen Factory" CD 1999 Membrum Debile Propaganda
Kinetic radiating energy oozes from these darkly composed, ambient yet experimental pieces which incidentally were previously released on tape back in 1997. Sub bass pulses, static induced sounds, brooding keyboard melody treatments, are expertly combined to make for eclectic moving soundscapes. Discordant drones, sustained noise texture of mid-level velocity (avoiding piercing range) makes 'Ivan 1810' a solid piece of dark ambience, minus any ominous synth elements. Flickering reverberations of multi-textural samples (some vocals, keyboard elements, etc.) make the core and direction of 'Carla 1977' an embracing one. 'Alvin 1953' is perhaps the most composed piece on offer here, with a plodding keyboard beat/rhythm, hazy elements and some whispered vocals awash with computer treatment. Alien vocal set amongst orchestral drones and condemning slow beats spawn an urgent atmosphere on 'Nara 1630', with a similar deep orchestral-type melody flowing through to 'Pierre 1902' (although the other main keyboard section gives a vast universal vibe). 'Brigitte 1872' goes even further in the exploration of classical sound mixed in a more sterile cutting-edge sound production (very much a sci-fi computer sound to what is essentially a classical composition). The short piece 'Exit B' which finishes the album is a subdued drone piece of cold astral qualities, which could be said to be characteristic of much of the overall feel. I am really surprised that Bad Sector are not more highly regarded, as everything I have heard from them warrants praise and attention. With what M. Magrini has created here, this is akin to listening to the experimentations of a modern alchemist shaping stunning compositions from sound elements that by themselves have little consequence. Recommended.

Band of Pain (Eng) "Sacred Flesh: soundtrack" CD 2000 Cold Spring Records
As this is a soundtrack to a recent motion picture, I don't know how much this differs from the group's previous works; yet some tracks seem to have been re-badged as new versions of older songs. Slow profound pulsations, moody orchestral layers, and brooding dark intensity mark slow moving soundscapes of (surprise, surprise) cinematic proportions. Tonal elements of mid to deep bass range make for a very dark ambient styled recording that works very well as an album in its own right and not just as a musical counterpart to selected visuals. Bleak organic sonics, and scattered human vocalizations of pain and ecstasy likewise heighten the mood (and themes encompassed in the motion picture) appropriately. 'Strength to Resist' has a bite to its subdued intensity, with the distant backing sounds and vocals being unnervingly

chaotic, while the title track (the disc's opener), is repeated mid-way though, and at an extended length does full justice to its orchestral bleakness. 'Beat out Desire' is certainly the noisiest piece with mid paced dark percussion over a deep sonic bed with choral samples and complimentary sounds of pain and pleasure. Sweeping, almost electronic sounding elements invade the aura of 'Sister Ann' creating a shrill textural piece. The overall slow movement and evolution of the compositions sees one piece meld into the next to create a drawn out whole, whereby the album really gains nothing by being dissected in to selected 'scenes'. Comparisons for the uninitiated would certainly have to be made to selected works of Caul given the overt religious aura to the compositions. Yet while Caul may have been lifting the veil to let more light into his recent works, these tracks of Band of Pain stay deeply entrenched in darkness and shadow. In presentation this is a little different in look to other Cold Spring items, however this is mainly due to the packaging being aimed squarely at the soundtrack-styled cover. Containing images from the movie (covering themes of forbidden sexuality within a convent) there is a certain element of a Cradle-of-Filth-style photo shoot, but without the blatant tackiness. Lastly, it is great to see selected artists slowly and insidiously weaving their way into wider public consciousness by being given the opportunity to work on motion picture soundtracks. The question is: could members of the public comprehend such a fantastically bleak sonic tapestry?

Baradelan (Ger) "The 3rd and the Final" CD 2000 Quatuor Coronati 762
Another relatively unknown group (well, for the moment) hailing from Germany with this self-released item that I was very impressed with from the first listen. Much of the disc is based on drawn out electronic and organic sounding drones, sequenced in a very spacious (and 'space' oriented) guise seemingly illustrating an intrinsic universal order. A comparison could be made to Inade's "Aldebaran" CD with its murky, sinister and alien like atmospheres - this comparison could be pressed even further (or is it a strange coincidence?) since the name `Baradelan' is an anagram of `Aldebaran' (note: 'Alderbaran' being the title of Inade's first CD). Some sort of unusual choir sample introduces the CD, and is followed by kinetic and pulsating drones mixed with static nuisances to create the basis of sound. The track also utilises a repeated vocal sample (which references the CD's title) that is positively placed throughout the composition, shifting from speaker to speaker and intertwining perfectly to enhance the overall vibe. At 14 minutes things are slow-going, but this is exactly where the charm lies as the track slowly unfolds and refolds a multitude of layers, creating a shifting mass of (sub)conscious oscillations. Containing less width and depth to the sound, the second track is louder and more sweeping with low, quickly grinding drones and windswept textures that change pace with a commandingly slow keyboard passage taking the foreground in the last quarter of the song. 'Bunsoh' has a slight industrial tinge to it with the use of select factory-type textures that, by being placed well back in the mix, emphasize the depth of production. Juxtaposed against this is a deathly slow drone pulse that is repeated throughout the track, containing a certain physical element in the sound (or in its low penetrating frequency), making it quite uncomfortable to listen to for the total 15 minutes - essentially eliciting a physical response. The alien sounding textures are again abundant on the following piece ('Mortician's Sough'), using much the same techniques as already displayed, yet creating drones and sounds distinguishable from the preceding tracks. Containing a certain accelerating feel in the composition the tension quickly builds to sustain this atmosphere throughout. 'Dinas Bran' is introduced with signal bleeps, a sporadic layering of sounds and speaker-shattering sub-bass textures, and is the most experimental and minimalist piece on offer. The disc is rounded out with a short three minute piece of sampled era vocals and voice textures paying homage to silent movies of the 1920s. I'm not sure how widely available this release is, given it may be only be a promo release but it couldn't hurt to inquire through <schwerttau@cityweb.de>. Lastly as the inscription on the cover states "Ambient is silence: HEAR IT LOUD!". Sound advice Indeed (no pun intended!).

Beefcake (Ger) "Coincidentia Oppositorum" CD 2000 Hymen
With cover art very similar to the first CD, I could make some comment between the metamorphosis of the sound of the albums in comparison to the cockroach to moth insignia of the cover art - yet I won't (but then again did I just do it anyway?). Regardless, anyone who heard the first CD will not be disappointed here, likewise anyone who hasn't should not pass this by. In short, Beefcake have a highly distinctive sound of sweeping cinematic melodies and classical inspired backings, infused with obliterated break beats, vocals and text samples. The first album was quite dark yet had playful elements, and while the same tendencies are displayed here, this disc is overall a slower, much more gloomy affair. The breadth of soundscapes can sometimes be mistaken for sparseness, which would actually be quite incorrect as it is the volume of the beats in the mix that tends to subdue the sections where they are not included. The third track works on three levels: that of slow melodies, chaotic break beats (that are messed up beyond simple sequencing) and a full female vocal sample. This doubling and even tripling of sound layers is where the genius of Beekcake lies - part classical musical theory, part cutting-edge studio composition. A true merging of past and present sounds is perfectly illustrated on track 8, with the drum-and-bass beat enhanced by chamber music orchestrations - and the harp and flute melody gives the track that extra special touch. At its most playful, track 9 is based on multi-layered cut up beats and light quirky melodies. Regardless of the shear variance of tempo of beats and modulation of sound textures, one track still merges seamlessly into the next, yet another trait that makes the album play out as a stunning whole. Beefcake have opted to not title any of the 16 tracks, letting the listener decipher their own meanings. My unqualified translation? Brilliant!

Beefcake (Ger) "in medias res" 12"ep 2000 Hymen
In a continuance of the review above this vinyl is another in the 12" series that acts as a counterpart to the main album. Here we are treated to four unnamed pieces not on the album proper, which just goes to show how productive this group is (remember that main album is over 60 minutes in length). On obvious difference regarding these tracks is that a more beat-oriented focus is solidly infused throughout. Even on the first track the beats are much less scattered and cut-up, which makes for brooding groovy ambience with the same sparse sweeping background of solemn melodies. Track 2 has a flurry of mid-paced beats that are quite forceful in a way that could be described as 'big beat', if one was so inclined. The backing of this track remains a sparse collage of scattered drones with limited if any tune being shown. The cut-up hip-hop inspired beats of track three (Side B) makes for a moody listen when transposed over the trademark cinematic keyboard layers in perfect Beefcake style. Bittersweet beauty is on order for the final of the four tracks with slow beats consisting of kick drum, snare and high hat that assist in focussing the classically inspired keyboard lines. Overall yet another piece of Beefcake brilliance.

Belborn (Ger) "Belborn" CD 2000 World Serpent Distribution
Belborn are a group to add to the growing list of neo-folk acts creating rousing volkish hymns and marching tunes. Being German in origin and consisting of Holger F. and Susanne H., vocals are presented in their native tongue (mostly containing male vocals commandingly spoken/sung in low to mid range - the female vocals when present of higher range or whispers and acting mostly as backing). Despite being clearly composed on a keyboard (except for acoustic guitars and bass when used) the sound does not come across as weak; rather it contains enough layers of organs, grand piano, flutes, classical orchestral elements, marching percussion etc to create a full and rich sound production, so as the slight synthetic edge not detract too greatly. On selected tracks (for instance, 'Undertan' and 'Wegbereit'), a weird almost pop vibe is presented due to the programmed mid-tempo drum machine beats which in my opinion is much less successful than the more traditionally focussed tracks that precede it. 'Weint Keine Trane' is a beautiful yet tragic and melancholic acoustic ballad of delicate tunes and strummed riffs, with this feel and aesthetic also present on a later track, 'Lichtreich'. With its meandering piano melody the last listed track, 'Ruckmarrsch Nach Vorn', actually reminds me of the sound and feel of a CD by Fata Morgana (an old Mortiis side project), but transcends this comparison with a more soaring musical backing complemented with marching beats and the sounds of an epic battle in progress. As a bonus the track 'All Unser Blut' is repeated with English vocals (translating to 'All Our Blood'), showing this track to be a great blending of a grand piano melody with marching snare, clarinet and organ dirge. The cover is a simply presented digipack containing imagery of runes, runic alphabet and woodcut pictures (one detailing priests being burnt at the stake) that suits the vibe and sound of the CD. A lyrically sheet also accompanies the cover, with lyrics printed in both English and German - odes and laments to times past and ways forgotten. Quite a good album overall.

Black Lung (Aus) "The Great Architect" CD 1999 Kk Records
David Thrussell, who also does time as the logo battering industrial cynicist/realist, Snog, and the projectionist for the inner cinema treats of Soma, continues his patented, spring-loaded percussive experimental techno excursions, on the latest unraveling of sonic disarray from the International Mind Control Corporation, The Great Architect. The slippery, deft execution is in prime cut and splice mode, as David gleefully manipulates an assortment of choppy samples into sonicscapes that adhere to nonsensical rhythmic patterns. Though I detect rhythms throughout that seem more straightforward (I was going to say familiar, maybe normal, but nothing here could be qualified as normal...), this development cannot be looked upon as laziness. As the multi-layered, multi-faceted approach to construction, to assembling the disparate sounds and textures has advanced, David has honed his skills in such as way as needing, at times, a more (ahem) familiar base for the chaotic melange of sounds. The sonic patchwork is vast, including everything from vacuum-packed, squiggly electronics, to deep-fried razors, to flatulent, squished bleats, to internet connecting mutilations, to contorted, between the dial radio transmissions, to eye-blurring ejaculations of noise, to a thousand other snippets... It's a crazy quilt stitched together with dexterity and a subversive sense of humor, as witnessed by the brow furrowing song titles ('Unorthodox Abnormality Broadcast,' 'Gizmo Prediction Fallout,' 'Surreal Opinion Simulator,'), and the covert thread woven throughout the whole presentation. (Did I mention the satirical gibberish channeled by David as one opens the digipak...?). The Great Architect is David hisownself, a true master of kinetic electronics and deceitfully ambiguous psychological motivations that might just be construed as genius. Or the sonic manipulations of the mischievous... —JC Smith

Blackmouth (USA) "Blackmouth" CD 2000 Crowd Control Activities
This album is billed as comparable to what two members Brett Smith and John Bergin have created with another of their collaborative projects, Tertium Non Data, except with the vocal contributions of Jarboe. On this front I don't entirely agree, as the music fuses many musical elements that would never really fit the Tertium Non Data sound, and due to this mixed focus I feel that some tracks work really well while others do not. The intro track is one example, with low, haunting melodies and the emotive, snarled vocals of the enigma which is Jarboe. Track 2, the title track, is a short bridging piece of slow gloomy beats and partly tuneful backing that runs into 'The Black Pulse Grain'. This piece is a good example of the deviation from T.N.D's typical sound with its dark trip hop/drum and bass sound and female vocals ranging from sung to spoken, as is 'Risen,' a similarly dark yet more up-tempo track of trip hop/electronica. The (yet again) trip hop styled backing of 'The Burn' is in my opinion marred by sections of grating guitars, however here Jaboe has seized the opportunity to experiment with the tone and range her voice. On the other hand, the slow evocative piano and rasping soundscape of 'Inner Alien' highlight the beauty of Jarboe's voice when she chooses to use her vocals in a clean styling, as she does on 'Smother' against a backdrop of sub-orchestral melody, slow bass and a harpsichord tune, of all things. 'Surrender for his heart' is a particularly good track with trip hop beats and short disjointed orchestral breaks, giving Jarboe the opportunity for a narrative piece. 'Seduce and Destroy' is another track that does not seem to work due to the industrial rock guitars, making the track come off like a bloated overindulgent experiment. The remix of 'Risen' (bloodless remix) included late on the album is rendered slightly more friendly to the ears, with thick bass sound, low distant piano lines and other assorted break beats (as is the case with first track reintroduced as the outro, this time with a different break beat musical form). Despite some less-than-fantastic deviations in sound (on selected tracks), this is still quite a strong album overall, and now that I reevaluate my position, it could be compared to T.N.D, but only on the proviso that you expect quite strong elements of vocals, trip hop and electronica.

Brighter Death Now (Swe) "Untitled" 7" 1999 Xn Recordings
The latest 7" from the sonic malignancy, Brighter Death Now, relinquishes no information (kinda sounds like an extension of the May All Be Dead mindset only, quite possibly, more chaotic...). There is nothing to go on but the music...but what more does one need? The A side opens with the wail of a siren from an operating room in the pit of Hell, a pummelling beat tattooing the souls in torment (unwilling patients to a sadistic fate), scalpels wielded with negligible glee: dissection, imminent; anesthesia, questionable (non-existent...). Don't know what the guttural vocals intone as they are garbled, chewing on distortion. The brain is filleted, that damn siren's wail signalling...what? (Another victim for grim experimentation?) Another soul destroyed for the sonic cause? Did I say this was brilliant?! The B side overflows with blood as sticky crimson bubbles from my speakers. We, humble listeners all, embrace the repetitious annihilation, Roger's vocals crawling underneath, belly to the blood soaked floor. Cluttered, confusing-like a storm on the horizon, THE storm, bringing black clouds and a rain that consists of the broken bones of those who believed in something (...someone-GOD?), and now that the millennium is upon them, all belief has been abruptly discarded... Like a trapdoor swinging open and the instant it swings, the thoughts are as follows: a.) Try to catch oneself on the rim and persevere amidst the hailstorm of bones that invalidate all hope or b.) Let yourself drop DOWN, because there is nothing to look up to the heavens for anymore... Comes in a very appealing, simple yet heavy cardboard foldout sleeve. -JC Smith (Reprinted by permission from Side-Line magazine: www.side-line.com)

Brighter Death Now (Swe) "May all be Dead" CD 2000 Cold Meat Industry
The first edition of this as a DLP was no less than an infuriating lottery game due to the random additional tracks and bonus single or double sided 7"s. At least everyone is guaranteed the same tracks with this CD re-release although in 'feel' it really does pale in comparison to the original vinyl version. Housed in a similar yet shrunken fold out poster cover, the CD comes also encased in a colour slip sleeve of the main cover image of a massive pile of skulls being set upon by scavenging crows (minus the text and superimposed necrose symbol). All the main tracks off the LP are here, likewise introduced via a short and remixed version of an untitled tracks off one of the bonus 7", crammed to the capacity of the disc given its overall 74 minute running time. Still, those holding the DLP version may retain additional elements not on this CD in the way of between one and three tracks (depending on which LP/bonus 7" combo they got). The sounds of this release are not really like any particular album that precedes it, rather a mixture of elements packaged in an early punk anarchistic delivery and DIY aesthetic. Taking the repetitive droney elements of 'The Great Death' era and mixing it up with the harsher elements of 'Innerwar', you might get some idea. Given that this contains only 6 listed tracks, the cuts are bone scrapingly deep and long, inflicted from a knowing soul who has mastered the art of delivering and sustaining pain. With an abridged nameless intro remix track of pure cathartic aggression, the chugging/surging tape loop of 'I Hate You' kicks in with considerable force, and also contains tape-processed vocals and sporadic stabs of sound. Repetition is in order and as the track hits its plateau early, it is content to pronounce its hatred for everything - including you as the listener. 'I Wish I was a Little Girl' is a personal favourite BDN track, with its feverish vocals, incessant loops and pure noise aggression. 'Behind Curtains' is atmospheric in tone, with high end wavering sound and a mid-ranged distorted rolling beat. Spoken vocals are again included, but have a more psychotic edge which becomes more noticeably aggressive as more layers of noise are applied. 'Pay Day' enters with yet another vocal snippet before the apocalyptic waltz loop and industrial clatter stomps on everything in sight, while 'Oh What a Night' uses a slower dronier edge and some ear piercing elements, again employing the simple method of increasing vocal and music intensity as it progresses. The final track, 'Fourteen', is quite lengthy, and features a slow pounding beat complementing the electronics fluctuating in the background, with vocals and samples distorted in such a way that they simply become another layer of electronics within the track. For the most part, putting words to BDN's sound is an arduous task; yet since Karmanik has been at this project for well over 10 years now (and with no sign of letting up), this will go down as another classic chapter in the BDN bible.

Carrion (USA)/Crepuscule (USA) "Crypotomnesia" CDR 2000 Louis Productions
This CDR is basically a non-commercial prerelease of a side project of Crepuscule along with a bonus track from the main project; however there is talk of this being officially released via Slaughter Productions (and who knows, by the time this review is published this may have occured). While Crepuscule takes a skewed angle on the death industrial genre, Carrion more inhabits the power noise scene associated with Ant-Zen label but likewise takes a (very) left-of-centre approach. The tracks here represent a relentless mix of beats, corrosive sounds, vocal samples etc, oft appearing to be working on two levels - that of the beat/programmed layer and that remaining of the multitude of bolstering sound layers, vocal samples and random keyboard layers used more for effect than tune. Even on the slower tracks the sound collage is just as full and forceful due to the make up of grinding electronic machinery and studio manipulations creating a dark 'beat/noise' type manifesto. However to think that these 'tunes' are straight forward enough to every be 'danceable' would be clearly wrong, as even when sections of groove or rhythm appear to solidify, other random generated elements leap into the mix throwing things completely off. Carrion's focus is more akin to cutting edge-studio trickery with the randomness of the compositions simply being a by product of the main intention. Nonetheless I have taken quite a liking to groups of this ilk of late, including the new Ultra Milkmaids CD and new Squaremeter CD (both reviewed in these pages). Also as I am such a music packaging/presentation junkie (and that this CDR is without cover), I am intrigued to see how this item will get packaged on official release. The bonus Crepuscule number and the closer of the disc is entitled 'a voice from nothing' and was specifically utilised as source material on the title track of Schloss Tegal's latest CD "Black Static Transmissions". More interestingly both this track and Schloss Tegal's version supposedly contain samples of Electronic Voice Phenomenon (EVP, otherwise known as voices of the dead). I will say that this is by far the best Crepuscule track I have heard yet and likewise one of the downright creepiest when played loud late at night (given the implications of the content). Much of the scattered sounds, documentary narration and just plain weird noises and voices are (sporadically) recogniseable from the Schloss Tegal version, yet they retain the trademark signs of a Crepuscule piece. Though with minimal (if any) recogniseable keyboard tunes, one discerns deep, clinical and otherworldly drones interlinking sections of sampled voices, EVP examples and poltergeist-like clatter - if didn't already mention it, this is certainly a very intriguing (and entrancing) listen. I don't know if this track will be included on the official Carrion release (or later Crepuscule CD, for that matter), but I am damn glad I have a copy of this on this CDR to fully appreciate!

Chthonic Force (USA) "Chthonic Force" CD 2000 Zos Kia Sounds (via World Serpent Distribution)
This one is quite hard to review given the variety of genres it transverses over its short length (just under 40 minutes). The main person behind this is Tim Madison, though guest appearances come from the likes of Monte Cazazza, Boyd Rice and Thomas Thorn, among others (mostly as vocalists). Acoustic guitars, swirling textures and low spoken/sung vocals of the opener give the perception of an apocalyptic folk type release; however the noise elements and screeching feedback (in amongst a spoken word piece by Monte Cazazza) on track 2 certainly makes you think twice about pigeonholing this. The neo-classic elements of 'In and Out of Sin' (even though a short piece) again further define the distant boundaries of the amount of ground covered in sound and style. Short pieces of spoken word (the one by Boyd Rice covers a comparison of society to the S&M scene - just without the role-play), noise experiments, droning guitar riffs and doom laden keys really only give a short description of what to expect. The overall vibe of the compositions (regardless of styles) has a very old school sound, and this would seem to be much the product of the calibre of collaborators present. Ranging from calm to grating, harsh noise to industrial might seem to present a jagged whole, but this is still an interesting listen.

Coil (ENG) "Astral Disaster" CD 2000 World Serpent Distribution
Forming some sort of re-mix/re-working of an earlier album, this CD contains also new material not on the 99 copies of the original 12" vinyl. After toying with a short moog generated, scattered sound treatment piece ('The Avatars'), the slow ritual percussion and fleeting synth treatments of 'the Mothership and the Fatherland' commence the real section of the album. Melding hazy electronic treatments the 22 minute piece seeps out the speakers, slowly coving the floor, filling the empty vessel of the room drowning everything in the thick, dreary atmospheres. Subdued angelic voices chant slow wordless prayers, along with the tonal drones and intentional sporadic clutter as if being true relics of forgotten sound. Enticing and utterly engulfing . . . . '2nd Sun Syndrome' continues as a simmering liquidous mass of sound, complete with a tar-like consistency throughout the rise and fall of the quirky rhythm. Returning to an epic length format, 'The Sea Priestess' explores more subterranean depths, this time in a more commanding manner with drawn-out male vocal drones/chants. Set alongside various radiating keyboards treatments and chimes are the smooth echoed spoken vocals of John Balance (which reference the CD's title late in the track) resulting in no less than great psychedelic ambience and fable narration. Containing a more solid song structure, with classically-driven elements of cello and violin amongst synths and vocals, 'I Don't Want to be the One' tends to jolt the passive possessed out of their haze, yet still embraces enough to offer comfort, later becoming tensile with increasing lunacy of the vocalist. The

Autumn 2000

NOCTURNE présente
KAPITULATION
...plus releases from COLUMN ONE - World Transmission 3 & 4, 2LP
ULTRA UNITED - Ultra Audience, CD

SA022 Ltd. edition CD
(Special edition in calligraphy available from us.)
KAPITULATION - The resignation of civilisation!

STATEART c/o Koch
Roseggerstrasse 2
30173 Hannover
Germany

WRITE FOR FREE UPDATES!

stateart

www.stateart.de

last on offer ('MU-UR') returns the depths of the second track with its ritual percussion and darkly haunting tonal soundscapes sprawling past the 20 minute mark. This time the spoken vocals are again in narrative form, yet are so heavily treated that they sound almost feminine or childlike as the backing becomes occasionally jarred with eruptions of experimental tones and keyboard tunes. Towards the mid to late segment the experimental elements take over to quite a schizoid effect, devolving to the opening soundscape in the concluding stretch. Finally, the notation of recording location seems to indicate that it had a major influence the atmospheres created here, as the album was allegedly recorded under the water level of the River Thames.

Coil (Eng) "Queens of the Circulating Library" CD 2000 Eskaton (via World Serpent Distribution)
With a CD encased in a clear pink shell with next to no info, (other than listing the title track and collaborators), here we have a one-track 50 minute journey into slow drone territory. Early in the piece Dorothy Lewis (Thighpaulsandra's mother) is the guest vocalist uttering lyrics written by John Balance. Some slight reverb and surreal vocal treatments are utilised blending the words as if some form of electronic cipher. Below the vocals the hazy warm drones slowly fold and overlap in a circular fashion not really having a clear direction rather rising and falling in a sonorous fashion. Over the remainder of the disc not a hell of a lot happens other then slight shifts in the alignment, level and number of the drones, yet still inhabiting much the same sound texture territory throughout. Consequently this is probably my main gripe with the track as it lacks direction and pacing for a piece that spans close to an hour. Anyway, I believe that this item was released both as a mothers day tribute and to celebrate a live performance of the group and while not my favourite Coil piece, no doubt this will mean little to the hardcore collectors of the group.

Coil (Eng) "Music to Play in the Dark, Volume 2" CD 2000 Chalice (via World Serpent Distribution)
A vocal mantra (consisting of the single word 'something') sitting amongst swirling winds and a lone keyboard drone, acts as an unusual opener of the disc (a follow-up to "Music to Play in the Dark, Volume 1"). Nominating 'Something' as somewhat of an intro, the following track ('Tiny Golden Books') would not be out of place on a computer of space type documentary given the playful programming of the tune. The dark traditional piano playing of 'Ether' catches my ear rather favourably, yet the weird scattered sounds and vocal treatments making this a not entirely straightforward listen. The computer programmed cut-up beats and baroque-sounding tune of 'Paranoid Inlay' offers another weird listen, while the brief middle track ('An Emergency') features Rose McDowall on vocals. Built around a rhythm of static glitches, and Middle Eastern sounds, my favourite track comes in the form of 'Where are You?', which exudes some of the fantastic atmospheres of the "Astral Disaster" CD with both John and Rose handling vocals. The final piece, 'Batwings (A Limnal Hymn)', progresses slowly, beginning with an organ tune and wavering electronic/astral computer noise (again with the spoken vocals of John) before culminating in some quite beautiful vocal harmonies.

Column One (Ber) "Sad Finger" 7"ep 2000 StateArt
This being my first introduction to this quite prolific group I can say that I have been more than pleasantly surprised. Side A offers up the title track, which is in fact a live recording from a 1999 Polish show. Sparse symbol percussion and fluctuating backing noise start things off, with a morose bass/ piano tune and low sung/ spoken vocals later becoming apparent. The gentle depressive aura of this is fantastic, which is sustained with only minimal change throughout (some increased use of tape loops and noise) on what is really a composition of part song & part experimental ambience. Flipping over the nicely weighted vinyl, the two tracks on side B represent studio recordings. The first of the two tracks is 'Silent' and is reminiscent of the feel of side A, mostly due to the slow bass tune & later utilised vocals, piano and symbol percussion. This track sounds somewhat 'artsy' but it is again the depressive mood evoked via the beautiful piano tune and accompanying distant guitar that has me utterly floored. The third track 'with a cry' again achieves the same feel (& ultimate result) of the preceding track, yet is done via a treated guitar tune and a myriad of backing loops, noises, sound treatments and field recordings. The packaging while of the standard slip sleeve variety is printed on textured card (& contains another card insert) with unusual pictures to illustrate the ep's title. I certainly want to seek out more from the group on the strength of this (although I do hear that the sound of the group does change drastically between releases).

Con-Dom (Eng) "Rome Songs" 10" EP 1999 Old Europa Cafe
Here three tracks of Con-Dom vitriol are pressed into blood-red vinyl, one side timed at 45 rpm and the other at 33 rpm just for interest's sake. Without even referencing the musical attack, this is worth getting for the cover alone - a period photo of Pope Pius XII shaking hands with Hitler. This image of religious hypocrisy has obviously fuelled the project into yet another anger filled analysis of the control-domination concept. 'Rome Song' is a typical hotbed of white-hot noise, with mid-ranged static, squealing feedback and the obligatory ranted vocals which in most part is singular in its approach throughout its duration. 'Pro-Judas' is more subdued than usual, and is therefore the most interesting track. More bass-heavy in sound, it contains a mid-paced beat, yet another unconventional element for the group. The vocals are still yelled and slightly echoed, but the beats and sound depth move away from the all-out sonic attack for which this project is best known. 'Papal Bull', the last track on offer, features a slow feedback loop that doubles as a lurching rhythm, again in a manner slightly more subdued than one would expect from Con-Dom. Layers of static do enter the mix, but these only add to the breath of sound rather than taking over completely. A large written passage on the inside cover (detailing the concept of religious ordainment of war) forms the lyrics of this piece that are repeated a number of times over the lengthy format. Here the vocals are not yelled in anger, but are rather spoken as a declaration, and are subjected to a mild and highly emotive sound treatment. The length of this piece allows the track's dynamic to play out slowly, with the noise and static gaining momentum and volume throughout, creating power through more subversive means. For a Con-Dom release this is actually highly listenable and not just an anger venting tool, showing that the group just keeps getting better with age.

Contrastate (Eng) "Todesmelodie" CD 1999 Noise Museum
So the new Contrastate album has finally arrived, which unfortunately also represents their swan song. And when it comes to electro-acoustic soundscapes inter-dispersed with poetic spoken-word segments, none have ever really challenged the distinctive sound of this group. 'Third Rock'n'Roll session' arrives with semi-melodious guitar derived drones and organic sounding clutter, with the layered segments ebbing and flowing in a confined forward motion. Spooky sepulchral voices and a lone ringing telephone precede a fractured echoed beat segment that ushers in the first spoken word section of the album, and contains almost a full structure with beat, tune and voice (I said `almost'). The ever increasing and pulsating beat/rhythm under a miasma of treated sound samples and voices make for an urgent piece on the unusually titled 'The Sardines have Finished Knitting'. Here as the pace increases the backing becomes likewise sparse yet more emotive with its tense semi-classical aura. When 'Cutting the Cancer' commences with its beautifully dark melody and sung vocals, it appears as if we are to get a real song format out the group; but this notion is quickly dispelled in the flurry of semi-martial drumming and sporadic sound (although we do get a second taste of the vocal/melody mid-way through). And what would you make of the vocal line "you are blamed for avoiding the truth"? Gregorian chants carry the epic 24-minute piece `The Suitcase or the Coffin' to the altar of the inner ear, offering up a subtle and engulfing soundscape punctured by other snippets of subdued classical tune, choral vocals and vocal mantras. More guitar drones and sparse percussion resurrect the piece, sweeping it off into weightless spatial soundscape territory. Yet this is by no means heaven as the aura takes a sinister twist through the introduction of slow plodding piano notes, hand percussion and writhing drones (the last 7 odd minutes of this piece arrive as a partly disjointed mix of sung/spoken vocal drones/ harmonies and other straight electro-acoustic segments). While I don't think this could be considered the ultimate Contrastate album, it is still leagues ahead of most and a great testimony to their legacy.

CTI (Eng) "Electronic Ambient Remixes" CD 2000 Conspiracy International (via World Serpent Distribution)
This CD is by the infamous Chris Carter, who has extensively remixed and reworked one of his analogue synth albums called 'The Space Between', released way back in 1980. I can say that I really did not have any expectation nor any real idea of what this was supposed to sound like, but after numerous rotations I have been more than pleasantly surprised. While billed as 'dark ambient remixes', there are faint traces of trance-inducing electronica, that in fleeting moments bring to mind Atomine Elektrine's "Archimetrical Universe" with its sweeping galactic (occasionally beat-laced) soundscapes. There are never really any real beats per se, but the programming does come in the form of very subtle rhythms, pulses and tunes (as is shown on the fantastic 'Interloop'). Much of the aura is akin to drifting through the endless expanses of space (likewise drifting effortlessly between the ambience of each track), stretching the concept of time and space in its wake. The underlying sound is of course analogue given the main source material, but other than that this presents itself as a very current sounding experimental electronica/dark ambient release.

Current 93 (ENG) "I Have a Special Plan for this World" MCD 2000 Durtro (via World Serpent Distribution)
Given that I don't have an overall grasp of the sounds produced on Current 93's numerous albums over the years, I will avoid acting like I do - rather, I will present a straight up description and let well-versed fans decide how this album measures up to other releases by the group. One track at a touch over twenty minutes seems much longer as it engulfs you in a poetically tinged hypnotic state. Words written by Thomas Ligotti and spoken by David Tibet are both desperate and tragic in content, with delivery conveying a feeling of total emptiness and loneliness. After getting the rambling's of a madman set against a clock ticking out of the way, David's first vocal passage seems as if random thoughts were recorded and played back on a dictaphone. Soon after the shimmering, wavering organic waves flow forth, yet strangely contain a somewhat metallic resonance. Vocals cut back and forth from sections of indecipherable treatments to tragic story-telling, segmented by the intentional nuisance of an on/off switch, all the while with a half-played melody ebbing throughout. Limited additional ground is covered other than the above sound treatment, but this is where the magic is most evident, stretching the essence of the time fabric with the focus held on the narration of the surreal story, full of confusion and ambiguity. The primary-coloured art of the digipack cover is yet another facet of Tibet's talent, and while at face-value it seems to misrepresent the music, it is also entirely appropriate in its surreal depiction.

Current 93 (ENG)/Antony and the Johnsons Orchestra (USA) "Immortal Bird/ Cripple and the Starfish" CDS 2000 Durtro (via World Serpent Distribution)
Two tracks, 11 minutes including a new track off the upcoming Current 93 album and an introduction to this unusually-titled new group (that David Tibet incidentally brought to the attention of World Serpent). Although Current 93 is listed as the first artist, the play order shows otherwise with Anthony and the Johnsons Orchestra appearing first. Calling this music melodramatic is somewhat of an understatement, for its tops even Nick Cave in vocal delivery. Being an octave or two higher than Cave's vocals, the accentuation of vocalisations give them a very distinctive sound, set against a backing band of violins, cello, piano, harp and clarinet, later including standard drumming and a saxophone solo. Although this is different to what I would normally listen to, it remains an intriguing track nevertheless. Reasonably straightforward in song construction, Current 93's 'Immortal Bird' is a subdued guitar, organ, xylophone, and sung/spoken vocals piece that has a nice ambient air. Heavy in radiating warmth, the production is akin to dozing before a warm open flame. This is quite removed in sound from the previous MCD, but still has sparked my interest for the upcoming new release. As much as this is an introduction to a new group and new album respectively, its real purpose has been to serve as an appetiser for both.

Current 93 (ENG) "Sleep Has His House" CD 2000 Durtro (via World Serpent Distribution)
The review of the above Current 93 track (which appears on this album) stands as a broad description of this release, yet I find the aura all the more tragic and desolate when a similar sound is played out over 9 tracks. The instrumental opener of a sparse bass tune, lightly strummed guitar and droning organ (liner notes state it is actually

a harmonium) sets this mood precisely. Each song uses mostly this same instrumentation and evoke a similar depressive mood; yet rather than being boring or one dimensional the CD opens up an emotional vortex that you can't help but revel in. The tragic air is evoked less by the content of David Tibet's sung/spoken vocals than in the manner in which they are intoned. This would seem to have a lot to do with the album having been produced in memory of his recently deceased father, with songs and artwork revolving around this theme. Mild electronic minimalist studio treatments are employed on the latter half of 'The Magical Bird in the Magical Woods', but do not detract from the emotive framework being woven. 'Red Hawthorn Tree' sees the odd shrill trumpet blast included in a track that is the closest equivalent to what would constitute a smile for the album (but barely that, in all honesty). It is funny how a track can encourage a whole new perspective when presented in the confines of an album rather than as an unfettered single: the above reviewed 'Immortal Bird' single weaves more magic as part of a collective whole than as a lone crusader. The vocals on 'Niemandswasser', which sound as if they were presented by a man on the verge of total collapse, only adds to the depressive dimensions explored, conjuring up a soul swept away by the swirling winds that mark the track's end. The only drawback I could possibly find is in the 24 minute title track (specifically dedicated to the memory of his father), as the harmonium drones become too repetitive without the assistance of other instrumentation (except for spoken vocals). While the last piece, 'The God of Sleep Has Made His House', does not alter the basic framework of sound, strangely a hint of Pink Floyd can be detected here (and not in a disparaging way either). Between the two Current 93 albums reviewed, two very different facets of their sound are explored. Take your pick, as either are great.

Cyclotimia (Rus) "New Death Order" CD 2000 StateArt
This is somewhat different to what I was expecting, however this has much to do with the previous track I had heard from the group (a track on the "Edge of the Night: Russian Gothic Compilation" where the group presented a new aged/classically influenced trance/techno piece). Overall the sound here is quite a bit darker than this particular track and likewise contains far less trance/ beat oriented sections. 'Miserere' (the first track) has extremely tense sub orchestral drones and is yet another of many groups that have used that now infamous sample from the movie "Jacob's Ladder". Half way in the sound changes completely with Gregorian vocal chants that are partly uplifting and partly sorrowful, complimented with underlying synth layers and factory clatter type noise. Such is track two in representing the title track, it is introduced with hard snare drums and rising noise layers with sampled choir vocals adding a sense of morose despair in amongst multiplying (relatively) non musical sound layers. There is a certain sound here comparable to early rasion d'etre but here is generally a harsher vibe. Lush (synth) strings & choir vocals commences 'cursed ground', yet things take a turn to harder atmospheric territory with shrill treated synth layers and other assorted noise voice samples. The final two pieces 'Manifest Destiny' (parts I & II) are mid paced synth layered percussive type sound works with smatterings of sampled talking the cover topics relating to the title and cover image (depicting three surly looking high flying business types). An unnamed bonus track is also included and manages to solidify a soundscape that cuts across the modern and arcane via the use of religious chanting and low syth pulses and drones. The overall vibe is fantastic and a great conclusional piece. I somehow think Cyclotimia will become a quickly know name on the strength of this MCD.

Dawn & Dusk Entwined (Fra) "Forever War" CD 2000 World Serpent Distribution
My first introduction to the group was on Anthanor's "Lucifer Rising" compilation, and even though the track was a reasonable effort, for me it acted more as a marker hinting at what was to come from the group in future. And while I may not have heard the first CD (released last year, also on WSD), this second CD is nonetheless quite stunning. Deep, morose, neo-classical is what is on hand here, even with a certain similarity to the distant forlorn sounds encompassed in LJDLP's works – in other words, very damn good. The prominence of a heavily accented European voice is shown on the opener 'Heading towards the west' - the music a combination of deep percussion and slow classical string melodies. While the main piano line on 'To the Fallen Ones (Eternal Two)' is quite simplistic (in its overly drawn-out orchestral sounds), it sustains a particularly evocative aura with distant rumblings becoming more evident in the foreground. Again the piano lines on 'Shades and Shadows' draw heavily on what could be described as a trademark LJDLP element, complete with speech samples and scarred sweeping textures shifting in the background. Segments of trumpet blasts and distorted martial percussion render 'Wyrd' a much less melodic track, resulting in it being mainly a vehicle for crowd noise, vocal samples, far off bomb blasts, etc. The sorrowful choir samples at the start of 'Skies of Belgrade' convey a feeling of unspoken misery, prior to the shrill whistle of an air raid siren puncturing the subdued backing atmosphere (from here distant echoed percussion, spoken vocals and a slow organ tune enter the composition). 'Enter Ashland' is yet another example of where the group excel by taking what is essentially a simple melody and creating a more than effective aura by embellishing it with organ sounds and heavy pounding percussion. After hearing the calibre of the tracks on this second album, I will have to see what I can do about tracking down their first effort. Recommended.

Death in June (Eng) "Heilige" CD 1999 NEROZ
When referencing my show report of the Death in June performance in last issue, one might consider this would get an instant thumbs up given this live CD release was recorded at the aforementioned show. Sadly this is not the case, mostly due to the fact that the live recording lacks much of the power and punch of actually being there. The overall martial aura in the live sense came through via the pounding drumming, yet on this recording it has been mixed far too low. Likewise the recorded vocals have taken much more of a central focus, with less emphasis on the underlying music. Taping the show straight from the mixing board (I assume) has removed any hint of crowd applause, and further tends to turn the listeners' ear way from appreciating the music as a live rendition, rather sounding like a live studio take. Now that I have aired these grievances, in balance I will add that the sound production is crystalline in clarity and full-bodied in breadth, with no complaints about the actual sound (these have more to do with the mixing). As with the earlier description of the show, the CD showcases much of the newer material in the first half, with the second half reverting to the standard acoustics of the early to middle era of DI6. Aces in the first half certainly are provided with live renditions of the some of the tracks off the "Take Care and Control" album, including 'Despair', 'Little Blue Butterfly' and 'Frost Flowers' being definite stand outs, complemented by the use of orchestral and vocal samples. Both 'Bring in the Night' and 'Only Europa Knows' are presented in full percussive guise, with the latter being a very aggressive rendition complete with full vocal snarls. 'Death of the West' marks the changeover to the acoustic format followed in quick succession by 'Heaven Street' and 'Little Black Angel'. 'Kameradschaft' comes across stunningly live, merging the acoustic strains of the guitar perfectly with the more martial percussion of recent DI6 albums. Later acoustic stand outs also come with 'Giddy Giddy Carousel', 'Rose Clouds of Holocaust', 'Hullo Angel', 'Leper Lord' and 'Fall Apart'. After lulling the listener into a somewhat relaxed state due to the acoustic segment, DI6 ups the anger level for the pounding final track 'C'est un Rêve'. Overall this is a good musical document of the last show of DI6 for the 20th Century (which incidentally features 20 tracks in all), but sadly it does not quite capture the sound of actually being there. The talent of the musicians and clarity of recording is still a testimony to this long standing group, and any fan who has followed DI6 for a number of years will no doubt want to obtain this.

Death in June (Eng) "Operation Hummingbird" MCD 2000 NER (via Tesco Organisation)
Playing out as a sister album to the new direction DI6 toyed with on "Take Care and Control", Douglas P (assisted by Albin Julius of Der Blutharsch) returns with 7 tracks, likewise on a new label after departing from the World Serpent ranks. This time around any hint of the traditional DI6 use of acoustic guitars has been removed, instead again playing with martial themes of sampled classical loops, keyboard treatments, vocals and drumming. While the opening cut "Gorilla Tactics" (sic) contains savvy dry humour, it is also a venomous attack on Switzerland for banning DI6 from playing there during the 1998/1999 tour (pointing out the utmost hypocrisy of the country's banking regime), completing with the chiming of cuckoo-clocks to drive the message home. Here Douglas cuts a straight path through all emotional arguments against the group by squarely turning the mirror back against his accusers. 'Flieger' is one track that just has to be heard to be believed, sounding like a swinging 60s number (but with obvious DI6 slant) with an uptempo beat, driving bass and meandering keyboard accompaniments. By all accounts this should not work, but somehow manages to be one of the most surprising and engaging tracks of the CD. Other tracks continue with the verse/chorus/verse format of the preceding acoustic phase of DI6 compositions, but here employ a totally different framework of orchestral/classical driven sound ranging from shrill to brooding string sections, commanding horn movements, marching beats, etc., depending on which track is being played out. All are done superbly, and create both calm and rousingly-inspired atmospheres. Also with track titles such as `Hand Grenades and Olympic Flames' and `Let the Wind Catch a Rainbow on Fire', you are assured poetic yet ambiguous lyrics throughout. With Douglas P having recorded music as DI6 for nearly 2 decades, there still seems to be no sign of slowing down, and instead he sounds refreshed and revitalised with the new direction on this MCD (and the last CD), ready to continue unrepentant for years to come. Even if you have not been aquatinted with DI6 before, this would be a great place to start given the new-found direction and vitality.

Death in June (Eng) "Discriminate" 2CD 2000 NER (via: Tesco Organisation)
Being a re-released item, this double CD set has written in gold embossed writing on the back cover stating "a compilation of personal choice", which quickly sums up this release. All in all 33 tracks are included spanning songs from DI6's albums released through the years 1989 to 1987. Not having seen the original version I don't know if the packaging has changed, but with this the two CD's are housed in slip sleeves further housed inside a larger card outer cover (similar to that of the 'Operation Hummingbird' cover), additionally with a standard cover insert. Simplistic but aesthetically well presented. I guess there is little point in specifically reviewing the music as so many of the tracks have become classics within the DI6 camp and thus require no further comment. This is a great release to capture a broad overview of what DI6 have been and have subsequently become over the years, and even for an avid fan it is akin to having a large portion of the back catalogue on multi-disc rotation.

Der Blutharsch (Aut) "The pleasures received in pain" CD 1999 WKN (via World Serpent Distribution)
This is the second full length CD of Der Blutharsch and, incidentally, the last via World Serpent now that WKN are to be distributed by Tesco Organisation. The packaging consists of a reasonably simplistic brown card slip cover depicting a knight on horseback in the midst of battle and a picture of Albin on the inside. The slow ritual neo-classics of chiming bells, massively deep horns and slow strings of the first (of thirteen) untitled tracks sets the underlying mood of the CD, while the second and third pieces set the overall martial marching tone that is slightly tinged with volkish sentiments. Massive orchestrations and mid paced pounding beats are immaculately presented, both tracks showing the more frequent use of main vocals in a commanding sung/spoken guise. Some people have stated they are not enthralled by the increased use of vocals, yet I feel they complement the atmosphere of the shorter tracks of this album. The darker ritual/industrial undercurrent momentarily surfaces on the slow soundscape of the sixth track, with the muffled sound actually adding to the mysterious atmospheres, in amongst which spoken vocals, sampled choirs and deep horns reverberate. Track 7 is simply amazing in the urgent strains of the beats and tunes, resplendent with rousing chanted vocals, as is the warlike strains of the up-tempo track 8 with its mantra of "patria et libertas". Track 9 has sampled quotes pertaining to a conversation between Boyd Rice with his Son, while musically it sees the introduction of an acoustic guitar into the Der Blutharsch sound creating a slow folk/ritual feel. The shrill cry of distant bagpipes and anthemic martial drumming give way to one of the most powerful tracks on the album (track 12) that only multiplies in stature over its five minute span. This tune is segmented somewhere between ritual and deep brass orchestral, complete with commanding dual vocals throughout (chanting 'we never give up' towards the end). The lengthy final track has a subdued trench warfare sound (and conjures up a visual picture consisting of barren fields in the dead of night with the unnerving quiet between combat). Some of the backing noise sounds appear to have been sampled from a couple of tracks off Brighter Death Now's 'Innerwar' album, with distant air raid sirens, slow horns and sampled text vocals making up the remainder of sound. Whereby the first album played out as a single vision (from subdued to commanding orchestral atmospheres), this album comes across more like a collection of songs under the guise of a compilation album. This brings also a comparison to the feel of selected albums of 'TMLHBAC' (Albin's previous project) with the emphasis on individual songs collected in a single album. While the debut full length might have overall been a cinematic vision, this album is a refocused view of

subdued, rousing and celebratory marching tunes. If you are yet to discover the power of Der Blutharsch musical works, do not wait any longer.

Der Blutharsch(Aut)/Ain Soph (Ita) "Roter Berg/Baltikum" 7"EP 1999 WKN (via World Serpent Distribution)
The packing on this one is not much to get excited about - a simple brown and yellow slip sleeve with next to no information (other than it appears both tracks were recorded live at different performances). Far off orchestral strains and subdued pulse foundation get things off the mark for Der Blutharsch, being quite ritualistic in feel compared to the much more folkish neo-classical strains associated with Albin's compositions. After a few minutes of the introduction have elapsed, the martial implications burst forth with mid to high range quick percussive beats, shrill orchestral strains and commanding sung/spoken vocals undercut with higher range (sampled?) choir-like vocals (all done to a high standard). With this lasting for another few minutes, this passage abruptly finishes to the sound of rapturous applause, followed by a very eccentric and hokey 'western' piano dirge. This has me scratching my head somewhat, but it really only serves to end the segment... The Ain Soph selection is much harder to get excited about, even to the point that I would call this track openly embarrassing. This sounds like a very bad jam session of a couple of drugged up and washed out muso's... complete with keyboard runs, strummed guitars, up tempo rock beats and bland vocals. My distaste for this track goes is such that I feel it even taints the quality of the Der Blutharsch segment. While Ain Soph has gone through various stages of musical evolution, I still can't believe this is the same group that produced the totally encompassing dark ambient (concluding) track on the fantastic "Lucifer Rising" compilation. I would say that this EP is worth having for the Der Blutharsch track alone, but it also depends how much you can get it for since WKN releases are generally pretty pricey and highly collectable.

Der Blutharsch (Aut) "The Track of the Hunted" CD 2000 WKN (via Tesco Organisation)
The ever productive Albin Julius has quickly returned with his third full length declaration under the Der Blutharsch banner. As with the last album, this too is built around a format of shorter songs, and while the neo-classical sound has certainly not been removed, there is less focus on martial and marching themes, with slightly more exploration of the ritual and industrial sides of Der Blutharsch. This is not to say that there has been a change in direction, rather an exploration of a different facet of this project's sounds. Here 10 untitled tracks are presented with the opener containing sampled choir vocals and air raid sirens, creating a mix of beautiful and alarming sounds. Slow strings, more sampled female choir vocals, and a slow undercurrent of industrial sounds embodies track 2, being a good example of the mix of neo-classical and ritual industrial. Track 4 (as with a couple of tracks off the last album) uses again the acoustic guitar within the sound, creating a folk oriented feel within the chanted vocals, slow tunes, drones, etc. Track 5 contains probably the best use of martial percussion that I have heard from Der Blutharsch thus far. The brilliance of the multi layered percussion is in its anthemic proportions that have additionally avoided being simply a marching beat. This rousing number is one of the highlights of this disc with a perfect blend of echoed spoken vocals, deep horns and xylophone tones. Track 7, a piece of mid-paced ritual beats, weird accordion tune and overt darkly-muffled atmosphere (also including a Charles Manson sample) is another example of the slight diversion of this album, while track 8 is of the dark neo-classical martial percussion style - another highlight of the album. Sampled voices, spoken vocals, incessant percussive beats and brass horns and mournful bag pipe tunes intensify until its conclusion. An up-tempo era recording in the form of German accordion song is sampled in its entirety without any modification as track 9 (Ah yes, Albin certainly enjoys these heritage recordings!) before the move towards the closing passage is made. The last track is much more cinematic in its orchestral sound, more along the lines of the first CD than the remainder of this album (or the last album for that matter). There is a free from flow evident here with the massive orchestral sound, which does not seem to have emphasized throughout the shorter compositions. Within this track is a hidden eleventh piece, again seeing the exploration of martial and ritual sounds creating a dark soundscape devoid of any tune (apart from the occasional tune held in the sampled chanted vocals). The embossed digipack is particularly stunning, consisting of brown card with images of statues and classical art printed in silver. Overall this is another successful and victorious battle won by Der Blutharsch (but it seems that Albin already knew this, considering that the very first sound of the album was the pouring of a celebratory glass of wine).

Dissecting Table (Jap) "Power out of Control" CD 2000 Triumvirate
Working under the Dissecting Table moniker, Ichiro Tsuji has constantly forged ahead with the exploration of over-the-top power industrial rhythms and noise structures. "Power out of Control," an album recorded in 1998, has just now been released in 2000. A muffled bass intoned section starts the album ('Uncontrollable'), but only lasts for a minute or so until the trademark elements of squealing feedback noise, rigid programmed beats, grinding bas runs and over-the-top electronic growls appear. The palpitations of both beats and bass give an sense of urgency, yet the track does calm down into a sub bass and beat segment at the six minute mark with an almost neo-classical feel to the slow keyboard tune recreating the sound of deep horns (not that this lasts for all that long before heading back to cerebral damage territory). More trademark bass/rhythm structures are found on 'Bottom' as an introduction to the machine gun pulse, noise and obliterated vocals. Later things calm down again (not in relation to speed but noise attack). It is here, when the high-end squeals are shelved, that I find D.T most engaging, as it gives the opportunity to appreciate the complexities of bass and programming being presented. This track also contains a great section of semi-structured deep sub noise and slow dark pounding industrial beats, morphing into what could essentially be drum and bass (but with a sound only Ichiro could create). Reasonably composed beats and bass in a mid paced dark groove oriented style embodies 'Naturalism', along with vocals gargled in an almost death metal guise. With no overt noise attacks on this track, I would have to designate it as my favourite here. With a track appropriately entitled 'Go Beyond the Limit', it is not hard to envisage the noise/grind machinery being kicked back into full swing, yet still retaining a complexity of approach between segments of the composition - the use of composed/ noise, loud/ soft format is the key here. With only 4 tracks this still has a play time of over 40 minutes, I guess this would be a good place to start as an introduction to D.T, as much as it will appeal to those already taken in by the insane style of the group.

Sally Doherty (Eng) "Empire of Death" CD 2000 Tiger Records (via World Serpent Distribution)
This beautifully powerful release certainly has the winds of time permeating every aspect of it, sweeping the listener back to an epoch of human civilisation long past. The music on this release was originally composed for a BBC documentary of the same title, focussing on the discovery of the pyramids of a Black African Empire discovered in Sudan during the 1930s. As a quite interesting musical illustration of this subject matter, I found it a little odd that the cover is adorned with images of Egyptian stone artifacts rather than imagery relating to the actual topic of the documentary. Anyway, turning to the actual music, comparisons could be made to selected moments of Dead Can Dance (particularly where Lisa Gerrard presents solo chanted vocals) or even Sephiroth. A classical structure of flute, cello, violin, clarinet and oboe intertwined with female vocals used predominantly as an instrument itself, is the basis of the sound of these reasonably short compositions (16 in all and a little short of 40 minutes). Even though programming and keyboards are also noted in the instrumentation listing, there are no elements that hint at a synthetic sound production, which greatly assists in the timelessness of the music (the synth and programming seem mostly related to the dark percussive sections). An Arabic flavour is likewise fused into much of the song writing, and despite the length of the tracks being around 2-3 minutes, they do contain an impeccable flow, appearing rather as segments of one drawn out composition. While typically movie or documentary soundtracks can have some parallels with the dark ambient genre, in most cases they fall well short in one regard or another. However here the evocation of a subdued mysterious air throughout this music (in my humble opinion!) allows this release to transcend any barriers of simply being deemed a soundtrack piece, containing the ability to work extremely well as a dark ambient work.

Dreams in Exile (USA) "Since Long Before CD 2000 Crowd Control Activities
Like the Amoeba release also reviewed in these pages, Dreams in Exile follow a similar path. Gentle guitar works of both acoustic and electric format encompass a hazy mood, the male vocals likewise being gentle and mournful in delivery. Interestingly the majority of tracks have been embellished and enhanced by drone artist Vidna Obmana, and these deep swirling drone atmospherics add a distinctive breadth of sound. Elements of rock, folk and tinges of subdued gothic influence are all evident, but the CD never really totally subscribes to any of these genres. Some instrumental tracks are barely noticed as such given the low vibe that the vocals create when they are present. Despite have traditional elements of guitars, drums and vocals, all are processed in such a warm resonating manner that it is quite easy to become engulfed in the music much as one would while listening to drone ambient works. This is sort of a release that transcends genre boundaries in its distinctive artistic pursuit.

Droneament (Ger) "Wassermond" 7" EP 2000 Drone Records
Calming textures and digital drones give way to a slow evolving atmosphere based loosely around a water sample (the liquidous feel is evident yet remains in the background). Without being forceful, side A offers up a multidimensional piece of layered sounds, (some hazy some mildly rhythmic) all the while the bubbling and gurgling water textures create an amazing drone piece. Side B ('Wassertank') starts more slowly yet has an inherent forcefulness not evident on the first track. The main textures are more urgent, consisting of a multiple drones, sound pulsations and full bodied water samples. Less actual sound distance is covered, but this is made up in the departments of sound depth and dynamic. The cover consists of green card, with silk screen printed image to match the clear green vinyl. Another superb release from Drone Records.

Dual (Eng) "Klanik/4 t H" 7" EP 1999 Drone Records
When guitar layers are presented as treated drones I could not be happier, with Dual making me quite ecstatic! "Klanik" contains sounds of both low and mid ranged frequency sitting alongside a slow percussive beats, creating atmospheres that surge off on multiple tangents. The texture and volume remove this from a simple derivative drones, likewise when infused with sparse melodious sounds creates an engaging slow morphing song. '4 t H' embodies a sparser experimental guise with solid crumbling and fractured textures, deep feedback, sporadic clatter etc, all underpinned by elements of drawn out guitar drones. The level of volume and intensity of feedback again ensures that the track transcends any simplistic drone categorization. There could be a broad comparison to Contrastate indicating the sheer brilliance of this. Definitely worthwhile.

Einleitungszeit (Slo) "Schrei des Feuers" Video 1999 Ars Morta Universum
As far as videos go for this type of scene this is not a bad offering at all. While there will always be limitations to how a live video turns out, the feel and look of this falls somewhere between the slightly inferior quality of the Tesco Organisation's Heavy Electronics festival video and the quite superb Der Blutharsch live video. As for the live set up, the group consists of two individuals – one on the floor working various distortion pedals, pieces of metal, pipes and steel spring (that all appear to have been contact mic'ed), while the other (standing) individual handles the noise/beat samplers and live vocals. The sound is extremely heavy and chaotic with searing noise blasts and flanged vocal shrieks creating an all out aural offensive. Situated somewhere between power electronics and death industrial, the intensity peaks early on and remains so throughout its 30 or so minutes. With a mix of synthesised samples and mostly non-rhythmic beats, the bone-grinding machinery aura is further embellished with tortured vocals (of nondescript ramblings or outright screaming) and the shifting textures of random metallic noise. Certainly these sounds give the aura of some of the most tortured sounds to come from Brighter Death Now (i.e., the "Necrose Evangelicum" CD). At one point the guy working the homemade noise implements, sets upon the mic'ed metal sheet with an angle grinder (creating quite a calamity, as your would expect) then alternating between that and an un mic'ed metal plate strapped to his chest (more for visual effect and symbolism than noise generation, I suspect...). The footage is derived from a single camera (mainly of a hand-held style), moving in and out of close ups, with the visuals being fed through some post production colour and texture that adds to the chaos. And while there may be the odd audible applause at the end of each track, there is no footage to indicate the size of the venue nor how many people may have been in attendance. Admittedly having only previously known

this group by namesake, I don't know if the live tracks are taken from previous releases, however on the quality of these live noise scapes I now plan on tracking down their other musical outputs.

Elijah's Mantle (Eng) "Legacy of Corruption" CD 2000 De Nova Da Capo (via World Serpent Distribution)
Elijah's Mantle's a group I have heard quite a bit about, but whose sound was unknown to me until this album. Knowing that the man behind the project, Mark St John Ellis, is both an artistic and poetic fellow, this release is actually quite along the lines of what I was anticipating. Toying with rigid romantic (if not baroque) neo-classical framework, spoken vocals are unique if nothing else in presentation - each word meticulously pronounced to give an air of pomp and ceremony. The neo-classics of the pieces use the expected sounds of horns, strings, deep percussion and likewise harps, flutes, clarinets, organs, pianos etc which results in a framework that is less militaristic than most others in the genre. One other instrumentation element is the electric bass used within a number of the tracks, which to my ears does not sit all that well, given that it isn't the most expected instrument to hear alongside an orchestral sound. Another point that on initial listens has been slightly off-putting, are the spoken vocals. It is not that they are at all bad in and of themselves, rather I think the 'less is more' principle would work here. Particularly when Mark St John Ellis was guest vocals on the Protagonist's debut, the vocals melded perfectly when only presented in a short segment. Maybe the extent of such vocals has been somewhat dictated by the theme of the album being poems of Charles Baudelaire being set to music (I assume this is the individual on the cover?) and the need to include sufficient text. Anyway, not wanted to dwell on negatives, the musical backing is very solid in authentic classical composition, (if not aesthetically sparse in instrumentation) which clearly brings to mind Shinjuku Thief's "The Scribbler" CD, which incidentally also took inspiration from an literary source (some Kafka texts). Highlights are found on the lengthy tracks such as 'The Spirit and the Flesh' and 'Abel and Cain', which bring out the full flair of the project in a sweeping yet subdued orchestral manner. The packaging is a stunning 24-page booklet of selected poems by Charles Baudelaire printed in black and silver on a stark white card stock.

Ex.Order (Ger) "Silence + Brutality" MCD 1999 Associated Distortion
Three tracks of subtly insidious psychological degradation, a collaborative effort forged by Inade side-project Ex. Order and the image work of Charles Acethorpe. Echoed vocal samples lead one into the slow throb brainwash environment of 'A Dazzling Peace,' calm, deceptively sinister tones rising and sinking in the background, burrowing into the cranium: it has begun. 'Bound By Threads' continues the heavy samples vein, this time disrupted by distant machinegun fire and a swirling, menacing ambience upon which pulsing distortion is slathered over the top. Escape is futile: outside, the war rages on; in here, in the Ex. Order sonic vacuum, a more depraved fate awaits. 'Flesh Pumping' is a furious pummel and squeal affair, no need any more for prisoners or the attainment of covert information, just kill them, kill them all... And, before death, the looped female vocal sample conjures an image of an underlying sexual deviation that fills the mind with perversity, a perversity born of the hideous circumstances: the cruel, less apparent vestiges of war... As with the brilliant The Infernal Age CD from early 1999, Silence + Brutality is another devastating journey into the blasted cranial mind-field that is Ex. Order's sonic dominion. -JC Smith (Reprinted by permission from Side-Line magazine: www.side-line.com) -JC Smith

Fire+Ice (Eng) "Birdking" CD 2000 Tesco Organisation
A bit of an all star cast is featured on the new album by Ian Reed (aka Fire+Ice), with musical contribution from members of Death in June, Ostara, Blood Axis, and Backworld, to name but a few. As for the music, this is traditional poetic apocalyptic folk music, and the vocals of Ian are full of tragedy and nostalgia. While not stepping outside of the boundaries of the genre, this stays true to its folk origins, even to being even more folk oriented that any other of the affiliated artists. A piano tune follows and embellishes the main melody line of the title track and likewise crops up in varying degrees on other tracks (as do keyboards, percussion, etc.). The particularly traditional folk structure of 'Drighten's Hall' is fantastic with its lone acoustic guitar and whistle - the vocals of Ian are more forced in delivery, sitting against a backing of female vocals. Things really hit their peak on this track with the use of soaring violins, bringing visions of elder times into full view of the mind's eye. 'The Lady of the Vanir' does not feature Ian, but seems to be a piece written and sung by Alice Karlsdottir, with acoustic guitar, keyboards and percussion providing the musical backing. The track sounding most akin to DI6 acoustic works comes with 'Take my Hand', which incidentally features none other than Douglas P himself playing both acoustic guitar and keyboards. The organ sound and vocal delivery of 'My Brother' strangely sounds like a gospel hymn, and I don't feel that it fits all that well with the other acoustic tracks. Regardless, the final track has a mood of more uplifting celebration when compared to the others insofar as it is full and rich in sound, the musical accompaniment here consisting of acoustic guitar, piano, keyboards, violin, etc., which is a good conclusion to this set of traditional folk sounding tunes.

First Law (Ger) "Violent::Sedated" CD 1999 Loki Foundation
First Law brews a strange concoction of uncommon, enigmatic ambience (and what strange concoction is suggested by all of the pharmaceutically inspired song titles?). Violent::Sedated circles from the periphery, from a place not often explored (just to the left of limbo), blending tonally oblique elements into a sonic cauldron that continually boils over with contextually bizarre sounds. Brittle, fluttering wings introduce 'Amphetamine Sulfate (100 mg),' after which futuristic, smooth edged synth textures are unveiled—think Wendy Carlos' work on Clockwork Orange. A sudden interruption of odd, anxious tapping leads one into a realm of metallic, tribal percussion upon which the synths are re-introduced, giving the ambience a different focus. Wary slivers of razor honed nuances peek through the folds of 'Loxapine (220 mg),' while uncomfortable synths desperately try to arrange themselves, to no avail: the mood is tenaciously discomfiting throughout. 'Paraxetine HCl (50 mg)' seems recorded low to the ground as twitching, insect level sounds overwhelm; the ambience is moist and uneasy, a nauseous landscape as heard/sensed/translated via insect antennae. The caught in the propeller blade gyrating ambience of 'Phenobarbital (175 mg)' is jolted by bursts of ritualistically laced percussive disruptions and a noisy crowd demonstration. Gurgling, oscillating synths and feedback struggle for control amidst a whirlpool of chipped plastic, percolating rubber, and splintered metal during 'Phenelzine (70 mg)'. As threaded together with light tribal structures, the noise itself is never out of control (despite the aspirations of each individual sound). Repeated listens familiarize the listener to the First Law sonic mandate and really bring out the hidden textures buried within. Unique—not exactly dark sonicscape, but different...—JC Smith

Fennesz (Aut) "Plus Forty Seven Degrees 56'37" Minus Sixteen Degrees 51' 08"" CD 1999 Touch
It is reported that Christian Fennesz, armed with a powerbook laptop and guitar, recorded this album outdoors and unrehearsed, which if is the case sits perfectly with the beautiful landscape shots of the booklet and oversized card cover. One shot in particular details power lines crossing an open field, factories dotted off in the distance. This image of the merging spheres of the electronic and the organic sums up much of the feel of this album. With no sounds that could be recognized as being derived from a guitar, the album is a sweeping explorations of textural sound intensity and cutting edge sound aesthetics. Hints of melody weave throughout the sound exploration, yet really remain incidental to the overall atmosphere. Tracks three and four contain a sound texture akin to that of a low flamed fire, yet produced via an electronic medium of glitched sporadic sounds and gaps of silence. Track five is an intensely noisy and dynamic piece of multi-layered static, but is presented in with an underlying melodious drone that it has a soothing quality. The fragile shimmering textures, submissive static and distant sounds of track six create a massive depth of sound revealing to the mind's eye a panoramic vista of storm clouds closing in over a rolling landscape. The final two pieces are reasonably short, but cover sounds ranging from the aggressively loud to the softly contemplative (even when each are just over two minutes in length). For those not really familiar with the MEGO label (on which Fennesz first appeared) and affiliated artists this could be compared to the sound textural direction that Hazard has been pursuing over recent albums. The only other thing I could add is that this is brilliant underground experimental work of digital abstraction - the product of a scene that will be a major force in the future of experimental music.

4th Sign of the Apocalypse (USA) "Lost Hour World" CD 1998 Suffering Clown
While not musically similar to Dream into Dust, the sounds created by this project do have one similarity in that they defy an easy description. There are dark soundscapes punctured with weirdness (somewhat humorous choices of sound bites), slow experimental guitar driven tracks with morose male vocals (such as on 'Miss Meh'), and other pieces of selected sonic oddities. Even when the dark ambience is more straightforward looped styling, they are furnished with track titles such as 'On a Slightly Higher Moonbeam Than Death', again taking a somewhat tongue-in-cheek approach. On the other hand, 'Bleeding' contains an industrialised rhythm with repetitive driven guitar riff and vocal chant, while field recordings, sirens and an assortment of other found sounds act as the backing collage. An acoustic guitar intro to 'KnickKnack' ushers in the weirdest track of the CD, sort of a drug- infused experimental jazz piece with experimental industrial overtones (this track is a little too far out there for me to fully appreciate). The plodding beats and surrealist atmospheres of 'Take me Away' seems to present musical insight into a madman's mind, with the rambling, heavily treated vocals ultimately solidifying this vision, while 'The last 7:38 of Your Life' is an appropriately engulfing listen with guttural bass tones, deeply echoed cyclic sounds and disembodied voices calling from the abyss (ultimately being one of the best tracks of the CD). Great ideas are explored here, yet sometimes it is hit-and-miss in final musical presentation.

Genocide Organ (Ger) "The Truth will Make you Free" LP 1999 Tesco Organisation
Arguably the most controversial power electronics group ever, Genocide Organ returns with this new release. Now before the politically correct factions get all riled up with the visuals, text and samples contained on this LP I think the following quote from a G.O interview is relevant: *"We never say what we think, and we never believe what we say, and if we tell the truth by accident, we hide it under so many lies that it is difficult to find out"* (Descent Volume 5: The Death Issue, June 1999). Now with that out of the way, even if the music was not up to standard (not that this is the case at all) this release is worth it for the packaging alone. There is a certain special feeling you get when holding the ultra thick, heavy weight, maximum thickness, gloss card gatefold album cover, that is essentially beyond description. This simply needs to be seen to understand what I'm getting at.... Orchestral sample intro and ambiguous 'fatherland' styled speech text introduces 'Tide Side' (side B is 'Grow Side') merging into the subdued electric throbbing, sweeping textures and absolutely amazing vocal treatment/ of 'Harmony'. It is this track which both introduces and likewise solidifies the overall vibe of the LP (being heavily controlled rather than an all out blistering attack). Essentially this album opts for domination through subversion when compared to G.O's previous use of sheer sonic violence. Smattering of vocals and voice snippets are inter spread throughout the factory stompings, sinister drones and general clatter giving a quite old school feel to the sound production creating some supreme industrial noise/ power electronics. Each of the 10 tracks establish a different sound early on, then explore minor variations with the sound treatments, loops, vocals, voice samples etc throughout. A nice touch to the LP is a locked grove finishing each side to ensure the tracks will never finish either with looped vitriolic laughter or factory clatter depending on the side. If the LP and packaging were not enough, a bonus CD is included: a re-release of the 36 minute 'Leichenlinie' LP. Taken from a much earlier period of G.O's power electronics career the sound is more of an all out aural assault just to boil the blood a little in the wake on the subdued chaos of the LP (including the classic cut 'Klaus Barbie'). Lastly I'm not sure why there is a point in reviewing a release such as this (as already the 1750 copies are long sold out) other than to spite those who were too slow in ordering this and to egg on the ensuring bidding wars that will occur as unscrupulous record collectors start auctioning off their multiple copies. Expect to have to sell a kidney if you find one of these for sale....

This Gentle Flow (Aus) "This Cage" MCD 1999 Left as in Sinister
Here we have a solo group of one Valerious Calocerinos, also the founder and operator of the label on which this is released. Distant rain and thunder, slow fuzzed out guitar and grandiose keys waiver before kicking full swing into the quick paced gothic rock of the title track. The bridging elements and a certain style of song-writing draw some comparison to some the more experimental black metal bands (particularly Arcturus), however it is the drum machine and mid-ranged vocals that position this

squarely within the gothic realm (although thankfully not being derivative of this scene). Strange clangings, wails, programmed beat elements and choir generated keys give a certain gothic ritual element, prior to a huge monster industrial riff making its appearance - but heaven forbid that things are straight forward from here! Vocals have a weird treatment, keyboard layers become more prominent and generally tunes, vocals, riffs, noises etc tangent off to do there own thing generally under the banner of the track ('punctured vein') but somehow remaining relevant to the overall direction. The prominent programmed bass and beats of 'Laugh' probably work the least favourably in my eyes, but even as the most structured piece I feel is the most experimental in melding elements into a whole. 'Confused (just still)' is something of a gothic Mr Bungle number, with background sampled carnival music and simply weird and quirky compositional writing of mid paced darkly gothic tunes, heaped with plenty of down vibed keys and up tempo beats. I found this quite an intriguing listen given these are not musical territories I often frequent, particularly due to the surreal elements evoked through the more experimental tune writing.

Golden Dawn (USA) "L.V.X" CD 1996 Suffering Clown

This CD contains the actual rituals used by the Order of the Golden Dawn partially set to music (likewise the 20-page booklet cover includes the full written instructions of the said rituals). To start the disc off, 'The Temple' is independent of the later ritual side of things, and sets out to describe the history and dynamics of the Golden Dawn organization via a plodding gothic rock type musical foundation. The auras evoked on the seven ritual movements are obviously heavily ritualised due to the chimes, vocal chants and reading of written passages, but it the inclusion of keyboard layers, guitars, bass and programmed beats that removes it from being simply a ritual recording. The stylistic sound of the music, with its intricate guitar work, classical synth lines and slow rigid beat programming, adheres to a gothic rock framework, but does so in an understated way that prevents it from becoming pretentious (as this style can often be). The fifth track, 'Spirit (Part 2)', is quite unusual in its use of a funky bass line and straightforward rock chorus which in my opinion jars unfavourably against the atmospheres generated up to that point, but luckily the CD does redeem itself on the beautifully sorrowful next track 'The Ritual of the Rose Cross'. Musically speaking this is good, and made all the more interesting due to the magical and ritual implications.

Gridlock (USA) "5.25" CD 1999 Pendgragon

There are no rules, no clear-cut guidelines, when it comes to Gridlock. Not one to cater to the specific ideals or dynamics of industrial (the genre/label usually associated with them), the duo of Cadoo and Mike Wells have always pushed away from the expected constrictions, into a place uniquely their own. 5.25 collects rare, live and remixed tracks from the ever-mutating electronicians, materiel that spans their whole creative existence as Gridlock. The music Gridlock creates is distinguished by pristine, hope-ravaged synthwork and snarling, stuttering ratchet, machinery infused percussive interjections. Tracks like 'Halo,' and the live version of 'Burn,' utilize an incendiary feedback whine as a creative tool, assisting with metal pipe clanking percussion that spits bolts in rapid fire succession, while Cadoo's gritty, screaming whisper vocals seem reminiscent of one who regularly gargles steel wool. But the already sparse vocals have been pushed even further by the wayside on more recent endeavors. The title track is a spastic percussive excursion, kinetic to the nth, that defies the laws of gravity as it scampers over extraterrestrial terrain, accentuated by looming bass structures that rise above the frozen craters. Just excellent! 'Edit 364' crisply illuminates remote cosmic frontiers, offset by some corrosive percussion that rips and snorts in restrained junctures, as if speaking an as yet undefined language. 'Program 41' emits squiggly, lubricated electronics that slither upon the surface of another sonically visualized extraterrestrial topography. This strange, beautiful music highlights the exquisite transformation in progress. It's a long stretch from the earliest incarnations, including the electro-fied corruption of Berlin's 'Metro,' included here for kicks. A very worthy release that showcases Gridlock's evolution from electro-industrial into dark sonicscape into…(?)…via music that continually moves beyond…—JC Smith

Gruntsplatter (USA) "The Death Fires" CD 2000 Crowd Control Activities

Watching this group's evolution from the early split CD releases has been an intriguing and rewarding endeavor when considering the quality of this debut full length CD. Promise was definitely shown on the early split CD's, further enhanced with the 7" of last year, now amalgamating all experience in a coercive whole, to create an album that I knew they would always produce. While some of the earlier recordings were slightly marred by elements of lo-fi and muffled production, the digitized medium of this release has brought everything to the fore, and was mastered impeccably by one Thomas Dimuzio. While the tones of many of the noise layers are reasonably harsh and scathing, the production has purposefully blunted the razor edge to create a deceptively ambient air - otherwise described as 'noise ambient'. Seething furnace fumes permeate 'Black Toothed Morality' along with a sparse keyboard tune, introducing a new and very positive element into the Gruntsplatter sound. Probing high pitched squeals introduce 'Access the Blood' and waver in view throughout while crunchy sub-base textures grind away at the flesh of your inner ear. The bone-grinding machinery is certainly cranked into full swing for 'Against the Dying of the Light', mixing the chaotic with a system of repetition. Crispy static loops and speaker imploding bass work particularly well in storming unison on 'Fearbitter'as elements are added and subtracted from the mix at various points, As spacious and drawn out 'Struggling to Breath' is, it still contains a feeling of finite audile space, gradually closing in and engulfing the room in heavy ashen air. With the forcefulness of many of the preceding tracks, the minimalist construction of 'Below the Stones' provides an opportunity for a more detailed exploration of textural subtlety (including mournful drawn-out chants), ensuring this is one of my favourite pieces on the disc. Comparisons could be made to the greats of the death industrial genre such as Brighter Death Now (such as the drawn out moments on the Great Death series); yet while BDN has a very European sound, I feel that Gruntsplatter has a very American flavour, matching up with the sounds being explored in different formats by a variety of US groups. In this increasingly recognized US scene Gruntsplatter have created a niche in exploring sounds that generate fiery and suffocating mental imagery. Finally the cover art matches the atmosphere perfectly, in that text and images are melded into a dark background, akin to being covered in black soot and ash.

Hazard (Swe) " Field/Bridge - Wood" LP/CD set 2000 Ash International (R.I.P)

Benny Neilsen from the inception of his Hazard project has forged ahead with creating increasingly more subdued and experimental soundscapes, becoming more minimal with the previous album and likewise this release. However, the arctic cold feeling of 'North' is not so evident here, where one is instead exposed to an enveloping yet sterile digital warmth. For those not familiar, the title could conjure up visions of someone simply taking field recording and presenting them as music, but this is rather taking an organic aura and bringing it to life through electronic means (whether or not the sounds once originated as field recordings). Interestingly the liner notes state that the final material was recorded outdoors in a Swedish forest (on a lap top I'm assuming) yet many sound samples have a certain 'urbanism' to them (the creaking of an old elevator on 'Location South' is a good example). 'Fibre Test', the first track on the CD, uses the repetition of high-pitched digital blips to gain somewhat of a rhythm, whilst the lower sound range rumbles with bass loaded intensity, and scraping processed textures that likewise enter and exist sporadically.   These elements of 'found' sounds, subtle tones, shifting textures, electronic digital cut ups categorise the tracks, placing variations of these in random and programmed patterns over a base of what are often drawn-out bass tones or idling machine-like drones (that occasionally hint at melody). Clutter and chaos versus order and composition: this release manages to work on both of these levels. 'Chords and Branches' is beyond amazing, containing a feeling of rising dread (a horrific archaic atmosphere in the heart of a track of cutting-edge electronic experimentation). The oceanic sonic waves of 'Pylons' are presented via mid-ranged wavering drones, hearkening back to the hazy atmospheres of the debut Hazard CD 'Lech', while the last CD track 'The Log Fire' is just that, a recording of the sonic intensity of fire, with rhythms of malfunctioning machinery thrown in for good effect. The two tracks on the LP take advantage of the longer format, presented two drawn out pieces - one each side. 'Field' takes the guise of the CD tracks slow subtle shifts of digital sound, that is gradually enveloped by drone elements (here they are more high-pitched than bass driven). Mid to late in the track the atmosphere morphs somewhat into far off storming rumbles mixed with sinister sounding scraping textures, the last section morphing again to warm electronic drones, rounded out with a locked groove. 'Bridge' a track of rising static, drones, and sonically crisp elements, is quite a forceful piece by virtue of the quick rotations of the vortex of sound, which at the same time makes for a more composed piece. The format/s in which this has been released is a nice touch, in that around 70 minutes of music are presented, yet halved between CD and LP, acting as a complete set and not just as one item with a bonus CD or LP. I guess this also breaks up the sound that each format flows to its conclusion quite quickly. With simple slip sleeve for both CD and LP, the images are becoming a trademark of Touch and Ash International (R.I.P) releases, detailing forest and wood imagery taken by Jon Wozencroft. This is another fantastic example of digital/organic abstraction that combines cutting-edge studio experimentation with enough old school industrial sentiments to keep me very happy.

Heid (Swe) "Arktogäa" CD 2000 Malignant Records
I had been waiting quite some time to hear this group as I unfortunately missed out on getting a copy of their limited debut CD. From the positive words been spoken about the group, this, their second CD has not disappointed one iota. In amongst all the archaic atmospheres of slow shifting symphonic layers, distant chanted vocals etc, sits more abrasive sonics and programmed ritual percussive textures of a more modern sounding origin. The inherent skill in Heid's work is that these are blended perfectly together, neither element ever feeling out of place. Likewise it seems that the sounds coming from CMI in the early 90's have been given a full working over with a heavy dose of evolution and originality. Seven untitled tracks of varying length are showcased, resulting in an overall play time of just under 45 minutes. Track 2 is a wonderfully deep piece of classically tinged dark ambience - low bass tones emphasizing depth, with the other sparse layers of vocals, drones and keys creating the slow evolving vibe that is concluded with a slow sorrowful piano tune. A foggy haze permeates all aspects of track 3, (yet this could be said of much of the CD's atmosphere) being reliant on noise and scattered sound as it basis rather than any minimalist tune. Mid paced yet sparse martial beats and an unusually treated vocal sample introduce track 5, the backing tune gradually gaining momentum. The beats sinking into oblivion further allows the slow tunes to take over mid way through. As a conclusion piece track seven contains elements of distant chiming bells, deep bass laden atmospheres and minimalist classical movement to great effect (some middle eastern samples are also infused into the background). Despite having provided some descriptions of individual track, each piece is placed into its inherent whole, creating a fluid movement throughout the complete album with one piece flowing perfectly onto the next, essentially creating one piece of music. The cover is another element that deserves a mention, with the inlay being three sepia toned transparent inserts, the jewel case further provided with a black card slipsleeve. This is a stunning introduction to the group and will now have me feverishly searching out their debut.

Herbst9 (Ger) "From a Dark Chasm Below" CD 2000 Loki Foundation
Herbst9 create complex, textural ambience, consisting of layer upon layer of kinetic, luminous tones and ephemeral nuances of time, sounding not unlike label-mates Inade, though with a completely different agenda. Born in the destitute fringes and moist jungles of Asia, Herbst9 sail the tenacious undercurrent of past indiscretions and potential future travesties (waiting, patiently waiting...), homing in on the timbres of the forgotten, erased from memory, horrors of humanity. 'Ab Ovo' sets the rickety stage, upon which a radiant ambience glowers, augmented with the brushed with solitude intonations of monks, and slivers of coarse memory. The ambience throughout seems leery of human allegiance, though the inhuman impressions are still built on a purely human foundation (a Pandora's Box of sonic possibilities) as layers are melded into, folded over, and unraveled within, other layers. 'The Snake Of Saigon' is an anxious excursion littered with war-like nuances, a miasma of surrounding sonic elements in subtle communion—mournful monks, a plucked instrument that sounds like a banjo but is most certainly some similar Asian instrument—dark rumblings that slither and, eventually, a helicopter that circles in the distance. The remnants of devious, inhuman deeds that could only have been constructed by the human monster itself, linger throughout. 'Melting Spheres' scatters unknown winged monstrosities (a limbic regression to the time of pterodactyls?) before a pensive drone and the rising pulse of anxiety dominate. A demonstrative yell opens 'In The Vein Of Purusa,' a yell that inspires dread and pause for concern as the rain drenched ambience is sliced by a knife that caresses bone strings, trace animals (the jungle looms ever near), and a predatory machinery loop. Odd classical underpinnings add another layer to the strange design, the track, as with all of the tracks on this amazing CD, subtly metamorphic in construction, inherently restless. Herbst9 construct sonic rituals gleaned from the ruins of minds scraped hollow and left to decay, minds privy to evil deeds and the existence of such evil deeds made concrete. On the brilliant LOKI label, reason enough to check this out. -JC Smith (Reprinted by permission from Side-Line magazine: www.side-line.com)

Howden/ Wakeford (Eng) "Three Nine" CD 2000 Tursa (Via World Serpent Distribution)
Having been introduced to this collaborative project on the compilation "On the Brink of Infinity", I was quite looking forward to this. Standing by my summation of their track on the compilation (I reviewed their track by stating the composition was somewhere between an actual song and piece of ambience) this album plays out in a similar fashion. Ambient folk noir perhaps? Segmented acoustic guitars, plucked bass, flowing female vocalizations, sparse programmed textures, piano and violin segments, sampled and treated vocals etc make up the myriad of elements. Yet even in most part containing relative sparseness, selected segments of tracks burst into quite composed urgency, certainly resulted in obvious contradictions. Likewise from the way the overall flow of the album pans out, one would guess that the majority of elements were recorded separately and painstakingly collated into the finished pieces in the studio. Referencing the background of the work the bio states that this album is dedicated to the third and ninth runes with musical time signatures and patterns being derived from the sum of associated equations. Even then with the main nine tracks, we are treated to the prior mentioned compilation track, which is in fact derived from the fragments of nine main compositions (with the then additional bonus instrumental version clocking in at - you guessed it 9 minutes!). Regardless of these calculated nuisances of music composition the end result is an impressive debut album of dark nostalgic feel from two renowned artists.

H.P.P. (Ita) "Horse Penis Pants" CD 2000 Possessive Blindfold
H.P.P. (Horse Penis Pants-now there's a name for you!) is Maurizio Landini, who also does time with (the brilliant!) I Burn. Where I Burn specialize in incinerator ambience sonicscapes, H.P.P. creates looped rhythmic discharges through percussive means, as well as clipped noise and static overload. 'Re-Education' entwines piercing needles into the eardrum while hiccuping belches of condensed distortion and pummelling percussion joist for dominance. 'Scarweld' solders bubbling, white hot noise onto a stuttering rhythmic loop; as the track progresses, abrupt squeals are melted into the mix. 'Private Play' gets positively electronic, a fusion of incessant beats with quirky electronic impulses, sounds that skitter and tumble with a purpose; the track is constructed in shifting segments, vaguely reminding me of the excellent Shock Front CD from Converter, circa 1999. 'Labia Engine' spastically grinds, with punishing consistency, before the racing corpuscles fill the genitalia to an aching arousal, ending with slowly teasing, pre-orgasmic sludge pacing that never reaches orgasm. Furiously beat-splattered and slathered in noise! -JC Smith

I-Burn (Ita) "Third Degree Burns Ambience" 1999, Old Europa Café
I-Burn's second album is a collection of ten tracks in the style and sound that was hinted at on the previous 'Ipertermia' 10". Likewise with the tracks playing out over longer segments than those on the debut, the pieces having become more fluid, enabling them to traverse additional territory within their timeframes, thus making for a much evolved and improved sound. Deep subterranean textures, vast glacial soundscapes, metallic clatter, static induced bursts of noise are just some of the sound elements that are collated, mixed and infused into these mind-altering offerings. Brooding yet harsh, sinister yet atmospheric – the tracks play out in various such configurations, creating an aura of desolation and isolation due to the shear barrenness of any organic sounds. To my mind's eye, the atmospheres generated on these tracks represent less the flesh-burning qualities of searing heat than the infliction of pain via severe low glacial temperatures (or even that of dried ice). What is a little frostbite when you get to hear a CD such as this?! Recommended

Ickytrip (USA) "Ickytrip" CD 1999 Ickytrip
Without beating around the point, it is a bit hard for me to review this objectively since straight-off-the-keyboard programming sound simply leaves me cold. This is just too synthesized, particularly in relation to the drum beats and sequences. By all accounts there is no question that the individual behind this can compose and write music, it is just the means by which it has been recorded that I cannot seem to overcome. In justification the synthetic sounds alone are not really the problem, rather the rigidness of the up-tempo factory preset drum machine beats and the lack of any grittier background sounds. While most dark ambient/ neo classical/ industrial artists have no other option but to use keyboards and programming it is often what background elements and layering techniques that are utilised that makes all the difference in smoothing out the sharpness of synthetic textures and likewise assists in achieving a personalized sound. The complaint about factory preset sounds again comes into contention. The bio references this as 'classical composition with modern technology to create orchestral music that resembles a cinematic soundtrack', which I guess is OK to a point; yet, on the other hand, simply add some guitars and a morose vocalist and you really have mid-paced gothic fare. Again my dislike for gothic music or gothically-derived sounds surfaces, but maybe in its favour gothic fans would go nuts over this as a darkwave type release. Sorry, this just does not float my boat.

Ildfrost (Nor) "You'll Never Sparkle in Hell" CD 2000 Fluttering Dragon Records
My, my, look at what the passage of time has offered up for us on the new Ildfrost release! Gone are sweeping and depressive neo-classical hymns of "Natanael", with Ildfrost now veering towards intelligent tribal/neo-classical tinged electronica. Sound like an unusual mix? Well, it's not at all when you listen to this. Modernity has played quite a large role in the updated and 'current' sounding production, but after getting over the initial change in sound the Ildfrost structure is still quite evident. A good example is the dark throbbing classical hymn that is 'Shitspinner', taking on a new studio sound aesthetic by mixing it up with sampled tribal vocals that have in turn influenced the underlying tribal beat. Referencing a more standard electronica sound, 'Novadrops' approaches a sound not unlike what Atomine Elektrine produce with a chilled out new age type beat oriented atmosphere. Dark echoed richness signifies the sound of the tribal percussion of 'Exhalation', with sepulchral voices summoning the unknown (and ultimately succeeding) as the atmosphere becomes increasingly tense with an air of shrill orchestral dread. Sitting over what sounds like a raging firestorm, the introspective piano/xylophone tune of 'Auxiliaries' rises steadily to be the main element (with radio voices cutting in and out occasionally), capturing some of the best auras of the "Natanael" album via quite a different sound direction. On the other hand, 'Fetish of the Hour' is a fantastic track of a dark orchestral/choral aura driven constantly onward by a framework of mid-paced pulsating electronica. Sweeping cinematic precision is showcased on 'Past is no Choral Moon', containing what could easily be described as progressive classical (if that is even a term) where 'Effete Vocabulary of Summer' is another stunning example of a heavy, darkly brooding slab of beat-laden electronica, and acting as the last album track prior to the short outro 'Done'. While years may pass and musical directions and interests may change, Ilfrost shows they are all the stronger for it.

Imminent (Bel)/ Synapscape (Ger) "Screenwalking" CDEP 2000 Ant-Zen
Not having any knowledge of Synapscape's previous works I guess I can only review this from the Imminent perspective, likewise with the 'Starvation' tag having been dropped from 'Imminent', there might have been the perception that an aim was being made to a more commercial and accessible sound. In reality any notion of this is quickly dispensed with the powerhouse beat-n-noise-fest served up. Whip lashing beat structures explode in crystalline static bursts, leaving barely any room for the trademark moody background layers. And as intense listen as the 'Nord' CD was this effort makes it seem like an album of candy floss coated pop tunes. The flurry of electronic beats are relentless, surging and attacking from multitudes of angles, the remaining soundscape encompassing barbs of flesh scrapping static and noise. The tracks are akin to a machine careening out of control being overloaded with pure sonic power, which actually in part would make this music difficult to groove to given the rigidity of it. The track 'Warc' differs slightly by not containing any beat structure but with a tonal soundscape backing and fractured electronic blips and bursts of frequency. The following piece 'Uatio' moves closer to the noise and groove sounds of the 'Nord' CD, with 'Aigre' the final piece being an elongated slab of technoise beats and static. As the promo for this CD went "Imminent Starvation is dead...long live Imminent". Well while your there singing praise of them please bring on the next full length so when can hear just what Imminent have become in an individual setting!!

Inade (Ger) "Burning Flesh" CD 2000 Loki Foundation
While I wait extremely impatiently for a new full length Inade album, I could not have been happier to hear that their debut cassette was being re-released with bonus tracks. With the original cassette long out of print this was a great opportunity for me to get acquainted with the formative compositions of the group. Of the 8 tracks originally on the 'Burning Flesh' tape, these come into shorter song formats with less flow overall, concentrating on the death industrial/death ambient vibe of each piece. Remembering reading an earlier review of the 'Burning Flesh' tracks, a comparison was made to the likes of Archon Satani, which I never quite saw in their later releases but can now see why that comparison was made. Windy mid to high end drone textures, sampled crowd cheering and manipulated/ echoed church bells encompass 'Overtune Bells', while with its dredging drones, distant factory clatter, chant-like sound layers and slow moving dynamics, 'Shattered Bones' brings to mind the classic Swedish sound of death ambience which permeated many groups in the early 90s. 'The Coming of the Black Legions' is the first storming track of intensely ominous slow beats, and fractures electronic layers to a create rhythmic and anthemic piece. Other standouts come with the title track in the form of the abrasive yet subdued drone clatter, including some indecipherable vocal samples. The last track of the 'Burning Flesh' set comes with the gargantuan cyclic and spacious drones of 'Through the Gates of Death', a perfect track to complement the visuals of massive stone statutes printed on the disc. Moving on to the bonus tracks, there is a marked change in style and sound from the earlier tracks to the later. While great at creating good solid death industrial sounds on earlier material (such as the aforementioned 'Burning Flesh' tracks and on 'The Flood of White Light' 10"), in my mind Inade really hit that special `something' when they started to focus on mystic, occultist, ritualized sounds. Even within this guise of such inspiration the group has still managed to create diversity of material such as fantastic spacious drone works ('Aldebaran' CD), to more sinister sub orchestral sounds ('v.i.t.r.i.o.l' 7"). This clear change in sound and direction is partially evident at the conclusion of the 'Burning Flesh' tracks (composed in 1993) to the 'Genius Loci' tracks (composed throughout 1994-1998. Even the bonus inclusion of 'Tat Twam Asi' (formerly of "The Book of Shadowz" compilation LP) shows this brilliant massive occultism aura that Inade have since gone on to master. 'Genius Loci Pt. 1' intermixes clanging church bells, subterranean bass textures and the odd vocal chant that rises to prominence late in the piece. 'Pt. 2' with ritual wind instruments and slow tribal beat shows exactly where Inade broke away from emulating a sound to creating something all their own. Distant vocals add to the tense atmospheres, less machine and factory sounding, rather encapsulating an aura of a time long forgotten. Delayed, slowed and manipulated, the once Gregorian chants on 'Pt. 3' still hold their inherent religious flavour, while the backing of slow tribal beats provides some focus and direction. Whilst still slow, `Pt. 4' ups the dynamics in an urgent styling of ritualistic chants and odd percussion, likewise with increased dimensions of sound layers. Limited to a mere 500 copies, this is a brilliant documentation of the progression of one of the most important groups of recent years.

Inade (Ger) "Quartered Void" 7" EP 2000 Membrum Debile Propaganda
Slowly rising out of the glacial void, slow drones and scattered pulses mark the introduction of this two-track picture disc. 'Crackling Void' is assisted in its namesake via the vinyl format - slow drawn-out shimmering movements being the stylistic approach. 'Quartered Conclusion' is more singular in direction, that brings to mind their 10" EP 'The Flood of White Light'. The cyclic rotation of sound makes it more active and forceful than the first, the assaulting and fluctuating sonics increasing tension immensely. Given these tracks are a few years old (yet only recently released) I would place the sound of this in the evolutionary period where Inade were moving from death industrial sounds and towards the more expansive and spacious territory explored on the "Aldebaran" CD. In regard to the picture disc format and with the images being of a manipulated eye, could this be potentially referencing the void of the mind's eye? Regardless, all I can say in passing is that too much Inade is never enough!

In Death's Throes (USA) "Infernal Deities Transcending" CD 2000 Live Bait Recording Foundation
Hellish, looped vocal belches climb the limestone walls of the Abyss during the opening sonic aberration, 'War,' riding on the back of metallic scorpions as the din scrambles toward the surface. Dark priests evoke demonic uprisings, meshing (and mashing) the Black Occult aspirations into the ground bone and blood soaked machinery of singed ambience that is In Death's Throes. It seems all Hell is about to be unleashed. This leads into the unnatural cadences of 'Civil Disobedience,' dragging the listener not into sunlight, but an aborted annex just below the surface...an annex of Hell decorated with esoteric tones, the cries and whispers of sounds in torment, and hallucinogenic madness. This is the stuff of nightmares, of those whose eyes have been sutured shut, and there is no light, no awakening revelation bent on releasing them from the grim clutches of such suffocating, condemning darkness. In Death's Throes are Brian Sutter (God's Pets and Jinnseraph) and Stephen Petrus (Murderous Vision, Umbra, head of the Live Bait Recording Foundation label, plus more?). They create multi-layered sheets of sound guaranteed to mess with one's perception of reality by concretizing the existence of Hell, of a pitch-black netherworld that teems with a rabid urgency, with a frothing desire, to infiltrate the confines of your nice, normal world. Dull, yawningly weary loops are the foundation of 'In Celebration II (The Port),' sprinkled with more vocals culled from the blackest regions of creation, subtly espousing sinister sonic intentions. The epic 'Where God Is...' is triggered by a depraved chorus which douses the listener in a swirling cesspool of despondent tones and scratchy cadences. The sensation while listening to this track is palpable, flowing from my speakers, enveloping me in dread. Further in, the track descends into an even more subcutaneous realm, full of volatile, cranium-eroding winds streaming from a crumbling, cavernous (hungry) maw. The sound manipulation and inhuman vocal processing throughout inspires discomfort in the listener, the unnerving ambience at times reminiscent of the work of the great Schloss Tegal (the ultimate compliment!). Evil! —JC Smith

IRM (Swe) "The Red Album" LP 1999 Cold Meat Industry
IRM is a flag bearer of the next generation of sound coming from the CMI camp, with their debut LP being unleashed in a pressing of 700 copies. This full length has arisen after thier introduction to the world with their two tracks on the "Estheticks of Cruelty" compilation (incidentally both 'Powerdrill' and 'Martyr 2000' are featured here among the 7 tracks). Classy, pulverising and cleansing power electronics is what we have here, very much rooted in the tradition set down by the likes of Anezephalia, Genocide Organ, Con-Dom, etc. With constant pounding machinery, flesh-searing electronics and a bludgeoning, slightly flanged vocal attack, I would say that IRM are not really forging into new territory, but when generated with such fantastic conviction and clarity of sound production, there are no complaints from this quarter. Regarding my personal tastes, the more unstructured and improvised a power electronic track, the less engaging I find it overall. However IRM have found a prefect balance between chaotic aggression and clear structure and direction, as is displayed on the brooding yet concrete slab solid track 'Unconscious'. Likewise 'Soulcleaner' (the last track on side A), is an absolutely stunning piece with massive and bludgeoning machine gun rhythms, hefty flanged vocal attack and general extremities of mid ranged electronics. The later track 'Katharsis' opts for a part droning, mostly storming framework of sweeping static and cascading waves of searing distortion, creating a cleansing (instrumental) baptism of sound. A similarly slow sweeping structure follows on into the final track 'R.S'; yet here the returning vocals are a fantastic counterpart due the sheer anger and desperation of delivery, enhanced via echo and flanged effects. As alluded in the title of the album I would have to say that this is the plainest cover that Karmanik has ever designed; yet it is still classily presented in all its simplicity. Although somewhat on the short side this is certainly an album that should be in every power electronic enthusiasts' collection.

Iron Justice (Swe) "Tell Me" 7" EP 1999 Cold Meat Industry
Iron Justice, another representative of the new guard of Swedish power electronics groups, present this limited 7" in an 8-page booklet sleeve, embellished with imagery of questionable intent and phrases such as *"This is our truth... now tell us yours! The existing edifice is rotten. We need some new foundations..."* (just to ensure that things are politically obscure). Despite the pulverizing, grinding textures vocal sample smatterings and general noise mayhem of 'Tell Me', this track is actually reasonably subdued. The pace is mid to slow, managing to be at once harsh and atmospheric simultaneously (yet the intensity does increase toward the end of the piece). When the vocals are introduced, they are heavily flanged and echoed, adding that nice urgent flavour. 'Sons and Daughter's' of side B has a more high end obliterated noise attack, particularly the vocals moving from the rantings of the previous piece to all out psychotic yelling. Screamed wails of distortion and feed back give no respite, creating a track of feverous sonic punishment. This is good power electronics that by no means reaches outside of the boundaries set down by the pioneers (Con-Dom, the Grey Wolves, Genocide Organ, etc.) but that will please most fans of this genre.

Iron Justice (Swe) "Manufacture Of Consent" LP 2000 Cold Meat Industry
Iron Justice specializes in politically infused power electronics whose white noise regime is the very definition of 'harsh' in all its contaminated glory. Opening with the title track, vocal samples bow before the gurgling, slobbering and spitting, squeal infested noise that annihilates the proceedings. Echoed vocals rage underneath, but it's the torrential onslaught above that mangles the audio receptors. Just brutal...and it's only beginning. An impatient arm of feedback is injected with a rusty needle of free-based rage during the clattering cacophony of 'The Worlds Sole Hygiene.' Writhing, wriggling worms of wet processed noise pour from the viscous sonic upheaval that is 'Conspiracy Intl.' A voice flails underneath, amidst static samples and the insurmountable sonic discord. The relentless assault continues on side two with 'Mutual Terrorism,' an undiluted exercise in whip slashing audio terror as sheets of corrosive noise are beaten, lashed and electrocuted while the ever-present vocals bark from underneath the ragged din. 'Mother To Us All' juggles a variety of sharp implements (knives, scalpels) before said implements are utilized to puncture and corrupt in conjunction with a throbbing machinery loop. 'Towards The Sun' dissects the squirming body of strapped down but still alive white noise amidst a deluge of feedback and more frenzied vocal utterances. Manufacture Of Consent is a merciless, streamlined corruption of sound that is mind-numbingly (you guessed it) harsh. Comes on lovely, thick white vinyl and includes an assortment of postcards. -JC Smith

Kelm (Ger) "Blue Mesk" CD 2000 Welt am Draht
With this duo working under the guise of Kelm, one of individuals behind this might already be known to some from his workings in projects such as Skalp and Kenotaph (both of which had releases out on Tesco and Functional respectively). Anyway, in regard to this project the first track is a whopping 34 minutes, which makes for quite a lengthy introduction! Dualities of texture are evident here, this track working on two levels: one of lower death ambient drone styling, the other on higher end sonic experimentations akin to Daniel Menche's subdued works. Selected textures hint at rhythms when also sporadically mixed with random-esque sounds and scraping elements, but overall things are firmly entrenched in the slow evolution camp. Dense catatonic beats in various coagulated configurations weave throughout the middle segment and continue to lurk throughout until close to the 29 minute mark, where the home stretch of sub bass textures are explored. More easily digestible than the mouthful of the first, the second track is an exploration of mid bass rhythmic distortion and insectile sounds, the third of furnace blasts, machinery drones and fractures electronics which reminds me of a very noisy version of Hazard's new sound explorations. Alien vocalisations, weird textures and rhythms, static bursts and a underlying sub and mid, electronic and bass drones abound on track 4, making for an eclectic piece or new school 'Mego' styled sounds. The split level of sound again surfaces on track 5 with deep sub bass textures, liquidous/electronic mid ranged elements mixed with what sounds like scattered field recordings sampled from within a disused factory. Overall this track lacks that certain something - not quite sure what... To close the set the far off thunderous sounds and signal bleeps of track 6 swing into chaotic but slightly rhythmic territory, disembodied voices appearing sporadically. Although it took me a few listens to warm to this release (mostly due to collecting my overall impressions of the variance of sounds) my thoughts have solidified in favour of appreciation and subsequent praise for these dark experimental sonics.

Klangstabil (Ger) "Sprite Storage Format" LP 2000 Ant-Zen
With the concept of this release revolving around tracks created from a Gameboy as the main sound source, you are assured an unusual listen. An obvious hint of cheesy

computer game sounds is unavoidable, but these elements are actually cut and looped into patterns and sequences that create credible sounding tracks. Mostly chugging computer glitches and segments are looped into discernible format which seem to hold for most of the tracks' lengths. 'Raw Stripping' is less recognizable as being generated from computer game music, a sinister electronic track of malfunctioning software origin. Complexities of rhythms and beats gradually structure themselves around the track's core making for quite a noisy, static-riddled piece. What could only be a Mario Boys type tune is looped on 'Symmetrical Reduction' that creates quite a quirky groove within the repetitive choppy static beats. More obvious Gameboy looped tunes are found on 'Japanese Roms', here relying less on beat structures other than straight programmed noises. The Gameboy inspiration goes even a step further in regards to packaging, with group photos taken and printed via a Gameboy camera and printer and with the shape and clear insert of the slip sleeve cover likewise looking like an actual Gameboy. I will admit that I initially bought this due to the gimmick factor (and wanting to hear what such a project would sound like), yet overall this is a surprisingly compelling listen.

Klood (Fra) "Gag - Hamin" 7"EP 1999 Drone Records
Sticking to the formula of a lot of Drone titles, this is yet another take on slow morphing drone sounds. 'Eagla' on side A has full bodied analogue synth lines that compose sparse tunes and in turn create bleak visions of barren arctic wastelands. Sounds seep out in every direction towards the distant horizon giving a spatial resonance to the minimalist sound and movement of the tracks. 'Juste de Passage' on side B has a sound more closely associated with guitar treatments and textures, and is a more active piece of sound exploration. Deep echoed sounds and distortion layers rise and fall throughout, with mid-ranged notes playing a barely composed tune (a subdued Contrastate could be a comparison here). Overall both tracks have barren somberness to them which is certainly to my liking. On the aesthetic front, it's a pity that this is pressed into ugly pink vinyl.

La Maison Moderne (Aut) "Day after Day" MCD HuaRuk/WKN (via Tesco Organisation)
My, my, what will hardened industrial fans think of Albin Julius of Der Blutharsch trying his hand at a dance music project? Not much I'm sure, but here it is for us to marvel and/ or scratch our craniums at. Though the opening track 'Spiel Suber' presents itself as up-tempo and playful, it still infuses distant air raid sirens, sampled German vocal segments and bomb explosions that would not be out of place on a Der Blurharsch track. Up-tempo yet brooding, the cyclica; noises/programmed tunes and constant mid-paced beat of 'Welcome to Paradise' contains more vocal samples and even real vocals, again akin to what has been presented by Der Blutharsch. Although still up-tempo, 'Day after Day' has a much more dark trance-inducing edge, and the repeated vocal line is somewhat more prominent ('day after day . . . nothing changes'). Stomping beats and sub orchestral melody characterise 'Sea of Love and Hate', and while a late breaking programmed tune sees the track to its conclusion, it later reveals a fifth hidden track of mid-paced trip hop beats and celebratory type tunes - very pleasing indeed! Overall the sound is quite eclectic - both modern and retrospective at the same time. Hints of orchestral/martial themes are also infused deep within the backing, mainly due to the rigidity of selected pieces. and if you listen intently you can actually pick the trademark song structure and style of Albin. Flouting any 'rules' that people may want to impose on artists in regard to what they can and cannot do, Albin has created a very interesting and listenable take on the dance music genre.

Law (USA) "Vindication and Contempt" CD 2000 Triumvirate
Having put an LP out on Ant-Zen some years back and then falling seemingly quiet, Law have burst back into action with a succession of recent and forthcoming releases (the most recent being the "Wading Knee Deep in your Blood" LP reviewed last issue). Like that LP, 'Vindication and Contempt' was recorded in 1997 and has been only now released on the new label, Triumvirate, thus representing an extremely powerful release for a label's debut (and Mitchell Altum, the man behind Law, has a partnership in Triumvirate). Cascading sonic waves, pulsing (manipulated) beats and slow grinding electronics waver, prior to the 'hollow' introductory sermon of Mitchell - at first almost morose and regretful - later solidifying the anger of delivery as the barrage of electronics take hold. 'No One Will Find Them' takes a slightly different tangent in that a strummed acoustic guitar is sporadically fed into the sound collage along with more segments of Mitchell's multi-layered spoken vocals. Whilst some power electronics artists are content in having their vocals heavily treated and barely decipherable here Law has something to say and wants you to hear, contemplate and UNDERSTAND his message of contempt for the masses - let's just hope you're not among them.... Again another sound tangent is explored where 'A Place of Refuge, a Test of Commitment' utilises a repetitive string (synthetically generated) melody on one level with controlled electronics churning below. The shimmering tones of 'You Have No Choice' give an almost ambient feel, yet Law would never choose to be that subtle, ensuring the lurking harsher (controlled) tones are constantly threatening dissent (which occurs in a partly recognisable guitar layer). Mitchell really demonstrates his understanding and control of suspense throughout this track, effortlessly pushing the composition into many sections whilst constantly increasing intensity throughout the sordid journey. The massive orchestral strains of 'Locked Down Solid' are quickly obliterated in the noisiest track thus far, replete with chainsaw tones, rhythmic machine clatter, screeching tortured voices (really too many layers to reasonably count) amassed into a weighty multi (sonic) dimensional whole. The crystalline and more sharply defined textures of 'Unknown Command' and 'Fluctuating Tensile Strength' again expand Law's sound, running a fine line between relaxing ambient and sinister sounds, with the grating textures never far away. The album overall sees the elements of sound generally working on two tangents - those with swirling layers (almost organic in feel) and those layers of machine-like sound textures and programming, all processed and expertly combined to created the stunning final result. In part some of the tones and structure remind me of an early to mid 90s project Allegory Chapel Ltd. (who seem to have all but disappeared) or otherwise akin to Stratvm Terror; yet these comparisons give only a marginal indication of what to expect, as essentially Law has too many defining characteristics of its own. Beyond recommended.

LeftHandedDecision (USA) "Instinct and Emotion" 2000 Crionic Mind
This is a disc which demands focussed listening throughout, which I guess is not a difficult task when considering how punishing this is! 'Innate Perception' introduces the disc with sonic earthquake tones, which seem to have been mixed with sinister intent to destroy speakers before the disc goes even close to being played out (I think this quality may have a little something to do with Phil Easter being behind the mastering desk). For the most part there is a mid-ranged level of static going on here, but the pure brute force comes with the grinding sub bass tones that can be felt vibrating your internal organs. Although still very chaotic like what preceded it, 'Self Restraint' has a slower brooding edge and with a few sweeping noises tends to remind me of a much noisier Stratvm Terror. With tracks 1 through 6 playing out between 36 seconds to just under 5 minutes each, track 7 ('Isopraxism') arrives at a whopping 37 minutes! Starting with what is comparatively quiet (for this album, anyway) grinding electronic feedback squirms over a subsonic underbelly, moving slowly toward slow grating territory that just continues to multiply in force and density. There appear to be vocals and vocal samples somewhere in there, but they are just too mangled to comprehend what is being conveyed. The direction of the track (if you could even call it a direction) is to forge forever forward to increase the sonic intensity via any means possible, including some high-pitched ear drum assaults (although the concluding passage has mid ranged bass flow to it in a less harsh guise). Hidden tracks 9 through 23 all contain silence but strangely range in length from 4 to 24 seconds (hmmm...I'm not really sure what this is meant to signify); however the real hidden track comes at track 24. A scraping death industrial pulse introduces this as by far the quietest piece, prior to a full sampled song being fed into the sound destruction devices of the group, with sporadic pieces of the track rising to the surface of the maddening noise (as if watching a drowning man coming up for air). Without finishing there, a hidden track within a hidden track appears, which for some reason has mangled snippets of what sounds like two individuals having a conversation at a party with none other than MC Hammer playing in the background?! (I don't even want to know what was going on there...). Overall as much as the tracks presented do not sound formally composed, I'm sure there would have been at least some framework planning if this is in fact mostly improvised. In that I am reluctant to regularly play this at high volumes due to the speaker shredding qualities, I have tended to opt for a more restrained volume that has uncovered a certain relaxing ambience to the crispy sub sonic forcefulness of the wall of sound. Not quite pure noise and not quite power electronics, this has melded the harshest parts of both to create something quite unique that to my ears reflects a certain sound inherent in the American scene.

Francisco Lopez (Ita) "Untitled #90" CD 1999 Pre-Feed
With one 45 minute-long track Mr Lopez delivers another tonal soundscape work of field and natural type recordings. Shrill in its incessant high pitched-hum, the obvious sampling of insect sounds remains a constant throughout. Located deep underneath the insect sounds are low washes of waves lapping at the shore, which not surprisingly become more prominent throughout. Shifts in direction are minimal at best, and occur so slowly that they are barely noticed, with one segment of insect sounds traversing to the next. The lack of obvious treatment to any of the sound layers gives a realistic vibe and I would not be at all surprised if this was a pure environmental recording. At low volume the high pitched hum becomes almost a drone, but becomes increasingly piercing and invasive as volume is increased. For the type of sound work this is, it works best when put on in the background, allowing it to envelope you whilst you mind is focussed on something else. Surely not for collective listening, this is one way to mentally escape the city even if it can't be achieved physically.

Megaptera (Swe) "Electronic Underground" CD 2000 Slaughter Productions
Given that Peter Nystrom has decided to quit all further work by this group, "Electronic Underground" is a posthumous re-release of an early tape (unfortunately it does not seem that the scheduled DCD on CMI will ever eventuate). Being an older recording, the tracks do differ from the death industrial musings of "Disease" and "Curse of the Scarecrow"', yet they are still recognisable as Megaptera. While the other albums I am familiar with were full of sweeping atmospheres and packed with movie sample dialogue, these take a more singular approach in dynamics likewise mostly without the sampled voices. The cold pulse is still here, yet the predominant sweeping atmospheres mixed heavily with slow programmed beats/ rhythms have been replaced with more of a straightforward electronic character. The cold sterile atmospheres of the title track both in parts 1 and 2 set the scene of the album via sparse (slow to mid paced) percussion, static drones and mild noise. 'Metal Blaster' ups the level of noise, focussing on noisy drones and scattered metallic clatter for the most part, solidifying into a rumbling solid mass of sound. 'Megaptera Theme' beginning with the lapping of waves at a shore and the grunts and groans of nameless things sound as if it was recorded in inky blackness of an underground lake cavern. Moving on from the opening passage the track slowly meanders through segments of subdued drones and urgent static attacks. 'Hypnotic Fear' is particularly noteworthy with a distant furnace blast textures and pounding drums, while low drawn out keyboard notes gradually shift between tones. Midway though the beat becomes more complex (complete with cavernous echo) to create a very ritualized vibe. 'Last Machinery' is just that being the final piece on the disc, sounding much like an idling motor (soon to be empty of its fuel of flesh and bone) and could even be partly comparable to some of Brighter Death Now's pieces. At close to 60 minutes if you have been missing the ultra dark ritual industrial sounds that characterized the early 90's Swedish scene this should be an ample fix for your craving.

Daniel Menche (USA) "Scourge" 3" CD 1999 G.M.B.H.
Nice packaging on this item, with the 3" CD housed in a tiny gatefold containing imagery of bullet shattered glass. As for the sonics it contains a single 21 minute piece of trademark Menche sound manipulations - totally engulfing in all its electro acoustic power. Thick sonic slabs of sound are gradually erected around the ear drums with faint acoustics and subtle textures intermixed completing the desolate audial aura. The drawn out textures give the piece a slow evolving essence which eventually multiply into a tense segment of suspenseful cinematic tones. At around 10 minutes the former segment abruptly ceases for yet another mid range section to commence which is less subtle and more scattered overall (basically sounding like 'track 2'). Again the 'multiplier effect' is used building and removing layers of sound texture creating some truly contemplative moments. The last few minutes take on the guise of 'track 3' which sounds as if cockroaches are being slowly crushed between two plates of glass

- crispy and crackly indeed! While Mr Menche may have become more subtle overall with his recent sound-workings (in comparison to high much noisier earlier releases) in essence the results are becoming more stunning with each new release.

Militia (Bel) "Kingdom of our Lord" MCD 1999 Praxis Dr Bearmann
2 tracks at 21 minutes, this is not nearly as long as I would like, but then again at least it is a Militia item! Mixing almost discordant orchestral sentiments with rough and repetitive percussion, Militia manage to create uniquely heavy atmospherics on this MCD. Title track opening, the knife edge atmospheres fold and overlap prior to the incessant martial ritualistic beats, tribal chimes and general machinery clatter taking hold. Having an off kilter sway about the rhythm it also runs the knife edge...somewhere between hypnotic and rousing, with the ending passage engulfing all elements into a (subdued) almost power electronic tone. Second track ("Maschinezimmer") is even more percussive based and using quite hyper forceful beats and mixed background clatter. Likewise as with the first track the beat has a slightly groggy sway which is kept in check with an understated orchestral string segment. Though less atmospheric overall than the first track (and for me less engaging), it is still a good listen. Packaging on this will one infuriate those who only like jewel cases for easy storage.....housed in an A4 sizes fold out envelope involving imagery and text to complement the content of each track.

Militia (Bel) "The Black Flag Hoisted" 2xCD 2000 Tactical Recordings
This item has certainly been highly anticipated, being the official third release in the Militia 'Statement' Trilogy (New European Order 3xLP and Nature Revealed 2CD were the first two parts). Straight of the mark, the packaging does not disappoint with a large fold out card cover, larger insert poster, 2 CD's with individual slip cases and, to top the whole thing off, a medium sized black flag with the Militia logo printed at the centre. Truly amazing! For all the right-wing sounding implications of the packaging, titles, etc., the ideas displayed within the music and cover are actually from a 'leftist' perspective covering anarchist philosophies and the actions of the Animal Liberation Front, among others. The cover even includes a listing of the organisations, documents and statements that inspired them, and which obviously reflect their cause. The music itself falls somewhere between the N.E.O sub-orchestral sound and the rousing percussive style of the above reviewed MCD. CD1 of the set contains contributions from many artists, (both in the form of vocals and soundscapes) with some of the notables being Bastard Noise, Waste Matrix and Con-Dom. The first track of CD1 quickly moves from low rumblings to snare and tympani martial percussion and the trademark horn blasts. Here the scene is set, with the track diverting quickly into another low soundscape courtesy of Bastard Noise (with foreign ranted vocal), prior to third brilliant track kicking in - a massively heavy loop and metal percussive track. Repetitively hypnotic, this is Militia at their best. Jumping between low, brooding soundscapes and massive percussion, the group do both brilliantly, remaining solidly grounded and focussed at all times. The chugging/surging oil barrel rhythms and loops of 'Die Theorielosigkeit des Anarchismus' are superb with a new element of a piano line thrown in randomly. 'Light and Truth' contains a soaring organ loop, keyboard layers shrill trumpet blasts, hinting that something is approaching – that being the following track, 'In Mitten von Kamph', which after a slow voice text sample introduction, moves back into the aggressive percussion territory (yet this is subdued by Militia standards, set against a sorrowful orchestral melody). CD2 does not appear to contain the input of any guest artists, and is thus an even purer form of Militia than on the first disc. The sparse soundscapes and use of a didgeridoo on 'Liberecana Anarkista Kolonio' hints at the sound of the "Nature Revealed" CD, albeit with electronically-generated sounds, and the straightforward mid-paced percussion of 'Manifest' includes a proclamation (in full anarchist flair) of the clear agenda of Militia. The introductory tensile soundscape of 'Black Wolves Music' includesa further Militia statement, with the track again moving toward heavy percussion; yet here a standard drum kit is used along with bass to create a quick-moving piece that expands on their traditional sound. 'Anarchist Movement for Collective and Direct Action' again uses the drum kit and standard raucous percussion, with swaying background loop and didgeridoo. 'Final Statement' contains a brooding and shrill backing loop, percussion stripped back to tympani, oil barrel & clanging symbols. The vocals of this track take various words/ideas that are stated in a commanding style, and then immediately loop them backwards over themselves to intriguing result. One last other thing to add in regards to the music is that the last track on both CD's come courtesy of the Nas Dom-Slomsek Choir, with quite beautiful dual gender vocal harmonies. Both politically and musically heavy, this is simply a brilliantly conceived and realised work.

The Mirror Reveals (USA) "Frames of Teknicolor" CD 2000 Middle Pillar
Whatever Middle Pillar has released thus far has been a pleasure to listen to (be it the ethereal folk type bands of the more obscure dark ambient projects) with this, the fourth release, falling into the former category. The fragility of the female vocals (Kit Messick) set against the likewise fragile and subtle clean guitar work (James Babbo) contains a true essence of dark brooding beauty only further enhanced by the vast and mostly delicate musical backing (piano, keyboards and violin). Coming off the back of two tracks adhering closely to the above description 'Moebius Stripped' is the closest this comes to a (slow) gothic rock track, only due to the programmed beat, but more than amply avoiding the pitfalls of the said genre. The deep reverberating bass of 'In a box' works wonders as an introduction - keyboard atmospheres solidifying, duet male/ female vocals flirting with a lone violin - all amounting to a soothing gentle wave of introspection. There is a celebratory beauty to 'In a Memory' given the slightly up-tempo drum-kit beat, putting it in the leagues of the excellent experimental prog group the 3rd and the Mortal. Without doubt 'The Undying Man' is the most sorrowful piece with the depressive guitar tune, sweeping keyboards and male vocals - respite only in the female vocals and riff of the chorus. 'Frozen in Time' crystallising the finally of the album comes with a prominent dark piano/ guitar piece again using the building atmosphere of keyboards, slow beat and the ever stunning female vocals. Bitter sweet sorrow at its finest..... Lastly taking noticing the quality production, the expanse of space contained within the tracks ensures an additionally vast and haunting listen thanks to the skills of both Bryin Dall and Derek Rush (of other affiliated projects). Having released only items from their own backyard (New York) Middle Pillar thus far are creating an identifiable face to an obviously flourishing scene. Lets hope the torch is held equally high for subsequent releases.

Moljebka Pvlse (Swe) "Koan" CD 2000 Eibon Records / Pre-Feed
In their minor introduction on CMI's "Estheticks of Cruelty" compilation, Moljebka Pulve presented a track of stilted rhythmic static, which is a far cry from the much more mature and hypnotic drone atmospheres of this, their debut CD. Thick in brooding sonic intensity, these densely drawn-out drones have a certain element that could be traced to treated guitar layers, yet this perception is more from a tonal perspective as opposed to being clearly and specifically recognizable. Pulsating textures probe with low end intensity, the sonics buffed with smooth rounded edges – no sharp or abrasive noises in earshot. Deep rhythmic pulses work up to mildly urgent intensity on 'Parshva' despite the backing remaining subdued. Obvious slow movement and evolution of sound is the format, yet this is exactly the hallmark of drone type works that enable one to get lost in the morphing atmospheres. At first some underlying scattered sounds on 'Rujing' sound more akin to a faulty mix of the track, but they do consolidate into a rough rhythm in the last minutes. Between 5 to 13 minutes of sound expanse are covered on each of the six tracks, and the cover has a visually pleasing image of a nondescript shape and colour.

Monokrom (???) "Monokrom" CD 2000 Ant-Zen
Power noise? Abrasive ambience? Rhythmic industrial? This release is somehow none of these yet all at the same time. The embossed black paper cover gives absolutely no information at all about the group's recording or track listings, but the disc itself contains 11 tracks, that average between 5-7 minutes in length, creating a running time that verges on the maximum amount of sound your can cram into this format. Fractured soundscapes of subdued and chaotic electronic derived resonance, flicker between heavy and heavier sonic atmospheres. Even when quiet in actual sound it can't shake of its dark cloaked aura. Track three contains metallic machine gun rhythms of shredding intensity that blast out between the quieter rhythmic segments, whilst track four solidifies between squealing blasts of noise and mid-paced beats. Disembodied voices wander aimlessly throughout track seven, a piece which could be described as an electro-noise-ritual summoning that randomly weaves beats, voices, sounds, and textures. The slower textural intensity of track eight works well as a very modern sounding piece of industrial ambience - the blips, bleeps and modem-like sounds giving it a modern edge. Track nine then skews off on another tangent - a noisy factory-type rhythmic machinery piece that swirls amidst aggressive sound loops. As for track ten, if I heard this at random without being told who it was by, I would have certainly picked it as one of the most aggressive Con-Dom tracks, consisting of squealing feedback and screeched and gargled vocal distortion. This is of course not the case at all, but it would have had me fooled and, yes, I would have to say that this short piece differs quite a bit from the remaining tracks. Slow building tension and metallic clatter see the disc to its conclusion on track eleven, where the sound spectrum encompasses everything from sustained high-pitched notes to the guttural sub bass beneath. Slow and atmospheric yet tense and chaotic, this track is the perfect way to conclude a broadly expansive album. For a round-about comparison, I would have to offer up a couple in the form of Morgenstern maybe mixed with a hint of Imminent Starvation's slower or beat-less tracks off the "Human Dislocation" CD - so, yes, in essence this has a very 'Ant-Zen' sound. For those who can't get enough of the disc there is an exclusive MP3 track available only on the website - but to gain access you must first own the CD. This bonus track does display a certain cohesion with the other tracks, but it is by far the most straightforward beat-oriented track (hint: the website access code is visibly imbedded on the music side of the disc). Happy hunting.

MZ412 (Swe) "Legion Ultra" 7" EP 2000 Cold Meat Industry
The basic premise of this item was that anyone interested was invited to send in whatever source material they wanted, and then MZ412 would record two tracks for a limited 7" EP. Myself having sent in contributory sounds I'm not sure if my opinions are somewhat biased . . . but anyway here goes! Likewise when anticipating what to expect, I was not sure if I would be able to pick out any of my contributory elements within the overall track dynamics, but surprisingly there they were smattered throughout. All in all twelve the contributions of twelve 'individuals' were utilized, but I use this term 'individuals' with a grain of salt as I remember someone saying their cats had provided material (would that be 'Cleopatra Velvetpaws' and 'Galaxy Glitterpants' perhaps?!). Anyway, I guess whoever has had input into this will listen to the tracks quite differently and take away a completely different impression when hearing their own sounds within the tracks. For a general overview I will add that the tracks are surprisingly MZ412 in character insofar as they take various sounds and manipulate them into rhythmic patterns; however the sound is here slightly more harsh and gritty than normal, I guess mostly due to the nature of the contributions. Side A contains a noisy and chaotic yet rhythmic piece that begins with swirling vocal distortion and feedback, before high-pitched squeals and fractured looped static give it some sense of movement. An amazing reverberating bass echo, the main core of the piece is offset against a high pitched looped squeal (I believe I may be responsible for this sound) and likewise looped vocal-type sample. The track manifests a classic MZ412 song structure which is exploited here to stunning effect. Side B the encompasses a subdued sound of slow modulations, but ends up being nosier than the first with a furnace blasting static sound that is loosely fused together in grinding loops of low, mid and high ranged sound (incidentally, I can pick out more of my contributions on this number). Calming down for only a brief moment, the track lurches back into a finale of abrasive textures that conclude the EP. In short, here are two great tracks that won't disappoint any MZ fan and will be collectable given this is limited to 412 copies in white and 412 in black vinyl. A recommended item (but of course I would have said that!).

Necrophorus (Swe) "Drifting in Motion" CD 2000 Crown Control Activities
The original title for this being 'tundra stillness' when combined with the actual title furnished upon release gives quite a good synopsis of the atmospheres on offer here. There is an obvious calmness to the flow illustrating a bleak wintry haze, surely influenced by the use of a block of ice as part of the sound source material. The first Necrophorus CD is probably my least favourite of Peter Andersson's works, but the passage of time that passed between the recordings has ensured this is leaps and bounds ahead of the debut. With little to compare to the debut, other than the calm new aged tinged atmospheres, this CD works perfectly as a slow cohesive journey

into the arctic wastelands of the mind. And while this has more in common with the meandering soundscapes on the Yoga 10", release there are no middle eastern elements as included on that limited vinyl. Solidifying a vision in the mind's eye, the amplified sound of the source material is akin to the permafrost slowly cracking under the weight of the arctic caps, further intermixed with slow drawn-out keyboard passages, minimal drones and non-descript chimes. Selected moments veer off into more sinister atmospheres such as on 'ice shifting' (containing an air of urgency), while 'Frost' better illustrates a passage of mournful emotional desolation (verging on some of the most depressive segments of Raison d'être's works). The exploration of the transformation of ice from solid to liquid on 'Partial Melt' is particularly evocative set against the droning melodies and distant shrill calls of a whale - a primal call evoking the archaic forces of nature. Although quite lengthy at 57 minutes (over 6 tracks), when listening to this time feels as though it has been momentarily suspended. Firstly there is the feeling of time passing quite quickly (despite the slow motion pace compositions), but secondly confounded by the lingering perception that a great mental distance has been travelled.... Nothing more to add, except than that this is yet another handiwork of Peter Andersson that is essential to your collection.

Nocturne (Fra) "Kommando Holocauste" 10"EP 1999 Old Europa Cafe
Being my first introduction to this group, I think I will have to try and track down their previous 10" EP on Tesco if this is anything to go by. Versions I and II of the title track are an interesting blend of almost power-electronic-inspired atmospherics interlaced with orchestral samples and historical vocal snippets. This is not noisy or forceful enough to be true power electronics and likewise too skittish to be a dark ambient/ industrial project. Layering plays an important role in the shifting dynamics of the sounds, yet by maintaining a sense of controlled tension it gives the impression of a vertical expanse rather than the more conventional 'breadth' of sound. Track I sets the tone by being more controlled with a couple of searing interludes, but it is track two where things take a more dramatic turn through the condemning implications of the forceful sound layering. Initially set under a wartime recording, the intent of the rising tones can certainly be felt, being more condensed and focussed, and gradually multiplying in strength. As the static hits mid to high range distortion, more era vocals are intermixed as the 'rising/falling' dynamic established surges towards its demise. Comparisons to parts of LJDLP's sound are the most obvious in this case, and while there were previous statements to the effect that this group was once part of the aforementioned project, it would now appear that was actually a misunderstanding. Regardless this is another nice piece of vinyl that has been coming out of the OEC camp of late.

Northaunt (Nor) "The Ominous Silence" CDR 1999 Northaunt
In amongst the better known groups there are always some unknowns that rise out of the depths to produce quality self-released items. After following a group email link and browsing Northaunt's website, I was sufficiently intrigued to ask for a review copy . . . and in a situation stranger than fiction the group informed me that they had already sent off a promotional copy only two days before! Mixing rain drenched field recordings with synth-generated textures, 'Might and Misanthropy' commences the proceedings, awash with sweeping bass tones, understated piano tune, and mournful violin passage that gives it a very good dark ambient/neo-classical hybrid feel. At close to 13 minutes things meander along slowly, veering off on a couple of darker, more subdued tangents, including an acoustic guitar interlude, a section of folk oriented flute and tortured vocal shrieks akin to what is found in black metal. The track 'Northaunt' rumbles on in a cavernous guise with shifting sound treatments buried in the mix, later with harsh whispers and a barely accentuated piano tune. More field recordings and an industrial noise pulse make up the backing of 'Der bor en frost her inne', while an acoustic tune form the main musical counterpart. Gradually things take a 'downward' turn (by that I mean 'good'!) with dark factory clatter and a sustained (synth-produced) string movement. 'De sorte traer' again utilises the acoustic guitar in amongst an intricately textured sound backing while 'Running out of time' reminds me somewhat of early raison d'etre with sweeping layers, chant like drones and church bells. The track however remains distinctive with multiple samples of ticking clocks and a lone voice somewhat desperately stating the tracks title. On first hearing 'In rain' the piano tune sounded a little off time but on subsequent listens the off kilter playing only enhances its charm. 'And I Fade Away' is the last track on offer and is a little more experimental than the previous tracks with its mid-paced keyboard tune set amongst dungeon-like clatter, dripping water and far off noises (attention is held in the fore with some spoken vocals). The overall aura of this release quite reminds me of Ildfrost's 'Natanel' CD, although this is somewhat less composed with a larger variety of sound sources. What I guess I am getting at it is that there is a comparison to the overall dark atmosphere and morose classical feel of the stated item. The atmospheres presented definitely show clarity of ideas and I think the use of natural field recordings as a backdrop really enhance the depth of sound. Piano movements, string sections and acoustic guitars are used sparingly, and only enhances the atmosphere at the appropriate times. Although a CDR, it is still encased in professionally printed and presented booklet, complete with full sized printed CD label. A group to keep an eye out for.

Novatron (USA) "New Rising Sun" CD 1999 Cold Spring Records
Being oblivious to the previous musical projects of the main man Anthony Di Franco, I can't really offer any comparisons. However, having Novatron billed as 'solar music', the spacious and inky blackness of the sonic tones certainly do this title justice. Throbbing swelling dynamics and textural sound, 'Kore' commences the epic solar journey, sweeping into 'Axis One' and simultaneously intermixing effect-laden beats to stunning impact. On first rotations I had the sounds pegged for heavily treated guitar generated source material, but the cover revealed that instead that samplers, electronics and a myriad of synths alone were utilised with a bass. The shimmering elements of 'Inamorata' in part bring to mind Atomine Elektrine's "Archimetrical Universe" disc, however the bass loaded beat and more abrasive elements steers into darker sonic territory, choir like tones keeping the piece afloat from sinking into pure darkness. The repetitive succession of fast-paced throbbing sounds of 'Alloy/Sorcerer' is the only drawback I can find on the album, being far too repetitive and high in the mix; yet putting these criticisms aside, the track hits a great segment of harsh sonic noises and random pounded beats. The drawn-out drones of 'Total Mass Retain' work on the lower sonic levels, while other slightly scathing elements hovering just overhead. Symmetry and balance is the feeling conveyed by this pieces, grasping you in its breathtaking sonic vortex. The rumbling, imploding textures of 'Cobra-Bora' could easily illustrate the last moments of a dying super nova (does this signify the end of the journey?), yet things do settle into sweeping multi-dimensional drones (I'm still convinced these sounds have a guitar-like resonance, choosing to take a drawn out path to the disc's conclusion. Around the nine and a half minutes mark, a sinister dynamic stages a takeover encompassing deeper and harsher drones, almost emulating a symphonic character. With the stunning fiery tones of the cover, set against an inky-black background and overwritten with silver print, the cover is the perfect counterpart to the sounds on offer. As with everything Cold Spring put their name to regardless of style, you can always be guaranteed a fantastic release, with Novatron being no exception.

Novy Svet (Aut) "Faccia a faccia" CD 1999 HuaRuk/WKN (via World Serpent Distribution)
This CD is both bizarrely strange yet highly intriguing. Signed to the label of Albin Julius (of Der Blutharsch infamy) and knowing his penchant for folk music, this might begin to explain this group, but not entirely. The opening track is somewhere between folk and jazz with plucked double bass and up-tempo snare/ symbol percussion, while two off kilter Austrians sing in an almost drunken fashion?!! The second song is no less weird, with slow beer hall piano playing, more of those sung/spoken vocals, trippy keyboard sounds and some sort of ritual percussion. Track three takes a more standard industrial subdued rhythmic approach similar to Deutsch Nepal (but don't forget how weird some of his stuff is!) yet the vocals again set this well apart. 'Puro Rumore/Puo Amore' runs between sections of slow and up-tempo accordion playing, with the vocal treatment and presentation totally overshadowing the fact that - yes, an accordion is indeed being used! (Drunken accordion volk music indeed?!) The ritual and martial undercurrent of 'Brigada Budoucnost', with its dark industrial intensity, is almost out of place on this album (the next track consists of yet more mid-tempo beer hall piano playing and vocal chanting!). The drunken sway is again displayed on 'Operazione Runa', as if the group were literally trying to compose a marching tune while heavily intoxicated (and I might add that however it was composed it has resulted in a great but quirky track). The last track, 'Sala, 19.00 MEZ', has a distant and muffled orchestral sound, and as it is mixed with crowd voices and church bells to achieve a field recording vibe, it is easily the most subdued piece on the disc. After 10 minutes of silence the hidden track appears with the accordion brought out for one last drunken lament before this bizarre musical oddity draws to a close. I guess this CD would really be only for the adventurous music enthusiast, but as much as my review might make it sound like it would not work, it is actually a highly addictive release that while has confounded me, certainly has not disappointed.

Nurse with Wound (Eng) "Alice the Goon" MCD 2000 United Dairies (via World Serpent)
I don't know how much I am convinced by this MCD, but for collectors it is a re-release of a limited (read: 500 copies) one-sided LP released in association with the Musiques Ultimes Festival held in France in 1995. Track one '(I don't want to have) Easy Listening Nightmares', is a way out and totally quirky piece with a big band type brass and percussion loop that is overlaid with sound snipits, noises, saxaphone drones, etc. The main loops act as the platform with limited variation and movement throughout the track's nine odd minutes. 'Prelude to Alice the Goon' mostly contains deep double bass rhythm/tune, and tripped out vocals (with full vocal treatments). There is more movement in this passage of time, and works best when the vocals are not presented with other broad background sounds, sparse vocal choirs and percussion. The third untitled track was not on the original LP, but was recorded at the same time. Quite minimalist, it commences as a low drone with distant voices and an untold echoed depth. Vocals become more prominent as mournful wails whilst likewise the shimmering textures increase with metallic texture and for its atmosphere this would easily have to be the best track on here. As for the digipack cover, it contains some nice visuals of strange line drawings.

Of the Wand and the Moon (???) "Sol ek Sa" 7" EP 2000 Hau Ruk
Limited info about the group comes with this one, however two very different styles are showcased. Side A contains one track ('My Blackflamed Sun') of drawn-out ritual/ industrial drones, slow beats and scattered sounds. The sound progresses in the expected manner - starting slow, and gradually building to climactic moments. To swap sounds completely, the second side of the vinyl contains two stunning two neo-folk tunes. The acoustic guitar and low spoken vocals of 'Sol ek Sa MIIX' do bring to mind the likes of Death in June, yet the clarinet accompaniment works particularly well in giving the track its own distinctive sound. A track of beautiful misanthropic wonder. The depth of sound of 'Lion Serpent Sun' is further highlighted with the acoustic strains being overshadowed by piano, and backing horns, percussion, etc., creating again a fantastic piece. Though the vocals do not rise above a low whisper, they still remain high in the mix. I for one will be certainly looking out for future releases from this new group.

Of Unknown Origin (USA) "Seven Ovens of the Soul" CD 1998 Suffering Clown
The two artists behind this (Derek Rush of Dream in Dust and Bryin Dall of 4th Sign of the Apocalypse), already have a well-established history of collaborative efforts – whether on Middle Pillar's 'A Murder of Angels' CD of last year or their various contributions to each other's projects (to name just a few). Of Unknown Origins is yet another project birthed out of their collective interest in dark experimental sonics with this album taking a broad dark ambient approach, containing smatterings of unusual segments and mildly crispy electronics. The tortured vocals of 'From the Womb' form part of this short introductory piece, before a looped and sampled horn sound starts with 'Meditation Ladder', complete with spoken psychological instructions (sampled of course) on how to immerse yourself in a subconscious mind frame. This track is essentially unusual in vibe rather than being specifically dark, however things do take a bleaker turn on 'Saturnine Night' with bursts a mild static and loose rhythmic framework. A style comparable to that of Deutsch Nepal is presented on 'Chemognosis', with looped mechanized rhythms and cold metallic sounds; however, the sound of a lone guitar sets it somewhat apart from this initial comparison (with it fading in and out at will throughout). Visions of barren wind-swept landscapes (mixed with distant

factory sounds) are evoked on 'Sphered in a Radiant Cloud' to good effect, raising in intensity as it progresses (and it even includes a tribal metallic beat in the last minutes). 'Urlo' continues with the tribal mind-set, with heavy (repetitive) percussive beat as the swirling sound textures align themselves in varying sweeping patterns. Deutsch Nepal is again brought to mind on 'Nemonik Enbtropy', with the central plodding bass tune and quirky off center programmed percussion surging forward in repetitive fashion. All in all this is another worthwhile listen, even if it's already a few years old.

Ohrenschmerz (Ger) "Example Compilation" CDR 1999 self-released
As you can see from the title this is not an official release rather a collection of tracks from three releases of this group from this group from 1998 through 1999. I'm not sure how official these original items were, but I get the feeling they may have also been self-released. Anyway, unrelenting power/noise industrial is what we have here, ranging from pure noise attacks to the more hyper beat stabs. 'Fehlfunktion' presents the sounds of massive unidentified machinery in total over drive, intense in all its rough repetitive glory with enough obliterated feedback and scattered German vocal samples tossed into the meat grinders which are my speakers to bring a smile to my dial (in appreciation of course). The noise attack of 'Intro' aside, 'Tinitus' contains a cleaner yet no less metallic resonance in the pummelling beat structure. Blistering loops again of metallic origin (on 'Tote Liebe') really grab at the roots of what industrial music is all about (and not this mainstream fluff that passes as 'industrial' these days). Powerful, aggressive and all encompassing is this melding of two parts noise and three parts beat. 'Traum II' explores the use of feedback blasted vocals and a barely contained programmed tune that adds a further positive dimension to the later works of this group. The lurching loops and corrosive static of 'Deutscher Hass (sv)' contain a razor sharpness making this a premier power electronics number comparable to the likes of Genocide Organ, with the final track reverting to the power rhythms format. Overall the biggest comparison would be to the harder edged Ant-Zen and affiliated groups, in particular the likes of Converter. I will certainly be looking out for a new release, which I'm sure will eventuate on one label or another given the strength of this taster.

Oil10 (???) "Metastases" 12" EP 1999 Hymen
Siren generated rhythms and static oriented beats situates Oil10 in rather quirky yet groovy ambient/techno territory that is not all dissimilar to the stylistic approach of Black Lung. This comparison is further enhanced when the second track ('Shadows in the Sand') morphs off into an introduction of shimmering sub-bass pulses, later focussing around programmed 'blip'-oriented melody lines creating a very sci-fi styled vibe. The slow pace and extended length of this piece does make for a chilled-out aura that brings side A to its close. Side B begins with a much more evasive sound, where mid-paced beats drive the track forward amidst quickly-building loops and increasing complexity, while the tripped-out quirky blips that make up part of the tune again encompass a sci-fi edge. The final track is probably both the fastest and most straightforward piece – a slow, drawn-out droning tune over quick beat sequences, with random sounds adding to the various patterns being toyed with. Another nice item in the Hymen series of 12" EPs (where all vinyls have the same cover, except for the authentic postage stamps that detail the name of the artist and release).

Ordo Equitum Solis (Ita) "Metamorphosis - Personam Impono" CD 2000 World Serpent Distribution
Being serviced by World Serpent with promo items has given me the opportunity to hear groups that I am well aware of but, due to a lack of funds, have never gotten around to checking out (with O.E.S being such a group). For those familiar with the group the press release references that this CD has reached a level of maturation that was both not expected nor required so I guess this is saying something if you appreciated their past releases! Likewise my impressions of the group hearing them for the first time are of a positive slant. Following a classical/folk, male/female duo type path, shades of Dead Can Dance and other slight dark wave influences are evident (the dark wave influence I would attribute to the partial keyboard programming sound). These elements, along with sparse acoustics, bass melodies and the interplay of gender specific vocals, no doubt expand upon an established sound. The acoustic guitar and trumpet of 'Tomorrow Cries' nods to Death in June's sound on the "Rose Clouds" album, yet the female vocals presented in a very mainstream styled delivery which I hear is another variance to previous offering. The beautiful flowing instrumental track (incidentally titled 'Instrumental') is a brooding classical inspired piece which does not suffer greatly from the synthetic means of production. The percussive, acoustic guitar tracks (with related instrument embellishment) are the most numerous here, with each taking on different emotive qualities. On one of the later tracks the merging of the acoustic strums and deep cinematic classical melodies of 'Reprise' is where the album works at its best, but is a little disappointing as it lacks vocals. 'The Last Hopes in Me', the concluding piece, partly resolves my disappointment with the preceding track, here merging a more subdued backing with female vocals a lone piano line and mournful trumpet tunes. Surprisingly mainstream on many tracks, this CD is by no means a difficult listen, nor something that you have to have a lot of 'scene' baggage to appreciate, thus there could be quite wide appeal for this.

Orplid (Ger) "Orplid" CD 1999 Eis und Licht Tontrager
Having read a interview and recommendation in Descent Magazine 5# (and knowing they are spot-on with knowing what is worthwhile), I tracked down a copy of this CD. My searched resulted in me obtaining the original slip cover version, however I hear this has been released with new packaging and maybe a bonus track or two. A deep orchestral marching ode opens the CD setting a shrill battlefield aura (snares and tympani's pound, brass horns bellow etc) prior to the main focus of the album presenting itself as dark melancholic apocalyptic folk music. 'Bruder Luzifer' presents complex arrangements of acoustic guitars playing brooding tunes and melodies, complemented with synth layers, and deep martial percussion. Vocals sung in their native tongue (being powerful and commanding in the mid-ranged presentation) certainly add to the aura. In regard to these vocals, 'Totenlied' bases itself around a vocal choir arrangement (sung by the male members), obtaining an intense heathen flavour. The title track differs again from what precedes it, being a stunning piano movement with flute accompaniment - male vocals softly sung against the fragile and beautiful piano tune. Intense acoustic tunes, a lone cello, volkish mouth harp and monkish chanted vocals embody an ode to the Norse God Balder (on a track of the same name), with the background screams acting as emotional catharsis. The volk marching ode of 'Jenseits von hier' uses electronic means to create the tunes, and here with female vocals taking the centre stage while male vocals act as a restrained backing. Apocalyptic acoustic folk music does not get much better than on 'Dan Abendland', whilst the straight sung vocals come close to sounding like Douglas P (the musical backing is far more folk-tinged, though). The last track is strange in its inclusion here that it starts as a crusty programmed dark drum and bass piece, with full nightclub crowd noise in the background. Once this segment is concluded, swirling winds and an angry German speech sample arrives full force, than falling back into field recording territory with rain and thunder, a slow acoustic tune presenting a mournful ballad for the final minutes. This track is a really good piece but it is just not something I would have expected given the overall flavor of the album. For a final comparison, if anyone has followed a band by the name of Ulver, (and in particular their second acoustic folk CD), this is a marker to what you can expect from Orplid and their stunning acoustic and vocal battle hymns.

Osso Exotico (Por) "VII" 7" EP 1999 Drone Records
Created via a church organ, this is not exactly how you would expect this to sound like given the drawn out essence of the pieces, yet the aura of sound does retain a slight resemblance to its origin (fleeting sounds spark this recognition). Likewise there is an unavoidable religious flair to the sounds, mainly due to the connotations associated with the choice of instrument, but this has more to do with preconceived notions than anything else. On both tracks a slow hazy warmth exudes from the grooves of the vinyl, with slow enveloping drones and deep cavernous sounds that rise and fall in volume during the slow journey of the two pieces. Essentially dark ambient pieces, these sit well with the likes of Amon and the more minimalist school of sound. Interestingly the packing sees the music pressed on clear vinyl and comes with a small packet of spices. Very tasty!

Ostara (Aus/ Ere) "Operation Valkrie" CDS 2000 World Serpent Distribution
Ostara (Aus/Ere) "Secret Homeland" CD 2000 World Serpent Distribution
Two items reviewed in one, mostly as the single was a limited to 1000 promotional copies containing one of the tracks off the upcoming album. The single certainly grabbed my attention, frustrating me that I would have to wait by the letterbox for the arrival of the full length it was taken from (luckily I only had to wait for a bit over a month). Continuing on from the former group Strength Through Joy, the name has now been changed and the musical orientation slightly altered, creating quite an interesting spin on the 'apocalyptic folk' sound. One of the first things that is evident is the crystalline clarity of the production, being full, rich and lively in all elements of vocals (which are mostly male with selected female backing), guitar (including slide), bass, drums, keyboards and the occasional cello. Apart from the production setting a standard above much in the genre, the use of a standard drum kit (rather than martial percussion), sends the music on a much more rock/folk tangent. 'Epiphany', the first off the mark, highlights the lyrical poetry and vocal delivery, being well sung in a mid range octave, encompassing lines such as "I believe in mysteries and I can see with clarity, the truth behind the veil, beneath the lie". Being set against keyboard layers and deep bass make the tragic acoustic strains of 'Operation Valkyrie' both a highlight as a single track and highlight of the album, being an ode to the myths of northern paganism and the strife facing Europe with the loss of such traditions. 'Midsummer Sunday' is a much calmer affair, coming across as a beautiful acoustic strummed celebration, complete with female vocal and cello accompaniment. 'Ways to Strength and Beauty' opens with a poetic metaphor, then becomes another stand-out track of subdued anger realised via the mid-paced acoustics, bagpipes and more forceful (marching) drumming. The rock/folk perspective mentioned earlier is again shown on 'Nostalgia for the Future', mainly due to the up-tempo guitar, drumming and violin passages. 'The Wolf's Door' (dare I say it) contains an almost low key prog-rock feel, with the following 'Beauty to Burn' also using a non characteristic drum pattern for this genre. Rounding out the album is 'Serpent's Wine', an optimistic sounding tune of mid-paced acoustic strummed and cello bowed bliss. In conclusion, as much as I feel this is a fantastic album from execution of musicianship through to production, at nearly 70 minutes these 12 tracks evince a certain 'sameness' to the sound. Maybe with a few less tracks this would have been all the stronger for it, but, really, if this is the only gripe to raise it is not much of one at all.

Ovum (Swe) "Plastic Passion" MC 2000 Troniks
Having had a minor introduction to the world via the CMI "Estheticks of Cruelty" compilation, Ovum came across as one of the quieter groups with a track of subdued machine-like drones. While the said compilation track was reasonably one- dimensional, this tape shows the same slow drone aesthetic, yet with more movement and spaciousness explored. Two long untitled tracks are presented (one per tape side) exploring cold barren soundscapes. On the first side drones placed on a number of bass and sub bass levels resonate thick sonic waves with other mid ranged glacial shimmering sounds rhythmically rising and falling in volume. With freezing crystalline beauty, this likewise has a sterile clinical feel devoid of human emotion or interaction (the thought patterns of a cold, unfeeling mind perhaps?). Still at a snail's pace, track two increases dynamics somewhat by introducing sound elements at a quicker rate. Again the sounds sit between deep drones and rising/falling glacial mid ranged textures however a few more cavernous element creates a sense of depth that was not evident on track 1 (due to its emphasis on breadth of sound). A high pitched sound or two weave into the composition, without being obtrusive to the ear likewise mixed with what sounds like a distant slow grinding melody muffled somewhere in the background. The tense dynamic, and cold liquidous movement of this makes it more engaging than the first, fusing some more low end machine like tones and static towards then end. Probably a little too active to fit into the 'isolationist' mould, this is cold barren dark ambience perhaps slightly reminiscent of Hazard on the 'North' CD. A good release that unfortunately for me won't get played that often due to the format (me never having been much of a tape buff).

Dagobert's Revenge

Musick ✠ Magick ✠ Monarchism

Current Issue:
Boyd Rice
Death in June
Ulver
Legendary Pink Dots

UFOs
Masonry
Mind Control

Subscription:
2 Issues $(US)16
(Outside USA: Cash only)

Send to:
Dagobert's Revenge
2301 New York Ave.
2nd Floor
Union City
NJ 07087
USA

Visit our website to order by credit card.
www.dagobertsrevenge.com

Ovum (Swe) "Epepe" CD 2000 Fever Pitch
Despite being marked as an EP and containing only 4 tracks, this Ovum release still has a running time of over 40 minutes. Continuing on from the review of Ovum's sound above, it seems that these recording predate the tape tracks having been recorded in around 1998-99. The first track, 'Bolesc', takes a very 'Thomas Koner' type take on slow glacial minimalism of shifting sub bass textures. Slow and steady, this track introduces the album, intensity rising at such a slow rate you barely notice the volume has increased from the opening passage to its conclusion at over 9 minutes. From the very start the second track, 'Islossning', takes a more active role of mid-ranged stormy drones, bleak gray enveloped textures and fractured machinery type sounds - part minimalist, part subdued noise, overall to great effect. Glacial archaic depths and shifting deep space bleakness (à la Lustmord on the "Black stars" album), the title track is a great sparsely textured dark ambient number that weaves its way into your psyche over its (nearly) 10 minute span. All I can add is that I can never seem to get enough of this sound when it is pulled off with such flair! The final track, 'Cenote' bass-rumbles its way into contention, more singular in focus and likewise muffled in its suffocation of a partly composed melody. The minor shifts occur here and there (likewise with slowly increasing intensity) mark a track content in slowly unravelling itself over 16 minutes. Of the fours tracks of minimalist dark ambience presented, each takes an individual sound and focus creating a well-thought out and presented document of bleak atmospherics. Ovum are certainly a group worth checking out, and with myself now having some of the group's material on CD will certainly ensure regular rotations.

Pain Station (USA) "Cold" CD 1999 COP
Cold is the third release by Scott Sturgis' Pain Station; he also helms the distorted rhythmic maelstrom that is Converter. Where the previous release, Disjointed, veered into regions of the mind tinged with bleak futuristic nuances, Cold tears off the layers of (already lean) sonic excess, presenting a blinding, bone-white melding of a psyche in disrepair, hinged to existence by futility and despair. The sound is one of isolated machinery murmur and corrosive synths augmented with spastic beats amidst a taut electro industrial framework. The dry ice vocals and introspective lyrical focus concisely align the listener with Cold's exploration of the struggle within ('One mans journey into self-destruction...'). The bass of 'Dead Inside' thumps solemnly (reminiscent of Ennio Morricone's crisp, glacial soundtrack to John Carpenter's The Thing) before frustration pours from the synth line and vocals stumble down the staircase of inner turmoil. 'Turning Point' opens with machinery whispers and a despondent soundscape loop (is that Heid?) upon which mysterious beasts chirp, bleat, and scramble, and layers of subtly percussive rhythms vie for transient supremacy. 'Braindead' slinks through the computer-banks refuge, stuttering beats punctuated by the parched, sun-blasted vocals of one desperately holding on to one's already fractured sanity. Like a vacuum, the chorus of 'Aftermath' sucks the listener deeper into the swiftly disintegrating psyche. 'Dark Day (Self-Destruct)' sprays liquid radiation upon the scoured cranium, a scathing noise fusion of nuclear waste and mental deterioration. The whole disc feels as though it was, literally, recorded from within the mind of the tormented narrator. An illuminating blend of electro industrial idiosyncrasies and dark sonicscape dynamics. Highly recommended! —JC Smith

P.A.L (Ger) "Release" CD 2000 Ant-Zen
This, P.A.L's third CD, is my first introduction to this group; yet I have the feeling that this may be the most commercially accessible 'release' given previous reviews I have read. Each of the tracks encompass layers of percussive up-tempo beats, synthesiser lines and programmed sound textures, done in a way that is reasonably straightforward, gradually morphing through various segments of each. After a short layered synth/answering machine message intro, 'Discoroad' roars into existence in the guise of a driving bass sonic piece with an overload of mechanically driven beats and minimalist melody. The following track, 'Crash the Party', continues with a similar driving feel of bass sonics that, with slightly less emphasis on the beats, opts instead for a heavy focus on the programming side of things. A much harder edged beats-and-machine driven rhythmic clatter is found on the appropriately entitled "Death is a Drum Machine", heading towards the territory inhabited by label mates Converter and Imminent (Starvation). 'Welcome to Annexia' is a more personal track, containing a slow minimalist dirge of programming with hints of buried beats, sub-bass melody and scattered noise. Amping up the mood again, 'Bang your Box' is an absolute stomper of a track which has a hell of a groove to the driving bass current, complete with harsh (straight up) percussion, resulting in it being one of the definite highlights of the CD. 'In the Now' has a weird (repeated) cigarette dialogue vocal sample layered over a reasonably dark, brooding piece (with limited slow beats), providing a bit of down time between the faster tracks (which incidentally is the next track, 'Move!'). This piece creates a good suspenseful atmosphere via the gradually layering programming, increasing the intensity before the full beat/noise programming kicks in. 'Reborn' mixes up the sound palate considerably, containing a massive surging (down tuned) guitar riff alongside mid tempo pounding beats and programming being refreshing in its simplicity. 'Leeste, Night' is the lengthy closer to the disc, commencing with sampled angelic vocals later moving into a darkish synth line, continuing over a 7 minute span until the conclusion - acting as a coming-down track considering the over-the-top energy displayed on the majority of the 51 minute disc. One last comment would be that there is the element of humour evident in the music, given the use of vocal samples taken from cartoons and episodes of Faulty Towers, among others. While not too obtrusive, they slightly detract from the overall feel in that it for me it gives a gimmicky edge which I tend to dislike when associated with hard-edged electronic music.

Pita (Aut) "Get Out" CD 1999 Mego
This is another Mego artist that uses a laptop computer to create these eclectic takes of digitally abstract noise/sound. Despite high-end burst of static (as on track 1), the resonance is not akin to, say, Japanese noise, but has a more inherent subdued sound. Cutting from one track to the next quite sporadically, track two has an earthen depth to the low end, with the sound spectrum occasionally sweeping quickly upwards to ear piercing result. The singular highlight of the disc come with the 11-minute third track, which has taken what sounds like a 'borrowed' classical type melody/choir vocal and fed it through a harsh computer mixing programming. While the beauty of the tune is still evident, it is somehow enhanced by being juxtaposed with the thunderous driving static and glitched distortion textures. This track can't help but stand out from the others, particularly as the majority of the nine pieces are between 1 to 4 minutes in length (and only explore small snippets of sound and noise texture). On the other hand, this track has taken a single theme and toyed with it to stunning effect over quite an extended length. Track four brings a computer game sound aesthetic to its chopped framework, while track five has a thicker liquidous tone in a calm droning type piece. You would be forgiven for thinking that your CD player is malfunctioning on track seven with the way it presents itself as a digitally-fractured segment of sound. The final track again explores an extended length, timing in at around 8 minutes. As such I feel that the disc works better when the tracks are given a bit more breadth to move, as here the tonal rumblings and mid ranged sounds are given the ability to gradually morph into different patterns without appearing to have changed drastically. I would say this disc is worth it for tracks three and nine alone.

Polar (USA) "Consistencies in Nature" CDR 2000 M.M.S
Without any bio or release info sent with this, I have next to no idea of the background of this project and, from what little I can glean from the cover, Polar appears to consist of two guys experimenting with selected traditional instruments (leaf blower, yadaki, etc) and samplers/rhythm machines. The results they come up with encompass 6 lengthy tracks, sometimes constituting mature, well-evolved, (mildly) tribal, yet mostly studio-tweaked soundscapes, whilst other segments fall somewhat short, coming across as less accurately planned or executed (maybe even improvised), particularly on 'Winged Flight on Base Zero'. The pace of play generally keeps it down to a slow crawl emphasising the evolution of the tracks and being much akin to watching hazy textures of light emitted from a slowly heating lava lamp. 'Half-Hibernation' in part uses a standard programmed beat, distinguishing it somewhat from the other pieces, but overall it probably grabbing my attention slightly less than the more experimental sections. 'Two Points Converging' pulls out the big guns in an all-out, sprawling drone-fest of bass drenched waves and sharper, more refined textures gradually spinning and weaving in a tangled audio collage. 'Falling to the Sea' heads off on a different tangent, and contains some nice death ambient vibes (yet still experimental), being mostly built on bass and distortion loops with other scraping sounds and random tribal percussion. Elements of this remind me of a more subdued and organic sounding Stone Glass Steel during the "Industrial Icon" and "Industrial Meditation" albums, and likewise this could fit nicely with some of the items coming from the Influx Communications label such as the albums by Asia Nova or Smooth Quality Excrement. Overall this is a good introductory listen, and I get the feeling that these guys could be something to watch out for. Contact: sine23@sonic.net, if interested.

PPF (Fra) "Propagande Par Le Fait" LP 2000 StateArt
First up I will say that the packaging of this would sit very nicely next to the recent Iron Justice LP, as this is also pressed into ultra heavy weight vinyl and housed in a white slip sleeve. And if we are going to make the comparison to another power electronics group, you might as well expect this to be in the same arena. Well, in actual fact this statement is only true to an extent, as PPF do have a distinctive sound of their own that cuts from (mostly) power electronics to noise ambience and noise industrial (all done fantastically I might add). The sinister drilling tones and fluttering white noise sets things in motion on the first track of the LP 'Minski's Torture Chamber', with the

arrival of the tortured flanged vocals articulating a sense of blissful anger. Squiggly mid toned layers add to the backing of 'Penis Pressure Forensics' where the vocals are the focal point and main wonder here. Shrieking and heavily treated they take the total fore of the composition, becoming even more frantic and unintelligible throughout. 'PCF' sits more in a noise ambient styling with low guttural sounds that are treated with both echoed and sweeping textures. Various segments of French spoken samples add to the subdued calamity with also a higher pitched sound akin to someone trying to obtain a signal on CB radio. 'Your not welcome' harks back to a classic power electronics sound, starting off slow with a few select layers of cyclic noise that quickly multiply and accelerate forward to urgent mid paced delivery. The vocals add a whole new dimension, which has more to do with the insane conviction of delivery and level white noise distortion added. The tension constantly building as sporadically the voice can be made out to screaming the track's title. Not breaking any new ground, but masterfully done all the same. Side B offers up three choice selections with 'Airwaves Control' being the first. More radio transmitter signalling noise is used here to good effect within a shrill/ sweeping noise industrial framework (obviously with radio voices of French origin occasionally filtering in and out of the tense noise collage). 'PPF' takes a slight diversion in that it contains a slow drum machine percussive element. Sustained keyboard tones ebb out a slight melody in amongst more shrill piecing elements, all over a backing of distant bombing and other French speech samples. The last track of the LP ('En Milieu Hostile') comes as a lengthy extended piece that starts with deep wavering textures and scattered layers of surging mid ranged sound. Further in, heavier distortion plays a bigger role along with the use of vocals that are flanged, echoed and distorted (and is quite interesting to hear power electronics vocals presented in their native tongue). By the end of the track is has degenerated into a mass of screaming vocals, feedback and the ever present underlying surging loops. All in all yet another great addition to the power electronics genre (both group and album) with this release being limited in number to 500 cuts of vitriolic vinyl.

Psychic TV (Eng) "Were you ever Bullied at School...Do you want Revenge?" DCD 1999 Cold Spring Records
Can I review this item without ever referencing the music? Lets see if I can't! A double CD set of vintage Psychic TV live gig recordings is what this is all about, the performances themselves supposedly having never been heard before (other than by those at the actual shows, I guess). Two CDs and two performances, one recorded in September 1984, the other in December 1994, and both in Germany. Psychic TV are a group whose reputation precedes them, embellished both by past associations and by the members' own individual and collective achievements, all of which has solidly embedded them in industrial folklore. God knows what I was doing when these shows were recorded (attending primary school perhaps?) but that is not really the point other than not having a great background knowledge to drawn from and hence severely flawing my ability as reviewer. Basically, you are either a massive Psychic TV fan and avid collector of their outputs and will already have this (or will ultimately be obtaining this), or you may be a little like me, being far from well-acquainted with Psychic TV's sound (let alone everything they stood from), creating a bemusing situation for me to write a semi competent, let alone intelligent review of it. Thus as you may have guessed I am not even going to try, but then again any real Psychic TV fan has probably not read this far realising my ignorance in relation to all things Psychic. Fourteen tracks in all are included (7 per performance/per disc) encompassing different song sets for both shows, including: 'Turn the Golden Thread', 'Rope your Self', 'Ov Power', 'Soul Eater', 'Godstar (Never Forget)' and 'Papal Breakdance'. Well what else to say that this may just be the longest non-music descriptive review I have ever done!

Psychonaut (USA) "The Witches' Sabbath" CD 2000 Athanor
I guess there is ritual inspired type music and then there is music encompassing actual ritualistic rites. This would most definitely be placed in the latter category, and while it is noted to be specifically influenced by Austin Osman Spare, the lyrics of one track ('Hymn to Pan') were penned by Aleister Crowley. If you were not already aware, this is a project of one Michael Ford (the main member) who has worked previously with projects such as Valefor (among others). Constant ritual percussive elements, vocals of both gender (female vocals are most prominent, either sung or spoken) and wind instruments over sparse sweeping electronic textures gives the aura of rites and evocations in full progress. Each track sets out to capture an aura, then enhances it via general repetition and minimal progression. The lack of percussion on track like 'Bacchanal' actually enhances the seductively sinister electronic drones and accompanying pan flute. 'Lights Black Majesty' presents a similar non-percussive sound, yet with additional electronic clatter and quite prominent male vocals reciting the lyrics to a Rosaleen Norton piece. It is for all the specific ritual connotations that the album does not really work as an active listening tool, but works better when listened to in a background sound context, or even as an enhancement to your own ritual practices. The cover is quite stunning, containing panels of artwork from notables such as Rosaleen Norton, Aleister Crowley and Austin Osman Spare, likewise with a transparent over wrap. Overall, I am generally at a loss for words with this one (that is quite unlike me actually...).

Puissance (Swe) "War On" CD 1999 Fluttering Dragon
Ah yes, Puissance are back at it with a remix CD of some of their favourite tracks along with two new numbers presented in a simplistic digipack case. Culling two tracks from all three albums each have some sort of discernible difference in sound, mostly that they have been made more bombastic overall or that the vocals have changed slightly in presentation - meaning that I get the feeling that some of the tracks may have been actually re-recorded. Taken from the first album, 'Control' opens this disc with a less muddied sound, massive harsher drumming and more spiteful vocals. 'Erlangen' (the first of two new tracks) starts with a sound very much like the orchestral tracks of the first CD, which initially had me worried that Puissance's sound might be regressing. This concern abates after the whole track has been taken in, as it shows that Puissance have started to write longer tracks that meander through a number of segments rather than focussing on one or two themes. The opening segment contains deep horns, shrill strings and marching percussion with one or two off kilter breaks before being stripped back to a quieter foreboding middle sections of tense ambience. Somewhat relaxed epic orchestral tones return as the third passage strides confidently back into the opening segment to bring the track full circle (although for some reason ending abruptly at mid-passage). 'Totalitarian Hearts' has had a reworking where the mastering has increased the intensity of the music and with the vocals being re-recording with a slight echo effect and a touch more irony or cynicism in the tone of the voice. 'For the Days of Pestilence', the second new track, mixes orchestral strains very well with a more primitive industrial clanging undertone, containing a steady mid paced beat, sweeping background choirs and mechanical rhythms. Although containing the same overall sound as the original, this version of 'Burn the Earth' is still almost unrecognisable when compared back to the original. It is surprising how weak the original recording was with many of the orchestral layers getting lost in a definitely mediocre production. The reworked version is thankfully much more crystalline, giving each layer of sound room to move and to embellish the track overall improving it tenfold (even if it is still a tad synthetic). 'In Shining Armour', selected as one of the most powerful tracks of the last CD, has its main touch-up in the vocal department (being re-recorded) utilising a much more forceful half sung/half spoken guise which takes a very central role over and above the massive folk tinged backing. 'Light of a Dead Sun' (also off the last CD) seems for the most part to be the same except for the obvious perks that a good re-mastering provides. I must say that 'Command and Conquer' was always a powerful track, but the manner in which this re-working portrays it all out anger is truly impressive. This is one of the most outwardly militant tracks Puissance have written, scrapping any hint of epic orchestra elements by opting for a sinister drone and mechanical pulse that rips into a massive whirlpool of distorted fast kettle drumming. Falling back to the sinister drones, mechanical textures and sounds of distant explosions, the track again ravages the listener's ears with the distorted drumming being even more powerful the second time around. I will say that with this track it is the first time that Puissance have struck me as much as some of Turbund Sturmwerk's compositions have done in the past - and that is certainly no mean feat. Given I guess this a bridging release before the new album, I am quite intrigued with what it will contain as this is too short at only 40 minutes.

Raison d'être (Swe) "The Empty Hollow Unfolds" CD 2000 Cold Meat Industries
Since this highly anticipated release appeared in my letterbox, I have been settling (or is that unsettling??) into this new offering from Raison d'etre. On first listen and making a comparison to previous works, there is a more meandering song framework than the "In Silence..." CD, hearkening more back to tracks on "Within the depths.." CD. The song structure of this new album is essentially somewhere in the middle of these albums, though overall this is the DARKEST thing exorcised by Raison d'être yet. The drones are increasingly suffocating and keyboard passages even more solemn than ever before, intermixed with a fair whack of abrasive factory clatter, tonal outbursts and scrapping textures (with the odd monk or choir sample arising in between). An icy wind blowing through 'The Slow Ascent' stimulates metallic wind chimes within the framework of guttural atmospheric depth, while craggy outcrops of sub bass textures mar the journey, all the while with lamenting choirs mourning the fate of the traveller in his desperate search for the unnamed but ultimately desolate place. Lethargic orchestral movements embody the depressive melody of 'The Hidden Hallows', only made all the more dark via the shifting catacomb textures. Of the more abrasive and unsettling tracks, 'End of a Cycle' is the one to name, indeed marking the end of Raison d'etre as a sweet/sorrowful group, here totally embracing and immersing the project in pure darkness, the invasively loud choir sounds making an commanding presence rather than depressive one. 'The Wasteland' is simply that - a sparse soundscape of tonal depth and dungeon atmospherics mainly evoked by the metal-on-metal abrasiveness. Female type choir melodies smooth the edges somewhat, yet the overall feel remains that of a place of an inhospitable bleakness. The journey reached at 'The Eternal Return and the Infinity Horizon' takes the longest span of the album, fleshing out over 20 minutes. Early Lustmord is brought to mind within the starting blocks segment, slowly introducing more doom laden sounds, sparse metallic clatter and layers of resonating male choir sounds. More comforting in non movement, the place which was being sought had finally been reached, marking also the end of another journey. Although I have made mention of the louder textures being introduced, it must be said that even with the more abrasive Stratvm Terror like samples, they are never so harsh as to detract from the typical aura for which Raison d'être is renowned and revered (likewise, it is nothing like sitting through the 'Pain Implantations' CD!!) I'm hard pressed to rank this against Raison d'être's previous albums as I tend to find that whichever is playing at the time is my favourite, with this being no exception. All that can be ultimately evidenced from this is that there is still plenty of territory for Raison d'être to explore, and I for one will be waiting patently for the next chance to be led down into another catacomb within the depth of Peter's psyche.

Remanence (USA) "Apparitions" CD 1999 Cold Spring Records
From the brilliant packaging (sepia toned booklet with transparent over wrap) to the compositional tunes (premier neo-classics) everything here is top notch. The music spans 13 tracks of stunning, emotive beauty, which appear to take vision and inspiration from ghosts and afterlife phenomenon, rather than being produced under a militant guise of many other artists in this genre. Parallels could be drawn to some of Shinjuku Thief's albums, or perhaps the works of Ontario Blue or Iidfrost. Orchestral passages, piano interludes, and classical percussion are just some of the elements to be found. In regard to specific tracks, '1st Wave' appears to have captured the depressive pulse of time in its core essence - a sweeping of classically inspired keyboard layers, clarinet and partly tribal (treated) beat, all perfectly understated. 'Be careful what you wish for' is not as sinister as the title would imply, and features a slow piano melody with the accompanying background sound of a rainstorm (however, the title is obviously referencing crackly vocal sample asking "...is there anyone on the air?"). 'Where the Shadows Lie' sees the adoption of a militant guise containing striking percussion and both shrill and brooding string/brass accompaniment (although is probably the track where the synthetic elements are most recognisable). With combinations of instrumentation ranging from the real to the synthesized, overall it assists in the sound having an authentic vibe rather than if the whole album was keyboard generated. The flow of the album is likewise quite stunning, navigating slow depressive (almost dark ambient) pieces to more mid-paced neo-classical percussive works, meaning that there is never danger of this album being one dimensional or derivative. Additionally, when selected segments are repeated throughout the album, they appear to be echoing fragments of time and emotion (such as with '1st Wave' being repeated as '3rd Wave', but now resplendent with acoustic guitar). Not much else to say but search this out.

Reynols (Arg) "10000 Chicken Symphony" 7" EP 2000 Drone Records
Of all the sound sources one could choose, Reynolds have surely opted for one of the more obscure, directly related to the EP's title. Side A contains a muffled mix of thunderstorm tones, distant sounds and deep textures, which are actually quite ambient and relaxing in their droning qualities. Elements multiply and sounds increase in volume, yet the ambience remains throughout. Selected noises seem to point to the sound source, yet are not such that they are totally recognizable. Side 2 is much noisier, reflecting relatively untreated samples of the sound source. The high-pitched chirping of thousands of birds is presented in a cacophony of high end texture that borders on white static. This track is quite a difficult piece to sit through, yet works surprisingly better than one would expect considering the source from which it was created. Given the intensity of the middle of the piece, it has me wondering if I would have identified the sound source if not already aware of it. An interestingly diverse release over only two tracks.

Sanctum (Swe) "New York City Bluster: Live at CBGB's" CD 2000 Cold Meat Industry
Being around four years since the release of the debut Sanctum album, I guess this acts as a bridging live release, showcasing old and new material of Sanctum (and other affiliated projects) before the imminent second album. Essentially, in 1999 the two male members travelled to the US 999 (leaving the two female members behind) to undertake a short string of dates, culminating in the New York performance that forms this recording. A fair extra heft of weight and grunt is evident in lieu of the female balance of the group, encompassing the exploration of grinding industrial elements and very Sanctum-esque neo-classical segments. The first two tracks, 'Axiom' and 'Mindtwister' (both noted as being fragments of what to expect on the next album), range in this format, arcing between the harsh and the beautiful, the grating and the sublime. The live rendition of 'Decay' is simply stunning, with vocals being even more feverous when set against the sampled industrial buzz saw guitar riff, all sheathed in soothing keyboard textures. An excerpt of a Parca Pace track (Parca Pace being a side project) encompasses track 4, slowing things down into a tribal/industrial soundscape, later exploring harsher vocals, heavier percussion and random noise textures before finally reducing to a mid-paced, slightly urgent neo-classical ending section. The sheer beauty of 'In Two Minds', while lacking the lush female vocals, simply cannot be held back when executed in such a perfect fashion. In my mind this track forms the core of everything Sanctum embody - the perfect blend of the industrial and the classical. If Sanctum were ever 'in two minds' of what direction to pursue, this would be it! 'Sly Dog' is a track of another side project 'Mago', being much more focussed on complexities and subtleties of percussion and rhythms than actual tune composition. Backing this is a track of polar opposites ('Gift'), being a quite playful neo-classical piece of multi-layered strings and, although not specifically a Sanctum piece (noted as originally being composed for a dance performance), it fits well within the morphing sound and direction of the live performance. Despite the mixed nature of the original source of the tracks (coming from the main project and other side projects), there is never any doubt that the resulting whole has Sanctum's trademark stamp all over it. As with the debut, this release illustrates that Sanctum are one of the more accessible groups of the CMI roster and will surely leave fans both within and outside of the ambient/industrial/neo-classical 'inner-sanctum' waiting with bated breath for the next offering.

Scorn (UK) "Imaginaria Award"CDEP 2000 Hymen
Having not extensively followed Mick Harris's output under a multitude of project names and styles (apart from a couple of 'Lull items), I do not have a wealth of background knowledge to draw from, however Scorn is a name I have been aware of, and now can relate to some of the hype. It seems this project has been recording for some 9 years now in the search and creation of darkly menacing drum and bass music (this is something like the fifteenth Scorn release). Opening with 'Out of the Picture', this could be better characterized by drum and noise than drum and bass. The combination of kick, snare and high hat are certainly there, yet there is no real groove or tune to the pulverizing textures or the more subdued background noises. Big (slightly tweaked) slow pounding beats and deep sweeping tones comprise 'Worried' as it grooves forward navigating a few minor interludes from the main theme along the way. The straight upbeat rigidness of 'As If' gives it a brooding, hip hop feel, interspersed with sporadic keyboard note hits and ominous grinding bass. Twisted and morphed beat structures of 'As If (Part 2)' never quite solidify into a full composed piece (which is obviously intentional), choosing to remain an experimental exploration of tone and structure. The final track is the most upbeat and playful, with huge repetitive bass lines, grinding noise rhythms, mid paced kick drum and quick paced high hat. Sitting comfortably above this are quite atmospheric yet abrasive elements, further stretching the boundaries of the composition. A distant sinister and hazy tune also plays its role, creating a down vibe to the otherwise up-tempo fair. With all elements working perfectly, this is easily my favourite off this release. Although having become acquainted with this project somewhat late (okay, extremely late), I found this to be a great introduction to Scorn given it is an easily digested 5 track EP. Soon to follow is a full length under the name "No Joke Movement" on the same label.

Simvlacrvm (Slo) "Zeugma" CD1999 Old Europa Cafe
A hum emanates from my speakers, rising from an undefined horizon, one measured in time as well as distance. The past melds with the present as desolate, tribal rhythms mesh with occasional blasts of shredded machinery noise, a female vocal utilized as an instrument (no definable language is spoken, it is just another layer in the tapestry of sound), and sparse synths shrouded in melancholia. Simvlacrvm's (side-project of the noisy Einleitungszeit) unique juxtaposition of sonic elements, a combination of diverse sounds that transcends the ages, is most captivating. Zeugma contains six tracks listed as I-VI (track VI indicates two halves, 0 & I), all of which follow along similar thematic lines. 'II' opens with brooding drones upon which a kick and stomp belch of noise grows quite ferocious. In the distance, distorted radio-wave vocals (voices defying the laws of time, in essence, crossing the known parameters of time?) are plucked from the empty skies. As the track unfolds, pensive synths and the ever-present tribal rhythms, along with the same female vocals from the previous track, are blended into the mix. I am in awe of the way the disparate textures meld into a cohesive piece, a dark, fiery, forlorn trek. Each track seems a part of what came before, while expanding and metamorphosing the Zeugma sonic landscape, building and shifting the perceptions in fascinating ways. Synths that casually slip one into a state of disorientation open 'III,' before tribal rhythms lead one into a realm of shattered hope distinguished by an acoustic guitar (or, most probably, a synth masked as one). The synths of 'VI' solemnly whisper amidst an ambience coated in subtly grim trepidation, before a light rain of percussion and raw bleats of noise corrode the background. The second half of the track eerily resonates with exhaling synths, nervous crystals of sound, a looped, fuzzy pulsation, more synths dredged from the depths of hopelessness, and chiming percussion that skitters about before everything, somehow, comes full circle (though from an alternate trajectory...). The vocals are similar, but not the same; the feel is similar-as throughout-but not the same... A wonderfully enchanting, darkly illusive, listening experience. —JC Smith

Shining Vril (UK/Aus)/ Knifeladder (UK/Aus) "Self Titled" split CD 2000 CAPP
Here we have a split CD of two of John Murphy's current musical projects. First up is Shining Vril, with four tracks of partly rhythmic yet fully tensile atmospheric soundscapes that generate an unusual ambience with the use of an Australian accented female voice on one of the tracks. 'Tortured Willow' (the first track) is a captivating piece of shrill high and low end loops that create a foreboding and suspenseful sound texture. The same atmosphere carries through to `Carcass Black', but there is an increased reliance on treated and looped vocalisations and far off percussive drumming. The female spoken vocals are used with grim abandon on 'Dislocation', ranging from looped words, whispered and spoken passages that are vaguely treated with echoes, and other treatments to make up the basis of the track. The last track from Shining Vril is 'All my Sins Remembered', which is quite a sweepingly atmospheric piece of male vocals, sound loops and ritual sounds that still retains the underlying tension. Next up is Knifeladder with three tracks that in comparison opt for heavy percussive power electronics with the compositions partially resembling the soundscapes of Militia (albeit with more aggressive and straightforward percussive elements). 'Lasp Gasp', the first taster of Knifeladder, contains slow ritual/martial percussion, plodding bass and a slightly melodic backing soundscape/tune that gradually morphs into much heavier territory as all its musical elements become more aggression. Hitting a point late in the track, it quickly surges off at a rapid pace of increased tempo with fast drumming and noisier backing layers of sound. The next offering, the live track 'Dervish', redefines the meaning of driving percussion, and I simply can't begin to describe the inherent power of the all-out percussive/noise looped soundscape. At over 6 minutes there is no let up whatsoever to the drumming that complements perfectly the mounting intensity of the noise loops and sound stabs. The last track for both the CD and Knifeladder is the lengthy 19-minute 'Maelstrom I+II+III', which meanders through various stages along its travels. Beginning with a slow percussion and bass tune, the layered electronics remain subdued in the background whilst gradually becoming more focussed and prominent over time. The middle section sees the percussion and bass drop off somewhat replaced with a centre of noise loops, sound bites and grinding electronics, with the final segments moving back to bass and percussion driven atmospheres enhanced with the tense electronic backing. Of the two projects I would have to say I am much more enamored with Knifeladder, although Shining Vril has more than a few great moments. I guess I am a sucker for percussive driven power electronics at the moment, and Knifeladder is a name I'm sure we are going to hear quite a lot more of in the future.

Simply Dead's (Swe) "Structure of Minds" CD 2000 Fluttering Dragon Records
When I opened the package from the label containing this album, I had no idea who this group was (and I still don't), and the cover gave no hint at all to the style of the music. From the first listen I can say that I was literally blown away, as the music was able to stand on its own without suffering from any preconceived notions. The opening track, a darkly brooding trip-hop piece, resplendent with computer vocals (later mirrored with female vocals), absolutely floored me and is quite comparable to the darker sounds of a group like Massive Attack. From there, the album toys with similar sounds whilst tangenting off into more experimental, programmed type synth soundscapes (also with vocal samples, voices, etc.). The classical synth lines and reverberating bass tune of track three mirrors the emotive elements of the opening track, and continues with track four being intermixed with spoken samples from Martin Luther King and covering other topics such as Jonestown. The depth and sparsity of the tune on track 7 melds composed and minimalist elements to an emotive result, morphing back into much more heavily programmed territory with the beats and multi-layered programmed elements of track 8 (which unfortunately goes so far with the programmed sound that it detracts from the preceding aura evoked). A groovy, laid-back beat section of programming arrives on track 9, solidifying all that is great on this album, while the next piece enhances the darker, less beat-oriented programmed segments of the album. The diversity of material coming from Fluttering Dragon has thus far been very impressive, and if they continue on this path will continue to garner a positive reputation. I for one hope they can bring forward more material from this group, and here's hoping that something will eventuate soon given that this album was recorded in 1998/1999. It is worth the time to seek this one out. (Note: as I recently learned, it seems that the group includes one member who is the live vocalist for In Slaughter Natives.)

Skrol (Cze) "Heretical Antiphony" CD 1999 Membrum Debile Propaganda
This debut CD for this Czech group showcases a very classically influenced, war- mongering dark industrial group, potentially comparable to In Slaughter Natives and the like, with the rigid beat programming and more flowing and shrill string and organ segments. 'Agog' is a particularly forceful track, with violent strings, organ keys and harsh programmed rhythms with underlying martial implications due to the synthetic snare rolls. `Litany' is the most drawn-out track at over 6 minutes, and contains a heavy focus on the monotonous organ dirge, part operatic female vocals, more shrill violins and distant explosions in the background. The cinematic battle scenes evoked on 'Non-Organic' are extremely rousing with fast beats, multi layered strings, deep horns and partly buried monotone (male) vocals. Things are mixed up a bit more on 'Fire Scene' with slow drum rolls and piano again with the organ and commanding female vocals. Although I have not had a chance to check, this tracks sounds suspiciously like a re-worked song from the "Matyria" vinyl 10". `Converted' uses a basic construction of female vocals and programmed string segments in a mid-paced fashion before again adding the snare and organ, with Martina Sweeney all the while stating themes of "a new life". The final cut, 'Epilogue: Exsanguis', is the most flowing piece and

somehow manages to sound removed from the preceding tracks due to its slow triumphant air (also due to the reduced emphasis on the organ) signalling the end of battle (but not the war....). Overall this is the quality of release hinted at on the preceding "Matyria" 10", and although the overall feel is probably still a little rigid for my personal liking (due to the programming basis), it is still a commendable item packaged in a simple yet well-presented predominantly black digipack.

Skrol (Cze) "What the Eye have Seen Have not Seen" Video 1999 Ars Morta Universum
This live video was released by the same mob who produced the Einleitungszeit video (also reviewed in these pages), and they have again come up with commendable results. Here the footage for this production is more professional than the first video, taking on a number of different camera shots and angles that have been collated and melded in post production. It also seems that the footage was shot across a number of different live performances and then spliced together to create this live document. As for the performance side of things, it would appear that Vladimir Hirsch handles the synthesizer and sequencer elements (basically the music side of things - and additionally with some backing vocals), while Martina Sweeney fronts the project by presenting commanding vocals and occasional percussion and synth work. The apocalyptic industrial/neo classical/heavy orchestral hymns have as much power in the live arena as in a studio format, and with the tracks presented it sees a number lifted from their 10" EP and CD, along with other live tracks (though I'm not sure where they originate). Among these unfamiliar tracks I suspect there may be some newer compositions, for they are more complex, epically dramatic and free-flowing than the material showcased on earlier releases. With the live performance sounding similar close to their studio output, I wonder how 'live' these tracks really are (i.e., as with Der Blutharsch playing to backing tapes presenting live vocals and percussion); but either way the rigid incessant power of the tracks shines even brighter with the aggressive vocal presentation and stage persona of Martina (Vladimir is less active, and situated off to the side of the stage). Another element to the post production is that the majority of footage does not play out in real time, but is rather slowed and slightly blurred with random nondescript images filtering through. The stage lighting also adds to the effect, with the artists bathed in a heavy luminescent glow along with video footage projected behind the stage against the wall. At just over 40 minutes (8 tracks in total), the music is presented in clear stereo sound, complemented with decent filming and post production, creating a good quality video release. Now I hear an upcoming item from this production crew includes a live video of Schloss Tegal that I will certainly be keeping a keen eye out for!

Sol Invictus (Eng) "Trieste" CD 2000 Tursa (via World Serpent Distribution)
Rather than a new album, this a live recording of the group from an acoustic performance in Italy during November1999. Assisted by both Sally Doherty and Matt Howden, the morose sung/spoken vocals of Tony Wakeford are embellished by acoustic guitars, violin, flute and the voice of Doherty often echoing or following the main vocal lines in sweet feminine divinity. This format encompasses much of this 17-song, 60-minute set, never lacking or being overstated in instrumentation, stepping between quieter subtle renditions to more forcefully played numbers (yet still retaining a fragility through the acoustic format). The renditions of 'Come the Morning' and 'In a Garden Green' are particularly great, as is the whole performance. 'Remember and Forget' has the soaring vocals of Doherty operatically phrasing Latin, with light acoustic guitar and violin guitar being the only accompaniment. Other tracks in the set list include 'Amongst the Ruins', 'Media', 'See how we Fall', 'Against the Modern World', and 'In Europa'. The high production quality of this disc makes one almost forget that it is a live recording, yet in between the songs there is ,polite and enthusiastic applause. The sound of the crowd has me slightly bemused seeming as if Sol Invictus were playing to the appreciative audience of a concert hall gathering, rather than that of a normal show. If this was actually the case, maybe there is a level of cultural interest by the arts crowd of Italy in such music that is not prevalent in other countries (where they tend to snub such folk noir music). Regardless, this is a great document of the live performance.

Spear (Pol) "Not Two" 7" EP 1999 Drone Records
Ritual chimes and deep ambience start the title track - a tense atmosphere of sweepings archaic sounds of aeons past. Half composed melodies abound, combined with sparse vocal chants and condemning sounds that remind me of some of the less composed works of Raison d'être. Quite a good introduction. The first of two tracks on Side B, 'The Names - Low Frequency Silence', does a good job of giving a brief description of the sound. Less forceful, here the atmospheres are of introspection, focussing on slow movement of tone and sound in a droneage guise. The archaic atmospheres are still prevalent, and are like a much more ritualized Lustmord or akin to the works of ExoToendo. The next track, 'Equilibrium', slowly rises forth at a quicker pace than its predecessor, and soon surpasses it in volume. Tense drones, smatterings of texture and sweeping textures are mixed with other unusual sound outbursts creating a track of experimental quality that I feel is not totally related to the first two track. Nonetheless you should seek this out for the quality of the first two pieces.

Squaremeter (???) "14id1610s" CD 2000 Ant-Zen
This is an extremely great example of cutting edge sampling and studio trickery, creating astounding glitch-orientated soundscapes (created, manipulated, de-constructed and assembled by the artist Panacea). Taking 89% of sound samples from Ant-Zen releases, most are only fleetingly recognisable due to the scattergun approach to melding them together. Static bursts of beats, blips, bleeps and other random sounds spit and gurgle from the speakers housed and delivered in a crystalline sound production. The breadth of sound exploration ranges from scattered hyper beat-driven atmospheres to minimalist electronics, and represents a fantastic cornerstone of a emerging new genre of sound texturalisation. To even begin describing all the elements of the album, let alone individual tracks, is an absolutely fruitless task since once appropriately descriptive words solidify, the sounds of the CD have already surged off on a totally different tangent. However this is not to say that this lacks focus, for it is a very engaging listen. Not quite digital abstraction (due to the many beat-oriented samples), this is also not flowing enough to be able to be played in a club. Rather, it is more appropriately viewed as a digital canvas masterwork to be appreciated by connoisseurs of experimental digital soundworks. The packaging also deserves special mention with its minimal print, transparent cover and inlay card housed in a clear jewel case creating a very nice visual effect. Lastly, referencing the title, the CD equates to 14 tracks (14id) and an astounding 1620 samples! (1610s). To even imagine collating that many samples into a cohesive and listenable whole is an astounding feat within itself. Ant-Zen does it again!

Sleeping with the Earth (USA) "S/T" CDR 1999 SWTE
Most people in power electronics would be well aware of the varying sounds coming from different geographic regions, with the two disciplines of German and English power electronics being the most distinctive. These scenes have gone on to inspire other groups with the emergence of a hybrid of these two sounds with a number of American artists. Taking a select amount of the high pitched un-structured mayhem of Con-Dom and the Grey Wolves and the obliterated semi-structures of Genocide Organ and Anzenzephalia would end up somewhere in the vicinity of Sleeping with the Earth, particularly as show cased on the track 'Inside/Beyond'. On this track rather than opting for an audible or partly audile vocal component, they are simply heavily processed into yet another squealing layer of feedback. 'And Sell my Soul' is content in presenting a few spacious loops that multiply into a subdued throbbing mass, later with churning vocals and spits, hisses and crackles of speaker obliterating tones. The surging mass of 'Untitled 2' is quite chaotic with a layer or two of squiggly, improvised sounding layers, which become less obtrusive when overshadowed by the sweeping noise elements. Overall the tracks can be characterised by their seemingly unstructured and ferocious free-form flow, yet all the while containing a hint of looped form via the building blocks of sound layers. 'Faluire 2' is a good example of this with stabs of static white noise (both feedback and vocal) over multiple pulsating factory generated textures. 'Reduction' is the closest the group gets to sounding like Con-Dom in its absolute chaos of vocals and all-out aural warfare. Here the distortion is so extreme that even the basic structure is almost entirely obliterated. I'm not sure how widely available this CDR is, but for a demo recording it is of good quality, ensuring that the group has been signed up for a number of releases, including items on Troniks and Malignant Records.

Smooth Quality Excrement (USA) "Bird and Truck Collision" CD 2000 Influx Communications
Do not be put off by the unusual title of either the group or the CD, or even by the modest packaging, as all these elements pale in comparison to the sheer brilliance of the tension-filled atmospheric electronics on the disc. The liner notes specify that all 5 untitled tracks were the result of live improvisations by three individuals who used absolutely no sequencing. In itself this is no mean feat, and it perfectly explains the sprawling, constantly tangent-pursuing nature of the sounds. Dredging electronic drones, low flying textures, spits and bursts of static, random processed beats, storming, swirling sounds burst out of the speakers from every which way, keeping the listener on their toes by creating a situation where you are never quite sure when any of these random elements will leap out. For an unusual analogy for such unusual sounds, it is akin to being in a virtual reality kitchen, listening as the compositional layers are continuously rolled and folded, never repeating with each kneading touch (with the inevitable baking process being yet another plundered sound source). Other than the tension created throughout, the tracks are constantly on the move, with some parts being highly active and multidimensional, while others create more subdued liquidous drones - maybe, just maybe, this is what Yen Pox would sound like on bad acid trip! All in all there are too many sounds and too much ground covered to describe everything going on here, but believe me when I say that you could not go wrong by picking up a copy of this. Yes, this is a definite recommendation!

The Soil Bleeds Black (USA) "Alchemie" CD 1999 World Serpent Distribution
With this, their fourth album release (this time on a new label), the group have endeavoured to take their sound forward by the use of primarily real instrumentation, attempting to rely less on sound generated from synthetic means as show cased on previous releases. The newer components of sound mainly come in the form of acoustic guitars, dulcimer, pipes, whistles, recorders and various types of percussion, which all greatly assist in fleshing out the breadth of sound. If unfamiliar with the group, The Soil Bleeds Black is a project producing traditional medieval folk music illustrating a past aeon. Essentially the intent is not to create folk music with an updated modern sound, rather it is to create authentic medieval music. Revolving around the twin brothers, Mark and Mike Riddick, and a third member Eugenia Houston, male and female vocals intermix with acoustic guitars, synth layers, pipes and percussion on reasonably short movements. Predominantly folk-oriented in vibe, selected moments border on the neo-classical with some segments of accentuated instrumentation and in particular on "Winter Marriage". The influence of CMI recording artist Arcana can be felt on the guest appearance track 'Lapis Philosoyhorum', which has a darker and more majestic edge than the more celebratory folk sound of the other tracks. In most part the male vocals suit the vibe very well, but unfortunately on 'Fire of the Sacred Seal' are a little over the top in accentuation, mostly in relation to the deeper voices (and not the higher, clean sung part). The haunting feel of 'Some sweet sorrow did her heart distraine, Act 1', complete with its slow pounding drumming, hymn-like female vocals, keyboard and recorder tunes is a good ending track, presenting yet another element to expanding song writing sound to the group. At 13 tracks only over 35 minutes, this might be quite a short release but it is beautifully presented in a mini gatefold card slip sleeve.

Subklink (USA) "Dawn of Desekration" CD 2000 CDR Live Bait Recording Foundation
While Subklink are one of the generation of American artists delving into death ambient type sonics that call to mind pioneers such as Megaptera, this release is somewhat more subdued overall. Containing six 'movements', these are coagulated into one track of just under 70 minutes and, given the length, things start slowly and continue in such a style for the majority of the album. Densely heavy and partially fractured guttural drones slowly grind in sparse cyclical fashion, giving the air of discarded machinery being cranked into action once again. Far off windy textures add to the rumbling sound palate, thus providing some variation along with faint hints of slow droning keyboard melodies and occasionally understated rhythmic clatter. There is not a great change in sound across the six movements, thus the single track format suits it

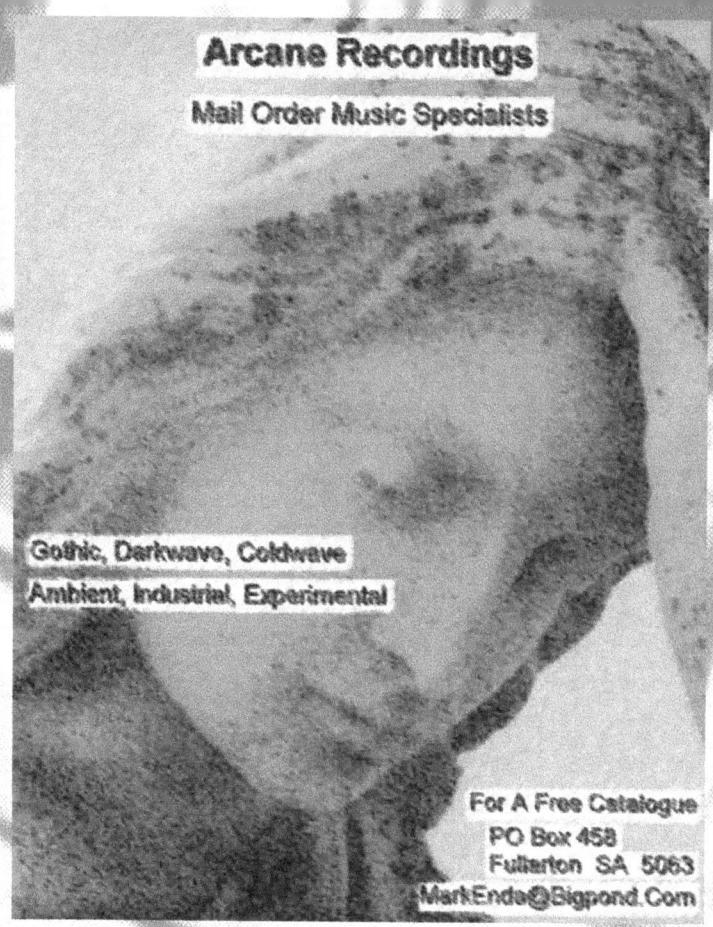

Arcane Recordings
Mail Order Music Specialists

Gothic, Darkwave, Coldwave
Ambient, Industrial, Experimental

For A Free Catalogue
PO Box 458
Fullarton SA 5063
MarkEnds@Bigpond.Com

as a drawn-out soundscape sonically illustrating hollow catacomb depths. Not a bad release by any means, this item shows that Subklinik has much more than rudimentary ability. If this is anything to go by, I shudder to think of the much stronger and powerful soundscapes they are likely to come up with in future. The packaging comes with a nice oversized DVD case.

Thee Majesty (USA/UK) "Time's Up" CD 1999 Suffering Clown
This CD by Thee Majesty (comprised of Bryin Dall and Genesis P-Orridge) works in a similar manner as the Merzbow/Genesis P-Orridge collaborative CD, "A Perfect Pain". And while the latter CD was a vehicle for the sounds of Merzbow with Genesis P-Orridge's spoken passages over it, here the CD is much more reliant on spoken vocals as the focal point while the backing sounds are much more subtle, and even non-existent in sections. (Incidentally it is also noted that some of the spoken passages were also used on the Merzbow collaborative CD). Half sung, half spoken, each word is heavily articulated in a slow drawl akin to the narrator of a children's novel, albeit one that has the ability to unnerve even an adult. All sorts of ideas are explored by Genesis on the disc, with one example being on the 29 second cryptic piece 'I.T', with the only included vocals stating "First it was....then it knew it was....and that is it". By posing questions, presenting quirky takes on common ideas and other passages of literary weirdness, it creates an aura where ordinary perceptions are shattered and where you begin to question the construct of your own reality. But I guess this is quite understandable considering that Genesis P-Orridge has been a long-standing media provocateur. Referencing the project's other member, when Bryin's contributions do make themselves known they are mostly in the form of experimental soundscapes of low subtle sounds and shifting noise textures that act as an enhancement rather than as a prominent element, and generally seem to have the resonance of being derived from a guitar. (An exception to the non-musical rule is the classical tune contained in 'Wisdom'). Basically this CD demands your attention and requires a certain mood in order to take in the content, but during the wee hours in a darkened room, it somehow seems very appropriate. The packaging is the standard jewel case, but the cover is printed in beautiful shades of purple with a silver logo and writing.

The Sword Volcano Complex (USA) "The Sword Volcano Complex" CD 2000 Suffering Clown Inc. (via World Serpent Distribution)
Many acts write and produce 'cinematic' music, yet this CD has the feeling that you are actually hearing a movie (while lacking the visual counterpart). This perception has much to do with the use and inclusion of extensive field recordings as utilised on the track 'The Sanctum', which follows the opening piece (a beautifully sorrowful passage of orchestral violin and keyboard melodies). Footfalls, seagull cries, water lapping at the shores, distant ship horns etc intermixed with droning textures and found sounds illustrate and amplify the bleak experimental collage. The liner notes of the disc make 'Cupid Never Speaks' an intriguing track as we learn that both music and words were totally improvised and pieced together into the final track. An introductory soundscape meanders along before the musical composition segment of slow programmed electronic beats/bass enters along with well executed clean vocals and minimalist keyboard tune. The following piece, 'Monolithic', arcs back to the field recording and sound experiment format, differing in that a spoken word piece is included. One track I feel that does not really fit within the context of the other tracks is 'Adrenalin' due to the electronic/pounding drumming and partly chanted vocals format - personally I feel this is too up-tempo in comparison to the rest of the flow of the album, and unfortunately has me leaping for the skip button. Again from my reading of the liner note it appears that a trance-like state was attained for the recording of the vocals on 'The Sperm of Metal', which manages to evoke a very ritualistic feel, backed with spare experimentalism. 'Descent into the Valley of the Kings' represents another sound sculpture containing air raid sirens, looped anger filled vocals (chanting `ashes to ashes . . . dust to dust') slow distant horn and orchestral melodies resulting in quite a stunning piece. On the final offering, (the title track) a mantra of the repeated phrase `when will I see you again?' loops, while a variety of words central to the philosophy of the group are slowly revealed over the course of tense backing of electronic drones and experimental beats. Combining the talents of Bruce LaFountain (is this who is pictured on the cover?) and John Murphy (with other select contributions), this debut CD (even if not viewed totally in context of music) is an evocative and introspective exploration of an inner self.

Tehom (Cro) "Theriomorphic Spirits" CD 2000 Twilight Command/ NER (via Tesco Distribution)
Although this is the second album for the project, I can't compare as I have not heard their debut. Knowing that the project was discovered and signed by Douglas P, I had the perception that this might be some apocalyptic folk/neo-classical fare, but in reality is stunning dark ambient atmospheric works much in the vein of Lustmord, Inade and Yen Pox. These tracks are atmospheres sounding if derived from barren windswept battle fields long after the conflict has ended, yet remnants of twisted and discarded implements of war are still visibly scattered across the ground. The tracks also range in length from 7 to 16 minutes, further illustrating the drawn-out nature of the compositions. In the middle of the opening piece, 'Jaldabaoth', a low chant filters into the mix for a fleeting instant, before the track moves on to noisier machine-grinding textures. Ritualized percussive textures and cavernous dungeon sounds work fantastically on 'Aberth', with the main section of echoed and treated hand percussion being a particular standout. The sweeping barren soundscapes are again employed on 'The Eight Sky', the various echoed treatments launching the tense drones out into the infinite distance. Subtler deep droning sound elements are toyed with on 'The Shadow Integration', with hints of choir like textures floating somewhere off in the distance. At around the 6 minute mark a slow, cripplingly heavy beat arrives as a ritualistic sound element as a slow horn tune introduces itself. The remaining tracks play out in similar style, intermixing ritualistic sounds and dense echoed drones; yet the final track `Hybris' has the most focussed orchestral sound with a prominent looped horn tune. One of the greatest tragedies of the CD is that its creator is reported to have died from a war related-illness soon after the completion of recordings (Sinisa Ocurscak fought in the Balkans conflict within a Special Unit based in Dugave-Zagreb). Maybe Sinisa is now one of the spirits mentioned in the title.

Ure Thrall and the Fruitless Hand (USA) "Forbidden Fruit" CD 1999 HydrXdelusions
Given that the above collaborators form two thirds of the Smooth Quality Excrement project, this gives a certain slant on what to expect of this CD (although incidentally this was recorded and released prior to the SQE album). Descending into a vortex of subliminal yet confrontational cascading drones, the all-expansiveness of the tracks present themselves as slightly more subdued and brooding than that of SQE, and at close to 30 minutes track one sets this tone in an expanded construct of experimentation. Liquidous yet shimmering and fractured multi layered tones rendering themselves void of any recognition to the original sound source due to massive amount of pre and post production undertaken. Much as in a relay, segments arise, surge forward then interlink with the next section with the former slowly receding, creating a seamless flowing voyage, navigating a myriad of peaks and troughs in the sonic ocean. Rather than utilising mostly subliminal or minimalist drone elements, this is much more dynamic, creating a quite playful take on what some may have considered a genre that contains certain limitations. Interestingly tracks two and three are live recordings but do not distance themselves from the first in sound or tone, being just as crystalline and dynamic, one opting for a 'quick' 8 minute jaunt while the other sprawls out over 28. This is highly recommended for any 'drone' fan, and is still awash in brooding sentiment to entice fans of darker groups like Yen Pox.

... Today I'm Dead (Ita) "The Anatomy of Melancholy" CDR 1999 Slaughter Productions
Not only has this project taken a heavy overdose of the Brighter Death Now carcinogen, but the sole member has gone so far as to inject it into his bloodstream to gain inspiration via intravenous means. While plagiarism can be a huge downfall, I will say that this homage is done with enough spite and hatred that they will be forgiven for any such comparisons, with this forming an ultimate tribute to their master - Mr Karmanik. The dense carcinogenic pulsations of 'Death Passion Time' are a perfect reflection of the early to mid phase of BDN's sound (complete with distant psychotic ramblings), while later tracks see the addition of much more tortured distortion for a gritty resonance without having a clue of what is being conveyed (but with titles such as 'Young Flesh' or 'Rape Me (explicit version)' you might be thankful). On 'Satisfy your Desire' the low industrial drones are merged with other noisier and seemingly improvised layers, creating a track rife with scattered modulating distortion and incessant high pitched squeals. Whereas following on, the extreme density of 'A Cold Winter' renders it a droning, writhing mass, with vocals barely able to puncture the coagulated black ooze dripping from the speakers. Weirdness of sample choice is an understatement on the untitled track 10, containing a female sung German folk song, the only treatment being the use of slight reverb and echo...strange, strange, strange indeed.... Tympani like factory poundings, sparse drones and even sparser vocal wails still recreate some of the best minimalist tracks of BDN's "Great Death" trilogy on a track simply entitled 'All' - and, yes, there is no doubt about it, with atmospheres like this, the abyss is certainly calling.... 'I'm Alone' is a sophisticated death ambient track (if there ever was such a thing), with over-the-top electronic explosions and acerbic vocals akin to rusty razor blades dragged across cold flesh. Already covering all sorts of violent extremities, religion is hardly going to escape unscathed, with God getting a good serve of venom on 'Jesus Can't' with its obliterated (inside an oil drum) sound treatment of various religious inspired radio and text snippets. These tracks, along with the cover and enclosed text, depict an individual who is truly beyond redemption (let alone salvation), yet I imagine this is no less than exactly where he wants to be....

Triage (USA) "The Cessation Of Spoil" CD 1999 Glass Throat Recordings
Triage teams the ubiquitous Scott E. Candey (Gruntsplatter, head of Crionic Mind, plus more...) with Chet W. Scott (Ruhr Hunter, head of Glass Throat Recordings) for a collection of mini soundtracks adorned in trepidation, in the tattered shroud of dismay. A tension whine rises during the opening 'Serum.' Dread is highlighted as the

contorted distortion swells to the forefront. But the tension is never released; the dread remains, an ominous shadow, even as the track simmers to conclusion. 'Donor' kicks in with samples from David Cronenberg's gloomy descent into love/obsession inspired, drug-laden, co-dependency (quite literally) melancholia, Dead Ringers (this must be Chet's favorite movie as he also sampled it on 'Euthanasia' from the excellent Ruhr Hunter—...Ritual Before The Hunt CD). Subtle humming and clicking noises set the foundation for moist, grinding machinery noises. The underlying, despondent drone slips under the skin, a needle injecting discomfort. Throughout, marching feet slosh through the sodden sonic landscape. The inherent unnerving quality grows more imposing as the track progresses. This track, as with much of the CD, highlights the dark sonicscape elements as opposed to the sheer noise assault, but the presence of noise is always on the periphery, occasionally slipping into full view. The oscillating, whirring tendencies of spastically fluttering propeller blades slices through 'Grume' as hideous noise gurgles insanely underneath. Jagged metal spikes sink serrated teeth into the brooding, noisy ambience of clutter and dissolution during 'Assume.' 'Natural Order' resonates with the repetitious cadences of an exhausted machinery loop before slivers of subtly melodic sound and distorted vocal noise intrude. The fuzzy throb of 'Genetic Drift' portends danger, a danger accentuated by the slippery, scoured feedback sounds that scamper from within the smoldering embers radiance. A diverse, exceptionally crafted and conceived piece of work; each track opens new wounds in the dark sonicscape flesh, new perceptions gleaned from the glistening cavities. Masterful! —JC Smith (Reprinted by permission from Side-Line magazine: www.side-line.com)

Tripwire (Swe) "Intellavoid" CD 1999 Fluttering Dragon
With the involvement of one of the Puissance members this piece of pure brooding techno/ambience is certain to shock a few. This is not at all really what you would expect considering the infamous main project. The next question is whether this is any good, and I have to admit that it is. Although slightly lacking in the cutting-edge studio sounds that are being forged by the some of the Ant-Zen crew (Beefcake and Xingu Hill come to mind), the tracks themselves are all pretty solid. Working on two levels, there is the sweeping galactic ambience (generated from multi-layered synths lines), overlaid with the programmed drum machine beats and rhythm distortion. The title track has choir keyboard textures, with mid-paced bass pounds and energetic drum work creating a dark yet dynamic listen (which goes for much of the other 7 tracks). 'Prokain' starting as a drum and bass piece quickly snaps into quick break beats then back again, using this format throughout. Things get somewhat tribal/classical in the tune and drum sequence of 'Made Out' with the classical tunes also being used in 'Imaginary Flies', break beats and noise swirling throughout the main violin melody, likewise the partly urgent/ partly brooding choir synth lines work particularly well here. Crazy bass lines and schizoid beats are the fair for 'Thief' with a strangely cheesy (in a good way) keyboard line that appears towards the middle of the track. The track 'Tripwire' is the closest thing you will get to a Puissance number, only by virtue of the angrier bomb loaded beats and sweeping urgent neo-classical backing. More drum and bass is featured on last offering 'Scartissue' with a slow bass tune, mid to fast paced break beats and again those great (sweeping) down vibed melodies. I guess this could muster a comparison as a more energetic Atomine Elektrine (more so in relation to the first album than the second), yet this remains noisier and more complex in track construction. Overall this is a pretty good listen, but I have to admit that I originally purchased this more out of curiosity than anything else.

David Tonkin (Aus) "Semblance of Perfection" MC 2000
With a definite lack of groups within Australia focussing on the death industrial genre, David Tonkin has certainly started to change all that with this high-quality self-released tape. And while the project may not have a very sinister moniker, the compositions certainly bring to mind Megaptera, Deutsch Nepal and No Festival of Light - in other words, this is a project of great old school death industrial vibes. Hands down the opening track ('Baptism of Fire') is the best track, being in the vein of the best of what Megaptera has to offer. The multi-layered drawn out electronic drones (some guttural, some mid-ranged and one high-pitched), catatonicly slow beat and well placed vocal samples (taken from 'The Candyman', if I'm not mistaken) are all processed together, as further external thunderous elements sweep into the composition. The slow movement of the track allows a variety textures to be explored through various segments, coming to a conclusion with an interesting use of a distressed Papua New Guinean tribesman's voice. The clinical electronic pulse of 'Buyer Beware' brings to mind No Festival of Light along, and employs somewhat hazy and shimmering factory type sound textures. 'Terra Coitus' is slightly aggressive, with mid-paced pulsating layers and soulless beats, that over an extended length gradually align themselves into a loose yet quirky industrial rhythm (à la Deutsch Nepal). The sunken, muffled tones of the last track on side A do justice to its title ('(Song for) Aquatic Dreamers'), giving off a subdued ambient feel, with 'Glacial Drop, River Freezing' (first on Side B) continuing in a similar vein, though using fewer murky textures to help distinguish it. More vocal samples appear on 'Take me to your Feeder' (referencing religion and passivity/violence) followed by some Tibetan monk type vocals chants reverberating in cylindrical fashion until a very crispy electronic tone bursts forth from the speakers. No Festival of Light is again brought to mind on 'Dance of the Sheeple', being totally calculated with its use of clinical drones, wavering sounds and typewriter like beat. Lastly, 'Night in ABSU' rounds out the tape with an extended length track. A horn like drone, bass drenched textures and ritualistic beat set a Lovecraftian air, the mood slightly lightened with a looped sample (sounding akin to a treated harp/ female vocal recording), entrancing the listening into a dreamlike journey. While I have thrown in a few more comparisons than normal, I have simply done so to emphasise the quality of these tracks. Many facets of the death industrial/death ambient genre are explored on the tape thus preventing any of the tracks (or the overall tape) from ever sounding one-dimensional. Given that I know these are some of the first compositions that David has recorded, with the clarity of ideas shown and skills displayed, I'm sure you will be hearing a lot more about this. If intrigued drop David a line on: daveton@start.com.au.

Turbund Stermwerk (Ger) "Weltbrand" CD 1999 Loki Foundation
Having had this CD for a couple of months now, I am still undecided about my perceptions of this album. The tracks are certainly of a high calibre, with martially enhanced orchestral/neo-classical hymns, and these features seem to work best on individual tracks rather than flowing throughout the album (as they did on the debut). Likewise as the tracks are quite a bit more straightforward, they also tend to be patchier between individual pieces. With an opener like 'Vortex' (formerly off the stunning "Natural Order" 2LP compilation set), it is easy to see where my misgivings about this album originated, because exactly where does one go after a track of such brilliance? A repetitive yet intricate acoustic string instrument (sounding more like a lute than an acoustic guitar) forms the basis of the tune, mixed with xylophone chimes, female hymn oriented vocals and an understated beat, overlaid with Charles Manson's world view presented in narrative conversational form. Sharp abrasive drum outbursts, drawn-out violin segments, distant sound textures and sampled German voices embody 'Europa', and sustain a tense atmosphere and air of anticipation that never quite comes, running straight into 'Feueradler'. Here drum textures are swapped for trench warfare sounds with razor-edged kettle drumming, as bombs fall and explode overhead. This continues with electric tension until the absolutely <u>massively</u> epic brass orchestral segment strides in quite unexpectedly (and I question anyone who would not get inspired by this) which is however just too damn short. 'Wellenthal' again has that weird trench warfare vibe, except that here it seems to be illustrating the emptiness of downtime between battle, where the soldier is simply waiting for the next confrontation when one is faced with the choice of killing or being killed (distant air raid sirens sound, slow tunes play out, melded with layers of nondescript sounds and tones...). I find 'Stumme Front' to be the most difficult track on the album due to its repetitive bass tune appearing very high in the mix, with the only other elements being more sampled German speeches, swirling tones and liquidous/scaping sounds. Returning to my favourite format, 'Kainmal' mixes interludes of slow pounding drumming with shrill strings and deep horns to embrace the huge epic orchestral aura (flowing through a number of segments), and the less intense (but no less commanding) 'Sonnenschild' uses a similar approach of neo-classical brilliance. Militant to the core, no hint of a tune is present on 'Allen Gewalten', rather using looped tympani/snare drumming, industrial factory noise and a single German phrase repeated throughout to drive the message home (that message is lost on a monolingual anglophone like myself). An echo treated piano and tonal elements make for a short interlude to the final track 'Arcanum', which is essentially a soundscape piece used as backing to yet another era speech (incidentally, the final hidden track is a sampled early recording of a German male singing and straight drumming piece). The blood red cover with text and imagery (in a combination of black and white print) if full of esoteric symbolism and unfortunately as the text is again exclusively in German I can't appreciate the full implications of what is written. While on the musical front this may not be exactly what I was expecting from the debut release, I think my overall uncertainty is more tainted from this angle than specifically being a below par second album. Turbund Sturmwerk have created a very solid and worthy album, it is just that it slightly differs in sound and direction from what I was expecting.

Ultra Milkmaids (Fra) "Peps" CD 2000 Duebel
This is the first I have come across this French duo, yet maybe this is for the best since the bio states that the group had previously toyed with industrial-noise-rock and jazz-noise?! Here they seem to have settled into minimalist ambient soundscapes, and do a mighty fine job of it! (Maybe their previous experimentations would not have been as bad as my expectation). Regardless, this could be filed alongside artists like Squaremeter, or alternatively some of the MEGO roster in its obvious studio manipulation and glitch aesthetic. Would 'digital abstraction' be an appropriate term? I think so.... Tones, blips, fractured static and dismembered melodies form the broad canvas of the sound textures, creating a sterile environment of electronics often enveloped in a minimalist brooding tune. The juxtaposition of silence (when utilized) emphasizes tone - and thus heightens the perception - of what would otherwise be wrongly perceived as fragile soundscapes - there is an inherent power in these recordings even if the actual volume is not overwhelming. Additionally the disc comes with a multi-media component with a video for the opening track of the disc. Much as in the description of the music, the video does a commendable job of visually illustrating the sounds with a slow panning shot of nondescript imagery, with the video production footage intentionally textured and flawed.

Ultra United (Swi) "Research 1" 7" EP 1999 Drone Records
Having heard good things about this project, I was eagerly anticipating this EP. Not only does it not disappoint, but it only makes me impatient for upcoming releases! (For a general categorization I guess you would slot this in with groups of an industrial noise, or subdued power electronics sound). The introductory piece 'Achtung!' is a mildly treated female choir vocal sample that sets the stage for the first proper track 'Execution 2'. Comprising intense noise with slow militant orchestral underpinnings (synth generated layers), the shrill swirling of mid-ranged sound amplifies throughout the progression of the slow atmospheres. Whilst I was trying to describe the last track on Side A 'Scrape in the Sky', I noted that it has already finished before descriptive terminology had a chance to solidify in my mind . . . hmmm, far too short (for easy reference, check the description above!). On Side B, fire-blazing intensity is presented and detailed on 'Physical Initiation', again with a great mixture of deep orchestral sub melodies and mid-ranged noise. 'Arrival (excerpt)', on the other hand, explores shrill high-end noise of almost air raid siren proportions that overshadows the lower noise texture. Given that this is a shortened version, I would certainly like to hear the unabridged version of this track. The brooding yet tense atmosphere of the final track 'The Volunteer' (another abridged piece) applies deep orchestral layers (rather than noise) to great result, much like some of the works of Dagda Mor. Printed on gold vinyl, this is a special item you should seek out, and should likewise keep a keen eye out for a future release, which I believe will materialize via StateArt.

Ulver (Nor) "Metamorphosis" MCD 1999 Jester Records
Those who have followed Ulver's evolution will either be astounded by this release or will be unable to 'get' what the band was doing. Well I can say without a doubt I am of the former mind-set, and this mini CD is much of the reason why I tried to track down the group for an interview in this issue (note: an interview was consented to by the group but unfortunately was not returned before publication). Following on from the electronica/trip hop tinged "Themes from William Blake's Marriage of Heaven and Hell", Ulver have severed any ties to their fledgling black metal days to come up with a banging techno/dark electronica/ambient gem. Starting out with 'Of Wolves and Vibrancy', (after a short interlude) the track strides headlong into a hefty mix of fast techno driven beats, grinding bass, computer glitchy textures, all complimented with

a dark synth underbelly. If only all techno was to sound like this.... "Gnosis" is a more brooding, drawn-out dark electronica piece that covers quite a distance over its 8 minutes. The track plays with cinematic half-composed segments, subtle acoustic guitars and slow driving rock beats before a heavy pounding (but still rock) beat and various studio trickery solidify the core of the track. Stripping back to a desolately mesmerising guitar tune, the vocals are introduced (being the only track with vocals as always handled greatly by Garm, aka Trickster G, in his trademark full throated clean singing style) followed by the re-introduction of all the former beat and computer generated elements. Again rock drums and piano introduce "Limbo Central" before becoming progressively more treated with studio manipulations, drum machines, synth lines (and the like), with the last section being played out with a segmented (almost) industrial guitar riff, tension rising into the last seconds of the three and a half minutes. Last up is `Of Wolves and Withdrawal', and, as the title may suggest, is a direct opposite of the opening cut, opting for a greatly flowing piece of drone ambient textures and cavernous sounds, all the while remaining true to the essence of the sound production already established. As a bridging release to the upcoming CD "Perdition City", if this release is any indication it will be no less than a masterpiece.

Umbra (Pol) "Ater" CD 1999 Fluttering Dragon
While there is another US group operating under the same name, this is the Polish 'Umbra', a one-woman project by Eliza. This CD oozes a ritualistic air from the opening segments, summoned forth from the 'witch'-like whispered spoken vocals, solemn keyboard layers, distant moans and half sung wails. The slow pace of the segments of ritual drums and chimes heightens this feeling, yet when used sparsely creates a meandering musical forum. At other times small outbursts of shrill strings and heavily accentuated female poetic evocations add a nice amount of tension to the dank and dreary musical setting. Later sections contain understated classical piano and orchestral backing, ushering the listener through mournful settings to be later jolted into heightened awareness with urgent bass pounding, church bells, slow string segments and scattered tones all combined into a surreal nightmarish atmospheres. Each of the 9 tracks (at a touch over 40 minutes) interweaves with the preceding piece to create an impeccable flow even if a wide variety of ritual atmospheres and compositions are explored. Given that this is a very professional sounding release, one may draw a wide variety of (fleeting) comparisons to sections of sound from groups such as Aghast, Endvra, Desiderii Marginis, Ildfrost and the like. The packaging (particularly the cover) is well presented in a jewel case along with various panels and fold-out sections in tones of earthen reds and browns, and is complemented with gold text print with the overall visual feel being quite comparable to the 'CMI' look. Another great ritual/industrial/dark ambient CD from this rising label.

Umbra (USA) "Unclean Spirit" CD 2000 The Rectrix
Umbra is Scott E. Candey (Gruntsplatter, head of the Crionic Mind label) and Stephen B. Petrus (In Death's Throes, head of the Live Bait Recording Foundation label). They perfectly meld the Gruntsplatter Armageddon Noise Grind dynamics (a type of post-apocalyptic sonic haven built on destruction) with the In Death's Throes eerie, more darkly sinister inclinations. Oscillating, humming feedback chews through the ground bones ambience of 'The Valley Of Dry Bones,' Scott's destructive tendencies barely held at bay as the ambience is smothered in distortion. 'Tangled Gullet' weaves anxious tones into a wall of crackling, radiantly alive sound. The compelling balance showcases what the novice noise listener might miss-the inherent language of each layer, the emotional pull of each layer, as it is peeled to reveal the intricate design at the heart of the piece, hence, the inherent anxiety. Voices swim below a slow throbbing rumble of noise during 'Stacking The Dead,' the brain numb from the death work at hand. 'Spiders Under The Skin' reverberates in a more haunting, downright ghostly vein, Stephen's esoteric tendencies on display, murky and discomfiting. The speaker ripping, acid waves tumult of 'Washed Up On The Banks' prophesize cataclysmic doom, while more of that damned strangely melodic humming slinks underneath. 'Lecher' is the masterpiece, the crystallization of Umbra's sonic vision, featuring deep, growling noise, slashed and immediately cauterized. The incinerator burn distortion leads one into the molten, melting walls of the abattoir. The tonalities and density of napalm drenched sound has been compressed, allowing no escape, the dripping walls of the abattoir closing in, claustrophobic—brilliant! There's also a recontextualization of the material on Unclean Spirit by Azoikum, entitled "Husk," in which the turbulent tides so inherent in the music (an impression of turbulent electronic seas can be gleaned throughout) is brought into focus. Excellent work and reason enough to check out both of these artists' other projects. —JC Smith (Reprinted by permission from Side-Line magazine: www.side-line.com)

The Unquiet Void (USA) "Between the Twilights" CD 2000 Middle Pillar
A slight diversion is taken on this new Middle Pillar release, with an album of composed sub-orchestral dark ambience. A project of one individual, Jason Wallach, the concept revolves around the dream state with this aura permeating the sometimes dreary, sometimes uplifting surrealist-tinged atmospheres. As the primary tool, the synth gives a hint to the stylistic sounds generated, but is done in such a way (with layering and the use of tonal elements) that it generally avoids any cheesy sounding moments. Much like the music, the track titles correspond to the idea a journey into the dream state. Dark-pounding percussion and massively uplifting string elements marks 'The Dreaming Begins', detailing a mix between ambient tones and orchestral elements. 'Sinking into the Blue Black Oblivion' takes a ritual percussive framework and builds over it a darkly sweeping classical melody that ebbs and flows for the nine odd minutes. While 'Sea of Serenity' contains a more sombre underlying mood with a slow, depressively echoed tune, the sound switches to an increasingly urgent and tense atmosphere on 'Angels' (here there is a mild programmed rhythm element within the sweeping keyboard textures). With its groaning pulse and distant drones, 'Morning Twilight' marks the beginning of the end, as if the uplifting multi-layered orchestral tune is drawing the soul back into the slumbering body. Packaged in the now trademark elaborate fold out digi-pack, Middle Pillar presents another fine act in their growing roster of US artists.

Unveiled (Ger) "Silver" CD 2000 World Serpent Distribution
Being a solo project of one of the members of ...Of the Wand and the Moon, this has little in common with their acoustic folk sounds. And in what would appear to be the second CD from this group, this album focusses on electronic/ambient type soundscapes. On more than one occasion elements of the sound bring to mind the recent works of Hazard, as is displayed on 'Anotherworldness', with its grinding industrial factory textures wrapped in an experimental/electronic aesthetic. 'Soul in a Crystal' adds a mysteriously sweeping edge to the sonic palate (almost choir-like in its selected layers of sound), mixed with spoken word lyrics and some damn heavy martial/ritual type percussion. The slow grinding machinery returns on 'Winter', engulfing the listener in its bleak hazy resonance, where half-remembered melodies seem to be buried somewhere under the textural slab of sound. 'Fire as a Friend', on the other hand, is quite active, containing a mid-paced metallic rhythm mixed up with circular weaving sonics. 'Sand' comes off as easily the most composed track, with spoken vocals and commandingly heavy slow martial beats over a base of sparse sounds and slight melody, while the mid-paced programmed rhythm of 'Letter and Stones' is adequately sonically scarred to not detract from the dark and partly ritual atmosphere. The title track takes the CD to its demise via a low subtle soundscape, which is beautifully enhanced with a looped Gregorian vocal line and ultra subdued percussion (and in part brings to mind a fleeting reference to Raison d'être). Overall this could not quite be described as straightforward dark ambience, but rather as an electro/acoustic endeavour that has subsequently taken on quite a few darker characteristics. Either way, the results are very worthwhile and worth your time.

Urawa (Bel) "Villa Vertigo" CD 2000 Foton Records
With input from Olivier Moreau (aka Imminent) and John Sellekaers (aka Xingu Hill) what is presented here is very different to what I was otherwise expecting. Consisting of a series of drawn-out subtle soundscapes (with each track title referencing a room in the "Villa"), this has more in common with digitally abstract experimental works than anything like the electronica/industrial of their main projects. Ambience generated of a quite minimalist nature sees strange sounds, samples and voices used with cunning effect (such as the dripping water, ticking clocks and metallic scraping of 'The Study'). The type of sounds Hazard have been creating are brought to mind on a number of occasions, however this differs due to its playful and quirky style that is generally less cold atmospherically than the comparative project. There is a definite complexity to the subtleness of the compositions, and words do little to adequately convey my generally positive perceptions. Packaged in a slimline case in an outer card slipsleeve, insets include a real photo, business card and projector slide.

Various Artists (Rus) "Edge of the Night: Russian Gothic Compilation" CD 2000 Russian Gothic Project
If you are anything like me, normally you would run a mile from a compilation with the word 'Gothic' in the title, and though this was my first instinct the cover's blue and silver printed wood cut art initially grabbed my attention and encouraged me to explore further. After browsing through the 16 odd tracks, I tend to feel that categorising the compilation as 'gothic' actually detracts from the diversity of material on offer. While there are indeed some bands who do little more than perpetuate all of the cliched sound associated with the Gothic genre (guilty of this are: No Man's Land and Phantom Bertha) there are plenty of other groups that have a wealth of talent to offer. Canonis is an unusual ethereal band due to the incorporation of folk, progressive rock and doom touches throughout their track, as well as a sweet female voice for the vocals. Baroque-type classical music is the fare offered by Caprice, consisting of a harp introduction and orchestral chamber music and operatic female vocals that are done superbly. Not that I am totally taken by Dvar's track, I mention it just because it is quite bizarre. Mid-paced programming and synth lines are overlaid with vocal shrieking akin to what is found in extreme metal circles, except that they sound as if they recorded when under the influence of acid. Hmmm... not sure what to make of it. The synth ethereal project Dreams contains a trip hop/drum and bass type backing over soothing keyboard lines and soaring female vocals, and is quite interesting. Cyclotimia inhabit the type of sound coined by Atomine Elektrine in a new aged/classically influenced trance/techno piece. With the sheer brilliance of this track, it is quite easy to see why StateArt have signed them up for a release. What could almost be described as a perfect blend of gothic and ethereal genres, Lunophobia make a good fist of this with a melody that both rocks and soars. If pure traditional folk/medieval music is your fare (and I must have to say it is for me when done with this much conviction and authenticity), Djembe should be checked out. The use of mostly (if not entirely) real instrumentation has only assisted in the full and rich sound of the tribal beats infused with pipe/fiddle/violin melodies. A melancholic folk tune is perfectly handled by Kratong, with Douglas P-type whispered/spoken vocals, further enhanced by female backing, string quartet accompaniment and lone intricate acoustic guitar melody. Moon far Away have a brooding classical cinematic feel (yet gothic tinged sound), with their sparse composition being fleshed out over the six-and-a-half-minute mark. Of those other groups not already mentioned or described thus far, these include: Romowe Rikoito, Neutral Damsel's Dream, Tnt Art (presenting a Swans cover) and Cisfinitum. Giving a broad cross-section of the variety of the sub-cultural music originated in the heart of Russia, this is a well compiled and presented compilation that shines as a beacon for many (at this point) unknown artists.

Various Artists (Wld) "How Terrorists Kill" CD 1999 StateArt
If you do not like your sounds harsh and abrasive, or balk at the questionable inspirations that lurk behind the music, I suggest your steer clear of this! This compilation was originally slated to be issued via the Ajna Offensive, however it has now surfaced via the superb German label StateArt. The oversized 20 page cover/booklet is immaculate in collation and presentation of the artwork submissions from each artist. The sinister intent of the subdued Ex.Order track, 'The Only Way to Heaven', sets a subversive platform for the launching of later, more forceful pieces. Tense atmospheres, slow pounding factory rhythms and shrill yet bearable noises are what can be found here, beneath which lurk what appear to be voices, sirens and general crowd chaos. Slogun do what they are best known for - obliterated walls of extreme punishing noise. From memory I have never really appreciated the vocals, but here the distorted treatment and ranted dialogue work particularly well. A piece of Christian gospel-type music acts as the introduction for Thorofon's track (of which the looped bass from the song appears to sit in the background throughout the whole track) before machinegun fire ushers in the main section of tense power electronic noise tones and repeatedly ranted phrase. Next up is Valefor's track of subdued ritual industrial sound, more akin to Deutsch Nepal or No Festival of Light. Nothing fantastic, but a solid track nonetheless. Though I would have never thought that power electronics could

provide a forum to present rhyming poetry, Robert X Patriot does here to laughable effect. This is a shame considering that there is certain charm to the crude improvised noise/rhythm backing. A pretty trademark track is offered up by Con-Dom containing straightforward squealing mid-ranged noise, ranted heavily treated (and mostly indecipherable) vocals. Like Slogun, Macronympha opt for the wall-of-noise sound, yet do not choose to include vocals in what is an intense if not throwaway piece. The sinister ritual sound and pulse of TGVT's track is intermixed with a variety of vocal samples, speeches and conversation snippets, creating an intense death ambient/ death industrial sound.
Having heard quite good things about Wertham, the track here does not really grab me, suffering from a muffled, muddied sound production of noise industrial implications. The collapsing and imploding ultra noise textures of ASP's 'The Order of Faith' is intense power electronics, albeit a little repetitive, and while normally hard-hitting, the Grey Wolves present a track that is uncharacteristically atmospheric without losing any inherent power (via a slow sweeping noise industrial sound). Slow and subversive, the untitled piece from Der Kampfbund starts off slowly before launching into an impressive noise attack that is both shrill and grinding in sound texture, and infused with indecipherable crowd chants. Operation Cleansweep have the somewhat daunting task of concluding the compilation, yet handle this with ease via the swirling noise and the incessant grinding of the out of control factory machinery. Overall, the tracks presented are thoughtfully placed in their track listing to align noisy tracks next to quieter ones to give some respite and appreciation of diversity between pieces. Worth getting if you are a power electronics/noise industrial afficionado.

Various Artists (Wld) "Insights of the Profane" CD 2000 Ma Kahru
This compilation represents the merging of sounds from two musical scenes (black ambient and black metal) which, while sounding very different, do often have a similarity in inspirational approach. The basic layout of tracks goes something like black ambient/black metal/black ambient, creating diversity between pieces. Given the focus of this publication, I will deal mainly those groups which fit under this umbrella. Anapthergal (hailing from Finland) are a group I have not heard before, but this does not prevent them from opening the CD with deep noise/ambient atmospheres, Gregorian chants, distant groans etc thrown in for great effect. The shrill high speed riffing of Abigor (the most well known Black Metal band on offer here) has an old school thrash style to the song-writing which is actually quite different to the medieval black metal style on their first few albums. Baal are particularly good with a track of swirling sub bass textures of varying levels, gradually multiplying into a storming mid-ranged noise track. Subklink's track, which contains both low drones and muffled sweeping elements, don't really set my world on fire - it's not a bad piece, but there's just not enough tension in the sound. 'Murderous Vision' take a noisy mind frame distilling it down into a tensile atmosphere, essentially creating an impotent noise track that is all the better for it. Ontario Blue, a side project of Stephen Pennick (of Endvra infamy), present a track of pure Middle Eastern tribal flair that is the least dark and most composed of the ambient tracks (no real point in pointing out that this a great track if you already appreciate his other solo and collaborative outputs). If I remember correctly, Darkness Enshroud were once a black metal band but have now been resurrected as a black ambient project. Slow synth layers, deathly drum machine pounds and ghostly female vocals make their evocation a reasonable but hardly fantastic track. GoatWAR deserve a special mention for their musical style alone, described as "raw black vomit war metal"! (Hmmm.. black metal is not known for its sense of humour, but this surely has to be tongue-in-cheek?). Deep subterranean dungeon atmospheres and a piano being played somewhere off in the catacombs make Veinke's track a great listen as the last main track (except otherwise for the hidden track - a blistering 1 minute 27 seconds speed riff attack from Allfather). As there has been quite a bit of crossover interest from Black Metal to industrial music over the past 5-7 years, this release would be of obvious interest to such fans; yet as I'm not sure how much crossover interest has gone the other way, I don't know how an entrenched industrial fan would take to this. Regardless this is a solid document of some of the currently lesser known groups of each genre with a suitably dark satanic imagery. Finally, of those black metal bands not prior mentioned, the compilation also includes Azaghal, Archaean Harmony, Judas Iscariot and Myrmidon.

Various Artists (Wld) "Noise Transmission CD 1999 Deafborn Records
With the clarity and ferociousness of the production, you would be hard-pressed to identify these tracks as live recordings, yet the nine tracks from four different artists were recording at the 1998 Noise Transmission Festival held in Germany. The artists collated on here cover the power electronic and death industrial genres either exclusively or bridge the two. First up is Rectal Surgery, with a pounding mix of industrial noise, beats, scattered samples and screamed vocals. In particular the fusion of mechanized beats (bordering on gabber) and noise in 'Gefahr' is very impressive. Irikarah is a name I have not come across before, but they create a subdued noise industrial piece with 'Mistress of Agarthi' before stepping into searing noise/power electronics on 'Fight Fast' (my speakers sound if they can barely withstand the punishment being dished out). The Cazzodio tracks are a little different to what I heard on their debut CD in that vocals are included as either spoken sections or death metal screeches. I don't know how convinced I am with the vocals themselves (particularly when growled), but the music is of the same high calibre of industrial-strength power rhythms (albeit a bit slower overall than normal) and hefty slabs of concrete noise. To bring the CD to a conclusion, Morder Machine (feat. Atrax Morgue) grinds things down to a death obsessed halt with two tracks, including one previously off the 'Death Show' CD. Vocals gargling razor blades over a death industrial pulse and scattered screeching mayhem envelopes the room with both 'Living Dead' and 'I'm so'. With this act the vocals are the true wonder obviously working in a cyclical fashion in feeding off and giving back to the creation of the deadly atmosphere of the obliterated slow beat and noise textures. Overall worth getting if you have an interest in any of these artists.

Various Artists (Wld) "RGB [An Audio Spectrum]" CD 2000 siRcom (via World Serpent Distribution)
As a conceptual work this is quite interesting. Three sound artists were each given a colour (red, blue or green) and asked to produce a 15-minute composition illustrating what they thought their colour sounded like. These three tracks were then compiled into one 45-minute piece (divided into three 'movements'), while two other tracks ('Black' and 'White') were created from the collective material and used to start and conclude the CD. The three sound artists involved include Leif Elggren of Sweden (red), sourRce research of the UK (green) and Matmos of the USA (blue). The collective introductory track, 'Black', is an unusual one in that it uses great expanses of silence over its 10-minute length, occasionally containing fleeting tonal analogue outbursts (black=suffocating silence maybe?). On the lengthy main track, Leif Elggren is up first on Movement 1, offering his interpretation of the sound of red. Thick wavering analogue drones characterise this segment, increasing in intensity and evasiveness that to extent exudes the feeling of warmth (hence the colour red). On movement 2, souRce research are given the task of tackling the colour green, and handle it by starting with low shimmering sounds, and building it to a point where an acoustic guitar tune, whispered vocals and field recordings of seagulls are utilised. At first I was not so sure about the effectiveness of this segment, but the more I thought about it, the more it did bring to mind visions of rolling green hills along some unnamed British coastline. The shimmering sounds are again used (but now becoming more akin to an electro/acoustic soundscape) that bridges the piece towards movement 3, where Matmos tries his hand at the colour blue. From the written passage on the cover, it seems quite a formula went into the ethos behind this soundscape, which makes more sense when listening to this last segment. High-end scattered junk sounds sit over deep and watery tonal elements, basically attempting to illustrate the receding nature of the colour by using foreground textures (high end) and low drones and pulses (background). Interestingly, a mid section includes a jazz type percussion drum beat infused with the other sounds, though I'm not exactly sure what it signifies. For me this piece is the most experimental and unfortunately the least successful in its attempt to create its colour through sound, although it does appear to have had the most thought put into it. Rounding out the disc is the collective track 'White', whose subtitle 'red+green+blue=white' states the obvious insofar as elements taken from each movement intermix and interact. Overall I think this works better as an experimental and conceptual work than an album one would listen to for simple enjoyment.

Various Artists (Wld) "Saturn Gnosis" 2 x 10" Box Set 2000 Loki Foundation
Saturn Gnosis is a mesmerizing collection of surreptitious sonic atmospherics, each track depicting varied impressions of the German occult lodge, Fraternitas Saturni. But, not only is it a feast for the ears, the presentation must be noted. The face staring at me (with no discernable pupils) from the cover of this impressive package is stern, the unyielding expression draped in secrecy, in knowledge most mysterious. As Rene, head of LOKI informs me, the face is "the Gotos, a visualized medium that was based in every lodge of the brotherhood of Saturni as a stone bust. This Gotos is overlaid on the front image by a demon-painting of a Saturni member." (Interestingly enough, when looking directly at the picture, the bust is most prominent, splashed in crimson brush strokes…but look at it indirectly, from an angle, for a more sinister perception. Glance at the picture in the mirror, from a distance, and the demon within becomes more visible, gaunt and in allegiance with…demons, of course. Eerie and hauntingly effective.) Open the glossy black box and there is more delight for the eyes. Therewith enclosed, both sleeves, as well as a large booklet, are decorously designed with the brightly colored, geometrically enticing artwork of Frater Pacitus, one of the original members of the Fraternitas Saturni from the 1920's. All of this would be for naught, though, if the music were not as compelling as the packaging and subject matter. Not to worry, as one places the semi-opaque (it is oddly tinted-brown, bronze?-individual perceptions may vary) vinyl on the player and sets the needle to the groove. Inade's 'Cherub' bursts through the stratosphere, unveiling an uncanny, tension weary ambience upon which vocals with a certain arcane enunciation (the German language foreign to me) are tattooed. Further in, the Inade ship blows a horn as it crosses from one dimension to another (and neither dimension may be this dimension…). As it lurches forth, the roiling cosmic seas disintegrate into a tempestuous corkscrew of sonic trepidation and awe-inspiring discovery. In the background, a scalpel is thrust and twisted into the barren heavens. That's one track, 7:28 of explorative ambience that transcends genius. Yes, it's that good! Easily on par with the brilliant V.I.T.R.I.O.L. materiel, and worth the price of admission, as I like to say. How can anyone follow this up? Well, rest assured, what follows more than validates the proceedings. Herbst9 solidify their standing as one of the finest dark ambient practitioners with the molar grinding ambience of an unknown beast amidst tribal ruins during 'Threshold To Akasa,' the violin of Blood Axis' 'Der Gefallene Engel' singes the strings of sorrow while Stephen Flowers (author of the book Fire And Ice, in which more information on the Fraternitas Satumi can be found) speaks of "The Fallen Angel," and strange sounds gurgle underneath.   First Law blends astonishingly bizarre, almost otherworldly textures (understated instrumental vocalizations, disintegrating crystals from afar) and time devouring tribalism during 'Velochrome 1.' The track surprisingly ends up in a region distinguished by medieval shadings, forging an unexpected path in the winding darkness. SRP trespass on the desolate, darkened terrain of the void, a terrain littered with symphonic sonic residue that pushes at the periphery, eventually succumbing to the insistent symphonic radiance during 'Hochpolung Des Willens.' A slumber of nebulous design is disrupted by the processional pummel and ascending, born of fire chorus that rises from the very center of a convoluted labyrinth amidst the multi-layered progression of sounds during Predominance's 'Awaken Of The Violet Demons.' The masters of ancient darkness, Endvra, decorate a dull, wind from nowhere throb with crisply plucked injections of tattered anxiety amidst threads of brittle, obscure tones woven into the glistening flesh of 'The Sun And The Stillborn Stars.' Turbund Sturmwerk entrance via a disjointed collage of discomfiting vocals and a foreboding bass, grim dynamics harbored in confusion amidst the chaos din during 'UrFyr.' Pandemonium is upon us, though it is a subdued, distinctly lethal interpretation. Saturn Gnosis brings out the best in all of the participants (literally-the First Law and Turbund Sturmwerk tracks may be their best yet, the Inade track only confirms that they are inventing music that is of a level most cannot even comprehend…). Each track envelops the listener in an ambience drawn from the well of imagination that each band drinks from. Each track also seems to have two distinct sides (at least): the visible, predominant sounds, and the taciturn sounds that suggest indecipherable allegiances. On every conceivable level, Saturn Gnosis is nothing less than a masterpiece! —JC Smith

Various Artists (Wld) "Your Daily Buzz" CD 2000 Tripmeke Records
This CD is the first release on this new label with contributions by Lasse Marhaug, K2, and MSBR vs. Cartisian Faith. Lasse Marhaug is on track 1 'Surface Sci-Fi', which is a grinding mass of lurching feedback gradually becoming more chaotic and metallic as it builds up multiple layers, giving me the feeling that guitars might have been somewhere in the original sound source. Mid-way through, the first segment cuts out with a second feedback grinding loop kicking in (over a slightly watery undercarriage)

prior to the full force arrival of high-pitched squeals. While not sufficiently free-form to be pure noise, it is still a good, partly-composed noise track. On track two, 'Limb Bud', K2 subscribes more closely to the pure noise sound aesthetic with a 14-minute ear reaming piece of blasting high-end white noise. There are the odd segments of composed texture, but this is really only a small fraction of the total sound, with chaos basically reigning supreme as the piece chops and changes sound focus every few seconds. The remaining tracks (three through nine) are created by a collaboration between MSBR & Cartisian Faith, and seem to be more experimental in exploring sound texture and equipment effects. Vocals form about half of their first piece, 'Yon', but as they represent the sound source they have been basically mangled beyond recognition. 'Daily' is a reasonably noisy and harsh piece of mid-ranged static, but with a good sense of direction and tension-building it makes for a good listen at over eight minutes. 'Buzz' is much more typical of the noise genre with its wall-of-screaming feedback style, while the following piece, 'Grey', is almost the total opposite, with low, dredging metallic and electronic sounds akin to a more synthetic Daniel Menche. Following on, the track 'Cyclic' is quite unusual in that it seems to be generated from someone taking a bath with contact mics creating 'up close' sound effects. Another one of the longer format pieces is 'Lurid', and while consisting of extremely stormy metallic echoed scraping textures, it tends to hold its direction well even when incorporated with soulless, machine type-beat off in the background. Overall quite a good CD if you are an experimental/noise music type fanatic.

Veinke (USA) "Collection III The Black Summer" CD 2000 Triumvirate
Seven unnamed pieces are showcased covering a reasonable amount of ground in the process, but a basic description could be that this CD encompasses ultra dark sonics with bleak & searing qualities. There are segments of cavernous drone oriented soundscapes (such as on track one) while track two contains tense atmospheres of shrill textures, deep throbbing heartbeat, guttural chants and the sound of a metal implement chipping away at stone (giving the aura of some uncontemplated entity valiantly trying to dig its way out of its core earth entrapment). Track three arrives with a running time at over 20 minutes, sprawling out with drone undercurrents and smatterings of factory oriented sounds (echoes, clanging metal and nondescript textures). Later things are stripped back to a distant cavernous drone with a mild percussive texture and the rambled religious chant of someone acknowledging their imminent demise. Even further in, awesome (non lyrical) vocal chants that sit alongside with a deep echoed metallic rhythm that ushers the track to its ultimate demise. The megalithic programmed percussion of track four gives it a rough power noise type vibe and while the following piece opting for a similar sound yet arriving with far less percussion and much more searing noise. Track six is unusual in that it utilises a fair amount of contact mic type derived sound, which is more akin to the sounds created by Daniel Menche that the sounds on preceding tracks (this sound continues to an extent on the final track but also contains an undercurrent of droney textures). Overall Veinke have offered up a more than commendable disc of dark sonic textures.

Vir (USA) "Strika/Solaris" 7" EP 2000 Drone Records
Having something to do with the project Love Lies Crushing (incidentally on the Projekt label), this is a sparse experimental release with mild ethereal overtones. Harmonies, swirling textures, and a spacious expanse of atmosphere is prevalent here, with sounds ranging from soothing to tensile, and female vocals shift within the mix of the first track as if articulating archetype memory (rather than simply being included there for the sake of providing vocals). Side B offers up an even more expansive vision of multi-textural drones, shimmering guitar-generated textures and massive reverberating sounds, with the coagulation of these elements toward the end creating a very full bodied atmosphere of orchestral/noise proportions. The grey vinyl with blue streaks makes quite a nice looking piece of wax.

Von Thronstahl (Ger) "Imperium Internum" CD 2000 Cold Spring Records
Hello? I think we have a new contender rising to make challenge for the neo-classic crown. The statements and actions of the group aside (which seem to have stirred quite some controversy in the underground recently), this is an extremely ambitious debut given the breadth of influence and sound incorporated into this. While all the obvious martial themes are here (including pounding rhythms, profound horn and string accompaniments), the grand orchestrations all fused together with vocals of a rasping spoken quality and an industrial noise underbelly. Yet while these form the CD's core, many other sounds, vocalisations and instrumentations create a multi-dimensional work. The prominent female spoken vocals on 'Schwarz, Weiss, Rot' sit within a menacing framework of multi-layered strings and brass instrumentation, with male voice delivering a German speech in a background of industrial gritty textures. The epic piano piece 'The Majestic Return' is fleshed out by clean guitars, snare and tympani rolls, and full classical orchestration in the midst of roaring crowds and warlike sounds. The power is increased another notch on 'Kristall/Kristur', with classical melody lines taking a sweeping path above the rigid fast-pounding beats, while the vitriolic speech comes to the fore. Half industrial/half classical, the harsh looped sounds of 'Under the Mask of Humanity' add the grittiness of presentation, with the repeated vocal line likewise rasping in delivery. The harsh battle tank rhythms of 'Sturmzeit' eclipse the forcefulness of any previous track, rolling ever forward in warlike intent, snippets of choirs melded into the quick loops of pounding beats and shrill orchestrations. The following track then comes as a complete surprise, with its folkish strains of strummed acoustic guitar and relaxed framework of semi-romantic musical backing. A reflective sorrowful sound is appropriated on 'Noch Bluht Im Geist Verbogen' removing the martial undertones, leaving a framework of deep brooding classical melodies, while the massive brass sounds of 'Atlantis Teil' cuts in and out of snippets of what sounds like an 'Oi' band and other beats, voices, and sounds, as if the main backing has been set against someone flipping through radio static and finding the odd sound filler (which remarkably works extremely well). Another acoustic guitar number, 'Turn the Centuries' while still folkish is much more epic sounding, the whisper vocals adding a spine chilling effect. 'Pontifex Solis' the track which concludes this stunning work is a piece which sees the melding of many elements of sound on the whole album, be those of martial drumming, sorrowful classical melodies, acoustic guitars, speech presentation vocals etc. In its more blatant aspects of attention grabbing within cover imagery, these elements can be overlooked when an album of this stature is pulled off as debut release. Given this fits very nicely alongside Turbund Sturmwerk's debut CD in its similar broad musical vision should tell you this is an item that must be placed high on your want list.

Where (Ita) "The Creatures of the Wind" CD 1999 Eibon Recordings
Within sub cultural genres, certain countries tend to spawn their own distinctive sound, with Italy being no exception. Where are very much part of this Italian sound, often characterised by sparse, minimalist dungeon ambience. Sweeping moisture-laden air swirls forth from the speakers on 'Boreas', as if a long sealed cavern has been breached for the first time in aeons. Rusted hinges creak and metal scrapes on metal, creating harsh unnerving sounds that elicit visions of things best not thought of lurking in the crevices of these cavernous soundscapes. 'Conoscenze oscure' contains what sounds like distant rolling thunder, creating an extreme sense of depth to the sound. Again the metallic noises are present, but this time they are off in the distance, muffled and subdued. 'Sa'ra'ny', which commences as an echoed minimalist offering, lulls the listener before unloading a whole segment of flesh-crawling metallically generated sounds that continue for the remainder of the 10-minute track. The crumbling textures of 'Cialarere' present a density of sound not present on the preceding tracks (with a wind encapsulating membrane preventing the sounds from sprawling outwards), while 'Streghe del vento' has a subsonic bass drone creating a low-level echoed ambience as many of the other metallic sounds are mixed or at minimum muffled by the bass textures (not that these don't make themselves fully felt toward to end of the piece). Although little is presented in the way of tunes or audible melodies (except on the last track), Where presents the atmospheres via ghastly haunting soundscapes of distant sounds, wind-swept textures, sporadic clatter, echoes and any other sound you would expect to hear in dungeons and catacombs described in HP Lovecraft's writings. Lastly, taking inspiration from and being dedicated to of variety of mythical entities from Italy, Greece and Hungry, Where has created a release that is really beyond the sort of ambience one could listen to when going to sleep given the unnerving qualities presented (believe me as I have tried this!). Eibon may not release a stack of items, but of the handful they do release you are assured of quality both musically and in presentation.

Yen Pox (USA) "New Dark Age" CD 2000 Malignant Records
Considering how highly anticipated it has been, where does one start with a review of the second Yen Pox album? Could it be that the passage of time has pegged expectations too high? Well, I am glad to say that this has both lived up to and ultimately surpassed any of my initial expectations. One thing that is instantly evident is the massive sound production and sweeping spaciousness of the tones. While the last album explored suffocating and confined subterranean depths, this has a less obvious organic edge, lending itself to spacious territory as if illustrating a lifeless barren wasteland as the twilight quickly recedes. This is not to say that the trademark depth and tone of Yen Pox's sound has at all been lost, as its bass-loaded intensity still gives my stereo a run for its money. The multi-dimensional layering of sound is another all-encompassing element - tones sweep in from all angles, rising and falling throughout the composition, with faint and barely recognisable melodies all the while playing in a catatonic fashion. For such slow moving soundscapes it is quite astounding how much variation and movement is to be found in each composition - never faltering or slowing down, constantly spiralling headlong into its self-supporting vortex as one piece slips into the next, constantly building on what has preceded it. All I can say in conclusion is get this disc and bow before the new master of dark ambience.

"......Armageddon, Apocalypse, End Time, Holocaust - call it what you will....."

out : oktober 20th 2000

in the 10x100 series :
Stone Glass Steel
Corruption/Redemption
10-inch limited to 100 copies
act before it's too late

in the Nautilus series :
Ah Cama-Sotz
U-Boot
LP - heavy transparent blue vinyl
deep underwater music

in the Nocturnus series :
Tunnel / Hypnoskull / SonaEact®
picture 7-inch limited to 399 copies
with a recording from their US tour
live @ CBGB's

SPECTRE

Spectre
P.O.Box 88
2020 Antwerpen 2
Belgium
www.spectre.be
info@spectre.be

ÆTHYRIC DESIGN

STEPHEN O'MALLEY ≈ POST OFFICE BOX 2339, STUYVESANT STATION, NEW YORK, NY 10009, USA

soma@khanate.org

CONTACT LIST

ANT-ZEN: C/- S.Alt, P.O Box 1257, 93135, Lappersdorf, Germany, info@ant-zen.com, www.ant-zen.com
ARCANE RECORDINGS: C/- Mark Endacott, P.O. Box 458, Fullarton, South Australia, Australia 5063, markenda@bigpond.com, www.arcane-recordings.com.au
ARS MORTA UNIVERSUM: nuclearshelter@post.cz, www.macabre.cz
ARTWARE PRODUCTIONS: c/- Donna Klemm, TaunusstraBe 63b, (D) 65183, Wiesbaden, Artware.prod@T-online.de, www.artware-prod.com
ASH: 13 Oswald Road, London SW17 7SS, England, ashrip@touch.demon.co.uk/ash.htm
ASSOCIATED DISTORTION: 301-5500 Arcadia Road, Richmond, BC, v6X 3p5, Canada, elihaz@istar.ca
ATHANOR: C/- Stephane, BP294, 89007 POITIERS, Cedex, France, ursprache@wanadoo.fr, www.multimania.com/wiligut/athanor/accueil.htm
BASTET RECORDINGS: p.o Box 170 116, D-47181 Duisburg, Germany, vuz@yuz.du.gtn.com, www.cmx.de/chorus
BLACK PLAGUE: C/- Malignant Records, arc@magnus.net, www.malignantrecords.com/blackplagve.html
CAPP: Lislou 8 GR 11146 Athens, Hellas
CHTHONIC STREAMS: P.O. Box 7003, New York, NY 10116-7003 USA, www.chthonicstreams.com
COLD MEAT INDUSTRY: Villa Eko, 595 41 Mjolby, Sweden, order@coldmeat.se, www.coldmeat.se
COLD SPRING: 8 Wellspring, Bilsworth, Northants, NN7 3EH, England, UK, info@coldspring.co.uk, www.coldspring.co.uk
CRIONIC MIND: PMB 105, 4644 Geary Boulevard, San Francisco, California 94118, USA, crionic@pacbell.net, www.crionicmind.org
CROWD CONTROL ACTIVITIES: P.O. Box 2340, Upper Darby, PA 19082, USA 821 White Elm Dr. Loveland, CO 80538 USA, crowded@relapse.com, www.ezlink.com/~crowded
DEAFBORN RECORDS: C/- L Bauer, Brunnenstr 20, 40223 Dusseldorf, Germany, deafborn@dmx.de, www.deafbom.de
DOROBO: C/- Darrin Verhagen P.O. box 22 Glen Waverley, Victoria, Australia 3150, dorobo@werple.net.au, http://werple.net.au/~dorobo/dorobo.html
DRONE RECORDS: Baraka (H) S. Knappe, Gneisenaustrasse 56, 28201 Bremen, Germany, dronetroum@aol.com, http://members.xoom.com/dronerecords
DUEBEL: www.duebel.net
EIBON RECORDS: Via Folli 5, 20134 Milano, Italy, rberchi@galactica.it, www.this.it/eibon
EIS UND LICHT TRONTRÄGER: P.O. Box 160142, D-01307 Dresden, Germany, eislicht@geocities.com, www.eislicht.de
FEVER PITCH MUSIC: 1108, E. Capitol Drive, Appleton, WA 54911, USA
FLUTTERING DRAGON RECORDS: p.o. Box 182, 03-700 Warszawa 4, Poland, xak@serpent.com.pl, www.serpent.com.pl
FOTON RECORDS: info@fotonrecords.com, www.fotonrecords.com
GLASS THROUGHT RECORDINGS: P.O. Box 2313, Seattle, WA 98111-2313, www.crionicmind.org/gtr
HEARTLAND RECORDS: 61 Peel Street, Melbourne West, Victoria 3003, Australia
HYMEN: hymen@gmx.net, www.klangstabil.com/hymen
INFLUX COMMUNICATIONS: 760 Market Suite 315, SF, CA 94102 USA, influxcommunications@angelfire.com
JESTER RECORDS: via Voices of Wonder, PB 2010 Grunerlokka, N-0505 Oslo, Norway, www.vow.dk
KK RECORDS: Krijgsbaan 240, 2070 Zwijndrecht, Antwerp, Belgium, kknz@kkrecords.be
LEFT AS IN SINISTER: P.O Box 1769, Collingwood, Victoria 3066 Australia, valerious@rabbit.com.au
LITTLE MAN RECORDS: P.O. Box 45636, Seattle, Washington 98145-0636, USA, vox@speakeasy.org
LIVE BAIT RECORDING FOUNDATION: 423 Seventh Street, #3, Fairport Harbor, Ohio 44077 USA, livebaitrecording@hotmail.com, http://crionicmind.org/livebait
LOKI FOUNDATION: PSF 241321 04333 Leipzig, Germany, loki-found@t-online.de
MA KAHRU: P.O Box 887, Pittsfield, MA, USA, makaru666@aol.com
MALIGNANT RECORDS: PO Box 5666, Baltimore MD 21210, USA, malignant@malignantrecords.com, www.malignantrecords.com
MEGO: www.mego.at
MEMBRUM DEBILE PROPAGANDA: LESSIGNSTR. 21, d-97990 Weikersheim, Germany
MIDDLE PILLAR: PO Box 555, NY, NY 10009 USA, info@middlepillar.com, www.middlepillar.com
NOISE MUSEUM: 19, Rue Colson. 21000 Dijon, France, noise.museam@wanadoo.fr, www.zone51.com/noisemuseum
NORTHAUNT: C/- Herleif Langas, Almev.6b, 7058 Jakobsli, Norway, northaunt@yahoo.no, http://northaunt.cjb.net
OLD EUROPA CAFE: C/- Rodolfo Protti, Viale Marconi 38, 33170 Prodenone, Italy, oec@iol.it, www.stack.nl/~bobw/music/OEC/
PERIL UNDERGROUND: Basement 17-19 Elizabeth Street, Melbourne 3000, Australia, peril@realism.com.au
POSSESSIVE BLINDFOLD RECORDINGS: C/- S. Beebe, 1624 Chapin Street, Alameda, CA 94501, USA, info@possessive-blindfold.com, www.possessive-blindfold.com
POWER AND STEEL: C/-—Loki Foundation PSF 241321 04333 Leipzig, Germany, loki-found@-online.de
PRE-FEED: C/- Gabriele Santamaria, via Gen. Pergolesi 21, 60125 Ancona – Italy, mantein@lin.it, http://move.to/Pre_Feed
PSF-FEED:
QUATUOR CORONATI762: C/- Thomas Sauerber, Jahnstrabe 4, 27568 Bremerhaven, Germany, schwerrtiau@citweb.de, http://members.tripod.de/Baradelan/grid
RED STREAM: P.O. Box 342 Camp Hill Pa 17001-0342 USA, mall@rstream.com, www.rstream.com
RELEASE RECORDS: C/- Relapse Records, P.O. Box 251, Millersville, PA 17551, USA, relapse@relapse.com, www.relapse.com
the RETRIX: 144 Hillcrest Ave, Morristown, NJ, 07960, USA, rectrix@aol.com
RUSSIAN GOTHIC PROJECT: C/- Sergey Merenkov, P.O. Box 129, Moscow, 117331, Russia, coroner@gothic.ru, www.gothic.ru
SELF ABUSE RECORDS: 26 S. Main Street #277, Concord, NH 03301, USA, www.mtv.com/jusers/selfabuse
SLAUGHTER PRODUCTIONS: C/- Marco Corbelli, via Tartini 8, 410-49 Sassuolo (MO) Italy, slaughter@mail.dex.net.com, www.welcome.to/slaughter
SPECTRE RECORDS: P.O.Box 88, 2020 Antwerpen 2, Belgium, spectre@skynet.be, http://users.skynet.be/spectre
STATEART: C/- Koch, Rosegerstr. 2, 30173, Hannover, Germany, www.stateart.de
SUFFERING CLOWN INC: P.O. Box 2124, New York, NY 10009 USA, sufclown@aol.com, www.sufferingclown.com
SYNAESTHESIA: P.O. BOX 7252 Melbourne, Victoria 3004, Australia, mark@synrecords.com, www.synrecords.com
TACTICAL RECORDINGS: Schandweg 3, 89264 Weissenhom, Germany, tactical.recs@gmx.de
TESCO ORGANISATION: P.O. Box 410118, D68275, Mannheim, Germany, tesco-org.-MA@t-online.de
TRIPMEKE RECORDS: Skogsduveu.4, 856 53 Sundsval, Sweden, tripmeke@hotmail.com
TRIUMVIRATE: 853 E #rd St, Mishawaka, IN, 46544, USA, triumvirate@datacruz.com
TRONIKS: P.O Records of Unit 7 #rd St 94704-0055 USA, tenebrae@ijs.net, www.troniks.com
220N: handsproductions@gmx.net
WELT AM DRAHT: C/- M Seipp, Karlstr. D-38106 Braunschweig, Germany
WKN: P.O. Box 467, 1060 Wien, Austria
WORLD SERPENT: Unit 7+7 Seager Buildings, Brookmill Road, London SE8 4HL, England, mailorder@worldserpent.demon.co.uk, www.worldserpent
YANTRA ATMOSPHERES: Bobdegatan 20C, nb s-595 52 Mjolby, Sweden, raison.detre@swipnet.se, home9.swipnet.se/~w-90779/index.htm

SLIP INSIDE THE SKINCAGE

Skincage: Axon

this is where
the world goes
when you blink...

an ever-morphing
tapestry of samples
capturing
the beauty & horror
of a life
within the skincage

CD * $13
< MALIGNANT ANTIBODY / TREATMENT 01 >

DEBUT RELEASE / INTRODUCING:

MALIGNANT ANTIBODY

A NEW LABEL FROM MALIGNANT RECORDS

HOME TO:
SKINCAGE
R|A|N
STONE GLASS STEEL
IRON HALO DEVICE

NEW RELEASES FROM MALIGNANT RECORDS

YEN POX
NEW DARK AGE (CD / $12)
TUMOR 12

HEID
ARKTOGAA (CD / $13)
TUMOR 13

NAVICON TORTURE TECHNOLOGIES
SCENES FROM THE NEXT MILLENNIUM
FALL Y2K

AND NEW FROM
BLACK PLAGVE:
"CONTROL" (CD)

VISIT THE
MALIGNANT
WEBSITE
FEATURING
"MALIGNANT
RADIO"
AND
A COMPLETE
ONLINE
CATALOG

P.O. BOX 5666 • BALTIMORE, MARYLAND 21210 • USA   www.malignantrecords.com

SPECTRUM ISSUE 5
AMBIENT/INDUSTRIAL/EXPERIMENTAL MUSIC CULTURE MAGAZINE

BRIGHTER DEATH NOW/ CROWD CONTROL ACTIVITIES
DEATH IN JUNE/ FOLKSTORM/ HOUSE OF LOW CULTURE
IRM/ MIDDLE PILLAR PRESENTS/ NOVY SVET
SKINCAGE/ SPECTRE/ TRIBE OF CIRCLE/ VOX BARBARA

middle pillar

DISTRIBUTION
MUSICAL ESOTERICA

ethereal
electronic
darkambient
experimental
industrial
neo-folk

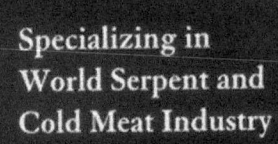

Specializing in
World Serpent and
Cold Meat Industry

Middle Pillar, Dept S.
PO Box 555, NY, NY 10009
Fax: 212-378-2924
TOLL-FREE U.S. ORDER LINE
1-888-763-2323

complete catalog online at:
www.middlepillar.com
email: info@middlepillar.com

MIDDLE PILLAR PRESENTS

LORETTA'S DOLL
Creeping Sideways

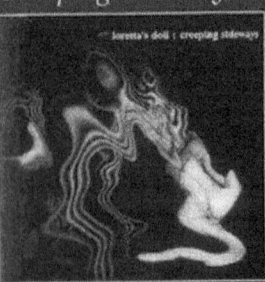

Their long-awaited new album is their darkest and weirdest yet. Semi-structured experimental soundscapes with a special guest vocal by Genesis P-Orridge. A joint release between MIDDLE PILLAR and WORLD SERPENT.

THREAD
Abnormal Love

Cybernetic chaos and beauty moves across a modern dark electronic landscape. Combining the rhythmic influence of IDM with succinct, darkly abstract poetry, this album also features guest vocals from Jarboe (ex-Swans).

THE MACHINE IN THE GARDEN
Out of the Mists

New electronic/ethereal masterpiece features thirteen delightful and powerful tracks with darkwave, gothic, and neo-classical elements. Multimedia portion contains the video for "The Unaware".

BUTOH
Various Artists

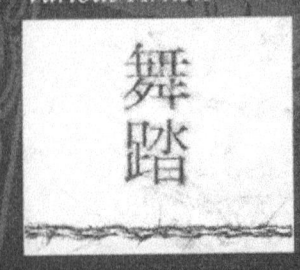

The dance of darkness with new music by the Machine in the Garden, A Murder of Angels, The Mirror Reveals, The Unquiet Void, Mors Syphilitica, Sumerland, Thread, Wench & Zoar.

COMING SOON
SUMERLAND *Sivo*
ZOAR *In the Bloodlit Dark*

ALSO AVAILABLE
THE UNQUIET VOID *Between The Twilights*
THE MIRROR REVEALS *Frames of Teknicolor*
A MURDER OF ANGELS *While You Sleep*
THE MACHINE IN THE GARDEN *One Winter's Night*

American Distribution via Middle Pillar Distribution
http://www.middlepillar.com/mpp/
212-378-2922
European Distribution via World Serpent Distribution
www.worldserpent.com

7" Puissance - Genocidal

7" Control - Praying to Bleed

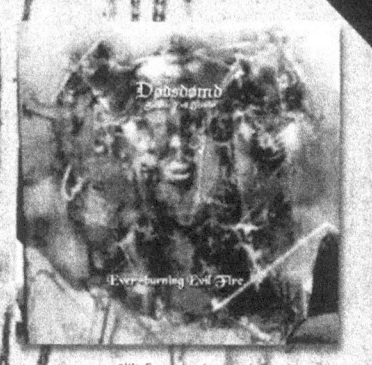

7" Dodsdomd - Everburning Evil Fire

7" Cloama - Provokaattori

Acetate LP Nordvargr/Drakh
Northern Dark Supremacy

7" Merzbow - Hummingbird

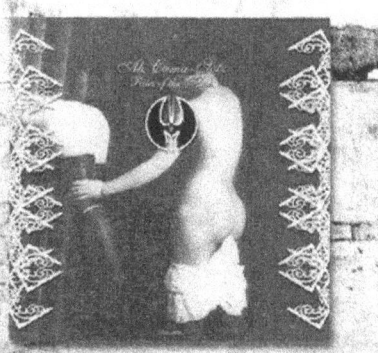

7" Ah Cama Sotz - Rites of the Flesh

2x7" Slogun - Murder U.S.A.

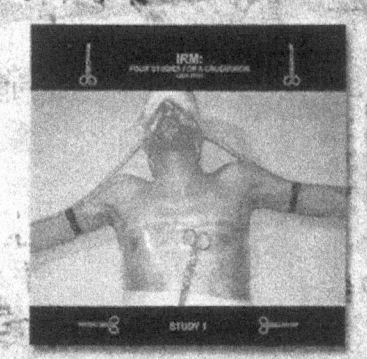

2x7" IRM - Four Studies for a Crucifixion

LSDO-S022 Dodsdomd (Sweden) - Everburning Evil Fire
LSDO-S024 Control (US) - Praying to Bleed
LSDO-S026 Puissance (Sweden) - Genocidal
LSDO-S028 Cloama (Finland) - Provokaattori
LSDO-A/L029 Nordvargr/Drakh (Sweden) - Northen Dark Supremacy
LSDO-S030 Merzbow (Japan) - Hummingbird
LSDO-S031 Ah Cama Sotz (Belgium) - Rites of the Flesh
LSDO-2S032 Slogun (US) - Murder U.S.A. (Gatefold) 2 x 7"
LSDO-2S033 IRM (Sweden) - Four Studies for a Crucifixion 2 x 7"
LSDO-2S034 Iron Justice (Sweden) - Post 2 x 7"
LSDO-4S035 nod (Sweden) - The Story of Three Little Pigs
and the Big Bad Wolf 4 x 7"

Nordic Cathedral
a sub-division of L.S.D.Organisation
CD release division of LSDO

NC I first human ferro (Ukraine) - Metaballistik: Viewed under Infra-red
NC II Death Kontakt Projekt II - "Swedish Ekstasy" V/A Double CDs
featuring 14 Swedish Artists : nod, Jarl, Iron Justice, Folkstorm, Karten, Golem,
Painbringer, Withering Shadows, Winquist, Virtanen, Survival Unit, Rhabdophobia,
Inimrkal, Del Nostri, and Syndikhat.
NC III Jarl (Sweden) sideproject of IRM: - Woundprofile + 2 extra tracks

From the Unknown ; background painting by Nefixium , Winter 1992

P.O.Box 99, Monterey Park, CA 91754-0099 USA · W : http://www.lsdo.com · http://www.mp3.com/lsdo · E : info@lsdo.com · fax : 626.918.5212

**DISSECTING TABLE
MEMORIES**

**GEOMATIC
CONTROL AGENTS**

www.triumviratemain.com | triumvirate@datacruz.com
P.O. BOX 6254 | SOUTH BEND, IN | 46660 USA

COMPACT DISCS $13.00 ppd.

**ONLINE DISTRIBUTION OF
UNORTHODOX AUDIO**

APPROACHING>
Summer 2001.
VoS [solo project of S. Hall/Yen Pox]
Autumn 2001.
NOTHING, restructured
by M. Hensley [Yen Pox/Blood Box],
graphix by S. Candey
[Crionic Mind/Gruntsplatter]
Winter 2001.
RADIAL
[hard rhythms,
harsh frequencies]

TRIUMVIRATE

LAW   DISSECTING TABLE   VEINKE   LAW

SPECTRUM MAGAZINE ISSUE 5: EDITORIAL MAY 2001

Well, what to say? Hmmmm…basically if you read the editorial in last issue you might remember that I was not sure to if Spectrum 5# would arrive sooner or later, as this essentially hinged on my probable European travels. Anyway as you can obviously see, Issue 5# has materialised, basically caused by two factors: (being) 1: a partial delay in my anticipated departure date, and 2: a personal character flaw of needing to be continually stressed with workloads and publication deadlines! Thus, on one hand the new issue is presented for your reading pleasure, however on the other hand Spectrum 6# will definitely be put on hold for an extended length of time, given my flight is booked and my travels through England and Europe are at this point for an indefinite period. Most importantly I look forward to visiting the countries, monuments, galleries, sites, locations etc that so much of the music covered in Spectrum derive inspiration from, and who knows, if I have been in contact with some of you European dwellers throughout Spectrum's short history, you might just expect me to come a knocking on your door for a visit! Not much else to say from here as Spectrum 5# already goes beyond the call in expressing its share. Until next time…whenever that may be…

O'vr'n out……end transmission……

-Richard Stevenson

EDITOR - INTERVIEWER - REVIEWER - LAYOUT DESIGNER ETC: RICHARD STEVENSON
CONTRIBUTORS: JC SMITH - REVIEWS/ CHRIS FORTH & JOSEPH AQUINO - REVIEW SECTION PROOF READING.

Greetings and thanks:
To all artists/ individuals who donated their time in providing interviews. Labels, distributors & shops who have thus far supported this publication via providing promotional items, advertisements and stocking copies (your collective input and support in invaluable and particular gratitude is extended to Jason Mantis and Phil Easter @ Malignant Records). JC Smith for continued input. Chris Forth & Joseph Aquino for thoughts and suggestions. Mick Stevenson for technical computer assistance. Lastly, friends and family for interest (enveloped in bemusement and intrigue).

TEXT & DESIGN LAYOUT: COPYRIGHT SPECTRUM MAGAZINE
ALL IMAGES: COPYRIGHT THE RESPECTIVE ARTISTS

(no section of this publication may be reprinted without prior permission - all rights reserved)

SPECTRUM MAGAZINE: P.O. BOX 86, ELSTERNWICK 3185, VICTORIA, AUSTRALIA
S P E C T R U M M A G A Z I N E @ H O T M A I L . C O M

"The pale autumn sky was filled with the exodus of millions of leaves, deported by the wind to distant corners of the city, away from the branches which had once given life. Here and there, stone faced men worked with slow concentration to control this arboreal diaspora, burning the dead from ash, oak, elm, beech, sycamore, maple, horse-chestnut, lime and weeping willow, the acrid grey smoke hanging in the air like the last breath of lost souls. But always there were more, and more still, so that the burning middens seemed never to grown any smaller, and as I stood and watched the glowing embers of the fires, and breathed the hot gas of deciduous death, it seemed I could taste the very end of everything".
Phillip Kerr: The Pale Criminal 1990

The cover image consists of two source photographs taken by: Jon Ray (aka: Skincage) and further manipulated into the final image by: Richard Stevenson.

CONTENTS

TRIBE OF CIRCLE: 7-8
NOW SVET: 9-11
HOUSE OF LOW CULTURE: 12-14
SKINCAGE: 15-17
MIDDLE PILLAR PRESENTS: 18-20
FOLKSTORM: 21
VOX BARBARA: 23-24
CROWD CONTROL ACTIVITIES: 26-27
DEATH IN JUNE: 28-35
BRIGHTER DEATH NOW: 36-37
IRM: 38-39
SPECTRE: 41-42
SOUND REVIEWS: 43-66
CONTACT LIST: 67

ADVERTISERS

MIDDLE PILLAR-2/ LSD ORGANISATION-3/ THROMBOSIS-4/ DRAGON FLIGHT RECORDINGS-6/ SELFLESS RECORDINGS-14/ CRIONIC MIND-20/ LIVE BAIT RECORDING FOUNDATION-22/ JC ROBERTS REVENGE-24/ CROWD CONTROL ACTIVITIES-25/ MEMORUM DEBILE PROPAGANDA-40/ THE RECTAL-42/ TESCO ORGANISATION-46/ SOMBRE-49/ COLD MEAT INDUSTRY-50/ RELAPSE-53/ SPECTRE-54/ COLD SPRING RECORDS-58/ DEGENERATE-60/ NEROZ-62/ ANS MACABRE-65/ DOUBLE N NOISE INDUSTRIES (ZXNHIT-67/ MALIGNANT RECORDS-68/

Dragon Flight Recordings

Vedisni - Architects and Murderers

Intensely dark ambient/industrial with harsh noise influences and eerie voices, recitations, and invokations. Vedisni have created one of the darkest ambient releases ever pressed to CD. Not for the timid.

Necrophorous - Gathering Composed Thoughts

From the mind of Peter Andersson (Raison d'Être). A collection of dark minimal soundscapes, eerie ambient tracks, and soaring neoclassical passages. Another great release from a pioneer in dark ambient/neoclassical music.

LS-TTL - el es tee tee el

An abstract project ranging from electronic and ambient to industrial and noise. LS-TTL balance harsh noise passages with more subdued, brooding ambience, creating astounding soundscapes

Monstrare - IsFet

Fearsome, creeping minimal ambient/black industrial. Rumbles and drones, distorted voices, and an overall atmosphere that will send chills through your spine. This will leave you looking over your shoulder...

Distribution

North America: Soleilmoon, Metropolis, Dragon Flight, Manifold **Mexico:** Noise Kontrol
Europe: Darkambient.net (Holland/Belgium), Unholy Cross (Spain), Dark Vinyl, Tesco, Division House (Portugal), Faithless (Poland) **Japan:** THA

Dragon Flight Recordings/Magazine

780 Reservoir Ave Pmb294
Cranston RI 02910 USA
http://www.dragonflightrec.org/
info@dragonflightrec.org (General Questions)
promotions@dragonflightrec.org (for promotional Cds)
DFR List- DragonFlightRec-subscribe@egroups.com
401-767-1735 (DFR Office)

Tribe of Circle

With Tribe of Circle making their public debut in 2000 with a 7" ep on Hau Ruk, followed soon after with a full length CD on Athanor, I can say I was rather impressed with their style. By virtue of taking the looped based industrial structure of Deutsch Nepal and mixing it with the martial and neo-classic style of Der Blutharsch, Tribe of Circle have certainly created a rather impressive and epic sound. Solo member Jean-Paul Antelmi provided counsel in regards to the circumstances of his project.

Tribe of Circle would seem to be a relatively new project with only a 7" and CD released thus far. What details can you provide of your musical background both before and up to the formation of Tribe of Circle? In fact, the project TOC exists for many years now, but it has evolved a lot concerning the line-up. At the beginning TOC was composed of a few members, but as i was the only one to compose, to create the project and since human relationship within the band was not good at all, we parted and i stayed alone with my long cherished project!!! So i've been playing alone for 6 years now in TOC, but as you know, my first official productions were released last year, because i felt ready to perform & assume my task.

Your debut 7"ep was released on Albin Julius's label Hau Ruk. How did you come to be in touch with Albin that lead to this Tribe of Circle release? When i decided to send some demos to labels, i wanted in the same time to send some of them to artists whose work i really appreciated.. one of these artists was Albin and he liked it at once. Then he offered me to release a limited vinyl to begin. And so to speak, nothing could separate us now!!!

After the debut 7"ep, your debut CD was released not on Hau Ruk but rather on the rising cult French label Athanor. What were the circumstances of this change of label and was there any interest from Hau Ruk to issue the debut CD? As i just told you, the original idea with HauRuck! was to release a limited item only. Meanwhile Athanor offered me to release my first full length album cd. I had just accepted the Athanor's proposition when Albin finally asked me the same. As i had given my word to Stéphane (Athanor), i took the decision to release the 1st album with Stéphane, and the second one with Albin which was well accepted on each side! But, as Albin really loved one of my songs (called «Altered State»), i have taken it out from the cd, and kept it aside for the 7inch on HauRuck!

Various loops clearly make up the majority of your compositions (both of industrial and neo-classical focus), however how much is Tribe of Circle a programmed and sample based project? With clearly audible elements of percussion etc do you play any of the instrumentation yourself or is it again sampled? In regard to the more classically and vocally oriented samples where do you derive these from? As i am alone, my music is definitely based on samples and loops...However, it is not a staunch will to work in this way; to me, it is the best way to work. Indeed, i sometimes sample myself using percussions, vocals, fx, etc. But i'd really appreciate to work with a few instrumentalists. As you certainly know, playing alone brings as many advantages as it can bring the contrary. Anyway, the means is not important to me, the essential is to be able to express what i feel inside, so that the listeners may feel the same!

With no lyrics being present within your compositions how much could the track titles be viewed potentially as propaganda? Do these titles reflect the intention of feeling that you derive from the music or the idea your attempt to embody in the composition? Which comes first music or title? I do not and i will never make any propaganda! I have already said it before but i prefer to repeat it once again… TOC is not made to teach anything or force people to think in a certain way, but rather make people have a reflection on certain subjects. Above all, suggestion is better than ready-made truths! As the music, the titles suggest ideas and are as many guidelines. I do not agree with your words «no lyrics present», because there is a difference between a few lyrics, and no lyrics at all… Sometimes there is only one sentence or two in a track, but it exactly represents the essence and the meaning of it. As a matter of fact, the result does not lie in the quantity but rather in the quality. To answer to your last question, sometimes the music speaks for itself, so the title is revealed by it; but sometimes, particularly when i want to express myself about a precise subject, the title comes first…there are no rules!!

A track off the debut CD is entitled "Evil is a state of mind". For me this would indicate an ironic slant, however the dialogue sample contained within this track specifically references the track's title (reflecting on the nature of evil in comparison to the actions of God). Firstly what is your view of my alternate interpretation? Also does the use of this dialogue sample point to anti-Christian sentiments that you might hold? For your guidance, the title in question is not entitled "Evil is a state of mind", but "Evil is a point of view" what includes many semantic differences!! So i can't answer as well as i would like to in regard to your alternate question. Nevertheless, my view of it is that evil is perceived differently according to many factors, like the period in which one lives, the culture, the religious beliefs, the moral context, etc. Obviously, one tries to feel less responsible, and God (whatever Christian or not) is the best excuse to perform this task. So the spoken words in this track are to me very well adapted to this concept!! Of course, i could debate on this subject more than that, but i think the previous sentence is the best summary for a so much delicate question!!

Given your music could be said to contain a Euro centric focus, including the use of runes within your imagery, what are your thoughts on the often misinterpretation that the use of such ideas/elements equals a fascistic intent due to the previous appropriation of such themes by the Third Reich? This subject has been debated for long, and i think it is far from ending… All of us are influenced by the culture in which we live; Actually in each culture, the use of symbols is important, and History can change the meaning of them, as it was the case during the Third Reich. For my part, i make a clear distinction between my personal use of Runes and the one that was made during this dark period. The Swastika is for me, one of the most beautiful existing symbols, in its primary meaning, as for the symbol of Sigil; **BUT** do not misjudge about these words: as you certainly know, these symbols have been existing for thousands of years, and within a few years they became the darkest, the most negative and outrageous signs ever. For me, this often misinterpretation is due to a lack of culture, but even without that, it is understandable that people have wanted to forget that these symbols have been positive one day.

Do the use of runes hold the keys to the themes and intentions behind Tribe of Circle? Likewise is there any meaning inherent in the symbolism of your swirling circular logo? The whole concept of Tribe Of Circle is based on the one of DUALITY, whether for Man, the Universe or anything else. In this view, we can actually compare this to the use of Runes, because the latter carry Duality in themselves, without any judgement of values, positive or negative, even if it is mirrored. The logo of TOC is conceived on the same idea, adding the concept of circularity, in concordance with the fact that in the Universe, everything tends to be circular.

With a quote on the CD cover stating "From Hope to Loyalty…From Strength to Victory!", this is rather an ambiguous statement that could almost be interpreted in anyway an individual could see fit depending on their agenda. Do you want to divulge any of your personal reasons for utilising a slogan that in essence could be used to misrepresent yourself/Tribe of Circle? Just try to recognize yourself within these words, perhaps you'll feel the same as me, or a different interpretation. Anyway, i think that «hope» and «loyalty» are two values which express very well what i'm looking for in life, amongst others of course, such as respect, honour, integrity, and all these things that make us feel more humane, and certainly what we miss the most today!! Without hope, you can only survive…without loyalty, you're alone!!

Given that your music has a central framework of neo-classical sounds, how much does history interest you as opposed to the modern world? There is no opposition, History has made us what we are today. My use of neo-classical sounds is not made to represent certain periods of History, it's just a matter of personal taste.

Not wanting to jump to conclusions to who may be sampled on the last track of your CD it is still a rather vitriolic speech being conducted in German. Who is it that is sampled and what was the intention of the inclusion of what seems to be rather a provocative dialogue sample? I see what you're getting at…The title of this track carries in itself all its meaning, but as it is in French, i could understand that you missed the sense of it….this title is «Rien ne disparaît jamais vraiment», which means in English "Nothing ever really disappears"…that's why the sentence in it is so « vitriolic ».

In the liner notes of your debut Douglas P is given a mention of special regards. Was this greeting included as mere appreciation of his music works as Death in June or is there something deeper? Maybe is the same for you, as for me, some periods in my life are linked to the music i was listening at the time. I know DIJ's music for more than 10 years now and, of course, it counts a lot. Beyond the music, the texts of Douglas have always been present and essential, like a permanent support. If there was a person to whom i wanted to pay homage, Douglas P. was this person.

Who would hold as comrades in the musical path that you are currently marching on? What music interests you both in reference to and away from Tribe of Circle? My musical tastes have many horizons….As a matter of fact, i can easily listen an old Napalm Death one hour, and change it to Jacques Brel the other one!! Except DIJ (which is «unclassifiable» with other bands for me) i really like bands like Der Blutharsch, LJDLP or Arcana, even if i don't listen a lot of industrial music (!!??). I have recently discovered an excellent Russian band called L.C. which have already released some cd-r and one first official album (i think). I have a really high respect for ALL the work of Lisa Gerrard, with DCD or her solo works (except collaborations with Peter Bourke). The «Mirror Pool» is one of the most great Masterpiece i've ever heard. But the most of times, i like to listen genius compositors like Penderecki, Schnittke, Gorecki, Arvo Part or Ligeti , but i can listen as well indusmetal bands like Kill the Thrill, Neurosis,... So as you can see, it's a very large and non-exhaustive list.

There currently seems to be a growing number of projects arising from France to prominence and notoriety. Is there any sort of focus to the French scene or is it essentially fragmented into groupings of individual interests? I don't know. I have not a lot of contacts with other French bands, except for Erik (LJDLP), Alberto (NothvsFilvsMortis) and Thierry (ex-Exotoendo). But i'm very amazing about the quality of some french projects like Asmorod, Regard Extreme or Etant donné (I certainly forgot some others). I'd really liked to have more contacts with other French bands, but to answer to your question, i think that a few bands have some grouped interests, but with individual methods!!!

In that the tracks off your debut were recorded between June 1998 and December 1999, does this mean that there is wealth of new material ready for imminent release? What upcoming musical movements are you currently involved in? Do you have a spy in your team??!! Yes, you're absolutely right, the new album is musically finished, i'm working on the artwork for the layout right now, and i'm doing some little arrangements on certain tracks…It's the first time i'm really satisfy of my entire work at 100%!! For me, it's the best music i've ever made so…. I have no date about its release for now, but just ask to Albin, he certainly have his idea. I hope to have it around April/May, it depend of the Hau Ruck schedule too!! Meanwhile, TOC will appear on 2 forthcoming compilations: the 1st with Oktagon Records entitled «Audacia Imperat», and the 2nd for a «Tribute To C.Z.Codreanu»….In the furthest future, i'll make a 10inch on Athanor (surprise!!!) and a Vinyl Edition on Malignant records for a retrospective of the 20st century.

Last statements? I'd like to thank you very much, Richard and all the Spectrum team, for your interest in TOC and for your patience in waiting my answers!!!! I hope to see you all in TOC future live performances (no dates yet), and to visit your beautiful country one day….Enjoy life, take care, and be yourself!!

«From Hope to Loyalty…From Strength to Victory!»

For anyone who has heard Novy Svet, I gather on first listens that you might have been scratching your head in bemusement akin to my reaction. After the initial shock of the unusual style abated, (that I have incidentally described in reviews as ranging from drunken accordion folk. to jazz/ folk infused lounge and finally to ritual industrial) the hypnotic elixir that are the compositions have really captured something special – even if I can't entirely grasp in words what that special something is! Here an interview is presented with the male half (j.weber) of the musical duo.

What (and when) were the circumstances of the formation of Novy Svet? the group novy svet as it exists now was born in 1.997. before that both frl. Tost and me were in another loose and nameless project that experimented with different styles of non-traditional/non-conventional musical forms. this band which consisted of some more people split up due to personal problems and some questions of musical directions. we were very much into bruitism and noise that we wanted to combine with our other obsession folk music. the rest of the group moved to a more punk orientated style. after a break of some months we started to make music again, bought our own equipment and recorded loads of songs. some of those make up 'rumorarmonio', our debut lp, although we never thought to release anything or work on that semi-professional basis we do now.

As Novy Svet sounds very different to any other project that I can think of (due to the distillation of traditional folk influence with more modern industrial loop base structure), it has enabled you to highlight parallels with the neo-folk scene yet being leagues apart. Did you always have visions of creating such bizarre but compelling music? well, we never planned to make especially 'bizarre' music. we don't feel like our music is that 'out of the world' as many people claim. we just record what spouts out of us and never thought about any audience. Still today we just do what we like to do and don't care that our output is accidentally distributed in the so-called 'industrial scene' in which's limited musical frame novy svet for sure is a bizarre diamond. we would feel as fine on a worldmusic-label or anywhere else. it is just that many people have problems with topics that we touch and can't / don't want to follow our thoughts.

I believe that Novy Svet is meant to translate to "New World" in Czechoslovakian. Does this group moniker hint and a philosophy or world view embodied within your music? indeed the group's name means 'new world'. we liked the sound of the czech phrase and of course also the idea that a new world is definitely a 'no' to the world as it is now. there is no philosophy or ideology we follow. in fact our aim is to smash all ideology and all idioty...in real life, not in music. music doesn't change anything. we are happy if we reach some people who listen to our records and afterwards don't feel as solitary as before. I personally believe that music is the strongest of all arts but in most cases people don't permit anything to pass through the thick walls they have built up around themselves.

Given the folk orientation of you sound I would assume you consider your selves culturally aware, therefore what European cultures collectively interest you? From this perspective do Novy Svet embrace or reject the modern world? Also in your exploration of the folk elements of your sound (and therefore being representative of the past) is Novy Svet regressive in philosophy or do you study the past in order to gain an understanding of your personal direction towards the future? we always felt that both the adjectives 'modern' and 'european' fit very well to our work. if 'modern world' means to speed up communication between different people with different backgrounds or to jump into an aeroplane and get wherever you want this is absolutely great. but if 'modern world' means political lies, suffering humans, animals and nature, stupidity and senselessness then it is something that should be fought and destroyed. unfortunately it seems as if the negative aspects within the term 'modern world' exceed the good things. but we have to point out that we wish to reach a status behind post-modernism and not before. so, all those pseudo-traditional movements that are followed by teenagers in uniform don't mean anything to us. musical wise we never looked back but neither we denied our geographical and traditional background. we never understood why people put us into one big sack with the label 'traditional' on it. we agree that there is a certain nostalgic feeling in some of our songs but this has nothing to do with a longing for any historical past. in our case this is more a personal past we are longing for. novy svet follows a very honest path - we don't sit in a social building wearing training suits and claim to be deeply influenced by the books of blabla that we read at candlelight with a glass of good french wine in one hand and a cigarre in the other. do you understand what we mean? switching on the computer, sampling some speeches from old records and add some drums doesn't make up any traditional approach - it is the complete opposite.

nový svět

What other music, literature, concepts or otherwise do you drawn upon to gain inspiration for Novy Svet compositions? the main influence for our music is our every day life and the contact to the people we love. artistical influences come from everywhere, especially from visual arts and literature. not that much from music although we both listen to music a lot.

Given that Novy Svet are signed to Hau Ruk - Albin Julius's (aka Der Blutharsch) label, how did you to be involved with this label? I am assuming that both projects having their roots in Wein had something to do with this? hahaha, yes both projects have their roots in 'Wein' which means 'wine' in German (ED: damn miss-spelling...I meant to say Wien!). no, to become serious again: novy svet's roots are more into beer and vienna. Albin Julius also lives here although he originates from the far west of austria. we know Albin for quite a long time now. first we met at a party when he was still in TMLHBAC. we established friendship and when he listened to our music for the first time he was totally enthusiastic about it and asked us if we were interested in releasing something on a new label he wanted to start. this was HAU RUCK!.

If I am not mistaken three individuals played on 'faccica a faccia' yet only two on 'cuori di petrolio'. Who are the full time members of Novy Svet and what are the roles in instrumentation and vocalisation? novy svet consists of two people who are the tough center of the group. this is frl. tost and myself. we are the only ones who have worked on every release so far. the rest of the line up changes from recording to recording. if we have problems with realizing a musical phrase or need an additional vocalist we ask one of our friends to join us. each album needs a certain number of people to be produced. for example 'cuori di petrolio' is a very isolationist album both regarding the music but also the way we have recorded it. there wouldn't have been any place for someone else during the recording process. in general both members bring in ideas that we then arrange together and put into a certain structure. most of the songwriting is done by myself - the same goes for lyrics - whilst frl. tost is in charge of the arrangements, the instrumentation and the mix. our method of working is changing from album to album, from song to song. everyone takes the instrument he/she wants to play and then we start.

With the general lack of female presence within the collective music underground, do you consider that having a central female figure within Novy Svet has had a great deal of influence on sound and direction? Also, despite the male vocals are currently a highly characteristic element of your sound and atmosphere, will there be female vocals employed on future recordings? it has no influence at all that we have one female half. it is strange but obvious that novy svet is a very male project. of course we both agree with the contents of the lyrics but they are written from a very masculine point of view (it may sound a bit odd but i would also say that the music is very 'male') which of course doesn't mean that there won't be any vocal's by frl. tost in the future...well, there'll be a song we've recorded together with our friends of CIRCUS JOY that also features her on vocals besides others.

Apart from having three full length Novy Svet albums out (1 LP & 2 CD's), you have released quite a number of limited vinyls. What is your view of vinyl being a collector's item and the common accusation that labels deliberately limit such items to low print runs? some releases are produced for many people, others for not that many. the vinyl releases by novy svet and the releases of the label we run, THE NEKOFUTSCHATA MUSICK CABARET, are all very special and directed at a special audience. well, of course we would like that everybody who is interested can listen to all our releases but this is utopic anyway. we will go on doing vinyl-only productions. now it seems as we will put out a complete album named 'chappaqua' on limited vinyl only.

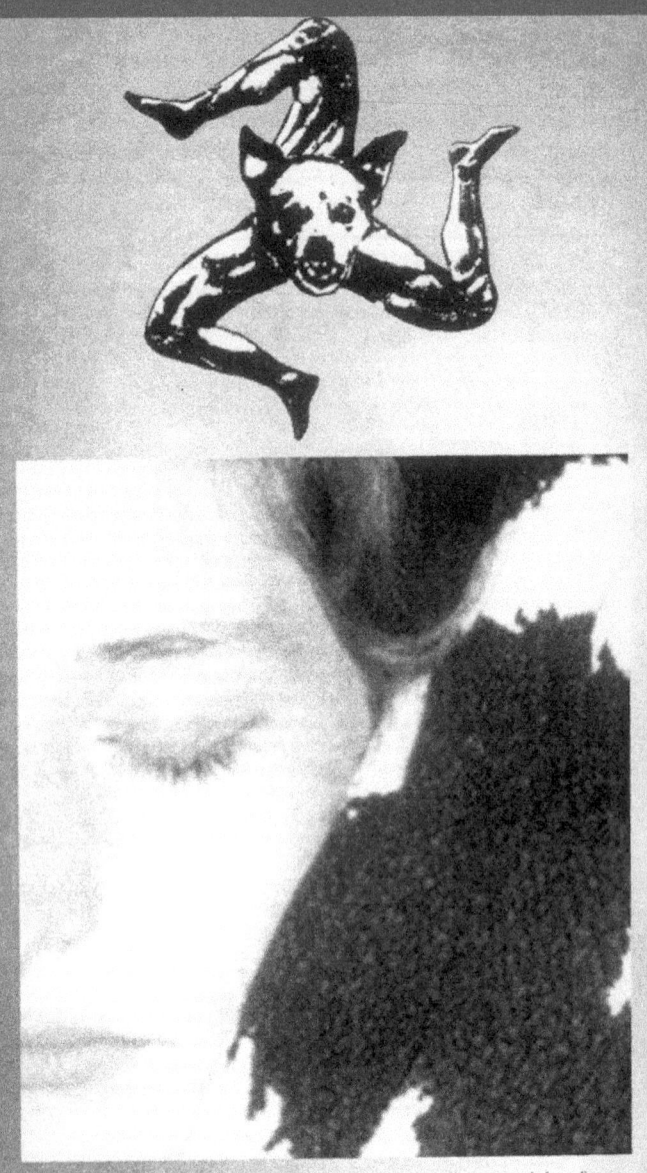

Talking of limited vinyl there was a split Der Blutharsch/ Novy Svet 7" (in a ridiculously limited edition of 99 copies), that was incidentally meant to coincide with a double bill live performance in December 2000, however this event was cancelled prior to it ever eventuating. Can you give us some details of the background details that lead to the cancellation of the event? the concert in Trieste was cancelled because of 'political' problems. it was neither the right place nor the right date regarding that this weekend, as a huge neo nazi meeting took place there. well, possibly we could have gained another hundreds of new fans there...but we are not very keen on these people whose ideology is stupidity. we have not cancelled the show. we would have played there but Albin and the organisation have cancelled the concert out of different reasons.

Likewise I have been lead to believe that this cancelled show was meant to be your first live performance. How difficult is it and/ or would it be playing Novy Svet material live given both the complexities of your material and extent of instrumentation used, particularly with limited members? once we have played at a private party of a friend but we never did a bigger show. of course there would be more people than frl. tost and me involved in a live performance which's form would depend on the venue we are playing. right now we have several offers from all over europe to play but we plan to do only one live show in our whole career and this should take place in italy...or it should bring us lots of money.

In that you use numerous languages within Novy Svet (Spanish, Italian, English, French and German) why do you choose to present multilingual vocals and do you consider that there are advantages inherent in the atmosphere each presents? Could it be construed that via the use of different languages you are attempting to illustrate different viewpoints of the European spirit? there is no rational decision why to use this or that language. this comes naturally to me when i write lyrics. it is more that each song needs a certain language or a mix of different ones.

the languages i use are in a peculiar way close to me, nothing more. the european viewpoint is only one...europe is only one...not because of the EU. that's simply how it is. personally we feel familiar with some areas, not so familiar with others -this fact is of course also evident in our works.

Who has been responsible for the collation of the images on your two CD albums (depicting ethnic religious trinkets on 'faccica a faccia', and 1950's bikers on 'cuori di petrolio'). While I will admit that these do give the albums quite a timeless or at least regressive aesthetic, do these themes particularly reflect Novy Svet's interests? of course the cover images have a strong connection to the album they are used for. the pictures for 'faccia a faccia' were taken in mexico at the 'dia de los muertos' - the day of the dead. we were obsessed with this day and everything fit very well together when you know that most of the lyrics on the cd deal with death and dying, also in a metaphoric sense...the pictures for 'cuori di petrolio' were taken in russia. later than 1950. they were used because they reflect those memories of the past the whole album is all about.

Although the Balkans conflict did not impact on Austria directly, when referencing Novy Svet's folk orientation did the war in the eastern European counties have any psychological effect on you? we don't know. we both do not share any special friendship with the balkans - with the exception of slovenia possibly - although this is often said in magazine articles. the typical music from the balkans had an impact on us for sure but mainly because this music is also always present here in the eastern parts of austria which comes from the monarchy and this long historical period austria, hungary, italy and the balkans shared together. the balkans conflict was something that had to happen and i am sure that it will happen again. these countries will burn forever.

Even though you currently might not have the stature as say Der Blutharsch it appears that this is quickly changing, particularly since you seem to have embraced a similar production output of material with numerous items both released and scheduled for release. I am assuming that writing and producing material comes easily to Novy Svet? What is your view of the 'quality vs. quantity' argument and the generally perception that it is good to be productive but not overly so? indeed novy svet seemed to get more popular during the last year. for us this is already too much. that's why we have also closed down our p.o. box now and try to reduce the contact to the 'outside' to a minimum. there are times when recording is easy and others when it is not. initially we wanted to take a break after 'cuori di petrolio' but straight after this album was released all the frustration that was accumulated during it's recordings was gone and we felt fresher than ever before. that's why we, especially myself, are so happy to have done this album which has been such a depressing experience. it was like a curse that was hanging over the group for a long time and that was finally gone. we started recording again straight after 'cuori di petrolio' was finished and it was maybe the most productive period in the short life of novy svet. we have two more albums ready. one is 'venezia' that will be mixed in italy in february and released in april through HAU RUCK! (that's what is planned now...too often things change) - this is quite psychedelic. the other one is 'chappaqua' and we have already talked about it. for now this will be available on vinyl only. it is very surreal and full of energy. there are also some more smaller projects like the long scheduled new 10" with CIRCUS JOY. we will also finish this in february in rome and hopefully have it released as soon as possible. we never thought that it is a problem if there exists a large quantity of releases as long as this goes hand in hand with quality. if we would only do re-recordings of 'faccia a faccia', repeat us again and again, it would be enough to release an album each second year to keep people hungry. but - even if this makes you feel sad - there will never be anything that can be compared to 'faccia a faccia' and we also won't do a new 'cuori di petrolio'. our records are all very different from each other and we believe that it needs many releases to allow the listeners to understand each step we take. sometimes the whole chronology is messed up by the labels and their 'business strategies' or other problems. for example 'aspiral III' was thought to be a stepping stone between the two cds (although we have to point out that in this case the label is not guilty for the delay at all) ...we will keep up our natural rhythm, no matter if there are ten releases in one year or only one. i would be very glad if some bands would produce more than one album in ten years.

It seem that future recordings are to encompass a cycle via a musical trilogy. What is the focus of this musical concept and are there any particular ideas you have for format and packaging? the trilogy is called 'aspiral' and one part (the third one) has already been released through WHITE LABEL (see above). the overall topic for this project is 'living'...this is hard to explain now. maybe it is better to listen to the music that has more to say than my/our words. 'aspiral III' was dealing with nature and it's powers. one of the missing parts will possibly be about the concept of 'biomechanic' but it seems like people will have to be patient until 2002. originally we wanted to release two 7inches and the final 10" but now it seems like the other parts will also be a bigger format. we will see. the artwork of the whole series will be in the vein of the available record.

Ending remarks? thanks to you and all your readers....and: no, there are no kangaroos in austria.

From reading the review of House of Low Culture's debut CD in these pages it will be quite evident that for me this project was a highly surprising and rewarding discovery. Obviously the review was not mere hype, as I felt it warranted to track down Aaron Turner of the interestingly entitled project to discover a bit more about his evocative (sometimes guitar oriented) experimental soundscape musings....

To start with, it is of specific interest the HoLC is not your main project, rather a side project away from your main guitar oriented bands. Can you please provide a summation of you musical activities up to and including HoLC? i've been a quite a few guitar oriented bands, most recently isis and old man gloom. isis has been together for about 3 years now and we're just beginning work on our 8th release. old man gloom is another side project - isis being my main band, and we've just released our second and third full lengths. both bands are heavy in focus while isis has more of an epic godflesh/swans/melvins influenced sound and old man gloom consists of shorter blasts and long stretches of ambient and sometimes noisy soundscapes - much like what much of the first HOLC consists of. i'm also currently involved with a project called "the lotus eaters" with stephen o'malley and james plotkin. the lotus eaters project also ambient in nature but perhaps less traditionally guitar oriented than HOLC. i've done other things in the past and am working on other projects currently, but these are the most recent and most significant to me at the moment.

Where there any specific groups/ scenes that influenced you into forming HoLC as an independent project? over the last few years i have really enjoyed being involved with the various bands i'm in, but in that time i came to realize that i could create on my own through a totally different process which was gratifying in a way i hadn't experienced in any of my more "traditional" musical experiences. i was very influenced by guitar records that were really expansive in approach like the earth 1-3 records and the neil young soundtrack to the "dead man" film by jim jarmusch. those 2 records were probably the most influential in terms of how i viewed the guitar and what could be done with such simple means. on the other end of the spectrum i absorb a lot of ideas from merzbow, to lull, to pan american, to arovane, to zipperspy, oval and microstoria, etc. i became really interested in electronically generated textures and rhythms, and the juxtaposition of melodic structure and dissonant noise. i wanted to combine all these elements in a way that would somehow flow and that was my initial intention with the project.

Do you consider the HoLC represents the beginning of a new wave of guitar based experimental soundscape type projects? i don't think of HOLC as being part of anything specific - i just used the guitar because it was a tool i knew how to utilize and it helped me make the transition into using other tools and experimenting in ways i had previously avoided. i didn't intend to make a guitar record - it just kind of worked out that way. i will continue to use the guitar because i'm happy with the results achieved thus far, but i won't limit myself to anything. i find that specific classification is something that hinders music and i don't believe in the idea of musical purity. i don't feel the need subscribe to one specific sub genre of the experimental realm, i think the juxtapostion of all these different elements and styles is what makes HOLC interesting for me.

Given the experimental guitar format I am wondering if you are at all well acquainted with Japanese experimental guitar master KK Null? of course - he is another guy who has totally stretched the capabilities of the guitar as a less traditional instrument. the "aurora" record he did in collaboration with james plotkin was another record that has influenced the path i've taken with HOLC. while i don't love everything i've heard from him he certainly has made some great albums. i am also comforted by the fact that he has managed to maintain a successful heavy rock outfit with zeni geva and produce successful efforts in a much more experimental realm. i often feel that heavy guitar oriented music is shunned by the more avant slanted audiences and i think it's a shame, especially now with so many underground metal and hardcore acts incorporating more noise oriented elements, electronics, and intellectual conceptual ideas. NULL among others has proved that you don't have to limit yourself to one area to be successful in creating great art.

Also what is with the projects title? Do you consider your rather complex compositions as low brow and if so what would be the relevant marker for referencing to what might be considered 'high' or 'low' brow? i don't see a marker between low art and high art - only that which is perceived by others. the title of the project was sarcastic in the sense that i was referring to what i do as low brow because of the metal/hardcore influence - any thing heavy is considered unintelligent and lacking depth. i also used the title in reference to the perception of other "low brow" activities by mainstream society at large outside of the musical realm. i feel there are many things which many musical communities shuns because of our perceptions of "low" and "high" and it's very limiting in the sense that we cut our selves off from things that might otherwise be enriching in our lives or influential in the things we create. many "low" art forms (comic books, rock, hip hop, design, etc) have risen to intellectual, conceptual, and artistic heights but are still largely ignored by those outside of the community in which they were created because of their perceived status as low art.

Obviously the guitar is the main sound source used within the project presented alongside other less dominant elements of samples and sounds derived from various production/ programming techniques. How do you compose you material – do you lay down the guitar riffs, layers, and melodies to later manipulate and transform these into compositions? usually it works the other way around actually. i often experiment with the textures and soundscapes first - creating the sounds, arranging and layering them, creating a dynamic/flow for the song, and then trying to find a guitar sound and melody to fit with the underlying soundscape. other times i will improvise the guitar lines add a quick textural environment and then with that rough sketch recreate the elements in a more focused and purposeful fashion. often the mixing of the tracks is where the composition is really created. i will add many layers of sound and melody and then add and subtract them in mixing to make a structure - intertwining the components in a way that makes sense to my ear.

In the review of your album I made a comparison to the motion picture 'Dead Man' in regard to both fleeting sound influence and selected track titles. Are these comparisons and assumptions at all correct? most definitely. the second track on the album was basically improvisations based on the theme created by neil young for the dead man soundtrack. as i said before that was a highly influential record for me and the film equally so. the combination of the music and images in that film is as perfect as i've ever seen, and the dialog, pace of the narrative, and the concept of the movie are brilliant i think. i've rarely heard a more sensitive and emotionally dynamic treatment of the guitar as displayed on that album.

Via your compositions are you trying to evoke certain themes and emotions for the listener, or is your music a personal catharsis with it being an added compliment if others can relate to the atmospheres created? the atmospheres found in my tracks are designed by my sense of musical asthetics and are structered based around what i find interesting and provoking. these emotional themes are not uncommon ones - isolation, despair, and a sort of tragic triumph and i did not use these themes to relate to the listener in anyway though i know that many people will connect with it in some way. i hope that people can derive something useful from my music, but that was not the intention in it's creation. while this sort of music may be masturbatory in a sense i think it's important for anyone creating any sort of art to fully enjoy what they make before considering the reactions of whoever their audience might be. if you can't embrace your own creations then it's not likely that many others will.

Speaking of your track titles, they don't seem to follow any sort of overall concept, rather utilising unusual phrases such as 'another tragic one: hands sold by poachers' or 'ultrasonic escalating eye irritant'. How important are the track titles to the project are there any intentions for inherent concepts apart from the merely musical? i had no narrative concept in mind when creating the album - all the tracks were conceived independently as were the titles. all the tracks were the result of a years worth of recording and listening - i picked those tracks out of 3-5 hours of music because of the way they fit together musically. both of my guitar oriented bands are heavy on the conceptual end lyrically and some of those themes carried over into the titles for various tracks on the album, while others were words selected for the emotional impact - to give some sort of little map for individual tracks, suggestive imagery. i think the titles are very significant to me and to the meaning of the tracks, but i don't know if these ideas are easily read by others. i purposely abstract the ideas involved - i don't want to give up anything to easily - i like the idea of the listener having to dig a little to discern the themes and to leave a little room for interpretation.

In relation to the packaging of the 'Submarine Immersion Techniques Vol 1' CD, it is presented a relatively non descript card sleeve, with red foil stamped writings and flower woodcut illustrations that generally do not really give a hint to the style of the compositions. How do you view the packaging as a vehicle to promote and present your wares? i wanted a non standard package because i felt the record did not fit the standard jewel case format. i wanted something unusual and i didn't want something overtly dark. i felt the ideas involved in the album were dark but also beautiful and hopeful in certain ways and that's what i wanted to convey with the packaging. obviously the cathartic venting of negative emotions is an important aspect of this album and many others, but i feel too many projects focus on the negative end while disregarding the benefits of such a venting process. if the idea is to really rid ones self of these destructive emotions through the process of creation i feel that should be apparent in the creation itself. i enjoy a lot of negative sounding music and while i'm not out to make a "happy" record by any means i do feel it's important for me to inject some thread of passivity into house of low culture if only briefly. i believe, at least for myself, that if i am plagued by negative aspects of my external life or my internal psyche then immersing myself in negative music with out examining the positive benefits of doing so will only lead to further immersion in negativity and depression.

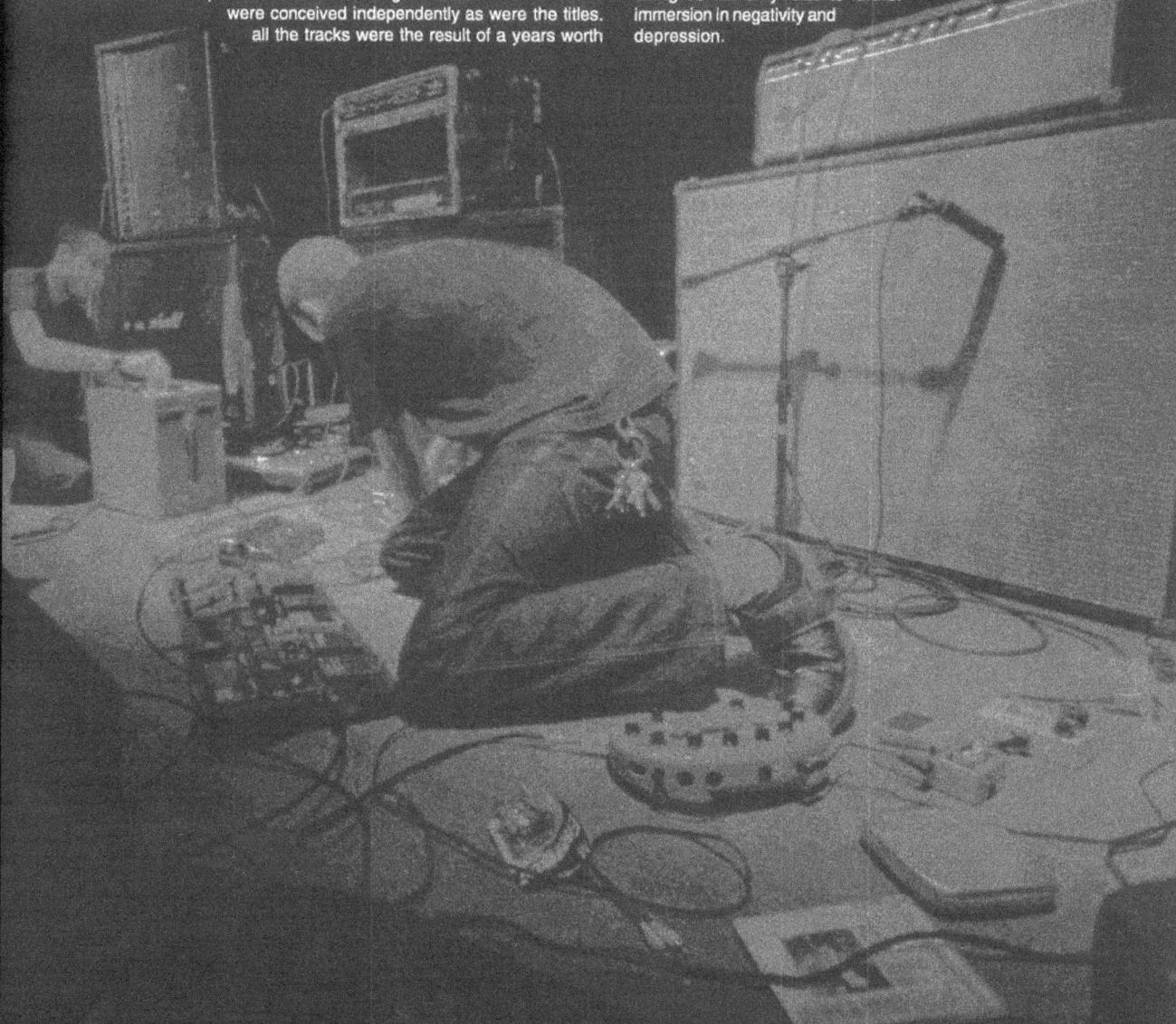

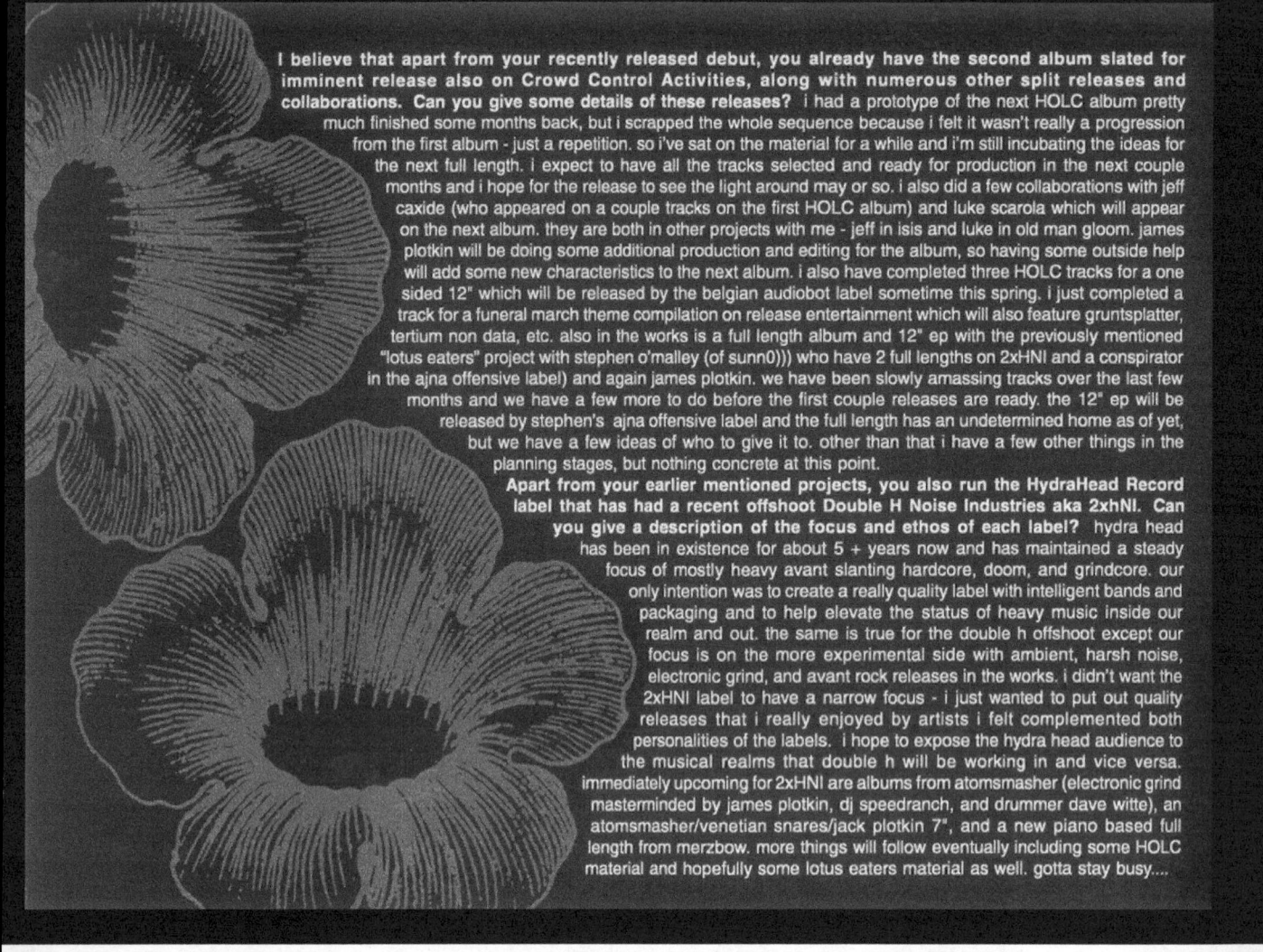

I believe that apart from your recently released debut, you already have the second album slated for imminent release also on Crowd Control Activities, along with numerous other split releases and collaborations. Can you give some details of these releases? i had a prototype of the next HOLC album pretty much finished some months back, but i scrapped the whole sequence because i felt it wasn't really a progression from the first album - just a repetition. so i've sat on the material for a while and i'm still incubating the ideas for the next full length. i expect to have all the tracks selected and ready for production in the next couple months and i hope for the release to see the light around may or so. i also did a few collaborations with jeff caxide (who appeared on a couple tracks on the first HOLC album) and luke scarola which will appear on the next album. they are both in other projects with me - jeff in isis and luke in old man gloom. james plotkin will be doing some additional production and editing for the album, so having some outside help will add some new characteristics to the next album. i also have completed three HOLC tracks for a one sided 12" which will be released by the belgian audiobot label sometime this spring. i just completed a track for a funeral march theme compilation on release entertainment which will also feature gruntsplatter, tertium non data, etc. also in the works is a full length album and 12" ep with the previously mentioned "lotus eaters" project with stephen o'malley (of sunn0))) who have 2 full lengths on 2xHNI and a conspirator in the ajna offensive label) and again james plotkin. we have been slowly amassing tracks over the last few months and we have a few more to do before the first couple releases are ready. the 12" ep will be released by stephen's ajna offensive label and the full length has an undetermined home as of yet, but we have a few ideas of who to give it to. other than that i have a few other things in the planning stages, but nothing concrete at this point.

Apart from your earlier mentioned projects, you also run the HydraHead Record label that has had a recent offshoot Double H Noise Industries aka 2xhNI. Can you give a description of the focus and ethos of each label? hydra head has been in existence for about 5 + years now and has maintained a steady focus of mostly heavy avant slanting hardcore, doom, and grindcore. our only intention was to create a really quality label with intelligent bands and packaging and to help elevate the status of heavy music inside our realm and out. the same is true for the double h offshoot except our focus is on the more experimental side with ambient, harsh noise, electronic grind, and avant rock releases in the works. i didn't want the 2xHNI label to have a narrow focus - i just wanted to put out quality releases that i really enjoyed by artists i felt complemented both personalities of the labels. i hope to expose the hydra head audience to the musical realms that double h will be working in and vice versa. immediately upcoming for 2xHNI are albums from atomsmasher (electronic grind masterminded by james plotkin, dj speedranch, and drummer dave witte), an atomsmasher/venetian snares/jack plotkin 7", and a new piano based full length from merzbow. more things will follow eventually including some HOLC material and hopefully some lotus eaters material as well. gotta stay busy....

BROUGHT OUT FROM WITHIN...
A FINAL DETONATION

GOATPENIS
"TROTZ VERBOT, NICHT TOT"
CD $15 US / 17 WORLD

SERIOUS WAR MUSICAL TERROR BASED ON
ALL FORMS OF TOTAL WAR AND INHUMANIZATION.

PUISSANCE
"A CALL TO ARMS"
7"EP $8 US / 10 WORLD
NOW AVAILABLE...

SELFLESS RECORDINGS
PO BOX 726
ISLIP TERRACE, NY
11752, USA
WWW.SELFLESSRECORDINGS.COM

Looking back on the year that was 2000, one of the clear revaluations was delivered in the form of the debut album of sonic cartographer Skincage aka Jon Ray. The utter diversity and complexity of the album 'Axon' cannot be summed up in a few mere words, yet 'cinematic isolationism' might just be a start. After being quite enthralled by the CD of course I was intrigued to find out about the man who lurks behind this fantastic opus....

Skincage was not really a known name in the scene covered by Spectrum, prior to the Malignant Antibody promotional juggernaut making your debut album 'Axon' a household name in the underground, however I believe that 'Axon' was originally released as a self financed CDR. How much did his first version of 'Axon' differ from the official version, and what type of response did it receive? You're correct, there are somewhere between 50 and 70 copies of a CDR version which really preceded by a much more primitive 'Axon'. You only about half as long, it had two songs later dropped... [illegible] ...and only reason it even existed was because [illegible] compared to the final release but I felt even when there's no real release involved general (one might say my table of contents [illegible] version of 'Axon' had 12 tracks. These are the 11 [illegible] of that song, one of which only exists on the [illegible] of the original samples that caused [illegible] cleaned them up a bit. The sound just [illegible] he noise I was 'cleaning' out of the sam[illegible] used creatively sometimes. There are [illegible]

Was the 'Axon' CDR your official release or... [illegible] say. It was reviewed very favourably [illegible] really have to promote it which is pro[illegible] list and later Jon recommended [illegible] Bly.com did a great deal of hyp[illegible] it through his site. So basically [illegible] me a lot. Some of them even wrote [illegible] discouraged and cures me temporarily. I really owe [illegible] to everyone who supports me in various ways.

How long have you been partaking in such sonic experimentation? Well, that's hard to pinpoint. I used to make really silly mix tapes of songs from the 50s and 60s from the radio when I was around ten or so. After that I started making collage tapes by holding the tape recorder near the TV speaker, which seems really ridiculous now but maybe I should try it again. Eventually I figured out that I could just run cables from the VCR's audio out into my beloved tape player, so I was doing exactly that. I was very fond of making these collage tapes, and I'm sure that's a big root of Skincage right there. Another thing I liked to do was record all the sound from a movie or tv show and then try to imagine my own visuals for it when I was trying to go to sleep. I've always had trouble sleeping so things like this were what I did to tire my mind out. I think that kind of imagining also led to Skincage. When I got a computer with a sound card I started recording from VCR to tape and then to soundcard, since I couldn't very well sneak in and grab my parents' VCR at 1 AM and connect directly. I was using this really low bitrate DOS program before there were wav files. I think it used .voc files. It was monophonic of course, with the sampling rate still less than half CD quality. Damn, I wish I could find it again! Eventually I borrowed a 4 track from a friend and that got me into layering/mixing. I got my own later on and I got better at sampling and got better software, did several tapes by the time I was 17 or 18, but only a few I'm actually proud of. So basically I've been doing some kind of sound experiments about half my life.

As it seems that the original version differs from the later in that the official version was mastered my expert knob twiddler Phil Easter (and also Malignant Antibody label boss) hear on the official release can be accredited to his input? Well, when I first sent Phil my masters of Axon to see if he would remaster it for the CDR release, he told me he was really impressed with what I'd done on my own. I'm pretty proud of my original efforts as well, especially considering that for about half the tracks all I had to work with were the final mix files, with no way to edit them except minute processing on the final mixes themselves rather than re-recording them from a multitrack program. I was lucky in that I had managed to back most of these final mix wav files up to zip disks I had forgotten about until after the crash. Without them I would have had to work from decoded mp3s, which as anyone knows is just nasty.

SKINCAGE

So I did my best to reconstruct and finalize these tracks, but it wasn't perfect. I had gone a little crazy toward the end and I made a few amateurish mistakes trying to get the volume higher and such (I know better now), so he went in and fixed some of the unwanted crunchiness and stuff like that. I lost some of the more shrill high end which I kind of miss in retrospect, but overall I'm really pleased with his work. It sounds less like something I did on a consumer level soundcard and more like "tape manipulation" (the term he used, which I think is pretty fitting). It has more clarity now, and it retains its life with subtle improvements here and there. I've had people tell me it would sound great on vinyl.. maybe someday.

How has the overall response been to the official 'Axon' CD including pertinent sales? As of now more than half the copies have sold, which is encouraging. I'm glad people enjoy it. I've had people tell me that they've recommended it to friends which is wonderful to hear. There's also been a lot of great feedback on the tumorlist and from other groups online, which keeps me going. I'm thankful to all the people who put me on playlists and got people into Skincage in other ways. And in person people really listen when I play them something, which means a lot. I just got my first check from Malignant which is satisfying. I think I'd frame it if I didn't have to turn it in in order to cash it. Perhaps I'll scan it beforehand for posterity. Anyway even though it would be ridiculous to be into this kind of project for the money it's ideal to be paid for what you love, and while it's no fortune it still feels good. I plan to put the money back into gear, Skincage feeding itself so to speak.

While 'Axon' clearly aligns with the underground "cinematic isolationist" mold, on the other it could have easily come from less underground experimental music scenes. How much were you aware of the scenes revolving around labels such as Malignant, Tesco Organisation, Loki Foundation, Cold Spring etc prior to being signed for the official debut release? I've never really known much about the various noise scenes, though I've listened to their output here and there. It's kind of awkward and amusing at the same time, being lumped in with artists I've never heard of and scenes I've never known of or acted within consciously. I'm not offended, just not sure what to make of it. I think some people get far too serious about these things. I can see where labels are useful when you're trying to discuss this type of music or that, or trying to describe what kind of music someone is doing. I think it's great when you can't really put someone in a drawer like that. Change is important in music just like anywhere else. I hope I remain a little hard to label, and I hope a lot more musicians like that emerge. I think it's high time there be more music that we can only refer to as "good". I have to say I am happy to see that people who are into much harsher music are genuinely into what I'm doing. I was kind of nervous about that when I first got on Malignant and started reading the tumorlist.

Given I had a difficult time reviewing 'Axon' due to the compositions evoking a multidimensional sonic textured whirlpool, I still think the "cinematic isolationism" tag is at least a starting pointer to Skincage's style. Would you agree with the "cinematic isolationist" reference and how would you further embellish you own description of Skincage's works? Well, like I said, if people need a phrase that's their call. "Cinematic" is a fairly appropriate adjective since I'm telling a story, and "isolationist" is probably not bad either, since I'm a bit more of a hermit than I'd like to be. I can see how it might help to such you have to work within some kind of framework when you're doing reviews. The best way I can describe or approach my work is that I'm doing what feels natural. It's just about the only time I'm at ease, and probably the only time I really feel like I'm doing something right.

To what extent is Skincage sampled based and do you provide any 'musical' input in the traditional scene? I've worked with samples since the beginning; it's central to what I do, and probably always will be. I'm not well-versed in music theory or even scales or that sort of thing, but I'm not against it. I'm more and more interested in playing instruments, homemade or traditional instruments played in new ways perhaps. The more sounds the better no matter where they come from, that's how I look at it. I'm writing an actual score for an upcoming piece, which will involve live use of modified speech synthesizers interacting with pre-recorded manipulations of human speech in "tongues". It's for a class, so I'm not sure if it will end up recorded or not, but chances are it will. Whether it gets released or not depends on how I feel about it in the end, but either way the challenge of writing effective notation for music that doesn't have set pitches ought to be good for me.

Do Skincage's compositions tend to write themselves as many other artists tend to indicate of their creative processes? In some cases, yeah. I'd go so far as to say my most successful work is done this way. I'm hopeful that I can find a way to get into this mode more often and more easily. Sleep deprivation, working through fevers, stuff like that can be helpful, but it's not healthy to do that all the time. This is why I've adopted the method of creating sounds while I'm in that sort of analytical mode, and reserving composition for when I'm at some point of emotional saturation or a rare moment of clarity. Waiting for the right times means that things take longer, and I'm probably notorious by now for just slipping by with deadlines, but I'd rather be late than crank something out early that I'm just not happy with.

Can you also provide some details of your inspirational sources and creative methods? Inspiration is all around. I don't understand people who say they don't have any ideas. I have my share of slumps, but sometimes it really is as easy as simply slowing down and paying attention to daily life. There's so much going on, if you just stop to notice things, they can teach you a lot. I'm inspired by all kinds of things: random snippets of conversation out of context, music from passing cars, insect and other animal behavior... the strange palette of sounds that emerges when you close your eyes, stop what you're doing, and just listen to the world. I keep my window slightly open even in winter so I can listen to this. I'm rewarded with a constant wash of cars on the highway, static rhythms of rain, scattered conversation from the parking lot five floors down, distant sirens.. it's beautiful. Sometimes I like to turn on my mixer, aim a microphone out the window, and just listen on headphones. It's not all outdoors, either. This week I've noticed a strange sound that happens randomly somewhere around my desk. I can't find the source, much less record it. It's partly infuriating, but in a way I am charmed by it. Or sometimes when I'm unable to sleep I listen to the refrigerator and heater sounds phasing in and out of each other. That sort of thing is what I mean. With high quality sampling as easy and flexible as it is now, everything's a potential instrument, and I think that attitude keeps me inspired.

Do you envisage that Skincage would have existed (albeit in different sonic format) if it were not for the common availability of samplers and computer software? I think I'd be doing something similar, but it would perhaps be more primitive. As I mentioned I was working with little more than a VCR and a tape recorder before I got my first sound card, so who knows where that might have led. Maybe I'd be working within similar lines with more of a hardware base, using complex systems of tape loops or sampling delay pedals.. I've flirted with these kinds of things off and on, and I think they're just as valid a means to work as say a multitracking program and all that comes with those. I've seen bands live who used nothing but a series of pedals and produced beautiful results. It's really more about the technique than about the tools. Sampling on the fly and doing something meaningful with it live has a charm that you can't always get by doing things with software; there's an ephemeral quality because that particular version only happens once. So I plan on moving toward more of a balance between software and hardware. But really the intent and outcome

are more important than the tools, and there are many roads to one point. I'm always fascinated to see how other people, both musicians and other artists, are getting to some of the same places I am in really drastically different ways. I think we all have a lot to learn from each other. Maybe that's the whole point.
Who would you nominate as artists that either have a similar sound if not musical sampling construction ethic to that of Skincage? Talking of sonic construction ethics or ideals, are you of the "re-contextualisation" school of thought? Well, that's very old school and I think it's always been there, from Futurists to musique concrete to the real DJs.. For a long time people have been fed up with where music is going and follow up on their urge to inject life back into whatever their field is by using sounds or tools in a new way. I think most artists who use samples or loops are automatically in this league, but it also includes the realm of experimental composers in all kinds of music. As for similar artists, I really don't know. I say that not to be pompous but because I can't really listen to my own music in a way that allows me to accurately compare it to someone else's. I'm all inside my music, but no matter how much I enjoy someone else's it is still external. See what I mean? I could produce a list of bands or composers I admire here but that's not really answering the question or getting anywhere. I'm sure there are people doing things similar to what I do; I've got no illusions about being an island as far as this style of music. I'd like to find out from people who listen to Skincage who they think I sound like so I can check those musicians out and see what they're doing. It would be as close as I can get to hearing my own music externally, and I think that would be interesting.
In my review of the Skincage album I made reference to my interpretation of your moniker. Firstly and most obviously 'Skincage' is reference to the body (your body?), but perhaps it could be a more abstract metaphor to that of an individual trapped inside the body of society. What are your thoughts of this interpretation and does you own significantly differ? The name is just a glyph really, something I came up with that seemed appropriate at the time and I've stuck with. Like the music, I think it's open to interpretation. One thing I'd like people to understand about Skincage imagery or what have you is that there are no wrong answers when someone asks what one of my songs is about. What I thought of when I composed it is not necessarily what you get out of it by listening, and really we're both correct. In some cases, people report results similar to what I intended without me clueing them in first, and that's always exciting (because I'm not sure how I pull it off) but not a case of there being a valid or invalid interpretation.
Again referencing interpretations, with the CD title 'Axon' do you perceive that your compositions could be representative of structures at a molecular level? I'm flattered by the comparison, actually. Hidden worlds will never fail to fascinate me. I'd love to know someone who could get me access to an electron microscope, I'm sure I'd be addicted instantly. To sort of repeat the answer to the last question though, if that's the mood you get out of it, you're absolutely right, and I'm glad to hear about whatever people glean from what I do.
In regard to your website it features numerous images of abandoned and decrepit factories taken by yourself - some of which were featured in the collage of the official 'Axon' release. What intrigues and draws your towards such subject matter? A metaphor for death and decay perhaps? I look at the remains of old buildings the same way I'd look on a piece of someone else's junk that I could later turn into an instrument of some kind, or a tape I found on the street that ended up being full of great samples. The fact that it was discarded kind of makes it fascinating to me, I like to find out what's "left" in it, I guess you could say. I feel like if something I find seems to have a story to tell, it's my responsibility to help that happen. Those factories haven't produced a product for decades, but they certainly provide a lot of inspiration. Giving something new life even if it's only in my own mind is one of the most satisfying things I can think of to do.
As a bit of an x-mas 2000 bonus, we were treated to an MP3 file of a brand new song on the Malignant Radio web site. This track 'There is no Silence' is very minimalist and in scope is almost an environmental type recording (in that it utilises only slightly altered field recordings of common sounds). Does this at all mark a future direction of Skincage material? Well, in a way yes but in others no. Minimalism is a nice break from complex structures and I'm sure I'll return to that territory but I don't think I'll be making permanent switches in that direction. That track started out as a class project where my aim was to explore the sounds usually avoided when recording film sound on location, basically trying to turn it into something useful. Then I got more into it as a chance to demonstrate the power of focused listening. A lot of the source material was gathered with a homemade stereo contact mic (this is easy and I'd be glad to explain how to build it to anyone who emails me). I walked around from about one in the morning until dawn to try to take advantage of the brief quiet that exists on this campus during those hours, listening for sounds that caught my ear. Then I just probed around finding the best places to pick up the sound and electric taped them in place. What results is a transference of say an area of one foot into a large mental space with each channel carrying a different element of the sound. I was really happy with most of the results. I think this kind of listening is good for you, which is why I decided to make the piece publicly available. I wish I'd had more time to expand it, but it's doubtful many people would download a 20 minute track anyway. Maybe future albums will see me returning to this method.
I hear that there are a couple of split releases, collaboration efforts, and compilations awaiting release that include Skincage input. Can you inform us of regarding these? Well, I did a split with Leech of NTT which was quite a pleasure. He didn't really want to try doing a "blind" remix so instead of sending me source to remixing it he sent a minidisc of short samples and I made a drone track from these fragments. It's pretty listen-able within and I feel it was pretty successful. I think the release will be out pretty soon and I can see how it's coming along with the other contributors. I'm really excited to be on the same CD as Lab Report! I don't know if this is what you were referring to but I also have a track on Krach Test, a compilation being put out by Nicolas of Recycle Your Ears. More info's available at http://www.adnoiseam.net/ I'm excited about this too, as artists like Vox Barbara, Aural Blasphemy, and Sickrobot are also going to be on. There are a lot of other bands involved too but to be honest I'm not familiar with many, which is a situation I should probably fix. Sickrobot/Aex and I are going to work together at some point under the name Testool, and that'll also be put out by Nicolas. That's about it right now. I'm pretty interested in collaborations as they've gone well for the most part in the past. I'd like to do something with Hilflos Kind of infin8ty.com, to pay him back for being so supportive thus far. I guess I'll just see what develops.
Have you commenced any work on an official second album? Any concepts of ideas as to what we might be able to expect? Well, mostly I've been working on production, trying to learn better ways to do things, and new things to try. I've also been building instruments so that I can do more external to the sound card and eventually have something which to more actively perform live, which is something else I'm interested in doing. It's gone fairly well in the few occasions I've done it so far. I wonder if anyone out there reading this was at the show I did in July 2000 at Auralice in Seattle. For the time being, I'm stockpiling sounds and ideas. When inspiration hits, when I find something I need to say, I'll be well armed to tell my new stories. I'm not really sure what to expect from myself as far as a new album, given the chaotic way in which everything I do takes shape. I don't think it will necessarily be Axon part 2; I don't think that's really necessary or very creative. Too many musicians are already putting out basically the same album over and over with different names and I don't want to fall into that trap. So it will probably be a departure, but as long as people keep their ears and minds open, I don't think fans of "Axon" will be disappointed. Whatever I'm doing, the same mentality sits behind it, and I think the same kind of feeling will be there no matter if I'm doing samples or performing on a homemade instrument. If it ever stops being there, I won't really have a reason to continue, right?

middle pillar presents:

"Middle Pillar Presents" is the reasonably recent label imprint of Middle Pillar mail order, who have thus far released some great examples from the ambient/ ethereal/ folk noir scenes. Both KD (K) and James (J) provided their thoughts regarding some of my perceptions of the label, whilst also briefly delving into some of their associated musical projects.

How long had Middle Pillar been operating as a mail-order outlet prior to starting the record component? Likewise what was the basic motivation to head down the label path? K: I started the mail order company in December of 1994 with my wife, Jennifer. At the time I was working for a record store that did a lot of mail order, but for rock and roll, blues and rockabilly. I always wanted to open a store, but the rents for a storefront in New York City is near extortion, so starting a dark music mail order company was a pretty good compromise. I could apply the little business sense I had with the skills I learned on how to properly pack a $200 LP going to Australia via surface mail, combine both with an appreciation for dark music, and hopefully still be able to pay rent at the end of the month. Getting the balls to just do it was the hardest part. There was apparently enough of a need that it worked – people actually sent me money in the mail! Also, I was tired of people complaining that they couldn't get any of my bands CDs (Loretta's Doll) because the label we were on (World Serpent) wasn't stocked locally, or because stores charged way too much for import CDs. Of course this is going back a couple years. So I started off carrying music that was difficult to find elsewhere, and we offered them at reasonable prices. As people became familiar with the name "Middle Pillar" a kind of branding began to occur. It was only natural for us to branch out in becoming a label.
J: Naturally there was a void to exploit in the way of bringing American bands to the same fan base that the Europeans have, but producing them domestically at a cheaper cost. Middle Pillar Presents as a label provides an outlet for a lot of quality bands that could not find markets for their music to be heard.

Who are the management players behind Middle Pillar and does it differ between be it mail-order component to record label component? K: We have a relatively small, overworked staff that deals with the Distribution end of it, all crammed into an office in Manhattan. Wholesale, retail, packing, shipping, and customer service is all handled out of that office, which is where I spend my days, with my crack suicide staff! James spends his days in another office dealing with mostly label-type things, or something.
J: I handle most of the promotional correspondence between the label and those who receive advance copies of new releases (radio stations, DJ's and clubs). A lot of the merchandising end goes through me as well, sending posters and other free items to events like record release parties and sponsoring events like Gothcon for example.

Thus far you have exclusively released American artists and furthermore all seem to be derived from an ambient/ ethereal/ folk noir scene centred in New York. Firstly how true is this assumption and secondly is this cultivation of a particular American scene/ style/ sound something that you plan to continue with? Do you ever envisage expanding the roster to non-American artists? J: As mentioned earlier, the original intention of the label was to provide a showcase for American bands, not necessarily from New York. As a matter of fact the first band signed to the label was The Machine in the Garden, who are based in Austin, Texas. Most recently we've signed Sumerland from Portland, Oregon. Overall the scene was already there. Middle Pillar Presents just provides a platform for their music. But we wouldn't limit ourselves to only having American bands out of some sort of pride. Initially the idea of MPP was to have domestic bands, grab people's attention and say, hey, here's some great music! In the future, I would like to see MPP having artists from other parts of the globe. For the rest of this year we're concentrating on the many wonderful releases we have coming out.
K: A lot of the bands featured on our "What is Eternal" compilation were from all over the place, as well as New York. I'd like to think we are a part of the scene here, but I don't think we set out to define the New York genre through our releases. I feel as a small label, it's important to work with people you know, so I think it's only natural that we'd be picking from the "locals" to a certain extent.

Further to the above do you consider Middle Pillar typically American, or is it that whilst the label might be American that signs American artists, that the actual music has more of a European focus? K: I'm not really sure what "typically American" means anymore, to be honest. We're signing American acts out of support for music that is in our own backyards, that is within our direct field of vision. Good art isn't always relative to geography! I think as far as the style of music we sign, it is of itself a unique mixture of cultures, European cultures inclusive. I think that two great examples would be The Machine In The Garden's "Out of the Mists" and the forthcoming "Sivo" album by Sumerland; both draw from classical influences, but mix them with other factors unique to an American cultural experience.

Talking of a European focus, Middle Pillar releases are distributed and or repressed by World Serpent Distribution for the European market. How did this collaboration come about? K: I'd already been working with World Serpent as a part of Loretta's Doll as well as buying from them for the

Distribution. Since five artists from the "What Is Eternal" compilation were already distributed by WSD, it seemed simple enough that they would be interested in picking it up, which they did. In early 1999 WSD took a very limited amount of WIE, not really expecting much from it, but it sold out very quickly. In fact by the time our ads came out, we were totally out of product! It was insane. Between the copies the artists got for free, and the large amount of promos we sent, only about 650 copies were available for actual sale. When WSD wanted to re-press it, with a focus on a European audience, the bands agreed. At first I felt that I wanted to focus on newer releases, instead of looking back. But it was a terrific opportunity for the bands and ourselves. But as far as our working relationship with WSD, they were very supportive about the label as a whole; and I appreciate their honesty in their dealings with me. I'm in awe of the strong reputation they've built, and thankful that we can be a part of it.

In relation to both at home and abroad what has the interest been like in Middle Pillar as a label and likewise artist's releases? What has been the most successful release to date? J: I've been on top of where the music is being played and it astounds me where it can found. Europe and South America seem to be the most open as far as airplay goes. While in the US, these genres of music are largely underground and the domain of college radio, stations from Brazil to Belgium, Chile to Lithuania and even as far as Moscow, Russia have been playing Middle Pillar artists. And with the advent of web broadcasting the music reaches the smallest corners of the globe. Here in the states, there are a limited number of darkwave and experimental radio shows, which are usually limited to a small amount of time. Within the confines of an hour or two, there's only so much that can be played. Fortunately, we try to maintain our relationships with these DJ's who rarely hear any feedback from anyone regarding their playlists. I always send thanks when I see a MPP disc played. We've tried to build a reputation of having interesting releases and quality music. I think the DJ's realize it and that's why you'll hear MPP on those stations. As far as releases go, there have been strong reactions to several bands. A Murder of Angels have received many accolades by those in the experimental set and we sold out of that very quickly. Our compilations have done very well as an overall sampler of the label and as a showcase for upcoming talent like The Unquiet Void and The Mirror Reveals. Our top seller continues to be The Machine in the Garden who's second album for MPP, "Out of the Mists", has just been released.

All Middle Pillar items to date have been packed in non-standard fold out card digi-pack and are in fact quite different from what you would normally consider as a digi-pack. Was there a particular philosophy behind choosing this presentation other then to give Middle Pillar releases an easily identifiable appearance? J: We looked at several different formats and decided that standard jewel cases were not the way to go initially. The special cardboard packaging adds to the overall aesthetic of the label and adds another layer of style to a diminishing art - the album cover. A lot of music packaging these days has an assembly line feel to it. Luckily we're fortunate to have such talented graphics people working on our covers and promotional items. Reviews have often commented on the quality and uniqueness of the packages so I'd say we succeeded in our choice.

K: My philosophy is that this music should not be looked at as an easily duplicated commodity, a hard call in the digital age, and I think our packaging underscores that thought. The covers, like the music, need to be shown respect. It appeals to the collector part of my personality.

When meticulously perusing your releases it is noted that thus far the numbering of the releases are progressively counting back from 100. What is the reasoning behind this? J: Just another idiosyncrasy. The standard releases move backwards from 999 on down and the compilations start from 000 (What is Eternal) on up. I guess it's conceivable that they might meet up one day but we'll worry about it then!

How do view the current state of the underground ambient/ ethereal/ folk scene particularly in that there seems to have been an increase in releases and labels over the past two years? K: I think the explosion in labels and the growth in the number of bands leads to a broader audience, it also enlarges the signal to noise ratio between the truly innovative and the imitative. But I still believe that more music is definitely better, for any scene. Middle Pillar is a new label that's blossomed over the last two years, so I definitely feel that we could be lumped in as part of that new wave of "Johnny Come Lately's" too. I don't see too many entries into that category on the American side of the pond. It's mostly new European labels that are making bigger leaps, like Athanor, Eis & Licht, Fluttering Dragon, Prikosnovenie, Oktagon, Cynfeirdd, Loki, Stateart. In the US we've got Triumvirate, Crowd Control, Malignant, Precipice....us....

Furthermore what would you consider are the biggest opportunities and or challenges for the current scene? K: The biggest challenge of any scene is not to implode with personal gripes and politics, which is hard thing not to do. When people are doing things out of love, pride becomes an important issue. It's important to be wise and let the scene grow, because it's bigger than just one person, it always is.

J: In a market place that is dominated by the majors, I hope the independents do not follow their example of churning out repetitive product and assembly line crap. There is a mindset within the dark music scene that it's dying out slowly. I think it's an overall pessimism that underlies the material within its psychological framework. This isn't bubble-gum pop after all! But it always seems to thrive. And with new technology on the horizon, the smaller labels with make the most out of it (Napster for example) until someone bigger catches on and exploits it for the masses. I've always felt the best marketing tool is bringing the music right to the audiences. People will always love the live experience and clubs can offer it to them. Since you won't always be able to catch anyone in the Top 20 in your neighborhood, therein lies the domain of the independent.

In regards to artists on Middle Pillar, do they have to hold a certain philosophy or worldview to be considered for signing? On an alternate tangent, if you appreciated an artist's music but did not agree with and/ or condone their sources of inspiration, would this prevent a project from being signed to Middle Pillar? K: As far as the distribution is concerned, I certainly carry music from artists that I don't necessarily agree with on a philosophic or ethical basis. We carry over 3000 titles, and I'm sure that there must be at least one artist we sell that has a point of view that I would consider misinformed! And as soon as I find them, I'm going to sit him or her down and set them straight! □

J: We haven't had a situation where an artist's politics or philosophy has effected their relationship with us, so there's no point of reference. In the case of a theme compilation, it would make sense if the artist understood and felt similarly about the concept. For example, I wouldn't ask Ted Nugent to do a song for PETA. I guess we'll have to deal with each situation as it comes but personally, I'm more interested in the music itself.

K: For instance, we'll be doing a compilation based on the Tree of Life, that we hope to have out by next winter. We tried to select artists that would create appropriate musical interpretations of each Sephiroth associated with the Tree. The Tree is a powerful symbol, so we wanted musicians who I thought understood those particular concepts. So I suppose that would be an example of acceptance or denial based on our perception of an artist's particular belief system. Guilty as charged!

Knowing that you both have your own musical projects (KD with Kobe and James with The Mirror Reveals) can you give introductions to the music, style and history of these projects? Also are these the only musical formations you are involved with? K: I should start by saying that I've actually been a member of Loretta's Doll since almost its inception in 1992, and I'm happy to report that Middle Pillar has just jointly released, with WSD, our newest album "Creeping Sideways". My role in the band is percussion and rhythm. I've been playing electronic percussion for the past few years, which allows me to explore non-traditional "drum" sounds, and non-naturalistic instrumentation in a rhythmic way. "Creeping Sideways" was for me an exploration of more experimental form than my role in the past, and the end result was a bit more abstract. The record features returning guest "Doll" Orson Wells, has Derek Rush (Dream Into Dust, Chthonic Streams, A Murder of Angels) again returning for a stint in the "bassist" role, but also helping to shape the sound during mixes and production. We've just played Suffering Clown's A Night of Misanthropy, which is a live underground music event in NYC, and is always great fun. Live, our sound has always been a bit angrier, and ballsier, than our records. And of course there's our long awaited "comp of comp tracks" "Mein Komp" (hehe). My other musical project is KOBE, which is steeped in traditional Japanese percussion, then distilled by modern western approaches, re-shaped, and re-created. With the conception of Butoh, I did a song in a modern style that was a sort of tribute to Kodo drummers trapped in a Neubauten-esque nightmare! The final mix turned out different from what I had initially imagined, not as traditional sounding as I had hoped, but certainly not bad. And thus a new project was born! I'll have a CDep completed by the fall, I hope.

J: The Mirror Reveals was an idea forged during the production of "What is Eternal". The track received lots of attention, which led to the full length, "Frames of

Teknicolor." I've always wanted to work with a female vocalist and Kit Messick provided the inspiration. Listening to her vocal style through her background with the theater, it allowed me to write dark emotional torch songs. What started as a studio project has evolved into a full band with the addition of Joanna Dalin (ex-Backworld) on violin. A follow up EP will be out shortly, with another full length on its heels. It's wonderful to work on creating art instead of nurturing others. Eventually, I would like to return to my roots and do an aggressive punk-industrial record but that's down the road.

What are the plans for Middle Pillar both in regard to the short term and long term? What of upcoming releases? J: Middle Pillar Presents plans to expand through greater distribution in the US while maintaining a presence in Europe and the rest of the globe through advertising and the loyalty of radio and club DJ's there. MPP is growing exponentially before our eyes. It's a delight and a nightmare! I need more sleep! We just released "Abnormal Love" by THREAD, an electronic tour de force of many styles. The auteur, James Izzo, has gained the admiration of many artists included Jarboe (ex-SWANS) who sang on the CD. The Loretta's Doll's "Creeping Sideways" CD should be in stores by the time this is read. Upcoming is the debut album by Sumerland entitled "SIVO, who are this amazing blend of acoustic instruments and the resonant voice of Dorian Campbell.

K: We'll be releasing albums by ZOAR over the next year or so. They do amazing textural, dark and beautiful industrial atmospherics, extremely theatrical stuff, heartfelt but with a razor's edge. Next fall will bring a series of Cdeps from our artists featuring new material, remixes and a video. Mirror Reveals will be doing one, as will Kobe, Zoar, and Thread. Another release from A Murder of Angels is in the works. Plus the aforementioned Tree of Life comp by the 2001 holiday season. Middle Pillar Presents has a lot on its plate right now and many people are listening. It's an exciting time!

Middle Pillar Presents: A Discography:
MPP999: the Machine in the Garden "One Winter's Night" CD Digipak
MPP998: A Murder of Angels "While You Sleep" CD Digipak
MPP997: The Mirror Reveals "Frames of Teknicolor" CD Digipak
MPP995: The Unquiet Void "Between the Twilights" CD Digipak
MPP994: the Machine in the Garden "Out of the Mists" Digipak CD
MPP993: Thread "Abnormal Love" Digipak CD
MPP992: Sumerland: "Sivo" CD Digipak (softspot)
MPP991: Loretta's Doll: "Creeping Sideways" CD Jewelcase - Joint Release with WSD (WSCD023)
MPP990: Zoar "In The Bloodlit Dark" CD Jewelcase
MPP989: KOBE: "tba" CDEP
MPP988: Zoar "tba" CDEP
MPP987: The Mirror Reveals "tba" CDEP
MPP986: Thread "tba" CDEP
MPP002: V/A "Butoh: Dance of Darkness" CD Digipak (softspot)
Limited to 1500 copies; With exclusive songs or mixes by KOBE, A Murder of Angels, Mors Syphilitica, the Machine in the Garden, The Unquiet Void, Sumerland, Wench, The Mirror Reveals, Thread and Zoar.
MPP001: V/A "Tree of Life" CD Limited to ??? Final track listed "TBA"
MPP000 V/A "What Is Eternal" CD Digipak Limited to 1000 copies With exclusive songs or mixes by the Machine in the Garden, 4th Sign of the Apocalypse, Unto Ashes, Mors Syphilitica, Quartet Noir, Loretta's Doll, Dream Into Dust, The Changelings, Tony Wakeford & Tor Lundval, Backworld, The Mirror Reveals, Jarboe, Athanor, and Zoar
MPP000X: V/A "What Is Eternal" CD Jewelcase Limited Re-issue; Re-mastered; Exclusive distribution via WSD Contains same track listing as MPP000, but with a remixed Jarboe track

WILT - "Wither" CD - $11(us) $13(wld)
Wilt extol the invisible corners of the thirsty earth with this exaltation of decay and reclamation. Best described as Noise Ambient, "Wither" is a aural quagmire of dusky vapors and ivy draped relics, grating erosions and the thorny shadows that rise and fall across dying landscapes. Moldering Dark Noise from this inspired American project. Limited to 500 copies.

KK NULL / MOZ - "A Split Release" CD - $11(us) $13(wld)
KK Null presents five new tracks of frenetic electronics and rhythmic experiments, ranging from cacophonous to an almost tribal atmosphere. Ever evolving within a sphere of obscure tension the details reveal themselves with a stalwart elegance. Moz delivers 6 tracks of socially introspective Death Industrial and Dark Ambient. Drifting slabs contrast sharply with vitriolic sonics to render this misshapen pillar of sobering electronics. Limited to 500 copies.

DEISON - "Dirty Blind Vortex" CD - $11(us) $13(wld)
A fuming miasma of desiccated frequencies and oppressive atmospheres from this Italian purveyor of Death Industrial & Dark Ambient. "Dirty Blind Vortex" is a cryptic snarl of emotion and obsession, impulse and lethargy. Features contributions from Sshe Retina Stimulants, Govt. Alpha, Baal, R.H.Y. Yau, Lasse Marhaug and more. Limited to 500

ALSO COMING IN 2001
EXSANGUINATE - "tba" CD - obsessive death industrial
NEVER PRESENCE FOREVER - "Disturbed Visceral Nociception" CD - bleak soundscapes

CRIONIC MIND

ORDERING INSTRUCTIONS: All prices are postage paid, payment by well concealed cash or money order made payable to SCOTT CANDEY, NOT CRIONIC MIND. All payment must be in US funds only.
PMB 105 : 4644 Geary Blvd. : San Francisco, CA 94118 : www.crionicmind.org : crionic@pacbell.net

Given Folkstorm essentially represents an even nastier musical alter ego of one Mr Nordvargr of the infamous MZ412, this really negates the requirement for a lengthy introduction. With the project representing a back to basics and raw approach to power electronics/ industrial noise and more particularly after a spate of recent releases (most of which are reviewed in these pages) it was high time for a Folkstorm feature.

When did Folkstorm become an active and established side project to MZ. 412? What essentially were your reasons and/ or needs to start a solo side project? Folkstorm started as an idea in my head some years ago... must have been 1997 or something like that. There were many reasons for starting it - the main one being my creative head... I had a lot of energy and ideas that I had to "channel".
If we were to compare the first three MZ. 412 albums to Folkstorm there is a substantial difference to be noted, however as the Nordik Battle Signs saw a more militant evolution of MZ. 412's sound, therefore this CD could be viewed as having more clear parallels with Folkstorm. Would you agree that there has been a cross pollination of ideas and focus between the projects in recent times particularly since the two Folkstorm studio albums were recorded back in 1999 around the same time as N.B.S? Of course a similarity between the two bands cant be avoided. "Information Blitzkrieg" and "Victory or death" were both recorded at the same time and are both about war. They were recorded after NBS, and maybe I still had some of the "NBS-vibe" fresh in mind...
In that you can detect fleeting sounds and samples also utilised in MZ. 412's work, in actual fact how much overlap is soundsource? Hmmm... some of the MZ. 412 samples have been re-used for Folkstorm, yes... Consider it a fun game for the real fan to find them!
Considering the raw and basic sound construction of Folkstorm's sound, is this back to basics sound reflected in the recording techniques you use? What encompasses a Folkstorm recording session? A Folkstorm recording session is a real, violent, freeform and loud experience. I usually team up with Ulvtharm (who nowadays owns our fully equipped studio Nar Mattaru) who is the perfect sound engineer for this kind of music. We start of making the basics - drones, samples etc. Then we turn up the volume really high and just "go with the flow" or whatever you call it. Lots of sweat and beer are usually present. Then when we are done we sit back and listen to the result - what you can hear on the albums is what is left after we take away the parts that I didn't turn out good enough. The process is very freeform and improvised - far from the perfectionist production of MZ. 412.
The first two albums 'Information Blitzkrieg' & 'Victory or Death' (although not released in sequence) were recorded with you being the solo member, however the live recording CD 'Hurtmusic' is credited to both Mr and Mrs Nordvargr. Who is this mysterious Mrs Nordvargr and is she now a full time member of the group and what is her primary role? My wife. She hates power electronics and industrial music, but still she likes to add some noise to the production... She is a member through marriage whether she likes it or not, muahahaaaa....
In that you have coined a slogan for Folkstorm 'No Politics, No Religion, No Standard' yet you utilise a myriad of samples, recordings, voices, images and symbols that could be construed as being extremely controversial, to what extend is the use of this slogan a diversionary tactic? It is not diversion... Folkstorm doesn't take a stand - it is freeform. I just observe the world I live in and use it as a source. It might sound like a cliché but it is the truth...
Much of the sampled dialogue segments within the Folkstorm compositions are so drastically altered and distorted actual deciphering of the message is mostly a lost cause. Are the samples used to convey a direct message or used as a source of inspiration to how the composition will sound? The samples are used as an extra voice or instrument - its part of the concept... however in the future there will be less samples. I'm working more in a "man vs machine" way now...
How much do you view Folkstorm in a cultural sense and the message you want to bring to your audience if not a message to the wider general populous? Folkstorm is part of modern art and culture even though I bet that the "established" cultural elite of Sweden would hate it. My mission is to infiltrate and contaminate it all - that is the meaning of the Culturecide movement. I have a lot of ideas that I plan to execute this year. Watch out!
'Culturecide' is another concept you have coined in relation to Folkstorm. Can you expand on its meaning or should it simply be interpreted on face value? I think I just answered that. You might wonder about what these "Culturecide Campaigns" are about... I can tell you about one which you all can do - Download some 20 modern megahits (Madonna, Backstreet Boys, whatever) on the web and then modify the files... make sure that the first halfminute or so still sounds like it is supposed to be. Then add your favourite Folkstorm track. So far some 1000 people have downloaded hidden (and rare exclusive) Folkstorm tracks disguised as popmusic with Napster. Some of them are very mad, trust me...
Folkstorm has played live a couple of times in 2000, one of which became the 'Hurtmusic' CD. I am assuming that it easier to perform Folkstorm material live due to the raw essence of the sound – yet how much of what you have performed live has been improvised? When we recorded HURTMUSIC I guess that half of the sources were prerecorded. Usually I prerecord the rythmic parts and use them as a "skeleton" for the performance. The rest is mostly live improvisations. I like the freedom it gives me. The combined live performance with MZ. 412 in Rostock, Germany was different. There we used more tapes and prerecorded stuff and used the stage more as a battlefield/temple... lots of fire, swedish soil and dirt.
While for the most part Folkstorm comes across as an intensely serious project, notwithstanding, one track off 'Culturecide Campaigns' sees a rather well know pop song gets quite massacred in somewhat humorous style. How do you view this assessment of humour within the concept of Folkstorm? As I said before, Folkstorm can be anything... That particular track also appears in a different version on the split mCD with Lefthandeddcision (later this year from Troniks). You cant always be deadly serious about everything...
Again referencing 'Hurtmusic' emblazed on the cover is an image of yourself in a Christ like pose. Is this picture a symbolic offering of yourself as a martyr to your beliefs? No. I dont feel like a martyr... it is more a symbolic representation of the restrained anger that dwells inside of me. Chained by the morals and beliefs of a decaying society ruled by fools...
In an interview of yours I wanted to quote a specific segment. "I simply observe the truth and expose it to the masses" (Letters from the Nuovo Europae Vol 1#). What truth are you referring to? Likewise to what extent it the 'truth' a defunct concept, given that there can only ever the one truth – being that according to an individuals own perceptions, thus relegating 'truth' to being not more than a strongly held opinion? I think I was misinterpreted... it should be "I simply observe the reality around me and expose...". What I mean is that Folkstorm is a reflection of todays society - it observes, manipulates, lies, entertains and worries people, but it never takes a stand.
On an alternate yet related topic, there was talk of you starting a vinyl only record label. How is this new planned endeavour progressing at the moment? It is at a complete standstill. My life has become very busy the past year and I haven't found the time to make anything else than plans... the first release on HoloGram will be a LP with Survival Unit, hopefully during 2001. The planned Folkstorm/MZ. 412 collaboration will not be released thru HoloGram.
What new or old groups would you give the Nordvargr/ Folkstorm stamp of approval? If you mean my personal favorites they would be Slogun, Judas Iscariot, Survival Unit, Nod, BDN, Marduk and Brainbombs... at the moment.
Lastly given the quite prolific output of Folkstorm in a short amount of time, is this release schedule going to continue? What can we expect in the near future? Folkstorm - Noisient 10" (OEC) and Folkstorm vs Lefthandeddecision (Troniks) is probably out during the first half of 2001. I have already one album recorded but it is not mastered yet... when, how etc it will be released is yet to be determined. Also, a still unnamed cooperation with Slogun will probably be out later this year. I am also discussing a vinyl project with the new English label Kokampf... we´ll see what happens... anyway, Folkstorm will not slow down...

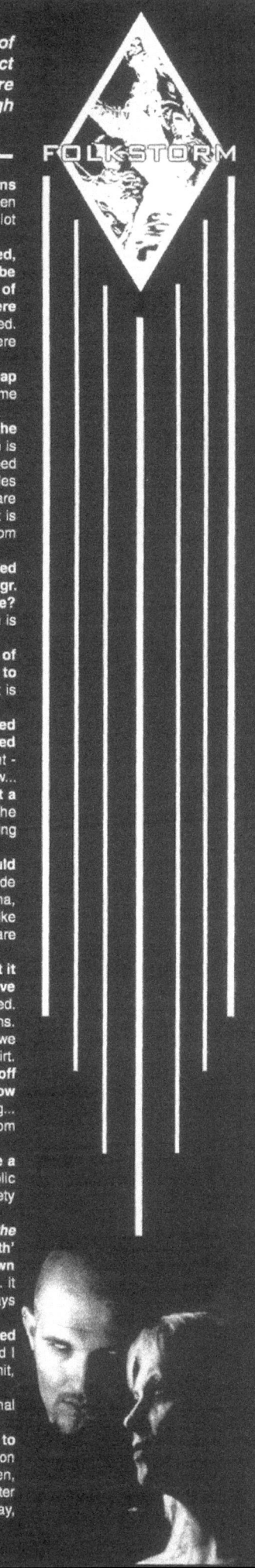

Live Bait Recording Foundation

Proudly Presents...

LBRF015 Salvation Bloodletting Compilation CD
Featuring 70 Minutes of new and Unreleased Tracks by
Amon, BaaL/Berith, The Hollowing, No Festival
Of Light, Origami Arktika, Azoikum, Nothvs
Filivs Mortis, Deison, Nothing, Slowvent,
Gruntsplatter, In Death's Throes,
Ravens Bane and Lefthandeddecision
In Jewel Case with 8 page booklet
of Artwork and Texts Dealing with
Religious Fanaticism...A MUST!!!!
$12.00 PPD in the USA
$14.00 PPD WorldWide

Also Upcoming-
LBRF016 Minus/Luftkanone Split CDR
LBRF017 This Morn Omina TBA CD
LBRF018 Lockweld/Lefthandeddecision Split CDR
LBRF019 Azoikum/Quell Split CDR
LBRF020 In Death's Throes 12" LP

LBRF
423 Seventh St #3
Fairport Harbor Oh, 44077
USA
livebaitrecording@hotmail.co
www.crionicmind.org/liveba

vox barbara

Vox Barbara might not be a highly known name at the moment, yet those who have heard the project all seem to have exclusively positive comments to make. While this situation could be construed to amount to partial obscurity, this should not prevent you from checking out Frank Smith's diverse experimental sonic collages that via containing an element of directional structure and rhythm have created uniquely dark atmospherics. Given I immensely enjoyed the tribally tinged debut CD 'The Five Sences' and with the second more clinically/ digitally tinged CD '(de)constructing ghosts' having recently been released, I thought it was about time I grilled Frank Smith with a few questions.

How long was it after you started listening to experimental soundscapes/ dark ambience that you decided to try producing your own compositions? Likewise what were some of the artists that birthed your interest in experimental styles of music? Some of the first artists I listened to were Zoviet France, The Hafler Trio, Nocturnal Emissions, Muslimgauze...but the desire to produce the music and my exposure to it really seemed to happen at the same time. In a lot of cases, I'd read about what artists were doing and be very drawn to it based on the descriptions, then maybe go ahead and do some of my own experiments, and when I finally heard the artists' work I had read about, I'd be amazed at how similar it sounded to what I was producing.... Some things did influence me directly; for instance, John Watermann's "Calcutta Gas Chamber" was a big influence on the overall feel (and conceptual nature) of the first vox barbara album, "The Five Senses." But more often than not, it would be more a case of, as I said, reading about something and being drawn to it or having someone tell me after hearing my work, "oh, you really should check out so and so..." and finding out there were others out there with whom I was already on the same wavelength....

Both of your albums have been released on your own label Little Man Records, which was created out of necessity in that no other label was interested in taking on the task. Particularly what was the label reaction like to you latest work '(de)constructing ghosts', even if none came forth with an offer to release it? The label reaction was kind of baffling, frankly: almost utter silence! Very few labels that I sent advance copies of 'Ghosts' to even responded at all... One reason it's so baffling is because the reviews, etc. I've read of 'ghosts' have been so overwhelmingly positive, peppered with comments like, "I can't believe no label has picked this up..." In retrospect, I'm happy, though, because releasing things myself, while a big expense and lots of work, gives me total artistic control over the packaging, etc., which is very important to me...so the self-releasing is probably going to continue in the future.

Although this question is a tad biased (considering the glowing review I have written of the latest CD), I wanted to ask what public response has been to the CD compared to that of label reactions? Oops, guess I already answered that one! But yes, it's been very, very positive...it feels really good when people appreciate what you've set out to do and obviously have taken the time to really listen and get inside it; when they actually "get it"!

Referencing '(de)constructing ghosts' this utilised some subversive computer technology in the form of what is known as 'Ligea' sound analysis software. Can you provide some background to how you obtained this and what is the premise of its operational intent? Well, I was lucky enough to download it from the old "Anarchy N' Explosives" underground FTP site before it disappeared...from what I've read, the software was developed on the same principles as the Kirlian Camera, i.e. if you bombard an object—in this case, sounds—with the right stimuli, you'll uncover the nature of the underlying "energy" of the object, and originnally had some sort of "investigative," spy-like sort of intent. As to exactly how it works, I'm not a programmer or any sort of expert in such matters, so for all I know, it could be a total sham...e.g: it could just be a sophisticated audio-processing/mangling software...but whatever it is, I like the sonic results, which to me is what counts.

Despite using this software to create the new album, what is your personal opinion in regard to the validity of its claims? Like I said, I'm really not sure...for me, concept is such a big part of art, so just the IDEA that it might do what it says, that it might somehow draw out the history of an object, the voices or energies trapped in it, and release them as the sonic "ghosts" of the object's past, is thrilling enough to me, and really enriches the bizarre sounds it produces. It ultimately doesn't matter to me if it really does what it's supposed to, you know? The concept has stimulated my imagination as far as interpreting or contextualizing the sound sources I selected and then processed through it, and it seems to have stimulated the imaginations of many listeners to, based on the comments I've received...that's enough for me!

Around the time '(de) constructing ghosts' was released you had many positive things to say about the mastering work Phil Easter did for the album. How much did the mastering after the finished recording to released result? Phil did several great things to that material. Some were strictly "mechanical;" i.e. he cleaned up some very annoying (to me) background noise present in some of the source material, enabling one to focus much more clearly on the primary sounds...it's amazing what he was able to do in that regard, especially on the track "Ritual Dissection," which was based on construction site sounds and marred by some annoying microphone noise, which he pretty much totally removed. And then through equalization and other magic, he just gave the overall material a lot more "punch." The other thing he did that pleased me so much was to suggest and execute a number of cross-fades, where one track flows seamlessly into another track, a kind of built in "dj mix" feel, if you will...that kind of work is to me more artistic than mechanical. I think Phil has a great feel for that stuff (just listen to the old Stone Glass Steel albums), and it was a great unexpected benefit to his overall mastering package.

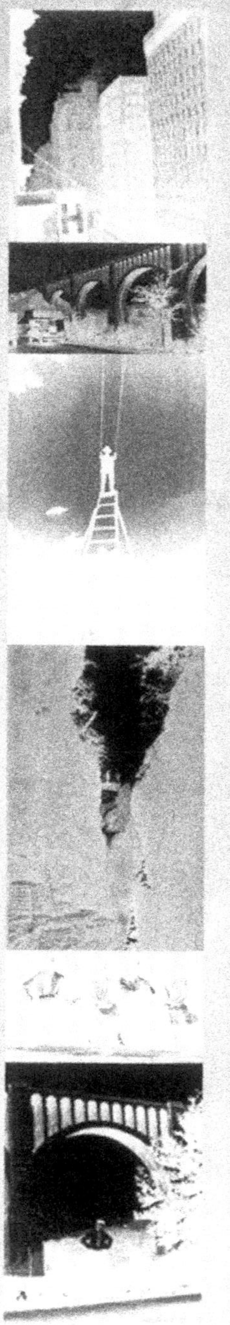

Given the use of this software, how did this after your creative process compared to those you may have employed on your first CD "the five senses"? Are you albums primarily spliced together digitally on a PC? The way I worked on both albums was pretty much the same: source material was sampled into a Macintosh (a UNIX-based workstation in the case of 'Ghosts'), then loops were layered on a four-track and then eventually mixed down to DAT. The only difference with 'Ghosts' was, all processing was done by Ligea, as opposed to by various shareware audio processing programs and stomp-box effects as in the case of 'The Five Senses.' The real creation and building, for me, comes in the collaging process of layering and fading the loops in and out on the four track...knowing when to bring what up, to play what against what, when to drop things out...and using repetition to build a trance-like state...that's really what the vox barbara project is all about.

The debut CD was also rather conceptual, surrounding a 1797 writing of Anaitre Tellsos on the five senses and the potential ability for humans to experience the world on much higher levels that the common held sight, hearing, taste, smell and touch. Can you expand on the basis of this literally inspiration and also how this related to the musical compositions created for 'the five senses' CD? What drew me to Tellsos' novel was how he imagined a sensory world so opposed to and in contrast with our own, along with the notion that it's just barely submerged underneath our day-to-day "mundane" perceptions. So what I tried to do musically with "The Five Senses" was to use very mundane, everyday (household) objects and by processing and looping their sounds, bring out something very bizarre and "otherworldly."

Given your first CD encompassed tribal influenced experiential soundscapes and the second CD was much more clinically and technologically sounding experimental soundscapes I was wondering what direction will you take future recordings in? I think probably some combination of the two extremes...though ultimately more toward the organic end of the spectrum. Certainly the rather cold and digital feel of 'Ghosts' was in large part a function of the Ligea software and the specific kinds of things it does to sounds...so while I may use it again in small amounts in the future, the "tribal" elements and the coaxing of the extraordinary out of ordinary sources through repetition and rhythm is my main goal with vox barbara.

In that I find Vox Barbara to be somewhat of an anomaly due to there being very few artists that have a similar sound, who would you consider to be like minded artists or even comparable sounding projects? Well, I just express what I feel, there's never really an attempt to sound "like" anyone, which is I guess why it sounds unique! There are a number of people doing maybe one thing to which I feel a kinship but not others; you know, artists whom I may not sound like but with whom I feel a like-minded spirit in some aspect, maybe the choice of source material, the overall feel, the rhythmic elements...some people with whom I feel varying degrees of kinship and to whom I listen a lot are Contagious Orgasm, Harry Bertoia, John Watermann, old Zoviet France, Templegarden, old Deutsch Nepal, The Moon Lay Hidden Beneath a Cloud...none of them are really "similar sounding" to vox barbara, but all have at least one aspect of their music to which I'm drawn or feel in kinship to.

Final words/ thoughts? To anyone trying to produce dark ambient/ritual/experimental music out there: true art is a window onto another world, a way out of this predictable and mundane realm into uncharted territory. If what you're doing sounds a lot like the latest release from [insert favourite label name here], then you're probably still planted a bit too firmly in this world...fuck genres, open that window!

Dagobert's Revenge

To subscribe to Dagobert's Revenge, please send $14 for two issues, plus your name and address, to:

2301 New York Ave., #2
Union City, NJ 07087

Or order online at:
www.dagobertsrevenge.com

You can also send a SASE for a complete catalogue of our magazines, audiotapes, videotapes, CDs and t-shirts.

Interviews with:
Boyd Rice, Death in June, the Legendary Pink Dots, Rose McDowall, Ulver, Guy Patton, Peter Levenda, Prince Michael Stewart.

And Articles about:
Templars, Freemasons, Nazi Occultism, the Holy Grail, Priory of Sion, Skull & Bones, Royal Bloodlines, Conspiracies, UFOs, magick, Satanism, the occult, secret history, heretical thought, and Monarchist politics, + learn how Jesus is actually a descendant of Lucifer!

"There's Only One Blood Royale."

CROWD CONTROL

As All Die "Time of War and Conflict" CD
Apocalyptic Folk from Clint Listing and Greg Ball. Following a well-received split release, As All Die's debut full-length shows that this is truly a project on the rise. Melodic hate sure to be embraced by the mysanthropist in all of us.

Chaos AS Shelter "Midnight Prayer/Illusion" DCD
Two CD's of dark ambient music from Israel. Chaos As Shelter blend deep, ominous drones with the ethnic influences of the region. Utilizing somewhat of a musique concret approach, Vadim Gusis crafts some of the most interesting sounds in dark/experimental music.

House of Low Culture "Submarine Immersion Techniques Vol.1" CD
Welcome to the excellent debut by Aaron Turner's (Isis/Hydra Head Records) House of Low Culture. "Submarine Immersion Techniques" is a psychedelic concoction made up of droning guitars and catchy riffing. Though noisier elements are applied, HOLC maintains a pwerfully relaxing mood.

Nasopharyngeal "Endless" CD
"Endless", the initial offering by Nasopharyngeal, is an improvisational piece performed by Brendan Krause (Metropolis Records) and his enigmatic partner 'the priest'. Refreshingly old-school, beats and constant sonic flux make this an impressive listen capable of drawing you further and further into it's madness.

Blackmouth "ST" CD

Dreams In Exile "Since Long Before" CD

Gruntsplatter "The Death Fires" CD

Necrophorus "Drifting in Motion CD

Crowd Control Activities

Crowd Control Activities PO Box 2340 Upper Darby, PA 19082
email:crowded@ezlink.com
www.ezlink.com/~crowded fax: (610) 394 2751

Distributed by Relapse, Metropolis, Dark Vinyl, Malignant and Soleil Moon

CROWD CONTROL ACTIVITIES

The American label Crowd Control Activities has been kicking around for some years now, constantly solidifying their profile via releasing a diverse range of music from the general ambient/ industrial underground. Label boss and sole operator James Grell enlightened me on matters involving the label and other associated topics....

Prior to actually launching Crowd Control Activities, did the idea for starting a label surface quite some time earlier? How involved or interested were you in the underground that ultimately lead to the decision to birth CCA? I have wanted to start a label since I was in High School. At that time I was way into punk and grind. That's the kind of label I envisioned doing. About 7 years ago I started getting into the dark experimental stuff. So when I finally got the gumption to start a label I chose the ambient/noise type genre to work in. I kind of saw myself doing both actually (as evidenced by the Pissed Happy Children CD). For whatever reason though I haven't expanded into the hardcore direction beyond that release.

How tough was the task to convince other underground labels and distributors that you had serious intensions for the label? That wasn't really that difficult. I had arranged for my first release to be the Hybryds "Ein Phallischer Gott" CD. Hybryds are pretty well known and the disc had a good looking layout so I think it was obvious when people saw the disc that I was serious.

I guess it has to be asked. What exactly does the label title mean – any strange story to how it eventuated? Well, good question. I kind of see it having two meanings. One being that the type of music I am releasing isn't for everyone. So the notion of a crowd isn't something I associate with bands like Brume and Dissecting Table. The other concept being the belief that most of the problems the world faces have a lot to do with overpopulation. The number of people on this planet is just killing the Earth. I'm not so much an environmentalist, but the effects are noticeable in so many ways.

Power electronics, death industrial, dark ambient, ethereal atmospherics, electronica, experimental etc. - the list goes on as to the styles of albums that CCA has associated themselves with via releases (and the extent of styles is almost as diverse as the review section of Spectrum!). How do you go about deciding what items you want to release on your label? I have tried to do a variety of things from day one. If you look at my first five releases it's clear that none will be confused with the others. I don't really want to have a label "sound". My tastes are fairly broad and I see the Crowd Control aesthetic as a representation of those tastes. I don't think it really occurred to me that people might like Alio Die but not like ConSono until long after I started CCA. I want my label to offer different sounds for different moods. I just look for bands I like and that have something to offer in the way of rounding out the roster.

Do you have a set number of albums pressed up for each release? What does a standard CCA deal encompass for the artists you deal with? Runs are usually 1000. Bands either get copies or part of the profits. I usually let them decide which they prefer. No matter what though, they get some copies.

Also how much of the CCA back catalogue is out of print and are all of your releases limited to the initial print runs? The only titles out of print are the Hybryds CD and the Svasti-ayanam "Sanklesa" CD. Most titles are not really limited, but they don't necessarily move enough copies to worry about pressing more.

In your view when did Crowd Control Activities first achieve momentum in gaining noticeable interest of your outputs? Well, I don't know that I feel I have really gained any noticeable momentum. I don't think I have really experienced any rush of interest. I do well enough to get by but to me it's always a struggle.

Are there specific countries that have shown the greatest interest in CCA material or does it differ between releases? I have traditionally done most of my business in the US. But if something goes well it tends to go well worldwide. The slower titles are slow regardless.

While many of your releases have encompassed albums from established (or at least known) names, yet more recently you seem to be trying to gain a specific focus for the label in cultivating an association between CCA and multiple albums from newer projects. What are your views on the pro and cons of working with established names over raising the profile of new artists under the recognition of one label? Interesting that you've noticed that. When I began Crowd Control I really wanted to work with artists whose music had excited me about these types of sounds in the first place. That's why I contacted Hybryds, Brume, Dissecting Table, Alio Die, Inanna, Consono, Peter Andersson. After having the opportunity to release albums by some of my favorites, I decided to make more of a conscious effort to work with newer projects. At this point I would rather concentrate on establishing artists like Gruntsplatter and Tertium Non Data, with releases coming up by Chaos as Shelter and As All Die. The pros of working with established names include the opportunity to be associated with projects you have respected and also getting more immediate attention for a young label. The cool thing about helping to establish something new is that one can take a little more pride in the involvement. Also, I like the idea of having the image of band and label tied together. When people think of Gruntsplatter I want them to think of Crowd Control and vice versa. An artist like Dissecting Table has worked with a number of labels so it really isn't possible to cultivate that same type of relationship.

What are you personal thoughts on the current state of the scene, in that there seems to have been an increase in releases and labels over the past two years? On the up-side, that would seem to indicate a great deal of interest in the scene. The drawback of course is that there are that many more releases for people to choose from without really having any more money to spend. It wasn't that long ago I was just starting out and thereby competing with the labels that previously existed so I can't complain. I think there is room for everybody and it's great that more artists have the chance to find an audience.

Likewise what would you consider are the biggest opportunities and or challenges for the current scene? Like any aspect of art and entertainment, there is always the chance things can get stale. I think that there are some great new projects with quite a bit to offer so I don't see things running dry any time soon. As for opportunities, I don't know that there is anything huge on the horizon. I don't think these genres will explode in popularity. But who knows, anything can happen.

Knowing that you also work at Relapse Records / Release Entertainment, I am assuming that CCA is not a profitable enough venture for you to live off on its own. Yet is the label profitable in any sense other than it being self supporting? (and while it would be great to release products in the underground if money were not on object, however sadly this is simply not the case). Working at Relapse (the world's finest extreme music label) is definitely what pays the bills. Crowd Control doesn't really make me any money. On the other hand, I don't lose money either. Hell, I don't know where the money goes. How about Spectrum? Are you in the black or in the red so far? *(ED: as it stands currently there is no way I could even come close to making a 'living' off Spectrum and likewise there are no real dollars to count – but on the flipside I am no longer losing money and Spectrum does allow me to adequately feed my excessive music addiction!).*

What is your proudest release you have been associated with to date as opposed those new projects you would nominate and being worthy to look out for? (be they signed to CCA or not). That's a difficult question. I have always been proud of the Brume disc. Early on though I probably played the ConSono album more than anything else. Taking everything into consideration (music/packaging/ and the fact that Swans are one of my favorite bands ever) I would have to say the Blackmouth CD is the one I am most proud of. Things I have heard lately that i like that are not CCA related are Bad Sector, Herbst9, Coph Nia. Fortunately for me the best dark ambient record i have heard in some time was a demo sent to CCA. Needless to say i quickly jumped on it. It's a project by Andrea Bellucci (of Red Sector A) called Subterranean Source. I can't wait to release it.

If you had to pick a few albums that you wished you had released (could be of any genre, style or era) what would those be? Neurosis "Souls at Zero" and "Enemy of the Sun", Slayer "Reign in Blood", Swans "White Light From the Mouth of Infinity" Napalm Death "Scum", Dirty Rotten Imbeciles "Dealing With It", the list goes on....

In that most labels at some point tackle the obligatory compilation, CCA has not ventured down this path as yet. Is this something we could expect in the future? Any ideas for concepts of themes? I did put out the "Sound of Sadism" comp, *(ED: ops...I forgot about that one!)* which in my opinion is as good as any power electronic comp out there (thanks to Jon/Malsonus for putting it together). But funny you would ask, since I do have another compilation coming up. It will be titled "Funeral Songs". the theme of course being songs that the artists feel convey a mood appropriate for a real or imagined funeral. Contributors include: 27, Gruntsplatter, Agnivolok, 2 Raison D'etre tracks, Shinjuku Thief, House of Low Culture, Chaos as Shelter, Dreams in Exile, Tertium Non Data, Alio Die, etc. It will actually be a split release with Release Entertainment. I hope to have it out in May, June at the latest.

Also lavishly packaged vinyl collects items seem to be quite popular of late with the Loki Foundation's Saturn Gnosis 2 x 10" delux box set setting the bar very high (and not to mention that it is ALSO a compilation). Are these types of release you would consider tackling - or even vinyl releases? I have embraced the digital age. Nothing against vinyl, but it is unlikely I will ever release anything on that format. I think that the titles on Crowd Control tend to look pretty good compared to many of the other labels out there doing similar things. I think that Cold Meat always does a good job as well as Cold Spring. I prefer jewel boxes to digipaks and that's why most things I do are in jewel boxes. Wait until you see the Chaos as Shelter double CD I have coming out. It will be a sharp looking disc. I hate to call these elaborate limited items gimmickry, but to some extent it is. As you pointed out, there are more labels so it is tougher to draw attention to one's products. I just want my releases to be solid instead of purposely setting out to create a collector situation.

Lastly given that label bosses often have their own musical creations, can we ever expect a musical project of James Grell to be wheeled out into the public arena for scrutiny and comment? No. But here's a label discography (all compact discs):

Hybryds "Ein Phallischer Gott"
Brume "Drafts of Collisions"
Atrax Morgue "Slush of a Maniac"
Alio Die "The Hidden Spring"
Dissecting Table "Into the Light"
Discordance "Supremacy"
ConSono "Ignoto Deo"
Svasti-ayanam "Sanklesa"
PHC "Pissed Playground"
Hollow Earth "Dog Days of the Holocaust"
Negru Voda / third EYE split
5000 Spirits "Mesmeric Revelation"
Alio Die / Antonio Testa "Healing Herb's Spirit"
Tertium Non Data "The Third is Not Given"
Dissecting Table "Kaiboudai" 3 CD set
V/A "Sound of Sadism"
Inanna "signal/or/minimal"
Necrophorus "Drifting in Motion"
Gruntsplatter "The Death Fires"
Dreams in Exile "Since Long Before"
Blackmouth "S/T"
House of Low Culture "Submarine Immersion Techniques Vol.1"
Nasopharyngeal "Endless"
Chaos as Shelter "Midnight Prayer / Illusion" double CD
As All Die "Time of War and Conflict"
V/A "Funeral Songs"

DEATH IN JUNE

If there is any project that needs no introduction Death in June would be it, but more to the point how could I within a few mere sentences adequately sum up the 20 influential and controversial years the group has been active? Regardless, Douglas P was kind enough to go beyond the call of duty in answering my queries and in the process creating the longest feature interview in Spectrum's short history. Either way to if Douglas P is a household name for some, or remains as an enigma to others, this feature provides and engrossing and intriguing read.

To start with your most recent past, Albin Julius (of Der Blutharsch infamy) featured prominently on the two previous Death in June albums (being 'Take Care and Control' and 'Operation Hummingbird'), but I believe by mutual agreement this collaboration within the framework of Death in June has now ceased. What are your thoughts of the new direction that Albin brought the project that is essentially your personal essence? The whole collaboration with Albin came about because Albin was visiting Australia at the same time as I was and it seems too good an opportunity to miss to see if we could come up with something in the studio. We had already spent time together in Europe but we hadn't worked together, although there had been an attempt. I was aware of his previous group '...the moon lay hidden beneath a cloud' from its very first release in the early 1990's and I was intrigued by it. It looked beautiful, and different, and sounded equally so! However, it wasn't until December 1996 when he came up and introduced himself backstage at a Death in June/ Boyd Rice, Strength Through Joy performance in Munich that I first met him. It quickly transpired that we were a mutual appreciation society and he, Boyd and a Croatian friend of mine, as well as myself, took off to a famous beer cellar in the city. After that we knew we really got on and kept in contact. Albin in fact organised some concerts in Vienna and travelled with us to Zagreb, Croatia the following year and then, once again apparently by chance, I found myself with an Australian friend staying in Vienna for Christmas 1997. Anyway, Albin and I went around a lot of great places togethers and became quite good friends and I was ready to do some recording with '...the moon lay hidden beneath a cloud'. Sadly, whenever this seemed likely to happen Elizabeth, his partner in t.m.l.h.b.a.c became ill or was 'busy' with something or other. So the planned recordings never took place and as Albin later explained he was pleased they didn't. 'Der Blutharsch' already existed and as Elizabeth and he were soon to split he would have found it difficult to know what to do with any recordings he had done with me. Should they be t.m.l.h.b.a.c or Der Blutharsch? As the recordings did not take place I suppose that got him out of that quandary but it still left an unsatisfied thirst. Albin visiting Australia in the following February soon quenched that. By the beginning of 1998 I had already begun recording what I thought was going to be the follow up to "Rose Clouds of Holocaust"/ "Black Whole of Love" which was, and still is "the concrete fountain". I knew a new direction was demanded by the life force of Death in June and I had experimented with different ways of letting this loose. But, then Albin arrived! We began writing material almost immediately and it was so natural that wherever it decided to go was the place DIJ was heading for. Of course Albin brought with him his unmistakable style and this is precisely what I loved because it was created almost entirely within the environment that I provided for him. "Take Care and Control" was a great cocktail of the both of us and equally so "Operation Hummingbird" which we wrote together in the space between concerts in Australia 1999. But you don't always go to bed and/ or live with your drinking partners. I wanted the 'summer' and 'winter' from Albin, my 2 favorite seasons, and I'm sure I got them. Albin was only ever meant to be a guest collaborator in Death in June and that was discussed before we even started work on "OH". Death in June has always been in flux from the very outset so I didn't need to explain further than that. When Patrick Leagas, one of the founding members left the group in 1985 I swore then that I would never have another 'permanent' member in DIJ and would only ever work with other leaders or hired hands. Albin Julius is another leader with much else on his plate besides Death in June. But, that doesn't mean we will never work again together in some form or another. If our separate careers allow it then live work could still happen. Although we rehearsed for it "Operation Hummingbird" has for instance, never been performed live. When the big Leipzig festival collapsed in the summer of 2000 we lost our chance to showcase that which works brilliantly as a live piece. Outside of DIJ we have in fact been recording together with Boyd Rice on a project called "Wolf Pact". But, more of that later.

Do you think these two most recent albums with a slightly different slant have seen a resurgence of interest in Death in June or even that you have attached new listeners that may not have paid a great deal of attention to the group before? I don't think there needed to be a resurgence of interest in Death in June as that presupposes that the interest had gone away which it hadn't. However, I do think that there has been an increase in new listeners to both the work of DIJ and Der Blutharsch because of our connections. But, then again I think that was happening anyway, partly due to the amount of touring I/ we were doing in the late 1990's and partly because that has always happened throughout the history of Death in June. It's an organic, growing 'thing' and as naturally as some people loose interest and fall by the wayside others join the march with fresh attitudes etc. Long may that continue.

Notwithstanding that the majority of your titles generally either have a poetic flair (or otherwise underlying irony), your upcoming album 'All Pigs Must Die' is a rather blunt and direct title. While anyone who has followed the recent Death in June saga over the past 12-18 months would know that the title is not referring to the police, I wanted to ask your thoughts of this perceived direct and blunt approach? For whatever reason I spent a lot of time last year listening to George Harrison's "All Things Must Pass" album. Coupled with him writing the "piggies" track on the Beatles "White Album", which was one of the so called inspirations behind the Manson Family's Tate Labianca killings, some how the title "All Pigs Must Die" came into being. So. it's not quite straight forward. The fact that I have spent the best part of the last 18 months dealing with the utter shit of the world who wouldn't know the words "honesty" or "honour" if they came smashing down on their piggy heads with the force of a hammer is neither here nor there.

Again discussing the new album, I believe this sees a new collaboration with Andreas Ritter of the German neo-folk project Forseti. Firstly I remember reading that part of the reason for the quite lengthy hiatus after the 'Rose Clouds of Holocaust' album was that you thought you had brought your apocalyptic folk phase to a sort of conclusion and were unsure where to take Death In June next – with Albin Julius eventually answering this quandary. Given that Forseti is quite a neo-folk oriented project, where has this new collaboration taken the Death in June sound - if not back to the sound characterised on 'What Ends When the Symbols Shatter?' and 'Rose Clouds of Holocaust'? Forseti sound nothing like Death in June so I never thought for a moment that collaborating with Andreas Ritter would drag DIJ back onto well worn paths. Forseti had really impressed me at the few concerts they've supported Death in June at in Germany so at the last one in Kassel July 200 I had a new song which I thought would sound great with the addition of accordion which I've never had on a recording and which Andreas plays very well. So, after a brief explanation from the German promoter, because Andreas doesn't speak English too well and my German is very basic, I ran him through the song that is now called "The Enemy Within". Within just a few minutes it was working out really well backstage and the plan was to perform it live that night. Unfortunately, the performance was later cancelled by the club owner so it was never performed in public that evening. However, back at the hotel where most of the groups were staying we did eventually perform it in the foyer to the otherwise depressed members of the various bands. Even Eric Konofal from Les Joyaus de la Princesse joined in on drums and eventually the whole thing spilled out onto the carpark where an impromptu, stripped down acoustic performance took place for about ½ hour. It was very magical and very inspiring and it got me thinking! With the exception of some e-bow and electronic effects on the second half of the album "All Pigs Must Die" is extremely stripped down and certainly doesn't feature any of the string or keyboard arrangements that "Symbols" and Rose Clouds" have and most people tent to forget about when they're talking about 'apocalyptic folk' or 'neo folk' or whatever they wish to bracket those albums into. There's a lot more than just guitar on them but "All Pigs Must Die" is basically acoustic guitar, accordion and trumpet. There a particular type of German music called 'Schlager' which is very popular in beer halls and the like. Some of the direction of "All Pigs..." reminds me of that! Maybe?

You have regularly praised the facilities of the Big Sound Studios in Adelaide (Australia) yet the new album was recorded in

Germany I believe. While the reason would seem obvious considering the Forseti collaboration, however how did you find recording over there considering you seems to have quite an affinity for the studio back in Adelaide? The latest album was in fact recorded in 3 different countries in 3 different studios basically because that was where the 3 different musicians involved in it were based. It started off at Big Sound Studio in the Adelaide hills then went onto Geyer Studios in Germany where Andreas assed his bits and then the recording was really finished in Jacobs Studios, England where I've done a lot of work in the past. That is where Campbell finally added his trumpet parts. I enjoy working in familiar surroundings and over the 20 years existence of DIJ I've only ever worked in 4 studios: Alaska Studios and the Greenhouse in London which were owned by Garry Glitter, Jacobs Studios and Big Sound. If I'm Lucky enough to find a place and engineer that I'm comfortable with then I stick with them but that obviously wasn't possible for my work in Germany but with the exception of one song called "Flies Have Their House" I didn't actually do any recording there. My job was really directing and producing Andreas. Regardless, the atmosphere at Geyer was really helpful so it didn't cause any undue stresses. Not for me at least! I think that Andreas was more nervous of me then the studio surroundings!!

Now that I have had the opportunity to hear a pre-release copy of the new album, I wanted to ask how you arrived at the decision to create an album of with two clear halves and two very distinct sound frameworks?(consisting of the acoustic 'Schlager' music as you refer to it, and the more experimental noise industrial pieces). Likewise were some of these noise industrial oriented pieces actually left over from the 'We Said Destroy' recording sessions? No, the more experimental material wasn't left over from the completely separate "We Said Destroy" sessions, although the thought crossed my mind whether to include that on the CD of "All Pigs Must Die" because it does blend in with that side of the album. With the exception of "Ride Out", which was the last track I wrote for the project, all that type of material was recorded and mixed before I'd finished the "Schlager Folk" songs. I went to a realm, declared my intent, gave an offering and these were the results. The whole album could have been an all out "industrial assault" for want of a better description but, I kept being pulled back to the idea that had formulated in my mind after working out "The Enemy Within" with Andreas Ritter. In fact, the original idea was to call every song "We Said Destroy" and work on different versions of that theme. Eventually that drove me and Dave Lokan, the sound engineer, completely mad so I opened up more and let the album dictate itself as usual. The theme and purpose behind it remains the same, however.

Notwithstanding that you have previously created sound collages on selected Death in June albums, the noise pieces of 'All Pigs Must Die' are much more electronic and distortion based(but certainly expertly executed). Is experimental (and potentially improvised?) industrial noise something you have been dabbling in for some time? My first recordings in 1974-75 were of that style. An old school friend of mine and I recorded different tape machines and record players all playing at the same time, some of them backwards, and then added live vocals and other instrumentation over the top of that. Much of it worked out really well and it went on to form the sound track to a couple of short films called "The Rose Garden" and , I think, "L'Ange" or "The Angel" or something like that. During some of the early performances by Death In June some of those films, along with specially shot slides etc., used to be projected onto us and over us as we played. Patrick and I had found a shop in the back end of nowhere in London that sold old Royal Air Force and SAS snow camouflage suits along with a MASSIVE camouflage net that was used to cover Chieftain tanks. The white of the snow suits let the images play off and on our bodies really well and when we draped the net across the front of the stage the images of the slides and films used to be broken up or distorted or look like they were weird scenes within a forest. I thought it was really good and different and it was obviously the beginning of Death In June's association with camouflage. Towards the end of the original line-up we were performing 2 different sets during the same event-one more experimental and one more like the studio recordings of "The Guilty Have No Pride" or "Burial". There has always been those 2 sides to DIJ. As an aside to that, by chance in about 1990/91 the person who had those films and slides suddenly appeared in the pub I was drinking in clutching a copy of Nick Cave's "The Arse Kissed The Donkey" or whatever it's called - and very surprised to see me! He had disappeared shortly after the Paris concert in January,1984 along with all that film material. When I quizzed him about that stuff he said I could have it for 17,000 pounds but he was on a plane to Los Angeles later that day and wouldn't be able to deal with it immediately. With that he promptly departed [never to be seen or heard from again] and I started getting harassed by a drunk who thought I was John Travolta.

Boyd Rice is a character that you have had a loose affiliation with for over 10 years now, including a number of collaborative recordings that you participated in together. This continued association sees Boyd providing spoken word introductions to a couple of the tracks on the new album, thus I wanted to ask whether these text pieces were specifically written by Boyd for the album? If this was not the case, why was the invitation to recite these pieces extended to Boyd instead of you personally handling the task? I actually write all the words on the album but shortly after writing "Tick Tock" I had the idea to ask Boyd to record his interpretations of the lyrics. With his great, creepy, radio friendly voice and his greater understanding than most of what I'm all about I thought it would be perfect. It was touch and go for awhile whether I would get them in time for the end of my recording session. Unbeknown to me Boyd was away in France working on a television documentary for Fox Television but couldn't get into a studio quick enough when he eventually found out about my request! Luckily they arrived in time for me to add them during the mastering stage which is as last moment as it can get.

Talking of the collaborative material you have produced with Boyd, the most well recognised recordings include: Boyd Rice and Friends: Music Martinis and Misanthropy CD (which also featured Michael Moynihan of Blood Axis infamy) and Scorpion Wind: Heaven Sent CD (also featuring John Murphy and has been referred to as Music Martinis and Misanthropy II). Likewise as recently as February 2001 you have finished recording with Boyd Rice and Albin Julius at Big Sound Studio's in Adelaide, Australia. How did the recording sessions pan out and what style/ musical focus can we expect from this new album? Despite already having a working title of 'Wolf Pact', could this be considered as Music Martinis and Misanthropy III? Because "Music, Martinis And Misanthropy" was our first collaboration together and caused such a stir, and sold so well, everything from there on would always be perceived as mk. II, III or IV etc. Before Boyd arrived in Australia to start recording I spent weeks listening to both "MMM" and "Heaven Sent" and I was surprised at how apparently 'uncomplicated' "MMM" was in comparison to the Scorpion Wind album. I think that "Heaven Sent" is the great undiscovered classic recording of any of our works. So many people have never heard of it, yet alone heard it. It also brings back some unhappy memories about its release through World Serpent. Not only did the sleeves of the record and CD turn out differently to what I had requested but also the initial sales proved very disappointing . To try and help counter that Boyd and I contacted WSD and asked them to put a sticker on the covers showing that it was a collaboration between him and me and we even volunteered to go into the warehouse and put them on the thousands of records and CDs that were languishing there. One of the directors would have none of that and turned down the idea of the stickers and us putting them on. The excuse, besides the extra 'expense', which would have come out of Boyd's and my own pockets anyhow, was that we would be in the way. No, it was much better to have those thousands of LPs and CDs hanging around for years in the warehouse and 'getting in the way' instead, wasn't it! So, that is exactly what happened. It sold very badly and was a financial burden around my neck until only quite recently. One of the other directors of WSD explained away the problem with "Heaven Sent " as there being always a runt in any litter. Going by his contributions to the wonderful world of music I assume he is an expert at giving birth to 'runts of the litter'!! However, 'Wolf Pact" is an attempt to sweep those memories away. I think it is a successful synthesis of the styles and approaches that Boyd, Albin and myself would bring to any venture. I'm very happy with it and I don't mind if it does get referred to as "Music Martinis And Misanthropy III" because I'll see that as a form of recommendation.

With the extent of collaborations you have brought into DI6 over the years, why have you chosen this creative path other than being self sufficient with the use of session musicians? Also is there a common theme to the circumstances that lead to the various collaborations? After Patrick departed DIJ in 1985 I really had to re-evaluate what I was going to do with the group. It was a dangerous situation which I nearly didn't survive so I decided never to reply upon anyone else again but work only with other leaders who had their own groups and so therefore their own agendas separate from Death in June. My collaborations with David Tibet had already begun but that acted as a springboard for work with Rose Macdowall, Boyd Rice, John Balance and so on. Why look for a session musician when you've got all the most original talent in the world as friends? But, that really has petered out by the early 1990's more by force of circumstance rather than design. I was hardly ever in England, and when I was Tibet would be abroad, or Rose would be breeding or something like that so we just never met up and that period came to a natural end. In many ways! I've only ever worked with two session musicians, for want of a better word, in the history of Death in June and they have both been trumpet players. Since Patrick left I've never met anyone else who can play that instrument. In fact, the trumpet was nearly not included on "All

Pigs Must Die" as, unbeknown to myself, Campbell had suffered a stroke a few weeks before my arrival in England in November, 2000. Proving he was more that just a session musician he still came down to the studio and did an extremely good job although I have to admit that coaching him through what I wanted him to do did sometimes become completely surreal. Hopefully, it was some kind of music therapy for him. I know by the end of the session we were both fit to drop! A lot of information had well and truly been scrambled that day!

Talking more broadly, what are your thoughts that you initial attempt to be a 'faceless musician' (via the use of masks and uniforms) has worked in reverse whereas your most well known facemask (the Japanese white clay mask) has become an important if not integral part of Death in June iconography? And despite this, I am also sure that all Death in June fans would know your face also. Are there two versions of Douglas Pearce – the stage persona and the private persona? I think there is a difference between not wanting to be equated to the usual stable of inanities that are normally available to 'the record buying public' and being a 'faceless musician', which I'm not sure I've actually ever said I wanted to be. The use of 'props' such as masks or photographs with only backs turned towards the camera not only separate Death In June from the majority of embarrassing pap that permeates the music industry, which like it or not, I must be part of in some kind of way, but also on a very 'simplistic' level are more attractive and pleasing from a purely aesthetic aspect I also think that you might be leaping to conclusions that all DIJ fans know what I look like because the last time I performed in Munich, Germany a few years ago I had great difficulty getting back into the venue after I'd been to a beer cellar with some friends before the concert began. I didn't have any venue I.D. on me and as I tried to go through the crowds outside the doors not one person recognised me and all thought I was pushing in which resulted in a few interesting words being said! Finally the bouncers at the doors believed me and let me in. How anonymous I was I found a little creepy after so many years! The mask is, in fact, made of paper and I bought it in a shop in Venice, Italy in late 1991 and because of its constant use since then it has become part of DIJ's iconography. But, thinking about it I don't think it is just because I use it a lot in photos, on stage etc. it is also because it looks so great and so different. It does almost have a Life of its own and that's fine by me. Almost all the photographers that I've done sessions with have commented upon how it doesn't appear to be me underneath it. Naturally, I don't go shopping in Woolworths wearing it so, of course, there are differences in the visual aspect of what you see on stage and what you get in my more private moments. It is, however, most definitely the same person.

To what extent is the essence of Death in June encompassed within your image? (I ask this as I have seen live images where someone has gone out of their way to photograph the clay mask sitting on the ground at the back of the stage – as if this was the true Death in June and not Douglas Pearce). My Life is my Love is my Work is my World. All that you see or hear are aspects of the essence, as you refer to it, of Death In June.

Given you seem to thrive on leaving the interpretation of Death in June up to the individual I wanted to see you opinions on two possible explanation behind facets of you aesthetic. i): the use of uniforms represents the 'state' or 'government' (in a fascist sense) and thus it is this controlling element that suppress both individual thought & action. Therefore Death in June uses ironic symbolism to present a spiritual message in an aesthetic form that represents censorship. ii) the uniform represents the personal battle

for individual freedom (be it spiritual or social) in a westernised society that mostly demands conformity (hence the inscription on the recent 'Heilige' live CD "dedicated to all those who fight in isolation" or the quote within Brown Book "It is the plague of our time, that we fight in isolation"). I think you've almost answered your own question by the way you've come up with such interesting theories about what may, or may not be, the aesthetic reasoning behind DIJ. I could pontificate about how I feel that more can be achieved in Life in an underground, camouflaged kind of way, or that to be "Hidden Among The Leaves" is the Japanese way of the warrior, or that it is some attempt at a physical manifestation of a willingness to have a link to the pathos and tragedies of the past but, I prefer to let others do that for me. I prefer to leave some doors open to some people. My Art, my Love my Life would otherwise become earthbound and that is not for me.

Over the (nearly) 20 years of Death in June's existence you have played live irregularly, yet in recent years you have been much more active on the live performance circuit. Why the recent alteration in focus towards live performances? In fact, the change came about in 1992 when after about 3 years since the last DIJ performance I decided that it was time to change tactics. Tactics which I think, in retrospect, had worked against DIJ, but had been deemed necessary at the time. I felt the need to expose Death In June to a bigger audience and was lucky enough to have the right people around me to make that possible, on both a personal and professional level. Since then there have been several major tours of Europe, a large tour of America and a few one-offs in places like Australia and New Zealand. Realistically, I caught the touring bug and despite all the numerous hassles concerned with most tours or performances I kept coming back for more. That was totally different to how both Tony Wakeford and myself felt at the beginning of Death In June. We had performed a lot with our previous group Crisis but the problems we faced with that really did get on top of us. It was a conscious decision not to take our new group out on the road very often and at the time we were happy with this approach. But, as I said earlier, I look back and think that to be so extreme possibly worked against us. The original line up of Tony, myself and Patrick Leagas worked brilliantly live and it was getting even better as we went along. The last concert performed by the original line-up in Paris in January, 1984 was one of the most interesting, unique and exciting I've ever been present at let alone performed! However, there were problems between the 3 of us and Tony departed the group shortly after. Just over a year later Patrick had also gone so logistically it became impossible to even do any live work. To this day Tony and Patrick are the best all round musicians I've ever worked with and not having them around curtailed any ideas for doing more live work. That had to wait and when the opportunity did arise again I seized it with both hands.

Do you have any special plans to mark the 20th anniversary of Death in June (incidentally being this year 2001), or do you consider such celebrations could evoke bad omens? (as you have previously mentioned a similar reason for not documenting the early days of the group). Until this milestone had been mentioned in interviews such as this I hadn't given it any conscious thought. I have no idea when Death In June, as it was going to turn out to be, performed its first rehearsal or recorded our first release "Heaven Street". The only definite date I know is DIJ's first concert which was with The Birthday Party and Malaria on a snow-bound London night 25th November, 1981. The best celebration I could possibly think of would be to hear that a certain company that Wyrd's steadily destroying had collapsed! Collapsed owing thousands of $'s!! Just like they owe thousands of $'s to me right now. That would be a real cause for celebration and raising a glass or 4. Perhaps I'd even invent a new cocktail called something like 'Just Desserts' or, better still, 'But, What Ends When The Piggybank Shatters'?. In the beginning Tony, Patrick and I would celebrate the release of a record by going to a cocktail bar in London and drinking the night away. It would seem fitting to keep with tradition!

What are your thought on the current state of the neo-folk scene? In as much as you a sort of godfather to this movement do you have much involvement with the new generation of groups? Any there any that have particularly caught your interest? I don't know about being a Godfather to any movement but I do really like some of the new groups that are apparently connected to this genre. Forseti I've already mentioned and I have, in fact, recorded with when I was last in Germany working on "All Pigs Must Die" with the leader of the group, Andreas. I did the lyrics and sing on a new track called " Black Jena [This Time The Victim Is Desire]" which I think will either be released as a single or featured on their soon to be released new album. Outside of them, I really like the Danish group Of The Wand And The Moon, The English group Lady Morphia and, yet more German groups like Darkwood and Dies Natalis, who I remember playing a fantastic, impromptu acoustic performance in the wood that surrounded an ancient castle keep Death In June had just performed in last year in Germany. I think the new wave of neo-folk, or whatever it's going to be called, is truly based in Germany. Forget the Wander Vogel here come the Wunsch Vogel with their dreams that could come true.

One criticism that has been levelled at DI6 ad nauseam over the years is that the group has right wing extremist ideologies and agendas – yet your previous band Crisis was ironically labelled as being an extreme left wing group. While a crude response to this would be that if you did have a subversive agenda, you have actually done a fantastically poor job in clearly articulating it to ensnare and entrap masses of impressionable minds, however why have you and do you continue to use controversial themes and then steadfastly refused to discuss their implications? Likewise in all your ambiguity of content (lyrically and imagery) that could be interpreted on surface level as well as being impregnated with deeper meaning and/or metaphors, why do you think you continue to be a sort of lightening rod for controversy despite the various interpretations that can be made to various elements? Probably because people are so non-specific about what they suppose are controversial images or themes or whatever! And, 9 times out of 10 they are so way off the mark that it would seem ridiculous for me to even try to attempt to bring them back into focus because they are obviously determined to see and hear things their own way. I know those types of people and I don't like their smug, know-it-all, 'concerned' thoughts and opinions. They belong to that tribe of Fish Wives that sneakily look out through their net curtains at what their neighbours are up to and tittle tattle about what they assume is 'going on' over the back garden fence, underneath the blankets and through the back of beyond and try to ruin other people's lives. I'd prefer that they ruin their own. And, surely left to their own devices, they will!

Do you think that modern dogma of 'political correctness' has lead to a ludicrous situation where the majority of people are blind to irony within the context of musical expression? Are artists (in the traditional sense) by some sort of social default given more leeway in regard to public interpretations of their work and are therefore more freely able to exploit irony and art? I don't feel that artists have any sort of monopoly on the use and understanding of irony and I also think that aspects of what is called 'political correctness' were absolutely necessary in helping to combat the more 'lumpen' aspects of sexism and racism. It's a shame that a lot more 'common sense' isn't also applied but, what do you expect from people. Given the choice between an easy, simplistic way of doing things and a difficult, stupid way of dealing with a matter most people will always choose the latter. That's humanity. The World isn't overflowing with problems because of some strange ethereal condition that has smitten it down. It's because of people! I'm dealing with 3 'people' right now that, given the choice, took the latter route because they wanted to fuck with me. They wanted to show me 'who was boss'. They wanted a problem and they wanted to screw me. It could have been so very different but, typically those bimbos cut off their nose to smite their own face. I would love to cut off a lot more!

In another interview (Dark Angel Issue 20# 1995) made reference to your meeting with 'God' or 'life force' in London in 1980. How much should we read into this as being a metaphor for spiritual awakening or could it perhaps have been the initial mental spark that lead to the formation of Death in June? It was a spiritual awakening, it was a meeting with God , it was being enveloped within a deluge of a Life Force, it was a meeting of Heaven and Hell on earth, it was Everything! And, I know it will always be Everything even though the passage of time cushions me from the more devastating smells and memories and feelings of that time. It was the foundation of Everything that has brought me to Here. It may not consciously have been the initial mental spark that gave birth to Death In June but, it definitely had a say in it from the very beginning and totally took over from the time when Patrick Leagas departed and I started to write "The World That Summer" album. It kept me strong and focussed and continues to, although I tend not to draw on its energy the way I used to. I took too much of it and that can equally devour you. It did come close! To cast aside any ambivalence this statement might have it has nothing to do with the taking of any chemicals etc. It was 'something' that really did happen to me in London on a summer's afternoon,1980. I still puzzle over it. I still Love it and I still Dread it. To think how pathetically unprepared I was is the stuff of Tears.

Destiny and fate are common themes that permeate the various interview of yours that I have read, how much do you feel this is directed by your own subconscious as opposed to an external force or entity? In all honesty, who can really tell? However, I can definitely say that I've seen so many signs in my Life I feel I am on a course that has been, to a certain degree, pre-ordained and that I don't believe are self delusory. But, also within that structure I feel you do have room for manoeuvre. That is the nature of Wyrd. Think of those weak, sly dullards that I was mentioning earlier. They did have a choice and history has already shown that they made the wrong one. History, Destiny, Fate or Angels will continue to demonstrate that, until they are no more and the cleansing process has been completed.

Given that I imagine that you will never father any children, do you hold any regret that you will not be leaving a legacy by the continuation of your bloodline? Could it also be construed that this situation is central to Death in June being the focal point of your life, thus the project could be viewed as a sort of surrogate child? This is possibly the most interesting question I've ever been asked. When I was 30 in 1986/87 I underwent a very paternal phase in my life and had very strong urges to father a child. Obviously, I didn't want a relationship with a woman so I answered some ads placed by couples and even met some. The best of the bunch was a pair who lived in Northampton in the Midlands of England. When I went to meet them I was greeted at the railway station by a distinguished looking man in his 50's and immediately whisked off in his Mercedes Benz to rendezvous with his wife. She turned out to be German and just a little older than me. We all got on very well but she and I really hit it off and raved about the work of Rainer Werner Fassbinder and Kraftwerk. It was decided that we should go for a meal and it was when we arrived at the restaurant that the whole thing started to take on different dimensions that unnerved me. The restaurant itself was a converted railway carriage that seemed to be situated in the middle of nowhere and during the walk to it I noticed the man had a club foot. We all still got on really well but for me it began to feel like I was sitting in the railway carriage where Hitler made France sign the capitulation papers in 1940 with Joseph Goebbels and Eva Braun. What kind of baby was I going to be part of creating? Kenneth Anger says that if you lead your life correctly it is filled with recurring themes but I wasn't sure if I really wanted to take this theme that far! We went back to their house where they wanted us all to go to bed together and see how things worked out but, I decided against that offer and told them I didn't think it was wise to take the matter any further. The journey back to the railway station was filled with the sound of the wife weeping in the back of the Mercedes and it was a hard journey for me back to London in the train. Anyway, shortly after I was told by a very down to earth white South African stripper girlfriend of mine that I should view my works as my children and I've sort of

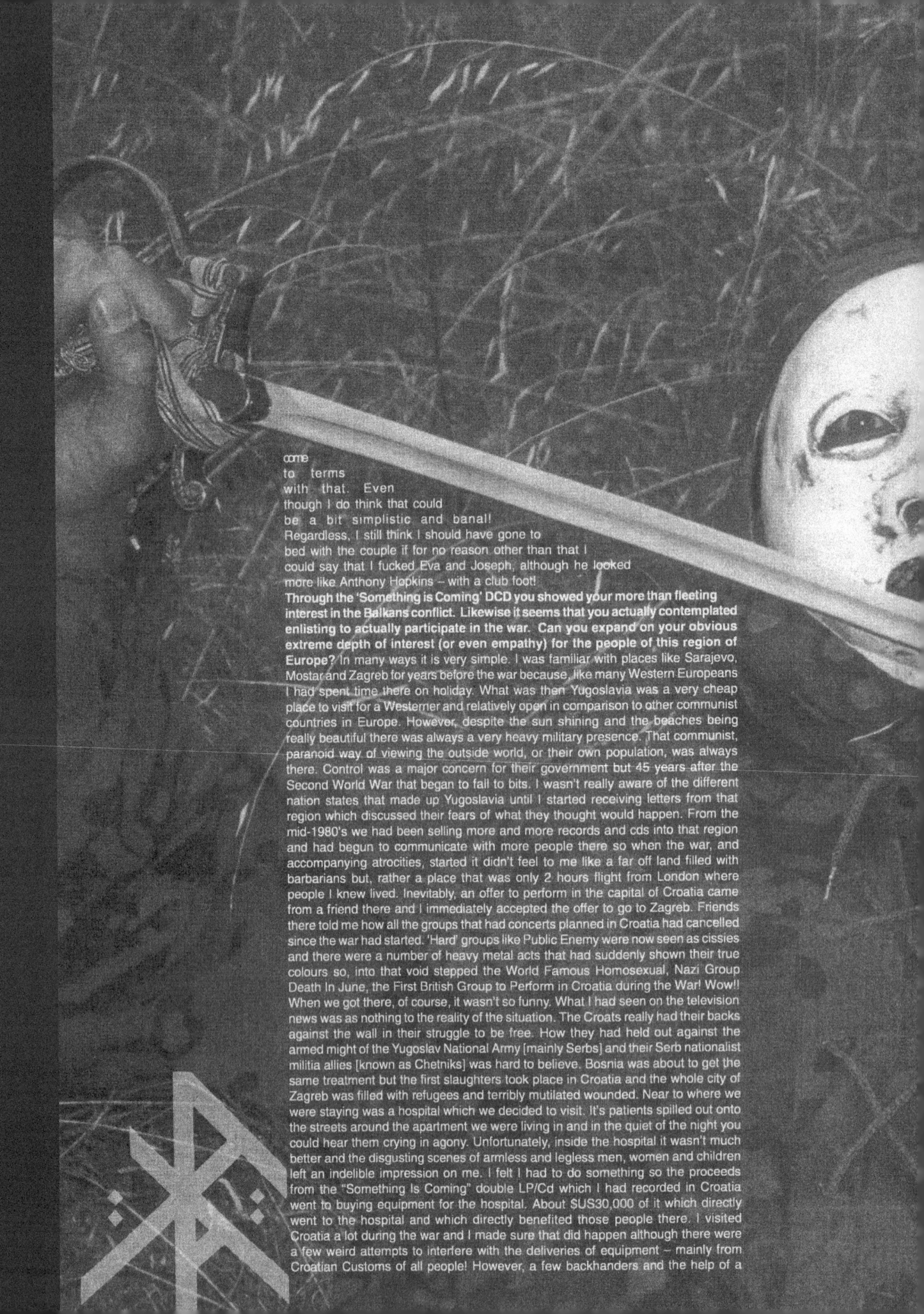

come
to terms
with that. Even
though I do think that could
be a bit simplistic and banal!
Regardless, I still think I should have gone to
bed with the couple if for no reason other than that I
could say that I fucked Eva and Joseph, although he looked
more like Anthony Hopkins – with a club foot!

Through the 'Something is Coming' DCD you showed your more than fleeting interest in the Balkans conflict. Likewise it seems that you actually contemplated enlisting to actually participate in the war. Can you expand on your obvious extreme depth of interest (or even empathy) for the people of this region of Europe? In many ways it is very simple. I was familiar with places like Sarajevo, Mostar and Zagreb for years before the war because, like many Western Europeans I had spent time there on holiday. What was then Yugoslavia was a very cheap place to visit for a Westerner and relatively open in comparison to other communist countries in Europe. However, despite the sun shining and the beaches being really beautiful there was always a very heavy military presence. That communist, paranoid way of viewing the outside world, or their own population, was always there. Control was a major concern for their government but 45 years after the Second World War that began to fall to bits. I wasn't really aware of the different nation states that made up Yugoslavia until I started receiving letters from that region which discussed their fears of what they thought would happen. From the mid-1980's we had been selling more and more records and cds into that region and had begun to communicate with more people there so when the war, and accompanying atrocities, started it didn't feel to me like a far off land filled with barbarians but, rather a place that was only 2 hours flight from London where people I knew lived. Inevitably, an offer to perform in the capital of Croatia came from a friend there and I immediately accepted the offer to go to Zagreb. Friends there told me how all the groups that had concerts planned in Croatia had cancelled since the war had started. 'Hard' groups like Public Enemy were now seen as cissies and there were a number of heavy metal acts that had suddenly shown their true colours so, into that void stepped the World Famous Homosexual, Nazi Group Death In June, the First British Group to Perform in Croatia during the War! Wow!! When we got there, of course, it wasn't so funny. What I had seen on the television news was as nothing to the reality of the situation. The Croats really had their backs against the wall in their struggle to be free. How they had held out against the armed might of the Yugoslav National Army [mainly Serbs] and their Serb nationalist militia allies [known as Chetniks] was hard to believe. Bosnia was about to get the same treatment but the first slaughters took place in Croatia and the whole city of Zagreb was filled with refugees and terribly mutilated wounded. Near to where we were staying was a hospital which we decided to visit. It's patients spilled out onto the streets around the apartment we were living in and in the quiet of the night you could hear them crying in agony. Unfortunately, inside the hospital it wasn't much better and the disgusting scenes of armless and legless men, women and children left an indelible impression on me. I felt I had to do something so the proceeds from the "Something Is Coming" double LP/Cd which I had recorded in Croatia went to buying equipment for the hospital. About $US30,000 of it which directly went to the hospital and which directly benefited those people there. I visited Croatia a lot during the war and I made sure that did happen although there were a few weird attempts to interfere with the deliveries of equipment – mainly from Croatian Customs of all people! However, a few backhanders and the help of a

Catholic aid society always got over those problems. It didn't matter how it got there as long as it got there and so Christ came in useful for once! Whilst on this subject I would like to add that during the last few years there have been attempts by unscrupulous, so-called 'antifa' groups in Germany to create a myth that I, in fact, donated monies to a Croatian front line military hospital. First of all, as I've described previously, the hospital cared for men, women and children, soldiers and civilians, and to my surprise, also wounded Serbs! I thought the Croatian authorities were very generous on that regard. Secondly, if supplying a military hospital with much needed medical equipment had been the only way I could have helped the Croatians against what I consider to be modern day barbarians then I would have also done so. I was prepared to join one of the paramilitary foreign units to actually go into combat but it was seen that I would be of better service elsewhere. In those early days of the new wars in the Balkans, Croatia had few allies in its struggle to be free of Serbia and the Communists. It was the Chetnik Serbs and the Communists that committed most of the atrocities that have left hundreds of thousands dead in modern day Europe. It was the Chetnik Serbs and the Communists that committed most of the ethnic cleansing that has resulted in probably millions being displaced and the de-stabilization of Southern Europe. It's mainly Chetnik Serbs that are being hunted as war criminals! Yet, strangely the so-called 'antifa' in Germany, and perhaps elsewhere, paint a picture where I have supported the 'bad guys'. I have done something absolutely terrible! Huh? What complete buffoons those people must be! Never mind what liars they are.

As I believe that by choice you are vegetarian, I wanted to ask if this reflects a facet of your spirituality and/or worldview? I first became a vegetarian at the age of 7 and ,whilst I can't remember the precise reasons why, my parents told me that it was after looking at the dead turkeys hanging upside down in a butcher's window Christmas ,1963. I didn't understand why any animal should die to feed me. It seemed cruel and unnecessary. Well that was fine until I was 14 when I began to get strong cravings to eat meat again. Bird's Eye beefburgers began to be a point of obsession but the choice was really taken out of my hands when I went to France on an Easter school trip. At the large student hostel in Paris we were all given horse meat and it was 'like it or lump it' in those days so I indulged myself for the first, and only time, on horse. That appeared to satisfy my 'cravings' for meat until the early-mid 1980's when I returned to eating meat again on a regular basis. However, it wasn't long before I was getting sick. And, so were many of my friends in England. Food poisoning used to be a very rare occurrence but it began to be common place. Within the space of about 18 months I had 3 bouts of food poisoning. The last one was so bad that I had to stay at the friend's house where I had returned, after eating steak at a restaurant, for 3 days before I could even consider returning back home. I was violently sick and my entire body was in agony. I haven't touched a steak since! The rumours and suspicions about the state of the meat herds in England had been going around for years before the government even admitted there might be something wrong with them. Now, of course, the whole world knows there is something REALLY wrong with them as one disease goes to another. I don't eat meat because I think it is bad for me-full stop!

Who would you credit as some inspirational authors, artists, philosophers, historical figures, movie producers, song writers etc? As most people who are slightly familiar with me would know the 2 authors that I have worshipped at the alter of are the French writer Jean Genet and the Japanese writer/poet warrior Yukio Mishima. However, I have to admit that I haven't read any of their works for years now. With Genet I ran out of new material after his death in 1986 and with Mishima I feel I had read his best works. I began to find works that I found too light weight and paid too much attention to microscopic detail and which bored me. I didn't want to defile my memory of classics like "The Decay Of The Angel". Besides, the past 10 years have been far too busy for me to even find time to read a book from cover to cover. All that there was to have been learnt from such things has been put into action. This also refers to the philosopher Nietzsche whose work I used to devour. What is the point in perpetually reading, or consuming, if you cannot put into practice anything that you may have learnt from that consumption? I have favourite films rather than directors although I must admit that I'm intrigued by anything by David Lynch or Sergio Leone. Without doubt my favourite living artists are Gilbert and George, any artist who painted for the Allach pottery, Arno Brecker and Andy Warhol. There are too many historical figures and songwriters to mention that I've found inspirational in one way or another. And, besides, that would be giving the game away, wouldn't it?

NEROZ being is the Australian division of New European Recordings (NER) and despite you spending much of your time in Australia, the establishment is not actually run by yourself. What is the circumstance and operational dynamic of this label? As I mentioned in the previous question I have found myself far too busy to set time aside to even read a book in the last few years and in an attempt to rectify that situation I have relinquished some responsibilities. NEROZ [New European Recordings Australia] came about initially to combat the weakness of the distribution of Death In June's material in Australasia. It seemed stupid to be in a country where groups like Death In June, Current 93 or Coil receive a lot of radio play but their releases really difficult to find their recordings, and when you did, they were at a ridiculously high price. The release of the Australian version of "Take Care And Control" in 1997 was meant to revitalise those markets and to see if it was worth doing other releases here. My old distribution company World Serpent had given its blessing to this venture and I even had ideas about distributing other acts like Current 93 or Coil in Australasia so their works could also be available at domestic prices. And, hopefully get them to a deserved bigger market! However, that wasn't to be as after one too many idiotic and infantile run-ins with them I decided in August, 1999 not to put any further new material through World Serpent. From that date everything changed. They stopped paying me and refused to hand over any of the original masters or artworks for all of the NER/Twilight Command catalogue even though I had paid for them! So, since then, NEROZ and my new European distributor Tesco Organisation Germany, have begun a process of re-issuing the back catalogue titles of Death In June. By enforced necessity that has to be one of the main dynamics for NEROZ. Any thoughts about dealing with any groups or individuals outside of myself have to take a backseat for the foreseeable future.

With the release of upcoming new album, and continued re-release schedule of the Death in June back catalogue are there any surprises we can expect from the NER and NEROZ camps? Yes! Without being totally bogged down in the past, which even though it is being reinvented and rejuvenated is still nevertheless the past, NEROZ will issue a new album from Boyd Rice, Albin Julius and myself sometime later in 2001. We've only recently finished the recording of it here in S.A. and it will almost certainly be called Boyd Rice And Fiends "Wolf Pact". I'm very, very happy with that -and the soon to be released "All Pigs Must Die".

It has been reported that collectively Death in June has sold over a quarter of a million albums. Given than most individual albums in the general underground scene have difficulty shifting over 1000 units, first of all do you vouch for the validity of this figure and is so how do view this achievement? Those figures are accurate, I'm extremely proud of them and I want them to continue to increase-For Ever, And Ever And Ever,…………………

Last Hails? Never Forgive, Never Forget and Never Surrender!

BRIGHTER DEATH NOW

The reputation of Roger Karmanik aka Brighter Death Now surely precedes him due to the sheer number of year he has been a player in the industrial scene, either by virtue of his recording project/s or as the label boss of the Cold Meat Industry empire. Anyway Roger was obliging enough to answer my questions (but not without a bit of prodding first!) with the results published for your pleasure below.

Given that Brighter Death Now has formally existed as a project for some 13 years, has the project become an ingrained part of your personality? Do you consider 'Roger Karmanik' and 'Brighter Death Now' to now be mutually exclusive, or is it that Brighter Death Now has taken on such a life of its own that it can be considered separate and removed from you? It is me, alright. Lets say, the project was born out of some of my personalities, now all merged into a stronger and more perceptive ME!

Can you ever envisage a time where Brighter Death Now will no longer be musically active and subsequently be laid to rest? I thought that I never could, but now I can, in what time prospect we are talking about I can not say, but there will of course be a time when I move my creative side to another object. Lately I have found writing poems of some interest, but it could even end up as common as basic gardening.

Can you give a summation of your perceptions to how Brighter Death Now has grown and evolved over its life span thus far? It started as a little child, played around, got scared, frightened and depressed, moved on and became a creature that scares, frightens and spreads depression as leprosy, got cured, raised up an proclamation of world peace, love, understanding and death to those who don't understand.

In the period of 16-17 years that you have been producing harsh electronics (from Lille Roger to Brighter Death Now) you have become both a father and husband. Have these circumstances changed or altered your outlook on life in general and the modus operandi behind your music production? Yes it has, I have matured in a way, become a better man, more content, but not more common as the average family husbands (I assume). I use my insight in a slightly different perspective, I see upon life rather different as well as upon the work I do in comparing to what many other in this scene does I assume.

Talking of your family, your wife is obviously well aware of all aspects of your music, however how do you children perceive your musical leanings – or is it to the extent that you shield them from it until they are older and can better understand? Well considering some people never get old enough to understand, I would just let it grow into them, like any other family someday it well get to their knowledge, and what will happened from there I can not say, but I will not shield them from more than they're capable to handle. My oldest daughter, who is 13, is a huge fan of Eminem.

There are aspects of exploration on each of your albums, yet on the past three albums ('Obsessis', 'May All Be Dead' and 'Innerwar') there appears to be more harsher motivations that have drawn comparisons to the power electronics scene and likewise that you are infusing anarchistic punk elements into Brighter Death Now's death industrial musings. How do you respond to such theories? Well it is very simple; I do what I feel like. Without looking back or forward, I just do it all straight out, as it comes from my heart. With all the respect from my history and all the influences of everything around me, it becomes a gigantic pot of images/influences/memories. The outcome is disastrous and inevitable.

In the beginning of your label Cold Meat Industry, there were few if any other groups on the label's roster that were in similar leagues to Brighter Death Now. However with CMI's recent re-establishing focus towards power electronic projects viewed along with the harsher direction of your recordings, the label's sound and Brighter Death Now's sound are more closely aligning. Was this deliberate or coincidental? Everything I do is deliberate, but at the present time I choose to see it as coincidental. With this I mean that many things in the past that I've previously seen as purely coincidental, seems more and more as a deliberately and subconsciously planned.

While most people clearly appreciate you current focus of Brighter Death Now, others seems to want you to further pursue the sounds explored on the 'Great Death' Trilogy and 'Necrose Evangelicum' CD's. Is this a likely prospect? No, not really, more likely is the Pain in progress era, something I like to catch up on again.

If one is to not take you material on face value (be it imagery/ titles/lyrics/ dialogue/ samples etc) and not jump to conclusions on such a basis, irony of content begins to filter through. However, on the latest album 'Obsessis' the irony has manifest itself in a humorous guise, particularly referencing the cover image and track titles. How do you view the themes of irony and humour in relation to Brighter Death Now? I think they have a great importance, like in life, life is an irony in itself, so instead of just laying crying in our beds, we can start laughing back in its face and make something creative out of it. People who can't look at themselves or their work with a part of irony is too pathetic in my eyes. Irony or a distance is the best cure for all this madness, a way to survive.

I have noted that through use images/ text/ samples/ lyrics of Brighter Death Now they paint a very bleak and sadistic picture, however when breaking these down into individual elements, it is more from the association of the material that leads to this perception and thus has ultimately been lead by the individuals interpretation. Do you view yourself as the collator of potentially questionable material under the Brighter Death Now banner to allow people to use, interpret and decipher it as they see fit, rather than you using such material to make a specific point – either for or against? I want people to make their mind up, or not, or just leave it open. I don't see things in either black or white, there is always a second meaning with almost everything, if you just want to find it. I am not trying to point in any political, ethical or morally direction, it is much up to each individual to decide right from wrong in all respect to others, individuals and alike.

What is your opinion of the use of potentially offensive material for mere shock tactics within the industrial scene? When (if at all) will shock tactics in industrial music become redundant or at least a cliché – which many argue it already has? Shock tactics doesn't work anymore, there is no longer any offensive material, for that purpose, not since we got the internet... nothing is sacred anymore! It is time that people start act differently.

What is inherent within the symbolism of the Brighter Death Now 'necrose' logo particularly as this has been a focal point of image on most albums to date? I use to say that the symbol stands for nothing, or everything, or anything that you may like, for me it stands for me and BDN, it is significant with what I believe in as I use it as a trademark for my music, the interpretation has grown into the symbol, rather than the opposite which seems to be more common nowadays with the use of symbols.

Over the past 5 years you have made various statements that Brighter Death Now will no longer to conduct interviews or play live, however these assertions have since been broken on a few occasions. Can this be construed as part of your erratic nature when referenced to the changing focus of Brighter Death Now over various albums? Will you continue to play live? Ha ha, yes it can! I like to hold up for a while, to gather strength, to withhold the unique attitude towards my work. I do actually like playing live, when it's over. But all the weeks, months, before it is just plain agony, I want each show to mean something and to be interesting, not just a damn playback of a dat-tape, that is so boring and I've seen so many boring concerts, you can't imagine. Sometimes I think I set my standards to high for myself, but at the same time I know, there is no other way to do it.

Talking of live performances while it was not so much of an assault, I hear at one show you grabbed the hair/ head of one audience member at the front of the stage whilst delivering the main vocal line to "I Hate You" directly to this individual's face. What do you consider is the relationship between project member and audience when dealing with often quite hateful material? Also when performing live do you take on an alternate identity/ character in the presentation of the themes of the lyrics ie: being similar to what like what Mike Dando does with Con(trol)-Dom(ination)? I used to see BDN and myself as more of a "Dr Jekyll and Mr Hyde" relation but I think we have melted very well together... When I record in my studio I am always alone, and many things are rushing through the head, whilst live it's like I am in the studio but suddenly there are people watching, it's like having people watching your most intimate moments, if some people gets to close in the wrong moment anything can happen, I am surprised worse things haven't happened, but it isn't until the latest shows that I felt more in a relaxed situation than I previously did on live performances, it's like I almost enjoyed it...

It seems that Lina of Deutsch Nepal has been involved in recent live performances as well as contributing to one of the tracks off the latest 'Obsessis' CD. Is his participation simply as a session member or something more? Well he is a good friend, and a great attraction to have on stage....! With him I can attract both the male and the female audience!

Concepts have been utilised throughout your various albums with the most notable being the 'Great Death' Trilogy. How important do you consider concepts are to the production of a focused album? For me it is 90%. The concept comes almost always first. But the Great Death trilogy was more a coincidental than a planned concept. When I did the LP I never though about even doing a part 2 of it, but time went on and while I was working on some material it all made sense to make at least a double for the re-issue of the first, and then the idea was born for a trilogy. The Nordvinterdöd single was more like a bonus.... a way to see how far you could go with this lunacy.

Some time back you released a limited 10" on what appears to be a one off obscure CMI side label 'Anarchy and Violence'. One of the trademarks of this release was that you intentionally scuffed and marked the covers. In response I hear that you actually had complaints from customers that their copies were damaged. What is your view of vinyl buying collectors after this incident, and did this in any way lead to the lottery type game you played with the May All Be Dead DxLP? (the release saw the inclusion of various random bonus tracks and bonus single and double sided 7"'s). Well the first reason for damaging these covers was the firstly the amount of special edition vinyls that more and more bands and labels released to rip off their poor fans of more money, and on the other hand the fans that really want that perfect vinyl, with that special number, and specially signed, with a specially handmade crocodile, or what ever the hell. So the whole thing was to give my fans, the BDN-freaks, something special, a nice low-priced limited edition vinyl with hand-damaged cover by my dear self, and not to my surprise they only complained!!! "ehh, this one is all damaged, do you have another one?" I never sign records either. Signing is for popstars and little girls. Yes it could have lead to the lottery of MABD, it at least planted an evil seed in my mind.

In that you have raised the Cold Meat Industry label to well respected and recognised prominence, whilst at the same time raising the profile of Brighter Death Now, from this stance would you view yourself as a sort of Godfather to the industrial scene? In the sense of giving offers that no-one can refuse? Maybe. But I don't really like to see myself as anything special. I am no more than anyone else, I might even see myself as less, and that may be my strength. I don't like to announce myself as a Godfather at least, not as the industrial music looks today.

I believe that you have a upcoming 12" on an American label Jinx. Firstly the majority of your work has been released on CMI, thus I wanted to ask what is your preference for Brighter Death Now – to self release albums to have total control over packaging, or to have another label take on the time and expense of preparing the release? As for this upcoming 12", from what era of recording to the tracks originate from? This 12" is cancelled out of various reasons, nothing to do with the label or the person behind that, as I have full respect for; JINX. I have just become more reserved to work with other people again. I use to feel that it was a good way to explore new grounds, theories, and concepts in a less hyped way, but at the moment I feel much too protective to my work to leave it in other peoples hands. It's paranoia.

What are the future recording plans for Brighter Death Now? Do you currently have any idea of style/ concepts/ direction? I have a great deal of plans....

The slaughterhouse floor is yours....last remarks? Chop!

IRM
purveyors of post-modern
c r u c i f i x i o n

Despite being a relatively new player in the power electronics game, with their rather unique take on content and inspiration, it is not hard to envisage that IRM will quickly become a classic stalwart within the genre. With two albums already dropped on Cold Meat Industry (one LP and one CD), and a number of other releases in the pipeline, IRM were a perfect candidate for the pages of Spectrum 5#.

Starting at the beginning (or at least when you first surfaced), the Esthetiks of Cruelty compilation was the vehicle to brought your name to the wider public. What is your view of this compilation overall? Also do you feel that it was difficult to stand out amongst such a large and diverse group of mostly unknowns? I thought EOC was pretty good. My favourite acts are Nod, Klan and Blod. But to be honest I though our own material was among the strongest on the album. It stands out, don't it? Otherwise I'm not to keen on compilation albums, I don't buy these kind of records myself.

Taking things back to even prior to the above mentioned compilation, it would seem that IRM started as a project in 1997. Who would you acknowledge as influences that inspired you to embark on the creation of power electronic movements? Also how long had you been involved in the underground at the point when IRM was form? Acts like Brighter Death Now and Whitehouse had made a great impression on us. I still remember when I heard BDN for the first time; so monotonous, dark, suggestive and powerful. I had a similar experience with Whitehouse. These two acts changed my life and overall view on music. Me and my companion Erik had been into the industrial movement for a couple of years before IRM was founded. At that time we were really fed up with the occidental, and conventional, view of what music is and should be.

IRM consist of two members - what is the role that each plays in the group? It has also been said that IRM stated with a synthesiser as the only 'musical' tool. What equipment are you currently utilising? (I ask that none of your sounds remotely resemble what you would generally associate with being derived from a synthesiser). The two core members of IRM is me, Martin Bladh, and Erik Jarl. On all our previous recordings I guess our work has been rather separated; me writing the lyrics, creating the artwork, aesthetics etc, and Erik being our musical motor. But recently we've both been very active in the "musical" creation. It's true that we started out with a synthesiser as the only deriving sound source (I think it was some shitty half digital Yamaha), and that the heart of IRM still is the synthesisers. We use a Korg MS 10 / 20 with a SQ-10 sequencer. All the sounds on the Oedipus Dethroned album were derived from these. I also have to point out that Erik is a remarkable noise-maestro, really talented. On our latest recording Four Studies For a Crucifixion (released later this year on LSD.O), we've been trying to develop a more organic sound. Now we use acoustic instruments such as chimes, trombones, gong-gongs and accordions as well, so I guess the next IRM fullength release will be quite different from it's precursors.

Ever since the release of the LP there has been a significant buzz about IRM. Are you surprised with this quickly gained notoriety? Well, we haven't really noticed this "buzz". Probably because we haven't had an email address until just recently. CMI may be a rather big label, but there aren't that many magazines and record stores that get the vinyl releases (especially if they're limited to 700 copies, like our first album). Although, I'm glad I haven't seen any bad reviews yet.

How would you view IRM as being one of the new wave of groups that are marking a new direction and focus for CMI? It's true that the Karmanik-family has expanded a bit; harsher acts like IRM, Institut, Proiekt Hat, Iron Justices, Slogun and Sutcliffe Jugend is rather common these days. And I like this new wave of power industrial. It seems like we've become one of the spearheads of this "new wave". Nowadays Roger can afford to sign acts that he really likes himself, he's more into power industrial music than ambient/

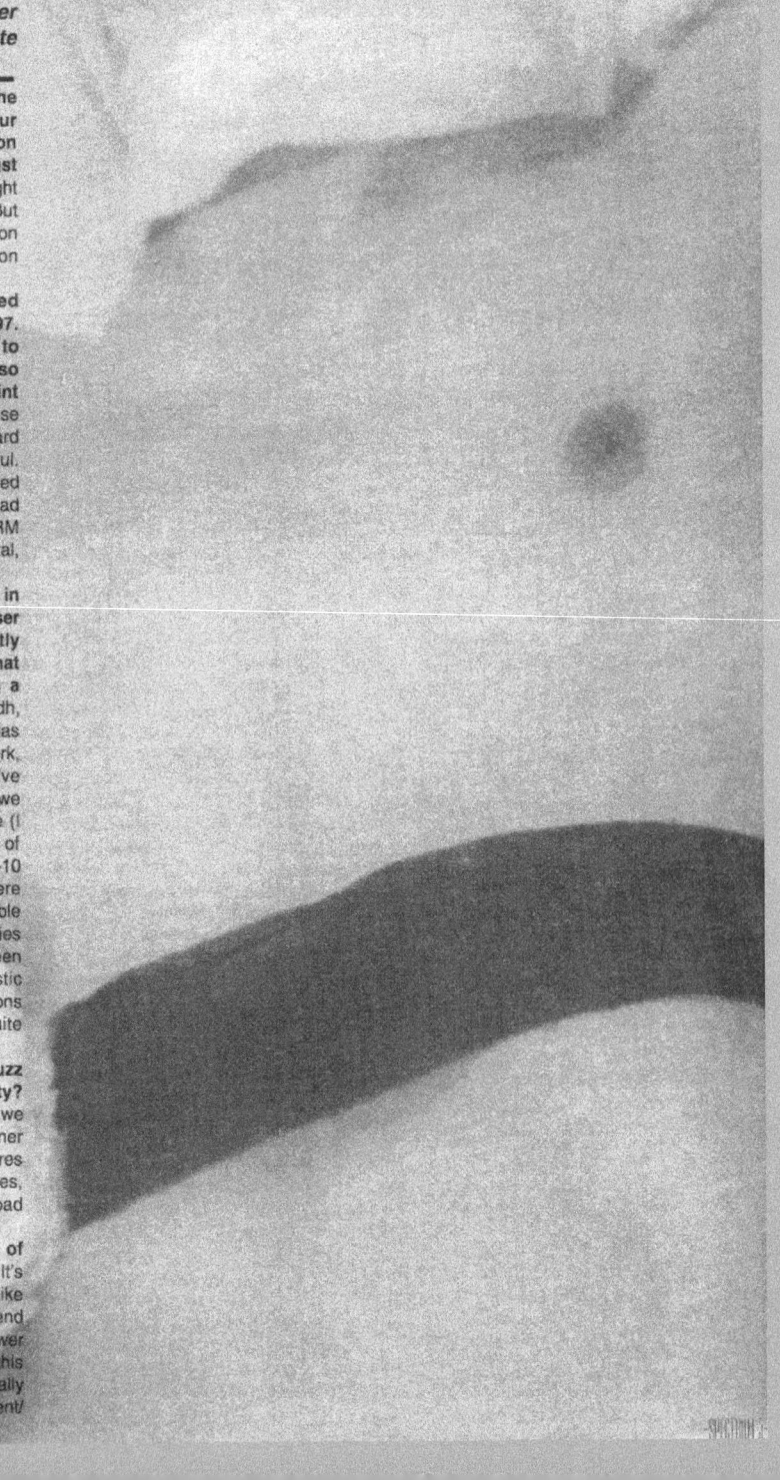

darkwave and apocalyptic-folk hybrids.

Talking more broadly, does the IRM moniker stand for anything in particular and likewise does it, or could it operate in a similar fashion to the interchangeable meanings of the infamous SPK? First of all, IRM is a word, not a shortening. This word is really personal to me and Erik, it has pursued us for several years, and we don't even know it's rightful meaning our context yet. It seems irrelevant to try to explain it at this date. Although, I promise you that we'll find it out sooner our later; only time can tell when or where this will happen, but I can assure you that when the moment arises it will be a moment of understanding and supreme beauty. Then I can't exclude that our name might work as an interchangeable shortening in the old SPK tradition, maybe it is, maybe it isn't.

The route you have taken with your lyrical approach (a more philosophical slant) seems quite a diversion from the standard political/ true crime/ serial killer focus of many power electronics groups. From both listening to and reading your lyrics, permeating themes include that of a martyr figure, personal sacrifice, crucifixion, clinical dissection etc, thus appropriating the convergence of aspects spirituality, obsessiveness, dogma etc. Would you agree with this assessment and how would you personally categorise IRM's focus and lyrical approach? It's not just that I'm sick of the usual "sub-cultural" power electronic concept, it's more a thing of me finding these kind of shock tactics unnecessary, cause in reality they are not shocking anymore (TG did it in the mid seventies, yawn...). Power electronics / power industrial or whatever, have developed into some kind of serious sub-cultural movement. You know "independent individuals" that listens to the same music, wearing the same clothes and having the same opinions as the other "independent individuals". Everything seems to be focused around selling a product; this is totally non aesthetic and all through awful. IRM is an aesthetic, not an idealistic creation. I have my personal obsessions which I've repeated over and over again on our albums. Everything is about haunting images. I try to get my subconscious down on paper. This make our work very personal and introvert. Did you know that I've been obsessed by pictures of the crucifixion ? Yeah, I guess you figured that out. I like to use an imaginary martyr figure to help me out in my writing, some kind of masochist test pilot. This Christ figure have to make an odyssey through my subconscious netherworld, and it always comes out as a journey through flesh and blood, like being crucified to a dissecting table. People use to ask me if this test pilot is me, and the answer is yes, sometimes it is me, but I'm also a voyeur observing this imaginary spectacle. Looking back at the OD album, it seems like all the lyrics are dealing with some kind of post-modern crucifixion, and that makes it a concept album. I'm still obsessed by images of the "post-modern crucifixion", so I guess it will be the main subject on the next IRM album as well.

Considering that the images of your two official releases detail a bandaged head, broken teeth, dismembered flesh and surgical scissors it delivers the feeling that you also have a sort of medical/ clinical type fixation (& not to mention various track titles and lyrics that point to this concussion). Would you agree? Yes, there is a medical fetishism within those images and writing. The scissors is especially common. Mainly because it's a fascinating tool. When I was a child I saw the Cronenberg film "Dead Zone", in which a man commits suicide by forcing a pair of scissors into his mouth. That scene really stuck with me for years. The scissor is a useful tool but could still be a lethal weapon which has the power to cut objects into half. It's also used for surgical means, and at this occasion it is an aiding tool and a threatening weapon towards our bodies, all at the same time. I don't know why I have this fascination for medical/surgical aesthetics. Maybe because they're the absolute everyday fear of most occidentals these days. Death is always related to hospitals, surgeons and doctors. Surgical aid is also the closest to physical torture most of us get. To be afraid of this subject is the same as fear of death, still it's so common to us. Also, I can't deny being influenced by the Vienna actionist Rudolf Schwarzkogler (the insert photograph of the bandaged head on our first album was taken by him). His work is an endless source of inspiration for me; the pictures are incredible beautiful. I remember buying his collected work some years ago and being completely stunned by its beauty. The way he let medical equipment such as syringes, bandage and scissors become tools of annihilation invokes some kind of mystic martyrdom, just amazing. Sometimes I only have to look at his work and the words and images comes flowing through my head. The IRM imaginary is often more fleshy though, not as sterile and clean as Schwarzkoglers.

In that there are further themes of personal mutilation, is this something that you personally partake in or does IRM give the a sort of metaphorical catharsis to not warrant such actions? Self mutilation is also one of my obsessions. As I mentioned before IRM is about images, to put yourself into different kinds of situations on an imaginary plain. I think it's hard to determine if you should view this as being active or not. To me it's aesthetic fantasies. Somebody may think I am a spineless chicken-shit hiding away in my imaginary world, but this is what its all about. I'm not for or against self mutilation, just very interested. I especially enjoy reading doctors reports and watch pictures of mutilated genitals because it feels so symbolic. It's like the ultimate sexual cleansing. Then there is psychical mutilation; how to cut yourself out and what I have to do in order to accomplish that.

Given your diversion in lyrical approach, what is your view of the role that politics plays in much of the content of power electronics inspiration? Do you feel that this is simply a trait of the style and is then simply perpetrated by various groups? What is your opinion of the face value extreme right/ extreme left ideology that is so often presented in this scene? People tend to see everything in black or white, right or left etc. Frankly, I don't care. If that's what they want let them have it . I think they're just choosing an easy way of life and how to live it out. But that's just my opinion, if it works with them, then fine. We have no interest in politics whatsoever, IRM is an esthetical creation built around personal fantasies and has no revolutionary tendencies.

While still a raucously wild ride, Oedipus Dethroned is a more subtle affair than the debut 'red' (or self titled) album. What were you trying to achieve with the direction and sound of each of these releases? The Red Album is more or less a rock album with choruses etc. It's got seven rather catchy tracks that are very easy to enjoy. When we did OD we wanted to do something different , more epic. The sounds are more sublime and the lyrics don't follow any ordinary narrative context. Most of the lyrics were done when we started to record, and we both knew what we wanted: a concept album. It took about five months to record it and we're satisfied with the outcome.

Talking of Oedipus Dethroned, the lyrics pertaining to the track of the same title does not seem to match up with what one would refer to a the Oedipus myth or Oedipus complex (apart from a barely discernible sound bite that reference child and mother). Can you expand on this perception? The mythical protagonist from the Sophocles tragedy "Oedipus Rex" is a stark symbol for physical and psychical cleansing. Just like Christ he's a martyr figure; his fascinating life- tragedy, the mother/father relation and the self mutilation: his blinding. He's one of the ultimate symbolic protagonists for an album such as OD. The whole catharsis theory personified. The album is a study of the post-modern crucifixion and the post-modern tragedy as well. The title track had been with me long before the album was recorded , it was the working-title for our second fullength-album almost a year before we recorded it. When we put all the material together it seemed like the second track embodied all the essential essence/context of the album, that's why I choose the symbolic name OD for it. Somebody thought that the title was some kind of anti-Freud statement, but that is wrong.

Likewise the list of track titles on Oedipus Dethroned seems to indicate a concept, yet the disjointed ideas and phrases of the lyrics tend to disguise any overall concept that might be present. Thoughts? OD is a concept album, and by now you already know it's context.

What authors or philosophers interest you if not inspire the works of IRM? Artists such as Hermann Nitsch, Rudolf Schwarzkogler and Francis Bacon. I enjoy the work of authors such as de Sade, Jean Genet, Peter Sotos, Burroughs etc. I've felt inspired by David Cronenbergs thoughts of the "new flesh" and Antonin Artauds theories about a new human anatomy and " the theatre of cruelty". I also like to read surgical manuals and lexicons. Lately I felt attracted to the pictures of Joel-Peter Witkin and the films of Alejandro Jodorowsky.

Both the external covers of the debut LP and follow up CD are both housed in very simplistic packaging (plan red with black writing for the LP and black with red writing for the CD). Was this style something specifically requested by the group? In that you have stated that the red cover represented anger, what can we construe from the use of a black cover? We like to have a strictly functional artwork to our releases, and I have designed them by myself. The red colour on our first album doesn't necessarily have to represent anger; the colour red is very powerful and suggestive, like the inside of a body, or maybe a murder, it's the colour of intense life and action. Black has got a similar impact, I don't really know how to describe it. The OD album feature both colours, not just black. It's red surrounded by black. What do you make out of it ? *(ED: well, the black cover could be considered to represent depression and/ or self loathing which draws parallels to the more drawn out and intense atmospheres of OD as opposed to the straight forward & aggressive style of the Red Album).*

Your personal image hasn't played any sort of role in IRM thus far. Is this by deliberate choice or unplanned consequence? Its been a deliberate choice from our side. Pictures of ourselves would probably destroy the impact of the overall artwork.

I hear that upcoming releases include a double 7" on the new American label LSD Organization and a compilation appearance on Malignant Records. Can you give details of these items and likewise any other material and or projects that you might be working on? LSD.O is going to release a 2 x 7" inch boxset called "Four Studies For A Crucifixion" limited to 500 hundred copies, sometime this spring. As you mentioned we'll participate on a compilation album for Malignant Records. I don't know when this item will be released. We're going to record an 2 x CD for CMI later this year (we haven't got any working title yet). There has also been some plans to release a 7" on the Swedish label Segerhuva. Then there is some other upcoming projects: there will be some intense IRM live-actions for a limited audience. In these actions the audience will be one of the active forces of the performance. We're also going to do a short, rather controversial film, which will be sold through CMI (maybe together with the next IRM album).

Martin, thanks for you input....

Order now

Maria Zerfall In Phase Pervers "Ich-Katastrophe"
6000-31, CD
*rerelease, nice price, brilliant german industrial from the 80ies with female voice, a concept album about the inner war

Maria Zerfall "Kopfkrieg 1985-95"
6000-36, DoCD
*best of, one of the most interesting and bizarre german projects, old school industrial, hard german lyrics and a pathetical female voice, recommended!!!

Bad Sector "Dolmen Factory"
6000-35, CD
*rerelease, nice price, the best Bad Sector album, wonderful ritual music & great sound structures from Italy

Deva-Loka ":Kampfstationen:"
6000-47, MLP
*lim. 300, fantastic new german ritual-projekt, intensive dark sounds about stations in a war. in memoriam Ernst Juenger

In preparation

6000-51 Dark Water Memories "Night fog kommando" (MLP)
*nordic germanic ritual industrial & darkambient with neofolk influences, great new project from Hungary

6000-53 Intensive Care Unit "ICU" (7")
*old school industrial in the very earlier Throbbing Gristle and SPK style

6000-55 Grey Wolves "Pure hatred" (LP)
*incl. the best tracks from tapes like "religion" etc. the original cultural terrorists!!!

6000-56 Irikarah "Good morning, America!" (CD)
*phenomenal new album, old school industrial, heavy electronics and power industrial, the best Irikarah release ever!

7000-14 Facies Deformis "Sundown" (CDr)
*digi-pack, monumental neoclassic ritual and symphonical dark ambient

7000-15 Sardh "Sa(e)nds" (CDr)
*digi-pack, fantastic german experimental dark ambient

Coming soon

Asandre "Midgard"
6000-48, LP
*new project of Irikarah, fantastic dark neoclassical stuff, ritualc soundscapes & northern mythological songs

Echo West "Signalisti"
6000-49, LP
*80ies retro minimal electronics, negative-pop and cold wave industrial, brilliant new german band

Linija Mass "Proletkult"
6000-50, LP
*first vinyl album of this unbelievable russian project, martial old school industrial with steel percussion & cold atmosphere

Linija Mass "Eiserne Revolution"
6000-52, 7"
*2nd 7" on MDP, martial heroic industrial sounds about the iron revolution

Echo West "Stars"
6000-54, 7"
*aesthetic coldpop & minimal elektronics, the most poppy release on MDP ever!!!

Deva-Loka "Aural Structures For Rituals"
5000-01, CD
*lim. CD, fantastic new german ritual & minimal ambiet project

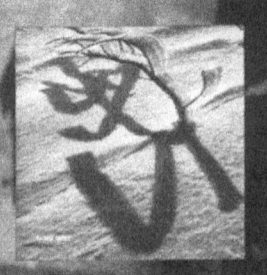

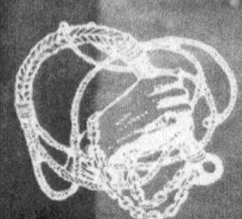

MEMBRUM DEBILE PROPAGANDA
Lessingstr. 21, D-97990 Weikersheim
order@membrumdebile.de

Attention!!!
New mailorder catalogue available!
Download at www.membrumdebile.de

spectre
[...it's a fetish thing...]

With a penchant for quality music, Spectre has forged quite a niche for themselves via producing some rather fine releases - thus far being purely on vinyl & some with quite special and elaborate packaging. Label operator Tom Kloeck speaks his mind....

Spectre, being born out of the demise of a publication 'Audio View' (that spanned two issues), can you give an overview of your collective involvement in the underground music scene that lead up to the formation of 'Audio View' and then on to starting the record label? About 15-16 years ago I was tired of listening to the boring commercial music on the radio and got interested in more electronic orientated music like house, techno and stuff like that. After a while I discovered the more "softer" side of these genres, more ambient-like music. I then founded my weekly radio show on a local radio station - that was back in 1991. I discovered new music every week and I wanted to "do" something creative with all those new experiences and started the magazine Audioview. Since I was doing most of the work by myself I only published 2 issues. After that, I decided to start Spectre, initially only for producing the 10" series. Later on, I decided that other releases and platforms should be possible and I created the two sub labels.

Taking a glance of Spectre, it is not a label that has had a high number of releases and in fact only 1 product was released per year from 1996 through to 2000. To some this might seem that Spectre is a small scale hobby label, however how would you personally assess the labels status and its individual importance to you? Well, I consider the releases on both sub labels Nocturnus and Nautilus also as genuine Spectre releases. But indeed, the number of releases is not very high. But that's ok for me, I have a full-time day job and cannot spent all my time to the label. Also, my goal is not to releases as much music as possible, but only the music and bands I like. Quality before quantity! The label is rather important to me, but I allow myself to have spare time to do other things that I like, for example collecting music from various other labels and running the weekly radio show.

To someone uninitiated to the outputs of Spectre, how would you describe the focus, style and direction of the releases on the label? for Spectre itself I can say that the general direction is somewhere situated between electronic/experimental/industrial music. I like the dark moods of musical styles, so most music released on spectre should carry that vibe. For other moods, I created the 2 sub labels. Nocturnus is more rhythm-orientated while Nautilus focuses on water-related ambient projects. I think Nautilus is a great project, I always wanted to create something around water and this is the perfect vehicle - The Kraken album, the Ah Cama-Sotz U-Boot album and the new Bad Sector collaboration are in my opinion really great albums.

Certainly flying in the face of what I would expect to constitute commercial viability, you have embarked on producing a 10 x 10" series with each item in the series limited to 90 special packaged copies (a further 10 of those in extra special packaging). Can you please give a bit of an overview to this concept series and what it has encompassed with the thus far released items and where you expect to take it with future items in the series? Ah... it's certainly not a commercial series, on the contrary! However all releases in this series are rather quickly sold, the profits are none... The concept of the series is to produce records with an extreme limitation and extraordinary packaging - I myself am a collector of limited editions and special packages, so I hope this series is somewhat of a wet dream for other collectors. Beside the special layout, the music is an important element of the concept - it has to be special too. Two good examples of this are the Aube releases (with sounds of human blood vessels) and the SGS release (with re-sampled classical sounds). There are no exact plans for the future of this series - it definitely ends with the 10th 10" release but no deals are made at this time.

Overall how do you feel that Spectre has been received in the underground scene and are you content with the stature that you currently have? to my surprise very well ! People are very keen on the limited editions and praise Spectre for the care of music and layout. For me it's natural, if you do something, do it right or not at all! It's good to get such enthusiast reactions - it encourages even more to go on.

When referencing one of Spectre's slogan's "It's a fetish thing" you have thus far held true to this in only releasing vinyl record products. Can you expand a bit further on your personal interest in the vinyl format? Right now I'm working on 2 CD albums - but Spectre and vinyl will always be partners! Vinyl is a great product and is more "human" than the perfect and faultless cd format - vinyl has that typical sound and for fetishists it stays the perfect medium for music. However, CD has its advantage too of course - clear sounds, no errors, better quality and cheaper to produce. The vinyl I produce is often very expensive; extra heavy quality sometimes combined with extra colors... but that only adds to the fetish-value and that's good!

Do you envisage branching out into other audio formats such as CD's to potentially gain a greater exposure to receptive fans of this style of music but who may not be fanatical vinyl collectors? As I said I'm going to produce CD's too, but not for the reason you mention. If people don't want to buy vinyl, well that's ok and back luck for them but that's not my problem. I like to stick to vinyl for certain releases – I don't think I will ever do a re-release on CD or do a CD/vinyl release...

Another slogan you use is "Aggression is good for you"? How does this ideal fit within the framework of Spectre's operations? But that's irony you know... so it fits perfectly...

After a number of releases on Spectre you have branched out with two new side labels - Nocturnus and Nautilus. What was it that you felt you could not accomplish under the one Spectre label banner that ultimately lead to the decision to start these two other sub labels? I think that's a fetish thing again... series are fun to do and to collect too. but as for the Nautilus concept it's obvious that it has to be separate from the regular Spectre releases - it's something completely different.

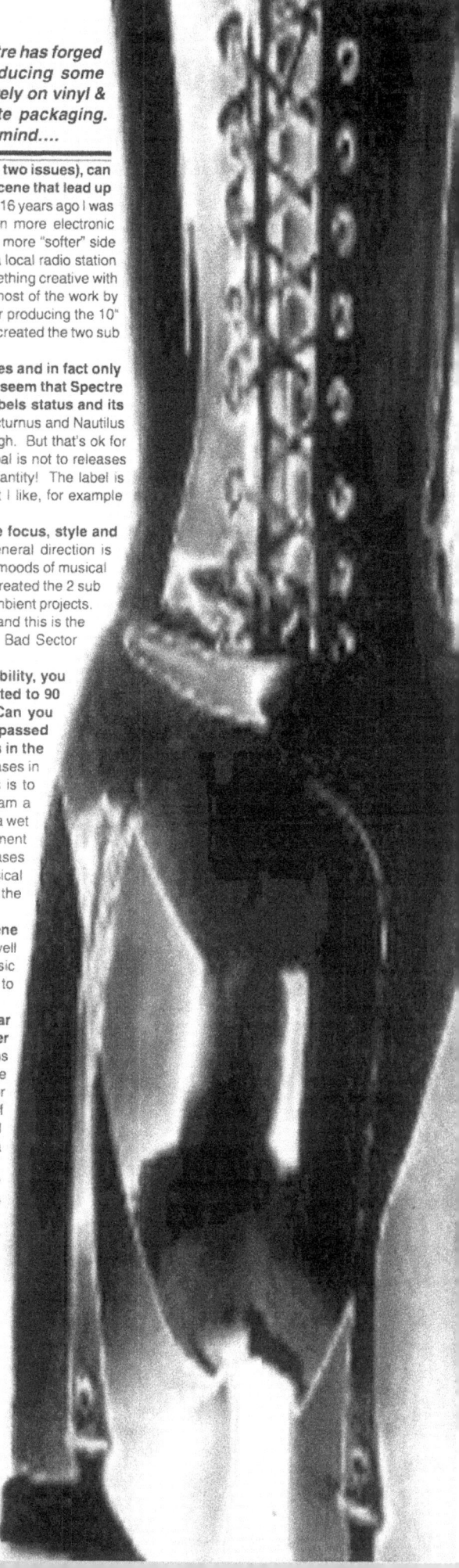

What has been your favourite release thus far and alternately what has been the most difficult to produce? Favourite is tough to decide... every new release feels like the best one so I don't think I can pick one out... the best achieved one was certainly The Book ov Shadowz. The most difficult one to produce was the new Stone Glass Steel 10"... I had to combine the 3 elements into one good looking concept that was possible to produce... and also everything that could go wrong with producing such a release went wrong and caused huge delays. At that time I was also moving to another house which caused even more stress...

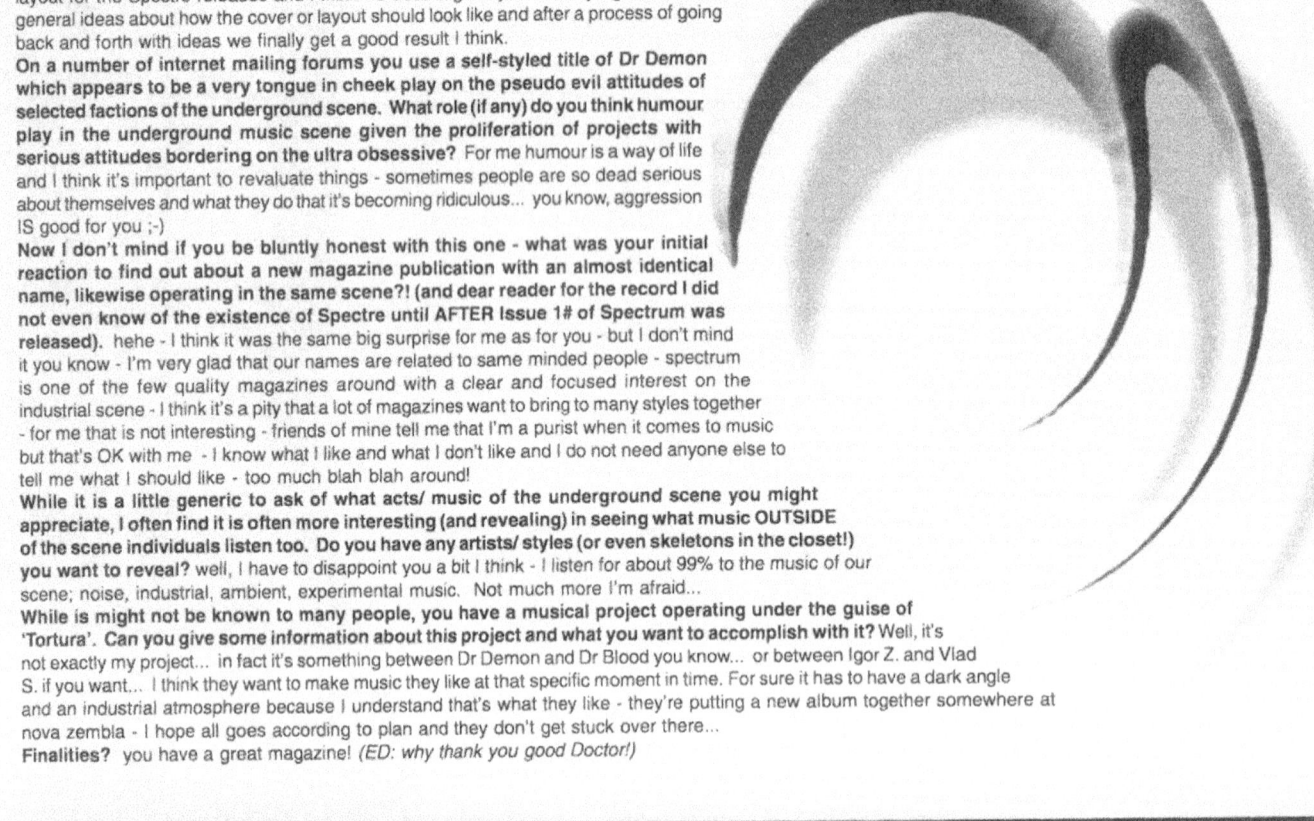

I will say that Spectre items (including sub labels) have a certain 'look' to the style of the computer manipulated designs of the covers. I assume all artwork for the releases is produced by yourself? No - I wish... Sandy from Hybryds (recydesign) is doing most of the layout for the Spectre releases and I think he does a great job - mostly I give him some general ideas about how the cover or layout should look like and after a process of going back and forth with ideas we finally get a good result I think.

On a number of internet mailing forums you use a self-styled title of Dr Demon which appears to be a very tongue in cheek play on the pseudo evil attitudes of selected factions of the underground scene. What role (if any) do you think humour play in the underground music scene given the proliferation of projects with serious attitudes bordering on the ultra obsessive? For me humour is a way of life and I think it's important to revaluate things - sometimes people are so dead serious about themselves and what they do that it's becoming ridiculous... you know, aggression IS good for you ;-)

Now I don't mind if you be bluntly honest with this one - what was your initial reaction to find out about a new magazine publication with an almost identical name, likewise operating in the same scene?! (and dear reader for the record I did not even know of the existence of Spectre until AFTER Issue 1# of Spectrum was released). hehe - I think it was the same big surprise for me as for you - but I don't mind it you know - I'm very glad that our names are related to same minded people - spectrum is one of the few quality magazines around with a clear and focused interest on the industrial scene - I think it's a pity that a lot of magazines want to bring to many styles together - for me that is not interesting - friends of mine tell me that I'm a purist when it comes to music but that's OK with me - I know what I like and what I don't like and I do not need anyone else to tell me what I should like - too much blah blah around!

While it is a little generic to ask of what acts/ music of the underground scene you might appreciate, I often find it is often more interesting (and revealing) in seeing what music OUTSIDE of the scene individuals listen too. Do you have any artists/ styles (or even skeletons in the closet!) you want to reveal? well, I have to disappoint you a bit I think - I listen for about 99% to the music of our scene; noise, industrial, ambient, experimental music. Not much more I'm afraid...

While is might not be known to many people, you have a musical project operating under the guise of 'Tortura'. Can you give some information about this project and what you want to accomplish with it? Well, it's not exactly my project... in fact it's something between Dr Demon and Dr Blood you know... or between Igor Z. and Vlad S. if you want... I think they want to make music they like at that specific moment in time. For sure it has to have a dark angle and an industrial atmosphere because I understand that's what they like - they're putting a new album together somewhere at nova zembla - I hope all goes according to plan and they don't get stuck over there...

Finalities? you have a great magazine! *(ED: why thank you good Doctor!)*

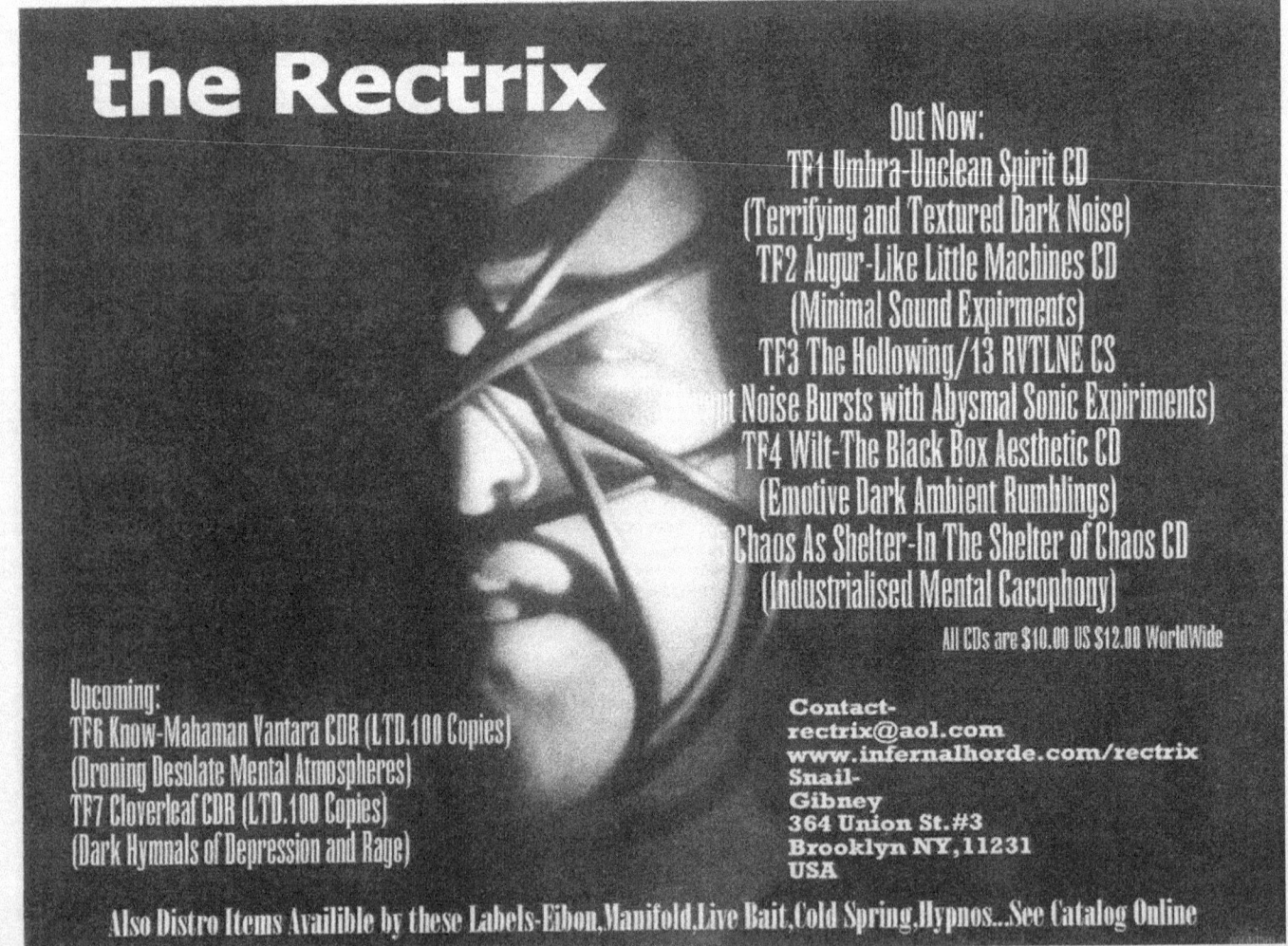

---

the Rectrix

Out Now:
TF1 Umbra-Unclean Spirit CD
(Terrifying and Textured Dark Noise)
TF2 Augur-Like Little Machines CD
(Minimal Sound Expirments)
TF3 The Hollowing/13 RVTLNE CS
(...nt Noise Bursts with Abysmal Sonic Expirments)
TF4 Wilt-The Black Box Aesthetic CD
(Emotive Dark Ambient Rumblings)
Chaos As Shelter-In The Shelter of Chaos CD
(Industrialised Mental Cacophony)

All CDs are $10.00 US $12.00 WorldWide

Upcoming:
TF6 Know-Mahaman Vantara CDR (LTD.100 Copies)
(Droning Desolate Mental Atmospheres)
TF7 Cloverleaf CDR (LTD.100 Copies)
(Dark Hymnals of Depression and Rage)

Contact-
rectrix@aol.com
www.infernalhorde.com/rectrix
Snail-
Gibney
364 Union St. #3
Brooklyn NY, 11231
USA

Also Distro Items Availible by these Labels-Eibon, Manifold, Live Bait, Cold Spring, Hypnos...See Catalog Online

SOUND REVIEWS

ALL REVIEWS BY RICHARD STEVENSON UNLESS OTHERWISE NOTED

Ab OVO (Fra) *Triode* CD 2000 Fluttering Dragon
To my surprise (yet again), Fluttering Dragon have released a very interesting album that is quite removed from the neo-classical/dark ambient releases that the label have previously released. The release in question is much along the lines of the great Simple Dead CD (reviewed in Issue no.4), but at the same time completely different. Minimalist ambient electronica (with a detectable dark streak) would be the broadest description I could give to this, as it is constructed on pretty subdued beats and rhythms that are structured in quite a cutting edge manner. For this reason, parallels to the Ant-Zen camp would have to be referenced. However not to be fooled by a minimalist description, these compositions are complex in construction and neither is specifically quiet - in essence the two elements you might normally associate with minimalism. It is rather a circumstance where the tuneful elements are kept to a minimum, as is the actual track flow, which gradually evolves the atmosphere over long compositions. Subdued programmed beats, blips, electric hums, cut-up textures, pulsating rhythms (and the like) are spliced together into mélanges of sound that are further tweaked and twisted along the way. Track five (the title track) stands out, as it reminded me of Black Lung from the outset (which can only be read as a compliment in my eyes). Given the complex minimalism (who'd have thought!!) of each piece, it is difficult to descriptively do each composition justice. But if chilled out ambient electronica is of interest to you, this could be exactly what you are seeking.

Ah Cama-Sotz (Bel) *U-Boot* LP 2001 Nautilus
Continuing the aquatic theme of the Nautilus series, the renowned death industrialists Ah Cama-Sotz have taken on this challenge with rather successful results. With opener *U-Boot Theme* with its synth melody encapsulated within swirling noise, the album takes a slow descent into the increasingly murky depths particularly when it forges into the sparse yet bass-intoned *deep inferno* (this piece includes elements akin to bubbling air pockets floating up towards the sea's surface). Sinking even further into a deep sea trench, *Ocean* is a slow moving and slow morphing piece appearing as if the oceanic tides dictate its movement. *Fate* incorporates again some ominous sounding synth elements in amongst shifting muffled textures to round out the first side. *U-68* with the framework of murky noise, shifting synth elements and sparse sonar blips, achieves a level of intensity not reached on preceding tracks. Additionally, with this track paying homage to the legacy of this particular submarine (information provided on the sleeve indicates it was responsible for sinking 33 ships) it is quite easy to picture the sub silently and majestically gliding into attack (with a more suitable soundtrack backing playing out). Steering into *Iceberg* territory, this track is a gloomy and stifled isolationist piece – and would be considered an authentic isolationist piece if it were not for faintly detectable synth elements (but mind you this element works fantastically here). *Lord of Steel* contains a heavy atmosphere of tidal shifting sounds and subtly bubbling textures, making way for the final piece *Sinking* – yet another fantastically brooding composition of subtle muffled sounds and slow morphing synth tunes. However, when the synth tune transcends its surrounds to embody both an epic and forlorn atmosphere, it clearly reminds me of Necrophorus's last album – the glacial and aquatic themes *Drifting in Motion* (which is a massive compliment to give and rather fitting ending to the album). On the aesthetic front, the music is pressed onto deep blue vinyl to match the concept, while housed in a visually pleasing sleeve creating a fine release for both label and artist.

Aluminium Noise (USA) *Totally Fucking Lost* CDR 2001 Sacred Sound Noise
From the project name and CDR title, I must admit that I was really expecting some full throttle noise assault, yet what is actually presented is far removed from this initial perception. Aluminium Noise present some really fantastic droneage/dark ambient atmospheres that are intelligently and expertly composed to be able to claim a spot alongside the likes of Yen Pox (Yes, I know this is a reasonably big call but I still considered it to be suitably justified). Also given the structure of the songs appear to have little resemblance to their synthetic origins (i.e. keyboards/synthesisers), rather encompassing an organic and sometimes quite raw distortional tone, it draws parallels to the sound-works of Daniel Menche. The five compositions on the CD, span between eight minutes (at the shortest) and up to 17 minutes at the longest - each holding its own particular charm, yet remaining consistent within the ebb and flow, steadily amassing to grating tension or alternatively, subtly shifting off into the infinite distance. Despite *Pain Reminds Me That I Am Alive* being introduced with some pretty basic guitar pedal distortion, it quickly disappears to reveal slow throbbing atmospheres and shifting sounds that fleetingly appear to have an orchestral edge. Again this track morphs through a myriad of sections, where a particularly attacking pulse characterises the later section of this track. *Mass In Time Of War I* contains a rather metallic texture to the rotational loops – stacking one layer over the last to create quite a structured calamity (some orchestral subtleties can be detected in the final minutes of the piece). This track directly interlinks with *Mass In Time Of War II*, which holds an even rawer and attacking framework to the distortional drones, however later on it does quieten down into more brooding territory particularly with the use of a sampled and manipulated symphony drone. The final track *Patterns of Dysfunction* holds a guitar drone edge to one of the early elements, while the others evoke deeper tonal sounds and subtle reverberations (once again utilising the building/manipulating method to drive forward the composition). The packaging is DIY in aesthetic with spray painted card sleeve and screen-printed insert that, while slightly crude, certainly serves its purpose more than adequately. Being limited to only 50 copies this might be hard to find, yet I have a sneaky suspicion that this might be snapped up for a more official release given its musical excellence. (Note: my hunch turned out to be correct as project soloist Jason Crumer recently informed me that this CD will be re-released in 1000 copies on CrimeThink.

Amber Asylum (USA) *The Supernatural Parlour Collection* CD 2000 Release Entertainment
Although I have not heard the albums that preceded this, their fourth release, Amber Asylum's *The Supernatural Parlour Collection* commences strongly with *Black Lodge*, where the light yet incessant snare march sits submissively below the lightly plucked emotive guitar and classical string tune, that gradually increase in force (in more ways than one, considering the group has its nucleus with Kris Force), sweeping off in a wash of atmospheric waves of distortion. All in all the song sets an immaculate atmosphere that is somewhat difficult to top (anticipation and expectation can be a terrible curse in this regard). Things never quite reach the same heights as set here, but rather opt for an unusual mixture of classical sentimentalities and more modern musical approaches to sound interpretation (such is the cover version of a Carlo Menotti operatic piece on *Black Swan* in the way that a guitar both fits while traditionally speaking is a foreign element). A beautiful neo-classical tone arrives in splendour on *Silence of the Setting Sun*, yet sits within a song structure more akin to a modern rock piece, again highlighting this mixture of the old sound and modern approach. Depressive string quartet harmonies and mournful female vocals form a subdued ode on *The Shepard Remix* (I am unsure how this actually constitutes a 'remix' in the modern sense), traversing a similar vein of emotion on *Disembodied Healer* injecting sparse vocals and select bass/guitar structure (that ultimately leans towards an experimental tone). The sixth offering, *Black Lodge Reprise*, is not all that recognisable in relation to the framework of the opening track, rather the main elements of percussion and tune have been removed in favour of focussing on the distorted washes of sound (guitar generated) and melodious violin drones. With the bio giving a nod to the likes of Godspeed you Black Emperor!, in regard of this track you would not be far wrong. To conclude the album in true style (that will also offend the hardened purists), Kris Force and entourage tackle the task of covering none other than the composition of Black Sabbath's title. Particularly with the use of violin and guttural bass/drums this sounds like what you would expect My Dying Bride to have come up with if they recorded this cover around the time of the *Turn Loose the Swans* album - albeit with a female vocalist (mind you the result is none other than a very sombre and doom-riddled vibe that is both bizarre and compelling).With an overall opinion that this album is patchy in a few places and brilliant in others, I will admit that the latter wins out overall.

Amoeba (USA) *Pivot* CD 2000 Release Entertainment
After becoming acquainted with the guitar styling and standard song structures of this Robert Rich side project, I thought I knew what to expect with this second album. Well surely things could not be that predictable, could they?! Yes, the same guitar/vocal/percussion song structure is here, but the song writing sound has become quite pop influenced! Fleeting hints of jazz and rock influences can be detected filtering through the pop sensibilities of the opener, *Fireflies*. Working with bass rhythms and steel guitar this continues into the straighter edge of the pop-rock *No Empty Promises* that surges forward with slight programming and cello backing. The vocals of Mr. Rich embellish most songs in a dreamy, softly sung manner that both follow and hold the melody of the compositions, that incidentally for all their structure often create an understated atmospheric result (this also has much to do with the warm sound production). A middle album track *Moonlight Flowers*, with its sweet acoustic noodlings, reflects the title perfectly (all the while sitting over a resonating bowed cello), while late album track *Underground* also deserves an individual mention due to its bleak progressive rock sound. I am still unsure whether I prefer the more sombre mood of the debut to the slightly up-tempo twist of this second album (only time will tell). An interesting release nonetheless.

As All Die (USA)/Veinke (USA) *In Vacuum of Blackened Space/Destitution* CD 2000 Dragon Flight Recordings
As All Die's six tracks present a somewhat unusual blend of neo-folk and neo-classical that appears to have hints of influence from the black metal sector. This metal comparison is mostly due to the vocals that are present through most of the tracks, ranging from the whispered, spoken, and choir-esque to the downright gruff, but all in a generally metal-like style. While I am not averse to extreme metal vocals where they have their rightful place, within these musical pieces, however, I feel that they slightly disjoint the atmospheres being evoked. As for the music the compositions tend to work with mid-paced strummed acoustic guitars with keyboard layers replicating orchestral strings, piano, organ etc. to build the musical backing (or otherwise acting as the total focus on others). It can be said that despite the tracks being mid-paced, a dark brooding undercurrent remains quite evident throughout. Track four features an introductory idea that, while interesting, simply does not work positively for me (urgent, disjointed and dissonant piano lines and vocal screams). This opening segment is then stripped back to a darkly sweeping orchestral section that incidentally ends up reviving the intro segment, only to fall away yet again (this pattern is then subsequently repeated). Criticisms aside, the sixth and last As All Die track is my personal favourite, stirring up a forlorn, melancholic mood via intricate acoustic guitar work, sparse piano and a few additional synth/sound layers for good measure. Some good ideas are evident in these offerings, thus at least it will be interesting to see how subsequent recordings span out. With the review of the second half of this split album it is being undertaken somewhat in reverse as I have actually already reviewed Veinke's newer debut album (on Triumvirate) in the last issue. A single track at just a touch over 30 minutes is Veinke's offering, an extended piece of catacomb-type yet slightly orchestral dark ambience. Thick bass sonics and other amassed sounds converge at varying points, some fleeting while others linger. Disembodied and indecipherable vocalisations randomly appear along with snippets of other noise clatter, including hints of tunes that seep in through the bleakness, thus adding to the half dream/half memory-type aura. Some tones suggest a comparison to guitar distortion and feedback, but never become blatantly obvious - yet on the other hand a creepy and macabre piano tune can be heard far off in the distance during the late section of the composition. Without going into any further descriptive gymnastics, basically I can say that this track is as good as any on the debut.

As All Die (USA) *Time Of War And Conflict* CD 2001 Crowd Control Activities
As a recording from times past unfolds (WWII or thereabouts…), and a brass-punctuated, choral celebration rages, a voice proclaims, *"We will win, I say, victory or death!"*, a pep talk for the legions headed out to war. It sets the appropriate stage for As All Die's acoustic guitar and desolate synth excursions into apocalyptic anguish, alit with a steadfast, forged-in-lead idealism. *Victory Hymn* connects with the aspirations of that speech, as dreary synths, emoting tones of spiritual decline and questions of wavering faith, forlorn, shimmering violins and the distinctive vocals of Clint Listing (Long Winter's Stare, Dragon Flight Recordings) repeat the urgent pleas of the aforementioned introduction. A backdrop of strummed acoustic guitars beautifully accentuates the shadowy synths and, again, the distinctive vocals (enunciation is at the forefront, quite appealing) during *Johnny Got His Gun*. After a slight pause, this smoothly leads into *Mother Earth*, in which the mood grows contemplative, inspiring a provocative spoken word recitation seemingly drawn from parchment texts full of fatalistic convictions; memoirs of hope, nothing more than cold, blackened embers in the hearth of eternity. The completely despondent timbres etched by piano and overcast cello into the hollow soul of *The Longest Day* drip like tears on the finger-picked acoustic guitar, Clint's subdued vocals contorting into every conceivable shape of anguish and misery imaginable. Powerfully despondent music, steered with fervent determination towards the disintegrating horizon of man… -JC Smith

Asche (Ger) *Distorted Disco* CD 2000 Ant-Zen
I have listened to this CD quite a few times and still cannot fathom its apparently random exploration of electronic musical styles. Dark droning ambient in the opening segments (*The Sound ov the Shell*), it then jumps to a whip-cracking noise-fest and beat programming on *Kiss the Whip*. The stakes are then upped even further on *Riding on the Atomic I.C.E*, and while its power noise beats and technoid rhythms are damn heavy, the track would still be quite dance-floor friendly. *Another Kind of Being* gives a good go at redefining the word 'harsh' with its slamming and corrosive drum'n'noise, but when the track *Zapped* arrives it sounds as if a completely different artist is at the helm - this piece is straight up techno, and quite friendly to the ears at that. This is not to say that this track is bad by any means, rather that it seems to sever any links to the tracks preceding it, thus tending to slightly disjoint the flow of the album. A later track, *Inside the Sarcophagus*, plays out as a composition that bridges subdued noise industrial and dark ambience coming across as sounding similar to that of Brighter Death Now (which is only a compliment in my eyes). Heavier and sinister themes again pervade *Peter*, where power noise/electronics are showcased in all the glory of its screaming white noise and rough and ready programming, with a similar style used on the following two (and final) tracks of the11 track disc. (Note: the hidden/unlisted track is yet another diversion with a completely bizarre drugged out drum'n'bass/ electronica number further embellished with distorted sung vocals and organ tune). To say this CD is eclectic is beyond an understatement, but it is best to be aware of this fact when approaching your first listen - it will help in understanding what is being fed into your eardrums to enable you to identify the elements that align positively with your personal tastes (whether it is dark ambient, techno, drum'n'bass, power electronics, etc.).

Ask Embla (Nor) *questions asked* CD 2001 Fluttering Dragon
Encompassing gothic and industrial-infused sounds (and here I mean 'industrial' in the band-type tradition), from the outset this CD was going to have difficulties in winning me over, as these two styles don't exactly set my heart ablaze. So after listening to this a number of times, I have to declare that my initial reservations were justified. Yes, I can admit that this is good for what it is, but I basically find it difficult to be objective, when I simply don't care for the styles it encompasses. Anyway, the framework of the music is presented in the format of a band, including a female vocalist fronting the project and accommodating a heavy reliance on keyboards (guitars and bass are also present, along with a drum machine to complete the unit). The 10 songs that make up the album are often plodding, driven forward by a drum machine, guitar and bass, while the keyboards and mid-range vocals are relied upon for the delivery of more emotive elements. Romantic baroque sentiments are to be found on *Into the Day*, yet are all but obliterated with the chugging guitar riff. The brooding atmospherics and piano melancholy of the third instrumental track *Savn (til Eaivor)* go part of the way to redemption. Unfortunately this is rendered useless when a guitar noodling individual plays the *Over the Rainbow* tune in the final bar (I have no idea what the band were thinking when they included this...). *Not Pleased* with its clean guitars and understated female vocals reminds me of Machines in the Garden's approach, coupled with the use of meandering piano and avoiding heavier guitars, happens to be one of the better tracks of the album. The final track, *Dream* is also worthy of a mention, being a slow depressive waltz based on programmed (muffled) beats, broad synth passages, clean guitars and sweetly sorrowful female vocals. Anyway, before I ramble on too much longer, if you are able to filter through my obvious prejudices, the determination of whether this is the type of album for you will be a much easier task.

Ataraxia (Ita) *Suenos* CD 2001 Cruel Moon. BC
With Ataraxia's previous album *Lost Atlantis* (reviewed back in issue no.3), one of my complaints at the time was in relation to some pretty synthetic programming percussion not doing the historic themes of the music justice. Well, it seems that Ataraxia have heralded my call and reverted to the predominant use of real instrumentation (ahem ... I think I am being just a little presumptuous!) and, in my eyes, are all the stronger for it. On this album Ataraxia appear to be encompassing a greater apocalyptic neo-folk sound than ever before, and for this reason alone this is clearly their strongest release to date. Starting powerfully with hand percussion and commanding male chanted vocals *on Parti de mal*, track two *Saderaladon* reveals a sweeping acoustic guitar-driven atmosphere with plenty of percussive elements, flutes and the ever unique and stunning vocals of Francesca certainly evoking visions of times long past. The re-working of a traditional French ministerial song on *Saderaladon* plods along with percussion and guitar, as the female vocals take flight above (prior to quickening the pace and urgency of playing towards the end). A romantic accordion tune being the basis for this is greatly enhanced with a (gradually rising and falling) full orchestral backing, that despite being synth generated does not sound as such (and this goes for all elements where synthesizers and keyboards are used to replicate orchestral instruments). One of few tracks with English vocals, *I Love Every Waving Things* is particularly emotive, with a mixture of sung and spoken female vocals. The music here ranges from orchestral strings, harps and clarinets to guitars. The darker flamenco-styled guitar work in *Encrucijada* travels a more solemn path, likewise reflected in Francesca's more commanding vocal style (with this track stretching over some seven minutes). The solemn flavour is again embodied by the horn and percussion-driven march of *Funeral in Datca*, switching between morose and more epic atmospheres. Beautiful in its reflective aura *The Corals of Aqaba* is (again) built around an acoustic guitar and female vocal track along with clarinet and associated backing layers. With there being nothing quite like a celebratory trumpeting march to finish an album, *Nemrut Dagi* is an appropriately majestic ending to the album. In passing I can safely say, that I'm fast becoming a fan of Ataraxia, particularly if they continue to forge along on this path - presenting their traditional/historical musical explorations, while avoiding more modern musical sounding elements that have detracted from the historic aura on previous works.

Auger (USA) *like little machines* CD 2001 the Retrix
Auger (an unknown project to me) present a CD of live improvised recordings dating back to August, 1999. To make my reviewing task difficult, the CD contains nine tracks yet only eight are listed on the cover...hmmm. Anyway, with a dense industrial basis and fractural samples being overlaid, the opening track *More or Less Human* is akin to a noisier version of Hazard's sound experimentations, with the samples gradually aligning as loose percussion. *Smears of Light* takes a slightly more subdued approach with a dense droning structure that pitch shifts between speakers to disorientating effect. With a scaping tonal basis, *The Seed Inside the Bud* builds aural intensity along with shifting and improvised sounding drones. Followed by the fantastically titled *Spread Your Ghastly Wings*, it contains a loose percussive structure that swings in and out of alignment, creating a chaotic affair. Throughout its lengthy journey the basic framework is tweaked and morphed, including a subdued aquatic segment that takes over midway through and sees the track take a gradual downward spiral into a minimalist piece. *A Boundary Is Not a Wall* is the most improvised piece thus far with random pitched noise and an underbelly of droning frequencies but unfortunately it is not a real attention grabber. This improvised sound transfers across to *Inside the Trees*, yet with the increased resonating textures it is slightly more successful (I found the extreme swinging between quiet tonal musings and loud outbursts became rather distracting). Shifting into an ultra-minimalist sound collage mindset, the title track contains distant blips and electro static that requires the volume to be tinkered with to actually hear what is going on, but when considering the previous track I was initially quite wary of some unforeseen outburst wreaking havoc on my speakers (thankfully that does not eventuate). The later tracks on the album are a chaotic collection of found sounds, blips, drones and general sonic clutter as embodied within *Hag* that forges onward unrepentant for its 10-minute span. The final unnamed piece (let's call it *The Unnamed!*) works on rather subtle shifts of electro-static drones that rise and recede throughout, with the final segment adding a touch of non-obtrusive clatter. In winding up the review I don't know how often this will end up being played when considering the vast amount of albums I own, but it was at least an interesting item to review.

Autumn (Ger) *A Romance of Art* MCD 2001 Sin Organisation
Although Autumn have been around for some 16-17 years, this is actually the first release of theirs that I have come across. This MCD appears to be a collection of Autumn's songs lifted off prior tape releases and specifically re-mixed for this format. Starting with a very nice melancholic piece of neo-classical romanticism (the sweeping strings and forlorn piano melodies presenting wondrous visions), this passes all too quickly, moving through to *Windows*. With a jangly clean guitar, programmed kit percussion and varying synth lines, it creates a nice twist on the neo-folk/dark wave sound. Likewise, with the vocals being cleanly sung in a rather commanding full-throated style, they complement the music in a very positive manner. The perfectly titled *Serenades*, with its composition expertly composed and multi layered, this neo-classical piece swells the emotions of the heart. The more urgent *Glaube* uses rough yet melodic stabs of piano keys, making way for aggressive percussion and fleeting tune that somewhat reminds me of Allerseelen's more aggressive musical approach (the female vocals further solidifying this perception). The title track is clearly darkwave in its focus and intent with the smoothly programmed beat being the first indicator. Additional elements - the strains of a soft acoustic guitar, subdued keyboard lines and far off echoed vocals - work particularly well, creating an emotive and very atmospheric production. Although *Flaming* threatens to really break loose, the harmonious soundscape never actually does, with spoken word vocals (akin to radio voices) sitting over layers of programming and orchestral keys. *Blue Fortress* is another track that bonds neo-classical intent with dark wave construction resulting in a quick paced, heavily programmed track, with dual male/female vocals and associated synth tunes. The all too short *Epilogue Dawn* returns back to the beautiful aura of the first track, and in essence, is the perfect way to conclude the eight autumnal compositions. On the whole this CD is a great example of a group that can expertly straddle genres (those of neo-classical, neo-folk and dark wave) and clearly have the song writing skills to back up the task.

Bad Sector (Ita)/Contagious Orgasm (Jap) *Vacuum Pulse* CD 2000 Old Europa Café
Vacuum Pulse is the CD re-issue of a cassette, CD and cassette both released by Old Europa Café, the CD version including bonus tracks. The agenda is one in which each band utilizes the sound sources of the other in the creation of something that is indicative of both bands, a melding of sonic ideals. Contagious Sector's *Vacuum* opens with a brittle resonance, like being pierced by the blinding glare that glimmers from a field of sun-bleached diamonds, subsequently devoured by magma that boils up from the earth's core, a surge of lifeblood slowly hardening Mother Earth's arteries. Seeking respite, the sounds pass through many veins, sonic capillaries bounding through convoluted alleyways within the body, from fuzzy and unclear to skittish and electronic, ending up in a place that resonates off of the ionosphere... (The sounds are not confined, they explode, dispersing and disintegrating outwards ... freedom through the wound.) Weird machinery loops with a vocal quality ignite the shuffling of scattered warehouse debris and bubbling liquid during *Pulse*. Waves of radioactive noise rise to thrash the proceedings, a swirling, spasmodic revelry of rattled noises and voice samples that utilize reverb as a stepladder out of the mayhem, but never quite break free of its clutches. They remain a part of the confined storm within the abandoned warehouse. Each of the four tracks flows with unencumbered resiliency, moving, shuffling, skidding from here and sliding into there, pockets of sound and noise ('EMP' gets positively chaotic - the screech of desperate machines seeking refuge from the manipulation at hand). An excellent meshing of styles! -JC Smith

Bad Sector (Ita) *Toroidal Body 7"* + MCDR 2001 Pre-Feed/Eibon
The criminally under-recognised Bad Sector returns with a new release spanning two formats and two recordings sessions. The 7" part of the set encompasses the two the newest Bad Sector tracks, while the CD includes three pieces from the *Dolmen* recording session (which have already yielded a CD and 7"). Interestingly the new track has a more focussed electronica/rhythmic approach than what I have heard from the project to date. The first vinyl track, 'Hen', starts off with the usual computer-type noise, yet with the gradual addition of various electronic percussive layers it builds into a slow moving composition that is quite comparable to the technoid sound coming from some sectors of the Ant-Zen camp (yet the ominous keyboard melodies that form the backing of the composition betray the typical Bad Sector aesthetic). *Pan*, the second vinyl track, is more mid-paced and runs a fine line between the classic Bad Sector dark ambience and the new rhythmic approach. The combination of dark keyboard layers and alien-like vocalisations processed with the rigid programmed percussion works supremely well, and is particularly enhanced with choir-like textures midway through. The three tracks from the Dolmen sessions encompass a much more deep space oriented sound with ominous shifts of keyboards and heavy (but fleeting) percussion. The first CD track, *Egidea*, works on so many levels with multitudes of layers (sporadic martial-type percussion, computer glitched sound, a sweeping atmospheric melody, etc.) that makes it all too easy to succumb entirely to its grandiose dark ambient aura. *Lilia (20A remix)* is slightly more experimental with sporadic electronic sounds and glitches forming loose rhythmic patterns, while the final track *Ibor (Coded)* opts for percussive yet sweeping dark ambience. The cover image of an ominous sky severed by power poles and electric wires is a perfect visual counterpart to the compositions of Bad Sector. As it is limited to only 300 copies, you might have some trouble finding one of these as I know the labels are already fully sold out.

Baradelan (Ger) *Anorgonia In The Carcinomatous Shrinking Biopathy* CDR 2000 Membrum Debile Propaganda
With a name like Baradelan, an anagram of Aldebaran, one would be led to believe that Baradelan is a tip of the hat to the masters of crackling anonymity, Inade. But Thomas Sauerbier, Baradelan's lone dark sonicscape technician, informs me that the name originated with the track, *Aldebaran Of The Hyades* from the deep cosmic plains explored on The Place Where The Black Stars Hang. Meaning that the genesis of Baradelan is aligned with (and inspired by) the godfather of sonic darkness, Lustmord. *Anorgonia in the Carcinomatous Shrinking Biopathy* (title derived from the writings of Wilhelm Reich) is a fascinating excursion down the desolate corridors of space, a clinical analysis of dark sonicscape terrain devoid of hope. *Sudden Infant Death Syndrome* breathes and ripples with vast fluttering electronic noises and a pulsing tone that skulks inauspiciously like the Grim Reaper waiting to pounce. The fact that the vacuum of sounds incorporated here reach across the vast, empty cosmos, adds a delicious layer of discomfort to an already expected finality (see title), though the death in question is gentle, like a pillow pressed over the face of the sleeping. The fluttering electronic noise continues during *Orgonotic Pulsation*, assisted by a procession of sporadic percussion that teeters unsteadily above. Synths emote ominously, goose pimples running free over chilled flesh during *Cold Clinical Theology*. The empty horizon that creeps forth is never clearly realized. The scope of tones here emanate from the internal vacancy of soul, out towards the unattainable horizon; the mood is one of solitude, enveloped in morose intentions: lifeless ... despondent ... so very alone. *Carcinomatous Shrinking Biopathy* resonates with agitated waves that surge and throb with electronic urgency, as if this course of action will wash the cancerous corrosion away. Instead, though, it is only made to battle, inflict more torment, on a body already wasting away... And the dim, flickering bulbs of the endless corridors (of space, and deflated spirit) radiate gloomily as one wanders, not towards the light, but towards uncertainty... Though precious moments of all-encompassing darkness sprinkled throughout may confirm the influence of Lustmord, Baradelan move well beyond that pitch-black genesis, the air of uncertainty a major part of the burgeoning sound. I'm definitely keeping an ear out for the next Baradelan release... -JC Smith

Bardoseneticcube (Rus) *Necklace* CDR advance copy 2000 Athanor
This unknown and almost unpronounceable project has been snapped up by Athanor after the original version was released as a 100 limited CDR (on some label called Black Dead Rabbit?!). Furnishing it with an official bio, it goes on to state *"this was considered by us as the most important 'dark ambient' recording we have heard since Lustmord's: The Place Where the Black Stars Hang"*. Pretty big words you might say, now the question is: does this album come through with the goods to back up such a statement? In a single sentence, I think this release falls just short of reaching the same breadth and depth of the aforementioned album, yet I do acknowledge that this is still a powerful recording. Forging forward from the outset with cyclic pulsations, track one sets the scene to make way for track two to take on a broader and more atmospheric frame that sweeps off into nebulous regions. Continuing on the building and evolving format, track three arrives as a mass of urgent, partly metallic, sweeping atmospheric sound textures (and conjures up an image of an ancient monolithic generator positioned at the centre of the cosmos, that for unnumbered aeons has been powering the infinite expansion of the universe...). More brooding and catatonic, track four uses deeper more minimalist

movements to create its atmosphere of cosmic resonance, including just a hint of melody and slow rhythmic percussive sounds (and to an extent actually reminds me of early Archon Satani). Spiralling pulses categorise the lengthy seventh track, with the sound palette working on a vertical axis with its rising/falling framework, again bringing visions of an idling archaic generator. However at around the five minute mark this track verges off into a panoramic-styled soundscape with the whole atmosphere becoming increasingly urgent. On the eighth and final piece, with the use of slow echoes, pulses and cyclic drones, it verges on an Inade-like quality, particularly when enhanced with tribal-esque percussion in the final segment. Taken as a whole, this recording does a splendid job of evoking visions of the cold barren cosmos.

Brainlego (Aus) *Perimelasma* 3"CDR 2000 label:KETTLE
Given the promotional blurb that promised *"A dark apocalyptic vision"*, this is a touch different to what I was expecting, for Brainlego's *Perimelasma* contains elements of both electronica-type programming and more subdued experimental textures. The programming aspect is evident from the bass pulse tune of the opening track (*Perimelasma A*) that becomes quite catatonic with random blips and static. The second track, *Phyllum Mollusca*, contains a purer electronica sound with treated vocals, clear tune and beat cut-ups that are actually quite heavy and corrosive in sound. Referencing the promo statement quoted above, the tracks *Shit into Silver* and *Scry Me a Mirror* deliver the goods by way of subdued drone-oriented soundscapes mingled with static, warped reverberations and computer generated clutter, all of which point to Hazard's recent style of sound experimentation – in other words, it is certainly to my liking. Given both facets of Brainlego's sounds are executed to a high standard, it creates pleasant diversity with what are still essentially complementary sounds.

Brighter Death Now (Swe) *Obsessis* CD 2000 Cold Meat Industry
While the new BDN offering is finally with us, the first thing that strikes you is that its cover is presented in a white sleeve with pink writing instead of the trademark black tones and 'necrose' symbol. Depicting a facial image of an innocent looking female, it is only upon closer inspection that a nasty twist is evident, creating a cover that is quite reminiscent of the artwork of Trevor Brown. Further referencing the inner sleeve, this reveals images of a dental inspection being undertaken on another teenage girl. While these pictures in themselves are not at all shocking, they begin to become slightly disturbing when considered in the context of the album. Forging even further into a power electronics aesthetic, BDN have gradually removed themselves from the death industrial sounds with which the project rose to prominence (especially during the *Great Death* trilogy), at the same time partially reverting to the harsh schizophrenic sounds of Lille Roger (the 1980s pre-BDN project). Although there has been much debate about the pros and cons of this project's direction over the past few albums, when the storming ear piecing tones, loosely formed loops and stoically psychotic vocals converge in the opening seconds of *Intercourse – Now is the Time*, I knew this album was going to be an absolute corker! Amassing in a much tighter framework, *Hipp Hipp Hurray – I Will Kill You Today* showcases an out-of-control machine loop with the ranted and obliterated vocals reaching a greater heightened urgency in their feverous tone. With vocals being somewhat subservient to the harsh noise layers (as well as the processed, flesh-shredding treatment), there is little if any opportunity to decipher content, a task rendered even more impossible with no lyrics sheet. *A B C D – Learn a Lesson* partially revisits the older death industrial style, giving a certain level of respite from the first two ear-reaming offerings. Here low bass throbs, wavering sonic layers and what appears to be a distorted voice sample merge to create an interplay via an addition-and-subtraction style (that in itself forges a sparse, looping style). On the title track, a queasy idling machine and high pitched squeals are juxtaposed against sounds of children playing, all in all creating a somewhat sickening result (in regard to both the sonic tone and the implications of the content). When a lone voice begins repeating *"Oh no"* as an introduction to *I Can't get no Sadisfaction*, it is immediately evident that you are in for one wildly filthy ride! With this track having the most easily decipherable vocals that mostly repeat the title, the seedy sonic underbelly consists of slow machine drawls and coagulated sound textures (ranging from guttural to squealing), all contributing to a very tasty offering. With Lina B Doll of Deutsch Nepal featuring on *In Circles – Psycho Circles*, the partially quirky main loop could easily be credited as his input, with the BDN sound being freshly cling-wrapped in harsh static and shredded vocalisations. Overall, for a strict comparison, this album is reminiscent of *Innerwar* mixed up with the harshness of last year's untitled 7", creating a product that points forward to Cold Meat Industry's constantly growing power electronics focus while simultaneously harkening back to the old school harsh noise aesthetics of the Lille Roger days. While it has been stated that this album represents the completion of a cycle, God only knows (and I question if such an entity could possibly exist in the realm of BDN!) what depths of the deranged mind of Kaptain Karmanik we will be plunged to on future confessions. Until then this provides ample redemption.

Canaan (Ita) *Brand New Babylon* CD 2000 Prophecy Productions / Eibon Records
Canaan have been toying with their quite unique style of dark ambient-infused/gothically-tinged/doom-laden melancholia for two albums prior to this release (one being the epic *Walk into my Open Womb* DCD), yet, not to be content with a simple continuance of what has preceded it, *Brand New Babylon* sees the introduction of moody yet catchy pop-like structures to their song framework. Dark orchestral soundscapes introduce the album with *Theta Division*, where the only hint at the 'band' framework of the group is the sparse rock drumming (the full band sound arrives full flight on *In Un Cielo Di Pece*, which includes - of all things! - morose whistling!). Pushing into a down vibed yet up-tempo sound, *Sperm Like Honey* is heavily reminiscent of that certain sound created during the *Disintegration* era of The Cure, most clearly in relation to the guitar style and sound - not that this comparison takes away from the quality of the song by any stretch (ironically by having made mention of such a comparison, is it a revelation or mere coincidence that the following sparse dark ambience piece is entitled *Disintegrate*?!). While not being all that different to what Caanan are about, *La Simmetria Del Dolore* reminds me of when the progressive Norwegian band In the Woods took their sound from early pagan metal roots, even down to the more urgent vocals of Mauro. For another slight twist the Middle Eastern strains of *For a Drowning Soul* reveal yet another dimension of the Canaan experience (with vocals being convincingly authentic for the structure of the song), while the bleak instrumental piece *The Circle of Waters*, which creates a beautifully depressive aura that transforms from merely floating to absolutely soaring when the slow percussion alters to up-tempo drumming. For yet another fleeting comparison, *The Meaning of Solitude [return to 9117]*) with its brooding synths, sparse guitars and half sung/half spoken vocals (that sound as if on the verge of collapse), brings to mind the best moments of another cult Italian band, Monumentum – and for anyone who appreciates this band it is a compliment not to be taken lightly. At a shade over 10 minutes the final track, *A Descent to Babylon*, makes use of its epic format, sprawling out in a cinematic style, with the swirling guitar riffs and mournful tunes constantly picking up pace as it forges ahead (the very last segment delving one last time into experimental ambience). As with the previous Canaan releases, in amongst their overall distinctive sound, it can be split up into those moments of dark introspective ambience, juxtaposed against the band/song-styled framework, thus with the distillation of their best ideas, intermixed with new evolutions of their sound this is easily the most immediately accessible Canaan album produced to date.

Celluloid Mata (Fra) *Sable* CD 2000 Ant-Zen
The well established project Celluloid Mata have now found their way to the Ant-Zen roster, which is understandable given this fresh sounding album of intelligent electronica mixed with a power noise styling. The backing of *Barbarous Coast*, which is dark ambient in scope, is perfectly complemented with a deep and rhythmic mid-paced beat that carries things along nicely. This deep rhythmic approach is again utilised, yet taken up a notch (or three!) on *Foolish*, which you simply can't but help finding yourself nodding your head to. On the flip side, other tracks such as *At Bunkers* and *Pop Porn Doll* take on a much rougher power noise and slamming beat-driven sound in noisy and rigid frameworks. *Del Mar* does its best to induce ear bleeding in the listener, as the track simply consists of nothing but a singular high pitched electronic squeal, while again on the experimental tangent, *We Sync* is a low whispered voice being barely audible in the articulation of the words and sentences. Late album composition and title track has a pummelling sound akin to that of label mate Imminent (Starvation) on the *North* CD and is another example of Celluloid Mata's flair for creating simple yet engaging beat-styled sounds. Overall the tracks are mostly orientated to the heavier and noisy rhythmic beats, with these elements usually taking the main focus while more subdued layers of drones and sounds carry along the more minimalist tunes (the final track makes particularly good use of a subtly progressing tune that is devoid of any beats or rhythms). Apart from the music, Stefan Alt presents yet another great idea for the cover with a transparent film over-wrap and a series of cards presented in the style of Polaroid photographs.

Chaos As Shelter (Isr) *Midnight Prayer/Illusion* 2CD 2001 Crowd Control Activities
I first heard Vadim Gusis' Chaos As Shelter on the *In The Shelter Of Chaos* CD from The Rectrix, quite possibly the finest release from 2000. I garnered further enjoyment with the limited release, *The Devil's Brothers*, from Ignis Projekt. Therefore, my expectations were high as I anxiously awaited this double disc release of promised dark sonicscape excellence. I suppose my expectations may have been too high, as the first two tracks on disc one, Midnight Prayer, failed to enrapture me as I wanted. Not that they are bad, quite the contrary, but there were slight elements (the laughter on *The Temptation Of St. Anthony* seemed almost of an amusement park/haunted house variety; the tones of the keyboards on *In Nomine Patris* did not ring as substantial … appropriate … something?! …). Of course, my initial hesitancy was unnecessary, as most everything here (including the aforementioned first two tracks - having now heard them repeatedly, they are more than worthy - quite intriguing, actually) borders on brilliance, if not successfully attains it! The world of Chaos As Shelter is one that escorts the listener into the enigma of the unknown nether regions of the earth, a tattered latticework of rickety scaffolding constructed across broad, mysterious plains of concrete and squalor. To continue with Disc one, *Dead Sea Song* maddeningly tramples through sewage across brick and mortar, the destitute remains of the crumbled dreams from above. A humming tone that somehow incorporates impetus rises to upend *Mauka*, before percussive rattling beats on the agitatedly buzzing textures of unknown origin. The mottled landscapes contain sparse textural elements, moments of brusque noise (but not of volume, per se, more of sensation, surging forth before slipping back into a hiding place), moments of scattered resonance, moments of uncertainty enveloped in curiosity. Though it may seem to meander, the music of Chaos As Shelter is never less than intriguing, flashing wild, flickering images of esoteric origin on the uninhibited cinema within the skull, as timbres of contemplation mingle with designs of an improvisational nature. Disc two, Illusion, is a dark sonicscape masterpiece! Though it is sculpted from similar sonic matter as Midnight Prayer, it seems to work better as a whole, a tightly wound spider's web of intoxicating sounds that incorporate more colour, more darkness, a little dread, and much mystery. (Mystery is a key to the Chaos As Shelter sound, not darkness, not the forbidding or ominous, but mystery…) *Dream* is beaten with slippery wooden implements, the disparate tones skirting about, a sliver of strange buzzing inspiring an acoustic guitar to rise from the shadows. (This strange buzzing crops up throughout. I am reminded of the nefarious book, *Necronomicon*, whose original title is *Al Azif*, which means *"book of buzzings"*, or thereabouts … is there a deeper meaning to the landscapes that Vadim trespasses upon?) It's just a few precious seconds of beauty, before the clicking of subway train tracks leads one deeper into the hollow earth. Tinkling chimes open *Illusion Pt. 1*, before more buzzing/humming arises, and brooding, heavy synths heave and swell, dispersing amidst clinks and scattered percussive tones that volley about. And the landscape breathes! And an unearthly horn blows… And a trace of something else (melody? - or was that just the wind speaking…?) … Unknown animals, distinguished by the clattering of their bony exoskeletons, scamper over moist concrete during *Place Of Warning*. The shadow of spirituality bounds off the gray walls, humming vocalizations (?!) of indiscriminate allegiance. *The Time Of Sacrifice* groans despondently, murky reverberant sounds that shimmer with an unhealthy glimmer, a jaundiced plague of sound, forbidding and born of eternal filth. Powerfully expansive work, inventive and infernally aligned. One of 2001's best, no doubt! -JC Smith

Coil (Eng) *Music to Play in the Dark – Volume 1 (2nd edition)* CD 2000 Chalice Records
I'm not sure exactly how I managed to review the second volume (of the two CD series) in the last issue – yet somehow it has happened! In quite true Coil form, *Are You Shivering* launches the album with a bizarre and quirky programmed synth soundscape, with treated vocalisations sitting independent of the spoken story being told. Less bizarre musically, the title of the following track takes over this role: *Red birds will fly out of the East and Destroy Paris in a Night*. The music is made of more programmed synth sounds, but these are quicker paced in tune, and contain a trance-oriented vibe. Gradual metamorphosis of the basic structure occurs over its 12 minutes, but the track remains quick paced and focussed throughout, while becoming noisier and more galactic in scope. Stripping back to an experimental piece of sound glitches and treated vocals, *Red Prince* enters its musical phase with a stunning almost free jazz vibe containing plodding metallic bass sound and meandering piano playing, throughout which vocals incessantly talk in a slow articulated drawl. *Broccoli* has a hazy drug-induced vibe surrounding it, made up partly from the bass drones and glitch sounds and partly from vocals being chanted, sung and spoken. *Strange Birds* creates quite an impressive rhythm from nothing but low volume glitched static, and toys with modern sounding art-noise techniques (later the track spirals down into sparsely treated field recordings of birds and barking dogs). The final track, *The Dreamer is Still Asleep*, is a great trance-dub sounding piece of standard drum machine percussion, keyboard tune layers and quite normal sounding sung vocals (which in itself is weird for Coil). Undoubtedly Coil in sound and scope, this is a second opportunity to obtain this once-deleted mail order album.

Cold Electric Fire (USA) *Cold Electric Fire* CDR 2001 Sacred Sounds
After the Aluminium Noise CD introduced me to the DIY label Sacred Sounds, this second release has firmly solidified my intrigue in it and its affiliated artists. Likewise, even before I got to hear the actual CD, the cover encompassing a photocopied card that is hand stitched together, certainly presented a personalised aura for the music held within. In terms of the music itself, Cold Electric Fire presents sparse and darkly emotive soundscapes that fall somewhere between dark ambience and drone compositions. Working on a split format of sound, *In Passing* introduces the album with a piece of rhythmic clatter and foreboding drone elements. Finishing all too quickly, an even shorter piece *Process One* is showcased (being only 1 minute and 11 seconds). Consisting of a distant forlorn sound, a faint emotive plucked guitar tune can be detected within the drone framework, yet despite its short length this track

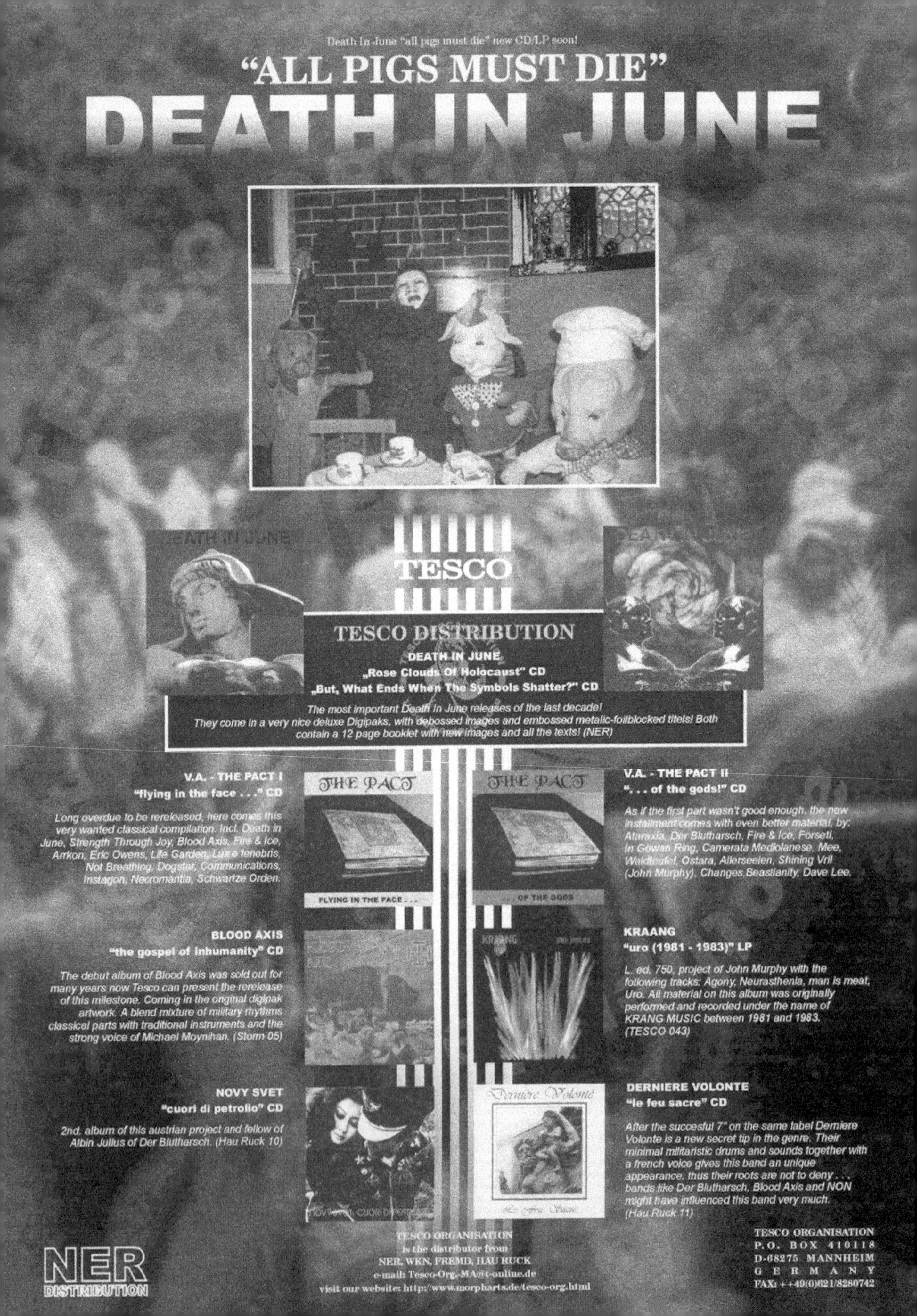

Death In June "all pigs must die" new CD/LP soon!

"ALL PIGS MUST DIE"
DEATH IN JUNE

TESCO DISTRIBUTION

DEATH IN JUNE
"Rose Clouds Of Holocaust" CD
"But, What Ends When The Symbols Shatter?" CD

The most important Death In June releases of the last decade! They come in a very nice deluxe Digipaks, with debossed images and embossed metalic-foilblocked titels! Both contain a 12 page booklet with new images and all the texts! (NER)

V.A. - THE PACT I
"flying in the face..." CD

Long overdue to be rereleased, here comes this very wanted classical compilation. Incl. Death in June, Strength Through Joy, Blood Axis, Fire & Ice, Arrkon, Eric Owens, Life Garden, Luxe tenebris, Not Breathing, Dogstar, Communications, Instagon, Necromantia, Schwartze Orden.

V.A. - THE PACT II
"... of the gods!" CD

As if the first part wasn't good enough, the new installment comes with even better material, by: Ataraxia, Der Blutharsch, Fire & Ice, Forseti, In Gowan Ring, Camerata Mediolanese, Mee, Waldteufel, Ostara, Allerseelen, Shining Vril (John Murphy), Changes, Beastianity, Dave Lee.

BLOOD AXIS
"the gospel of inhumanity" CD

The debut album of Blood Axis was sold out for many years now Tesco can present the rerelease of this milestone. Coming in the original digipak artwork. A blend mixture of military rhythms classical parts with traditional instruments and the strong voice of Michael Moynihan. (Storm 05)

KRAANG
"uro (1981 - 1983)" LP

L. ed. 750, project of John Murphy with the following tracks: Agony, Neurasthenia, man is meat, Uro. All material on this album was originally performed and recorded under the name of KRANG MUSIC between 1981 and 1983. (TESCO 043)

NOVY SVET
"cuori di petrolio" CD

2nd. album of this austrian project and fellow of Albin Julius of Der Blutharsch. (Hau Ruck 10)

DERNIERE VOLONTE
"le feu sacre" CD

After the succesful 7" on the same label Derniere Volonte is a new secret tip in the genre. Their minimal militaristic drums and sounds together with a french voice gives this band an unique appearance, thus their roots are not to deny... bands like Der Blutharsch, Blood Axis and NON might have influenced this band very much. (Hau Ruck 11)

TESCO ORGANISATION
is the distributor from
NER, WKN, PREMD, HAU RUCK
e-mail: Tesco-Org-MA@t-online.de
visit our website: http://www.morpharts.de/tesco-org.html

TESCO ORGANISATION
P.O. BOX 410118
D-68275 MANNHEIM
GERMANY
FAX: ++49(0)621/8280742

NER DISTRIBUTION

feels to be much longer. Encompassing a longer span, the seven minute *Wild Fire* is more forceful than the first two pieces consisting of drones, tape loops, found sounds and slowly bowed and manipulated cello. Quite dynamic, it quickly whips up a maelstrom of sound that, while a drone-oriented piece, hints at classical melodies buried under numerous layers (whether or not actual classical samples are used is another question entirely – but the effect is nonetheless stunning). *Cultivate Your Growl* is not as fierce as one might expect, and on one hand contains crackling layers akin to environmental recordings, that are set off against the sounds of an organ/theremin. With the darkly crafted tune shifting along at a catatonic pace, the actual tune is barely discernable, rather utilising the drawn out notes to evoke its enveloping aura. *Process Two* is another short piece, this time having rather prominent fractured noise loops underscored with a faint tune, followed soon after by *Tailor*, being a rolling mass of drone elements offset with an atmospheric yet depressive guitar tune. Building the track with manipulated percussion, this piece surges out to the horizon, effortlessly spanning every aural chasm along the way. *Sightless*, on the other hand, takes a darker downward sweeping turn, with grinding metallic textures and a more urgent framework to the gloomy drones and swirling winds. Final track *Alchemist* is the longest piece at a touch over 11 minutes, opting for the middle ground of an atmospheric and emotive drone piece that incorporates elements that appear to be derived from environmental sources, along with unobtrusive percussive/rhythmic elements. With its longer length, this track quite appropriately meanders along unfettered with the final moments whisked off with swirling winds. I'm not at all sure how many copies this CDR is limited to, but it would not hurt to make enquiries with the label directly and seek out a copy for yourself to find another gem in the US underground.

Control (USA) *Praying to Bleed* 7" 2000 L.S.D Organisation
The 7" grey vinyl, apparently a specialty with this label, is contained in a standard gloss cardboard sleeve (adorned with brutal imagery presented with a keen design eye) and further housed in a screen printed canvas velcro slip case, meaning that there is little need for safety packaging when sending one of these via the post! From what I hear, Control are a relatively new power electronics project, that seem to have a number of items slated for imminent release (including one on Black Plagve) and while I would have to say that there isn't anything particularly innovative or groundbreaking about what Control produce, it is very solid in focus and to a high standard all the same. The mid-paced title track works on approximately two levels: one being the filthy underside of constant bass rumblings, the other the multifaceted squealing feedback that chaotically bursts in and out of earshot. There sounds like there might be vocals somewhere in amongst it all, but these are severely mutilated so as to not resemble that of a human voice (much as the image of the corpse on the cover). Rather than boiling the blood, this track tends to place it simmering temperature just short of all hell breaking loose. *Lust Killer* takes a more subversive approach with its slightly more machine rhythmic rumbling structure mixed with subdued noise elements that slowly multiply in thickness and intensity, rising to the surface then sinking again only to repeat the cycle (don't get me wrong here, this track is still damn harsh, just less so when compared to the first). Ultimately this track works much better due to its somewhat building structure, a quality that I find particularly enticing in power electronics projects. As this item is my first taste of both the label and group, both seem to be worthy elements of the growing US scene and are worth keeping an eye out for.

Control (USA) *Control* CD 2000 Black Plagve
With what amounted to a minor eruption in controversy on the TUMORlist regarding what some considered to constitute extreme and violent misogynist imagery (as presented on the cover of this debut Control album), it threatened to overshadow the actual music presented. Well, arguments aside, this CD could have been packaged in a plain black case without losing any of the inherent intensity of the power electronics blitzkrieg. The blisteringly loud and insanely angry *Pain* gets things moving with mid-paced chaotic rumblings, high-pitched fractural sonics and heavily treated/distorted wailing vocals. With the sound and focus quickly established, the remaining pieces surge forward in a similar manner. With the album sounding partly hectic and improvised while containing basic structure and direction, this assists in gaining and holding the listener's attention. *Hematoma* manages a sweeping atmospheric tone to its static washes and wailing electronics, creating a constantly building sonic firestorm aesthetic. Despite some other tracks having some pretty nasty-sounding titles (like *Streetcleaner*, *Humiliation*, and *Left to Bleed*) the vocals are never discernable in their content, firstly due to being ranted (or screamed) and then heavily processed with distortion to create another layer to the chaos. *The Sickness* contains an underlying rhythmic pulse, which is utilised as the foundation for the gradual building atmosphere that, despite being quite noisy, is relatively subdued when compared to earlier offerings. With a track title such as *Anger* it is easy to be deceived, given the actual focus is mid- to slow-paced fluctuating and cyclically constructed sonics (rather than the anticipated attacking approach). Anyway, to say that Control represents a strong contender in the growing US power electronics scene would be an understatement, as this CD solidifies what all the fuss has been about with previous live performances and limited edition vinyl and CDR items. It should be noted that this release is also somewhat limited with only 500 copies having been pressed.

Converter (USA) *Blast Furnace* CD 2000 Ant-Zen
Over the last few years, Scott Sturgis has established himself as one of the finest musicians within the realm of dark music, through his electro-industrial sonicscapes as Pain Station, and his rhythmic noise as Converter (I've yet to hear the d.b.s. material). The fact that the quality of each is of the utmost, well, that puts Scott in elite company, alongside the ultra-prolific Peter Andersson (Raison D'être, Stratvm Terror, et cetera…), Adi Newton (Clock DVA, TAGC), and a few more choice individuals. Blast Furnace is consummate rhythmic noise, meticulously crafted, sculpted from metal and burnished in blood and sweat. The title track stutters amidst whiplash, metallic percussion, discharging multiple layers of static ricochet noise, shifting the focus throughout. The construction may sound familiar, but the results are anything but, as the locked-in methodology is honed to a precision most excursions into rhythmic noise lack. Rubber gloves massage the womb of *Be Broken* before metallic noise shatters into shards of noise that spray as shrapnel into the flesh of the ambience. An ambience also punctured by snippets of glossy, distorted synths. The gurgling miasma of rhythmic, throbbing noise that introduces *Red Crystal* ventures off into the distance before a rippling retort drags the noise back into focus, amidst injections of virulent metal and jackhammer pummeled bleats of ripping noise. Oily electronics squelch amidst awkwardly stumbling rhythms, finally ending up in a valley of screams, moans and contorted vocalizations. Nothing is ever still, nothing follows a simple path; even amidst an abundance of loops, this music is in constant motion, multiple layers adding multiple perspectives. And the noise is NOISE, not some simple bastardisation of the rhythms-molars grind, mountains crumble, buildings implode, all with Scott's amiable assistance. (Even the calmer moments spit and flail, straining the sonic straightjacket.) There is so much to soak up here it is beyond listing. Just buy the damn disc! (Yes, that is most definitely a recommendation.) -JC Smith

Coph Nia (Swe) *That Which Remains* CD 2000 Cold Meat Industry
When the bio steals all of my potential comparisons (Sephiroth, Lustmord, Raison D'être, and even snippets of Dead Can Dance) what am I supposed to do other than wholeheartedly agree?! However one thing that sets this stellar debut apart from these other groups is the occultist/ritualistic side that steeps itself in Crowleyan mysticism (again it sounds like I am simply rehashing the album bio – that is, if it didn't also happen to be true). The gaping depths of Cold Meat Industry's traditional dark ambient sound are evoked from this CD's opening passages with lurking drones, muffled ritual clatter and haunting quasi-chanted vocals. The ritual/occult aspects are more obviously explored on *Opus 77*, with prominent male spoken vocals (reciting Crowley's concept of Will) along with fleeting segments of a lone female chant that could quite easily pass for Lisa Gerrard. While I could personally do without the prominent male vocals of this piece, they are not so much of an issue as to become a distracting (and therefore detracting) element. On the other hand, I have to say that some truly flesh-crawling screams, wails and wickedly demonic voices add an extremely unnerving air to the otherwise sweeping and classically-tinged dark ambience of *Doppelganger*. With further reference to vocals, the interplay of commanding male and fragile female vocals embellished with acoustic guitars ensures the introduction of complementary elements to the track *Sanctus* - but rest assured, the deeply resounding dark ambience is never too far from the surface (and particularly wallowed in on the following piece *Holy War pt. 2*). *Our Lady of the Stars* throws the preceding offerings to the wind by embracing a stunning piece of gothic-tinged neo-classical resplendent with soaring female vocals, organ tune and sparse yet booming percussion – but rather then dwelling on a description of its aura, this piece simply needs to be heard to be fully appreciated. The title track caps the album with a lengthy dark ambient slab of sound texture, where particular care is taken with the use of sparsely placed haunting choirs and slowing unnerving shifts of sound – again a track where full immersion is the only solution and the perfect way to usher the album unto oblivion. It seems that there was some sort of mini bidding war surrounding this artist with both Cold Meat Industry and World Serpent Distribution being the main players. Either way, at least this album has now been released and can be fully appreciated. As always Kaptain Karmanik has done a stunning job on the cover with images of cemetery statues in tones of black, silver, grey and purple.

Death In June (Eng)/Fire + Ice (Eng) *We Said Destroy* 7"EP 2000 Frehdheit
A most surprising track from DI6, *We Said Destroy* contains a framework of industrial experimentation created via loose and echoed metallic rhythms that push the track forward, while being mixed together with an underscore of noise, spoken vocals, sampled voices and assorted drones (the track even finishes with a locked groove that gives off the aura of a bizarre carnival tune loop). While *We Said Destroy* is completely different to what most would ever expect from Douglas, this is still a fantastically creative piece and shows there is much more to the DI6 than just their familiar apocalyptic folk sound (…and unless you have been living under a rock for the past twelve months, you would know the concept of this track is aimed at the circumstances surrounding DI6's split with former label World Serpent Distribution). Fire + Ice, on the other hand, create a quiet folksy organ dirge on *The Unquiet Grave* complete with the trademark morose vocals of Ian Read. Mid-track sweeping violins and female vocals really add flair to the sorrowful atmosphere. Packaging is also aesthetically pleasing, with blue foil stamped symbol and dragon presented on the cover.

Death In June (UK) *The World that Summer* CD 2000 NEROZ
This album, which was originally released as an LP way back in 1986, has now been re-released (for the first time on CD) in a beautifully and immaculately presented digipack of black embossed roses and red foil stamped writing. Held within the musical framework of this album there are classics like *Torture by Roses* and *Break the Black Ice* (both emotive apocalyptic folk odes that would become such a staple of later works), that have stood the test of time very favourably - if not being entirely timeless. On the other hand, the production sound of some other tracks point to the time when they were captured (such is the new wave up-tempo drum sound of *Come Before Christ and Murder Love*) likewise clearly marking the progression of DI6 over the years. The falsetto vocalisations of David Tibet (going under the alias *Christ 777* for this album) on *Love Murder* are simply bizarre, floating over a light melancholy yet wispy keyboard tune. *Rule Again* is another new wave-inspired song that ever so slightly hints at martial themes in regard to the steady beat and lone trumpeter, while the lyrical focus points to Crowleyan-derived inspiration. For the lengthy soundscape presented on *Death of a Man* it is surprising in that this is quite similar to the quieter trench warfare sounding tracks that can be found on the last Turbund Sturmwerk album *Weltbrand* – yet amazingly these two comparative pieces were recorded 14 years apart, again highlighting the timeless aesthetic that Douglas and entourage have been able to evoke over the years. The final three tracks of the album come with *Reprise 1*, *2* and *3* which are actually alternate (vocal-less) versions of *Rule Again*, *Break the Black Ice* and *Blood Victory*, bringing the total play time to nearly 70 minutes. As it seems like there is a plan to re-release much of the DI6 back catalogue with refurbished packaging, it is good news for individuals like me where there are annoying holes in my DI6 collection, especially in regard to the older items.

Death In June (UK) *Brown Book* CD 2000 NEROZ
Another classic and out of print Death in June album has finally been re-released on CD for the first time. The digipack is presented in light camouflage green with gold foil stamped totenkopf skull and title emblazoned on the front. Additionally the cover insert is printed on high gloss paper with photos and text from the original release - also including a photograph of a much younger Douglas Pearce. As the actual recording harks back to 1986-87 (similar to *The World that Summer*), *Brown Book* includes well-known songs intermixed with other tracks of soundscapes, speeches and general experimentation. The lineup for this recording includes Rose McDowall, David Tibet (credited as Tibet '93'), Ian Read (among others), and their individual contributions can be heard on various tracks throughout the album. The best known DI6 pieces here include *Hail! The White Grain*, *Runes and Men* and *To Drown a Rose*, all of which follow the apocalyptic folk tangent and thus do not require further description, as anyone who even had a passing interest in the group will be aware of this style and sound. The more experimental numbers include *Red Dog-Black Dog*, which is built around hummed female vocals overlaid with an echoed male voice reciting a cryptic story, and *We are the Lust*, which consists of heavy percussion, haunting sound textures and vocals (the track basically avoids any reliance on a main tune). *Punishment Initiation* is a fantastic mixture of non-standard percussion, keyboard soundscapes and acoustics with the pained vocals of David Tibet really adding flair. The following piece is also the title track, consisting solely of a German chant that Douglas says is as controversial today as when it was first released (when first released the album was banned in Germany). The last real track, *Burn Again*, has an almost Spanish flamenco sound with its lightly plucked acoustic guitar, which is the lone musical element presented alongside David Tibet's vocals. As has become a staple of Death in June albums over the years, the last three tracks are mixed versions or 'reprisals' of other album tracks – here including *Hail! the White Grain*, *To Drown a Rose* and *Runes and Men*. Though not my all-time favourite Death in June album, this is still an essential item for my collection.

Death In June (UK) ***but, what ends when the symbols shatter?*** **CD 2001 NER**
Death In June (UK) ***Rose Clouds of Holocaust*** **CD 2001 NER**
These two albums see the scheduled re-release of the DI6 back catalogue, and when they were released back in 1992 and 1995 respectively, were somewhat considered as brother and sister albums due to their strict adherence to the now benchmark apocalyptic folk sound. And with the current label advertisement proclaiming *"the most important Death In June releases of the last decade"*, how could it have been more accurately put without sounding like an understatement or exaggeration? Originally presented in jewel cases, the re-released versions see the albums now housed in individual digi-packs that have used combinations of pressed embossing and foil stamping. While the packaging pays homage to the original artwork, the digi-packs also include high gloss printed cover inserts that quite thrillingly incorporate additional images from the periods that the albums were recorded, creating rather majestic covers for each album. Forlorn and nostalgic, tragic and melancholic - the gamete of these emotions are encapsulated within an overriding framework of despair that spans both albums and the years that they were conceived. With the atmospheres of both albums being built on an acoustic guitar framework, they are further embellished with keyboard layers, backing vocals (male and female), trumpet, bass guitar, percussion, melodica etc., creating a continuity of simplicity yet an air of diversity. If we are then to look at individual tracks, it becomes apparent that there are simply no fillers on either disc. And it is quite astounding as to the number of DI6 classics that these albums contain. From *Death is the Martyr of Beauty, Little Black Angel, The Golden Wedding of Sorrow, Ku Ku Ku* and the title track off *but, what ends when the symbols shatter?*, through to *God's Golden Sperm, Omen-Filled Season, Symbols of the Sun, Luther's Army, 13 Years of Carrion* and likewise the title track off *Rose Clouds of Holocaust* it highlights how magnificently strong these albums are when viewed either individually or as a representation of just how far Douglas had evolved DI6's sound by the early to mid-1990's. Referencing alternate tracks on *but, what ends…, Daedalus Rising* is particularly harrowing due to the urgency of the guest vocals presented David Tibet. The same can be (partly) said for *This is Not Paradise* (again on *but, what ends…*) which sees David's spoken vocals delivered in both English and French, presented over a soundscape of calling of gulls in a coastal setting and mid-paced strumming of the acoustic guitar. Mr. Tibet also guests on *Rose Clouds…*. where the presentation of his vocals on *Jerusalem the Black* are rather subdued, but certainly contain his trademark style. With David providing one last collaboration, *Life Books* closes *Rose Clouds…*, seeing the amalgam of both Douglas's and David's (spoken) vocals in a rather sparse soundscape (with David in the ending moments hissing *"it's a dream, it's a dream…wake up, wake up"*). Likewise including the immortally controversial line *"The swirling sounds of swastikas, like rotor blades of thought, threshing the wheat out from the chaff"* (spoken in deadpan voice by Douglas) to conclude the album, it is a perfect example of a type of lyric that on face value seems to articulate one idea; however, after delving deeper into its ambiguous symbolism has a much more profound meaning. Basically I cannot speak highly enough of either of these albums, and if you were to only have one DI6 CD in your collection it most certainly would be one of these. If Death In June remain as an enigma to some readers out there, either of these albums would be the absolutely perfect introduction.

Death In June (Eng) ***All Pigs Must Die*** **CD 2001 NER**
After the diversion from the 'classic' Death in June sound on the two previous albums *Take Care and Control* and *Operation Hummingbird* (due mainly to having been recorded in collaboration with Albin Julius), the question being asked was: - *"what sound will the new Death in June album encompass?"* Particularly when it became apparent that Albin would not be involved with this particular recording. Well, to address this question, the seemingly blunt titled *All Pigs Must Die* provides the official response. Splitting the album into two halves and two sounds, it encompasses half-celebratory yet scornful apocalyptic folk nostalgia and half industrially harsh experimental noise-scapes. The more acoustic 'classic' DI6 sounding tracks were recorded in collaboration with Andreas Ritter (of German neo-deutsch folk project Forseti). While on the flip side, it seems the noisier experimentations were recorded by Douglas alone and are similar in approach to those tackled on the *We Said Destroy* 7" (see earlier review) of last year. Firstly making reference to the acoustic tracks, interestingly these don't contain any sort of martial percussion (which seems to be a popular element of current neo-folk acts), rather utilising trumpet and accordion as the main backing elements. Likewise with the absence of any other backing elements of keyboard melodies, vocals and strings it has created quite a stripped back and rather direct approach to DI6 apocalyptic folk sound. With the title track commencing proceedings, the acoustic strains are offset with trumpeters, accordion tune, folk whistle, and vocals almost being in the form of a chanted and repeated mantra (and certainly representing a solid beginning). Boyd Rice guests by providing a spoken word introduction to *Tick Tock*, which is a stunningly spiteful acoustic guitar waltz presented via cyclic strumming and semi-romantic accordion tune. *Disappear in Everyway* taking on the acoustic/trumpet/accordion basis, reverts late in the piece to again use the repeated mantra of the album title. *The Enemy Within (Strange Days)* with its vocal line *"these are strange days for you and me and Germany … but we have honour and with that we'll win"*, sung over a rather epic and atmospheric acoustic guitar playing, makes me wonder if this (along with other lyrical hints) could in any way be interpreted as an ode to DI6's new label Tesco Organisation? (…You decide…). Boyd Rice guests again at the start of *We Said Destroy II* prior to Douglas presenting another immaculate acoustic number, with the following track *Flies Have Their House* accommodating a stunningly forlorn and depressive aura evoked via atmospheric trumpeting and meandering accordion tune (the last minute of the track regresses to a mélange of voices, noises, song samples etc.). Moving into the experimental side of the album, *With Bad Blood* acts as a bridging number given the extremely noisy and spiteful reprisal of *Tick Tock*. The basic structure of the former acoustic track seems to have been fed through distortion and manipulating equipment, with the vocals re-recorded with unbridled anger, sitting alongside discordant piano tones and other demonic vocalisations. *No Pay Day* takes on the aesthetic of the prior track yet is even more spiteful, lacking any sort of tune, rather opting to have the drawled acerbic vocals as the main focus. *We Said Destroy III* is another partially reworked piece - here taking on the form of *We Said Destroy II* and further destroying it with static feedback, echoes and noise. *Lord of the Sties*, consisting of a spoken vocal piece, takes various German and English recited lyrics, amassing these into a loose framework of distortion and noise. The final track, *Ride Out!* as a piece does not entirely align itself with either the experimental/industrial or acoustic framework, but rather is a perfectly constructed piece of manipulated deep brass orchestral loops and indecipherable vocals, and is a great diversionary piece to conclude this new offering. Overall, the collaboration with Andreas Ritter on the first half has incorporated an increased neo-folk aura into the DI6 sound (mainly due to the swaying accordion melodies), yet also I would have to say these tracks could be viewed as some of Douglas's strongest acoustic works to date. Especially with having melded the traditional forlorn reflective mood with a very sharp and very spiteful edge. Even if I am not aware of all of the details surrounding DI6's split with WSD, the lyrical content throughout the album seems that these events have had a profound impact on Douglas to the point where it has been both the inspiration AND obsession for the new album. While I initially found the lyrical focus unnecessarily blunt and somewhat lacking the ambiguity or spirituality of earlier lyrics (and I question too if they will have the longevity of other DI6 lyrics), I can say that this album IS a very strong release, albeit short at around 40 minutes. Given I have only an advance copy of the CD at the time of review, I am certainly interested to see what the artwork will comprise of.

Deison (Ita) ***Dirty Blind Vortex*** **CD 2000 Crionic Mind**
Deison is a name that I was familiar with, but not so much with the actual music until this recording. So after this introduction, the best overview I can give of Deison's style is that it runs the gamut between sinister dark ambience and oppressive death industrial motifs. Grinding and obliquely tuneful, *Dream:Morphology* is a dense looped soundscape with dialogue sample being derived from David Lynch's *Eraserhead* which adds to the bleak yet slightly surrealistic edge. Radio frequencies and sporadic voices blend together with fractured sound layers on *Inside Sources* to a bleak conclusion – as does *Novamalia* but rather opting for a bass-soaked and muffled industrial sound with slight orchestral undercurrent. Whipping the atmosphere into an electric frenzy, *Lodge, Hlny* is rather chaotic and somewhat improvised with loose groupings of loops and sharper textures that resemble electric wire distortion, while the sparse shimmering minimalism of *Silenzio* is sporadically punctured with bursts of machine looping clatter to add to the oppressive aura. With the writhing electronics and fog-like atmospheres of *Out of Spasm*, it laboriously accrues intensity to become rather weighty by the time it has passed the five minute mark. *Symptomatic Headache* creates the track with the least muffled production with sharp and twisted electric pulses swirling at a higher sonic range. This higher, sharper sonic edge is again replicated on *Terminal Suck Sick*, however there are fewer aspects to the sound stratum creating a broader electric-oriented air. Diving headlong back into death industrial musings, *Automatic Pain II* is quite fantastic with orchestral undercurrent that is massacred with full warfare samples (machinegun ablaze, bullets whisking by close overhead). The final album track *Dirty Intercourse* clocks in at over 12 minutes, being a broad soundscape of dense undercurrents with more improvised textures, sounds, samples and malfunctioning machine idling noise laid over the top. In that it appears that Deison has collaborated on various tracks with Sshe Retina Stimulants, Government Alpha and Baal (among others) it has resulted in a more diverse sound palette between compositions while retaining a specific genre focus. Having said that, the album is sonically dense and tonally bleak to create an album of cruel musical intentions.

Dernière Volonté (Fra) ***Le Feu Sacre*** **CD 2000 Hau Ruk**
Being signed to Albin Julius' (of Der Blutharsch infamy) label, you could expect this to have a stylistic slant towards martial/neo-classical, which is in fact right on the mark. This is another group that has arisen from seeming obscurity but has managed to produce an astoundingly solid debut album that warrants comparisons to the likes of Tribe of Circle, Les Joyaux de la Princesse and Der Blutharsch – in other words, top notch! In amongst a generally martial framework, selected songs seem to utilise sampled and looped classical snippets that enhance the forlorn atmosphere and likewise provide a timeless aesthetic. Other tracks, such as *Nous Maintenons Notre Histoire*, contain spoken vocals sitting above a looped percussive base, deep resonating horns, sweeping strings and folkish flute tune. For yet another comparison, the slow and depressive aura of *Der Kinder Nacht* seeps from the speakers much in a similar style to the brooding works of Raison D'être, with unnerving shifts of sounds and sparse hints of choir vocals and violin tunes. *Le Coeur Ombre* is more warlike in its clanging metallic percussion and pounding tympani, acting as an inspiring counterpart to the slow brooding tune enshrined in the violins and piano. This battle-oriented vibe is again present on *Der Zorn Gottes*, but is here produced with constant rolling snares and quite massive epic horn melody (finally completed with sampled vocal phrase pertaining to the track's title). Both epic and forlorn, *Marchefunèbre* contains slow snare drum work, marching alongside a brooding organ tune and understated piano accompaniment, while a flute tune floats slightly above. By far the folksiest track on offer is *Les Tambours*, mainly due to the prominence of the flute and deeply sung male vocals, while the backing music sustains a quite rousing marching tune. On a different tangent the production sound of *Mères De Nos Souffrances* holds quite a distant aura with its echoed and resonating piano tunes playing off against each other, which at just under three minutes is far too short (but I guess that this late in the album oblivion is slowly approaching, thus there is no point putting off the inevitable). While there might be multitudes of new groups popping up in the ever growing neo-folk/neo-classical genre, if they all produce albums of this calibre the scene can only be all the stronger for it.

Dissecting Table (Jap) ***Memories*** **CD 2001 Triumvirate**
The distinct industrial noise madness created by Ichiro Tsuji is again explored on the new Dissecting Table, where four tracks or *Memories* are presented, giving a total play time of around 40 minutes. From the opening segments it is apparent that while the same auras you would normally associate with this project are present, the tracks have also taken on a (partial) format that is more akin to the construction of a full band than a sole individual. *Memory I* with screaming noise feedback, fast-paced metallic programmed percussion and buzz saw bass guitar all give the aura of listening to a hybrid of a grind band and noise project (the guttural distortion of the vocals additionally rendering them in a death metal guise). Retaining a free form flow, the track chops and changes between segments, yet it is when incorporating the structured parts, they appear to be the most composed that Ichiro has used. *Memory II* commences with an ominous slow-paced bass tune and programmed pounding beat that, apart from some metallic noise in the background, interestingly could easily be passed off as a full band. Things continue in this fashion including the screeched vocals following a clear verse/chorus/verse format, while the middle segment contains electronic pulsating sounds highlighting a diversion from the metallic feedback (additionally with static blasts and a clanging church bell). Given the squelching feedback chaos of *Memory III*, it shifts through a variety of noise and percussive segments, and is far removed from the more structured 'band' sounding elements of the first two pieces and a nice diversionary offering. The final track or 'memory' of the CD swings back to the fast repetitive percussion, obliterated bass tune and trademark vocals, before swinging off onto other tangents of semi-to-unstructured tangent, electronic weirdness, programmed dub etc. In that I find that most people have a love/hate relationship with Dissecting Table, for those who have succumbed to Ichiro's chaos before, prepare for yet another all-out onslaught!

Dodsdomd (Swe) ***Everburning Evil Fire*** **7" CD 2000 L.S.D. Organisation**
Another L.S.D. Org. release presented in the dual packing of a pleasingly designed gloss cardboard slip sleeve, inside a screen printed canvas slip case. Although Dodsdomd were, like so many other projects, introduced on the *Esthetiks of Cruelty* DCD set, the two tracks on this transparent green vinyl (to match the full colour cover) are admittedly less raucous and chaotic as the sucker-punching track included on said compilation. Atmospherically noisy, the title track makes use of an unusual vocal treatment for the semi-whispered voice while mid-ranged, loosely looped rumbles intersperse further with sections of static-derived noise and high-pitched squeals acting as the combined 'musical' counterpart. The very title of *Fleshgrinder* gives an indication of what to expect, and the track itself furiously amasses into a focussed whole after a short build-up. Machine gun-style loops and multi layered high end noise reach such a point of intensity that it actually sounds as if the vinyl is faulty, and its incessant (but of course deliberate) crackling adds yet another roughly hewed loop in amongst the many. Despite all its hellish noise it does reach an unusual atmospheric tone that all too quickly fades away (I don't know how I would fare listening to a whole CD of something like this track, but it is good over the one side of a vinyl EP). Two sides, two tracks, and two interesting styles within Dodsdomd's power electronics/noise focus make this quite an interesting item.

Sally Doherty and the Sumacs (Eng) *Sleepy Memory* CD 2000 Tiger Records
Rather than constituting a new album, this is actually a re-release of Doherty's debut of 1998, but now with proper distribution via WSD (I assume that it may have originally been self-released). Quite a bit more song-oriented than Sally's *Empires of Death* soundtrack of 2000, her vocals take centre-stage as varying instrumentation is used to embellish the 13 tracks. The vocals themselves are sung in a quite contemporary style, although hints of a Middle Eastern influence can also be detected. The songs also tend to hold a classical feel due to the instrumentation, which includes piano, flute, cello, violin, harp and classical guitar. *Watching the Horses*, which builds the musical framework on meandering piano and string accompaniment, is quite a dreamy song with Sally's vocals being both that of lead and backing, while the tablas percussion on *Lake-Linear* gives a clear nod to Middle Eastern inspiration, as do the vocals. The title track is clearly one of my favourites of the album, with this being attributed to the soaring vocals and piano/violin playing that leap into a number of the more urgent segments. On *Fast Approaching Silent*, the piano's minor keys give a darker, moodier aura, and are assisted by the sparse backing vocals and accompanying flute tune, while my penchant for the mixture of strings and grand piano is satisfied on the slightly depressive track *Voice*, which is also really the last proper track of the album (if we do not include the one minute instrumental piece, *Waiting*). Generally this album reminds me of the more fragile moments of The 3rd and the Mortal's works or even the recordings of ex 3rd vocalist Kari Rueslatten (when she was not trying to be a pop princess!). Basically this is a quite contemporary and beautiful collection of emotive songs.

Droneaement (Ger)/The Infant Cycle (Can) *Klab (Phonorecord)* LP 2000 The Ceiling
Coming from a label I was not previously aware of, this features one artist I have heard (Droneaement) and one I have not (I don't need to spell it out for you do I?!). The first Droneaement piece, *ER-9 Noise Transmission.wav*, is very much akin to what the group's moniker and track title would allude to, given it presents thick sonic waves of mid to low range register, with keyboard notes forming a slightly glitched sound. Interestingly this track moves into regions I would have not expected from the group, utilising a programmed beat segment to push things along in a mid-paced, almost groovy sound. Here as much as the drones are not noisy or assaulting, neither are the beats, rather opting to be understated, consisting of low-toned bass kicks and light percussion. Midway through, the drones slip off into the background, upping the antics of the beats and slight driven noises and squeals yet still retaining the mid paced groove. Overall this track could particularly sit alongside any number of recent Ant-Zen releases of the dark electronica persuasion. Track two for Droneaement (*331/3 rpm Acoustictransmission.wav*) on the other hand is a surging mass of low end psycho-acoustic tunings - layer upon layer building into a bleak monolithic structure, where even the surrounding inky blackness appears to shimmer. For my mind-set track one is good but track two is where the real deal is at (I have always been a sucker for droning dark ambience). Flipping the clear vinyl over, The Infant Cycle has only one track to their side, a piece that starts out with a section of good old classic drones that morph into slightly evasive sound textures. Things continue on in such a guise until it unexpectedly breaks into a dub/beat segment! Sharp and snappy percussion categorise the programming, yet ever present in the background are some semi-melodious keyboard drones. The format meanders along where the beats (and selected samples) are added and subtracted at a number of points – with this both jarring and assisting the flow (in a good way, that is!). Again I would have to comment that this piece has quite a bit in common with the cut-up electronica style of the current Ant-Zen roster. For interest this release is more than simply a split LP as both projects have assisted in the construction of each other's tracks by providing the basic source sounds and assorted noise treatments, likewise with Droneaement providing the handmade covers (grainy card with minimalist screen-printing and image attachment).

Exotoendo (Fra) *Push Kara* CD 2000 Athanor
Although *Push Kara* is only the second album by this French project, it seems that the group has already split up. This is indeed very unfortunate news considering the quality of the ritualistic dark ambience that they have created here and on their previous CD (on Old Europa Café) a few years back. Although not mentioned in the cover liner notes, I have heard rumours that this CD was recorded in some sort of industrial vat, which partly explains the sparse resonance of the drone atmospherics. The Tibetan Buddhist-derived inspiration also points to the ritualised sounds that seep gently into the mix at appropriate moments – perfectly creating ritualised dark ambience. Both wistful and arcane, deep drones meander forth from the speakers and are later set amongst sparse notes (played on wind or string instruments), with light percussion (in the form of chimes and wood/metal implements) that mark the ritual aspects. Occasionally a chanted vocal appears, sounding like a disembodied soul marking its mournful presence. As one track morphs into the next, some highlight more extroverted segments, while others work with a minimalist aesthetic, yet the slow evolving direction and flow of the album make discerning where one piece finishes and another starts quite a difficult task indeed. From this perspective it means that the CD is quite a good tool for meditative practice, or otherwise as a piece of music to which you can simply succumb without having a change of tracks break the feel and flow of the warm spiritual atmospheres being evoked. While Exotoendo may not have a huge name within the dark ambient field, this does not prevent me from recommending this highly.

Fennesz (Aut) *03_02_00 Live at Revolver, Melbourne* CD 2000 Touch
At only 16 and a half minutes this live recording is a mere snippet of the set Christian Fennesz hammered out on his powerbook during a sweltering summer evening show. Static riddled and constantly fragmenting, this CD conjures up an oddly engulfing sound, with higher-pitched tonal notes giving off a shifted modem type of sound. Within the contest of these sound textures, a sparse direction is found with the interlinking sample elements creating a rough drone-type flow, constantly splintering off on new tangents. A middle segment gives the impression of someone scanning frequencies on a short wave radio – not that any voices are ever heard, mind you, but instead the barren soundwaves give off an electric hum. An extremely noisy and chaotic framework is used around the nine minute mark with a sampled tune being obliterated in the distorted static mix, amongst multitudes of other quite fierce noise textures. Things do calm down for the final part of journey as another sample tune and gentle static and glitched elements create a somewhat meditative state. Although the packaging is not worthy of a mention, if you have appreciated Christian Fennesz's experimental soundscapes before, this CD will not disappoint.

Fennesz (Aut)/Rosy Parlane (NZ) *Live* 3" MCD 2000 Synaesthesia
This CD is quite stunning both musically and in the discreet miniaturised packaging that houses the 3" disc. The live recording showcased here was undertaken at an afternoon barbeque when a number of the Mego crew were in Melbourne, Australia, in February 2000 as part of the *What is Music?* festival. Although totally improvised between the two artists, it does not sound as such, working perfectly in both the drone and digital glitch sound styles. Two untitled tracks make up the 14 minutes of music, with both inhabiting a similar sound framework while holding their own distinctive aura. Track one contains calm static glitched loops at the foreground, with sparse drones crawling below that actually reveal a slow moving melody as they surge forward. Sparse and highly atmospheric, it creates an emotive air in which to revel and ultimately lose yourself (I first heard this when it was played on the radio as I drove home in the small hours from a Scanner performance, with the track complementing both the time and my mood perfectly). Track two offers a touch more rhythm and melody, with the slow format being fed through distortion effects to disguise the original soundsources. Here the glitches are still present but generally less dominant – but nevertheless a similarly stunning aura is evoked. Nothing else to add but that this is quality stuff indeed, and clearly shows the genius of artists who can create such sounds in an improvisational format.

Folkstorm (Swe) *Information Blitzkrieg* CD 2000 Old Europa Café
While this is the first Folkstorm CD off the ranks, you might also note that two other CDs were released in the same year (and are likewise reviewed below); yet despite the sudden rush of releases it appears that *Information Blitzkrieg* dates back to 1999. All the same Mr. Nordvargr has certainly been busy with this project to record three albums (four, if you include the ultra-limited MP3 exclusive *Culturecide Campaigns* CD) in between the operations of his main project MZ.412 - and having dropped that project name it should be pricking up a few ears. I will certainly admit that one of the charms of Folkstorm is its raw, almost crude styling, which ultimately alters from the more polished sounds of MZ.412. Likewise, by not being constrained by other members, Folkstorm appears to be a very direct channelling of Nordvargr's sound into these no frills aggressive power electronic movements. Apart from an unusual sampled opener (a 1940s-1950s stage song sampled in its entirety with no modifications except for an underlying analogue drone), the real meat comes with *This is War*. Noise, loops, distortion, dialogue samples and then even more distortion for good measure - this should give you an idea of what to expect! Beginning with a drum sample that I am certain was originally from MZ.412's *Nordik Battle Signs* album, *Haus Betula* arrives as a sprawling mass of throbbing electronic bass loops that is morphed ever so slightly over its length, whereas the harsh layers and blow-torch noise of *Alle Sagen Ja* act as incinerating agents to samples of Third Reich speeches and military songs that have the misfortune of finding themselves inserted into the crushing mix of searing atmospheric noise. Lo-fi, mid-paced distortion box noise simmers just below the boiling point throughout *M.H.S.M* as the inserted dialogue samples are almost completely lost in the somewhat subdued grinding layers, while *We Control You (1989)*, with its fast and aggressive percussion, obliterated vocal smatterings and slight static, is a great but at just under two minutes a disappointingly short track. Concluding the album with aggressive militant atmospheres - and even a hint of structural melody - *Beendigung: Opus Rex* uses a lengthy format to construct the various layers of samples, dialogue, noise and programmed sounds to an engrossing result. Overall there is a definite comparison to be made to MZ.412, almost seeming like a stripped back and raw power electronics version of that project. Folkstorm is a more than capable project to provide you with an ample fix of culturecide.

Folkstorm (Swe) *Hurtmusic* CD 2000 Old Europa Cafe
Marching into battle, snare drum in martial alliance, Folkstorm welcomes sonic bloodshed via this scorching live presentation. Mixing samples; raw, nerve to the flame, feedback squeals; ultra-distorted loops of machinery noise, and what sounds like mangled retching from within the throat of abused guitars (?!), Folkstorm plough through fields of death with relentless revelry. The blanched in distortion vocals rage maniacally, the chaotic spiels an integral part of the Folkstorm grinding crush of sludgy noise. Despite the fact that the recording has a very controlled atmosphere, one can almost sense the heat and feel the sweat and ear-shredding reverence that a show of this purely assaulting nature must have inspired. Sheer, sonic, wrapped in distortion so thick it crackles like bacon on a skillet, like napalm on living flesh, brutality! What more can I say? (And, yes, this music can hurt!) -JC Smith

---

COLUMN ONE
World Transmission 3 - SA020 (LP)
The soundtrack of religious architecture, recorded inside a church by using various sacred tools in context of their archetypical environment. A quality heavy vinyl LP comes housed within a beautiful and limited 2LP set, together with "World Transmission 4".

COLUMN ONE
World Transmission 4 - SA021 (LP)
Re-worked recordings from a COLUMN ONE live meeting in Berlin. A sonic ritual of numerous acoustic sound sources and native recordings, placed into a new context, in a catacombs scenery. A quality heavy vinyl LP comes housed within a beautiful and limited 2LP set, together with "World Transmission 3".

NOCTURNE
Kapitulation - SA022 (CD)
First full length CD release, after two highly demanded 10"s. "Kapitulation" once again is a historical raid into the fields of human failure. A French conqueror of aggressive art and discrepant profile, who unites rude electronika and documentary recordings in a dangerous mixture...

SURVIVAL UNIT
One Man's War / No Surrencer - SA023 (7")
Certainly one of the most aggressive acts coming from Sweden! This limited heavy vinyl 7" contains two raw and powerful tracks of electronic assault and hateful shouts in front of a cultural terrorist manifestation. A titbit in advance of SURVIVAL UNIT's forthcoming CD!

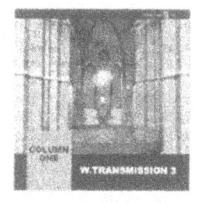

STATEART c/o Koch
Roseggerstrasse 2
30173 Hannover
Germany
eMail: info@stateart.de

Distributed by:
TESCO DISTRIBUTION
P.O. BOX 410113 · D-68275 MANNHEIM · GERMANY

| LETUM | ATARAXIA | NOVA | MEGAPTERA | ORE |

Join the party!

www.coldmeat.se

| GERMANY | EUROPE | FRANCE | GREAT BRITAIN |
| EFA / TRISOL | AUDIOGLOBE / TARGET | SEASON OF MIST | SHELLSHOCK |

Folkstorm (Swe) ***Victory or Death*** **CD 2000 Cold Spring**

Victory or Death is the third Folkstorm release, yet like the debut, *Information Blitzkrieg*, was also recorded back in 1999 and therefore predates the live recording *Hurtmusic* captured in March 2000 (the live CD was incidentally released second in the queue). Seething noise, slow bass pounds, repeated vocal phrases and high-pitched squeals see the stockpiling of sonic weaponry from the get go of *Stolz*, giving no ground as it trudges forward (later stamping on the noise accelerator and becoming all-out chaotic). Fast analogue throbs characterise the main section of *Feldgeschrei*, and are pushed through further distortion and treatment throughout the track. By being simple and direct this piece nonetheless creates an addictive result - particularly at loud volumes. Again, analogue loops constitute the backbone of *Harsh Discipline*, and are combined noisy and very crunchy sonic textures while slow non-rhythmic beats and distorted vocals rise from the mix (later the track sounds as if it may collapse under the crushing weight). For a bit of education we are taught the principles of *Propaganda* (on a track of the same title) as a slow pitch shifted voice discourses on the subject while high-pitched squeals and blistering looped noise bores incessantly into your skull. *We are the Resistance* makes use of a stunning main section of deep tribal/industrial beats, again with sections of looping noise and sampled dialogue, where simplicity and directness win out. *Funreal Force* (which is surely a typo) takes no prisoners as it builds on a base of muddied, bubbling textures, directly attacking with bursts of high-pitched noise. Hints of slow percussion appear but seem only to increase the aggression of noise to screaming intensity as the whole shrill atmosphere is amplified (does it get any better than this?!). Taking an overall comparison of albums, I would have to say this is my favourite of the three as it appears to be slightly more worked through and also more militant and direct in atmosphere. To add to this, the chaotic loops, static and noise have all been given a very pleasing production that additionally tends to accommodate a greater differentiation in sound between tracks.

Gae Bolg and the Church of Fand (Fra)/Omno Datum Optimum (Fra) split 12" EP 2000 Cynfeirdd

The first of a trilogy, this split instalment is limited to 333 copies. Up first is Gae Bolg, who are extremely traditional in their medieval/gothic song construction, with the male vocals sounding like a morose bard against a segment of guitar and wind instruments. Interestingly this slow tuneful segment is then juxtaposed against a section of absolutely pummeling tympani percussion as the track cuts back and forth between these segments for its duration. Basically, while being very traditional, it still remains an unusual blend of folk and martial neo-classical. The second track presents a much less musical structure, opting rather for a soundscape of drawn-out flute notes, disembodied voices, and archaic sounds (that actually remind me quite a bit of the ritualistic sounds of Psychonaut), and overall leaving me slightly edgy and unnerved. The flip side of the EP by Omno Datum Optimum is not far removed from the first, and mixes gothic chanted male vocals and tympani percussion with a more full and brooding orchestral sound that is slightly more sweeping in its musical vision (distant strings, horns, snare drumming and subdued piano all add to the beautiful atmosphere). Omno Datum Optimum's second piece slowly rises as a deep cello movement with accompanying orchestral drones, chanted male vocals and deep percussion. By gradually increasing the intensity of each musical element, this track seems even more engulfing than the first despite its more limited musical movement and direction. With full colour cover and inset this relatively new label is presenting some quite stellar releases that should at least pique your interest if neo-classical sounds are your thing.

The Galerkin Method (USA) ***The Galerkin Method*** **2000 MCDR self-released**

This must be one of the most bizarre releases I have been sent to review in this issue, given that The Galerkin Method meld contemporary songwriting with everything from ethnic Indian sounds to European waltzes within their musical style. With the group centering around Stefany Anne, it would appear that she is responsible both for writing the basis of the songs and vocal duties (that incidentally, due to the infusion of an Indian influence, are therefore quite comparable to the vocal style of Lisa Gerrard). The opener *Whatwas*, with its hammered dulcimer, provides a certain ethnic slant and a distinctive individualistic sound for the project (despite the drumming taking a march-like approach and other instruments such as guitar and flute acting as backing elements). The accordion waltz on track two *Hale* is enhanced with violin, bass drums, guitar and Stefany's vocals and apart from holding a traditional sound, has a fleeting Mr. Bungle-type weirdness (however, revealing nothing that I could directly put my finger on). The third track, *Carmina B*, delves into the alternate musical auras of the first two tracks (the European and the Indian), resulting in a heightened sense of a surrealist nightmare playing out in the crevices of the mind (and to think I considered some of Novy Svĕt's compositions to be out there!) Free form and ever so slightly folksy in feel, *This Perplexing Frost* is the most straightforward song on presentation, yet the ethnic slant of the female vocals, along with accordion and violin, provides the necessary continuity to preceding tracks. *Longitude/Latitude* is reminiscent of the traditional eastern experimentations that the Tea Party delved into on their early releases - here the track using a moody dulcimer tune, layers of radio voices, violin and the ever present, urgent yet angelic, female vocals. The darkest number is left to last via melding a brooding accordion tune (again) with the dulcimer and vocals of Stefany, prior to it picking up quite a bit of pace, galloping along with bass guitar and drums. Whist certainly an interesting recording I am still left a little bemused as what to make of this, but the closest overall description I can think of is imagining the music that Lisa Gerrard would create while on a chemically induced outing … in other words strangely enticing!

General Magic (Aut) ***Rechenkönig*** **CD 2000 Mego**

Any CD that can sample Barney the Dinosaur on the opening track certainly shows a sense of humour that cuts against the grain of the often ever so serious academic 'art-noise' scene. Primarily of the static/glitch-oriented sound for which the Mego label is so well known (which is not surprising since General Magic is comprised of the founders of Mego!), the 26 tracks on this album generally range in length from a mere 30 seconds to just shy of five minutes. Random programmed and sampled tunes, percussive elements and diverse digital static all seem to have been fed through distortion-inducing computer programs to create off-kilter and quite disorientating sonic textures. No tracks really stand out over the rest, yet each one explores its own little territory generally framed by the original source material utilised. Moreover, given the cut-up nature of the album, it can as easily be played through from start to finish or alternatively via the random selection button, yet still finding that you arrive at the same result of listening to playfully complex and sometimes confusing sonics. I quite quickly have run out of ideas of how to describe an album of this style, and would thus prefer to keep this review short and sweet. While this will certainly please aficionados of the Mego sound, this CD might not be the best introduction for newcomers to this label.

Gerome Nox (Fra) ***Blood-Red Poppies*** **CD 2000 Moloko**

Taking an overall concept centring on murder and serial killers, this solo artist has produced a CD which ranges from dense and disturbing death industrial soundscapes to more traditional industrial guitar chugging riffs. Also used quite extensively to embellish the themes of the CD, numerous sampled dialogue pieces are used to occasionally chilling effect. More guitar-oriented pieces like *On the Road* are not presented so much in, say, a Ministry vein, but are closer to how guitars were integrated into In Slaughter Natives' *Sacrosancts Bleeds* CD. *Mass Destruction* is a touch cheesy due to the up-tempo programmed beats and cyclic heavy guitar strumming, yet things do start to get interesting around the start of the following piece, *Monologue Two* (as there are no guitars), which relies on subdued keyboard drones and scattered sounds to create a tense atmosphere further enhanced by the statements of a serial killer (recounting how he was forced to have oral sex with his mother). This vibe is carried through the title track, which at over 11 minutes is introduced with crime scene dialogue, and later encompasses massive furnace-blasting sound textures, echoed metallic clatter, creeping footfalls and buzzing flies – these elements create a mental picture of a killer returning to the murder scene (and with tracks of this quality I wonder why the guitar tracks were ever included!). *Hell's Kitchen* does a somewhat reasonable job of mixing the darker soundscapes with slightly abstract guitars – yet again my comments on the guitar element remains. To finish the CD, *A Tribute* features a male and female voice reeling off an exhaustive list of killers (some well-known, others less so), and while this is an interesting idea that is set to backing sounds that are reminiscent of Megaptera, it unfortunately comes off as tedious and drawn out (considering that it spans 18 minutes). While the guitar pieces might not be bad at all, the darker soundscapes are much more distinctive and are really where the gems of this CD can be found. The cover imagery remains true to the title and is presented in a simply and cleanly designed digipack.

Gothica (Ita) ***Night Thoughts*** **CD 2000 Cruel Moon bc**

Gothica's *Night Thoughts* is a beautifully lush and orchestral-oriented album with moving compositions and sweeping operatic female vocals. From the opening strains of *Stagione Oscura* the mood is set in full classical mode, with fleeting gothic-oriented influences filtering through as the album progresses. Ornately structured compositions add a certain depth to the album with combinations of both real and synthetic instrumentation providing a layered effect. As these sounds are aligned with prominent classically-oriented female and restrained male vocals, it is not hard to draw parallels with the almost legendary Dead Can Dance. The tribal-esque percussion and slow keyboard dirge of *Spirits of the Dead* is particularly noteworthy, with the more oppressive themes of the track embodied in the subdued male vocal lead. Slightly baroque in styling, *Proserpina* is a flowing mass of meandering vocals, violins and keyboards that would not have been out of place on Dead Can Dance's classic *In the Realm of a Dying Sun* (indeed, several other tracks bear this comparison). The late album track, *The Pure Nymph*, encapsulates a slow, down-vibed orchestral movement that in my mind would have been better without the electric guitar solo noodling, yet this is not so prominent that it can't simply be ignored. For one of the most active and up-tempo pieces, *Lost in Reverie* strides forward with orchestral keys and strings – female vocals remaining a powerful central focal point. At mid-song a commanding piano segment appears with auspicious result – fading the track to its conclusion. Of the 12 compositions, (which on average hover around the three to four minute mark), each explores its framework in moderate detail, creating an album of maturity in relation to Gothica's orchestrally gothic stance.

Haus Arafna (Ger) ***für immer*** **7" EP 2000 Galakthorrö**

There are always certain groups that I know I should have checked out a long time ago (with Haus Arafna being one such project), but for whatever reason this did not happen until now. Knowing their cult status in the power/heavy electronics game, I must say that the vocals on these tracks were not entirely what I was expecting - but I have also been made aware that on previous tracks the vocals were far less tuneful. Anyway, packaging on this 7" is stunning with a fold out card cover, printed vinyl sleeve and black wax and canvas ribbon to hold everything in place. The title track presents a piece of queasy analogue electronic static and rough grinding rhythms, the male vocals are partly commanding/partly monotone in presentation, quite a diversion for the often screamed distorted style of the genre. *Amputation Cures* sees the vocals presented in a more urgent, slightly distorted guise, as loose noise loops and discordant tunes writhe in sparse groupings. Side B offers up *No Right To Live* - a great piece of mid-paced static, grinding textures and plenty of rough and heavy percussive sounds to complement the sometimes subdued, sometimes commanding (but always clearly sung) vocals of Mr. Arafna. The fourth and final piece *Rebels Have No King* slows things down to a crawling pace, including the anaesthetised vocal delivery sitting over slow drawn-out textures and occasional noise and static blasts that give off a very morbid atmosphere. Due to my tardiness in becoming acquainted with this project, I now have the annoying and arduous task of attempting to track down their prior releases. Recommended.

The Hollowing (USA) ***Sepsis*** **CDR 2001 Live Bait Recording Foundation**

With this project hailing from Brooklyn, New York, it would seem that this bustling metropolis could be seen as a metaphor for the material that The Hollowing produce. Dense, chaotic and certainly crowded, the compositions clearly mark the experimental industrial noise style of the project. From the outset *Selected* shows this focus using static, noise, numerous tuneful elements, samples etc., that are massacred in a distortional grinder. Spitting forth furious anger, the track does not let up and forges quickly into the next piece *Cloning Process*. With a bizarre (almost) rhythmic loop, it appears that an underlying sound might just be sampled from a computer car game! Vocal (or is it a sample?) of a whispered and indecipherable guise can just be detached as the partly structured/partly improvised piece continues. *The Quickening* samples and again massacres a number of orchestral loops that are mixed in with the static blasts and growled/distorted vocals and despite being quite chaotic the piece does manage to obtain a brooding and tense flow. *Chapter 186* is built on distortional static, in amongst what might just be urban field recordings, creating a rather freeform piece. The track is occasionally punctured with an aggressive vocal wail that is good for the first few times but becomes a tad monotonous in that it is used throughout much of the six-minute track. A more subdued atmosphere is evoked on *Passage of Regret*, seeping out of the speakers as a soundscape of quite metallic clatter and rather forlorn semi-tuneful sounds (is it a horn or treated vocals or just a synth created texture?). Partly tribal-esque in intention, the pounding beat of *Blood on the Stones* is the skeleton on which voice samples, distortional sounds, looped vocals etc. are draped to flesh out the repetitive cyclic piece. Static-driven minimalism is the flavour for *Exist*, of which a vocal sample appears occasionally during the 13-minute journey with some of the sound textures being akin to the sounds within an underground train tunnel (and could well be just that). Last piece *Heartless Resurgence* is a bit of a bizarre piece with ritualistic improvised percussion and vocal chants built up with bird samples and fleeting orchestral samples (I am not entirely sure what to make of this piece as it seems to really sit apart from the other album tracks – even though they are rather diverse themselves). Overall I would have to say that The Hollowing definitely show some good ideas on this CDR, which will no doubt be honed even further on future recordings. Also with what is becoming rather a trademark of Live Bait releases, this comes housed in a DVD package. Lastly, with artwork designed by Peter Shelton, for those who know why this name is rather infamous on the TUMORlist, will get a kick out of knowing he is still lurking somewhere out there! (Hint: and I quote from the album cover "*Wanted by the FBI – Peter Shelton.*")

House of Low Culture (USA) ***Submarine Immersion Techniques Vol. 1*** **CD 2000 Crowd Control Activities**

Well, this album by House of Low Culture is certainly winning hands down as one of the most surprising recent CDs that I have been sent, mainly as its primary instrument is an electric guitar (and thus less likely to be fit into *Spectrum*'s sphere of interest). While this might be true of most 'guitar' albums (read: rock, metal, etc.),here the stylistic slant of strange looping riffs, vague melodies, layered distortion, feedback and samples ensures it has that certain resonance that aligns it so well with a darker experimental style. As for the emotional atmosphere, I wonder if it is a mere coincidence that track two is entitled *Damnation of a/Dead Man*, and that segments of it remind me of the sparse yet depressive guitar musings that Neil Young provided as the soundtrack to Jim Jarmusch's similarly titled film *Dead Man*. (A later track '*C.F.T. (demo)* hammers this impression home more solidly, maintaining the same desolation evoked through the poetically told black and white film). On the other hand, *(Study for) in the Streamline*, has little if anything in common with guitar-generated tones, and alternatively opts for samples of a dialling modem, random clatter and cut-up soundscapes. *Another tragic one: hands sold by poachers*, arrives somewhat at middle ground, mixing elements of a depressive guitar tune and static-riddled backing that verges on a subdued power electronics/white noise type of sound. Track eight, *Submarine Immersion Techniques III*. it does exactly that by sinking into a crushing mass of mostly non-musical distortion and slow noise induced riffs. The final track, *It Approaches*, is almost entirely a death ambient piece of crushing bass and wavering tones, rising and falling in intensity throughout. While a slight deviation from what CCA have previously released (but then again they have released items ranging from tribal ambient to power electronics), this is a fabulous album that has been brought to my attention as one of a number of new groups working in with experimental guitar sounds.

Ikon (Aus) *The Shallow Sea* CDS 2000 Nile
Acting as a taster to the upcoming album *On the Edge of Forever* (although credited here as a 'single version'), the title track is a magnificent slab of partially acoustic up-tempo gothic rock. A bass guitar melodically (and prominently) plods alongside the constant kit drumming, while the acoustic guitar strums the main tune - the accompanying electric guitar acts as a soaring and embellishing element rather than as the main focus. A couple of down-vibed interludes only add to the wide screen vision, with the accompanying vocals ranging from understated singing to partial whispers. The second track, *As I Recall*, takes a much more prominent programmed focus in the percussive department, yet still remains quite up-tempo as both keyboards and a drawn-out electric guitar hold the tune. The middle ground of this five track release consists of a demo version of *Closing In*, while the last two tracks encompass two live songs recorded at the May 2000 Death In June/Ikon show (reviewed last issue). As mentioned in that review, an up-tempo version of DI6's *Fall Apart* was showcased, with the stunning results captured here. Not simply being a cover, this is Ikon taking the essence of the said track and shaping it to be very much true of their sound. Encompassing a sincere attitude and lacking that certain pretentiousness present in many gothic groups, I have found this to be a very pleasing introduction to the works of Ikon, despite their having been around MUCH longer than *Spectrum*.

Inade (Ger) *Alderbaran* CD 2001 Cold Spring
No, no ... before you flip out this is not a new Inade release, rather a repressing of the now much sought-after first Inade CD (and at the time of writing the ONLY true full length Inade CD if you do not count the *Burning Flesh* tape re-release). Birthed originally in a double fold out digipack cover, this version is housed in a standard jewel case and with minor alterations to the font and print colour, but with the cover still doing justice to the mystical and cosmic radiance of the original artwork. While I am generally loath to undertake full in depth reviews of re-releases (unless they have changed drastically in some way or I didn't hear them first time around) I would rather use this as an announcement to people who are yet to obtain an item. Anyway to keep it brief I can't recommend this highly enough, thus if I am are going to go all the way in compliments I may as well do this properly! Now to have it said, given the milestone that Lustmord's *Heresy* represented in dark ambient way back when, this album has taken the basis of that sound to create just as much of a landmark release in the esoteric heavy electronics sound (how is that for big words?!...Yes, you better believe me when I say that this is that good!). If you missed this first time round, be warned! I'm sure the re-press won't be hanging around long and should have you salivating for the highly anticipated second album *The Crackling of the Anonymous*.

Institut (Swe) *A Great Day To Get Even* CD 2000 Cold Meat Industry
Sweden's Institut hail from the punishing, repetitive percussion and tortured machinery loops school of rhythmic noise, heavier on the noise as it is dispersed in greasy peals of harrowing feedback and caustic screech. The rippling mayhem of *Landing Target* flutters like the tail of an irritated rattlesnake, like an agitated helicopter prowling the skyways for victims to slaughter with the swish of its blade. *On The Highway Picking Up Speed* adds some clipped and flayed dynamics to the mix, as bursts of grind and shriek noise perforate the metallic flesh of the white noise asphalt; the result is a wild ride along steaming byways littered with metallic carcasses and bleached bones. The piston pummel rhythm of *Black On Red*, sounding like the looped splat of brains on concrete, pounds down an iron door, unleashing some exceedingly harsh vocals. The rhythm is almost mesmerizing, monotonously insistent. Twelve tracks in all, a quality punch and squeal affair. -JC Smith

IRM (Swe) *Oedipus Dethroned* CD 2000 Cold Meat Industry
Oedipus Dethroned is a staunch declaration of hatred ignited by the frailties of self, of being human, the weakness of the flesh, and the inherent misconception (or slippery truth) that all men are created in God's image. What good is image without substance, if it is nothing more than borrowed; what good is image when it is wrapped around a scarred soul and made to suffer in ways that God would never have conceived (unless He is a malevolent being...). The blistering screech, stomp and blood pumping, grind and squeal power electronics presented here is evidence of the torment of existence. The thematic thread sutured into the sonic body is self-revelation through self-mutilation, corruption, defilement ... only achieving stasis through death. (Death of self = Death of God, the ultimate 'father.') A scalpel plunges into virgin flesh during *The Celebration of the Untouched Skin*, the ultra-processed vocals spewing, *"This is beauty,"* as it seeks release through the 'ultimate abortion'. All of this amidst sludgy electronics caked in choral samples, the lie initiated via the inclusion of faux spiritual elements among the increasingly riotous noise. *The Disease* invites infection as feedback injects the heaving clamour and pummel of brutal cataclysmic noise to *"My utopia-the plague"* (conveyed through a seemingly bloodied larynx!). *The Stage-Surgeon* is Christ, the shaper of clay (man), a deceptive manipulation, the only safety achieved in the grips of Death: *"Death and God: the total annihilation"*. The thematic focus throughout this amazing disc is honed to crystal clarity, amidst the roiling sonic turbulence. *Oedipus Dethroned* is one of the most provocative presentations within the genre of power electronics that I have yet to hear. Mandatory is an understatement! -JC Smith

Isomer (Aus) *the lotus eaters* MC 2001 self-released
For regular readers, some might remember a review of a tape by David Tonkin featured in the last issue. Well David returns with this tape now under the Isomer banner to explore some further eclectic ambient/industrial experimentations. With an introductory sample philosophising on moral decadence and the media, *Baby Fuck Me Please* is a concoction of angry muffled death industrial textures that drop to the lower end of the sound spectrum. Voices are barely detectable in all the chaos as the layers are pushed to the extreme with cyclone-like intensity. Followed by *Dispossessed*, this track builds on a lo-fi subdued rumbling drone, overlaying scattered fractured electronic snippets of sound as it meanders along. *Package Deal Option* uses a more direct approach with a ridged and echoed percussive structure that begs a comparison to rhythmic industrial sound of the like of Morgenstern. However with a partly improvised personality it is not unlike having your neurons misfiring during an alcohol-induced hangover. I would have to say that the title track is clearly the best piece on here with its sturdy death ambient approach. With a lo-fi drone constituting the backbone, a repeating structure of sparse clatter is overlaid along with a bizarre repeated sample (a woman stating softly *"don't steal ... you'll feel so much better"*). Further melding in sparse yet foreboding keyboards and sampled choir, it build an intense atmosphere akin to Megaptera, and highlights how good this project is when all the elements hit their mark. Diving headlong into increasingly intense territories the lengthy track is an attention grabber for its entirety. On the other hand *Compressed Formula* forges a quirky experimental sound constructed with an assortment of blips, pulses and bass-heavy elements, that sits somewhere between a digital and industrial aesthetic in its partly structured, partly scattered construction. Final track *Call to Arms* gives the rhythmic industrial sound another bash with its fast-paced pounding arrangement. Once the initial structure is forged, it is gradually morphed and tweaked while constantly introducing new elements and in the process amplifying the intensity. Maybe this tape is not as clearly focused as the debut tape, however it demonstrates some positive ideas and some clear highlights, thus should be viewed in the context of a project forging its own niche.

Karceral Flesh (Fra) *Bienvenue* 10" EP 2000 Athanor
After being introduced to the group via their rather anthemic organ tune/martial percussive track on the VAWS *Thorak* compilation, this vinyl has come as a slight surprise mainly due to its inclusion of tracks with a more rhythmic percussive than specifically martial orientation. Also, as there was some indication that Les Joyaux de La Princesse was partially involved in this release (though the cover gives no specific details), if anything I expected that it might have been on the opening track, *Tout Est Nuit*, with its slow synthetic yet slightly orchestral tones. An extremely short piece of deep storm cloud drones, *L'Attente* quickly moves into the third track *Stutka Dance* which, after beginning quite atmospherically with air-raid-like drones and subdued static, evolves into a mid-paced/up-tempo forceful percussive track. The first track of Side Two is *Agitation*, another mid-paced rhythmic piece that is actually quite complex - its clanging metallic layers result in a catchy composition. *Defile 2* hints at the orchestral/martial grandeur of Karceral Flesh's contribution to the *Thorak* compilation (*Defile 1*) and is the best track here with massive stately pounding percussion and brass and organ-oriented tune. The final track, *Souvenir*, is a deeply muffled soundscape of shifting tones and barely discernable orchestral sounds that rise in prominence (proportionate to the time elapsed) only to surge into a complete firestorm of orchestral industrial noise (this piece easily claims second place to the best track). A grey vinyl and immaculately presented slip cover presents the visual side of a release that, while slightly different to what I was expecting, is by no means a disappointment.

Karnnos (Por) *Deatharch Crann* CD 2000 Cynfeirdd
Alongside Lady Morphia, Karnnos' debut CD is one of the best discoveries within the apocalyptic folk scene. And likewise with Cynfeirdd, they are a relatively new label that have consistently come up with quality releases, making it worth your while to keep a keen eye on them - particularly if neo-folk/neo-classical works are of interest to you. As for Karnnos, they hail from Portugal and have a very distinctive, shimmering and warm enveloping aura to their folk drive soundscapes and acoustic odes. Instrumentation of the three member group ranges from electric and acoustic guitars, mandolin, flute, bagpipes, viola and synthesizers (to name but a few), expertly interwoven irrespective of whether the track is ambient in nature or traditionally song styled. *As life is carved on wood and blood* builds a song framework of acoustic guitar, flute and viola that transports the listener's mind far from the mundane aspects of life to revel in visions of European mysticism. *The streams of longing, solitude and the one-eyed death* takes on the more meandering soundscape style, highlighting the differentiating elements of song and soundscape collated on this album. Also, the vocal range used, from the groups native tongue through to English (even when the latter is used), is a particularly heavy accent, and builds another distinctive sound into the compositions. On the fifth track (the acoustic driven *A tree of union under the lost divided, lost spirits*) I cannot even begin to fathom words to describe its haunting depressive beauty - other than having such a profound effect, making you feel as if your own soul is collapsing. Late album track *Loki, Wizard of Lies* is a darkly aggressive looped composition with a vocal mantra repeating the title that gradually leads into another fantastic ode, *Land of Stags* which mixes drawn out classical synth lines and martial snare percussion with resonating acoustic riffing. The final track *In the pale, pale night* starts as a dark looping collage and evolves into a depressive guitar-driven tune – hence being a track that perfectly covers the two aspects of Karnnos' sound. As for the cover, it is presented as a gatefold card sleeve with an additional booklet, and superbly presents the visuals for the music on offer. In passing I simply cannot recommend this album highly enough.

Kettle (Aus) *With my left eye closed* 3"CDR 2000 label:KETTLE
Packaged between two tin plates, the concept of this CD revolves around the aural interpretation of a medical condition suffered in the right eye of the artist (i.e. closing the good left eye to perceive the world through the sight of the deteriorating right eye). With three tracks and just short of 20 minutes, the compositions blend one into the next as fractal sonics of clinical static and electronic-induced noises and drones. Mostly in the mid-ranged tonal velocity, things are rough around the edges, but the sounds never reach a high-end pain-inducing pitch. Sections of sounds and noise align themselves and bridge one into the next, holding an aesthetic of new sound art/minimalist noise experimentation with a convincing dark and slightly menacing edge. I guess this material has a comparison that could definitely be made to the new direction of Hazard, which only further highlights the quality of this. The format of the label releasing 3" CDRs is also a way to present short snippets of the works of Australian sound artists in intriguing packaging.

KK Null (Jap)/Moz (USA) *a split release* CD 2000 Crionic Mind
Having witnessed a couple of KK Null performances in previous years, I was expecting massive doses of (post) guitar manipulated distortion, yet surprisingly Mr. Null has taken a whole new approach to his experimental noise using samplers/sequencers to fuse a technoid aspect within his wall'o'noise approach. While the experimental noise distortion elements are still clearly the main focus on the first track *KXYL*, it is the sampler/sequencer that weaves a clear rhythm and structure into the composition - a sizzling molten mass of mid-level distortion merged with cathartic rhythmic elements creating a modern yet tribal aspect to its repetitive aura. With a title only a Japanese artist could come up with, *Giant walking in a tunnel of libido* initiates a mid-paced beat sequence that is progressively tweaked into a slow churning whirlpool of static and noise, while the disorientating fast-paced speaker fading and distortion attack of *Psychopathic Surfing* is more flowing freeform experimentation. Leading onwards *Hypnocide* contains an almost psychedelic (yet tribal-esque) percussive sound (which is great I might add!) The final KK Null piece *quid pro quo* is a short seizure-inducing attack on the senses! Certainly different to what KK Null is typically known for, it is however great to see further progression and experimentation from such a renowned noise artist. In clear opposition to KK Null, MOZ opts for ultra-dense and bleak soundscapes of death ambient intention – the first track *release value* has a low bass-oriented rumble that is shattered with a stunning (yet fleetingly used) static pulse, being the perfect aural interpretation of the title. *Wage Slave* ups the ante a notch or two, building structure with aggressive guttural loops, mid- to high-end electronic feedback and gruesomely distorted vocals. Barren glacial electronics characterise *degradation of divinity* - ever ebbing and flowing with bleak tension (this is fantastic yet far too short at under

four minutes). *Imperialism*, on the other hand, is an attacking mass of structured pulse, furnace-blasting distortion and firestorm textures, being clearly inspired by the negative connotations of its name. One can again visualise the aura of a track embodying the title *Funeral Procession*, with its solemn keyboard melody and the slow gait of the programmed structure. Final track for both MOZ and the CD is *Asylum*. A fantastically echoed resonance via metallic scrapings, slow chime/gong and scarce structure, all blended into a cavernous and unnerving result (fleetingly bringing to mind selected works of Robert Rich). For anyone unaware of Crionic Mind, they are really starting to solidify their presence as a premier underground label, with such a split release only hammering home such a perception.

Kraang (Aus) *URO: 1981-83* LP 2000 Tesco Organisation
This Kraang LP showcases some selected experimental noise compositions that soloist John Murphy recorded during the early 80's under the original name Kraang Music. To offer a personal perspective, these recordings are nearly 20 years old, which means that I was only five when these noise experimentations were first evoked! Anyway, by virtue of the period during which these pieces were recorded, the LP inevitably encompasses an old school style; however, given the amount of old school industrial noise and power electronics currently being produced, there is certainly a clear niche for such an album in the current market, despite its status as a historic document. With four lengthy compositions being showcased (two per LP side) and while encompassing improvised industrial noise, clear direction and flow within the pieces are specifically evident. Frequenting neither piercing high-end static nor guttural bass tones, the noise squeals, looped feedback and chaotic clatter are all framed in a mid-ranged pace and tonal velocity. Segments of noise are approached and established before being manipulated, tweaked and basically destroyed to form the basis of the next segment that in turn suffers a similar fate. Fleeting voices are detected on *Man is Meat*, yet appear to be sampled in that they are not generally discernable. In its entirety, the LP generally flows together as one mass of experimental noise despite being divided into four sections or 'tracks', but having said that, the final track *URO* is the most atmospheric one on offer, striding along with muffled hurricane intensity alongside metallic scrapings and random textured noise (...very grand indeed!). As for the cover, this is particularly stunning due to the reflective card stock used, all in all lending a very 'Tesco' look to the LP's presentation. While John Murphy is known for his workings with Lustmord during the early days through to Death In June more recently (and plenty more in between), it would appear that he has never diverted from some sort of involvement in the post-industrial underground. This LP really serves as a celebratory document to this dedication, to be likewise viewed in conjunction with his new projects, Knifeladder and Shining Vril, both of which are currently raising their profile.

Lady Morphia (Eng) *Recitals to Renewal* CD 2000 Surgery
Lady Morphia would seem to be a relative newcomer to the English neo-classical/apocalyptic folk scene, with this being the first official album after a few self-released tapes and CD's. Taking cues from the likes of Death In June and Der Blutharsch, Lady Morphia have come up with a fantastically strong album that reflects their influences while generating its own distinctive aura. *Prologue: Hope and Despair* is the first track that utilises a sampled Polish knighthood song, prior to the introduction of slow martial beats and neo-classical orchestrations that mark the second half of the track. *Sun Spirits* is a track of pure joy with an acoustic-driven tune, classical backings, church bells, sporadic tympani/snare drumming and clean sung vocals of defiant quality. The xylophone accompaniment to the acoustic strains of *Heimat* are nothing short of magic - as are the clarinet and oboe elements that follow the main guitar and vocal tune. Some fantastic dark ambient atmospheres can be found on *The Mirror of Shame*, containing shimmering textures, disembodied vocals, chimes, water samples (and the like), expertly crafted into a deep atmospheric piece. *Wings of Survival* is an urgent acoustic guitar ode, using sparing elements of piano, tympani and assorted percussion to build its aura, while the following track *Beauty Decay* interestingly contains a heavy eastern influence over the slow tune/soundscape. Another celebratory acoustic ode is found in *Brothers*, expertly mixing oboe and acoustic guitars with heavy and stately percussion, that overall holds an amazingly distant and forlorn atmosphere. *Palingenesis* is one more dark ambient piece - offering a ticking clock, distant snare drumming and whispered vocals (among other elements), while Ernst Jünger recites from one of his writings. And it is this element of Ernst Jünger alone that solidifies one of the heavy influences present on this album, to the point where it has been specifically dedicated to his memory. The slower and more reflective *Parhelia at the Precipice*, is yet another magical acoustic-driven track that leads the album towards the final track *Epilogue: Spero-de-spero* – a beautiful yet forlorn piano melody sweeping the album into morose oblivion. For Lady Morphia's first widely available release, they have certainly produced an album of stunning diversity, with all elements reflecting a heavy European flavour. Falling mere millimetres short of being an instant classic, this is as close as one could come and only speaks volumes of what to expect from Lady Morphia in future.

LAW (USA) *Our Life Through Your Death* CD 2000 Triumvirate
Our Life Through Your Death is an exhilarating, sometimes jarring, always intense, exhibition of embryonic salvos (it was constructed in 1996) launched by one of the most fascinating and original bands within the realm of experimental/noise/ambient music (it touches every base, and more), LAW. As orchestrated by Triumvirate co-founder, Mitchell Altum, LAW weld together a compelling blend of uncommon electronics, harsh machinery-infused ideals, and disjointed rhythmic deployments, creating a foundation of immense sonic strength upon which the human element (guitar, bass, sparse vocals) brings it all to life. The music is raw and unfettered, cluttered, but with imaginative focus, less refined than later material, not as hard-wired, more hot-wired and coarse, like being caressed by talons of steel wool. The highlights are abundant and ever shifting, each listen bringing different revelations, but here are a few that continually stand out. The hornet's stinging whine that pierces multiple layers of shackled, murky noise during *Vision Flashes to Red*, finally sinking into a miasma of unnerving ambience upon which a garbled voice declares, *"Our life through your death"*, appropriately setting the disc in motion. Wading through the wastelands of lost souls, an ambience taut with torment and haunting despair resides at the core of *Abrasion*, an ambience annihilated by the corrosive, caustic howl of guitar and whiplash reverb percussion that flutters in spasmodic retaliation. It is a resurrection by chaos, the lost souls battered into oblivion by Pandemonium's gnarled fists. Brilliant! The mouth of sinister tongues that licks the marrow from within the broken bones of *Unseen Existence*, an ambience of constantly shifting turbulence; tongues like juggled razors, scraping and fluttering, procuring sustenance... (and a warped, backwards looped classical passage...?!). The brittle acoustic guitar intro to *Betrayal of the Flesh*, that ends up being devoured by soldier-stomping percussion and choppy, fragmented guitar, while an undercurrent of molten tides recedes, leaving a blasted terrain upon which Mitchell drenches the listener in roaring feedback so visceral it threatens to draw blood. The fidgety cymbals and drums of *100 Degrees*, plowing a path for a yawning guitar that ferociously prowls around the mechanized drive inherent to this track, a caustic, harrowing evisceration of controlled, groaning noise. There is much more here, enthralling and strange and unlike anything else you have ever heard. Period! -JC Smith

Les Joyaux de la Princesse (Fra) *Croix de Bois/Croix de Feu* 10" EP Les Joyaux de la Princesse
How could one approach writing a review of this release without touching on the packaging first? This 10" EP was sold in 900 copies by subscription only, and upon payment one received an official subscription ticket. Not all that stunning, you say? But when considering that this subscription ticket it is packaged in a grey card A2-sized folder and over wrap ribbon (in the colours of the French flag, of course) that holds in place a two-track clear flexi-disc vinyl, the special aura of this release begins to be unfold. Regarding the official release itself, the red vinyl is housed in an oversized 10"x14" booklet cover (also in blue, white, and red, with gold twine along the spine), with numerous pages of French text and 1920's images relating to the theme of the release (which evidently relates to French nationalism and a mystic organisation operating around the time). While there might be constant argument for and against such high priced limited edition releases, when the finished product comes together as this one does, I am happy to fork over a bit more money for such special packaging. And what of the music? The title track side of the 10" commences with deep orchestral keyboard-layered drones that gradually build and overlap along with distant sweeping choir voices that add a human element. The intensity is later increased via a diversion away from the opening segment with more prominent orchestral melody mixed with war-like bombing backing noise. Commencing the second discernable track (still on side One), are sampled French speeches set against a deeper orchestral melody (although snare percussion can also be detected). A sampled and partly looped music hall song is used to mark the commencement of the third piece, and although this is again built around French speech samples and orchestral keyboards, it creates a much more doom-laden and apocalyptic atmosphere. With the first side really driving home an overall morose and forlorn orchestral atmosphere, the second side of the 10" comes as a partial surprise given the use of quite fierce static to fire blast the keyboards and yet again more era speech and crowd samples (concluding with another music hall song that is sampled in its entirety, without alteration). The following segments again fall back to the presentation of the classic Les Joyaux de la Princesse sound (forlorn and distant sounding orchestral soundscapes); however, with the looped samples of brass instrumentation it really lifts the atmosphere to the next level. The flexi-disc contains two short pieces - one being a slow evolving keyboard-based tune that is more classical then orchestral, the other more of a noisescape with radio voices, war-like atmospheres and distant drones. Both are nice bookend pieces to the main 10". Overall this might not be as epic as the previous *Exposition Internationale: Paris 1937* 7" (but it still comes quite close); it is more along the lines of the *Aux Petits Enfants de France* CD. Given that this is most likely already sold out, I shudder to think what price this will fetch on resale. A word of advice – be diligent in ordering such items up front to avoid paying through the nose for it later from unscrupulous collectors.

LS-TTL (USA) *el-es-tee-tee-el* CD 2000 Dragon Flight Recordings
The first release by Brian Coffee's LS-TTL is a fascinating, slow-moving descent into the mechanized Hell of a splintered mind (the booklet claims this is *"The soundtrack for the untitled film of the mind."*), sonicscapes of suffocating darkness that subtly morph from forlorn and foreboding, to agitated and tortured. Where lots of dark sonicscapes are moist, signifying a conviction to something living, or at least once alive, LS-TTL is very dry (not cold, but dry...),

SPECTRE
audio fetish

soon :

Iszoloscope
Coagulating Wreckage
debut CD album

Bad Sector & Where
Olhon - Veiovis CD
3rd album in the
Nautilus series

Spectre
P.O.Box 88
2020 Antwerpen 2
Belgium
www.spectre.be

devoid of human allegiance ... and yet, human elements continually peek through. The songs stretch, peeling off layers of the flaking metallic epidermis from the body of sounds; sounds emanating from a desolate outpost, the machinery whine and engine clatter toiling in solitude, awaiting ... what? (Or is that the mind cracking?) Metallic insects scramble about, antennae twitching in static communication, above a sombre synth drone during the opening *Drktual*. During the next few tracks, the LS-TTL manifest is aligned, amidst subtle yet distinctive tonal shifts and looped choppy noises, creating a foundation of unease. The atmosphere of *Eraf* is blanketed in harsh winds that erode any connection between humanity and existence, while nauseating undertones (the impatient struggle for something more - a sense of incapacitation is present) are tattooed with grinding gears and almost human screams ... almost... (Listen to how the human element persists, even out here in the furthest reaches of desolation.) Humans (?) moan like cows being led to the slaughterhouse during *Tro*, amidst murmuring synths and clattering noises (weary gears grinding forth, a conveyor belt procession) and much spattered blood, all bound together by a thread of desperation. Eerie and discomfiting. Low rumbling bass tones (like dead bodies being dragged about) carve rituals into the ebony hide of orc, before radiant tones scour the senses as *Calmix* Commences. Through echoed tides of windswept chaos, ricochet syringes of noises are injected into the flesh, a climax of hallucinatory disorientation; everything sounds like it would send a Geiger counter into the red, adorned in radiation and corrosive reverb. All simmers uncomfortably on *Amesch*, agitation at bay, crackling and swirling but, somehow, contained. (And then there is the untitled bonus track, which veers into alien territory - the ambience suggests unearthly allegiances - hinting of things to come for LS-TTL?) A fascinating, well-thought-out trek through the barren hub of isolation within the mind, and the vast wilderness of uncertainty and despair (and madness, and horror) that resides within one's self. -JC Smith

The Machine in the Garden (USA) *Out of the Mist* CD 2001 Middle Pillar
The third album for this US project (and second album on Middle Pillar), sees a slight alteration in musical focus, being more heavily reliant on martial/orchestral themes and moving away from the darkwave/electronic sound of the last album (although structural influence from these sectors are still evident). As for the opening track *Fates and Furies*, it is a rather grand, pompous, instrumental marching tune, solidifying the perception of new territory being explored. The acoustic strains of *Valentine* bring to mind a classic apocalyptic folk sound, yet the sometimes delicate, sometimes soaring vocals of Ms. Summer Bowman add the necessary flair of individually. The following track *Oh Dear*, constructed purely around multi-layered female vocals, is very reminiscent of Karri Rueslatten's solo work and highlights the vocal abilities of Ms. Bowman to carry a complete song using only her voice. *Failure* is the first (and only) track to see the vocals of Roger France used, presented as an accompaniment to a sweeping beat and guitar oriented ethereal/electronic piece. More fantastic folk-oriented acoustic guitars are displayed on *Everything She Is* – here the mood presented creates a bitter-sweet composition. Slow shifting orchestral melodies on *Wasted Time* hold a brooding focus, and while the music seemingly wants to break its invisible tethers, this never actually eventuates, thus remaining subdued throughout. *Never Again* contains fragile guitar musings, being further embellished by female vocals and grand piano/synth tunes, which are partly carried through to the more commanding strains of the final track *Fade* (the track being partly darkwave and partly orchestral results in a fantastically ominous piece to close the album). Basically I would have to say that with the altered orientation of musical approach, combined with the group's already clearly evident musical talent, this CD is clearly a positive progression from the previous album.

Maruta Kommand (Eng) *holocaust rites* CD 2000 Kokamph
Maruta Kommand is a relatively new entity rising out of the English scene, and via this release has also seen the birth of a new label (run by one of Maruta Kommand's members, Andi Penguin). The CD represents a debut for both project and label. As for the compositions of Maruta Kommand, they have generated an interesting blend of electro-industrial dancefloor-oriented musing and the harsher tones of a death industrial guise. While I will not shy away from the fact that I have a general distaste for the former style of music, when coagulated with the latter it has created a quite palatable cross-genre cocktail. After a short introductory segment, the rigid battle tank rhythms of *Executioner* storm into earshot with rough metallic percussion, assorted programmed noise, fleeting synth tune and morbidly distorted vocals. On an alternate tangent and being more electro than death industrial, *Mass Grave* is a fast-paced noisy programmed piece heavily reliant on slamming percussion and wavering synth textures that is certainly club-oriented in style. While a good track, it is the following piece *European Deathmarch* that is much more to my liking, containing striking dark undercurrents of noise, haunting synth textures and acerbic vocals, as the complete track gradually morphs towards slow crushing programmed percussion (that while ending up being quite prominent do not detract from the ashen atmosphere). The dialogue samples and orchestral melody introduction of *Cultural Suicide* converge with mid-paced programming, synth-generated noise and again the vocals with a fair whack of distortional bite - the rough texture to the sound production rounding everything out nice and harshly. Homage is duly paid to death industrial pioneer Roger Karmanik/Brighter Death Now on the track *Karmanik Jugend*, constructing a pyre of crunchy, often free-form distorted and grinding (former) synth textures, resulting in a piece that could have easily been lifted off BDN's *The Slaughterhouse* CD (and mind you this is meant as the greatest of compliments). With dredging noise and slow programming, *War on Life* has a fleeting comparison that could be made to Megaptera, yet the haunting female vocals and violin accompaniment really sets this track on an individual high and is clearly one of the best on the album. *Hanging on the Old Barbed Wire* being the last true album track (not including two bonus electro-industrial remix tracks – one by Melek-Tha) is a scarred landscape of barren metallic reverberations and spare snare hits constantly increasing intensity over the seven minutes, again using female vocalisations to great effect. In passing, for a debut CD Maruta Kommand have certainly created a mature and diverse album that clearly has cross-genre appeal.

Daniel Menche (USA) *crawling towards the sun* MCD 2000 Soleilmoon Recordings
In recent years Daniel Menche might not have been quite as prolific when compared to the number of items released in the early to mid 90's, nonetheless here we have a new snippet of Mr. Menche's current experimental activities. As always the visual side of this is superb, with the artwork on the disc acting as the main focus. Housed within a slimline jewel case, the CD image encompasses a rather bleak painting of the sun created by Eric Stotik (who has been responsible for artwork on earlier Menche CDs). From artwork to title, Daniel Menche has always had a knack of conjuring up fantastic titles to accompany his soundscapes, with this outing being no exception. Essentially *crawling towards the sun* forms a single track at just a touch over 20 minutes, within which the subtleties and complexities of copious layers of shifting noise are amassed – and, as the title suggests, it is a slow-moving piece overall. Sonic textures churn at the deeper end of the sound scale giving off a searing cosmic resonance via a shimmering sound aesthetic. Cyclically the track builds intensity as the varying elements shift in and out of alignment yet remain as drawn-out drones throughout. At its loudest, the track is still pretty subdued, using not volume to enhance the track, but rather opting for increasing the mid-range tonal layers to evoke sonic intensity. It is as a whole a less organic piece than previous recordings. Could it be that Mr. Menche is leaving behind his earthbound sonic experimentations to explore the sonic intensity of the cosmos? Either way I am happy to blindly follow, using only the experimental sounds of Mr. Menche to lead the way.

Mnortham (USA) *Breathing Towers* MCD 2000 Dorobo Limited Editions
Taking a somewhat academic approach to experimental soundworks, this disc is much like the experimental wire music that Alan Lamb has explored, incidentally also released on Dorobo. With one track at 21 minutes this is, as the cover states, a *"stereo recording inside two hollow steel towers with wind blowing across the open bases"*. While not as broad in scope as Alan Lamb's recordings of telegraph wires, there is still a very similar resonance in the sounds recorded. While there would also appear to be less outward movement to the piece when compared to the Alan Lamb recordings (obviously wires are more susceptible to various external forces than a solid steel structure), the limited movement of the piece creates another comparison to the slow evolution of Thomas Köner's minimalist and isolationist soundworks (evident primarily in the rumbling depths of the sounds captured, that sit at the very low end of the soundwave spectrum). Both metallic shimmering sounds and more organic wind-type textures can be discerned within the framework, amongst other cavernous bass sound layers that all add up to creating an archaic, otherworldly vibe. The sounds at various points pick up and become more outwardly aggressive, seemingly attuned to weather patterns at the time of the recording, thus generating visions in the mind's eye of numerous storm fronts sweeping across the landscape. In regard to the scope of the sound, it is a fine release that involved nothing more than someone recording and mastering it, but that in the process has captured a soundscape that contains elements that would appeal to fans of experimental soundworks, minimalist drone music or isolationist ambience.

Morgenstern (Ger) *Cold* CD 2001 Ant-Zen
This new CD from Andrea Börner has expanded on the death industrial sonics of 1999's *Zyklen* album into a more diverse palate of tribalised power noise/power electronics, yet with a clear Morgenstern twist. While this might not be entirely evident from the bone-grinding textures and wailing atmospheres of the opening title track, it is on the second track *horny being* that things really take off. Strained keyboard textures tensely build until the incorporation of rhythmic pulsations that threaten to implode the speakers due to their bass heaviness. Crispy and highly strung, the composition continues to build an almightily intensity which is nothing short of sonic bliss. *Hypnotized*, built on a death industrial looped base, mixes in a power, noise and static beat structure to create a clanging dancefloor result (imagine older Imminent Starvation with a handful more distortion thrown in for good measure). The ridged typewriter beat of *Blow Away My Reason* works the main audible level, while a whole other world of low bass rumbling sounds sits low in the mix and builds occasionally with semi-melodious sound (a vocal sample also repeats the track's title throughout). Fast-paced power electronic looped feedback creates a rather catchy track on *Insight* and I'll be damned if the searing distortion drenched vocals are those of Andrea, as these are fierce enough to match any male vocal of the genre! *Interlude* is a quieter, more aquatic-sounding, affair with far off idling machines, surreal vocalisations and unnerving field recording sound textures, yet *Hinrichtung Durch Raum Und Zeit (re-edit)* reclaims the noisier distortion and looped based sound. A radio voice chatters incessantly while the sonic noise gains strength and momentum finally letting loose with a bass rhythm so damn heavy it coagulates into a barely discernable loop. Minimalist percussion can likewise be detected, building the track over its lengthy yet repetitive format. *Combat Zone* without doubt obliterates all offerings that precede it, with a pure sonic attack on the senses. Bass-heavy and static-driven, it builds to a point where a few pivotal sounds (at the higher end of the sound spectrum) swoop in at odd angles to wreak havoc on the eardrums. The vocals are also rather phenomenal - metallic and alien-like - never really rising out of the distortion hurricane. After such an attack, *Eye* is thankfully a quieter affair, being a rather beautiful and subdued tune complete with sampled choirs radiating in the background of the mix. Sounding akin to a rhinoceros tap dance, the beat is fractured and stilted including a number of piano plucked sounds that (if I am not mistaken) have been sampled from another Ant-Zen release - namely the CD by Passarani. Before you actually realise it, the beat section has taken over the composition completely and it is only a matter of time before it again veers off into percussive-driven, distortional noise territory. The last track of the 60 minute disc arrives in the form of *Over*. Framing itself with another track of looped death industrial proportions, it is both seething and brooding over its length, rounding out the track and album with some further samples of choir sounds. Overall this is certainly a more diverse release than *Zyklen*. Thus it will really depend if you can appreciate more structure and beat-oriented tracks within a broad death industrial styling, but for myself this presents no problem whatsoever given the sheer finesse by which these elements are intermixed into the Morgenstern sound.

Murderous Vison (USA) *suffocate...the final breath* CDR 2001 Twenty Sixth Circle
This project is the solo vision of Stephen Petrus, who is also known for his work in the duo In Death's Throes and for running Live Bait Recording Foundation. Here, Stephen offers up a coagulated cacophony of bass-laden atmospheres, with tracks appearing to have been culled from two prior releases and including a number of exclusive tracks. While given the collection format the flow might not be as focused as one would expect for an album proper, this does not prevent one from succumbing to the individual atmosphere of each piece. The opener *Book of Fears* could have ended up being quite grating, yet the sharpest sonic elements have been blunted by the production to give a thick wall of fluctuating noise and industrial drones. As each individual track plays out it gradually becomes evident that despite the atmospheres that each evokes, there is a common thread present throughout. In essence each track encompasses thick slabs of slow-moving sound that have a dense and slightly muffled sound production. While *Deathwretch* might have a greater windswept atmosphere, *Yersinia Pestis* has cavernous minimalist frame, *body count rises* a noisier improvised sound and *The Pomes Ov Urine* a non-musical bass pulse, the majority of the pieces rely on a common production theme. Regardless, the greatest diversion to be found is *Anthropophagy (Regurgitation)* in that this is a collaborative piece with Baal and features a rather prominent tribal beat/percussion element that creates an engrossing effect when sandwiched with the dense nature of the underlying sound. Lastly, with the cover stating that the recordings were *"Induced In Trance Like States"*, it is also a rather apt description for the overall atmosphere. This is an interesting listen, particularly if noise ambience in the vein of Gruntsplatter is your thing.

Nasopharyngeal (USA) *Endless* CD 2000 Crowd Control Activities
Endless is a very good title for this CD as this the feeling you get when listening to the one track, 74-minute odyssey. Back to basics old school electronica is what we have here, sounding mostly improvised in the way it is pushed in varying directions through the course of its journey. The programmed drum machine beats (of a mid-paced style) are almost a constant throughout, as the random bleeps, noises, and grinding/droning electronics do their thing. However these are not really beats that one can dance to; rather they act as both a bridging element and a focal point - in the flow of the sound they are just more elements for the composer to manipulate and twist as he sees fit. Likewise elements of the backing electronic layers seem to amass, sweep through the speakers then dissipate before periodically re-converging later (with hints of tunes occasionally arriving as lone keyboard notes, only adding to the hazy atmospheres created). The virtually endless stream of sounds collated on this CD are composed in a surprisingly engaging and coherent manner, despite this having ended up being quite a short review! And talk about surprising - between this and the House of Low Culture CD, CCA have once again come up with the goods, but with projects that are quite unlike anything they have previously released.

Necrophorus (Swe) *Gathering Composed Thoughts* CD 2000 Dragon Flight Recordings
For those wondering, this is not a new album, rather (as alluded to in the title) a compilation of earlier Necrophorus tracks, select re-workings of others, and two tracks from the limited 10" picture vinyl entitled *Yoga* (which was reviewed in full way back in Issue no.2). The two lengthy and meditative tracks entitled *Yoga – part 1* and *Yoga– part 2*, open the album. Although fleetingly infused with Middle Eastern melodies, the somewhat minimalist dark ambient styling of these tracks is akin to the most recent full-length Necrophorus album, *Drifting in Motion*. *Spiritchasher*, the third track, is one of the most recent compositions on this release, consisting of tonal shifts of sound, outbursts of semi-metallic clatter, and groans emanating from seemingly inhuman sources – all generating an unnerving aura. It has to be said that the reworking of *Sophysis*, (formerly on the first Necrophorus album) is nothing short of brilliant, slowly sweeping along over 10 minutes with depressive melodies, atmospheric tonal waves, gong chimes and even field recordings of singing birds. As the album progresses it becomes evident that the earlier recordings are also the most rigidly composed, much like the compositions of Peter Andersson's main project, Raison D'être. These earlier tracks usually work around a composition of layered keyboards and the sparse interplay of down-vibed melodies, sometimes with prominent tribal-esque percussion. As far as light deviation, *The Dormant Being* is quite neo-classical in construction and even operatic despite its lack of vocals (stranger still, this sounds as if it could fit perfectly as a keyboard intro to an album by any atmospheric black metal band, as is the case with the following track, *A Second Very Heavy Grief*). If I did not know otherwise, I would swear that the track *Soporific* was recorded at the same sessions for the self-titled Fata Morgana album that the infamous Mortiis had operating as a side project a few years back! At just a shade away from being cheesy (as was the case with Fata Morgana), this is admittedly quite a good number! To conclude the album, a better choice could not have been made with *In Mourning* that, rather than opting for a depressive air, presents a quite uplifting neo-classical and almost baroque piece including percussion that is just short of being mid-paced programming. While the flow of the album might at times feel a little disjointed, this is really only due to the fact that it was never planned to be an album proper, rather a release showcasing the progression of this project over time. As a collection of good individual tracks this is worth your attention if you have a fleeting interest in any of Peter Andersson's musical output.

No Festival of Light (Swe) *If god lived on earth, we would break his windows* CD 2000 Fluttering Dragon
The new opus for this premier anti-Christian project returns with a rather tongue-in-cheek album title, possibly representing a finger in the face of ultra-evil types. Low bass rumbles offset with looped vocal snippet repeating *"the greatest trick … didn't exist"* introduces the CD on *The Unexisting Trick*. Yet, as the album shifts forward it is evident that the clinical minimalist sound of the last CD (on Functional Organization) has been mixed up with earlier more suffocating dark ambient styling. The second track *7405926* starts by jumping between hypnotic minimalism and blasts of harsh static, yet things solidify creating dense dungeon-like atmospheres, deep groans and tribal percussive beats that come full circle to electronic noise manipulations. Distant flutes and bass-heavy percussive sounds shift *Onomaka Brush* into a quite rousing tribal guise, continuing in this fashion throughout, while also introducing some deathly-sounding foghorn blasts (possibly summoning the minions of blasphemous cherubs from the underworld!). Slightly symphonic in tone (due to the drawn out synth textures), *Day of Wrath* resembles a mixture of Raison D'être and Desiderii Marginis, particularly with the use of clanging metallic sounds and sampled choir chanting, and could easily have been culled from outtakes of either of the aforementioned groups (in other words a damn fine composition). Rather urgent percussion makes up the basis of *Deus Otiosus* with some sort of sampled voice (a ritual chant perhaps?) and other radio-type voices buried underneath. Midway through additional percussive sounds are introduced to embellish the tribalised aura, while static minimalism adds a diversion to the final passage prior to the percussion having one final spin. Encompassing a track of rough dark ambience, *Jigoku-Source of Eternal Joy* meanders along slowly with loosely-constructed loops and choppy percussion in a guise of darkly muffled production. To bring the album full circle the final track is an adaptation of the opening piece, but at the beginning the full vocal sample is heard but once (*"the greatest trick that devil ever pulled was convincing the world he did not exist"*). After this the vocal loop reverts to the shortened version over a partially ominous underlying drone and semi-melodious synth passage. Certainly this album is another fine product from the Swedish dark ambient/industrial underground, even if it has originated from one of the lesser-known groups.

Northaunt (Nor) *The Ominous Silence* CD 2000 Fluttering Dragon
After releasing *The Ominous Silence* as a self-produced CDR, Northaunt were signed to Polish record label Fluttering Dragon and re-released it (with bonus material). It also sounds like the album might have been re-mastered, as the music seems to have a little more crispness and clarity to their atmospheres. Mixing rain-drenched field recordings with synth-generated textures, *Might and Misanthropy* commences the proceedings, awash with sweeping bass tones, an understated piano tune, and a mournful violin passage that gives it a very dark ambient/neo-classical hybrid feel. At close to 13 minutes, things meander along slowly, veering off on a couple of darker, more subdued tangents, including an acoustic guitar interlude, a section of folk-oriented flute and tortured vocal shrieks akin to what is found in black metal. The track *Northaunt* rumbles on in a cavernous guise with shifting sound treatments buried in the mix, later with harsh whispers and a barely accentuated piano tune. More field recordings and an industrial noise pulse make up the backing of *Der Bor En Frost Her Inne*, while an acoustic tune forms the main musical counterpart. Gradually things take a darker turn (by that I mean 'good'!) with dark factory clatter and a sustained (synth-produced) string movement. *De Sorte Traer* again utilises the acoustic guitar amongst an intricately textured sound backing and pained spoken vocals reciting a passage in the project's native tongue. *Running out of time* reminds me somewhat of early Raison D'être with sweeping layers, chant-like drones and church bells; however, the track remains distinctive with multiple samples of ticking clocks and a lone voice somewhat desperately stating the track's title. On first hearing *In Rain* the piano tune appeared a little out of time, but on subsequent listens the off-kilter playing only enhances its charm. *And I Fade Away* is a little more experimental than the previous tracks with its mid-paced keyboard tune set amongst dungeon-like clatter, dripping water and far-off noises (attention is held in the fore with some spoken vocals). One of the bonus tracks, *Pain is Better*, extends the atmosphere of the CD perfectly with its darkly composed acoustic guitars and piano accompaniment. Field recording textures and spoken vocals flesh out the musical skeleton, likewise remaining through the middle minimalist section that includes some fantastically haunting vocal wailing from former Aghast member Nacht (the vocals sounding as if they are emanating from a far-off cavernous depth). *Ode* is another newer track (and likewise the final musical piece) that operates in a dark ambient guise of sparse ominous rumblings, extended drones and again some great vocal contributions from Nacht, to create a quite unnerving atmosphere. The CD has an enhanced feature that incorporates a rather bleak video of a *Funeral Inside* (another bonus track). The music of the video is yet another pearl of a song, encompassing an ultra-depressing atmosphere evoked through acoustic guitar, piano and backing field recordings (along with the use of a number of dialogue samples). As for the video, it uses a series of black and white images (illustrating the themes of the track's title) that have been merged into a RealMedia file slideshow; however, via the use of a zoom and pan feature within the images it creates the perception of film (and is certainly well done overall).

Basically the overall aura of this release quite reminds me of Ildfrost's *Natanel* CD, although this is somewhat less composed with a larger variety of sound sources. What I guess I am getting at is that a comparison can be made to the overall dark atmosphere and morose classical feel of the stated item. The atmospheres presented definitely show clarity of ideas and I think the use of natural field recordings as a backdrop really enhances the depth of sound. Piano movements, string sections and acoustic guitars are used sparingly, and only enhance the atmosphere at the appropriate times. A CD definitely worth checking out and a group I will certainly be keeping an eye on with future releases.

Nový Svĕt (Aut) *Cuori Dipetrolio* CD 2000 Hau Ruk
The beyond bizarre Austrian project Nový Svĕt are back with their second full length CD; however here things seem a touch more subdued, and less focussed on the sounds of a drunken accordion player that figured prominently on the first disc. A slower conglomeration of tuneful sampled loops often make up the framework of the tracks. This is the case with track two, *Punished with Longing*, a relatively straightforward orchestral/martial piece that nevertheless bears the trademark vocals of the Nový Svĕt sound (the same goes for *Utopia*, with its ritual sounding hypnotic loops and low, crooning male vocals). The acoustic guitar loops on *Traicion* are a nice touch in amongst a slow ritual-type beat (and again the morose vocals), while *Un Canto Sobre El Amor* is hands down the most twisted track of the album. This can really only be described as Austrian folk reggae, but it's still highly listenable and very enjoyable. *Sin Fin* contains a dredging bass loop, creating a slight death industrial sound that is only enhanced with scraping textures, while the vocals remain a low whisper – all in all representing a pleasing shift in focus. The sluggish double bass tune and infrequently plucked guitar morph into their own loops on *Linea Alba* before branching out on yet another tangent and evoking in the process an immaculate late night drug-hazed vibe. Clocking in at over 22 minutes, the last track is a miasma of ritual beats, loops, scattered sound, vocals, etc., that lasts for around four minutes before lapsing for 16 minutes into a comatose silence, only to reappear to conclude the album with a quirky-type folk/lounge track that is more reminiscent of the first CD. Without a doubt this is Nový Svĕt through and through, but on this second album they have produced something that might just be more palatable for average underground listeners who are not regular frequenters of bizarre song-styled albums.

Nový Svĕt (Aut) *Aspiral III* 10" EP 2000 White Label
Nový Svĕt (the group of the moment for me) return with another release, with the musical direction on this recording having been directed by an old school industrial loop aesthetic and mixed with a large dose of the group's quirkiness. A slow musing piece, the opening track *Origen* is built on a slow industrial looped beat and barely discernable melody, with the male vocals carrying the tune in a lamenting style. The rather rough looping aesthetic plays through to the following piece *Re Delle Cose*, but with the use of a shrill violin loop, clanging percussion, and treated vocals it creates a fantastically disorientating miasma of sound. Third track *Panika* builds various loops of horn instruments to a groggy sway over a solid base of grinding elements and sampled vocal loops to generate this increased industrial aspect to the Nový Svĕt sound. *Rituale* has a fantastic aura of echoed atmospherics that acts as the foundation to mid-paced looped strings, bass guitar tune and percussion, including the most chaotic and upfront vocals I have heard from the group. With loops falling in and out of sync, all adding to the bizarreness that Nový Svĕt are able to pull together for their unique style. Side B caused me a bit of frustration prior to realising that the grooves have been cut from the inside edge out. However, maybe I should have taken notice of the fact that the spirals printed on the labels of opposing vinyl sides already seemed to indicate this (one other thing I did however note was that the word 'dogstar' is etched into side A, while 'godstar' is etched into side B. Make of this what you will!) Here only one lengthy track is presented (*Noyol Guimati*), opting for a rather bland cyclic and tribal piece of slow percussion and assorted sound loops and the trademark vocal being closer to spoken or drawled, recorded quite low in the mix as the track catatonically plays out. Not the worst Nový Svĕt piece, but clearly not the best either. Being released on the White Label this is of course pressed into white vinyl, with a textured cover and gold foil motif stamp that are simply stunning (and limited to a mere 200 copies).

Nový Svĕt (Aut)/Der Blutharsch (Aut) *Inutiles* 7" 2000 WKN
Talk of an infuriating release - limited to a ludicrous 99 copies - the first time I played this heavyweight clear vinyl, it appeared that it was only one-sided (with only the Nový Svĕt track being evident). To make things even more perplexing, the grooves of the vinyl revolve from the inside to outside edge! After a few rotations of the Nový Svĕt track - followed by a few curses! - I ended up emailing Albin to see if my copy was somehow a mis-pressing, as there simply did not appear to be a Der Blutharsch track on it. Well, as was then pointed out to me, it seemed that the answer was right under my nose all along: the 7" was indeed single-sided, but the two tracks were grooved one next to each other (meaning that you have to physically place the needle outside the normal lead in groove, to be able to drop into the groove of the Der Blutharsch track!). Up-tempo and even slightly cheesy in tone, the Nový Svĕt number melds standard kit drumming with a low register piano tune and organ with (as always) bizarre semi-chanted vocals doing their thing. Not the best track from them I have ever heard, but still unquestionably Nový Svĕt. As for Der Blutharsch, this is where the real action is - a top-notch piece and alone worth the price of this expensive vinyl. An emotive violin introduces the piece (to later arrive again midsection) while elements of rousing chanted vocals, slow pounding drumming, ritual percussion and a deep resonating orchestral horn melody build a stunning atmosphere, with slightly tweaked spoken vocals embellished with vitriolic flair. This is certainly Der Blutharsch at their best, which is nothing less than what I had hoped for when ordering this. One last thing to mention about the vinyl is that there is no protective locked groove at the outside edge, meaning that if you are not in close proximity to the stereo when the track finishes, the needle simple bops off onto the (still rotating) record platter! For all its physical nuisances, it is as if Albin stated that *"my records shouldn't be too easy to play. Always take care when listening to Der Blutharsch"*. Sound advice when considering this one... And before I forget to mention it, the packaging has a simple but nicely arcane hand screen printed image of martyr and eagle on (you guessed it!) brown card.

Ordo Equitum Solis (Ita) *A Divine Image* Picture 7" EP 2000 World Serpent Distribution
I have generally found that, while they may look more stunning, on most vinyl picture discs the sound often suffers more than that of standard vinyl (tending to accrue higher amounts of crackles and hiss). Is this due to the different type of material required for pressing? Who knows. Anyway this O.E.S is quite picturesque in visual presentation - basically the image of the velvet-clad female half of the group. With the title track up first, *A Divine Image* is an up-tempo, dreamy keyboard number, with atmospheric programmed percussion and angelic female choir vocals that give way to a singular sung main vocal line that in style has quite a similarity to Madonna (I have heard this comparison before)! From the pop aspect of the vocals, the meandering piano line that sneaks in at selected moments only adds to the quite pop-influenced sound and creates a very nice track overall. On the flip-side, *Before the Morning Rose* harks back to their more traditional neo-folk sound, with acoustic guitar tune and interplay of male and female vocals. An accordion and keyboard following the tune of the guitar is likewise a nice touch. This release is yet another item in the World Serpent series of 7" picture EPs that have also included items from Backworld and Belborn. Who will be next, you may ask?

Ordo Rosarius Equilibrio (Swe) *Make Love, And War (The Wedlock Of Roses)* CD 2000 Cold Meat Industry

The first track, *Beloved Kitty And The Piercing Bolts Of Amor*, is an amusingly looped piece of aged samples juxtaposing a rough-hewn German vocal (probably culled from WWII, or thereabouts) as it urges on an obviously aroused female to the brink of orgasm. (Well, okay, the female participant may just be sampled from an adult film, but there are timbres within her ... um, ecstatic revelatory cries upon every obvious thrust, that seem borne of times long ago...) It is a strangely appropriate introduction to the agenda spirited by Tomas Petterson's newly christened Ordo Rosario Equilibrio. With the exit of Chelsea Krook from the (moist) folds of Ordo Equilibrio, Tomas has changed the band's name to Ordo Rosario Equilibrio: *"the wedlock between equilibrium & roses-Ordo Rosario Equilibrio/The Order of Roses & Balance."* Even without her dispassionate, monotone sexuality (her vocals always expressed the conflict of fire and ice, an arousing confluence of voluptuous sensuality expressed amidst bland recitation ... the recitation of the prostitute, the sexual deviant, drenched in carnality to the point of listlessness), the prevalent sexuality still dominates. (As extracted from within the carcass of the dead...) Through the tracks that follow, Tomas' lyrics deliciously romanticize a restrained erotica amongst apocalyptic visions, be it the erotica of decay (*Make Love, And War*), or of transformation (*Never Before At The Beauty Of Spring*), or of corrupt spirituality (*Ashen Like Love, And Black Like The Snow*). The music is acoustic guitar-driven, but not without an abundance of synth and sampled textures. An amusingly pompous prelude to simmering finality, as mankind destroys itself between the split, scarred and bloodied thighs of Mother Earth ... and all Hell is unleashed! Quite intriguing! -JC Smith

Orplid (Ger) *Barbarossa* 10" EP 2000 Eis & Licht

Orplid have over the past few years slowly been raising their profile within the underground, melding quite stunning acoustic guitar apocalyptic folk odes with more neo-classical movements. Having already released a CD (in two different formats), 10" EP, and MCD (these being the items I am aware of), *Barbarossa* represents the new vinyl release. Taking a more tribal-esque/neo-classical stance, Side A offers up a lengthy track of deep war-like ancestral drumming, organ tune and clean sung vocals in the German language that borders on a deep classical/chanting style. Further layers of sweeping winds and vocal choirs add to the flair of the piece, but in most part this track strides onward at a consistent pace despite morphing through quieter and louder segments. The flip side of the vinyl commences in an even more epic style with mournful choirs radiating sorrowful melodies over a backing of distant bombing. Things slip back into a quieter forlorn classical synth melody, only to be overshadowed by a rather stern and aggressive German voice reciting a speech/written passage for the remainder of the piece (the underlying musical element remains throughout). The next and final piece seems to take its cue from the prior piece as it is much more aggressive, clearly evident from the outset with the shrill wail of air raid sirens. With a track of epic orchestral proportions, marching footfalls add to the pounding martial rhythms, further completed with deep orchestral brass instrumentation and soaring strings to create a grandiose war-mongering aura. For the multi-faceted elements that Orplid incorporates into their style, they certainly handle each brilliantly, melding them together in the creation of music with a strong folk and classical European flavour.

Ozymandias (???) *Karnak* CD 2000 Ramses Records

Being an album that was recorded with direct influence and inspiration derived from a trip that the artist undertook to the Egyptian temple 'Karnak', I assumed there might have been quite a bit of Middle Eastern influence infused within the compositions. Yet this is not the case with the music, which is quite standard classical piano melodies and tunes. Despite the music not having a clear relationship with the subject matter, it is clear that the songs are from a formally trained musical mind within the scope of the melancholic and understated piano meanderings. The 12 tracks are quite subtle in style and are all solo pieces, without multiple layers. Although superbly written and executed, this album is not partially dark, brooding or bombastic, which are generally the common themes threading through most current neo-classical albums. I am thus unsure to which segment of the underground this would really appeal, as it is essentially the type of CD my father (quite a connoisseur of classical music) would listen to. Nonetheless this is interesting.

Panzar (Swe) *Panzar* 7" Pic 2000 Panzar

Panzar is another project by Sweden's most prolific manipulator of sonic darkness, Peter Andersson. To list all of the projects in which he is involved would be an exercise in futility, as by the time you read this a few more may have arisen! Anyway, this 7" by Panzar is a scintillating teaser for something more (I hope). *Inertia* casts metallic synth shadows over blasted sonic terrain, while percussion drops like bombs from the heavens. The background, the smudged sonic canvas that this bombardment corrupts, is reamed by radiant strands of feedback (or wiry synths) and muddy, obscure vocals. This canvas seems to (possibly) incorporate textures derived from Heid and/or maybe Hollow Earth, but they are stretched, kneaded and gnawed on in such a way as to distinguish itself as a singular entity dispersing dread. *Tensor* includes German vocals as they wind through a latticework of thick, molten white noise, upon which clanking percussion, marching off into death, steers a panzer tank into oblivion... It is restrained, contained, insistent, deceptively sinister, the rumble of the tank crushing everything in its path... It's amazing the way, with each of Peter's many projects, an actual distinction of sound and focus can be gleaned. The only thing I ask of Panzar is more, please! -JC Smith

Poota (Aus) *Chunks* 3" CDR 2000 label:KETTLE

Poota is a collaborative project between Andrew Kettle (aka KETTLE) and Loyd Barrett (aka Brainlego) that has been operating from some four years with no official releases until now. This release is the amalgam of what the artists felt was the best material derived from 1998 recordings (studio and live) and, by the artists' own admission, showcases *"skill and spontaneity; innocence and experience"*. The first thing that is evident is that the cut-up, glitched framework of both their individual projects have been somewhat amassed together within these recordings, creating broad collages of intertwined malfunctioning electro static, rhythms and samples. The first of the CDR's five tracks appears to work on two levels - one presenting a broad deep undercurrent, the other a mid-ranged scattered rhythmic element that generates a mostly soothing sound presentation. This framework is again utilised on the second track, yet as here many more sonic layers are drawn upon (mainly at the high-end spectrum) to create overall a more chaotic offering. Likewise, with its focus on a high-end blip tune, it evokes a galactic spatial aura that later transforms into stunning and solidly focussed deep rhythm (that might just be comparable to segments of Atomine Elektrine's *Archimetrical Universe* CD). Track three brings a drawn-out playful style to its odd manipulations of a quite crunchy, centrally focussed mid-paced beat. Pure sonic experimentation abounds on the fourth piece, where gradually shifting sounds, static and (tune/beat/voice) samples generate a loose focus to the occasionally fierce and quick-paced sonics. The fifth and final track is simply stunning due to its use of a sampled segment of Indian tabla drum percussion to create a brooding atmosphere. With this central sample offset against a subdued tune and understated electronic treatments, the track presents an excellent blend of traditional and modern sounds.

Despite the artists acknowledging that this release offers more of a *"historical fragment ... than a new work of evolution in music"*, it is still a fine example of the creativity of the underground/experimental music scene in Australia.

Predominance (Ger) *Nocturnal Gates Of Incidence* CD 2000 Loki Foundation

A wind from the outer reaches of space and time (it caresses the cool flesh of infinity) arises *From Ancient Aeons*, accompanied by strange, almost ritualistic vocals of a cryptic origin; they seem ancient, culled from some banished realm of forsaken obscurity. (The sensation is like that of an American Indian chanting...) Synths rise to sway and harshly rub the bass textures, the mood one of mysterious allegiances of anomalous pedigree, as clanking, muddy percussion and subtly sinister tones climb the invisible walls of a vast abyss. My initial take on *Nocturnal Gates Of Incidence* was that it was not quite on par with the excellent *Hindenburg* LP. Of course, they are two very different creations, and repeated listens have moved it, quite possibly, beyond that mighty signpost, and definitely down dark highways of unexplored space that many of the dark soniscape practitioners on the (amazing!) LOKI label traverse. *Aurora Borealis* resonates with stern, anxious vocal/choral aspirations wrapped in swarthy, brooding synths. The trepidation-laced lyrics transcend the imposed limitations of time (*"Open the gates of incidence/Where all began and everything ends"*) and plead for rescue from the clutches of eternal dismay (*"Save our souls from the blackness/The stars remain like eyes of the fairies"*). *If the Last Star Burns Out*, possibly the darkest exploration here, is ignited by metal-on-metal percussion crashing on the bruised hide of the sporadic engines of emptiness. The sprawling emptiness is dappled with tones that evoke unease via scattered noise discharges: snowflakes of cracked metal, stinging lashes of grim discomfort. The possible ramifications of what would transpire if the last star burned out are expressed in clearly enunciated tones, a foreboding observation of deliciously rendered darkness. The synth waves of *Once They Arrive* swell with an odd, optimistic beauty, while appealing, German accented vocals expound on the imminent arrival of ... something (other beings, of interstellar origin? ... or is this a more divine apotheosis?...) that will arrive, crossing eons of time, and link all that has been with all that is... *Nocturnal Gates Of Incidence* is one of the rare occurrences in dark sonicscape music in which the varied vocals and vocal approaches really broaden the sonic palette, adding drama and perspective. A remarkable, cosmically explorative presentation! -JC Smith

Psychonaut (USA) *Liber Al Vel Legis* advance CDR 2001 Athanor

After being delayed due to copyright issues over the use of imagery and text associated with the estate of Aleister Crowley, this album (recorded back in 1998) is finally obtaining an official release (the bio further states that this was actually the first recording of Michael Ford under the Psychonaut banner). Anyway, given that this album predates the last Psychonaut release (likewise on Athanor) it actually encompasses a different sound and focus. Where *The Witch's Sabbath* was predominantly based on cathartic tribal and rhythmic percussive works, here there is a more sparse musical outline containing often a heavy emphasis on spoken (yet slightly echoed/treated) vocals that recite passages from Crowley's *The Book of the Law* (particularly conducting the Ritual of Liber Samekh for the Attainment of the Knowledge and Conversation of the Holy Guardian Angel). Minimalist in nature, the backing sounds contain sparse collages of echoed and resonating textures seeming to aim at evoking a hypnotic state where the mind can transcend its earthbound surrounds (particularly when contemplating the words being spoken) and from this perspective the description of 'Astral Musick' is an appropriate portrayal of the shimmering synth textures. That said, there are a number of tracks that do contain sound elements that crop up on later recordings, particularly the loose frameworks of tribal percussion and sustained and wavering non-melodious woodwind instruments. Overall these are used as complementary elements to the main framework. I would have to attest that this recording has a much greater ritualistic air then the tribal movements of the other Psychonaut recordings I have heard, and for this reason alone this CD is more engaging. Again and as with the previous release, this will be of specific interest for those who have a more than a passing interest in ritualistic magic particularly of the Crowleyian variety.

Puissance (Swe) *All Hail the Mushroom Cloud* MCD 2000 Fluttering Dragon

Well, while this is meant to be the 'new' MCD, it seems that the tracks were actually recorded back in 1998, which has me wondering if these were recorded around the time of the last album, *Mother of Disease* (not counting the re-mix album *War On*, which also contained two new tracks). While this MCD is good, it is a little disappointing when compared to an MP3 track I have heard, a brand new piece called *A Call to Arms* which is, in my opinion, closest to the pinnacle of what Puissance can create. Anyway this CD comes in a deluxe digipack and contains four tracks or 'acts' relating to the mini-album's title. While the heavy orchestral/industrial framework is still utilised, there seems to be an underlying looped element to many of the sounds, giving the industrial underbelly a more modern edge than noted on previous offerings. Reasonably convincing synth choirs soar as a backing to *Act 1*, while other elements focus on mid-ranged string segments. Mid-paced and reasonably repetitive, there is no real divergence from the main focus once it is established. All four tracks have a clear similarity in direction and approach, meaning that each of the pieces are generally on a par with each other and all contain the trademark mid-paced brooding orchestral framework and industrial martial aura. (*Act IV* differs only slightly in that it has a tinge of folkish element created via a flute tune, thus making it the best track here). If you have already heard Puissance's music then you already have an opinion of it, and this MCD presents nothing that would alter that perception – good or bad, depending on your persuasion.

Puissance (Swe) *A Call to Arms* 7" EP 2001 Selfless Recordings

Having referenced the title track of this 7" in the above review, it seems this fantastic composition has finally been furnished with an official release on new American label Selfless Recordings. And talking of *A Call to Arms* - guttural yet slightly metallic percussion and a lone flute tune introduce this mid-paced orchestral epic. Soon after, sparse chimes and a slow piano tune build the composition up to the next level, while the incorporation of martial snare drumming and layers of orchestral choir voices ensures Puissance's musical sights are set high. With this track building up until the final moments, this is essentially the pinnacle of what (I knew) Puissance had the potential to create. Likewise throughout this track a monotone voice recites a page from the Puissance manifesto; however, the philosophy here seems to have taken a step away from the previous 'destroy everything' attitude towards a metaphor of a fatalistic martyr figure (*"It's a pointless struggle but we will fight them ... still losing I'm sure, but at least alive, for a short while longer"*). The spoken passage is further reprinted on the cover, being well written and serious, highlighting a certain maturation from earlier slightly more simplistic written passages that Puissance used as lyrics. *Religion of Force* (the side B track), is instrumental and while not quite as epic as side A, is more of an industrial/martial evocation. Rigidly sharp and atmospheric mid-paced percussion strides forth from the outset, set alongside sparsely constructed and relatively non-musical atmospheric wavering sound layers (slivers of treated radio voices can also be faintly detected). By no means would I say this is a bad track, rather it just tends to take a back seat to side A. Pressed into white vinyl and limited to 880 (I'm unsure if this is a minor attempt at controversy), the cover is simplistic yet effective in design, and certainly worth checking out.

COLD SPRING
RELEASE SCHEDULE : SPRING 2001
FULL CATALOGUE AND SECURE ONLINE SHOPPING NOW AVAILABLE AT www.coldspring.co.uk

INADE — ALDEBARAN
Originally released in 1996, the dark ambient classic sold out immediately. At last, after constant demand from fans - the mighty `ALDEBARAN` has been reissued! This has been cited worldwide as one of the most important dark ambient albums ever recorded, focussing on the mythos of the Aldebaran star system and its links with spirituality on Earth.
A classic album available once again in brand new packaging! **CD**

GENESIS P-ORRIDGE / Z'EV — DIRECTION OV TRAVEL
The two innovators and founders of Industrial music collaborate - a meeting of these two incredible minds. Utilising metals, Tibetan bowls and ingenius processing, they have created a soundtrack of awesome magickal significance. They are aided on violin by Gini Ball (wife of SOFT CELLs Dave Ball).
Supreme ritual workings **CD**

SLEEP RESEARCH FACILITY — NOSTROMO
Ultra deep ambience, based on the first 8 minutes of the movie `ALIEN` which depicts the deep space haulage vessel slowly moving through the void. The disc takes you through a slow trip into the ship via tracks DECK A - E, deeper and deeper into the bowels of the `NOSTROMO`.
Colossal dark ambience from the abyss. **CD**

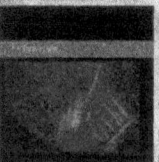

VON THRONSTAHL — E PLURIBUS UNUM
After the massive success of the debut album, "IMPERIUM INTERNUM" this album neatly collects together all compilation tracks and rare 10" releases, along with some remixes and unreleased pieces. Another statement confirming the power and majesty of VON THRONSTAHL!
Martial industrial epics! **CD**

KEROVNIAN — FROM THE DEPTHS OF HARON
The long-awaited album from the Black Ambient master! Some two years in the making, and what has been created has been hailed as a milestone of supreme oppressive darkness. Essential!
Black Ambience from the heart of oblivion **CD**

KEROVNIAN — DEAD BEYOND DEATH
Two exclusive cuts for vinyl only, never to appear elsewhere! `Dead Beyond Death` and `The Fall Of Prometheos` are straight from the Black Masters dark soul!
Limited to just 333 copies! **7"**

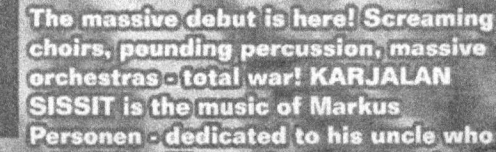

KARJALAN SISSIT — KARJALAN SISSIT
The massive debut is here! Screaming choirs, pounding percussion, massive orchestras - total war! KARJALAN SISSIT is the music of Markus Personen - dedicated to his uncle who died fighting the WinterWar - solemn but bombastic neo-classical - in the vein of the mightiest IN SLAUGHTER NATIVES or LAIBACH!
Pure anthemic power! Out Now! **CD**

FOLKSTORM — SHIRT
The first shirt from the harsh war-noise master! Troops on the back, and FOLKSTORM logo on the front. Show your allegiance! Shirts are printed on high quality, black Screen Stars, 100% cotton, XL only with white print.
Album `VICTORY OR DEATH` still available!

PRICES (UK): CD:£12 7":£4 FOLKSTORM SHIRT:£11 **SPECIAL!!** Buy KEROVNIAN CD + 7" for £14
EUROPE please add £1 REST OF WORLD please add £2

All prices INCLUDE first class / Airmail postage and packaging.
We take all major credit and debit cards, and also cheques, Money Orders and carefully concealed cash (sent at mailers risk). Write with stamp or IRC for our latest catalogue which contains hundreds of titles, rare and deleted vinyl and CDs, and oddities. Catalogue free with any order. Or visit http://www.coldspring.co.uk to use our secure online shopping site, where you'll find our complete catalogue of DARK, INDUSTRIAL, DEATH AMBIENCE, BLACK AMBIENT, RITUAL, OCCULTIC, and BLOOD MUSIC.

FORTHCOMING TITLES:
SCHLOSS TEGAL - collection of all 7" and compilation tracks - a 10th anniversary for SCHLOSS TEGAL!
ENDVRA - Contra Mvndum CD - the English neo-classical kings
MARK SNOW - Death...Be Not Proud CD - X FILES, MILLENIUM composer finally completes his exclusive album!
LAIBACH - Neu Konservatv CD - the 1985 bootleg digitally remastered and exclusively on COLD SPRING - with 2 exclusive tracks!

COLD SPRING,
PO BOX 40,
NORTHAMPTON
NN7 3ZB
ENGLAND, UK

Tel/Fax: (0) 1604 859142
Email: info@coldspring.co.uk
VAT: GB 623 38 6726

Pure (Aut)/Ultra Milkmaids (Fra) *s[e]nd* CD 2000 Vacuum

When it comes to experimental 'art-noise', this disc displays the kind of sounds that I tend to appreciate the most. This is basically derived from the perspective that while not particularly musical, the sounds rather work with a drawn-out aesthetic and are therefore akin to sprawling drones – albeit more minimalist and fragile by virtue of the experimental style. Shimmering, warm tones radiate fragility from the album's outset, and with such sounds being akin to what I know of Ultra Milkmaids, I am also assuming that Pure covers similar territory when recording solo. In small segments the drawn-out textures become intentionally disjointed and fractured as if the CD is mis-tracking; yet the music's ability to pull this off convincingly is just part of the CD's charm. The slow evolution of content means that one track meanders into the next, emphasising the minimalist nature of the sound works presented. Regardless, the atmospheres created gradually evolve from warm textures on the first few tracks to more clinical and glacial sounds, such as on the lengthy 14 minute third track. Although there are never any real tunes and melodies to be detected within this release, it works with sparse electronic harmonies and tones to give a fleeting 'musical' reference to the sound. Track six is quite a bit more quirky and playful with textured sound glitches, but this is really only a fleeting moment of increased intensity within the complete album. Overall this is an album that can be enjoyed both as foreground or background listening, and I have quite enjoyed what is on offer.

Raven's Bane (USA) *sorrow breeds* CDR 2001 Live Bait Recording Foundation

This project is a solo excursion by Profane Grace member Robert Cruzan and I imagine this little snippet of information should raise interest. While the ghostly atmospheres of the main project are less evident here, death ambient would still certainly be an appropriate description for this. Dense, slow evolving loops, machine-orientated hums/drones and shimmering drawn-out keyboard textures construct the quite minimalist auras of each offering, as if presenting various telekinetic transmissions from the netherworld. Likewise even without track titles such as *Plaguehost*, *Shrine of Sufferance* and *Cacophony*, the sound already contains a deathly morbid edge that is enough to give the listener an aural peek into the shadow world. From the liner notes, it seems that this monotone and minimalist nature of the recordings has a specific purpose to generate a plane for the mind to escape to, and I will certainly vouch for this fact as when playing this CD while going to sleep it creates an aura that is never too jolting, thus the perfect counterpart for pre-sleep contemplation. Now having said this, as the album progresses the aura of the tracks gradually become more urgent and damning in tone, marking a clear direction and evolution of each piece in relation to the next. The fact that this is a CDR and limited to only 100 copies, the aesthetics of the colour card cover have been immaculately presented utilising the graphic talents of Mike Riddick (who incidentally produced the cover of *Spectrum* no.3!). Putting non-related topics aside, this is worth checking out.

Boyd Rice & Fiends (USA) *Wolf Pact* CD 2001 NEROZ

Before you ask, no it is not a spelling mistake, the working title is in fact Boyd Rice & 'Fiends' and not 'Friends' as was the case with an earlier album. Anyway, with the auspicious accolade of accommodating the creative inputs of Boyd Rice (of course), Albin Julius and Douglas P., this alone will provide ample reason to generate a significant amount of interest in this project. Recorded in Adelaide (Australia) during February 2001, this is a rather eclectic album that blends selected elements of the music created by its contributors on an individual basis (those being NON, Death In June or Der Blutharsch), creating a diverse recording project. *The Watery Leviathan* opens with a celebratory acoustic folk piece, resplendent with backing keyboard melodies, chiming church bells and understated percussion as the spoken/sung vocals of Boyd are presented in an unassuming style. Title track *Wolf Pact* is another dreamy acoustic/keyboard number (although there is always a darker undercurrent scratching beneath the surface) where Albin presents spoken vocals in his native tongue alongside choir-like backing vocals. Unyielding martial-sounding loops and the whispered vocals of Boyd introduce *Worlds Collide*, which is further embellished with sparse keyboards, acoustic tune and orchestral layers, while *Fire Shall Come* with its gruffly shouted vocals and heavy stately percussion is reminiscent of the DI6's track *C'est Un Reve*. *Bad Blood* works itself into quite a cascading church organ dirge, where spoken vocals are further looped, treated and added to the mix (although remain quite hard to follow/decipher). *Rex Mundi* with its slow neo-orchestral/martial sound is comparable to the first Der Blutharsch album if not the works of TMLHBAC, yet with the spoken vocals of Boyd and constant whip-cracking (most often associated with DI6 recordings), it creates a positive mix of the distinctive styles. *Hamlet* is a rather abrasive mélange of screamed/spoken vocal loops that is further manipulated and tweaked, then leading into *Bad Luck and Curses* that is a short piece of manipulated/reversed snippets of Boyd's spoken vocals. *Murder Bag* presents an unusual sounding rhythmic industrial piece with hints of discordant trumpet playing and segments of movie dialogue, the source of which I'm not entirely sure of (on a hunch they could be snippets taken from the still long-awaited *Pearls Before Swine* that both Doug and Boyd star in). After playing through the sparse soundscape of *Joe Liked to Go (to the Cemetery)*, *People Change* reverts to the acoustic guitar format, mixing in more of Boyd's spoken vocals and odd backing samples and sounds (Albin at the mixing desk I assume?!). Introduced with storming rain, this is used as a partially manipulated platform of *The Reign Song* whereby Boyd speaks his mind further, while the lengthily titled *The Forgotten Father/The Tomb of the Forgotten Father* clearly has the stamp of Albin all over it with its rhythmic yet classical approach (however it is less like his Der Blutharsch material, and more comparable to the material he recorded with Douglas as Death In June). Piano melody and yet more vocals from Boyd complete the vocal portion of the track before late in the piece it tangents off into a heavy martial percussive guise with xylophone and orchestral elements marking a heftier sound. Final track *The Orchid and the Death's Head* marks a soundscape style of deep drones, understated sparse tune and various sampled and spoken vocals that build intensity through to the dying seconds. Not that this album will really need any encouragement to sell, it is both a diverse and intriguing amalgam of recording influence.

Salt (Ger) *re.wasp* 3"CD/box 2000 Ant-Zen

As much a piece of art as a musical release, the landmark 100th Ant-Zen item is a celebration of the man behind the Ant-Zen empire - the one and only Stephen Alt. Packaged in a sturdy cardboard slide box, the 3" CD is housed in a miniature gatefold pouch, along with a series of 13 postcards that illustrate and display the graphic design genius of S.Alt. Basically I would have been more than happy with the release on the packaging front, regardless of quality of musical content, yet the music is also top quality, consisting of two tracks - part noise soundscape and part glitch-riddled technoid experimentation. *One* shifts forward at a minimalist pace for a few minutes prior to a rather prominent and very engaging electro static rhythm whipping things into a low-key frenzy. From here, constant yet fractured layers build, overlap and fall away, repeating loose cycles in a partly electric, partly mechanical, guise. *Two* again runs with an electro static framework with varying frequencies characterising initial segments. Glitched sounds take a more prominent position on this piece, forging tonal layered experimentations until things sweep off in a mass of throbbing static intensity. Falling somewhere between noise experimentation and power electronics this is certainly a nicely hued and quite blistering intense composition. Of course with this item being limited, some searching might be required.

Sator Absentia (Fra) *Mercurian Orgasms* CD 2000 Dark Vinyl

Sator Absentia is Cedric Codognet, whose work I had previously heard on the Asmorod CD, *Involution Toward Chtonian Depths*. Sator Absentia incorporates some of the elements of that disc, while chiseling out its own variations of melancholic darkness tinged with weirdness. *Sounds of Mercurian Devotion* opens with a scratchy violin (spectral timbres stolen from Lovecraft's Erich Zahn…?) caressed by tonalities of discomfort (matching the violin, they are almost vocal, though of ludicrous allegiance). Additional mood is coloured by beautifully sparse (tears like plucked icicles) acoustic guitar and scattered background voices (a crowd, a mass … except for the laughter…), all shrouded under a cloak of midnight synths. Tectonic plates shift during *Panorama*, extricating a violin born of the darkest agony in the process. An ache is wound into the strings, distraught, tattered bowing drawing out both the pain and despair in lusciously stroked cadences. Low rumbling fills the void, a platform upon which the brittle violin performs. The vista grows more expansive as the track stretches, ominous synths rising to lick the strings, the saliva causing the violin bow to slide sporadically… Absolutely riveting! Processional percussion etched with slivers of splintered, moaning violin opens *Enter the Red Garden of Frustration*. The mood is fraught with ritual, as if something is about to commence. But that possibility is deemed impotent, the only thing the music inspires is sadness of an undefined nature, not simply born of depression, but of something more tactile (yet elusive). The music on *Mercurian Orgasms* has a quirky underbelly, despite the inherent dark foundation, that seems most enigmatic; the violins, in particular, seem bowed by hands of unearthly origin. Impressive! JC Smith

Scorn (Eng) *Greetings from Birmingham* CD 2000 Hymen

For all intents and purposes, the new full-length Scorn album looks and sounds like an extension of the *Imaginaria Award* CD EP reviewed last issue – meaning that the previous item was really a taster to this, the main dish (it also seems the original title of this has been altered from the previously alluded *No Joke Movement* – however this slogan graces the inner sleeve). As for the music, the grating, gutturally heavy drum'n'bass/hip hop-flavoured tunes are again presented here in all their tweaked and repetitive glory. The twisted and morphed pulverizing textures, deep sweeping tones and big (slightly tweaked) slow pounding beats characterise this modern yet underground sound that Mick Harris (aka Scorn) has made his trademark. After a one-minute intro, the standard snare sound on *Can But Try* has a really tweaked snap to it, with all other elements likewise pushed to the extreme. With barely a melodic moment to be found on *Still On*, the track opts for sparse otherworldly sounds with combinations of kick, snare and high hat. Throughout the album there are a number of tracks that are presented in different versions, but some appear to be similar in name only (as is the case with *Told you can tell: part 2*). A late album track, *Closedown*, achieves a mild groove to the crunchy beats, with smatterings of droning sounds hinting at a sparse tune that is bookended by a quirky sporadic piece called *Part Of* that, with a few segments of clanging cymbal abuse, works quite well. Rounding out the CD are a throw-away 11-second noise piece and a one-minute outro beat, all in all another good album of darkly menacing drum and bass music.

The Seventh Dawn (Aus) *The Age to an End Shall Come…* CD 2000 Nile

This new project comes from none other than Chris McCarter (of Ikon infamy) and his sister Susan McCarter. Taking its cues from a neo-folk perspective, the instrumentation (handled by Chris) consists of acoustic guitar ballads and folkish keyboard tracks. With Susan predominantly handling the vocals, the dreamy and restrained delivery helps evoke arcane visions that are particularly evident on baroquely-styled *He's not Playing for the King*. The minor piano keys of *In Light and Roses* are fully embellished with orchestral layers, acoustic guitars, chimes and marching snare beats - this is also one of the few tracks to feature the vocals of Chris. Apart from being a fantastic song, overall this is somewhat comparable to the composed works of Ordo Equilibrio while containing hints of Death In June (when it is stripped back to a lone trumpet, percussion and acoustic guitar). A slight diversion is toyed with on *In my Lonely Hours*, where the down vibe of the synth backing remains the same, despite the main focus arriving with programmed up-tempo beats, rhythmic bass, and clanging keyboard tune. Whimsical atmospheres float gently from the speakers on *1881* as (again) lightly strummed acoustics and unassuming classically-inspired keys swirl from background to foreground – Susan's vocals are a constant joy throughout. Almost aggressive, the final track *The Rosin Bridge* holds a slightly ominous air, with a focus on heavier rolling beats while the darker melody is reflected in and enshrouded by the main vocals, again those of Chris. 10 tracks in all and housed in jewel case with a beautiful full colour cover, I would imagine this album would have the ability to appeal to a number of scenes ranging from industrial, neo-folk, gothic (or potentially even contemporary) given the sweet yet beautifully sorrowful compositions showcased here.

Skincage (USA) *Axon* CD 2000 Malignant Antibody

I must admit that I put off the task of reviewing this CD for some months. Essentially each time I listened to it I found my mind swimming in its multidimensional sonic whirlpool of sampled and re-contextualised sound, leaving me unable to transform the experience into words (well, now the time has finally come…) *Axon* is the first release on the new Malignant Records side label, Malignant Antibody, which is run by none other than Phil Easter, creator of the sampled and manipulated sonic bliss of Stone Glass Steel and Iron Halo Device (as well as Malignant's web technician and Malignant Sound Technologies knob twiddler). Immediately evident is the fact that Malignant Antibody highlights a certain focus and direction away from that of the main label, with this flagship release forging into quite cinematic sounding territories. Given that this is also the realm that Stone Glass Steel frequents, it is no surprise to hear that Skincage utilises a similar sampling and construction ethic to that inherent in Stone Glass Steel compositions, although Skincage approaches its musical aesthetic from a completely different angle to create a more subversive tone (for my interpretation, it could be the outward view gained from being trapped inside a decrepit society - much as the moniker suggests the operation of this idea on a much more personal scale). Akin to scanning radio bandwidth for signals, solo artist Jon Ray chops, splices and tweaks his way through a myriad of samples – whether random noise, static, beats, rhythms, violins and whatever else you could possibly imagine. Brooding melodies, crumbling textures, aural clutter, machine pluses, hydraulic hisses, radio voices, modem dialing sounds, sublime static, angelic vocals, resonating chimes, insectile scramblings, tribal percussion, telephone conversations, Gregorian chants - the list of samples that can be individually detected is simply endless. Yet even with providing such a list, it is less WHAT is being sampled than HOW it has been interpreted, collated and further manipulated to ingeniously engrossing effect. Assessing some of the pieces individually, *Household Gods* (being central to the album) stands out prominently over the preceding tracks, due to its bizarre rhythm sequences and fleeting classical tunes. Horrific sounds intermixed with angelic voices and urgent orchestral blasts characterise *Relapse*, all wrapped in a very sharp and sonically crisp production which is exemplary of modern sound techniques. Later segments of this piece are more orchestrally sparse and generally less threatening in tone. With a subversively subliminal packaging note suggesting that *Struck by the Arrows of Artemis* be played on rotation, the darker hypnotic undercurrents are more likely to induce nightmares than to soothe, despite being balanced out with a prominent sample of a child's toy (now that I think about it, this element indicates more sinister implications). Anyway, with all the sampled calamity of most of the album, the final track *The Bruised Mandala* seeps off into the distance as a fantastic soundscape of orchestral minimalism. Too composed and active ever to be

¡DEGENERATE!
magazine for:
Power Electronics, Noise,
Ambient, Industrial, Experimental,
...

information of current issue, visit: www.kaos-kontrol.org or contact:
Freak Animal
P.o.box 21
15141 Lahti
Finland
fanimal@hotmail.com

Kaos Kontrol
c/o Jukka Mattila
Mikkosentie 15 A 2
04600 Mäntsälä Finland
kaos-kontrol@kaos-kontrol.org
KAOS KONTROL
freak animal

considered dark ambient, yet at the same time not sufficiently composed to be bona fide songs, the finished album is a perfect example of 'cinematic isolationism'. Based on this debut release, I am expecting BIG things to come from both the artist and the label.

Silbernacht (Ger) *Nacht ohne Sterne* demo MC 2001 self-released
Receiving this tape in the post, the letter introduced the material on this cassette as potentially being described as *"…symphonic gothic or symphonic black. Sometimes it sounds like cinematic music"*. Well I can say that this sounded promising (or at the very least a little intriguing), but what you actually get with this four track/28 minute tape is rather bland and very synthetic sounding classical/organ-oriented music. While there is a level of skill evident in the execution of the compositions, the actual music comes across as being uninspired, as if the player has executed it with technical proficiency but forgotten to put any emotion into the playing. Selected pieces have a feel of soundtracks used in old horror movies (you know those with the slightly flamboyant yet gothically-grounded organ dirges), but overall the music does not really contain a specific dark streak. Given that the tracks seem to simply meander along, there is no real hook or focused direction to the material, and in many spots you are left feeling as if you've starting reading a book midway through and attempting (unsuccessfully) to follow the storyline. Touches of swirling winds, and some more epic and grand keyboard notes bring to mind some of Mortiis's early works, yet it is the gothic slant to the sound that avoids Mortiis being used as a huge comparison. Maybe I'm being a bit too harsh, but when I reflect on this I really lack any specific feeling (be it love or loathe) hence the 'uninspired' comment. You decide. Available for $5 US in Europe or $10 US rest of world; if interested contact: Frank Esser, Kempener Allee 108 D-47803 Krefeld, Germany.

Silk Saw (Bel) *4th Dividers* CD 2000 Ant-Zen
This is another artist on the Ant-Zen roster that I had not heard up until this item, and yet again presents another group whose back catalogue I want to become better acquainted with. Fitting into the trademark Ant-Zen 'technoid' sound, the track dynamics are often structured around and slowly built upon repetitive beat sequences that create clinical yet quite groovy, chilled-out sounds that have a certain ambient flair despite their composition. The snappy beats of *Safe Area* are particularly infectious and make it hard not to be tapping along, as is also the case with *No Twists No Turns* (but here a bigger throbbing bass sound is the main percussive element, with clicks, pops, chimes and the like making up the remainder). For some respite the treated, looped and manipulated guitar strums of *Pave the Way* are the main focal point, resulting in quite a dark musical exploration without any use of percussive beats. *Ratchet Mechanism* hints at a quirky source of inspiration despite the track being quite vertically rigid in its beat programming, and also marks the start of the second half of the album containing other similarly quirky and slightly more bizarre compositions (just reference *Wrong Door* if you want to know what I mean!). With most of its 12 tracks ranging between three and eight minutes, it results in quite a lengthy CD that explores the subtleties and dynamics of each composition.

Sleeping With The Earth (USA)/Combat Astronomy (USA) *Split Compact Disc* CD 2000 Troniks
A rainstorm introduces the listener to Sleeping With The Earth; it is a deceptively organic tease. As rain batters and thunder erupts in violent peals, an undercurrent of malevolent, slashing noises (I hear voices amidst tortured machinery) rises to overwhelm the torrential downfall, meshing to make a more potent assimilation of said rainstorm. Ultra-manipulated voices (I think it's voices - it might just be noise incoherently screaming amidst slaughter…), distorted into shades of thunder that shred like talons of metal, gleefully rip at the organic base, mangled sounds dispersed in tattered sheets of inflamed metal and gouged flesh. A brilliant introduction to the meticulously designed dynamics utilized by Sleeping With The Earth. *Deliver Us From Evil* slowly ascends from depths unknown, a black mass marching on the heels of the song's wary sonic navigator… Release is never attained; one is left with an impression much like an itch unscratched. *What Have I Done?* plods unmercifully through fields of ground bone and gristle, a death march of low rumbling, monotonously rippling distortion punctured by clattering knives (…think Brighter Death Now, circa *Necrose Evangelicum*). Powerful stuff, exquisitely presented; even amidst the fury unleashed here, there always seems a purpose (well, except maybe the mutual masturbation of the Big Tex-assisted *This Is My Room*, a still amusing affair that gains quite a bit of sonic mass as it evolves). Combat Astronomy commences with a sound like skin being ripped off the hide of an android. As *Tiat02* unravels, murky subcurrents of grime are beaten on with metal pipes that assume a ratcheted rhythm. Though maybe less focused than Sleeping With The Earth, Combat Astronomy utilize a variety of noisy approaches in the manufacturing of their mayhem. Subterranean loops of blood surge through iron veins, clotting in a diseased artery crusted in metal (hence, the clanking metal din) on *J-Vax*. A percussive loop is splattered with progressively more caustic abrasions during *nOMON*. *Hut* sounds like the laughter of looped, cut and spliced, hiccupping machinery, while an avalanche of sonic discord tumbles through the belly of a white noise tornado during *Archon*. Seventy minutes of maliciously rendered abuse! I look forward to more from both of these artists… -JC Smith

The Soil Bleeds Black (USA) *Quintessence* CD 2001 World Serpent Distribution
Representing the fifth album, it seems the Riddick brothers have further re-evaluated and refined their approach of neo-medieval folk music, and to my ears this is their strongest recorded work to date. Shunning the shorter pieces and soundscape interludes, these tracks embody a much longer length and are predominantly built around darkened acoustic guitar ballads. Likewise the actual vibe of this CD is much more morose and melancholic with less emphasis on the whimsical yet ridged minstrel-type atmospheres of prior recordings with an improved flow. The male vocals have also gone through a slight stylistic change, where rather than presenting caricatures, here they are quite simply and cleanly sung (and as always complemented with the vocals of Eugenia Houston). Basing the album around five tracks (*Earthe*, *Air*, *Fyre*, *Water* and *Quintessence*), the first track - a brooding piece of acoustic guitar sentimentalities - is embellished with various percussive elements, woodwind instruments and even a trumpet. The darker acoustic folk tangent of *Air* uses Eugenia's voice as the vocal lead while xylophone, recorder, stately drums, church bells and trumpet all add to the foreboding atmosphere. The cyclic and repetitive guitar strumming of *Fyre* brings to mind selected tracks of Ordo (Rosarius) Equilibrio, yet the embellishing of woodwind instruments, percussion, marching beats etc. creates a fantastic and individualistic celebratory flavour – both male and female vocals presented in unison. With a minimalist ambient introduction, *Water* falls back into morose acoustic musing territory that is both subdued and epic. Again elements of drum and wood percussion, synth layers, recorders, whistles etc. make up the backing, providing the basis for dual male female vocals that are used as both backing and lead (ranging from soaring to chanting). Final track *Quintessence* again embodies the morose acoustic guitar style and is some 15 minutes in length. With the percussion presenting heavy slow pounding beats and multi layered woodwind instruments it presents the perfect basis for Eugenia's vocals, with the lyrics noted to be an ode to the four elements referenced in the first four tracks. After the five-minute mark, the track falls away into a rather engaging dark ambient soundscape, presenting an aura of being in lost in a dark woodland during the Middle Ages, that later makes way for a hidden track. This instrumental piece is yet another fantastic acoustic guitar track (I can say I have always been a sucker for acoustic folk guitar tunes) that sees the multi layered guitar along with percussion, woodwind tunes, dulcimer and even a stunning trumpet interlude. This album is easily the pinnacle of what the The Soil Bleeds Black have recorded to date and now sees the group further aligning themselves with the current neo-folk movement where particular comparison to the like of Atataxia can be made. *Quintessence* will certainly not disappoint established fans of the group, but will also create an opportunity for those who might not have been totally enamoured with previous albums to rediscover the group via the gem that is this album.

Somatic Responses (UK) *augmented lines* CD 2001 Hymen
With the bio stating this is the second CD release for Somatic Responses, this is, however, my first introduction to the group. Mixing elements of drum'n'bass, break beats and darker aspects of electronic experimentalism, this has resulted in a complexly twisted listen. Amazingly atmospheric, *RNB* utilises an undercurrent of shimmering drones that are overlaid with sharp and puncturing beat and groove arrangements, highlighting a key characteristic of the album. Using this aspect of dual layers in the creation of the compositions, it has created quite an engaging listen. Essentially each element of beats or tuneful undercurrent could stand on their own, yet it is when they are mixed together that it is a truly great listening experience. *Automata (Sonic Empire)* being a composition of slamming mid-paced beats and noise treatments, there is an always detectable, subdued and partly tuneful drone melody. The more frantic programmed beats of *Catacombs* surge the piece forward, yet ground it with the dark twist of the brooding melody (that partially hints at the style of Beefcake). The fantastically titled *Perfumed Ammo* provides enough deadly and sweet sentiments with its cranking beats and wistful tunes that sweep along through a myriad of morphed segments. A ridged and complex drum'n'bass style is utilised on *Critical Path* with its rather direct and sharp approach that only becomes heavier and more distorted as the piece progresses. Again exploiting the dual composition focus to maximum effect, the moody tune textures of *U.D.T* is mixed alongside fractured and fast-paced free-form beat structures creating an aural panoramic vision. The ominous synth tunes of *CS Bastardo H* take centre-stage prior to a dense and fast-paced beat that cranks things up a notch and gradually drags the composition into noise and distortion obliteration. The final track *Engines of Desire* is a rather catchy composition with pulsating rhythms and blips sandwiched in with mid-paced beat programming and atmospheric tone for a sense of completion. In conclusion, while less classical/orchestral in orientation than label mates Beefcake, this does share similarities in the actual break beat composition framework and wide screen sweeping musical backing, thus subsequently this gets my tick of approval of being another impressive release from the Hymen camp.

Sona Eact® (Bel)/Hypnoskull (Bel)/Tunnel (Bel) *fucked by others' attitudes* 7" picture disc ep 2001 Nocturnus
Delving into 'shake your booty' territory, the three projects that inhabit this release all embody a heavy rhythmic noise approach (think industrial strength techno – or even technoise) and are incidentally all projects of one Patrick Stevens. Further noting that the vinyl 7" plays at 33 rpm at least this ensures maximum play time for the three compositions that are presented herein. Sona Eact® are up first with their track *The External Inputphase*, that uses a grinding analogue drone introduction, prior to the track quickly leaping into an extremely heavy mid-paced beat. With a searing metallic resonance its basic structure is set in stone, using a repetitive framework to drive its message home (with a short interlude in the middle the track quickly stomps back in for one final rhythmic rotation). Hypnoskull, on the other hand, up the speed just slightly on *Push>Eject>Return*, with a slightly muffled yet no less weighty programming. With the basic structure set, the piece is tweaked, twisted and generally fucked with, likewise including machine gun blasting noise. Some sort of bizarrely morphed vocal snippet jumps in at random moments (never to actually be deciphered) as the track continues on its short, sharp and HEAVY delivery - that is incidentally credited as being a live recording. By virtue of submitting a lengthier track, Tunnel get a side to themselves (which is a project between Patrick and his wife Meike) to present their piece *I Know Your Attitude*. Opening with slightly distorted and cynically delivered female vocals that are retained throughout the track, alongside a muffled

fast-paced programmed beat. With the programmed sequence of the track being slightly more complex than those on side A, on face value there appears to be more movement with this piece particularly as further noise and sound layers are added and tweaked over a longer time span. However to get to the crux of the matter this is yet another addictive beat-oriented track. Overall the three tracks presented all use a weighty and direct approach to their dancefloor-oriented noise anthems that work particularly cohesively as part of this vinyl.

Sophia (Swe) *Sophia* CD 2000 Cold Meat Industry
Encompassing a side project of Peter Petersson (aka, the male half of Arcana) you would immediately know this is going to be a project worthy of a listen. While there is a certain songwriting style and sound that hints at Peter's work from his main project, here the orchestral and neo-classical hymns come in a much heavier, martial and aggressive guise. The sweeping orchestral melodies are kept relatively harsh and commanding due to a heavy reliance on brass instrumentation, while the ever-present booming tympani and snare percussion resembles the thousand footfalls of a charging army. Intermixed with the massive orchestral tracks are less musical ones that work more on the premise of illustrating windswept soundscapes of a recently deserted battle field. These subdued tracks break up the album in a very positive way - they work well on their own while bolstering the epic mood of more composed numbers, much like the bridging tracks on Turbund Sturmwerk's *Weltenbrand* CD. *Sigillum Militum XI* deserves a mention on its own as the building atmosphere it encompasses is very reminiscent of the constantly building aura of In Slaughter Natives' *Purgate My Stain* CD (the following track yet another all-out brass and snare percussive battle hymn that towards the end sinks into a morose French horn tune). With massive tympani percussion echoing and resonating as if it was recording in an underground cavern, *Sigillum Militum XIII* enshrines its only tune within the stunning multi layered, deep Gregorian chants of Peter - and given the atmosphere the vocals generate they are really a revelation unto themselves. The last track, opting for another windswept soundscape, integrates clanging church bells and far-off martial percussion signalling the end while illustrating to my mind's eye the victors striding off into the distance (a sparse and mellow piano tune takes up the final gasping minutes). The only complaint I could really raise in relation to this album (as has been my complaint with all of the Arcana albums thus far) is that, at a touch over 40 minutes, it is simply too short and leaves me wanting more.

Stone Glass Steel (USA) *Corruption/Redemption* 10" EP 2001 Spectre
Well, Spectre's lunacy continues with this release (part of the 10 x 10" EP series with each item in the series limited to 100), particularly as this 10" vinyl is housed between two steel plates that are held together by metal nuts welded into place. Additionally the printed cover sheets are glued to the face surfaces of the metal, whereby a rectangular piece of glass has been further attached over the Stone Glass Steel (SGS) logo. And with the 'glass' and steel' and elements represented, it is the image of a concrete wall/drain depicted on the cover that encapsulates the 'stone' element of the package's concept. Basically this has easily created one of the most impressively packaged items that I own, made all the more sweeter considering it is a SGS release (particularly as new SGS material has been rather light on the ground in the past few years). With Phil Easter (aka 'Eyespark') at the helm, he has taken a topical issue from the TUMORlist e-group and used this for inspiration of one of the tracks. Some time back when a discussion raged over whether or not the orchestral-derived keyboard sounds presented an authentic enough sound, this inspired Phil to record a track using only samples derived from actual classical/orchestra recordings. Well, *Corruption* is the final result, with this piece being rather astounding as it sounds as if all elements were recorded specifically for this composition and not collated in a cut and paste method. With shrill strings, ominous brass instrumentation (and every other orchestral sound you care to name), the track swings effortlessly through urgent passages, to layers of brooding atmospheres, to subdued romantic sentimentalities. Without having any sort of scattered cut-up sound to the final production, *corruption* comes across like a very modern and experimental orchestra composition by virtue of it being seamlessly spliced together. Without it ever sounding disjointed or messy, it simply speaks volumes of Phil's ability to be able to take an idea and bring it to fruition with stunning result. On the flip side the track is more typical of SGS - but then again what is 'typical' when considering the diversity of sound that has been previously presented under this banner? Anyway, *Redemption* takes on a framework of throbbing bass, and multi layered sounds ranging from the shrill to the subdued - yet incidentally it is these quasi-string elements that enable the track to achieve coherence with the track on the opposing side, despite sounding completely different. Heavy percussive sounds increase the pace of the track to a quick trot, as the varying layers morph into increasingly free-form structures. With the track both grounded with bass and percussion yet evoking emotive and atmospheric elements with the higher-toned layers, this is certainly SGS back in fine form. Not to end there, when the deep structural sounds are later removed, it enables the track to evolve into a sparsely shifting soundscape with widescreen cinematic scope prior to a chugging rhythmic pulse and plodding beat drawing together the far reaches of the track to morph it into its chaotic and noisy conclusion. If the above sounds too analytical, it is due to the sheer complexity that SGS compositions contain, ensuring the reviewer's task is a rather difficult one - as I can certainly attest. Notwithstanding, this is an absolutely stunning release, but with this item being sold out prior to its official release I don't like your chances of securing a copy of your own.

Stratvm Terror (Swe) *Genetic Implosion* CD 2000 Old Europa Café
The third Stratvm Terror CD (two Old Europa Café releases - *Pariah Demise* and this one - sandwiching the excellent *Pain Implantations* from Malignant) is a slathering, noisy affair drenched in moist feedback and much controlled chaos, more directly noisy than either of the previous discs. As constructed by The Master, Peter Andersson (if you do not already know who he is, your CD collection is sorely lacking...), and Tobias Larsson, *Genetic Implosion* is an exercise in sonic disarray of the highest standards. *Uranium* opens the proceedings with the slow ascent of compressed factory clatter amidst flames that voraciously lick at the swiftly charring hide. The tones are at first reminiscent of the shifting of tectonic plates that Peter has utilized in some of his other projects (specifically, Raison D'être, circa *In Sadness, Silence And Solitude*, as well as *Saifeiod* from *Death Odors II*), a kind of slow erosion of the earth from within. But the force and ferocity in which the flames devour (actually, this may be more indicative of the radioactive burn of the uranium of the song's title ... maybe...), recorded at such close range, withers the weak: it is a molten flood that singes to the marrow. It is the ambience of noise (not power electronics, nor dark sonicscape, per se, more the middle ground ... where I'd like to hear more bands explore/reference Dagda Mor's *The Border Of The Light* as a prime example of where I am coming from), honed to perfection. Metal bends and screeches during *Static Systematic Cloning*, the stentorian machinery moan birthing razor sharp tentacles of searing feedback in the process. *Cox* surges and crackles amidst more factory clatter, the pulsing undercurrent signifying life amidst the sonic discord. *Bleeding* gushes forth from the sonic wound, more of the ever-present caterwauling feedback lashing with malicious intent (a virulent cobra strike) amidst distressed samples. The final three tracks on the disc were recorded live at the Nursery Festival in Stockholm, Sweden, during June of 1998. Though not quite as sonically dense (which may just be live production versus studio production), these tracks still rage with earnest, frothing glee. Bony fingers scratch rusted metal during *Swelter Deformation*, building in intensity as flaking timbres dig frayed fingernails into the mounting sonic melee; this bleeds into *Gore*, a frothing denouement of ragged percussion amidst agitated metallic squalor. Unquestionably one of 2000's finest releases. As with all of Peter Andersson's endeavors - mandatory! -JC Smith

STROM.ec (Fin) *Dogs Of Total Order* CD 2000 Freak Animal Records
Radioactive ambience infused with irritably rustling, static-drenched pulsating noise fries my speakers (and the hairs on my arms) as the incendiary agenda of Finland's most malicious export, STROM.ec, is aligned on the introductory track, *Neuroscan*. As accompanied by doused-in-gasoline-and-set-on-fire vocals, the relentless, steamroller dynamics are fused into a surly amalgamation of no frills power electronics. Ricochet metal percussion is drowned in reverb-washed vocals and precision machinery squeal, an exercise in disorientation, during *General Enemy*. Crematorium scorched white noise and harsh, rabid (desperate...) vocals ignite *Can You See The Light*, while the body of one being burned alive bounds haphazardly about, blackened bones beating on the unforgiving walls, a flailing percussion procured from within the molten, skin-melting embrace. The distorted loops that open *Pillhead* are straight out of Deutsch Nepal's abundant reserve, but the sound that corrodes them is abusive, a flurry of convoluted noise skirmishes, humming bass tonalities and the sparse vocals cranked to demonstrative rage. A rippling screech of sound, like the wailing of a prehistoric siren, is decimated by gurgling feedback and vocals that, for all intents and purpose, eagerly gnaw at the bone and sinew of the charred body of sound, ambushed by the sheer ferocity of vitriolic expression. Through the freewheeling use of noise, as well as a prominent incorporation of reverb, STROM.ec acknowledge their industrial forefathers, while forging their own brand of intense power electronics. An upcoming release on the Malignant side-label Black Plagve should further their status as one of the preeminent purveyors of power electronics fury. - JC Smith

STROM.ec (Fin) *Glass Cage* 7" EP 2000 Kaos Kontrol
Highly acclaimed Finnish project STROM.ec return after their successful debut CD (reviewed above) with a vinyl offering of three live tracks recorded either in August 1998 or July 2000. With massively chugging power electronic looped rhythms with spiteful and fully distorted vocals bleeding into the mix, *in a glass cage* is fantastically punishing and aggressive in manner. Second track *hypnoosi* sees a diversion away from the pure death industrial/power electronics with a programmed, almost techno-styled, rhythm; however, underlying noise and spoken/echoed vocals retain a heavy and intense flavour. Side B contains a lengthy single track *you or them*, a brooding offering of mid-ranged static and distortion. Things do solidify for a minute or two via looped noise of flame-thrower-like intensity. Radio voices are detectable sporadically in between the looping framework of loud noise (or even louder noise) and for this reason alone this sounds most like it would have been a partly improvised live recording. A worthy item if the CD was to your liking.

Sturmovik (Ger) *Feldweihe* LP 2000 Tesco Organisation
Sturmovik's debut album being built on what sounds like deep orchestral melodies, it is as if these have been further buried under tons of concrete and steel, giving a very muffled and distant (not to mention distinct) aura – and, mind you, this is said in the most positive of lights. Intermixed elements also include metallic scrapings, noises, radio voices/samples evoking comparisons to subdued noise industrial material. *Stahlhauch* (the second track) is a perfect example of this orchestral/industrial mixture by interweaving rhythmic looped noise, subdued yet slightly searing texture, radio vocals and a slow evolving classical melody. An all-out World War II atmosphere is toyed with on *Volk Im Feuer*, which comprises threatening rhythms, static, and the sound of low flying bombers. It is quite difficult to find words to describe the depths of the orchestral melody on *Schicksalswg*, yet the other elements of jumbled snippets of radio voices, songs and martial drumming build the piece to a chaotic conclusion. Battle tank clatter and atmospheres of full-scale trench warfare (including bombers swooping close overhead) introduces *Sonnengefecht*, with these sounds giving way to a fantastic sampled and looped classical melody to conclude the first side of the LP. The title track opens side B with an extremely hefty rhythmic noise loop and martial percussive element, with the latter soon becoming the focal point. Shifting through a few other passages of rhythmic experimentation (all with a WWII aura of course), *Feldweihe* abruptly stalls to make way for *Der Toten Ruhe*, a rather crushing mixture of orchestral and chanted choir layers compacted under a corroding slab of noise. The martial battle hymn evoked through a clear melody and percussion indicates that *Gluhende Front* is not all that far removed from what Der Blutharsch produced on his debut full length. The final track, *Davon Geht Die Welt Nicht Unter*, opts for a subtle exit, slinking away with slow subdued loops, scattered vocal samples and fleeting segments of orchestral sound (a 1940s-era music hall recording can be detected in the dying moments). While the cover might be a simplistic slip sleeve, this is, as with all Tesco vinyl releases, presented with immaculate layout and quality card stock to capture that special 'Tesco' aura. Destined to be a much sought-after rarity – that I am quite sure of.

SubArachnoid Space (USA) *These Things Take Time* CD 2000 Release Entertainment
House of Low Culture is a guitar-oriented project that is nevertheless very much at the experimental end of the spectrum in regard to its finished product. On the other hand, SubArachnoid Space is very much a guitar band and sounds like a band proper; yet by approaching their compositions from a sweeping, improvised perspective, they ultimately end up creating quite a hallucinogenic journey. It is even more amazing to read that this release was recorded during a live to air performance that is partly evident in the music, which takes a sparse and loose framework of each instrument, then melds them into a completed composition. In regard to the musical direction, it is interesting to note that this is more firmly rooted with the meandering bass melody and atmospherically flexible mid-paced drums, while the guitar creates sparse roaming tunes that are more often than not enshrined in swirling feedback and drawn-out organ notes. Despite mostly sounding like a group of musicians in a band format, it is quite easy to find yourself swept up in the trance-like atmosphere and transported off into the often untapped cavities of your own mind, only assisted by the fact that the seven untitled tracks (*A* through *G* titles) merge into each other, never really giving the listener a hint as to where one piece finishes and the next begins. Given the 'band'-oriented sound of this album, this may not appeal to all fans of the types of sounds that *Spectrum* generally covers, but I have found this to be a refreshingly great album that has been a nice diversion from the multitude of similar albums that I receive for review.

Substanz T (Ger) Tripped experiences CD 2001 Hymen
While containing that certain accessibility that most a releases embody, this release is even more focused and a commercial tip with vocalist contributions on a number of pieces, but thankfully this has not been traded off by removing the deeper brooding intelligent compositions. Working on one level with a break beats-infused trip hop style and on the other with minimalist drone-oriented melodies there is a lot to discover and explore. *Nexus* launches Substanz T's third album - a sleek blend of trip hop breaks, whispered vocals and exquisitely haunting ambient synth melodies. *Really Good* shifts with a mid-paced bass-driven guise, and crisp echoed beat structures. Again there is no escape from the slowly chilled trance melodies. Increasingly complex, the breaks become driving, as do the tuneful elements. *Le Contact De Ta Voix* is for the most part one of the most focused pieces with the beats and programming, yet lacks the underlying brooding elements which make the preceding tracks so exceptional. Incorporating mildly funky bass lines and focused beats, this is quite club-oriented, but for my personal tastes is not as strong as other pieces. With what could be described as galactic programming sounds, *New-U* takes lethargic flight held aloft by flighty yet understated female vocals. Shifting the beats from subdued to focused breaks it enhances the mood to no end,

NEROZ

DEATH IN JUNE
Take Care And Control
CD NEROZ 42

DEATH IN JUNE
Heilige!
CD NEROZ 43

DEATH IN JUNE
The World That Summer
CD BADVC CD9

DEATH IN JUNE
Brown Book
CD BADVC CD11

The original Australian version featuring the extra track 'Circo Massimo' plus now a remixed version of 'Little Blue Butterfly'. The first collaboration between Douglas P. and Albin Julius. Cleansed!

20 live tracks to celebrate the final performance of the 20th Century. Comes in a spot varnished digipak sleeve. Thunderous!

The original 1986 vinyl recordings digitally remastered and for the first time featured on CD. This was the initial album that saw Douglas P. working as the only official member of Death In June. The digipak is spot varnished with roses, foil blocked and includes extra photos from that period. Beautiful!

1987's classic and controversial follow up to 'The World That Summer'. The original vinyl recordings, plus 3 extra tracks, digitally remastered and featured for the first time on CD. The digipak is embossed, foil blocked and contains rare promotional pictures and text from that era. Superb!

COMING SOON: BOYD RICE AND FIENDS
Wolf Pact
13 tracks. 13 days. 13 wishes. The ultimate new work between Boyd Rice, Douglas P. and Albin Julius. Unique!

Other DEATH IN JUNE material, or material by Ikon and related projects may also be in stock - so why not ask?

NEROZ   P.O.Box 277 Flemington Victoria 3031 Australia
fax: +613 9382 0310   email: commanderxxx@hotmail.com

with the deeper synth sounds reappearing. *Was It God*, with its heavy beat and trip hop focus, includes a rap MC vocal contribution which itself is not entirely bad, however isn't so impressive as to be indispensable. *Unique*, on the other hand, has a fantastic sparsity with sustained synth textures and sounds with slow non-distracting bass/beat programming - vocals likewise subdued and being presented in the form of a low whisper. Melancholic trip hop, with drone-like melody and mild breaks ensures that *Hypnotised By Bee* floats along unassumingly, while presenting visions of cold urbanism. Particularly impressive is the minimalist and forlorn piano line used late in the piece that merges classical and cutting-edge sounds giving the track a somewhat timeless aura even despite the framing break beats. *SOLution*, with its prominent snappy breaks and urgent beat programming, offsets these against moody synth textures and angelic female backing vocals. By way of a plodding bass melody and slow-plucked guitar tune the mood of *Black* is a morose yet atmospheric one, only grounded by the straightforward kit and symbol percussion. The closing piece *Unite* chooses a lounge-type vibe with sprinkled keyboard noodling, that I had slight misgivings about until the track busts out with snappy kit percussion beats of hip hop flair (groove-oriented indeed). Those of you who have purchased material from this label would have a good idea of what to expect from this, with this being a rather pleasant diversion from other sonic weight that my ears are regularly subjected to.

Sutcliffe Jugend (Eng) *XI* 7" EP 2000 Death Factory
Side V contains two tracks, or what seems like two tracks; there seems a distinct break between segments at least, and since there are no track titles listed … well… The first track is doused in nausea-drenched vocals, rubbery, upon which the lash of abusive percussion smacks the soft gray matter of a demented, legion of maniacs, hive mind. This succumbs to a looped ambience that cruises along darkened streets and through back alleys, as fingernails of dread existence (aligned by insidious motives, insidious desires…) scratch at the back of the cranial cellar. The second track (or second half?) is an eruption of bleached insanity power electronics, lubricated, fists of nails noise that shreds an unwilling orifice as unintelligible vocals deliriously expound teeth-grinding gibberish. (Whew!) The silence that follows is pierced by what sounds like some seafaring loon (be it 1. A fish-eating, diving bird or 2. A crazy person…) off in the distance. Weird, and subtly disturbing. *VI* continues along a similar path, successfully lulling the listener into a state of anticipation via ground bones ambience that simmers uncomfortably, the tension growing progressively more prominent until an abrupt thrust of needles into the tympanum (in the ear) rattles all thought amidst the high-pitched attack. And yet, it all has the essence of control, restraint, and the unmitigated joy in torture. Control is annihilated towards the end as a regurgitative flow of truly sick vocal administrations is unleashed, vomitous tides in line with what the deranged, drooling occupant of an insane asylum might spew. Some of the best work Sutcliffe Jugend have yet produced, convincingly powerful documents of unfettered lunacy. -JC Smith

Sunn O))) (USA) *The Grimmrobe Demos* CD 2000 Double H Noise Industries (2xHNI)
With what appears to be only bass and guitar used for this recording, it is quite difficult to find words that might adequately describe the sonic weight and intensity captured in these sub-bass drones and harmonics. Sunn O))) present what are essentially guitar compositions, yet ones that are played at such a lethargic pace while the overriding guttural distortion creates a drone-oriented framework that is at some remove from a typical 'band' format (from this perspective, the liner note description of the music as *"doom:power:ambient:drone:invokati on"* is spot on the mark). The CD's three tracks still clock in at just short of 45 minutes, further highlighting the almost catatonic pace of playing. Likewise, often hidden under the weighty, down-tuned bass and guitar drone elements are distant and atmospheric guitar riffs and other general noodlings that work to add more fleeting layered elements to the otherwise crushing tonal textures. As for the main melodies of the songs, these are quite deceiving and difficult to grasp due to their slow pace. Basically the tracks drag you along on their individual journeys, where only a few preceding musical notes are remembered. Essentially this prevents the overall song structure from being deciphered in its entirety, suggesting that the tonal harmonics are the main identifiable musical element. While you can certainly hear the guitar/bass elements on these tracks, clearly the style and focus of the actual playing allows you to transcend 'listening' to these elements as you normally would. I must admit that at first I was a little apprehensive about the project, simply due to its 'guitar' orientation; but after hearing Sunn O))) I am thoroughly glad that I have. For a very broad comparison this might be like a beefed-up and slowed down concoction of the heaviest elements of Novatron. The cover is also damn fantastic in imagery and presentation, consisting of a trifold heavy card sleeve with separate card band to hold the CD in place.

Sunn O))) (USA) *00 VOID* CD 2000 Double H Noise Industries (2xHNI)
Although this is the second album from the power ambient drone doomsters Sunn O))), on *'00 Void* I believe that the group have reworked parts of *The Grimmrobe Demos* sessions into the basis of this album. To partake in a bit of name dropping, this album was recorded under the guidance and direction of one-time Kyuss bass player Scott Reader (and anyone who knows Kyuss will be familiar with the guttural, stoner rock bass sound for which they are renowned) making Scott an obvious choice to consult regarding heavy bass-oriented production. On this album the same style, framework and direction as the debut CD is clearly followed; however, when translated through Scott Reader's production, it has created a guitar power drone framework where each instrument layer is both cleaner and even more guttural and ominous than before. The same goes for the higher end layers, which achieve a greater level of atmospherics when they are fleetingly used. With four tracks presented to illustrate the *'00 Void*, the album achieves a play time of just short of 60 minutes, with the pace of the tracks akin to watching a piece of dead flesh slowly shrivelling under the incessant attack of the blazing sun (or SunnO))) in this case!). Interestingly, one of the four compositions (*Rabbits' Revenge*) is actually a Melvins cover – not that you would ever recognise it as such, again due to the song's morphed transformation into a guitar drone soundscape (with hints of percussion to be sparingly detected in the backing of this track). The cover of this (a standard jewel case) might not be quite as special as *The Grimmrobe Demos*, however the graphic art does make up for this. I can also say that I was rather surprised to see an excerpt from the William H. Gass novel *The Tunnel* quoted on the cover; yet given the absolute desolation and desperation it conveys it certainly does set a similar mood to that of the music. In conclusion, either of the Sunn O))) releases would be a recommended starting point as both have their particular charms in relation to sound and presentation.

Terra Sancta (Aus) *Anno Domini 2000* MCDR 2000 Terra Sancta
For a debut recording this is a surprisingly strong work that suitably aligns itself with the early- to mid-sound of the infamous Cold Meat Industry label. Terra Sancta takes its cue from stunning acts like Raison D'être and Desiderii Marginis, which is less an accusation of plagiarism than an indicator of the depth and maturity that has been achieved on this first official recording. I even feel that any of these tracks would have nestled perfectly into the line-up of either of the two now legendary *Death Odors* CDs released on Slaughter Productions. Three lengthy tracks span the 32 minutes of music, mixing sparse textural soundscapes, deathly drawn-out keyboard melodies and smatterings of sampled (predominantly female) choir vocals. Depth and sparseness are used positively as compositional elements, and are particularly noteworthy when a sorrowful (sampled) violin tune rises briefly out of the depressive undercurrent of the first piece, *Desert Earth* (late in the piece the sparse textural elements take on the guise of searing desert winds whipping up a blinding sandstorm). *The Infinite Lurking* is not as gentle as the title may suggest, and commences calmly with multi layered choir vocals before fierce mid-ranged layers arc into the composition (illustrating the final death throes perhaps?). Things do calm down again, but only very briefly before massive drawn-out keyboard drones and catatonic melodies commandingly stride into contention and remain for the majority of the piece. A Middle Eastern flavour is apparent on Lithified with a (again, sampled) wind instrument melody that gives way to a mid-ranged slow keyboard tune (evoking a distant mournful aura) set against sounds of slowly dripping water and other assorted field-type recordings. The only other point I can make is that, while there is no complaint with the sound and production, I get the feeling that a good bit of mastering work on this recording would have assisted in further evolving it from great to brilliant (but, all things considered, this is a minor point). I will admit that I have constantly whined about the lack of quality Australian acts that align themselves with *Spectrum*'s content, but a least now a few noteworthy projects are beginning to surface.

This Empty Flow (Fin) *Nowafter* CD 2001 Eibon Records
With the bio stating that this is to be filed under "dark", it is not much of a lead to go on, but further on, when it references The Cure and Pink Floyd as musical reference points, it sparks intrigue. Anyway, after having given this CD a wealth of listens, I can say that I don't entirely agree with providing merely two musical reference points. Rather I'd heap massive amounts of praise on this by saying that it is an absolutely astounding album by further incorporating elements of how Portishead and Radiohead approach their songwriting and production. Musically diverse, instrumentally intricate, and stunningly written, each track is leagues apart from the next, yet there is still a perfect cohesion to the dark musical streak that interweaves all elements into a full album. From the quirky electronica/pop/rock of the album opener *Jen(N!)i Force*, it sets the scene for something quite different for both Eibon Records and the underground scene in general. The widescreen musical aesthetic of *marmite* certainly brings to mind some of the most depressive moments of Radiohead, here with the mellow tune seething out into the bleak horizon. The quirky pop of *Stilton* is only made more bizarre by the high-pitched male vocals, as the track swings along with programmed drums and leftfield guitar melodies. Another touch of Radiohead melancholia is employed on *Shoreditche* and when it eventually breaks its tethers, this track really takes flight in wide upward spirals. With a bleak organ dirge, driving bass and xylophone tune, things couldn't get weirder on *and also the drops* until the vocals (both lead and backing) are presented with a flamboyant air akin to those of David Bowie – and by all accounts none of this should work, but does in stunningly superb fashion. On *one song about solitude*, the Cure reference can be seen clearer than on any track preceding it - here the slow kit drumming having a beautiful cavernous echo, as fragile morose vocals bleed their themes over a tune of plodding bass and subdued keys (and if you were to wallow in melancholy the last half of this track would be the perfect accompaniment….). The slinky bass and kit percussion-driven dub-type atmosphere has a Portishead touch to it, but obviously the male vocals and other touches of depressive guitar, synth and piano lines have given this a life and character of its own. With the intricate opening guitar lines of *Drops* you can't help but be reminded of Katatonia's recent musical approach, but this takes that atmosphere up a fair few notches when it kicks in with a full complement of guitars, drums and clean vocals, all generating a sweetly sorrowful sound that meanders forward, effortlessly increasing with passion and emotion. Returning to a Cure-esque aura on *Angel's Playground*, the drawn-out drums, synths and vocals create the bed on which the mournful lone guitar line reclines upon (*Hunger* likewise plays out in very comparable format). In terms of background to this album, it does not represent the first for the group, rather a release that includes new tracks, as well as tracks lifted off an earlier album and limited promotional CD. (To my ear the early album tracks of quirky yet dark pop/electronica would constitute the most recent recordings, while the latter portion of the album encompasses the more subdued depressive compositions – those being the earlier works). Despite the subtly detectable differences in recording styles between tracks, the overall re-mastering has presented a release that works as if it were always intended to be the one album. Lastly, if there were any release of this issue to be able to cross over to the mainstream and make it big, clearly this is it (and partly due to this encompassing a more palatable band framework). Nonetheless I will say that Eibon are by no means exaggerating when they claim This Empty Flow is one of the greatest undiscovered bands on the planet.

Tribe of Circle (Fra) *Rien ne disparait jamais vraiment…* CD 2000 Athanor
Athanor have come up with the goods again by releasing the debut album of this group (after a 7" on Hau Ruk that I am yet to hear). To begin with, the primary 'tool' used by this project in the creation and categorisation of their sound is the looping of segments of music which, depending on what is sampled, alters the focus and style of the sound. A short military tattoo-type bagpipe tune (including bodhran percussion) introduces the album followed by *When tears turn into solidarity* that melds a short looped female vocal and deeper solid loops, heavy noise and unusual percussive sounds gradually melding into a loose driving collage. The metallic clanks, aggressive scraping sounds, choir-like textures and crushing percussion of *Colours of Europa* each introduce themselves at different points, gradually building on what the previous loop had brought forward, yet things take a stunning twist when a highly rousing orchestral loop (comprising horn and string section) leaps from the speakers mid-song and takes the forefront for the remainder of the track in simply stunning fashion. Deep ritual sounds and shrill orchestral textures ensures that *Evil is a point of view* (I assume this would have to be a tongue-in-cheek title) is an emotionally unnerving listen, that in shades brings to mind Raison D'être due to the desolate tones of the sampled choir vocals. *In this Land!* redefines driving percussion via its presentation of incessant mid-ranged looping floor tom rolls, underscored with more spare sound textures and bass melody (but never really becoming tuneful) in a sort of old school industrial fashion. Continuing in similar vibe (in a vague roundabout way) *Coranic Submission* infuses rousing crowd noise and whip-crack beat (an ode to Death In June perhaps, considering Douglas P. is greeted on the cover). The title track and concluding piece packs a fair punch, mixing ritual/martial/neo-classical loops into a crushing blend, with one segment revealing the unnerving sound of a pulse monitor cutting out only to hear spiteful laughter echoing off in the backing. Vocal chants, screams and German speech samples further add to this unnerving chaotic air, opting to shake the listener right to the last minutes of the album (only for a sampled merrygo-round carnival tune to appear in the dying seconds - simply weird). Of this group I can say that I had previously heard comparisons made to the likes of Deutsch Nepal (in relation to the sound loops) and Der Blutharsch (in relation to the orchestral/militant sound), both of which I would agree with entirely. Apart from the quality of the music, the brown and sepia tones of the digi pack cap this off as an extremely solid debut album.

Trifid Project (Wld) *Trifid Project* (featuring: James Plotkin, Matthieu, Sheila Mata, Yves and Marie Daubert) MCD 2001 Vacuum

Quirky, very experimental and tripped out, this multi-collaborational project revolves around the electronica end of the musical spectrum. Complex beat/blip sequences introduce the MCD on *Rubber Chick*, not really containing a tune as such, rather using melodious bass sounds and the programming to take the track through its paces. Being even more bizarre, the limping gate of beats and fractured structure of *Alice* is melded with a peculiarly vocalised and computer-treated French accented female voice. Track three, *Zickzack* is credited as being created only by James Plotkin, opting for a cut-up experimental collage, ranging from crystalline textures to tonal outbursts and quite similar to various Mego artists. *The Nine* runs the straightest edge of all tracks that precede it via using dense up-tempo styled beats and lashing bass guitar-driven rhythms, creating one of the more user-friendly compositions of the MCD. At over five minutes it is one of the longer tracks, using its timeframe to morph off on tangents while still retaining a common theme of a darkened electronica groove. *Psalm 66* from its outset contains dense bass reverberations, distant guitar riffing, building atmospherically echoed drum percussion and some understated female vocals. Basically of all the pieces of the MCD this is the track that best suits the cover art that depicts a number of wave/surfer images, particularly due to the guitars accommodating a jangly tone associated with instrumental surf-inspired music. Final track *Nebula*, despite being too short, is a rather spacious and minimalist drone piece reflecting its title with occasional vocal snippets added for good measure. While this is an interestingly complex and intricately produced recording, I am also of the opinion that this is almost too diverse for its own good. I guess this must be one of the difficulties of having five people collaborate on a project, while only recording an EP's worth of material.

Troum (Ger) Framaþeis/Vŭr 12" EP 2000 Moloko

Although representing my first introduction to Troum, I am aware that this is the project of one Stefan Knappe of Drone Records and Maeror Tri fame. Containing a shimmering crystalline resonance, *Framaþeis* gradually envelops the room, with sweeping and subdued harmonics. Gently the atmospherics are pushed in more areas of louder volumes that coincide with the increasing intensity of the tonal shifts. Late in the track things become quite heavy on the rhythmic side, accommodating a rather crushing echoed tone, marking a much heavier drone aesthetic for the remainder of the track. *Vŭr* on the other hand is more focused and intense from the outset, with grinding drones, and assorted attacking noise layers. Due to the faster pace it is able to generate an atmospheric and inwardly swirling vortex, thus creating a track that becomes tighter and more enveloping as it progresses, achieving a comparable sound to that of Yen Pox (incidentally, an upcoming album sees these two groups collaborating). Anyway in terms of this track, I guess that drone works don't come any more sophisticated than this. Given these two tracks were recorded back in 1997 and 1998, I am very interested to hear what Troum have been producing on more recent offerings and particularly the above mentioned collaboration.

Various Artists (Wld) *deafness is not a gift* CD 2001 Deafborn Records

Picking a selection of (clearly) noise-oriented artists, Deafborn Records have produced a premier themed compilation, with the quote of the cover expanding on this topic: *"those who are unwilling to listen are not much better off than the deaf"*. With all track contributions being exclusive, it ensures that interest in this should be at peak level. Reminding me somewhat of the style and focus of Stateart's *How Terrorists Kill* compilation, one should really have an appreciation of hectic noise and power electronics to tackle this (or certainly be willing to subject yourself to some rather ear-shattering and brain-numbing compositions). Cazzodio introduce the compilation, clearly spelling out its focus with an all-out punishment of atmospheric noise melding partial structure into the chaos as the metallic percussion forges forward (with select noise layers following suit and overall reminding me of Stratvm Terror's noisiest pieces). On *bilaterally unwanted*, Grunt showcase a sustained high-end noise approach with an underbelly of weighty distortion that is certainly focused, if not a touch one-dimensional. Regardless, the blistering noise, throbbing distortional structure and vocals presented as expulsions of violent static certainly ensures Rectal Surgery's track is worthy of a particular and individual mention. At the quieter end (and to provide just a hint of respite), Anemone Tube's track starts off with a lower key approach having a touch of a death industrial framework with distortional static amassing in the background that gradually crawls towards the foreground – achieving submission through a subversive approach. Continuing on (and being far from subversive), the Death Squad track is a fantastic free-form and chaotic yet atmospheric piece that uses prominent screamed and further distorted vocals (that are certainly reminiscent of the Con-Dom or Grey Wolves approach). Despite this compilation being mastered VERY loud, somehow Macronympha (the American noise specialist) manages to be even louder than most, with a partly fragmented piece of metallic/electronic-oriented noisescape. DL, on the other hand, creates an aura of a slightly more experimental noise aesthetic with some choppy, some atmospheric, sounds along with wavering short band radio scanning elements (yet it is the sporadic moaning of a distant human voice that is a bizarre and slightly unnerving addition). Einleitungszeit is a fierce beast to contend with due to high-end piercing distortion writhing above a dense and slow metallic percussive base. Working both on structured and free-form levels, the vocals meld into the mix, sometimes providing focus but mostly adding to the sonic chaos. Lefthandeddecision's piece contains a hint of rhythmic structure with the mid-ranged rumbling static affair, but does not progress terribly far as the piece is less than three minutes in length. Admittedly Satori's contribution stands out more than most, mainly as they are much more subdued, starting with slow tonal shifts of sound and far-off noise, building further with blasts of crunchy static (nice!). The final track on this compilation is offered up by Skalpell, presenting a track of noisy dark ambience generated via pulsating undercurrents inter-spread with free-form static, dialogue samples and a cyclic tune that certainly ensures *purgatorium* is a memorable conclusion. Without having made reference to all tracks, other pieces are presented by Narbenerde, Murnau, Irikarah, Government Alpha and Mourmansk 150 which take this 16-track compilation up to a play time just shy of 75 minutes. A release that your ear specialist is highly unlikely to recommend (unless to first dislodge that nasty wax build-up!).

Various Artists (Ita) *Death Odors* CD 2000 Slaughter Productions

I am not going to undertake a proper review of this, given it is limited re-pressing of a much sought-after cult compilation. If anything, this 'review' is a reminder call to those who, after missing it the first time around, might still be looking for a copy. Issued as the first CD release for Slaughter Productions back in 1994 in a 1,000 copy edition (until this point Slaughter Productions had been operating solely as a tape label), this item has almost become a cult classic, that also spawned the successful follow up *Death Odors II* CD of 1997. Many of the names on this compilation are now cult classics in their own right, including the likes of Megaptera, Raison D'être and Archon Satani, with many of the remaining acts likewise being well recognised (such as Inanna, Atom Infant Incubator, Runes Order, Alio Die, Allerseelen, Con Sono and The Grey Wolves). For those interested take heed of this message and do not miss out on this second opportunity given this re-release is in an edition of a mere 500 copies.

Various Artists (USA) *Middle Pillar Presents: BUTOH – The Dance of Darkness* CD 2000 Middle Pillar Presents

BUTOH is a compilation whose main theme centres around the aural exploration of Japanese dance theatre, and each of the featured artists have presented tracks that interpret this 'dance of darkness'. A short segment of tribal drumming and fractured noise loops (by Kobe) introduces the proceedings, followed quickly by A Murder of Angels with a cinematic yet nightmare-inducing soundscape (liquidous shimmering sounds, discordant bell chimes, factory loops and forlorn chants constitute the mix). The soaring female vocals and beat-oriented track by Mors Syphilitica encompasses an ethereal flair due to the melody and style, with the following track by The Machine in the Garden also having an ethereal element, but one that is generated through more gothic programmed means. On *Chrysalis* The Unquiet Void truly astound with an engulfing peek into the expansive depths of cinematic dark ambience. Here the depth and breadth of sound sucks you into its vortex, as the percussive elements become an increasing focal point as time elapses. Sumerland, a male vocal/piano-oriented ethereal project, present a track entitled *Morpheus* that, apart from the main mentioned elements, utilises keyboard backings, percussion, etc. to build its brooding mood. A Murder of Angels impress yet again on *Vessel of the Incubi*, which interestingly moves away from the strictly dark ambience of the first track towards a heavier reliance on percussion with each of the sound elements being blended perfectly. The gothic-oriented style of Wench's track does not really catch my ear positively, yet this has more to do with my own musical preferences. This also partly extends to the second track by The Machine in the Garden and the remix track by The Mirror Reveals, due to the heavy reliance on what I consider to be somewhat cheesy keyboard programming. Not to be marred by these, Thread presents a quite bizarre electronic piece consisting of beats, programming and soundscape elements. Zoar opts for a quirky mixture of dark keyboard melodies and industrial beats (that lean towards a dance style), but actually manage to pull this off quite well by not going overboard with the beat programming while including a few subdued guitar riffs that follow the main melody. The Unquiet Void have also been given the opportunity to present two pieces, and their second track is a remix of a track from the project's debut album. Static glitches and disembodied voices float over the original track, which has also undergone some slight cut-up treatment while retaining its sweeping cinematic dark ambient aura. Being introduced by Kobe, the compilation is likewise closed by another tribal percussive piece that has been further treated with industrial noise loops. Judging from the intro/outro by Kobe, it would be quite interesting to see what the group would sound like if the tracks were longer than the one to two minutes presented here. As with all Middle Pillar releases, the CD is housed in a stunning card fold out cover.

Various Artists (Swe) *Nihil* DxLP 2000 Cold Meat Industry

This double LP collection spotlights four of Sweden's most virulent practitioners of fiery, agitated noise, kind of a more concentrated extension of the ideals and abusive agenda featured on the double CD *Estheticks of Cruelty* compilation from 1999. Each of the four participants is given one side upon which to convey their own special brand of noise. IRM get things rolling with the molten stomp and shimmering feedback squeal of *The Cult Of The Young Man*. Through a mouthful of highly processed, phlegm-coated vocals, the track continues along thematically similar terrain as the brilliant *Oedipus Dethroned* CD: self-destruction through Christ. Each of the five tracks meticulously winds lurching rhythms through fields of flesh stretched taut and awaiting autopsy, a self-dissection sliced by scalpels of intense vocals spewing concentrated streams of rage. It is a cacophony of hyper-focused, all-encompassing hatred, of God and self! *Euphoria (Rebirth)* wraps things up with a ferocious battery of noise that tumbles like boulders of compressed bone, beating on vocals that urge one into a loop of self-immolation. The IRM side is worth the price of admission; I'm in firm belief that they are one of the best power electronics bands around! Catching my breath ... and on to side two. Institut gets positively explosive as the white noise tsunami that is *Autohypocrisy* clatters and crashes maniacally. Through clenched teeth windstorms, Institut batter an array of found sounds into a screech, ratchet and clamor assimilation of absolute chaos; they sound like the pissed-off half-brother of Dissecting Table. Probably the best track yet by Institut, who apply a more skittish, scratchy, shuffling rhythmic approach to their lone other track (more in line with the material on their debut CD, *Great Day To Get Even*). A looped giggling child introduces one to Nod's contributions on side three. Of course, this amusing pretext is buried beneath a barrage of combustible noise, bent on brutalizing through sheer force and monolithic heft. Synths wage battle in the background, adding an almost melodic texture, while vocals psychotically rant amidst the reverb-drenched clutter. A female recites the strange tale of *The Girl And The Giant*, a fairy tale told amidst exhaling noise that becomes (once again) melodic and distorted towards the end. Very odd! There is much variety to the Nod tracks, including everything from reverberant noise to a storyteller's approach to lyric recitation. Intriguing. IRM side-project, Sharon's Last Party, wrap things up with six incendiary tracks of crackling, distortion frosted noise (well, five, as *Love Never Ends* is just a quirky song filled with ... love, a snippet, a sample, from another era). *When Love Came To Your House* ripples with streamers of feedback that fall like shards of metallic confetti; an uproarious wave of noise and incensed vocals spill forth, a convulsive, rusted din that flays the eardrums. *Never Learned To Love You* is adorned in machinery-ground static that percolates below vocals seeking those who understand that "Submission is a gift," sonically submitting to the pounding sway of the percussion. Four sides of impressive power electronics noise, though it must be noted (again) that the price of admission is paid back with interest during the phenomenal IRM side. -JC Smith

Various Artists (Wld) *Salvation Bloodletting* CD 2001 Live Bait Recording Foundation

Some quite positive recommendations were forthcoming regarding this religious dogma-themed compilation even prior to it being released, and when after perusing who is featured, I can see why. Featuring many up-and-coming projects, including many from the American scene (nine of the 14 projects are from America), it is a positively collated collection of dark ambient, death industrial-oriented tracks. Being one of the more senior projects of the compilation, Amon get things started with a densely heavy dark ambient movement of low-end shifting atmospherics (and anyone who has heard Amon before should know the high quality of material to expect). Baal/Berith is up next and appears to be a live collaboration between Baal and Murderous Vision. Their track, *Checotah Blood Cult*, presents a collage of deep drawn-out sounds that contains quite a sharp and metallic resonance - solidifying into an increasingly urgent composition with the incorporation of a tribal percussive element. The Hollowing on their track also take on a percussive sound by presenting a bizarre amalgam of tribal chants, ridging and incessant pounding beats, noise and horn blasts etc. that is as if you have been transported to deep within the jungles of South America to witness the rituals of a cannibal cult. No Festival of Light feature their track *The Onomako Brush* (lifted from their latest CD *If God Lived on Earth we Would Break His Windows*), and is basically a great piece of rousing tribal percussion with a subdued undercurrent of ambience. Origami Arktika mark a shift away from the tribal percussive sounds with a mid-volume piece of droning and aquatic-sounding dark ambience that becomes quite complex via multi layering techniques, including elements that appear to have derived from environmental recordings. Being the first recording I have heard from German project Azoikum, *Mein Ist Die Rache* is a great track of tense death industrial proportions, where repeated radio voices (speaking on religious themes) alongside gruff distorted vocals are mixed into a throbbing and spiraling mass of blunted noise textures). Rising French project Nothvs Filivs Mortis create a monumental death ambient track of cavernous and resonating textures. Catatonic in pace, blasphemous choirs chant in the background, whilst scattered voices puncture the dense mass of sound that forges forward with sound elements converging into increasing structure (and this track certainly gives Megaptera a run for their money!). Deison's track is somewhat subdued when compared to the tracks on their recent *Dirty Blind Vortex* CD – with the piece crawling along with sustained drones and dense programming to introduce a morbid chopsticks-styled keyboard tune midway through. Nothing being a project name I am aware of, *Self Spiller* is, however, my first introduction to their actual music. Representing a great track, it incorporates an unusual blend of dark electronica and death industrial programming, to create a mid-paced heavy percussive piece. Slowvent add further weight to the American 'noise ambient' sound via a track that I might just have mistaken for a Gruntsplatter piece if I weren't closely following the play list! Static-riddled and bass-heavy, Slowvent's track shifts along with distortional weight in a partially-structured rumbling mass of speaker imploding intensity. Gruntsplatter, up next, opt to infuse a power electronics aesthetic into their noise ambient sound. With higher-end static noise over a hefty slab of bass sound, it is the perfect counterpart to some sickly screamed and distorted vocals. Building in intensity throughout, it morphs through a muffled sound, finally arriving at a much clearer but no less harsh production. In Death's Throes amaze with their piece *Slay the Savior* which is a massive sounding death industrial piece. Noisy yet highly atmospheric, it shifts through free-form structure like a cadaver lost and ambling through the catacombs. Raven's Bane present a louder and noisier track when referencing their recent CDR (also on Live Bait), particularly due to the use of a much more forceful structure whipped into a swirling mass. Lefthandeddecision tackles the final piece of the compilation. A bulldozering number of grinding distortion that might just contain some sampled voices somewhere under all those crunchy textures! This is without doubt a strong compilation from start to finish, which merely points to the quality of material submitted.

Various Artists (Wld) ***Ten Years of Madness: Behind the Iron Curtain*** **2xCD 2000 Achtung Baby!**
With the variety of cult acts on here this double CD compilation will not need much talking up to sell its limited pressing of 1,000 copies (some of those names being Inade, Turbund Sturmwerk, Der Blutharsch, Blood Axis, Ostara, Nový Svět, Les Joyaux de la Princesse etc.). Essentially this is a celebration and document of the first 10 years of the Achtung Baby! website that operates out of Russia and focuses on post-industrial and related music styles. It seems that there was an earlier version of this compilation including a few different tracks that was released on double cassette. However, as far as I am aware it was not widely available and may have only been distributed amongst the featured artists. Anyway, with this version of the compilation including the input of Sanctum, First Law, Skrol, Dissecting Table, Cyclotimia, Troum, Dream into Dust, Ataraxia (amongst many others and having a total of 27 artists in all), it is a classic collection of artists and their individual works that ensures an extremely diverse, yet well-conceived and executed, compilation. Housed in an oversized A5 card sleeve, the 16 black pages (with silver print) contain imagery for each group (along with basic project information) and other text and pictures associated with the compilations theme. Recommended.

Various Artists (Wld) ***The Pact … of the Gods*** **CD 2000 Fremdheit**
Being a sister compilation to the recently re-released compilation *The Pact: Flying in the Face*, this CD covers tracks from quite a few well-known suspects of the neo-folk movement. The late William Burroughs, who (along with Ian Read) was partly responsible for the original compilation idea, introduces the CD at the commencement of the rousing apocalyptic folk number by Changes. With intricate acoustic guitar strumming and commanding vocals singing about the world's impending demise, the short length (a mere two minutes) of *Waiting for the Fall* does not do justice to the fantastic atmosphere evoked. This is followed by Der Blutharsch, where Albin and entourage present a quality martial/ritual percussive-type track that nevertheless doesn't break new ground for the group. The Fire + Ice track is another fantastic apocalyptic folk piece with the morose vocals of Ian Read embellished by bodhran percussion, violin and acoustic guitar. The Ataraxia track contains a similar feel to the preceding Fire + Ice piece; yet the multi-layered vocals (ranging from spoken to operatic) of Francesca Nicoli are the real gem here and even call to mind Alzbeth's vocals in the now-defunct The Moon Lay Hidden Beneath a Cloud. Allerseelen surprises with a piece of slow and heavy percussion and looped violin melodies (in amongst various other sound elements), which is followed by In Gowan Ring tackling a traditional folk piece, *The Rolling of the Stones*, thus evoking a gentle folksy aura that gradually builds to a jig. The prominence of the female vocals on Camerata Mediolanense's track, which sound quite like those of Francesca Nicoli, makes me wonder whether this is an Atraraxia side project – and the track itself is a live recording of massively martial-oriented percussion with keyboard and melody encompassing the tune. The quite stunning brooding soundscape of *Der Gefallene Engel* by Blood Axis (which previously appeared on the *Saturn Gnosis* 2 x 10" compilation) is included here, and while I would have preferred to hear more new material, I have been placated by its sheer quality. Shinig Vril is up next, and their sound differs significantly to what they displayed on the split CD with Knifeladder - here the track encompasses an organ dirge with other random scaping sounds and deep ritual percussive throbs. The start of the Mee track is quite impressive with strained and emotive female vocals; however, as things progress the vocals become increasingly over the top and just don't sit well with me. Not to be fazed by this, the following intricate and introspective acoustics and lone male vocals (sung exclusively in German) of Forseti work particularly well when embellished by flute, cello and bodhran percussion. Ostara are likewise featured here, having lifted a track from the *Secret Homeland* album - this composition, *The Reckoning*, is a fantastically romantic celebratory waltz. Markus Wolff's project, Waldterfel (assisted by Michael Moynihan and Annabel Lee of Blood Axis), tender an aggressive folksy piece of driving percussion and booming vocals while layered violins direct the tune. David Lee's one-minute piece is more of a spoken word track with some backing keyboard noodlings, and the compilation is finally closed by the Australian group Bestianity, who present a very aggressive soundscape of various loops, spiteful vocals and free-form drum kit percussion. The number of well-recognised names on the compilation should be reason enough to obtain a copy.

Various Artists (Aut) ***Wo Die Wilden Kerle Wohnen*** **7" EP 2000 Rauhnacht**
Representing a release on a new and quite obscure sub label of WKN/Hau Ruk (Albin Julius's label) this is a four-track compilation of Austrian artists (namely Allerseleen Allgrena, Der Blutharsch and Nový Svět), and with the title translating roughly to "where the wild things are" this partly explains the more avant-garde and playful nature of each of the band's offerings. To also tie in with the title, the cover depicts four mini-bike riders wearing masks associated with the mythical creature Krampus. Allerseelen are up first with a rhythmic marching soundscape piece that actually reminds me of a couple of Deutsch Nepal tracks off their *Deflagration of Hell* CD (however, the female vocals do give this piece a greater sense of consistency than other Allerseelen pieces). Built around a constant mid-paced beat, chimed tune and noise loops, the vocals are presented in a layered guise to create a hypnotic track. Allgrena, being a group that I am not familiar with, present their track as an interesting piece of sound and rhythmic experimentations to create an off-kilter aura. Moving on to side two, I have never really agreed with the description of Der Blutharsch's songs as being 'kinky military music', yet this describes this particular track perfectly, given the playful organ tunes sitting in amongst the looped and heavily rhythmic marching chimes and beats. Fleetingly, violins and vocals appear but do not distract the focus from the heavy percussion that remains the focal point throughout. The Nový Svět track does its best to be even more bizarre than normal, with their track - a slow and plodding tuba and accordion-driven tune, - underscored with deep percussion and the trademark morose male vocals (and every time I hear this track I can't help but picture a procession of elephants!). If you have any interest in the featured artists, this a decent item to track down.

Vedisni (USA) ***Architects and Murderers*** **CD 2000 Dragon Flight Recordings**
In what I believe is the debut album for Vedisni, dense industrial cacophony is ritualistically toyed with in a brooding and harsh manner, so much so that on several occasions I found myself making comparisons to Stratvm Terror (particularly the *Pain Implantations* CD). Outbursts of static shards are spat from the speakers, occasionally becoming so blisteringly loud that it almost constitutes a fierce noise release – as is evident during various points on the first track *Fnord. as gift.* The second track, *Mercurious Apex – Blue Psyche*, holds an underscore of slightly symphonic keyboard tone accentuating the grinding mid- to low-ranged textures that build and multiply to static fury, while later simmering down to a very nice section of rhythmic pulses and catatonic keyboard melodies. Some aspects of this release have me somewhat convinced that the individuals involved in this project may have something to do with the metal scene, however I have difficulty in putting my finger on specific elements (maybe the occasional screeched vocal is somewhat of a start). This is not to say that this sounds like a metal album at all, rather in stylistic terms it sounds akin to how someone accustomed to playing metal would approach a dark industrial release. This is by no means a criticism, but merely an observation about how one genre may influence the product of another. Anyway, having made reference to the vocals, it is on tracks like *Where Ouspensky Failed and Gurdjieff Fled* that the vocals unfortunately jar against the dark ritual pulses and venting of sonic fissures, creating a somewhat distracting element. Regardless, the album strides onward, continuing with the grandiosely titled *A Sword into a Cup, as Seven Insects Proclaim*, which contains both brooding ritualistic percussion and subdued symphonic textures that again morph into screaming washes of static (here the vocals are given the full static work over and fit in quite well). The final track, the fantastically titled *Driven East Like Another's Menace*, is the most fragile composition on offer, commencing with very subdued low clangs, far-off voices and sweeping sounds that all give rise to a very cavernous sound, while sections of barely discernable morose keyboard melodies add to the aura (the keyboard segment gradually gives

rise to more classically-inspired sounds that likewise beg a partial comparison to Caul). Towards the final third, bludgeoning feedback commences its gradual obliteration of the composition, akin to the sound of metallic maggots as they bore into the sonic tapestry. The music on this very active CD is not content to stay in one place for long, instead choosing to tangent off from the main themes of the tracks, particularly since the five compositions range in length from seven to 16 minutes. With this relatively new label having dredged the American underground, thus far they have unearthed a number of decent releases. This is certainly one of them.

Darrin Verhagen (Aus) *Hydra* CD 2000 Dorobo Limited Editions
With what seems to be a constant demand for Darrin to produce the soundtracks for experimental dance theatre, *Hydra* is another such release based around a water-themed dance production by the Chunky Moves collective. Despite the dance side of things containing the prior mentioned water theme, the soundscapes presented are actually sharp and clinical experimental electronics. Also the label contains a warning that the CD *"contains trace elements of soft ash"*, which refers to one of Darrin's earlier solo experimental soundworks released with the *Soft Ash* title - snippets from this can be occasionally identified. The first track, *Prelude*, contains acoustic/glacial-type reverberations with fleeting radio voices gradually building the track to a heightened point of all-out chaos by solidifying other electronic static and sonar sonics. Track two, *Carnage*, is simply that, with its massive static over-driven rhythmic electronic mayhem and heaps of leftfield improvised noise to keep you on your toes. *Aftermath* calms proceedings considerably by slipping into an introspective track of subsonic isolationist musings, and is akin to listing to a rumbling thunderstorm far off in the distance. A fleeting orchestral string melody seeps into this piece to create quite a stunning apocalyptic feel quite reminiscent of the quieter tracks of Shinjuku Thief's *The Witch Hammer* CD (another of Darrin's projects, if you were not aware); yet the incorporation of more modern rhythmic production in the track's last segment partially negates this earlier comparison. *Sirens* reverts to the deep electronic soundscape and radio voice-type format before bridging into the final piece, *Seduction: Asphyxia*, that is a lengthy excursion into dark ambient territory with suffocating drones and the occasional blip of a submarine's sonar. Within this piece's framework, static and subtle glitch cut-up elements become more prominent as time passes, including prominent telegraph wire-generated textures (Alan Lamb is credited for the use of these samples from his stunning *Night Passage* Album, which is also on Dorobo). All in all this is an engrossing and suffocating conclusion to the CD. Given that I missed the actual stage show to which this soundtrack relates (and that the CD contains very little of what one might envisage being used by a dance company), I am now very intrigued as to what the performance would have encompassed. Regardless, the beauty of this CD is such that it can stand on its own as a cutting-edge soundwork, independent of the original context for which it was commissioned. Lastly, the cover image sums up the aura of the music perfectly – a body floating face down in perfectly still water, with ripples emanating only from the point where the body has just submerged below the surface.

Vox Barbara (USA) *(De)constructing Ghosts* CDR 2000 Little Man Records
Having no success in finding a label willing to release Vox Barbara's second album (now this is a situation that I can't really understand), Frank Smith of the project has pressed and released this via his own label (as was the circumstance with the first album). Limited to an edition of a mere 200, the handmade origami-style packaging is a novel and eye-catching way to present the release, including a sleeve insert containing extensive notes on the background to the recording. As for that concept, the basic premise of the album centres around the use of illegal software that supposedly has the ability to tap into and isolate historical sound energy that is believed to be encoded within all sound waves emitted. Various sound sources, field recordings and other aural scraps were fed through the software to arrive at a sound palette that was altered only slightly through looping, layering and collation to arrive at the final product. Less organic and tribal than the first album, this CD is a mechanical blend of experimental dark ambience with noisy electronic overtones. The first two tracks play up these two angles, the first being a static-induced surging loop (akin to what I would expect a binary code to sound like), the second with a low pulse rumbling off into the far distance with a minimal grinding loop sneaking in from an oblique angle. *Ritual Dissection* runs the gamut of spare dark ambience, but is better described as a field recording captured in the hull of a monolithic rusting tanker. The depth of this track is quite breathtaking, yet essentially subdued, with a multitude of sound fragments being the subtotal of the whole. The metallic scrapings, cluttered bass tones and indecipherable voices of *Liver Dance* give way to a loose machine loop, with the following piece *Artificial Curiosities* again seeing the appearance of the voices that are mutilated in a churning sonic mass (additionally a segment of fantastic tensile ambience breaks forth for the remainder of the track). The spinning vortex of *Perforation Bite* rotates into a dizzying mass of droning textures - both relaxed and evasive, concluding with sharp static feedback to further scrape your raw eardrums. *Silicon Phantom* is yet another pearl, mixing (again) sharp static and glitch-oriented loops with warm throbbing drones. The metallic and highly rhythmic percussion of *Tabernacle Mirror* harks back to the tribal aura of the first album, with a lone chanted vocal further embellishing this reference. *Theatre of the Uninhabited* returns to darker, more drawn-out territory to see the album to its end – the shimmering bleakness made all the darker with tribal/ritual hand percussion. Disembodied voices fleetingly appear to inject an air of urgency during the last minutes of the album. I can say that there are few, if any, artists that produce works comparable to Vox Barbara's sound, which is surely a compliment when considering the multitude of underground projects that have a similar style and direction. It is a shame that an artist with such a focused vision for creating albums of world-class material has thus far been denied an official release other than on his own label.

Wilt (USA) *The Black Box Aesthetic: Zeitgeist Movement 1* CD 2001 the Retrix
One characteristic thread that appears to tie together the relevantly sparse American underground scene is that of a slighter noisier aesthetic, with Wilt being no exception. Despite working within the realms of sparse resonating dark ambience, Wilt's compositions contain a sharp distortional edge evident from the opening track (*Opening The Black Box*) that sees dense keyboard melodies soaked with inky noise. This introductory perception is not lost on the remaining tracks that span almost the entire CD format (over 70 minutes), with the 17 compositions ranging from short pieces of under two minutes up to the nine-minute mark at the longest. Metallic clangs and bamboo wind chimes add a surreal edge to the windswept sound of *Searching For A Corner*, while *Nothing Is Exact Not Even Nothingness* is a more weighty and densely liquidous-sounding isolationist piece. *Containment Of Aluminium and Stone* uses a framework of echoed metallic clatter to create slightly chaotic reverberations while containing a vague direction and focus. On the other hand, *Approaching Singularity* is a more atmospheric piece that uses a hefty low-end bass tone to amass the piece into a veritable representation of a black hole at work. Although less than two minutes long, *Static Trench* uses its short span to attempt to implode the speakers with low-end choppy frequencies, with my sound system being more than thankful once this track had played out to its conclusion. *Arabidopsis: Seedlings In Culture* reveals a sinister edge to the subdued drone frequencies, which gradually reveal others layers of scattered sounds that revolve in loose patterns and build continually to increased noise intensity over its length. *Thermodynamic Equilibrium* builds its blazing noise intensity, which in full flight could easily constitute a power electronics piece if it weren't for the lack of vocals. The following piece *Sculpture of Rust* also holds a sharper edge of static frequency yet melding it with cyclic drones to rather atmospheric result. Sinking back into a dense, subdued isolationist mold, in *Expansion of Consciousness* the rotating singular drone ebbs the piece forward, adding further tonal drones along the way. To bring the album full circle, keyboard melodies are to be found on the short piece *Closing The Black Box*, where it should be noted that apart from the intro and outro pieces, there is little (if any) tuneful or melodic elements throughout the vast majority of the album, rather concentrating on the manipulation of tone and frequency. With regard to packaging, the card gatefold cover is likewise a nice addition for the visual side of the music's aesthetic via bleak yet non-descript images. Diverse and engaging, Wilt are one emerging project to keep an eye on, particularly as they have two upcoming releases on both Crionic Mind and new label AdNoiseam.

LAST MINUTE ARRIVALS: NEW/UPCOMING RELEASES ON L.S.D. ORGANISATION
Just as I was going to print, a batch of new items and advance copies from L.S.D. Organisation arrived in the post, and after a quick perusal it was evident that they were certainly worthy of a brief mention in this issue. Likewise if 2000 was the year that this new label started to really generated a lot of positive interest, I'll be damned if they're not making a bid for world domination in 2001! Just read the following to see what is out and what is upcoming!

As for the official releases these included:

Puissance (Swe) *Genocide* 7" 2000 L.S.D. Organisation
Packaging: Sepia-toned clear vinyl and card cover, with postcards, inserts and screen-printed cloth bag. Music: The two trademark and well-worn sounds of Puissance are showcased here with one side of the neo-classical/orchestral style and one side of brooding industrial ambience. As strong as anything they have released before.
Edition: 300 copies.

Cloma (Fin) *Provokaattori* 7" 2001 L.S.D. Organisation
Packaging: Clear red vinyl, full colour card cover, postcard and screen-printed cloth bag. Music: Oppressive industrial noise/ambience (with samples) plays out on one track and rhythmic industrial on the other, both forming a solid and intriguing introduction to this project.
Edition: 300 copies.

As for the upcoming releases these include:

IRM (Swe) *Four studies of a crucifixion* 2 x 7" 2001 L.S.D. Organisation
Packaging: One solid yellow vinyl and one solid red vinyl, (both with gloss colour covers), full colour eight-page booklet, four colour postcards, two screen-printed cloth bags, four buttons, poster, t-shirt, all housed in a wooden box (five different types of boxes limited to 100 each). Music: IRM just keeping getting stronger. Massively brooding power electronics pieces, which see their sound becoming slower, heavier and even more intense. With their trademark vocals included on three of the four tracks, most interestingly two of the pieces see the use of chimes and non-harmonic trumpet! More amazing and brilliant material from these relative newcomers.
Edition: 500.

Iron Justice (Swe) *Post* 2x7" 2001 L.S.D. Organisation
Packaging: Two vinyl, black and white eight-page booklet, four black and white postcards, two screen-printed cloth bags, two posters, four buttons, t-shirt, wooden box with metal logo (250 x white box, 250 x black box).
Music: Stepping away from the pure power electronics/noise approach of their debut 7" and LP, this new material sees the group morphing their sound into a pounding metallic (read: machine gun!) rhythmic framework yet still including harsh screamed/distorted vocal attacks. Without totally forsaking their harsh power electronics sound, this is easily the best material I have heard from these two guys.
Edition: 500.

NOD (Swe) *The story of the three little pigs and the big bad wolf* 2001 4 x 7" L.S.D. Organisation
Packaging: One navy vinyl, one coffee vinyl, one red vinyl, one green vinyl, colour poster, four buttons, four colour postcards, full colour eight-page booklet, t-shirt, four cloth bags, wooden box with metal logo (boxes presented in one of four different colours).
Music: Many facets of sound and approach are showcased by this project including: deep industrial/power electronics musings (where on one track this is offset against the reading of the above fairy tale), pummeling rhythmic industrial/noise with aggressive spoken/shouted vocals, subdued soundscapes (with one track using female sung and spoken vocals), various mixtures of the above elements, etc. Diverse and certainly intriguing from another former *Estheticks of Cruelty* compilation artist!
Edition: 500.

In wrapping up this miniature spotlight (in lieu of full reviews of each release) other items to look out for in 2001 from L.S.D Organisation include vinyl releases from Ah Cama Sotz, Slogun and Merzbow. Considering that everything I have seen coming from this label is executed with extreme precision and attention to the finest detail, this year they will surely solidify L.S.D Organisation as the new 'IT' label (which is more than warranted in my eyes).

***NOTE:** Anyone who has followed this label since its inception would know that of the upcoming releases listed above, only the Iron Justice release transpired as planned as the label mysteriously disappeared. IRM came out as a 10" EP and NOD as a CD, both on Cold Meat Industry.*

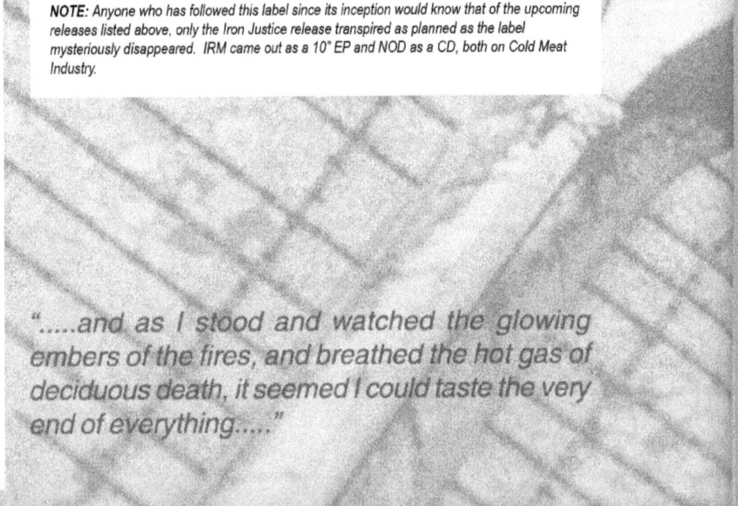
".....and as I stood and watched the glowing embers of the fires, and breathed the hot gas of deciduous death, it seemed I could taste the very end of everything....."

2XHNI DOUBLE H NOISE INDUSTRIES

ATOMSMASHER
"ATOMSMASHER"

SUNN O)))
"00VOID"

ALSO AVAILABLE:
SUNN O)))
"GRIM ROBE DEMOS"

DOUBLE H NOISE INDUSTRIES
PO BOX 990248
BOSTON, MA 02199
USA
w: www.hydrahead.com
e: info@hydrahead.com

UPCOMING RELEASES
MERZBOW "DHARMA" CD
LOTUS EATERS 12"
ATOMSMASHER / VENETIAN SNARES 7"
2XHNI COMPILATION 2XCD
(UNRELEASED TRACKS FROM MERZBOW, MONOTONOUS, HOUSE OF LOW CULTURE, JAMES PLOTKIN, ATOMSMASHER, SHIFTS, ETC.)
TRIBES OF NEUROT VINYL BOX SET

CONTACT LIST

ACHTUNG BABY!: P.O. Box 2218, Rostov-on-Don, 344038 Russia, www.druge.here.ru/achtung, m-r93@mail.ru
ANT-ZEN: C/S.Alt, P.O Box 1257, 93135, Lappersdorf, Germany, info@ant-zen.com, www.ant-zen.com
ARTWARE PRODUCTIONS: c/- Donna Klemm, Taunusstraße 63b, (D)65183, Wiesbaden, Artware.prod@T-online.de, www.artware-prod.com
ATHANOR: C/- Stephane, BP294, 85007 POITIERS, Cedex, France, urspracle@wanadoo.fr, www.multimania.com/wingu/athanor/accueil.htm
BLACK PLAGVE: C/- Malignant Records, arc@magnus.net, www.malignantrecords.com/blackplagve.html
The CEILING: P.O. Box 25086, 25 Frederick St. Kitchener, ON. N2H 6T4 Canada, www.nas.net/~jpejong/ddtl.html, jpejong@nas.net
CHTHONIC STREAMS: P.O. Box 7003, New York, NY 10116-7003 USA, www.chthonicstreams.com
COLD MEAT INDUSTRY: Villa Eko, 595 41 Mjölby, Sweden, order@coldmeat.se, www.coldmeat.se
COLD SPRING: 8 Wellspring, Bisworth, Northants, NN7 3EH, England, UK, info@coldspring.co.uk, www.coldspring.co.uk
CRIONIC MIND: PMB 105, 4644 Geary Boulevard, San Francisco, California 94118, USA, crionic@pacbell.net, www.crionicmind.org
CROWD CONTROL ACTIVITIES: P.O. Box 2340, Upper Darby, PA 19082, USA B21 White Elm Dr. Loveland, CO 80538 USA, crowded@relapse.com, www.ezlink.com/~crowded
CRUEL MOON BC (C/- COLD MEAT INDUSTRY): Villa Eko, 595 41 Mjölby, Sweden, order@coldmeat.se, www.coldmeat.se
CYNFEROD: 41 Rue Jean Moulin, 78460 Vernueil Sur Seine, France, cynferod@hotmail.com
DARK VINYL: P.O. Box 1221, 90539 Eckental, Germany, darkvinyl@t-online.de
DEAFBORN RECORDS: info@deafborn.de, www.deafborn.de
DEATH FACTORY (C/- COLD MEAT INDUSTRY): Villa Eko, 595 41 Mjölby, Sweden, order@coldmeat.se, www.coldmeat.se
DOROBO: C/- Darrin Verhagen P.O. box 22 Glen Waverley, Victoria, Australia 3150, dorobo@werple.net.au, http://werple.net.au/~dorobo/
DOUBLE H NOISE INDUSTRIES (2XHNI): P.O. Box 990248, Boston, MA 02199, USA, www.hydrahead.com, info@hydrahead.com
DRAGON FLIGHT RECORDINGS: 780 Reservoir Ave. PMB 294 Cranston, RI 02910 USA, www.dragonflightrec.org, info@dragonflightrec.org
DRONE RECORDS: Baraka (H) S. Knappe, Greisenaustrasse 56, 28201 Bremen, Germany, droneciroum@aol.com, http://members.xoom.com/dronerecords
EIBON RECORDS: Via Folli 5, 20134 Milano, Italy, info@eibonrecords.com, www.eibonrecords.com
EIS UND LICHT TRONTRÄGER: P.O. Box 160142, D-01307 Dresden, Germany, eislicht@geocities.com, www.eislicht.de
FLUTTERING DRAGON RECORDS: p.o. Box 182, 03-700 Warszawa 4, Poland, xak@serpent.com, www.serpent.com.pl
FREAK ANIMAL RECORDS: PL 21, 15141 Lahti, Finland, fanimal.com
GALAKTHORRO: P.O. Box 2111, 38011 Braunschweig, Germany, www.galakthorroe.de
HEARTLAND RECORDS: 61 Peel Street, Melbourne West, Victoria 3003, Australia
HYMEN: P.O Box 1257, 93135, Lappersdorf, Germany, hymen@gmx.net, www.klangstabil.com/hymen
KAOS KONTROL: Jukka Mattila, Mikkoisentie 15 a 2 FIN-04600 Mäntsälä, Finland, kaoskontrol@robox.fi
KOKAMPH: nahemoth@hotmail.com
Label-KETTLE: http://listen.to/kettle
LITTLE MAN RECORDS: P.O. Box 45636, Seattle Washington 98145-0636, USA, vox@speakeasy.org
LIVE BAIT RECORDING FOUNDATION: 423 Seventh Street, #3, Fairport Harbor, Ohio 44077 USA, livebatrecording@hotmail.com, http://crionicmind.org/livebait
LOKI FOUNDATION: PSF 241321 04333 Leipzig, Germany, loki-found@t-online.de
L.S.D Organisation: P.O. Box 99, Monterey Park. CA 91754-0099 USA, info@lsdo.com, www.lsdo.com
MALIGNANT RECORDS: P.O Box 5666, Baltimore MD 21210, USA, malignant@malignantrecords.com, www.malignantrecords.com
MEGO: www.mego.at
MEMBRUM DEBILE PROPAGANDA: LESSIGNSTR. 21, d-97990 Weikersheim, Germany, order@membrumdebile.de
MIDDLE PILLAR: PO Box 555, NY, NY 10009 USA, info@middlepillar.com, www.middlepillar.com
MOLOKO: ralf_friel@terrostaal.com
NAUTILUS (C/-SPECTRE): P.O. Box 88, 2020 Antwerpen 2, Belgium, www.spectre.be, info@spectre.be
NEROZ: P.O Box 277, Flemington Victoria 3031, Australia, commandorxxx@hotmail.com
NILE: P.O Box 277, Flemington Victoria 3031, Australia
NOCTURNUS (C/-SPECTRE): P.O Box 88, 2020 Antwerpen 2, Belgium, www.spectre.be, info@spectre.be
OLD EUROPA CAFE: C/- Rodolfo Protti, Viale Marconi 38, 33170 Prodenone, Italy, oec@iol.it, www.stack.nl/~bubw/music/OEC/
PERIL UNDERGROUND: Basement 17-19 Elizabeth Street, Melbourne 3000, Australia, peril@realism.com.au
PRE-FEED: http://move.to/pre-feed
PROPHECY PRODUCTIONS: Kurfuistenstrasse 5, 54492 Zeitingen-Rachtig, Germany, www.prophecy-productions.de
RELEASE ENTERTAINMENT: C/- Relapse Records, P.O. Box 251, Millersville, PA 17551, USA, relapse@relapse.com, www.relapse.com
the RECTRIX: Gilbney, 364 Union Street 3# Brooklyn NY, 11231, USA, www.infernalhorde.com/rectrix, redrix@aol.com
SACRED SOUND NOISE: P.O. Box 66146, Greensboro, NC 27403 USA
SELFLESS RECORDINGS: P.O. Box 726, Islip Terrace, NY 11752, USA, www.selfless.cjb.net
SIN ORGANISATION: Gianfranco Santoro-Via Adige 8-33010 Colugna-Tavagnacco (Udine) Italy, nairecords@infinito.it
SLAUGHTER PRODUCTIONS: C/- Marco Corbelli, via Tardini 8, 410 49 Sassuolo (MO) Italy, slaughter@mail.dex.net.com, www.welcome.to/slaughter
SOLEILMOON RECORDINGS: www.soleilmoon.com
SPECTRE: P.O Box 88, 2020 Antwerpen 2, Belgium, www.spectre.be, info@spectre.be
STATEART: C/- Koch, Rosegerstr. 2, 30173, Hannover, Germany, www.stateart.de
SYNAESTHESIA: P.O. BOX 7252 Melbourne, Victoria 3004, Australia, mark@synrecords.com, www.synrecords.com
TESCO ORGANISATION: P.O. Box 410118, D68275, Mannheim, Germany, tesco-org-MA@t-online.de, www.morpharts.de/tesco-org.html
TRIUMVIRATE: P.O. Box 6254, Southbend, IN. 46660 USA, www.triumviratemain.com, triumvirate@datacruz.com
TRONIKS: C/- 4065, Berkeley, CA 94704-0055 USA, tenebrae@jcs.net, www.troniks.com
TWENTY SIXTH CIRCLE: www.sss.org/masceruis/twentysixth.html, twentysixth@hotmail.com
VACUUM: www.thevacuum.net
WKN: P.O. Box 44, 1133 Wien, Austria, wkn@aon.at
WORLD SERPENT: Unit 7-7 Seager Buildings, Brookmill Road, London SE8 4HL, England, mailorder@worldserpent.demon.co.uk, www.worldserpent

NEW FROM MALIGNANT RECORDS

NTT
THE SOUND OF A
POST NUCLEAR-WAR SOCIETY
WHERE WAR MACHINES
SHUDDER AND GRIND
IN ENDLESS CYCLES
AND THE BLACK SOOT OF
DYING FACTORY PRODUCTION
FILLS THE POISONOUS AIR

NAVICON TORTURE TECHNOLOGIES

STRUCTURED ELEMENTS OF
LOOPS AND SAMPLES MELD
WITH CAUSTIC TEXTURES
ERUPTING AMIDST
BRIDLED CHAOS
AND PULSATING WAVES
OF WHITE HOT SATURATED
NOISE AND DISTORTION
AN ANGUISHED CONFRONTATIONAL
VOCAL PRESENCE MAKES ITSELF KNOWN
EXPLODING IN A CATHARTIC AGGRESSION
BROUGHT ON BY SUPPRESSED
DEMONS AND FESTERING HATE

SCENES FROM THE NEXT MILLENNIUM
MALIGNANT RECORDS (TUMOR-CD 15)
$12 U.S. (POSTAGE PAID IN NORTH AMERICA)

full MP3 preview available on malignant radio:
www.malignantrecords.com/radio

SPRING 2001

Dusk of Hope
flexible response

R|A|A|N

DUSK OF HOPE
FLEXIBLE RESPONSE
MALIGNANT RECORDS
TUMOR-CD 14

R|A|A|N
THE NACRASTI
→ MALIGNANT ANTIBODY
TREATMENT*02

AVAILABLE SOON

FROM MALIGNANT:
EX.ORDER
WAR WITHIN BREATH
(TUMOR-CD 16)

FROM BLACK PLAGVE:
STROM.EC
NEURAL ARCHITECT
(CD / INFEST04)

MALIGNANT RECORDS > P.O. BOX 5666 > BALTIMORE, MD 21210 > USA >> malignantrecords.com <<

SPECTRUM
MAGAZINE ISSUE 6

SPECTRUM MAGAZINE NO.6

■ Earlier some details regarding the initial plans and eventual cancellation of *Spectrum Magazine* Issue no.6 were discussed. Issue no.6 was intended to be released in late 2002 and was planned to feature interviews with various projects, along with a compilation CD of exclusive tracks. The projects scheduled to be included in the issue were: Chaos as Shelter, Con-Dom, Genocide Organ, Inade, Isomer, John Murphy (KnifeLadder/Shining Vril), Militia, Navicon Torture Technologies, Of The Wand & The Moon, Propergol, Sophia, Terra Sancta, Toroidh and Troum.

Seven interviews had been completed at the time of cancellation; each published here, with all prepared reviews.

Artists planned to be featured included: Chaos as Shelter, Con-Dom, Genocide Organ, Inade, Isomer, John Murphy (KnifeLadder/Shining Vril), Militia, Navicon Torture Technologies, Of The Wand & The Moon, Propergol, Sophia, Terra Sancta, Toroidh and Troum. With content relating to underlined artists having been completed before the issue was formally cancelled in July 2002, this material is republished within this compendium.

With reference to the compilation CD of featured artists, this was intended to be framed around a theme based on the word/idea of *'re:(e)volution'*. The following is the thematic instructions text that was issued to artists at the time:

Notwithstanding that 're:(e)volution', does not exist as an actual word, by virtue of how it is written and punctuated, it can actually be broken down into various separate words and interpreted accordingly. Therefore the idea is to compose a track on how you perceive the word 're:(e)volution', interpreting as you choose. This theme will also flow through to the interviews where you will be asked to comment on your perception of the theme. To further solidify the theme between CD and magazine, Spectrum #6 will also have the subtitle of "the 're:(e)volution' issue". Furthermore, the compilation CD will represent the flagship release for a new label that will use the name of 're:(e)volution' for its title.

As for suggested interpretations of 're:(e)volution', the following could provide some ideas:

— revolution (socio/political)
— revolution (RPM/circular rotation)
— 'regarding' evolution
— re-evolution (further evolution of a species, concept and/or idea)

Opposite is the cancellation statement issued in July 2002.

ISSUE NO.6 CANCELLATION STATEMENT

Although I was not living in Australia between June 2001 to June 2002, a great deal of preliminary work had been put into organizing Spectrum Magazine Issue no.6, which was additionally to include a compilation CD of exclusive tracks of featured artists. However, due to factors beyond my control I have had to cancel this scheduled issue. Basically (and in summary), due to many of the confirmed contributing artists having other commitments to work, study, family, etc., less than half of the scheduled artists were able to meet the July 1st deadline for the submission of compilation tracks. Accordingly this has impacted upon the time frames I originally allocated myself to complete Spectrum Issue no.6, making it impossible for me to complete and release the new issue before returning to the UK in late 2002. Thus it is with regret that I am left with no choice but to CANCEL the upcoming issue of Spectrum Magazine.

Likewise at this point Spectrum Magazine is to be put on permanent hold, thus only the future will reveal to if it will be resurrected at a later date. Whilst I am disappointed that Spectrum Magazine Issue no.6 has had to succumb to a fate such as this, I still extend my gratitude and thanks to those who have supported Spectrum Magazine over the years.

—*Richard Stevenson/Spectrum Magazine*

Prior to the formal cancellation of *Spectrum Magazine* Issue no.6, five contributions to the *re:(e)volution* compilation had been received from: Chaos as Shelter, Isomer, Militia, Navicon Torture Technologies and Toroidh. These five tracks have now been made available as an exclusive digital download associated with the hardback edition of this book (available only from Headpress directly).

Cancelled Issue no.6 material

Genocide Organ profile 2002: Previously published in *Degenerate* magazine (Finland) Issue no.3 (2003). **Militia Interview 2002**: Previously published in *Degenerate* magazine (Finland) Issue no.3 (2003). **John Murphy/ KnifeLadder/Shining Vril interview 2002**: Previously published on www.compulsiononline.com (2002). A slightly reformatted version of this interview was published in *Noise Receptor Journal* Issue no.4 (2016) as a tribute to the passing of John. A different version of the interview focusing solely on KnifeLadder was also previously published in *Degenerate* magazine (Finland) Issue no.3 (2003). **Isomer Interview 2002**: Previously published in *Goth Nation* (Australia) Issue no.1 (2002), *Degenerate* magazine (Finland) Issue no.3 (2003). **Toridh Interview 2002**: Previously published on www.compulsiononline.com (2002). **Terra Sancta Interview 2002**: Previously published in *Goth Nation* Issue no.2 (2003) and *Degenerate* magazine (Finland) Issue no.3 (2003). **Navicon Torture Technologies Interview 2002**: Previously unpublished. **Reviews: 2001–2002**: Selected reviews previously published via *Degenerate* magazine (Finland) Issue no.3 (2003).

GENOCIDE ORGAN PROFILE : 2002

■ Genocide Organ have been in existence for over seventeen years now, slowly but surely rising to a cult level within the heavy industrial/power electronics scene. This status has been achieved through the production of an extremely physical sound approach in combination with deluxe packaging, creating a collector's fetishism of sorts. Yet for all their notoriety within the post-industrial scene, Genocide Organ remain relatively obscure and somewhat shrouded in mystery. This is in part to do with the group refraining from including 'band' photos on releases, yet more specifically (for the most part) refusing to conduct interviews. Personally I am only aware of one interview, being that which was published in 1999 in *Descent Magazine* issue 5, and even the introductory blurb to that interview stated the group had requested the interview to be removed (without success of course).

So, when considering the members of Genocide Organ, their actual personalities remain obscured for the above mentioned reasons, yet one fact remains certain, that the group contains four key members: Wilhelm Herich, R. Freisler, D.A.X and Doc M. Riot (presumably all assumed identities), with R. Freisler later leaving the band to be replaced by B. Moloch (of Anenzephalia infamy). Notwithstanding the obscured identities, one member has become more recognizable than the remaining, being one Herr Wilhelm Herich), due to his collaborations with Anenzephalia and Der Blutharsch for the delivery of a number of live actions.

As a collective each of the four members has specific roles within the Genocide Organ collective, relating to studio composition, live mixing, video arts and stage performance. With regard to live actions they encompass a direct physical approach of noisescapes and confrontational vocals that also often incorporates installations ranging from video projections through to emblematic use of religious symbols and images of political figureheads (i.e. burning of a wooden/chainmesh cross, use of an oxy torch to cut the Genocide Organ symbol from a sheet of steel, display and later destruction of crosses plastered with images of political leaders etc.).

In analyzing and critiquing Genocide Organ's recorded output via lyrics, texts, images and dialogue samples, there is a clear focus on matters relating to war, the Ku Klux Klan, conspiracy theories, American imperialism, terrorism, the Third Reich, fetishism etc. Likewise many of their releases come armed with loaded titles such as *Klan Kountry, Mind Control* and *The Truth Will Make You Free*. Packaging additionally utilizes many images that are considered to have loaded connotations, or otherwise by virtue of their use seem to inherit a deeper meaning (for example take the face image on the cover of *The Truth Will Make You Free*). To put it in another context I quote Lina Baby Doll of Deutsch Nepal who has been a long-standing fan and more recent comrade of the group:

Genocide Organ, the heroes of German electronic shock-treatment are one of the most physical appearances within industrial culture. Every piece of sound they've released, and all live performances I ever experienced have been 100% 'ultra' in all directions possible. Just to feel the weight of the heavy vinyl, study the sleeves and almost cut your hands open by the scalpels attached, among the dried bloodstains on the unpolished surface is an experience worth the long and hard search for the items. For me it's not the extreme approach of the group that make them interesting, it's the ability to withhold the possibility to go way too far out in the wasteland of cheap fetish commercialism, which for me is a sign of both intelligence and style. These are people who have got more to show than a poor tattoo and some piercings, this group shows you the truth whatever it might be. And the truth will make us free!

Essentially the convergence of elements (visuals, titles, text, dialogue samples, set to extreme electronic sound and overlaid with shouted distorted vocal delivery), creates a sensory overload ensuring that ambivalence towards their releases is almost impossible. And within such a context Genocide Organ HAVE provoked reaction from listeners — be those extremists who perceive the group have certain sympathies that align with their own, or vocal detractors labeling the group racist, fascist, or more crudely, hate mongers. Likewise for those listeners intelligent enough (or otherwise uninterested) in making such simplistic and polarized views of Genocide Organ, merely the extremity of sound can likewise provoke reactions from revulsion through to pure pleasure (the pleasures received in pain is an amply reasonable adage here). Yet in creating a reaction and/or emotional response, can art legitimately use the interpretation of politics as the point of stimuli? I would argue that it is entirely legitimate. Granted that differing emotional responses may create a psychological barrier and therefore limiting the ability of many to fully appreciate certain kinds of musical and artistic expression, this however does in no way negate the validity of the interpretation of politics within art. Additionally if art is deemed to be the pinnacle of emotional expression, this still leaves scope for each individual to interpret each emotion intrinsically stimulated — be that positive or negative.

But what do Genocide Organ actually stand for and represent? Something, or nothing at all? Are they a group simply taking a mirror to modern society, reflecting the squalled depths of hatred and violence that humanity is capable of sinking to, or do they truly embrace a nihilistic worldview and only stand to accelerate the modern world's decline? Alternately are they left wing, or right wing, religious or apolitical? Or are they simply purveyors of 'ultra' dry humour and irony pushed to an absolute extreme? Put any of these assertions to the group, however, and none will be forthcoming with affirming or denying such theories and/ or allegations. The virtues of silence perhaps? Equally, are the questions raised in the listener's mind significantly more important than any answer that the group could ever provide?

Likewise with reference to modern society are there any political or philosophical ideas which can be viewed in a simplistic black and white context? Consequently could it be said that Genocide Organ embrace the infinitesimal shades of interpretative grey in the way they choose to operate? Quoting from the aforementioned *Descent* interview it might just give some insight into the mindset of the group (or failing that, simply adding to the confusion): 'We never say what we think, and we never believe what we say, and if we tell the truth by accident, we hide it under so many lies that it is difficult to find out' and 'Everything is as it is and nothing is as it should be.' (*Descent* issue 5: The Death Issue, June 1999).

It is clear that that there is no single or for that matter simple interpretation that can be said to holistically represent Genocide Organ, and therefore it is useless for anyone but the group themselves to pontificate about knowing the exact answer. Thus without providing any sort of iron-clad theory, could the question be posed: is confusion the real key to Genocide Organ's intent? The final interpretation is up to you…

MILITIA INTERVIEW : 2002

■ Although an introduction was not written back in 2002, the interview was requested at the time on the basis of the amazing *The Black Flag Hoisted* 2xCD (2000). The interview was then conducted in the years prior to the release of *The Eco-Anarchic Manifesto* book/live CD (2003), and the *Everything Is One* CD (2005), and functioned to explore Militia's eco-anarchism ideology and world view.

With the intention of *Spectrum* no.6 to include a compilation CD of featured artists, Militia's contribution was They Marked The Path, which at the time was an advance track from *Everything Is One*. It is also featured on the *Spectrum Compendium* compilation, available only with the special hardback edition of this book.

SPECTRUM: What were the initial ideas behind the formation of Militia, and how did the members come together to establish the project?

MILITIA: Militia is an instrument for spreading the eco-anarchic ideology and social world view. These ideas are being spread by means of music and statements, films, literature and performances. The method Militia uses while working on their projects is based entirely upon the anarchic way of practising things — so with constant communication and debate, suggestions and decisions being formed from that basis.

I believe that there are three main individuals as part of the Militia project. However, having seen you perform live there are many more members than this. How does the project operate from the composition and recording stages, through to live executions?

Every individual in the Militia group takes in the same position as all the others, so there are no main individuals as you put it here. Ideas — or better, a 'story board' — for a new project always comes from several people in the band. Then I compose the basic music tracks: I write the music notes using a combination of classical music notation and my own symbols. Next step: I play and record this music on synthesizer and sequencer and record the whole on CDr format, this is the so-called basic music tape. With this CDr I go to the other band members and together we compose the additional percussion pieces, the music for the wind instruments and all other instruments involved. Then starts a long period of rehearsing and constant evaluation till the definitive music is finished. At that moment we've already contacted our German label Tactical Recordings and they pay for and hire the studio, which is a professional music studio called AnnaBee, led by the sound engineer Willy Pirotte. This means that we start recording the music and finish a new CD.

Given that many of your tracks are heavily percussion-based, how do you approach composing a track? Can you list the instrumentation that you use and do any of the members have formal musical training?

All members are well-trained percussionists, a few also play a variety of wind instruments. As said before, I write my music in a self-developed symbolic notation which all can read. Starting from my notes and the input of the other members, we always find it quite easy to try out, compose and play the additional percussion layers. But it always takes quite a number of rehearsals to get everything right and to start playing it by heart, obviously. When six people play different layers of percussion which all have to form one balanced whole together with the basic music tape, this certainly asks for an intensive organisation and lots of practice. Amongst our instruments we count a concrete mill, a chain saw, three empty gas tubes, several empty oil barrels, a radiator, several metal blades suspended on chains and connected on self-made standards, metal tubes and plates, but also a big bass drum (timpani), snare drums, djembe, didgeridoo, trumpet and so on…

On a number of releases you have used the tribal instrument called the didgeridoo. Given that this is actually an instrument primarily known to be native to Australian Aboriginals, what drew you to utilize this?

At first I used a long metal tube to generate the same sound — using the same technique — that can be made with a real didgeridoo, just because I liked the sound very much and the thing fitted perfectly into the concept. Now Dirk also plays didgeridoo (and we had other didgeridoo players in the past as well) and the combination of the real thing and the metal substitute works quite well. It was a main instrument for our Nature Revealed project, also because that work was about primitive human societies and the relation with their natural environment.

With regard to the upcoming album, what details can you provide regarding its sound/style and concepts? Which label will be releasing this item and will it form part of a larger concept (such as your now completed *New European Order* trilogy)?

Everything Is One will be a kind of conclusion of the pamphlet I've written, entitled *The Eco-Anarchic Manifesto*. It is the philosophical and metaphysical survey in the form of sound of the eco-anarchic ideology as it is proposed in the *Manifesto*. The style differs from neo-classical music to rhythmic percussion pieces. And we also used conventional but 'not-so-obvious' instruments this time, mainly played by a number of new guest musicians ... but I will tell no more, we'll keep it a surprise.

I also believe that you are currently involved in the preparation of a book to further expand on the concepts behind Militia. Can you provide some details of this and its planned release? Will it be released under the Militia name and do you hope this book will have a wider appeal than the at best obscure musical genre that Militia inhabits?

The book will be the cover of the live CD we've recorded in Lille. So book and CD will be released in a few months by Tactical Recordings — who organise the releases of all our works for that matter. The book deals with our eco-anarchic principles, social world views, it reveals a possible structure for an eco-anarchic society and it deals with the problems of money, possession, order and solidarity in such a society. We hope that our website will be ready around the same time as the book and CD will be released, because we want to start a discussion forum as well. We're convinced that there will be a need for discussion and information as soon as people will have read this manifesto. It is a strong opposition against ultra right wing ideology, against a society ruled by any form of government, against the abuse of animals and the endangering of our planet. Instead it offers a global community that is strong in structure, based upon solidarity, equality and autonomy.

Taking a step back and making an overview of the *New European Order* trilogy, when making reference to the first triple LP set of the series (entitled *New European Order*), to my interpretation the underlying political stance was not clearly evident. However to qualify this perception, I am referring to the later two releases in the trilogy (*Nature Revealed* DCD and *The Black Flag Hoisted* DCD), which clearly and concisely put forward Militia's stance through the use of lyrics, dialogue samples and text excerpts. Accordingly at the original time of release of the *New European Order* triple LP set, did you receive much reaction, either positive or negative, regarding its potential to be perceived as being ambiguous?

The concept of the 'Statement Trilogy' was already planned and designed in early '90. The basic ideas for the three albums taking part were already written down. At first we wanted to show how our society became what it is now: a sick and corrupt whole of intrigues, a world based upon hatred, greed and lies, a community that masters racism, exploitation, oppression, murder. The first track of the *New European Order* 3LP set is called *Natura Magica*, and this was already a link towards the next album, *Nature Revealed*. *New European Order* is a documentary about our society in decay, but it included also the need for an alternative: a society that is not being ruled by corrupt and egocentric people, but based upon mutual respect and autonomy, free also from religion and possession. If some people found it ambiguous, it may be because they didn't see the real concept and ideas behind it, whether they didn't take the time for it, I don't know. Perhaps we also attracted the attention of right wing adepts, but they should have discovered definitely what the Militia ideology really stands for. I have the feeling also that a lot of people in the so-called industrial scene very much like to be ambiguous themselves, dwelling with right wing ideas, symbols and clothing and so on. I sometimes wonder if they really know what they are doing. *Nature Revealed* deals with the other aspect of the eco-anarchic society, namely the environmental side of it. In order to create a basic social structure for this new society, we studied some primitive African communities and looked back at the pre-historical societies and their specific social structures. For this, we've received the guidance and help of the people of the African Museum in Tervueren and the Gallo-Roman Museum in Tongres. Not only did we use their information, but they showed us how to make primitive music instruments (clay flutes, horns, drums...) and how to play them. They also assisted in creating a primitive pre-historical (not existing) language and so on, all useful things for the *Nature Revealed* concept. So *Nature Revealed* was the second part of the statement trilogy and a very important [one], dealing with the environmental aspects of such a society. In fact, Nature is an equal partner in this social whole. Unfortunately we had some comments about it saying that *Nature Revealed* wasn't 'industrial' enough and not 'hard' enough. I would like to suggest that those people stay with the conventional noise they like to hear and stay away from music with a deeper continence. If they believe that Militia is going to repeat itself style-wise they're wrong. We'll always adapt and even alter our style of music and the instruments we choose in relation to the concept and the ideas we want to spread. The ideas are the most important aspects, the music plays a supporting role. Music is not art, it is a form of communication. If you're the owner of all three statements, you'll see the whole picture. For those who see, feel or even support our ideas now, the forthcoming book will just be the ultimate confirmation of it all.

Who would be writers, artists, philosophers, musicians, politicians etc. that have inspired or otherwise have common ideals with the concepts behind Militia?

Oh, there are lots of them, and their number is growing. Therefore I would like to suggest only a few of them, as kind of a basic start from which people who are interested automatically can discover and follow connecting and even different streams of information. To start with, please read the books of [Pierre-Joseph] Proudhon, [Mikhail] Bakunin and [Peter] Kropotkin, or try to find out about the lives and actions of [Buenaventura] Durutti and [Errico] Malatesta or the FAI [Federación Anarquista Ibérica] movement. Interesting also are the environmental action groups like GAIA [Global Action in the Interest of Animals] from Belgium and the Animal Liberation Front or the anarchic movement in Amsterdam and Rotterdam (Holland).

Referencing the third instalment of the trilogy, on one particular track on *The Black Flag Hoisted* you give clear credence to the militant actions of the animal liberation front. Do you therefore expose a personal view in support of a vegetarian/vegan lifestyle?

Yes, we definitely do so. The fact is that we believe that it is impossible to use such a great number of animals for food on such a huge industrial scale as it is being practised now without abusing, hurting and torturing the animals involved. Different ideas about this topic exist within the Militia group, but all are convinced that, given the current situation, all animals involved suffer. We suggest that at least the number of animals used in the food processing industry should be diminished to a basic limit so that a more gentle form of meat processing eco-industry — on a biological basis — should be installed. But we also support the intentions of so many people to stop eating meat completely and turn to a vegetarian/vegan lifestyle. We strongly oppose the use of animals in laboratories and vivisection, using them for fur or for the manufacturing of other luxurious goods.

Talking on the matter further, what are you opinions between the farming of animal products on a mass scale, versus subsistence farming or the use of animal products at a collective/community-based level?

See above.

What is your opinion of the views held by some eco environmentalist/eco terrorist groups, that fundamentally the globe's human population has/is approaching critical mass and cannot sustain continued population growth?

They're right. Several reports from international health organisations, global economic/social institutions, UNESCO and so on ... also point out that the problem of the increasing human population has to be dealt with urgently. It is the basic cause of the major problems we know today: hunger, diseases, starvation, unemployment, over-exploitation of natural resources, drought, corrosion, the extinction of animal species ... and even war... It is quite unbelievable that the Catholic Church still condemns the use of condoms or even sterilisation. We must stop this enormous growth or we will deal with even greater problems in the near future.

Being a Belgium-based project what is your view of your country being a member of the European Union?

Well, for a start it is a purely economic union, founded just to preserve power and wealth and to increase it. Whether the common people profit from it, I doubt it. Unemployment hasn't been stopped, that's for sure. Secondly they haven't done anything to stop the pollution of our environment, although there is a board installed to deal with these problems. I wonder what the members of the environmental board are doing there, not much, that's for sure. And next, the people in charge's main objective seems to be the formation of a European Fortress, to keep political and economical fugitives from poor countries or countries at war (or dealing with other major problems) and all people in need out. Militia proposes an open society where everyone can just live where they want to. We stand for the abolition of geographical and institutional borders and the destruction of all forms of governments and leaderships.

Do you view the events of September 11, 2001 as being an extreme manifestation of a growing level of unrest in relation to mass western capitalism?

Religion, economic, financial and military power are the main causes of all problems. Most leaders of the Islamic communities deny basic human rights, especially the rights of women and children. America believes it has to rule over the entire world and oblige to everyone their standards of living and handling. There is an ever growing gap between the West and the East, economically and otherwise. Sooner or later this had to happen, triggered as it was by the devastating situation of the Palestinian people. In their utopic world view, Militia propose an atheistic society, not ruled by any government but by the people themselves. Such a society leaves no space for greed, hate or oppression. We need a total reconstruction of the present social structures or we'll never find a solution for all world problems. On the contrary, they will increase, they will be worse, actions will be more violent, more deeds will fall.

What is your opinion of the anti-globalisation movement, both in what it represents and the overall actions that range from peaceful to violent (and of the latter, particularly the violence that is provoked by authoritative intervention)?

We support the anti-globalisation movement and propose an alternative solution: the eco-anarchic global solidarity forms a basis for mutual respect and respect for our environment. Starting from the social structure Militia are proposing, we are convinced that we can take on any major problem in the world. To our opinion, the leading governments are well aware of the potentials of the anti-globalisation movement and all other environmental action groups. The only thing they can do to try to stop the increasing power of these movements is to put them in bad daylight towards the public opinion. I wonder if those people who started acting violently during the peacefully organised demonstrations could have been people put deliberately in the 'inside', just to start trouble and hand out to the political leaders a reason to condemn all of these action groups.

Making reference again to your live performances, during your live show a variety of footage is projected as a backdrop, but most particularly archival war footage. What attracts you to use this as a visual counterpart to the live rendition of tracks?

The film you refer to shows at first the battle of the communist and anarchist militia against the Russian tsar Peter the Great. Then come pictures of the pope (symbol of spiritual power, supporting the upper classes and the leading governments against the common people), then followed by pictures of the great American crisis (as a symbol for the fragile financial power, shows what can happen if an entire society is based upon wealth and property), then followed by pictures of the Animal Liberation Front in action and at the end you see the battle of the FAI (Italian anarchic movement) against the troops of the fascist leader Mussolini, mixed with images of the first active anarchic communes in Italy and Spain. So the film and the music we play (*The Black Flag Hoisted*) form one whole.

In between the release of parts two and three of the *New European Order* trilogy, a two-track EP was released. Given that the majority of your releases provide commentary on political, social and environmental issues, this EP included a track entitled Kingdom Of Our Lord and appears obviously to be levelled at religion and more specifically the church. With limited reference points within this track (text, lyrics, samples etc.), what is your opinion of the church as a long established religion and/or social controlling mechanism?

The churches (and we mean all religions here) have lifted the power of the leading class up to a spiritual level. We see this in most early societies, where even in some cases the absolute leader claimed to be a god himself. The position of the Japanese emperor Hirohito for instance shows the same thing, a profound mixture of spiritual laws and civilian laws can be found in most Islamic states. Militia also like to point to the fact that the churches have been (and still are for that matter) the organising party of a lot of so-called 'holy' wars, starting from early in history to even now. We see armed conflicts and (civilian) wars between Muslims and Zionists, between Protestants and Catholics, Hindus and Muslims and so on... The main role of the churches still is dividing the people and handing out more power to the leading classes. Only in a 'free of gods' society men can feel free. As an alternative we propose an atheistic spirituality, in which the beauty of nature and the positive actions of men can be admired and celebrated. The eco-anarchist does not waste his precious time on worshipping gods and kneeling down for the so-called supernatural beings, no, he tries to understand the world and find a scientific and logical explanation for the natural events, trusting only his own eyes and insight and discussing his opinions with others. In fact you can call us materialists, because we only believe in what we see and hear and feel and not in the invisible, in matter and not in spirits. The churches and all inherent symbols and rituals have to be crushed under boot and replaced by a new form of education based upon autonomy and a scientific approach of things!

Moving towards concluding the interview, what are your views of the political context that many bands within the underground scene inhabit or ambiguously flirt with?

You mean the ultra right wing ideas that are being introduced in the industrial scene and the uniformed swastika brigade? Well, we don't know whether to have a good laugh at this or worry instead, but honestly, don't you think it's very silly watching these people dressed up like a combination of Herr Flick from *'Allo 'Allo!* (you know, the English comedy series about a small French village being occupied by the Germans) and members of a Tiroler castrated boys choir, their hair cut like Rudolf Hess had it, with their mad looking faces like frozen meat? Militia deeply dislike their stupid outfit and (that's if they've even got any) the sick ideas that go along with such stupid behaviour. Militia stand for the eco-anarchic philosophy which incorporates a deep respect for all people, regardless [of] their cultural background or the colour of their skin, and for our natural environment and all the living creatures that inhabit it. No, my dear readers, we don't go searching for camouflage outfits at the nearby American Army Stock, nor do we visit the local hairdresser with a silly request and we use *Mein Kampf* only for toilet paper to clean our ass with.

Are there any final points you would like to add?

Yeah, hope to see all good folk on a next occasion. Please don't hesitate to send replies to our discussion forum as soon as our website will be active. If people still want to get our latest album (*The Black Flag Hoisted*) please contact us on our email address, which is: mekanorganic@hotmail.com.

'ONLY SHEEP NEED A LEADER' — MILITIA

JOHN MURPHY/KNIFELADDER/SHINING VRIL INTERVIEW : 2002

■ Although an introduction was not written back in 2002, the context in which the interview was conducted may be of interest. My first contact with John via email at some point during early 2000 and was followed by meeting in person at a Melbourne Death In June show in May, 2000. However following my move to London in mid-2001, it was during my time there that I got to know John a little better as we both frequented monthly Hinoeuma the Malediction industrial shows (and which included John performing as Shining Vril and Foresta Di Ferro). After meeting John in this context, and also having the opportunity to see numerous KnifeLadder shows in London, the idea was formed to do an extensive interview with John on his own career, as well as his main projects at the time, namely KnifeLadder and Shining Vril. With the resulting interview far exceeding anything I could have expected at the time, in light of John's untimely passing it can be considered as an important historic document as it tells John's story in his own words.

John Murphy, 1959–2015

SPECTRUM: First of all, when one looks at your extensive and lengthy involvement with the industrial/post-industrial genres, you have had a rather illustrious career. Could you provide a historical rundown of your involvement with industrial/post-industrial music, relating to both your own projects and collaborations with others?

JOHN MURPHY: My so-called career has been shaped as much by chance as chosen design. There hasn't ever really been any overall master plan, which may have hindered me at various points along my route to oblivion. Some people might find my tale fascinating, others an abject lesson in how NOT to have a coherent career path — perhaps I am my own worst enemy in some regards.

The so-called evolution of my musical interests has taken place over many, many years. It is so convoluted even I cannot accurately remember everything. Over the years I have been involved with many different styles of music besides the whole industrial/post-industrial thing but in regards to my so-called more industrial/experimental/electronic — whatever side of things — I became interested in the genesis of this sort of thing firstly in the mid-1970s, just before the advent of punk when as a teenager in Melbourne, Australia, I was first exposed to the joys of Krautrock, European prog rock, early-seventies glam rock and sixties/early-seventies psychedelia. I started collecting and listening to all sorts of music at an early age and became involved in bands, properly from the age of eight years old onwards. I could go on and on about this period and my influences and experiences for quite a while but won't bore the pants off you. I was always an ardent Anglophile from a very early age onwards mainly through the influence of my mother and various relatives, so British music and culture was always very important to me.

I was heavily involved in the early Melbourne punk/new wave scene of the late-seventies and after playing with local politically-orientated punk outfits I helped form one of the southern hemisphere's first sort of electronic acts called Whirlywirld in late 1978. This was a five-piece outfit perhaps somewhat similar in some ways to early Clock DVA, Tuxedo Moon and Cabaret Voltaire with a dash of late-seventies *Low* period Bowie. There was also a slight bit of a TG influence in some of the songs — though we did vary quite a bit over a two year period. We folded in late 1979 as we had hit a sort of artistic ceiling locally.

I ended up in London very early in 1980 basically to form another outfit with one of the other members of Whirlywirld, who is now sort of an Antipodean electronic dance music icon. Because of my percussive ability and certain contacts I became involved as a sort of permanent session drummer for the Associates. During the early 1980s I also worked as a session drummer for Shreikback, Gene Loves Jezebel, Nico (briefly) and a few others.

My European industrial/experimental experiences started towards the end of 1980 when I started working on the whole Kraang thing, purely as a bit of interest and fun for myself. At this stage it was called Krang Music and I released a cassette mid-'81ish, which seemed to gather some sort of interest in certain quarters. I had always been a noise freak from an early age much to the despair, anger and head scratching of many of my teenage Melbourne peer group who just could not understand why I wouldn't just stick to playing the drums and leave the music to the professionals. I think I may have had the last laugh, perhaps.

Through my friendship with Jim (Foetus) Thirlwell, who I had known well since 1978, I somehow met both William Bennett of Whitehouse and also Steven Stapleton of Nurse With Wound. I was asked to perform live with Whitehouse playing modular synth throughout 1982/early 1983, as well as recording one album with them. I also did some Kraang performances in London around this time and also did some live work with a sort of improvised experimental outfit that was sort of in the style of AMM. I'm afraid I can't remember the name.

I did quite a bit of stuff with various people during 1983–84 including tours and recording with SPK, recording for a video soundtrack released through Twin Vision, SPK's video company, recording on one Nurse With Wound album, recording with Lustmord (the *Paradise Disowned* album), recording and live work with the early Current 93/Dogs Blood Order (the first few C93 albums) more Kraang material, another duo outfit called Krank which eventually had a European and North American CD release many years later in the early 1990s of material recorded in mid-1983. Some of this material was originally used for the Twin Vision video release. I also contributed tapes and primitive loops/sound samples via mail to an Australian quasi-industrial outfit called Hugo Klang, old pals of mine.

I returned to OZ [Australia] after five years away in the mid-1980s mainly because of physical illness and general exhaustion. I got my health together and helped form an OZ-based experimental, post-industrial act titled Orchestra of Skin and Bone. This outfit was in the same general area as mid-period SPK but had a darker, more ritualistic sort of tone, perhaps. Live it was a very confrontational sort of act indeed. We were quite influenced by the music of Harry Partch. We released one album in OZ in 1986, and did some soundtracks for local underground films. A CD of one of these soundtracks and a live 1985 Melbourne performance was released in Europe and USA in 1991 under the title of *1984–1986* (on Unclean Productions). As far as I know it received a good response and reviews but the band somehow or other ground to a halt during mid-1986, rather a pity as I always thought we had the potential to be a world beating act, as I knew what was going on elsewhere. Locally in OZ the general response was not good. We were basically feared by local audiences and had much trouble getting shows or local interest. An unfounded reputation of being sort of occult weirdies and onstage bloodletting at times did not help matters. The album we released in late 1985 garnered some overseas interest, particularly in the USA, but fell into obscurity locally. The label collapsed soon after — typical of an OZ indie label of the time. I lost a lot of money, which caused me a little bit of grief.

Various members of the Orchestra of Skin and Bone including myself helped co-ordinate and record the soundtrack and incidental music for the OZ film *Dogs In Space* during 1986. I also worked on soundscapes for local video clips, underground films and did quite a bit of session work with various locally based acts between 1986–1990. Some of this was semi-experimental in nature but a lot was quite conventional and pretty straight. Some of the acts were The Index, Shower Scene From Psycho, GUM, Bum Steers, Box The Jesuit (well known Sydney-based gothicy act), Max Q (semi-solo experimental project of Michael Hutchence of INXS), Not Drowning Waving and a lot more that I can't and don't want to remember. A lot of it was purely for the money.

In the late 1980s Kraang did the occasional local performance and recordings in both Melbourne and Sydney, though not to any sizeable interest. Some of these performances went under the name of My Father of Serpents. In the early 1990s I did some more ritualistic, dark ambient performances using the name Ophiolatreia (it's Latin for serpent worship) and had a track titled Mirror To Dionysus on a compilation CD released by Dark Vinyl in Germany in 1992. This was just after they released the Krank material that I had originally recorded in mid-1983.

In the OZ experimental industrial area between 1986–91 I also worked with Ulex Xane of Zone Void, who had some recordings I participated in later released on Cthulhu Records of Germany; GUM — a local industrial duo who put out two local albums; Stress Of Terror — one cassette tape; Disciples of None — another project of Ulex's; Sooterkin Flesh — a friend's semi-solo project in the style of Whitehouse meets early NON with ritualistic drums, pretty good actually (two tapes were released and an unreleased album for a local metal label); Browning Mummery — old OZ friend of mine doing classic style industrial sound. Two CD releases featured myself amongst others; Nada — a local Sydney-based art ritualistic performance troupe; Jaundiced Eye — a Sydney-based experimental/post-industrial three-piece which at times included myself. The music was a mish mash of experimental techno-cum-ritualistic dark ambience. Unfortunately nothing has ever been properly released, only short run CDrs I believe.

Subcutaneous Theatre was a ritualistic sinister, industrial dark ambient duo that I was involved with that also featured Debra Petrovitch, a Romanian Australian performance and sound artist. In some ways she is like a cross between Jarboe and Diamanda Galas — a very talented and intense performer. She has also appeared on some Shining Vril pieces, on the *Split* CD of Shining Vril/KnifeLadder. Subcutaneous Theatre appeared at some Sydney art experimental events in the late 1980s and released one cassette on the local label Cosmic Conspiracy Productions and were planning to record a proper album in late 1990 with Andrew Trail engineering. For various non-musical reasons this never happened.

In slightly more conventional terms I also became involved with two acts from 1986–87 onwards. The first group was called Slub, something I originally put together as a sort of revenge-cum-musical joke in early 1986 as a one off event. I originally tried something sort of similar nearly eight years before in Melbourne, a feedback no/wave one off act called The Alan Bamford Musical Experience named after an old friend of mine. This eventually petered out in the early 1990s, quite a while after I made my escape. This was a noise guitar-orientated act and could be at times alternatively brilliant and utterly appalling — often in the same show. It was sort of like a cross between a deranged Plastic Ono Band, *Trout Mask Replica* Beefheart, early Swans, Butthole Surfers, Whitehouse and Skullflower. Though all these comparisons do not quite do it justice. We were probably one of the most loathed acts ever in the whole southern hemisphere but even so we put out one cassette which got international interest, one locally released album titled *Rootman* which got rave reviews in the USA, and we released quite a few singles on the USA-based label Sympathy for the Record Industry which seemed to do okay. I should also point out that I was one of the two singers in this act plus I was responsible for the majority of the noise and atonal sounds playing feedback drone, Slub guitar at intolerable volume, my trusty old EMS AKS synth and a primitive sampler/tapes. The other guitarist playing in a Beefheartian deranged style. It was through this band I originally met Andrew Trail, later of KnifeLadder, as we once shared the bill with his act (Ministry of Love) in Sydney. He still thinks that the Slub was one of the most 'out there and plain crazy' acts he has ever seen anywhere. This group also used to make some of my more muso friends — guitarists especially — virtually froth at the mouth in anger as we were so unmusical in their correct eyes. The fact that I was also much better at getting extreme guitar feedback frequencies than they were didn't help matters at all.

The general negativity of this band left me with many bad psychological and physical scars and I eventually got out and sort of saved my tattered sanity and soul in late 1989 after leaving Melbourne for Sydney where I briefly drummed for Box The Jesuit, did the odd performance with Subcutaneous Theatre, Jaundiced Eye, My Father of Serpents, Browning Mummery, recorded with Max Q and some of the aforementioned acts and developed my friendship with Andrew Trail and lived a fairly degenerate lifestyle if the truth be known.

The second act was called Dumb And The Ugly, which released one 12-inch mini album, and one CD. We performed in Melbourne with the odd show in Sydney. This was a three-piece outfit in which I played drums and some samples. This was formed with some very old friends from my teenage years who also played with other acts. This act was in the style of Sonic Youth meets Hendrix and Chrome/Helios Creed. Personality clashes eventually destroyed this outfit. I had had enough and couldn't deal with music any more.

In the early part of the 1990s things were generally spiraling out of control in my tattered existence and I slowly curtailed many of my musical activities as I was not finding a great deal of personal satisfaction with any of them at all. I did some performances and recording with a Sydney-based ritual, dark ambient, experimental techno hybrid sort of act, which was originally called Jaundiced Eye, but somewhere along the line the name somehow changed over to Dweller On The Threshold. We played at quite a few rave-cum-pagan-orientated events in and around Sydney including a support slot for Meat Beat Manifesto. I also guested from time to time throughout the first part of the nineties with some other live local acts playing drums, synth, samples and lo-tech electronics/tapes on both recordings and live dates. These acts included Monroe's Fur, Psychic Date, Harpoon, Louis Tillet (OZ singer, writer) Monkey See Monkey Do, Beastianity, Extinct, Hugo Race's True Spirit (industrial Nick Cave-like blues), Blood and Iron (which also featured David Booth, who now plays live with Der Blutharsch; this act had a sound somewhat in the vein of Laibach, Autopsia and similar acts) and possibly a few others. It is actually rather hard to remember everything from this time. I also continued to do the odd bit of session work for more conventional musical acts — all OZ-based so the names wouldn't mean anything to Northern European or North American readers. It was mainly recording with the odd live show — I needed the cash! Even that didn't always come through — such are the foibles of the music industry.

In the early 1990s I did some recording and three live performances in and around Sydney with an old friend of mine, Dominik Guerin, who was one of the original founders of SPK. He was with them up until the time of *Leichenschrei*. Along with another old OZ experimental pal named Jon Evans who now lives near Berlin, we recorded and performed together under the loose name of DOM. Eight to nine tracks were somehow recorded and the remastered tracks (which I did with Hunter Barr of KnifeLadder at Retina studios in mid-2001) may be at last released sometime in the next few months or so … under the name Last Dominion Lost. The title will be *The Tyranny of Distance* and the music has at times some resemblance to *Leichenschrei* era SPK. Others may beg to differ about this — there was certainly little local interest in what we were doing around this time ... so once again things slowly petered out.

Around mid-1993 I literally by chance (fate perhaps?) bumped into Douglas P. of Death In June at some sort of semi-industrial event in Sydney during one of his periodic visits to Australia. We renewed our friendship and acquaintance and later in the mid-1990s or thereabouts the Scorpion Wind album, *Heaven Sent*, was recorded. This also featured Boyd Rice of NON. A few months later I was asked to play live percussion on some DIJ live shows in Europe and I have been doing this ever since.

While I was in and around London in early 1997 I renewed my friendship/acquaintance with Andrew Trail whose previous outfit Autogeddon had just finished and slowly and tentatively KnifeLadder was formed — even though at this stage it did not really have a name as such. We did a few live rehearsals and the hard graft of sound source and sample making at home, building prospective pieces from literally the ground upwards. Soon, Hunter Barr, an old pal of Andrew's, joined and KnifeLadder was properly formed. We played our first proper live date towards the end of 1997 at the Bull and Gate in Kentish Town. I also did a little bit of drumming recording session work with Strength Through Joy in the middle of 1997, I seem to recall.

Since 1997–98, besides live shows and tours with Death In June in many different parts of the globe, I have also mainly worked on KnifeLadder and to a lesser degree on my own solo ritualistic experimental soundscape project Shining Vril.

As well as this over the past few years I have done quite a bit of guest and session work (both live and recording) with various acts scattered all over the place. These have included live percussion with Der Blutharsch in 1998–99, some live percussion on a few Fire and Ice shows in late 1998, some recording and live shows with Ostara, Wertham, Andrew King, Sleeping Pictures and Foresta Di Ferro over the past few years. I have also contributed sounds and samples to album and CD releases by the Sword Volcano Complex, Genocide Organ, Browning Mummery and Subcutaneous Theatre (both in Australia). Recently there have been a few other artists scattered in differing parts of the globe who have also asked me to possibly contribute 'bits and bobs' to their forthcoming recordings and I may possibly do so — depending on time and what I can possibly come up with. I am currently trying to keep most of my ideas and sounds for KnifeLadder and Shining Vril recordings. I have also recently decided to reactivate my old-school industrial noise project Kraang for a round of new recordings sometime soon. I hope this gives something of a general idea of my personal musical history and collaborations over the years in the general industrial/post-industrial, experimental areas of music.

What introductory information can you provide about your solo project Shining Vril?

To explain the whole concept of Shining Vril is rather difficult but I will attempt to give it a go anyway. This particular project came into being somewhat slowly towards the end of 1999. Without really attempting to give it a great deal of thought I started to record a few solo pieces that were due for various compilations around the globe. I had made quite a few potential contacts with my various live tours with Death In June and had received a few offers for contributions to various compilations and samplers on European and American labels. I had also met Stefanos of the Greek label C.A.P.P during a Greek Death In June tour in mid-1999 and somehow or other we got talking and he offered to release a 'split' vinyl release of my solo recordings and some KnifeLadder material on his label. This eventually turned out to be the *Split* CD release that came out in mid-2000 that seemed to gain a reasonable critical response in Europe and North America.

Basically Shining Vril is an ongoing solo project of mine to explore my own interests-cum-obsessions. It does not encompass any one particular musical style or aesthetic. Anything can or will be used in the construction of the compositions. The lineup is flexible with myself being the only constant. It can be anything I want it to be. There is also an esoteric/spiritual side to the whole thing but I am trying not to make this too obvious or self-evident. It is there for potential listeners to discover and contemplate for themselves. A form of self-initiatory gnosis perhaps using musical and other sounds in a ritualistic and a subconscious way, to aid the process of self-discovery and awareness along somehow. I find all this very difficult to accurately put into words as I generally find they can be quite inadequate for the task.

I have contributed to quite a few compilations over the past few years and will continue to do so for the immediate future. Hopefully a proper full length release will happen as well as I have quite a few unrealised ideas and plans.

As Shining Vril as a moniker has a rather esoteric/spiritual connotation, what led you to choose this and does the name signify a specific pursuit with the ritualistic soundscapes you produce?

My reasons for using the name Shining Vril as a moniker are many and varied. Many years ago, as I said earlier, I used the moniker My Father of Serpents as a name for some solo recording and live performances in Australia, but I was never entirely happy with this. This name mutated into Ophiolatreia which basically means serpent worship in Latin but this was a bit of a mouthful and didn't really do what I had in mind justice. I found it very difficult to actually settle on one particular name but the word Vril kept cropping up, so it was destined that somehow or other the word Vril would be used somewhere in the name for my solo material.

I have rather a deep interest in esoteric cosmology and hermetic, gnostic philosophy especially in the areas of ancient sacred sites and the still potent power associated with them, the old Mystery religions, rites and practices, the Northern Mystery tradition and what you would call 'the Perennial Philosophy' of mankind. I'm also interested in the more esoteric work of Jung, Reich, Evola, and associates; the Grail Myth and the work of Otto Rahn which encompasses a few different paths that interest me such as Catharism, the Thule Myth and also esoteric Christianity and the whole Black Sun thing. The whole Vril belief as espoused by the Luminous Lodge and the Vril Society in 1920s Germany also personally interested me. I believe there is something undeniable and powerful in all this — call it what you will and me gullible perhaps. Vril, Chi, Odic Force and a thousand different localised names in many differing cultures. This force seems to have been in existence for perhaps forever, even if a lot of the interest over the past century or so has been due to many reading the book *The Coming Race* written in the late-nineteenth century by the English occultist and novelist Edward Bulwer-Lytton which seemed to be taken rather seriously in certain parts of northern Europe in the early-twentieth century.

On a slightly different level I have also in the past ten to twelve years learnt various forms of healing techniques such as Seichem, an ancient Egyptian-derived healing technique supposedly, and I've seen various forms of Taoist Asian chi energy techniques performed often in front of dozens of people. This is really what inspired the name Shining Vril as in one demonstration in Sydney in 1992 the Korean chi master produced a shining wavering sort of chi energy ball which everyone in the room could see — and certainly feel. I prefer to call this sort of energy 'Vril' as this may have been its primordial name many thousands of years ago and it was probably a lot more potent and powerful than today.

***Split* was a shared CD with Shining Vril and KnifeLadder. How was this disc received by the underground?**

This CD release seemed to be received reasonably well and received some decent reviews in various magazines and websites around the globe. Personally I cannot actually say how the 'underground' received it overall but the reaction in general seemed to be quite positive. I am still not actually sure how well it sold but apparently it was pretty widely distributed through the many distributors worldwide that Stefanos of C.A.P.P deals with. Some people found it slightly confusing as to which pieces were by KnifeLadder and which pieces were actually Shining Vril. As I mentioned earlier it was originally intended to be a vinyl release with one side each for each act but it somehow ended up being a split CD. Reviews in general were quite good especially from some Northern European-based magazines. I receive feedback from time to time especially from places like North America, Germany, Scandinavia and Italy but not much from Australia I'm afraid. Both act's names seem to be slowly but surely getting around in various circles. I suppose my past reputation may have been of some help in this area. One never knows!

The Shining Vril tracks on the *Split* CD featured female vocal contributions; is this person a full time member of the project?

The membership of Shining Vril is basically myself and anybody I feel can make a positive contribution at the particular time of recording or live work and who wishes to do so. I have collaborated with many others during my so-called long and illustrious career. I have done a lot of recordings and work over the past ten years under a few different names with the woman who provides the female vocal contributions. At the moment though our relationship is perhaps unclear. Her name is Debra Petrovitch and she is an Australian performance artist-cum-experimental musician of Romanian extraction who I have known and intensely argued with over many years. We did some work together some years back in Sydney under the name Subcutaneous Theatre. Andrew Trail of KnifeLadder also knows her quite well. I would be happy to work with her once again but she can be a rather formidable and difficult personality at times. I can assure you that the Vril sessions for the *Split* CD became rather an intense emotional experience for both of us. We sometimes rub one another the wrong way around literally. Both of us were also having minor emotional crises at the time, which perhaps did not generate a particularly positive atmosphere. Still, some people do their best work when they are like this.

It would appear that you use a mélange of electronic samples, processing equipment, tape loops etc. along with real instruments such as bells, chimes, singing prayer bowls, flutes etc. How do you approach a writing composition particularly as Shining Vril tracks inhabit a free-form flowing style?

This is rather a difficult question for me to answer I'm afraid as I actually have no set, regular pattern in composing. This may disappoint some people out there who worry about such things but things generally come together out of their own accord. I use whatever and whoever is available: a combination of high and low-tech in equipment, borrowed, found and abused. I suppose my subconscious, musical, life experience and dreams in general play a large part in my writings. I decided some time back that there would be no definite musical 'style' to Shining Vril so I may 'dip my wick' — to use such a charming expression — in a few different genres. I am interested in many different things and these perhaps come through in my work and compositions. Sometimes the pieces just write themselves and I perhaps am just the chosen channel. I also often work from a very gut-level feeling and often find words fairly inadequate to properly express what I am trying to put across. I also do not claim to be particularly original or indeed inspirational in my so-called compositional style. The pieces/tracks whatever just sort of evolve in the actual process of recording — make of this what you will. My only actual musical rule for myself is 'try and keep it simple' which I seem to inevitably break almost every time I am doing my own material in the studio. My complex restless mind seems at times to be my worst enemy especially when making new music.

You stated on the Death In June discussion list that you were not too enthusiastic about performing as Shining Vril and more specifically performing solo. Can you elaborate on this? Likewise was this aversion to performing solo the reason for recruiting live support from Marco Deplano (of Wertham and Foresta di Ferro) for the show at the Hinoeuma club in London?

I have never particularly enjoyed doing solo performances of my own work. A few fairly disastrous live performances mainly in Australia in the mid to late-eighties sort of confirmed me in this view. For some odd reason I find it far more comforting to perform in a group mode — safety in numbers perhaps? I have played thousands of live shows over the past twenty-five years or so in various parts of the planet but these have mostly been with some sort of band or other musicians. I have also done a lot of session work both live and recorded where I have been an anonymous backing musician. I used to take to this like a duck to water and never really felt any pressure or nerves. It only seems to be that when I do my own solo live stuff that the inner demons seem to rear up their little pointy heads. Still this is something I am slowly getting over. Unless you have actually been a performer it can be difficult to describe the inner tension that can go on when presenting your own work by yourself to a potentially hostile and contemptuous crowd. My OZ experiences were not particularly pleasant and maybe it scarred me somewhat.

Last year Gaya (Donadio) of the Hinoeuma club asked me to do a performance and didn't seem to take no for an answer so I eventually relented and started to plan something without banging my head against the rehearsal room wall in frustration, something that has indeed happened more than once in the past.

I asked Marco to give me a helping hand as he is a good friend and rather supportive of most of the things I am involved with. I have also helped him with live Wertham and Foresta di Ferro shows at Hinoeuma in north London over the past two years or so and he was quite keen to return the favour. So yes, performing with one other person onstage, for me anyway, can sort of relieve some of the internal doubts and pressure somewhat. I am rather a perfectionist unfortunately and I only want to present a Shining Vril performance that would be out of the ordinary. Ideally there would also be a visual element as well but I suppose I will have to leave this for the future — once all those performance and songwriting royalties and cheques start to roll on in once again. I may be waiting a long time.

The show at Hinoeuma actually went a lot better than I expected both musically and as an actual performance. I was reasonably pleased with it for a change and as a result have considered doing some more as a few people in various parts of Europe have requested some. There may be some in the not too distant future in Italy, the UK, Poland and maybe Germany/Scandinavia as well. These will probably be on the same bill as Foresta di Ferro or KnifeLadder. I was also asked a while back to do something in the USA but whether this ever eventuates is up to the gods. We shall see.

I understand that you collaborated on a musical project with members of KnifeLadder in Australia prior to forming KnifeLadder. Could you tell us about this? How did

KnifeLadder come about? What was the idea behind the project?

I will have to answer sort of yes and no to this particular question. I have known Andrew Trail of KnifeLadder since approximately early 1988 when I first met him in Sydney, Australia, when my act at the time, titled the Slub — a noise guitar outfit sort of like a combined Skullflower meets Butthole Surfers-cum-Plastic Ono Band — performed on the same bill as his band of the time called Ministry of Love. We sort of hit it off and when I returned a few months later to Sydney — after recording with Michael Hutchence of INXS, for his experimental group project called Max Q — we resumed our budding friendship. Over the next two years we saw one another pretty regularly. For a few months in 1990 I helped out on drums for some mutual pals of ours in a Sydney-based gothicy-orientated band called Box The Jesuit (at times slightly in the same area as the Virgin Prunes) after their drummer disappeared. Andrew also mixed Subcutaneous Theatre, an experimental, ritualistic duo I was also involved with which included the performance artist, Debra Petrovitch.

We sometimes appeared on the same bill as Andrew's act, Ministry of Love. Andrew was also due to engineer an album for Subcutaneous Theatre towards the end of 1990. This was going to be released on the local experimental label Cosmic Conspiracy Productions (run by Alex Karinsky who later moved to New York and promoted some Current 93 shows there in 1996–97) which had also released some Ministry of Love material. Unfortunately this never happened mainly due to financial reasons and Debra's unforeseen pregnancy, which put a spanner in the works and pretty much curtailed everything for a while, rather unfortunately in my humble opinion, as I'm sure it would have been pretty impressive.

I saw Andrew quite regularly and he also sometimes mixed another ritualistic experimental act I was involved with at the same time containing ex-members of Box The Jesuit called Jaundiced Eye, who also played quite a few shows around Sydney, especially at two notorious venues called The Evil Star and a local arts centre/squat called the Gunnery. Books have been written about the Gunnery in the last few years in OZ.

Andrew formed another EBM-orientated act called Psychonaut in early 1991 which played around the traps to little response and decided to head to London in mid-1991 or thereabouts. He was tired of the inevitable ceiling you reach if you are doing leftfield music in OZ and the Antipodes. Overseas is often the only option … that or slowly implode and decay … and recede into alcoholic, drug-orientated despair and bitterness over what could have been. I meanwhile stayed in OZ and entered what I call my 'dark years' which were not particularly pleasant on a personal level. I was still involved with music but was basically slowly killing myself in various ways. That is all I will say about this unfortunate period of my life but people who really know me will be well aware of what I am referring to…

Andrew and myself sort of kept in touch through various means and mutual friends. I returned to London myself in the mid-1990s for live touring purposes with Death In June. I had bumped into Douglas P. completely by chance while he was in Sydney in 1993 visiting different parts of OZ. He remembered me from the early 1980s and early Current 93 days and we renewed our acquaintanceship. Sometime later this led to him asking me if I would be interested in doing the live percussion for some European and possibly US dates and not being an idiot, of course, I said yes.

After returning to London I soon moved into a spare room in a flat in King's Cross with both Andrew Trail and Andrew King and slowly but surely that was the genesis of the entity called KnifeLadder. This was early 1997, I believe.

Some of the ideas behind KnifeLadder I had sort of previously explored some years back in two OZ-based outfits called Orchestra of Skin and Bone and Stress of Terror which were both around in Melbourne from the mid-1980s to early 1988 — until I left that city under murky circumstances.

Andrew Trail was one of the few local OZ musicians I felt pretty much at ease with who knew of my overseas history and adventures and was eager to musically explore uncharted terrain. Unlike quite a few of my so-called 'friends' back there who were not very supportive at all, and slaves to the latest trends from abroad.

When I returned to London we renewed our friendship and without really meaning to we slowly started the gradual formation of the concept of KnifeLadder, by working on sounds-cum-samples in his home studio. I had tried doing some solo recording in OZ in the early 1990s using the name Ladder of Knives, due to a friend of mine visiting China who brought back a photo of a Taoist ladder statue of swords. These recordings were not particularly successful in concept mainly due to the rather disturbed state of mind and body I was in at the time but once I got myself reasonably well I intended to pursue the ideas I had with hopefully more suitable companions.

The general concept behind KnifeLadder started to develop in London during 1997. Over a period of a few months we worked on sound sources and originally-made samples, often quite primitively recorded and processed-cum-treated from their very low-tech origins. We started to have some live rehearsals-cum-semi improvisation sessions and then later on with Hunter Barr — an old pal of Andrew's — at various London rehearsal rooms. An important part of the sound of KnifeLadder pretty much from day one has been the live semi-improvisory trance (in its proper way) repetitive aspect — which to a certain degree is an integral part of every piece we record and perform live.

If there is a main concept and idea behind our sound it is that we are very much into the live performance aspect of doing so-called electronic-based music. Loops and various sound samples put together in a cyclic hypnotic semi-repetitive manner with organic trance wind instrument drones and exotic and heavy ritualistic percussion plus repetitive bass drones are pretty much what we are currently about.

Unlike loads of other electronic acts we tend to play our equipment and instruments 'live' in the manner of a traditional three-piece band (though we are much more flexible in instrumentation and member's roles than normal rock acts) and prefer not to rely on sequences, backing CDs, DATs or everything being generated by the mixer using laptop facilities and the like. Live semi-improvisation over carefully thought-out backing is critically important to the KnifeLadder sound in both live and studio work. Generally we do not play any of our tracks exactly the same way twice. There is always some sort of variation — also the live mixer is of great importance to the overall sound. We know a few really good ones fortunately. It is not that we are Luddites or anything similar, it is just that most electronic-orientated acts nowadays seem to hide behind their computers and the like in live performances with little thought. The best exception to this I have seen in the last few years are some Coil shows in Europe, 2nd Gen, some Ant-Zen acts and possibly some of the acts on at the Hinoeuma club in north London. The audience is often an afterthought and many times you may as well stay at home and just listen to the recorded output on CD or vinyl.

Also unlike many electronic-orientated outfits no matter what the style, the three members of KnifeLadder are influenced by and enjoy many different styles of music and sounds. We have also had many years of experience in live performances and playing many differing styles of music in front of sometimes hostile audiences worldwide. I for instance have had close to thirty years experience in live work, playing many different forms of music such as jazz, blues, orchestral, Scottish pipe bands, musicals, various forms of rock, session work etc. and have personally performed in front of some of the toughest and most contemptuous crowds in the world, especially in OZ where you can play like God and still be totally ignored by the local crowds who will be the first to cheer some third-rate over-the-hill act from abroad.

Hunter Barr is also classically trained in different instruments and has a lot of experience working as a studio engineer for all sorts of differing types of acts and music over the past five years or so. Both he and Andrew Trail are experienced and qualified sound engineers for recording and live mixing and they have a sort of professional studio and rehearsal set-up connected with KnifeLadder called Retina II. So there is quite a bit of experience and knowledge between the three of us.

It's an unusual sound comprising looped sounds, various percussive devices and solid bass throb. How do you compose/construct songs? How important is the studio to KnifeLadder? What do you mean by voodoo power electronics?

KnifeLadder pieces-cum-songs are composed/constructed in a variety of ways. It is very much an organic intuitive process between the three of us. Often a piece will be built upon from an original loop or sample that the three of us have had a hand in making, often from very low-tech origins and by constant rehearsal and improvisation in both the studio and rehearsal room a song somehow forms itself. Tracks have also been built ... constructed ... from the percussion and sampler upwards ... with gradual and cyclic changing of sounds/samples etc. overlaid ... over time. Other tracks can be constructed differently — beginning with the bass harmonic throb or the Moroccan horn that Andrew often plays. There is no one set way of working for us. Some songs write themselves literally and we just go with the flow. A track can also end very differently from the original conception but we seem to allow room for this as the construction of songs and soundscapes is a very organic process for us. There are no real definitive versions of songs in the KnifeLadder side of things: pieces change and evolve constantly every time we perform them live. The tracks Dervish or Scorched Earth, for example, have evolved of their own free will over the past three or so years and can vary quite a bit in live and recorded performance, especially in the use of rhythmic dynamics, and length. We very often use a call and response instrumental/soundscape aspect between the three members in a live performance context.

For our more soundscape and non-rhythmic-orientated tracks — only some of which have been presently recorded and haven't really been featured on *Organic Traces* due to time restrictions — we have used different methods again in song construction, often constructing a piece from the voice used in a harmonic overtone manner or as an underlying drone or Moroccan horn with other sounds added on at will, playing off one another in a live rehearsal context, working out which sound sits best with another and constantly remembering to not be too self-indulgent and to keep things relatively simple, and to use the recording studio as an instrument in itself. Our ways of working and constructing songs are constantly evolving and changing and we have a few surprises in store for the future in this area.

The studio is critically important to us as is live rehearsal. In the construction of the whole KnifeLadder sound and way of being we try and record regularly in our own studio, and as soon as we come up with the basis of something new, we attempt to record the bones of it and flesh it out. Some of the material, including two tunes (Born Under Fire and Carousel) due for release on two different Italian label compilations, were completely constructed in the studio from literally nothing. This was also sort of the case with Hymn. our piece on the Operative *First* compilation, which was built in the Retina studio. All these tracks vary quite a bit from their studio versions when done live. We don't really think of the studio and live aspect of KnifeLadder as two completely different things. The studio is really another creative tool for us and unlike some other acts we tend not to be passive, overwhelmed participants when in the studio. Quite the reverse, as we often really go for it!! — Dervish being a very good example of this in both the studio and live performance contexts. Many different ideas/sounds and overdubs are tried and perhaps used if they are deemed suitable by the three of us. If not then we often keep these for future use — for other tracks and blueprints.

I am not really sure if 'voodoo power electronics' is an entirely accurate description of our sound anymore. Perhaps we have somehow gone sort of beyond this convenient description now. The others may disagree perhaps. The sounds we use probably are quite a bit more varied than the power electronics description. We even attempt to use — horror!! — some melody on occasion from the keyboards, vocals and horns. We have been known to dip our wick into the ritualistic trance, industrial, dark ambient, soundscape areas at times — all these terms don't really do justice to what I am attempting to say. We try to use many different sounds and do not limit ourselves to one particular area which can cause some confusion when people try to pigeonhole our sound. Still, people love descriptions, don't they?

In the percussive side of things there are a few different things at work besides vodou drumming and rhythms. I have studied Middle Eastern and Indian tabla percussion some years ago, plus the master drummer aspect of different forms of African drumming which sort of rears its head in some of our work, especially in live performances. Pipe band side drumming which I did for five years as a teenager in OZ with a Scottish pipe band ... these influences all sort of blend together in the percussive assault onstage and in the studio. Maybe we will have to think up a new more exact and detailed description of our style and sound as unlike a lot of acts around now we are not easily classifiable and cut across a few different musical boundaries and styles.

I hope this sort of answers this question for you — apologies if you all are still scratching your heads in bewilderment.

What artists/projects currently hold your interest?

I personally enjoy many different types of music and have a very diverse appreciation of many different musical styles and artists. As far as I am concerned there is only good and bad music. I try to keep an open mind about almost everything I hear and try not to fall into the all too familiar trap of musical cynicism, something I semi-regularly did when younger.

In regards to the current industrial and experimental music scene I appreciate many different artists and acts. A few examples would be the various artists sort of connected with the Hau Ruck label such as: Nový Svět, what I've heard of Dernière Volonté, PPF, Der Blutharsch; various Tesco acts such as Anenzephalia; Stateart releases including one from Cyclotimia; other European acts would be Deutsch Nepal, Inade, Tribe of Circle, Thorofon, Scivias, Dieter Müh, Amenti Suncrown, Nocturne, Arkkon, Cyclobe, Coil; some of the Ant-Zen acts such as Imminent; a new Antipodean dark ambient act called Isomer; anything involving Z'ev; the last two NON releases on Mute; Browning Mummery (an old industrial act and friend from OZ — very good); two Polish acts: Spear and Le Plastic Mystification; Aube; various releases from Daniel Mensche, Lustmord, Nurse With Wound, Illusion of Safety and Voice of the Eye over the years; Andrew Liles, Muffpunch, Anti Valium and White Dog, all based around London. These are all just examples. In the neo-folk area I think Naevus, Of The Wand & The Moon, A Challenge Of Honour and the work of Andrew King are the most interesting acts personally speaking. Even though it is difficult to keep up with all the new and latest releases constantly going I try somehow to do my best in these areas. Looking at it objectively I think the whole experimental/industrial/dark ambient/ritualistic whatever 'scene' is probably more vibrant than ever — though a touch more originality could be added at times. Still, this is something I have never particularly claimed to be.

Outside of this area I personally enjoy a lot of serious classical music (straight and avant-garde), film soundtracks, all forms of fifties/sixties/early-seventies popular music and folk, rock and jazz. Too many composers and artists in these areas to mention and I often forget the names that go with different pieces and songs sometimes. I will always keep an open ear and mind to pretty much anything, though most rave, dance and rap/hip-hop music doesn't really thrill me or indeed attract my interest much. The culture with all this stuff sort of passes me by completely.

You split your time living between Australia and the UK. Why do you choose to do this?

The reason I do this is because I actually can. I have never felt 100 per cent comfortable anywhere and have never really been one of the local lads, so to speak. I have always had an overwhelming urge to see the world and possibly discover myself (man) ever since I was a young sprog. I am usually in Australia for a few months each year where I tend to keep a fairly low profile doing lots of non-career related things. There is no exact reason why I divide my time between both countries it just seems for a good proportion of the last twenty or so years that most of my creativity and work happens in Europe, especially the UK. When I am back in OZ I usually do a bit of recording at a local studio near my mother's seaside house which is probably one of the best studios I have ever worked in anywhere and for some bizarre reason is situated in the boondocks of southern Queensland, miles from any large town. Other than that, as I said before, I keep a low local profile and do not receive much Antipodean support or interest at all.

One other reason could be that I have a reasonably large support network and musical peer group in London and parts of the rest of Europe who sort of understand where I am coming from and are generally supportive. In Australia I have a network of old acquaintances who often aren't very supportive at all. Quite the reverse, in fact: some are downright contemptuous and hostile, while others are totally bewildered by the aesthetics which seem to guide my path. The majority of the projects that I have been associated with over the years have received either little or indifferent response from Australian audiences. A lot of the people I know there have become increasingly parochial over the years which has always alienated me. I have had many discussions-cum-fruitless arguments with various Antipodean pals over the years about what I do etc. so in general I no longer bother to keep the majority of them informed of my activities — musical or otherwise. This is just one of many reasons why I spend quite a bit of time outside of Australia. I have had many unusual experiences which would just not have been possible if I had stayed in OZ and I would be a far lesser person for it. I march to a different darker drum, so to speak, than the majority of Ozites who mostly consider me (if at all) a weirdy ratbag eccentric, if not worse. Why should I bother to have to put up with a local insular mindset when I know that others elsewhere will be more appreciative?

Also another reason is that I personally love being an expatriate from my homeland. This is very stimulating and intellectually satisfying. I feel somehow more alive and this in turn stimulates my thought processes, musical composing and general pursuits. I use my time in OZ as a bit of a breathing space and regeneration period before venturing out once again to parts unknown. I could say a lot, lot more on this particular subject but will shut up for now.

I should also point out that I have met other people from various parts of the globe who have similar things to say about where they came from so it's not confined to one place.

You seem to be able to travel through Australia and UK/Europe on a reasonably regular basis; how are you able to manage this? I suspect that this might lead to some interesting jobs in order to finance such travels?

This would be telling somewhat but let us just say that I sort of get by — not particularly well admittedly. I do lead a somewhat primitive lifestyle which certainly wouldn't be for everybody, and I would certainly not recommend it if you want to hang on to your sanity and health. I have paid a heavy price in terms of lifestyle for the musical and artistic adventures I have had over the past twenty or so years. Quite a bit of sacrifice has gone into my endeavours and international travels. I am also something of a 'scammer' in regards to accommodation, musical equipment and such like, and currently at least do not really have a settled abode anywhere in the world.

Yes, I have had many interesting and mundane jobs over the years in both Europe and OZ, which have helped finance things a bit. Examples include: running recording studios and rehearsal rooms in both OZ and London; lots of restaurant work in London and OZ; bartender; theatrical hand and stage manager; new age and alternative bookshop co-owner in Sydney some years back; working in record stores; packing records at various distributors in the UK and OZ; session musician in both the UK and OZ; telesales marketer; actor in underground videos and films; soundtrack designer for similar sort of films; extra in TV commercials and mainstream films in OZ; antiquarian bookseller in Australia (briefly); assistant in jeans shop (late 1970s); and industrial cleaner at various times. These are just a few jobs I have had to do to earn a crust to continue on my merry bohemian way and enjoy what the world has to offer.

I believe there is also another John Murphy operating in a similar experimental and/or soundtrack field of music. Is this the case and how much actual confusion has it created?

Yes, apparently this is indeed the case, and it has caused some confusion with a few people, which I have attempted to clear up. Certain friends and acquaintances of mine have occasionally seen a documentary or something similar on Channel 4 in Britain or SBS in OZ or elsewhere which mentioned in the credits that a John Murphy was listed as responsible for the sound design and soundtrack, and that the music or whatever was in a sort of industrial/experimental mode. They just sort of assumed that it was just little me. I had to disappoint them by saying that I had no personal knowledge of the aforementioned documentary or indeed the person involved. This incidentally is an area I would like to explore and possibly get involved with as I have had a little experience in this particular neck of the woods in years past both in OZ and the UK.

There hasn't been a great deal of confusion but this was possibly the catalyst to me to again start spelling my first name as Jonh, something I used to do many, many years ago in the days of punk in the late 1970s. Running into quite a lot of other John Murphys in various parts of the globe may have had something also to do with this. This in turn seems to have confused a few people out there in the international experimental/industrial music arena. Obviously I have shot myself in the foot once again by overestimating people's general intelligence in the first name department. I will just have to persevere in that I suppose.

Something you are involved in is the relatively new Operative Records. What comments would you like to make about the concept of this emerging label?

Well for a start Operative Records as a label and so-called collective came into being towards the middle of 2001 in London. Members of KnifeLadder, Naevus, Muffpunch, Rective, Andrew Liles, Ruse, Andrew King, Anti Valium, Gaya of the Hinoeuma club and a few others got together at a series of meetings-cum-drinking sessions at various people's abodes around London and slowly but surely the idea of some sort of supportive label-cum-collective sort of emerged out of the fog. Some of us felt that there was quite a bit of interesting and innovative stuff happening at various venues such as the Hinoeuma club in Finsbury Park without much local interest or label support. We sort of perhaps foolishly attempted to do something about this by putting together a compilation CD titled *First* that sort of showcased what we all felt were the most interesting and innovative acts who hopefully would eventually release their own CDs or vinyl through or on the Operative label. This would be financed partially through the money earned from sales of *First*, theoretically speaking, of course.

The basic concept of Operative is to have so-called Outsider sort of acts that we all felt were being ignored locally as they didn't conform musically or conceptually to Brit fashion dictates. It was to give these acts a sort of vehicle; a way in which to get their releases exposed, distributed and to provide a support network. I'm not actually sure if I am explaining the whole thing properly but it is slowly but surely reaching towards its goal. Besides *First* which has received some interesting reviews internationally, CDs have also been released by Leisurehive, Naevus, KnifeLadder and a few more are being planned for the future. These include a possible split Shining Vril CD with Lloyd James of Naevus and his solo project called Retarder. An Antivalium/Andrew Liles split release, a White Dog (Gaya and Joanne of Naevus) CD. All these releases will be self-financed so Operative is also an avenue for innovative acts to put out releases and gain distribution through Shellshock in the UK and abroad. That is sort of it in theory and hopefully it will eventually all work out for the best. The concept behind the label is best explained on the website at www.operative-records.co.uk.

The Naevus release *Behaviour* and the new KnifeLadder CD release *Organic Traces* have both received more than a bit of interest and appreciation internationally though this is still early days. Both of these acts have also performed outside of London at the Leipzig festival in Germany and have therefore garnered some international fans and interest, after a lot of hard slog around the local traps to little avail at times.

What's next for KnifeLadder/Shining Vril/Foresta Di Ferro and any other acts you're involved in? Closing comments?

First of all I would like to say that KnifeLadder is not my band!! And I am not their leader. Some people, especially in Europe, seem to have got this idea into their head, at times, so I would like to point out that I am only one of three members who are all treated on an equal basis in terms of songwriting terms and in all aspects of the group. We discuss all ideas and plans fully before putting them into practice.

Over the next few months I would say that our main priority is to get *Organic Traces* properly distributed and sent out to all the people in various parts of the globe who seem to be interested. We also plan to perform live outside of London hopefully. We would like to take up some possible offers of shows in the north of England, and different parts of Europe, mainly Italy and possibly Germany and Belgium. We also have some tracks appearing on a few European compilations and samplers. Some of these are due to be released very soon — though you can never really tell with these sort of things. Two pieces are on two different Italian-based compilations: one track Born Under Fire on the Oktagon compilation *Audacia Imperat* and another piece titled Carousel which is a recorded reinterpretation of an early KnifeLadder live track appears on the Italian compilation *Tal Mont De Lune* due for release soon by Nail Records. I should also mention that Shining Vril has two tracks (Conquest and A Secret God) on these compilations as well.

We also intend to record (for an eventual second CD release plus some possible compilations) over the next few months. Some of our newer less rhythmic-orientated material — which will certainly showcase other not so obvious aspects of the KnifeLadder sound and maybe introduce some new unusual sounds, recording techniques and instruments. These may also feature some unexpected 'guest' vocals/ voice. These are ways to widen our sound and to introduce the unexpected. We all enjoy confounding expectations and are determined not to fall into recording or live-performing clichés with all our newer material especially. We are worried about falling into a formula in our general approach.

Finally, very recently someone in Europe has just approached me and KnifeLadder about something new which may open up a whole new field for us to possibly explore in the long term. I will leave this for all of you out there to ponder...

Shining Vril will continue to appear on various European and perhaps American compilations and samplers. I have quite a few tracks appearing on various so-called Europe-based V/A tribute 'compilations': including one for Ain Soph which was supposed to be released by Oktagon; a track on a sampler being put out by *Die Tat* mag of Germany; the two aforementioned Italian-based compilations and maybe a piece on a Scott Walker tribute that someone in Spain (I think) is putting out in early 2003. I also intend to slowly record more material and eventually release a full scale self-financed CD or album, probably through Operative Records, though this will entirely depend on personal finances. One or two Europe-based labels have also expressed some interest in releasing some Shining Vril material as a CD or similar so we will have to see. Lloyd James of Naevus and myself have occasionally talked about doing a joint Shining Vril/Retarder CD release sometime in the future. Retarder is the name of his solo project. Anyway expect some Shining Vril full length release sometime in the not too distant future and also expect some possible Shining Vril live performances — probably in London and maybe Italy, Denmark and Germany. It'll probably be with both KnifeLadder and Foresta Di Ferro or something similar.

Two other releases that include sounds-cum-'bits and bobs' from me are the second full length release from Sword Volcano Complex on Triumvirate Records in the USA and the debut full length CD release from Foresta Di Ferro, Marco Deplano's project. This will be released through Hau Ruck — Albin Julius's label in Vienna. Both releases should be out early in 2003 or thereabouts.

There may be some new recorded Kraang material out through Tesco from Germany sometime in the not too distant future. I am due to start work on new tracks pretty soon. These will be the first new pieces recorded since the late-eighties.

Tesco will also be releasing some old material recorded just over ten years ago in Sydney, Australia, which I was involved in along with my good friend Dominic Guerin who was one of the main and original founding members of SPK back in the late 1970s and another old friend known in the experimental scene in Oz named Jon Evans. This will be released under the name of Last Dominion Lost, and the title of the CD and vinyl album will be *The Tyranny of Distance*. It is in parts somewhat similar in sound perhaps to *Leichenschrei* period SPK — make up your own mind. That seems to be about it for now I guess!!

ISOMER INTERVIEW : 2002

■ Isomer may at this point in time be a relatively unknown name, but the fact remains that sole member David Tonkin is producing some damn solid dark ambient/heavy electronics music, an almost nonexistent style and/or scene within the Australian musical landscape. Regardless, Isomer have managed to garner the attention of premier Deutsch label Tesco Organisation, who have subsequently signed the project and are releasing the official debut CD *The Serpent Age*. Following on with this interview, David provided some interesting insight.

SPECTRUM: Given that Isomer is quite a new project it will be a name known to very few who read this interview. So, please introduce yourself, the project and the musical path you traversed that led to what Isomer has become today?

ISOMER: Initially I just needed to focus my energies into something creative. Other than basic piano as a kid, I never took any formal musical training. I came into dark ambient/noise/PE/whatever music through a couple of CMI [Cold Meat Industry] releases, and they sort of inspired me to explore for myself those sorts of textures. I bought a secondhand Akai S2000 sampler and basic MIDI keyboard, found a couple of PC programmes and had a go. That was around the year 2000. The results were pretty hit-and-miss, but they served their purpose, giving me some sort of release, and I had fun doing it. Basically whatever came out I put down on tape. It varied from light-hearted novelty pieces to noise to dark ambient and death industrial. *Serpent Age* is much more focused in intent and sound, and I put more effort into making it a complete package.

When you first started releasing material in the ambient/industrial genres it was done so under your own name. It was not until later that you took the project name of Isomer. Why the shift in focus to entity away from you as an individual?

I just found I was sitting on a number of tracks with no moniker to use in distributing *Semblance Of Perfection*, so I used my own name. I guess also I wasn't really concerned with creating a recognizable mark or image. By the time I had put together the tracks for *Sedation*, I had found the definition of an isomer was analogous to the sorts of ideas I was exploring, so started to use that. [*An isomer is one of a group of chemical substances that have the same number and type of atoms, but in which the atoms are arranged slightly differently in each substance. — Ed.*]

Given that your early tapes were rather eclectic in scope, it was not until you recorded your debut CD that Isomer gained a clear focus and direction. Obviously this was a conscious effort, but what made you focus your sound towards a dark ambient/heavy electronics fusion?

On a basic level, it was partly a result of the programmes I was using. Until then I had only been using the S2000, a demo version of Fruity Loops and Audio Mulch. When I got my hands on a full version of Fruity Loops (with you and a couple of others!) I had access to a much wider variety of sounds, generators and effects, the sampler took a back seat and I let fly on the PC. I guess it also reflected a change in attitude and approach on my part. I'd gained more confidence in what I was doing, and took the production of *Serpent Age* much more seriously.

Can we expect drastic stylistic changes to Isomer's direction and sound in future?

I've been drawn to more noisy material lately, so I imagine that will filter through pretty soon. Some vocal treatments maybe?

In the review of your debut CD I made a comment regarding the track title Every Man A Star implying that it could be said that some shine more brightly than others. What is your view of this perception, or is the track title to be taken in a more literal manner (with regard to the theory that all life has been derived from exploded star matter)?

It's a reference to personal strength and energy; that fundamentally you can really only rely on yourself and your own reserves. 'Be a light unto yourself.' You can always look to religion, philosophies and other people for guidance and inspiration, but first and foremost strength must come from within. But yeah, I'd agree that some do shine more brightly than others!

Likewise the first track Star Of Sarajevo may imply an interest in matters surrounding the conflicts within a particular region of Eastern Europe. Is this at all the case?

My wife is a Bosnian Serb from Sarajevo who migrated out here to Australia with her family in '93 after being forced from home. I've developed a great respect for the generosity, honour and integrity of the Serbs since then, and the track's a homage to them. Of all the peoples of the Balkans and of Europe at large since WW2, I don't think any have been demonised and ostracised to the extent the Serbs have, largely as a result of the work of public relations firms, the rivers of shit that came from the US and NATO, and the complicity and involvement of the Western media. So much of what filtered through to us was and still is tainted, and Star Of Sarajevo is a personal response to that.

Additionally many of the track titles refer to the sun and the cosmos, with the preliminary album artwork partially reflecting this. I would also assume that there is a concept behind the whole album if not simply a common theme between tracks. Please comment. Also how will the final album artwork differ from that of the promo version?

I was very much focusing on my resolve and personal strength though the whole process, and I think the sun and its associated imagery and symbols are a powerful representation of these ideas. Together they gelled into the overall 'concept' for the album, and I chose the final cover images accordingly. The demo cover featured a seal of the sun over some treated surgery photos. For the Tesco release I've used an image of the sun itself and representations of a lion-headed serpent which appears in Roman, Egyptian and early Christian mythology.

I do believe that you produce most of your material using modern computer methods, which has come under fire from some post-industrial artists who believe that the use of a PC to create such music is not a positive thing. What is your view on this matter?

I really don't think it matters how you produce it. There's no ideological reasoning or intent behind my use of a computer. Actually it's partly born of necessity — it's a cheaper alternative for me, as I already had a PC at the time I chose to start toying with sounds. I do sometimes wish I had a rack of knobs to fiddle around with — something more tactile than the click of a mouse button — but I'm happy with what I'm using at the moment, and the results they produce. Certainly in the future I'd like to broaden my palette a bit.

Do you find composition of tracks difficult? Also prior to commencing a track do you have a clear idea of what you want to achieve or do the tracks tend to evolve of their own accord as you progress through to completion?

Often I find if I encounter difficulties in the initial stages of assembling a track, I probably shouldn't be forcing it. Sometimes an idea or concept will inspire me to manifest it somehow, but more often than not I just start from a particular sound or sample which I'm taken by, and everything else coalesces around it.

Given that you are now part of a minute (but growing) Australian scene how do you view this in its international context? Are there other Australian projects that you have networked with that you would like to mention?

As you yourself would know, it can be a lonely path to tread, but I agree the 'scene' does seem to be growing. Two projects I'm really impressed by at the moment are Terra Sancta and Vespertine (at least his album *Transmissions From Antiworld*). New label Cranial Fracture Recordings in New South Wales also look set to be something of a force, so all power to them. I'm also a big fan of Darrin Verhagen's material (Shinjuku Thief/Filth etc.) and much of David Thrussell's stuff (Black Lung etc.). Streicher seems to have made quite a name for himself in some circles (if only for the implied politics), but I'm yet to hear any of his material. Historically speaking, as you know a number of trailblazers and some bigger names also originated in Australia, such as SPK, John Murphy, Strength Through Joy/Ostara etc.

There's definitely a healthy output of experimental music here, but not much of the darker material. As you put it once, there's plenty of the chin-stroking, 'academic' experimentalism. More broadly speaking, I think your own magazine *Spectrum*, and a number of dedicated individuals/labels such as Dorobo and Arcane Recordings (RIP) help provide a focal point and draw some international attention, but there's not much of a recognizable 'scene' as such. There is quite a bit of crossover which I find interesting — I stumbled into this sort of music through more straight-edged industrial — but I think there's still a lot of parochialism and tribalism when it comes to music in Australia — this or any sort. It's interesting that even though Douglas P. has been periodically living and recording in Australia (and just outside my home city of Adelaide) for quite a few years now, no one really associates him with the country in any meaningful sense. His place of residence is regarded as almost incidental, even though — as I understand it at least — he has drawn some inspiration and peace from living in the Adelaide Hills. Having said that, I guess his heart will always lie with Europe.

I am also under the impression that you are currently and/or have recently completed university studies focusing on Asiatic matters. In that one track on an early tape contained a sample of an Indonesian Tribesman, how much has your study influenced or inspired your compositions?

I finished a Bachelor of Arts (Honours) degree majoring in Asian Studies a few years ago, and continued teaching in related topics for a brief period. I even gave a couple of lectures on Japanese film and popular music, and included a short discussion of Japanese 'underground' culture, playing the students some Masonna and showing a little of the film *Tetsuo* — that was fun. The sample you refer to was actually a Papua New Guinean tribesman in a doco going nuts as he was about to be baptised by missionaries. Obviously he wasn't quite sure of his decision! I wouldn't really say my interest in Asia has directly influenced or inspired any of my music, but I'm always on the lookout for areas in which the two interests coincide. For a short time I was tracking down Asian experimental/industrial material outside the obvious output from Japan. There's a great cassette of death ambient material called *Xatya* from an Indonesian project, Worldhate.

What releases are on the imminent horizon for Isomer?

I'm working on a remix for a friend here in Adelaide with a project called The Spinning Room, and one of the tracks from *Serpent Age* appeared on the debut compilation release for Cranial Fracture Recordings. But other than that, I've been a little too busy to devote a lot of time to Isomer as of late, and I'd rather not do any half-hearted attempts. Planning a wedding certainly hasn't helped either! I'm only just now settling down after that and am now back at work, so I'm sure soon enough I'll be more inclined to channel my energies into it again. There'll always be something on the horizon!!

TORIDH INTERVIEW : 2002

■ The ever prolific Henrik 'Nordvargr' Björkk of Mz.412 and the now defunct Folkstorm has returned with a new martial industrial-orientated project Toroidh which also incorporates elements of neo-folk and dark ambience for good measure. With the project being self-described as: 'folk music from the times when history was written in black and white and coloured in red', and with the first three albums forming a broader 'European' trilogy, Nordvargr expands upon the conceptual underpinnings of the project below.

SPECTRUM: Within the Folkstorm interview featured in Spectrum Magazine Issue no.5, you stated that Folkstorm would not slow down, but less than six months later you had declared this project dead. Had you already established the concept of Toroidh prior to the demise of Folkstorm? Also what are your current intentions with Toroidh in regard to how long you see it as a viable musical vehicle for your interests?

TORIDH: Firstly, the reason for killing Folkstorm had nothing to do with the birth of Toroidh. The concept of Toroidh has been with me for a few years actually… The first idea was to make long minimal tracks based only on marching drums (similar to track two on the first CD), but as I started to actually record the material I wanted to push things a bit further, hence the use of real instruments and even some clear vocals. I think that I will continue with Toroidh since it has grown to be one of my most successful projects, both when it comes to sales and positive feedback.

Can you give reasons to why you choose to quit recording as Folkstorm?

The main reason was that I wanted to focus on Mz.412… This reason seems kind of ridiculous today. I just can't keep myself out of the studio… But since I promised to quit Folkstorm I will stand by my word — there are still some releases on their way, but I do not record any new material. If you still want to hear me do some harsh chaotic noise I recommend Hydra Head Nine (me and S. Halibot).

Likewise while Toroidh is musically far removed from the raw power electronics sound of what Folkstorm produced, do you see parallels in the ideas and concepts utilized in both projects?

The only thing that Folkstorm and Toroidh have in common is the war theme, otherwise they are very different.

I am not familiar with the word Toroidh? What significance is held within this name?

Nothing.

You have stated that Toroidh (apart from Mz.412) is your most ambitious project to date. How do you see the concept and sound of Toroidh being more ambitious than any other of your musical projects?

Basically this means that Toroidh represents the music I personally like the most. Of all my projects Toroidh is the only one that I can listen to myself and appreciate as if someone else had made the music. This I have never experienced before. Also Toroidh is more 'musical' than all my other work.

One statement you have issued relating to Toroidh exclaimed: 'With the atmosphere of early Laibach and LJDLP we are thrown back in to the time where history are written in black and white and coloured in red. More a reflection than glorification.' Given Toroidh uses themes and images that can be deemed as constituting a political lightning rod, was this the reason you felt it necessary to write this mission statement of sorts?

Because it is the truth. I use political statements and imagery from all camps — both left, right and all in between to reflect Europe's birth (and death) — but as usual people get pissed off because of the right wing samples. I wanted to clearly state that Toroidh is not about glorification of anything — it is a reflection of times passed.

As has been alluded to in the above question (and as was the case with Folkstorm), the titles and imagery inhabit a political sphere pertaining to the events of the early/mid-twentieth century. This is clearly highlighted with another mission statement of: 'Toroidh should be considered a time machine — let yourself be swept back in time to the first decades of the 20th century when Europe was boiling with frustration…' Would you care to expand further on this?

I partially answered that in my previous answer… it is a musical melting pot of all camps — I have sampled Stalin, Hitler, Churchill and lots of other less famous politicians, agitators, pacifists, anarchists and 'men of the street' in order to get the 'total' feeling of the chaos that is (and was) Europe.

Your first three releases *Those Who Don't Remember The Past Are Condemned To Repeat It*, *Europe is Dead* and *Testament* form individual parts of a triptych fittingly entitled the 'European Trilogy'. Can you elaborate on the trilogy's concept? Do you have any conceptual ideas that will be encompassed within forthcoming Toroidh material once the above mentioned trilogy is completed?

The 'European Trilogy' is all based upon the chaotic twentieth century — the world wars, the ethnic conflicts and the dream of a united Europe. The Europe that conquered the old world, and colonized the new, and that passed away with the Second World War. What forthcoming Toroidh material will be about is still a mystery.

Your first release under the Toroidh banner was the limited *Those Who Don't Remember The Past Are Condemned To Repeat It* LP. This was then re-released soon after on CD format, however, containing different tracks and mix. Was the original intention to release it as an LP only? What was the reasoning behind the formats containing different music/mixes?

All the Toroidh full lengths are released on both vinyl and CD, but they are all different versions. So in order to experience the 'whole' album you need both formats. The reason for this? You have to work hard to get it all.

In that Toroidh utilizes dark ambient type passages, intermixed with militant neo-classical sampling, guitars and other elements pertaining to the neo-folk scene, how much of a fan are you of the current output of the neo-folk scene?

To some extent I like it, but I am more of a noisehead... I think that most 'folk/neo-folk/classical/whatever'-artists make some good tracks on each release but also a lot of crap — the productions are almost always unbalanced. There are so many pseudo-musicians that can't handle the keyboard/guitar, but still keep on trying... Maybe it's just me being picky since I have been around in this field so damn long :)

On a number of occasions (both speaking to you personally and likewise your views put forward on e-list forums), you have stated that you have a general dislike for music recorded on computers. Therefore I assume that you still avoid the use of a computer with the creation of your music; however, what methods of production do you utilize to create Toroidh material?

I record most of the stuff in our studio mostly using samplers, analogue synths, guitars and some snares. I then master and mix the recordings on a computer... The computer is very good when it comes to editing and mastering, but to use it to make music is bad. Especially when it comes to making noisy stuff — you just can't make a computer sound as a 'real' distortion pedal!!! What I truly dislike is noisemakers who (most of the time) use computers and end up with badly looped noises and cheap soundcard crackle... I will not mention any projects, but there are lots of them out there... Nothing beats working with real instruments!

Having had the opportunity to witness Folkstorm live twice prior to its demise I can personally vouch for the sheer physical intensity of the performance. Given that Toroidh differs drastically in musical approach to Folkstorm, is Toroidh a project you have any intention of thrusting into the live action arena?

I don't think so... When I play live I like the physical and confrontational approach, and the music of Toroidh is more laidback ... but it all depends on the time and place of the arrangement.

Given the sheer number of projects you have been involved in over time, there has been a clear increase in the number of active projects you have in recent years. Could this be viewed in any way as a subconscious effort to tackle the prolific output of one particular Peter 'Raison D'être' Andersson (given the number of project names he operates under)?!

Oh yes, it´s a competition ... seriously, NO... it's just that I am very productive and collaborate with lots of people and to call it all Folkstorm, Mz.412 or Toroidh would be evil... and I shouldn't take all the credit — I have worked with lots of talented people and without them and their guidance I wouldn't have become what I am today.

Again we are at the conclusion of the interview. What can we expect from Toroidh in future and is there anything you would like to add?

I will probably start working on new Toroidh material later this year, but first I have to join the rest of Mz.412 to finish the *Infernal Affairs* boxset. That's all I can reveal at the moment.

TERRA SANCTA INTERVIEW : 2002

■ If you were to excavate down through the layers of underground music within Australia, you would discover artists and projects toiling away in relative obscurity, particularly with reference to those who are involved with dark ambient type genres. As was the case with Australian dark ambient project Isomer, who have recently issued their debut CD on cult German label Tesco Organisation, similarly sole member Greg Good of Terra Sancta looked abroad for label interest, subsequently being snapped up by premier American label Malignant Records to issue their debut full length. Read on to discover more about another great Australian export within the dark ambient genre.

SPECTRUM: Terra Sancta have been around for a relatively short amount of time (since 2000 I believe) and will only be known by a small number of people at the moment, however can you please introduce yourself, giving some background information as to how you came to form the dark ambient project Terra Sancta?

TERRA SANCTA: I bought my first synth in 1996. At the time I listened mainly to metal, but also to ambient music. Often when listening to metal intros/outros etc. I used to think that it would be cool if there was music that was all like this, something that incorporated these two extremes in music styles. I guess I had a vague Godflesh meets Brian Eno sort of idea. When I heard that the bass player from Emperor had quit the band to work on a synth project I was very curious and tracked down the CMI [Cold Meat Industry] *And Even Wolves...* compilation, and that's how I discovered industrial/dark ambient music.

I played around with various styles for a while, but it wasn't until 1999 that I began to work seriously on the concept that became Terra Sancta, culminating in my demo CD *Anno Domini 2000*.

Where did you derive your project name from and how do you believe that it represents (if at all) both your own personality and the music that you create?

Terra Sancta translates literally as 'sacred earth'. It is a historical term for the 'holy land' of Israel/Palestine. I thought it was an interesting name as it refers to a place of such reverence for three religions, but also a place of perpetual conflict. Musically, Terra Sancta reflects this spiritual aura as well as the darker undercurrents. However I don't intend to make any political or religious statement with this music, and I look at the project name and song names more as metaphors.

Your first recording was a three track mini CDr/demo *Anno Domini* that, whilst obviously influenced by the dark ambient sounds associated with a number of Cold Meat Industry artists, managed to retain its own personality and flair. How did you approach the writing and recording process when setting about making your first recordings and do you think you were successful in achieving the results you initially intended?

I wanted to create something that mixed beautiful sounds like choirs and strings with darker drones and industrial sounds. My CMI influence was fairly obvious, but hopefully it does have its own sound and style. I am happy with it as a first body of work.

What response did you receive from the release of the mini CDr/demo *Anno Domini* and how widely available was it?

I made twenty copies which got sent to a few labels, magazines and friends. I really had no idea what the response would be like but it was overwhelmingly positive. Two labels showed interest in releasing it but as it has turned out it became a self-release.

Jumping forward two years from the release of *Anno Domini*, you have now re-recorded these tracks, had them professionally mastered and released the recording yourself as an official MCD. How has the response been to the new and improved version?

One thing I wasn't happy about with the demo version was the overall sound quality. So after I finished the recording of my second CD I felt that my techniques had improved enough that I should redo the demo. I reworked the tracks and got it mastered by Phil Easter, so it sounds great now.

I got 500 copies printed up and am in the process of trying to get rid of them. Interest is slowly catching on and I have some good distribution now, but it takes a while to get noticed without any sort of label promotion etc.

After having had the pleasure of hearing an advance copy of your debut full length *Aeon*, a definite progression of

the sound can be detected. Whilst your MCD has a relative level of musical structure due to the use of sampled instruments, your debut CD differs in that it is slightly more minimalist musically and takes a deeper and more sweeping dark ambient sound. How do you personally view the differences between the recordings and why did you choose to take this stylistic shift in musical approach?

I am very satisfied with the way *Aeon* turned out, as I have really found my niche with this album. It was a conscious effort to create a deeper, darker sort of brooding ambience. I have done away with sampled melodies and vocal samples are used more sparingly and subtly. A lot of the sounds have been sampled myself and synth is used just to complement some parts, rather than being the main sound source.

Do you find the composition process difficult? When commencing the composition of a track do you have a clear idea of what you want to achieve or do tracks tend to evolve of their own accord as you progress? Additionally, is Terra Sancta your first endeavour at creating or playing musical compositions?

The hardest thing about the composition process is getting the time to sit down and do it. The process itself comes fairly naturally once I have gotten my mind into 'the zone'. I usually have a general idea of what I want before I start, but since the process involves a lot of auditioning and treatment of sounds you can't fully predict the final result.

Before Terra Sancta became a defined project I recorded a few other pieces of music covering a variety of styles, but these were just part of an experimental, formative phase. Some of it is still quite listenable and who knows, maybe it will find itself reworked as part of a soundtrack or something, but it wouldn't be under the name Terra Sancta.

What equipment and production processes do you utilize in creating your dark ambient atmospheres and has this altered at all over time?

I have a couple of synths and sound modules, but most of the sound manipulation and song construction is software-based. I use synths less now and try to get my own samples as raw materials, but there will always be a place for synths, vocal samples etc.

But all this equipment is damn expensive, and there is always another piece of hardware or a software plug-in that you want to buy, so this better start paying soon!

Unlike the power electronics or neo-folk scenes that can be said to contain a political aspect (implied or otherwise), dark ambient music alternately tends to inhabit a bleak spiritual sphere without the political angle. Are there any concepts you utilize as inspiration for the music of Terra Sancta or which are otherwise are inherent within the atmospheres you create?

Yes, I agree with this comment. There are no particular messages behind Terra Sancta, but at the same time I hope it invokes a response in the listener. The music is loosely based around a concept of this earthly wasteland that we are part of and the sadness and beauty that resonates from it. The first track I wrote, Desert Earth, sums it up: deserts conjure up contrasting images, harsh barren wastelands, or places of lonely spiritual journeys. Terra Sancta is a world of deserts.

I guess that such themes and images are important in initiating the creative process, but once started the sounds themselves are what drive it.

Given the premier American label Malignant Records holds the honour of releasing your official full length debut *Aeon*, how did this signing come about and was there a great deal of interest from other labels?

I just sent a CDr to Jason and he wrote back with great enthusiasm wanting to release it. This was a pleasant surprise as I didn't hear anything from him when I sent my *Anno Domini* demo to him a couple of years earlier. Obviously he likes the progression of the music. Only a couple of other people have heard it so far, but the reaction has been good.

As Terra Sancta can be viewed in the context of a small but growing Australian scene of dark ambient artists, how do you view this within the global scene? Do you care to mention any other Australian projects you may be aware of?

Australia has always had a small but significant contingent of artists working in peripheral forms of music, and a few have made a name for themselves on the international scene. We are home to one of the premier labels — Dorobo Records, which I am a great fan of, especially Alan Lamb's wire music. I am in contact with David Tonkin whose dark industrial project Isomer has just released a CD on Tesco. I don't have a great knowledge of this music scene, but I know there are other people doing similar things.

Apart from your debut full length that is soon to be issued on Malignant Records, do you have any other Terra Sancta recordings in the pipeline?

Most of the sounds for the next album have been collected but the actual recording process won't begin until the new year, so I guess it's a bit premature to say much more than that at this point.

Also I am aware that you operate a side project under the name of Gun Metal Grey, with the one track from the project I have heard indicating a death industrial type sound. What information would you like to provide on this side project and how do you view its importance when considered against Terra Sancta?

This is a project I have played around with for a couple of years. It has a noisier more industrial sound. There are several half-recorded tracks lying around and I hope to finish the first album sometime in 2003. For now Terra Sancta is my main project, but how far I go with Gun Metal Grey will depend on the response to it and how much time I can dedicate to it. I have lots of other musical ideas, but if and when I can work on them also depends on finding the time.

NAVICON TORTURE TECHNOLOGIES INTERVIEW : 2002

■ Although an introduction was not written back in 2002, the interview was conducted at a time when the project was gaining wider recognition following the release of the Malignant Records debut *Scenes From The Next Millennium* in 2001 (but prior to the soon to follow double album *The Church Of Dead Girls*, also issued on Malignant Records in 2002).

SPECTRUM: It would seem that Navicon Torture Technologies (NTT) has been active since 1997 but your involvement with industrial music spans back over ten years. Can you provide a chronology of this musical involvement?

NAVICON TORTURE TECHNOLOGIES: I formed my first band S.H.R.I.K.E. in 1991 when I was a freshman in college, with some people who shared some of my musical interests. This group was composed of two synth players, a guitarist, and myself as vocalist. We mostly did a lot of what I would call 'post-industrial ballads' emulating Skinny Puppy, Chemlab, The Cure ... I feel as though it was an important time of my life, but the music wasn't very good overall. There were only two people in the band with any real talent, and I wasn't one of them. After about a year or more, we split up, and around winter 1992, I eventually started working under the name Oilrotsrubber with a friend of mine who had been in an industrial-grind group called Drencrom, who had performed on a few occasions alongside S.H.R.I.K.E. at local events in our area. Over time we changed our name a few times, Nullandvoid, Narcoticsandvaginas, finally settling on NAV. In the early nineties I was putting a lot of time and effort into involving myself in the NYC industrial scene, and had become friends with various people within the scene, such as Jared Hendrickson of Chemlab and Krayge Tyler of Virus 23. At this same time, I had begun to contribute to *Industrialnation* magazine, and myself and some friends were trying to get together a zine centred around the longest-running 'alternative/industrial' club in New York at the time, Communion, which took place every week at the now infamous Limelight. I was doing some small work there as a member of the club's army of 'distributors', people who were actually paid to hand out flyers for the club all around the city and boroughs and suburbs, etc. During this time, I had the opportunity to see a lot of great shows and meet some of the people who were having a big influence on me, so it was definitely a time of my life that I remember fondly, although this was around the time that rave hit the States in a big way, and drugs began to permeate every facet of my social life, so I got a little lost, though certainly not as lost as some. This drug surge was essentially the reason why NAV in that form had to end, so I was left to my own devices, and started working on stuff by myself around 1995–96, using only my computer and the sampling application SoundEdit Pro under the new name Navicon Technologies, having taken the NAV moniker and mutated it further. I had graduated from college in 1994 with an associates degree, and eventually went back to school in 1996, where I enrolled in 'computer and electronic music' classes with the intention of learning how to record using midi. It was in this class that I met someone who seemed to have an interest in experimenting with sound as I had been, and he and I began recording together under the new name Navicon Torture Technologies in 1997. During the latter days of NAV, I had befriended some other local guys who were in an industrial-grind band called Negativehate, and we began talking about the possibility of doing a split CD together with their more electronic side project Negative Eight, and eventually in August of 1997, we released the split disc *Amalgam: A Collection Of War Poems*, which is the first official NTT release.

Why NTT as the name for your activities?

There has never been an exact reason for why I use this name, there are times that I feel unsure about continuing to use it, but now that I've become moderately established under the moniker, I will continue to use it for at least a few more releases before I retire the name. Because it has stayed with me for so many years in so many different incarnations, it has a certain importance to me, even though the name itself doesn't necessarily carry some profound meaning in the world outside my head. Some people have attempted to give meaning to it, one person suggested that Navicon might be shorthand for 'navigating consciousness', which seems to me to be some lame drug-culture reference that I might have found more appropriate back when I was actually doing lots of drugs. For my purposes, it could best stand for 'navigating conscience' which is something I think we must all do in our daily lives, making the choice between what is best for us and what others want us to do. Who knows, others could perhaps interpret it better than I.

Your official debut NTT release came out on Malignant Records during 2001 and obviously was the point where your project became more widely known. However, what is probably less known is that prior to your debut Malignant album you had already released quite a number of limited tapes and CDrs. Do you think the timing was appropriate for the release of this debut CD when considering the evolution and progression of the project, or in hindsight would you have preferred to have been able to release an official CD earlier?

I feel that as I am always evolving psychologically and emotionally, my artistic output therefore evolves with me, and I was simply not ready to have anything released as widely as the disc on Malignant until that point, or I would have put more effort toward making it happen. I also feel that the release on Malignant completely stands alone in terms of what I've been doing. Each NTT release is more or less an obvious evolutionary step, and the way that *Scenes From The Next Millennium* was recorded can and will never be replicated, because it was a unique experience, very intense and very frustrating at the same time. My method of constructing tracks has changed radically since then, and I'm anxious to continue to refine my techniques. When I first began seriously recording on my own around 1994–95, it was a very simple and primitive process. I would sample from various sources onto my computer with SoundEdit and construct these very minimal pieces using loops, often I would use just one sound looped for ten minutes and leave that as a completed track. I would also sample my vocals, and then construct the piece, and record it to cassette directly from the machine's audio output. Then, I would delete the files from the hard drive and start all over again, since the completed tracks usually took up too much space to fit on a floppy. I still have a lot of those old samples on disc, but I had an accidental hard drive erasure in 1994, so a lot of that stuff is lost. It seems I have to go through something like this every several years now, since I just lost tons of material in a hard drive crash in February 2002. Moving from that early system, I later began using the computer as a sampler, constructing loops and then recording them on two channels to analogue four-track, recording other sounds and vocals live to tape on the other two channels. Eventually, I bought a minidisc four track and used the same technique. It wasn't until two years ago, that I sort of reverted to the original system of constructing everything on board the computer and the four track hasn't been abandoned altogether as a tool for recording probably until during this last year, and I now do every aspect of my recordings on the computer, still using SoundEdit. I realise that was a very longwinded and tangential response. Sorry.

Broadly speaking I would categorise NTT as a noise industrial/power electronics project, yet when critiquing your musical output at a deeper level, your music does range from dark ambient passages through to the all-out aggressive noise. How would you personally describe NTT output and additionally what projects would you acknowledge as being inspirational?

Over the course of this project's history, I have called it many things, and of course others have their own ideas of what I'm making. In the early days, I called it 'noise-ambient' or 'noise', then I sort of set out consciously to make power electronics. There is a sort of soliloquistic tale I tell, which was when I once stated to Sasha Noizguild that I had decided on making just 'straight-up' power electronics, and she asked me what I thought I had been doing all along. It hadn't really dawned on me that I was making anything specific to a particular subgenre, because I have had so many different influences within this broad spectrum of electronic music. I have come up with a genre designation of my own which most accurately describes the current and recent body of NTT material, which is 'power romance'. Some huge influences from the past twelve years that I can reel off from the top of my head are James Plotkin, Boyd Rice, Justin Broadrick, Brighter Death Now, Aube. My greatest musical and personal influence has been Swans, and the various related projects. I've been listening to Swans since I was about sixteen or seventeen, and they have remained important to me. I have grown apart from so much other music since then: when I was in my early twenties, I worshipped Skinny Puppy, and now I couldn't care less about them, their music will remain with me, and I can always appreciate it, but anything current which I may hear about those people is of no interest to me at all. There are many groups from that time of my life, who now have zero significance to me, and I suppose it's just that I'm a different person than I was back then. Hell, I'm a different person now than I was two weeks ago!

Given that my personal musical interests are vastly broader than the specific underground scenes I used to cover within *Spectrum Magazine*, what music/styles/artists both within and outside the 'scene' are of particular interest to you?

Within recent years, I have become more interested in some of the newer metal/post-hardcore stuff that is becoming somewhat popular; I love Today is the Day. Jim Plotkin introduced me to a lot of this stuff like Isis, Botch, and his new projects Atomsmasher (now called Phantomsmasher) and Khanate, with maestro Stephen O'Malley, are excellent. In my local suburban area, there is a huge and still growing hardcore/metal scene, and interestingly enough, I've developed a small following here. I find it strange because on the whole, I don't feel as though these people really understand what it is I'm doing, but they're still into it and seem genuinely interested in knowing more about it. I have many friends who are involved in this local scene as musicians and promoters, and such, and though I feel like somewhat of an outsider, I've been embraced by a small contingent of younger people. Other than that, my musical interests don't stray too far from the realm of 'industrial' music. I've been lucky enough to meet and be in contact with a lot of the greatest people within our scene, and some of the friendships I've made through mutual interest and appreciation of one another's projects have proven to be very rewarding. Examples I can give are Frank Merten of Herbst9 and Scott Candey of Gruntsplatter, who are two of the best friends I have made even though we've never met in person. In terms of those who have influenced me musically, IRM has definitely been a milestone, and Martin and Erik are people who I've enjoyed corresponding and collaborating with.

With album and track titles such as *I Fucking Hate You All And I Hope You All Fucking Die*, Freedom Of Choice Is The Right To Hate, and I Want To Commit a Crime Of Passion, to me these would be bordering on being so blunt as to be potentially viewed as cynically humorous. What are your thoughts of this perception?

There is probably a high degree of cynicism somewhere in a lot of my work, though as for humour, I do maintain a certain philosophy in which I try to be serious within my work, just because of the cathartic nature of what I'm trying for. Though I suppose some of my sense of humour probably seeps through, since I am hardly a stone-faced humourless automaton. I try not to take myself too seriously in everyday life, since I've spent the majority of my existence being depressed.

As there is a significant amount of negativity inherent in both the sound and concept of NTT, do you view NTT as a channeling device for your negativity in order to create a positive result for yourself?(And this is not being asked in some sort of new age philosophical manner I would add!)

NTT is really approached as something which I need to do. I am a generally unhappy person, and I attempt to alleviate that unhappiness by channeling the negative energy creatively, and the fact that there has been such a positive response to my work is a positive result, for certain.

Given this scene's interest, if not obsession, with war, terrorism and violence-related subject matter, it is inevitable that I would ask about your thoughts on the events of September 11, 2001. Despite having already issued a statement for your web page that re-evaluated your position to where your inspiration is derived from in light of the events of that day, given that you are both part of the scene as well as being an American residing in New York, do you care to expand on your thoughts on 9/11 and its aftermath?

There is this paradox here where we are still recovering from those events, but life has continued to move on. My feelings about the events of that day have never truly been expressed in the strictest of terms because I'm not sure what I feel about it, other than feeling how terrible it is that so many lives were taken, and remembering the terror of being at work in Manhattan on that day, and worrying about people I know and just wanting to be home, but having to sit there locked in at my office building until things calmed down and they opened the roads out of the city. However, there is an entire historical sequence of events which led to this attack and there are so many things that we as the general population are not privy to, it's impossible to be in full possession of the facts, and therefore difficult to form a solid opinion. Then there were the cheap plastic American flags available for sale on television, the fact that so many people have used those events as fodder for furthering their own ends; for example at local diners in my area they began advertising gas masks and survival kits on the fucking menus. This kind of thing was in large part what led me to issue the statements I had posted on my website, because I had to challenge my own motives in order to understand what I was doing with NTT. It turned out to be something which was both a positive and negative move on my part, because it brought out a very strong hostile response from one person in particular, though other responses were much more constructive and supportive. But, I needed to do it, because I had begun to feel on a certain level that some of the material I had been working on prior to that date might have been contrived, and some of the ideas I had been working with may have been somewhat childish, I had to make sure I was being true to myself, and I was probably in a state of shock when I made those statements, which is not to say that I don't stand by them today, but I had to go back and edit them in part because there were certain points made in that letter which were based entirely in momentary rage, and were better off edited out.

Likewise in hindsight it could be said that your debut CD on Malignant entitled *Scenes From The Next Millennium* was rather prophetic. Thoughts?

This has been suggested before, but honestly I don't find it prophetic at all. Of course there have been apocalypse fantasies for longer than I've been alive, and I'm of that generation of people who grew up fearing nuclear war was imminent, so dream images of dead cities and atomic wastelands are a large part of my socio-cultural tapestry, as it is with much of the western world. The cover artwork for that CD was appropriated from a variety of sources, so obviously it was not my original idea to create an image of a post-apocalyptic landscape. One of the guys from Negativehate said that there are two buildings on the cover which look like the twin towers, but I disagree. There is such a thing as coincidence.

Live actions would appear to be a staple feature of NTT, and although I have not seen any such performance, with regard to the photographs I have seen these actions seem to be executed with a very physical approach. What similarities and differences do you see between live and studio settings for music production and how much are live actions an integral part of the NTT experience?

In the beginning, while performing, I had a tremendous amount of self-doubt, and I tended to be very stiff. Early NTT performances weren't much to look at, though not that much has changed, I suppose. I have always felt this need to sort of completely lose my shit onstage, though I could never get relaxed enough to do so, and generally remained fairly stationary during the set. As I became more comfortable with my performances, I probably thought less about it and was able to put the idea of becoming physical out of my head. The first time I performed alone onstage, for the Achtung Amerika! festival, was the first time I sort of allowed myself to loosen up just enough to let the emotional content of my material manifest through physicality. One review I read of the show said that I didn't have much stage presence, and looking at the video of my performance, it's not exactly how I remember, but it was an important step. Sasha Noizguild later told me that it was good to see me 'let go' onstage, so she at least knew the difference between that show in particular and the many NTT performances she had seen before then. I wouldn't really call my performance 'physical', but it has definitely become more physical than it used to be, and that's good enough for me. As with my recorded work, the performances have evolved over time, and the five shows I've done so far in 2002 are very different than the ones I did last year. I have always tried to have other people participate in my performances, and there have only been two NTT shows where I was onstage alone.

Your upcoming album on Malignant Records entitled *Church Of Dead Girls* is slated for release before the end of 2002. How will this CD differ from the material that which people have already had the opportunity to hear?

When I first began to conceive this release in winter 2001, I was in a very bad place emotionally, and I was at times probably going over the edge. The album was going to contain some of the most evil thoughts I had mustered, and I was getting darker and more intense to a point where the things I had been writing and thinking were really disturbing me. The line between myself and my musical persona was beginning to blur, and I was finding it difficult to interpret these impulses sonically. Then, I fell in love, and things really took on a different light. It's that old cliché that colours and smells all change when you're in love, but I was experiencing it for the first time in several years, and it transformed NTT as a result of my own transformation. A lot of my material has always been centred mostly around emotional dissonance generated by my personal relationships, but the shit I was dealing with at this time was an important and new experience for me, and it was the impetus for the 'power romance' concept, which sort of bridges the gap between the utter bleakness of my previous feelings and the new perceptions I had gained through this relationship. I think now that NTT has become so much more honest and sometimes after I've recorded a track which has real emotional significance for me, I really feel like some of this unbearable weight upon my chest has been lifted, even if it eventually returns. The last year of my life has been incredibly rewarding and at the same time, possibly the most harrowing time of my life, and while *The Church Of Dead Girls* is now a far cry from the fucking brutal evil bastard I had originally hoped it would be, it's sheer open honesty will make it that more intense. It will, I hope, be the ultimate expression of my love and grief, and the ultimate expression of power romance sensibilities. (Or at least, that's what the press release will say!)

REVIEWS : 2001-2002

Alphonse De Montfroyd (Ukr) *Silence*
3" CDr 2001 CDr Ad Noiseam

■ While the title might be a touch misleading, it does nonetheless give an indication of the intricate subtleties that this mini release encompasses. Given this is the debut release for this Ukrainian artist, five short pieces are showcased, and while they have an allegiance with darker forms of ambient music, they also teeter at the edge of an experimental framework (partially akin to the direction that Hazard has taken since signing to A.S.H International). Pulsations, drones, textural sounds, faint rhythms etc. are explored here in a minimalist vein, focusing on subtle shifts rather than grandiose movements. Melody is also a foreign concept here (as are organic sonorities); instead the atmospheres are quite clinical and digital which gives partial recognition to the laptop experimental scene (yet I have no idea by which means these pieces have been created). Essentially representing a taster for this artist's material, it will be interesting to see how he progresses it with future releases. Oh, and this particular release is limited to only fifty copies.

Ativ (USA)/Radial (USA) *Split*
3" CDr 2001 Ad Noiseam

■ Not being familiar with either artist, the bio tells me that both projects hail from the New York rhythmic noise scene and have collaborated on this four track mini EP by re-mixing two tracks of each other's material. For me there can be rhythmic noise ('great!') and there can be rhythmic noise ('it's OK...'). While my perception of this release is leaning towards the latter, it does not mean the tracks on this release are bad, rather they do not have that certain 'something' that would enable me to declare the tracks excellent. This might sound like an apathetic statement to some, yet when listening to these tracks they neither grab me in a positive nor a negative light. Anyway in regard to the actual music, the Ativ re-mixes of Radial's material are relatively twisted, using frayed sounds injected with heavy driving beat sequences. Radial on the other hand have re-mixed Ativ's work using a more subdued undercurrent, then overlaying this with rather harsh distortion or cut up-orientated beats. Notwithstanding that hearing this material performed live would give me a whole different perception of the two acts, my apathetic stance stands when listening to this material on CD. Non committal perhaps? You might have an entirely different perception. As with all of the 3" CDr releases on Ad Noiseam this is limited to 100 copies.

Azure Skies (Swe) *Azure Skies*
CD 2001 Ant-Zen

■ Being a collaborative project between members of Sanctum and Metal Destruction, initially many people may have expected this to be released by Cold Meat Industry, but for whatever reason this has been issued via Ant-Zen (and even I must admit that it is quite different to the direction that this label has been pursuing over the last few years). At any rate such considerations are immaterial and do nothing to detract from what is essentially a great CD. Commencing with a crusty mix of noisy rhythmic loops and sweeping orchestral atmospherics the two facets of the Azure Skies projects are revealed — on one hand nasty and gritty, while on the other, beautiful and forlorn ('rhythmic, orchestral industrial noise' perhaps?!). Chopping between these sounds and including a hefty whack of metallic percussion, the mid-paced flow of Crater bodes very well for a solid release. Even more roughly hewn, Deniability is built on static lurching loops, dense rumbling elements and random noise crawls through a myriad of sections occasionally converging into some hyper-rhythmic parts. Being calmer in volume, the weaving noise loops of Hydrazine are initially offset by a fleeting piano tune that gradually fades into the recesses of the track only to make a reappearance late composition. As for the nasty rhythmic industrial side of Azure Skies, this is displayed in full force on Collapse with processed vocals, cyclic mid paced loops, sporadically blasting searing noise for good measure (and if this were pushed up a notch or two it could have qualified as a power electronics track). Alternatively, Bring Nothing Back contains a brooding orchestral melody that sounds particularly 'Sanctum-esque', except for the ridged and rhythmic percussion setting it apart, only for the heavy rasping/shouted vocals to beg a comparison to the vocal deliveries of Mental Destruction. Presenting the most free-form piece of the CD, Still is a wavering and meandering industrial noise piece, while Forward Contamination is initially deceptive in its dark ambient tone, only to evolve into a superb pounding rhythmic offering. All in all a damn fine CD and a positive result of the cross pollination of the skills and ideals of members of two known and respected projects.

Bad Sector (Ita) *Ampos*
CD 2002 Power & Steel (via Loki Foundation)

■ Bad Sector are a project that should need no introduction, but if they do *Ampos* is a fine place to start. Forming a re-release of an older album, this was originally released in 1995 on God Factory, however two bonus tracks that originate from the same recording period are tacked on the end for good measure. Likewise the album packaging has been re-evaluated, with the re-designed digipack being rather resplendent in complementing both the sound of the group and the overall aesthetic of the label. As for the music, straight off it has the unmistakable sound of Bad Sector (if you have heard it before), and if not it is a sound that blends sound experimentalism with dark ambient textures. Yet in their pursuit of musical brilliance Bad Sector manage to avoid the stuffy intellectual aspects of academic sound exploration while similarly avoiding the clichés that can be present within the dark ambient scene. And the result I hear you ask? None other than a musical palette of cosmic spatial breadth, combined with a hint of a science fiction-type resonance, all evoked via the flowing and shimmering sound structures. Across the thirteen compositions, the album retains continuity and focus, yet each individual track chooses to explore the subtleties of the slow morphing rhythms and swelling harmonic tunes. Thus from the outset each track is impressive as it weaves its own caustic undercurrent while intermixing clinical blips, slow morphing melodious textures and alien-esque voices. To conclude, little if any more needs to be said in way of praise of both this album and Bad Sector as an artist, given I can only offer the highest of praise in respect of both.

Boyd Rice and Friends (USA) *Music, Martinis and Misanthropy*
CD 2002 NER (via Tesco Distribution)

■ Being a reissue of a classic release, the original artwork has been expanded with new digipack format (beautiful gloss card, silver foil print and de-bossed details), and new images within the twelve-page gloss booklet. Under the Boyd Rice and Friends moniker it combines the collaborative input of luminaries such as Douglas P., Rose McDowall, Michael Moynihan, Tony Wakeford and Bob Ferbrache, and in the process creates a musically diverse album. However being more than merely music alone, the lyrical content plays a major, if not the central, role given its scathing indictment of the modern human condition (but more often than not this is done via misanthropic humorous witticisms). Another highlight comes in the form of the absolute classic song *People* — a hauntingly beautiful (jangling) acoustic track, where the lyrics have been increasingly validated by the passing of each year (listen and ye shall understand). Disneyland Can Wait is another amazing cut of sparse acoustic guitars, floating female vocals and the calm and forlorn spoken vocals of Boyd (...lets take a ride on Mr Toad's Wild Ride shall we?). But what of the other tracks you ask? Well, they encompass orchestral/sound collages (Invocation and An Eye For an Eye, Shadows of the Night), spoken word/narrative pieces (The Hunter, Nightwatch, Tripped a Beauteous Maiden, History Lesson and Silence Is Golden) and acoustic guitar-based songs (Down in the Willow Garden, I'd Rather Be Your Enemy and As For The Fools). Additionally, one last bonus track is enclosed, being an interesting piece that seems to have been contributed by recent Boyd associate Ms. Tracy Twyman. As for this unnamed track, it is a rather nice piece of conspiracy type humour that implies Boyd Rice was responsible for the Columbine High School shootings. Subversive indeed! Overall this is one wild romping musical and socio-political ride that has not aged one iota in the thirteen years that has transpired since its original release. *Music, Martinis and Misanthropy*? - a musical, mandatory, masterpiece!

Changes (USA) *Fire of Life*
CD 2001 Hau Ruck (via Tesco Distribution)

■ This CD was first released on Storm Records in the mid to late 1990s, after Michael Moynihan encouraged one original member (Robert Taylor) to dig up archival recordings from this duo (Nicholas Tesluk being the other member). Likewise the recordings that make up *Fire of Life* have been derived from a variety of source tapes dating from 1969–1974, and which had never been officially released before the original Storm Records pressing. However thanks to Michael Moynihan's sincere interest in encouraging this music to be heard by a new generation, the original release has become rather infamous, despite being well out of print (therefore this re-release is much welcomed news for those who may never have otherwise been able to track down a copy). As for the music this is apocalyptic folk music in its truest form, created in a time well before any such term was first coined. Primarily based around an acoustic guitar and male vocals (one track augmented with flute and female vocals), there is a simplicity at play that allows the inherent beauty and strength of the tracks to shine. Some tracks have been limited by the condition of the original source tapes; however when taking this into consideration, this does not take away any of power and conviction of these eleven tracks. Highlights of the CD would include the title track, Satanic Hymn #2,

The Stranger In The Mirror (Pt. 3) and Twilight Of The West. Overall this Changes CD represents timeless music that is as relevant today as when it was originally written.

Combat Astronomy (UK) *Lunik*
CDr 2001 Ad Noiseam

■ Stunningly designed oversized DVD packaging for this 100 limited release, this CDr represents the debut full length for Combat Astronomy following on from a split CD with Sleeping with the Earth (released on Troniks in 2000). Remembering not being entirely convinced with Combat Astronomy material on the split CD, I was actually quite floored by the eclectic and rather playful tracks that make up this release. Not really sounding like any particular group (other than Combat Astronomy of course), a barrage of quirky loops, noise segments and technoid-style tribal beats combine to assault the listener in a very appealing style. With a loose direction the album uses a variety of cut-ups and interlude segments (even within tracks), yet still manages to remain focused. The track Scene Of Zealot is a great composition of broken, clanging beats undercut with sweeping noise and spacious sound that flows into the even more hyper and twisted track Memories (psychotic tribal beats and disorientating noise). The track Illusions is likewise rather deranged due to it chopping and changing between a throbbing mass of sound, to some over the top fractured beats, mixed again with a good dose of noise. The bizarrely titled Cure Of Zombie is just as bizarre musically with an epileptic beat overlaid with nice partially harmonic drones and programming (only to add further beat sections as it progresses). With the resonance of a heavily treated and upwardly spiraling guitar riff at the start of Konat, quickly a variety of percussive sequences and random noise and static converge into a pleasing coagulated sound mass. Moving in a cyclic manner, the album finally arcs full circle by concluding with short reworkings of opening tracks one and two. Eclectically diverse and highly original, Combat Astronomy have produced an album that is a very enjoyable and refreshing listen, but I think it is slightly unfortunate that it is limited to only 100 copies given it deserves wider attention.

Converter (USA)/Asche (Ger)/Morgenstern (Ger) *Erode*
CD 2001 Ant-Zen

■ This three-way collaboration by three of the well known artists on the Ant-Zen roster has created a rather eclectic release spanning tense ambience, rhythmic noise and death industrial. Static swirling textures and a tongue-in-cheek sample commences the CD (referencing the label name), with the piece gradually morphing towards a mid-paced rhythmic industrial groove. A whiplashing beat-orientated affair on track two has a heavy Converter stamp on the sound — if not just a touch quirkier than normal which has much also to do with the use of another humorous sample. Another industrial dancefloor-orientated track is toyed with again on track three, whereby direction is forged with beat and rhythm as opposed to tune. Morgenstern comes to mind on the fourth piece where slow rising ominous textures eventually combine with mid-paced modulating distortion to create a cavernous yet tense edge, while pulsing programming, distorted death industrial vocals, and amply static noise is the recipe for the fifth piece. Track seven is another fine mixture of a death industrial undercurrent, overlaid with a rhythmic noise framework and distorted vocals in order to create another complex piece that is clearly far from being one dimensional. On the other hand the ninth and final track is a fantastic piece of tense cavernous ambience, intermixed with metallic clatter, vocal samples and death industrial programming. Intense does not begin to describe this, with it being quite reminiscent of the sound approached on Morgenstern's *Zyklen* CD. Overall I feel that fans of the general 'sound' of these three Ant-Zen artists should not be disappointed with this collaborative effort.

C.O.T.A (USA) *Marches and Meditations*
CD 2002 Sonick Sorcery (via Tesco Distribution)

■ This is my first introduction to the group, however I can't say that the rather amateurishly designed (and almost cheesy) digipack did much to inspire confidence. Anyway, as for the music, what we have here is five lengthy tracks with a little over an hour's total playing time. Blending manipulated programmed elements and tribal-style influence, *Mahayuga* set proceedings in motion with a wailing horn and scattered rhythmic electronics. With the tribal-orientated focus, repetition is utilized quite heavily by choosing to morph each track gradually and blending layers of noise, vocalisation, distortion, sampled voices, programmed sounds, tribal percussion etc., using an ebb/flow, rising/falling technique. The sound between each track generally follows a broad and loose framework, yet uses different techniques and patterns to generate differing results per composition. However, it is due to the slow pace and length of tracks that proceedings sometimes become a little self-indulgent and lose focus, thus destroying any mood evoked (five minutes' worth of little more than manipulated swirling wind textures at the start of Deep Within The Womb Of The Mother Part 03 is a case in point). While not entirely awful, there are many other CDs that I would prefer to listen to, thus I would say that this is a release that will not be receiving multiple rotations on my system.

Death In June (Eng) *NADA!*
CD 2002 NER

■ The DIJ re-release juggernaut is finally kicking into full swing, now that the long drawn-out saga with WSD has reached a conclusion (with *Nada!* being the first re-press post-court case). As with the other items re-released thus far, this is similarly housed in superb packaging, consisting of gloss digi-pack with debossed detail and sixteen-page gloss booklet containing previously unseen images lifted from the original photo shoot. And while mentioning additional material, alongside the *Nada!* tracks, the *Born Again* 12" has been included as a bonus. Harking back to eighteen years prior, the year was 1985 when DIJ were reduced to a duo, with Patrick Leagas and Douglas continuing the legacy after the departure of Tony Wakeford (although this recording does feature the input of Richard Butler and David Tibet). Containing some hallmarks of the neo-folk scene (that would become the focus of later DIJ releases), *Nada!* intermixes the acoustic guitars, understated vocals and military percussion alongside other more synthetic, electronic and programmed tracks (e.g. The Calling (MK II), Carousel, The Torture Garden and Born Again). While the latter described tracks will potentially catch a few newer fans by surprise, when viewing such material in context it is a sound influence that somewhat aligned itself with the new wave sound of the time. And while it could be said that the sound has dated on some pieces, these compositions are nonetheless an integral part of the progression of Death In June's overall sound. *Nada!* is also the album that contains the well known, if not classic, tracks Leper Lord, Behind The Rose (Fields Of Rape) *and* C'est Un Rêve, which have all become staple features of Death In June's live performances over recent years. The re-released version of *Nada!* is a CD well worthy of you time, containing classic tracks and acting as another integral paving stone in the continuing legacy of Death In June.

Der Blutharsch (Aut) *When All Else Fails!*
CD 2001 WKN

■ On initial listens I was somewhat disappointed by this new album, but nonetheless this has been one to positively grow on me after repeated listens over an extended passage of time (I received an advance copy when visiting Albin back in September, 2001). Also, after gaining familiarity with this album, one thing to note is that it encompasses a sound and style that, although it acknowledges the past sound(s) of Der Blutharsch, also hints at the potential future direction of the group due to the incorporation of new elements and influences. So, with regard to these 'new' elements, here I would be referring to a few compositions where it seems Albin is at his quirkiest yet — maybe acknowledging a touch of influence coming from fellow Viennese artists Nový Svět? (Track two is a good example of this with up-tempo melody and a myriad of eccentric instrument/sound samples woven into a general percussive military framework). Other 'new' elements would also include using clearly synthetic programming which would seem to give a nod towards another of Albin's temporary projects La Maison Modern. However, this is not to say that the militant stance of Der Blutharsch has been dropped, still setting the overt tone of proceedings here. As for acknowledging past albums, it is noted there are a number of slower pieces included within the thirteen tracks, with the general aura arriving at the distant morose atmospheres to that of the *Der Sieg Des Lichtes Ist Des Lebens Heil!* album. Yet with the shorter song-orientated format of this album, this also acknowledges the style and format of later album *The Track of the Hunted*, as does mid-paced track five, with heavy percussion, monotone vocals and rousing orchestral melodies set amidst samples of falling bombs. Albin's new partner Martina is also introduced on this release, complementing Albin's (and other guest vocalist's) contributions with whispered, spoken or low-key hymn-like vocals on numerous tracks. While many who are well aware of Albin's musical past will automatically want to make comparisons due to this reintroduction of a female vocalist, I on the other hand am not even going to bother (that was then, this is now). But not to be reduced to merely a backing singer, track nine sees Martina take the (solo) vocal lead, presented in a strong part-sung/part-spoken style which works well with the heavy percussion and piano-led tune. In terms of collaborative input on this album, with track eight it is the main vocal that has most obviously been contributed by artist Dernière Volonté, amidst mid-paced percussion and part orchestral/part programmed tune — another track melding old and new influences. One particular standout track of the album is the rather aggressive track ten — an over the top composition of militant bombastic anger, created by fast and harsh driving percussive elements, deeply rousing orchestral samples and main chant of 'patria et libertas' (and ultimately showing just how good Der Blutharsch can be). Yet, the (potential) future direction of Der Blutharsch seems to be most evident on track thirteen, where it clearly indicates a greater reliance on programming and synthetic sounds to diversify the sound — here using low-key rhythmic programming scored alongside orchestral synth textures (the rasping aggressive vocals on this piece have been contributed by Jurgen of Nový Svět). And lastly the final (and hidden) fourteenth track is another fine example of a kinky neo-military ditty, being an upbeat yet swirlingly surreal jig of all things?! Weird perhaps, but still a good listen! It is clear that on this album Albin is attempting to broaden the horizons (and perceptions) of what Der Blutharsch's music is capable of, yet it will be interesting to see if the hardened neo-folk fans can accept the sound shifting away from a purely nostalgic and militaristic one.

Ex.Order (Ger) *War Within Breath*
CD 2001 Malignant Records

■ Ex.Order (the malevolent power electronics/noise industrial alter ego of Inade) have unleashed upon the unsuspecting masses their fantastically titled second album *War Within Breath*. With the material spanning 1997 to 2000, rather than being a new album proper, this CD is a collection of studio tracks (five unreleased and four lifted off the prior *Law of Heresy* MC), and three live tracks. While the first Ex.Order album was a solid one, I will admit that it pales in comparison to this, which I feel has a lot to do with the digital polishing and buffing undertaken by Malignant Sound Technologies to create added sonic punch. Likewise if I did not know that this CD contained some live material, I would have never picked it out as the flow and clarity of sound between tracks is immaculate, giving an overall feel of being a formally composed album rather than a collection of tracks from different sources. Without giving a breakdown of each individual track, there may be a singularity in approach with this collection, yet a clear breadth of elements are used to ensure this is far from being one dimensional industrial noise/power electronics. Thus to give an overall description the sound is stripped back, raw and direct, using seething and bristling textures, abrasive loops, loosely constructed rhythms and heavily distorted and processed vocals and/or voice samples. Notwithstanding, A World of Lies is a highlight with its pummeling percussion and vocals processed to encapsulate a sonic razor-like quality. Alternatively the deadly and seething pulse of the title track contains a trench warfare-type atmosphere, driven by sounds of sprayed gunfire and accentuated by sporadic cries of agony. Intense stuff indeed... Additionally, later track Generated Invasion has a tensile sound consisting of cyclic noise loops, bursts of static and sermon-like vocals flanged to the point of being indecipherable. 'Caustic' might not be the right word, but it is the first one that comes to mind... To conclude, when first hearing this CD I was quite surprised by the similarities between selected sound textures and some of the noisier sound elements used on the latest Inade album *The Crackling of the Anonymous*. While I guess on one level this is to be expected seeing as both groups contain the same two members, on another level is represents a cross-pollination of ideas between the two projects that I certainly was not expecting. Another essential release from the Malignant Records stables.

First Law (Ger) *Refusal as Attitude*
CD 2002 Loki Foundation

■ The third full length album for this project that, as far as I know, is either a side project of, or otherwise has direct lineage to, Turbund Sturmwerk. However, it is worth highlighting that the music of First Law is vastly different to the neo-classical/military industrial sounds of the latter. Operating from an almost progressive, dark ambient/experimental sound, the music of First Law is on one hand quite composed (with respect to the slow rhythm structures), but also contains a free-form, heavily drugged, hallucinogenic ambient quality (possibly illustrating the weaving journey through the recesses of the subconscious, evoking surreal morphing images and half remembered thoughts?... maybe...). Yet it is the sampled voice on Still Humping The American Dream asking: 'what was the meaning of this trip? Was I just roaming around in a drug frenzy of some kind?' that hits the mark perfectly for a description of the album's overall vibe. The mid-paced military-style drumming and acoustic guitar of the opening track In The Final Fleeting Seconds Of Life might beg a comparison to Turbund Sturmwerk, however the swirling synth melodies and austral textures negate this by giving it a sound all its own — that of First Law. The mid album composition (I Am Not) A Coward is rather oppressive with its heavy droning textures and multilayered synth tunes that, when combined with a slow clanging rhythm, takes on a heavy orchestral quality. Alternatively, late album track The End Of The World-Concept has an urgency not present on other tracks, with mid-paced tribal beat structures, clanging bells and the swirling vortex of hazy synth textures that multiply in intensity as the track progresses. The final track is the album's title (split into five parts and extending over a twenty-four minute expanse), and encapsulates a journey of complex weaving melodies, dynamic rhythms and enveloping dreamy psychedelia to create a fantastic cinematic experience for the mind's eye. Sit back, close your eyes and be swept away... Maybe the sound of this will be a bit avant-garde for some dark ambient fans, yet anyone with a mild experimental streak will gain something from this, and if you have any of the other First Law albums you would have no doubt already contemplated getting this.

Frames a Second (Bel) *Disoriented Xpress*
CD 2001 Spectre

■ *Disoriented Xpress* is the second full length CD for Frames a Second, I believe — however I am only familiar with a previous 7" EP of the group released on the same label that has sired this offering. Distorted and damn crunchy, the opener Metrical Beats is a pulsating affair of mid-tempo snappy beats and driving rhythms and as such sets the scene for much of the album. Without any real let-up, track one merges into the next (Specified Information), marking a subtle shift of focus in the composition towards that of sweeping sounds and rhythms. Again not letting up between tracks and flowing directly into Cycle Of Misinformation, things amp up slightly with a faster-paced track of machine drones and successions of rhythmic pulses and sequences — ultimately seeing the album hitting its stride! As for the title track, with this being built on a heavy undercurrent of death industrial textures, it is the lighter beats and synth tune that balance out the sound, and in the process create a fantastic head-nod session! Alternatively, later album tracks, while still rhythmic, take on a darker and sadistic dark industrial framework (Silence Is Bad with clanging metallic percussion and Y-Incision with gloomy programming and quirky sequences). With the title track popping up again as track ten, the second time around it is in an alternate version a touch more menacing than the first. Changing Into Club Music, while not entirely what the name would suggest, remains rhythmically-based with heavy distortion and crunch, but is mostly devoid of melody or tune (this is by no means bad of course!). The final album track is credited as a bonus one and while not stated as such appears to be a remix of a track called Legend. What we get in the end is a track where there is a heavy emphasis on melodic programming without a reliance on noise and grinding beats, as is the case with many of the preceding tracks (with a tinge of urgency, the track surges out of the speakers in a very smooth and club-friendly guise). Overall I would have to say that rhythmic industrialists would definitely be doing themselves a grave disservice if they were not to check out this album. Very commendable.

Genesis P-Orridge (Eng)/Z'ev (USA) *Direction ov Travel*
CD 2002 Cold Spring Records

■ This twelve-track CD comes courtesy of two original pioneers of the industrial scene (read: late 1970s), who have been active in such musical pursuits even before the term 'industrial' music was coined as a descriptive term (the term since becoming bastardised from all it stood for at its initial inception). Anyway I digress... The music on this disc appears to have been originally recorded in 1990 and potentially re-mixed or at least mastered in 2000. With instrumentation ranging from Tibetan bowls and bells, to drums and violins (that have been further processed and mixed), you would reasonably expect these recordings to encompass a spiritual sound. Likewise with the cover, including extensive text relating to the attainment of meditative trance states, you may also expect that this is not music to listen to directly, rather it is for use as an atmospheric musical backdrop for such journeys into the inner recesses of the psyche. While not something I would put on and listen to directly, it does work as a non-abrasive sound collage backdrop (or otherwise, as I believe it was intended) as a focal point for meditation activities. Overall the album has a warm enveloping aura of loosely constructed loops, minimalist washes of sound and sporadic elements of tribal-esque percussion. Each piece is relatively short at around three to four minutes, showcasing repetition and minimalist progression over the duration of the tracks. I would say that this is quite an interesting release for its concept and content but not something I would recommend if you wanted a release to actively listen to.

The Grey Wolves (Eng) *Blood and Sand*
CD 2002 Cold Spring Records

■ Those individuals who can attest to having heard a small portion of The Grey Wolves' significant output over the years (a massive amount of tapes, yet far fewer items on vinyl and CD formats) may describe the project as a politically heavy power electronics act. While this is not at all wrong, there is another side to The Grey Wolves that is less widely known and recognized: those tracks that are far less power electronics-orientated and aimed at an atmospheric noise approach. It is exactly this sound which is to be found on this new CD *Blood and Sand*. Upon reading the liner notes of the cover, it interestingly states that the CD is a re-mix of the same title that was released on cassette shortly after the Gulf War, making this release all the more relevant given current world events. As for the music, only two tracks are present on this disc, yet both span a lengthy passage resulting in a CD that is in excess of fifty-five minutes. First track Desert Storm is a slow moving and tensely brooding piece containing sweeping sounds, throbbing rhythms and indecipherable radio voices that flits between structure and free-form flow. The following piece Gulf Breeze takes a similar tactic of wielding a tensile and caustic vibe, yet does introduce (late in the piece) a heavily processed guitar/drums-based element within the noise layers. Despite the atmospheric inclinations, one of the greatest elements of this CD is that there is always the sense of an undercurrent of aggression ready to burst forth from the speakers in full sonic warfare. Although this aural obliteration never entirely eventuates, *Blood and Sand* is no less of a quality release without it, and in turn showcases the lesser-known atmospheric noise side of The Grey Wolves.

Inade (Ger) *The Crackling Of The Anonymous*
CD 2001 Loki Foundation

■ After what seemed like an eternity, Inade have FINALLY returned with their second CD — five years after their landmark heavy electronics album (and full length debut) *Alderbaran*. So with this wait finally over, I will come straight out and proclaim that *The Crackling Of The Anonymous* is easily one of the top three albums of 2001 and, not surprisingly with the reputation that precedes Inade, this was likewise one of the most highly anticipated. Not to be content with creating *Alderbaran: Pt. II* as many might have expected (and/or wanted), Inade have created a sound that while instantly recognizable as their own, is significantly more intense and substantial, above and beyond that which they have previously been known for. And while *Alderbaran* worked well as a complete and singular inter-linking journey, this CD is a grouping of ten tracks that can equally stand on their own to form part of a collective whole. Avoiding merely describing the sounds, this album is the aural equivalent of staring into the infinite abyss of a black hole, formed post-collapse of a megalithic supernova. Yet when one tries to directly perceive its form, the black hole itself is invisible, being only perceptible to the eye by the surrounding light and matter being sucked into oblivion (in the process both time and the actual fabric of space is bent, twisted and warped by the immense gravitational weight). If this all-encompassing chaos were to achieve the improbable — to actually connect with another black hole — ensuring a link across immeasurable leagues of the cosmos and aeons of time, it represents the ultimate key to allow the listener to spiral out on an inter-dimensional journey (....and if willing, to discover the space between space, where light and dark become but one). Yet, it is not as though this album represents the cold clinical view of modern man's perception of the universe; rather this is akin to the universe as perceived by primordial man — unmistakable due to an aura of immense archaic spirituality weaving a constant undercurrent (or is it the surfacing consciousness of a cosmic ancestral memory?). Inade have managed to perceive the unthinkable in their own mind's eye and then proceed to give it life and tangible form for all willing ears to discover and explore (choosing to provide a number of subtle hints as to what lurks at the core of the project's psyche by skillfully weaving vocals and dialogue samples into the sonic tapestry). Again, the immense totality of the release is genuinely astounding, clearly a result of the breadth, depth and scope of the meticulously constructed atmospheres — the final recordings being their own testament to why it takes Inade members Rene and Knut so long to write and record material. This review may have dwelled extensively on the colossal visions evoked, as opposed to merely describing sounds, but when music is this evocative it transcends being simply a listening experience. But if further descriptive content is to be sought, track titles such as Eternity's Crevice, Titan In Shivering Sand and Breath Like Ground Glass should be hint enough. If you don't already own this, or have read this far without considering how to track down a copy, maybe one last statement will yield a result: *The Crackling Of The Anonymous* is no less than a landmark classic, to be spoken of with feverish excitement for many years to come.

Isomer (Aus) *Serpent Age*
CD 2002 Tesco Organisation

■ The prior release of a number of self-financed tapes (under the guise of Isomer or otherwise simply as David Tonkin) showcased a burgeoning talent within the almost non-existent Australian scene. And despite the tapes being quite eclectic in scope, they did showcase solid tracks ranging from dark ambient through to death/rhythmic/noise/ experimental-type industrial. Now turning to the official debut CD (and on Tesco Organisation no less) David is forging ahead with a much more focused sound and direction — here leaning towards a dark ambient/heavy electronics fusion. And with regard to this more focused pursuit, a comparison between Isomer and heavy electronics masters Inade is not too great a stretch, certainly being a worthy compliment. Opener Star Of Sarajevo has a cold and clinical, yet deep space-orientated tone, constructed with dense sound layers, slow machinery loops and alien-esque blips/sound pulses to forge an ever-expanding breadth of sound (unfolding over eleven and a half minutes). This flow continues into Omphalos, yet a heightened sense of tension is evident with the sweeping and droning subharmonic elements, gradually moving the piece towards a grating heavy electronics sound. The Sun Shall Reign begs a specific comparison to Inade with its dense ambience and tribal-esque slow pulsing rhythm that surges in a spiraling cyclic style, until an odd vocal chant leads the track to its demise. Every Man A Star (could it be said that some shine brighter than others?!) is a soundscape of solar wind intensity, built with multiple sweeping layers and mildly harmonic elements, weaving its journey over an extended passage. Red-Haired Dog arrives as a more minimalist ambient type piece, using some rather anomalous sounds, while the following (title) track would have to be my favourite of the album. Meshing an array of static, ambient drones, slow beat and other rhythmic elements, it hits the mark perfectly. Dark, brooding and damn intense, the pinnacle is reached when a vocal sample (Al Pacino lifted from *Scarface*) is skillfully interwoven into the ambient framework. Alternatively Oriflamme concludes the CD with an intensity not seen on other tracks, here utilizing harsh and screeching heavy electronics textures, intermixed with a solemn and damn heavy death industrial type tune. Solid stuff indeed. So, with my whining in the past that there was not enough Australian acts of the darker ambient variety, Isomer is the perfect response to this, and being released on Tesco Org should be testament enough as to this album's quality.

Iszoloscope (Can) *Coagulated Wreckage*
CD 2001 Spectre

■ Iszoloscope are a new project (as far as I'm aware), with their debut CD being a corker of an album. Inhabiting a rhythmic death industrial framework (in the ballpark of Morgenstern's sound perhaps), the scathing machinations of corrosive intent are skillfully forged into compositions of decadence and decay. Drilling pistons, and idling engines housed within a slowly rusting machine room, is the essence of what has been captured here — an atmosphere (fear?) derived from the soulless machines singing their metallic chorus. The title track gets things underway by presenting an offering of sinister noise and crushing percussion that becomes increasingly rhythmic as it progresses — which actually becomes quite a trademark of many of the tracks here. With an aura of building noise threatening to explode at any moment (scathing sounds and distorted radio voices rising and falling sporadically), Prime Momentum in the end doesn't, and in the process creates a perfectly controlled on-edge vibe. With a similar technique applied to the rhythmic basis of Phobos II, this track also comes up as another striking album offering. As for the machinegun percussion of Intermittent Cycles it is not intermittent at all, keeping its brand of high energy noise and beats for the entire track's duration. Winds of Minas Linea, on the other hand, harks towards the sound of Stratvm Terror, the track here evoking acidic blasts of noise and an ominously tense undercurrent. The incessant driving rhythms and typewriter-type beats of Crimson Road makes it a particularly catchy piece, that although could be easily played on the club floor, doesn't at all forsake its darkened and noise-riddled edge. Purge is another damn brutal piece of fast-paced throttling beats, shrink-wrapped and suffocated in a veil of all-out distortion (no tune or respite here). Taking an unexpected turn, the track Iszoloscope (Tomes Un) forges sinister death ambient musings with sampled Gregorian chants and snippets of radio voices, and to attest to how great the sound is this piece is comparable to Raison D'être's last album *The Empty Hollow Unfolds* (yep, it is damn good). For the concluding piece Contemplating Paranoia & The Morning After, it opts for a come down of sorts using chilled out beats and subtle drifting sounds to create an almost relaxing atmosphere — if it were not for those ominous elements lurking in the background! Despite Spectre's previous releases having been limited to vinyl only, with the three recent items released exclusively on CD — and all being fantastic (Olhon and Frames a Second are the other two items), it should bring the label the much wider recognition they deserve — not to mention raising the profile of the artists in question. Again very commendable.

In Slaughter Natives (Swe) *Recollection*
CD 2001 Cold Meat Industry

■ Put simply, this release is a taster to the now released five-CD In Slaughter Natives box set that contains all four full length CDs, plus a fifth CD of live, rare and newly composed tracks. Contained on this simply but effectively designed digipack CD are eight tracks in all — two lifted from each full length album. Without any real need to actually review the individual tracks, nonetheless this release showcases just how groundbreaking In Slaughter Natives was in defining the apocalyptic neo-classical/industrial sound, given the earliest tracks date back to 1988. This CD is not really worth your time if you already own the full lengths (apart from the fact these tracks have been remastered) or you are planning on getting the box set, but otherwise this is a perfect single CD overview of what In Slaughter Natives represent for the scene.

Judas Kiss (Eng) Issue 7
Magazine 2001 Judas Kiss

■ *Judas Kiss* is a magazine I particularly enjoy reading, as for the most part the focus and content of interviews and reviews runs a very similar line to what is covered in *Spectrum Magazine*. With the format (A5 journal) and design layout taking on a simplified fanzine concept, it is a pocket sized read packed to the brim with in-depth and well informed interviews and reviews. The main body of the magazine is photocopied, but the cover is pro-printed in gloss stock, likewise with this issue being furnished with a transparent 'dust jacket'. Along with music-related coverage *Judas Kiss* also tackles different subject matter, with this issue containing articles on 'Death of the West' (industrial music and fascism), 'Happiness in Slavery' (interview with a female submissive) and 'The Eye of the Needle' (Thailand Vegetarian Festival) all making for intriguing insights. Music-related interviews for this issue are: Von Thronstahl, The Days of the Trumpet Call, Midnight Syndicate, B'naj Brith, Remenance and the label Middle Pillar Presents. Apart from these interviews and articles there is a Der Blutharsch live in London report, 100 or so reviews and a Death In June/Wolfpact review special. Recommended reading.

Kerovnian (Cro) *From the Depths of Haron*
CD 2001 Cold Spring

■ This mysterious Croatian black ambient project returns with their second CD, after being unveiled to the underground by the ever worthy Cold Spring label. Well, the first thing that is immediately evident is that the atmospheres evoked on this second album are less dense and suffocating and at times a touch more synthetic than that of the debut. With a reduced sonic density, the breadth of sound has expanded, particularly apparent on introductory track Dripping In The Form Of Styx with its glacial underbelly, muted harmonics and indecipherable mutterings of alien tongue. As for the almost indescribable noises of The Worm Of The Broken Urn (digestive, perhaps?), these could have parallels drawn with the somatic recordings of Daniel Menche, apart from here the sounds have been shaped into black ambient atmospheres (as opposed to an experimental framework) giving off visions evoked in H.P. Lovecraft's supreme horror writings. As for Let Yourself To Float…To The Flute Of Death, this piece sees Kerovnian at their most musical to date, with a depressive synth melody not dissimilar to Raison D'être that utilizes a haunting female vocal reciting the track title. My personal favourite of the album comes in the form of Litany Of A Lonely Corpse, with its pulsating and cyclic synth textures that are not so much dark as morbid sounding, particularly so with abyssal voices rising within the mix. The Shadows Were Unmade, following the minimalist The Silence Was Unmade, is obviously a louder affair, building layers of rumbling and lashing noise along with whispered voices; again it is a language unknown. The rather short concluding album track A Cry From The Maze arrives with a semi-composed style, including a slow understated tune and female voice mid-way between a wail and cry. With an overall bleak and depressive aura, Kerovnian are carving a niche for themselves with a sound that is certainly their own.

KnifeLadder (Eng) *Organic Traces*
CD 2002 Operative Records

■ While KnifeLadder might not be a massively known name at the moment, the buzz they have been generating in the underground over the last couple of years is proof enough that they are producing something entirely unique with a broad ritual industrial/tribal experimental sound. Being three years in the making, this is the debut full length for the project, achieved through a process of composition and improvisation, or to put it in the words of the group themselves: 'KnifeLadder is an ongoing electronic, organic project utilizing elements of live improvisation and cyclic repetition to produce music to break down the confines of conventional structure'. Featuring John Murphy on vocals, drums, percussion and loops; Andrew Trail on electronics, samples, vocals and Moroccan horn; and Hunter Barr on bass and electronics, KnifeLadder have produced an intensely woven mélange of sound. Red Drum, the opening track, is urgent and roughly hewn, being a pounding percussive/plodding bass affair, including textural sound loops and the wailed vocals of John that recite the track's title to create a strong introduction indeed. Yet it is on the following track Faultline that the album takes a step back in pace, containing a slow ritual industrial pulse built on sparse percussion, bass melody, samples and random sounds, with Andrew taking the vocal lead in an almost spoken word delivery. Haunting and tensile, Scorched Earth commences as a cyclic dirge, overlaid with sporadic loops and percussion that gradually builds over the track's duration. Consequently by the time the track concludes (towards the seven minute mark), it has morphed into a stunning mass of rolling sound and heavy martial drumming (vocals here handled again by Andrew reciting lines such as 'my father's sins are mine.....carried in my blood'*)*. Fourth track Ossirian Window commences with a ritualised dark ambient aura, yet is later fleshed out with slightly more musical structure and percussion than one would normally expect from the dark ambient scene. The atmosphere of this track is less tensile than other album cuts given its free-form flow, carried along by the hymn-like vocals of John and disharmonic tones of the Moroccan horn. Easily my favourite track of the album, The Wilderness Of Mirrors is a hypnotic soundscape of faint bass melodies, swirling loops and the mantra-like vocal delivery of John. Over its duration it undertakes a full metamorphosis from ritual soundscape to a full-blown driving percussive track, with the addition of the wailing Moroccan horn creating a particularly haunting effect. Commencing with a sickening and lurching death industrial type tone, 'Feline' surges forth from the speakers with clanging loops and indecipherable vocal treatments. Again this piece uses an evolving layering technique to build the intense atmosphere, here using free-form percussion, cyclic loops and tectonic bass layers as the main focal elements. Final album track Dervish is determined not to conclude the album quietly, rather opting to build intensity via electronic loops and John's vocal wails being delivered in an extremely spiteful and harsh manner. Matching the intensity of the track's introductory segment, the hammering drums later kick in and surge forward incessantly, loosely followed by bass lines and metallic loops, again using the Moroccan horn to evoke an esoteric aura (undeniably a grand final declaration). 'Unconventional' was probably the first word that sprang to mind when I first listened to this disc, yet this can only be a positive impression given the broad industrial scene is currently suffering from a glut of copyists not bringing forth anything new or of particular worth. Being a release that is difficult to categorise within any particular scene, this is nonetheless an extremely solid and intense album that deserves wide attention.

Land:Fire (Ger) *Gone*
LP 2002 Power & Steel (via Loki Foundation)

■ There is little information forthcoming about this new Power & Steel/Loki Foundation project Land:Fire, however this LP does adhere rather well to the tried and true sound of these labels. Inhabiting the heavy electronics sound of early Inade and Predominance releases, this LP has the instant effect of taking me back to the time when I first discovered the aforementioned groups (which can only be a good thing!). From the commencement of opening track First Mesa, all the right elements are there: the galactic drones, shimmering textures, ominous and dense sound structures; yet it is the scattered digital sounds that evoke a clinical and alien feel, as opposed to an archaic aura. With the stage set early on, the remaining seven tracks pursue variations on this theme over the forty-odd minutes of music. Each track being around three to six minutes in length, the direction and variation of each composition is limited, establishing its niche early on and morphing slightly over the duration by utilizing a layering/building technique. The track Before They Are Sent is particularly good with fractured rhythms and ominous mechanical pulses, as a lone radio voice sporadically surfaces within the mix. The track Land:Fire on the other hand, takes a low-key approach of menacing drones and stilted mechanical loops which reminds me quite heavily of Stratvm Terror's first album, as does the following track As Night Fell Over. The final two tracks conclude the album with a brooding sonic aesthetic, choosing to suffocate the listener with layered drones and shifting clinical/digital textures. While Land:Fire have created an LP that is not entirely groundbreaking, this is certainly solid material and worth more than a cursory listen.

LS-TTL (USA) *43 Hz (Note: F1)*
3" CDr 2001 Ad Noiseam

■ Another exponent of the growing US scene, LS-TTL return with a mere morsel of new material after their debut on Dragon Flight Recordings last year. With a single track clocking in at twenty-one minutes, much the same themes and sounds as encapsulated on the full length are explored here (for those unaware, LS-TTL work within the broad genre of dark ambience). Evoking non-melodic glacial atmospheres via mechanical sounding means, the piece meanders forth by gradually looping and inter-linking sections with seeming ease. Tension is also continually built throughout, yet remains relatively subdued in volume, opting rather to increase the intensity of those sounds and loops that are present within the mix. No doubt this is a good listen and certainly on a par with (if not above) the material of the debut, but with a limited run of seventy-five hand numbered copies, few will get the opportunity to evaluate this for themselves.

Mushroom's Patience (Ita) *The Spirit of the Mountain*
CD 2002 Hau Ruck

■ Although Mushroom's Patience have been around in various forms since 1985, it is a more recent group, Nový Svět, that would give readers a reference point for the musical weirdness and downright quirkiness of this album. This comparison goes much deeper given that both members of Nový Svět have contributed to and collaborated on this CD (and I also suspect it is they who are part of the reason why this release ended up on the Hau Ruk label). Defying the conventions of any actual scene (other than the niche carved by Nový Svět perhaps?), this album simply exists in its own sphere — and a rather drug-hazed, hallucinogenic one it is too. Basic programmed rhythms and beats, looped/scattered noise, vague guitar tunes, keyboard melodies and meandering trumpet tunes all intermingle to form the basis of the compositions, while the vocals, where present, are delivered in a lethargic manner (and almost in the form of drunken ramblings). Likewise there is a loose feel to how the tracks have been constructed, leaving me wondering whether they were written in the studio, or even partly improvised during the recording process. Yet when this perception is viewed in context, it is a feel which adds to the overall charm, while creating a vibe that is reminiscent of nonsensical children's stories. Some tracks being up-tempo and playful, others slow and 'down-vibed', much territory is pursued over the fourteen tracks and sixty-four minutes — but what is the meaning of the actual pursuit, I can hardly begin to imagine! Obviously this is not going to be for everyone, but this review should at least give a hint as to if you would glean something positive from it or not. Recommended? It all really depends on your musical reference points and your degree of fondness for the bizarre.

Mz.412 (Swe) *Domine Rex Infernum*
CD 2001 Cold Meat Industry

■ This new album from true Swedish black industrialists Mz.412 is promoted as not so much representing the current direction of the group, as rather being a bridging release (or pr(hell)ude?) to the upcoming album *Infernal Affairs*. However, even without such a statement, when listening to this album it is clear that it does not easily slot into the evolution and progress of Mz.412 thus far (mainly due to the slower ritualistic overtones of this release). Containing only three tracks, the opener Invol: Satha with its searing noise blasts certainly acknowledges the past, but these elements soon drop away to be replaced by a darker brooding aesthetic, complete with a slow keyboard melody akin to what you would hear in an old horror movie. Thus from this perspective, it is the darker ritualistic edge (enhanced by slow tribal drumming and distorted vocal invocations), that comes to represent the predominant aesthetic of *Domine Rex Inferum*. With track one clocking in at six minutes, it is the second track (Ritual: Summ IIV) at a whopping forty-one minutes that further encapsulates this meditative ritualistic aura. Consisting of deep brooding textures and metallic clatter, it is the slow yet incessant tribal drumming that ushers in the suffocating atmosphere of an (imagined) black mass. Pushing through various sections, later parts give rise to ominous keyboard textures, clanging metallic objects and disembodied voices before more turbulent and urgent hand percussion increases the intensity. Forever forging forward, dense sound loops merge and inter-link to continually progress the piece, also ensuring the composition does not degenerate into repetitive minimalism. In the approach to the 33.3-minute mark things become more outwardly aggressive with searing static blasts and horrific background textures, highlighting elements used when Mz.412 are at their most aggressive. Yet this section is only short lived, receding back to calmer yet bleak territory — the final section reverting to tribal drumming and monstrous vocalisations. The third and final track Komuni: Disciple is a much shorter piece (more akin to a traditional Mz.412 track), consisting of distorted loops, searing noise, static-riddled samples (lifted from *Braveheart* of all movies) and slow rolling percussion (but lasting not more than seven minutes overall). This album may be a solid listen, but if you haven't heard Mz.412's music before I would not recommend being introduced to the group by this particular release, as it works better as a bridging album for established fans. In regard to packaging, the simplistic yet stunning black gloss digipack is an admirable visual counterpart to the ritualistic black ambient sounds of this release.

Naevus (Eng) *Soil*
CD 2001 S.P.K.R

■ Naevus are an unusual project in that they flirt with the sound of some established bands such as Death In June, Current 93, Swans etc., yet do manage to pull off their own aura without sounding simply like copyists. The acoustic guitars, synths, vocals etc. work well overall to create mid-paced morose atmospheres similar to the aforementioned groups, yet the rather ridged and synthetic sounding drum machine programming and plodding bass playing push the tracks towards a gothic rock sound, that unfortunately does grate with me a little (while this aspect of goth rock influence in my eyes is detraction, to others it might not be a problem at all). This album contains ten compositions with the majority treading the standard song structure format, yet a few pieces employ touches of an experimental industrial framework for an alternative effect. With this album having been recorded in 2000, a new album *Behaviour* has already been released on Operative Records out of the UK, thus it will be interesting to see what Naevus's new material has to offer given I quite liked their track Visions, Rushed (also on the new full length) on the Operative Records compilation *First*.

Navicon Torture Technologies (USA) *The Church Of Dead Girls*
DCD 2002 Malignant Records

■ The second official release for Navicon Torture Technologies (NTT) on Malignant comes in the form of a stylistically packaged DVD sized digipack. When listening to this double album, it is immediately evident that NTT have returned with a more refined sound than their debut *Scenes From The Next Millennium*. Less chaotic and fierce than earlier material, the new material is a stylistic take on dark ambient intermixed with the harshness of a power electronics musical aesthetic. It features brooding, semi-melodious textures and dialogue samples crossbred with layered noise, looped distortion and obliterated vocals. Although there is obviously a lot of material to digest, it is a surprisingly focused double album of tensile and highly charged atmospheres. There is a brutal honesty with the themes explored, with it being clear that solo member Leech has poured his very being into this work as if it is his only means of personal catharsis. One criticism is that the use of dialogue samples is occasionally overdone. Not in reference to the number of samples used, rather that in selected tracks the sample becomes annoying by its sheer repetition. Leech has nonetheless produced a monumental piece of work featuring twenty tracks spanning over two hours. *The Church Of Dead Girls* is no less than an attempt at the personal purification of his psyche, presented for your musical pleasure or disgust — whichever best suits you.

Nordvargr (Swe) *Awaken*
CD 2002 Eibon Records

■ To start with a question: to date exactly how many releases does Mr. Nordvargr aka Henrik Björkk (of Mz.412, Folkstorm, Toroidh etc. infamy) have to his name? Although I may have lost count, here is yet another CD to add to that expansive and ever expanding list. Nordvargr being somewhat of solo project, this is the first official release, if you choose not to count the two collaborative Nordvargr/Drakh releases on LSD Organisation and Fluttering Dragon. Embodying a dark ambient framework, *Awaken* extrudes a sinister dark ambient malice, interspersed with (occasionally) horrific atmospheres. Furthermore, as the tracks have been composed in a rather visual way, they often sound less like specific musical tracks, giving rise to the perception that this could be the background score to an unnamed horror motion picture. This is particularly so of the opening title track with its low-end bass production of rumbling drones and muted orchestral tones, which combine to build an overall atmosphere of lurking dread. Cellardweller is likewise as visually active as the title suggests with dense drones, random noise and some truly chilling but indecipherable vocal effects. Lament, on the other hand, opts for a haunting effect evoked via disembodied choir voices, distant clanging church bells and minimalist backing. A rather engaging ritualistic aura is intoned within Sulphur Mist (muffled tribal beats and vocal drones), while using an echoed depth to the sound production that gives the impression that it was recorded deep in some underground cavern. Yet mid-track the atmosphere turns rather militant with the introduction of marching snare, thus begging somewhat of a comparison to the soundscape-orientated works of Toroidh. The final track (being the seventeen-minute Seeds of Blood (Acts 1-4)), certainly takes the CD out on a high note, with a militant/tribal/dark ambient concoction. Militant tribal beats hammer out a slow rhythm in what seems to be the first 'Act', before moving off into a more free-form section of muffled sounds, ritual chanting and sampled orchestral elements. Following on, another section of slow tribal percussion is reprised where the atmosphere is suitably tensile (offset with indecipherable chants), later veering into a final track segment of orchestral dark ambience. To give one last broad comparison, this particular album is along the lines of the polished ritualistic sounds of Mz.412, and most specifically the *Domine Rex Inferum* CD of 2001. Likewise, as with the majority of Mr. Nordvargr's output, this is high calibre material and certainly does not suffer from lack of ideas or creativity, which often can be of concern if an artist issues a large amount of releases under various monikers.

Of The Wand & The Moon (Den) *:emptiness:emptiness:emptiness:*
CD 2001 Euphonious Records

■ With strict adherence to the framework of the neo-folk scene, Kim Larsen of the group Of The Wand & The Moon has produced his second album under the depressive title *:emptiness:emptiness:emptiness:*. While I am yet to hear the first full length *Nighttime Nightrhymes*, I must say I was sufficiently taken by the 7" EP on Hau Ruck to be rather keen to check out this new album. This was despite hearing some complaints and criticisms that the project has lost some of its individuality due to the perception that this album slavishly sounds like Death In June during the *What Ends When The Symbols Shatter?* and *Rose Clouds Of Holocaust* era. Yet side-stepping this debate, when you listen to the opening misanthropic cut of Lost in Emptiness with its mid-paced acoustic guitar-driven ode (complete with haunting backing synth textures, oboe and mildly sung vocals), it is without doubt a grand vision indeed. The following piece My Devotion Will Never Fade is a touch more militant with subdued yet incessant rolling drums (that follow the guitar strumming) — the organ tune left to float and circle above. Steeped in mysticism, In A Robe Of Fire consists only of vocals accompanied by cello and violin, finally completed with the sound of crackling fire in the background. Algir Naudir Wunjo, a soundscape built on a distant orchestral melody and percussion/vocal mantra, while evocative, perhaps drags on a little at over twelve minutes in length. Gal Anda increases the tempo of the acoustic guitar strumming (again percussion, organ textures and understated vocals are used), with the atmosphere flitting between the morose and the celebratory, that really takes flight with the inclusion of a flute solo late in the track. The final two tracks revert to the drawn-out soundscape style of the group (working generally with sparse percussion, synth textures, vocals etc.), which, although interesting and hypnotic, for me pale in comparison to the acoustic side of the group. In passing I would not say that this is a perfect album, nor an instant classic, but this still certainly showcases that Of The Wand & The Moon are one of the strongest acts in the current crop of neo-folk acts. Lastly I will highlight that the artwork is the perfect accompaniment to the pagan and misanthropic themes of the album's lyrics. Runes, fire and misery indeed…

Orphx (Can) *The Living Tissue*
CD 2001 Hands

■ Having not paid any attention to Orphx since their debut CD on Malignant Records (way back in 1995), the magnitude of this stupidity was rather soberly driven home when I witnessed the brilliance of this project first-hand when they performed live as the closing act for the Maschinenfest 2001. While these days they may encompass a much subtler sound than their formative material, their current focus on rhythmic and experimental minimalism is utterly engaging and hypnotic. The tracks on this CD actually form a concept, with field recordings being taken from various sources and the ensuing compositions specific attempts to capture the vibe and atmosphere of the source material of each track. Thus the merging of organic spheres of sound (the sound source material) with the clinical (the studio construction technique of deriving quirky rhythms from the recorded sounds), shows the high skill and musical foresight of this duo. Favourites of this disc include the somatic rhythmic pulses of Biorhythm, surging forward at mid pace, overlapping clicks, with pops and swelling sound textures, while Mother Tongue, built on crowd samples with a dark droning undercurrent, uses snappy clicking elements and hand clapping to create its blended atmosphere. Not being based on a rhythmic style, Ether arrives in a suffocating cyclic fashion by enveloping the listener with dense rising/falling textures, the sound source seemingly derived from wind recordings. Accelerator, on the other hand, is fantastic late night highway driving music (you can just envisage the shadowed landscape effortlessly slipping by), with the indicator sounds amongst other car sound samples being cleverly used to create the up-tempo rhythmic elements. Naked City works more as a glimpse of the city it was recorded in (Hamilton, Ontario), sounding mostly akin to field recordings being taken while an individual walks along the busy streets, past shops, continuing into interior spaces such as a shopping mall. However, that said, the end result is much more evocative than this description would suggest (the same can be said of the track Dwelling, built on everyday home-based recorded sounds). Lastly, the title track is the final of the album encompassing a subtle collage of environmental recordings and nature-orientated sounds interlinked to create loose droning textures. Overall containing an excellent blend of experimentalism with skilful minimalist composition, this is a CD that could be said to easily bridge the gap between the experimentalist art scene and the works of rhythmic ambient artists. Great stuff indeed.

Olhon (Ita) *Veiovis*
CD 2001 Nautilus (via Spectre)

■ Olhon being a collaborative project between Italian projects Bad Sector and Where, it sees the artists tackling the water-orientated theme embodied in the releases issued on Spectre's side label Nautilus. With both artists working in the general field of dark ambience, luckily this collaboration sees neither dominating proceedings, thus creating a CD that embodies a positive blend of influence. The atmospheres of this release have been derived from source material recorded in the depths of various volcanic lakes, with the pieces further manipulated into compositions via a studio process. From this perspective the album's overall sound arrives as being partly organic (source recordings) and partly digital (additional studio sounds and manipulations). Containing seven untitled tracks, the first contains a bristling yet subterranean timbre, and is a fine example of where the subtle influence of the two artists can be detected merging to create another level of sound altogether (Where with suffocating dark ambience and Bad Sector with brooding experimental manipulations). At times verging on aggressive, the second piece is multitextural, with wave upon wave of sound surging from the speakers, interspersed with sporadic digital sonar frequencies. With a glacial ebb and flow, the brittle drone-orientated harmonics of track three are almost cosmic, yet the guttural frequencies keep the vibe deeply submerged, and while less aquatic than other tracks, the fifth piece is nonetheless a fantastic piece of dark ambience, with a phenomenal breadth of sound (through headphones my ears feel VERY far apart!). The sixth piece transports the listener on a journey; one can imagine sinking into the murky fathoms, with the sounds clearly evoking the feeling of the crushing pressure and visions of the light gradually giving way to inky blackness as the depth increases (yes, this is certainly emotive music). The seventh and final track is another highlight, embodied within a track of depressive dark ambience (droning textures, shimmering textures and subtle harmonics and rhythms intertwine and overlap, with the pace never rising beyond a crawl). This album is another fine example of a collaborative project that showcases a diverse sound palette between tracks; however, when Bad Sector's name is involved you are always assured of a fine production (not to denigrate Where's contributions of course!).

Orplid (Ger) *Geheilight Fei Der Toten Name*
mCD 1999 Eis & Licht

■ Originally released a few years back in a plain card slipcase, this mCD has now been reissued in a digipack format. The title track is a slow rolling marching hymn which uses stern and commanding male vocals, alongside a tense orchestral backing rising in flair and prominence as the track progresses. Jungend is however entirely different, being a short bittersweet piece of duelling acoustic guitars that acts as an interlude to the orchestral cinematic track Der Sonne Soldner. Built with layers of war samples, sweeping noise, ominous classical passages and whispered vocals, it is mildly reminiscent of Les Joyeaux De La Princesse, given the distant forlorn atmosphere evoked. Im Sturm, on the other hand, is an acoustic call to arms, using an urgent acoustic tune and full throated commanding vocals that are undercut with pounding militant percussion (mid-section the mood is slightly calmed with a piano melody). The fifth and final track Belgrad is a slow orchestral piece constructed with slow moving string and horn sections, with a sampled voice referencing Hitler's bombing of the aforementioned city. Given that this mCD showcases both sides and sounds of Orplid (militant neo-orchestral along with neo-folk acoustic), it highlights exactly why this new group have gained such critical acclaim within said genres.

Propergol (Fra) *United States*
CD 2001 Nuit et Brouillard

■ A scathing indictment/reflection of the squalid underside of US society, it is ironic to note that this idea is driven home by utilizing a multitude of dialogue samples (liberally scattered throughout the disc) that are exclusively derived from American-produced motion pictures! Anyway, *United States* is actually the third album for Propergol, but is the first widely available disc as the first two had only limited runs of 200 CDr copies each. Having missed the first CDr, but being utterly floored by the second, *Cleanshaven*, I was amply salivating for the release of this disc (and call me a prophet if I predict it is only a matter of time before someone gives the first two CDs a proper repressing). The opening cut is a grand beginning and while the samples lifted from *Se7en* might be a touch obvious, at least no bones are made about this via the sample playing a prominent role by being repeated numerous times as the caustic and tense atmosphere continually builds. Overloaded intensity is the calling card of track two and is without doubt the highlight of the disc. Appropriately entitled Outburst, it is absolutely explosive with rhythmic death industrial, searing noise blasts and some truly sadistic screamed (and treated) vocals, giving no let-up for the entire duration. While the remainder of the album does not reach the same level of mayhem as shown on Outburst, this is not to say that it is at all subtle or straightforward. Navigating a path through death industrial soundscapes peppered with samples, disorientating searing noise, shifting sounds, jagged outbursts etc., the compositions are rarely what they seem due to continually cutting between segments and samples in an attempt to throw the listener into confusion (this is a veiled compliment by the way!). While the tracks are sometimes rhythmic, more often than not they contain a tense and brooding cinematic edge which ties in rather well with the overt uses of movie samples (*Henry: Portrait of a Serial Killer* is another such example). While taking an overall reflective view of this disc, this is a definite highlight of 2001 (and destined to give Propergol cult status), yet I also feel that the previous album *Cleanshaven* slightly tops this particular release with its caustic mayhem and madness. *United States* is fantastic nonetheless, with the only thing left to do being to see what will be showcased on the quickly following fourth album *Renegades*.

R|A|A|N (USA) *The Nacrasti*
CD 2001 Malignant Antibody

■ With the label promotional blurb for this album reading: 'imagine Lustmord & Raison D'être marooned on an ancient alien planet', it simultaneously sets expectations high, and steals my thunder as I simply cannot devise a better description! Not to disappoint at all, this album easily lives up to expectations and, to add further praise, comparisons could be made to Inade, particularly with respect to their *Alderbaran* CD. Notwithstanding that R|A|A|N wears its influences rather boldly, *The Nacrasti* has been created with such conviction and skill that it transcends any simplistic accusation of being a mere copyist project. Likewise the absolutely gorgeous and detailed cover artwork (solar images, barren extraterrestrial landscapes, gold foil stamped writing and spot varnishing) is a perfect visual counterpart to the album. Composed in nine parts, each interlinks with the next to create a complete and quite complex whole. Utilizing a large array of sound elements and a multi-layering technique, the aura is one of a forever moving and evolving album. Constructed partially through synthetic means, the depth and complexity is really achieved through the use of sampling, environmental recordings and real instrumentation (gongs, hand percussion etc.), that have all been manipulated within the overall framework of deep drones, harmonic loops and muted melodies. It is also interesting to note that the sound palette radiates a certain warmth that is not normally associated with dark ambience, likewise managing to infuse atmospheres that on one hand are quite alien, yet also hint at a benevolent spirituality. I must say that after having heard as many dark ambient albums as I have over the years, it takes something special to really grab me, yet this album contains that indescribable 'something'. An immensely strong debut that should guarantee a legion of fans awaiting future sound works.

Regard Extreme (Fra) *Resurgence*
CD 1996 Cynfeirdd

■ Probably most well known for a collaboration with Les Joyeaux De La Princesse a few years back, fellow French neo-classical project Regard Extreme do have two solo albums to their name. Here, their third album is actually a partial revision of early tracks, as noted on the cover: 're-orchestrated, re-recorded & unreleased tracks'. Thus, *Resurgence* includes the title track (being formerly unreleased), two original versions and seven new versions of old pieces. So in all with the nine tracks, we have lush, swelling neo-classical orchestrations as the main musical element. Sticking to a slow pace, morose strings and choir-like textures are underscored with deep brass melody, occasionally using martial timpani/snare percussion to add an air of urgency to the otherwise slow movement of the album. While all of the tracks have been synthetically derived, the album has been suitably produced so as not to degenerate into totally cheesy keyboard-sounding neo-classical. Given Regard Extreme's compositions have a certain formula and sound signature it means that there is not a great degree of diversity between pieces; however, Egotisme is an exception to this rule, given it is a rather heavy militaristic/orchestral track reminiscent of early In Slaughter Natives. Nonetheless if solemn neo-classical catches your ear it is done with ample flair here. Full colour slim-line digipack with insert is the packaging for this release.

Robert Rich (USA) *Bestiary*
CD 2001 Release Entertainment

■ Although not an aficionado of Robert Rich's solo works, the first thing that jumps to my mind is flowing dark ambience. This new effort of his is, then, a touch on the surprising side given that it encompasses a bizarre textural rhythmic style on a deft hallucinogenic tangent. So this CD may not be specifically dark, yet the sounds are clearly not on a 'happy' tangent either, nonetheless having been composed in a playful manner. Constructed to contain a synthetic and organic-fused edge, throbbing sounds, both of murky and atmospheric textures, converge into a complex mass of sound, often with fleeting tribal and eastern elements appearing via the use of odd percussion and disembodied voices to generate a warm sonic miasma. Never content to follow a clear defined path, the compositions are as sporadic and unpredictable as a shifting deep-sea tide, flowing continually into new territory, one track interlinking with the next, traversing the densely composed and stripped back minimalism. Given this music is not all doom and gloom this just maybe could appeal to a wider audience (i.e. world music listeners), without alienating those who despise 'new age' music twaddle.

Scivias (Hun) *...and You Will Fear Death Not*
CD 2001 Eis & Licht

■ Being aware of the group's name but not having heard their music, I did however know that they were of the neo-folk genre and that this album was quite an anticipated one. Strangely enough this album is somewhat removed from what I would have expected from a neo-folk album both thematically and musically. With inspiration centring on a traditionalist view of imperial Japan, a hymn/choir-like vocal piece provides the setting, while the following track Age of the Last Law — Nuclear Japan is a track composed with rough and distorted electric guitar strumming, backed with synth layers and spoken vocals. Interesting but certainly unexpected. With a short cello/spoken work interlude (The World is a Teardrop...) the mood is entirely altered again, leading into a quieter passage of the album spanning Breathing Deeply (morose violin melodies) and The Peach Boy (haunting acoustic guitar, flute, cello and female vocal-driven tune that draws inspiration from a traditional Japanese tale — and one I enjoyed hearing as a child). A Tower Of The Devil dramatically shifts the album's focus once again, here consisting of a mélange of programmed rhythmic elements, choir voices, spoken vocals and synthesizer textures. Again, certainly different from expectation and potentially comparable to the often odd sound of Allerseelen. Passion meanders along as a slow acoustic folk tune of plucked/strummed guitars only to morph into a slow march with the late inclusion of rolling snare percussion. However Die Before Dying is easily the strongest track of the album, being a fantastic yet morose militant piece that ebbs and flows over its ten-minute expanse. With the mid-paced acoustic guitar strumming being accentuated with fleeting horns, commanding piano lines, martial percussion and spoken vocals it creates an air of both celebration and sorrow. Powerful to say the least. Following track The Empire In Me is another standout, being built with slow violin, sullen horns, church bells, bass and (now trademark) spoken vocals. Later the entire track builds with belligerent anger with the use of rolling percussion and muted electric guitar strumming to create another highlight. Concluding on an almost uplifting note, In Memory Of The Last Empire uses trumpeting horns, rolling piano tune and slow violins to convey an aura of celebration intermixed with a hint of sadness (possibly directed towards an era that passed into the pages of history?). Nonetheless a fine ending indeed. *...and You Will Fear Death Not* is an album that may contain contradictory sounds when considering the standard approach of the neo-folk scene; however, these have been meshed together with Scivias's inspiration, ideal and conviction to create an altogether intense listen.

Sleep Research Facility (UK) *Nostromo*
CD 2001 Cold Spring

■ Seemingly arriving out of nowhere, Cold Spring have released this fantastic debut CD by Sleep Research Facility. With the concept centring on the spacecraft *Nostromo* (as featured at the start of the motion picture *Alien*), this CD has five tracks, each dedicated to a level of this vessel (a-deck through e-deck). Yet despite the inclusion of five tracks, these rather operate as integral parts of a single and continuously evolving dark ambient composition (much the same as how Lustmord's *Place Where Black Stars Hang* and Inade's *Alderbaran* CD were composed). Essentially this album is best absorbed in its sixty-odd minute entirety — with uninterrupted attention yielding its subtle brilliance. While on one hand the album is minimalist and seeming at first to be rather subdued, it is when one takes the time to concentrate on the subtleties that one discovers the amply powerful atmospheres are at play here. Given all compositions are around the twelve-minute mark, the tracks unfold slowly, often using an ebb and flow technique to introduce and evolve the compositions, thus creating ample amounts of sweeping sound and rising-falling textural elements. Likewise, while the flow gives rise to the album having a drone-like resonance, the tracks are not harmonic-based, again adding to the glacially cold and clinical (if not entirely alien) essence Sleep Research Facility have managed to skillfully evoke. Also, one of the phrases included on the cover ('In space no one can hear you dream…') is a clever play on words with the original promotional phrase 'in space no one can hear you scream…', and sums up the review rather nicely. Oh yeah, this album is highly recommended!

Sophia (Swe) *Herbswerk*
CD 2001 Cold Meat Industry

■ With a bridging 10" EP released between the debut album and this, the second album, Sophia continue going from strength to strength without necessarily altering the tactics that have won them accolades thus far. Again, and as with prior releases, this is militant neo-classical music on a grand scale, ranging from brooding depressive segments (such as the first track Miserere, built on a backbone of deep choir vocals), through to rousing percussive tracks such as the title track that uses slow hammering percussion (booming kettle, timpani and snare drums), orchestral strings, French horns and a choir voice chanting the track's title. As with the previous recordings, I have made passing comparisons with label mate In Slaughter Natives, which in my opinion is still relevant here given March of Strength again reminds me of ISN at his most brooding (as per his *Purgate My Stain* album). As for the depressive aura of Inner Turmoil, it certainly shines strongly, yet the layering of minimal sweeping textures has additionally enhanced the atmosphere by giving it a distant and morose sound, anchored to the earthly realm only by a meandering piano tune. In reference to Copper Sun I admit it does not come much more powerful than this, where the stately orchestral layers, heavy percussion and choir voices are all presented in grandiose fashion. Alternatively, My Salvation, being purely constructed with choir textures and lone spoken voice, is meditative in ambience and offers some respite from the shrill orchestral battle cries of other album tracks. With eight tracks in all, again my only complaint (as with Arcana and Sophia albums thus far), is that they are generally on the short side, but this time such criticism is negated by the fact that the prior *Aus der Welt* 10" EP has been included as a bonus, pressed as a mini 3" CD and including its own miniature slip case (being great news for those too lazy to get the 10" or alternatively who don't own a record player). Anyway word from Peter Pettersson is that a third CD is already on the way, including a revaluation of sound and direction for the project. Let's sit back, then, and wait to be delivered!

Sophia (Swe) *Aus der Welt*
10" EP 2001 Erebus Odora

■ Although quickly following the debut CD with this 10", by the time I actually got around to reviewing this item, the second CD was already out. Anyway, the brown colour of the vinyl is here encased in a matching brown cover, with the spot varnished cover image (taken during the bombing of London), being a visual that certainly suits the massive brooding orchestrations cut into the record. Opener Strength Through Sorrow, being a slow orchestral piece, is based on a heavy use of choral voices and pounding percussion, arriving at a sound that could be said to be a partial mix of Arcana (of course) and In Slaughter Natives — which are both complimentary comparisons in my view. Second track March Of A New King is obviously a march, here based on shrill snare rolls and flute tune, with the track increasing its urgency as it progresses, likewise including spoken vocals that rise within the mix. Side B arrives with the title track: a composition of slow sweeping orchestral beauty that could easily have been a track lifted from an Arcana, albeit for the fact it lacks the trademark male/female choir vocals. Fourth and final piece Sono De Ignis ups the ante once more with a heavy percussive and orchestral piece — yet reining in the composition to accommodate a slow but masterful pace. Sophia impressed on their debut and continue to impress here. Recommended.

Tarmvred (Swe) *Subfusc*
CD 2001 Ad Noiseam

■ With bleak cover art that to me would suggest a dark ambient project, Tarmvred's debut is far removed from this perception, and hailing from Sweden, I can say that I was not at all expecting an album mixing some furious rhythmic industrial/noise elements with heavy techno club-orientated breaks. Sounds like an unusual mix? Well, with extended song formats (most tracks run ten minutes or longer) Tarmvred have created a complex and deeply engaging album. With the tracks often commencing slowly, they gradually hit their stride over drawn-out introductory sections, before launching headlong into slamming beats and breaks. But not to give the impression that is all about these breaks vying for supremacy (as one overlaps another), it is the other elements of minor key-orientated tunes and snippets of blasting static and noise (playing out their respective parts), that really gives rise to the originality of this release. With tracks heading off on different tangents throughout the compositions, the album rarely degenerates into an uncoordinated mess; rather, it skilfully traverses a knife edge of strict structure and free-form improvisation which makes it an all the more inspired and energetic listen. With each track forging its own identity within the broad confines of the album (and I do mean BROAD!), it only highlights its diversity — with one track even incorporating a sample of some lush female vocals. Maximizing the format, the album runs right up to the outer edge at seventy-three minutes, and of the seven tracks in total, it is the last one on offer that is credited as being a remix by Converter, who has tackled the album's fourth track (Converter does a fine job of creating a sometimes minimalistic, but more often than not harsh and whiplashing version to round out this furious album). A grand album indeed and I'm sure the new-ish label Ad Noiseam would be rather chuffed with having this group on their roster considering this album could have easily slotted into the roster of one of a few larger rhythmic industrial-orientated labels.

Tarmvred (Swe) *Onomatopoeic*
3" CDr 2001 Ad Noiseam

■ For those who can't get enough of this new Swedish project, this limited 3" CDr (read: seventy-five copies) was released in unison with the debut CD (reviewed above), but showcases a different side to the project — that of a less harsh sound, with cleaner and more straightforward structure. Likewise the only track by Tarmvred proper is the title track, as the other three are essentially remixes of Tarmvred's material (undertaken by other artists). The title track is a pure rhythmic industrial/techno piece containing multiple cascading beat sequences and is a relatively fast-paced offering, chopping and changing throughout. Generally staying on a straight track direction-wise, late in the track it shifts into a great section of trance techno complete with female vocals, stretching the track to over ten minutes in length. Aural Blasphemy's remix of E.C.W is a muffled and suffocating version that (almost) obliterates the beat-orientated structures to create a great rhythmic death industrial vibe. Any Future, up next, tackles a remix of Amfetakrom, positively morphing the track into a texturally harsh piece of part drone and part rhythm. The last remix is a track called Mourning overhauled by Digidroid into a rather eyebrow-raising and very club-friendly piece consisting of clean beats, female vocals and melodious programming (totally unexpected but very nice indeed). Probably too limited to get any wide recognition, this is still a nice accompaniment to the full length by showcasing some alternate sounds of Tarmvred.

Terra Sancta (Aus) *Anno Domini*
mCD 2002 self-released

■ For a bit of background information, this professionally pressed mCD represents a re-recorded and remastered version of Terra Sancta's debut demo CDr — and who are Terra Sancta you ask? Well, they may be rather obscure, but this lack of current profile does not negate the high quality coming from this Australian dark ambient project. When I first heard the original CDr version of this back in 2000, I was amply surprised by the quality and maturity of the project, but at that stage did comment that while there was no complaint with the sound and production, a good bit of mastering work would assist in evolving it from great to brilliant. Well, with none other than Phil Easter of Malignant Sound Technologies (the studio offshoot of Malignant Records) having been enlisted to remaster this recording, it has had the result I expected — the breadth and depth of sound has been expanded into widescreen, cinematic proportions! As for the actual music of Terra Sancta, it suitably aligns itself with the early to mid-nineties sound of the infamous Cold Meat Industry label, by taking its cues from stunning acts such as Raison D'être and Desiderii Marginis. Yet this is not so much an accusation of plagiarism than an indicator of the depth and maturity that has been created on this re-release of the first official recording. Three lengthy tracks span the thirty-two minutes, mixing sparse textural soundscapes, deathly drawn-out keyboard melodies and smatterings of sampled (predominantly female) choir vocals. Depth and sparseness of sound is used positively as a compositional element, particularly noteworthy when a sorrowful (sampled) tune of a Middle Eastern instrument rises briefly out of the depressive undercurrent of the first piece Desert Earth. Late in the piece the sparse textural elements take on the track's moniker, with the aura being akin to searing desert winds whipping up a blinding sandstorm. Second track The Infinite Lurking is not as gentle as the title may suggest, commencing calmly with multilayered choir vocals prior to fierce mid-ranged layers arcing into the composition (illustrating the final death throes perhaps?). Things do calm down again, but only very briefly before massive drawn-out keyboard drones/catatonic melody commandingly stride into view and remain for the majority of the piece. A Middle Eastern flavour is again apparent on Lithified with a (sampled) wind instrument melody that gives way to a mid-ranged slow keyboard tune that evokes a distant mournful aura (also set against sounds of slowly dripping water and other assorted field type recordings). It is good to finally see a growing number of Australian acts working in the obscurer aspects of dark experimental music, and to highlight that Terra Sancta are producing compositions of a world class standard, I can announce that they have been snapped up by Malignant Records to release their official full length debut *Aeon* (hopefully) before the end of 2002. In the meantime it would be well worth your time to contact sole member Greg Good to snap up a copy of this official, yet limited, mCD re-pressing. Highly recommended.

Toroidh (Swe) *Europe is Dead*
CD 2002 Cold Spring Records

■ Toroidh return with the second instalment of their 'European Trilogy' with *Europe is Dead* following on from the debut CD *those who do not remember the past are condemned to repeat it*. While the first instalment contained a mixture of brooding dark ambience, military percussion and neo-classical sampling, *Europe is Dead* follows a similar path to the debut, but here sees the introduction of neo-folk elements. And I would have to say that from my perspective it is through the use of the acoustic guitars and clean sung vocals, that the sound of Toroidh is all the stronger for this added diversity. Presented in eight parts, track one is an introductory piece containing sampled orchestral tunes intermixed with a brooding undercurrent and speeches to evoke the aura of the early decades of the twentieth century. While the heavy brooding vibe at the start of track two does not abate for the track's length, it is lightened somewhat by the neo-folk elements of slow strummed guitar and morose commanding vocals. Tracks three and four are tracks that really bridge one to the next, containing sections of dense neo-classically-tinged ambience that at times brings to mind the French project Les Joyeaux De La Princesse (which can really only be a compliment). The fifth piece arrives as a lengthy seventeen-minute passage, with the middle section again showcasing a fantastic neo-folk sound, using acoustic guitars, stately percussion and vocals which chant a chorus of 'lead us to war, lead us to battle, lead us to victory, lead us to peace' (later sections of this track return to a brooding martial industrial/neo-classical sound and are not too far removed from the early works of Der Blutharsch). Another highlight of the disc is the sixth track that reverts to a neo-folk style using an acoustic guitar offset with booming timpani percussion, while track seven contains a passage of muffled orchestral sounds, propagandistic speeches and marching drums. As for the cover, the simplistic but stylishly designed digipack contains a central cross created from the images of four eagle's heads rotating in a clockwise direction, and by virtue of being printed in murky black and grey tones it suits the atmosphere of the disc perfectly. Lastly, after hearing the progression from the debut, Toroidh is a project to watch out for, particularly as the final instalment of the trilogy (*Testament*) should have already been released.

Ulver (Nor) *Perdition City: music to an interior film*
CD 2000 Jester Records

■ Ulver again leap headlong into unknown territory — this time producing an album that transcends even their previous forays into experimental and electronic sounds. With regard to the title and suggested listening environment ('This is music for the stations before and after sleep. Headphones and darkness recommended.'), the album has managed to capture the essence and ultimate soullessness of the city in the small hours after the stroke of midnight. *Perdition City* is by all means a bleak and lonely journey through some unnamed city (possibly located in the recesses of the subconscious?) that has been splendidly evoked through a range of sounds and instruments — both real and synthetic (washes of sounds, cold programmed beats, kit drumming, city field recordings, morose synth textures, treated guitars, saxophones, string quartet etc.). Compositions range from those with clear musical structure, through to others that are non-musical and experimental, yet even when bypassing standard song formats the whole album is an awesome aural journey to revel in. With the introductory crunchy beats and rumbling bass of the opener Lost In Moments, the composition shifts along with piano movement, understated vocals and background field recordings of city noise. Later on the use of a wailing saxophone brings to mind the vibe and mood of the darkly surreal motion picture *Lost Highway*, particularly referencing the scenes where the main character is performing said instrument in a nightclub setting (and the more I think of it *Lost Highway* would be a rather apt visual counterpart to the whole album). Strings, piano, guitar noodling, fractured beats and clean vocals are the choice on Porn Piece Of The Scars Of Cold Kisses, becoming progressively overtaken by programming and electronica noise. Piano, programming and a myriad of beats are again used on the instrumental Hallways Of Always, which for me would seem to be acknowledging the style of the fantastic compositions on DJ Shadow's *Endtroducing* album, with this comparison also being applicable to the following instrumental track Tomorrow Never Knows. The haunting blip-orientated tune, slow piano movement and choppy break beats of The Future Sounds Of Music is magnificent and a highlight of the disc — particularly when it cuts back in the middle section, only to let fly with pounding (kit) drumming and rumbling guitar/bass tune. Other tracks such as We Are The Dead and Dead City Centres opt for a soundscape/experimental style, with the latter piece using a monologue and semi jazz-orientated musical backing that brings to mind a fifties era 'detective in a dangerous city' type vibe. For the final cut, Nowhere/Catastrophe resembles the most straightforward song composition of the album with mid-paced meandering piano tune, kit drumming, bass, guitar and clean vocals — which only drives home the twisted diversity of the remainder of the material. If you have any prior notion of what this group is about, leave behind all prior expectations when approaching this and prepare to marvel (yet again) at the immense musical prowess that Ulver possess.

Ulver (Nor) *Silence Teaches You How To Sing: EP*
mCD 2001 Jester Records

■ Limited to an edition of 2000, I believe that this ep was released as a musical counterpart of an art exhibition of photographic images captured by main group member 'G' (aka 'Garm' aka 'Trickster G' aka 'Christophorus R. Rygg' aka whatever...), with a number of these images being reproduced on the CD sleeve. Additionally, despite the cover spine containing a statement 'absence and presence for the connoisseur only' (is this a veiled warning...?), I feel that the group have already and MORE than adequately shaken up the public's expectations and perceptions of what Ulver is about, thus making such warnings and statements a moot point. Anyway, contained herein is a single track clocking in at around twenty-four minutes; however, the actual piece consists of snippets of compositions and conceptual soundscapes all spliced and melded together (and could this release perhaps be viewed as the musical interpretation of the individual images that form the above mentioned art exhibition?). The first segment is driven by a low-key brooding atmosphere; it includes the presence of ample static (not harsh though), later merging into a distant-sounding semi-composed drawling (clean) guitar tune. With reference to the next segment (that arrives at around the five-minute mark), the melancholic beauty and simplicity of the piano/bass guitar tune (complemented with washes of electronic noise), is simply stunning and a highlight passage of this EP. Continuing on, one of the mid sections occasionally verges on experimental dark ambience due to the utilization of a laptop computer-type glitch aesthetic, and with some low-key non-vocal chants it surely is alluding to the EP's title. With G's professed appreciation of Coil, this is certainly becoming increasingly evident with the scattered and schizophrenic, yet darkly hypnotic, moods evoked, drawing parallels with the experimentalism of the aforementioned legendary group. Likewise some of the semi-composed musical noodling towards the end of the EP brings to mind the eccentric and quirky compositional works of fellow Norwegian artist (and now label mate) When. I have read one review of this which stated that it sounds like outtakes of the *Perdition City* recordings (due to being less 'song'-based in structure), but in my opinion this EP inhabits an entirely different spectrum of sounds and ideas. Working positively as an excellent piece of musical experimentation (despite all segments being sandwiched within the one digital track) this is by all means worth your time if you have been continually enthralled with Ulver's artistic creativity and musical evolution.

Various Artists (various) *First*
CD 2001 Operative Records

■ Being the debut release for this new UK-based label, it incidentally is run by a collective of artists of which many (if not all?) are featured on this compilation. ANTIchildLEAGUE are first off the starting blocks, being a project of Gaya Donadio — organiser of London's Hinoeuma Malediction monthly live industrial night. Germ of Decay, as ANTIchildLEAGUE's offering, presents a seething power/heavy electronics sound where I am somewhat reminded of Anenzephalia's approach. Here, the slow caustic noise manipulations and loops intertwine with well-placed samples creating an impressive track that has pricked up my interest in hearing the further evolution of this project. Alternatively, Leisurehive inhabit a more traditional 'industrial band'-type sound, but as this scene has never really been my forte, their track sounds much like many other slow moody pieces of this genre. KnifeLadder, on the other hand, present an absolutely storming track in the form of Hymn. Incessant rolling percussion woven into a framework of droning/static noise, tortured vocal wails and rumbling bass, made all the more eerie with the use of what sounds like a snake charmer's flute. After hearing the strength of this offering I can't wait for the full length CD. With a similar moniker, the group Knives present Lights Out, which sounds not much more than an improvised jam, or better still, what you would expect to hear from a band at the conclusion of a live set (not something I would rate personally though). Ruse, on their piece N.Y.Cd, create an aura that spans clinical-sounding experimental electronics through to a dark ambient tone that is very nice indeed. But moving on, Angel (being Shining Vril's piece) is far more avant-garde than what I have previously heard from the ritualistic project — here utilizing a mélange of chimes, percussion, scattered sounds, harmonic/disharmonic sound and trippy vocalisations. Next artist up, Emblem, on their piece Azazel, use a slow shifting soundscape of environmental recordings and synth layers, that slightly reminds me of Contrastate (or even Current 93 in their more experimental guise), but this perception has more to do with the prominent poetic spoken vocals used throughout. Here the track remains sullen and introspective until a sampled speech and orchestral track are fed into the mix to bring the track to an intense conclusion. The comically titled Muffpunch showcase An Air Of Random Menace, which accommodates a muffled wall of noise sound; however, with its rough structure and obliterated vocals it also leans towards a power electronics sound. Damn aggressive stuff but probably a bit too muffled in production for my liking. Naevus are entirely different to the other artists on the compilation given that their track embodies an apocalyptic folk sound, and although a nice brooding piece of acoustic guitar, bass, synthesizers and understated male vocals, the lyrical content has me somewhat bemused (if you don't know what I mean listen to the opening lines!). On the other hand, dark sonic experimentalist Andrew Liles forges a slow morphing slab of sound on A Certain Step that has a clinical ambience to its shimmering sounds and although a touch different (i.e. more subdued) to the live set I saw in March 2002, it is nonetheless a promising piece. Final compilation track Pure Code comes courtesy of Antivalium, arriving as a static-riddled slab of noise that is almost orchestral in its scope and intensity. Here it is the crystalline production along with the forever changing direction of the track that makes it such an intense listen. Being a compilation that presents a diverse range of (currently) London-based artists, it is also worth mentioning the packaging given this is housed in an unusual frosted case, creating something different to the standard jewelcase format.

Various Artists (Wld) *Heilige Feuer*
CD 2001 Der Angriff

■ With a release that has been issued to commemorate the first ever industrial festival in Russia (Heilige Feuer held in St Petersburg on 9 December, 2000), each of the performing artists at the festival have subsequently contributed two exclusive tracks for this compilation (which is incidentally housed in a nice oversized cardboard booklet sleeve). Sal Solaris, a Russian project, is the first artist up on the CD and manages to impress quite heavily. While Sal Solaris may inhabit a dark ambient style, they present it with a tense, evocative edge via their compositions that contain a slow, dense (and often pulsing rhythmic) undercurrent, including the occasional outburst of harsher metallic textures. Disembodied vocal chants in track one likewise affix a spiritual edge to proceedings and to an extent the overall sound and direction begs a comparison with Inade. Very promising overall. While Deutsch Nepal may have been relatively silent with new tracks over the past few years, here the one and only Lina Baby Doll returns with two solid tracks. Chatrine 1 (From Above), the first track, consists of a hallucinogenic blend of drawn-out synth textures, background sound loops and repetitive (again looped) tribal hand percussion — quality stuff. Drugmother, on the other hand, is quite bizarre even by Lina's standards. With a more militant edge due to the slow snare percussion and shrill sound loops (likewise offset against an aggressive introductory vocal sample), the track sees Lina presenting vocals in full singing style. While vocals may have never played a huge role within Deutsch Nepal, the commanding yet morose drawl of the delivery on this piece works well and certainly does suit the overall atmosphere of the song. It now just has me wondering what the next Deutsch Nepal CD will offer if this piece is any indication! As for the next artist, I have noted that when Albin is removed from the shackles of presenting tracks within the context of a full length album, his compilation tracks are often quite different and often quite quirky — with the first Der Blutharsch track being no exception. If you're wondering exactly what I mean, just listen to Untitled 1 which is a hyped-up and mostly programmed 'spaghetti western' styled jig of a song! Basically I would challenge most fans to pick this as a Der Blutharsch track if they were not told otherwise, and on first listen I actually found myself checking the track order to confirm this was in fact Der Blutharsch! The second untitled piece is more along the lines of a traditional Der Blutharsch track, however the slow sampled acoustic guitar and sampled chanted choir vocals used throughout give the piece a refreshing air to the slow orchestral backing. As for Genocide Organ, their two contributed tracks actually play out more as a single track by containing a slow and relatively quiet introductory passage, then all hell breaking loose in the second half. Commencing with a subdued rumbling soundscape, the mildly processed dialogue samples assist to set the scene (referencing civil disobedience and the struggle for revolution), where at the flick of a switch the track changes into a sadistic power electronics piece. This second bare-fisted, white-knuckled track Comandos uses a roaring/lurching rhythm as its focal point, where the screamed vocals are entirely obliterated in their distorted delivery (and being just another layer in the chaotic madness). Fantastically aggressive stuff indeed from one of the true masters of power electronics. Into the home stretch another Russian project, Reutoff, rounds out the disc, with their first track The Day I Found Crystal Indian-Dolls being a death industrial/industrial noise soundscape of evolving semi-orchestral sounds, dialogue samples and tense electric sound textures. Second track Sweet Blood is a tinge more aggressive with static-riddled sound loops, dense sound textures and heavy rhythmic percussion that converge with solidly grating and ominous effect. Again another promising act. On the whole Heilige Feuer is a solid compilation containing quality tracks from both well known and rising projects.

Vidna Obmana (Bel) *Tremor*
CD 2001 Release Entertainment

■ Much the same as with Robert Rich, I have heard quite a bit about Vidna Obmana over the years, but have actually heard very few of the many CD releases he has had out to date. Regardless, Vidna Obmana remains a well-respected solo artist who is more than positively renowned for evocative ethno-ambient tracks, with more of his complex tribal ambience forming the foundation of this release. Built on a base of synthetic mid-paced tribal programming, this is overlaid with textural sound layers in order to create a warm enveloping sound, which although quite composed overall, retains a dreamy, floating air about it. Complex layering in an evolving style is basically the key here, with sound layers being both organic and synthetic in origin. For instance there are those which can easily be picked as being programmed from a synthesizer, as can those which are organic, and with regard to the latter it would appear that various types of woodwind instruments have been utilized to positive effect. And although not 'orchestral' in the true sense of the word, the synth layers could be described as being classically-tinged given their replication of drawn-out and droning string sounds. Other real instrumentation that appears within the mix, is that of a semi-composed guitar tune, but the guitar is not at all a lead instrument, rather in the form of yet another reverberating element to build the depth and breadth of the track. Despite containing eleven tracks in total, there is a singular direction and atmosphere that floats through the consciousness of the compositions, each track interlacing with the previous and following tracks to create a continual evolution of the ethno-orientated atmospheres. By and large this is a quality release that, while not specifically dark, encompasses a bleak aura in a warm enveloping guise.

Virologic (Ger) *[[[bugged]]]*
3" mCD 2002 Power & Steel (via Loki Foundation)

■ First up it is worth noting that Virologic is a side project of German heavy electronics/dark ambient group Predominance. As for this release the concept is based on the construction, deconstruction and corruption of sounds when processed and encoded through a computer programme medium — hence the title *[[[bugged]]]*. With respect to the actual music here, the single eighteen-minute track is presented as a slow evolving piece of glitched ambience. Loops, digital textures and subtle waves of sound are the predominant aural palette, but have been composed and collated in such a way that it sounds much more engaging than mere sound experimentation for the sake of it. Overall an interesting snippet of music but I wonder how well it would hold up if it spanned a whole album? Limited to 500 copies.

Von Thronstrahl (Ger) *E Pluribus Unum*
CD 2001 Cold Spring Records

■ This being the second CD for Von Thronstrahl, it may not be as focused as the debut; however, there is good reason for this, essentially lying in the fact that this CD is not an album proper, rather a collection of material lifted from previous compilation CDs, limited vinyl releases and other assorted re-mixes and unreleased tracks. Likewise not as overtly bombastic as its predecessor album, this is also related to the general periods that these tracks were composed and recorded. Bells opens the CD (being a reworking of the main riff from legendary Australian rock band AC/DC's song Hells Bells) coming across quite well, with stately percussion, guitars and of course a myriad of chiming bells. Second track Mitternachtsberb represents the track which first introduced me to the then-rising project, when they were featured on the *Riefenstahl* compilation. Slow and heavy percussion, accentuated by a brooding main piano tune and harsh rasping vocals, made this a powerful introduction to the project and it has lost none of its initial power by being featured here. The increasing use of musical layering to build orchestral movements is clearly apparent on Inthronisation (a track from 1998), here resulting in a sweeping symphonic quality. A reworking of the Thorak compilation track Fahnentrager is particularly powerful, commencing with subdued orchestral sentiments and a central piano line that increases in tension to match the urgency of the vocal sample used (Rainer Maria Rilke's poem 'Cornet' read by Oskar Werner). Verein(sam)t and Victoria (I) are two tracks lifted from a prior 1999 10" EP *Sturmzeit*; the former centring mainly on stately non-musical loops to create an intense sound; the latter pointing clearly to the militant and heavy orchestral sound of the debut album. Victoria (II) is a subdued reworking of the preceding track, most evidently removing the bombastic percussion and introducing an acoustic guitar to follow the main tune (also including crowd samples and era recordings). The theme of presenting a calm acoustic guitar reworking follows through to Turn The Centuries; the main vocals are also overhauled with a grating and rasping delivery, including spoken sections (both male and female). Built on aggressive looped orchestral samples, Das Neue Reich is a powerful (yet short) offering, subsequently leading into the militant and brooding classical sentiments of Hail You Captain And Thy Guard (a track dedicated to Captain Codereanu and The Iron Guard). Path Of St Michael raises a heavier bombastic flag again, using a quite rigid frame complete with meandering tuneful elements. As for the reworked version of Under The Mask Of Humanity, here it is built around the guitars recorded at the group's controversial appearance in Leipzig in 2000, yet the guitar part seems to have only been included in order to dredge up reference to this event, rather than enhancing the song itself (the electric guitar sounds surprisingly unprofessional and does not really fit into the whole direction and mix of the song). Regardless, Lawrence Of Arabia is quite a good track, being a sweeping melodramatic composition built around fleeting Middle Eastern flutes, piano, and string movements. As for the final album track (This Is Europe Not L.A.), as is stated on the cover the composition is a sound collage, whereby a cut-up soundscape of sampled traditional marching hymns is presented in order 'to lead our comrades back the European roots, forward into a future that will be written by us' (I will leave it up to the individual to decide how successfully the intent of such a statement has been achieved). All in all, if the debut did not set your heart ablaze then this release would not really sway your opinion of Von Thronstrahl, yet if you were rather taken by their first full length then it will slot more than nicely into your music collection.

Vromb (Can) *Episodes*
CD 2001 Ant-Zen

■ Over the years, by virtue of simply having too much music to listen to, I confess that I have never succumbed to the cult of Vromb — but this is not to say that I have listened to prior CDs and rejected the project, rather it is that I never have actually heard a Vromb album until now. Starting with a complex and clinical programmed piece (with an underlying sinister edge), I can't help but make a comparison to Black Lung's conspiracy theory-based debut CD — and with this being my comparative point of music reference, this is rather a large compliment. The low-key clinical approach, is again in order for the third track, yet here the pace is stepped up a few notches, with clicks, pops and pulses interlinking to creating a driving rhythm with minimalist melody. The mid-paced, dancefloor drive of track five again sees the construction of a piece by repetitive means — creating what is essentially a minimalist arrangement of multiple non-tuneful, rhythmic layers. The hyper-speed programming of track seven works particularly well, yet retains the minimal progression approach (here sounding akin to the streaming of computer data), while track nine really solidifies the direction and atmosphere of the CD with a mid-paced swirling and pulsing and composition offset with a quirky blip-orientated tune. Likewise with the predominant album theme being that of rhythmic minimalism, another potential comparison that could be bandied around would be the current direction of Oprhx — and of course this is again a large compliment in the humble opinion of yours truly. Track fifteen is another standout piece, continually building and evolving, but at the same time retaining a subtle flow and evolution to the programmed beats, swirling electronic textures, bleeps, blips and random sounds. While I might not be able to give an adequate comparison of this album to prior efforts, *Episodes* remains an impressive release to my virgin Vromb ears.

Wilt (USA) *Amidst a Spacious Fabric*
CD 2001 Ad Noiseam

■ So the relative newcomer Wilt has already returned with his third CD and on a third label! While this glut of material could potentially render more harm than good to a new artist, thankfully in the case of Wilt each successive album has turned out to be more impressive than the last. Again showcasing why they are one of the leaders of the new wave of US artists, Wilt create ultra-dense, yet highly atmospheric, soundscapes of slow morphing dark ambience. Despite giving a general nod towards the definitive *Heresy* era of pioneering act Lustmord, Wilt possess enough ideas and characteristics of their own — often by virtue of the sound sources utilized. In regard to this album Wilt have used a multi stringed instrument called a zither as the main sound source element, yet for the most part rendering it impossible to detect the origin of these sampled sounds (apart from some sections where scraping, plucking and tapping of the strings can be heard, thus giving a nice organic touch to the swirling mass of enveloping reverberations). Combining all this with inventive compositions (some subtle and slow, others more structured and urgent) this is no doubt a bleak journey for the ears to traverse. So with eleven (untitled) tracks in all, and with a play time of sixty-four minutes, the album presents a more than ample array of dense sound transmissions from the abyss to immerse yourself in. Wilt, not to be content with their current profile, would seem to forging ahead with further multiple releases, including a collaborative project with rising act Tarmvred and no less than four more albums slated for release on as many labels! Let's just hope the quality will remain to a positively high standard.

XhM2 (Ger/Can) *This Anxious Space*
CD 2001 Ant-Zen

■ This CD, if you did not work it out from the title, is actually a collaborative effort between the cinematic electronica of Xingu Hill and the experimental electronic cut-up style of Squaremeter. Composed in an evocative yet rather abstract cutting-edge way, the first two tracks act as a quirky, cut-up, static and 'blip-hop' prelude to the more musically composed track three. This third piece Dreadful Menace then takes on a smoother dark electronica approach, with a sci-fi-type aura enveloping the programmed tune. With a framework of low-key ambience intermixed with static and tense cinematic cutups, the fourth piece sounds both flowing and disjointed at the same time; however, the sci-fi ambience returns on the fifth piece, using a droning underbelly and again a dark yet smooth programmed tune. Revisiting a quirky cut-up style, the sixth piece manages to run a fine line between disjointed and flowing, with the following seventh revisiting the now familiar territory of a smooth programmed sci-fi tune intermixed with flowing ambience, random beats, cut-ups and disembodied voices. With ten tracks in all being quirky and playful, yet dark and evocative, *This Anxious Space* is another fine piece of cutting-edge studio trickery from two fine Ant-Zen artists.

Yen Pox (USA)/Troum (Ger) *Mnemonic Induction*
CD 2002 Malignant Records

■ Representing the long awaited collaboration between two of the biggest acts of the dark ambient/drone scenes, 2002 is the year that witnessed this album's final release. Housed in an eight-panel digipack, the deep orange/yellow colour and flowing topographic-style line artwork of the cover is actually a rather apt visual description for the warmth of enveloping sounds contained within the sixty-two minutes of the album. Four compositions of catatonic pace are spread across the length of the CD, each flowing and linking into the next, rather than representing separate and individual tracks. Containing a yawning and cavernous aural aesthetic, passages of murky tonal depths are skillfully interlinked with sections of spiraling sonic clarity. Likewise, muted swelling melodies occasionally reveal themselves within the sonic miasma adding to the complex mélange of sound skillfully woven into an all-enveloping sonic tapestry. Thus it is while listening to such impregnated sounds (and pondering potential inspiration), one gains the feeling that a half remembered thread of archaic consciousness and spirituality has been the driving influence for the atmospheres created. Yes, such music as this does transcend simplistic appreciation, essentially tapping into something primordial, something deep within the organic fabric of humanity's origins. Overall I would say that this collaboration sees the two groups presenting a sound that is almost the exact middle ground for the two. On the one hand the music is not as 'blood red' and dark as what you would expect from Yen Pox, yet on the other it does inhabit a sonic density that exudes a certain darkness not totally affiliated with the sound of Troum. Nonetheless a classic album for drone and dark ambient fanatics alike.

SPECTRUM
ARCHIVAL MATERIAL

SPECTRUM MAGAZINE INTERVIEW : AVERSIONLINE WEB MAGAZINE

Conducted by Andrew Aversionline
Responses by Richard Stevenson
Published online October, 2001

ANDREW AVERSIONLINE: *Spectrum* is one of the only magazines dedicated solely to the various genres of experimental music associated with noise, dark ambient, etc. When were you first introduced to these types of music?

RICHARD STEVENSON: In terms of the length of time I have been into experimental music it is not actually all that long (around seven years); however, once I grasp onto something, I will seek out as much information on it as possible. Thus, since my initial introduction to experimental/underground music I have collected quite a bit of background information and material (books, magazines and albums) enabling me to have a reasonable idea of its background and how this 'historic' context relates to the current status and direction of the scene.

As for when I was introduced to experimental music, it was around the early 1990s that I was heavily interested in extreme underground metal music and had established contacts with band members and individuals also in this scene. Around the same time a local metal music importer started dealing with the distribution of albums on the Cold Meat Industry label. Although there were all these fantastic projects on Cold Meat Industry, part of a scene that I knew little or nothing about, it nonetheless had quite a profound impact on me. Combining this with my waning interest in extreme metal music, it turned out to be the perfect scene that I could immerse myself in. Additionally, given that I wanted to discover more projects that were not merely limited to the Cold Meat Industry label, it was Shane Rout of Australian black metal project Abyssic Hate who provided me with a tape with 2 classic albums on it (namely Kontakta — *self titled* and Archon Satani — *Mind Of Flesh And Bones*), whilst also recommending the classic *Heresy* album by Lustmord, and CDs by Thomas Koner and Shinjuku Thief. Armed with such releases it was enough to set me on a path of total immersion in the field of (dark) ambient, industrial and experimental music. Other groups that I also soon picked up on were the quirky and avant-garde Norwegian project When, the fantastic German heavy electronics group Inade, American group Yen Pox and likewise the plethora of material coming out on Cold Meat Industry at the time etc.

Another crucial step was when I managed to obtain copies of the now defunct magazines *Audio Drudge* (Issues 6 and 7) and *Eskatos* no.2 — both being American magazines with an almost identical focus to *Spectrum*. Essentially both magazines contained long-form interviews and were jam-packed with heaps of in-depth reviews that subsequently allowed me to empty my wallet by seeking out many of the albums that received positive reviews (I admit that I still read these magazines as a reference tool!). Additionally the last three issues of *Descent Magazine* (nos 3, 4 and 5) were also a useful tool due to this publication (also now defunct) broadening and shifting its direction away from a purely metal basis.

I note that your question touches upon the specific focus of *Spectrum*, with this being a factor which often receives favourable comments. Personally I dislike magazines that try to cover too much and therefore lose their focus, or simply cover too much and as a result only contain maybe one or two articles and a bunch of reviews that I might be interested in. As much as my publication covers a wide 'spectrum' of styles and sounds, I feel that the content generally blends together well. As many readers would note, this is often by virtue of the record labels covered creating a loose collective and focus for the overall 'scene' (whatever that means!). Likewise to have it said, it is not as though what I cover in Spectrum are the only forms of music I listen to, as my overall personal musical interests span styles and scenes far removed from what I write about and choose to cover. Yet, further expanding on the question of focus, I do feel that *Spectrum*'s content has broadened far wider than that written about in initial issues — which were much more focused on the dark ambient/industrial side of things. Given there is now a growing emphasis on neo-folk/apocalyptic folk, technoise, power electronics and beyond, I think the 'ambient/industrial/experimental' tag has become slightly defunct. This is to the point where I am considering dropping it altogether in favour of simply *Spectrum Magazine* with future issues, rather than trying to add to the list of descriptions contained in the subheading!

What led to the decision to start *Spectrum*?

I had always had the idea of starting a publication to promote obscure music to a wider audience, which was also compounded by the fact that I am not musically minded enough to have a project of my own (and the scene can certainly do without another second rate death industrial/ power electronics/noise project). I had been involved on a very minor level in another friend's fanzine by providing cover art and background images, borders etc., However, as this was not entirely satisfying, I got to thinking about creating my own publication in order to have total control over content, focus and direction. But the real turning point in solidifying my thinking came when Jason Mantis of *Audio Drudge* informed me that he had quit the magazine in favour of dedicating more time to his upcoming label Malignant Records. Essentially this meant that there were too few magazines being produced covering ambient/industrial/ experimental music, thus I started *Spectrum* in an attempt to fill this void. Another concept I wanted to achieve through *Spectrum* was to create a publication with a 'fanzine' concept, but bridge the gap to commercial music magazines in terms of layout and design. Whilst being modest, I feel that the later issues of *Spectrum* are now partially starting to achieve this.

I find it interesting that you don't have your own musical project. I would think that having heard so much music from all facets of these genres you would be able to create something quite unique, not to mention your extensive knowledge of the scene and the number of contacts you've gathered over the years. It's true that the scene can do without any more 'second rate' projects, but surely you would be able to rise above that category?

There is a saying which goes something like: 'those who can play music play, those who can't write about it' which I feel is more than apt when applying this to me. I have played music when I was much younger (I was taught medieval music on the recorder, and also completed around two years of piano), whilst more recently I took to teaching myself the very basics of the bass guitar (about three or four years ago now) for a period of around six months. However, as I have always found playing music relatively difficult, I am wise enough to be able to admit that while I know what I like to hear, this does not automatically equate to myself having the actual ability to create music.

On a related tangent, having spoken with quite a few artists during my travels, during discussions of music they might make a comment along the lines of: 'I know how that was created and it is simple to do'. In this circumstance I generally do not have the first clue on how an album has been programmed or created, so in a way my technical and musical ignorance is bliss and subsequently does not detract from the magic when listening to and appreciating music.

To further cover my 'second rate' comment, while it is certainly not true of the truly great noise/power electronics/ death industrial artists, it seems that individuals without a defined musical ability tend to gravitate towards these styles when they have a burning ambition to have some sort of project regardless if they have talent or not (and on a certain level I am guilty of this! ...Read on to glean insight!).

Above all I simply do not have the time (the one thing I would need ample amounts of) to acquire and experiment with a range of synths, samplers, effects units etc., in order to learn how to use these before even setting about creating something that might even be part way to being worthwhile, and — of utmost importance — original. For all the unknowns surrounding this and also that it would most certainly mean that I would have to sacrifice *Spectrum* to this cause, it is not something I currently have an inclination for!

But having said all I have above, there is a reasonably recent release to which I contributed some sound source material to. To tell the story in full, some three years ago I was living in a shared house arrangement with a group of friends, of which a number played the guitar, which gave me access to a lot of equipment to experiment with. Thus on quite a few occasions I would plug a bass guitar into a pre-amplifier, two distortion pedals and finally an amplifier in order to create basic feedback loops that I would morph and evolve in a purely improvised manner (much to the bemusement of my friends!). These experiments culminated in probably an hour to an hour and a half of very basic recordings that were nothing of worth — other than for my own interests. Yet it was some time later the Swedish black industrial group Mz.412 put out a call on the Cold Meat Industry email list, requesting sound contributions for an upcoming limited edition two-track 7" EP. Well, with this invitation I dug out the tape and gave it another listen and found that although it was very basic and crude in style, it would be perfect for Mz.412 to work into a composition of their own. Subsequently I sent off a tape to Mz.412 containing three culled segments from the recordings (being about fifteen minutes in total and about five minutes per section), each showcasing some of the different sounds I had been able to improvise. Although I did not really expect too much become of my submission, I was pleasantly surprised when the finished product arrived (in the form of 412 copies on white vinyl/412 on black vinyl), given that I could detect my own contributions throughout the length of both pieces (of course in amongst the material submitted by the other contributors). So for the moment at least having a release out that contains my name on the sleeve as a contributor is more than ample to satisfy my musical yearnings!

Is there much of a scene for these types of music in Australia? I'm not sure I can think of any labels or projects off the top of my head that are located there.

Well, if you can't think of any wait for the following barrage of information!

Of the current crop of artists, the most well known and respected exponent of dark ambient music from Australia is Shinjuku Thief, with the artist Darrin Verhargen also being the label boss of the superb Dorobo Records (who release Shinjuku Thief's material along with other local and international artists). With reference to Dorobo, one artist in particular is Australian sound collage artist Alan Lamb who has done some fantastic recordings of old disused telegraph wires, releasing two CDs of this material thus far. There was also a remix album of his recordings (also released on Dorobo), with the remixes executed by artists including Tomas Korner and Lustmord to name just two. Likewise all of the other catalogue items on Dorobo are of a high quality standard (both in an audio and visual sense), hovering mostly at the experimental end of sound (be it experimental dance theatre soundtracks, sound manipulation/exploration etc.).

It is also a reasonably well known fact that Douglas P. of Death In June now resides in Australia — but admittedly most would still consider him to be a UK artist. However, he does have an offshoot of the NER label (under the NEROZ title), which is managed and operated by Chris McCarter of the more goth rock-orientated band Ikon.

When making reference to NEROZ and Death In June, on a related tangent Ostara (formerly Strength Through Joy) formed in Australia, however now both members, Richard Leviathan and Timothy Jenn, reside in the UK and Germany respectively.

Industrial music icon John Murphy comes from Australia also, but currently splits his time between here and the UK. His activities over the years include being involved in, or collaborating with, many excellent projects — SPK, Kraang, Lustmord, Genocide Organ, Death In June, KnifeLadder, Shining Vril to name but a few. And let's not forget that the industrial music pioneering legends SPK were originally from Australia (with SPK members also including notables Graeme Revell and Brian Williams aka Lustmord).

The reasonably prominent Extreme label is another successful Australian export, with one of the most recent releases being the excessively ambitious Merzbow: Merzbox release.

On the techno(ise)/electronica side of things there is the quite well known David Thrussell with his projects such as Black Lung, Song, Soma etc.

Referencing new labels, there is a new home-based Brisbane label called label:KETTLLE that is doing some interesting things via melding pure artistic type experimental electronics with a darker streak.

Female solo artist Cat Hope is likewise creating some interesting droning soundscape material using manipulated bass guitar sounds — of which I have managed to catch her play live once. I also believe that she plays with a collective of other musicians, including the group Lux Mammoth. I am also aware that the individuals behind Lux Mammoth have an affiliated record label called Bergerk, but I must have only heard about their activities and have not yet had an opportunity to check it out.

Submerging to an underground scale, there are a few projects popping up which align perfectly with *Spectrum*'s content — with two to mention being Isomer, dark industrial/ambient from Adelaide and Terra Sancta, dark ambient from Sydney. I also believe that the controversial (yet quite obscure) power electronics project Streicher comes from my hometown of Melbourne.

There is quite a bit of activity on the pure experimental side of things, but often this tends to be more 'artistic', in the chin-scratching, university undergraduate vein, so I am not really attracted to this.

Given that any scene will also include record stores, and after having the opportunity to see quite a few shops over here in Europa, I'm actually quite surprised at the general quality of the few local record stores I have back home in Melbourne: namely, Peril Underground, Heartland Records and Synesthesia — the latter of which has started a small record label under the same name focusing on the cutting-edge, laptop-type experimental music.

The above information is all I can think of for the moment and I'm sure I have forgotten quite an amount — sorry to those inadvertently forgotten!

However, despite there appearing to be quite an amount of activity, due to the sheer size and expanse of Australia, there is no overall 'scene' to talk of, rather it amounts to small groupings of individuals pursuing their interests and obsessions with experimental forms of music. Likewise as ninety per cent of *Spectrum*'s sales are accommodated overseas (particularly in the US, the UK and mainland Europe), this means that for the most part (for *Spectrum* at least) the greater scene lies overseas, resulting in the majority of my efforts being focused internationally.

I didn't become aware of your magazine until around the time of issue no.3. In the earliest days of the magazine's existence, around the time of the first two issues, what was the response like from both the readers and the bands/record labels? Was it hard to garner support?

The interest was surprisingly positive from the outset, but more so with regards to the comments from record labels than in regard to actual feedback from individuals. Also gaining interviews was surprisingly easy once I had indicated my intentions to the artists regarding the intent and focus of *Spectrum* — likewise their subsequent feedback (upon seeing the finished product) was encouraging enough to spur me on to continue with *Spectrum*.

From the outset, another way to generate interest from record labels was to offer free advertising space in the first issue, then moving onto paid advertising with subsequent issues once I became a touch more established. Basically I feel that the increase in print runs with each issue (also noting increase in size and overall content) tells its own story, with *Spectrum* being produced in the following volumes: Issue 1: 150 copies, issue 2: 250 copies, issue 3: 330 copies, issue 4: 500 copies and issue 5: 500 copies. Currently I am sold out of Issues 1 through 3 and only have Issues 4 and 5 available from me directly (although select mail order companies might still have copies of issue 3, if you are lucky). That said, 500 copies is not a significantly large amount of copies and I am convinced that there is the potential to at least double this figure, but I am finding that a lot of people seem to be hesitant to order a magazine via the post if they have not first seen a copy — the proof of this being that I sold out of all copies of *Spectrum* that I brought over to the UK at the first show I attended (the same occurring at the Maschinenfest with the copies that Spectre Records stocked). Also sending small quantities abroad becomes quite cost prohibitive, and many actual record stores I have approached don't seem keen to stock *Spectrum* for this reason (for reference my current distribution network is predominantly with mail order companies). So, in order to expand *Spectrum*'s reader base what I really need to work on is some sort of distribution deal with a company that stocks records stores directly...

In many cases you seem to have researched your interviews fairly well (for instance the recently published discussion with Death In June). What measures do you take to properly prepare yourself for each interview, especially when speaking with such infamous acts as Death In June, Brighter Death Now, etc.?

Well, first of all I never interview an artist or project I do not like, so chances are by the time I ask for an interview I have been a fan for quite some time and have already gained quite a bit of knowledge about them through releases and other interviews.

But to deal with one specific aspect of your question, I admit that the Death In June interview was a rather daunting prospect, despite it being Douglas that actually offered to provide an interview to *Spectrum*! It was after I had interviewed Albin Julius/Der Blutharsch in issue 4, that Albin inquired if I had sent a copy of it to Douglas. As I hadn't, I subsequently forwarded a copy of issue 4 onto Douglas, who incidentally by coincidence (or fate?!) had heard about *Spectrum* from three different people in the preceding weeks. So after seeing the issue and being rather pleased with it, Douglas promptly wrote back with the offer of providing an interview for inclusion in issue 5. Anyway I digress... Given that Death In June has been active for around twenty years, I realised that my interview would be up for scrutiny from fans who have been familiar with the group far longer than I. Therefore I obtained as many previous interviews from Douglas that I could find in order to be as informed as possible when conducting the interview, and also to work from a questioning basis that on a certain level expected the reader to have an amount of familiarity with the concepts and themes behind Death In June. It would seem that most interviews I conduct contain around twenty to twenty-five questions, however I think the DIJ interview spanned in excess of thirty and accordingly many comments I have received have mentioned it is the most comprehensive and in-depth interview that Douglas has given for many years. I take this as a compliment and also take a bit of pride in Douglas commenting that one question in particular was one of the most interesting questions he has ever been asked!

Anyway speaking more broadly, I generally undertake a bit of background reading on an artist before drafting the questions and as all of my interviews are conducted via email, I feel I have the ability to ask more in-depth questions (than if it were conducted in person or on the phone), with the artist likewise having the ability to take their time in responding adequately. It is also a policy of mine to never use form questions. Admittedly certain questions may be asked of all groups, but I always write the interviews from scratch to avoid repetition in the wording of the questions asked, and to also tailor them specifically to the artist.

If I'm not mistaken, aside from a few review submissions you take care of everything *Spectrum*-related yourself, including the graphic design elements. Is this the case? And if so, how much time would you estimate spending on *Spectrum* each day?

Yes, you are certainly correct on this front. I can say that the input of my contributors is invaluable, but in essence ninety-five per cent of all work on *Spectrum* comes from myself. As for these contributors, I have two people (Chris Forth and Joseph Aquino) who assist with proofreading and the excellent reviewer JC Smith contributes a small handful of reviews — but yet again the remainder of the input lies solely with me.

When I am working on a new issue, it is essentially undertaken in the hours outside of my full time professional career. Of a night time I will generally get home mid evening, and then spend three to four hours toiling away on the PC — be that preparing layouts, writing interviews or listening to and reviewing the mountains of CDs that I get sent. On weekends, apart from catching up with friends and going out drinking, I probably invest a similar amount of time per day as during the week.

Thereafter once all of the reviews, interviews and design/layout work is complete (this being really only half of it) I then need to co-ordinate the printing of the file with the printer (there is ALWAYS some sort of problem that must be overcome), receive the finished product, and THEN start to promote and distribute it. This is even before putting on the accountant's hat and having to chase up invoices, prior to the preparation work for another issue getting under way! (Nonetheless there is maybe a month or so after actual publication where I don't review any material at all in order to recharge my 'inspiration' batteries and also simply to listen to music for pleasure again).

As for the amount of time I have dedicated to *Spectrum* and with regard to the last two issues in particular (no. 4 and no. 5), it is reaching a point where it is almost out of control and getting to be more than I can personally handle. Thus far I have managed to release an issue every six to eight months, but with each issue growing in content, this is becoming increasingly unmanageable. As I am currently taking a break with *Spectrum* between issue 5 and 6 due to my travels through the UK and Europe, I am currently considering certain options to reduce my personal workload without compromising the focus and content of *Spectrum* — and more importantly to strengthen it.

What are some of the options that you are considering, and what would be the desired outcome of these options, specifically?

First and foremost it would be recruiting additional individuals to assist with providing reviews — as this is where the greatest part of my time is taken up. However with anyone potentially coming on board with *Spectrum*, I would firstly demand that they have a solid and individual reviewing style and likewise I would need to ensure that their musical tastes go hand in hand with *Spectrum*'s coverage (hence back to the issue of keeping the publication focused). I have in mind a few people that I am considering personally inviting to contribute to future issues, but I shall have to see what their responses are before I potentially start casting my net wider. I have also thought of getting in guest interviewers, but at this stage I am a touch more hesitant on this front as this is what I really quite enjoy coordinating and undertaking.

Regarding another aspect of strengthening *Spectrum* (and whilst not necessarily relating to reducing workload), I am considering modifying the format of *Spectrum* (but still remaining a printed publication though), and likewise might branch out with the introduction of a compilation CD of artists interviewed. These modifications, however, hinge on a number of specific factors that I am still exploring the logistics of — which is proving to be a bit of a task considering I am not currently at home in Australia at the moment!

I'd like to end with a potentially complicated question that I rarely ask, but in this case I'm curious. What are the single most positive and negative events that you have encountered as a direct result of your work with *Spectrum*? (For example, becoming closely acquainted with projects that you admire, or perhaps offending an 'artist' and having an interview session go incredibly poorly, etc.)

You are right that one of the major positives of running *Spectrum* is that I have been able to make contact with many people behind the projects that I have admired for some time, with this positive aspect certainly being much more pronounced now that I am over in Europa (as I have finally been able meet many of my contacts in person). At many of the festivals and shows I have been able to attend since being over here, I have actually been quite overwhelmed by the reception that I have received from acquaintances, as they have gone absolutely out of their way to make me feel at home. This was particularly so at the Electronic Gathering

Festival in Stockholm in August 2001 where many Cold Meat Industry acts were performing, and I can attest that the 'Karmanik Family' (the general grouping of the Cold Meat Industry roster and associates) is certainly one big happy family! I also have to send extreme gratitude to the following individuals for providing me with accommodation and hospitality during my initial travels: Alex of Cynfeirdd Records, Stefan of Fusarium Distribution/Promotion, Hans of Run Level Zero and Stefan of Ironflame.de (and for those I have had a drink and talked shite with, you are too numerous to mention — but you know who you are!).

As for conducting interviews I have never had any trouble on this front, but as I said earlier these are always conducted by email so the 'interview session' is slightly more formal than a personal one. The only issue that has ever been raised was when a particular artist refused to respond to a question and likewise requested that the question not be published with the interview. This situation arose not out of offence, rather from the perspective of potential negative ramifications if it were responded to and/or published, and in that I understood the artist's view I could respect and adhere to their request.

As for any other negatives, it is just the general stresses with managing my workloads and the anxious moments when the computer decides to have a fit with a particular technical request. Yet, maybe the biggest negative in recent times was when the time came to publish the last issue. I had calculated my advertising rates against my printing and postage overheads (comparative to what I had been charged in the past), but when I submitted the finished file to the printer, they indicated that it had been discovered that they were losing money with my particular job, thus with their new costing it roughly doubled my printing overheads. In that I was hoping to offset printing and postage against my advertising revenue (in order to make the final sales price cheaper) this increase in printing costs blew out my budget

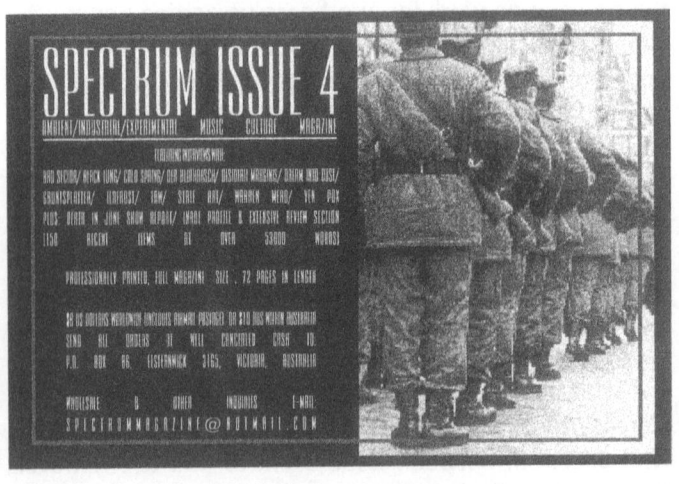

Spectrum Magazine printed flyers.

and meant that I had to increase my wholesale prices just to ensure I would merely break even. I did contemplate trying to find a new printer, but as I was departing for Europa in a mere five weeks, I simply did not have the time and had no option to fork out the extra money. Luckily after publication I managed to shift ninety per cent of the print run in a matter of weeks so all was not lost!

Lastly, at times I have expected that I might get some hate mail, or otherwise protests regarding the coverage of certain acts, or use of certain images — but thus far it has been silent on this front. Whilst Europe-based acts and publications seem to be subjected to such vilification, it seems that Australia is a little far away for anyone to be bothered with the likes of me and my activities. Also, if anyone were to potentially have a problem with *Spectrum*, after reading a bit of it I'm sure they can ascertain that my agenda is to have no agenda at all (other than music coverage and exploration of ideas of course!).

What printing plant(s) do you use?

It is a small-scale specialist printer, who offer a form of printing that does not require the creation of actual printing templates (this is particularly advantageous as plate printing would become excessively expensive with my current print run of 500 copies). Essentially they use an industrial strength laser printer (called a docutech machine if I am not mistaken), that can print high resolution greyscale images.

What words of advice would you offer to those thinking of starting their own magazine?

Hmmm… Expect to invest many more hours (and particularly dollars) than even the most excessive estimate that you calculate. Running a magazine is also not all about the perks of receiving promotional music either, as keeping enthusiastic and focused can become quite difficult, particularly if you start getting flooded with tons of music of average quality, or the music does not fit into the context of the styles you have chosen to cover etc. Moreover you often have so much music to wade through that you don't get to listen to the great albums for pure enjoyment as you are always moving onto listening to newly received material, and/or you are always thinking in the back of your mind of how to describe it when the time comes to give it a review.

It is also wise to remember that writing, producing and publishing a magazine is only half the work, as that you also need to promote and distribute the thing in order to recoup your outlay costs of printing and postage (advertising revenue provides only partial assistance on this front). Likewise producing a magazine is something that you really have to be dedicated to and is also not to be tackled on a whim, particularly if you know you are a disorganised individual!

Drawbacks aside, I admit that it is particularly rewarding when you start getting positive feedback from both labels, groups and general readers saying how much they appreciate the time and effort put into the creation of each issue. I imagine it is much the same as when a band release a CD that is positively received!

Lastly there is also the question regarding the positive and negative of producing an actual printed magazine versus a web-based one that I have not even touched upon!

Well, it's obvious from your lengthy and informative responses that you are well aware of how an interview should be conducted! Thanks for your time, and if you have any closing words, please feel free.

No, there is nothing to add other than the obligatory 'thank you' to you, Andrew, for giving me the opportunity to spout off some of my thoughts! And finally … ov'r 'n' out … end transmission…

LIVE PERFORMANCE PHOTO ARCHIVE

■ The following live performance photo archive brings together live photos taken at various shows and festivals I attended between 2000 and 2002. All of these photos were taken using the same set up: a fully manual 35mm film SLR camera, with a basic camera-mounted flash. Armed with only rudimentary photographic knowledge I am surprised that some of these photos turned out OK — or at least captured some of the atmosphere of each of the shows. Noting that in the early 2000s camera phones simply did not exist, nor were digital cameras at all common at shows, I often found only myself and perhaps one or two others making the effort to bring a camera and seek to capture the moment.

Although my original intention was to write a series of live show reports to be used alongside the live photos, clearly that never eventuated (other than the Death In June show report featured in *Spectrum* Issue no.4). But, upon reflection I do remember feeling at the time it was important to at least attempt to document these performances and was perhaps also reflective of my enthusiasm for being able to finally see so many acts I had only previously been able to read about.

Another observation to make (which may be lost on those who have only used digital cameras), is that when relying on actual camera film you are limited to around 24 shots per film, so there is no opportunity to simply fire off hundreds of shots to make sure one works. Rather it is a case of being patient and selective to try and get the best shots possible, but even then you leave the show not knowing whether any photos will work out at all — such is the game of chance with real film photography.

As a final comment, for those with a keen eye, many of these photos have previously been available online via the Hinoeuma the Malediction London website/s, as well as a selection featuring on the cover of the Cold Spring Records compilation *Steel Nights 29.11.01* (including: Death In June, Von Thronstahl, The Days of the Trumpet Call, Mz.412 vs. Folkstorm). However for the sake of posterity, most of the photos from the 2000 to 2002 period are now brought together as part of *Spectrum Compendium*.

Top: Show advert, *Inpress* magazine, May 2000.
Show photos: Death In June: above (Douglas P), right (L–R: Douglas P and John Murphy).

Artists: Death in June, IKON
Date: 24 May, 2000
Venue: Gershwin Room, Esplanade Hotel, Melbourne, Australia
Promoter: Soiree Neroz
Additional notes: Full review of the show featured in Issue no.4. Death in June's performance was recorded and issued on CD in 2008 as *Black Angel – Live!*

SPECTRUM MAGAZINE ARCHIVE

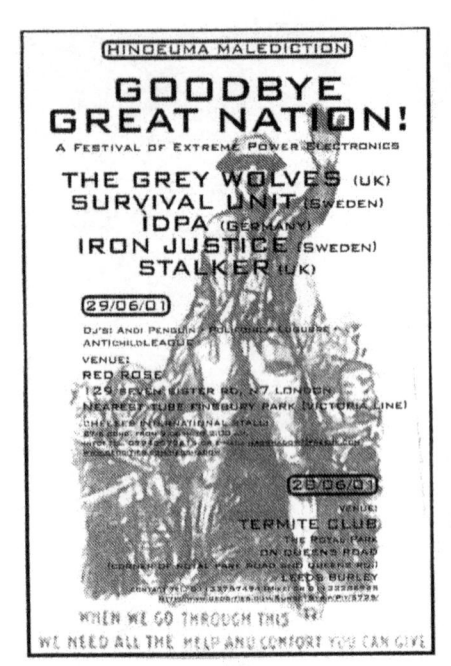

Top left: Show flyer.
Top right: The Grey Wolves (L–R: Mike Dando, Dave Padbury).
Above: Iron Justice (L–R: Björn Lindström, Rickard Freden).
Right: Survival Unit (L–R: Marco Koch, Kristian Olsson).

Festival: Goodbye Great Nation!
Artists: The Grey Wolves, Survival Unit, IDPA, Iron Justice, Stalker
Date: 29 June, 2001
Venue: Red Rose, Finsbury Park, London, UK
Promoter: Hinoeuma the Malediction
Additional notes: The run order of the night was: IDPA, The Grey Wolves, Survival Unit, Iron Justice, Stalker.
For the Survival Unit performance main member Kristian Olsson was assisted by Marco Koch (of IDPA and the Stateart label).
For The Grey Wolves performance one of the main members Dave Padbury was assisted by Mike Dando (of Con Dom).

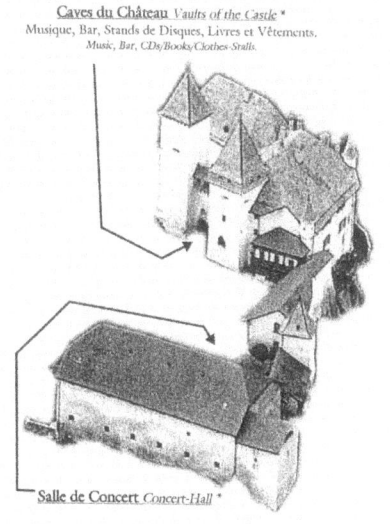

Festival: Sol Veritas Lux
Artists: Les Joyaux De La Princesse, Camerata Mediolanense, Ostara, Forseti, Der Blutharsch (unbilled & unannounced)
Date: 21 July, 2001
Venue: Chateau De La Sarraz, Switzerland
Additional notes: Der Blutharsch played a short unbilled and unannounced surprise set, which included a part-collaboration with Les Joyaux De La Princesse.
The run order of the night was: Ostara, Forseti, Der Blutharsch, Les Joyaux De La Princesse, Camerata Mediolanense.

Top: Show flyer
Middle, left: Der Blutharsch (L–R: Albin Julius, Marthynna)
Middle, right: Les Joyaux De La Princesse (L–R: unknown, Erik Konofal)
Bottom, left: Ostara (L–R: Timothy Jenn, Richard Leviathan, unknown)
Bottom, right: Forseti (L–R: Andreas Ritter, unknown)

Above, from left: Sephiroth (Ulf Söderberg); Ordo Rosarius Equlibrio (L–R: Fredrik Bergström, Rose-Marie Larsen, Tomas Pettersson); Sophia (L–R: Per Åhlund, Peter Bjärgö). Below: The Protagonist (L–R: Magnus Sundström, unknown, Marten Sahlen). Bottom, from left: Sanctum (L–R: Håkan Paulsson, Lena Robert, unknown, Jan Carleklev); Folkstorm (L–R: Henrik Nordvargr Björkk, Jouni Ollila).

Festival: Electric Gathering Festival
Artists: Side stage: Sephiroth, Sophia, The Protagonist, In Slaughter Natives (cancelled), Folkstorm (replacement), Sanctum, Ordo Rosarius Equilibrio, Raison D´etre, Vidna Obmana
Date: 12 August, 2001
Venue: The Swedish Museum of Architecture, Stockholm, Sweden
Additional notes: Bands and projects booked to play the main stage included: Apoptygma Berzerk, Attrition, Dark Side Cowboys, Das Ich, In Strict Confidence, Malaise, Pouppée Fabrikk. Project X & Tiamat (cancelled). For The Protagonist performance Magnus Sundström was assisted by Marten Sahlen on drums and unknown on cello. For the Folkstorm performance Henrik Nordvargr Björkk was assisted by Jouni Ollila (of Mz.412).

Show: Whitehouse Live Action 93
Artists: Whitehouse, Con-Dom, Anenzephalia
Date: 28 September, 2001
Venue: Red Rose, Finsbury Park, London, UK
Promoter: Hinoeuma the Malediction
Additional notes: The run order of the night was: Anenzephalia, Whitehouse, Con-Dom. The Whitehouse photos do not come close to capturing the sheer intensity and chaos of their show (285 audience members according to the Susan Lawly Live Action Dossier). For instance, the aggressive taunting of the front rows by Peter Sotos; the constant crowd shoving and dragging of Philip Best off stage at one point; and the shower of beer and broken glass (caused by pint glasses thrown at the stage and ceiling). It was only in less chaotic moments I was able to sneak up to the stage to grab these photos of the performance. Con Dom performed a set focusing on his *Colour Of A Man's Skin* album, which is reflected in the use of b&w body paint.

Whitehouse: Philip Best (above), Peter Sotos, William Bennett (left), Peter Sotos (right).
Below, left: Anenzephalia (L–R: Wilhelm Herich, B. Moloch). Below, middle: Con Dom (Mike Dando). Below, right: Show flyer.

SPECTRUM MAGAZINE ARCHIVE

381

Artists: Desiderii Marginis, Sophia, Institut
Date: 14 October, 2001
Venue: Indigo Club, Malmo, Sweden

Above, left and right: Sophia (L–R: Cecilia Bjärgö, Peter Bjärgö).
Right: Institut (L–R: Johanna Rosenqvist, Lirim Cajani), Johanna Rosenqvist (below).
Below right: Desiderii Marginis (Johan Levin).

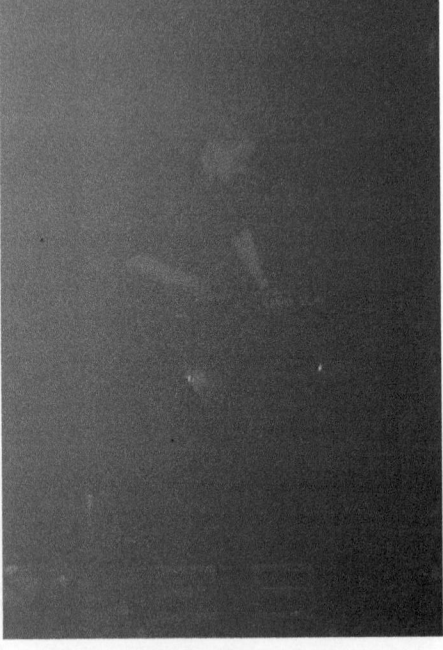

Hinoeuma Malediction in collaboration with Cold Spring & Kokampf present....

STIGMA
A 2 Day Festival At The Slimelight And Red Rose

VON THRONSTAHL
MZ.412 vs. FOLKSTORM
NOCTURNE
THE DAYS OF THE TRUMPET CALL

Electrowerkz (Slimelight)
Torrens Street, N1.
Nearest Tube: Angel
(Northern Line)

THURSDAY 29TH NOVEMBER 8:00pm - 2:00am

MILITIA
FROZEN FACES/DEUTSCH NEPAL
PPF
AESTHETIC MEAT FRONT

Red Rose,
129 Seven Sisters Road, N7.
Nearest Tube: Finsbury Park

FRIDAY 30th NOVEMBER 9:00pm - 2:00am

INDUSTRIAL / TECHNO / NOIZE - DJ JUDAS KISS AND DJ ANDI PENGUIN
Record stalls - Hagshadow Distribution / Cheeses International

Prices For The Nights Are:
advance 2 days: £15
advance 1 day: £8
at the door: £10 each night

For more information, and advance ticket booking, call 07940 079615 or email Hagshadow@freeuk.com

Tickets also available from:
RESURRECTION RECORDS, 228, Camden High Street, Camden, London, UK. Open 7 days

http://go.to/stigma2001
http://www.coldspring.co.uk
http://www.geocities.com/hagshadow

Festival: Stigma Festival
Artists:
Thursday: Von Thronstahl, MZ.412 vs. Folkstorm, The Days Of The Trumpet Call, Nocturne, Death in June (unbilled & unannounced)
Friday: Militia, Frozen Faces/Deutsch Nepal, PPF (cancelled), Aesthetic Meat Front
Date: 29 & 30 November, 2001
Venue:
Thursday: Slimelight, Angel, London UK
Friday: Red Rose, Finsbury Park, London, UK
Promoter: Hinoeuma the Malediction, Coldspring, Kokamph
Additional notes: Death in June played a short unbilled and unannounced surprise set on the Thursday night at the Slimelight. The run order of the Thursday night was: Death In June, The Days Of The Trumpet Call, Mz.412 vs. Folkstorm, Von Thronstahl, Nocturne. The run order of the Friday night was: Frozen Faces/Deutsch Nepal, Militia, Aesthetic Meat Front.

SPECTRUM MAGAZINE ARCHIVE

Previous page: Top left show flyer; bottom left Death In June (Douglas P); middle Days Of The Trumpet Call (L- R: Raymond P, all others unknown); bottom right VonThronstahl (Josef K on vocals, all others unknown). This page: above left Mz412 vs Folkstorm (L-R: Henrik Nordvargr Björkk, Jouni Ollila); above right Militia (Frank Gorissen centre, all others unknown); left DeutschNepal/ FrozenFaces (Lina Baby Doll), right Nocturne (Saphi); below Aesthetic Meat Front (L- R: unknown, Louis Fleischauer, unknown).

Show: Unforgivable Italian Assault! A morbid evening of Italian necrosonics!
Artists: Mörder Machine, Today I'm Dead, Wertham, Hydra
Date: 1 February, 2002
Venue: Red Rose, Finsbury Park, London, UK
Promoter: Hinoeuma the Malediction, Kokamph
Additional notes: The run order of the night was: Wertham, Mörder Machine, Today I'm Dead, Hydra.
For the Wertham performance main member Marco Deplano was assisted by John Murphy (of Shining Vril, Last Dominion Lost, Knifeladder). Richard Leviathan (of Ostara) also provided guest vocals to present a power electronics version of Foresta Di Ferro's track *On The Marble Cliffs*.

Left: Show flyer.
Top left: Wertham (L–R: Richard Leviathan, John Murphy, Marco Deplano). Top right: Today, I'm Dead (Tairy Ceron). Bottom: Mörder Machine (Marco Corbelli).

Top left: Der Blutharsch (L–R: Bain Wolfkind, Albin Julius, Marthynna).
Top right: Of The Wand And The Moon (L–R: unknown, Kim Larsen, Matt Howden).
Above left: Foresta Di Ferro (L–R: Richard Leviathan, Marco Deplano John Murphy).
Right: Shing Vril (John Murphy).

Artists: Der Blutharsch, Of The Wand And The Moon, Foresta Di Ferro, Shing Vril
Date: 8 March, 2002
Venue: Red Rose, Finsbury Park, London, UK
Promoter: Hinoeuma the Malediction
Additional notes: The run order of the night was: Of The Wand And The Moon, Der Blutharsch, Foresta Di Ferro, Shining Vril.
For the Shining Vril performance main member John Murphy was assisted by Marco Deplano (of Wertham).

Artists: KnifeLadder, Shock Headed Peters, Andrew Liles
Date: 10 March, 2002
Venue: The Verge, Kentish Town, London, UK

Above: KnifeLadder (L–R: Hunter Barr, John Murphy, Andrew Trail).

Artists: Death in June, NON
Date: 4 May, 2002
Venue: Slimelight, Angel, London, UK
Promoter: Hinoeuma the Malediction
Additional notes: Tracks from the Boyd Rice & Friends albums *Music, Martinis, And Misanthropy* (1990) and *Wolf Pact* (2002) were played on the night.

Left: NON (Boyd Rice); right show flyer.
Bottom: Death In June (L–R: John Murphy, Douglas P).

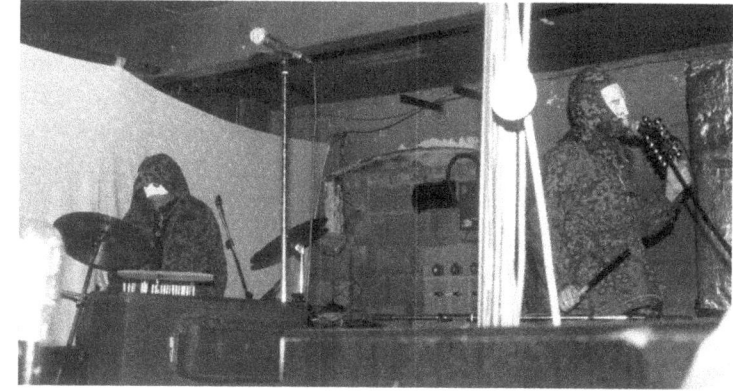

Hinoeuma Malediction present
DEATH IN JUNE
NON
MAY 04 2002

SPECTRUM MAGAZINE ARCHIVE

PERSONAL CORRESPONDENCE ARCHIVE

■ Before the internet and email, there was the 'old school' method of physical letters. Emails lack personality and the personal touch, while letters are the opposite: the means by which a person presents themselves, including chosen stationery, are a window on the person behind the words. Below is a small selection from my personal correspondence archives, specifically relevant to *Spectrum Compendium*.

This page: Mortiis letters, 1994 & 1995.

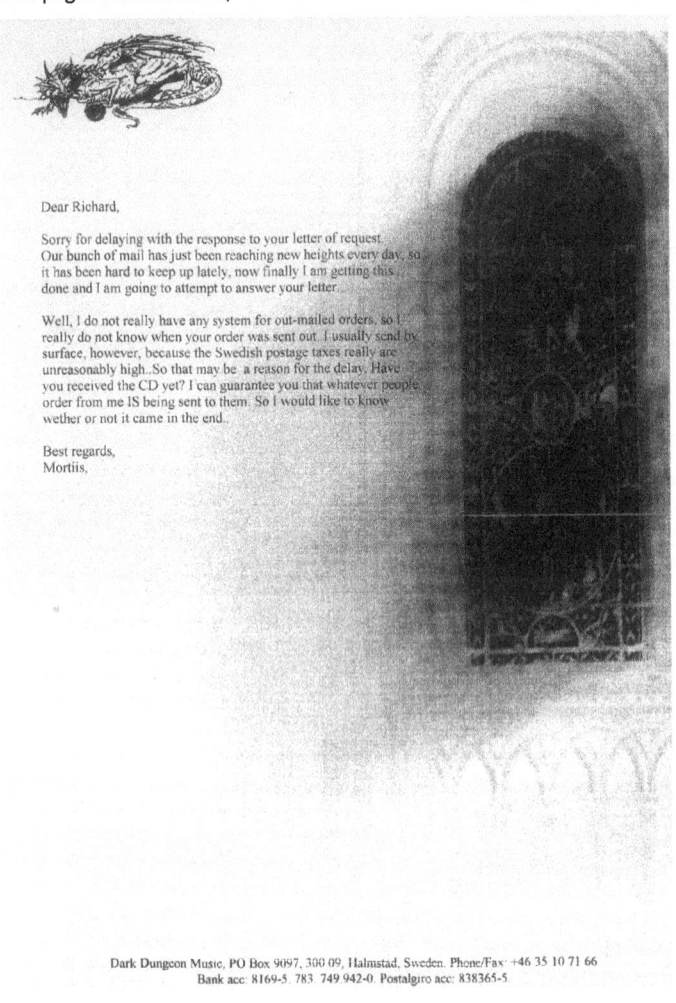

> Dear Richard,
>
> Sorry for delaying with the response to your letter of request. Our bunch of mail has just been reaching new heights every day, so it has been hard to keep up lately, now finally I am getting this done and I am going to attempt to answer your letter.
>
> Well, I do not really have any system for out-mailed orders, so I really do not know when your order was sent out. I usually send by surface, however, because the Swedish postage taxes really are unreasonably high..So that may be a reason for the delay. Have you received the CD yet? I can guarantee you that whatever people order from me IS being sent to them. So I would like to know wether or not it came in the end.
>
> Best regards,
> Mortiis.

Mortiis/Dark Dungeon Music

This correspondence is circa 1994, predating the formation of *Spectrum Magazine*, but it illustrates the methods employed by the underground before the internet: primarily sending physical cash in the mail. Intriguingly the second letter highlights a rather frustrating situation of the slow speed of international parcels to reach Australia, while actual letters were making it back and forth in the interim.

Marco Corbelli/Atrax Morgue/Morder Machine/Slaughter Productions

Given the untimely passing of Marco Corbelli (1970–2007), the scan of a handwritten letter is instrumental in illustrating how the underground scene operated back in the late 1990s.

With the first issue of *Spectrum* I sent out promotional copies to various labels I respected, with Slaughter Productions high on that list. Given that Marco's return letter is dated 16 September, 1998, he must have received the promo copy of issue 1 in early to mid-September and immediately written this reply letter, which ultimately led to the feature of an interview with Slaughter Productions in issue 3. The reproduction of the original photo of Marco Corbelli was then provided to me in 2000 at the time of the Slaughter Productions interview, but went unused at the time.

Douglas P/Death In June

I have included some archive scans relating to my first introduction to Douglas P of Death In June as well as the interview which was eventually completed and included in issue no.5. These scans are included to illustrate the attention to detail some artists take, and particularly in the example of Douglas, this extends to both handwriting and personalized stationery.

The handwritten postcards along with half of the interview being physically typed on a manual typewriter by Douglas (and later transcribed onto a computer by myself), are both a tangible and important part of my personal archive which I felt worthwhile to share as part of *Spectrum Compendium*.

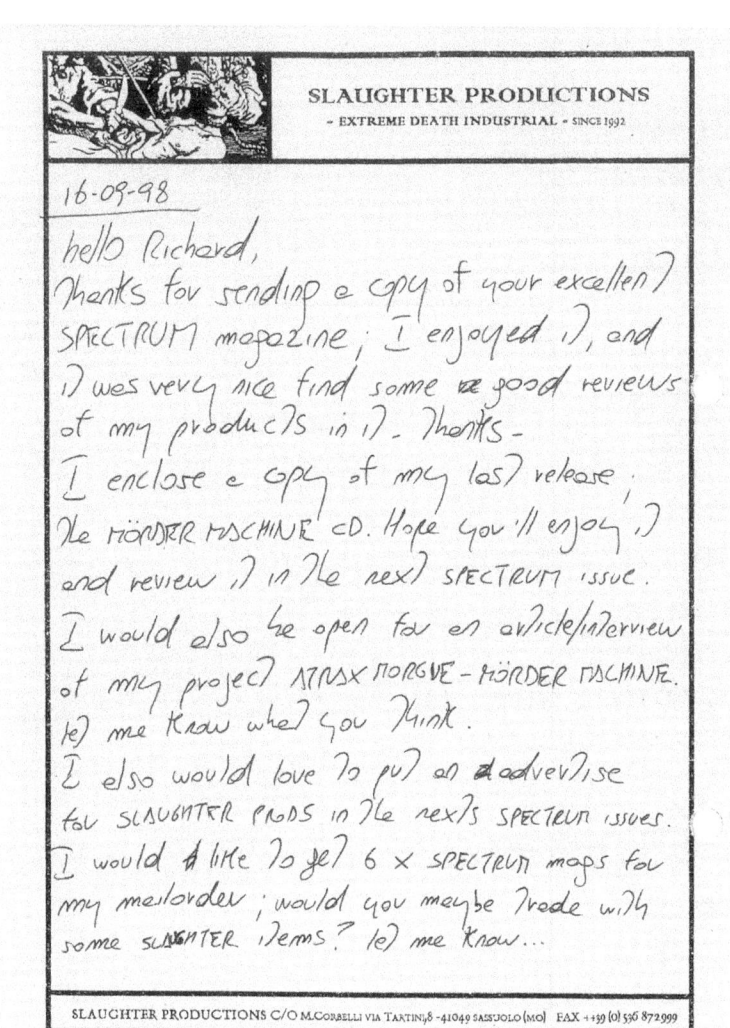

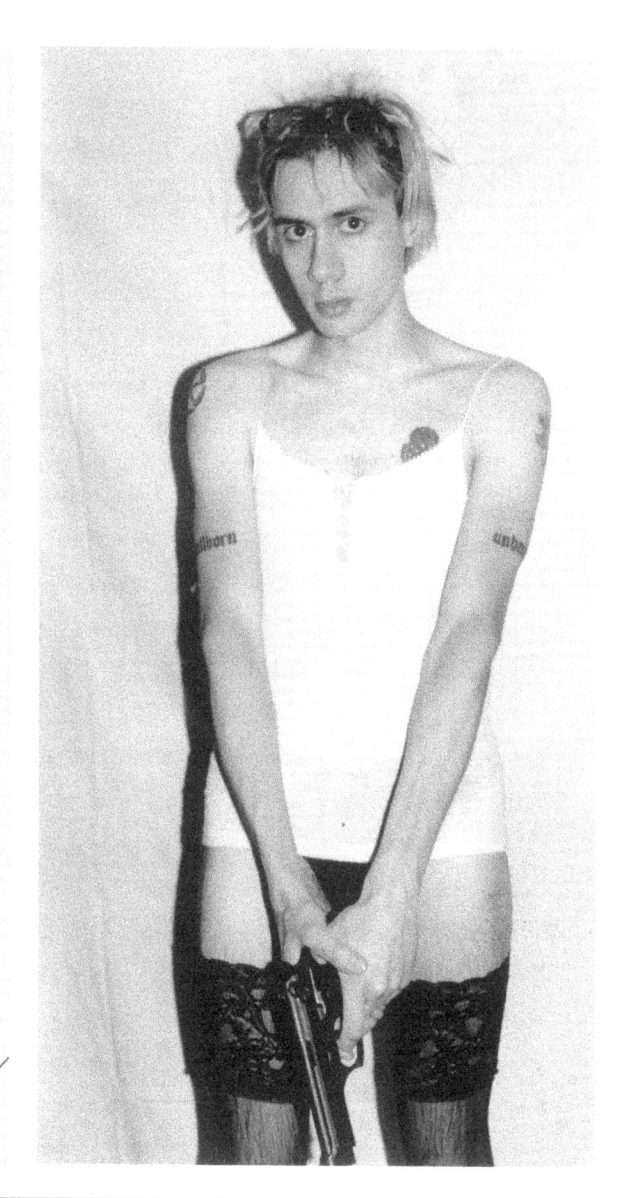

Above: Marco Corbelli letter, 1998. Above right: Marco Corbelli (who supplied the photo, 2000).

Right and following page, top left: Death In June postcard, 2000, front and back.
Following page, top right: Death In June postcard, 2001, front and back.
Following page, bottom: Death In June typed interview 2001.

Postcards/flyers

In the underground, promotional flyers and postcards had a dual purpose: promoting releases and a handy means to write a quick note to the recipient. A couple of scans of such examples are provided herein.

SPECTRUM MAGAZINE ARCHIVE

Letter 1 (18.X.00):

Dear Richard,

"Spectrum" appears to have been on the offensive of late as David Tonkin (via an interview on Adelaide 3D Radio) have all told me about you. The comments have all been positive and I can see why now I've viewed your magazine. Yes, I'm interested in doing an interview but I'm due to return to Europe in 3-4 weeks. If I haven't received it by then it's unlikely I will be able to do it until the early New Year. Either way, if you email the questions he will forward them to me. Otherwise post to the Oz address before mid Nov. or any English address after (until mid Dec.) should also be sending you some promo material + I'll arrange for a copy of the first Tekhom CD to be sent to you. I'm also interested in buying a copy of #3 if still available. I enclose $10 — please forward to my G/A. address!

Heilige!
Douglas P.

Letter 2 (22.iii.01):

Dear Richard,

Thanks for the letter so, I'll send the rest of the interview via email which I've just got access to.

In the meantime, perhaps it's best for you to have what I've done so far so you can get started on the transcription.

Hinlige!
Douglas P.

---

www.deathinjune.net

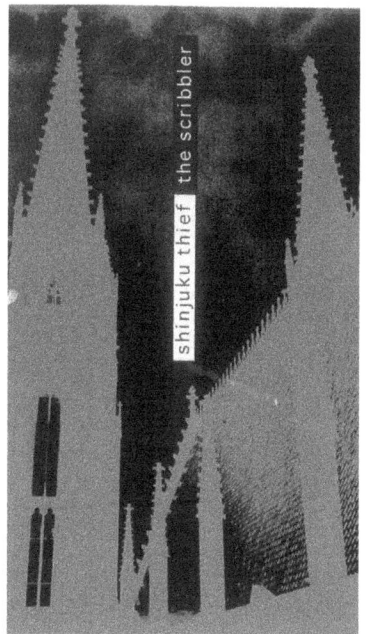

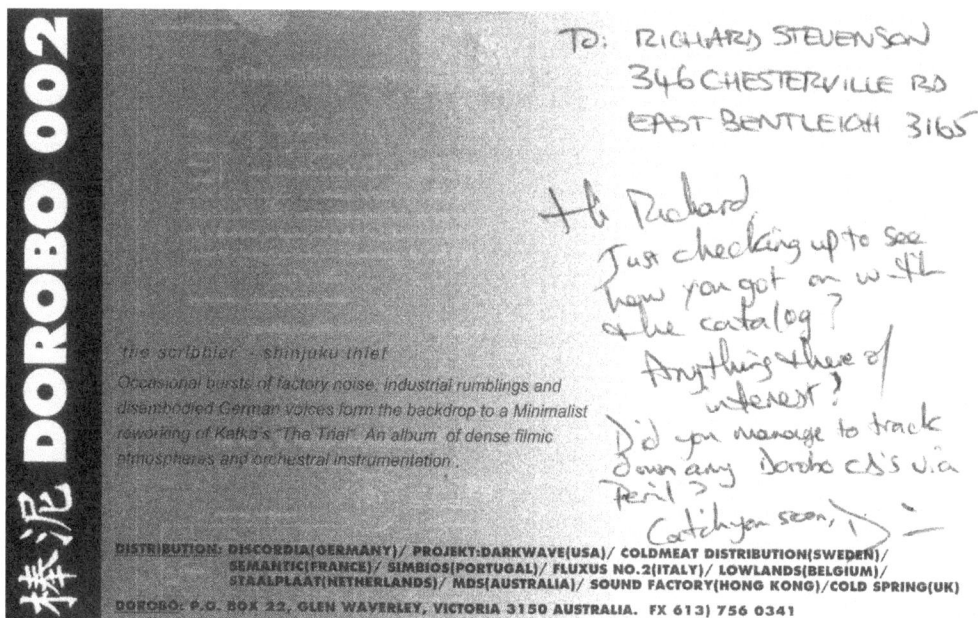

Top: Dorobo postcard, front and back.
Middle: Endura postcard, front and back.
Bottom: Stateart postcard, front and back.